Jewish American Literature

A Norton Anthology

Jewish American Literature

A Norton Anthology

Jules Chametzky
University of Massachusetts, Amherst

John Felstiner
Stanford University

Hilene Flanzbaum, *Coordinating Editor*
Butler University

Kathryn Hellerstein
University of Pennsylvania

W · W · Norton & Company · New York · London

Printed in the United States of America
First Edition

The text of this book is composed in Fairfield Medium, with the display set in Bernhard Modern. Composition by Binghamton Valley Composition. Manufacturing by R. R. Donnelley & Sons.

Editor: Julia Reidhead
Developmental Editor: Carol Flechner
Permissions Manager: Kristin Sheerin
Editorial Assistant: Christa Grenawalt
Production Manager: Diane O'Connor
Associate Managing Editor: Marian Johnson
Cover Design: Debra Morton Hoyt

Library of Congress Cataloging-in-Publication Data

Jewish American literature : a Norton anthology / [compiled and edited by] Jules Chametzky . . . [et al.].
p. cm.
Includes bibliographical references and index.
ISBN 0-393-04809-8
1. American literature—Jewish authors. 2. Jews—United States—Literary collections. I. Chametzky, Jules.

PS508.J4 J45 2000
810.8'08924—dc21 00-055393

W. W. Norton & Company, Inc., 500 Fifth Avenue, New York, NY 10110
http://www.wwnorton.com
W. W. Norton & Company Ltd., 10 Coptic Street, London WC1A 1PU

1 2 3 4 5 6 7 8 9 0

Contents

Preface

Jewish American Literature: A Norton Anthology has been a collaborative venture for its four editors from the beginning. While the anthology is organized in exactly dated and neatly titled historical periods, in fact the decisions about where period breaks should occur and what those periods should be called, along with the choice and placement of writers and works to be included, were much debated. Space constraints and permissions restrictions meant that important writers had to be excluded—another topic of intense debate. All four editors participated in these collective decisions and likewise contributed to each other's individual work on selections, introductions, headnotes, footnotes, and bibliographies.

Even though the anthology is a collaborative endeavor, the reader should be aware of the particular responsibilities of each editor. Jules Chametzky prepared the introduction to and is responsible for most of the writers in *From Margin to Mainstream in Difficult Times, 1924–1945;* he also edited the selections for Abraham Cahan, Sidney L. Nyburg, Horace M. Kallen, Edna Ferber, and Norman Mailer, wrote and edited the section on *Jewish Humor,* and, with diplomatic and editorial skill, wove together the General Introduction to which all contributed. John Felstiner had primary responsibility for *Achievement and Ambivalence, 1945–1973* and created the section *Jews Translating Jews,* where his translations of poems by Paul Celan appear. Hilene Flanzbaum edited the first seven writers in *Literature of Arrival, 1654–1880* and wrote that period's introduction in collaboration with Kathryn Hellerstein. She edited selections for Kate Simon, Gerald Stern, Philip Levine, and John Hollander. She prepared *The Golden Age of the Broadway Song* and *Wandering and Return: Literature since 1973*. Kathryn Hellerstein selected the final nine writers in *Literature of Arrival* and wrote the introduction to *The Great Tide, 1881–1924*, as well as editing that section. She also edited the Yiddish-language writers throughout the anthology, the Hebrew writer Ephraim E. Lisitzky, and the Sephardic writer Emma Adatto Schlesinger. Her translations of Yehoash, Moyshe-Leyb Halpern, Joseph Opatoshu, Celia Dropkin, Anna Margolin, Fradl Shtok, Jacob Glatstein, Berish Vaynshteyn, Malka Heifetz Tussman, and Kadya Molodowsky are anthologized here.

Following the model of other Norton anthologies, the editors have written period introductions, headnotes, and annotations designed to make the anthology self-sufficient and accessible to general readers and students new to Jewish American literature. In the same spirit, we have modernized most spellings and (very sparingly) the punctuation in *The Literature of Arrival* so that archaic usage does not pose unnecessary problems. We have followed, though not slavishly, the YIVO system of transliteration of Yiddish and the *Prooftexts* style sheet for Hebrew in the introductions, headnotes, and footnotes. When authors or translators use Yiddish, Hebrew, or Ladino in their texts, we have left their transliterations. We have used square brackets to indicate titles supplied by the editors for the convenience of readers. Whenever a portion of a text has been omitted, we have indicated that omission with three asterisks. After each work, we cite the date of first publication on the right and the date of composition, when known, on the left. We have used the *JPS Hebrew-English Tanakh,* second edition (1999), as the standard reference for biblical citations.

Acknowledgments

Among our many advisers and friends, the following were especially helpful in shaping our conception of *Jewish American Literature: A Norton Anthology* by providing critiques of our initial proposal for the book: Robert Alter (University of California, Berkeley), Joyce Moser (Stanford University), Sanford Pinsker (Franklin and Marshall College), and Michael Shapiro (University of Illinois at Urbana-Champaign).

We wish to thank many people for their contributions to our individual efforts. Jules Chametzky gives special thanks to Anne Halley for doing basic research and writing headnotes for several poets, and for her sharp editing of all of his manuscript. He also thanks his assistant, Wendy H. Bergoffen, and Doris Newton at the University of Massachusetts at Amherst, Susannah Rebekah Rankenberg for her assistance during a Fulbright year at the University of Copenhagen, and the many contributors of old and new jokes found in the *Jewish Humor* section: Haim Gunner, Anne Halley, Bruce Laurie, Paul Lauter, Paul Levine, Jerome Liebling, Lillian Robinson, Howard Ziff, and the comedians who played the Sha-wan-ga Lodge in the Catskills when he was Assistant Stage Manager in 1949.

John Felstiner thanks Chris Hale and Jonathan Ivry for their research efforts.

Hilene Flanzbaum acknowledges with gratitude her students and former students at Butler University, especially Elizabeth Barrett, Kim Campanello, Lesley Carroll, and Dana Sullivan Kilroy, Mari Kozlowski, Matthew Marietta, Annie Pierros, Lesley Blumthal Wallace, and her English Department colleagues Larry Bradley, Lynn Franken, Andrew Levy, Carol Reeves, William Walsh, James Watt, and William Watts. Special thanks to Paula Geyh, Virginia Gillette, Stuart Glennan, Peggy Golnick, Paul Hanson, Arkady Plotnitsky, Paul Valliere, and the Indianapolis Hebrew Congregation, especially Rabbi Eric Bram and librarian Evelyn Pockrass. She also extends thanks to Andrew Furman, Lou Harry, Rabbi Sandy Sasso, the Center for Advanced Judaic Studies at the University of Pennsylvania, Abraham Karp, Laura Myran, Tom Myran, and Geoffrey Sharpless.

Kathryn Hellerstein wishes to thank Dianne Ashton, Norman Buder, Ann Greene, David Hellerstein, Elisabeth Hollender, Lisa Katz, Alan Mintz, Anita Norich, Catherine Rottenberg, Jeremy Singerman, Michael Steinlauf, Liliane Weissberg, Shira Wolosky, and Linda Zisquit for their conversations and correspondence. For kindly granting permission to publish her translations of Celia Dropkin, Moyshe-Leyb Halpern, Joseph Opatoshu, and Kadya Molodowsky, she thanks John J. and Ruth Dropkin, Isaac (Ying) and Pat Halpern, Daniel Opatoshu, and Ben Litman and Edith Schwarz. Thanks to her colleagues Simon Richter (University of Pennsylvania) for encouragement and photocopying privileges and Emily Budick (Hebrew University of

Jerusalem) for facilitating an appointment as Visiting Lecturer, and to the Guggenheim Foundation for a fellowship. At the University of Pennsylvania, the Van Pelt–Dietrich Library and the Library at the Center for Advanced Judaic Studies, where Judith Leifer was especially generous with her time, were essential resources, as were the Jewish National and University Library at the Hebrew University of Jerusalem and the Bloomfield Library for Humanities and Social Sciences at the Hebrew University, Mount Scopus. Finally, she gives heartfelt thanks to David Stern, who translated selections in *The Yankee Talmud* expressly for this anthology and provided immeasurable encouragement, pragmatic help, and inspiration, and to Rebecca and Jonah Stern, who kept her smiling.

The editors feel privileged to have worked with the superb staff at W. W. Norton. We thank vice president and editor Julia Reidhead for her constant support, wisdom, and enthusiasm for the project; developmental editor Carol Flechner, whose sharp eye and kind heart urged improvement; and editorial assistant Christa Grenawalt, associate managing editor Marian Johnson, permissions manager Kristin Sheerin, and production manager Diane O'Connor for helping to shepherd the book through to completion.

Jewish American Literature

A Norton Anthology

General Introduction

At the outset, the editors wrestled with the question of what to call this anthology. Similar collections have been about equally divided in using "Jewish American" or "American Jewish" in their titles, with no rationale given one way or the other. But the choice matters; each pair of words emphasizes something different.

The term "Jewish" in "Jewish American literature" matters because it distinguishes this literature from all other American literatures. Yet "Jewish," because it is an adjective, is also subordinate to—merely modifies—"American literature." And "Jewish American"—like "Irish American," "Polish American," and so forth—evokes that early period when immigrants were viewed askance. By the same token, "Jewish American literature" sounds nicely congruent with "African American literature," "Mexican American literature," "Asian American literature," and "Native American literature," filling a multiethnic and multicultural paradigm for what America has come to be.

Is that congruence accurate? After all, "African," "Mexican," "Asian," and (in a sense) "Native" denote place and nationhood. But Jews have not often been a nation dwelling in one place. Nor are they bound only by religion. They are a people, over many centuries and over all the globe.

During World War II and thereafter, synagogue Sunday schools used a textbook called *When the Jewish People Was Young*. It didn't take much precocity to hear something peculiar in that singular verb because *people* are plural, especially Jewish people. To assert the oneness of the Jews, their unity over time and place, counted vitally then and may still. But a somewhat discrepant idea has equal urgency: Doesn't Jewish identity center in Israel rather than in the Diaspora? There are good reasons to say yes; but, at the same time many American Jews, Zionists included, refuse to think of themselves as being tangential, contingent on Israel. America is the "land of our destiny," they say, that destiny being no less definitive than Israel's.

In Nazi-occupied Europe, one's Jewishness, however defined by Jews or their oppressors, determined one's fate; in the United States, being a Jew is a factor in one's life, but the degree of its significance varies considerably. In no other country in the world, from the beginning of its national existence, have Jews enjoyed such freedom of religion, movement, and the ordinary rights of citizenship in a republic—to be educated, to be part of the political and social life, to own property, to pursue liberty and happiness. Which is not to say that this freedom and these rights have not had to be fought for and defended against bigotry, prejudice, and intolerance almost continually. Nevertheless, the strongest arguments can be made for the uniqueness of the Jewish experience in the United States and the embrace by Jews, in the main and over time, of America as the golden land, the promised land. If those terms have sometimes been treated ironically—there was no gold in the streets for the hapless immigrants, nor was America's promise of meaningful work and equality always fulfilled—it was precisely because the originating and hopeful ideals of America were so strongly believed in. Much of the writing by Jews about their American existence reveals a prophet's urge to make the country live up to its best self. In that sense, the "Americanness" of Jewish Americans is paramount, and the title of this anthology is more than justified.

The other formulation—"American Jewish literature"—might also sound primarily American and secondarily Jewish. Or does that term point up a distinctively Jewish writing in its American incarnation? Can we discern an "American Jew" at the root of the phrase, someone as deeply akin to Russian or Argentine or Israeli Jews as to other Americans? Yes and no, depending on time and circumstance. On September 16, 1919, smarting from the Versailles Treaty's "stab in the back" to German nationalism, Adolf Hitler complained in a letter: "It's the Jew who never calls himself a Jewish German, Jewish Pole, or Jewish American, but always a German, Polish, or American Jew." Thus, what outraged Hitler ought to suit ourselves. To be an American Jew might mean (de)nominating oneself nounwise, while making one's national bond incidental. Again, a charged concept.

And how would we identify that common denominator, a Jewish kindredness? Not something racial, presumably, some geno-literary litmus test. Maybe something historical, religious, ethical, temperamental? Of course, if "all men are Jews" in suffering (Bernard Malamud) or "all poets are Yids" in alienation (Paul Celan), then Jewish distinctiveness gets either universalized or effaced, depending on your vantage point: the more Jewish, the more human and/or vice versa. Yet arrogance, even a pariah's arrogance, arrogating radical humanness primarily to Jews, will not do. It was Franz Kafka, after all, who wrote in his diary in 1914: "What have I in common with Jews? I have scarcely anything in common with myself." Was he then being quintessentially Jewish or merely, starkly, human? Kafka also wrote this in his notebook one day: "Writing as a form of prayer." But surely the People of the Book, as Jews have been called, are not alone in practicing that sort of prayer.

On balance, both potential titles for this anthology are questionable—which is to say, multifold and open, expansive. "Jewish American" risks a kind of literary assimilation, and yet behold the strong implantation of Jews in the United States—Nobel literature prizes, a poet laureate—and the richness of their American English. "American Jewish" implies a particularism, a genius and/or plight endemic to Jews everywhere, and yet witness the strength shared by Robert Pinsky with other poets, not Jews, such as Carolyn Forché and Robert Hass.

So both terms seem richly problematic. An idiosyncratic joke comes to mind. Two people bring a dispute to the rabbi. The first tells one side of the story, to which the rabbi replies, "You're right." The second tells the other side, and the rabbi says, "You're right." Then the rabbi's wife speaks up: "But, Rabbi, they can't both be right." Whereupon the rabbi says, "You know, *you're* right, too!"

From the earliest known Jewish American author, Abraham de Lucena, writing in 1656 to Governor Stuyvesant to claim basic rights, Jews have been expressing their distinct experience of America. But the questions persist:

Do these Jews writing in America make up a literary tradition, even without being particularly aware of their forebears? And, if so, what defines that tradition? As ever, it depends on who's doing the defining.

Scholar Leslie Fiedler sees an ethnic literature in which cultural and social traits form a distinctive voice, often ironic. Writer Cynthia Ozick speaks for a covenantal literature that is constantly reviewing the sacred texts of Judaic inheritance. Poet Jacob Glatstein believed that a poem on Buddha or a Hindu god was Jewish as long as it was composed in Yiddish—in effect, that Jewish literature is Jewish by virtue of its language. Some commentators have argued that Jewish literature evinces certain moral qualities, though this is slippery ground. Scholar Harold Bloom holds to the commitment of living in and through texts, wrestling to regain tradition. Finally, Jewish American literature may simply or strictly derive from the author's identity as a Jew. But this most reductive definition again begs the essential question—that of identity.

This anthology means to expand the question of identity to encompass all its turns and folds. "Jewish American literature" signifies an American literature that is Jewish: fiction, poetry, drama, memoir and autobiography, commentary, letters, speeches, monologues, song lyrics, humor, translations, and visual narratives created by authors who admit, address, embrace, and contest their Jewish identity, whether religious, historical, ethnic, psychological, political, cultural, textual, or linguistic.

It may be that in the past, Jewish civilizations survived by cleaving to the righteousness and difference inscribed in sacred texts. Some would hold that this spiritual tenacity is still necessary and sufficient. Possibly so. But with it come wit and self-deprecation, moral dilemma, verbal ingenuity, aspiration, tragedy and joy, families aplenty, nostalgia, satire—a full slice of human life at its most vocal.

Who are the Jews, and, more specifically, who were and are the Jews who settled in this country in greater numbers than they ever have in any other land, including Israel?

A LONG HISTORY BRIEFLY CONVEYED

Any consideration of Jewish American literature requires some knowledge of the history of the Jews. Jewish existence originated in the Middle East at least four thousand years ago. According to the Hebrew calendar, which is based on a lunar month, the year 2000 on our Gregorian calendar is 5760/61. Recorded Jewish history and literature as reflected in the Hebrew Bible—the Tanakh, or Torah, Prophets, Writings—begins more than three thousand years ago; as such, it has been one of the great underpinnings of the Christian and Muslim civilizations as well as of the Jewish people. The long and varied history of the Jews includes centuries of sovereignty over their own kingdoms during biblical times as well as a large presence in classical antiquity. It has been estimated that the Jews comprised 8 percent to 10 percent of the population of the Roman Empire (perhaps 4.5 to 7.0 million Jews) by the end of the first half of the first century. There were also long periods of subjugation and several exiles by foreign imperiums—Egyptian, Assyrian, Persian, Greek, Roman.

The destruction of the First (or Solomon's) Temple in Jerusalem in 586 B.C.E. resulted in the Babylonian Captivity. The destruction of the Second Temple by the Romans in 70 C.E. after the Jews rose in revolt did not result in an immediate diaspora, although some captive Jews were taken by the Roman legions to their camps in the Rhineland to be used as craftspeople, slaves, and concubines. The Jewish population and religious center did gradually shift to Babylonia over two centuries. Earlier than that, there were significant populations of Jews in the Greek-speaking Diaspora for centuries. The Jews came to Europe in significant numbers about 900 C.E., and from Babylonia to Spain beginning around 1000 C.E. Jews moved to southern Italy and then to France around 900 C.E. and north to Germany (*Ashkenaz* is a biblical term that in modern times denotes Germany). These Ashkenazim established significant settlements in Rhineland towns like Speyer, Worms, and Cologne, and, ultimately, a language of their own—Yiddish.

The Jews who settled in Iberia, called Sephardim, developed their own Judeo-Spanish language, Ladino, and their own variations on Jewish ritual. In time, they produced a flourishing civilization for several centuries, living in relative harmony with the Muslim and small Christian populations. During the eleventh and twelfth centuries, they created a golden age of literature, poetry, and philosophy, Maimonides being the most famous of that period's philosophers. The Hebrew poetry produced in Spain during this period was strongly influenced by Arabic models. Quantitative meter was introduced, and for the first time something like a secular Hebrew poetry emerged in the Jewish tradition, including idealized love lyrics, wine songs, satires, and homoerotic poems. In 1492, this civilization was crushed, the Jews being ruthlessly expelled along with the Moorish or African presence as the land was united under Christian sovereigns.

Christian persecution and massacres during the period of the Crusades and in the time of the Plague or Black Death in the fourteenth century made life precarious in Western Europe for the Ashkenazim, and large numbers of Jews responded to invitations from the ruler of Poland to settle in that land and serve as a progressive element in its development. These now–Eastern European Jews had carried with them the Yiddish language and devotion to their religion and sacred texts. In isolation from the development of Western and Central Europe, they developed over six hundred years a unique, dense, and complex civilization. These Jews spread into Lithuania, Russia, Galicia, Romania, and Austria-Hungary, residing for the most part in a network of small towns and villages—shtetls, or *shtetlekh*, and *derfer*. By the end of the nineteenth century, they comprised the largest body of Jews in the world: in 1900, there were 1,328,500 Jews in Western and Central Europe, 1,175,000 in America, and 7,362,000 in eastern and southeastern Europe. They had by then created significant religious institutions—great yeshivas and places of learning in Vilna (the city Napoleon had called "the Jerusalem of Lithuania") and elsewhere—and a vibrant secular literature in Yiddish, epitomized by the work of such early masters as Mendele Moykhr Sforim (1835–1917), Sholem Aleichem (1859–1916), and I. L. Peretz (1852–1915).

Yiddish, written with Hebrew letters, had developed from its Middle High German origins, with about a 10 percent to 15 percent mixture of Hebrew and Aramaic plus some trace elements of Old French and Italian and, later, some Slavic influences, to become a veritable lingua franca of the Jewish people in Europe (and the immigrants to America). Despite the disdain of Hebraists and intellectuals, who regarded it as a "jargon," Yiddish was and remains the repository of one thousand years of Jewish culture and history, and the vehicle of a formidable literature. Although this literature, composed in the nineteenth and twentieth centuries, attempted to reach its audience in their own language, Yiddish, it built on a long tradition of earlier writing in Hebrew (in which the early masters of Yiddish literature were well versed)—the Bible, Talmud, Commentaries—as well as Yiddish precursors in translations of the Bible and in stories and prayers meant largely for women denied training in the sacred tongue.

Eastern European Jews were isolated until the mid-nineteenth century from the early enlightening forces unleashed in Western and Central Europe by the French Revolution and Napoleon's opening of Europe's ghettos. They never had a realistic hope of full citizenship and equal rights in the countries of the Russian czarist empire. Eastern European Jews remained, by and large, steadfastly traditional in religion and culture—overwhelmingly Orthodox, with many Hasidic groupings as well—and even the *maskilim* (the "enlighteners"), especially after the Dreyfus affair in "enlightened" France of the 1890s, were stimulated toward movements of Jewish self-identity and self-emancipation. From among them came the first major theorists of Zionism (not, however, the Hungarian-born founder of the movement, Theodor Herzl), the pioneers of Zionist settlements in Palestine, and the founders of Jewish socialism in the Bund of Jewish workers of Poland and Lithuania. While German, French, English, and Dutch Jews could aspire to citizenship in those countries, and with it the possibility or threat of full acculturation and assimilation, Jews in the east had less experience with such currents. Until, that is, their large migration—the largest in Jewish history (which embraced, ultimately, more than one-third of their number)—to the United States, beginning in the 1880s and lasting until the discriminatory Johnson Act of 1924 restricted immigration from Southern and Eastern Europe. That is where and when the story of Jewish American literature picks up its pace and takes on the dominant characteristics it has displayed up to the present.

THE DREAM OF AMERICA

America's newly arrived Jews were part of a vast number of European immigrants (about 23 million between 1880 and 1920) who were pushed by an explosion of population in the nineteenth century, impoverishment of land and loss of work, and various repressions, and were drawn to the United States by its expanding economy and promise of religious, political, and social freedom and equality. The first Jews in America, however, were twenty-three refugees to New Netherland who came from the Dutch colony of Recife, Brazil, retaken by the Portuguese and the Inquisition in 1654. They were descendants of the Jews driven from Spain in 1492—the "two-faced year" (one of tears, the other of smiles), as Emma Lazarus said in her sonnet *1492*—the same year as Columbus's "discovery" of America. They and their descendants were Sephardic Jews. As described earlier, the Sephardim had their own vernacular, Ladino, and followed a religious ritual somewhat different from that of Ashkenazic Jews, the other stream of Jews from German-speaking and Eastern Europe.

Emma Lazarus was the author, too, of *The New Colossus*, the inspirational poem inscribed at the base of the Statue of Liberty, welcoming the tired, the poor, the "huddled masses yearning to breathe free." Born in America in 1849, daughter of a well-off Sephardic family in New York—her grandparents had been in America at the time of the Revolution—she was an all-but-assimilated writer praised by Emerson in the 1860s. But in the later years of her life (she died in 1887), the horrors of pogroms against the Jews in Europe impelled her to become an ardent Spiritual Zionist—an advocate of a Jewish homeland. In 1882, the *American Hebrew* (a contemporary journal) published a small collection of her works called *Songs of a Semite*. In a sense, her intellectual and literary development reflects a continuity and connectedness among America's Jews generally and its writers specifically.

No matter how "at home" Jews may feel or be, often after considerable struggle with hostility from without and doubt within, what it means or can mean to be a Jew in America and in the world at large has always been an issue, a subject, sometimes a curse (*A klug af Columbus,* "A curse on Columbus," was the Yiddish expression occasionally uttered by dispirited immigrants), more often a hope and creative spur. Even in our time, when American Jews are more integrated in social and economic terms than at any other period in history, when the ample literature they have produced is varied and prized, nonetheless, the thought of the Holocaust and the fateful history shared to some degree by all Jews cannot be far from any Jew's mind—even when it is not mentioned—however assimilated, nonobservant, even nonidentifying they or their work may be.

At the time of the American Revolution, there were under 2,000 Jews in America—most of them Sephardic—comprising only about 0.05 percent of the total population. Immigration, though continuous, increased greatly only in the first third of the nineteenth century so that by the time of the Civil War the Jewish population was about 150,000 (0.47 percent of the whole country). The major source of immigrants between 1830 and 1880 were German Jews (in 1880, there were 250,000 Jews in America). After that, the numbers skyrocketed, mostly Jews from Eastern Europe, 2.3 million in all by 1924, when the total Jewish population was 4.2 million (over 3.00 percent of the U.S. total).

The German Jews had spread out into the Midwest and West, where there were many business and mercantile opportunities. Often starting as peddlers, filling a need in isolated communities, they rose into the middle class, acculturating quickly. They acquired in America or brought to that country skills as merchants and businesspeople, bankers and thinkers, philanthropists and theologians, journalists and editors. Levi Strauss supplied denims (the hardy blue cloth from Nîmes, France—that is, "de Nîmes") to California miners, and German Jews helped found many of San Francisco's major cultural institutions. German Jewish names were displayed on department stores in all the large cities: Boston, New York, Philadelphia, Pittsburgh, Cincinnati, St. Louis, Dallas, Tucson. Bankers and financiers like August Belmont and Jacob Schiff (a founder of the American Jewish Committee in 1906) played important roles in U.S. history during and after the Civil War and well into the twentieth century.

Rabbi Isaac Mayer Wise (1819–1900), born in Bohemia, immigrated to the United States in 1846, becoming the father of Reform Judaism in this country, founder of the Union of American Hebrew Congregations (1873) and the Hebrew Union College (1875). Reform Judaism became the dominant branch of the Jewish religion in America before the large influx of Orthodox Jews from Eastern Europe. Solomon Schechter (1850–1915) was instrumental in founding Conservative Judaism, a result of his studying in Vienna and Berlin the "Science of Judaism" (*Wissenschaft des Judentums*), which relied upon careful new biblical-historical scholarship; he also became president of the Jewish Theological Seminary in 1901. Conservative Judaism is now the largest of the four main branches of the religion in America. The others are Orthodox Judaism, Reform Judaism, and the relatively recent Reconstructionist Judaism, which was founded by Rabbi Mordecai M. Kaplan (1881–1983) in 1934 and which incorporates elements of all the other branches but regards Judaism as primarily a civilization—dynamic, diverse, evolving.

Besides their impressive institution building, German Jewish theologians produced journals and newspapers, which usually had a religious or spiritual orientation while addressing the contemporary problems of their parishioners and readers. Jews published essays, verse, and short fiction, but the literary output, relatively small, did not reach far beyond the Jewish readership. The literary emergence of American Jews, from the margins of American life and culture at the turn of the twentieth century into its mainstream by mid-century, was accomplished only after the mass arrival of Eastern European Jewry.

Numbering now about 5.5 million, Jews in America comprise only about 2.5 percent of the total population, but they have interacted with and affected the nation's life and thought at every significant point. Many of the works in our anthology will reflect this influence, presenting a literature that mediates between Jewishness and Americanness, broadly conceived, and that illuminates aspects of each, even as a creative synthesis is often achieved. But before turning to the literary presence of Jewish writers in American life and literature, let us look closely at the social, economic, and political participation of Jews as a whole.

JEWISH LIFE IN AMERICA

When Asser Levy, one of the small group of Jews who landed in New Netherland in 1652, applied in 1653 for membership in the colony's armed defense force, he was refused. Governor Peter Stuyvesant had not welcomed the refugees and was prevented from turning them out only by order of his superiors, the Dutch West India Company of Amsterdam, whose board of directors included several Jews. The directors felt that the new arrivals had nowhere else to go and had proven themselves loyal and most useful to Holland in the wars against their enemies. Stuyvesant had urged that "the deceitful race . . . enemies and blasphemers of the name of Christ" be expelled. Within a few years, the Jews won the Burgher Right, but the struggles for rights and equality—freedom to practice their religion—went on, to be renewed when the English, who lagged behind the Dutch in their treatment of Jews, won the colony and renamed it New York. Finally, in 1740, Jews, along with foreign Protestants and Quakers (but not Catholics), were allowed "naturalization" and could omit the words "upon the true Faith of a Christian" from their oath.

This act presaged the achievements of the American Revolution and the new Constitution and Bill of Rights that followed. In 1787, the Constitutional Convention decreed that no religious test would be required of officeholders, and two years later Congress ratified the Bill of Rights, whose First Amendment assures the separation of church and state as well as other fundamental rights—free speech, assembly, and petition.

In 1790, the Newport, Rhode Island, synagogue, the oldest Jewish congregation in the United States, grateful for "the blessings of civil and religious liberty" that they enjoyed, wrote to the new president of the nation, wishing him well as he assumed his duties. President Washington responded eloquently:

> The citizens of the United States of America have the right to applaud themselves for having given to mankind examples of an enlarged and liberal policy worthy of imitation.
>
> All possess alike liberty of conscience and immunities of citizenship. It is now no more that toleration is spoken of, as if it was by indulgence of one class of people, that another enjoyed the exercise of their inherent natural rights. For happily the government of the United States, which gives to bigotry no sanction, to persecution no assistance, requires only that they who live under its protection should demean themselves as good citizens, in giving it on all occasions their effectual support.

Good citizens Jews proved themselves to be, although calumnies and prejudices surfaced from time to time. They participated in the growth and struggles of the nation as best they could and were involved in the great issues of the day.

An early advocate of women's rights and an abolitionist, Ernestine Rose, a Polish Jewish immigrant, spoke ardently at the National Woman's Rights Convention at Syracuse, New York, in 1852, declaring, "I am an example of the universality of our claims; for not American women only, but a daughter of poor, crushed Poland, and the down-trodden and persecuted people called the Jews, 'a child of Israel' pleads for equal rights for her sex."

Jews played a role in the settlement of American frontiers, from Pennsylvania, Virginia, and Ohio in the early days to the more familiar American West. They participated in the creation of the Texas Republic in 1836 and in the Mexican War in 1846–48. They were an early presence, economically and militarily, in California. One of the best-known figures in military actions in California was Uriah Levy, a Naval Academy graduate who attained the rank of commodore, the highest in the U.S. Navy, before the Civil War.

Solomon Nuñez Carvalho (1815–1897), from a prominent Charleston Sephardic family, was recruited by Colonel John C. Frémont to be the official photographer on his expedition to find a railroad route across the Continental Divide. Carvalho had learned daguerreotyping from Samuel F. B. Morse and had become one of the earliest photographers of the Rocky Mountains and of American Indians. Other Jews supported Frémont in the founding of the

Republican party and in his candidacy for president in 1856. Frémont's abolitionist sentiments were actively displayed in August 1861, when, as a major general and commander of the Western Department of the Union army, he issued an order emancipating all the slaves in that department. He and his entire staff, including a Jew, Captain Isidore Bush, were then discharged from the army.

Three Jews rode with John Brown in "bleeding Kansas" in 1855 against the proslavery Missouri "border ruffians." August Bondi (whose family fled Vienna after the failed 1848 revolution), Theodore Wiener (a 250-pound Polish immigrant), and Jacob Benjamin (about whom little is known) participated in the battles of Black Jack, Osowatomie, and others. According to Bondi's later narrative of these events—*With John Brown in Kansas* and in the Kansas Archives—at Black Jack, while advancing up the hillside in tall grass, bending over as bullets from the Missouri sharpshooters whistled by, he turned to Wiener and asked in German Yiddish (as he wrote), "Nu, was meinen Sie jetzt?" (Well, what do you think now?), and Wiener answered in Hebrew, "Sov omon [sic] muves" (The end of man is death). They all survived, Bondi going on to a notable public career in Kansas.

Until the 1850s, the views of Jews toward slavery were similar to those of non-Jews North and South (Southern Jews comprised only 15 percent of all American Jews before the Civil War). In that decade, a large influx of German Jews who were decisively antislavery doubled the number of Jews in the country. During the war, some 6,500 Jews served in the Union army (1,300 served in the Confederate forces), hundreds became officers, seven won Medals of Honor. The Emancipation Proclamation was telegraphed on January 1, 1863, by a young immigrant Jew from Bohemia, Edward Rosewater. Despite this, there were occasional anti-Semitic incidents in the ranks—familiar to soldiers in all of America's wars through World War II at least—and an infamous General Order issued by Ulysses S. Grant in December 1862 expelled Jews "as a class" from the Department of Tennessee because he believed they were speculators and traded with the enemy. After many protests, President Lincoln rescinded the order within three weeks.

After the war, the Jewish and non-Jewish middle class in the North benefited from the expansion of the economy. The number of Jewish merchants and new businesses grew, and many of them prospered, especially in the ready-made clothing industries, which were given a boost during the war. A new class of bankers and financiers arose—Jacob Schiff, August Belmont, principals of the firm of Kuhn, Loeb & Co., the notorious Jay Gould—important but by no means as numerous or powerful as Morgan, Vanderbilt, Astor, Rockefeller, and the other non-Jewish titans of finance and industry of the period. They were, nevertheless, objects of suspicion and attack in times of economic crisis and depression, as in the 1870s and 1890s. Social anti-Semitism arose as well in the latter part of the century, although not as vicious or foundational for political movements as was the rise of ideological anti-Semitism in Europe. In 1877, for example, the Hilton-owned Grand Hotel in Saratoga, a fashionable resort at the time, refused to accept banker Joseph Seligman and his family as guests, which caused a great stir in the press. Boycotts and racial prejudice at resorts, in housing, in schools and universities became more common even as the social and economic conditions of Jews improved generally. All of this occurred just as the large wave of Eastern European Jewry was to break upon America's shores.

The older community of mostly German Jews had created educational, relief, antidiscrimination, and philanthropic institutions that were to be a great help to the new immigrants. But attitudes toward the newcomers were at first ambivalent. The largely acculturated and accomplished German Jews regarded with concern such a large influx of impoverished and seemingly backward brethren. Abraham Cahan, the leading Yiddish journalist of the new era, saw this group as lacking a fourth grader's knowledge of history and geography—they were a people, he said, whose Atlantic migration had taken them from a largely medieval existence to a modern one. Whether that was true or not, the urge to "Americanize" them prevailed; existing agencies tried to make them appear less "foreign" and less threatening to the well-established German Jewish community. In turn, the newcomers resented this condescension from the "uptown crowd." In time, friction between the groups abated as the newer immigrants created their own social patterns and accommodations.

Because of their numbers and dense settlements—mostly in New York initially, then in Boston, Chicago, and other large cities—these newer immigrant Jews established a notable culture and distinctive institutions. Overwhelmingly working class at first—largely in the apparel industries—they created a trade-union movement and a network of social, educational, political, and fraternal organizations. Starting often as "cockroach manufacturers" (a phrase of Abraham Cahan's), their entrepreneurs wrested control of the garment industry from the Germans, providing the basis for a progressive middle class.

A plethora of newspapers and journals appeared—mostly in Yiddish, though some were in Russian, Hebrew, and English—that answered to a variety of constituencies. By the time of the First World War, a vibrant Jewish theater challenged the prevailing sentimentality and melodrama of New York's mainstream. And pioneering Hebrew and Zionist literature emerged, accompanying a body of intellectuals, poets, and writers who made New York, rather than Warsaw or Odessa, the capital of a resurgent Yiddish literature. All of this generated a truly Jewish American literature.

Yet anti-immigration sentiment grew from the 1890s onward, much of it directed at Jews, to judge from the Anti-Immigrant League begun by Henry Cabot Lodge and others in 1896, the rise of the Ku Klux Klan, and virulent anti-Semitism in Henry Ford's newspaper, the *Dearborn Independent.* The Immigrant Acts of 1921 and 1924 restricted immigration from Southern and Eastern Europe by setting an annual quota of 1 percent of the national origins of those who had arrived in the United States in 1890, a year of little immigration from these regions. The effect upon Jewish immigration was pronounced and, ultimately, in the 1930s, when many Jewish refugees from Nazism sought admission to the United States, catastrophic. American prejudice proved fatal for hundreds of thousands.

This brake on immigration also meant the gradual demise of Yiddish as the principal medium of exchange among the mass of Jews. Pressures toward Americanization quickened, especially among the younger, American-born generation. More and more Jews began writing and publishing in English while entering American jobs, schools, and culture at its highest and lowest levels. Many went into vaudeville and the popular theater, Tin Pan Alley (from Irving Berlin to George Gershwin), Broadway and the legitimate stage, then movies and all arenas of American culture.

While thriving in these ways, Jews still struggled to maintain an identity beyond the immigrant generation. Despite pressures to "make it" in a relatively tolerant American society and to divest themselves of "foreign" or "ethnic" qualities, Jews as a whole did not "melt." Traditional values held out (to some degree) against or alongside Americanization and modernization. Yet most Jewish Americans adapted to the new culture—not necessarily abandoning tradition, but transforming it, learning to live as Jews and Americans.

Throughout the nineteenth century, as we have seen, Reform Judaism was the dominant strain among observant Jews. Then, with the influx from Eastern Europe, Orthodoxy took hold. From the end of unrestricted immigration through the final years of the twentieth century, Conservative Judaism, a kind of middle way, flourished along with Reform, while Orthodoxy and Hasidic practice enjoyed a renewal in many places. But, overall, Jewish religious observance today is in decline; more than 50 percent of American Jews have no synagogue or religious affiliation.

Religious affiliation was challenged early in the twentieth century by secular movements claiming a newer kind of Jewish identity. Thus, with the harsh realities of World War II and the establishment of the State of Israel, Zionism, which was moderately active after its founding in 1896 in Europe, has engaged many American Jews, religious or not. Likewise, Jewish socialism, especially among Eastern European workers and their descendants, has held messianic as well as practical appeal. In the 1920s and 1930s, Jewish social democrats such as Abraham Cahan, Sidney Hillman, and David Dubinsky (the latter two leaders of clothing workers' unions) fomented unionization and helped shape the policies of the Democratic party of Franklin Delano Roosevelt and his New Deal. These socialists clashed frequently with the Communist party, created after the Russian Revolution, which grew during the Great Depression and the rising fascist menace at home and abroad. Although few Jews were actually communists, as Gerald Sorin observes, during the 1930s they comprised 35 percent to 40 percent of the party (as compared with 15 percent in the 1920s), most of them leaving the party after the Moscow purges of 1936–38 and the nefarious nonaggression pact between the Soviet Union and Nazi Germany that opened the way for Germany's military aggressions.

Interestingly enough, the majority of American Jews, neither formally religious nor politically radical, consistently support the Democratic party and are more liberal than their high socioeconomic position might suggest. What's more, Jewish voluntary organizations abound. In the 1930s, for example, 17,000 organizations represented American Jews' political, social, economic, welfare, and defense needs.

What with secular and reformist elements and the wave of economic opportunity after World War II, plus ever-increasing rates of intermarriage, it seemed as if Judaism might rapidly vanish in America. But countervailing forces have arrested that possibility. The founding of the State of Israel in 1948, a growing awareness (around the 1961 Eichmann trial) of the Shoah/Holocaust that had nearly destroyed European Jewry, and a surge of affiliation with Israel during the 1967 Six Day War—all this galvanized Jewish American conscience and consciousness, both secular and religious, even as the radical postwar opening of society to Jews in all spheres ensured their Americanism.

At present, Jews are active in government, universities, finance, the media, and industries of all kinds. It is an American story, characteristically enriched by the persistent vein of self-critique and anxiety in Jewish American literature.

Many voices on the American scene—displayed in the writing of American Jews from Abraham Cahan to Saul Bellow and from Philip Roth to Grace Paley, Tillie Olsen, Cynthia Ozick, Allegra Goodman, Steve Stern, Mark Mirsky, and dozens of others—call upon Jewish Americans to examine who they are, where they came from, what fate they share, what spiritual, ethical, and other qualities they must cultivate as they make their lives in this world. If, as Henry James once put it, being American is a complex fate, how much more so is it to be a Jewish American?

LITERARY CURRENTS

Jewish literary creativity in America has existed throughout the history of Jews in America, and the present anthology documents these literary currents from the beginning. Our vision is one of inclusion, acknowledging the diversity of Jewish writing in the United States, especially by authors who wrote in the Jewish languages—ignored or given token representation in most other collections. Writers of Yiddish and Hebrew and those nurtured in Ladino or Judeo-Arabic environments expand our notion of Jewish American literature. So, too, do the earlier writers who could not possibly have grasped our current sense of ethnicity and multiculturalism. We have divided the anthology chronologically into five major sections: (1) *Literature of Arrival, 1654–1880;* (2) *The Great Tide, 1881–1924;* (3) *From Margin to Mainstream in Difficult Times, 1924–1945;* (4) *Achievement and Ambivalence, 1945–1973;* (5) *Wandering and Return: Literature since 1973*. In each period, writings by Jews have reflected the concerns and styles of their American surroundings. Here we add that, to our regret, for purely pragmatic reasons of length and questions of copyright, we have had to limit our selection to authors in the United States and thus have not been able to include the fine writers who contributed to the parallel tradition of Jewish Canadian literature in English, Yiddish, and Hebrew.

Literature of Arrival, 1654–1880, spanning the first 226 years of Jews in America, tells a story of the benefits and responsibilities of citizenship that European Jews experienced upon reaching the New World. Initially, Jews such as Abraham de Lucena and others in their 1656 petition to New Amsterdam's governor Peter Stuyvesant demanded political and civil rights in the colonies. Later, Rebecca Gratz in her letters and Isaac Mayer Wise in his editorial *The Fourth of July, 1858* extolled the equality afforded them by the democratic values of the United States. In contrast to patriotic exuberance, Isaac Leeser's sermon warned against the seductive assimilation that this same democracy promises. Writers such as Penina Moïse and Adah Isaacs Menken, for instance, translated or rewrote Hebrew liturgical and biblical texts; others, such as Nathan Mayer and Emma Lazarus, created fictional or poetic versions of Jewish history. We also find here writings that have no explicitly Jewish qualities but metaphorically reflect moral concerns that might be considered Jewish, such as the play by Mordecai Manuel Noah. These early figures found their way quickly and smoothly, it seems, into an idiom in English that marks them as American writers. Nowhere in this early literature do we find a sense of Jewish ethnicity.

The Great Tide, 1881–1924, covering the forty years of massive Eastern-European Jewish immigration, focuses upon questions of language. In contrast to the earlier immigrants, who published little in their native languages of Ladino, German, and Czech, the new immigrants from Eastern Europe wrote prolifically and insistently in Yiddish, the language they brought with them. These writers established a flourishing press and theater in New York, with smaller offshoots in Philadelphia, Boston, Cleveland, Chicago, Milwaukee, and Los Angeles. From these forums of popular culture, a serious literary endeavor grew. Yehoash, contemporary of the pragmatist Labor poets, turned his learnedness to literary rather than political ends and began the task of making Yiddish a literary language. The poets of two modernist movements, the Yunge and introspectivism, expanded and enveloped Yehoash's project through the first half of the twentieth century.

For many writers, though, the question of whether to write in English or Yiddish was a basic one. Those who chose English—Mary Antin, Abraham Cahan, and Anzia Yezierska, for instance—struggled to master an English prose style that could fulfill their artistic needs and portray the social reality of their experiences as immigrants. From these efforts came a new kind of American English, infused with Yiddish words, inflections, and syntax. Works like Antin's *The Promised Land*, Cahan's *The Rise of David Levinsky*, and Yezierska's *Hungry Hearts* drew in the mainstream reading public, which responded to the language and the stories of the immigrants' struggles and achievements.

This new Jewish American idiom was not at all desirable for Sidney L. Nyburg or Edna Ferber, who found their own American voices in works like Nyburg's *The Chosen People* and Ferber's *Fanny Herself*. Other writers appearing in this section chose to develop what both Benjamin Harshav and Irving Howe describe as the new American literature in Yiddish that at the same time kept its connections to movements in Warsaw, Vilna, and Kiev. Modernist poets Moyshe-Leyb Halpern, Celia Dropkin, and Anna Margolin, and fiction writers Lamed Shapiro, Joseph Opatoshu, and Fradl Shtok took on various subjects from American life, the vexed transitions of immigration, and the Old World seen anew, altering the texture of their Yiddish language to reflect cultural interchanges. Nonetheless, this Yiddish writing retained its Jewishness through its own linguistic and cultural independence from the American milieu. The Yiddish-speaking immigrant writers—both those who wrote in English and those who wrote in Yiddish—set the stage for the notion of ethnicity that is central to the idea of Jewish American literature in later periods.

At the same time, Jewish humor flourished. Fanny Brice on stage and Groucho Marx in the movies became famous precursors of later comedians, many of whom are discussed in the *Jewish Humor* section of this anthology.

From Margin to Mainstream, 1924–1945 begins with the Johnson Acts of 1921 and 1924, legislation that halted mass immigration, and ends with the conclusion of the Second World War. These cataclysmic years saw intensive literary production, when the literary (as well as literal) children of immigrants came of age and became a force on the American cultural scene. As more Jewish writers published in English for mainstream readers, the debate over which language to write in receded, yet modernist experimentation with language engaged the introspectivist Yiddish poets Jacob Glatstein and A. Leyeles as well as the English poets Charles Reznikoff and Louis Zukofsky, and fiction writers such as Gertrude Stein and Henry Roth. Two writers transformed Joycean modernism into a Jewish medium: Glatstein in his Yiddish poems, which break down the elements of language through memory and the senses, and Henry Roth in his novel *Call It Sleep*, which layers Yiddish, Polish, and English in a child's psyche. Roth also invoked Freud, as did J. L. Teller in his Yiddish poems. Political and social engagement emerged as a theme of Jewish American writing in Michael Gold's *Jews without Money*, a novel that directly descends from the Yiddish Labor poems of Morris Rosenfeld and David Edelshtadt. Tess Slesinger and Muriel Rukeyser explore social consciousness and feminism in fiction and poetry that unknowingly pick up the threads stitched by Yiddish writers Yente Serdatzky and Fradl Shtok. A palpable ethnicity can be sensed in the works of Edward Dahlberg, Meyer Levin, Clifford Odets, Delmore Schwartz, and Arthur Miller, whether or not their characters are called Jewish. And Isaac Rosenfeld's essay evinces an intellectual engagement typical of much Jewish American writing.

With *Achievement and Ambivalence, 1945–1973*, the defining lines of Jewish American writing are altered dramatically. Jewish American literature's ethnic stamp marks the characters created by Bernard Malamud, Saul Bellow, and Philip Roth, writers who also stretched the formal possibilities of American fiction. As much as their characters' ethnicity, the leftist and feminist politics of Tillie Olsen and Grace Paley define their work as Jewish American. Bellow protests the category of Jewish American writing entirely, yet his translation of Isaac Bashevis Singer's *Gimpel the Fool* erases the distinction between Yiddish language and Yiddish content, converting Singer's fiction about Eastern Europe into a new kind of Jewish American literature in English.

The translation of Yiddish literature into English grows sharply with the publication of short-story and poetry anthologies in 1954 and 1969, overseen by American intellectual Irving Howe and Yiddish poet Eliezer Greenberg; and Howe's 1976 *World of Our Fathers* recasts the American bicentennial as a moment of Jewish ethnic awakening. Cynthia Ozick's fiction and essays depict ethnic Jews through a prose thickened with Jewish texts (Hebrew, Yiddish, Ladino) in order to draw Jewish literature away from what she sees as the shallows of ethnicity into the depths of covenantal Judaism, attempting to convert English into a new tongue imbued with Jewishness.

Meanwhile, poets from various points on the compass—Carl Rakosi and George Oppen, David Ignatow and Howard Nemerov, Denise Levertov and Allen Ginsberg, Anthony Hecht and Irving Feldman—entered the stream of American poetry, both adding and conforming to it. Like Bellow, Malamud, Roth, Ozick, and others, and spurred in part by Elie Wiesel, they struggled somehow to integrate the Holocaust along with other legacies into Jewish American self-reflection.

Yiddish writers—Kadya Molodowsky, Malka Heifetz Tussman, Chaim Grade, and Isaac Bashevis Singer—continued to publish after the Holocaust, voicing their Yiddish stanzas and paragraphs against the immeasurable loss of Eastern European Jewry. Hebrew writing in America, which had begun earlier in the century, blossomed briefly in the prose and poetry of Ephraim E. Lisitzky and the modernist Gabriel Preil as well as in the works of Shimon Halkin and Naphtali Herz Imber, the Zionist who wrote *Hatikva*, Israel's national anthem. But as the Jewish community grew first in Palestine and then in the State of Israel, most of these writers immigrated to Israel, and Hebraic culture in America gradually diminished. New Sephardic writers began to publish, among them Stanley Sultan, Victor Perera, and Emma Adatto Schlesinger, whose writing in English, laced with Ladino and Judeo-Arabic phrases and flavors, expands Jewish American speech to include this other ethnicity.

In short, the ethnic nature of Jewish American literature, informed by echoes and translations from the immigrant Jewish languages, becomes linked to an idea of a Jewish American identity, fulfilling Horace M. Kallen's earlier attack on the notion of America as a "melting pot": in his view, to be democratic and American is to be ethnic.

This same era saw the rise of popular musical theater on Broadway. Many of the best composers, lyricists, and playwrights not only drew upon their Jewish backgrounds to create works that reflected Jewish experience in America, but were equally adept at imagining the nation's South and Midwest. The special section on Broadway in the anthology highlights this phenomenon in Jewish American literature.

Wandering and Return: Literature since 1973 shows the broad diversity of modern Jewish American literature. Questions of contemporary ethnic identity as well as attempts to reconfigure the experience and historical feel of the immigrant generation color the writings of E. L. Doctorow, Max Apple, Mark Mirsky, and Chaim Potok. As the children of survivors come of age, many write about the Holocaust they did not directly experience, thereby shaping contemporary Jewish awareness, as in *MAUS* by cartoonist Art Spiegelman. Some poets write from a political standpoint, extrapolating from the aims of the Yiddish Labor poets and socially conscious Jewish American writers in English of an earlier period. Politics of the Left and of feminism flow into a kind of Jewish American literary identity in the poetry of Adrienne Rich and Irena Klepfisz. But language as identity braids itself in here, too, as in Klepfisz's bilingual Yiddish-English poems, which also manifest a political point of view. Other poets return to Jewish subjects and texts, if not to the Jewish languages—even poets who, in most of their work, might subscribe to Lionel Trilling's "intellectual Jewishness," such as Robert Pinsky. Jerome Rothenberg sometimes reconfigures English as a Jewish language in his poems. Allegra Goodman writes fiction about modern Orthodox Jews from New York to Honolulu. Jacqueline Osherow's poems echo the Yiddish poets who populate the two major bilingual anthologies of Yiddish poetry of the mid-1980s: Benjamin and Barbara Harshav's *American Yiddish Poetry* (1986) and Irving Howe, Ruth R. Wisse, and Khone Shmeruk's *The Penguin Book of Modern Yiddish Verse* (1987). Notably, many of the translators in these volumes are English-language Jewish American poets and writers whose translations abound in several sections of this anthology as well, among them John Hollander, Adrienne Rich, Irving Feldman, and Cynthia Ozick.

Finally, with the section *Jews Translating Jews*, American Jewish poets bring their foreign predecessors and counterparts into the American bloodstream. When Emma Lazarus translates the German Heinrich Heine or Chana Bloch the Israeli Yehuda Amichai, we witness a transmission at the heart of tradition, an endlessly regenerative dialectic between Jewish literary identity and American literary creativity.

Literature of Arrival, 1654–1880

That the American colonies were founded in order to secure religious freedom for all is an often-repeated, often-criticized statement about the founding of the New World. Contemporary historians have objected to this generalization because it veils the fact that many colonists, such as the Puritans in New England and the Catholics in Maryland, while seeking their own freedom to worship, were intolerant of dissenters and those of other religions, and because many colonies were founded for economic, not religious, reasons. The accuracy of this statement, however, should not be overlooked when studying the Jewish settlers in the New World. The history of the Jews since the destruction of the First Temple in 586 B.C.E.—and the literature that recorded it—has been one of displacement, exile, and persecution. The earliest writings of Jews in America also record migration, yet they contain little of the misfortunes that the Jews of previous centuries had endured. This is a literature of arrival, and the term *arrival* should be understood literally as well as figuratively. The selections not only narrate the story of how the Jewish settlers arrived in the New World, but also document the euphoria of these immigrants upon arriving in a place that they would not soon have to leave, one where they would not be persecuted. In this land, Jews would flourish.

ORIGINS

What did it mean to to be Jewish in this early period? What did it mean to be American? How do these two identities fit together to form a literature and a literary heritage? These questions will reappear throughout the anthology. Because this period of Jewish American history is much less known than the later periods, we need to add another question to this list: Who were the first Jews to settle the New World?

The first Jews to arrive on American soil were Sephardic Jews, Jews of Spanish and Portuguese descent. The Spanish and Portuguese Inquisitions of the fifteenth and sixteenth centuries forced the Jews who had been living and prospering in Spain and Portugal for eight hundred years to convert, to become secret Jews (Marranos, Conversos, or "New Christians"), or to leave. Many of those who left found their way to the Netherlands, where the expanding Dutch Empire welcomed them for their wealth, their trade connections, and their skills and professions.

The Dutch tolerated the Jews' religious practices and permitted them to participate freely in the economic community. This freedom allowed the

Jews to take part in the Dutch colonization of the New World. Thus, the first Jews came to the Americas not to flee persecution, but, like their Gentile counterparts, to seek their fortune. From Amsterdam, Jews set out for Jamaica, Curaçao, Suriname, Brazil to establish trade routes. Persecution, however, did follow them when the Portuguese conquered these colonies and extended the Inquisition to the New World. In the autumn of 1654, twenty-three Jews sailed for another Dutch colony: New Netherland in North America.

These Sephardic Jews were joined in New Netherland by a handful of Ashkenazic Jews, Jews from Poland and Germany. Between 1654 and 1820, more Jews arrived from Europe and settled in other new centers: Newport, Philadelphia, Baltimore, Charleston, Savannah. In 1776, at the start of the American Revolution, some 2,500 Jews were living in the American colonies, including many who had come from Central and Western Europe to escape war, poverty, and persecution. After 1820, more Ashkenazic Jews immigrated and soon greatly outnumbered the original Sephardic settlers, who, nonetheless, maintained their positions of leadership and power in the original Jewish settlements.

In 1825, there were 3,000 Jews in the United States, a number that doubled by 1840. Only eight years later, that number reached 50,000, and by 1880, approximately 240,000 Jews lived in America. Still, Jews made up less than 1 percent of the general population, which was now moving westward across the country in large numbers. Jewish immigrants, too, headed for the larger midwestern and western settlements of Cleveland, Chicago, Omaha, San Francisco, and the agricultural regions of Minnesota and the Dakotas. While the earliest settlers—especially the Sephardim—had largely been prosperous merchants, by midcentury the picture of the typical immigrant was of a poor, young, single, and unskilled person. Whether in cities or in the countryside, Jews typically became peddlers. The more successful of these peddlers graduated into small businesses, becoming shopkeepers and entrepreneurs.

These original settlers came to the New World with their own set of literary traditions. In Europe, Jewish life was governed by the sacred texts of Judaism—the Tanakh (Torah, Prophets, and Writings—that is, the ancient Hebrew Bible)—the Talmud (ca. 500 C.E.), and vast numbers of legal, ethical, and exegetical literature composed in Hebrew and Aramaic from the early Middle Ages (ca. 1000 C.E.) through the eighteenth century. Both Ashkenazic and Sephardic Jews added to this body of sacred literature by writing liturgical and secular poetry, philosophical and mystical works, as well as sacred martyrologies that recounted the decimation of Jewish communities by Crusaders and Inquisitors. By the mid-sixteenth century, the Jews of Western and Central Europe were publishing popular religious literature in their vernacular—the Germanic-Jewish language that had originated in the tenth century and that later became known as Yiddish. This literature included translations of the Hebrew Bible, epic poems embellishing biblical stories such as the *Shmuel Bukh* (1544), and literature for women such as Rabbi Jacob ben Isaac Ashkenazi's 1590s *Tsenerene* (Ze'enah U-Re'enah), a homiletic interpretation of the Bible, and the *tkhines*, supplicatory prayers for and often by women.

Holding fast to their religious beliefs, the Jews in Europe lived under severe economic and political oppression. Their survival as a people was in constant jeopardy as, century after century, church and state attempted to convert or kill them. As a result, Jewish writing reflected their main concern: to keep their faith and tradition alive. For these Jews, literature had a clear, pragmatic function. They did not write for individual expression or to explore the imagination; rather, they intended to influence, to teach, and to promote the welfare of the Jewish people.

THE CHALLENGE OF EQUALITY

The earliest literature of the first Jews in the American colonies and the new nation reflects the excitement of opportunity and good fortune as well as the responsibility to the larger community. In Europe, anti-Semitism had a debilitating effect on the livelihood of the Jews; in America, anti-Semitism ceased to be the defining structure of a Jew's life. While there may have been occasional expressions of anti-Semitism, these feelings—whether expressed publicly or privately—had no legal force. As early as 1656, Peter Stuyvesant (governor of New Netherland) was rebuked by the directors of the Dutch West India Company, the corporation that financed the business venture that opened the settlement of New Netherland, when he had attempted to forbid colonial Jews to buy property or participate in the militia. The first entry in this section of the anthology, *To the Honorable Director General and Council of New Netherlands,* was written by several newly arrived Jewish traders who protested unequal treatment. In 1657, Jews in New Netherland were granted the Burgher Right, somewhat equivalent to citizenship.

These equal rights continued when the British captured New Netherland in 1664 and renamed it New York. With the exception of exclusion from political life (that is, holding office or voting), Jews in the original thirteen colonies were the victims of no government-sanctioned anti-Semitism. This milieu of religious tolerance encouraged many of the Jews to fight the British in the war for American independence. Two of our selections describe the participation of individual Jews in the American Revolution. A diary entry by Mordecai Sheftall, a soldier in Washington's army, describes his capture and imprisonment by the British. Another selection, a letter from "a Jew Broker" to a Quaker lawyer and Tory, is attributed to Haym Salomon, one of the principle financial backers of the Revolution. Even Haim Karigal, a visiting rabbi from Palestine who preached the first sermon at Newport's synagogue, could not help but get involved in issues of revolution. Karigal, however, warned the congregants in the primarily Tory-sympathizing audience that one needed to bow to the forces of authority, divine or otherwise.

When the new nation achieved self-governance, the unequivocal commitment to religious tolerance advocated by George Washington and even more by Thomas Jefferson secured the Jews' rights. By 1820, American Jews could hold office and vote, thus making them full citizens in the new republic. Their commitment to nation continued through this period and is evidenced in Rebecca Gratz's mid-nineteenth-century letters to her brother and sister-in-law in Kentucky. Gratz, writing from Philadelphia, extends her sympathies to them for the death of their son, a Union soldier in the Civil War. She anguishes over the division of the nation and her Confederate cousins. In fact, Jews from the North fought Jews from the South. National loyalties superseded religious and familial ties for Jews, just as they did for other Americans.

Gratz's letters highlight one of the greatest challenges that the New World presented to the Jews: How could American Jews balance their religious practices with their national culture and allegiance? Because they were offered—and ultimately guaranteed—the complete rights of citizens, American Jews identified as fully with their new nation as with their dispersed and migratory people. This attachment presented them with the tensions, the collisions, and the benefits of being Jewish Americans and American Jews.

When the Jews arrived in America, they needed to establish organizations that would enable them to observe the Jewish rituals and laws that had defined their lives in Europe. Through the mid-nineteenth century in Europe, the most fundamental necessities of Jewish life—the availability of kosher food, a sanctified cemetery, a place of worship, as well as the performance of circumcision and marriage rites, and the organization of schools, law courts, business associations, and charities—were organized by the Kehillah, the internal government of each Jewish community, led by the Kahal, its elected officials. The Kahal also acted as an intermediary between the Jewish community and the often-hostile Christian government. In the New World, the Kahal was never reconstituted: the democratic American government and the more hospitable reception of Jews made such intervention unnecessary. However, Jews still needed to establish community organizations that would provide them with the practical means to fulfill the traditional religious obligations that defined their lives as Jews.

To an extent, the American synagogue became responsible for maintaining these rituals. Sephardic merchants in Newport, Rhode Island, erected its earliest synagogue in 1763. In subsequent decades, other major centers would erect synagogues for their populace. Yet not every Jew who arrived in the United States would or could (because of geographical constraints) join a synagogue. Some gave up religious practice. Others started to define their religious obligations differently. Jews of German descent had been introduced to the Enlightenment theology of Moses Mendelssohn (1729–1786) that argued that Jews "should adopt the mores and constitutions of the country" in which they lived. Mendelssohn's ideas resulted from the new political situation of German Jews, who had recently acquired the status of citizens. German rabbis and laity sought to make Judaism more compatible with citizenship; from this desire, Reform Judaism would be born in the early 1800s.

Reform Judaism was uniquely compatible with life in the United States. In the mid-nineteenth century, the American Reform movement adapted Abraham Geiger's scientific ideas that perceived Judaism as an evolving organism and Samuel Holdheim's theology that retained Judaism's monotheism and morality but rejected the "ceremonial law" of the ancient Temple and nation. The Pittsburgh Platform of 1885 declared that "all such Mosaic and rabbinical laws as regulated diet, priestly purity, and dress originated in ages and under the influence of ideas entirely foreign to our present mental and spiritual state. . . . Their observance is apt rather to obstruct than to further modern spiritual elevation." Jews who would settle in small communities in Ohio or Nebraska faced almost insuperable obstacles observing the laws of kashruth. Shopkeepers could not afford to close their stores on the Jewish Sabbath and lose Gentile customers. Nor was it possible, without a sizable Jewish community, to build and sustain the ritual purification bath (mikveh). Thus, Reform Judaism spread rapidly in the country as the laity instituted changes in ritual that Americanized the practice of Judaism: congregations decided to translate parts of the Hebrew liturgy into English and shorten the service; they seated women together with men; they played the organ to accompany prayer; they eliminated the need for a head covering (yarmulke) and prayer shawl (tallis). Rabbis who had been paid to emigrate from Germany or England in order to lead the nascent American congregations were often disgruntled by this hodgepodge of reform and sought to rationalize these changes. Rabbi Isaac Mayer Wise, a leading moderate spokesman for reform, founded and edited the *American Israelite* in Cincinnati, an organ for the Reform movement. His editorial *The Fourth of July, 1858* is reprinted in this section.

While many Jews moved away from traditional Judaism by affiliating with Reform Judaism, others stopped practicing their religion entirely. Even in the eighteenth century, as much as 17 percent of the Jewish population intermarried; those who did were exiled from the Jewish community, and 87 percent of that group no longer identified themselves as Jews. Intermarriage constituted a threat to the survival of Judaism, as did the many other lures of life in America. In a nation where Jews were citizens equal to others and able to take part in all aspects of national life, remaining Jewish became a personal choice and a commitment rather than a condition imposed by prejudice and persecution.

Many immigrants sought Jewish fellowship outside the synagogue by creating lodges, clubs, and benevolent societies such as B'nai B'rith, founded in 1843. Such organizations strengthened Jewish communal life while they also reflected the growing secularization and acculturation of American Jews. In addition, they introduced in this country the idea of Jewishness as an ethnic as well as a religious entity. The Reform movement had made it possible for Jews to identify themselves primarily as citizens among other citizens and to leave their religion at the synagogue door. Paradoxically, these new institutions of the community were based on a principle of individuality—that is, given their own choice, Jews would seek out the company of other Jews. Jews desired to join together with their coreligionists both because they were newcomers, immigrants, and because they found strength in numbers to help augment their social, political, and economic power.

THE BEGINNINGS OF JEWISH AMERICAN LITERARY CULTURE

Jewish colonists immediately recognized the freedom, civic equality, and dignity that the new land promised them, often describing it as the promised land or the new Jerusalem. "Collect together thy long scattered people," Moses Meyer exclaimed in Charleston, South Carolina, in 1806, "and let their gathering place be in this land of milk and honey." Similarly, Jacob I. Cohen's *A Prayer for the Medina* suggests that America may indeed be the promised land.

From the start, the Jewish experience in the New World was a joyous and liberating one. The Jews' sense of exultation found in this early literature is notable, especially in contrast to that of their Gentile counterparts. While all the settlers in the New World felt that they, too, had found the promised land—a land of opportunity and plenty—early Puritan literature from this period also records trials and disappointments. The hardships that the early settlers faced—difficulties planting and harvesting, hostile Native Americans, sickness, and famine—do not appear in the documents of the earliest Jewish settlers in the colonies. The Jews of 1654 arrived two generations after the first English settlers of 1607; much of the Jewish population would not arrive for another 150 years. In addition, since most of these early Jews earned their livelihood as merchants, peddlers, and small entrepreneurs, they lived in cities and towns, and were not subject to the vicissitudes of agricultural life. Neither the economic nor political adversity that they had endured in Europe followed them to the colonies.

The improved political situation of the Jews in America naturally produced a new kind of Jewish writing. The experience of equal rights helped bring about a secular literature written in the national language. The ability to express freely their thoughts and grievances, and to have those grievances remedied by the emerging civil law, allowed the earliest Jewish writers to produce a Jewish literature that was pragmatic, idealistic, goal-oriented, and exuberant. When Jewish Americans protested the injustice of a law or attitude, that inequity was corrected through civil remediation. In the case of Jacob Henry, a Jew who, because of his religion, was asked to give up his seat in the North Carolina House of Commons, the entire House rose to support Henry's speech and his right to hold office. Thus, Jewish American writing originated from civic and social interaction, and the ability of the Jews to secure their place in the larger civic hierarchy. This literature combines the new sense of civic power with the inherited assumption that a Jew writes to represent the Jewish people. Added to this combination was one of the founding principles of burgeoning democracy everywhere: the importance of individual rights and identity. Letters like those of young Rebecca Samuel to her parents in 1791 illustrate the components of Jewish American writing at this time. Samuel worries about those Jews around her who are no longer observant; at the same time, she frets about prospective beaux. Her freedom to dream and to feel optimism about her future, an American luxury, couples with her sense of communal responsibility.

The Jewish American method of appealing to civic government in the voice of reason complements the prevailing mode of American discourse in the eighteenth and early nineteenth centuries. Jewish American playwright Mordecai Manuel Noah, author of *The Fortress of Sorrento*, believed in the compatibility of Jewish and American interests, held political office in New York City, and was a leading orator for the Jewish community. Rebecca Gratz's letters illustrate her connection as a Jew to the mainstream of American political, cultural, and literary life.

Yet the American environment shaped Jewish cultural life, too. Penina Moïse's hymns, published in Charleston, South Carolina, in 1856, Americanize the Reform Jewish liturgy by adapting rhythms from the Protestant hymnal to Jewish worship. Isaac Leeser's sermon of 1845 urges his congregants in Philadelphia to protect themselves against the proselytizing of Christian evangelists and the lures of an American education by teaching their children Jewish law, religion, and history.

Almost as if in response to Leeser's call, Nathan Mayer, a physician and a soldier in the Union Army during the Civil War, serialized his novels on Jewish historical subjects in the Jewish press to educate American Jews in their people's history. Flamboyant actress and writer Adah Isaacs Menken also published in the Jewish press in the 1850s and 1860s. Her poems reinterpret Jewish themes and figures with an individualistic passion contrary to organized religion and in free verse, learned from her friend Walt Whitman, that challenges the tidy stanzas of Moïse's hymns. Yet Menken's unconventionality, perhaps a form of American individualism, was laced with a transcendent devotion to Jewish learning and prayer. The anonymous poem *Miriam,* published in the *American Israelite* in 1858, like Penina Moïse's poem *Miriam* and Adah Isaacs Menken's *Judith,* reinterprets a biblical character in the style of poems by mid-nineteenth-century American Protestant women who used these legendary figures to assert their right to speak up in American religion, politics, and culture. Such a sense of entitlement to make one's voice heard and to claim a place in Jewish and American literature informs the poems and translations of Emma Lazarus in the second half of the nineteenth century. Lazarus's work brings together seemingly unrelated traditions—those of nineteenth-century American writers Henry Wadsworth Longfellow and Ralph Waldo Emerson; of German writers Johann Wolfgang von Goethe and Heinrich Heine, the latter a Jew; of the medieval Hebrew poets; of the Hebrew Bible; of classical Greek art and literature—and makes of them a new Jewish American poetic voice.

This period of the earliest Jewish American literature, often overlooked by anthologists and literary historians, is instructive for several reasons. First, the literature collected here registers a high level of rejoicing. In subsequent years, as Jewish Americans grew more accustomed to their civil liberties, they did not express such pure praise for their new nation.

Second, this early literature takes its Jewishness from a religious standpoint rather than an ethnic one. In other words, after great numbers of immigrants arrived from Eastern Europe, the tendency to see Jewish Americans as an ethnic group was overwhelming. In the earliest settlements of Jewish Americans, their differences from their fellow colonists derive solely from religious practice and belief—a unique period in Jewish American history.

Finally, these early works are related to the literature that follows because they ask the most pressing and persistent question that all Jewish Americans ask: How does religious identity combine, collide, or coexist with national interests, allegiances, and obligations? The following selections, including sermons, diaries, prayers, letters, editorials, and speeches, as well as texts more conventionally literary—a play, poetry, and an excerpt from a novel—show the earliest American Jews postulating answers.

ABRAHAM DE LUCENA ET AL.

This petition, dated March 14, 1656, resembles several others of the period wherein the earliest Jewish settlers of the New World requested the lifting of certain restrictions against them. Among those rights petitioned for—and granted—were permission to own a house, permission for the right to travel and trade, permission for the right to establish a cemetery, permission to join the militia, and permission to be admitted to the Burgher Right. Initially, Peter Stuyvesant, the governor of New Netherland, refused several of these petitions, though the Dutch West India Company had instructed him to ease the restrictions against Jews. Stuyvesant first denied the petition reprinted below, yet the persistence of the Jews in asserting their rights as well as the name Joseph d'Acosta, a principal shareholder in the Dutch West India Company, appearing on the document finally changed his mind. Three months later, on June 14, the Dutch West India Company rebuked Stuyvesant. Thereafter, Stuyvesant could no longer deny the Jews equal rights in the New Netherland colony, despite his conventional anti-Semitism, which consisted primarily of a medieval contempt for those who he believed had killed Christ. His beliefs, however, conflicted with the much more practical philosophy of the Dutch West India Company, which was primarily interested in financial returns and not religious issues. The company sanctioned the Jews' presence in the colony as long as they did not become a burden to the community.

The writers of this petition—Abraham de Lucena, Jacob Cohen Henricque, Salvador Dandrada, Joseph d'Acosta, and David Frera—had been leading Sephardic merchants in Amsterdam and were among the first colonists to settle in the New World. They were valued in New Netherland for their wealth and their trade connections.

To the Honorable Director General and Council of New Netherlands

[March 14, 1656]

The undersigned suppliants remonstrate with due reverence to your Noble Honorable Lords that for themselves, as also in the name of the other Jews residing in this Province, they on the 29th of November last past exhibited to your Noble Honorable Lordships a certain Order of the Honorable Lords Directors of the Chartered West India Company, dated February 15, 1655, whereby permission and consent was given them, with other inhabitants, to travel, live and traffic here and to enjoy the same liberty, and following which they humbly requested that your Noble Honorable Lordships should be pleased not to hinder them but to permit and consent that they, like other inhabitants of this Province, may travel and trade to and upon the South River, Fort Orange and other places within the jurisdiction of this Government of New Netherland. Regarding which your Noble Honorable Worships were then pleased to apostille:[1] For weighty reasons this request, made in such general terms, is declined; yet having been informed that the suppliants have already shipped some goods they are for the time being allowed to send one or two persons to the South River in order to dispose of the same, which

1. To annotate.

being done they are to return hither. Also your Noble Honors were pleased, under date of December 23d following, to refuse the conveyance of a certain house and lot bid in by Salvador Dandrada at public auction, and as a consequence to forbid and annul the purchase, so that the said house was again offered for public sale anew on the 20th of January following, and sold to another. And whereas the Honorable Magistrates of this city have been pleased to demand, through their secretary and court messenger, of the undersigned suppliants, individually, the sum of one hundred guilders, towards the payment for the Works of this city, amounting alone for the undersigned, your Worships' suppliants, to the sum of ƒ500,[2] aside from what the others of their nation have been ordered to contribute. Therefore your suppliants once more humbly request hereby that your Honors permit them if, like other burghers, they must and shall contribute, to enjoy the same liberty allowed to other burghers, as well in trading to all places within the jurisdiction of this Government as in the purchase of real estate, especially as this has already been consented to and permitted by the Honorable Lords Directors, as can be seen by the aforesaid Order shown to your Honors on November 29th. Then they are willing and ready, with other burghers and inhabitants, to contribute according to their means. Which doing, etc.

Below stood: Your Worships' Humble Servants:

Was signed: Abraham de Lucena, Jacob Cohen Henricque, Salvador Dandrada, Joseph d'Acosta, David Frera.

The above request being read, the same, after consultation, was disposed of with the following apostille:

The subscription was requested by the Burgomasters and Schepens[3] of this city and by the Director General and Council, for good reasons, for the benefit of this city and the further security of the persons and goods of the inhabitants, among whom the suppliants are also counted and included; therefore it is necessary that they, together with others, shall assist in bearing the burden occasioned thereby. In regard to the Order of the Lords Directors mentioned and exhibited, the Director General and Council are of opinion that pursuant to the same the Jewish Nation enjoy such liberty here in the city as the Order implies. Regarding the purchase and ownership of real estate, it is advised that the broad question be once again put to the Lords Directors, and pending the answer the last [request] is refused.

Thus done in our Assembly held at Fort Amsterdam, in New Netherland. Dated as above.

Was signed: P. Stuyvesant, Nicasius DeSille, LaMontagne.

1656 recorded 1893

2. 500 florins.
3. Two classes of elite citizen in the Netherlands and then in New Netherland. Roughly, they are equivalent to mayors and town comptrollers.

HAIM ISAAC KARIGAL
1729–1777

Rabbi Haim Isaac Karigal, a visitor to the colonies from Hebron, Palestine, who also visited Italy, England, Curaçao, and Barbados on this trip, delivered the following sermon to the congregation at Touro Synagogue in Newport, Rhode Island, on May 28, 1773. In the eighteenth century, Newport had a large, thriving Jewish community, and Touro Synagogue, erected in 1763, was one of the earliest in the United States. (New York's oldest congregation, Shearith Israel, had erected its synagogue in 1729.) Isaac Touro, the rabbi of the congregation in Newport, was a formidable presence, yet Karigal's address was awaited with much excitement by the whole community.

The sermon (excerpted below) must have been either instructive or infuriating to the Rhode Island colonists. Although it begins in a traditional manner and supposedly commemorates the anniversary of the giving of the law at Mount Sinai, Karigal very quickly alludes to a more pressing problem for the colonists. Delivered on May 28, 1773, the same year as the Boston Tea Party and only three years before the colonists would declare independence, the sermon becomes an object lesson in obedience to the crown. Karigal uses biblical teachings to decry "public commotions and revolutions" and warns the congregation that only God "establishes and destroys kingdoms."

One can only imagine the controversy that followed Karigal's sermon: Would the Jewish settlers support a revolution in a land that had treated them so well? In fact, most of the Jewish colonists in Newport were, like Rabbi Touro, staunch Tories; and after the Revolution, the community dispersed. The excerpt below picks up as Karigal's sermon begins to allude heavily to the political turmoil in the American colonies.

From A Sermon Preached at the Synagogue in Newport, Rhode Island

* * *

In the precepts of the decalogue is exhibited an epitome of the divine Law, consisting of the fundamental principles of religion, both respecting our faith or belief in the ONE SUPREME BEING, the creator of the universe, and respecting the institutions of morality. Those precepts in respect of the *Deity* and *morality* are entirely out of the present question; it being indubitable that neither of them can be subject to the least change or alteration in any time or place. The moral, part of its own nature, would be constant and permanent and of unchangeable obligation, even without the additional circumstance of having been dictated by the divine wisdom and authority: Since all morality consists in loving our neighbor as we do our own selves—*but thou shalt love thy neighbor as thyself*, Leviticus xix.18. This admits of no change, unless human nature be altered. Here I might conclude this subject, being certain that every one, who will keep the moral law with exactness, not only because it is consistent with reason, but because it is a divine and unalterable institution, there will be no doubt but that he will also observe all other precepts—both those whose reasons are comprehensible by us, and those which, on account of their obscurity, are not to be investigated; considering that they are all permanent at all times and places, except when the divine legislator commands the contrary;—as in the precepts relating to the sacred worship of the temple, and others that depend on our residence in the holy land; the observation of which is, by our wickedness, put in suspense, although they are not for that reason intirely abolished; because our restoration depends upon ourselves, if with a true contrition, repenting of our crimes and abominations, we promise amendment,—and consequently, of us only depends the approximation and renewal of the observance of those precepts again.

There have been some authors, who, touched with a vehement desire of finding out new methods of commenting upon the sacred scriptures, instead of illustrating them, have involved them in obscurity by expositions full of imaginary conceptions, remote applications, and expressions so excessive high and refined, that they cannot leave the least impression. I shall explain myself more clearly by repeating the following texts of the royal psalmist.[1] He says: Would you know when the divine law delights and tranquilizes the foul? It is only when that law is interpreted in its genuine sense, purity and perfection, without any mixed opinions and conceptions founded in air; *The law of the Lord is perfect converting the Soul*, Psalms xix.7.——Do you know when the divine testimony instructs the ignorant? It is only when justly explained according to its true principles, *the testimony of the Lord is sure making wise the simple*.[2] Then only do the sacred statutes rejoice and cherish the heart, when commented with rectitude and sincerity: *The Statutes of the Lord are right, rejoicing the heart*.[3] The divine precepts then only enlighten the eyes of the understanding, when the explanation thereof is pure and clear—which is not to be expected unless it proceed from the fountain of tradition; *the commandment of the Lord is pure, enlightening the eyes*.[4] Through the interposition of all these things the DIVINE FEAR will be constant and abiding, because it will be then purified, refined and freed of all alloy or human invention; *the fear of the Lord is clean enduring forever*.[5] This is the method which the inspired David[6] points out to us as a true manner of instruction, and as a natural way of attaining the divine fear. Upon this subject all preachers ought to employ their time, and to this matter all instructors of congregations ought to conform themselves. But there have been professors, who instead of teaching their auditories and disciples the essential [points] of religion and [morality], have employed their time in doctrines and discourses, (or at least in amusements and vanities) and subjects that are entirely out of our reach, and beyond human comprehension.

Thus, my noble and kind hearers, have I displayed before you the excellency of the *divine* study.

The *Calamities* we have endured have not been casualties or accidents. In the Talmud *(Sabbath)* we read the following remarkable sentences, written upon the destruction of the HOLY TEMPLE! "The famous ULA[7] says, that this ruin proceeded from the principle that the people in those times did not know what it was to be ashamed before each other, committing in public, and without any reserve, the most horrible and heinous crimes——*Were they ashamed when they bad committed abomination?* Jeremiah vi.15. But what is

1. Identity unknown.
2. From Psalm 19.8.
3. From Psalm 19.9.
4. From Psalm 19.8.
5. From Psalm 19.10.
6. Second king of Israel; reigned ca. 1010–970 B.C.E.
7. Possibly a variant spelling for "ULLA," a third-century Palestinian rabbinic scholar. Karigal frequently invokes early Talmudic scholars, though his exact references are not certain.

the wonder that it should so happen?—When they despised every manner of instruction, and when the word of the Lord was esteemed by them as a shame, contempt and baseness! Rabbi *Isaac* says, we need not wonder that in those times, there should be no shame, when we might see that the small and poor aspired to be in every thing on a level with the great and powerful, all order and regulation being lost, no respect paid to age, no regard to the dignity of employments, and the whole in confusion. The ecclesiastic ministers would give their vote upon civil matters: Princes and magistrates would not only interfere in religion, but take upon them to decide the most difficult points of it. In short, every one would step out of his bounds, and consequently the whole was public disorder and mismanagement; which is so wisely described to us by the prophet Isaiah—*As with the people, so with the priest.*[8] And what was the consequence of such disorder and confusion? That pointed out by R[abbi] *Hanninah*[9] in the following words, 'There was not one single person who would dare to rebuke his neighbor, and exhort him to the right way.' The same is confirmed by R[abbi] *Febudah*[1] saying, 'That the loss of Jerusalem was owing to the contempt and ignominy with which they treated every one who applied himself to the DIVINE STUDY.' These same opinions of those learned and eminent men, instead of contradicting one another, are very similar and consistent: It being certain that wherever any of the mentioned vices exist, they must of course be accompanied with all the rest."

We have thus clearly described the abominations that caused the destruction of the TEMPLE, and ruin of our holy country. There have not been wanting some critical men, who, because they know something of the ancient histories, think they are able to penetrate the natural cause of the rise, increase and decline of empires and republics. This they dare to utter, not thinking at the same time, that such public commotions and revolutions are effects proceeding from the council of the divine creator, who establishes and destroys kingdoms and empires for reasons reserved only to his infinite wisdom. *And he changeth the times and seasons; he removeth Kings and seteth up Kings*, Daniel ii.21. With the same liberty and arrogance with which these men talk of the misfortunes and calamities of other nations, they have been bold enough to speak of those of ours. And indeed there have been at all times some that have considered such events as casualties and natural accidents, and as happening without any interposition of the divine providence. To confute however opinions so heretic and ill grounded, I shall proceed, according to the promise made at the beginning of my discourse, to cite for that purpose some passages of history. I shall not allege any sacred historian, nor shall I produce any rabbinical authorities, being confident of the high degree of credit they would meet with, but will only relate some facts delivered by the most authentic Roman historians.

* * *

1773

8. From Isaiah 24.2.
9. Probably a reference to Hanina Ben-Dosa, a sage and a contemporary of Jesus.
1. This may be a reference to Jehu, king of Israel (ca. 843–816 B.C.E.).

MORDECAI SHEFTALL
1735–1797

The Sheftalls were a prominent family in Savannah, Georgia, in the eighteenth century. Mordecai's father, Benjamin, had emigrated from London in 1733 with the first group of Spanish-Portuguese Jews, though he himself was a German Jew. Like other early pioneers, Benjamin Sheftall struggled to feed his family. Mordecai, however, became a well-to-do merchant. By the time he was twenty-seven, he owned a thousand acres and nine slaves. He used his substantial community influence and assets to secure land for the first Jewish cemetery in Georgia and later contributed heavily to the construction of the first synagogue in that state. He is most remembered, however, for his participation and leadership in the American Revolution.

Although many Georgians hesitated to rebel against England, the Sheftalls organized the colonists' cause; Mordecai became chairman of the rebel Committee of Christ Church Parish, a crucial parish because it included Savannah. This committee operated as the de facto government after the British government broke down. Sheftall joined the army when war broke out; he became the commissary general for Georgia troops, then deputy commissary of issues for the Southern Department.

It was unusual for a Jewish colonist to rise to a position of such prominence, especially considering that there were only six Jewish families in the entire community. Acutely aware that the leaders of the Georgian revolt were Jewish—a fact that seemed to add insult to injury—the British protested the Sheftalls' role in the Savannah uprising. "The conduct of the people here is most infamous," wrote the governor of Georgia to his superiors in 1775, "and Sheftall, a Jew, ordered captains to leave port without unloading their cargoes." In subsequent years, the Savannah Jews were forbidden to return to the colony because the governor feared their extremism.

At the fall of Savannah to the British in late December 1778, Sheftall and his son were captured. This excerpt from Sheftall's diary not only demonstrates the revolutionary fervor of its author, but supplies historical information about conditions for prisoners of war.

From Diary

[December 29, 1778]

This day the British troops, consisting of about three thousand five hundred men, including two battalions of Hessians,[1] under the command of Lieutenant-Colonel Archibald Campbell,[2] of the 71st regiment of Highlanders, landed early in the morning at Brewton Hill, two miles below the town of Savannah, where they met with very little opposition before they gained the height. At about three o'clock, P.M., they entered, and took possession of the town of Savannah, when I endeavored, with my son Sheftall, to make our escape across Musgrove Creek, having first premised that an intrenchment had been thrown up there in order to cover a retreat, and upon seeing Colonel Samuel Elbert and Major James Habersham endeavor to make their escape that way; but on our arrival at the creek, after having sustained a very heavy fire of musketry from the light infantry under the

1. German soldiers that the British hired to help them fight the Revolution in the colonies.

2. Throughout, Sheftall names many of his fellow revolutionaries as well as his British captors.

command of Sir James Baird, during the time we were crossing the Common, without any injury to either of us, we found it high water; and my son, not knowing how to swim, and we, with about one hundred and eighty-six officers and privates, being caught, as it were, in a pen, and the Highlanders keeping up a constant fire on us, it was thought advisable to surrender ourselves prisoners, which we accordingly did, and which was no sooner done than the Highlanders plundered every one amongst us, except Major Low, myself and son, who, being foremost, had an opportunity to surrender ourselves to the British officer, namely, Lieutenant Peter Campbell, who disarmed as we came into the yard formerly occupied by Mr. Moses Nunes. During this business, Sir James Baird was missing; but, on his coming into the yard, he mounted himself on the stepladder which was erected at the end of the house, and sounded his brass bugle-horn, which the Highlanders no sooner heard than they all got about him, when he addressed himself to them in Highland language, when they all dispersed, and finished plundering such of the officers and men as had been fortunate enough to escape their first search. This over, we were marched in files, guarded by the Highlanders and York Volunteers, who had come up before we were marched, when we were paraded before Mrs. Goffe's door, on the bay, where we saw the greatest part of the army drawn up. From there, after some time, we were all marched through the town to the course-house, which was very much crowded, the greatest part of the officers they had taken being here collected, and indiscriminately put together. I had been here about two hours, when an officer, who I afterwards learned to be Major Crystie, called for me by name, and ordered me to follow him, which I did, with my blanket and shirt under my arm, my clothing and my son's, which were in my saddle-bags, having been taken from my horse, so that my wardrobe consisted of what I had on my back.

On our way to the white guard-house we met with Colonel Campbell, who inquired of the Major who he had got there. On his naming me to him, he desired that I might be well guarded, as I was a very great rebel. The Major obeyed his orders, for, on lodging me in the guard-house, he ordered the sentry to guard me with a drawn bayonet, and not to suffer me to go without the reach of it; which orders were strictly complied with, until a Mr. Gild Busler, their Commissary-General, called for me, and ordered me to go with him to my stores, that he might get some provisions for our people, who, he said, were starving, not having eat anything for three days, which I contradicted, as I had victualed them that morning for the day. On our way to the office where I used to issue the provisions, he ordered me to give him information of what stores I had in town, and what I had sent out of town, and where. This I declined doing, which made him angry. He asked me if I knew that Charlestown was taken. I told him no. He then called us poor, deluded wretches, and said, "Good God! how are you deluded by your leaders!" When I inquired of him who had taken it, and when he said General Grant, with ten thousand men, and that it had been taken eight or ten days ago, I smiled, and told him it was not so, as I had a letter in my pocket that was wrote in Charlestown but three days ago by my brother. He replied, we had been misinformed. I then retorted that I found they could be misinformed by their leaders as well as we could be deluded by ours. This made him so angry, that when he returned me to the guardhouse, he ordered me to be confined amongst the drunken soldiers and Negroes, where I suffered a great deal of abuse, and was threatened to be run through the body, or, as they termed it, skivered by one of the York Volunteers; which threat he attempted to put into execution three times during the night, but was prevented by one Sergeant Campbell.

In this situation I remained two days without a morsel to eat, when a Hessian officer named Zaltman, finding I could talk his language, removed me to his room, and sympathized with me on my situation. He permitted me to send to Mrs. Minis, who sent me some victuals. He also permitted me to go and see my son, and to let him come and stay with me. He introduced me to Captain Kappel, also a Hessian, who treated me very politely. In this situation I remained until Saturday morning, the 2d of January, 1779, when the commander, Colonel Innis, sent his orderly for me and son to his quarters, which was James Habersham's house, where, on the top of the step, I met with Captain Stanhope, of the Raven sloop of war, who treated me with the most illiberal abuse; and after charging me with having refused the supplying the King's ships with provisions, and of having shut the church door, together with many ill-natured things, ordered me on board the prison-ship, together with my son. I made a point of giving Mr. Stanhope suitable answers to his impertinent treatment, and then turned from him, and inquired for Colonel Innis. I got his leave to go to Mrs. Minis for a shirt she had taken to wash for me, as it was the only one I had left, except the one on my back, and that was given me by Captain Kappel, as the British soldiers had plundered both mine and my son's clothes. This favor he granted me under guard; after which I was conducted on board one of the flat-boats, and put on board the prison-ship Nancy, commanded by Captain Samuel Tait, when the first thing that presented itself to my view was one of our poor Continental soldiers laying on the ship's main deck in the agonies of death, and who expired in a few hours after. After being presented to the Captain with mine and the rest of the prisoners' names, I gave him in charge what paper money I had, and my watch. My son also gave him his money to take care of. He appeared to be a little civiler after this confidence placed in him, and permitted us to sleep in a state-room—that is, the Rev. Moses Allen, myself and son. In the evening we were served with what was called our allowance, which consisted of two pints and a half and a half-gill of rice, and about seven ounces of boiled beef per man. We were permitted to choose our messmates, and I accordingly made choice of Captain Thomas Fineley, Rev. Mr. Allen, Mr. Moses Valentonge, Mr. Daniel Flaherty, myself and son, Sheftall Sheftall.

1778

HAYM SALOMON
1740–1785

Born in Poland in 1740, Haym Salomon arrived in New York City when he was thirty-two. He married Rachel Franks, the daughter of Moses B. Franks, a wealthy New York merchant.

The legend that has surrounded Salomon—that he financed, or helped to finance, the American Revolution—bears only a small relationship to the truth. From the ashes of this legend, however, a more realistic description of Salomon's activities can be drawn. Salomon was a broker during the Revolution; thus, he loaned and transferred money to individuals and countries. He sold Dutch and French bills of exchange and loaned money to several members of the Continental Congress, including James Madison and Edmund Randolph. He also worked with Robert Morris, superintendent for the Office of Finance, and was permitted to sell provisions to the troops stationed at New York's Lake George. Although Salomon did not finance the Revolution, he did play an active role in the financing of the emerging nation. A scrupulous broker, a dedicated patriot, and a generous benefactor, Salomon was highly esteemed by his fellow citizens.

In 1784, Miers Fisher, a Quaker lawyer and former Tory, appeared before the Pennsylvania legislature to obtain a charter for a new bank, the Bank of Pennsylvania. Potentially, this bank would compete with the Bank of North America, the bank with which Robert Morris and Salomon were affiliated. Fisher argued for the new bank on the grounds that it would reduce the rate of interest, thus protecting the people against the usurious rates of Jewish brokers. Salomon, among others, felt the sting of the accusation and, along with the non-Jewish newspaper editor Colonel Eleazar Oswald, purportedly wrote the following response. This public letter to Fisher appeared on March 13, 1784, in the *Independent Gazeteer*, a Philadelphia publication.

The exchange between Fisher and Salomon is notable for several reasons. First, Fisher's comments rely heavily upon a historical anti-Semitic view that Jews and usurers were one and the same. As far back as the Middle Ages, a time when taking a fee for the lending of money was illegal, Jews were universally denounced for engaging in the practice—a paradox since this was one of the few businesses in which Jews were permitted to engage. In the seventeenth century, however, the restrictions against moneylending disappeared, and the term *usury* was applied not to those who charged fee a for their services, but to those who charged fees that seemed too high. There is nothing to back up Fisher's claim that Salomon's, or any other Jewish broker's, rate was higher than the rates that non-Jews were charging. It is commonly believed that Fisher was trying to distract the legislature from his earlier pro-Tory activities by uniting the group in its common—or so he believed—hatred of Jews. This tactic failed, and Salomon's defending himself so publicly and vehemently proved a victory not only for the Jewish community, but for the emerging American democracy as well.

[Letter from "a Jew Broker"]

To Miers Fisher, Esquire:

I must address you, in this manner, although you do not deserve it. Unaccustomed as you are to receive any mark of respect from the public, it will be expected that I should make an apology for introducing a character, *fetid* and *infamous*, like yours, to general notice and attention. Your conspicuous *Toryism* and *disaffection* long since buried you in the silent grave of *popular* oblivion and contempt; and your extraordinary conduct and deportment, in several other respects, has brought and reduced you to that dreary dungeon of insignificance, to that gulf of defeated spirits, from which even the powers of *hope* "that comes to all" cannot relieve or better you.

In this most miserable of all situations, principally arising from an obstinate, inflexible perseverance in your political *heresy* and *schism* (so detestable in itself, so ruinous and destructive to our country, and obnoxious to all around us), you are now left quite destitute and forlorn! Unhappy and disappointed man! Once exiled [September, 1777] and excommunicated by the state, *as a sly, insiduous enemy*; severed and detached from the generous bosom of *patriotism* and *public virtue; shunned* and deserted by *faithful friends*, in whom you once so safely trusted; since, debarred and prevented from *your practice* by rule of court as an attorney at the bar; *and excluded* from every other essential and dignified privilege of which the *rest of citizens* can boast—with the wretched remains of a *wrecked* reputation—you exhibit so complete a spectacle of distress and wretchedness, as rather excites one's tenderness than vengeance, and would soften and melt down dispositions more relentless and unforgiving than mine!

But whatever claims of mercy you may demand, on these accounts; whatever I should think, were I to judge of you as your *personal* enemy in *private* respects; yet the *forward* and unexampled advances and steps you have lately taken in the concert of *public* affairs; the high-cockaded air of *fancied* importance you now assume; the petulant, discontented humor you have manifested for establishing *a new bank*; your longings and pantings to approach our *political vineyard*, and blast the fruits of those labors for which you neither *toiled nor spun*; and more particularly, the indecent, unjust, inhumane aspersions, you cast so indiscriminately on the *Jews* of this city at large, in your arguments of Wednesday week, before the honorable legislature of the commonwealth—these circumstances, if my apprehensions are right, preclude you from any lenity or favor, and present you a fair victim and offering to the sacred altar of public justice.

You are not therefore to expect any indulgence, because you merit none. I daresay you experience it not in your own feelings; nor have you any right whatever to hope for the least tenderness from me. You shall not have it; and if you are cut and smarted with the whip and lashes of my reproach and resentments, if I lay my talons and point out the *ingrate*, if my tongue is clamorous of you and *your odious confederates*, and I should pain the tenderest veins of their breasts—remember, you first gave birth to all yourself, that it arose entirely from you; and in tracing of events hereafter to the source you will, perhaps, find to your sorrow and cost that you are only blamable for whatever consequences have or may arise on the occasion.

You not only endeavored to injure me by your unwarrantable expressions, but every other person of the same *religious* persuasion I hold, and which the laws of the country, and the glorious toleration and *liberty of conscience*, have allowed me to indulge and adopt. The injury is highly crimsoned and aggravated, as there was no proper reason or ground for your invectives. The attack on the *Jews* seemed wanton, and could only have been premeditated by such a base and degenerate mind as yours. It was not owing to the sudden sallies of passion, or to the warmth of a disconcerted and hasty imagination. I cannot, therefore, place it to the account of mere human frailties, in which your *will* and understanding had no concern, and for which I am always disposed to make every compassionate allowance. And though an individual is not obliged to avenge the injuries of particular societies and sectaries [sects] of men, he is nevertheless called upon, by every dear and serious consideration, to speak his mind freely and independently of public transactions and general events, to assert his own share in the public consequence and to act his part fairly on the social theater.

Permit me, then, with this view of things, to take notice of these terms of reproach and invective which, considering you as a friend to good manners and decorum, you have heaped on our nation [religious group] and profession with so liberal and unsparing a hand. I am a Jew; it is my own nation and profession. I also subscribe myself a broker, and a broker, too, whose opportunities and knowledge, along with other brokers of his intimate acquaintance, in a great course of business, has made him very familiar and privy to every minute design and artifice of your *wily colleagues* and associates.

I exult and glory in reflecting that we have the honor to reside in a free country where, as a people, we have met with the most generous countenance and protection; and I do not at all despair, notwithstanding former obstacles [the disabilities imposed by the Pennsylvania Constitution of 1776], that we shall still obtain every other privilege that we aspire to enjoy along with our fellow-citizens. It also affords me unspeakable satisfaction, and is indeed one of the most pleasing employments of my thoughtful moments, to contemplate that we have in general been early uniform, decisive Whigs, and were second to none in our patriotism and attachment to our country!

What but Erinnys [the name of the Furies of Hell] itself could have thus tempted you to wander from the common path of things, and go a stray among *thorns and briars*? What were your motives and inducements for introducing the Jews so disrespectfully into your unhallowed and polluted lips? Who are you, or what are you (a mere *tenant at sufferance*, of your liberty), that in a *free* country you dare to trample on any sectary whatever of people? Did you expect to serve yourself, or your friends and confederates [Tories and pacifist Quakers]—these serpents in our bosom, whose poisonous stings have been darted into every *patriot* character among us?

In any other place, in managing another cause, you might have had patience to attend to the consequences of such unpardonable rashness and temerity. But here you thought yourself safe, and at full leave to take the most unlicensed liberties with characters, in regard of whom you can in no respect pretend to vie! You shall yet repent, even *in sackcloth* and *ashes*, for the foul language in which you have expressed yourself. And neither the interposition of some well meant though mistaken Whigs who, I am sorry to think, have joined you, "nor even the sacred shield of cowardice shall protect you,"[1] for your transgressions. Who knows but the beams of that very denomination whom you have traduced may, on one day, perhaps not very remote,

1. A vague allusion, perhaps, to Book V of Aristotle's *Ethics*.

warm you into the most abject servility, and make you penitentially solemnize what you have done?

An error is easily remedied, and there may be some compensation for actual injuries. But a downright insult can neither be forgiven or forgot, and seldom admits of atonement or reparation. It is our happiness to live in the times of enlightened liberty, when the human mind, liberated from the restraints and fetters of superstition and authority, hath been taught to conceive just sentiments of its own; and when mankind, in matters of *religion*, are quite charitable and benevolent in their opinions of each other.

Individuals may act improperly, and sometimes deserve censure; but it is no less unjust than ungenerous to condemn all for the faults of a few, and reflect generally on a whole community for the indiscretion of some particular persons. There is no body of people but have some exceptionable characters with them; and even your own religious sectary [the Quakers], whom you have compelled me to dissect in the course of this address, are not destitute of *very proper subjects* of criticism and animadversion.

Good citizens who nauseate, and the public who contemn, have heard your invectives against the Jews. Unhappily for you, a long series of enormities have proved you more your own enemy than I am. To you, then, my worthy friends and fellow-citizens (characters teeming with strict candor and disinterestedness), do I turn myself with pleasure from that sterile field, from that *Grampian*[2] desert, which hath hitherto employed me.

It is your candor I seek; it is your disinterestedness I solicit. The opinions of *Fisher* and his adherents, whether wileful[3] in their malignity, or sincere in their ignorance, are no longer worthy of my notice. His observations are low; his intentions are too discernible. His whole endeavors center in one point, namely, to create a *new bank*.

To effect this end, he has spared neither pains or labors. He has said every thing that artifice could dictate, or malice invent. He has betrayed himself in a thousand inconsistencies, and adopted absurdities which, supposing him a man of sense and observation, would have disgraced the lips of an idiot.

And for whom is the new bank meant and intended? For the benefit of men like himself, who have been in general averse and opposed to the war and common cause: for the insurgents against our liberty and independence; for *mercenary* and *artful* citizens, where selfish views are totally incompatible with the happiness of the people; for bifronted political *Janus[e]s*,[4] the mere weathercocks of every breeze and gale that blows.

Who traded with the enemy? Who first depreciated the public currency? Who lent our enemies money to carry on the war? Who were spies and pilots to the British? Who prolonged the war? Who was the cause of so many valuable men losing their lives in the field and *prison-ships*? Who did not pay any taxes? Who has now the public securities in hand? Who would not receive our Continental money? Who has purchased *Burgoyne's* convention bills?[5] Who depreciated the French bills? Who depreciated the bills of the

2. The Grampians are the hills between the lowlands and highlands of Scotland.
3. Willful.
4. In Roman religion, Janus is the spirit of doorways. As such, he is two-headed or two-faced and thus symbolizes hypocrisy.
5. John Burgoyne (1722–1792) was a British general best remembered for his defeat in the battle of Saratoga (1777). To buy his "convention bills" means to financially support the British in their war efforts.

United States on Paris? Who slandered the institution of the *Bank* of *North-America*? Who refused taking *banknotes* when they fi[r]st issued? Who discouraged the people from lodging money in the bank? And are these the characters who talk to instituting a bank for *the good of the public*? Are these the people who want a charter from our legislature? Shall such a bastard progeny of freedom, such jests and phantoms of patriotism and the social virtues be indulged in their wishes? For shame! For shame! Surrender the puerile, the fruitless pretensions! Public honor and public gratitude cry aloud against you, and says, or seems to say, as earnest as your endeavors have been, you shall not have your charter.

From such a *medley* and *group* of characters (an impure nest of vipers, the very *bloodhounds* of our lives and liberties) we have every thing to hazard, and nothing to expect. Suspicion shakes her wary head against them, and experience suggests that the sly, insinuating intrigues and combinations of these persons are to be watched and guarded against as much as possible. Though the *proposals* are generous and captivating, their practices, I will venture to affirm, cannot correspond; and however *fascinating* they may be *in appearance*, their designs are *deep* and *wily*. With the soft and soothing voice of *Jacob* they may exercise the *hand*, the *hairy* hand of *Esau*![6]

I shall not inquire whether two banks in a commercial country would not clash with each other, and prove exceeding detrimental and injurious to the community. Having only ventured to give an account of the leading characters who compose the new bank, allow me in conclusion to rectify an error of Mr. Fisher's, who publicly declared, "the Jews were the authors of high and unusual interest." No! The Jews can acquit themselves of this artful imputation, and turn your own batteries on yourself. It was neither the *Jews* or *Christians* that founded the practice, but *Quakers*—and *Quakers* worse than *heathens, pagans*, or *idolaters*; men, though not Jews in *faith*, are yet Jews in *traffic*; men abounding with avarice, *who neither fear God, nor regard man*.

Those very persons who are now flattering themselves with the idea of a new bank, first invented the practice of discounting notes at five percent. I have retained an alphabetical list of names, as well as the other brokers, and can specify persons, if necessary. In the language of Naphtali [Nathan] to David, I have it in my power to point at the very *would-be* directors, and say: *"Thou art the man."*[7] I can prove that it were these people, unwilling to venture money in trade during the war, who first declined letting out money on the best mortgage and bond security.

Were they now gratified in their expectations, would they not display the same undue spirit and degrade the dignity of a bank with practices unbecoming a common broker? Is it not in their power to finesse at the bank, and refuse discounting notes on purpose to gripe [harm] the necessitous part of the people, and extort improper premiums out of doors [secretly]? And have we not reason to expect this would be the case?

A Jew Broker

1784

6. A reference to Genesis 27.11.

7. 2 Samuel 12.7.

JACOB I. COHEN
1744–1823

Written for the Beth Shalome Congregation of Richmond, Virginia, this *Prayer for the Medina* is typical of many that emerged from synagogues during the Revolutionary War period. Richmond's was a small Jewish community, having just been settled toward the end of the Revolution. When George Washington proclaimed the first annual Thanksgiving Day in 1789, Jewish congregations, even tiny ones like this, prepared for a service to be held at the synagogue in which all would unite to give thanks. It is believed that Jacob Cohen, a leader in the community and a partner in Cohen & Isaacs, a mercantile firm, wrote the following prayer.

Medina is Hebrew for "new land" or "new country." It is clear from this prayer that Jewish Americans joined their compatriots in their elation about the birth of the United States. The prayer combines the fledgling language of democracy with traditional words of Hebrew prayer. That "O Gracious God, thou has[t] delivered us from all our enemies" would, in this case, refer to the defeat of the British is an interesting rewriting of traditional biblical rhetoric. Most striking about this prayer—and others like it—is that it illustrates the commonly held belief at this time that for Jews, America was the new promised land.

A Prayer for the *Medina*

When we call on thee, O righteous God, answer us.
Hearken to the voice of our cry and show us grace.
Have compassion on us and hearken to our prayer.
For thou, Most High God, hast removed distress far from us.
O gracious God, thou has[t] delivered us from all our enemies;
Thou has[t] redeemed us from those who rose up against us;
Thou has girded us with strength to smite the pride of our enemies;
In shame and disgrace they fell beneath our feet.
O God of Hosts, thou has set peace and tranquility in our palaces
And has set the President of the United States as our head [ruler?],
And in prayer we humble ourselves before thee, oh, our God.
Unto our supplications mayest Thou hearken, and deliver us.
A *mind* of wisdom and understanding set in the heart of the head of our country;
May he *judge* us with justice; may he cause our hearts to rejoice and be glad.
In the *paths* of the upright may he lead us;
Even unto old age may he administer and judge in our midst.
Pure and upright be the heart of the one who rules and governs us.
May God Almighty hearken to our voice and save us.
We will prolong our prayer before God, our Redeemer.
May he guard and keep the Vice President, senators, and representatives of the United States.
May he give good sense and understanding to the officers of the courts.
May the hearts of our governors be upright and faithful.
May he prosper and bless our country,
And deliver us from the hand of outside enemies.

May our sons in their youth be like growing plants.
May our daughters be like [cornerstones?]
May our storehouses be full and bursting from end to end, multiplying in our streets.
May our cattle be fat and may there be no breach and no——in our broad places.
May our God bless all friends of our country and their judges,
And give glory to the Lord God, our Redeemer.
May Judah be saved and Israel dwell securely,
And may the Redeemer come to Zion, and let us say, Amen.

Signed
I, the small one,[1] Jacob son of R[abbi] Joshua Cohen(?),
Richmond, Virginia.

1789 1791

1. The term "the small one" is unclear. Perhaps Cohen refers to himself in relation to his father or older brother.

REBECCA SAMUEL
fl. 1790s

The writer of the following document was born Rebecca Alexander, the daughter of two German Jews. After marrying Hyman Samuel, a silversmith and watchmaker, she moved frequently and gradually became familiar with several of the Jewish settlements in the United States, including those of Baltimore, Maryland, and Charleston, South Carolina. Samuel's letter was sent to her parents from Petersburg, Virginia, the center of the tobacco trade. As is apparent from the texts, these communities contained few Jews and virtually no Jewish institutions.

These two letters are among the most significant documents we have from this period for a number of reasons. First, they address the tension between Jewish identity and American practices. Second, they convey Samuel's concerns about the hardships of observing Jewish ritual in the rapidly growing mercantile nation. Third, they offer a rare perspective—that of a woman—on the emerging nation.

[Letters to Her Parents]

Petersburg, January 12, 1791, Wednesday, 8th [7th?][1] Shebat,[2] 5551.

Dear and Worthy Parents:

I received your dear letter with much pleasure and therefrom understand that you are in good health, thank God, and that made us especially

1. As is indicated by most of the bracketed material throughout, this selection has been previously edited by Jacob Rader Marcus in *Early American Jewry: Documents*.
2. Variant spelling of Shabbat, which is Hebrew for the Sabbath.

happy. The same is not lacking with us—may we live to be a hundred years. Amen.

Dear parents, you complain that you do not receive any letters from us, and my mother-in-law writes the same. I don't know what's going on. I have written more letters than I have received from you. Whenever I can and have an opportunity, I give letters to take along, and I send letters by post when I do not have any other opportunity. It is already six months since we received letters from you and from London. The last letter you sent was through Sender [Alexander], and it was the beginning of the month of Ab [July 1790] when we received it. Now you can realize that we too have been somewhat worried. We are completely isolated here. We do not have any friends, and when we do not hear from you for any length of time, it is enough to make us sick. I hope that I will get to see some of my family. That will give me some satisfaction.

You write me that Mr. Jacob Renner's son Reuben is in Philadelphia and that he will come to us. People will not advise him to come to Virginia. When the Jews of Philadelphia or New York hear the name Virginia, they get nasty. And they are not wrong! It won't do for a Jew. In the first place it is an unhealthful district, and we are only human. God forbid, if anything should happen to us, where would we be thrown? There is no cemetery in the whole of Virginia. In Richmond, which is twenty-two miles from here, there is a Jewish community consisting of two quorums [twenty men], and the two cannot muster a quarter [quorum when needed?].

You cannot imagine what kind of Jews they have here [in Virginia]. They were all German itinerants who made a living by begging in Germany. They came to America during the war, as soldiers, and now they can't recognize themselves.

One can make a good living here, and all live at peace. Anyone can do what he wants. There is no rabbi in all of America to excommunicate anyone. This is a blessing here; Jew and Gentile are as one. There is no *galut* ["exile"—rejection of Jews] here. In New York and Philadelphia there is more *galut*. The reason is that there are too many German Gentiles and Jews there. The German Gentiles cannot forsake their anti-Jewish prejudice; and the German Jews cannot forsake their disgraceful conduct; and that's what makes the *galut*.

[Rebecca Samuel]

Dear Parents:

I hope my letter will ease your mind.[3] You can now be reassured and send me one of the family to Charleston, South Carolina. This is the place to which, with God's help, we will go after Passover. The whole reason why we are leaving this place is because of [lack of] *Yehudishkeit* [Jewishness].

Dear parents, I know quite well you will not want me to bring up my children like Gentiles. Here they cannot become anything else. Jewishness is pushed aside here. There are here [in Petersburg] ten or twelve Jews, and they are not worthy of being called Jews. We have a shohet[4] here who goes

3. Although this letter bears no date, it must have been written before 1796, for that is the year Samuel left Petersburg.

4. Hebrew for the person who does the ritual slaughtering of animals for food for those who observe the laws of kashruth (kosher—permitted—foods).

to market and buys terefah [nonkosher] meat and then brings it home. On Rosh Hashanah [New Year] and on Yom Kippur [the Day of Atonement] the people worshiped here without one sefer torah [Scroll of the Law], and not one of them wore the tallit [a large prayer shawl worn in the synagogue] or the *arba kanfot* [the small set of fringes worn on the body], except Hyman and my Sammy's godfather. The latter is an old man of sixty, a man from Holland. He has been in America for thirty years already; for twenty years he was in Charleston, and he has been living here for four years. He does not want to remain here any longer and will go with us to Charleston. In that place there is a blessed community of three hundred Jews.

You can believe me that I crave to see a synagogue to which I can go. The way we live now is no life at all. We do not know what the Sabbath and the holidays are. On the Sabbath all the Jewish shops are open; and they do business on that day as they do throughout the whole week. But ours we do not allow to open. With us there is still some Sabbath. You must believe me that in our house we all live as Jews as much as we can.

As for the Gentiles [?], we have nothing to complain about. For the sake of a livelihood we do not have to leave here. Nor do we have to leave because of debts. I believe ever since Hyman has grown up that he has not had it so good. You cannot know what a wonderful country this is for the common man. One can live here peacefully. Hyman made a clock that goes very accurately, just like the one in the Buchenstrasse in Hamburg. Now you can imagine what honors Hyman has been getting here. In all Virginia there is no clock [like this one], and Virginia is the greatest province in the whole of America, and America is the largest section of the world. Now you know what sort of a country this is. It is not too long since Virginia was discovered. It is a young country. And it is amazing to see the business they do in this little Petersburg. At times as many as a thousand hogsheads of tobacco arrive at one time, and each hogshead[5] contains 1,000 and sometimes 1,200 pounds of tobacco. The tobacco is shipped from here to the whole world.

When Judah [my brother?] comes here, he can become a watchmaker and a goldsmith, if he so desires. Here it is not like Germany where a watchmaker is not permitted to sell silverware. [The contrary is true in this country.] They do not know otherwise here. They expect a watchmaker to be a silversmith here. Hyman has more to do in making silverware than with watchmaking. He has a journeyman, a silversmith, a very good artisan, and he, Hyman, takes care of the watches. This work is well paid here, but in Charleston, it pays even better.

All the people who hear that we are leaving give us their blessings. They say that it is sinful that such blessed children should be brought up here in Petersburg. My children cannot learn anything here, nothing Jewish, nothing of general culture. My Schoene [my daughter], God bless her, is already three years old. I think it is time that she should learn something, and she has a good head to learn. I have taught her the bedtime prayers and grace after meals in just two lessons. I believe that no one among the Jews here can do as well as she. And my Sammy [born in 1790], God bless him, is already beginning to talk.

5. A large cask or barrel.

I could write more. However, I do not have any more paper.

I remain, your devoted daughter and servant,
Rebecca, the wife of Hayyim, the son of Samuel the Levite

I send my family, my . . . [mother-in-law?] and all my friends and good friends, my regards.

JACOB HENRY
1775–1847

Jacob Henry represented Carteret County in North Carolina's House of Commons in 1808. When he was reelected in 1809, Hugh Mills, from neighboring Rockingham County, moved that Henry give up his seat because "he denies the divine authority of the New Testament, and refused to take the oath prescribed by law for his qualification." After a day of debate—and Henry's rousing speech, reprinted below—the House voted to reject Mills's recommendation. Although Henry retained his seat, the House had ruled that even though Jews and Catholics could hold legislative office, they could not hold executive office. This law was not changed until the Reconstruction Convention of 1868.

Henry's speech, however, was a milestone for religious rights throughout the country. It was widely reprinted and quoted in similar debates. The rhetorical questions that Henry poses go to the core of the democratic experiment and demand that freedom of worship be an inalienable right. Because Henry's question "Shall this free Country set an example of Persecution, which even the returning reason of enslaved Europe would not submit to" seeks to establish more firmly the difference between Europe and the United States, his cause was met with support and acclaim.

An Address in the Committee of the Whole of the House of Commons of North Carolina

To the Honorable the Speaker, and members of the House of Commons.

I must confess that the resolution against me yesterday was quite unexpected, as I had a right to expect, that the Gentleman who introduced it, would have had the politeness to have given me notice of it.

The Gentleman has stated that I deny the divine authority of the old and new Testament.

However Gentlemen, I know not the design of the declaration of Rights made by the people of this State in the year '76 and one day before the Constitution, if it was not to consecrate certain great and fundamental rights and Principles, which even the Constitution cannot impair: For the 44th section of the latter instrument declares that the declaration of rights ought never to be violated on any pretense whatever—If there is any apparent ~~discrepancy~~ difference between the two instruments they ought if possible be reconciled. But if there is a final repugnance between them, the declaration of

Rights must be considered paramount: For I believe that it is to the Constitution as the Constitution is to a Law; it controls and directs it absolutely and conclusively. If then a belief in the Protestant religion is required by the Constitution to qualify a man for a seat in this House and such qualification is dispensed with by the declaration of rights, the provision of the Constitution must be altogether inoperative, as the Language of the Bill of rights is that all men have a natural and unalienable right to worship Almighty God according to the dictates of their own Conscience. It is undoubtedly a natural right, and when it is declared to be an unalienable one, by the people in their sovereign and original capacity, any attempt to alienate it either by the Constitution or by Law, must be vain and fruitless. It is difficult to conceive how such a provision crept into the Constitution unless it was from the difficulty the human mind feels in suddenly emancipating itself from fetters by which it has long been enchained: And how adverse it is to the feelings and manners of the *people* of the present day every Gentleman may satisfy himself by glancing at the Religious beliefs of the persons who fill the various civil offices in this State—There are Presbyterians, Lutherans, Calvinists, Menonists, Baptists, Trinitarians and Unitarians. But as far as my observation extends, there are fewer Protestants in the strict sense of the word used by the Convention than of any other persuasion; for I supposed that they meant by it the Protestant religion as established by Law in England. For other persuasions we see houses of Worship in almost every part of the State, but very few for protestants; so few, that indeed I fear that the people of this State, would for some time, remain unrepresented in this House, if the clause of the Constitution is supposed to be in force. So far from believing in the truths of the 39 articles, I will venture to assert that a majority of the people have never read them. If a man should hold religious principles incompatible with the freedom and safety of the State, I do not hesitate to pronounce that he should be excluded from the public Councils of the same; and I trust if I know myself no one would be more ready to aid and assist than myself. But I should really be at a loss to specify any known religious principles which are thus dangerous, it is surely a question between a man and his Maker, and requires more than human attributes to pronounce which of the numerous Sects prevailing in the world is most acceptable to the Deity. If a man fulfills the duties of that religion which his education or his Conscience has pointed to him as the true one; no person, I hold, in this our land of liberty, has a right to arraign him at the bar of any inquisition—And the day I trust is long past, when principles merely speculative were propagated by force, when the sincere and pious were made victims, and the light minded bribed into hypocrites.

The proud monuments of liberty knew that the purest homage man could render to the Almighty was in the sacrifice of his passions and in the performance of his duties; that the ruler of the universe would receive with equal benignity, the various offerings of man's adoration if they proceed from an humble spirit and sincere mind: that intolerance in matters of faith, had been from the earliest ages of the world, the severest torments by which mankind could be afflicted; and that governments were only concerned about the actions and conduct of man, and not his speculative notions. Who among us feels himself so exalted above his fellows, as to have a right to dictate to them their mode of belief? Shall this free Country set an example of

Persecution, which even the returning reason of enslaved Europe would not submit to? Will you bind the Conscience in Chains, and fasten conviction upon the mind, in spite of the conclusions of reason, and of those ties and habitudes which are blended with every pulsation of the heart? Are you prepared to plunge at once from the sublime heights of moral legislation, into the dark and gloomy caverns of superstitious ignorance? Will you drive from your shores and from the shelter of your constitutions, all who do not lay their oblations on the same altar, observe the same ritual, and subscribe to the same dogmas[?] If so which amongst the various sects into which we are divided, shall be the favored one? No Gentlemen, I should insult your understandings, to suppose it possible that you could ever assent to such absurdities. For you all know that persecution in all its shapes and modifications, is contrary to the Genius of our Government, and the spirit of our laws; and that it can never produce any other effect, than to render men hypocrites or martyrs. When Charles the fifth, Emperor of Germany, tired of the cares of Government, resigned his *Crown* to his son, he retired to a *monastery*, where he amused the evening of his life, in regulating the movements of watches, endeavoring to make a number keep the same time, but not being able to make any two go exactly alike, it led him to reflect upon the folly and crimes he had committed, in attempting the impossibility of making men think alike!!

Nothing is more easily demonstrated than that the Conduct alone is the subject of human laws, and that man ought to suffer civil disqualification for what he does and not for what he thinks. The mind can receive laws only from him, of whose divine essence it is a portion; he alone can punish disobedience; for who else can know its movements; or estimate their merits? The religion I profess, inculcates every duty which man owes to his fellow men; it enjoins upon its votaries, the practice of every virtue, and the detestation of every vice; it teaches them to hope for the favor of Heaven exactly in proportion as their lives are directed by just, honorable and beneficent maxims—This then Gentlemen is my Creed; it was impressed upon my infant mind, it has been the director of my youth, the monitor of my manhood, and will I trust be the Consolation of my old age. ~~Can this religion be founded upon the denial of the divine authority of the old and new Testament?~~ At any rates Gentlemen, I am sure that you cannot see, anything in this religion, to deprive me of my seat in this House. So far as relates to my life and conduct, the examination of these, I submit with cheerfulness to your candid and liberal construction. What may be the religion of those, who have made this objection against me, or whether they have any religion or not, I am unable to say. I have never considered it my duty to pry into the belief of my fellow citizens or neighbors, if their actions are upright and their conduct just, the rest is for their own consideration not for mine. I do not seek to make converts to my faith, whatever it may be esteemed in the eyes of my officious friend, nor do I exclude any man from my esteem or friendship, because he and I differ in that respect—The same charity therefore it is not unreasonable to expect will be extended to myself, because in all things that relate to the State and to the duties of civil life, I am bound by the same obligations, with my fellow citizens; nor does any man subscribe more sincerely than myself to the maxim, "Whatever ye would that men should do unto [ye], do ye so even unto them, for such is the Law and the Prophets.["]

With the highest respect I remain Gentlemen yours respectfully
J. Henry

1809

REBECCA GRATZ
1781–1869

Although she never published and was not a literary author, Rebecca Gratz, perhaps the most influential Jewish woman of her time, was a brilliant writer of letters. These letters provide an abundance of information about the private and public lives of wealthy Jews in the early nineteenth century.

Gratz was one of five daughters and seven sons born to Michael Gratz and Miriam Simon Gratz of Philadelphia. Her mother was born in Lancaster on the Pennsylvania frontier; her father, who had immigrated to America from Langensdorf, Upper Silesia, in 1755, became a prominent merchant in eighteenth-century Philadelphia. An American patriot, he protested the British Stamp Act in 1765 and took the oath of allegiance to the United States in 1777. Raised in affluence, Rebecca received her education in women's academies as well as in her father's library, where she read widely in literature, history, and science.

As a young woman, Gratz danced at the balls of Philadelphia's elite, wrote poetry, and was friendly with the writers Washington Irving and James Kirke Paulding. Legend has it that Irving described Gratz to Sir Walter Scott, who subsequently used her as the model for the dark-haired Jewess Rebecca in *Ivanhoe*, the first positive characterization of a Jew in British literature. Prominent American artists, including Thomas Sully, painted portraits of this young, beautiful woman. At nineteen, Gratz helped her mother care for her father after he suffered a stroke; she remained the family nurse for the rest of her life.

Around 1801, Gratz, along with her mother, sister, and other Philadelphia women, established a nonsectarian charitable organization to help impoverished women and children, and was appointed secretary of this organization. In 1815, she and others founded the Philadelphia Orphan Asylum, for which she was also secretary—for forty years. Later, in the 1830s, she advised her sister-in-law on how to establish the first orphan asylum in Lexington, Kentucky.

Gratz combined her concern for the welfare of women and children with her lifelong commitment to Judaism when, in 1819, she founded the Female Hebrew Benevolent Society, the first Jewish charity unaffiliated with a synagogue. With this society, Gratz wanted to counteract the proselytizing that Christian women engaged in while they provided charity for the poor. Later, in the 1850s, she founded the Jewish Foster Home to help the increasing numbers of immigrant Jews. As executive secretary of this organization, Gratz was instrumental in forming institutional policy; the reports she drafted were published to raise popular support, and she thus found a public.

Rebecca Gratz was a cosmopolitan, worldly, and very American Jew. A member of Philadelphia's Sephardic congregation Mikveh Israel, Gratz, like most other Jewish women, knew no Hebrew and prayed in English from prayer books in translation imported from England and, later, from those translated by Isaac Leeser, who led her congregation. An avid reader and promoter of Judaism, she collected the latest of the new Jewish American writings and translations by Leeser and others. In the 1840s, she publicized books by Grace Aguilar, the Jewish British writer who advocated the importance of Judaism to women. Her lifelong reading of British classic and contemporary writers such as William Shakespeare and Thomas Carlyle, as well as her conversations and letters with Christian friends and her beloved sister-in-law in Lexington, also contributed to her thoughts about religion.

Despite her celebration of the religious freedom and equality granted Jews in the United States, Gratz practiced traditional Judaism and insisted that American Jews know and observe their faith. While opposing the changes advocated by the Reform movement, Gratz initiated great changes of her own in Jewish religious education in America. In 1818, she organized a home-based Hebrew school for her nieces and nephews that, twenty years later, she developed into a coeducational, citywide institution. Independent of any synagogue, Gratz's Hebrew Sunday School was the first Jewish school where women could teach religion and determine curriculum. Two of its teachers, the sisters Simha Peixotto and Rachel Peixotto Pyke, wrote the textbooks; Leeser wrote and translated the school's Jewish catechism and publicized the institution nationally. In later years, the school chose and trained its faculty exclusively from the school's female graduates. The conventional Gratz was thus the first to give Jewish women the public means to shape and transmit American Judaism.

Of the twelve Gratz siblings, three of the daughters and two of the sons married. Gratz herself remained single. She lived with her three bachelor brothers and a sister, raising the six children of another sister, Rachel, who died prematurely. Gratz's older sister, Richea Gratz, was the first Jewish woman to attend college in America—Franklin College, in Lancaster, Pennsylvania, in 1787. Rebecca Gratz died on August 27, 1869, in Philadelphia.

The seven letters selected here show how Gratz's Jewish and American identities converged daily. Gratz addressed these letters to her youngest brother, Benjamin Gratz, his first wife, Maria Gist Gratz, and his second wife, Ann Boswell Gratz, in Lexington. Maria Gist Gratz, from a prominent Virginia and Kentucky family of Revolutionary stock, shared with her sister-in-law activities and interests in literature, culture, and philanthropy. After her death in 1841, Benjamin married Maria's niece Ann Boswell Shelby. Although both his wives were Protestants and their children identified themselves as Christians, Benjamin remained Jewish.

The letter to Benjamin Gratz dated February 27, 1825, describes the dedication of the synagogue Mikveh Israel, giving a detailed picture of how the Jews of Philadelphia worshiped. Writing to Maria Gist Gratz, Rebecca discusses her reading, which reveals her connections to both mainstream American culture and history and to the concerns of Jews in the United States and abroad. In the letter of June 29, 1834, she urges Maria to give the author of a new biography of George Washington details of the first president's unknown romance with Maria's aunt. In the letter of August 27, 1840, Gratz writes Maria about the latest translation of an obscure traditional Jewish text and about the American response to anti-Semitic riots in Damascus.

During the Civil War, Gratz wrote letters to Ann Boswell Gratz and to Benjamin Gratz, four of which are reprinted here. Grieving that her nephew Cary Gratz (son of Benjamin and Maria), a soldier in the Union Army, was killed in the battle at Wilson's Creek, Missouri, Gratz discusses how the divisiveness of the Civil War has reached into the very fabric of her own family. Details in these letters also reveal Gratz's patriotism in her outrage at foreign support for the South and at other Philadelphians' indifference to the danger. In her letter of March 11, 1863, Gratz mentions celebrating Purim, the commemoration of the ancient Persian Jews' defeat of their enemy, Haman. When she writes of conveying information from Ann's previous letter directly to President Lincoln, "where it might be useful to the country," Gratz unconsciously suggests that her own actions are like those of the heroic Jewish queen Esther, who saved the Jews of Persia.

From Letters of Rebecca Gratz

To Benjamin Gratz[1]

February 27th 1825

I scarcely know how to regret the defection of our brothers My dear Ben, since it has procured me the happiness of receiving a letter from you—I have never the less chid them for their neglect and as speedily as possible sit down to remove the evil of which you complain but I confess now that the pen is in my hand—I am at a loss where to begin. My heart and my eyes overflow at the idea of the long separation from my beloved brother—and a family record would be too full of feelings which have a home in every breast but may not be uttered without realizing what Byron[2] says of "the mirror which dashes to the ground, and looking down on the fragments—sees its reflections multiplied"—

I am not disposed though to indulge such sad thoughts in return for the grateful pleasure your letter afforded—lest I "weary you in well doing"[3]—and deprive myself of hearing again particularly as you mention your dear Maria[4] is not well and I shall anxiously desire to hear of her recovery.

I am surprised you have no account of the consecration[5] except from the newspaper as it was a subject engaging universal attention—the article you mention was written by your old friend Tom Wharton[6] who was a spectator on the occasion. I have never witnessed a more impressive or solemn ceremony or one more calculated to elevate the mind to religious exercises—the shool[7] is one of the most beautiful specimens of ancient architecture in the city, and finished in the Stricklands'[8] best manner—the decorations are neat yet rich and tasteful—and the service commencing just before the Sabbath was performed by lamp light—Mr. Keys[9] was assisted in the service by the Hazan[1] from New York Mr. Peixotto[2] a venerable learned and pious man who gave great effect to the solemnity—the doors being opened by our brother Simon[3] and the blessing pronounced at the entrance—the processions entered with the two Reverends in their robes followed by nine copies of the Sacred Rolls—they advanced slowly to the Tabah[4] while a choir of five voices chanted the appointed psalms most delightfully when the new Hazan had been inducted into his office and took his place at the desk. Mr. P in slow and solemn manner preceded the Sephers[5] in their circuit round the area of the building between the desk and the ark—whilst such strains of sacred songs were chanted as might truly be said to have inspiration in them—between each circuit, the prayers appointed (as you

1. Benjamin Gratz (1792–1884), the youngest brother of Rebecca Gratz, lived in Lexington, Kentucky.
2. George Gordon, Lord Byron (1788–1824), English Romantic poet.
3. "Let us not weary in well-doing" (Galatians 6.9).
4. Maria Gist Gratz (d. 1841), first wife of Benjamin Gratz.
5. The dedication of the new synagogue of Congregation Mikveh Israel in Philadelphia.
6. Thomas I. Wharton (1791–1856), a legal reporter and writer.
7. Shul (Yiddish), synagogue.
8. William Strickland (1787–1854), a Philadelphia architect, designed the synagogue in the latest neo-Egyptian style.
9. Abraham Israel Keys, rabbi at Mikveh Israel from 1824 to 1828.
1. Cantor (Hebrew).
2. Moses Levi Maduro Peixotto, rabbi of the New York City congregation Shearith Israel from 1820 to 1828.
3. Simon Gratz (1773–1839), the older brother of Rebecca Gratz.
4. The reading desk in the synagogue (Hebrew). "Sacred Rolls": the scrolls of the Five Books of Moses, the Torah.
5. The scrolls of the Five Books of Moses.

will see in the book our brother sent you) to be performed by the Hazan and the congregation were said and among the most affecting parts of the service—Mr. Keys in a fine full voice and the responses by Mr. Peixotto in a voice tremulous from agitation and deep feeling. I have no hope of conveying by description any idea of this ceremony—you must have seen the whole spectacle—the beautiful ark thrown wide open to receive the sacred deposit, with its rich crimson-curtains fringed with gold—the perpetual lamp suspended in front with its little constant light like a watchman at his post—and with the humble yet dignified figure of the venerable Mr. P. as he conducted the procession in its seven circuits and then deposited the laws—after which Mr. Keys recited with an effect amounting almost to eloquence that impressive prayer of King Solomon[6]—the whole audience was most profoundly attentive and though few were so happy as to understand the language—those who did—say they have never heard the Hebrew so well delivered as by Mr. Keys—the bishop expressed this opinion—and all who were there acknowledge there has never been such church music performed in Philadelphia—you will wonder where "these sweet singers in Israel"[7] were collected from—the leader, teacher and principal performer is Jacob Seixas and his female first voice his sister Miriam,[8] they were fortunately on a visit to their sister Mrs. Phillips and induced a class to practice for some weeks—Miriam and Becky Moses[9] contributed very considerably and all in the congregation who Mr. S. found teachable assisted—he is now resident here and we hope by his assistance to keep up a very respectable class of singers in the synagogue. The service continues to be finely performed and the congregation behave with the utmost decorum and propriety during the service. I scarcely know how to answer your questions concerning Mr. Keys—I do not believe he is a learned man—nor indeed a very sensible one—but he is a good Hebrew scholar—an excellent Teacher, and a good man, he is moreover very popular with the congregation and reads the prayers in a manner as to make his hearers feel that he understands and is inspired with their solemnity—perhaps his usefulness is not lessened by his diffidence—he is modest and unassuming, which suits the proud, the ignorant and presumptuous—these require most reformation and he is so respectable on the Tabah that he gives general satisfaction—Mr. P. is such a man as you describe, he was a merchant before the death of Mr. Seixas[1] but has since his clerical appointment studied and become as learned as he is intelligent—Mr. K. has had a congregation[2] which only required him to perform his shool duties—now that he is among more intelligent people he too will feel the necessity of study—he has a wife and three clever children and when he gets over his West Indian indolence he will shew what he can become—one very important talent he certainly possesses—he is a good Hebrew teacher—yesterday one of his pupils read a barmitzvah portion[3] very hand-

6. The passage of Scripture (1 Kings 8) customarily read at synagogue dedications.
7. An adaptation of 2 Samuel 23.2.
8. Jacob Seixas and Miriam Seixas were the son and daughter of Benjamin Mendes Seixas and Zipporah Levy Seixas.
9. Nieces of Rebecca Gratz.
1. Gershom Mendes Seixas (1768–1816), rabbi of Congregation Shearith Israel in New York City.
2. Mr. Keys previously led a congregation in Barbados, West Indies.
3. *Bar mitzvah* (Hebrew) literally means "son of the commandment." It is a Jewish religious coming-of-age ceremony in which a thirteen-year-old boy chants the weekly Torah portion.

somely although he had only a few weeks' instruction. Our brothers have all become very attentive to shool matters—Hyman is Gaboy[4] and they rarely omit attending worship. We all go Friday evening as well as on Saturday morning—the gallery[5] is as well filled as the other portion of the house—I think continually of you My dear Brother when I enter that temple and I pray that I may again see you worshiping within its walls—I know your faith is unchangeable and will endure even though you are alone in a land of strangers.[6] May God be merciful to us all and keep us steadfast to our duties. I love your dear Maria, and admire the forbearance which leaves unmolested the religious opinions she knows are sacred in your estimation. May you both continue to worship according to the dictates of your conscience and your orisons be equally acceptable at the throne of Grace. . . .

* * *

God Bless you and yours my beloved Brother—accept again my thanks for your letter and believe me always your attached sister

R G

1929

To Maria Gist Gratz

June 29th, [1834]

* * *

We are reading "Spark's Washington"[1] the 2 and 3 vols. only are out—the first will contain his Life—pray My dear, furnish him with that interesting portion of Washington's biography which relates to your Aunt for I fear he has slender materials of exhibiting the sentiment of his character—Mrs. Washington having destroyed all his letters addressed to her, shortly before her death—now everything great and noble, in the Soldier and Statesman may be presented to our respect and veneration—but it requires some touches of human affections and passions to complete the man, and give him a place in our hearts—he writes most affectionately to Col. Gist[2] and my imagination constantly runs on his fair Sister,[3] though Mr. Sparks is evidently ignorant of this attachment—he speaks of a humble attachment, which prevented his being endangered by the attractions of some inmates of the Fairfax family—and the letters which relate to his Marriage are so passionless that I am sure there was a corner of his heart locked up to the memory of his first betrothed—that generous self devoted being whose very

4. *Gabbai* (Hebrew), warden of a synagogue.
5. The women's section of the Orthodox synagogue.
6. Benjamin Gratz's first and second wives were Christians, but he never converted and was buried with Jewish rites.
1. Jared Sparks (1789–1866), American publisher, editor of the *North American Review*, historian, and educator. He edited *The Writings of George Washington* (1834–37) and *The Works of Benjamin Franklin* (1836–40), among other undertakings.
2. Colonel Christopher Gist, Maria's grandfather, who served with George Washington in Braddock's War in 1755.
3. Family legend held that one of Christopher Gist's sisters and George Washington had a romantic relationship in their youth.

rejection was a proof of superiority which could not have been lost on such a heart as Washington's—now Maria, if among old family papers you could find but a single note of his to your Aunt, or any record of their engagement—it would give such interest to the Editor's task—that you ought not withhold it—The mass of American biography now collecting will be a valuable addition to our literature—If you have not read "Gouverneur Morris"[4] I would recommend it as finely written and excellent letters—present My best love, to our dear Ben, and your lovely boys—charge a rainy afternoon with all this scribble—and believe I would not have been so unreasonable if a private conveyance had not offered—the sun now appears and an engagement abroad saves you from further tediousness which this fair sheet might invite—God bless you My beloved. . . .

I embrace you all with my whole heart and am devotedly

your Sister RG

1929

To Maria Gist Gratz

August 27th 1840

I received your letter from Canewood[1] My dear sister and was right glad to be carried back in idea to that delightful home scene of your family and the beautiful country I so much admired and enjoyed in the agreeable visit we made there together—I have a thousand times reflected on the bright moon light evenings we passed so quietly wandering about the lawn, or sitting in the shade of majestic trees conversing of one interesting matter or other, till the forest seemed peopled with their original inhabitants which the footprints of man rarely intruded.

I should like to have made one of your summer party—to have seen your namesake nieces, and heard your observations on the book of Jashar,[2] that extravagant chronicle of bible characters—there is a portion of it very agreeable to me—but so many improbable histories and some impossible exploits entirely destroy its credibility, and one cannot but wonder that the author or his translator, could expect it would ever pass for the veritable book of Jashar referred to in the Scriptures. An intelligent hebrew Scholar, raised my expectations so high, in favor of it before it appeared that I confess I was sadly disappointed, when I found it impossible, as I proceeded in the work, to class it with anything better than an old romance—It was very affecting to hear Abraham and Isaac conversing on the sacrifice, as they journeyed to Mount Moriah, and to find that Jacob shared the fortitude and faith that supported them—but the introduction of Satan, and his malignant effect on the life of Jacob is shocking—particularly as the next event recorded in Scripture history is the death of Sarah[3] it is true she had

4. Morris (1752–1816) was an American statesman, diplomat, and financial expert. Sparks's *The Life of Gouverneur Morris* was published in 1832.

1. The Kentucky estate of Maria Gist's mother.

2. The Book of Jashar is a lost ancient text of heroic songs, referred to in Joshua 10.13 and 2 Samuel 1.18. An English translation of a 12th-century Hebrew midrash was published under this title in New York in 1840.

3. A Biblical Matriarch, Sarah was the wife of Abraham and the mother of Isaac. "Abraham": the first of the three Patriarchs, father of Isaac, grandfather of Jacob. "Mount Moriah": the mountain to which God summoned Abraham in order to carry out his sacrifice of Isaac (Genesis 22).

reached a good old age and in the course of nature, might be called on to resign her life, and happily too, for as a wife and mother she was blessed, and triumphant, but we would rather think she had gone down peacefully to "the place appointed for all living,"[4] than to be killed by sudden joy—and the fallen angel the agent. Those who would take the bible history as the foundation of these works should be careful never to violate the spirit and influence of the Sacred book, nor assign motives for events not borne out by its authority—The beautiful history of Joseph too is spoiled in this book—and Moses[5] suffers so many adventures, that we scarcely recognize him as the plain man "meek" and "slow of speech" as he records himself to be—but enough of this, we are threading another passage in Jewish story as heart thrilling as any recorded since their dispersion—I mean the massacres at Damascus[6] and the still enduring sufferings of the poor tortured prisoners, who are accused of unnatural and unlawful crimes of which it is impossible they can be guilty—in Europe and America great exertions are making for their relief—there is a meeting to be held this Evening here, and I believe all the community feel an interest in it—Hyman[7] received a very gratifying letter from Dr. Duchesnel offering to cooperate with the Israelites in any measures devised, and saying had a general meeting of citizens been called, our Christian friends would have freely attended—but what can be done, unless the Governments of Civilized Nations combine to save them—the Jews have no representative powers, and can only act in their individual capacities, the support of the countries of which they are citizens—and the application of their wealth to purchase their brothers' lives is all that they can do—and perhaps this is as far as human aid can go.[8] God in his Mercy, may touch the hearts of their oppressors, or break their bonds when all visible means fail.

* * *

I have some doubts whether you will be able to read this letter, for all the materials are bad, and badly used, but may try to decipher enough to convince you of my real affection dearest Maria for you and all your dear family—Cary's[9] birthday does not pass us by unheeded—Horace claimed our good wishes on the same date—he is away and comfortably employed—. . . . God Bless you all with your heart's desire and make you happy prays yours true friend and sister R G

1929

4. Job 30.23.
5. In the book of Exodus, Moses freed the Hebrews from the Egyptian pharoah and, at Mount Sinai, delivered to them the Ten Commandments. "Joseph": Jacob's son, who, according to the Bible, rose to political prominence in Egypt after having been sold into slavery by his brothers.
6. Also known as the Damascus Affair or Damascus Blood Libel. In 1840, riots against the Jews of Damascus, Syria, were instigated by Christian authorities, who falsely accused Jews of murdering a monk in order to use his blood for Passover rites. In Europe and elsewhere, the use of Jews as scapegoats by politicians, both secular and religious, aided by an ignorant populace has a long history, extending from the Middle Ages through the 20th century.
7. Hyman Gratz (1776–1857), Rebecca Gratz's brother.
8. The Jewish communities of Europe and America protested the Damascus Affair and urged their governments to intervene. The British government officially castigated the Damascus violence.
9. Cary Gratz, son of Benjamin and Maria Gist Gratz.

To Ann Boswell Gratz[1]

August 23rd, [1861]

Thanks, what grateful thanks My dear Sister, do I owe you, for your most kind letters, over which I have wept again, and again—and prayed for my beloved Brother—whose grief I share, but cannot measure even by that which fills my heart—all human sympathy are but drops of comfort, in his great sorrow, but God in *his* mercy will open a fountain of consolation to his mourning spirit—the beloved son, whom "He gave; and hath taken away" will rise in an angel's form, to whisper peace—memorials of all his virtues and loveliness—his pure and innocent life, and brave qualities, the noble heart as tender, and full of filial love—all perfected and immortal—will in future be to him—his very son—his beloved Cary.[2]

You Dear Ann, and the treasures that are surrounding him, will win him from the indulgence of feelings which have so overwhelm'd him—and I trust restore his peace—experience has taught me, that it is thus God deals with us, we live on, cherishing those that are taken from us, as though they were only removed from sight—with the hope of reunion in another world. . . .

I hope My Sister, you can excuse my impatient pleadings—I had sent my letters before yours arrived—forgetting that though further away, we got information nearly as soon as you did.

Your second letter, which I have also received, gives me great comfort, as it tells me Ben is more composed—I trust the efforts of his friends will be successful in obtaining the dear remains—Frank Blair[3] is now on the spot to aid them—I pray most fervently that Kentucky[4] will not be involved in this dreadful strife—we live here in constant agitation—every day's account of wrongs and outrages perpetrated by kindred on each other—of familiar friends becoming bitter foes, is too appalling to be realized, in our late happy country—even members of the same family warring with each other. Lizzie Lee and her son are at Bethlehem—all the females of the family excepting your Aunt Blair,[5] are driven from their home—she will not leave her husband—though both are surrounded by troops and are uncertain of an hour's safety—

Give dear love for me to My Brother, and all the children. I am glad Bernard[6] is with you—his presence must be a comfort to his father—remember me most kindly to Judge Brown—and believe me always My dear Ann your grateful and affectionate

Sister RG

1929

1. Benjamin Gratz married his second wife, Anna Maria Boswell Shelby (a niece of his deceased first wife, Maria Gist Gratz), in 1843.
2. Cary Gratz, Benjamin's son and a soldier in the Union army, was killed in the Battle of Wilson's Creek, Missouri, on August 10, 1861, at the age of thirty-two.
3. Relative of Ann Boswell Gratz.
4. During the Civil War, Kentucky retained its allegiance to the Union North despite pressures to ally with the Confederate South.
5. A relative of Ann Boswell Gratz, still in the South. "Lizzie Lee and her son": relatives of Ann Boswell Gratz, in Bethlehem, Pennsylvania.
6. Son of Benjamin and the late Maria Gist Gratz.

To Ann Boswell Gratz

Philadelphia September 12th 1861

I have long thought of you My Dear Ann, and sympathized in the anxiety, which I knew must silently be preying on your peace of mind—on account of your Son Jo Shelby[1] whose name I have seen mentioned in the Southern Army, so fatal to our Beloved Cary—I heard previously to your letter, of the hopes entertained that we should probably recover his dear remains—and trust his good brother Bernard may have the consolation of bringing to his bereaved Father the privilege of depositing them in holy ground.

Dear dear Ann, what changes have taken place in our once happy country. One can hardly realize they are *at home*—in the U. S. of America—and are at war with each other—I have been reading some loving letters from some so near to me in blood and affections whose arms are perhaps now raised against the hearts at which they have fed—and the bosoms of those, who have cherished them—this I cannot but lament as among the horrors of war. The recent news from Kentucky is very cheering. God grant you may be successful—and retain your allegiance to the Union—such men as Holt and Anderson and Crittenden[2] must encourage your patriots to fight in the good cause. I hope the Governer will be true to his promise—

Just received your letter of the 9*th* thanks Dearest Sister, for your consideration of me, in the agitation of such a moment—I pray with you, that our beloved Ben, may be comforted, and like David,[3] resigned to the dispensation of the Almighty—hoping, though his beloved son, can no more come to him—they shall be reunited in another world—How I wish by sharing I could lessen My poor brother's grief!—

I sympathize with you, too My dear Ann, in the anxiety which is so harassing by the uncertain accounts the papers bring of the contending Armies—we may pray for Jo's personal safety—though we cannot for the success of his arms—Faith in Him, who in justice and in Mercy rules over the destiny of all, must give us patience! Tomorrow will be a holy day with us—Sabbath and day of Atonement,[4] when memorials of the dead mingle with petitions for the living—and we endeavor to purify ourselves by devotion, confession and repentance—you will all be remembered by me, in the house of prayer—

My health has greatly improved within a few weeks. I feel stronger than during the hot weather, and live very quietly. Miriam Etting[5] dined with me yesterday, and asked me to give love and sympathy to her Uncle and you—my tender greetings to all around you—and grateful affection to yourself My dear Ann

R Gratz

13th September [1861]

1929

1. Son of Ann Boswell Gratz from her first marriage, and a soldier in the Confederate army.
2. In December 1860, John Crittenden (1787–1863) introduced the "Crittenden Compromise" in the U.S. Senate as a gesture of conciliation between North and South. "Holt": i.e., Joseph Holt (1807–1894), U.S. secretary of war in 1861. "Anderson": i.e., Robert Anderson (1805–1871), who was in command of Fort Sumter, South Carolina, when it was attacked by Confederate forces in April 1861.
3. King David, who mourned the death of his rebellious son, Absalom (2 Samuel 19.1–5).
4. Yom Kippur.
5. Miriam Gratz Etting (1807–1878), daughter of Frances Gratz and Reuben Etting, niece of Rebecca Gratz and Benjamin Gratz.

To Ann Boswell Gratz

Philadelphia March 11th 1863

My Dear Ann

Your last letter was so full of interesting matter, and so graphic in describing the condition of Kentucky and its requirements that I could not resist sending it on a mission—where it might be useful to the country, so I enclosed it to Lizzie[1] and requested her to show it to her Father, who might make good use of it—on returning it to me she says, "I read what you said to Father, and he read carefully Cousin Ann's letter, which he will duly report to the President[2] in person—I return the letter as you desired and her name will not be used"—Lizzie mentioned our Dear Ben's letter to her father—you are working together in this holy cause, which may God prosper! and bring back to us peace throughout our beloved country—the part which most interests me at present is where you dwell because the immediate aid has been wanting and so much might be secured by a few good officers—I feel as if our turn would come, from the fleets preparing in Europe, in our unprotected harbors—England with her minister at our court, is in feeling acts and words doing all she can to aid our rebels—and is watching an occasion to do openly what it is easy to see she desires—The Lord Mayor's feast received Mason with honors—the illustrated News gives portraits of confederate Generals and Statesmen—and Punch[3] is full of satires on the U.S. and strictures on their great men—white and black

But my Dear Ann it is a happiness to hear that you are all well would I could relieve my beloved brother from some of his anxieties and annoyance— . . . . tell Dear Ben, our Purim[4] evening was celebrated this year on the 4th—his loving thoughts and good wishes were more precious than all else on the occasion. I pray it may please God to permit us to meet again in this world and the memory of the past be sanctified to us by blessings still in store to crown his life in his own happy household. Adieu My dear Ann, give my love to all around you, and believe me affectionately your

R G

1929

To Benjamin Gratz

April 15th 1863

I thank you My beloved brother for your most kind letter, which relieved me from much anxiety—I never for a moment doubted the good faith of your household—but was under the impression that Mrs. S. had come to reside with you and feared you might experience difficulties and incur responsibilities which would interfere with the harmony so essential to

1. Perhaps a reference to Lizzie Lee, a relative of Ann Boswell Gratz.
2. Abraham Lincoln.
3. *Punch: or, the London Charivari*: an illustrated satiric British political weekly magazine. England was sympathetic to the Confederate cause during the Civil War. "Mason": i.e., James Murray Mason (1798–1871), Virginia politician who, in 1861, was appointed commissioner of the Confederacy to Great Britain and France.
4. Purim, "lots" (Hebrew), is the Jewish holiday, celebrated on the fourteenth of Adar, that commemorates Queen Esther's rescue of the Jews of Persia from Haman's plot to murder them.

domestic comfort—I trust dear Ann[1] will pardon me if I give her a moments concern—my heart goes with her in the peculiar interest she has in this connection where her private feelings are so much in conflict with the condition we most approve and desire to accomplish—My love for Miriam[2] and her children makes me realize all she suffers for those so near to her—we heard that Miriam was in Virginia on account of the illness of her son, whom they had taken home to Savannah—but what their present condition may be is yet to be determined—one of Gratz's sons is in Canada with Sara,[3] sent there to keep him out of the way of mischief, but he seems tainted with the politics of his father—Sara and her husband are truly loyal, though it seems the community in which they live is full of southern sympathizers and no doubt ready to adopt any English measures—I am rejoiced that Kentucky is ably supported and I hope will be safe through all coming time—I marvel at the apathy of our community—with the knowledge of Fleets of iron clad steamers preparing abroad which might enter our rivers and lay our cities in ashes no movement of defense is made. Philadelphia is as full of idle people, the streets and shops crowded and except in the exorbitant prices asked for commodities and freely given the presence of war is unheeded—except indeed in the active works of charity for the sick and wounded brought to our hospitals. My Dear brother, I am too old to do any good, but feel deep interest in all this and pray for better times. . . .

Give My love to your sons and their families—and believe me, ever dearest and beloved Ben your affectionate Sister

R Gratz

1929

1. Ann Boswell Gratz, Benjamin Gratz's second wife.
2. Miriam Moses Cohen, daughter of Rebecca Gratz's sister Rachel, whom Rebecca raised; married to Solomon Cohen of Georgetown, South Carolina, in 1836; lived in Savannah, Georgia.
3. Sara Moses Joseph, Miriam Moses Cohen's sister who lived in Montreal. "One of Gratz's sons": Dr. Simon Gratz Moses, nephew of Rebecca Gratz, brother of Miriam Moses Cohen and Sara Moses Joseph, married Mary P. Asche of Wilmington, North Carolina, in 1838 and settled in St. Louis, Missouri.

MORDECAI MANUEL NOAH
1785–1851

Mordecai Manuel Noah was perhaps the most famous Jew in America during the early decades of the nineteenth century and the first person to grapple publicly with the tensions of being both an American and a Jew. By profession a highly visible politician and journalist, he was involved throughout his life with theater in the young and culturally independent United States and, as an avid and patriotic promoter of American literature, wrote four full-length plays and six shorter dramas between 1808 and 1840.

Born in Philadelphia to a father who had emigrated from Mannheim, Germany, and an American-born mother whose ancestry included both German Jews and a famous Sephardic rabbi, Noah was orphaned at age seven. He spent his boyhood shuttling between his maternal grandparents in Charleston, South Carolina, and other family members in New York City and Philadelphia, where he attended various schools, including New York City's only Jewish school. After an apprenticeship to a carver and gilder in Albany and work as a messenger and peddler, Noah returned to Philadelphia at age twenty-two, where he began his political career. Soon thereafter in New York City, he launched his parallel career in journalism by writing for the *Public Advertiser*, published by his uncle Naphtali Phillips. At this time, Noah also began writing and producing plays for a little theater company that he had helped found, and reviewed plays for a magazine that he helped edit.

Initially unsuccessful in his petition to President James Madison for a diplomatic post in 1810, Noah was appointed consul to the Barbary State of Tunis in 1813, a post from which he was dismissed in 1815 for purportedly stealing money, although the accusation was never proven. In 1819, he published *Travels in England, France, Spain, and the Barbary States in the Years 1813–14 and 15*, a travelogue based on his diplomatic stint that provides an invaluable portrayal of Tunisian Jewry. As editor of the *National Advocate*, Noah transformed this New York Democratic-Republican party organ into a lively, controversial newspaper. Appointed official city printer in 1818, he became deeply involved in the politics of the Tammany Society. He was elected sheriff of New York City in 1821 but lost reelection in 1822.

When the *National Advocate* was sold in 1824, Noah founded a rival newspaper, the *New York National Advocate*, and shifted his political alliances, breaking with Tammany to support De Witt Clinton for governor. In 1826, he established yet another paper, the *New-York Enquirer*, which he published until 1829. President Andrew Jackson appointed Noah surveyor and inspector of the New York Port, a salaried federal position that briefly provided the now married Noah with financial security. In 1829, Noah was elected to serve as a delegate to the New York City charter reform convention. However, he shifted his political loyalties to the newly formed conservative Whig party when President Jackson replaced him as surveyor. In 1833, Noah founded yet another newspaper, the influential (New York) *Evening Star*. Allied with the most conservative of the Whigs, Noah advocated temperance (but not prohibition), praised the rich for their discipline, opposed birth control and abortion, decried religious bigotry, and championed freedom of speech even for causes he despised. As an editor and journalist, he supported the Native American party of 1835–36 and the Texas revolt against Mexico of 1836 and vehemently attacked the cause of abolition. Noah was appointed a judge of the Court of Sessions in 1841.

As a Jew, Noah was committed to preserving Jewish uniqueness and, simultaneously, to helping Jews accommodate to the Christian world. In 1824, he attempted to establish on Grand Island, in the Niagara River, a haven for the persecuted Jews of the world that he aptly named Ararat, after the mountain on which the ark of the biblical Noah came to rest after the Flood. Despite the much publicized proclamation and ceremony in 1825, heralding "the establishment of the Jewish State of Ararat" "under the auspices and protection of the constitution and laws of the United States of America," Noah's efforts failed. He was active in the Sephardic synagogues of Philadelphia and New York, in the latter of which he supported a secession by Ashkenazic Jews. He championed Jewish education throughout his life, welcomed the founding of the Jewish periodicals the *Occident* and *Asmonean*, and was president of the philanthropic New York Hebrew Benevolent Society.

During the 1830s and 1840s, Noah wrote and published extensively in his newspapers on Jewish matters, ranging from synagogue dedications, journeys to the Holy Land, and the suffering of Jews abroad to answering personal anti-Semitic attacks by political and journalistic rivals and correcting more general slurs and distortions expressed in public, from Daniel Webster's Senate orations to university professors' books. In 1840, he joined the famous protest by Europe's Jewish communities and by Britain and other governments against the blood-libel accusation and subsequent anti-Jewish attacks during the Damascus Affair. He participated in the 1846 New

York protest of the abuse of Jews in czarist Russia. Shortly before he died in 1851, he protested against an American treaty with Switzerland that contained an anti-Jewish clause. As an American-born Jew, Noah sought to prove that one could be both a good Jew and a good American, cultivating the Jewish community and urging Americans to battle against the persecution of Jews everywhere.

Between 1819 and 1824, Noah's four feature plays were performed in New York City, and three were published. Two of these, *She Would Be a Soldier; or, The Plains of Chippewa* (1819) and *Marion; or, The Hero of Lake George* (1821), continued to play throughout the United States during the nineteenth century and were among the most important dramas written in America before the Civil War because they introduced episodes from American history (the War of 1812, the American Revolution) as legitimate subjects for the stage. *Yusef Caramalli; or, The Siege of Tripoli* (1820) dealt, like a number of contemporary plays, with the capture and enslavement of American sailors in the Mediterranean by the Barbary States (Algiers, Tripoli, Morocco, and Tunis) after the War of 1812. *The Grecian Captive; or, The Fall of Athens* (1822) was the first American play to present as a "just and holy" cause the contemporary Greek struggle for independence from the Turks.

Five of Noah's six shorter works were also performed on stage. *Paul and Alexis; or, The Orphans of the Rhine*, an adaptation of a French drama, was first performed in Charleston, South Carolina, in 1812 and later in London and throughout the United States. Others were occasional pieces, performed for specific celebrations, such as New York's new constitution in 1822 (*Oh Yes; or, The New Constitution*), Lafayette's visit to New York City in 1824 (*The Siege of Yorktown*), and the completion of the Erie Canal in 1825 (*The Grand Canal*). The last play, *Natalie; or, The Frontier Maid* (1840), based on events that took place during the American Revolution, was produced but never published. By his own admission, Noah was not primarily a playwright, saying that he had "no claim to the character of a settled, regular, or domiciliated writer for the green-room." Nonetheless, his plays were popular and influential in his day and helped to establish an American dramatic literature independent of Britain and Europe. None of his plays has a Jewish character or theme; rather, these works focus on establishing American themes and subjects in drama.

The play included in our anthology, *The Fortress of Sorrento,* was Noah's first, published in 1808 and never staged. Although Noah himself disavowed this work later in his life, calling it "a little melodrama" that was his "first regular attempt at dramatic composition," and commented that the publisher paid him in books rather than cash, the play has merit for our purposes. Derived from *Leonora*, a French opera, *The Fortress of Sorrento* lacks the bawdy comedy, the broader dramatic range, and the American theme of *She Would Be a Soldier.* However, *The Fortress of Sorrento* sets forth one of Noah's central devices—that of the heroine who disguises herself as a man in order to realize her goals of self-fulfillment and the restoration of justice. In *She Would Be a Soldier,* the heroine, Christine, dresses as a soldier in order to escape her father's choice of a husband for her and performs an act of military heroism. In *The Fortress of Sorrento,* the protagonist, Leonora, poses as the young Fidelio, a jailor's turnkey, in order to free her husband, Horestan, unjustly held prisoner and condemned to death by the evil governor of the fortress. Melodrama that it is, this short and readable play by a young man enthusiastically endorses justice and truth, and thus heralds the mature Noah. Notwithstanding its French origins, the play's setting in Sorrento, Italy, and mention of Seville, Spain, allude to Noah's own Sephardic ancestors—to his great-great-grandfather, Dr. Samuel Nuñez, and great-grandmother, Zipra Nuñez Machado, who were imprisoned and tortured by the Inquisition before they escaped to London and eventually to the colonies of Georgia and New York. Echoes of the Inquisition—for example, Leonora's prayer at the end of the first act, reminiscent of Hebrew liturgy, is delivered by the heroine while she kneels in the Christian manner—and the theme of political justice mark this play as more than simply an adaptation of a European popular work. Rather, this play, perhaps the earliest drama to be published in America by a Jew, resonates with Jewish American history.

The Fortress of Sorrento[1]

A Petit Historical Drama, in Two Acts

DRAMATIS PERSONAE

DON FERDINAND, *viceroy of Seville.*
DON PIZARE, *governor of the fortress.*
HORESTAN, *a prisoner.*
ROC, *the jailor.*
JACQUINETT, *the porter.*
GUARDS.
SOLDIERS.
LEONORA, *wife to Horestan, in disguise.*
MARCELINE, *Roc's daughter.*

Act I

Scene—a courtyard surrounded with buildings having grated windows—on each side is a grated arcade—at the bottom a large gate, near which a sentry-box stands.

MARCELINE *discovered netting*[2]—JACQUINETT *on guard.*

MARCELINE: Heigho! Fidelio does not return. Well, 'tis not surprising; for of late the poor boy has had so many errands to perform, I see him but seldom. Thank heaven the day will soon be fixed for our marriage, and my dear Fidelio will no longer be a turnkey:[3]—that duty hardens the heart until it becomes callous to the voice of pity.

JACQUINETT [*closing the gate*]: If I have not opened this gate at least a hundred times today, then is my name not pretty little innocent Jacquinett. Now, Marceline, let us chat a little. [*Knock.*] Again! can I never quit this cursed gate? [*Opens it.*]

MARCELINE: Now is he a-going to torment me once more with his love-sick tale. Would I were gone!

JACQUINETT [*without*]: Very well, it shall be delivered. Now my sweet Marceline, my little angel, I want to converse with you——

MARCELINE: Well, proceed—

JAQUINETT: You know how long I have sighed for you—

MARCELINE: In truth?

JACQUINETT: Ay, in truth. You know last night I refused to dance with every girl that asked me, for your sake—

MARCELINE: Indeed?

JACQUINETT: Ay, indeed; in short I love you, pretty Marceline.

MARCELINE: Hold, Jacquinett, why should I deceive you. I tell you with truth I do not like you.

JACQUINETT: Not like me, brazenface? 'tis all in vain, I know you do. Six months ago you encouraged me—

MARCELINE: What do you mean?

1. Commune, port, and church center in southern Italy on the south side of the Bay of Naples.
2. To knot, twist, or weave together in the style of a net.
3. Jailor or warden.

JACQUINETT: I was then your pretty little Jacquinett—you suffered me to walk with you, and to talk with you; and now you will hardly permit me to do either. Since that little varlet[4] Fidelio has been in the castle, your eyes are constantly on him; you converse but with him: and I verily believe you love him.

MARCELINE: 'Tis very true; I do love him.

JACQUINETT: A boy who comes from nobody knows where, and belongs to nobody knows who; whom your father has taken in from charity—

MARCELINE: 'Tis true, he is poor and an orphan; he does not conceal it, and I admire his amiable candor.

JACQUINETT: And do you think I shall suffer this beggar-boy to rival me? no, no, let me not see him look tenderly at you, or——

[*Enter* ROC, *the jailor*.]

ROC: How now! always disputing?

MARCELINE: Ah, father, I am glad you are here: Jacquinett has been teasing me to love and marry him, that's all.

JACQUINETT: Yes, that is all.

ROC: And what answer made you?

MARCELINE: I told him that the one was as equally impossible as the other.

ROC [*ironically*]: And so, my good master Jacquinett. I have but one daughter, and you would deprive me of her. My sighing swain[5] 'tis well; now to your post, and let me not hear you whispering your love-lorn tales again—[*knocking*] attend the gate.

[*Exit* JACQUINETT.]

Has Fidelio not yet returned?

MARCELINE: Not yet, father.

ROC: He must have been detained a long time at the forge.

MARCELINE: He is here.

[*Enter* LEONORA, *dressed in coarse garments. On her back a large basket—a belt around her waist, to which a tin box is suspended. She carries a heavy chain, which she lets fall as she enters*.]

MARCELINE: Ah, how fatigued he appears!

ROC [*assisting to remove the basket*]: My poor Fidelio, thou hast labored hard to day.

LEONORA: True; I am a little tired. I thought they would never have finished mending that chain.

ROC [*regarding it*]: And by the mass, I think the prisoners will never succeed in breaking them again. Have you the bill?

LEONORA: 'Tis here.

ROC: [*examining it*]: Marry, I cannot tell the reason, but since thou hast been with me, I have saved more for the six months, than I did a year before.

LEONORA: I do the best I can.

ROC: You cannot have more zeal and intelligence; and every day I become more attached to thee; thou art unknown to me, ignorant of thy birth and destitute of friends; still will I trust thee, cherish thee, and give my daughter to thee for a wife,—for I do believe thee honest.

4. Scoundrel; a base, unprincipled person.

5. Peasant; also, male admirer or suitor.

MARCELINE: How soon, dearest father?

ROC: As soon as the governor returns to Seville. He pays his monthly visit shortly to render an account of the prisons; till then be patient.

LEONORA: My embarrassment will sure betray me.

[*Aside.*]

ROC: Well, my children, you love each other, I believe truly; but love alone is light airy substance. Your old father will pinch himself; but you shall have gold to purchase happiness.

LEONORA: Nay, master Roc; the union of two hearts is the only source of true happiness; and conjugal love—ah, that must be the first of treasures! there is still, however, one which is no less precious to me; but all my efforts, I see it with grief, will not be able to obtain it.

ROC: A treasure? what is it?

LEONORA: Your confidence: forgive me this reproach. I often see you return from those dungeons exhausted with fatigue; why will you not allow me to accompany you? it would be grateful to me to assist your labors and partake of your fatigue.

ROC: Thou knowest well that my orders are most strict; and the heaviest injunctions are laid on me not to suffer any one to accompany me in my visits.

LEONORA: We must perform our duty, 'tis true; yet the fatigues daily experienced will one day exhaust you.

ROC: It is certain that I cannot long resist so many labors: the governor, notwithstanding his severity, must allow me to take thee in my visits to these dungeons.

LEONORA [*with sudden joy*]: Ah!

ROC: There is, however, one to whom (though I can confide in thee) don Pizare will never suffer thee to accompany me.

MARCELINE: Is it the prisoner of who we speak at times?

ROC: The same.

LEONORA: Has he been long confined?

ROC: Two years.

LEONORA [*hastily*]: For two years, say you?

MARCELINE: He must have been a great criminal.

ROC: Or must have great enemies, which is the same thing. We never could learn from whence he came, or what his name is; and oft as I conveyed him his slender pittance he begged to speak with me.

LEONORA: Well?

ROC: In my profession we can keep no secrets—I would not listen to him; but he will not trouble us long.

LEONORA [*with anxiety*]: How so?

ROC: Orders have been given to starve him.

LEONORA: Heavens!

MARCELINE: What crime can he have committed to occasion so dreadful a punishment?

ROC: For a month past don Pizare has ordered me to reduce his allowance: he has now but two ounces of bread, and a half measure of water in twenty-four hours; no light but the dull glimmer of my torch; no straw to rest his wearied head upon; his clothes are all decayed, and his appearance is misery itself——

MARCELINE: Ah! beware, my father; do not take Fidelio there. Such sights he is not accustomed to.

LEONORA: No, dearest Marceline! but in our calling we must be familiar with terrifying objects; and I have both strength and courage——

ROC: Right, my boy! I am pleased at your disposition: this will embolden me to ask the governor's permission for you to attend me in my visits to the dungeons.

[*A roll of drums is heard.*]

Hark! he is here.

[*Enter* DON PIZARE *preceded by* GUARDS.]

PIZARE [*speaking to the* CAPTAIN *of* GUARDS]: Three sentries on the ramparts; twelve men night and day on the drawbridge; as many on the side of the park; and let all who approach the walls be brought before me. Away! [GUARDS *disperse.*] [*To* ROC.] Is there any thing new?

ROC: No, my lord.

PIZARE: Where are my dispatches?

ROC: Here. [*Giving several letters, which he takes from a tin box.*]

PIZARE [*opening the letters*]: All commendations or reproaches! I have no time to waste on vile complaints. [*Regards a letter.*] Ha! methinks I should know this writing. [*Opens the letter, beckons* ROC *to retire, who removes the basket chair, etc. during the reading of the letter, and retires*—LEONORA *listens.*] "I inform you that the minister is acquainted that the prison you command contains several victims of arbitrary power: he sets out to-morrow to examine your conduct personally: take your precautions and endeavor, if possible, to evade his researches." Indeed! should he know that I now hold in fetters that very Horestan whom he thinks dead, and on whom I have such just cause for vengeance? Minister so vigilant? I shall find means once more to deceive thee! he arrives today; no time is to be lost.

[CAPTAIN *of the* GUARDS *crosses the stage.*]

Captain! [*leads him to the front of the stage and speaks in a low voice*] take a trumpeter, on whom you may depend, ascend with him the northern tower; you will attentively look on the road which leads to Seville.[6] As soon as you perceive at a distance a carriage with guards, give the signal by sounding the trumpet—do you hear? the signal must be given at the instant; be punctual, and above all, discreet: your head answers for it. Away!

[*Exit* CAPTAIN.]

Now to devise means to rid me of this Horestan. [*After a moment's reflection he casts his eyes on* ROC *who advances.*] There is but one, and it shall be adopted. Roc—

ROC: My lord!

PIZARE: I have something of consequence to relate to thee.

ROC: To me, my lord? [*With surprise.*]

6. In Andalusia, southern Spain. Long the cultural center and capital of Muslim Spain and, in the 16th century, the center for Spanish exploration of the New World, it became, in the 17th century, home to artists and writers, including Miguel de Cervantes, who conceived his novel *Don Quixote* while imprisoned there.

PIZARE: Ay, sir, to thee. If you will kindly condescend to lend me your hearing awhile follow me!

[*Exit* PIZARE and ROC.]

[LEONORA *and* MARCELINE *advance*.]

MARCELINE: Dear Fidelio, thou hast again fallen into a reverie: it is singular how quickly you pass from joy to sadness; imitate me—I am all gaiety.

LEONORA: Ah, dear Marceline! if, like thee, I had parents——

MARCELINE: Thou shalt have parents and those who love thee. Think not of thy misfortunes: and yet, dear Fidelio, I no longer marvel at what thou saidst in thy dreams.

LEONORA: Said! what have I said?

MARCELINE: Thou wert just returned from thy daily errands and exhausted with fatigue—was asleep in the courtyard beneath the trees. I drew near thinking thou wert deep in thought, but found thee agitated; heavy sighs issued from thy bosom, and these words escaped thee. "I shall yet discover him—yes I shall."

LEONORA [*agitated*]: Nothing else? be sure, dearest Marceline. said I nothing else?

MARCELINE: I heard but that.

LEONORA: Thank heaven! [*Aside*.] thou seest, Marceline, the effect of being ignorant of the author of my existence. It even haunts me in my sleep.

MARCELINE: Do not let it torment thee. Let us retire—this is the time the prisoners are permitted to take air in the garden. Come—let not unpleasant thoughts disturb thee; thy Marceline loves thee, and will never repent the choice her heart has made.

[*Exit*.]

LEONORA: What amiable candor, what engaging simplicity! how painful it is for me to deceive her! but everything forces me to it. And this impenetrable disguise which I have assumed is necessary to achieve my enterprise—achieve! ah, shall I ever be able! how many obstacles to surmount—how many dangers to encounter! let me not despair—the moment is near at hand when I shall penetrate those secret dungeons: everything tells me my dear Horestan is there confined; heaven has given me strength beyond my hopes; come what will I must proceed.

[*Enter* ROC, *hastily*.]

ROC: Fidelio, art alone? I must speak with thee.

LEONORA: How agitated you appear; what can have moved you thus? has the governor treated you rudely?

ROC: On the contrary he is all confidence, all familiarity. I enlarged upon thy fidelity, and he has granted thee permission to visit with me the secret dungeons this day.

LEONORA [*with joy*]: Today!

ROC: Yes; and we shall begin visiting this unknown of whom we spoke: he must in one hour——

LEONORA: Well?

ROC: Die.

LEONORA: Die!

ROC: And no vestige of his existence must remain.

LEONORA [*with emotion*]: Die! say you?

ROC: I at first shuddered, like thee; but don Pizare informed me the interest of the state depends upon it. And I have promised——

LEONORA: To assassinate this unhappy man——

ROC: No, not so. This plan we have agreed upon—

LEONORA [*hastily*]: Well, proceed—let me hear?

ROC: It is near three o'clock; the prisoners of the little pavilion are going to take the air.

LEONORA: Well—

ROC: We will avail ourselves of that moment to descend, unperceived, into the dungeon in which that man is confined; there, without exchanging a word with him, or answering a question, we shall begin to clear the rubbish from the mouth of a deep cistern which is near him: when our work is complete I shall give the signal which the governor has ordered. We shall open the door to a masked person, who will be introduced to the prisoner; and he will perform *the rest.*

LEONORA [*aside, who has listened with great attention*]: Yes, I understand that rest.

ROC: We shall afterwards ascend and divide this [*shows a purse*] which the governor has given me; it contains one hundred pieces of gold.

LEONORA [*with affected joy*]: Indeed! so much?

ROC: I was sure the sight would have the same effect on thee. Yes; there will be fifty for each of us: but it is on condition that not a word shall escape thee, that the governor has permitted thee to attend me. Thou knowest his disposition—his power, think well—we should both be lost.

LEONORA: Do not fear, depend on my discretion; and be assured that this important secret interests me as well as yourself. [*After a moment's reflection.*] Yes, I will attend thee; I am too proud of your confidence not to comply with your wishes. I have indeed, 'tis true, betrayed a little alarm at the idea of murder——

ROC: That's natural, I felt the same compunction. Nay, even now I think——

LEONORA: Yet after all what is it? to open a cistern, that's no crime—we are not to know its use.

ROC: Ay, that is it—that's what I said.

LEONORA: We dare not dispute the orders of the governor, even if their import is criminal.

ROC: Just what I said to myself. It is surprising how thy way of thinking agrees with mine. Come, we understand each other—[*giving her a bunch of keys*] hold—here are the keys of the little pavilion. I consider thee now as myself: when the clock strikes three, unlock those doors and let the prisoners into the yard; afterwards meet me at the house, where I shall wait for thee with all the tools prepared for our task. Come, Fidelio, rouse thyself; here is a good day's work, and we must profit by it.

[*Exit.*]

LEONORA: Yes I shall profit by it. Execrable Pizare! I shall find means to defeat thy plots and brave thy barbarity. What if I were to confide in Roc? though rude he has a feeling heart. If I were to discover to him who I am! perhaps my attachment—the singularity of my situation—but, no; he is too much attached to the profit of his station. Let me think—[*kneels*] o thou my only hope! avenger of the just, and punisher of the wicked! save at once, o powerful heaven, love, hymen,[7] and innocence; let not the sanguinary hand of assassins be raised against my husband; give me strength, and guide my steps to his dungeon. If I cannot restore him to light I can at least receive his last adieu, his parting embrace, [*clock strikes*] hark! the clock warns me of my duty. [*Rises.*] Let me perform my task—'tis pleasant to the grateful heart, for it relieves the unfortunate. [*Opens the prison doors.*] Come, thou abandoned by hope—the die is cast—let me save my husband, or perish with him.

[*Exit.*]

END OF THE FIRST ACT

Act II

Scene—a dark subterraneous dungeon, at the extremity of which a ruined staircase is perceived—large stones and rubbish are scattered about the whole; having the appearance of age and decay.

HORESTAN *is discovered chained to the wall and resting on a large stone: his visage is pale and emaciated: and his appearance bespeaks a long confinement.*

HORESTAN: Still no one approaches—God, what darkness, what eternal silence! am I separated from the world? am *I* alone in the universe?——is there no term, great heaven, to these sufferings? must I in the spring of life languish in captivity? can it be that slavery and galling tyranny should be the price of truth?—[*draws a picture from his bosom*] o thou, whose cherished image has witnessed my sorrows! dear Leonora! my friend! my wife! art thou well? dry thy tears—be firm, and say, "to his last moments, my husband was worthy of me." Alas, I am weak; cold and hunger freeze my senses. O death, death! [*Throws himself on the ground, and buries his face in his hands.*]

[ROC *and* LEONORA *are seen descending the stairs bearing tools and a lantern.*]

LEONORA: How cold it is.

ROC: 'Tis not surprising, this dungeon is so deep.

LEONORA [*casting a fearful glance around*]: I thought we should never have found the entrance.

ROC [*advancing towards* HORESTAN]: Here he is.

LEONORA: Where?

ROC: There—stretched on the earth.

LEONORA [*striving to recognize him*]: He appears motionless.

ROC: Perhaps he is dead.

LEONORA [*shuddering*]: Dead?—[HORESTAN *sighs*] no, no, he sleeps.

ROC: Come, let us begin our task; we have no time to lose.

LEONORA [*aside*]: It is impossible to distinguish his features—should it be him—

ROC [*placing the lantern on a stone*]: Under this rubbish the cistern is. Come, Fidelio, assist me to remove these stones.

7. Commonly, virginity, but here, marriage. "Avenger of the just, and punisher of the wicked": echo of the Hebrew liturgy.

[*He descends in a hollow, which is formed by the removal of the rubbish*—LEONORA *assists him.*]

ROC: Thou tremblest! art afraid!

LEONORA: O, no; the damp air chills me—

[LEONORA, *during* ROC's *employment takes advantage at intervals to regard* HORESTAN.]

ROC: Let us haste; he will be here anon——

LEONORA [*removing the rubbish*]: I am very active.

ROC [*raising a large stone*]: Fidelio, help me to remove this stone.

[LEONORA *assists him*—ROC *then descends into the cistern.*]

LEONORA [*in a low voice to* HORESTAN]: Whoever thou art, poor victim, be comforted——I shall save thee——

ROC [*raising himself from the cistern*]: What dost thou say?

LEONORA: Nothing. [HORESTAN *rises but still conceals his face.*] See, he awakes!

ROC: Awakes, say you? [*comes out*] yes, yes; he has raised his head:—he will perhaps ask many questions; we will reply now, for his hours are numbered.

LEONORA: Let us listen——

ROC: Well, thou hast rested awhile——

HORESTAN: Rested, say you?

LEONORA [*aside*]: That voice——

HORESTAN: Rather say exhausted nature has presented an image of the most frightful death——

LEONORA [*aside*]: The darkness still conceals his countenance—could I be satisfied——

HORESTAN: Are you still insensible to the voice of innocence? will you never have pity on the unfortunate Horestan?

LEONORA: Oh God! 'tis he! [*Sinks exhausted on a stone.*]

ROC: What can I do? I but obey my orders.

HORESTAN: I ask nothing of you contrary to your duty; but could you not tell me who commands in this fortress?

ROC [*aside*]: I risk nothing now to satisfy him.——Ay, I may tell thee. The governor is don Pizare.

HORESTAN: Don Pizare, say you? I am not now surprised at what I suffer: 'tis he then; he, whose abuse of friendship I have dared to detect, has found means to plunge me in this abode of death and terrors: he has obtained power over me but to exercise the most cruel vengeance.

LEONORA [*recovering*]: Monster! thy barbarity restores all my strength. [*Aside.*]

HORESTAN [*to* ROC]: If you would serve me, the most tender friendship—[ROC *listens with indifference*] the blessings of a whole family—[ROC *still indifferent*] your fortune—[ROC *starts—then listens with the utmost attention*] no, no; you are not made to be the accomplice of an assassin. Save me, then; take, o take me from this frightful dungeon.

ROC [*after a moment's reflection*]: No, it is impossible.

HORESTAN: If you will not break these chains, do not desert me, let not my only hope forsake me. Send to Seville—we cannot be far from it. Facing the public square stands the hotel which bears my name—there ask for Leonora Horestan——

LEONORA [*aside*]: He little thinks his Leonora is at this moment digging his grave!

HORESTAN [*agitated*]: Pardon me, if the mention of that beloved name moves me——let her know I still live: inform her of the place where I am in chains—the name of the barbarous man who thus has persecuted me: she will obtain my release. O save my life, and you will at once protect virtue, serve love, and rescue innocence.

ROC: Impossible, I should destroy myself without saving you.

HORESTAN: Alas! alas! since then I must end my days here, soften the bitterness of my sufferings; let me not expire with misery and want. The dampness of the dungeon cramp my limbs: for a whole day I have not tasted food. O could you feel my sufferings!

LEONORA [*supporting herself by the fragment of a large stone*]: Heaven! what trials!

HORESTAN: For pity sake give me a drop of water to cool my burning palate! a drop of water! it is but little, do not refuse it!

ROC [*aside*]: His distress unmans me!

HORESTAN [*in the most impressive tone*]: You do not answer me?

ROC [*with emotion*]: What can I say? to save your life is impossible. All I can offer is the remains of a bottle of wine.

LEONORA [*brings the bottle with haste*]: 'Tis here.

HORESTAN [*looking at* LEONORA]: Who is that youth?

ROC: My turnkey. Hold—[*presenting the bottle to* HORESTAN *who drinks*] it is but little, but I give it with a willing heart. [*To* LEONORA] Thou seemest moved.

LEONORA [*in great affliction*]: Alas! who would not? you also weep with me.

ROC: True; that devil of a man has such a melting voice! it goes to the heart.

HORESTAN [*after having drank part of the wine*]: I shall never forget those precious drops.

ROC [*in a low voice to* LEONORA]: Fidelio, we may assist him now without fear, for in a few moments he will die.

LEONORA [*aside*]: How I tremble! let me not betray myself.

HORESTAN [*aside*]: Could I but succeed in moving them—

LEONORA [*drawing a piece of bread from her pocket and says in a low voice to* ROC]: See here this little bread, which by accident I found—

ROC: Beware, Fidelio; should the governor——

LEONORA: O, do not deprive me of so great a pleasure!

ROC: I cannot consent to this extreme imprudence.

LEONORA: You said even now, without fear we may assist him, for shortly he must die.

ROC: Well, give it him.

LEONORA [*presenting the bread to* HORESTAN]: Here, take this.

HORESTAN [*seizing eagerly the hand of* LEONORA]: What soft voice is this? dear youth, suffer me to kiss thy hand and bedew it with the tears of an unfortunate captive.

LEONORA [*aside*]: Moment replete with horror and delight!

ROC [*to* LEONORA *after a moment's pause*]: All is ready—I will give the signal——

LEONORA [*aside*]: Now fortitude assist me.

ROC: Stay by him.

[ROC *retires to the back of the stage and whistles.*]

HORESTAN: What means that signal? is it for my death?

LEONORA: No, no; be composed, dear captive.

HORESTAN: Dear Leonora, shall I never see thee more,

LEONORA [*aside, repressing her emotion*]: My heart! my heart! nay, be satisfied, no harm shall approach thee: Providence will never forsake the virtuous.

[*She goes near the cistern*—HORESTAN'*s eyes following her.*]

HORESTAN: What does he mean? every word rivets my attention.

[PIZARE *descends the stairs disguised and masked.*]

PIZARE: Is every thing ready?

ROC: Yes.

PIZARE: Good—send that boy away.

ROC [*to* LEONORA]: Withdraw awhile.

[LEONORA *retires to the bottom of the stage, and unperceived draws near* HORESTAN, *attentively watching the movements of* PIZARE.]

ROC: Shall I unchain him?

PIZARE: No. [*Aside.*] That every thing should be buried in eternal silence, before night I shall rid myself of them all;—time presses; let me not think of it.

[*Draws a dagger, and at the moment he motions to strike* HORESTAN, LEONORA *screams and rushes before him.*]

LEONORA: Hold! I will defend him;—he shall not die!

PIZARE: How now? rash boy!

LEONORA [*with determination*]: He shall not die! or I will perish with him.

HORESTAN: Amazement!

ROC: I cannot overcome my surprise!

LEONORA: Yes, here, even here, will I remove the veil which shrouds me from your view. Know that this orphan whom thou hast protected—this turnkey, who for six months has served thee faithfully—is a woman, inspired by conjugal love.

ROC: A woman?

LEONORA: In a word, behold the wife of that suffering victim. [*Rushes in his arms.*]

HORESTAN: Heavens!

PIZARE: What do I hear?

ROC: Is it possible?

HORESTAN: O prodigy of strength and virtue!

LEONORA [*to* ROC]: Do not suffer the blood of my husband to be shed by that monster:—heaven has directed my steps to this abode of horrors to prevent the blackest of murders. Assist me, you whom he has chosen for his support, and obey the decrees of eternal justice.

PIZARE [*rushing between* ROC *and* LEONORA]: And wouldst thou yield to a woman? forget at once thy duty and thy fortune? see who I am, and recognize Pizare. [*Takes off his mask.*]

ROC: The governor!

HORESTAN: Pizare?

PIZARE [*with fury*]: Yes, Pizare!

HORESTAN [*rushing forward, but is detained by his chains*]: Monster!

PIZARE [*giving* ROC *a purse*]: Here are a hundred pieces of gold:—thou knowest my power—my credit[8]—my treasures:—wilt thou desert me? separate them!

[*Attempts to stab* HORESTAN—LEONORA, *throwing herself before him, and drawing a pistol from her bosom, presents it to*[9] PIZARE]

LEONORA: Advance, and thou diest!

[PIZARE *starts back with surprise: at that instant a trumpet sounds.*]

PIZARE [*with dismay*]: The minister here, already?

ROC [*aside*]: The minister, said he?

PIZARE: O fatal disappointment! what's to be done? I must instantly appear before him. Roc, follow me.

[*Exit.*]

LEONORA [*running after* ROC, *detains him*]: Ah, do not forsake us! do not betray us to that vile assassin.

[*Falls at* ROC'S *feet, who takes the pistol from her and exits—she screams.*]

HORESTAN: Leonora!—oh these chains!——

LEONORA [*with the greatest agony*]: And I suffered the pistol to be taken from me! It is done. I lose in a moment the fruit of all my labor—no hope remains. [*She falls.*]

HORESTAN: Leonora!—she is dying and I cannot help her—Leonora, dear Leonora!

LEONORA [*in a faint voice*]: Who calls?

HORESTAN: It is Horestan, thy husband—

LEONORA: Ah, that voice! [*Crawls to* HORESTAN, *who presses her in his arms.*]

HORESTAN: Is it no illusion? do I hold thee in these arms? delightful moment! it repays an age of sorrow. But say, or I cannot comprehend, by what prodigy didst thou discover me?

LEONORA: By the eagerness which don Pizare used, to make himself governor of this fortress. I was assured you were confined in it, I left Seville without imparting my project, and came alone on foot, and was admitted under this disguise as the turnkey of the prison, and succeeded in interesting the jailor, his daughter, and even the governor himself.

HORESTAN: Couldst thou bear so many fatigues?

LEONORA: Thou inspired me, and my strength was inexhaustible.

HORESTAN: And suffer so many humiliations?

LEONORA: That did I not:—nothing is humiliating when it exalts the heart.

HORESTAN: Never, oh never, was the heroism of love carried to this extent. Come nearer to me. [*With grief.*] Moment of delight, why art thou repaid with labor and pain. O had I that weapon of defense which the inflexible jailor deprived thee of, in spite of my chains I feel I could yet defend thy precious life. [*They hear footsteps.*]

LEONORA: Hark! they approach: these are our last moments.

8. Authority.

9. Points it at.

HORESTAN: There is no hope left;—but in suffering death my consolation will be to die in thy arms. [*They embrace.*]

[*Enter* DON FERDINAND, GUARDS, PIZARE *in custody*; ROC, MARCELINE, JACQUINETT—SOLDIERS *with torches.*]

ROC [*showing* DON FERDINAND, HORESTAN *and* LEONORA]: There they are, my lord; save them, save them.

HORESTAN: Whom do I see? don Ferdinand!

DON FERDINAND: Even so: I come to break your chains, and end your misfortunes.

LEONORA: Ah, my lord, your presence alone has effaced our evils. [*Falls at his feet.*]

DON FERDINAND: Rise, madam;—you at my feet! when I should be at yours, to express the respect which your virtue has inspired me with?

HORESTAN: If you knew what she has done for me—

DON FERDINAND: I know all. This man [*to* ROC] has informed me everything.

ROC: Pardon me, if seemingly I have betrayed; but I feigned to assist your persecutor to save you: and if I used violence in taking this pistol from *you,* it was through fear that in despair you would have attempted your life. I wished to preserve your precious days to avenge myself of the cruelties this man forced me to commit towards you. [*To* PIZARE, *drawing two purses.*] There is the gold thou gavest me:—I own I like wealth, but not when purchased by barbarous persecution. [*Throwing them down.*]

DON FERDINAND [*to* PIZARE]: And you abused my confidence to this extent—you announced the death of this unfortunate man, but to gratify the most cruel vengeance. O how I repent yielding to your perfidious counsel!—how the great are to be pitied when surrounded by such duplicity! [*To* ROC.] Unchain this victim of persecution—stay—give me the keys of these unmerited fetters. [*Presenting them to* LEONORA.] It is to you, heroic woman, the honor of delivering your husband is due.

[LEONORA *unlocks* HORESTAN's *chains.*]

MARCELINE [*apart*]: Who would have thought Fidelio was a woman!

DON FERDINAND [*embracing* HORESTAN]: How long, my worthy friend, have you been confined in this frightful dungeon?

HORESTAN: I cannot say—it was universal darkness; the days and nights were confounded, I could not number them.

ROC: My lord, it has been two years and some days.

DON FERDINAND [*to* GUARDS]: Let this monster be chained in the place of his victim—the laws condemn him to bear for the same time the tortures his barbarity has inflicted.

HORESTAN: Save him, my lord, from this terrible decree; his pains will be more dreadful, for he has not, as I had, an innocent heart to bear them.

LEONORA: Pardon him, my lord, pardon him.

DON FERDINAND: No; we can forgive false proceedings from error—from inexperience; but to spare this wretch who delights in the daily practice of cruelties; never, never! [*Taking* LEONORA's *hand.*] Come, model of women, honor to your sex.—O I shall everywhere publish what you have done! such virtues console us for sometimes meeting iron hearts like Pizare's: [*taking* HORESTAN's *hand*] and you, to whom my fatal confidence has caused such evils, come and retake near my person the place which is your due—come and partake of my friendship: the remainder of my life is too short to expiate what I suffered you to bear.

HORESTAN: So much goodness doubly repays all my pangs.

LEONORA: And thou, charming Marceline, if I have betrayed thy confidence and disappointed thy love—here is my excuse. [*Pointing to* HORESTAN.]

MARCELINE: O, I am not angry with you; but where shall I find a true Fidelio?

JACQUINETT [*coming from among the crowd*]: Here, if you will.

LEONORA: Whoever is the husband she chooses, her dowry shall be my care.

DON FERDINAND: Let us leave this abode of crimes and horrors;—let us hasten to efface the remembrance of these dungeons, by an immutable return of justice and truth.

END OF THE FORTRESS OF SORRENTO.

1808 1808

PENINA MOÏSE
1797–1880

In 1833, Penina Moïse published *Fancy's Sketch Book*, said to be the first collection of poems by a Jewish American to appear in the United States. All but forgotten today, Moïse was the best known of a number of Jewish women writing poetry in the United States in the nineteenth century. Among her predecessors was Grace Seixas Nathan (1752–1831), one of the first Jewish American women to publish poems, while Moïse's contemporaries included Adah Isaacs Menken, Octavia Harby Moses, and Rebekah Hyneman. Southern, impoverished, sick, never married, Moïse wrote with an energetic wit and irony, qualities not immediately associated with a woman who wrote hymns.

Moïse was born in 1797 into a Sephardic Jewish merchant family in Charleston, South Carolina, the sixth of nine children. Her father, Abraham, came from Alsace, her mother, Sarah, from a wealthy Jewish family from the island of Saint Eustace, in the Caribbean; Moïse's parents and their four eldest sons had fled to Charleston from a 1791 slave insurrection in Cape François, Santo Domingo. Moïse attended school until the age of twelve, when her father died. Thereafter, she pursued her studies on her own, living in genteel poverty while caring for her mother and an asthmatic brother. For a while, she earned money by embroidering and making lace. Charleston in the 1830s and 1840s was a burgeoning city—in 1841, it was the sixth largest in the United States—and its Jewish community, primarily Sephardic and one of the oldest in the country, was lively and diverse. Moïse became active in this community as a writer and a teacher. She hosted literary salons for both Jews and Gentiles, published in the Jewish and general presses, both national and local—in the *American Jewish Advocate,* the *Daily Times, Godey's Lady's Book, Southern Patriot*—and, like her contemporary Rebecca Gratz in Philadelphia, served as superintendent of the Sunday school at the Reform Congregation Beth Elohim. During the Civil War, which she spent in Sumter, South Carolina, Moïse went blind and contracted neuralgia, a painful nerve disease. Returning to Charleston after the Civil War, she, with her sister and niece, made a meager living by running a small private school for girls. She died in 1880 in Charleston.

Moïse published many poems and articles on current political and social issues. An American nationalist with great concern for the sufferings of Jews abroad, she wrote *On the Persecution of the Jews in Damascus* and, in another poem, called for Jews to immigrate to the United States after the 1819 anti-Jewish riots in Germany:

> If thou art one of that oppressed race,
> Whose pilgrimage from Palestine we trace,
> Brave the Atlantic—Hope's broad anchor weigh,
> A Western Sun will gild your future day.

In addition, Moïse wrote humorous and satirical verse on love, poverty, and death, as well as short fiction, such as the melodramatic *The Convict.* This short story appeared with her poem *Miriam* in *The Charleston Book: A Miscellany in Prose and Verse*, an 1845 publication of local writers that, following the fashion of the day, aimed to put Charleston on the cultural map alongside Boston and New York.

Perhaps Moïse was best known for the hymns with which she helped Americanize the Reform Jewish liturgy. Congregation Beth Elohim published 190 of her hymns in 1856 (*Hymns Written for the Use of Hebrew Congregations*) in a book that went through four editions. Thirteen of her hymns were still included in the 1932 edition of the Reform *Union Hymnal,* and some are still sung today. In *Hymn* ("I weep not now as once I wept"), included here, we hear diction and phrasing reminiscent of the Anglican *Book of Common Prayer,* yet the language expresses a particularly Jewish faith. Instead of bent knees, Moïse evokes hands lifted in prayer. At the same time that she echoes the U.S. Constitution ("Light, being, liberty, and joy"), she translates the phrase "Protector of the quick and dead!" from a Hebrew prayer, the Eighteen Benedictions. Reminiscent of the work of Emily Dickinson, Moïse's hymns lack the individual brilliance of the New England poet's poems. Nonetheless, with these hymns, Moïse, using a distinctly American voice, brings to life the Jewish liturgy more successfully than does Isaac Mayer Wise in his *Minhag Amerika*.

Moïse's poem *Miriam,* included here, along with the anonymously published poem, also called *Miriam,* from the *Israelite* and Adah Isaacs Menken's *Judith*, fits into the mid-nineteenth-century fashion, established by Protestant American women, of writing poems that reinterpret biblical characters, especially women, as a way of asserting a woman's right to speak about political and religious matters. These three Jewish poets may well have read *Women of Israel* (1851), by Grace Aguilar, a British Jew, which was very popular in the United States. The Jewish women's interpretations of biblical women are as various as those of their Christian contemporaries—ranging from pious (Moïse) to rebellious (Menken). This shows just how American these Jewish women writers had become.

Miriam[1]

Amid the flexile reeds of Nile a lovely infant slept,
While over the unconscious babe his mother watched and wept.[2]
Nor distant far another stood whose tears flowed fast and free,
'Twas Miriam the beautiful, the bright star of the sea.[3]

1. This name signifies star of the sea, lady of the sea, the exalted, the brightener, the enlightener [Moïse's note].
2. Yoheved placed her infant son, Moses, in a basket in the Nile River to save him from the decree of the pharaoh that all Hebrew male babies be killed; the pharaoh's daughter found and adopted him (Exodus 2.1–10).
3. Moses' older sister, who brought their mother to the pharaoh's daughter as a wet nurse for the foundling (Exodus 2.4–8)

With breaking heart that parent bids farewell to her doomed child,
Commending to Almighty God his spirit undefiled.
The sister lingers yet to mourn o'er tyranny's decree,
And bitter was thy agony, fair maiden of the sea.

The palace of the Pharaohs now sends forth a noble train,
Thermutis[4] comes, by Heaven led, to break her father's chain.
And who is she that homage yields upon her bended knee?
It is the graceful Miriam, the brightener of the sea.

Trembling she rose and timid stood upon the water's edge,
When lo! the princess marks the boy slumbering amid the sedge.
A fairy ark and foundling too? 'Tis Fortune's gift to me,
Joy to the heart of Miriam, the fair star of the sea.

A nurse for this deserted babe, cried Pharaoh's gentle daughter,
Whose name, my nymphs, shall Moses be, thus rescued from the water.[5]
A woman of the stranger's race I'll quickly bring to thee,
Said the delighted Miriam, the day-star of the sea.

She turned aside, nor tarried long, for soon her infant brother,
On the familiar bosom lay of his own Hebrew mother.
And bounding onward by her side, full of triumphant glee,
Went Miriam the beautiful, the bright star of the sea.

Time fleets—the child, to manhood reared, has left his proud abode,
And royalty's bold protégé has broken Egypt's rod.
The oracle of Israel has set his nation free!
Then sung melodious Miriam, enlightener of the sea.[6]

But why hast thou at Hazeroth thy timbrel cast aside,
And dared to lift thy voice against the legislator's[7] bride?
For this shalt thou be smitten,[8] till thy brother's prayer for thee
Restores again thy loveliness, rash lady of the sea.

A wail is in the wilderness, a deep and solemn wail,
The prophetess who soared beyond mortality's dark pale,
Has to the *spirit's promised land* departed pure and free.[9]
Farewell, inspired Miriam, thou lost star of the sea!

1845

4. The pharaoh's daughter, according to Josephus.
5. *Moses* means "taken out of the water," from the word *mashah* (Hebrew), "to draw out."
6. This verse summarizes the story of how Moses freed the Hebrews from enslavement to the pharaoh (Exodus 2.11–12.51). Miriam led the women in dancing and sang to them the *Hymn of the Sea* on the shore of the Red Sea (Exodus 15.20–21).
7. A reference to Moses as lawgiver.
8. In Hazeroth, during the Hebrews' forty years ofwandering in the desert, God afflicted Miriam with leprosy as a punishment for her and Aaron's speaking against Moses and his Midianite wife, Zipporah. God healed her only after Moses begged him to (Numbers 12.1–15).
9. Miriam died in Kadesh in the desert of Zin (Numbers 20.1).

Hymn

I weep not now as once I wept
  At Fortune's[1] stroke severe;
Since faith hath to my bosom crept,
  And placed her buckler[2] there.

Lightly upon this holy shield
  Falls sorrow's thorny rod;
And he who wears it, learns to yield
  Submissively to God.

It breaks the force of ev'ry dart,
  By disappointment hurled
Against the shrinking human heart,
  In this cold, callous world.

Wrestling with this, I have defied
  All that my peace assailed;
Passion subdued hath turned aside,
  And sin before it quailed.

How many wounds would now be mine;
  How many pangs intense!
But for the shield of faith divine,
  My spirit's strong defense.

Oh! when in prayer my hands I lift[3]
  To Thee Almighty God!
The excellence of this Thy gift,
  With fervor will I laud.

O God! to Thy paternal grace,[4]
  That ne'er its bounty measures.
All gifts Thy grateful children trace,
  That constitute Life's treasures.

Light, being, liberty, and joy,[5]
  All, all to Thee are owing;
Nor can another hand destroy
  Blessings of Thy bestowing.

None, save our own! for in man's heart
  Such passions are secreted,
That peace affrighted weeps apart,
  To see Thy aim defeated.

1. Luck, chance, fate (from the Latin *fortuna*). *Mazel* (Hebrew), a comparable concept, is rarely if ever found in Jewish liturgy.
2. Shield.
3. Adapted from "knees I bend," a phrase found in the Protestant hymns on which Moïse modeled her Jewish song.
4. Refers to the Hebrew liturgical phrase *Avinu malkenu* ("Our father, our king") but removes the idea of monarchy.
5. A paraphrase of the Declaration of Independence's "Life, Liberty, and the Pursuit of Happiness."

LIGHT is made dim by human guile;
EXISTENCE doth but languish;
and FREEDOM loses her bright smile
'Mid scenes of strife and anguish.

Father! though forfeited by sin
Are all Thy tender mercies;
There is a TRUSTING FAITH within,
That ev'ry fear disperses.

Honor and praise to Thee belong,
O God of our salvation!
Who will defend from shame and wrong,
Thy first elected nation.[6]

Protector of the quick and dead![7]
Thy love THIS WORLD o'erfloweth;
And when the "vital spark" hath fled,
Eternal life bestoweth.

1856

6. Moïse democratizes the Divine Covenant, in which God elected the Jews his chosen people.
7. A translation and adaptation of the Hebrew liturgical phrase *Melekh meimit u'm'ḥai'e* ("Our King who brings death and restores life") in the Eighteen Benedictions.

ISAAC LEESER
1806–1868

Isaac Leeser was a man of extraordinary energy and vision who, as rabbi, author, translator, editor, publisher, and activist, either founded or laid the groundwork for almost every institution, organization, and publication that makes Jewish life thrive in America today.

Born in Neuenkirchen, in Westphalia, Prussia, on December 12, 1806, Leeser lived with his grandmother in Dulmen, near Münster, from the age of eight, after his mother had died. He attended the secular gymnasium at Münster, where he studied Latin, German, and Hebrew; he also had a traditional Jewish education, including some study of Talmud. In 1824, Leeser immigrated to Richmond, Virginia, where his uncle, Zalma Rehine, sent him briefly to a private school to learn English. For the next five years, Leeser worked in his uncle's shop. During those years, he assisted the hazan (cantor), leading services in Richmond's one congregation, teaching children in the religious school, and thus mastering Sephardic liturgical practices.

In a series of columns published in the *Daily Richmond Whig* in 1828, Leeser defended Judaism against an anti-Semitic article. These columns brought him to the attention of Mikveh Israel, the Sephardic synagogue in Philadelphia, which hired him to replace the hazan who had died. He accepted the offer because, at that time, there were very few Jews in the United States who knew enough Jewish law and ritual to lead a congregation in prayer; in fact, there was no "ordained" rabbi in the country.

Leeser led Congregation Mikveh Israel from August 1829 until 1850. During this time, he introduced major innovations to help educate and unify American Jews, most of which his congregants resisted or objected to. He began to give weekly sermons in English in 1830 even though the congregation did not formally accept this practice for thirteen years. Seeing that there were no materials for instructing his congregation's children, Leeser translated from German into English a religious textbook, Joseph Johlson's *Instruction in the Mosaic Religion*. Despite the disparagement of his synagogue's officers and congregants (who included Rebecca Gratz), Leeser self-published the textbook and his own *The Jews and Mosaic Law*, developed from his newspaper articles in Richmond—the textbook in 1830 and his book in 1833—because no American Jewish publisher existed at that time.

Leeser's publications included many that were the first of their kind in America: his translations of the Sephardic (1837) and the Ashkenazic (1848) prayer books; his Hebrew primer for children (1838); his translation of the Torah (1845) and then of the whole Bible (1853) into English. He founded and edited *Occident*, the first successful Jewish magazine in the United States; it appeared monthly from 1843 until 1869 and was edited by Mayer Sulzberger for a year after Leeser's death. *Occident* linked the Jews scattered across the American continent, a number that grew from around 6,000 in 1824 to more than 150,000 at the time of his death forty-four years later. Including sermons, editorials, debates, and news, this journal provided readers with a forum in which to express their opinions on the pressing problems that the Jews of America and Europe faced. Less innovative and less literary than its competitor, Isaac Mayer Wise's *American Israelite*, *Occident* was the most important instrument for the dissemination of traditional Judaism in America.

Leeser also initiated many institutions of Jewish American communal and cultural life: the first communal Jewish religious school in 1839; the first American Jewish publication society in 1845; the first Hebrew high school in 1849; the first Jewish defense organization in 1859; the first theological seminary for Jews in America—Maimonides College—in 1867. These organizations became the foundations upon which his followers later established the institutions of Conservative Judaism: the Jewish Theological Seminary in 1886 and the United Synagogue of America in 1913.

Leeser was ousted from his rabbinical post at Mikveh Israel in 1850. In 1857, he became leader of a new congregation, Beth-El-Emeth in Philadelphia, a position he held until he died, on February 1, 1868. Unlike the more liberal reformer Isaac Mayer Wise, Leeser advocated a traditional Judaism. Yet by translating it into the American vernacular, he transformed it.

The sample of Leeser's writing that we include here is *Discourse XXIV: The Dangers and Defenses of Judaism*, which he published in his collected sermons, *Discourses on the Jewish Religion*, in 1867. Delivered on January 10, 1845, at Mikveh Israel, it warns of the dangers facing Jews in America: the programmatic attempt by evangelical Christians to convert them. Leeser urges his listeners to counteract this Christian proselytizing by educating themselves and their children in Jewish law, religion, and history so that when sons go off to American colleges and daughters to boarding schools, they will remain Jews. This sermon gives us a taste of how precarious the maintenance of a Jewish identity and of the Jewish community before the Civil War seemed to Leeser and his contemporaries.

From Discourses on the Jewish Religion

Discourse XXIV

THE DANGERS AND DEFENSES OF JUDAISM

Brethren![1]

No doubt you have often reflected on the singular spectacle you must exhibit to the world at large, who see not with your eyes, nor hear with your ears. They are the many, nations great and powerful, intelligent and wise, governed by all kinds of laws, living in every climate and on every variety of soil; yet they are different from you, and much as they vary from each other, they are all surprised that you should not become like some one of them. Men from among you have been appealed to, time and again, to forsake our standard,[2] because of the hopelessness of our situation; but they have tauntingly replied, "Whom shall we join, since you all claim to be on the only road of salvation, and each one of you insists that he alone is right, and that perdition is the lot of all who differ from his respective dogmas?" Still your opinions of the contradictions around you, and the absolute impossibility you labor under of making a choice among the religions offered to your acceptance, even if you were inclined to forsake Judaism, do not weaken in the least the astonishment of mankind at your existing as you do, a separate and distinct nation, strongly marked in all the walks of life, and tingeing as it were the current of human existence with the peculiar coloring which is so entirely your own. Voyagers tell us, that in approaching the mouth of some mighty river, like that stream which gathers in its bosom the floods that sweep down from the western side of the Allegheny mountains,[3] and those that flow in their solitude and distant courses from the eastern declivity of the rocky Andes,[4] they can perceive distinctly the current of the river as it rushes forth far into the deep bed of the fathomless ocean, remaining unmingled with the briny fluid, whilst the impetus lasts which the river has acquired in its prolonged course, swallowed up as it is by the waste around, yet distinct and marked in its nature. Even so, Israelites, are you; your state was dissolved; in its downward course it was compelled to mingle with the great mass, the ocean, so to say, of mankind; and yet your characteristic was not, is not destroyed, and onward you flow amidst the surrounding waves, and you are seen, and felt, and known, as the offspring of that race which took its rise far away in the gloomy days of antiquity, and which has rolled on, like the river, occasionally expanding into a wide lake, shone on by the bright sun of prosperity, then narrowed down by approaching cliffs into a contracted channel, overhung to darkness by trailing shrubs and trees, which almost hide your course; still always flowing on, flowing on, true to your source, diminished perhaps in volume to the outward eye, but flowing in a deeper channel, the same now as from the beginning, and charged with the same waters which you drew from the first spring, the origin of your being,

1. This sermon is addressed to the congregation of Mikveh Israel, Philadelphia.
2. In the 1840s, Protestant evangelists in the United States aggressively tried to convert Jews.
3. Part of the Appalachian Mountains that range through Pennsylvania, Maryland, Virginia, and West Virginia.
4. A mountain range extending along the western coast of South America from Panama to Tierra del Fuego.

from Ur in Chaldea.[5] Is this not a wonder? something to astonish the world around? And do you feel surprise that you are regarded with suspicion, with little love, by those who differ from you, who understand not your mission, who are ignorant of your modes of thought, and the influences which urge you on?—Still, even the calmest of us are occasionally staggered at the perseverance of the malignity which pursues us, even in this land of liberty, where all religions are alike in the eye of the law, where the constitution knows of no difference between Jew and gentile. The more surprising is all this, since they who differ from us themselves acknowledge, that no more than the river which runs its glorious course over many thousand miles, with its hundreds of tributaries, can with truth be said to have poured forth itself on its blessed mission, have the sons of Israel chosen their own portion; for equally with the powers of nature, which work ceaselessly and noiselessly in their calling, have they received their appointment to go forth over the face of the human world, to penetrate into every dell, to seek out the remotest peaks of the snowy mountains, to leave there a portion of their fructifying power, a trace of their benign influence upon the life and actions of others. And such are we, harmless in our lives, unoffending towards the state, whether we are free or enslaved; for we say it, and dare to say it boldly that, though our people are not always free from crimes against the state, as a class they are not found herding with the malefactors, nor have the penal institutions many of them within their walls or under surveillance; and withal, if one listens to the clamor concerning us, he would be led to suppose that not alone are our souls doomed to perdition because we are Jews, but every state also is bound for its own political safety to watch that no injury result to it from the presence of the few Jewish inhabitants within its borders. Do I speak the truth? Let history answer; let me appeal to your daily experience; let me call to witness the efforts of sectarian fanatics of all degrees and all ages to root up the vine of Jacob from the field on which the Lord's own hands have planted it!

But what is Judaism? that principle against which the world has warred so long, which has hitherto survived all the storms which have assailed it? What is it?—It is the spirit of light enkindled by the Most High in every age, when it pleased Him to make his will known to man; it is the code of peace, which teaches us to love our neighbor, to succor the needy, to aid the sick, to assist the enemy even when he needs our assistance; it is the true conception of the great Creator, which sees in all that exists but one Father, one God, one Ruler, and one Savior, to whom every thing is known, to whom every thing is possible. Judaism couples these sublime truths, these noble principles of morality, with outward signs, call them if you will symbolical acts, which distinguish its professors at first sight from other men, which point them out to each other as children of the same original parentage, as followers of the same belief; and this is all that we can expect our ceremonies to effect for us, as a people, and only this the world without can look to of right in their estimation of our character, and the shaping of their conduct, which they are justly empowered to assume towards us as a nation and individuals. But what is the offending of which we have been guilty? why is the

5. The ancient Sumerian city in southern Mesopotamia on the Euphrates River where the Patriarch Abraham was born (Genesis 11.28).

world inimical to us? Simply because we have persevered in our faith; simply because through good and evil report we have clung to our belief in a pure undivided unity in the Godhead;[6] simply because we have declared our invincible opposition to every system which can put any being alongside of our great Father to worship;[7] simply because we adhere to the observance of the divinely appointed day of rest;[8] because we declare as unclean what the Scriptures have taught us to be, those things which the Lord has declared unto us to be an abomination.[9] In not one thing do all these alleged sins against the world, as it is, affect in the least the prosperity of the commonwealth or the tranquility of kingdoms; in not one thing do our acts, our thoughts, our hopes, injure the peace or prosperity of any country under the sun: and yet we are looked upon with suspicion, deemed as outcasts from divine favor, avoided by the insolent fanatic as though the leprosy adhered to our flesh, and pitied, in tones of mock compassion, as though we were stricken with mental blindness, by those unwise ones who themselves have barely a glimmer of divine light to aid them in their painful struggle, to ascertain which is the right road to salvation among the many singular paths, which their system points out to the perplexed traveler. And such as these come to teach us! Such as these endeavor to tell us "Thus has the Lord spoken," when He has not sent them, and when they promulgate what has not entered into his counsels! But do they pity us for the persecution[1] which our brothers have to endure in countries where liberty is yet a theory, and where the will of a despot is the law of the land? Do they offer their aid to disabuse the minds of the prejudiced who combine to our injury? O no! they may perhaps, it is true, profess pity in words; but they will couple their false sympathy with some such expression, "See what the Jews have to endure in punishment for their willful blindness, in not adopting our religion instead of their own." It is truly grating on the ear to be compelled to listen to such sympathizers, who lament the victim and secretly applaud the tyrant, because he opens in this manner a wide field for their efforts, as they fondly believe, to induce many to forswear Judaism. And these men ask us to come and listen to their harangues in which they denounce our belief; and Jews can be found to go and hear them, and some even profess to be convinced by their appeals, and become—gracious God! apostates to thy law![2] and they go and swear fealty to a pretended revelation which thy prophets never promulgated in thy name! and they aver to see errors in thy law which require to be amended by a more spiritual legislation, as if there could be aught truer or purer, than what Thou didst announce in olden times as the evidence of thy will!

Yes, brethren, we have heard of these doings in our days, of systematic efforts at corrupting our people; but they have generally been directed either to those who desired to profit by the learning in worldly things which they had acquired, when to the professing Jew all offices are closed in illiberal

6. Monotheism, the basic tenet of Judaism.
7. Unlike the Christian belief in the Trinity (the Father, the Son, and the Holy Spirit).
8. Jews observe the Sabbath on Saturday, the seventh day, and are not permitted to work on that day.
9. Jews following the laws of kashruth do not eat pork, shellfish, or other animals declared ritually unclean (Leviticus 11.2–23; Deuteronomy 14.3–21).
1. In 1845, Jews throughout Europe and the Middle East suffered many kinds of discrimination and persecution, including the denial of their civil and legal rights, unfair taxation, religious oppression, limited access to higher education and the professions, false accusations, and violence.
2. Converts to Christianity.

countries; or to those who sought an alliance with the daughter of the stranger, who asked the change of religion as a token of the sincerity of the professed attachment; or, not to mention other cases, where the want of information[3] left the persons, against whom these attempts were directed, an easy prey to any argument which was urged upon the contested points at issue between us and the gentile world. *Children* even placed at *school* have been approached by their *teachers and friends* with appeals on religious subjects, and they have been drawn to churches to hear doctrines laid down adverse to the Jewish belief. That in the latter instance parents have been greatly at fault for exposing their offspring to such dangerous influences; that no plea of the necessity of a brilliant education, not attainable at home, can justify a father for putting his child away where his principles may, or, to speak more correctly, will surely be endangered; that no mother can ever claim any circumstance likely to occur in ordinary life as an excuse for depriving her daughter of maternal care and supervision, at the period when impressions are most readily received, and when they are but too well calculated to be so strongly impressed as to influence their whole afterlife; that, in short, the greatest blame is attachable to parents of every degree and station for leaving their offspring to imbibe such religious sentiments as circumstances may throw in their way,—is too self-evident to require any argument. But equally culpable with the negligent parents are all those, who do not apply all the means, which their talents or circumstances afford them, to enlighten the understanding of their fellow-Israelites, and to induce them by the power of persuasion, and, if possible, by argument, to remain faithful to our standard of religion. Some persons no doubt think, as parents do, for instance, when they, being faithful to themselves, admonish their children as they send them forth not to transgress too much, and never to forget that they are Jews, that they discharge their whole obligation if they themselves practice their duties, whilst they are perfectly indifferent to the wrong done by others, even should it be occasionally in their power to arrest the evil which they see before their eyes. But let these be told that they are not doing their duty. The gentiles among whom we live understand, or rather practice better, the exercise of wholesome influence. If they see one of their people doing what they deem an offense against their system, they endeavor to alarm his conscience; and though we may not altogether approve of the means resorted to, we must acknowledge that they leave nothing untried to impress all their members with their supposed duties. This office is not alone exercised by those who are appointed public teachers, but by many other, females for instance, who never expect to be other than mere humble and uninfluential members of their respective communities. Whenever also they believe that they can have any influence over persons not of their persuasion, for instance, to induce them to read a particular book on some doctrinal question, or to listen to a sermon of some powerful controversial preacher, or to witness some exhibition where a strong evidence of the effect of their system can be displayed: you will see them anxious and ready to improve the opportunity, after their own fashion, and endeavoring to say a word in season, which is more or less effective, especially with the weak and inexperienced.

3. Jews ignorant of the teachings of Judaism. "Illiberal countries": nations where Jews did not have full rights as citizens. "Daughter of the stranger": intermarriage between Jew and Christian.

But let me impress it on your minds, brethren, that we cannot afford to lose even such as these from our communion, though their adherence add ever so little strength to our cause. They are children of Israel as much as the strongest of us, and are bound by the same law as the wisest among us all. If they are ignorant, their ignorance is to be pitied, and you, who are better instructed, should endeavor to teach them, that they may be able to withstand the appeals of the gentiles, and become themselves defenders of the holy truths that are intrusted to us in the law. If they are weak and worldly, draw them to you by mild persuasion, and by those unceasing efforts of an untiring love, which deems no labor too great, no exertion too painful, which may by any degree of possibility confirm the wavering, and bring healing to a soul affected with the dangerous imbecility which knows not its own diseased state. Let us not deceive ourselves that nothing can be done. This woeful delusion has been the cause of several families having quitted the household of Israel; not because they were convinced of the truth of gentile doctrines, but simply because they had no intercourse with religious Israelites, and because their mind was absolutely uninformed of the ideas and duties which characterize us from other nations. Besides which considerations it must not be forgotten that, so far as the moral effects of such conversions extend, they are to the world at large almost as fatal, as if they took place among the really prominent members of our faith; and the triumph of those who bear no love for our race is equally great, though the changeling be one of the weakest and most worthless among us. By these means, also, family relations are, or should be interrupted; for I esteem it to be beneath the dignity of a sincere Israelite to hold any intercourse with an apostate who openly so declares himself.

Let us consider that we do not seek to make proselytes[4] ourselves, though for my own part, and I say it with due deferense to the opinions of wiser and better men than myself, I *cannot see any good reason for being opposed to receiving them if sincerity of their professions cannot be reasonably doubted*, as some of our people, nay the greater majority of them, are. At all events, though there can be no doubt that, if we resorted to the means gentiles employ, we could make large accessions to our numbers, it has become the settled policy of our brothers to reject even those who occasionally come forward of their own accord to claim a reception in the family of Jacob. It is evident, therefore, that we must decrease, if we do not take care that the influence from without do not rob us of a portion of our household; and it is also perfectly clear that too many, especially in this country, have formerly been left exposed to a corrupting influence strong enough to warp the judgment, if not equal to debase the reason (I speak in a religious sense) altogether. I fear that if we take a calm review of all the incidents in our own lives, I except not even myself, we may find some cause for self-accusation in not having been zealous enough in spreading the kingdom of Heaven, and preventing sin, when this was in our power. I will confess that apostasies are not so frequent, nor have those we heard of been of such a kind, that human means could in every case have prevented them; but I speak also of other grave transgressions, and therein I maintain we have not exerted our influence, nor borne a decided enough testimony to awaken and alarm the sinner.

4. Judaism forbids proselytizing.

Let us take counsel from the gentiles; we can easily avoid their obtrusiveness; there is no occasion to broach the subject of our salvation in season and out of season; but surely there are almost daily opportunities, when we mingle in society, to say or do something which will have a bearing upon our religion and the duties it enjoins. There is no demand for fanaticism, nor need we fear being ridiculed for our zeal. Perfect cheerfulness and appreciation of social pleasures can be combined with our serious conversation; and even in a jesting mood instruction may be conveyed the more striking, from the unexpected manner in which it has been uttered. But chiefly we must endeavor to place our younger branches under wholesome religious guidance, not to compel them to transgress by leaving them in situations where to live religiously is impracticable.

I know well enough that I shall be met with the objection, that in some places it is impossible for parents to educate their children commensurately with their wealth and standing; that their sons have no colleges to go to in their native towns, and that their daughters cannot obtain a sufficient knowledge of music, painting, the elegant sciences and modern and learned languages in their places of residence, distant from the centers of literature and refinement; and I shall be asked, "Are we to sacrifice the education of our children to the ceremonial observances of our religion?" I would answer "decidedly," if religion or science must be sacrificed, I say, sacrifice science; it is not the staff of life, much as it may embellish it. But there is no occasion to dread such an alternative. As far as my knowledge goes, there are high-schools of great distinction in all the larger towns of this country, where Jews are settled in considerable bodies, and in these both male and female children could be educated, whilst they are, at the same time, domesticated with Jewish families, even if there are no Jewish schools at which the children can be placed at once under the superintendence of the teachers themselves, for their mental as well as scientific cultivation. This much to parents who themselves practice in their houses the duties of their faith. But even to those who are indifferent in this great point, great we call it, for it was made the distinguishing mark between Israel and the other nations, we would urge this consideration: At home your children, it is true, do not live according to the law of Moses; your own example is injurious to their leading a pious life; but still they hear you speak in terms of respect of your belief, and they accompany you at stated periods to the house of God. All therefore is not lost, though a great defect does exist. But now you are going to send your son to a distant college, where the regulations of the school compel him to listen habitually to prayers and sermons propounded in the name of a belief more or less hostile to your own; he is constantly plied with arguments, even in the very class-books he uses, to prove that what you believe is false and erroneous. It may be that he has learned something at home, and will thus be able to withstand the appeals to apostasy, which the people he lives with and his school-companions address to him; but is it possible that he should return home to you after an absence of four years sound in his conviction, unflinching in his attachment to our faith? You may write to him constantly in the most affectionate manner concerning his Jewish birthright (we will assume in every thing the most favorable); he shall also occasionally come to pay you a visit during the vacation; but will all this be enough to counteract the not seeing the Sabbath sanctified, the absence of the Passover, and the non-observance of the Day of Atonement?[5] You see I leave out all minor points; but even thus how does the question stand? is your conscience at ease? have you discharged your whole duty?

Or take your daughter at the age of twelve or fourteen away from home; you have wealth, and she perhaps has beauty and intellect. You are determined that she shall be brilliantly educated, she must shine at all hazards; and you place her at a fashionable boarding-school, where the daughters of the great of the land receive their finishing education. You may accomplish your wish thus to introduce her into a more elegant circle than is found in your own house; she associates with those whose habits are refined and whose intellect is cultivated; she acquires in their society all the branches taught to the best families of the land; but her soul remains dark to all noble impressions; she has no moral guide, her gentile teacher is not able to prove one; and what she gains in elegance she loses in goodness of heart, in truth and sincerity, those bright ornaments of a virtuous female. But assume, on the other hand, that her spirit too is to be molded by her teacher, what becomes of the Jewish female? She is gentilized, and returns after a few years to your roof with anything but a Jewish heart, and pities you perhaps, after the gentile fashion, for your blindness in being Jews. At all events, it will take labor, and cost you much heartburning to make your loved child again fond of her religion, easy as its practice may be in your house, and years will perhaps elapse before the simple unity of God will again find a response in her rebellious soul.

There is one thing I have omitted, and that is the excuse occasionally made that a country-education is so beneficial to youth, especially the males, as it removes them during their age of susceptibility from the dangerous moral tendencies of a city-life; and as in most country college towns few or no Jews reside, it is requisite of course to place them with gentile families or within the walls of the college. But there is a great fallacy in this excuse. If it were that a child, after being once removed from the temptations of a city-life, would never be exposed to them again, the laziness of parents might find some palliation. But the fact is quite the reverse. The college-years are scarcely over, when the rusticated citizen is thrown with an amazing suddenness in the midst of the dissipation, which the large towns so abundantly furnish. He has been restrained for a long period, and now he will compensate himself for the time lost to pleasure. Besides this, it by no means follows that all country places are free from vice and allurement, and it is much to be feared that in a moral point the country is perhaps as corrupt as the city. But grant all in favor of the secluded village; still, as we have said, the college-life must end at last; and where is the safety of the candidate at his entrance into the great world? Only in the principles which have been implanted in him, to enjoy whatever good our earthly life may offer, but never to indulge to excess, or to enjoy if sin be the consequence. Where then is the danger? It is in the want of moral training, in the not instilling of a deep religious veneration for what is good, and a detestation for what is bad. But this is the province of the father, the duty of the mother: they are to curb the passions

5. I.e., Yom Kippur, a Jewish holiday observed on the tenth of Tishri with prayer and according to the rituals described in Leviticus 16. "Sabbath": Jews do not work on the Sabbath. "Passover": the eight-day spring holiday, beginning on the fourteenth of Nisan and commemorating the exodus of the Hebrews from Egypt.

in early years; they are to implant the silent monitor; they are to watch that the rank weeds of unbridled license do not choke the holy aspirations for what is good and noble; and if they neglect to do this, if they cannot succeed, can they believe that a paid schoolmaster, who has a hundred boys under his supervision, will or can do that for so many, what they fail to or cannot effect in one or two? Can they be so deluded as to imagine that in a school, where there are fifty boarders, an aged woman and five or six assistants can attend in the least to a proper training of the affections and the intellect, after they have been worn out to weariness with the hearing of recitations for eight hours during the day: when they themselves acknowledge that one or two girls cannot be managed at home, with ample leisure and servants to take from them all the laborious cares of a family?

I have not exhausted the subject, but only given you materials for reflection. Consider, then, that Israel as a people requires a union of laborers, who conjointly must aim to establish a holy sentiment of devotion in the hearts of all, and to elevate our character in the eyes of the world; so as to counteract, not by wordy demonstrations, but a silent and effectual effort, the inclination which the worldly-minded may wish to instill in many to forsake the standard of our religion. But not merely nominal conformists only do we want; we need intelligent thinkers, and faithful actors, who can guide others and promote good by their example. Thus can we best exemplify that we are a holy people, and thus can we show in our life how it could happen that, despite of our dispersion, we have been able to maintain our identity amidst the nations which surround us on all sides. Let us prove that we esteem highly the announcement which God made to Moses:

ולקחתי אתכם לי לעם והייתי לכם לאלהים וידעתם
כי אני ה' אלהיכם המוציא אתכם מתחת סבלות
מצרים : שמות ו' ז' :

> "And I will take you unto me for a people, and I will be your God; and you shall know that I am the Lord your God who bring you forth from beneath the burdens of Egypt." Exodus vi. 7.

When this promise was made we were marked as the bondmen of Egypt, whose every aspiration was suppressed under the heavy burdens which were laid upon us. But then the Lord became emphatically our God, by giving us his law and separating us from all the world besides. Nations since have warred against our state, overwhelmed our greatness; but we have continued undiminished, though always assailed. And now it is for us, the men of the present generation, to take heed that the blessed stream shall still flow onward, glorious, deep, holy! Be it then the study of all to aid in what concerns all; and thus only can we be accepted, and thus only can we fulfill our task, which each Israelite has received from his God and Maker. And may He strengthen and guide us safely. Amen.

1845 1867

ISAAC MAYER WISE
1819–1900

According to Jacob Rader Marcus, the great historian of American Jewry, Isaac Mayer Wise "was the most important man in the history of the American Jewish Reform Movement." Through his work as a rabbi, an educator, and an editor and journalist, Wise put forth the ideology and practical means of religious and cultural change that enabled the influx of Jewish immigrants from Central and Western Europe to acculturate and become Americans.

Isaac Mayer Wise was born in 1819 in Steingrub, a tiny village in Bohemia, part of the Austrian Empire. His father, an impoverished Hebrew teacher, died young, and at age nine Wise was sent to study Talmud in yeshivas in Prague and Vienna. A voracious reader and autodidact who lacked a formal secular education and perhaps even ordination, Wise became the rabbinical officiant in the Bohemian town of Radnitz, near Pilsen, in 1843. He married Therese Bloch in 1844, with whom he had ten children. In 1846, at age twenty-seven, he left Radnitz for New York City. His first rabbinical post was at an Orthodox synagogue in Albany, New York, where he began to make unorthodox changes such as mixed seating (traditionally, males and females were separated), sermons in German (the vernacular) rather than in Hebrew, a choir that included girls and performed modern hymns, and the confirmation of both boys and girls.

In 1847, he and Rabbi Max Lilienthal unsuccessfully tried to establish a single ritual for American Jewry and, in 1849, attempted to form a union of congregations.

Forced out of his pulpit in 1850, he and his supporters founded a new Reform congregation in Albany. In 1854, he became rabbi at Congregation B'nai Jeshurun in Cincinnati, a position he held until his death in 1900. That same year, Wise founded the *Israelite* (later the *American Israelite*), a weekly English-language newspaper, and its German-language supplement directed toward women, *Die Deborah*. Wise had begun to write for and publish in Isaac Leeser's Orthodox monthly, *Occident*, and in Robert Lyon's New York Jewish weekly, *Asmonean*, in the late 1840s. He saw that journalism was a powerful tool for disseminating his reformist ideas, ideas that would establish a distinctively American branch of Judaism. In 1855, Wise convened the Cleveland Conference in order to implement his program of reform. Even though the other rabbis and Jewish leaders, both Orthodox and Reform, defeated Wise's proposals for a new rabbinic authority, Wise published his radical revision of the Hebrew liturgy, *Minhag Amerika*, in 1856.

Although he was a stalwart Unionist, Wise did not support what he viewed as divisive pre–Civil War abolitionism. During the Civil War, he identified with the copperhead (pro-South) Democrats and in 1863 was nominated for the Ohio State Senate but did not run. After the Civil War, Wise continued his activism in reforming American Judaism. He laid the groundwork for the establishment of the Union of American Hebrew Congregations in 1873 and founded the Reform movement's rabbinical seminary, Hebrew Union College, in 1875, serving as president and ordaining more than sixty rabbis. In 1874, his wife died, and in 1876, he married Selma Bondi, with whom he had four children.

Wise wrote voluminously. Although best known for his journalism, reformist platforms, and theology, he also published his *Reminiscences* (1901) and (often pseudonymously) twenty-seven novels (eleven in English, sixteen in German), hundreds of poems, and several plays. One typical Wise novel, didactic and historical, was serialized in 1858 in the *Israelite* under the headline "*The Combat of the People: or, Hillel and Herod: An Historical Romance of the Time of Herod I*, by the American Jewish Novelist." In his memoirs, Wise writes:

> The leading characters were Bar Kokhba and Rabbi Aqiba, and their most prominent contemporaries. . . . I had to invent the female characters. . . . I described as faithfully as possible the customs, habits, views, the patriotism, the heroism, the victories and defeats, the joys and sufferings of that period of storm and stress. I had in mind the twofold object of awakening once again Jewish patriotism, and of popularizing an important portion of Jewish literature. . . . Thousands, as I knew well, read the novel eagerly, and it left a deep impression on thousands. . . . The novel was read more widely than anything had ever been read in American Jewish circles.

This novel, as well as two others that were serialized in the *Israelite*—*The Last Struggle of the Nation; or, Rabbi Akiba and His Time* and *The First of the Maccabees*—had, according to Wise,

> a telling influence on thousands of readers in the way of arousing patriotism and a desire for Jewish learning. They thus accomplished their purpose fully, although I never had any ambition to become renowned as a novelist. Thousands of copies of the last-named stories were sold in a second edition.

Wise's editorials in the *Israelite* are perhaps the most delightful and telling of his writings. In them, he writes about many issues of concern to Jews: the anti-Semitic boorishness of a Yankee boy; the statistics on Jewish and Christian criminals in Poland; the education of women; Jewish communities throughout Europe; the Sunday blue laws in California; why Jews should fast on Yom Kippur. Most notably, though, Wise unabashedly promotes American Judaism. For example, on March 5, 1858, he writes on the *Necessity of Studying Hebrew*, and on July 16, 1858, he calls for young, American-born Jews to become rabbis who will preach in English rather than Hebrew both to ensure the survival of Judaism in America and to enlighten all other faiths about the Jewish values that have influenced Christianity, Islam, and Confucianism.

In the editorial in this book, *The Fourth of July, 1858*, Wise lauds the coming "birthday of our independence" and calls it "the greatest" celebration of its kind, second only to Passover, "because it is a memorial of the triumph of liberty," "the second redemption of mankind from the hands of their oppressors." Using this as his foundation, Wise argues that the dual, interdependent identities of Jews and Americans represent the two poles of political history, marked by Moses and the American Revolution, that, through the establishment of Jewish law—the Ten Commandments—and of democratic law—the U.S. Constitution—have radically bettered the world.

The Fourth of July, 1858

Sunday next will be the fourth of July, the birthday of our independence, the eighty second anniversary of American liberty for all men who are desirous to participate in this boon of benign Providence. By common consent the independence day is celebrated this year on the fifth of July, on account of the Christian Sabbath; but it is not the day, it is the event which is celebrated; and immortal actions, like the minds who enacted them, are elevated above time and space.—Any time, at any place and by any class of friends of liberty, the event of the declaration of Independence may justly be celebrated, and the memory of the patriots and heroes be solemnized.

Next to the Passover feast[1] the fourth of July is the greatest, because it is a memorial of the triumph of liberty. Israel's redemption, God's direct interposition in behalf of liberty and justice, the first successful declaration of independence, the first birth day of the first free nation, free in truth and justice, which ultimately revolutionized the whole civilized world by the laws and institutions of the nation liberated on that day, to adopt right instead of might, law for despotism, justice for the arbitrary will of one or more men, and personal liberty in place of servitude—the fourth of July tells us the glorious story of the second redemption of mankind from the hands of their oppressors, the second interposition of Providence in behalf of liberty, the second era of the redemption of mankind, the second triumph of right over might, justice over arbitrary despotism, personal and legal liberty over the power of the strongest and most warlike.

We wrote on some other occasion: "Moses[2] forms one pole and the American revolution the other, of an axis around which revolves the political history of thirty three centuries,"[3] and we repeat it here fearless of contradiction. Impartial students admit, as they are bound to do, that the biblical theories revolutionized all the conceptions of the ancient world, and form the solid basis of modern society. They are not ready yet to admit, that the American revolution and the American republic are, politically spoken, the ultimate results of the biblical theories, clad in a form to suit modern society, and that the theories in this form will ultimately revolutionize the whole world. All coming revolutions, peaceful or violent, will change the form only; the theories, the vital principles will remain immutably the same.

We only need cast a glance on the progress of our doctrines, to be convinced of their ultimate destiny, to revolutionize all nations. During 170 years of dependency this country grew to three millions of inhabitants; during 82 years of liberty[4] the three millions of inhabitants multiplied nearly tenfold. This sounds fabulous, nevertheless it is true. Since 1776 the institutions of the middle ages as carried over from the Heathen times, died away more rapidly than in a thousand years previously. Old England verifies daily more her Carta magna,[5] emancipated Ireland, her colonies, the Jews,[6] and extends liberty to all parts of the world. France, Spain, Portugal, Belgium, Holland, Sweden, Norway, Denmark, the best part of Germany, Sardiny[7] and Switzerland witnessed the progress of the spirit of liberty, its rapid and irresistible march. Austria, Russia and Turkey felt its gigantic power, and none could prevent its incursions in Asia, Africa and Australia. The African Moor enjoys more rights and privileges this day than the German or French peasant did 80 years ago. The Persian native and the Indian

1. I.e., the Seder, the ceremonial meal eaten after sundown on the first and second days of the spring holiday of Passover, beginning on the fourteenth of Nisan, which commemorates the liberation of the Hebrews from slavery and their exodus from Egypt.
2. Prophet and lawgiver of the 13th century B.C.E. who liberated the Hebrews from bondage and then led them out of Egypt.
3. The estimated number of centuries between the time of Moses and American independence (1776).
4. I.e., the eighty-two years between 1776 and 1858. "170 years of dependency": the approximate number of years between the arrival of the first English colonists in North America and 1858.
5. I.e., Magna Carta, the "Great Charter" of liberties granted to the English people by King John in June 1215.
6. In 1858, Britain's House of Commons abolished the required Christian oath and admitted Jewish members for the first time, completing the legal emancipation of the Jews in Britain. "Emancipated Ireland": Britain ruled Ireland from 1171 until 1921. In the 1850s, the Fenians began demanding home rule. "Her colonies": the United States rebelled in 1776.
7. I.e., Sardinia.

Sepoy[8] are better protected now by laws and justice than the European operative was one century ago. So the genius of liberty crosses oceans, traverses pathless deserts, conquers mighty empires, and subjects arbitrary despots. So the genius of liberty marched onward and forward during the short period of eighty years; will it not in a-short time conquer the whole world? Yes! it has declared war to its opponents, its sword glitters already wherever God's sun shines, its friends and champions band together in legions, unconquerable and indefatigable. When hundreds fall on the great battle field thousands revive and rush to the glorious combat. It will not yield, not rest until it has crushed the thrones, crowns, scepters, and the depot's iron rod; and upon the ruins of its opponent's strongholds it will unfurl its glorious banner inscribed with the golden words: Liberty, equality and justice for all[!]

Hence we say, the fourth of July is the day of second redemption of mankind, the spirit of God as revealed through Moses and the prophets as far as this earth is concerned, was incarnated in a modern and suitable form and destined to conquer the nations, to break the chains of servitude, dispel the clouds of despotism, conquer the night of prejudice and superstition, that every eye may behold the sacred sun of truth and be delighted with its glorious rays, that every mind perceive the great laws of God, the path of truth and salvation. Hallelujah! we exclaim, for the birth day of liberty, when man came to the conviction, "Have we not all one father, has not one God created us?" Hallelujah! for the day when God's law was verified, "One law and one judgment shall be for all of you." Hallelujah! for the day, when man was restored to his rights, when conscience resumed its rightful throne and the dwarf of superstition was slain. Hallelujah! for the birth day of liberty to all nations!

1858

8. English spelling of *Sipāhī* (Persian and Urdu); a private soldier in the native infantry of the Indian army under British rule.

ADAH ISAACS MENKEN
1835–1868

A friend of Walt Whitman, Adah Isaacs Menken wrote poetry in a free verse that anticipated by a century the poems of Allen Ginsberg and Adrienne Rich. Notorious in New York, San Francisco, London, Paris, and Vienna for wearing a flesh-colored body stocking while strapped to a horse as the star of the melodrama *Mazeppa,* Menken, celebrity poet and actress, wrote poems as unconventional as her life. Unlike Rebecca Gratz and Penina Moïse, who worked with women and children in their Jewish communities, never married, were perceived as "true women"—that is, spiritual beings—and wrote within the conventions of their day, Menken defied the strictures of society and art.

Born in 1835 in Milneburg, Louisiana, to Auguste and Marie Theodore, Menken may have been a descendant of Sephardic Jews, although one source claims that her parents were freed slaves and another, that her original name was Dolores Adios Fuertes. She married four times in seven years, keeping the name of her first husband, Alexander Isaacs Menken, a Jew from Cincinnati. Her second marriage was to John C. Heenan, the heavyweight boxing champion of the world. She bore two sons, both of whom died in infancy, in 1859 and 1867.

As an actress (for a while, the highest paid in the theater) and a literary figure, Menken was friends with famous writers—Whitman, Bret Harte, Mark Twain, and Joaquin Miller in America; Charles Dickens, Dante Gabriel Rossetti, and Algernon Charles Swinburne in England; and Alexandre Dumas and George Sand in France. Sand, the baby's godmother, persuaded Menken to have her second son baptized.

Whether, as some believe, Menken was raised as a Catholic and converted to Judaism when she married her first husband or, as Menken once stated, she was born a Jew, the adult Menken was Jewish with a passion. She refused to perform in the theater on the Jewish High Holidays (Rosh Hashanah and Yom Kippur) and was visited by a rabbi on her deathbed in Paris. To whatever degree she was observant or traditional, Menken took a scholar's approach to Judaism, becoming fluent in Hebrew and studying classical Jewish texts when she lived in Cincinnati during her first marriage.

In that city in the 1850s, she began to publish poems in Isaac Mayer Wise's new weekly, the *Israelite.* (She also prayed from Wise's prayer book, *Minhag Amerika*, her copy of which is at Harvard University.) In some poems, Menken protested the persecution of Jews in Turkey, Italy, and England. In others, she expressed her individualism in terms of her deep and original commitment to Jewish texts and images.

In *Judith,* for example, Menken reinterprets the Apocrypha's story of the Jewish heroine of the sixth century B.C.E. who lures and decapitates Holofernes, the general who has laid siege to her city. Menken's Judith speaks as a prophet and a warrior, awakened by an angel bearing "the sword of my mouth" (Revelation 2.16). Judith, a conduit of "power that will unseal the thunders!" and "give voice to graves!" eschews the chaste, meek, and submissive roles for women ("I am no Magdalene waiting to kiss the hem of your garment") and recasts the voice of the conventionally male hero to reflect the voice of a woman. As she anticipates, with bloodthirsty sensuality, murdering Holofernes, Judith reiterates her power to give voice and her identity, "Oh forget not that I am Judith!"

In *Myself,* Menken considers the sweet fruit that lies within the bitterness of patience in love. The speaker, "decked in jewels and lace," laughs "beneath the gaslight's glare," while her soul waits "naked and hungry upon one of Heaven's high hills of light" for comfort or redemption. In section V, the poem shifts from an exploration of sensual love to a messianic vision. "When this world shall fall, like some old ghost," and "when God shall lift the frozen seal from struggling voices," then will she be able to speak out and "love will be mine."

In *Hear, O Israel!* Menken rewrites—"from the Hebrew"—the watchword of the Jewish faith, the Shema, in an American vein, using it and a passage from the prophet Jeremiah (32.38) to urge Jews to "rouse ye from the slumber of ages, and though Hell welters at your feet, carve a road through these tyrants!"

These poems and others were collected in *Infelicia*, published posthumously in 1868 in Philadelphia.

Judith[1]

Repent, or I will come unto thee quickly, and will fight thee with the sword of my mouth.—REVELATION ii.16[2]

I

Ashkelon is not cut off with the remnant of a valley.
Baldness dwells not upon Gaza.
The field of the valley is mine, and it is clothed in verdure.
The steepness of Baal-perazim is mine;
And the Philistines spread themselves in the valley of Rephaim.[3]
They shall yet be delivered into my hands.
For the God of Battles has gone before me!
The sword of the mouth shall smite them to dust.
I have slept in the darkness—
But the seventh angel woke me, and giving me a sword of flame, points to the blood-ribbed cloud, that lifts his reeking head above the mountain.
Thus am I the prophet.[4]
I see the dawn that heralds to my waiting soul the advent of power.

Power that will unseal the thunders!
Power that will give voice to graves!

Graves of the living;
Graves of the dying;
Graves of the sinning;
Graves of the loving;
Graves of despairing;
And oh! graves of the deserted!
These shall speak, each as their voices shall be loosed.
And the day is dawning.

II

Stand back, ye Philistines!
Practice what ye preach to me;
I heed ye not, for I know ye all.
Ye are living burning lies, and profanation to the garments which with stately steps ye sweep your marble palaces.

1. The beautiful, virtuous, widowed Jewish heroine of the apocryphal Book of Judith (written around 100 B.C.E.). She beheaded Holofernes, the general in chief of Nebuchadnezzar's army who had laid siege to her city, thus saving her people and their worship of God.
2. *Judith* is Menken's paraphrase of this verse, found in Revelation, a book of the New Testament. Revelation presents John the Evangelist's vision of heaven and of the defeat of the Roman Empire, using the imagery of the earlier Hebrew Book of Daniel.
3. "Valley of the giants" (Hebrew); southwest of Jerusalem. The Philistines more than once invaded and plundered this valley, rich in crops and animals, until King David repulsed and slaughtered the invaders so completely that the valley became a symbol of God's awesome judgment. "Ashkelon": an ancient city and port in Israel, west-southwest of Jerusalem, whose inhabitants surrendered to Holofernes and became his minions (Judith 2.28). "Gaza": a city and surrounding territory on the Mediterranean Sea whose inhabitants welcomed Holofernes' conquest. "Baal-perazim": "bursts of destruction" (Hebrew); the scene of one of King David's victories over the Philistines. "Philistines": inhabitants of ancient Philistia; also, figuratively, uncouth, uncultured, ignorant people.
4. The Book of Judith contains Judith's prayer to God (Judith 9.2–19) and her song of thanksgiving (Judith 16.1–21), but no prophecy.

Your palaces of Sin, around which the damning evidence of guilt hangs like a reeking vapor.
Stand back!
I would pass up the golden road of the world.
A place in the ranks awaits me.
I know that ye are hedged on the borders of my path.
Lie and tremble, for ye well know that I hold with iron grasp the battle axe.
Creep back to your dark tents in the valley.
Slouch back to your haunts of crime.
Ye do not know me, neither do ye see me.
But the sword of the mouth is unsealed, and ye coil yourselves in slime and bitterness at my feet.
I mix your jeweled heads, and your gleaming eyes, and your hissing tongues with the dust.
My garments shall bear no mark of ye.
When I shall return this sword to the angel, your foul blood will not stain its edge.
It will glimmer with the light of truth, and the strong arm shall rest.

III

Stand back!
I am no Magdalene[5] waiting to kiss the hem of your garment.
It is mid-day.
See ye not what is written on my forehead?
I am Judith!
I wait for the head of my Holofernes!
Ere the last tremble of the conscious death-agony shall have shuddered, I will show it to ye with the long black hair clinging to the glazed eyes, and the great mouth opened in search of voice, and the strong throat all hot and reeking with blood, that will thrill me with wild unspeakable joy as it courses down my bare body and dabbles my cold feet!
My sensuous soul will quake with the burden of so much bliss.
Oh, what wild passionate kisses will I draw up from that bleeding mouth!
I will strangle this pallid throat of mine on the sweet blood!
I will revel in my passion.
At midnight I will feast on it in the darkness.
For it was that which thrilled its crimson tides of reckless passion through the blue veins of my life, and made them leap up in the wild sweetness of Love and agony of Revenge!
I am starving for this feast.
Oh forget not that I am Judith!
And I know where sleeps Holofernes.

1868

5. A reference to Mary Magdalene, a woman who was healed by Jesus of evil spirits and who became his faithful, humble follower.

Myself

La patience est amère; mais le fruit en est doux?[1]

I

Away down into the shadowy depths of the Real I once lived.
I thought that to seem was to be.
But the waters of Marah[2] were beautiful, yet they were bitter.
I waited, and hoped, and prayed;
Counting the heart-throbs and the tears that answered them.
Through my earnest pleadings for the True, I learned that the mildest mercy of life was a smiling sneer;
And that the business of the world was to lash with vengeance all who dared to be what their God had made them.
Smother back tears to the red blood of the heart!
Crush out things called souls!
No room for them here!

II

Now I gloss my pale face with laughter, and sail my voice on with the tide.
Decked in jewels and lace, I laugh beneath the gaslight's glare, and quaff the purple wine.
But the minor-keyed soul is standing naked and hungry upon one of Heaven's high hills of light.
Standing and waiting for the blood of the feast!
Starving for one poor word!
Waiting for God to launch out some beacon on the boundless shores of this Night.
Shivering for the uprising of some soft wing under which it may creep, lizard-like, to warmth and rest.
Waiting! Starving and shivering!

III

Still I trim my white bosom with crimson roses; for none shall see the thorns.
I bind my aching brow with a jeweled crown, that none shall see the iron one beneath.
My silver-sandaled feet keep impatient time to the music, because I cannot be calm.
I laugh at earth's passion-fever of Love; yet I know that God is near to the soul on the hill, and hears the ceaseless ebb and flow of a hopeless love, through all my laughter.
But if I can cheat my heart with the old comfort, that love can be forgotten, is it not better?
After all, living is but to play a part!
The poorest worm would be a jewel-headed snake if she could!

1. "Patience is bitter, but is its fruit sweet?" (French).
2. "Bitterness" (Hebrew); the place where God enabled Moses to make the bitter waters sweet in order to quench the thirst of the Hebrews, who were wandering in the desert (Exodus 15.23).

IV

All this grandeur of glare and glitter has its nighttime.
The pallid eyelids must shut out smiles and daylight.
Then I fold my cold hands, and look down at the restless rivers of a love that rushes through my life.
Unseen and unknown they tide on over black rocks and chasms of Death.
Oh, for one sweet word to bridge their terrible depths!
O jealous soul! why wilt thou crave and yearn for what thou canst not have?
And life is so long—so long.

V

With the daylight comes the business of living.
The prayers that I sent trembling up the golden thread of hope all come back to me.
I lock them close in my bosom, far under the velvet and roses of the world.
For I know that stronger than these torrents of passion is the soul that hath lifted itself up to the hill.
What care I for his careless laugh?
I do not sigh; but I know that God hears the life-blood dripping as I, too, laugh.
I would not be thought a foolish rose, that flaunts her red heart out to the sun.
Loving is not living!

VI

Yet through all this I know that night will roll back from the still, gray plain of heaven, and that my triumph shall rise sweet with the dawn!
When these mortal mists shall unclothe the world, then shall I be known as I am!
When I dare be dead and buried behind a wall of wings, then shall he know me!
When this world shall fall, like some old ghost, wrapped in the black skirts of the wind, down into the fathomless eternity of fire, then shall souls uprise!
When God shall lift the frozen seal from struggling voices, then shall we speak!
When the purple-and-gold of our inner natures shall be lighted up in the Eternity of Truth, then will love be mine!
I can wait.

1868

Hear, O Israel![1]

(From the Hebrew)

And they shall be my people, and I will be their God.
—JEREMIAH xxxii.38

1. Translation of the opening words of the Hebrew prayer Shema, the watchword of the Jewish faith, which proclaims Judaism's monotheistic doctrine.

I

Hear, O Israel! and plead my cause against the ungodly nation!
'Midst the terrible conflict of Love and Peace, I departed from thee, my people, and spread my tent of many colors in the land of Egypt.
In their crimson and fine linen I girded my white form.
Sapphires gleamed their purple light from out the darkness of my hair.
The silver folds of their temple foot-cloth was spread beneath my sandaled feet.
Thus I slumbered through the daylight.
Slumbered 'midst the vapor of sin,
Slumbered 'midst the battle and din,
Wakened 'midst the strangle of breath,
Wakened 'midst the struggle of death!

II

Hear, O Israel! my people—to thy goodly tents do I return with unstained hands.
Like as the harts for the water-brooks, in thirst, do pant and bray, so pants and cries my longing soul for the house of Jacob.
My tears have unto me been meat, both in night and day:
And the crimson and fine linen molders in the dark tents of the enemy.
With bare feet and covered head do I return to thee, O Israel!
With sackcloth have I bound the hem of my garments.
With olive leaves have I trimmed the border of my bosom.
The breaking waves did pass o'er me; yea, were mighty in their strength—
Strength of the foe's oppression.
My soul was cast out upon the waters of Sin: but it has come back to me.
My transgressions have vanished like a cloud.
The curse of Balaam[2] hath turned to a blessing;
And the doors of Jacob[3] turn not on their hinges against me.
Rise up, O Israel! for it is I who passed through the fiery furnace seven times, and come forth unscathed, to redeem thee from slavery,[4] O my nation! and lead thee back to God.

III

Brothers mine, fling out your white banners over this Red Sea[5] of wrath!
Hear ye not the Death-cry of a thousand burning, bleeding wrongs?
Against the enemy lift thy sword of fire, even thou, O Israel! whose prophet I am.
For I, of all thy race, with these tear-blinded eyes, still see the watch-fire leaping up its blood-red flame from the ramparts of our Jerusalem![6]
And my heart alone beats and palpitates, rises and falls with the glimmering

2. Balaam, following the word of God, refuses to curse the children of Israel, as he was ordered to by the Moabite king Balak, and instead blesses them (Numbers 22.5–24.25).

3. The biblical Patriarch Jacob, also called Israel, represents the Jewish people who now welcome the repentant speaker of the poem.

4. A reference to Moses, who redeemed the Hebrews from slavery in Egypt. "Fiery furnace seven times": a reference to the three men who are thrown into the furnace for refusing to worship Nebuchadnezzar instead of God and who miraculously survive the ordeal (Daniel 3). This also refers to a parallel midrashic story in which Nimrod throws Abraham into the limekiln for refusing to help build the Tower of Babel.

5. Literally, "Reed Sea" (Hebrew), which God parted so that Moses could lead the Hebrews across it to escape the Egyptians (Exodus 14.21–28).

6. I.e., the fortification guarding the ancient walled city of Jerusalem. "Watch-fire": a fire kept burning at night for the city's guards or as a signal.

and the gleaming of the golden beacon flame, by whose light I shall lead thee, O my people! back to freedom!
Give me time—oh give me time to strike from your brows the shadow-crowns of Wrong!
On the anvil of my heart will I rend the chains that bind ye.
Look upon me—oh look upon me, as I turn from the world—from love, and passion, to lead thee, thou Chosen of God, back to the pastures of Right and Life!
Fear me not; for the best blood that heaves this heart now runs for thee, thou Lonely Nation!
Why wear ye not the crown of eternal royalty, that God set down upon your heads?
Back, tyrants of the red hands!
Slouch back to your ungodly tents, and hide the Cainbrand[7] on your foreheads!
Life for life, blood for blood, is the lesson ye teach us.[8]
We, the Children of Israel, will not creep to the kennel graves ye are scooping out with iron hands, like scourged hounds!
Israel! rouse ye from the slumber of ages, and, though Hell welters at your feet, carve a road through these tyrants!
The promised dawn-light is here; and God—O the God of our nation is calling!
    Press on—press on!

IV

Ye, who are kings, princes, priests, and prophets. Ye men of Judah[9] and bards of Jerusalem, hearken unto my voice, and I will speak thy name, O Israel!
Fear not; for God hath at last let loose His thinkers, and their voices now tremble in the mighty depths of this old world!
Rise up from thy blood-stained pillows!
Cast down to dust the hideous, galling chains that bind thy strong hearts down to silence!
    Wear ye the badge of slaves?
    See ye not the watch-fire?
Look aloft, from thy wilderness of thought!
Come forth with the signs and wonders, and thy strong hands, and stretched-out arms, even as thou didst from Egypt!
Courage, courage! trampled hearts!
Look at these pale hands and frail arms, that have rent asunder the welded chains that an army of the Philistines bound about me!
But the God of all Israel set His seal of fire on my breast, and lighted up, with inspiration, the soul that pants for the Freedom of a nation!
With eager wings she fluttered above the blood-stained bayonet-points of the millions, who are trampling upon the strong throats of God's people.
    Rise up, brave hearts!
The sentry cries: "All's well!" from Hope's tower!

7. A reference to Cain, the firstborn son of Adam and Eve, who killed his brother Abel and was marked by God (Genesis 4.15).
8. The formulation for reciprocal justice: ". . . life for life, eye for eye, tooth for tooth, hand for hand, foot for foot, burning for burning, wound for wound, stripe for stripe" (Exodus 21.23–25; Leviticus 24.20; Deuteronomy 19.21).
9. One of the twelve tribes of Israel that entered the promised land. Later, the southern kingdom of Judah was a rival of the northern kingdom of Israel.

Fling out your banners of Right!
The watch fire grows brighter!
All's well! All's well!
Courage! Courage!
The Lord of Hosts is in the field,
The God of Jacob is our shield![1]

1868

1. Translation from the Hebrew of two of God's names.

NATHAN MAYER
1838–1912

One of the first Jewish American novelists, now essentially forgotten, Nathan Mayer was a physician and a soldier in the United States Army during the Civil War. Born in Germany in 1838, Mayer came to America in 1849 with his father, Isaac Mayer, a rabbi originally from Alsace who had lost his property during the German revolutions of 1848. Nathan accompanied his father to his rabbinical posts in Cincinnati, Ohio (1849–56), and Rochester, New York (1856–59). The family finally settled in Hartford, Connecticut (1859–69). A rabbi opposed to the Reform movement and an advocate of Conservative Judaism, Nathan's father was also a writer: he published one of the first Hebrew grammars in the United States in 1854, translated *Sirach* (Ecclesiasticus, an apocryphal book of the Bible) into German, and produced a textbook for Hebrew and Sabbath schools, *The Source of Salvation*, in 1874.

After attending medical school, Nathan Mayer went to Europe in 1859 to serve as a surgeon with the French army during the French war with Austria. He came back to the United States at the beginning of the Civil War and joined Connecticut's Sixteenth Infantry as a surgeon. Captured by the Confederates, Mayer was interned in Libby Prison. When released, he was promoted to brigadier general and served as medical purveyor for the Union soldiers in North Carolina. After the war, Mayer settled in Hartford, where he practiced medicine until his death in 1912. As surgeon general for the state of Connecticut, Nathan wrote a report on the state's prisons and county jails in 1873.

Like his father, Nathan Mayer was a writer, but his writing was Jewish in a very different way. He published literary and music criticism in the general press. But most important for the purposes of this anthology, he published articles and serialized novels in the Jewish press. One of the novels, *The Count and the Jewess*, based on the legends of Rabbi Loew of Prague, was serialized in the *Israelite* in 1856. According to that weekly's founder and editor, Isaac Mayer Wise, Mayer also "conducted the department of belles-lettres and wove incidents from Spanish-Jewish history into articles" for the *Israelite*. A later issue of the *Israelite* (March 26, 1858), contains two pieces by Mayer. One is an essay on poetry and religion that characterizes Jewish poetry as the poetry of reason stemming from the revelation of God at Mount Sinai. The other is a spirited refutation of a slur that appeared in the *Cincinnati Weekly Gazette*, which stated that Jews are inherently incapable of owning and farming land. In this refutation, Mayer mentions, among other things, that Jews are bound to the countries in which they live, and he discusses their victimization and expulsions during the Middle Ages and their willingness to give up their freedom in order to stay in the lands "whose rights they had defended as soldiers, whose coffers they had enriched as merchants, whose literature and art they had developed as poets and painters," and from which they were forced out.

Mayer published at least two novels in book form. *Differences* (1867) provides a marvelous account of the adventures and problems faced by Jews in the South during the Civil War. *The Fatal Secret! or, Plots and Counterplots: A Novel of the Sixteenth Century* was first serialized in the *Israelite* in 1858. Set in sixteenth-century Portugal during the Inquisition and using an array of characters who are, in turn, wicked, innocent, seductive, and heroic, and whose stories are intertwined, this swashbuckling melodrama tells the story of how those last Portuguese Jews were saved from forced conversion and escaped to Amsterdam, the portal to the New World, becoming, in effect, the ancestors of the very first American Jews.

From The Fatal Secret! or, Plots and Counterplots: A Novel of the Sixteenth Century

[Hernando da Costa, son of a baptized Jew and a nonbeliever, has nailed blasphemous scrolls to the cathedral door, proclaiming the hypocrisy of the Church and the truth of the Jewish faith. The noble Gloria, disguised as a male page, observes Hernando, her betrothed, making love to another woman, the deceptive Donna Miranda, whose father, Sir Nuna di Perez, subsequently discovers that his daughter is pregnant. Miranda, spurned by Hernando, spies on a secret meeting of the Marranos, the hidden Jews, and betrays them to the Inquisition. The soldiers drag the Jews out of their synagogue on the eve of Rosh Hashanah. They are now in Santa Cruz, the prison of the Inquisition.]

Chapter XLVI

THE ESCAPE

All of the Isralites[1] had been hurried through a short trial, and many of them condemned to the stake, some to be maimed and imprisoned, and a few to penitence and banishment. The goods of all, as a matter of course, became the property of the King and the Holy Tribunal. The Cardinal Grand Inquisitor had deputed Pater Domingo,[2] the secretary, to take possession of the private property of the prisoners, and make a list of it, for the benefit of the royal officers. The King had entrusted the execution of a favorite plan to the Cardinal, which the latter also placed under Domingo's charge. It was, to distribute the children of the condemned New Christians on various African isles, where they might grow up without knowledge of Judaism, and become pious Christian settlers.

Pater Domingo had attended to both these commissions. Ships were provided which the Pater newly manned, in order, as he stated to be sure of good and faithful execution of the royal and Inquisitional orders.—For the character of the new crew he vouched.

They were drafted from various parts of the Kingdom, and with such celer-

1. Here, the Sephardic Jews masquerading as converted Christians, whom the agents of the Portuguese Inquisition have discovered, betrayed, and imprisoned.
2. *Pater* is Latin for "father," a monk.

ity, that four days after the trial of the Israelites each ship was manned; the children of the Israelites were placed on board of one vessel, and their most valuable treasures on the other. The first to be carried to African Islands; the latter to be conveyed to the King, who was journeying in the South of Portugal. At that time, even more than now, the conveyance by water was so much better and safer than by land, in Portugal, that things of value and importance were generally sent by ships. Therefore, Pater Domingo acted quite honestly in freighting a vessel with the confiscated treasures of the condemned Israelites.

On the evening of the day when they had received their cargo, both vessels stood out to sea. The Cardinal Grand Inquisitor, in very warm terms, expressed his thanks to Pater Domingo for the dispatch he had used.

There were two other vessels laying behind the rocks of Cintra[3] in a small bay full of dangerous cliffs and sandbanks, which seemed for some days past to be waiting the arrival of their cargo. The first was a ship of Dutch make; at its side lay a smaller one, though also of considerable capacity. The latter had great breath of beam, but a light and easy build.

They lay at anchor in a bay, where they could not be approached, but from which they could not emerge without foundering unless the most skillful of pilots held the rudder. Around them were raging breakers and shallow sandbanks.

We return to the palace of the Cardinal Grand Inquisitor, for the purpose of observing Pater Domingo, a few moments. He stands at a table glittering with goblets of crystal, silver, and costly wood. Selecting a large one of silver, worked in relief with crosses, and representations of the letter "S," he proceeded carefully to wipe the inside with a towel. Then having drawn a small case of tiny vials from his pocket, he chooses one and pours from it a whitish brown powder into the goblet. Again, the towel is used to rub the powder upon the inside of the cup. What remains is thrown away, for the Pater turns the mouth of the cup downwards, and shakes it several times. After he has seen that the powder upon the silver can not be noticed, he replaces the cup upon the table, and returns the case of vials to his pocket.

On the next day, which is the ninth after the capture of the Israelites, His Excellency the Cardinal Savelli falls very sick. Physicians and leeches[4] are sent for. They pronounce his disease without danger, but advise rest, and abstinence from any business. More than ever he had reason to congratulate himself on the abilities of his secretary. Everything is put into his hands, and the Cardinal retires to His chambers with positive orders not to be disturbed.

A new corps of familiars[5] has for some time been forming under Pater Domingo's management. They have arrived in town that very day. The Cardinal has been notified of it, and faintly whispered:

"Disturb me not. Pater Domingo will arrange all."

Pater Domingo has provided them with weapons, and ordered that, on this very evening they should begin their duty by guarding the Convent of Santa Cruz. The old familiars have partly been removed to the residence of Savelli, and partly been instructed to occupy a wing of the new palace of the Inqui-

3. I.e., Sintra, a town in the Lisbon district of western Portugal on the Atlantic coast; known for its beautiful mountain location.
4. Bloodsucking worms used in 19th-century medicine to treat mental illness, tumors, skin diseases, gout, whooping cough, and headaches.
5. Officers of the Inquisition.

sition, which has already been completed, while the main building is yet unfinished. Thus the convent of Santa Cruz is guarded by the new familiars alone, and their commander is Pater Domingo, the secretary of the Inquisition.

It is evening. Dusk in the city, dusk on the ocean, dusk in the frowning convent walls of Santa Cruz. The hazy light is about to disappear from the sky. And blazing up once more in hectic glory, it pours a bright red flush upon the handsome but swarthy face of father Domingo. He is standing at a dark, arching window, lost in thoughts. Oh those star-like eyes and regal brow were surely not made to hide beneath a monkish cowl!

The light disappears shooting a final flash over the white sails of a vessel far out at sea.

The hazy obscurity has disappeared, and, circled by azure night, the golden star of love and eve, the sweet glowing Hesperus,[6] rises and watches on the crystal hills of heaven.

The cowl of the monk has dropped over his brow and eyes. His form dilates. He approaches the door. Ere he has reached it, a thought seems to arrest his steps.

"God, God, eternal and almighty, merciful and just,"[7] he cries, throwing himself upon his knees, and raising his arms aloft; "God of my soul and my race, aid me!—Forsake not thy servant, thy devoted servant! Forsake not thy people, thy chosen ones! oh God, thou art Lord of Heaven and Earth, and the Disposer of fate! Turn not thy face from me!"

In his earnest supplication the hood had again fallen back, and the evening star smiled upon the monk's pure brow. Yet, for a moment he knelt there in profound silence. Clang, Tang! cried the bell of the convent beginning to strike eight.

With the words, "haste! haste!" the Pater arose, and leaving the apartment approached the prisons.

"Accompany me, and open the doors as we proceed," ordered Domingo to one of the familiars.

It was done.

Other familiars unlocked the chains of the prisoners. At Pater Domingo's command the men were led into the upper apartments of the convent, and provided with the weapons and dark uniforms of Inquisitorial familiars. The ladies were placed in ready sedans, well secured and carried by the men. They arranged themselves in the courtyard of the convent. The troop of familiars newly organized by Pater Domingo enclosed the disguised prisoners, who carried their ladies, on every side. They were all ready to issue forth at half past eleven.

"We will wait until twelve," said Father Domingo.

The priest had been indefatigable in his exertions to arrange every thing properly, to instruct and help every one. It was through his agency, thanks to him, that they were enabled to get ready in so short a time. He now made a sign for silence; not a sound was heard. All eyes were upon him.

6. The evening star, named after the son or brother of Greek Titan Atlas.

7. The opening words of a Hebrew prayer recited on Yom Kippur eve.

"Dear brothers," he said softly and calmly, "you may be uneasy about your children?"

A half stifled sigh from the ladies was the only reply.

"I have embarked them and sent them on to Amsterdam, under good care!" continued the priest.

A cry of joy rewarded this intelligence.

"And again you may be uneasy about your wealth and treasures, my brothers.—For to arrive in a strange land without means is a cheerless prospect."

A dark cloud upon the faces of the men replied to this.

"You can laugh at this care also. Your treasures have been sent on to Amsterdam, where you will find sufficient to begin life anew. Let me advise you, with the sword and plume to lay aside the high chivalric actions and thoughts of sunny Portugal.—Turn to the tradesman's counter—other employment is not open to the Hebrew. But in Holland[8] you will enjoy the inestimable privilege of professing your faith, your religion. Hark! it is twelve o'clock. Let us proceed to the vessel. Let all observe the deepest silence."

A murmur arose and rolled among the crowd.

"What is it?" inquired the Pater.

"Don Lionel Dian, our prince, where is he?" every one inquired. "He must be saved. The royal blood of David[9] may not perish."

"He is already in safety," replied Father Domingo.

"I see not my brother," whispered Enrique.

"Hurry on. I have thought of him. Ere you depart I will give you tidings of Hernando da Costa!"[1]

The convent gates were opened and the train proceeded to move out. Slowly, it crept through the streets of Lisbon, unquestioned, unchallenged. The ships which had been concealed behind the cliffs of Cintra in the rocky bay, had moved away and now lay a little distance below the city. On them the fugitives, together with the new corps of familiars, embarked.

Father Domingo had managed so well that the sailors of the vessels carrying the children and the treasure of the Israelites, were Hebrews. They had been ordered by him to carry both to Amsterdam, and were on the way already. The two other ships, one of which was Captain Sporaso's, were also manned by Hebrew sailors. The new corps of familiars, as the reader will already have suspected, was chiefly composed of Israelites from all parts of Portugal, desirous of emigrating and escaping. Soon as all were on board both ships made haste to get out into the open sea. The sails were spread to the feeble breeze, and aided by the ebb, good headway was made. It was three o'clock ere they could start, for thus long it took to get the fugitives on board.

Scarcely were they fairly in motion, when pater Domingo signed to a familiar behind him, who had, with four others, carried large bundles. They

8. Holland was a haven for Jews because it offered freedom of worship. "Tradesman's counter": even in Holland, Jews were prohibited from belonging to guilds or practicing trades and were permitted to be only merchants.

9. Dian, a hidden Jew and the lover of the widowed Portuguese queen Eleanor, is a descendant of the biblical king David.

1. Brother of Enrique and one of the hidden Jews; he has sacrificed his life at the stake in order to save the other Jews.

unrolled them and the white shrouds[2] taken from the Israelites on New Year's night were disclosed.

"It is the night of atonement,"[3] said Pater Domingo; "let each assume his shroud."

It was quickly done.

Aaron Rodow began his chant by seven times raising and dropping his voice. Soon all were lost in prayer.

1858

2. As a symbol of their purity, traditional Jews often pray in their white burial clothes on the Jewish New Year and the Day of Atonement. These hidden Jews were captured while praying on the New Year.

3. Yom Kippur, the Day of Atonement, begins after sundown of the preceding evening.

ANONYMOUS

Published anonymously in the *American Israelite* on July 16, 1858, *Miriam* may have been written by the weekly's editor, Isaac Mayer Wise, although its long, free-verse lines are reminiscent of the poems of Adah Isaacs Menken, who was being published in Wise's paper during the 1850s. This mid-nineteenth-century secular love poem imitates the verses of the Song of Songs. It celebrates Jewish women, both contemporary and legendary, as its speaker simultaneously addresses Miriam, the sister of Moses, and Miriam, a contemporary young woman. Miriam embodies medieval Jewish lore—she is "daughter of Akiba, beloved of the Faithful, and the Goyim"—and appeals to both Jews and Gentiles while collapsing all the biblical generations: her beauty is compared favorably to the beauty of Eve, the Matriarch Sara (here, Miriam's "aunt"), and Rachel, Hannah, Esther, Hagar, and Judith, among others; all these legendary women coexist in the anachronistic imagination of the speaker.

The identity of the poem's speaker is as ambiguous as the identity of the poem's author. In the opening lines, the speaker appears to be a man enamored of the beautiful Miriam, whom he praises in metaphors that echo the Song of Songs ("Pearl of the morning, gazelle of the palm-land"). The speaker tells of a dream in which he strolls by a river like the "purple" Jordan with Miriam and then kisses her. Despite the erotic quality of the kiss (lines 16–17), the love story is tempered by a sense of kinship between the speaker and the beloved: Miriam is "soul of my spirit," "love's sister," and "little sister." The hyperbole that characterizes Miriam's beauty ("Black eyes of endless fire") is modified by both spiritual hyperbole ("star-light eyes, blessed as the lamp of the Sanctuary") and the final paradox—"Thy bitterness, oh, Miriam, is sweeter than all their sweetness!" This final image brings to mind the story of bitter waters of Marah, which God enabled Moses to make sweet and potable for the Jews after their escape from Egypt (Exodus 15.22–25), and of the biblical Miriam, whose opposition to Moses' marriage to Zipporah brings upon herself God's punishment of leprosy (Numbers 12.1–10). By ending the poem with an image of the bitterness in the midst of this sweetness, the poet grants to the subject a complexity of character that makes her immediate and real. Whether this is a man's love poem to an archetypal Jewish woman or a woman's praise poem to a sister, *Miriam* is, like Penina Moïse's poem *Miriam* and Adah Isaacs Menken's *Judith*, a poetic reinterpretation of a biblical character modeled on the poems of Protestant contemporaries that assert the right of women to voice their views in the political and religious forums of the day.

Miriam[1]

Oh, Miriam! Pearl of the morning, gazelle of the palm-land, soul of my spirit,
Daughter of Akiba,[2] beloved of the Faithful, and the Goyim.[3]
Blue sea; sister of lilies and roses,
There came to me a dream, fresh on the wings of the morning,
Soft as the light of the silver Sabbath-lamp when it shines on the Pesach feast,[4]
Dear as thine eyes when loveliest beaming; love's sister.
I walked by thy side in a dream; we walked by a river,
Jordan[5] rolls not more gently; purple its waters;
Thine eyes were upon me, beloved, thy star-light eyes, blessed as the lamp of the Sanctuary,[6]
Black eyes of endless fire—oh, soul, thou art lovely!
Beauty of the East—the golden sequins and ear-rings—the antique gold of Judea,
Which hangs upon thy forehead with the golden ear rings from Damascus,[7]
Which thou had'st from Sara,[8] thy aunt—all the gold around thy dear face,
Is but the frame of a picture too fine for its setting.
My arm and thine twined like the vines in Spring,
Slowly we walked and slower, till trembling and pausing,
I kissed thee, oh, beloved—on the sand by the purple waters.
Anna, the gracious, is fair; fair, too is Sara, the mistress,[9]
Abigail, the joy of her father, and Ruth, the satisfied;[1]
Tabitha, the roe buck, light are her footsteps, and lovely,[2]
Deborah, the bee, and Rebecca, the plump and the lovely,[3]

1. Moses' older sister, who brought their mother to the pharaoh's daughter as a wet nurse for the infant Moses (Exodus 2.4–8).
2. Rabbi Akiva ben Joseph (ca. 50–135), the most prominent of the Torah scholars of Yavneh (Jabneh) in Judea after the fall of the Second Temple (70 C.E.). He was martyred by the Romans.
3. "Gentiles" (Yiddish); "nations" (Hebrew).
4. Hebrew for the Passover Seder, or ritual meal commemorating the exodus of the Hebrews from Egypt. "Silver Sabbath-lamp": candlesticks or a lamp lit before sundown on Friday, blessed in celebration of the beginning of the Jewish Sabbath.
5. The river that flows from the Anti-Lebanon Mountains through the Sea of Galilee into the Dead Sea.
6. Either the seven-branched candelabrum in the Temple in Jerusalem or the Eternal Light, the lamp that burns perpetually in every synagogue near the ark that holds the Torah scrolls.
7. The capital of Syria. "Judea": the ancient region in the land of Israel comprising the southern division of the country. It was ruled, at various times, by Persians, Greeks, and Romans.
8. The biblical Matriarch, Abraham's wife, who accompanied him from Ur to the promised land. Because she was beautiful, Abraham passed her off as his sister in Egypt (Genesis 12.11–20) and in Gerar (Genesis 20.1–14) to protect himself. As a result, he jeopardized his covenant with God.
9. Because Sara was barren (Genesis 11.30, 16.1), she gave Abraham her Egyptian maid, Hagar, who conceived and bore Ishmael but then scorned her mistress. Sara forced Hagar to flee to the desert. "Anna": a Jewish prophetess who, with the prophet Simeon, witnessed the dedication of the infant Jesus in the temple and spoke of him and the expected redemption of Israel (Luke 2.22–38).
1. The young, childless Moabite widow of Mahlon who accompanied her mother-in-law, Naomi, to Bethlehem, took care of her, and married Boaz. King David is descended from her. "Abigail": wife of the wealthy Nabal, who refused to acknowledge King David's authority and whose life she saved by intervening with the king (1 Samuel 25.2–35). When widowed, she married the king (1 Samuel 25.39–42, 27.3, 30.5, 18).
2. Tabitha is an Aramaic name meaning "gazelle." A Christian woman of Jaffa (Joppa), also known as Dorcas, who became famous for her good deeds and charity; she died and was resurrected by Peter (Acts 9.36–42).
3. The biblical Matriarch, wife of Isaac, daughter of Bethuel, sister of Laban, mother of Jacob and Esau. "Deborah": "bee" (Hebrew). The Israelite judge and prophetess (Judges 4) who accompanied Barak into battle against the Canaanite Sisera. The Song of Deborah (Judges 5) is her poem of victory.

Esther, the secret and silent, and Rachel, the sheep;[4]
Eva, life giving, Judith, praising, confessing,[5]
Jemima, fair as the day, Hagar, the stranger,[6]
Hannah, gracious and merciful, Huldah, all the world;[7]
Yes, all the world and its loveliness hath nothing like thine, little sister!
Thy bitterness, oh, Miriam, is sweeter than all their sweetness!

1858

4. Rachel means "ewe" in Hebrew. The biblical Matriarch, the favored of Jacob's two wives, mother of Joseph and Benjamin, sister of Leah, daughter of Laban. "Esther": "star," "Jewish maiden" (Persian). The Jewish queen of Persia (ca. 4th century B.C.E.) who rescued her people from annihilation.

5. Widow of Bethulia, she killed the Assyrian general Holofernes and saved her city from destruction. "Eva": "life" (Hebrew). The first woman created by God, designated "mother of all the living" (Genesis 3.20).

6. The childless Sara's Egyptian maidservant who was given to Abraham as a concubine. When she became pregnant, Hagar scorned Sara and was expelled into the desert (Genesis 16). She returned to Sara, who banished her again with her son, Ishmael. "Jemima": the first of Job's three daughters, born after God restored his good fortune. She and her sisters were exceptionally beautiful and, untraditionally, inherited their father's wealth.

7. A prophetess of Jerusalem (7th century B.C.E.), wife of Shallum, keeper of King Josiah's wardrobe. Huldah prophesied the destruction of Jerusalem (2 Kings 22; 2 Chronicles 34). "Hannah": "grace" (Hebrew). The wife of Elkanah, mother of the prophet Samuel (1 Samuel 1.2, 1.20), she dedicated her son to God (1 Samuel 1.26–28).

EMMA LAZARUS
1849–1887

Most famous for *The New Colossus*, her sonnet welcoming the hordes of immigrants to America, Emma Lazarus was a American-born Jew of colonial Sephardic and German-Jewish stock. Part of a literary circle that included Nathaniel Hawthorne's daughter, Emily Dickinson's proctor, and Ralph Waldo Emerson, and having written and translated poetry from girlhood, Lazarus evolved into a Jewish American poet who combined the contradictory forces of Jewish peoplehood and Puritan America, of Hebraism and Hellenism, to create a highly cultured expression of Jewish American identity for the new masses.

Born on July 22, 1849, the fourth of the seven children of Esther Nathan Lazarus and Moses Lazarus, a sugar merchant and descendant of the original Sephardic settlers in New Netherland, Emma Lazarus enjoyed the luxury of spending winters in New York City and summers in Newport, Rhode Island. Her parents hired private tutors, who taught the Lazarus children literature, music, and languages (French, German, and Italian). And Emma and her sisters were members of Julia Ward Beecher's Town and Country Club, where the members discussed science and literature. Her family belonged to Shearith Israel, a Sephardic congregation in New York City.

Lazarus's ambitions as a writer began when she was young. In 1866, when Lazarus was seventeen, her father privately printed her first book, *Poems and Translations: Written between the Ages of Fourteen and Sixteen.* Soon afterward, Lazarus met Ralph Waldo Emerson, and they began a correspondence as pupil and mentor that lasted until 1882, when Emerson died.

Lazarus's second book, *Admetus and Other Poems,* appeared in 1871 and her novel, *Alide: An Episode of Goethe's Life,* in 1874. She published a verse drama, *The Spagnoletto,* in 1876. Throughout the 1870s and 1880s, she published poems, essays, letters, and a short story in popular American magazines and newspapers such as *Scribner's, Lippincott's,* the *Century,* and the *New York Times.*

Between 1882 and 1884, Lazarus's essays appeared frequently in the weekly *American Hebrew*, her most famous one being *An Epistle to the Hebrews,* a series of open letters that urged American Jews not to take their privilege and security for granted and advocated that Eastern European Jews immigrate to Palestine. Her well-received book of translations, *Poems and Ballads of Heinrich Heine*, came out in 1881 and her own poems, *Songs of a Semite: The Dance to Death and Other Poems*, in 1882.

Lazarus toured England and France in 1883, where she met English poet Robert Browning and poet, artist, and socialist William Morris as well as other luminaries, including Jewish leaders. After her father's death, Lazarus returned to Europe in May 1885 and traveled in England, France, Holland, and Italy through September 1887. She died of cancer in New York in November 1887. Two of her sisters, Mary and Annie, published the posthumous two-volume *Poems of Emma Lazarus* in 1888, which includes a biographical sketch, the first published piece by her elder sister, the essayist Josephine Lazarus; Emma's translations of medieval Hebrew poets such as Judah Halevy; and her last work, prose poems entitled *By the Waters in Babylon.*

Lazarus's earliest poem with a Jewish theme, first published in 1867 and reprinted in *Admetus and Other Poems* (1871), *In the Jewish Synagogue at Newport* was written in answer to Henry Wadsworth Longfellow's poem *The Jewish Cemetery at Newport.* While Longfellow, speaking as a philo-Semite, stands in the cemetery and declares that the earliest New World Jews have left but dead monuments to a once-living faith and peoplehood, Lazarus, echoing Longfellow's quatrains but speaking with the collective voice of American Jews, enters the oldest extant American synagogue next to the graveyard. Although she finds it empty of present life, Lazarus nonetheless asserts the continuity of Judaism, for "the sacred shrine is holy yet" to the Jews living in America.

Most scholars agree that Lazarus's public identity as a Jewish writer emerged with the huge influx of Eastern European Jews after the 1881 pogroms in Russia. At this time, she began to study Hebrew seriously and worked for the Hebrew Emigrant Aid Society as an advocate for Jewish immigrants on Wards Island. And she became involved in establishing the Hebrew Technical Institute and agricultural communities for the immigrants in the United States.

Throughout her life, Lazarus balanced her American literary identity against her alliance with Jewish causes. In her essays on American literature (1881), Longfellow (1882), and Emerson (1882), she defended the new American literary tradition. Initially cautious, Lazarus became outspoken as a Jew in her writing. She protested, in *Songs of a Semite* (1882), both anti-Semitism and Jewish complacency in poems such as *The Crowing of the Red Cock,* in which she decries Christian anti-Semitism, and *The Banner of the Jew*, where she reminds unaffiliated Jews of their strong ties to their forebears Moses, King David, and the Maccabees. Her challenge as a poet was to combine her Jewish and American literary loyalties.

In *The New Ezekiel,* Lazarus, in her retelling of the messianic prophecy of the biblical Ezekiel in the valley of the dry bones, expresses her proto-Zionist vision.

Although her sister Josephine characterized Emma as "a true woman, too distinctly feminine to wish to be exceptional, or to stand alone and apart, even by virtue of superiority," Lazarus protested such a role. The sonnet *Echoes,* written around 1880, addresses the limitations put upon the woman poet, who, because she is "veiled and screened by womanhood," cannot sing "the might / Of manly, modern passion" or "the dangers, wounds, and triumphs of the fight." Despite these social limitations, the woman poet's "wild voice" echoes throughout nature, "answering at once from heaven and earth and wave," omnipresent and powerful.

The sonnet *1492* addresses the double-edged irony for the Jews of that famous year, when Spain's Jews were expelled from that land and Christopher Columbus discovered America.

In 1883, Lazarus was invited to write a poem for a literary auction to raise funds to build the pedestal for the huge statue *Liberty Enlightening the World* by the French sculptor F. A. Bartholdi. Her entry, *The New Colossus*, was published in the *Catalogue of the Pedestal Fund Art Loan Exhibition at the National Academy of Design* to raise more funds; only in 1903 was it inscribed on a bronze tablet and displayed inside the pedestal of the Statue of Liberty. The sonnet recasts the classical Greek Colossus of Rhodes, a representation of the pagan sun god, as the "Mother of Exiles," an American version of Deborah, the Mother in Israel in the Book of Judges. Rather than conqueror of the world, this mother is the welcoming, nurturing, and comforting presence of American democracy.

Venus of the Louvre, written during Lazarus's last European tour in 1885–87, brings out the dualism of Hebraism and Hellenism in her work through the figure of the famous Greek statue, the armless Venus de Milo, and the legend of the dying Heine's visit to it. According to Josephine Lazarus, Emma, too, visited the Venus de Milo when she was very ill in Paris. This poem and the poet's gesture reveal how Lazarus, Heine's American translator, identified with the Jewish German poet, "a pale, death-stricken Jew," seeking in a broken fragment perfection in art.

In the Jewish Synagogue at Newport[1]

Here, where the noises of the busy town,
The ocean's plunge and roar can enter not,
We stand and gaze around with tearful awe,
And muse upon the consecrated spot.

No signs of life are here: the very prayers
Inscribed around are in a language dead;
The light of the "perpetual lamp"[2] is spent
That an undying radiance was to shed.

What prayers were in this temple offered up,
Wrung from sad hearts that knew no joy on earth,
By these lone exiles of a thousand years,[3]
From the fair sunrise land that gave them birth!

Now as we gaze, in this new world of light,
Upon this relic of the days of old,
The present vanishes, and tropic bloom
And Eastern towns and temples we behold.

Again we see the patriarch with his flocks,[4]
The purple seas, the hot blue sky o'erhead,
The slaves of Egypt,—omens, mysteries,—
Dark fleeing hosts by flaming angels led.[5]

1. A seaport city and wealthy summer resort in Rhode Island. "Synagogue": i.e., Touro Synagogue, founded and built in 1763, the oldest extant synagogue in the United States.
2. The Eternal Light that burns above the Holy Ark, which holds the Torah in every synagogue. "Language dead": i.e., Hebrew, the language of Jewish liturgy and sacred texts.
3. Tradition has it that the Jews, expelled from Jerusalem twice—in 586 B.C.E. and in 70 C.E.—will remain in exile until the Messiah comes.
4. Abraham (Genesis 24.35), Isaac (Genesis 26.14), and Jacob (Genesis 30.38–43) all had flocks of sheep.
5. The Hebrews were enslaved by the pharaoh in Egypt until God appointed Moses to lead them to freedom. God afflicted the Egyptians with ten plagues, and, after the Hebrews were freed, he led them through the desert in a pillar of a cloud by day and a pillar of fire by night (Exodus 13.21–22).

A wondrous light upon a sky-kissed mount,
  A man who reads Jehovah's written law,
'Midst blinding glory and effulgence rare,
  Unto a people prone with reverent awe.[6]

The pride of luxury's barbaric pomp,
  In the rich court of royal Solomon—[7]
Alas! we wake: one scene alone remains,—
  The exiles by the streams of Babylon.[8]

Our softened voices send us back again
  But mournful echoes through the empty hall;
Our footsteps have a strange, unnatural sound,
  And with unwonted gentleness they fall.

The weary ones, the sad, the suffering,
  All found their comfort in the holy place,
And children's gladness and men's gratitude
  Took voice and mingled in the chant of praise.

The funeral and the marriage, now, alas!
  We know not which is sadder to recall;
For youth and happiness have followed age,
  And green grass lieth gently over all.

And still the sacred shrine is holy yet,
  With its lone floors where reverent feet once trod.
Take off your shoes as by the burning bush,
  Before the mystery of death and God.[9]

1867 1871

1492

Thou two-faced year,[1] Mother of Change and Fate,
Didst weep when Spain cast forth with flaming sword,[2]
The children of the prophets of the Lord,
Prince, priest, and people, spurned by zealot hate.
Hounded from sea to sea, from state to state,
The West refused them, and the East abhorred.
No anchorage the known world could afford,

6. On Mount Sinai, God gave the Ten Commandments to Moses, who read them aloud to the children of Israel, encamped below (Exodus 34–35). "Jehovah": English transliteration of the Hebrew name for God, YHWH.

7. King Solomon, who built the First Temple in Jerusalem (1 Kings 6), was famed for his enormous wealth and wisdom as well as for his many foreign wives, for whose sake he worshiped other gods (1 Kings 11.1–13).

8. After the destruction of the First Temple in 586 B.C.E., the Jews were exiled to Babylon.

9. God first spoke to Moses from within the burning bush (Exodus 3.2–4.17)

1. In 1492, the "two-faced year," the Jews were expelled from Spain while Columbus was discovering America. "Two-faced" also refers to Janus, the Roman god of beginnings and endings, who is represented in art as having two faces that look in opposite directions, symbolizing his knowledge of the past and the future.

2. A reference to the Expulsion from the Garden of Eden (Genesis 3.24).

Close-locked was every port, barred every gate.
Then smiling, thou unveil'dst, O two-faced year,
A virgin world[3] where doors of sunset part,
Saying, "Ho, all who weary, enter here![4]
There falls each ancient barrier that the art
Of race or creed or rank devised, to rear
Grim bulwarked hatred between heart and heart!"

1883 1889

The New Ezekiel[1]

What, can these dead bones live, whose sap is dried
By twenty scorching centuries of wrong?
Is this the House of Israel,[2] whose pride
Is as a tale that's told, an ancient song?
Are these ignoble relics all that live
Of psalmist, priest, and prophet? Can the breath
Of very heaven bid these bones revive,
Open the graves and clothe the ribs of death?

Yea, Prophesy, the Lord hath said. Again
Say to the wind, Come forth and breathe afresh,
Even that they may live upon these slain,
And bone to bone shall leap, and flesh to flesh.[3]
The Spirit is not dead, proclaim the word,
Where lay dead bones, a host of armed men stand!
I ope your graves, my people, saith the Lord,
And I shall place you living in your land.[4]

1895(?)

Echoes

Late-born and woman-souled I dare not hope,
The freshness of the elder lays,[1] the might
Of manly, modern passion shall alight
Upon my Muse's lips, nor may I cope
(Who veiled and screened by womanhood must grope)
With the world's strong-armed warriors and recite
The dangers, wounds, and triumphs of the fight;
Twanging the full-stringed lyre through all its scope.

3. America.
4. This invitation anticipates *The New Colossus,* lines 10–14.
1. The postexilic biblical prophet who told of the valley of the dry bones in which God infused his prophecy with the power to bring the dead back to life and return them to Israel (Ezekiel 37.1–14).
2. "Then he said unto me, Son of man, these bones are the whole house of Israel. . . . I will . . . bring you into the land of Israel" (Ezekiel 37.11–12).
3. A paraphrase of Ezekiel 37.7–8.
4. A paraphrase of Ezekiel 37.12. Lazarus transforms Ezekiel's prophecy into a call for a modern Jewish nation in Israel.
1. Songs, melodies.

But if thou ever in some lake-floored cave
O'erbrowed by rocks, a wild voice wooed and heard,
Answering at once from heaven and earth and wave,
Lending elf-music to thy harshest word,
Misprize[2] thou not these echoes that belong
To one in love with solitude and song.

ca. 1880 1895

The New Colossus[1]

Not like the brazen giant of Greek fame,[2]
With conquering limbs astride from land to land;
Here at our sea-washed, sunset gates shall stand
A mighty woman with a torch, whose flame
Is the imprisoned lightning,[3] and her name
Mother of Exiles.[4] From her beacon-hand
Glows world-wide welcome; her mild eyes command
The air-bridged harbor that twin cities frame.[5]
"Keep, ancient lands, your storied pomp!" cries she
With silent lips. "Give me your tired, your poor,
Your huddled masses yearning to breathe free,
The wretched refuse of your teeming shore.
Send these, the homeless, tempest-tost to me,
I lift my lamp beside the golden door!"

1883 1883, 1895

Venus of the Louvre[1]

Down the long hall she glistens like a star,
The foam-born mother of Love, transfixed to stone,
Yet none the less immortal, breathing on.
Time's brutal hand hath maimed but could not mar.
When first the enthralled enchantress from afar
Dazzled mine eyes, I saw not her alone,
Serenely poised on her world-worshipped throne,
As when she guided once her dove-drawn car,—[2]
But at her feet a pale, death-stricken Jew,

2. I.e., misprise: mistake, misunderstand.
1. Written in aid of Bartholdi Pedestal Fund, 1883 [Lazarus's note].
2. The Colossus of Rhodes, a giant bronze statue of Helios, the sun god, created by the ancient Greek sculptor Chares of Lindos in the early 3d century B.C.E., is said to have straddled the harbor of Rhodes. It was destroyed by an earthquake in 225 B.C.E.
3. Barak was the general who the prophetess Deborah urged to fight the Canaanite Sisera; his name means "lightning" in Hebrew (Judges 4.4–7). "Woman with a torch": the Hebrew phrase *eshet lapidot*, referring to the prophetess Deborah, "wife of Lappidoth," also means "woman of the torch."
4. Deborah is called a "mother in Israel" (Judges 5.7).
5. The Statue of Liberty stands in New York Harbor between New York City and Jersey City.
1. I.e., the Venus de Milo (Aphrodite of Melos), a famous ancient statue of the goddess of love now in the Louvre, Paris.
2. This Venus is displayed unrestored, its arms broken off and its original dove-drawn chariot destroyed.

Her life adorer, sobbed farewell to love.
Here *Heine*[3] wept! Here still he weeps anew,
Nor ever shall his shadow lift or move,
While mourns one ardent heart, one poet-brain,
For vanished Hellas[4] and Hebraic pain.[5]

ca. 1885 1895

3. Heinrich Heine (1797–1856), the German Jewish poet exiled in 1835 for his political satires, who, crippled in his later years by venereal disease, visited the Venus de Milo just before he died.
4. I.e., ancient Greece and its culture.
5. Heine reluctantly converted to Protestantism in 1825 in order to have a career in civil service, one of the many professions in Germany prohibited to Jews.

The Great Tide, 1881–1924

Early in this century, novelist Henry James, visiting the United States after having lived abroad for many years, was taken on a drive one June evening through the Lower East Side of New York City. There, he was struck by "the intensity of the material picture in the dense Yiddish quarter." Startled and repelled, he described, in his travelogue *The American Scene*, his feeling of being overwhelmed by the sense of "a great swarming, a swarming that had begun to thicken, infinitely, as soon as we had crossed to the east side and long before we had got to Rutgers Street. There is no swarming like that of Israel when once Israel has got a start, and the scene here bristled, at every step, with the signs and sounds, immitigable, unmistakable, of a Jewry that had burst all bounds." The cumulative presence of the Jews, whom James likened to large-nosed fish, ants, and "human squirrels and monkeys," made him perceive an " 'ethnic' apparition," a "spectre," the extent of the "Hebrew conquest of New York." James's host, Yiddish playwright Jacob Gordin, took him to the literary cafés of the Lower East Side, including the Café Royal, which James called "torture-rooms of the living idiom," for there he heard the "Accent of the Future," an ethnically altered language, no longer the kind of English "for which there is an existing literary message."

In the twenty years between 1883, when James had begun his self-imposed exile in Europe, and his August 30, 1904, return to New York, approximately 1.5 million Jews from Russia, Poland, and Romania had arrived in the United States; by 1920, that number rose to more than 2 million. According to Irving Howe in *World of Our Fathers* (1976), in the thirty-three years between 1881 and 1914, one-third of Eastern European Jews left their homelands because of violent and widespread anti-Semitism, which began with the assassination by revolutionaries of the so-called "liberal" Russian czar Alexander II on March 1, 1881.

His successor, Alexander III, enacted anti-Jewish legislation, imposing harsh taxes on Jews and restricting the schooling that Jews could acquire, the professions that they could follow, and the places where they could live; Jews were expelled from the Russian countryside by the May Laws of 1882 and from Moscow and other Russian cities in 1891. Russia's movement from an agricultural economy toward a manufacturing one resulted in nationwide economic hardship, and the Russian Orthodox Church as well as the czar's government did not discourage the popular scapegoating of the Jews. Beginning in 1881, the government instigated pogroms against Jewish communities throughout the Russian Pale of Settlement (an area established by Czar Alexander I in 1802, including provinces annexed from Poland, the southern Ukraine, Lithuania, and Belarus or White Russia, that endured until the Bolshevik Revolution of 1917). These government-organized burnings, lootings, rapes, and murders, along with their poverty, prompted hundreds of thousands of Jews who had for centuries inhabited *shtetlekh*, or towns, throughout the Pale to flee westward—initially into Austria-Hungary, then across Europe, and ultimately across the Atlantic to what became known as *dos goldene land*, the Golden Land: America. By the turn of the century, one-third of Romania's Jews had also fled for America's shores.

James's xenophobic attitude toward the powerful presence of these new immigrants reflected the attitude of many Americans. From the time the immigrants began to arrive in great numbers in the summer of 1881, American society was divided between the advocates of free immigration and those who wanted to restrict it. Howe lists five legislative acts for limiting the number of immigrants that Congress passed between 1882 and 1903. Across class lines, Americans were fearful because there were so many immigrants from southern and eastern Europe. They were not all Jews; in fact, Jews were only the second largest immigrant group, after Italians, who, along with other Catholics, the nativist Protestant Americans feared would take over the United States. Many immigrants arrived without money, skills, or English, which made life hard for them once they were crammed into the slums of East Coast cities (New York, Boston, Philadelphia) as well as the cities of the Midwest (Cleveland, Chicago, St. Louis) and, less so, the West. Because, during those first decades in which the immigrants arrived, the United States experienced a quick rise in industrialization and urbanization as well as economic depressions, many Americans felt that the immigrants compounded the problems.

THE JEWISH AMERICAN ESTABLISHMENT

Between 1881 and 1924, the Jews who had arrived from Germany and Central Europe in the mid-nineteenth century and those of Sephardic origins who had come even earlier were, as a rule, thriving as Americans, with well-established communities and organizations. Many had risen to the middle class, and some were very wealthy. Urban newspapers founded by Adolph S. Ochs, Joseph Pulitzer, and Edward Rosewater thrived. Jews made their fortunes in such commodities as jewelry, tobacco, and liquor. Many Jews were successful shopkeepers; others owned garment factories, where the immigrants found themselves exploited; some dealt in real estate; a few worked in banking or established department stores; and many aspired to a career in law or medicine. In national politics, Jews voted for the Republican party, in keeping with their families' mid-century alliance with Abraham Lincoln and the North during the Civil War, and some Jews were even elected to Republican seats in Congress.

From their position of affluence and stability, America's Jews extended aid to the Eastern European Jewish immigrants, albeit with ambivalence, wanting both to help and to subdue or "civilize" these foreigners. In New York City, the "uptown Jews" founded and ran "downtown" settlement houses and charitable organizations such as the Educational Alliance, a merging of the Hebrew Free School Association, the Young Men's Hebrew Association, and the Aguilar Free Library Society, which intended to help the impoverished immigrants survive in America by teaching them to help themselves. The benefactors' good intentions were complicated by their sense of cultural superiority, which many immigrants angrily perceived as condescension.

Despite their good citizenship and prosperity, American Jews still faced social anti-Semitism and discrimination. They were excluded from Gentile neighborhoods, certain hotels, summer resorts, college fraternities, and upper-class social clubs. Routinely, their choices were limited by quotas at private schools, colleges, universities, and professional schools. Jews were seldom hired for academic positions and often faced discrimination when applying for other jobs. Violent crimes against Jews occurred: more than two Jews were lynched in the South, the most famous case being that of Leo Frank, son of a New York merchant, in Georgia in 1915. In response to the violence and to the defamatory attacks on Jews in the press, the B'nai B'rith formed the Anti-Defamation League.

In these decades, the Reform movement grew powerful and distinct from Orthodox Judaism. From the 1897 World Zionist Congress until the rise of Nazism, a strong anti-Zionist position was adopted by many American Jews. In terms of literature, some German Jews published fiction and poetry in English and German in the 1890s, and a multitude of annuals, almanacs, and Jewish newspapers appeared in English. The Jewish Publication Society of America, founded by Isaac Leeser in 1845, published a definitive English translation of the Hebrew Bible. Between 1901 and 1906, the *Jewish Encyclopedia* was published. Although in terms of international culture all these achievements put American Jewry on the map, there was no coherent sense of a Jewish American literature in English during this time.

THE LIVES LEFT BEHIND

This was the new world that immigrant Jews were confronted with. They had come from communities in which their lives were organized by Jewish law, values, and religious practice as well as the Jewish religious calendar. They ordered their weeks around a Sabbath that begins at sundown on Friday and ends with the first three stars on Saturday night, their years around the cycle of holidays and fasts that starts with Rosh Hashanah and Yom Kippur (the New Year and Day of Atonement) in the autumn, continues with the festival of Hanukkah in the winter, with Purim and Passover in the spring, with Shavuoth at the beginning of summer, and concludes with the fast day Tishah-b'Av, the Ninth of Av, during the waning days of summer.

The European Jewish world was polyglot. Most Jews had some facility in at least three languages. They spoke Yiddish, *mameloshn*, the mother tongue of their inner culture; they read and prayed in Hebrew, *loshn-koydesh*, the holy tongue of their religion and law; and they could converse with their Gentile neighbors in the native Polish, Russian, Ukrainian, Romanian, Lithuanian, Latvian, Hungarian, or German, depending on the region they inhabited. Yiddish, their vernacular, had developed from the Middle High German of the Rhine Valley during the tenth century; it was transcribed in Hebrew letters as early as the twelfth century; and it moved with the Jewish populations as they were pushed eastward from the German lands into Slavic lands after the fifteenth century. While Yiddish was the language of the family, of the market, and of women, Hebrew was the language of religious culture. In the course of the centuries since the fall of the Second Temple in Jerusalem in 70 C.E., Jews had lived in *Goles*, the Diaspora, in both Christian and Muslim lands. There, their communal and economic existence was constantly threatened from the outside by waves of anti-Semitism, extending from the early Church period through the Crusades and up to the pogroms. In order to survive, the Jews strengthened the inner structure of their traditions based on the sacred texts and anticipated the messianic era, which would return them to Zion.

As a rule, the Jewish community focused its intellectual resources on educating boys in the sacred Hebrew language and texts. Most men attained at least minimal literacy from the heder, or primary religious school, where even the poorest boys, from the age of three, learned the Hebrew alphabet and to read the prayer book (siddur) and the Five Books of Moses (Humash). After the age of thirteen, when a boy becomes Bar Mitzvah, or an adult in the religious community, the more promising continued in the study houses and yeshivas. The communities did not educate girls systematically, although a significant number learned the Hebrew alphabet well enough to become literate in Yiddish so that they could read the devotional literature for women: the *Tsenerene*, the seventeenth-century Yiddish translation and adaptation of the Bible and commentaries for women; sermons; and the *tkhines*, the Yiddish supplicatory prayers written for and sometimes by women from the sixteenth century on.

When, in the mid-nineteenth century, the Jewish Enlightenment—the *Haskalah*—moved from its eighteenth-century roots in Germany, where Napoleon had emancipated the Jews in 1808, to Eastern Europe, the process of modernization began to change the culture and lives of the Jews. New secular ideas of citizenship, hygiene, science, geography, world history jolted the traditional Jewish view of life and forced Jews to look out at the natural landscape surrounding them rather than down at the flora and fauna they encountered in the pages of the Bible and Talmud. As a result, many Jews reevaluated their place in the world, becoming politically and culturally active. In particular, the anticzarist revolutionary movements, with their promise of a new social order upon the overthrow of the aristocracy, drew in many young Jews, male and female both.

In the preceding decades, the *maskilim,* proponents of the *Haskalah,* had attempted to spread the enlightened ideas to the general populace by writing didactic stories and novels in Hebrew, the language in which they had been educated religiously and which they associated with literacy and ideas. What these early writers found, though, was that they were unable to convey their new ideas in Hebrew to the less-educated manual laborers and artisans, and to the women who had not been taught Hebrew. They also found it difficult to manipulate this ancient Semitic biblical tongue and its offshoot, Aramaic, the language of the Talmud, to convey the contemporary reality that they hoped to change. Thus, they began to write in Yiddish, a language that everyone understood.

Because Yiddish was associated with women, who were considered ignorant of the sacred texts, and thus with the quotidian and the mundane, the early Yiddish writers felt shame as they turned to their vernacular. Scholar Dan Miron quotes the metaphor used by the "grandfather" of modern Yiddish literature, Mendele Moykhr Sforim, to describe his change from

Hebrew to Yiddish as a promiscuous affair with "a strange woman" that is only later redeemed by marriage and orderly procreation. Other mid-nineteenth-century popular Yiddish prose writers—Isaac Meyer Dik (1814–1893), Isaac Joel Linetsky (1839–1916), Shomer (Nahum Meir Shaikevich, 1850–1905)—also wrote in Yiddish out of necessity, ambivalently fond of the language's rich resources for depicting their society, yet scornful and even embarrassed for having to stoop so low as to write in this common tongue.

The complexity of writers' feelings toward the language they used gave rise to the use of pseudonyms. Of the three founding figures of modern Yiddish literature, two were best known by their pseudonyms. The first, Sholom Jacob Abramovitz (1836–1917), took on the name of Mendele Moykhr Sforim when he published *Dos kleyne menshele* (The Mannikin, 1864), a novel satirizing his hometown. The pen name gave the author both a mask to hide behind and a persona to develop in fictional terms. His Mendele the Bookseller, both humorous and familiar, reflected Abramovitz's "desire to penetrate minds and hearts of Jewish masses." The most famous Yiddish pseudonym was that of the second figure, Sh. Rabinovitch (1859–1916), who took the greeting "Sholem Aleichem"—literally, "Peace unto you"—as his pen name and created the hallmark authorial interlocutor that frames many of his fictional monologues, published between 1883 and his death in 1916. (The third giant of modern Yiddish literature, Isaac Leybush Peretz [1852–1915], published under his own name.)

Modern Yiddish poetry similarly came from both didactic roots and from the folk, not counting the sixteenth-century epic poems composed and printed in Western Europe: the anonymous *Shmuel-bukh* and Elijah Bokhr/Levita's *Paris un vien* and *Bovo bukh*, which were rediscovered by Yiddish writers and scholars in Vilna and Warsaw only during the 1920s. By then, modern Yiddish poetry was at its peak, having developed in the 1880s initially from folk songs and Purim plays into songs of the popular Yiddish theater, begun in 1876 in Europe by Abraham Goldfaden, and from the protest songs of the Jewish socialist movements.

HOW THE JEWS GOT TO AMERICA AND WHAT THEY FOUND

Typically, Jewish immigrants made their way to America by crossing the borders of Russia, often illegally, and taking trains or wagons or even walking west across Europe to the port cities of Bremen, Hamburg, Antwerp. These journeys were themselves perilous, and agencies organized by the Jewish communities of Western Europe were formed to help the immigrants negotiate their passage. From these port cities, the Jews crossed the Atlantic on steamships, spending from six to ten days in steerage, which situated them belowdecks in crowded and unsanitary conditions. Once the ships reached New York Harbor (or, before 1890, when the federal government took over supervising immigrants, Philadelphia, Boston, Baltimore), the immigrants, numbered and labeled, debarked in groups into Castle Garden, at the southernmost tip of Manhattan, which operated from 1855 to 1892; from 1892 to 1954, immigrants entered the United States through Ellis Island. At the immigration center, the newcomers were examined by doctors, who sorted out the healthy from the sick, the most common diseases being tuberculosis or trachoma, or with physical or mental defects. Then they were interviewed by inspectors about their personal life, profession, family, and character. If they passed these examinations, the immigrants were put on ferries to the Battery (from Ellis Island) or to New Jersey. Representatives of the Hebrew Immigrant Aid Society (HIAS) were often present to help the Jewish immigrants navigate entrance into America. Those who did not pass muster were either held on Wards Island or sent back to Europe. Both the difficult ocean journey and the dehumanizing arrival in America became the subjects of many memoirs and stories. Once the immigrants set their feet down in Manhattan, they made their way to the Lower East Side and its crowded tenements on Division Street, Hester Street, Canal Street—the Jewish quarter that Henry James decried. There they settled, a family squeezing into a tiny apartment, a single man or woman—a boarder—renting a bed in a corner of another family's apartment. The new arrivals, called derogatorily "greenhorns," were distinguishable from those who had come earlier by their old-fashioned European clothing, their inability to speak English, and their bewilderment at the fast-paced, chaotic, teeming spectacle of New York.

Generally, the new immigrants found one of two types of employment: as peddlers or as sweatshop workers in the garment industry. The peddlers were entrepreneurs of sorts, and some managed to work their way up from the meagerly remunerative door-to-door selling to pushcart sales and, finally, to small businesses of their own. Others left New York City for the Midwest or the South or New England. The sweatshop workers were exploited, working twelve to sixteen hours per day at very low wages, men earning slightly more than women. Often, the owners of the factories were American Jews of German origin whose families had settled in the United States in the mid-nineteenth century. Since such difficult working conditions proletarianized the immigrants, they, in turn, galvanized the American labor movement.

To ease the transition to America and to counteract the disappointments and hardships of immigrant life, the immigrants, with the occasional help of well-established American Jews, also developed many other kinds of organizations, ranging from the Workmen's Circle and HIAS to Beth Israel Hospital, the Clara de Hirsch Home for Working Girls, and the Hebrew Free Loan Society. The Workmen's Circle (*Arbeter ring*), founded in 1892 as a society to give socialist workers sick benefits and burial service, developed into a national organization of 80,000 members and provided diverse services: a tuberculosis sanatorium; classes and lectures for workers on topics ranging from Yiddish literature to free love to electricity; afternoon and high schools to provide children with a secular Jewish education by learning Yiddish language and literature. *Landsmanshaftn*, societies of people from the same town or district, were formed to support their members both emotionally and monetarily, offering sickness and death benefits, life insurance, help with wedding and other expenses. The Henry Street Settlement, founded by the middle-class German-Jewish nurse Lillian Wald, provided free medical help to Russian Jewish immigrants.

Despite many protests and strikes during the 1880s and 1890s, only a few stable labor unions formed among the Jewish workers until a massive strike by young women shirtwaist makers in 1909 initiated a series of strikes that brought the International Ladies' Garment Workers' Union (ILGWU) and the Amalgamated Clothing Workers (ACW) into full power. On March 25, 1911, a flash fire in the Triangle Shirtwaist Company killed 146 workers, mostly young Jewish and Italian women. The tragedy threw the Jewish quarter into mourning, and the demonstration of 100,000 people at the victims' funeral raised the awareness of the American middle and upper classes to the urgent need for change among urban workers. In the end, the fire enabled the ILGWU to become one of the most powerful unions in the country.

YIDDISH CULTURE IN AMERICA

For our purposes, the two most important cultural institutions established by the new immigrants were the Yiddish press and the Yiddish theater. The Yiddish press was the initial medium for Yiddish literature in America, where the First Amendment assured the press freedom from censorship. Because the Yiddish press was committed to promoting Jewish culture and knowledge, it regularly published poetry, fiction, and criticism and also provided a livelihood for many of the Yiddish writers. Yiddish newspapers became an essential part of the Jewish American experience—reading a newspaper was for the immigrants a mark of their urban Americanization.

The first Yiddish newspapers in the United States, published in the 1870s, were small weeklies that, for the most part, conveyed local Jewish news, were awkwardly written, and advocated traditional Jewish values. From one of these grew the popular Orthodox daily the *Yidisher tageblatt*, which had a large readership by the turn of the century. By 1890, other weekly papers, such as the *Arbeter tsaytung* (Workers' Newspaper) and the *Fraye arbeter shtime* (Free Voice of Labor), presented, through the radical perspectives of socialism and anarchism, a sense of the larger world and the growing secular, urban Jewish culture. The *Fraye arbeter shtime* in particular became famous for the high quality of its literary selections, and many of the Yiddish writers published poetry and fiction there.

Although these early newspapers were motivated by their ideological missions, whether Orthodox or radical, none was as effective in conveying or as directly formed by the practical needs of an ideology as the *Forverts*, the *Jewish Daily Forward*, founded on April 22, 1897, to give voice to the Jewish unions, as distinct from the larger Socialist Labor party. Abraham Cahan, the *Forverts*'s first editor, left the paper after eight months but returned five years later to produce the daily that dominated the Yiddish press from 1903 until his death in 1951; since the 1970s, it has continued to publish as a weekly. At its peak, in 1924, the *Forverts* had a circulation of nearly 250,000. Combining grittiness and vulgarity with Cahan's sense of Yiddish intellectual aspirations, the *Forverts* took a socialist stand without becoming a mouthpiece for the political party. It reported national and world news alongside articles on the most mundane aspects of immigrant life. Cahan edited the paper so its style was accessible to even the most naïve or ignorant reader. While he worked to strengthen the cultural and intellectual lives of the Yiddish-speaking immigrants, Cahan simultaneously "updated" the Yiddish language, adding Americanisms to the articles to reflect—and sometimes to effect—changes in actual usage. The most popular of the *Forverts*'s features was *A bintl briv* (A Bundle of Letters), the advice column from which we include a selection.

Several hundred Yiddish papers and journals started up between 1900 and 1920: the conservative *Morgn zshurnal* (Morning Journal); the Labor Zionist papers *Yidisher kemfer* (Jewish Fighter) and *Tsayt* (Time); the communist paper *Frayhayt* (Freedom); an intellectual journal *Naye lebn* (New Life); various cultural journals and periodicals such as *Tsukunft* (Future), edited by poet Abraham Liessin, and *Naye land* (New Country) and *Literarishe velt* (Literary World), edited by poet Avrom Reyzen; and satiric publications such as the *Groyser kundes* (Big Joker). But the most successful was the *Tog* (Day), a paper that bridged ideological rifts, avoided factionalism whether socialist, Zionist, or religious, and published many of the Yiddish writers presented here, including Joseph Opatoshu and Yehoash.

Yiddish theater in America began in 1882—the year Czar Alexander III banned Yiddish theater in Russia—with a production on the Lower East Side based on Abraham Goldfaden's operetta *The Sorceress*. Most early Yiddish theater was spectacle, a melodramatic mixture of "tragedy and vaudeville, pageant and farce," that diverted immigrants from their hard lives. The two rival theater companies of the 1880s—the Oriental Theatre, headed by Joseph Lateiner, and the Romania Opera House, headed by the self-titled "Professor" Morris Horowitz—produced great quantities of *shund* (trash), tearjerkers based loosely on Jewish history, bowdlerized Shakespeare or Goethe, reinterpretations of biblical stories, and dramatizations of current events. The actors—Boris Thomashefsky, Jacob Adler, David Kessler, Bertha Kalich—became popular stars, adored by the masses. In the 1890s, modern realism entered Yiddish theater as the playwright Jacob Gordin translated, adapted, and imitated the great European playwrights and writers: the German Hauptmann, the Norwegian Ibsen, the Russian Gogol, the French Hugo. Gordin wrote plays for Jacob Adler and became a dominant force in the Yiddish theater of the early twentieth century. His hits included plays that revised European classics in Jewish terms: *The Jewish King Lear* recasts Shakespeare's Lear as an old Jewish business tycoon; *God, Man, and Devil* sets Goethe's *Faust* in a Russian shtetl and gives it a proletarian theme; *Mirele Efros*, first entitled *The Jewish Queen Lear*, takes Shakespeare's plot and recasts it as the story of a matriarch gone wrong. After Gordin's death in 1909, Yiddish theater was divided into the profitable *shund* plays and the high-minded, literary financial flops. Even the initial efforts of Sholem Asch and Sholem Aleichem to put their works on stage soon after they arrived in the United States failed with the typical bad-mannered, disorderly, yet passionate Yiddish audience.

However, at the end of World War I, Yiddish theater experienced a revival of creativity and a new form, the Yiddish art theater. Although Jewish immigrants had done well during the war years and their prosperity resulted in higher cultural standards, the real force for this change came from the younger generation of actors (Maurice Schwartz, Paul Muni, Jacob Ben-Ami, Bertha Gersten, Celia Adler, Joseph Buloff, Molly Picon) and playwrights (Sholem Asch, Peretz Hirschbein, David Pinski, H. Leyvik), among whom were postwar immigrants who had been active in European Jewish theater companies and exposed to experimental theater in Moscow and Berlin.

From 1918 through the 1930s, several repertory companies arose alongside the Yiddish commercial theaters. In 1918, Maurice Schwartz formed a new company that evolved into the famous Yiddish Art Theatre, which survived until 1950 and produced nearly 150 Yiddish plays, ranging from *shund* to modernist experiments to translations of Russian, German, English, and French theater classics. The success of this eclectic and popular theater was based on Schwartz's deep connection with Yiddish culture. His most successful shows included productions of Leyvik's *Rags*, a serious play about American Jewish workers; an expressionist resetting of Goldfaden's *The Tenth Commandment*; an adaptation of I. J. Singer's novel *Yoshe Kalb*. Another important repertory company was Artef, which produced plays from 1928 until 1938. Framed by communist ideology, this avant-garde troupe, directed by Benno Schneider, trained factory workers to be actors and produced aesthetically sophisticated plays based on classic fiction by Mendele and Sholem Aleichem and stylized modernist works by leftist Yiddish writers like Moyshe Nadir as well as more standard revolutionary socialist realism. Artef appealed more to intellectual English-speaking audiences than to the Yiddish masses. Amateur companies formed, too, and one of them, the Folksbiene theater, has survived the decades and, recently revived, continues to produce new Yiddish plays.

A small but lively Yiddish film industry developed among independent producers in America in the 1930s and 1940s. Many of these films adapted fiction and plays by prominent Yiddish authors. Maurice Schwartz directed and starred in the 1932 film version of Sholem Asch's novella *Uncle Moses*, probably the first Yiddish talkie, and in the 1939 film *Tevye*, based on Sholem Aleichem's famous monologues. Other stars from the Yiddish theater appeared in film versions of Peretz Hirschbein's play *Green Fields* (1937) and Jacob Gordin's play *Mirele Efros* (1939) as well as in an adaptation of Mendele Moykhr Sforim's novella *Fishke der Krumer* (1939).

YIDDISH POETRY AND FICTION

Works in Yiddish, especially the poetry of immigrants produced during decades of the twentieth century, form a uniquely Jewish American literature, the heart and soul of all Jewish American literature that developed subsequently in English and the most distinctively modern of the Jewish literatures. Yiddish poetry arrived in America with the first wave of Yiddish-speaking immigrants in the 1880s and became an expressive medium for the nascent Jewish labor movement, influenced by Romantic poetry as well as by socialist political ideologies. The work of its poets—collectively known as the Labor, or Sweatshop, poets—expressed the plight of the Yiddish-speaking working masses. Couched in highly conventionalized rhetoric, both political and personal, and using standard symbols and predictable meters and rhymes, this poetry asserts the poet as spokesperson for the collective interests of the "folk" or the working-class immigrants. Of the major poets of this period, we include two: Morris Rosenfeld and David Edelshtadt. At the same time, several prominent writers transcended this utilitarian poetry in a turn-of-the-century effort to reconnect Yiddish writing with traditional Jewish culture, while reflecting the current concerns of Jewish socialism and nationalism. These writers had a more literary bent than the Labor poets in that they deliberately set out to enrich the texture and breadth of Yiddish literature, as we see in the highbrow poetry and translations of Yehoash and the popular writings of Avrom Reyzen.

A major change in Yiddish American poetry occurred when, in 1908, a group of younger poets and writers published an earnest little magazine, *Yugnt* (Youth). In contrast to the prevailing ideological and utilitarian orientation of the Yiddish press, *Yugnt* eschewed the issues of nationalism and socialism in order to focus on a program of aestheticism. Those who contributed to this short-lived journal and to its successors—*Shriftn* (Writings), *Literatur* (Literature), and *Inzel* (Island)—frequented the literary cafés on the Lower East Side, worked in sweatshops and at other menial labor, were young, mostly male, and new arrivals in New York. Avid readers of recent and contemporary poetry and fiction in German, Russian, French, and Polish, they sought to transcend the spokesperson role of the Yiddish poet by exploring the poet's individual sensibilities, the doctrine of art for art's sake, and the relationship between image and word. Abraham Cahan, of the *Forverts*, and other established members of the Yiddish press reacted to the social irreverence of these poets by labeling them derogatorily as *di yunge* (the young upstarts). To the Yiddish world, the Yunge seemed radical in their adherence to a poetry that "spoke" for no one but the individual poet.

The central poets of the Yunge were Mani Leyb, Reuven Iceland, Zishe Landau, and Joseph Rolnik. The works of these poets embodied the principles of musicality and romantic understatement to convey mood or eroticism through quotidian detail. Their experimentation was not formal, for most of their poems were written in conventional rhyme and stanza forms. Rather, their poetry appeared radical in subject, approach, and language as it played upon idiomatic Yiddish diction for unexpected melodious effect, excised rhetorical grandiosity or Germanic poeticisms, and relied on direct, sparse, concrete imagery. Introducing a 1919 anthology, their "theorist," Landau, defined the achievements of "pure" poetry as illuminating ordinary experience against what he scornfully called those of "the rhyming departments" of the socialist and nationalist movements. Three poets associated with the Yunge developed independently into major poetic voices. These were the acerbic, complex ironist Moyshe-Leyb Halpern, the visionary H. Leyvik, and the writer of the epic poem *Kentucky* (1925), I. J. Schwartz.

The fiction writers who initially published in and even helped subsidize the Yunge collections included Lamed Shapiro, Joseph Opatoshu, and Moyshe Nadir, although Opatoshu and Moyshe Nadir, more ambitious and politically minded, went elsewhere, and Shapiro drifted into alcoholism. These writers were instrumental in the maturation of Yiddish fiction in America, which occurred after World War I. Their work deepened and broadened the scope of Yiddish prose beyond the Old World richness of the three classic Yiddish writers Mendele Moykhr Sforim, Sholem Aleichem, and I. L. Peretz. The Yunge prose writers incorporated aspects of European modernism in their styles and approaches—in diction, in the presentation of imagery, in the focus on physicality, in the organization of narrative—and examined aspects of Jewish life and character that earlier writers had not touched upon—the criminal underworld, for example. They evoked the European shtetl from an American perspective, and they wrote, too, of Jewish experience in America with more subtlety and skill than the more widely read Sholem Asch.

The Yunge publications included only a few of the many women poets writing at the time. Among these stand out Fradl Shtok, Anna Margolin, and Celia Dropkin. Shtok's lyrics, especially her sonnets, were noted for their shocking imagery; her elegant, understated short stories were not appreciated by her peers. Anna Margolin, a major modernist voice in a truncated poetic career, wrote extremely complex poems that defuse the personal with dramatic personae. Celia Dropkin's poems are characterized by their condensed eroticism from a female point of view.

The Yunge were also avid translators. Inspired by Yehoash's example, they filled their journals and anthologies with translations of European and American literature as well as German or English renderings of classical Greek, Arabic, and Chinese works. Landau translated English ballads and Russian and German poems into Yiddish. Iceland and Halpern translated Heine's prose and poems. Mani Leyb translated a Scottish ballad and other poetry. I. J. Schwartz translated Walt Whitman as well as Bialik, classical Hebrew poets, Shakespeare, and Milton. This flurry of translations indicated the stepped-up effort of the Yunge to invent a tradition for their poetry. Even as they rebelled against their immediate poetic predecessors, they sought literary roots in world literature. The ballad form, consciously imported from other literatures, proliferated in their works (especially in Mani Leyb's and Halpern's) as an illusory artifice of folk poetry.

Inzikhism (instrospectivism) was a trend launched in 1919 as a theoretical and practical revolt against the dominance and the overly "poetic" quality of the Yunge. In 1918, Jacob Glatstein and Nakhum-Borekh Minkoff, who had met in law school at New York University, brought poems to A. Leyeles, whose first book, *Labyrinth*, had just appeared, and raised the idea for a new poetic movement that would take Yiddish poetry beyond the Yunge, whose innovations now seemed stalemated. Publishing in the Yiddish journal *Poezye* (Poetry), their poems struck a chord with American and European modernists. Unlike the Yunge, these poets did not labor in factories; they even had the advantage of American higher education. They read English and American poetry of the day as well. In 1919, these three poets stated their principles in their introduction to the anthology *In Zikh*. This introduction became known as the Introspectivist Manifesto, and the anthology soon evolved into the journal *Inzikh*, which appeared from January 1920 to December 1940. The poetic principles of the *inzikhistn* (introspectivists) opposed mimesis as the purpose of art and argued that poetry reflects an internalized social world, rather than serving as a vehicle to describe a political mood or humankind in general. These poets developed a full-fledged, sophisticated Yiddish modernism that, unknowingly, later Jewish American poets would parallel in English.

During the first six decades of Yiddish poetry in America, the poetic voice developed from one representing collective concerns to one expressing the individual poet, which may be explained by the shift in the role of poetry from a convention-ridden tool of political and national ideology to a poetry embracing and embellishing upon versions of the modernist notion of art for art's sake. However, the destruction of European Jewry during World War II wreaked havoc on this movement, and many Yiddish poets writing in America from 1939 on returned to the spokesperson stance and wrote a poetry that spoke for the collective people, although the collective intention was enhanced and informed by the previous lessons in modernism.

HEBREW LITERATURE IN AMERICA

Along with their vernacular Yiddish, the polyglot immigrants from Eastern Europe brought the sacred language of Hebrew with them. Among the newly arrived were some *maskilim,* adherents of the Jewish Enlightenment, who advocated Hebrew as a language of secular ideas and learning. They began a Hebrew-culture movement (*Tarbut Ivrit*) in America, which became active before and during World War I and matured in the years between the two world wars. Among the earlier *maskilim* and the later arrivals—young Hebraists with a nationalist agenda—were serious writers of poetry and prose. They wrote and published in literary and educational journals aimed toward small circles of intellectuals and founded teachers' colleges, summer camps, and schools to promote the revival of Hebrew as a modern language. At the time of World War I and the Russian Revolution, before the center of the Hebrew revival shifted to the land of Israel, the United States was the only place that could guarantee cultural freedom to Jews, and this freedom to write and publish drew the Hebraists to America. In our anthology, we include a small sampling of the Hebrew writers in America. The earliest example, *The Yankee Talmud,* presents pages from two Hebrew parodies written in 1892 and 1893 that imitate the form of a Talmud tractate in order to comment ironically upon Jewish life in America.

JEWISH IMMIGRANTS WRITE IN ENGLISH

When Henry James objected to the changes that the myriad Jewish immigrants were making to the English language, he would not yet have been able to read the fiction by three of the authors in this section: Abraham Cahan, Mary Antin, and Anzia Yezierska, immigrants whose primary language was Yiddish but who chose to write in English. Although these three are often thought of as the originators of Jewish American literature, in fact in their time they were transitional figures, lifting one foot out of their native Yiddish-speaking immigrant culture while, with the other, stepping toward the English-speaking American culture they aspired to.

Abraham Cahan stood firmly within the Yiddish world as a journalist and editor of the *Forverts.* Yet, having learned English in night school, he began publishing in English within a year of his arrival in America. When he resigned temporarily from the *Forverts* after helping to found it, Cahan worked as journalist in English between 1897 and 1902 with the American journalists Hutchins Hapgood and Lincoln Steffens. At this time, he was befriended by the powerful American novelist William Dean Howells, who encouraged him to write his short stories, novellas, and novels in English to reach a mainstream American readership. The paradox at the center of Cahan's writings pulled him simultaneously toward both Yiddish and English as he Americanized those who read his Yiddish newspaper and taught Americans about the cultural, social, and psychological forces driving the Jewish immigrants through their painful transformation. In fact, one might speculate that Cahan wrote his ironic American success story *The Rise of David Levinsky* (1917) in part to counteract the unmitigated optimism of Mary Antin's 1912 best-selling autobiography. *The Promised Land*, in portraying the metamorphosed immigrant girl as the perfect product of an American education, affirmed for its Gentile American readers the absolute goodness of their nation. The third of our immigrant writers in English, Anzia Yezierska, cultivated a high English prose style that was modeled on nineteenth-century British poetry; but she was rewarded for using the Yiddish-accented dialect of English that her 1920s Gentile American audience expected of her. It is fascinating that neither Antin nor Yezierska shows any awareness of the Yiddish literary culture that drew other writers of their generation.

Would James have been so scornful of Horace M. Kallen, a student of his brother, William? Because Kallen, a philosopher of ethnicity, arrived in America as a young boy of five from Silesia, in Prussia, where his family probably spoke German rather than Yiddish, it is not surprising that he wrote in English from the start. In fact, Kallen received an American education better than anything that even Antin could have imagined, for he earned a B.A. and a Ph.D. at Harvard and studied abroad at the Sorbonne and at Oxford. Although his field places him outside the other kinds of writings in this section, we include him because he articulated the problems of ethnic identity that inform this entire anthology.

And what would James have said about the American-born Jewish novelists Sidney Nyburg and Edna Ferber? Both Nyburg and Ferber wrote fiction in English because they were removed geographically and culturally from the Yiddish world of the new immigrants. Nyburg came from a German Jewish family well established in Baltimore for decades, and Ferber, of German and Hungarian Jewish background, was born in Kalamazoo, Michigan, and grew up in midwestern towns. Thoroughly Americanized, Nyburg, a corporate lawyer who published five novels, and Ferber, a Pulitzer prizewinning, best-selling novelist and playwright who was counted among the inner circle of the New York literary scene, wrote for the American public, not for a specifically Jewish audience.

Both the novels excerpted here—Nyburg's *The Chosen People* and Ferber's *Fanny Herself*, each author's only work on expressly Jewish themes—were published in 1917, the same year as Cahan's *The Rise of David Levinsky*. Although probably a coincidence, the confluence of these three English novels about being Jewish in America or about becoming American as a Jew deserves consideration. Why? Because these writers had nothing to do with each other, and, despite their similar themes, these works have no connection—in contrast to the works of the Yiddish poets and other fiction writers of the time. The point is that in English, as of 1917, there is no movement or perceived lineage of Jewish American literature, while in Yiddish, at that very moment, there existed a coherent, divisive, and ever-evolving culture and literature. During this period, there were, of course, Jewish journals being published in English such as the *Menorah*, a B'nai B'rith publication edited by the Sephardic American Benjamin Franklin Peixotto, and the *Menorah Journal*, a literary and arts journal edited by the college-educated sons of Eastern European Jewish immigrants. However, the great writing of this period is mostly in Yiddish.

Another American Gentile visited Lower East Side literary cafés around the same time as Henry James. Boston Brahmin journalist Hutchins Hapgood was escorted by Abraham Cahan through the Jewish quarter in 1901. Hapgood, recording his impressions in *The Spirit of the Ghetto* (1902), describes the cafés on east Canal Street as places "where excellent coffee and tea are sold, where everything is clean and good, and where the conversation is of the best . . . [among] the chosen crowd of intellectuals." And "the somber and earnest qualities of the race, emphasized by the special conditions, receive here expression in the mouths of actors, socialists, musicians, journalists, and poets. Here they get together and talk by the hour, over their coffee and cake, about politics and society, poetry and ethics, literature and life." Hapgood characterizes four of the poets he met there as "men of great talent," and writes with admiration about Eliakim Zunser, the wedding bard, or *badkhen,* famous as a Yiddish folk poet in Russia and New York; of the elite, refined Hebrew-revivalist poet Menahem Dolitzki; of Morris Rosenfeld, the Yiddish Labor poet famous to Hapgood's English-language readers through Leo Weiner's 1898 translation of his poems into English; and of a young poet, Abraham Liessin, a radical "Jewish bohemian," contemporary of Yehoash, who wrote verse essays on ethics and Jewish nationalism. Whereas James saw only the congestion of people and heard their voices as clamor, Hapgood observed the individuals within the crowd and, with the help of Cahan as his interpreter, spoke with and listened to many people, seeking out the scholars, the artists, and especially the writers. With such a positive, curious attitude, Hapgood discerned the immigrant culture as a part of the American whole and one that would enrich the American scene.

ABRAHAM CAHAN
1860–1951

Abraham Cahan was born in a small village near Vilna (the city that Napoleon had called "the Jerusalem of Lithuania") into an Orthodox family. His father was a *melamed* (teacher of small children), his mother a housewife, his grandfather a rabbi. He attended a teacher-training academy, studied secular subjects, learned Russian well, and read the radical anticzarist literature of the day. When the czar was assassinated in St. Petersburg in 1881, Cahan and his friends were in danger of arrest, so he fled his provincial teaching post and joined a group leaving for the United States at the very beginning of the mass exodus of Eastern European Jews to America. He was not to see his parents again until a trip to Europe in the 1890s, by which time the chasm between his and their ways of life was vast and unbridgeable. Although best known as an editor and journalist, Cahan wrote well-received fiction for twenty-five years, in which mediation and transitions between seemingly irreconcilable cultures among the immigrants of his generation were to be a major theme.

In the 1880s, Cahan rapidly became known as a political speaker (in 1882, he lectured in Yiddish on Karl Marx), trade-union organizer, writer, and editor in English and Yiddish for radical journals. He was a founder in the 1890s and, from 1902 until his death, the imperious editor of the great Yiddish newspaper the *Jewish Daily Forward* (*Forverts*). He took a sectarian journal of the Social Democratic party with 6,000 subscribers and made it the most successful foreign-language newspaper in America and the leading Yiddish paper in the world. At its high point in 1924, it had over a quarter of a million readers. Cahan combined sensational stories, human-interest features (*A bintl briv* was his invention), culture, and education within a humanistic, prolabor framework. The Yiddish used was "plain," Americanized (corrupted, according to purists), easy to read; it played a crucial role in the acculturation of America's Jews.

From 1892 until 1917, Cahan aspired to a literary career in English, although he still wrote some fiction and almost all of his journalism in Yiddish. He admired Tolstoy and Chekhov, but it was the American realist novelist and editor William Dean Howells who, in a sense, discovered Cahan and encouraged him to write about the life of the Jewish ghetto in New York. The result was his first book, the novella *Yekl: A Tale of the New York Ghetto* (1896), which won high praise from Howells and esteem for Cahan but did not sell well. Joan Micklin Silver's film *Hester Street* (1975) was based on this tale, so it still lives and resonates. It is the story of a callow young immigrant who sloughs off many of his Old World values (and the wife he sends for from Europe) while adopting superficial aspects of the new American life, ending with an uneasy feeling about his future.

The theme of losses, emotional and spiritual, that accompany the gains in the acculturation process was to appear in most of Cahan's stories and novels. Two years after *Yekl*, Cahan published a volume of five short stories called *The Imported Bridegroom and Other Stories of the New York Ghetto* (1898), which included *A Ghetto Wedding*. It is a story of two young sweatshop workers who plan an elaborate wedding they can ill afford, in the expectation that the value of the gifts they receive will exceed what they have laid out. But their invited guests are as poor as they are—it has been a slack season in the garment trades—and the results are disappointing. In the description of the wedding itself, Cahan gives us an unparalleled view of an Orthodox wedding ceremony as conducted on the Lower East Side of the period. After the wedding, the couple, Goldy and Nathan, forlornly walk the dark streets, tormented by street toughs (to add insult to injury), toward their meager apartment. But the pathos of the situation is surprisingly redeemed by an upsurge of love and joy in each other that they suddenly experience. Despite its gritty and bittersweet portrayal of the poor life of the Lower East Side, the story is one of Cahan's most charming.

The fullest expression of Cahan's major themes is *The Rise of David Levinsky* (1917), the story of a wealthy garment manufacturer looking back at his rise from immigrant rags to capitalist riches, who finds that he, too, is unsatisfied spiritually; the two halves of his life, he says, "do not comport well." Although Cahan wrote no more fiction after that ambitious book, which has been considered one of the very best American immigrant novels, he remains one of the most influential figures in Yiddish journalism, cultural life, and politics.

A Ghetto Wedding

Had you chanced to be in Grand Street[1] on that starry February night, it would scarcely have occurred to you that the Ghetto was groaning under the

1. Along with East Broadway, one of the leading thoroughfares and shopping centers on the Lower East Side of that time.

culmination of a long season of enforced idleness and distress. The air was exhilaratingly crisp, and the glare of the cafés and millinery shops flooded it with contentment and kindly good will. The sidewalks were alive with shoppers and promenaders, and lined with peddlers.

Yet the dazzling, deafening chaos had many a tale of woe to tell. The greater part of the surging crowd was out on an errand of self-torture. Straying forlornly by inexorable window displays, men and women would pause here and there to indulge in a hypothetical selection, to feast a hungry eye upon the object of an imaginary purchase, only forthwith to pay for the momentary joy with all the pangs of awakening to an empty purse.

Many of the peddlers, too, bore piteous testimony to the calamity which was then preying upon the quarter. Some of them performed their task of yelling and gesticulating with the desperation of imminent ruin; others implored the passers-by for custom with the abject effect of begging alms; while in still others this feverish urgency was disguised by an air of martyrdom or of shamefaced unwontedness, as if peddling were beneath the dignity of their habitual occupations, and they had been driven to it by sheer famine—by the hopeless dearth of employment at their own trades.

One of these was a thick-set fellow of twenty-five or twenty-six, with honest, clever blue eyes. It might be due to the genial, inviting quality of his face that the Passover dishes[2] whose praises he was sounding had greater attraction for some of the women with an "effectual demand" than those of his competitors. Still, his comparative success had not as yet reconciled him to his new calling. He was constantly gazing about for a possible passer-by of his acquaintance, and when one came in sight he would seek refuge from identification in closer communion with the crockery on his pushcart.

"Buy nice dishes for the holidays! Cheap and strong! Buy dishes for Passover!" When business was brisk, he sang with a bashful relish; when the interval between a customer and her successor was growing too long, his singsong would acquire a mournful ring that was suggestive of the psalm-chanting at an orthodox Jewish funeral.

He was a cap-blocker,[3] and in the busy season his earnings ranged from ten to fifteen dollars a week. But he had not worked full time for over two years, and during the last three months he had not been able to procure a single day's employment.

Goldy, his sweetheart, too, who was employed in making knee breeches, had hardly work enough to pay her humble board and rent. Nathan, after much hesitation, was ultimately compelled to take to peddling; and the longed-for day of their wedding was put off from month to month.

They had become engaged nearly two years before; the wedding ceremony having been originally fixed for a date some three months later. Their joint savings then amounted to one hundred and twenty dollars—a sum quite adequate, in Nathan's judgment, for a modest, quiet celebration and the humble beginnings of a household establishment. Goldy, however, summarily and indignantly overruled him.

2. Observant Jews have two sets of dishes (one reserved for dairy meals, one for meat) that they use only during the eight days of Passover, putting away the two other sets of dishes that they ordinarily use during the rest of the year (along with other *chometz*, or food and utensils not "kosher for Passover").

3. Hats and caps used to be shaped over blocks, usually made of wood, roughly the dimension of a human head.

"One does not marry every day," she argued, "and when I have at last lived to stand under the bridal canopy[4] with my predestined one,[5] I will not do so like a beggar maid. Give me a respectable wedding, or none at all, Nathan, do you hear?"

It is to be noted that a "respectable wedding" was not merely a casual expression with Goldy. Like its antithesis, a "slipshod wedding," it played in her vocabulary the part of something like a well-established scientific term, with a meaning as clearly defined as that of "centrifugal force" or "geometrical progression." Now, a slipshod wedding was anything short of a gown of white satin and slippers to match; two carriages to bring the bride and the bridegroom to the ceremony, and one to take them to their bridal apartments; a wedding bard and a band of at least five musicians; a spacious ballroom crowded with dancers, and a feast of a hundred and fifty covers.[6] As to furniture, she refused to consider any which did not include a pier-glass and a Brussels carpet.[7]

Nathan contended that the items upon which she insisted would cost a sum far beyond their joint accumulations. This she met by the declaration that he had all along been bent upon making her the target of universal ridicule, and that she would rather descend into an untimely grave than be married in a slipshod manner. Here she burst out crying; and whether her tears referred to the untimely grave or to the slipshod wedding, they certainly seemed to strengthen the cogency of her argument; for Nathan at once proceeded to signify his surrender by a kiss, and when ignominiously repulsed he protested his determination to earn the necessary money to bring things to the standard which she held up so uncompromisingly.

Hard times set in. Nathan and Goldy pinched and scrimped; but all their heroic economies were powerless to keep their capital from dribbling down to less than one hundred dollars. The wedding was postponed again and again. Finally the curse of utter idleness fell upon Nathan's careworn head. Their savings dwindled apace. In dismay they beheld the foundation of their happiness melt gradually away. Both were tired of boarding. Both longed for the bliss and economy of married life. They grew more impatient and restless every day, and Goldy made concession after concession. First the wedding supper was sacrificed; then the pier-mirror and the bard were stricken from the program; and these were eventually succeeded by the hired hall and the Brussels carpet.

After Nathan went into peddling, a few days before we first find him hawking chinaware on Grand Street, matters began to look brighter, and the spirits of our betrothed couple rose. Their capital, which had sunk to forty dollars, was increasing again, and Goldy advised waiting long enough for it to reach the sum necessary for a slipshod wedding and establishment.

4. The marriage ceremony for Jewish couples is performed under a *chupah*, or bridal canopy, which is a cloth covering with its four ends connected to poles that are usually held by honored relatives or friends of the family.

5. A belief that marriage or union was divinely foreordained.

6. A term used by caterers indicating places or meals for 150 guests. "Wedding bard": in Eastern Europe and among recent immigrants, a bard was often employed to spontaneously compose and recite rhymes and verses celebrating the couple, the families, the marriage; these might be as witty as they were lachrymose.

7. A patterned carpet made in Brussels of small loops of colored woolen yarn in a linen wrap. "Pier-glass": a long mirror that was set in the wall section (called a pier) between two windows.

It was nearly ten o'clock. Nathan was absently drawling his "Buy nice dishes for the holidays!" His mind was engrossed with the question of making peddling his permanent occupation.

Presently he was startled by a merry soprano mocking him: "Buy nice di-i-shes! Mind that you don't fall asleep murmuring like this. A big lot you can make!"

Nathan turned a smile of affectionate surprise upon a compact little figure, small to drollness, but sweet in the amusing grace of its diminutive outlines—an epitome of exquisite femininity. Her tiny face was as comically lovely as her form: her applelike cheeks were firm as marble, and her inadequate nose protruded between them like the result of a hasty tweak; a pair of large, round black eyes and a thick-lipped little mouth inundating it all with passion and restless, good-natured shrewdness.

"Goldy! What brings *you* here?" Nathan demanded, with a fond look which instantly gave way to an air of discomfort. "You know I hate you to see me peddling."

"Are you really angry? Bite the feather bed, then. Where is the disgrace? As if you were the only peddler in America! I wish you were. Wouldn't you make heaps of money then! But you had better hear what *does* bring me here. Nathan, darling-dearest little heart, dearest little crown that you are, guess what a plan I have hit upon!" she exploded all at once. "Well, if you hear me out, and you don't say that Goldy has the head of a cabinet minister, then—well, then you will be a big hog, and nothing else."

And without giving him time to put in as much as an interjection, she rattled on, puffing for breath and smacking her lips for ecstasy. Was it not stupid of them to be racking their brains about the wedding while there was such a plain way of having both a "respectable" celebration and fine furniture—Brussels carpet, pier-glass, and all—with the money they now had on hand?

"Come, out with it, then," he said morosely.

But his disguised curiosity only whetted her appetite for tormenting him, and she declared her determination not to disclose her great scheme before they had reached her lodgings.

"You have been yelling long enough today, anyhow," she said, with abrupt sympathy. "Do you suppose it does not go to my very heart to think of the way you stand out in the cold screaming yourself hoarse?"

Half an hour later, when they were alone in Mrs. Volpiansky's parlor, which was also Goldy's bedroom, she set about emptying his pockets of the gross results of the day's business, and counting the money. This she did with a preoccupied, matter-of-fact air, Nathan submitting to the operation with fond and amused willingness; and the sum being satisfactory, she went on to unfold her plan.

"You see," she began, almost in a whisper, and with the mien of a care-worn, experience-laden old matron, "in a week or two we shall have about seventy-five dollars, shan't we? Well, what is seventy-five dollars? Nothing! We could just have the plainest furniture, and no wedding worth speaking of. Now, if we have no wedding, we shall get no presents, shall we?"

Nathan shook his head thoughtfully.

"Well, why shouldn't we be up to snuff and do this way? Let us spend all our money on a grand, respectable wedding, and send out a big lot of invitations, and then—well, won't uncle Leiser send us a carpet or a parlor set? And aunt Beile, and cousin Shapiro, and Charley, and Meyerke, and Wolfke, and Bennie, and Sore-Gitke—won't each present something or other, as is the custom among respectable people? May God give us a lump of good luck as big as the wedding present each of them is sure to send us! Why, did not Beilke get a fine carpet from uncle when she got married? And am I not a nearer relative than she?"

She paused to search his face for a sign of approval, and, fondly smoothing a tuft of his dark hair into place, she went on to enumerate the friends to be invited and the gifts to be expected from them.

"So you see," she pursued, "we will have both a respectable wedding that we shan't have to be ashamed of in after years and the nicest things we could get if we spent two hundred dollars. What do you say?"

"What *shall* I say?" he returned dubiously.

The project appeared reasonable enough, but the investment struck him as rather hazardous. He pleaded for caution, for delay; but as he had no tangible argument to produce, while she stood her ground with the firmness of conviction, her victory was an easy one.

"It will all come right, depend upon it," she said coaxingly. "You just leave everything to me. Don't be uneasy, Nathan," she added. "You and I are orphans, and you know the Uppermost does not forsake a bride and bridegroom who have nobody to take care of them. If my father were alive, it would be different," she concluded, with a disconsolate gesture.

There was a pathetic pause. Tears glistened in Goldy's eyes.

"May your father rest in a bright paradise," Nathan said feelingly. "But what is the use of crying? Can you bring him back to life? I will be a father to you."

"If God be pleased," she assented. "Would that mamma, at least—may she be healthy a hundred and twenty years—would that she, at least, were here to attend our wedding! Poor mother! It will break her heart to think that she has not been foreordained by the Uppermost to lead me under the canopy."

There was another desolate pause, but it was presently broken by Goldy, who exclaimed with unexpected buoyancy, "By the way, Nathan, guess what I did! I am afraid you will call me braggart and make fun of me, but I don't care," she pursued, with a playful pout, as she produced a strip of carpet from her pocketbook. "I went into a furniture store, and they gave me a sample three times as big as this. I explained in my letter to mother that this is the kind of stuff that will cover my floor when I am married. Then I enclosed the sample in the letter, and sent it all to Russia."

Nathan clapped his hands and burst out laughing. "But how do you know that is just the kind of carpet you will get for your wedding present?" he demanded, amazed as much as amused.

"How do I know? As if it mattered what sort of carpet! I can just see mamma going the rounds of the neighbors, and showing off the 'costly tablecloth' her daughter will trample upon. Won't she be happy!"

Over a hundred invitations, printed in as luxurious a black and gold as ever came out of an Essex Street hand press, were sent out for an early date in April. Goldy and Nathan paid a month's rent in advance for three rooms on the second floor of a Cherry Street[8] tenement house.[9] Goldy regarded the rent as unusually low, and the apartments as the finest on the East Side.

"Oh, haven't I got lovely rooms!" she would ejaculate, beaming with the consciousness of the pronoun. Or, "You ought to see *my* rooms! How much do you pay for yours?" Or again, "I have made up my mind to have my parlor in the rear room. It is as light as the front one, anyhow, and I want that for a kitchen, you know. What do you say?" For hours together she would go on talking nothing but rooms, rent, and furniture; every married couple who had recently moved into new quarters, or were about to do so, seemed bound to her by the ties of a common cause; in her imagination, humanity was divided into those who were interested in the question of rooms, rent and furniture and those who were not—the former, of whom she was one, constituting the superior category; and whenever her eye fell upon a bill announcing rooms to let, she would experience something akin to the feeling with which an artist, in passing, views some accessory of his art.

It is customary to send the bulkier wedding presents to a young couple's apartments a few days before they become man and wife, the closer relatives and friends of the betrothed usually settling among themselves what piece of furniture each is to contribute. Accordingly, Goldy gave up her work a week in advance of the day set for the great event, in order that she might be on hand to receive the things when they arrived.

She went to the empty little rooms, with her lunch, early in the morning, and kept anxious watch till after nightfall, when Nathan came to take her home.

A day passed, another, and a third, but no expressman[1] called out her name. She sat waiting and listening for the rough voice, but in vain.

"Oh, it is too early, anyhow. I am a fool to be expecting anything so soon at all," she tried to console herself. And she waited another hour, and still another; but no wedding gift made its appearance.

"Well, there is plenty of time, after all; wedding presents do come a day or two before the ceremony," she argued; and again she waited, and again strained her ears, and again her heart rose in her throat.

The vacuity of the rooms, freshly cleaned, scrubbed, and smelling of whitewash, began to frighten her. Her overwrought mind was filled with sounds which her over-strained ears did not hear. Yet there she sat on the window sill, listening and listening for an expressman's voice.

"Hush, hush-sh, hush-sh-sh!" whispered the walls; the corners muttered awful threats; her heart was ever and anon contracted with fear; she often thought herself on the brink of insanity; yet she stayed on, waiting, waiting, waiting.

At the slightest noise in the hall she would spring to her feet, her heart beating wildly, only presently to sink in her bosom at finding it to be some neighbor or a peddler; and so frequent were these violent throbbings that Goldy grew to imagine herself a prey to heart disease. Nevertheless the fifth day came, and she was again at her post, waiting, waiting, waiting for her wedding gifts. And what is more, when Nathan came from business, and his

8. Essex and Cherry streets are on the Lower East Side of Manhattan, which was the primary area of residence for most Jewish immigrants to New York from the 1880s through the turn of the century.

9. An apartment house in a city, usually in a low-rent district, that barely meets minimum standards of sanitation, safety, and comfort.

1. A delivery person.

countenance fell as he surveyed the undisturbed emptiness of the rooms, she set a merry face against his rueful inquiries, and took to bantering him as a woman quick to lose heart, and to painting their prospects in roseate hues, until she argued herself, if not him, into a more cheerful view of the situation.

On the sixth day an expressman did pull up in front of the Cherry Street tenement house, but he had only a cheap huge rocking chair for Goldy and Nathan; and as it proved to be the gift of a family who had been set down for nothing less than a carpet or a parlor set, the joy and hope which its advent had called forth turned to dire disappointment and despair. For nearly an hour Goldy sat mournfully rocking and striving to picture how delightful it would have been if all her anticipations had come true.

Presently there arrived a flimsy plush-covered little corner table. It could not have cost more than a dollar. Yet it was the gift of a near friend, who had been relied upon for a pier-glass or a bedroom set. A little later a cheap alarm clock and an ice-box[2] were brought in. That was all.

Occasionally Goldy went to the door to take in the entire effect; but the more she tried to view the parlor as half finished, the more cruelly did the few lonely and mismated things emphasize the remaining emptiness of the apartments: whereupon she would sink into her rocker and sit motionless, with a drooping head, and then desperately fall to swaying to and fro, as though bent upon swinging herself out of her woebegone, wretched self.

Still, when Nathan came, there was a triumphant twinkle in her eye, as she said, pointing to the gifts, "Well, mister, who was right? It is not very bad for a start, is it? You know most people do send their wedding presents after the ceremony—why, of course!" she added, in a sort of confidential way. "Well, we have invited a big crowd, and all people of no mean sort, thank God; and who ever heard of a lady or a gentleman attending a respectable wedding and having a grand wedding supper, and then cheating the bride and the bridegroom out of their present?"

The evening was well advanced; yet there were only a score of people in a hall that was used to hundreds.

Everybody felt ill at ease, and ever and anon looked about for the possible arrival of more guests. At ten o'clock the dancing preliminary to the ceremony had not yet ceased, although the few waltzers looked as if they were scared by the ringing echoes of their own footsteps amid the austere solemnity of the surrounding void and the depressing sheen of the dim expanse of floor.

The two fiddles, the cornet, and the clarinet were shrieking as though for pain, and the malicious superabundance of gaslight was fiendishly sneering at their tortures. Weddings and entertainments being scarce in the Ghetto, its musicians caught the contagion of misery: hence the greedy, desperate gusto with which the band plied their instruments.

At last it became evident that the assemblage was not destined to be larger than it was, and that it was no use delaying the ceremony. It was, in fact, an open secret among those present that by far the greater number of the invited

2. Before refrigerators were invented and became commonplace, kitchens were supplied with ice-boxes, a kind of two-level cabinet that required blocks of ice in the upper compartment that kept the food in the lower compartment from spoiling.

friends were kept away by lack of employment: some having their presentable clothes in the pawn shop; others avoiding the expense of a wedding present, or simply being too cruelly borne down by their cares to have a mind for the excitement of a wedding; indeed, some even thought it wrong of Nathan to have the celebration during such a period of hard times, when everybody was out of work.

It was a little after ten when the bard—a tall, gaunt man, with a grizzly beard and a melancholy face—donned his skullcap,[3] and, advancing toward the dancers, called out in a synagogue intonation, "Come, ladies, let us veil the bride!"

An odd dozen of daughters of Israel followed him and the musicians into a little side room where Goldy was seated between her two brideswomen (the wives of two men who were to attend upon the groom). According to the orthodox custom she had fasted the whole day, and as a result of this and of her gnawing grief, added to the awe-inspiring scene she had been awaiting, she was pale as death; the effect being heightened by the wreath and white gown she wore. As the procession came filing in, she sat blinking her round dark eyes in dismay, as if the bard were an executioner come to lead her to the scaffold.

The song or address to the bride usually partakes of the qualities of prayer and harangue, and includes a melancholy meditation upon life and death; lamenting the deceased members of the young woman's family, bemoaning her own woes, and exhorting her to discharge her sacred duties as a wife, mother, and servant of God. Composed in verse and declaimed in a solemn, plaintive recitative, often broken by the band's mournful refrain, it is sure to fulfill its mission of eliciting tears even when hearts are brimful of glee. Imagine, then, the funereal effect which it produced at Goldy's wedding ceremony.

The bard, half starved himself, sang the anguish of his own heart; the violins wept, the clarinet moaned, the cornet and the double-bass groaned, each reciting the sad tale of its poverty-stricken master. He began:

> Silence, good women, give heed to *my* verses!
> Tonight, bride, thou dost stand before the Uppermost.
> Pray to him to bless thy union,
> To let thee and thy mate live a hundred and twenty peaceful years,
> To give you your daily bread,
> To keep hunger from your door.

Several women, including Goldy, burst into tears, the others sadly lowering their gaze. The band sounded a wailing chord, and the whole audience broke into loud, heartrending weeping.

The bard went on sternly:

> Wail, bride, wail!
> This is a time of tears.
> Think of thy past days:
> Alas! they are gone to return nevermore.

3. A small, light cloth skullcap, called a *yarmulke* in Yiddish, is often worn by observant Jewish males, who must keep their heads covered, especially during prayers.

Heedless of the convulsive sobbing with which the room resounded, he continued to declaim, and at last, his eye flashing fire and his voice tremulous with emotion, he sang out in a dismal, uncanny high key:

> And thy good mother beyond the seas,
> And thy father in his grave
> Near where thy cradle was rocked,
> Weep, bride, weep!
> Though his soul is better off
> Than we are here underneath
> In dearth and cares and ceaseless pangs,
> Weep, sweet bride, weep!

Then, in the general outburst that followed the extemporaneous verse, there was a cry—"The bride is fainting! Water! quick!"

"Murderer that you are!" flamed out an elderly matron, with an air of admiration for the bard's talent as much as of wrath for the far-fetched results it achieved.

Goldy was brought to, and the rest of the ceremony passed without accident. She submitted to everything as in a dream. When the bridegroom, escorted by two attendants, each carrying a candelabrum holding lighted candles came to place the veil over her face, she stared about as though she failed to realize the situation or to recognize Nathan. When, keeping time to the plaintive strains of a time-honored tune, she was led, blindfolded, into the large hall and stationed beside the bridegroom under the red canopy, and then marched around him seven times, she obeyed instructions and moved about with the passivity of a hypnotic. After the Seven Blessings[4] had been recited, when the cantor, gently lifting the end of her veil, presented the wineglass to her lips, she tasted its contents with the air of an invalid taking medicine. Then she felt the ring slip down her finger, and heard Nathan say, "Be thou dedicated to me by this ring, according to the laws of Moses and Israel."

Whereupon she said to herself, "Now I am a married woman!" But somehow, at this moment the words were meaningless sounds to her. She knew she was married, but could not realize what it implied. As Nathan crushed the wineglass underfoot, and the band struck up a cheerful melody, and the gathering shouted, "Good luck! Good luck!" and clapped their hands, while the older women broke into a wild hop, Goldy felt the relief of having gone through a great ordeal. But still she was not distinctly aware of any change in her position.

Not until fifteen minutes later, when she found herself in the basement, at the head of one of three long tables, did the realization of her new self strike her consciousness full in the face, as it were.

The dining room was nearly as large as the dancing hall on the floor above.

4. Rituals often performed in Orthodox marriage ceremonies. The bride is blindfolded (i.e., heavily veiled) since she is not supposed to look upon the groom until the ceremony is completed. Her walking around the groom demonstrates the absence of any ties, while the Seven Blessings or benedictions emphasize the religious character of marriage, give thanks for granting the glory of married life, offer prayers for the bride and groom's happiness and the restoration of Jerusalem. The wineglass that is broken is thought to represent and remind the happy assemblage of the destruction of the Temple in Jerusalem by the Romans in 70 C.E.

It was as brightly illuminated, and the three tables, which ran almost its entire length, were set for a hundred and fifty guests. Yet there were barely twenty to occupy them. The effect was still more depressing than in the dancing room. The vacant benches and the untouched covers still more agonizingly exaggerated the emptiness of the room, in which the sorry handful of a company lost themselves.

Goldy looked at the rows of plates, spoons, forks, knives, and they weighed her down with the cold dazzle of their solemn, pompous array.

"I am not the Goldy I used to be," she said to herself. "I am a married woman, like mamma, or auntie, or Mrs. Volpiansky. And we have spent every cent we had on this grand wedding, and now we are left without money for furniture, and there are no guests to send us any, and the supper will be thrown out, and everything is lost, and I am to blame for it all!"

The glittering plates seemed to hold whispered converse and to exchange winks and grins at her expense. She transferred her glance to the company, and it appeared as if they were vainly forcing themselves to partake of the food—as though they, too, were looked out of countenance by that ruthless sparkle of the unused plates.

Nervous silence hung over the room, and the reluctant jingle of the score of knives and forks made it more awkward, more enervating, every second. Even the bard had not the heart to break the stillness by the merry rhymes he had composed for the occasion.

Goldy was overpowered. She thought she was on the verge of another fainting spell, and, shutting her eyes and setting her teeth, she tried to imagine herself dead. Nathan, who was by her side, noticed it. He took her hand under the table, and, pressing it gently, whispered, "Don't take it to heart. There is a God in heaven."

She could not make out his words, but she felt their meaning. As she was about to utter some phrase of endearment, her heart swelled in her throat, and a piteous, dovelike, tearful look was all the response she could make.

By-and-by, however, when the foaming lager was served, tongues were loosened, and the bard, although distressed by the meager collection in store for him, but stirred by an ardent desire to relieve the insupportable wretchedness of the evening, outdid himself in offhand acrostics and witticisms. Needless to say that his efforts were thankfully rewarded with unstinted laughter; and as the room rang with merriment, the gleaming rows of undisturbed plates also seemed to join in the general hubbub of mirth, and to be laughing a hearty, kindly laugh.

Presently, amid a fresh outbreak of deafening hilarity, Goldy bent close to Nathan's ear and exclaimed with sobbing vehemence, "My husband! My husband! My husband!"

"My wife!" he returned in her ear.

"Do you know what you are to me now?" she resumed. "A husband! And I am your wife! Do you know what it means—*do* you, *do* you, Nathan?" she insisted, with frantic emphasis.

"I do, my little sparrow; only don't worry over the wedding presents."

It was after midnight, and even the Ghetto was immersed in repose. Goldy and Nathan were silently wending their way to the three empty little rooms where they were destined to have their first joint home. They wore the wedding attire which they had rented for the evening: he a swallowtail coat and high hat, and she a white satin gown and slippers, her head uncovered—the wreath and veil done up in a newspaper, in Nathan's hand.

They had gone to the wedding in carriages, which had attracted large crowds both at the point of departure, and in front of the hall; and of course they had expected to make their way to their new home in a similar "respectable" manner. Toward the close of the last dance, after supper, they found, however, that some small change was all they possessed in the world.

The last strains of music were dying away. The guests, in their hats and bonnets, were taking leave. Everybody seemed in a hurry to get away to his own world, and to abandon the young couple to their fate.

Nathan would have borrowed a dollar or two of some friend. "Let us go home as behooves a bride and bridegroom," he said. "There is a God in heaven: he will not forsake us."

But Goldy would not hear of betraying the full measure of their poverty to their friends. "No! no!" she retorted testily. "I am not going to let you pay a dollar and a half for a few blocks' drive, like a Fifth Avenue[5] nobleman. We can walk," she pursued, with the grim determination of one bent upon self-chastisement. "A poor woman who dares spend every cent on a wedding must be ready to walk after the wedding."

When they found themselves alone in the deserted street, they were so overcome by a sense of loneliness, of a kind of portentous, haunting emptiness, that they could not speak. So on they trudged in dismal silence; she leaning upon his arm, and he tenderly pressing her to his side.

Their way lay through the gloomiest and roughest part of the Seventh Ward. The neighborhood frightened her, and she clung closer to her escort. At one corner they passed some men in front of a liquor saloon.

"Look at dem! Look at dem! A sheeny[6] fellar an' his bride, I'll betch ye!" shouted a husky voice. "Jes' comin' from de weddin'."

"She ain't no bigger 'n a peanut, is she?" The simile was greeted with a horse-laugh.

"Look a here, young fellar, what's de madder wid carryin' dat lady of yourn in your vest pocket?"

When Nathan and Goldy were a block away, something like a potato or a carrot struck her in the back. At the same time the gang of loafers on the corner broke into boisterous merriment. Nathan tried to face about, but she restrained him.

"Don't! They might kill you!" she whispered, and relapsed into silence.

He made another attempt to disengage himself, as if for a desperate attack upon her assailants, but she nestled close to his side and held him fast, her every fiber tingling with the consciousness of the shelter she had in him.

"Don't mind them, Nathan," she said.

And as they proceeded on their dreary way through a somber, impoverished street, with here and there a rustling tree—a melancholy witness of its better days—they felt a stream of happiness uniting them, as it coursed through the veins of both, and they were filled with a blissful sense of oneness

5. One of the most fashionable streets in New York City, then the site of many mansions of the very rich.
6. A derogatory term for a Jew.

the like of which they had never tasted before. So happy were they that the gang behind them, and the bare rooms toward which they were directing their steps, and the miserable failure of the wedding, all suddenly appeared too insignificant to engage their attention—paltry matters alien to their new life, remote from the enchanted world in which they now dwelt.

The very notion of a relentless void abruptly turned to a beatific sense of their own seclusion, of there being only themselves in the universe, to live and to delight in each other.

"Don't mind them, Nathan darling," she repeated mechanically, conscious of nothing but the tremor of happiness in her voice.

"I should give it to them!" he responded, gathering her still closer to him. "I should show them how to touch my Goldy, my pearl, my birdie!"

They dived into the denser gloom of a sidestreet.

A gentle breeze ran past and ahead of them, proclaiming the bride and the bridegroom. An old tree whispered overhead its tender felicitations.

1898

MORRIS ROSENFELD
1862–1923

Beloved by Jewish workers, who sang his lyrics, and scorned by fellow writers, Morris Rosenfeld had a career bounded by his impoverished labor in New York sweatshops and momentary international fame when a Harvard lecturer discovered his work.

Moyshe-Yankev-Alter Rosenfeld was born in 1862 in the small village of Boksha in Suwałki, Poland, the son of a military tailor. When he was a child, his family moved to Warsaw and then back to Suwałki, where he attended heder (an elementary Jewish school) and studied Talmud. He also read secular Hebrew books and Yiddish poetry as well as a little German and Polish. He married young, briefly visited America in 1882, and then worked in the sweatshops in London, where he began writing poetry, before immigrating to America in 1886. Toiling in the garment factories in New York, Rosenfeld wrote of the lives of immigrant workers. He became known for these, his best poems, not so much as a spokesman for the battle, but as a depictor of the pathos in individual lives.

What distinguishes his career from those of other Labor or Sweatshop poets is that he achieved brief fame outside the Yiddish world. In 1898, a Harvard professor of Slavic languages, Leo Wiener, translated a selection of his poems into English in a volume called *Songs from the Ghetto,* and Rosenfeld was taken up by American literati. But the taste for his brand of exoticism passed, and Rosenfeld later earned a meager living as an assistant at the Yiddish newspaper *Forverts* (Forward), resentfully blaming his humbled circumstances for his depleted poetic abilities. Critics concur that his later poetry, which relies upon the standard themes of protest and calls to arms as well as upon Jewish national themes, is more bombastic and less compelling than his earlier work. He also wrote somewhat stilted and conventional nature poems.

Rosenfeld is best known for poems that make personal and particular the universal sufferings of the workers. In *My Little Son,* a father tells of his love for his young son, whom he sees only when he returns from work late at night and the child is asleep. Rosenfeld draws on generalized characters similar to the shtetl types found in classic

Yiddish fiction, but here they are city types: the factory-worker father who has to punch the time clock and who works sixteen hours a day for meager wages; the exhausted wife and mother; the innocent son who is victim to his parents' circumstances. The poet tells us little about these characters besides their poverty, which necessitates the terrible working hours and depletes their only source of pleasure and sustenance: being together.

In *Corner of Pain and Anguish,* Rosenfeld makes the struggles of the working class vivid through pathos, while in *Walt Whitman (America's Great Poet)* he pays homage to Whitman's evocation of nature, another of Rosenfeld's themes.

Corner of Pain and Anguish[1]

Corner of Pain and Anguish, there's a worn old house:
tavern on the street floor, Bible-room upstairs.
Drunkards sit below, and all day long they souse.
Overhead, the pious chant their daily prayers.

Higher, on the third floor, there's another room:
not a single window welcomes in the sun.
Seldom does it know the blessing of a broom.
Rottenness and filth are blended into one.

Toiling without letup in that sunless den:
nimble-fingered and (or so it seems) content,
sit some thirty blighted women, blighted men,
with their spirits broken, and their bodies spent.

Scurfhead struts among them: always with a frown,
brandishing his scepter like a mighty king;
for the shop is his, and here he wears the crown,
and they must obey him, bow to everything.

ca. 1886–1896, 1909

My Little Son[2]

I have a son, a little son,
a youngster mighty fine!
and when I look at him I feel
that all the world is mine.

But seldom do I see him when
he's wide awake and bright.
I always find him sound asleep;
I see him late at night.

1. Translated by Aaron Kramer. The Yiddish poem is called *Der svet-shop* (The Sweatshop).
2. Translated by Aaron Kramer. *Mayn yingele*, set to music, was one of the most popular songs among Jewish workers.

The time clock drags me off at dawn;
at night it lets me go.
I hardly know my flesh and blood;
his eyes I hardly know. . . .

I climb the staircase wearily:
a figure wrapped in shade.
Each night my worn-faced wife describes
how well the youngster played;

how sweetly he's begun to talk;
how cleverly he said,
"When will my daddy come and leave
a penny near my bed?"

I listen, and I rush inside—
it must—yes, it must be!
My father-love begins to burn:
my child must look at me! . . .

I stand beside the little bed
and watch my sleeping son,
when hush! a dream bestirs his mouth:
"Where has my daddy gone?"

I touch his eyelids with my lips.
The blue eyes open then:
they look at me! they look at me!
and quickly shut again.

"Your daddy's right beside you, dear.
Here, here's a penny, son!"
A dream bestirs his little mouth:
"Where has my daddy gone?"

I watch him, wounded and depressed
by thoughts I cannot bear:
"One morning, when you wake—my child—
you'll find that I'm not here."

1887 1887

Walt Whitman (America's Great Poet)[1]

Oh, thou, within whose mighty poet-heart
two fathomless abysses intertwined:
the deepness of the pure, blue heavens and

1. Translated by Aaron Kramer. Walt Whitman (1819–1892) is the great American poet whose famous *Song of Myself* and *When Lilacs Last in the Dooryard Bloom'd* Rosenfeld alludes to here. Section 24 of *Song of Myself* was translated into Yiddish in *Shriftn* (Writings) in 1919 by L. Miller.

the softly cradled deepness of the earth;
within whose heart arose the sun, the moon,
and where, in all their bright magnificence,
stars without number blazed, whole worlds of stars;
within whose heart the buds of May awoke,
and where the harsh voice of the thunder sang
beside the twitter of the nightingale;
within whose overwhelming chant one feels
the pulse of nature, its omnipotence;

immortal bard, I honor thee: I kneel
upon the dust, before thy dust, and sing.

ca. 1895, 1909

DAVID EDELSHTADT
1866–1892

Considered an early hero of the Jewish working class, David Edelshtadt wrote poetry in Yiddish with the sole purpose of serving the cause of political protest.

Edelshtadt, the son of a Jewish veteran of the czar's army and one of seven siblings and half siblings from his mother's first marriage, was born in 1866 in the Russian city of Kaluga. Because Kaluga lacked any organized Jewish community, the young Edelshtadt received a Russian rather than a Jewish education. He began writing poems in Russian at the age of nine and by twelve had published in the local newspaper. At the age of fifteen, he went to Kiev and worked in his brother's shoe factory, where he encountered anticzarist revolutionaries and the stories and songs of their struggle. Traumatized by the Kiev pogrom of May 8, 1881, Edelshtadt was hospitalized and there met university students who introduced him to the Jewish territorialist movement Am Olam. He joined up and in 1882 immigrated with a group of them to the United States to set up farming communes. But he ended up in Cincinnati, Ohio, where his two older brothers had settled, and worked in a clothing factory as a buttonhole maker. Radicalized by his experiences in the sweatshop and by the bloody 1886 Chicago Haymarket Riot and its aftermath, Edelshtadt published impassioned protest poems in the Russian Socialist-Democratic paper *Znamia* in January 1889. A month later, Edelshtadt, by then unemployed and in New York, published his first Yiddish poem in the anarchist paper the *Varhayt* (Reality). Thereafter, he published his polemical verse in his acquired Yiddish and soon became a popular poet-spokesman for the anarchist movement. Beginning in 1890, he wrote for and was an early editor of the *Fraye arbeter shtime* (Free Voice of Labor). In 1892, at the age of twenty-five, Edelshtadt died of tuberculosis in a Denver sanatorium.

During his lifetime, Edelshtadt published not only protest poetry, but also translations of Russian poetry, prose sketches, short stories such as *The Suicide* (Warsaw, 1906), as well as some fifty newspaper articles, most of which are uncollected. Many collections of his poems appeared in book form after 1892 in London, New York, Warsaw, and Moscow, including *Shriftn* (Writings), published in London in 1909 and reissued in New York in 1911.

Although Edelshtadt's poems were sung as anthems by millions of Jewish workers in sweatshops, at demonstrations, and at meetings throughout the world, few are available in English translation today. One of Edelshtadt's best-known poems was *My Testament*. Typical of Edelshtadt, its ballad strophes convey the grandiose diction of revolutionary catchwords and romantic clichés, pitting good against evil and worker against capitalist. *My Testament* and *To the Muse* tend to romanticize the poet as the spiritually powerful, though physically enervated, source of inspiration for the working masses.

To the Muse[1]

Muse! is that you knocking again
at the door of my heart's bleak room?
Turn back, my child—you knock in vain—
my heart is crowded with gloom.

I'm sick and weary—see for yourself.
How could I sing tonight?
And how could a song of sorrow help
my people in their plight?

The world is tearing me limb from limb:
it's savage and depraved.
My song is no more than a sexton's hymn
over an orphan's grave.

I never learned how to polish my rhymes,
how prettily thoughts can be dressed.
The bloody dramas of these times
were staged within my breast.

Great is my sadness. A venomous snake
resides in your wretched singer.
She sits in my brain, asleep and awake;
she's writing now . . . with my fingers.

Stop knocking, Muse, at the door of my heart!
No lamps of hope are alive;
it's crowded with tears, and terribly dark.
—Go to the poets who thrive!

to them who know about golden noons,
who've reached the rapturous isle;
and me, with my fetters and my wounds,
leave me alone for a while!

ca. 1882–1892

1. Translated by Aaron Kramer.

My Testament[1]

Oh comrades mine, when I am dead
carry our banner to my grave:
the freedom-banner—flaming red
with all the blood that workers gave.

And there, the while our banner flutters,
sing me my freedom-song again,
my "Battle Song"—that rings like fetters
around the feet of workingmen.

And even in my grave that song,
that stormy song, will reach my ears,
and for my friends enslaved so long
there, too, shall I be shedding tears.

And when I hear a cannon sound
the final siege of want and pain,
my song shall trumpet from the ground
and set the people's heart aflame!

1882 (1889?)

1. Translated by Aaron Kramer. The Yiddish title, *Mayn tsavoe*, denotes the ethical will traditional Jews wrote for their children. Edelshtadt uses this term nontraditionally, referring not to religious faith, but to class struggle. Set to music, this poem became a popular song among early Jewish labor organizers and workers.

YEHOASH
1872–1927

Poet and translator Yehoash (Yehoash-Solomon Bloomgarden), born in Verzshbolove, near Suwałki, Poland, came to New York in 1890. Contracting tuberculosis, he resided in a Denver sanatorium from 1900 to 1909. He then returned to New York, where he remained for the rest of his life, except for a visit to Palestine and Egypt in 1914–15. A contemporary of the Yiddish Labor poets, Yehoash, considered an intellectual, wrote poetry that was less explicitly political or national than it was aesthetic. Anticipating modernism, he addressed the art of poetry on its own terms, combining in his lyrics the influence of traditional folk song and modern speech. When he wrote nature poems, he attempted to free them from the Romantic conventions and clichés accepted by his contemporaries.

Yehoash's main contribution to literature lies in his attempts to bring Yiddish poetry up to date by importing into it the themes, forms, and language of world literature. He both experimented with exotic subjects in his poems by writing about people, places, things, and experiences, such as the Chinese empress Yang-Ze-Fu, that were outside the realm of most Jewish Americans and anticipated the cosmopolitan interests of the Yunge poets (and also, strangely, of American modernists such as Ezra Pound). The first to translate European and American poetry into Yiddish, including

Henry Wadsworth Longfellow's verse narrative *The Song of Hiawatha* (1910), he brought Native American mythology and nomenclature into Yiddish, including an eight-page glossary of *Indian Names and Words,* along with Longfellow's distinctive narrative meter. As early as 1891, the first year his work appeared in print, Yehoash published translations of Lord Byron's *The Gazelle* and of Psalm 18.

His translation of Byron indicates Yehoash's commitment to enrich with European high culture the poetic and prosodic vocabulary of Yiddish literature. The early biblical translation was a harbinger of Yehoash's greatest literary achievement: his translation into Yiddish of the entire Hebrew Bible, the Tanakh, a lifelong project that appeared in its complete form posthumously in 1941. In contrast to centuries of earlier Yiddish translations of the Tanakh, Yehoash's rendering freed itself from religious doctrine in order to appeal to a progressive, modern, secular reader. His Yiddish style in this translation is elegant, spare, and exact.

Two of the poems we have included here—*Amid the Colorado Mountains* and *Woolworth Building*—allude to Yehoash's experiences in Denver and New York, with their imagery of nature and the city. *Lynching* shows his concern with social justice. *Yang-Ze-Fu* is an example of his project to expand the cultural range of Yiddish literature. The poem *Rachel's Tomb,* prefaced by Yehoash's note "From the Hebrew," is grounded in the classical Jewish tradition although it enrobes the biblical matriarch with modern Jewish secular nationalism.

Amid the Colorado Mountains[1]

I

High black mountain peaks conspire
to enclose the orb of light.
Through the clouds that billow densely
day's last flames defy the night. . . .

Unfamiliar shapes and colors
soon emerge and soon recede.
Great hands hidden in the mountain
shift the scenery with speed. . . .

But the valleys soon lie lifeless,
as the twilight fires fade—
for what audience, there, westward,
is the night-light drama played?

II

Beyond the peaks a thunderstorm
is ready to commence.
The black clouds, like attacking knights,
come on in regiments.

It flashes forth! The blades unsheathe,
a savage sorrow howls
and more than once reverberates
from the abyss's bowels. . . .

1. Translated by Aaron Kramer. Yehoash, suffering from tuberculosis, was in a Denver sanatorium from 1900 to 1909.

Already every dale can feel
a gruesome tumult rise.
And on my face the first warm drop
has fallen from the skies. . . .

So I am too am anointed now,
and feel at home with cloud
and titan-peak, with lightning-flash
and thunder roared aloud.

III

The quiet evening hour arrives
with streaks of gold and purple,
and summer-day and summer-night
are now a loving couple. . . .

The mountains loom up blue and large,
the vale grows small and darkens,
and there's a soundless melody
somewhere, to which one hearkens.

Like incense rises toward the sky
a scent of meadow flowers.
The world grows calm and holy in
the soft glow of such hours.

1900–1909

Rachel's Tomb[1]

From the Hebrew[2]

On the fields of Bethlehem
Where the road to Ephrath goes,
A tomb stands. Years and generations
Have passed since it arose.[3]

When everything around is peaceful
And the midnight hour draws near,
Pensively, a woman's figure
Rises from the grave.

She walks down to the Jordan River,[4]
Gazing long upon the waves,
And from her lovely eyes, a teardrop
Falls upon the waves . . .

1. Translated by Kathryn Hellerstein.
2. Yehoash's note. He translated this poem from an earlier Hebrew poem by K. Shapiro.
3. The Matriarch Rachel was buried on the road from Bethlehem to Ephrath (Genesis 35.19, 48.7).
4. This scene is geographically unlikely, for the Jordan River runs more than twenty miles east of Bethlehem.

One by one, the quiet tears
Flow, without lament or cry,
Falling in the Jordan's waters,
Merging silently.

1891, 1910

Lynching[1]

"Father of my soul,
Where shall I find You?"

Defiler!
Look at your work—
A black body striped bloody,
Eyes rolled back white in the black face,
And gleaming teeth trying to eat
The swollen red tongue.

"Father of my soul,
And Lord of all bodies,
Where shall I find You?"

Profanity!
He who shudders
In the blue webs
Of your holy twilight,
He who sways in your lament at night
And your song by day,
He who trembles in the corners
Of your unborn desires,
He who calls you, craves you, tears at you—
Has become black meat
With thick lips and strange hair.

And you dug you
Dug nails into his ribs,
Knives into the heart.

Spitting on his agony,
You left him dangling
On the tree.

1919

1. Translated by Raphael Rudnick.

Woolworth Building[1]

Home winds a remnant of the craziness of day,
the eyes aglow and feverish, the faces clay. . . .
Few wheels now—one car where there were twenty;
over the asphalt, ponderous and empty,
a heavy wagon rolls.
Evening falls
like a dead fly on the knot of blent
wire and mortar and cement. . . .
The roar becomes a murmur, as in sleep
a gasp through gritted teeth
after a smothered cry. . . .
And high above all spires that scrape the sky,
alone, erect, and straight—behold
the temple of the god of iron and gold!

1920

Yang-Ze-Fu[2]

The Empress Yang-Ze-Fu
Has palaces fourscore.
A hundred rooms each palace has,
Each room, a golden door.
Black, giant slaves guard over all
With iron shields and lances tall.
To her mirror Yang-Ze-Fu
Laughs—"Who is as great as you?"

The Empress Yang-Ze-Fu
To the white stream goes nightly.
She grows smaller than a nut.
On the stream a leaf is put,
Wherein she sails lightly.
And the oars the Empress has
Are two dainty blades of grass.
To the water Yang-Ze-Fu
Laughs—"Who is as small as you?"

1920, 1923

1. Translated by Aaron Kramer. A distinctive skyscraper in New York City built in 1913 as the headquarters for the now-defunct F. W. Woolworth Company, a multinational corporation of retail stores, incorporated in 1911 and headed by Frank Winfield Woolworth (1852–1919), founder of the five-and-ten variety stores that came into existence beginning in 1879 in Utica, New York, and Lancaster, Pennsylvania.

2. Translated by Marie Syrkin.

AVROM REYZEN
1876–1953

Avrom Reyzen was the consummate littérateur: wherever he went, he contributed to the growth and enrichment of Yiddish literature in Europe and America both in his extraordinary output of stories, poems, plays, and articles, and in his irrepressible talent as an editor and a publisher who established more journals than can be counted.

Born in Koydenev, White Russia, on April 10, 1876, Avrom Reyzen was one of three children from an illustrious literary family. His father, Kalman Reyzen, a proponent of the Jewish Enlightenment, the nineteenth-century movement to secularize European Jewish society, published poetry and sketches in Hebrew and Yiddish; his mother read religious texts in Yiddish; his brother, Zalmen, became a writer best known for his biographical encyclopedia of the writers and scholars of modern Yiddish; his sister, Sore Reyzen, published poetry, short stories, and translations.

Reyzen attended heder and learned Talmud with his uncle. His father taught him Hebrew, Russian, and German, and hired a private tutor for general subjects. Reyzen began to write rhymes at the age of nine and, under his father's influence, composed verses in Hebrew. He became a teacher in Koydenev when he was fourteen. As a boy, he read the works of the great Yiddish and Russian writers, and corresponded with the Yiddish writers I. Dineson and I. L. Peretz, the latter of whom encouraged his writing and published one of his first poems in 1891 in *Yudishe bibliotek*. While teaching in several neighboring shtetls, he began to write short stories. He then lived briefly in Minsk, where he became acquainted with the pioneers of the Jewish socialist movement. Groups of his poems were published with the help of Sholem Aleichem (1892) and Peretz (1894). In 1894, Reyzen published many of his poems as well as translations of Heine and Pushkin.

Reyzen was conscripted into the Russian army in 1895 and served in a military band in Kovno. He wrote and published poems there and read European writers in Russian, German, and Danish. After being released from the army, he returned to Minsk, published poems in 1899, and then went to Warsaw, where his literary career took off. In 1900, in the tradition of his mentors, Peretz and Sholem Aleichem, Reyzen edited and published *Dos tsvantsikste yorhundert* (The Twentieth Century), an anthology that showcased the works of new Yiddish writers of literature, scholarship, and criticism. With this publication, Reyzen took a stand in the culture wars of the day, promoting Yiddish as the language of Jewish culture instead of Hebrew, and Jewish salvation through the Diaspora-based socialism of the Jewish Bund instead of the nationalist return to Israel of Zionism.

His first book of poems, *Tsayt-lider* (Seasonal Poems), came out in 1902 and his first collection of stories, *Ertseylungen un bilder* (Stories and Pictures), in 1903. In 1903 and 1904, dissatisfied with the daily newspapers in Russia, Reyzen published a number of miscellanies and periodicals, which became important in the dissemination and encouragement of the new Yiddish writing.

From 1904 until 1908, Reyzen traveled in Europe, continuing his work as writer and publisher. He made his first trip to America in 1908 and published short stories in the *Forverts* but stayed less than a year. In 1911, he returned to New York. There, he founded the first American Yiddish literary weekly, *Naye land* (New Country), and in 1912 edited *Literarishe velt* (Literary World). Both these journals, although short-lived, aimed to elevate the literary taste of American Yiddish readers. Returning to Europe in 1913, Reyzen traveled extensively and founded yet another journal that published Yiddish writing from Poland and France. When World War I broke out, he returned to the United States for good.

In New York again, Reyzen continued his frenzy of literary activity. His stories and poems appeared in a wide range of Yiddish publications—from Cahan's daily *Forverts* to the satirical rag the *Groyser kundes* (Big Joker) to a literary magazine of the Yunge poets. From 1922 through 1923, he published his last journal, *Nay-yidish* (New Yiddish), which presented both established and lesser-known writers and artists. In the late 1920s, Reyzen allied himself with communism, writing for the newspaper *Frayhayt* (Freedom) and, in 1928, touring Western Europe, Poland, and the Soviet Union, where a number of his books were reissued. He broke with the Left in 1929, when *Frayhayt* refused to condemn the 1929 Arab pogroms in Palestine. From then on, he wrote for the *Forverts*. Between 1929 and 1935, three volumes of his memoirs, *Episodn fun mayn lebn* (Episodes of My Life), came out in Vilna, although later installments, published in newspapers, were never gathered into a book. In 1955, Reyzen edited a book memorializing his destroyed hometown.

Although a littérateur, Reyzen was beloved by ordinary people. Many of his poems, set to music, became popular songs. He appeared often at the Yiddish schools, and his poems and stories, included in textbooks, were known by generations of Yiddish students. Reyzen's one-act plays were performed by professional and amateur theater troupes. His Yiddish translations of modern and medieval Hebrew poetry and of Russian literature were read widely. He was also known in Hebrew. Although he wrote only three short stories in Hebrew, Reyzen's Yiddish stories were translated into Hebrew by the leading Hebrew writers of the day.

While fostering the younger modernist writers, Reyzen wrote lyrical poems of more pathos and less new language than those of his younger colleagues. In his stories, he developed a concise style that depicts the small dilemmas of ordinary Jews—in the shtetl and in the American city—in such a way that with a stroke here, a nuance there, and a glimmer of irony and humor, the uniqueness of each character tells volumes about the larger clashes of tradition and modernity. The story included here, *Equality of the Sexes,* was originally published as *Glaykhkayt* (Equality) around 1911 and collected in Reyzen's *Gezamlte shriftn* (Collected Writings) in 1916. This quintessentially American story, characterized by Reyzen's typical use of ironic understatement, considers the price paid for progress.

Equality of the Sexes[1]

For almost a year now Harry has been going out with Ida. Harry is tall, slim, dark-haired and twenty-four. Ida is petite, comely and twenty. Their love is secure, firm and already encircled by a small, five-dollar gold ring which Harry gave her as a present, and it is further tied together with a 49-cent necktie which Ida bought him in return. Neither one of them has parents here to push them into marriage. They themselves believe that *khosn* and *kalleh*,[2] lover and sweetheart, are much more beautiful words than "man" and "wife." "Man" doesn't sound too bad, but "wife"—that is a word neither of them can stand.

"An ugly word!" Ida exclaims charmingly.

"A vulgar word!" Harry agrees.

It is much more pleasant for them to meet several times a week at certain pre-arranged places—at an "Elevated" station, or on the corner of a quiet little street. Ida is never punctual. Usually she is ten minutes late, that is, in addition to the first ten minutes that Harry has learned to expect. By nature, Harry is a very impatient person. "A big fault, her tardiness. I really should

1. Translated by Max Rosenfeld (1995).

2. Bride (Yiddish). *Khosn*: bridegroom (Yiddish).

talk to her about it." But when he sees her coming he strides forward to greet her with a friendly smile on his face.

And when she asks him: "Have you been waiting long, Harry?" he always replies good-humoredly:

"It's nothing, Ida. I don't mind . . ."

Harry is convinced that his sweet expectation of her arrival will vanish once they are married. She will be waiting for him in a home where two beds stand close together, and people who come to visit them will immediately perceive everything and smile knowingly.

Isn't it better when he steals into her room, with its one sparkling-white narrow bed that he doesn't have the nerve to sit down on, even on the edge, until she assures him that she does indeed want him to sit there because the only chair her landlady put in the room will "shorten your years"?

Or what about the moment when he and Ida leave together, surreptitiously, and her cheeks are aflame from his kisses and from the ice-cold water she has just washed her face with, so people won't suspect—not that it does any good.

"My cheeks are hot as fire, Harry!" she says in mock anger.

And Harry assures her that she is only imagining things, that a thief always feels as if the hat on his head is burning.[3] She laughs her charming little laugh, and going down the stairs Harry falls in love with her all over again. A brand new love affair. And right there on the stairs he kisses her again, and again she is "angry" and lectures him: "Harry, you're not being careful! People can see us . . ." And suddenly she bursts out laughing in such a delightful way that you've got to be stronger than iron not to kiss her again. But now they are already out in the street and must be content with squeezing each other's arms and snuggling up to each other.

All this—they are both convinced—will cease abruptly the moment they get married. The happy couple therefore does not even want to think about it . . .

From the standpoint of practicality, it definitely does not pay for them to get married. Harry's fifteen dollars a week makes him a real "sport." He owns three suits, one of them "made to order" for twenty-five dollars. One suit he bought ready-made for fifteen dollars. And one, for which he paid ten dollars, he wears to work. As for neckties, in addition to the one Ida bought him, he owns six of them—they still look brand new—plus three others that only have to be ironed, except for the red one, which he wears on May First and sometimes when there is a strike demonstration.[4]

And collars? He must have two dozen of them. As soon as a new style of collar comes out, Harry is the first to buy three. Even dress shirts, which are a more expensive item—he has two that are part silk, and one a hundred percent silk, that he bought on sale. And shoes—he has two pair, black for winter, tan for summer, and sandals for sunny days when he goes to Coney Island.

For a single man, fifteen dollars a week is real money. You even have some left over for cultural things. Every day Harry buys two newspapers—a radical

3. From the Yiddish saying *Es brent dos hitl afn kop fun a ganef* (The hat burns on a thief's head).

4. The red necktie symbolizes Harry's socialist politics. "May First": May Day, the day on which the political Left, including the Jewish Bund, or Jewish Socialist party, and Communists, traditionally held demonstrations.

one, where they write about his working-class interests, and a "Jewish" one, where the interests of his mother and father in the Old Country are discussed. Sundays he buys *The World*, which costs more—a whole nickel. The World runs beautiful pictures, which he clips out and gives to Ida. For himself he takes the faces of pretty actresses and keeps them in his vest pocket to show to his friends in the shop.

In a word, as a single man, Harry lives comfortably. He has everything a "sport" of his status needs, and he still has enough left over to take Ida out a couple of times a week purely for pleasure.

And his greatest pleasure is to sit with Ida in a restaurant and order "the best"—strawberries with sour cream in the summer, or a baked apple with sweet cream in the winter . . . And when he gets the two checks from the waiter, he adds up the totals, which usually amount to no more than forty cents and no less than twenty-five. And like a true sport, he leaves a nickel on the table for the waiter. Then he lets Ida go out first, while he stops at the cashier's, which signifies, "Ida, you go on ahead. Paying the check is *my* business . . ." And after he pays it, Harry has a feeling of pride, as after a very important accomplishment.

Out on the street again, Ida's curiosity gets the better of her and she asks:

"Harry, did it cost very much?"

And he answers with a wave of the hand:

"A trifle . . ."

But in that very reply one can hear the pride of a man who can afford to pay for what his lady wants.

Then Ida puts her dainty hand in the crook of his arm and they take a leisurely walk to the moving-picture house. Here again he stops at the cashier's booth, puts down two nickels for two tickets and the treat is on him again.

This entire process of "treating" makes Harry feel not only proud but gallant, and he carries it off with ease, even with a certain grace.

Ida accepts all these treats as part of the natural order of things: of course the man should pay the bill. But afterward she comments:

"You know, Harry, sometimes I feel like I want to pay for *you* . . ." This comment is punctuated with a little laugh, and she adds: "Yes, sometimes I want to treat *you*!"

But for Harry, the idea is insulting. From the expression on his face you would think that a belief he holds sacred has been violated.

"That's nonsense, Ida! Out of your seven dollars a week you're going to treat *me*?"

"Well, of course," Ida stammers in embarrassment, "not now. Of course not. But later on, when I start working at dresses and earn fifteen dollars—"

"You? Fifteen dollars a week?" There is a trace of mockery in his tone.

"Certainly! Why not? You think a girl can't earn fifteen dollars a week?"

"Well," he grumbles, "maybe there are some who can, but what do *you* need it for?"

And when Ida starts telling about her future fifteen dollars a week wages, Harry listens, shakes his head, smiles, and as though jealous of this manly sum, he mutters:

"Get that nonsense out of your head, Ida."

"Why is it nonsense? It makes good sense to me!" And gazing into his eyes, she teases him: "Because then I will be the one to pay the cashier! I'd like to do that sometime."

Here Harry becomes really upset and cuts her off with an artificial smile: "Well, we'll see, we'll see . . ."

Finally Ida's day came. A friend of hers, after trying for a long time to get Ida into her shop where they manufacture dresses, finally succeeded and taught her the skill at which she could earn the long-hoped-for sum.

For about two weeks Ida kept it a secret from Harry. In the first place, during those two weeks she didn't even earn the full amount, since she was not yet able to finish the required number of dresses. But by the third week she had mastered the work and on Monday, when she opened her pay envelope, she counted out fifteen dollars.

That same evening she and Harry had a date. This time she was not late, not even by a minute.

Harry was amazed. "You're here on time! Is something wrong?"

"No! But I've got good news!"

"Good news? What happened?"

"Let's get something to eat first. I'm hungry . . ."

She took his arm and they headed toward a familiar restaurant nearby. On the way she stopped for a moment and, looking straight into Harry's eyes, exclaimed:

"Harry, today you're the one who's getting a treat—from me!"

Startled, he smiled feebly and said:

"Don't be foolish!"

"I'm serious, Harry." Her voice had a little heat in it. "Otherwise, this whole thing won't work. Today I am paying for our supper." And she couldn't help giggling.

Again Harry started to protest, but she interrupted him and continued nervously:

"And then I'm taking you to the theater, you understand? A real theater, not the movies. A serious play. You know where? Fifty cents a ticket. And I'm paying . . ."

Again she stopped walking and, with a happy grin on her face, took the envelope out of her pocketbook.

"Count it!" she said, handing him the envelope.

With trembling fingers he took it, opened it—a ten and a five.

"Fifteen dollars!" There was a hint of fear in his voice.

"Yes! I'm already working there! At the dresses!"

"You're a silly girl, Ida." He himself could not understand what was making him so angry.

"You're silly yourself!" she smiled. "But it's still my treat tonight!"

He trailed along after her, as if he had just learned of some terrible disaster. Ida kept laughing and joking. He could not find the right words to say to her in this strange mood she was in. Finally he muttered witlessly:

"You know something, Ida. In that case, we can get married . . ."

"Now you want to get married? Really?" She laughed out loud. "You like the idea of a rich bride? Well, wait a while. First let's save up a few hundred dollars, then I'll see whether it pays me . . ."

And looking at him to see what effect her words were having on him, she started laughing again.

This time he laughed too, but his heart wasn't really in it.

They entered the restaurant.

Still smiling, Ida beckoned to the waiter.

"It's not nice," Harry whispered into her ear. "The lady is not supposed to call the waiter. The man does that."

"It won't hurt," she said. "Today I'm playing *your* role. I've always envied you when you did it . . . Well, Harry, what do you want to eat? Get something special, for a change. I'm paying."

And although Harry knew she was only playing a game with him, he replied gravely:

"I'll just have some soup. I'm not hungry . . ."

"Whatever you wish," she said magnanimously.

After the meal she quickly picked up the two checks as soon as the waiter put them down on the table. She squeezed them triumphantly in her fist.

"All right, Ida, enough!" Harry objected. "Give me those checks."

Though there was a smile on her face, there was also a definite steeliness in her tone.

"Not on your life!" she said resolutely as she marched toward the cashier's booth.

Still smiling, Ida handed over the checks, along with a five-dollar bill. The cashier, a tall, slender brunette, stared at her quizzically. Then she looked over at Harry. The shadow of a smile passed over her face.

"For two!" said Ida, pointing to Harry. She took the change and walked proudly out of the restaurant with Harry behind her.

Outside, he was too angry to utter a word. They walked along in silence for a few minutes. Finally he blurted out:

"You just acted in such a—you insulted me."

"I did? How?"

"By paying for me."

"Then why have you been insulting *me* for such a long time?" She had stopped laughing.

"I insulted you? When?" He had no idea what she was getting at.

"Whenever you paid for me . . . You think it's really so pleasant? All the time, *you* pay? Sometimes I want the pleasure of paying. You begrudge me that pleasure? Oh, you egotistical little boys!" She was laughing again. "You still don't want us to have equal rights with you!"

Harry had no reply to this. He even smiled. Then he grew serious again. This equality business was so new and so radical that he felt threatened by it.

But that evening he held Ida in his arms tighter than usual, differently somehow, as if he were afraid of losing her.

1911, 1916

YENTE SERDATSKY
1877–1962

A prolific writer of fiction and drama, Yente Serdatsky was hardly appreciated in her day and forgotten in ours in part because she wrote with anger about desperate women—working-class women whose intelligence and energy were worn down by their dislocation in the world and their disillusionment with marriage, motherhood, politics, and intellectual pursuits.

Yente Reybman was born on September 15, 1877, in the town of Aleksat, near the city of Kovno (Kaunas), Lithuania, into a poor but respected family. Her father, a learned man who sold used furniture, provided a basic Jewish education for his daughters by sending them to an elementary school for girls taught by yeshiva students. At an early age, Serdatsky was reading widely in German, Russian, and Hebrew. Her parents' house was a gathering spot for the Yiddish poets and writers who lived in Kovno, among them Avrom Reyzen, and from these writers Serdatsky learned about modern Yiddish literature and began to read Sholem Aleichem, I. L. Peretz, and others.

At age thirteen, she was apprenticed to a seamstress and then worked in a grocery store. She married a young man named Serdatsky, had three children, and supported the family as the proprietress of a grocery store. In 1905, around the time of the first Russian Revolution, she began to write fiction. Serdatsky soon left her husband and children and went to Warsaw, where she published her first story, *Mirl,* in the daily Yiddish paper, *Der veg* (The Way). I. L. Peretz, the literary editor of that paper, encouraged her to write more and published her stories and novels in his pages.

Serdatsky left Warsaw for America in 1907, initially living in Chicago, then New York, where she set up a soup kitchen to support her prolific writing of sketches, one-act plays, short stories, tales, and dramatic pictures. She contributed to publications across the Yiddish political spectrum: the anarchist *Fraye arbeter shtime* (Free Voice of Labor), the socialist *Fraye gezelshaft* (Free Society), *Tsukunft* (Future), and Avrom Reyzen's *Dos naye land* (The New Land) and *Fraynd* (Friend). She was able to support herself with her writing when she was made contributing editor to the *Forverts* (Forward), which published her short stories regularly. In 1922, however, after a dispute over fees, Serdatsky left the paper. From then on, she lived on welfare and on monies received for renting out furnished rooms. (There has been speculation that Serdatsky survived her last years with the help of a paramour.)

Serdatsky stopped writing between 1922 and 1949, but picked it up again between 1949 and 1955, when she published approximately thirty pieces—short stories and memoirs—in *Nyu yorker vokhnblat* (New York Weekly). Her single book, *Geklibene shriftn* (Collected Writings), appeared in 1913 and contains novellas, one-act plays, short stories, tales, and legends, but its 270 pages represent a fraction of Serdatsky's oeuvre. Her later works were never collected even though, after her death, there was a call to do so by the poet Jacob Glatstein. And only one or two of her writings have appeared in English translation.

Unchanged, the story included here, is a dramatic monologue delivered by a woman on the verge of suicide. She narrates the episodes of her life, including her attempted suicide and supposed recovery, lashing out at her readers' efforts to understand the unhappiness that persists.

Unchanged[1]

You say that I haven't changed. My acquaintances say so too. Their venomous words freeze the blood in my veins. . . . They begrudge everything, often snapping, "All that pessimism just for a man." Last year, when I wanted to die, they watched my every step to keep me from doing it. Now that I want to live, they won't allow that either . . . misguided creatures!

Are you saying I now interest you? Well, of course I do. Writers in search of subject matter look for characters. A year ago, gloomy, barely able to drag my feet, I wasn't "material" for you. . . . "As if life doesn't have enough of these," you say, "haven't they poisoned the air enough?"

Shall I tell you about my life? My past? Specific periods in my life? Well, human existence is all very boring. But, I'll start like a writer.

Period number one: A summer night, a wedding in the village, I'm seventeen years old, my blond hair is loose and tied with a blue ribbon. A blue summer dress clings to my slender body. My face aflame, my eyes, blue like the dress, luminous. I soar, I dance.

A red band on the eastern horizon shines through the window. I grow tired and quietly leave the house. A bit further along is a grassy spot with a couple of trees. I lie down in the grass, lean my head against a tree trunk and fall asleep. But not for long. I feel a flash of light and open my eyes. They're bright and clear, and my heart . . . well, I ask you. Let's not talk about "heart"! How tedious the words "heart and soul" in modern talk and writing. . . . With clear eyes I see the sun unbraiding from the russet sky (even that is a cliché), the green field is flecked with gold, the village houses are like chunks of fire, the nearby lake a wine goblet. My hair is blown by a breeze and rainbow-colored by the sun. The wind makes my blue dress billow, revealing the white of a starched petticoat. . . .

But that's not all . . . not far from the lake on a large boulder sits Avrom, staring at me . . . and he looks so strange . . . so reverential. Aha, you'll likely find all kinds of comparisons: "He looks like an enchanted knight gazing at a dreaming goddess" and so on and so on.

Ha, ha! Avrom is the bridegroom's brother, a boy of about nineteen, tall, pale and very handsome. He gets up and slowly comes towards me. A ray of sun catches his hair. Lord, how beautiful he is! So, you'd like to know more?

Period number two: A large city, enormous houses, wide streets, public gardens, shops with large windows displaying an endless variety of all the good things in life. The streets are teeming: people from everywhere, decked out, shining, in their best. It holds little interest for me.

I live with three other girls in a garret. We study, we're preparing. For what? I really don't know. We already have four diplomas: one from high school, one for massage, one for administering inoculations, one for midwifery, and now, we're preparing for hairdressing. We wear misshapen shoes, shapeless hats, tattered dresses. A gas burner sits on a wooden crate in our room. Milk and bread are the greatest extravagance. . . .

I'm twenty-four now, I already have wrinkles on my forehead, around my

1. Translated by Frieda Forman and Ethel Raicus.

mouth; short-sighted, I wear pince-nez.[2] Avrom long ago faded into a "dream." He left for America to avoid induction, and married there. I scurry through the same few streets every day, but I see the life around in a fog. My head is full of textbooks and tutorials that I'm forever giving. The students are thick-skulled, their brains suspended in fat. I eat my heart out; my heart has withered and often the pain is piercing.

Well! Period number three: I'm twenty-seven. The same city, stormy days. I've been in the movement a couple of years now. I don't do anything momentous. I'm in the sanitation section.[3] Great events don't take place in our city. For every garnet-ring there are twenty hands. . . . Isn't that interesting! I go to demonstrations with ambivalence. The workers stick together; they sense I'm from another class. And the intellectuals gravitate towards the workers, particularly the women among them . . . I march with others like myself . . . well, that's human nature. . . .

The "storm" subsides. Apathy sets in. Sunflowers burst from every little corner; girls in bloom sprout as from the earth. . . . I am enveloped in darkness. An eerie fire sears my vision.

The fourth period: I'm on this side of the ocean, drawn here by Avrom. I didn't want to disrupt his family life, heaven forbid. I wanted only to glimpse at a shadow of my former happiness. And perhaps . . . who knows? Who can penetrate the hidden corners of the human heart . . . ! Avrom is "well off." Fat and handsome, he has a fat, beautiful wife, five fat, healthy children and a thriving business. Not a nerve trembled when he saw me. His nerves awash in fat as my happiness drowns in fat. . . .

I have no friends here, nor close acquaintances. A few girls from our "cell" work and study here; they dream of becoming "noyses". . . . [4]

I can't even learn the language. I'm stuffed to the gills with study. I can't work either, but I have to.

I wake when it's still dark. My clothes are the ones I brought from the old country, my shoes worn out. I slog three blocks through rain and snow to the tram, my lonely lunch under my arm. I'm uncomfortable in the shop.[5] My small hands are unsuited to the work and my nerves give me no rest. I produce very little and in the evening, I come back broken. I spend very little time in my room: the Missus is busy with little children and the Mister[6] goes to meetings every night.

I belong to no organization here. Fed up with them. There are lots of books on my windowsill but I can't read them. As if I haven't read enough! Every day I grab a couple of newspapers. Some days I seem to discover treasures in them, consume even the advertisements . . . and other times, I leaf nervously through one paper after another tossing them one by one to the ground.

2. Eyeglasses that clip to the nose. Circa 1905, the narrator has moved from her girlhood village to the city, where she and her friends struggle to survive on their own, learning a trade, fighting the restrictions that prevent Jews from attending the university, and joining the anticzarist revolutionary movement.

3. Probably a division or committee within the local chapter of the Jewish Bund, to which the narrator belongs. "Sanitation section" may literally refer to the menial tasks of cleaning up after a meeting or figuratively refer to an ideological "cleansing."

4. I.e., the Yiddish-accented pronunciation of the English word *nurses*.

5. I.e., sweatshop, factory.

6. The narrator's landlords; she is a boarder in their apartment.

I have few acquaintances and even these few avoid me. No wonder: their zest for life vanishes when they look at me.

But who owes me anything? Who actually denied me a rich, beautiful, golden past? I hold no-one responsible; expect nothing of anyone.

When you're young, there comes a moment to seize your fortune by the beard. Miss that moment, and it's lost. . . .

Suddenly, my few girlfriends begin to drop by morning and evening. They whisper secretively with my Missus . . . they've guessed my thoughts. . . . Ha, can they really hold me back?

The thought of suicide came to me like an old friend. Somehow, it seemed that I'd been living with it for years. I don't believe you literary types who think you can penetrate the insides of a suicide; you prattle mountains on the subject. I felt only dreadful fatigue, the strongest desire for rest. I wasn't even romantically inclined; I didn't deck my room with flowers nor dress myself in bridal clothes—as depicted in your novels. I hadn't combed my hair for days, hadn't taken off my shoes. The room, cluttered with books and newspapers, was neither swept nor tidied. My dress was still damp from the rain; I just dropped on the bed as I was. But not before I had carefully sealed all the cracks and turned on the gas.

And now the fifth period: They pried open the door and rescued me. After that, relatives turned up. One brought me a present, a dress; the other, a suit; the third, a blouse. And suddenly, I acquired girlfriends. They sprouted like mushrooms. And, listen to this: boyfriends too . . . ha, ha! And he, my current one, was among them.

Now, as you see, my room is decorated with white curtains and the "deadly" gas has a milk-glass shade that spreads a lovely glow. We live together. I am arrayed in my relatives' gifts.

I glow, you say. Well, of course. He's young and handsome. Tender and refined. I am his wife, his goddess, his ideal. He loves me with the purity and innocence of first love. His kisses would revive a corpse. His embraces. . . . You detect the shadow of sadness in my eyes? Well of course. One step beyond our happiness gapes the dreadful maw of disaster. Soon I'll again have to reach for the gas. This time, tragedy will come from my own circle. They didn't expect this: that he would fall in love with me, and so passionately. . . .

And now they all dislike me. Everyone dislikes the unfortunate, but the fortunate they dislike even more. . . . It seems I owe everyone something, particularly the girls. I, the pessimist, faded, no longer young, ought not to appropriate such a handsome young man.

This wouldn't bother me either; true happiness is beyond such trivia. But they crawl like worms into my very being; no sooner have they finished their supper than one by one they arrive. They fill my small room to suffocation. They smoke, they chatter; a sea of platitudes chokes the air. And should he touch me, they eye both of us with venom, scorn. They probe and criticize and hold forth and sit there half the night. . . .

Their main topics are love, "variety," and so on. He's still so young . . . he's often lost in thought. . . . He hasn't really lived yet. . . . And I! Oh, I'm so far from him . . . and so afraid of his awakening.

It's almost six o'clock . . . he's coming soon. . . . Go in good health; happiness is brief and tremulous . . . fearful of a stranger's eye. . . .

After all, it's not as though you are my friends. Let me be. Leave me alone with my small happiness . . . !

Yiddish, ca. 1910–1922

LAMED SHAPIRO
1878–1948

Modeling his work after Chekhov and Flaubert, Lamed Shapiro wrote compressed, metaphorical fiction that unsettled readers with its dispassionate juxtaposition of beauty and terror, illuminating the workings of the human psyche.

Levi Yehoshua Shapiro was born on March 10, 1878, in the town of Rzshishtshev in Kiev Province, the Ukraine, and spent his childhood there with his parents and two older half brothers. Although raised in a traditional Jewish setting, the young Shapiro wrote poems in Russian as well as Hebrew and Yiddish.

From the beginning, Shapiro's life was peripatetic. An ambitious writer, he went to Warsaw in 1896, struggled for two years, then returned to the Ukraine, where he taught, survived a pogrom, and fell in love. The romance ended, and Shapiro attempted suicide. He was then conscripted into the czar's army but was released and went to Odessa, where his first published work appeared—a joke in a Russian newspaper.

Returning to Warsaw in 1903, Shapiro, with the support of I. L. Peretz, published his first literary works: a short story, *Di fligl* (The Wings), in 1903; a longer story, *Itsikl Mamzer* (Little Isaac the Bastard), in 1904 in an annual edited by Avrom Reyzen; and another story, *Boom-boom-boom,* in Peretz's journal *Yudishe bibliotek*, also in 1904. These and other stories gave him standing in the world of Yiddish literature. As an advocate for Yiddish, he entered into the literary debate of the time between proponents of the two Jewish languages, Yiddish and Hebrew.

Because of the pogroms and unrest of 1905, Shapiro departed for America, sojourning in London, where he was befriended by the Hebrew writer Yosef Ḥaim Brenner. He arrived in New York in 1906, publishing there a series of shocking fictions about pogroms: *Der kush* (The Kiss, 1907); *Shfoykh khamoskho* (Pour Out Thy Wrath, 1908); *Der tseylem* (The Cross, 1909); *In der toyter shtot* (In the Dead Town, 1910).

After attempting to open a restaurant in Chicago and failing financially, he left America for Warsaw in 1909, where he worked for a year as a journalist and translated into Yiddish novels by Victor Hugo, Sir Walter Scott, and Charles Dickens. With his wife, Freydl, he opened a restaurant in Zurich, which soon failed, and returned to New York in 1911. There the Shapiros attempted yet another enterprise—a vegetarian restaurant, which his fellow writers of the Yunge frequented until it, too, went under.

In 1919 in New York, he published his two greatest pogrom stories: *Di yudishe melukhe* (The Jewish State) and *Vayse khale* (White Challah). Based on the postwar pogroms led by Symon Petlyura during the Ukrainian civil war in 1918–19, both appeared in a volume called *Di yudishe melukhe*. The title story juxtaposes a Jewish community in its idealized state before a pogrom with the corporeal and spiritual wreck of the individuals who comprise it after the catastrophe. *White Challah,* first published in *Shriftn* (Writings), one of the Yunge miscellanies, tells of the events leading up to a pogrom and of the pogrom itself from the point of view of the voiceless Gentile Vasil. Unable to articulate his own suffering as a brutalized child and as a soldier overwhelmed by the chaos of war, the victim, Vasil, becomes a murderer and devours the flesh of a Jewish woman.

In 1920, under the pseudonym Y. Zolot, Shapiro became literary editor of the communist journal *Funken* (Sparks). After moving to Los Angeles with his family in 1921 and in failing health, he attempted to invent a method of producing color film. Between 1921 and 1928, he completed only two short stories and a book of poems, *Fun korbn minkhe* (From the Women's Prayer Book), in memory of his wife, who died in 1927. In 1928, Shapiro, now an alcoholic, returned to New York, where he began to write again. In 1929, a second edition of *Di yudishe melukhe* appeared. A new collection of short stories, *Nyu-yorkish*, was published in 1931.

For about six months, Shapiro served as an editor of the new publication *Vokh* (The Week) and founded a quarterly, *Studio*. He was also involved with the Communist party in the 1930s and, in 1937–38, worked for the WPA's Federal Writers' Project. He returned to Los Angeles in 1939. His last book, *Der shrayber geyt in kheyder* (The Writer Goes to Elementary School), a collection of essays that delineates a sophisticated theory of Yiddish literature, was published in 1945. At his death in Los Angeles on August 25, 1948, Shapiro left an unfinished novel, *Der amerikaner shed* (The American Demon).

White Chalah[1]

1

One day a neighbor broke the leg of a stray dog with a heavy stone, and when Vasil saw the sharp edge of the bone piercing the skin he cried. The tears streamed from his eyes, his mouth, and his nose; the towhead on his short neck shrank deeper between his shoulders; his entire face became distorted and shriveled, and he did not utter a sound. He was then about seven years old.

Soon he learned not to cry. His family drank, fought with neighbors, with one another, beat the women, the horse, the cow, and sometimes, in special rages, their own heads against the wall. They were a large family with a tiny piece of land, they toiled hard and clumsily, and all of them lived in one hut—men, women, and children slept pell-mell on the floor. The village was small and poor, at some distance from a town; and the town to which they occasionally went for the fair seemed big and rich to Vasil.

In the town there were Jews—people who wore strange clothes, sat in stores, ate white *chalah*, and had sold Christ.[2] The last point was not quite clear: who was Christ, why did the Jews sell him, who bought him, and for what purpose?—it was all as though in a fog. White *chalah*, that was something else again: Vasil saw it a few times with his own eyes, and more than that—he once stole a piece and ate it, whereupon he stood for a time in a daze, an expression of wonder on his face. He did not understand it all, but respect for white *chalah* stayed with him.

1. Translated by Norbert Guterman. "Chalah": the braided loaf of bread baked especially for the Sabbath by Jewish women. It is made from refined white flour instead of the coarser, darker flour used to make the daily black bread.

2. From a church teaching, dating to the 4th century C.E., which held that Judas Iscariot's betrayal of Jesus Christ to Pontius Pilate, leading to the Crucifixion, bestowed a legacy of guilt upon all Jews in subsequent generations. This was the basis for many acts of anti-Semitic violence for centuries. In 1965, Pope John XXIII rescinded that teaching and exonerated the Jews from this charge. "Wore strange clothes": Jews in the Ukraine wore clothing that differed from their non-Jewish neighbors. Jewish men and married women kept their heads covered at all times; men wore long beards and earlocks (*peyes*), long, dark gabardine coats (*kapotes*), and knee-length trousers.

He was half an inch too short, but he was drafted, owing to his broad, slightly hunched shoulders and thick short neck. Here in the army beatings were again the order of the day: the corporal, the sergeant, and the officers beat the privates, and the privates beat one another, all of them. He could not learn the service regulations: he did not understand and did not think. Nor was he a good talker; when hard pressed he usually could not utter a sound, but his face grew tense, and his low forehead was covered with wrinkles. *Kasha* and borscht,[3] however, were plentiful. There were a few Jews in his regiment—Jews who had sold Christ—but in their army uniforms and without white *chalah* they looked almost like everybody else.[4]

2

They traveled in trains, they marched, they rode again, and then again moved on foot; they camped in the open or were quartered in houses; and this went on so long that Vasil became completely confused. He no longer remembered when it had begun, where he had been before, or who he had been; it was as though all his life had been spent moving from town to town, with tens or hundreds of thousands of other soldiers, through foreign places inhabited by strange people who spoke an incomprehensible language and looked frightened or angry. Nothing particularly new had happened, but fighting had become the very essence of life; everyone was fighting now, and this time it was no longer just beating, but fighting in earnest: they fired at people, cut them to pieces, bayoneted them, and sometimes even bit them with their teeth. He too fought, more and more savagely, and with greater relish. Now food did not come regularly, they slept little, they marched and fought a great deal, and all this made him restless. He kept missing something, longing for something, and at moments of great strain he howled like a tormented dog because he could not say what he wanted.

They advanced over steadily higher ground; chains of giant mountains seamed the country in all directions, and winter ruled over them harshly and without respite. They inched their way through valleys, knee-deep in dry powdery snow, and icy winds raked their faces and hands like grating irons, but the officers were cheerful and kindlier than before, and spoke of victory; and food, though not always served on time, was plentiful. At night they were sometimes permitted to build fires on the snow; then monstrous shadows moved noiselessly between the mountains, and the soldiers sang. Vasil too tried to sing, but he could only howl. They slept like the dead, without dreams or nightmares, and time and again during the day the mountains reverberated with the thunder of cannon, and men again climbed up and down the slopes.

3

A mounted messenger galloped madly through the camp; an advance cavalry unit returned suddenly and occupied positions on the flank; two batteries were moved from the left to the right. The surrounding mountains split open

3. Traditionally, a meat-based, beet soup. "*Kasha*": cooked buckwheat groats, often served with sour cream. A Yiddish idiom states, "Do not eat kasha with borsht" because the one is dairy and the other meat.

4. Jews, as well as all classes of Gentiles, were recruited into the Russian army to fight the Germans in World War I.

like freshly erupting volcanoes, and a deluge of fire, lead, and iron came down upon the world.

The barrage kept up for a long time. Piotr Kudlo was torn to pieces; the handsome Kruvenko, the best singer of the company, lay with his face in a puddle of blood; Lieutenant Somov, the one with girlish features, lost a leg, and the giant Neumann, the blond Estonian, had his whole face torn off. The pockmarked Gavrilov was dead; a single shell killed the two Bulgach brothers; killed, too, were Chaim Ostrovsky, Jan Zatyka, Staszek Pieprz, and the little Latvian whose name Vasil could not pronounce. Now whole ranks were mowed down, and it was impossible to hold on. Then Nahum Rachek,[5] a tall slender young man who had always been silent, jumped up and without any order ran forward. This gave new spirit to the dazed men, who rushed the jagged hill to the left and practically with their bare hands conquered the batteries that led the enemy artillery, strangling the defenders like cats, down to the last man. Later it was found that of the entire company only Vasil and Nahum Rachek remained. After the battle Rachek lay on the ground vomiting green gall, and next to him lay his rifle with its butt smeared with blood and brains. He was not wounded, and when Vasil asked what was the matter he did not answer.

After sunset the conquered position was abandoned, and the army fell back. How and why this happened Vasil did not know; but from that moment the army began to roll down the mountains like an avalanche of stones. The farther they went, the hastier and less orderly was the retreat, and in the end they ran—ran without stopping, day and night. Vasil did not recognize the country, each place was new to him, and he knew only from hearsay that they were moving back. Mountains and winter had long been left behind; around them stretched a broad, endless plain; spring was in full bloom; but the army ran and ran. The officers became savage, they beat the soldiers without reason and without pity. A few times they stopped for a while; the cannon roared, a rain of fire whipped the earth, and men fell like flies—and then they ran again.

4

Someone said that all this was the fault of the Jews.[6] Again the Jews! They sold Christ, they eat white *chalah*, and on top of it all they are to blame for everything. What was "everything"? Vasil wrinkled his forehead and was angry at the Jews and at someone else. Leaflets appeared, printed leaflets that a man distributed among the troops, and in the camps groups gathered around those who could read. They stood listening in silence—they were silent in a strange way, unlike people who just do not talk. Someone handed a leaflet to Vasil too; he examined it, fingered it, put it in his pocket, and joined a group to hear what was being read. He did not understand a word, except that it was about Jews. So the Jews must know, he thought, and he turned to Nahum Rachek.

5. This list of soldiers' names reveals the geographical and ethnic diversity of those conscripted to fight in the Russian army, including Chaim Ostrovsky and Nahum Rachek, the Jews.

6. The Russian front was in the Pale of Settlement, an area densely populated by Jews, whom the Russians expelled when the military situation became desperate. Jews were accused of disloyalty, profiteering, desiring to undermine the stability of the currency, and spying for the Austrian army.

"Here, read it," he said.

Rachek cast a glance at the leaflet, then another curious glance at Vasil; but he said nothing and seemed about to throw the leaflet away.

"Don't! It's not yours!" Vasil said. He took back the leaflet, stuck it in his pocket, and paced back and forth in agitation. Then he turned to Rachek. "What does it say? It's about you, isn't it?"

At this point Nahum flared up. "Yes, about me. It says I'm a traitor, see? That I've betrayed us—that I'm a spy. Like that German who was caught and shot. See?"

Vasil was scared. His forehead began to sweat. He left Nahum, fingering his leaflet in bewilderment. This Nahum, he thought, must be a wicked man—so angry, and a spy besides, he said so himself, but something doesn't fit here, it's puzzling, it doesn't fit, my head is splitting.

After a long forced march they stopped somewhere. They had not seen the enemy for several days and had not heard any firing. They dug trenches and made ready. A week later it all began anew. It turned out that the enemy was somewhere nearby; he too was in trenches, and these trenches were moving closer and closer each day, and occasionally one could see a head showing above the parapet. They ate very little, they slept even less, they fired in the direction the bullets came from, bullets that kept hitting the earth wall, humming overhead, and occasionally boring into human bodies. Next to Vasil, at his left, always lay Nahum Rachek. He never spoke, only kept loading his rifle and firing, mechanically, unhurriedly. Vasil could not bear the sight of him and occasionally was seized with a desire to stab him with his bayonet.

One day, when the firing was particularly violent, Vasil suddenly felt strangely restless. He cast a glance sidewise at Rachek and saw him lying in the same posture as before, on his stomach, with his rifle in his hand; but there was a hole in his head. Something broke in Vasil; in blind anger he kicked the dead body, pushing it aside, and then began to fire wildly, exposing his head to the dense shower of lead that was pouring all around him.

That night he could not sleep for a long time; he tossed and turned, muttering curses. At one point he jumped up angrily and began to run straight ahead, but then he recalled that Rachek was dead and dejectedly returned to his pallet. The Jews . . . traitors . . . sold Christ . . . traded him away for a song!

He ground his teeth and clawed at himself in his sleep.

5

At daybreak Vasil suddenly sat up on his hard pallet. His body was covered with cold sweat, his teeth were chattering, and his eyes, round and wide open, tried greedily to pierce the darkness. Who has been here? Who has been here?

It was pitch-dark and fearfully quiet, but he still could hear the rustle of the giant wings and feel the cold hem of the black cloak that had grazed his face. Someone had passed over the camp like an icy wind, and the camp was silent and frozen—an open grave with thousands of bodies, struck while asleep, and pierced in the heart. Who has been here? Who has been here?

During the day Lieutenant Muratov of the fourth battalion of the Yeniesey regiment was found dead—Muratov, a violent, cruel man with a face the color of parchment. The bullet that pierced him between the eyes had been fired by someone from his own battalion. When the men were questioned no one betrayed the culprit. Threatened with punishment, they still refused to answer, and they remained silent when they were ordered to surrender their arms. The other regimental units were drawn up against the battalion, but when they were ordered to fire, all of them to a man lowered their rifles to the ground. Another regiment was summoned, and in ten minutes not a man of the mutinous battalion remained alive.

Next day two officers were hacked to pieces. Three days later, following a dispute between two cavalrymen, the entire regiment split into two camps. They fought each other until only a few were left unscathed.

Then men in mufti appeared and, encouraged by the officers, began to distribute leaflets among the troops. This time they did not make long speeches, but kept repeating one thing: the Jews have betrayed us, everything is their fault.

Once again someone handed a leaflet to Vasil, but he did not take it. He drew out of his pocket, with love and respect, as though it were a precious medallion, a crumpled piece of paper frayed at the edges and stained with blood, and showed it—he had it, and remembered it. The man with the leaflets, a slim little fellow with a sand-colored beard, half closed one of his little eyes and took stock of the squat broad-shouldered private with the short thick neck and bulging gray watery eyes. He gave Vasil a friendly pat on the back and left with a strange smile on his lips.

The Jewish privates had vanished: they had been quietly gathered together and sent away, no one knew where. Everyone felt freer and more comfortable, and although there were several nationalities represented among them, they were all of one mind about it: the alien was no longer in their midst.

And then someone launched a new slogan—"The Jewish government."[7]

6

This was their last stand, and when they were again defeated they no longer stopped anywhere but ran like stampeding animals fleeing a steppe fire, in groups or individually, without commanders and without order, in deadly fear, rushing through every passage left open by the enemy. Not all of them had weapons, no one had his full outfit of clothing, and their shirts were like second skins on their unwashed bodies. The summer sun beat down on them mercilessly, and they ate only what they could forage. Now their native tongue was spoken in the towns, and their native fields lay around them, but the fields were unrecognizable, for last year's crops were rotting, trampled into the earth, and the land lay dry and gray and riddled, like the carcass of an ox disemboweled by wolves.

And while the armies crawled over the earth like swarms of gray worms, flocks of ravens soared overhead, calling with a dry rattling sound—the sound of tearing canvas—and swooped and slanted in intricate spirals, waiting for what would be theirs.

7. The more desperate the Russian military situation became, the more intense the government's scapegoating of the Jews. Before the Russian defeat and retreat in 1915, hundreds of thousands of Jews were expelled from their towns. Cossacks instigated pogroms against the Jewish populations.

Between Kolov and Zhaditsa the starved and crazed legions caught up with large groups of Jews who had been ordered out of border towns, with their women, children, invalids, and bundles. A voice said, "Get them!" The words sounded like the distant boom of a gun. At first Vasil held back, but the loud screams of the women and children and the repulsive, terrified faces of the men with their long earlocks and caftans blowing in the wind drove him to a frenzy, and he cut into the Jews like a maddened bull. They were destroyed with merciful speed: the army trampled over them like a herd of galloping horses.

Then, once again, someone said in a shrill little voice, "The Jewish government!"

The words suddenly soared high and like a peal of thunder rolled over the wild legions, spreading to villages and cities and reaching the remotest corners of the land. The retreating troops struck out at the region with fire and sword. By night burning cities lighted their path, and by day the smoke obscured the sun and the sky and rolled in cottony masses over the earth, and suffocated ravens occasionally fell to the ground.[8] They burned the towns of Zykov, Potapno, Kholodno, Stary Yug, Sheliuba; Ostrogorie, Sava, Rika, Beloye Krilo, and Stupnik were wiped from the face of the earth; the Jewish weaving town of Belopriazha went up in smoke, and the Vinokur Forest, where thirty thousand Jews had sought refuge, blazed like a bonfire, and for three days in succession agonized cries, like poisonous gases, rose from the woods and spread over the land. The swift, narrow Sinevodka River was entirely choked with human bodies a little below Lutsin[9] and overflowed into the fields.

The hosts grew larger. The peasant left his village and the city dweller his city; priests[1] with icons and crosses in their hands led processions through villages, devoutly and enthusiastically blessing the people, and the slogan was, "The Jewish government." The Jews themselves realized that their last hour had struck—the very last; and those who remained alive set out to die among Jews in Maliassy,[2] the oldest and largest Jewish center in the land, a seat of learning since the fourteenth century, a city of ancient synagogues and great yeshivas, with rabbis and modern scholars, with an aristocracy of learning and of trade. Here, in Maliassy, the Jews fasted and prayed, confessing their sins to God, begging forgiveness of friend and enemy. Aged men recited Psalms and Lamentations, younger men burned stocks of grain and clothing, demolished furniture, broke and destroyed everything that might be of use to the approaching army. And this army came, it came from all directions, and set fire to the city from all sides, and poured into the streets. Young men tried to resist and went out with revolvers in their hands. The revolvers sounded like pop guns. The soldiers answered with thundering laughter, and drew out the young men's veins one by one, and broke their bones into little pieces. Then they went from house to house, slaying the men wherever they were found and dragging the women to the market place.

8. An allusion to Exodus 13.21.
9. Although the names of the Jewish towns in this list are fictional, their authentic sound gives verisimilitude to this landscape and echoes the medieval Jewish chronicles of the massacres of the Crusades.
1. The Yiddish word here is *galokhim,* meaning Russian Orthodox or Roman Catholic clergy.
2. Another fictional place name.

7

One short blow with his fist smashed the lock, and the door opened.

For two days now Vasil had not eaten or slept. His skin smarted in the dry heat, his bones seemed disjointed, his eyes were bloodshot, and his face and neck were covered with blond stubble.

"Food!" he said hoarsely.

No one answered him. At the table stood a tall Jew in a black caftan, with a black beard and earlocks and gloomy eyes. He tightened his lips and remained stubbornly silent. Vasil stepped forward angrily and said again, "Food!"

But this time he spoke less harshly. Near the window he had caught sight of another figure—a young woman in white, with a head of black hair. Two large eyes—he had never before seen such large eyes—were looking at him and through him, and the look of these eyes was such that Vasil lifted his arm to cover his own eyes. His knees were trembling, he felt as if he were melting. What kind of woman is that? What kind of people? God! Why, why, did they have to sell Christ? And on top of it all, responsible for everything! Even Rachek admitted it. And they just kept quiet, looking through you. Goddam it, what are they after? He took his head in his hands.

He felt something and looked about him. The Jew stood there, deathly pale, hatred in his eyes. For a moment Vasil stared dully. Suddenly he grabbed the black beard and pulled at it savagely.

A white figure stepped between them. Rage made Vasil dizzy and scalded his throat. He tugged at the white figure with one hand. A long strip tore from the dress and hung at the hem. His eyes were dazzled, almost blinded. Half a breast, a beautiful shoulder, a full, rounded hip—everything dazzling white and soft, like white *chalah*. Damn it—these Jews are *made* of white *chalah!* A searing flame leaped through his body, his arm flew up like a spring and shot into the gaping dress.

A hand gripped his neck. He turned his head slowly and looked at the Jew for a moment with narrowed eyes and bared teeth, without shaking free of the weak fingers that were clutching at his flesh. Then he raised his shoulders, bent forward, took the Jew by the ankles, lifted him in the air, and smashed him against the table. He flung him down like a broken stick.

The man groaned weakly; the woman screamed. But he was already on top of her. He pressed her to the floor and tore her dress together with her flesh. Now she was repulsive, her face blotchy, the tip of her nose red, her hair disheveled and falling over her eyes. "Witch," he said through his teeth. He twisted her nose like a screw. She uttered a shrill cry—short, mechanical, unnaturally high, like the whistle of an engine. The cry penetrating his brain maddened him completely. He seized her neck and strangled her.

A white shoulder was quivering before his eyes; a full, round drop of fresh blood lay glistening on it. His nostrils fluttered like wings. His teeth were grinding; suddenly they opened and bit into the white flesh.

White *chalah* has the taste of a firm juicy orange. Warm and hot, and the more one sucks it the more burning the thirst. Sharp and thick, and strangely spiced.

Like rushing down a steep hill in a sled. Like drowning in sharp, burning spirits.

In a circle, in a circle, the juices of life went from body to body, from the first to the second, from the second to the first—in a circle.

Pillars of smoke and pillars of flame rose to the sky from the entire city. Beautiful was the fire on the great altar. The cries of the victims—long-drawn-out, endless cries—were sweet in the ears of a god as eternal as the Eternal God. And the tender parts, the thighs and the breasts, were the portion of the priest.[3]

1919

3. The Yiddish word here is *koyen* (from the Hebrew *kohein*), meaning a priest of the Temple in Jerusalem, a descendant of Aaron, brother of Moses (Leviticus 21.1–22.16). "Pillars of smoke and pillars of flame": an allusion to Exodus 13.21. "Altar": the Yiddish word here is *mizbeyekh* (from biblical Hebrew), denoting a sacrificial altar, first mentioned in Genesis 8.20. "Victims": the Yiddish word is *korbones* (from biblical Hebrew), meaning "sacrifice," "offering," "victim" (Leviticus 7.13).

JOSEPH ROLNIK
1879–1955

A decade older than the Yunge poets with whom he was associated, Joseph Rolnik was their precursor, using spare, concrete diction and imagery to create poems whose subjects were the stuff of daily life.

Rolnik was born near Minsk, in Belarus, in 1879. His father was the proprietor of a water mill, and he grew up in an isolated house in a field. He was educated at home by a heder teacher and later attended yeshiva in the city of Mir. Lured from piety by the Hebrew writings of A. Malpus, Rolnik began to write poetry in Hebrew, Russian, and Yiddish. While living in Minsk from 1895 to 1898, he sent a poem in each language to I. L. Peretz, who encouraged him to continue writing in Yiddish.

Rolnik arrived in America in the summer of 1899. A year later, he began to publish in the *Forverts*; his translations of David Frishman's Hebrew poems and twenty-five of his own poems had appeared there by the time he returned to White Russia in 1901. He wrote nothing between 1901 and 1905 but then moved from his parents' village to Minsk and began writing poems again. In 1906, Rolnik returned to the United States. Publishing poems, he survived by selling newspapers and working at other menial jobs. He was often ill and tells, in his memoirs (*Zikhroynes*, 1954), how his literary friends gathered money to send him to the Catskills to recover. In 1915, he took a job as proofreader for the newspaper the *Tog* (Day), which he held for many years.

Within a year of his return to the United States, Rolnik was publishing poems in newspapers such as the *Fraye arbeter shtime* (Free Voice of Labor) and in literary journals, miscellanies, and anthologies in New York, Warsaw, and Odessa such as *Yugnt* (1907), Avrom Reyzen's *Dos naye land* (The New Land), *Tsukunft* (Future), and *Di naye heym* (The New Home). Even though he published numerous poems and, in 1915, *Literatur un lebn* (Literature and Life), edited by the Yunge poets Mani Leyb and Reuven Iceland, devoted a special issue to his work, Rolnik felt an outsider. *Shriftn*, the Yunge miscellany, refused to publish his poems. He expressed his poetic malaise in the long poem cycle *Hafiz,* modeled on an English translation of this fourteenth-century Persian poet's works; the cycle appeared in Joseph Opatoshu and I. J. Schwartz's rival collection *Di naye heym* in 1919.

Rolnik's poems, in balladlike quatrains or rhymed couplets, portray a sensual life in both the Russian countryside, where milkmaids sit, knees apart, and mock a lascivious steward, and on the Lower East Side, where the poet drowses in the library of the Educational Alliance. Two of the poems included here, *Home from Praying* and *The First Cigarette*, convey the pleasures of transgression.

Poets[1]

We have such plain faces
and talk quite ordinary talk;
the glow from our eyes is sober,
our joy altogether commonplace.

When we go in to eat, we sit down
in work clothes at the table set for us,
and when we bury someone close
it's on a day like any other.

Half asleep in the cold dawns, we hurry
to get under the whip on time,
and we drive away the young little poems
like the house dog who tries to come running along.

ca. 1914, 1935

Home from Praying[2]

The air was always damp and cool
when we hurried from the house.
The sun beat on the mill roof,
but shadow still slept in the lanes.
In our Sabbath best, our cuffs rolled up,
we walked, away from the roads and over the fields
to the next village, the Jewish estate there,
to gather for holiday services.
And stumps of trees spread across
the meadows and tripped our feet,
but we sang our prayer book out
and leapt from stump to stump like boys.
Going back, we took the longer way,
over mountains and valleys, valleys and mountains.
And when we got home
with dusty feet and dry tongues,
at first sight
we didn't recognize the barn and bridge,

1. Translated by Irving Feldman. This poem is one of fourteen sections of a sequence called *Poetn* (Poets).

2. Translated by Irving Feldman. The Yiddish title, *Fun davnen*, means literally, "From Praying," as the translator has interpreted it; it could also mean "Of Praying" or "About Praying."

the mill and house,
coming as we did from a different side
and at such an odd hour.

ca. 1914, 1941

The First Cigarette[1]

My first Sabbath cigarette between my lips[2]
one frosty Friday night
didn't taste awfully good.
I snorted and I coughed
but had to give it a drag.
This I took to be my first transgression.

So too Shloime Raskoser's son
got up from his mother's Sabbath table
to eat pig at the Gentile's place.[3]
But that sensitive young kid
couldn't stomach stale pork—
he gagged and felt sick.

And all our young generation,
we were loud with foul talk
behind girls' backs and women's dresses.
We troubled the sleep of the pious,
knocking store signs over,
and did lots of things we didn't like,
all because we wanted to rouse God's wrath—
being pricked on by our sixteen years
the way ripe oats will prick a horse.

And God who watched over us all,
God against whom we talked with such impudence,
sat there on his throne in heaven
and laughed into his deep white beard.

ca. 1914, 1948

1. Translated by Irving Feldman.
2. Traditional Jews are prohibited by Jewish law from lighting a fire on the Sabbath since it is considered work (Exodus 31.14–15)—and, hence, from smoking cigarettes.
3. The laws of kashruth prohibit Jews from eating pork because, even though the pig has a cloven hoof, it does not chew its cud (Leviticus 11.3, 11.7–8, Deuteronomy 14.6, 14.8).

SHOLEM ASCH
1880–1957

A controversial figure in Yiddish literature and perhaps the most widely translated of the Yiddish writers (along with Sholem Aleichem and Isaac Bashevis Singer), novelist and playwright Sholem Asch wrote both naturalist works that pushed the limits of taste in Yiddish literature, with their examination of Jewish crime, sex, and greed, as well as romanticized versions of history that include shtetl characters, medieval Jewish martyrs, and New Testament figures.

Asch was born in Kutno, Poland, in 1880. His father, who was descended from a family of ritual slaughterers, was a scholar and philanthropist who earned his living as a sheep dealer; his mother, who came from a scholarly family in Łęczyca, was a much younger second wife. One of ten siblings and stepsiblings, who ranged from pious Hasidim to rough-and-tumble secularists, Asch was singled out by his parents as a potential rabbi and was sent to the best heder in town and then to the study house. At sixteen, he began to read Hebrew literature of the *Haskalah* (Jewish Enlightenment) and the German classics. When he was seventeen, rumors circulated that he had converted to Christianity, and Asch left home, taking refuge with relatives in a village, where he tutored children and observed how the Gentile Polish peasants lived. Two years later, he moved to Włocławek, where he earned his living as a letter writer for illiterates. These experiences taught him lessons he could not learn from books. He began to read Tolstoy and I. L. Peretz's Hebrew poems.

Reading led Asch to writing—first in Hebrew. Then he discovered Peretz's Yiddish stories *Shtrayml* (Fur Hat) and *Bontshe shvayg* (Bontshe the Silent). In 1900, he went to Warsaw to show his writings to Peretz, who convinced him to write in Yiddish. That same year, Asch published his first short story; over the next three years, other stories and sketches appeared in Yiddish and Hebrew periodicals. His first book of Yiddish short stories was published in Warsaw in 1903, the same year that he married Matilda Shapiro, daughter of a writer in Hebrew and Polish, who had a tremendous influence on Asch's subsequent work. In 1904, he published his first major work, the novel *Dos shtetl* (The Shtetl), in the journal *Fraynd* (Friend); it came out in book form in 1905 in Minsk and depicted traditional Jewish life in a highly romanticized manner. In 1904, he also published his first play, *Tsurikgekumen* (Return), in Hebrew and Yiddish; it was then translated into Polish and produced in Kraków. This play was published as a book, *Mitn shtrom* (With the Stream), in 1909. Asch's second play, *Meshiakhs tsaytn* (The Time of the Messiah), was published in Vilna in 1906 and was translated immediately into Polish, German, and Russian, and mounted in St. Petersburg and Warsaw. He published stories, sketches, and notes on the Russian Revolution of 1905. Asch's play *Got fun nekome* (God of Vengeance), published in 1907, was performed worldwide. It shocked its European audiences with its setting in a Jewish brothel and the explicitly sexual love between the proprietor's daughter and one of the prostitutes. The proprietor, hoping to preserve his daughter Rivkele's purity, buys a Torah and places it in her room, but God takes vengeance when Rivkele makes love to the prostitute, causing her father to desecrate the Torah. Although first performed in Berlin in a 1907 production by Max Reinhardt, this play had a strong effect upon the American audiences who watched it in English on Broadway in 1923 until it was banned and the producer and leading actor fined. In 1996, *God of Vengeance* was retranslated, and, in 1998, a new production was mounted in New Haven, Connecticut.

Another play, *Shabtay tsvi* (Sabbatai Zebi), about the seventeenth-century Jewish mystic who claimed to be the Messiah, was read by a group of writers in Berlin in 1908 but was considered too sexually controversial to stage. This was followed by a collection of short stories revealing Asch's raw realism, which contrasts with the romanticism of *The Shtetl*. In his later works, the two styles merged.

A versatile writer, Asch wrote travel sketches and historical biblical narratives, and translated the Book of Ruth into Yiddish in 1910.

He visited America for the first time late in 1909 and there produced his first comedy about immigrant life in America: *Der landsman* (The Countryman). He returned to Poland and, between 1910 and 1914, published numerous works of fiction, poetry, and drama. Two novels appeared in 1913 and 1914—*Meri* (Mary) and *Der veg tsu zikh* (The Way to Oneself)—which represent his efforts to establish the form of the Diaspora novel, presenting a broad social and cultural portrait of Jewish life in a variety of countries and cities. Asch traveled throughout Europe in these years, settling for a while in Paris, but he returned to New York when World War I broke out in 1914, becoming a naturalized citizen in 1920.

In New York, his fiction was serialized in the *Forverts*, and in 1916 his novel, *Motke ganef* (Mottke the Thief), appeared. In 1918, Asch published the novella *Uncle Moses*, which examines the meaning of America to immigrant Jews and the price they paid for becoming Americanized. In 1932, Yiddish theater actor and director Maurice Schwartz produced and starred in a film adaptation of *Uncle Moses*, one of the first Yiddish talkies. The novel was published in an English translation by Elsa Krauch in 1938. In his first American years, Asch also published fiction about the effect of the First World War on Jews in Europe, short stories about America, and more plays. His famous historical novel about the 1648–49 massacres of Jews in the Cossack uprisings led by Bohdan Khmelnytsky, *Kidush hashem* (Sanctification of the Name), appeared in 1919 in reaction to the 1918–19 pogroms led by the Ukrainian nationalist Symon Petlyura. An English translation was published in 1926. In 1920, twelve volumes of Asch's collected works were published in New York.

Asch returned to Poland in 1921, where his play *Mottke the Thief* was the season's hit, with hundreds of performances throughout Poland. He stayed in Warsaw for an extended period from 1924, where he was involved in political and cultural controversies. During the 1920s, he published five plays, three social novels about Jewish American life, and two historical novels about Jewish martyrdom during the Spanish Inquisition.

Living primarily in Poland and Germany during the 1930s, Asch published prolifically. He was honored with an award from the Polish Republic in 1932 and became honorary president of the Yiddish PEN Club. His trilogy of novels about all classes of Jewish life in Russia and Poland before World War I and the Russian Revolution appeared in 1929–31 and was followed by a psychological novel, *Gots gefongene: der goyrl fun a froy* (God's Captive: The Fate of a Woman), in 1933 and, in 1934, a novel of Jewish spiritual life, *Der tehilim-yid* (The Psalm Jew), which was translated into English under the title *Salvation* that same year. In 1937, Asch published a novel about Germany on the eve of Hitler's coming to power, *Baym Opgrunt* (At the Precipice), and in 1938 *Dos gezang fun tog* (The Song of the Day), about pioneer life in the land of Israel.

In 1938, Asch returned to New York, where he composed his Christological novels and his essays that argued for the shared historical and theological bases of Judaism and Christianity. With these works, Asch intended to expose contemporary anti-Semites as betraying early Christianity. His trilogy of novels about the life of Jesus was so controversial in the Jewish world that the books appeared in English translation before they were published in Yiddish: *The Nazarene* came out in English in 1939 and in Yiddish in 1943; *The Apostle* (1943) and *Mary* (1949) came out in English, only. The American press lauded the books; the Jewish press (Yiddish, Hebrew, and English) condemned both the works and their author as apostate, proselytizing, and traitorous. Asch defended his identity as a Jew and his freedom of expression as a writer in *What I Believe* (1941) but was shunned and kept from publishing in the Yiddish press.

Asch continued to publish prolifically. Two novels, *East River* (1946) and *A Passage in the Night* (1954), are about assimilated American Jews; the short stories collected in *The Burning Bush* (1946) tell of the Nazi atrocities; *Moses* (1951) is another biblical-historical novel, as is *The Prophet* (1955), which presents the spiritual life of the prophet in the Second Book of Isaiah.

Asch lived out his last years in Israel but died suddenly in London in June 1957. At least twenty-six of Asch's books were translated into English in the United States—from *America* in 1918 through *The Prophet* in 1955.

God of Vengeance[1]

YANKL TSHAPTSHOVITSH, *the "Uncle," a brothel owner*
SORRE, *his wife (a former prostitute)*
RIVKELE, *their daughter, a young girl of about seventeen*
HINDL, *first girl in the brothel, thirty-something years old, showing her age*
MANKE, *second girl, still quite young*
REYZL, *third girl*
SHLOYME, *a pimp, Hindl's bought fiancé, a handsome guy of twenty-six*
ELI, *a matchmaker and go-between for Yankl*
AARON, *an orthodox Jew, a scribe*
A STRANGER *looking for a bride for his son*
A JEWISH WOMAN *with one eye (among the paupers)*

TIME: The present.[2]
PLACE: A large provincial town in Russian Poland.

ACT ONE

UNCLE YANKL'S *private apartment is on the main floor of an old wooden house, over the basement, where his brothel is located. An exterior wooden stairway, from which footsteps and creaking can be heard, leads up to his home. The large living room has a low ceiling, and the furniture is in the chintzy, contemporary Warsaw style, clashing with the old house. The walls are covered with girlish embroideries of Biblical scenes, "Adam and Eve at the Tree of Knowledge," etc. The front door is in the rear of the stage; to the right, the door to* RIVKELE'S *room. To the right of the door, two beds against the wall are puffed high with bedding. To the left, two small, low windows with curtains and interior shutters, flowerpots on the ledges. Between the windows, a glass cabinet. Under one window, a chest of drawers. The room is in the last stages of tidying and cleaning—apparently, company is expected. There are extra benches and tables, the latter set with baskets of baked goods and other kinds of food. It is an afternoon in early spring.*

SORRE (*Tall, slender, graceful, her features quite hardened, yet with traces of her former beauty; there is something brazen about her tone. She wears a marriage wig over her coquettish curls, which slip out from time to time. Her matronly clothes, though subdued, are adorned with jewelry. In her movements, she is still partly rooted in the world she came from. She is standing with* RIVKELE.)

RIVKELE [*An attractive young girl with long braids, she is dressed very nicely*

1. Translated by Joachim Neugroschel (1996). 2. I.e., 1907.

and respectably in a short, girlish dress. She is just finishing up the room, attaching paper flowers to the curtains.]: There, Mama. Now I'll decorate the mirror. Look, Mama, won't it be beautiful?

SORRE [*Busy at the table*]: Faster, darling, faster. Father's already gone to arrange for some fine people to bring home the Torah scroll.

RIVKELE: It's going to be beautiful, guests will be coming. . . . We'll play music, we'll sing. . . . Won't we, Mama?

SORRE: Yes, my dearest. This is a dedication ceremony, it's an act of great piety, a great *mitzvah.*[3] Not everyone can afford a handwritten copy of the Torah. Only a respectable and affluent person, a man of distinction.[4]

RIVKELE: And there'll be girls coming too? We'll dance? Really, Mama? [*Pause.*] Then I'll have to buy a blouse, Mama, and a pair of white dancing slippers. [*Points to her gaiters.*] You can't dance in high-button shoes, can you?

SORRE: When you get married at Passover, with God's help, I'm going to make you a long gown and buy you white slippers. Girls will come, fine Jewish girls, respectable daughters, and you'll all become friends.

RIVKELE [*Stubbornly*]: You're always putting it off 'til Passover. I'm already grown up. [*Preens in front of the mirror.*] Look, Mama, I'm already grown up. [*Points to her hair.*] I've already got such long braids. Manke says— [*catches herself.*] And Manke's coming too? Really, Mama?

SORRE: No, my dearest. Only decent girls, respectable girls. You're a decent and respectable girl.

RIVKELE: Why won't she come, Mama darling? Manke drew a Star of David for me on the vestment for the Torah scroll. And now I'm stitching it with silk thread and I'm decorating it with leaves and flowers. You'll see how beautiful it is, Mama. [*Points to the embroideries on the wall.*] A hundred times more beautiful than those embroideries.

SORRE [*Startled.*]: Oh my God! Don't tell Father. He'll be furious, he'll hit the ceiling!

RIVKELE: Why, Mama? It's for the Torah scroll, isn't it?

SORRE: He'll have a fit! [*Footsteps are heard.*] Shhh, Rivkele, he's coming.

YANKL [*From the stairway*]: Do they think I'm gonna beg? The hell with them! [*Enters. A tall, tough man of about forty, with a potbelly and a trimmed round, black beard covering his face. His voice is loud, his speech vulgar, his gestures are coarse. When he talks to someone, he grabs the person's lapel. Yet there is something frank and open about his face and his entire person.*] If they don't come, who needs them? I've invited a whole slew of paupers. I'm not worried. We'll find enough customers for our cakes and our goose. [*Sees* RIVKELE, *sits down.*] Come to your papa.

SORRE [*Angry, but tries not to show it. Serves the food*]: Do they think they'll ruin their reputation by visiting you? When they need to hit you up for a hundred rubles for charity, they're not the least bit ashamed. A goy may be *treyf*, but his cash is *kosher.*[5]

3. Literally, commandment; here, a good deed (Yiddish, from the Hebrew).

4. That Yankl, the proprietor of a brothel, has commissioned a new Torah scroll to be handwritten by a scribe is an unusual undertaking. Only a whole community or an exceptionally wealthy and honorable man would have the means to pay for this immense task.

5. Ritually fit for use, in accordance with Jewish law (Yiddish, from the Hebrew *kasher*). "Goy": Gentile (Yiddish, from the Hebrew *goy*, "people," "nation"). "*Treyf*": nonkosher, forbidden (Yiddish, from the Hebrew *treifah*).

YANKL: Look how tense you are! There's no reason to be upset. Don't worry, nothing will be spoiled. [*Calls* RIVKELE *over.*] Well, come to your papa.

RIVKELE [*Goes over to him very reluctantly*]: What do you want, Papa?

YANKL: Don't be scared, Rivkele, I won't hurt you. [*Takes hold of her hand.*] Don't you love your papa?

[RIVKELE *nods her head.*]

YANKL: Then why are you scared?

RIVKELE: I don't know.

YANKL: Don't be scared of your papa. Your papa loves you, he loves you very much. I've ordered a handwritten Torah, it's costing me a fortune, but I'm doing it for you, my child, for you. [RIVKELE *remains silent. A pause.*] And when you get married, with God's help, I'll buy your husband a gold watch with a gold chain—half a pound of gold. Your papa loves you very much. [RIVKELE *drops her head. Pause.*] Don't be bashful. Marrying is perfectly proper, it's God's will. [*Pause.*] There's nothing to be bashful about. Everyone gets married. [RIVKELE *remains silent.*] Well, do you love your papa?

RIVKELE [*Nods her head, murmurs*]: Yes.

YANKL: Well, what do you want me to buy you? Tell me, Rivkele. [*She doesn't answer.*] C'mon, tell me, don't be scared. Your papa loves you. Rivkele, tell me, what should I buy you? [RIVKELE *remains silent.*]

SORRE [*Busy at the table.* To RIVKELE]: Well, cat got your tongue? Your papa's talking to you.

RIVKELE: I don't know. . . .

SORRE [*To* YANKL]: She'd like a silk blouse and a pair of white dancing slippers.

YANKL: I see. So you'd like a silk blouse and a pair of white dancing slippers? [RIVKELE *nods.*] You deserve them. [*Reaches into his pocket, pulls out a gold coin and hands it to her.*] Here, give this to Mama. She can buy them for you. [RIVKELE *takes the money, brings it to her mother. There is a commotion on the stairway, the* POOR GUESTS *are arriving.*]

YANKL [*To* SORRE]: See, you said [*opening the door*] you wouldn't have any guests. [*Calls.*] Well, come right in, come right in.

PAUPERS [*A whole gang of* PAUPERS, *men and women, file in, at first one by one, as if sneaking in, then more and more, shoving, crying out, some calling sarcastically to* YANKL]: Good day, Mr. Tshaptshovitsh. [*Turning to* SORRE] Good day to you, Mrs. Tshaptshovitsh. [SORRE *puts on an apron, fills it with challahs, rolls, cakes, and other food, distributes it to the* PAUPERS.]

A PAUPER: A long life to the mistress of the house. May God grant you many more celebrations.

WOMAN: May the Torah scroll bring blessings and prosperity to your home.

YANKL [*Throws pieces of challah to the poor, after* SORRE]: Give each one a pound of cake and a bottle of whiskey to take home. Let them know that I'm really celebrating today. Don't worry, we can splurge.

ONE-EYED WOMAN [*Praises the host and hostess to the other* PAUPERS]: What a place this is! So help me, no one ever leaves here empty-handed. There's always a bit of broth if you're sick or a shirt if you're needy.

You don't think you'll get anything from the rich people who live in tall buildings, do you? [SORRE, *as if not hearing the* WOMAN's *words, puts some more food into her apron. The* WOMAN *opens her apron wider and keeps talking.*] And when they throw a party here, then it don't matter who you are, it don't matter whatcha do.

OTHER GUESTS [*To one another*]: It's true, I swear. It's true, I swear. . . .

YANKL [*Produces a handful of change and puts it in* RIVKELE's *apron*]: Distribute it to these poor people. [RIVKELE *distributes the change to the* GUESTS.]

ONE-EYED WOMAN [*More boldly, pointing to* RIVKELE]: Just show me a more decent girl in the entire city. [*To the other* WOMEN]: Even rabbis ain't got such wonderful kids. [*More softly, but still loud enough for* YANKL *and* SORRE *to hear.*]: And God only knows how they got such a decent girl. Imagine being brought up in a home like this—may God forgive me for saying so. [*Aloud*]: And they guard her like the apple of their eye. They watch every step she takes. It's a joy looking at her. [*Goes over to* YANKL.] Don' worry, word gets around! [*Points to* RIVKELE.] I wish I had a son who was a rabbi, I'd have him marry her!

OTHER WOMEN [*Among themselves*]: You said it. . . . You said it. . . .

YANKL: Just wait and see when I lead her to the bridal canopy—with God's help! You'll get whole geese, whole live pikes jingling with rubles, I swear, or my name isn't Yankl Tshaptshovitsh.

ONE-EYED WOMAN: I tell you, it's like she grew up in a synagogue. . . . Chaste, beautiful, more decent than all the other respectable daughters.

OTHER WOMEN: You said it. . . . You said it. . . .

YANKL [*Handing out glasses of whiskey to the* GUESTS, *remarks casually, almost inadvertently*]: Even though her father is Yankl Tshaptshovitsh.

SORRE [*Distributing food*]: My, oh my, what a fine audience to boast to!

YANKL [*Talking all the while, he hastily fills the whiskey glasses*]: I don't care if you're rich or poor, everyone should know, the whole town should know. I am what I am. [*Points to his wife.*] And she is what she is. It's all true, all of it. But they'd better not say anything against my child, or I'll crack their heads open with this bottle. I don't care if it's the rabbi himself. She's purer than his own daughter. [*Points to his throat.*] Or you can slash my throat!

SORRE [*Stops distributing*]: C'mon, we've heard it all before. We've heard it before. [*Brushes off her hands and looks for the broom in the corner of the room.*] The place has to be tidied up for the fancy guests we've got coming. [*Turns to the* PAUPERS.] Not a bad idea, don't you think?

PAUPERS: No, Ma'am. Bless you and our very best to you. . . . [*They file out, offering their good wishes.* YANKL *tosses them more food behind his wife's back.*]

SORRE [*Speaks to* RIVKELE *loud enough for the* PAUPERS *to hear*]: C'mon, Rivkele, go and finish the vestment for the Torah scroll. Eli will be here soon, and so will the scribe. [RIVKELE *goes to her room at the right.* YANKL *is left alone with* SORRE.]

SORRE [*Alone with* YANKL, *she sweeps the floor*]: Some audience you were boasting to—the crème de la crème, I tell you. Do you think they wouldn't 've shown up anyway? Throw a party every day and they'll come every day. In decent homes, people know how to behave so they'll get respect. Not like you, letting people get chummy on the spot. How respectable is that anyway?

YANKL: You want respectable people coming here? I guess you've forgotten who we are.

SORRE: Who we are? Why? Who've we robbed? You run a business. Everyone's got a business. You don't force anybody. A man can run any kind of business he likes so long as he doesn't hurt anybody. Why don't you try and offer them some money—they'll take it by the handful.

YANKL: They'll take from you but they'll treat you like a dog. In synagogue you stand by the door, but you're never called up to read from the Torah.

SORRE: You really think they're better than you? C'mon, you don't have to suck up to them. That's what the world's like today: If you've got money, a devout and respectable Jew like Eli walks in and gets a nice big donation out of you. He doesn't ask you how you got your money. You can cheat, you can rob—so long as you've got it. Nothing else matters!

YANKL: Don't go climbing too high, Sorre—you hear me? Not too high. You might suddenly fall and break your neck. [*He wags his finger ominously.*] And don't be pushy, I tell you, don't try to force yourself on other people. You've got a place to live—stay there. You've got bread—eat it. But don't try to go where you're not wanted. Every dog should know its own kennel. [*Leaves the table. Waves his hand.*] I'm starting to regret getting involved in this whole business. I'm scared that it's all gonna come crashing down around our ears.

SORRE [*Stands still, arms akimbo*]: And you call yourself a man! You should be ashamed of yourself! I'm a woman and I can say that what's past is past, gone, flown away. We can face anyone without being ashamed. No one in the world is any better than us! People would have to walk around with lowered eyes. [*Approaches him.*] Once you've got enough money, you can shut your business down, and no one'll give a damn. Nobody has to know what you used to be.

YANKL [*Mulling*]: That would be best. . . . [*Pause.*] I could buy a stable of horses, export them like Ayzikl the trucker. . . . Be somebody. . . . So people won't keep gawking at me as if I were a thief.

SORRE [*Mulling*]: Too bad for the business. You won't make such a pretty penny with horses. Now at least you're raking it in hand over fist.

YANKL: True enough.

SORRE [*Goes into the other room, returns with a pile of dishes, places them around the table.*] And look, we have a daughter who's more decent than all the respectable girls in town. She'll marry, she'll have a decent husband, decent kids. . . . You see? It could be a lot worse.

YANKL [*Gets up to scold her*]: Oh yeah, if *you* keep watching over her! [*Angry.*] Go on, let Manke come up and visit her! Why don't you let her stay here with you!

SORRE: Just listen to him bellow, will you! I asked Manke to come up here only once—to teach Rivkele how to embroider. She's ready to marry, after all. We have to think about her trousseau. Is there anyone she can make friends with? You won't even let her out into the street. [*Pause.*] But if you don't want Manke up here, then that's fine with me.

YANKL: I don't want her up here—do you understand!? I don't want any mixing between my home and the basement. [*Points down.*] They have to be separated, like pure and impure, like *kosher* and *treyf*. Downstairs [*points down*] there's a brothel and up here there's a pure bride-to-be—do you hear!? [*Pounds his fists on the table.*] A pure bride-to-be! I want her separated from what's below! [*Footsteps can be heard mounting the stairway.*]

SORRE: Whatever you say! Just don't yell! [*Pricks up her ears.*] Shush! Someone's coming. It must be Eli. [*She tucks her stray curls under her wig, pulls off her apron.* YANKL *smoothes out his beard, adjusts his coat. They station themselves by the door, waiting for the visitors. The door opens wide.* SHLOYME *and* HINDL *enter.* SHLOYME *is a tall, powerful man of twenty-six. He wears high boots and a short jacket. His movements are coarse. When talking he winks roguishly.* HINDL, *a prostitute showing her years, wears clothing that's too youthful for her. Her face is washed out. They boldly swagger in as if they were at home.*]

YANKL [*To* SORRE]: Get a load of my guests. [*To* SHYLOYME.] I don't do business up here. Only downstairs, everything downstairs. [*Points to the basement.*] I'll go down.

SHYLOYME: Whatta ya carryin' on about, huh? You ashamed of us or sump'n?

YANKL: Well, what can I do for you?

SHLOYME: You're throwin' a li'l party today, right? So we stopped by to congratulatcha. We're old buddies, ain' we now?

SORRE: Some "old buddies!"

YANKL: That's history. As of today it's over. If you have any business with me, we'll take care of it downstairs. [*Points to the basement.*] Up here I don't know you and you don't know me, starting today. You can have a shot of whiskey, that's all. [*Fills a glass for each of them.*] But make it snappy, I'm expecting someone.

SHLOYME [*Takes the drink and says derisively to* HINDL]: Hey, marriage is a great institution, it turns you into a solid citizen, like all the others. You sponsor handwritten Torah scrolls, you don' hang out wit' pimps and hookers, the way you do. [*To* YANKL.] Listen, I'm followin' your lead. I got engaged today to this broad here. [*Points to* HINDL.] Won't she make a great housewife? You'll see, once she puts on her marriage wig, she'll look as pure as a rabbi's wife—so help us both.

YANKL: Let's hope for the best. So you two got engaged? And when's the happy wedding day?

SORRE: Get a load of who he's chatting with! What an honor! With scum—if you'll pardon my French. And the scholar and the scribe are gonna show up any moment.[6]

SHLOYME: You wanna know when the weddin's gonna be? When do guys like us get hitched? I'll find me a coupla broads, have a weddin', and start a brothel of my own. What else can a guy like me do? It's too late for me to become a rabbi. But she's gotta be special, she's gotta be as hot as hell. [*Winks at him.*] If not, why bother?

YANKL: And so what do you want from me?

SHLOYME: What do I want from you? Very little. [*Points to* HINDL.] She's

6. The scribe has written out the entire text of the Pentateuch on a vellum scroll, making no errors. When a Torah is completed, there is traditionally a ceremony to dedicate it before it is used.

your girl, right? And she's my fiancée. She's got a complaint. [*Takes* HINDL's *wage book from her.*] From now on, you'll deal with me. Today I only want a trifle. Ten rubles on account. [*Slaps the book.*] Don' worry, she's good for the money. [*Glances sideways at* HINDL.] She wants ta buy herself a new hat.

YANKL: Downstairs, I tell you, downstairs. I'll go downstairs, and we'll take care of all our business. Up here I don't know you. I don't have any business with you up here.

SHLOYME: It don' matter to me either way—upstairs or downstairs. The guy down there is no stranger and the guy up here is no stranger. It's all the same to me, ya know.

YANKL: [*Angry*]: Move your ass outta here! Get lost—do you hear? I'm expecting someone.

SORRE: The hell with them, God damn it—coming up and spoiling our party. [*Glares at* HINDL.] It's not worth getting upset over that chicken shit.

HINDL: [*To* SORRE] If you don't think I'm a good hooker, you can peddle your own ass.

SHLOYME: [*To* HINDL]: Tell her she can send down her daughter. [*To* SORRE.] She'll be great for business, I swear.

YANKL [*Goes over to* SHLOYME]: You can insult me, do you hear? [*Points to his wife*] You can insult her, we're all birds of a feather. But don't ever pronounce my daughter's name—or I'll slice your goddamn guts out. Do you hear? She doesn't know you, and you don't know her.

SHLOYME: Then I'll get to know her, we're in this together, we're family.

YANKL [*Grabs* SHLOYME *by the neck*]: I'll slice your goddamn guts out! You can slug me, you can kick me, but don't ever pronounce my daughter's name. [*They struggle.*]

SORRE [*Runs over*]: Goddamn it! Fighting with scum. Guests can come any moment. . . . Oh my God! Yankl! It's Eli and the scribe. Yankl, Yankl, for God's sake! [*Drags him away.*] What's wrong with you? [*Heavy footsteps are heard from the outside staircase.* SORRE *drags* YANKL *away.*] Yankl, Yankl, Eli is here, and the scribe is here. You're disgracing us in front of decent people!

YANKL: No, let's finish it right here and now! [*Still holding* SHLOYME.]

ELI'S VOICE [*From the door*]: Here we are, Aaron. This is where the sponsor lives. [*He appears in the doorway, first sticking his head in with his big pipe in his mouth.*] What's all this commotion? When a man sponsors a Torah that's handwritten by a scribe, his house should be filled with rejoicing, not fighting. [*Withdraws his head into stairway.*] Forgive me, scribe. [*Upon hearing* ELI's *voice,* YANKL *lets go of* SHLOYME. SORRE *hurries over and hands* SHLOYME *a banknote she's gotten from a stocking. Then she pushes* SHLOYME *and* HINDL *toward the door. There they bump into the* SCRIBE *and* ELI, *who recoil from touching a woman as they let the couple through.*]

SHLOYME [*To* HINDL *as he leaves*]: Getta load a' the kinda people he's hangin' out wit' now. Just wait, he's gonna become a councilman some day. [*He leaves, still talking on the porch.*]

ELI [*A short fat man, speaks quickly, with ingratiating gestures, at ease, bold, self-assured*]: If you please, Aaron, if you please. [*Softly, to* YANKL *and*

SORRE.] You ought to act a little more respectable, it's about time. Decent people are visiting you.

SCRIBE [*Enters, a tall, old, bespectacled man with a long, white, wispy beard, his lank, scraggy figure in a spacious coat. Remains aloof and mysterious.*]

ELI [*Pointing to* YANKL]: This is Mr. Tshaptshovitsh, the sponsor of the Torah scroll.

SCRIBE [*Holds out his hand while sizing up* YANKL]: Sholem-aleykhem,[7] Sir.

YANKL [*Holds out his hand uneasily.* SORRE *respectfully draws back.*]

ELI [*Sits down at the table after pulling over a chair for the* SCRIBE]: Go sit down, Aaron. [*To* YANKL.] Have a seat. [YANKL *remains standing, unsure of himself.*] This is the man I ordered the Torah for. [*He pulls over the liquor bottle and fills a glass for the* SCRIBE, *then for himself.*] He doesn't have a son, so he wants to serve God with a copy of the Torah. It's a Jewish custom, and it's good of him to observe it, so we ought to help him. *L'khaim*,[8] Aaron. Drink up. [*Extends his hand to* SCRIBE, *then to* YANKL.] *L'khaim*, Patron, drink up. After all, this is your day to rejoice. [YANKL *shakes his hand uncertainly.* ELI drinks. SORRE *comes over to the table and places some preserves near* ELI. YANKL *tugs at her jacket, signaling her to move away from the table.*] Drink, Scribe. Drink, Patron. This is a red-letter day for you, God has helped you. And if you sponsor a handwritten Torah, you are performing a pious deed, a wonderful mitzvah.

SCRIBE [*Holding his glass, asks* ELI *about* YANKL]: What sort of man is he?

ELI: What's the difference? An ordinary Jew. He's no scholar—does every Jew have to be a scholar? If a Jew wants to do something pious, a mitzvah, we should lend a hand. [*To* YANKL] Drink up, man. *l'khaim*, you ought to be celebrating.

SCRIBE: Does he know how to conduct himself with a holy book?

ELI: Why shouldn't he know? He is a Jew, isn't he? And what Jew doesn't know what a Torah is? [*Drinks*] *L'khaim, l'khaim*. . . . May the good Lord grant better times for Jews.

SCRIBE [*Shakes hands with* YANKL]: *L'khaim*, Patron. [*To* SORRE.] Remember, a Torah scroll is a wonderful thing, it holds up the entire world.[9] And every Torah is like the Tablets of the Law that were handed down to Moses at Mount Sinai. Every line is penned in purity and holiness. And if a home has a scroll of the Torah, then God is also there. For that reason alone, it should be kept free of all contamination. [*To* YANKL.] Sir, you should know that a Torah scroll—

YANKL [*Terrified, stammers*]: Rabbi. . . . Rabbi. . . . I'll tell the rabbi the whole truth. I'll tell him. . . . I'm a sinful man. . . . Rabbi, I'm scared . . .

ELI [*Cuts in, to* SCRIBE]: This man is a penitent, so we have to help him, the Talmud says so very precisely. And why shouldn't he know what a Torah scroll is? He is a Jew, after all. [*To* YANKL.] A Jew has to respect a Torah scroll, you have to revere it, just as if a great rabbi were in your home. You mustn't speak any insolent words if there is a Torah in your home, and you have to be pious and modest. [*Speaks to* SORRE, *looking*

7. Hello; literally, "Peace unto you" (Yiddish, from the Hebrew).
8. "To life," a toast (Yiddish, from the Hebrew).
9. Simon the Just, one of the last survivors of the Great Synagogue, used to say, "Upon three things the world is based: upon the Torah, upon the Temple service, and upon the practice of charity" (*Pirke Avot* [Sayings of the Fathers] 1.2).

toward her but not at her.] A woman may not uncover her hair if there is a Torah in the room. [SORRE *tucks her stray curls inside her wig.*] She may not approach the Torah with bare arms. If these rules are observed, then nothing can go wrong in a home that has a Torah scroll. The family always enjoys good fortune and prosperity, and they are protected against all evil. How can anyone say this man doesn't know? These are Jews, after all. [SORRE *nods.*]

SCRIBE: Sir, you heard him. The most important things in the world depend on the Torah, it contains the very existence, the very survival of the Jewish people. A single word, Heaven help us, a single word could disgrace the Torah, and then a huge calamity, Heaven help us, could descend on all Jews—God have mercy on us!

YANKL [*Gets up from the table*]: Rabbi, I'll confess everything. Rabbi [*walks over to him*], I know you're a holy man. I'm not worthy of your presence here, under my roof. Rabbi, I'm a sinful man, she [*points to his wife*] is a sinful woman. We don't have the right to even touch a Torah scroll. Rabbi, in there. . . . [*Points to the left-hand door.*] For her, Rabbi. [*Goes into* RIVKELE's *room and brings her out by her hand. In her other hand she holds a velvet scroll-vestment, on which she is embroidering a Star of David with gold thread.*] Rabbi, she has the right to take care of the Torah. She's as pure as the Torah itself. It's for her, Rabbi. I ordered the handwritten scroll for her. [*He points to her embroidery.*] Do you see, Rabbi? She's embroidering a vestment for the scroll. She has the right to do it. Her hands are pure hands, there's nothing *treyf* about her. I, Rabbi, [*taps his heart*] I won't touch your Torah scroll. She, Rabbi, [*points to his wife*] she won't touch your Torah scroll. But she, Rabbi, [*places his hand on* RIVKELE's *head*] she will take care of it. I'll place the Torah in her room. [*To* RIVKELE.] And when you get married and leave us, you'll take the precious Torah along to your husband's home.

ELI: So you're saying that when the time comes, you'll give your daughter the Torah scroll as her dowry, right?

YANKL: Eli, when my daughter marries I'll give her a huge dowry, a mountain of money, and I'll say to her: "Leave your father's home and forget. Forget your father. Forget your mother. And have pure, decent children, Jewish children, like every Jewish wife." That's what I'll say to her.

ELI: So you intend to present the scroll as a wedding gift to your daughter's bridegroom, right? [*To the* SCRIBE.] You see, Aaron? There are still real Jews left in the world. A Jew has a daughter, and he orders a handwritten Torah for her future husband. How beautiful this is, how wonderful this is. I tell you, Aaron, Jewishness. . . . Jewish. . . . Ahh. . . . Ahh. . . . [*Smacks his lips.*]

YANKL [*Takes* RIVKELE *back to her room and closes her door.*] Rabbi, I can speak frankly in front of you, we're alone, and my wife can hear it too. Rabbi, we are sinful people. I know that God will punish us—let him punish us, what do I care? He can chop off my legs, he can cripple me. He can make me a beggar. But not my daughter. [*More softly.*] Rabbi, when a son does something horrible, then the hell with him. But a daughter, Rabbi. . . . If a daughter does something sinful, then it's as if your own mother were sinning in her grave. So I went over to the synagogue and I walked up to the scribe and I said to him, "Give me something to protect my home against sin." So he says to me, "Commission a Torah and put the scroll in your home." Our souls already belong to the devil, Rabbi, so I'm going to place the Torah in her room. Let her take care of it. We don't dare.

[ELI *leans over toward the* SCRIBE, *whispering and gesturing, pointing to* YANKL *who waits with* SORRE *near the table. Pause.*]

SCRIBE [*After thinking briefly*]: And where are the other guests? Who else is going to pay their respects to the Torah?

ELI: Let's go to the synagogue. We'll get together ten men for the minyan[1]—we'll find some Jews who'll pay their respects to the Torah. [*Stands up from the table, fills the glasses, and slaps* YANKL *on the back.*] C'mon, c'mon. God will help. Enjoy yourself, Patron. God helps penitents. Don't worry, you'll find a scholarly husband for your daughter, a poor yeshiva student. You'll support them, and he'll devote himself to studying the holy Torah, and God will forgive you for the sake of the Torah. [*Pause.*] I've done a little thinking about it, and I've got a boy in mind, a wonderful boy, with brains. The father is a very decent and respectable man. [*Interrupting himself.*] Are you offering a big dowry?

YANKL: Rabbi, take everything from me. I'll give you the shirt off my back. Everything. Everything. And the boy doesn't have to deal with his father-in-law, his mother-in-law. I'll take care of everything on the sly. Here's your food, here's your drink. Just keep studying your holy books. I won't know you, and you won't know me.

ELI: It will be all right. The holy Torah will take care of it. C'mon, Aaron, c'mon, Patron, let's go to the synagogue. We'll gather a minyan and we'll rejoice in the Holy Book. [*To* SCRIBE.] Do you see, Aaron? Even if a Jew sins, he remains a Jew all the same. A Jewish soul is looking for a son-in-law, a Talmudic scholar. [*To* YANKL.] Don't worry, don't worry, God will help. God loves a penitent—but you have to make donations for the indigent scholars. If you can't be a scholar yourself, then you have to support a scholar, *al Toyre Oylem Oymeyd,* "the Torah holds up the world"—Isn't that so, Aaron? And why not? [*Referring to* YANKL.] Goodness, I knew his father, a very decent man. He was a drayman[2]—and a very good Jew. Believe me, God will help, and this man will become as good a Jew as any Jew in the world. [*To* YANKL.] But mainly, you must repent truly and fully—that is, you have to follow a different path from the one you were taking. . . . And you have to support scholars.

YANKL [*Approaches* ELI, *bolder*]: Eli, let me squirrel away a little money so I can give my daughter a nice dowry—and I'll close down my business, or my name isn't Yankl Tshaptshovitsh. I'm gonna start dealing in horses, the same business as my father, may he rest in peace. I'll set up a stable, I'll go to the Lovitsh market. And my son-in-law will sit in there, right in that room, and study the holy writings. And when I come home on *Shabbes,*[3] I'll sit down right here and I'll listen to my son-in-law murmuring the Talmudic passages. I'm telling the truth or my name isn't Yankl Tshaptshovitsh!

1. The group of ten men needed for communal Jewish prayer (Yiddish, from the Hebrew).
2. Wagon driver (*balegole*, Yiddish, from the Hebrew). Connotes an uneducated, rough class of person.
3. Sabbath (Yiddish, from the Hebrew).

ELI: Don't worry, don't worry, God will help you, God will help you. Isn't that so, Aaron?

SCRIBE: Who can say? Our God is a God of mercy, a God of compassion—but He is also a vindictive God, a God of vengeance. [*Goes out.*] Well, it's getting late. Why don't we go to synagogue? [*Exits*]

YANKL: What did the rabbi mean?

ELI: Don't worry, don't worry, God will help. He has to help. Come, Patron, come. Go pick up your Torah scroll and bring it home and celebrate. [*He starts walking.* YANKL *hesitates, at a loss.* ELI *notices his confusion.*] What? Do you want to tell your wife to prepare something for us when we come back with the scroll?

SORRE [*To* ELI]: It's all prepared, Sir, it's all prepared.

ELI [*To* YANKL]: Well, what are you waiting for? The scribe has already left.

YANKL [*Stands by the door, unsure, points his finger.*]: Should I walk through the streets with the rabbi?

ELI: C'mon, c'mon. If God forgives you, then we certainly forgive you.

YANKL [*Enthusiastic*]: Eli, you're a good man. [*Stretches out his arms to embrace him, but checks himself and holds back.*] A good man, as I live and breathe. [*They exit together. Dusk sets in.*]

SORRE [*Starts quickly straightening the room, setting the table. Calls to* RIVKELE *in the next room.*]: Rivkele, Rivkele, come and help me. They'll be here any minute with the Torah scroll.

RIVKELE [*Appears in the door, unsure of herself*]: Is Papa still here?

SORRE: No, darling, he's gone to the synagogue with Eli and the scribe to bring back some people. The rabbi will also be coming.

RIVKELE [*Holds up the scroll vestment*]: See how nicely I've embroidered it?

SORRE [*Busy*]: I see. Comb your hair, get dressed. The minyan's on its way. The rabbi. . . .

RIVKELE: I'll call Manke to come up and do my hair. I love it when she combs my hair. She does it so beautifully, my hair gets so straight. Her hands are so cool. [*She takes an object and taps on the floor, calling.*] Manke, Manke!

SORRE [*Frightened*]: What are you doing, Rivkele? Don't! Papa's gonna holler. It's not proper for you to be friendly with Manke. You're the daughter of respectable parents and you're gonna get married soon. You're being offered matches, fine matches with Talmudic scholars.

RIVKELE: I love Manke so much.

SORRE: It's scandalous for you to be friendly with Manke. You're a respectable child and you ought to make friends with respectable children. You're being offered matches, fine matches. Papa is having a look at a possible bridegroom for you. Eli said. . . . [*Goes into the other room*] You've gotta wash up and get dressed. The guests will be here any moment.

RIVKELE: A bridegroom? What's he like, Mommy?

SORRE [*From the other room*]: A darling boy, a treasure. And a marvelous scholar, from a wonderful family.

[MANKE *appears in the opposite doorway, first poking her head in, her finger coquettishly beckoning to* RIVKELE. RIVKELE *steals over to* MANKE, *winking at her. The room starts growing dark.*]

RIVKELE [*Hugs* MANKE, *while talking to* SORRE *in the next room*]: Is he good-looking, Mommy?

[MANKE *kisses* RIVKELE *passionately*]

SORRE [*From the other room*]: Yes, dearest, a good-looking bridegroom, with black earlocks, and he's got a satin coat and a velvet cap, he dresses like a rabbi. In fact, Eli said that his father's a rabbi.

RIVKELE [*In* MANKE's *arms, stroking* MANKE's *cheeks*]: Where is he going to live, Mommy?

SORRE [*From the other room*]: In your room, where we'll keep the Torah scroll. The two of you will live there and he'll be studying the holy Torah.

RIVKELE [*In* MANKE's *arms*]: Will he love me, Mommy?

SORRE [*From the other room*]: Very much, my dearest darling, very much. The two of you will have respectable children, decent children. . . .

[*While they're talking, the curtain slowly descends, with* RIVKELE *in* MANKE's *arms.*]

CURTAIN

Yiddish, 1907

SIDNEY L. NYBURG
1880–1957

A lifelong resident of Baltimore, Sidney Lauer Nyburg was born into a family long established in that city. As critic Sidney F. Chyet observed in an excellent introduction to a 1986 reprint of *The Chosen People*—the only novel of the five he wrote that was about Jewish issues—he was "a scion of a comfortable family," and he and his wife "belonged to the local gentry." *The Chosen People* received respectful attention in Jewish journals, and Nyburg displayed thoughtful views on Judaism in the *Menorah Journal* a year later, but his chief career was as a corporation and business lawyer.

He took his law degree at the University of Maryland after doing undergraduate work at Baltimore City College. Civic-minded, he volunteered his time and skills in a variety of cultural and service organizations, including the Associated Jewish Charities. He was sensitive to the inequalities of the American economic system and to the exploitation of labor, and especially decried the divisions in the Jewish community based on wealth and social status. These were themes he combined and explored in *The Chosen People*.

Baltimore had been, since the 1880s, the site of vicious labor disputes in its very important garment industry—an industry largely created and controlled by Jews. The workers in the large factories were mainly Eastern European Jewish immigrants while their employers were German Jews. After many years of struggle, the Amalgamated Clothing Workers of America succeeded in unionizing the industry, shortly before Nyburg wrote his novel. The labor-capital dispute and the German–Eastern European Jewish relationship are carefully interwoven in Nyburg's work. The upper- and middle-class German Jews were, for the most part, Reform and English-speaking, while the workers were Orthodox and Yiddish-speaking. Nyburg weaves this into his novel as well.

The novel opens with an idealistic young rabbi, Philip Graetz, who has recently been hired by the congregation, delivering a Yom Kippur sermon. He is well meaning but naïve as he tries in the course of the action to get his Reform congregation to be fair to the poor workers and to recognize their union. The lawyer for the union is David Gordon, who helps to educate Graetz in the realities of the situation. Nyburg is sympathetic to the union, but nonetheless attempts to give a fair account of the employers' positions. He is also ironic about elements of Reform Judaism.

Nyburg felt that there was more to Judaism than a rationalist belief in an abstract monotheism, a religion without the traditional rituals, ceremonies, history. He even believed in some kind of *racial* bond, though the loose use of that term, common at that time, would today probably be replaced by the term *ethnic*. Among Jews, Nyburg suggests, an inveterate streak of idealism might be part of it. Our selection shows Rabbi Graetz becoming aware of the need to overcome the gap between German Jews and Eastern European Jews. He might have been better served and been a better rabbi if his training had taught him Yiddish rather than the "Higher Criticism" (that is, exploring the historical rather than the revealed basis of Torah). Although the labor lawyer Gordon makes this acerbic observation, it was very likely Nyburg's view as well.

From The Chosen People

Chapter VI

THE BROTHERHOOD OF MAN

The first incident tending to unsettle Philip's faith in himself and his work was so totally irrelevant, so completely unrelated to his own life or to the interests of his congregation, that it might easily have left a man of more phlegmatic temperament absolutely undisturbed.

About eleven o'clock one night in January he was slowly and deliberately making ready for bed. Although weary of body he was more than normally pleased with himself. He had made, this evening, at a public Emergency meeting, held in the vestry rooms of Beth El, a well-conceived and beautifully delivered plea for funds for the Jewish Charities—whose treasury had been strained almost to the point of bankruptcy by demands resulting from the violent economic changes caused by the European war.[1] He had pictured eloquently the unendurable misery existent in the city,[2] although his only knowledge of its actual details had been obtained from the routine reports of the Society's paid workers. The tangible results of his words in Dollars and Cents had been amazingly gratifying—even to the Society's skillful managing director, who had shrewdly decided, as he put it, "to play the new Rabbi as a trump card." Philip had done a good evening's work. Many unfortunate creatures would escape lack of food and shelter, because of the compelling force of his thought and imagination. Incidentally, this virtuous deed had been one which would entail pleasant personal consequences to himself. There are few of us—however contemptuous in theory of the shallow admiration of our fellows—who could have returned home from such a meeting without a comfortable glow of self-satisfaction—and Philip was only twenty-four years of age—and had believed ardently in the lovable qualities of all

1. I.e., World War I (1914–18), which America entered in 1917.

2. Baltimore, Maryland.

men, even before they had begun to demonstrate these virtues by extravagant praise of himself.

The reaction after his speech left him unusually worn, and he had hurried home from the Temple to enjoy what seemed to him a well-earned night of sleep. Just as he was in that debatable stage where one is neither properly garbed nor disreputably negligee, the telephone bell rang sharply and he sprang to obey its summons.

It was a woman's voice who spoke. "Is this Rabbi Graetz?" she demanded.

When he assured her of his identity she continued in the measured tones of a competent subordinate, performing a routine duty—not unimportant—but one which demanded no display of undue excitement.

"This is the Johns Hopkins Hospital," she announced. "The Resident has ordered me to ask some Rabbi if he could come here at once to see a man in the accident ward. The patient's injuries will probably prove fatal, the doctor thinks. We know nothing of the man except that he keeps asking to see a Rabbi. Will you come?"

"Certainly," Philip answered, "immediately! I'll order a taxi. What shall I do when I reach the Hospital?"

"Go to the desk in the entrance hall and ask for Miss Watts," he was told, after which the voice extinguished itself promptly, with a business-like click of the telephone instrument.

It was certainly characteristic of Philip that he had not indulged in even an instant's hesitation before accepting his duty. There were many extenuating circumstances he might have urged as excuses for inaction. He was tired, not because of mere frivolity, but because he had been engaged in work for the good of others. It was a night of sudden and penetrating cold after a day of dull rain, and the streets were covered with a thin and treacherous sheet of ice. As a matter of fact, one of his older brothers in the Rabbinate had been given priority by the Hospital nurse in her telephoned request, and had promptly pleaded a convenient indisposition. It was to this worthy man's thoughtful consideration that Philip owed his present necessity for a hurried trip to the opposite side of the city.

After summoning a taxi-cab, by telephone, he hastily replaced his discarded clothing and descended to the vestibule of the Hotel, there to await the arrival of the automobile. It seemed abnormally long in making its appearance, but when it finally drew up to the curb, its chauffeur explained how impossible it was for any machine, even if it were equipped with chains, to make rapid progress on such a night. Philip peered through the frosty windows of the cab as it threaded its deliberate path through unfamiliar streets. He noticed with a sense of growing depression row after row of small, monotonous homes, each one exactly like its neighbor. Through his mind, in unison with the steady throb of the motor, coursed somber and unconnected fancies. He thought of his errand, and the next minute found himself wondering into which of these staid, uncharacteristic little structures Death would make his next raid, bringing into the drab lives of its occupants, perhaps, the only touch of dramatic dignity they would ever know; and next his imagination was deciding what words he could find to say by way of consolation to the strange man to whose aid he was hurrying, and who, perchance, by morning would be far wiser than himself and all other living men, with a new-found knowledge of the mysteries of Life and Death.

At last the machine came to a stop before the great pile of Hospital Buildings, and Philip dashed up the steps, and into the vast rotunda of the central building. Breathless, and taken completely by surprise, he found himself face to face with Thorwaldsen's[3] great white statue of the Christ, the arms outstretched, the face filled with Divine Compassion. So significant was this huge mass of eloquent marble that there was scarcely need for the chiseled inscription—"Come unto Me, all ye who are weary and heavy laden, and I will give you Rest."

The young Rabbi unconsciously paused, and paid full and heartfelt tribute to the memory of the Great Rabbi of Bethlehem, who has been chosen by millions as the symbol of Infinite Love, yet whose name has been invoked by myriads of false followers in justification of deeds of fiendish cruelty. "He too was a Jew, and a teacher of our faith," was the thought which flashed into Philip's mind, immediately to give place to his own characteristic idea. "After all, it is we, who will not believe Him to be more than He truly was, who understand Him best,—who can best teach the world what He meant it to know." Filled with such emotions, he remembered his own mission of helpful ministry, and making his way to the desk, introduced himself and explained his purpose. The night clerk promptly telephoned to some mysterious personage and very shortly thereafter a trim, tall, young woman, dressed in stiffly-starched blue, came to his side and beckoned him to follow her. It was difficult to believe one could walk so great a distance without passing beyond the confines of the Hospital. Along many corridors, Philip was led by his guide. Each hall, with its dim lights reflected upon the brightly-polished floor, seemed almost deserted, yet somehow pervaded by an uncanny air of being ever watched by tireless attendants. He had never before entered this, or any other great Hospital, and the impression created in his mind was almost one of awe. Behind each of the doors Science was at grips with disease and death. Every instant was pregnant with Fate for scores who lay in their neat, white beds, unaware whether they should return again to take up their petty, engrossing anxieties and ambitions, or mingle themselves with the dust from which they had sprung. Now and then, a nurse or orderly would glide swiftly and noiselessly into some patient's room. Once they passed a physician garbed in spotless white linen, hurrying quickly upon some duty of apparent urgency. They paused at the turn of a hallway to avoid interference with two orderlies bearing upon a narrow litter the inanimate form of a patient still drugged with ether, on his way from the operating table to some place where he would await the mysterious return of the soul, which had somehow left his body untenanted during its hour of supreme ordeal. Yet all this intense drama was enacted in an atmosphere of abnormal quiet, like the death struggle of a mouse imprisoned under the glass vacuum bell of an air pump. The Rabbi felt oppressed, impotent, his own importance completely crushed out among these silent creatures who dealt without a shadow of excitement with the issues of health and agony, existence and eternity.

During all this time the young nurse had spoken no word. Philip, as he followed her, gave another swift thought to the possibilities of the interview which lay before him. It was an unusual thing for a Jew on the threshold of

3. Bertel Thorvaldsen (1768–1844), Danish sculptor and a leader in the classical revival.

Death to seek the aid of a Rabbi. A teacher in Israel is not believed by the most credulous of his followers to posses any greater power than any other poor mortal, to pardon sin or to intercede on behalf of a conscience-stricken penitent, with an offended and outraged God. Some very practical errand, or last message, no doubt, was to be entrusted to him by a forsaken, friendless creature whose desire for a Rabbi was based upon the knowledge that in such a man he could not fail to find a Jew—and therefore, a brother.

Philip's opportunity for conjecture came to a sudden end, for his conductress turned suddenly from the corridor into a small office where at a study desk there sat, apparently awaiting the Rabbi's entrance, a vigorous young doctor dressed in the white Hospital uniform.

"You're Dr. Graetz?" he began, motioning Philip to a seat, and speaking in brisk but not discourteous tones. He did not give Philip opportunity to reply before going on to say:

"I'm Dr. Manning. I'm in charge here till morning. It's not such an appropriate night for being dragged across town, is it? Still, I thought I ought to do something about this chap. He's a Hebrew." The doctor paused slightly before using the word, as though he were anxious to choose a term bearing the least offensive significance.

At another time the minister would have explained tolerantly his preference for the word "Jew," and repelled the idea of anyone of that race being anxious to escape its implications; but now he merely nodded, and the physician continued:

"He's an accident case. Slipped tonight, on a crossing at Baltimore Street, and one wheel of a heavy auto-truck passed over his abdomen."

Philip struggled unsuccessfully to restrain a shudder of horror, and the man of medicine noticed it with professional contempt.

"You needn't get squeamish. You won't see anything to shock you. He's covered up all right!"

"It isn't that!" Philip protested feebly, but there was a definite lack of conviction in his tones.

"Well," Dr. Manning said, "they brought him in here and took him into the operating room, but the house surgeons said, at the first glimpse, he hadn't a chance. He's sure to 'go out' pretty soon, and meanwhile, all we can make out of him is the word 'Rabbi.' He says it over and over again. He's still conscious, but we can't learn his name or anything else. If he'd been an Italian or an Irishman and had called for a priest, he'd have got one, so I thought if he wanted a Rabbi I ought to try to find one for him."

"I thank you very much," Philip responded. "I hope I'll be able to make him more comfortable. Does it matter how long I stay?"

"Not a bit," the physician answered coolly. "He's got no chance anyhow. I took him off the ward and into a private room because I didn't want him to disturb the other patients too much. So make yourself as comfortable as you can, and if you want anything, ask Miss Watts to send for me. She'll take you to him at once."

The nurse, who had remained silently standing in the presence of her superior, and who would have been shocked rather than gratified had the doctor suggested her being seated during the interview, now betrayed prompt signs of returning animation.

She opened the office door significantly so that Philip would have had no reasonable opportunity for further questions even had he meditated them, and without delay, led him once more upon his quest.

A minute later she ushered him into a small room with one great window through which there was visible, against the cold brilliance of an electric street lamp, a great wind-tossed tree, every twig of which was covered with a beautiful garment of glistening ice. The gray walled room was utterly bare except for a bed, a chair, and a tiny table bearing upon it a glass of water and a nurse's chart.

The form upon the bed was covered to the chin with a white sheet, but a long, nervous, ill-kempt hand lay wearily on either side of the patient's body, and on the pillow was the head of a man whose every feature proclaimed the Jew. Not the Jew one would have expected to meet at Beth El Temple, or in Mrs. Frank's[4] elegant living-room, but one who had known misery and hatred in the Old World, and who had fled from it to experience hardship, privation and grinding poverty in free and boundless America. His long and untrimmed beard was coarse and of the blackness of charred wood. It accentuated to an almost ghost-like whiteness the deathly pallor of his brow; but his eyes, in his hour of mute despair, were fine—great, dark, intelligent eyes—which seemed haunted with a tragedy the man himself could never have expressed or understood, even when he had been vigorous and full of abundant life.

The eloquent eyes rested inquiringly upon the intruders, and the nurse spoke with the slow distinct accents one uses to children, and to men who cannot comprehend the only language one can talk.

"The Rabbi," she announced, pointing to Philip,—"the Rabbi."

The dying man's eyes lighted up with an expression of eager hope, unspeakably touching to his young visitor. This broken creature was poor, helpless and unlettered. The life he was yielding up had been sordid and unbeautiful, but still this forlorn immigrant shared with himself the wonderful traditions of the Martyr Race, and in his crude way had borne all too heavy a share of its agony. He hurried to the bedside, and grasped the weak, useless hand in his own.

Then the mangled man on the bed began to talk in harsh dry tones spoken almost in a whisper, but with headlong feverish haste. The nurse was about to leave them to their confidences, but Philip stopped her with a gesture of consternation.

He was unable to understand one single phrase the poor creature was racking his soul to utter!

Why had he not thought to ask what tongue this man could speak, or why had not the Hospital authorities made sure before sending for him, of his primary qualifications for the task? Now and then Philip caught the sound of some familiar, though mispronounced, word of Teutonic origin, but the sense of what was being told to him was utterly lost.

The Rabbi spoke German—bookishly, it was true—but nevertheless, fluently. With Hebrew also he was perfectly familiar. Of the Yiddish dialect he knew nothing at all. Had this immigrant's vocabulary been composed almost entirely of words borrowed or corrupted from the Hebrew

4. Wife of the surgeon Dr. Frank. They give a dinner party at the beginning of the novel, welcoming the new rabbi, Dr. Graetz, where he meets Ruth, Mrs. Frank's sister, who will, by the end of the novel, very likely become his wife.

and German tongues, Philip might have succeeded in piecing together the significance of the torrent of words which issued from the lips of the sufferer. But unfortunately, Yiddish is a varied and fluid mode of speech. In the mouths of wanderers from some sections of Europe, it may easily be mistaken for an ungrammatical and degenerate form of the German language.[5] Other Jews, however, speak the dialect with so many infusions of words and accents appropriated from the Russian, as to make it totally unintelligible to anyone uninitiated in its baffling perplexities.

The patient, who was now staring desperately into the Rabbi's face, had come to the scene of his death from the wrong Russian village!

Frantically, Philip began talking to the man in his own grammatical German and instantaneously, the light of intelligence left the patient's eyes, and a look of dumb, puzzled misunderstanding appeared in its place.

Again and again Philip tried his utmost to find some method of communication with the injured man. He only succeeded in awakening in his mind, to which he had intended to bring peace and comfort, a reflection of his own excitement. The guttural whisper became sullen,—almost angry—and the one word which the Rabbi could understand in the immigrant's outbursts of despairing protest was the contemptuous syllable "goy"—which he knew to be this dying man's pitiless judgment upon himself as one who was in truth no Jew at all—a stranger and an alien.

"It's no use," Philip said helplessly, turning to the nurse. "I can't find out what he wants to say. He speaks nothing but Yiddish. You should have sent for a downtown Rabbi—a Russian."

The nurse, quick to repel any blame which might be imputed to her in this unexpected dilemma, replied quickly:

"I had to use the telephone directory. Down-town Rabbis can't afford telephones. Besides, I thought any Rabbi would do."

Her voice expressed a polite contempt for a religion so loosely organized to aid its distressed communicants. Had the man been a Roman Catholic the first priest she had summoned would have been fully equipped to cope with the situation, or at least to find prompt assistance, if for some reason he had found himself unprepared for his task!

"We must find him a Rabbi who is a Russian Jew, at once," Philip announced.

"I'll take you back to Dr. Manning," replied Miss Watts, evidently determined to become entangled in no further responsibilities.

The dying immigrant had relapsed once more into his former state of despairing apathy. Philip cast upon him a last glance of mingled compassion and self-reproach and returned to Dr. Manning's office. There new perplexities confronted him. The young doctor apparently considered Philip to be disgustingly ill-equipped for his duties, and had neither comprehension nor tolerance for these delicate distinctions between various kinds of Jews. To Dr. Graetz's demand that a Russian Rabbi be procured at once, the physician responded by giving him *carte blanche*[6] to summon as many as he chose, but this permission merely disclosed

5. The author and his character express the mistaken belief that Yiddish is a dialect of modern German.

6. Literally, blank document (French); permission to do whatever you want.

another bit of deplorable ignorance on Philip's part. He was compelled to confess he did not know the name of a single minister of his own creed in the city, except those of the few fashionable up-town Temples—no one of whom he had a right to suppose more proficient in Yiddish than himself.

Dr. Manning's smile savored slightly of amused cynicism. Philip, growing more miserably embarrassed every moment, yet feeling he dared not ignore his debt to his dying brother Jew, continued to rack his brain for some available solution.

"It needn't be a Rabbi, then," he urged. "Surely there must be some one in this big Hospital who can understand Yiddish."

"There is no one of your faith on the resident staff at this time," the doctor informed him patiently, "in the day time one of the young women in the Social Service Department could interpret for you, but they're all off duty now, and even if I wanted to drag one from her home at this time of night, I wouldn't know for which one to send."

"There must be plenty of Russian Jewish patients here," Philip insisted.

"There certainly are," Dr. Manning agreed, "but we don't catalogue them by race; I can't send someone through the wards waking up sick people to ask if they can talk Yiddish. I'm afraid I've done all I can."

Philip remembered suddenly that Dr. Frank had told him how often he was called to the Johns Hopkins in the small hours of the night, and it occurred to him to announce his acquaintance with the surgeon and to suggest the possibility of his aid. The young resident thawed slightly at the mention of Robert's name.

"Dr. Frank is a member of the Visiting Surgical Staff," he explained. "He's only here when he's operating or giving after care to his patients. I'm pretty sure he isn't here now, but I'll make certain."

Miss Watts, once more pressed into service, soon reported that Dr. Frank had been in the Hospital earlier in the evening but was not expected again until morning.

The thought of Dr. Frank awoke in Philip's mind some recollection of David Gordon, whom he had not seen since the night of the dinner at the surgeon's home. Here was a man who was himself of Russian birth, who could doubtless speak Yiddish, and who would, in any event, know just what should be done.

He asked permission to use the telephone and after a few anxious minutes succeeded in awakening the lawyer, and telling him excitedly the whole distressing story. Gordon was silent for an instant after Philip had completed his narrative. The young Rabbi, fearing the telephone connection had been interrupted, exclaimed impatiently: "Hello! Hello! Are you still there? Can't you tell me what to do?"

"I'm here," was the reply he heard, "let me alone a minute. I'm only a lawyer, I have to think before I can give advice." Then a minute later he was told:

"Lubowitz would come. He lives on Albemarle Street near Pratt, but he's got no telephone, and his English is so bad you'd never make him understand what you wanted if you went for him yourself. Same thing with all the others. I could give you a dozen of their names. If you think it needn't be a Rabbi, I'll come myself."

Philip's thanks were almost incoherent in their fervid gratitude, but David Gordon cut him short with rude decision.

"All right," he snapped, "you needn't make such a fuss about it. Telephone for a taxi while I get into my clothes. My address is 1086 Madison Avenue. Sure you've got the number? Better write it down. I'll be right over."

The lawyer rang off without more formality, and Philip, after arranging for Gordon's transportation, reported to Dr. Manning the result of his efforts. The doctor had never met Gordon but knew of him as one of the city's most successful lawyers. He secretly wondered at the strange quality of these Jews who were willing to leap eagerly from their comfortable beds at the call of some pauper with no claim upon them except the tie of a common race. "And when they get here," he thought, "they haven't an idea what's to be done! Still it's odd how they stick together!"

If the dying man, less than a hundred yards away, could suddenly have awakened to health and intelligible speech, he might have expressed some doubts as to the accuracy of this Gentile generalization relating to the Solidarity of Israel. Or had the physician remained to chat with the Rabbi while they awaited Gordon's coming, he might somewhat have modified his judgment, but he had hardly motioned Philip to a chair before he was called away to a distant part of the Hospital upon some mission which appeared to permit of no delay.

"Help yourself to a book or a magazine," he suggested. "There are cigarettes on the table if you smoke. I'll be back as soon as I can. I'll tell the ward nurse as I pass, to keep an eye on your man."

Philip, left to himself, found the minutes dragged wearily. He had never learned the solace of tobacco, and the books on the doctor's shelf seemed painfully technical. He ran his eye hurriedly over their titles, only to find text books treating of every disease of which he had vaguely heard, and a few whose acquaintance he hoped never to make. Among all this mass of medical lore he found in a corner a volume written by William Osler,[7] bearing the title "Aequanimitas and Other Essays." It was impossible to have lived in Baltimore even a few months without gaining some hearsay knowledge of the great physician whose name and whose personality had become a tradition, no less potent since his removal to a foreign land than when he had been part and parcel of the city's life. Philip pulled down the book with its title so oddly at variance with his own mood. He tried to read, but the words made no impression whatever upon his confused, jarring thoughts. Equanimity seemed, like many other desirable attributes, a thing one might well exalt when one happened to have it, but which was not to be procured for the mere desire. Sometimes the dark face of the injured immigrant stared up at him with great accusing eyes from the printed page, as though asking what right he had to pose as a teacher in Israel who had no comprehension of the wants of those who would stand most sorely in need of aid. Sometimes Philip was swept by wholly ignoble emotions of damaged self-esteem. He had been made to appear supremely ridiculous, he felt,—ridiculous to himself, to this business-like sprig of a doctor, and to David Gordon, who would be none too sorry to confirm his previous scoffing beliefs regarding the inefficiency of preachers in general and himself in particular. It was unfair that

7. Sir William Osler (1849–1919), a Canadian-born physician and educator, once a resident of Baltimore.

he, who had meant so well, should be placed in such an absurd position. He had been fed on praise ever since he had entered this hospitable city, and had unconsciously learned to shrink from the very thought of mockery.

For a minute he forgot the plight of the sufferer he had come to aid, in his boyish resentment against every one and everything connected with his unheroic situation.

He tossed the book upon the table. Equanimity was not for him, he decided, as he began nervously to pace the floor. It certainly did take Gordon a long time to make the trip across town, he thought, until his watch convinced him to the contrary. He began once more to indulge in vain conjecture as to what this man who was about to die could have to impart. Nothing, in all probability, of any real consequence. Still, it would seem vital to a man about to set forth on this last mysterious voyage. To die among men whom one had never seen before and whose every action proclaimed their utter indifference to the personality one was about to lose—it *was* hard, it was worse than hard; it was robbing a man of one of those few emotional consolations which are the birthright of all of us—rich and poor—learned and stolid. Fantastic visions of his own death invaded the young minister's mind. He had always thought of his end as something impressive, dignified, as nearly approaching the sublime as was consistent with standards of restrained good taste. Now he could not repel perverse pictures of himself, stretched on some rude bed in a foreign country, dying as the result of some grotesque mishap, among strangers to whom his last words of profound significance and burning eloquence were merely a confused jumble of uncouth noises. Never before, since his childhood, had Philip feared Death. It was a climax, according to his faith, to a triumphant purposeful life. Now, however, as he strode from wall to wall, he felt actual terror at the thought. How could one sustain his beliefs in the supreme dignity of human life and death as one remembered the mangled mass of aching flesh in the near-by room, whose career had seemingly been a painful quest across half the world for bread to fill an empty belly, and whose end was the unnoticed and matter-of-fact death of a worn-out animal?

The minutes ticked themselves away. Philip, whose nights had never before been tempestuous, wondered why he had failed to realize what an eternity of time stretched between the hours of sleep and waking. Yet there were nurses here—mere girls—who kept solitary vigil every night! He stole to the door almost as though he were about to attempt some actual crime, and opening it, peered out into the long, silent corridor. If someone would only make a noise, something loud, discordant, human! But no, there was nothing to relieve this overpowering sensation of suppressed, watchful but coldly unsympathetic, activity. It was like an unearthly, hideous pantomime.

The Rabbi turned again into the office and the door swung silently closed. He was once more the solitary prisoner of his sense of duty. In the hope of distracting himself with a new sensation, he seized from the table one of the doctor's cigarettes and with some awkwardness, succeeded in lighting it. He drew into his lungs a few experimental puffs of smoke. The adventure only added to his discomfort. Without feeling actually ill, he was conscious of a slight sensation of uneasy dizziness and confusion. Remembering the necessity of possible action when Gordon should arrive, he tossed the cigarette into the ash tray and resumed his solitary pacing of the room.

It was in this state of mental and physical wretchedness that Gordon found him. The lawyer, seemingly as alert and as fully master of himself as though it were noon-day, instead of two in the morning, came briskly into the office with Miss Watts.

"Hello, Dr. Graetz," he said, "you see I'm here. Where's the patient?" he demanded of the nurse with a hint of sharp aggressiveness.

She seemed more deferential to David Gordon's crisp authority than to Philip's studious courtesy.

"I must see Dr. Manning first," she explained, almost apologetically, "then if he says so, I'll take you in at once."

But when the doctor returned, it was with unexpected news. He introduced himself to the lawyer, and without the faintest apparent emotion went on to say:

"I'm afraid you've had your night's sleep disturbed for nothing. I've just had a look at your patient. He's gone into coma. You might wait around awhile if you like, but I'm pretty sure he'll never come out."

David shrugged his shoulders without making any comment. He was, in fact, watching Philip narrowly, being perhaps more interested in noting his reaction to these tidings than in the information itself. The Rabbi was horrified, it seemed to David, out of all proportion to the magnitude of the event.

"You mean," Philip stammered, "he's going to die! going to die, without being able to talk again?"

"That's about it," Dr. Manning answered. " 'He showed more stamina, at that, than the average, else he'd never have rallied after the ether."

The three sat silent for a few minutes. Such an outcome of the night's sordid tragedy seemed incredible to Philip—now that he had succeeded in bringing the capable David to his aid. He had nerved himself to the thought of his apparent absurdity and incapacity. He was no longer able to think boyishly of himself as a being of almost supernatural power, scattering balm and spiritual peace among the poor and hopeless of his brethren—not without some remote resemblance to the compassionate Christ whose sculptured presence dominated the entrance hall below. But that it should all end in complete and final disaster—a disaster which left another to pay for his own ignorance—this was more than he felt himself able to endure.

"Pull yourself together," David ordered in a stern whisper. Then in his normal voice he said: "After all, if he's unconscious the poor devil isn't bothered about what he wanted to tell. Perhaps it's just as well."

Courteously declining the doctor's suggestion of cigarettes, and calmly proffering his own well-filled case of black cigars, he proceeded dexterously to entangle Dr. Manning in a long and intricate argument regarding the value and veracity of medical experts in legal proceedings, and the consideration—or lack of it—accorded them by courts and counsel. So absorbed did the doctor become and the lawyer appear that the Rabbi's silence seemed entirely unnoticed. Philip had only garbled impressions of what they were discussing. He was plunged into a passion of the deepest self-reproach. He knew how illogical, how morbid, he had become; but he was unable to free himself from the memory of the unhappy man who had weighed Philip and his whole life in a single instant, and condemned them with one burning word of scorn.

He never did know exactly how long the lawyer and the doctor went on talking, but at last a nurse made her way into the room with a whispered message to Dr. Manning, and Philip understood that the man was dead, and that he and David Gordon were expected to go home.

David managed the details of their departure with the same easy authority he had displayed from the minute of his appearance. It was he who expressed the appreciation of both of them, of the doctor's kindness; it was he who procured a taxi for their transit, and who piloted Philip safely through the mazes of his farewell.

When the two men were at last seated in the machine, rumbling away from the Hospital, David lapsed into silence, as he puffed meditatively upon his cigar. Perhaps he thought nothing he could say would be of much help to Philip, and the best service he could render would be to give him time to regain his poise; but when the machine halted for a minute in the bright electric glare of a street crossing, and the lawyer observed how drawn and pale was the Rabbi's face—almost as though he were in physical pain—he turned to the young man impulsively.

"Look here," he said in his decided manner, "don't let yourself get maudlin about this affair. It was neither you nor I, you know, who ran over the man, and if we'd chosen to spend the night in honest sleep we couldn't have been indicted. It's not your fault the people at your Seminary chose to teach you the Higher Criticism[8] instead of Yiddish—and maybe they knew what they were doing, at that. If your worthy President,[9] Mr. Kaufman, could know what you are thinking, he'd decide he was squandering your salary on a madman."

The Rabbi perceived the kindliness concealed behind the lawyer's brusque words, but he shook his head despairingly.

"I know," he answered, "you think I've behaved like a child——"

"Not a bit," David answered. "I think all the better of you because of the things you're ashamed of. Of course, you've no sense of humor, but if you had, you couldn't be a Rabbi at all."

Philip's eyes widened with distress at the idea of anything humorous being mingled with the night's grim happenings.

David laughed a curt, dry laugh as he read his companion's thought.

"Never mind," he said, "you'll feel better, remembering what a heathen I am."

Once more Philip shook his head.

"You can't see!" he began, "I didn't come here to talk only to rich men. I wanted to help. It isn't just this one poor fellow. I——"

"Never mind," David repeated, laying his hand on Philip's shoulder, as the machine drew up to the Hotel where the Rabbi was to alight. "I see what you mean, and you're a good sort. But there's more to it all than you thought. It wasn't only the Yiddish! You and this Russian never could have understood one another, anyhow."

1917

8. Historical study of the Bible and religion dealing with questions of authorship and dates, sources, historicity, and literary genres, rather than treating them as revealed truth. The Reform movement in Germany was deeply influenced by this movement.

9. I.e., president of the board of directors of Rabbi Graetz's synagogue.

MARY ANTIN
1881–1949

Author of *The Promised Land*, the first best-selling book, according to scholar Michael Kramer, "written by and about a Jew in America" (almost 85,000 copies were sold by the time Antin died in 1949), Mary Antin glorified the process of Americanization as a transformative rebirth and redefined the term *American* to include immigrants and their cultures.

Maryashe Antin, the second daughter among six children, was born in 1881 in Polotsk, a shtetl in the Russian Jewish Pale of Settlement. Her father, a shopkeeper, privately tutored his daughters in Hebrew until illness made the family business fail and, in 1891, he left for America. Mary served as a milliner's apprentice until 1894, when her father brought the family to Boston.

Upon her arrival in the United States, Mary immediately entered public school where she thrived, completing grammar school in four years. Quickly becoming proficient in English, Antin wrote compositions and poems that impressed her teachers, who helped her publish them in Boston newspapers. She became a famous example of American education at its best. In 1899, her first book, *From Plotzk to Boston*, was published. (Polotsk was accidentally misspelled in the book's title.) This account of her journey from the shtetl to America originated as a long letter in Yiddish that Antin had written her uncle in 1894 and, with the help of a local rabbi, later translated into English. The book sold well enough to allow Antin to attend the Girls' Latin School, an excellent Boston high school.

Before she graduated, though, she married Amadeus William Grabau, son and grandson of Lutheran clergy originally from Germany who had just earned his doctorate in geology and paleontology at Harvard. Accompanying her husband to New York City, where he joined the faculty of Columbia University, Antin, between 1901 and 1904, was able to take courses at Columbia's Teachers College and Barnard College but never completed a degree. Their daughter, Josephine Esther, was born soon thereafter.

In 1910, Antin journeyed back to Polotsk. This visit and the death of her friend Josephine Lazarus, Emma Lazarus's sister, who had long encouraged her to write her autobiography, stimulated her to begin writing *The Promised Land*. The autobiography was serialized in the *Atlantic Monthly* from November 1911 until it appeared as a book in 1912. It presents an optimistic, even inspirational, view of the Americanization of the immigrant. Through her own story, Antin contrasts the oppression of Jews in Russia with the seemingly endless opportunities that America offers them, of which education forms the heart.

Unlike her first book, *From Plotzk to Boston*, which, according to Werner Sollers, editor of the 1997 reprint, was aimed at a Jewish American audience, Antin addressed a Gentile American readership in *The Promised Land*. Like Abraham Cahan's novel *The Rise of David Levinsky* (1917), Antin's autobiography and her first published short story, *Malinke's Atonement*, set out to educate the non–Jewish American reader in the language and culture of the Eastern European Jewish immigrant. In both works, Antin, against the wishes of her editor, used Yiddish and Hebrew words, defining them in parentheses or in the glossary at the end of the book. She thus makes Gentile Americans sympathetic to the immigrants while praising non-Jewish America.

Antin published other short stories, editorial essays, and, in 1914, *They Who Knock at Our Gates*, a book that argued against proposed restrictions on immigration. In 1912, she campaigned for presidential candidate Theodore Roosevelt and, between 1913 and 1918, lectured to Jewish organizations throughout the country on ideas from *The Promised Land*, including Zionism. She socialized and corresponded with philosopher Horace Kallen and other writers and, until the outbreak of the First

World War, lived an active, harmonious life with her husband and daughter in Scarsdale, New York. By the end of the war, however, Antin suffered a breakdown when her husband, as a result of his outspoken sympathies with Germany, lost his position at Columbia and took a university job in Peking, where he spent the rest of his life.

Antin later lived in Massachusetts—at the Gould Farm in Great Barrington, a social-service community; at her family's home in Winchester; and in Boston. In her later years, she became interested in Christian universalism, the mysticism of Meher Baba, and the anthroposophy of Rudolph Steiner.

We include here Antin's short story *The Lie*. Typical of Antin, this story tells how an American education, as transmitted by a sympathetic Gentile teacher, helps a Jewish immigrant boy become American. In the process, the teacher herself learns that the Jewish desire for education exemplifies the highest level of American values, even if it depends on a lie. The episode of the immigrant father who lies about his son's age in order to ensure the child two more years of an American public education, then compulsory for children only until age fourteen, was part of an early draft of *The Promised Land* that Antin subsequently cut. The story compares the Jewish immigrants to the first immigrants—the Mayflower Puritans and the Founding Fathers—in order to refigure the meaning of America.

The Lie

I

The first thing about his American teachers that struck David Rudinsky was the fact that they were women, and the second was that they did not get angry if somebody asked questions. This phenomenon subverted his previous experience. When he went to *heder* (Hebrew school), in Russia, his teachers were always men, and they did not like to be interrupted with questions that were not in the lesson. Everything was different in America, and David liked the difference.

The American teachers, on their part, also made comparisons. They said David was not like other children. It was not merely that his mind worked like lightning; those neglected Russian waifs were almost always quick to learn, perhaps because they had to make up for lost time. The quality of his interest, more than the rapidity of his progress, excited comment. Miss Ralston, David's teacher in the sixth grade, which he reached in his second year at school, said of him that he never let go of a lesson till he had got the soul of the matter. "I don't think grammar is grammar to him," she said, "or fractions mere arithmetic. I'm not satisfied with the way I teach these things since I've had David. I feel that if he were on the platform instead of me, geography and grammar would be spliced to the core of the universe."

One difficulty David's teachers encountered, and that was his extreme reserve. In private conversation it was hard to get anything out of him except "yes, ma'am" and "no, ma'am," or, "I don't understand, please." In the classroom he did not seem to be aware of the existence of anybody besides Teacher and himself. He asked questions as fast as he could formulate them, and Teacher had to exercise much tact in order to satisfy him without slighting the rest of her pupils. To advances of a personal sort he did not respond, as if friendship were not among the things he hungered for.

It was Miss Ralston who found the way to David's heart. Perhaps she was interested in such things; they sometimes are, in the public schools. After the Christmas holidays, the children were given as a subject for composition, "How I spent the Vacation." David wrote in a froth of enthusiasm about whole days spent in the public library. He covered twelve pages with an account of the books he had read. The list included many juvenile classics in American history and biography; and from his comments it was plain that the little alien worshiped the heroes of war.

When Miss Ralston had read David's composition, she knew what to do. She was one of those persons who always know what to do, and do it. She asked David to stay after school, and read to him, from a blue book with gilt lettering, "Paul Revere's Ride" and "Independence Bell."[1] That hour neither of them ever forgot. To David it seemed as if all the heroes he had dreamed of crowded around him, so real did his teacher's reading make them. He heard the clash of swords and the flapping of banners in the wind. On the blackboard behind Miss Ralston troops of faces appeared and vanished, like the shadows that run across a hillside when clouds are moving in the sky. As for Miss Ralston, she said afterwards that she was the first person who had ever seen the real David Rudinsky. That was a curious statement to make, considering that his mother and father, and sundry other persons in the two hemispheres, had had some acquaintance with David previous to the reading of "Paul Revere's Ride." However, Miss Ralston had a way of saying curious things.

There were many readings out of school hours, after that memorable beginning. Miss Ralston did not seem to realize that the School Board did not pay her for those extra hours that she spent on David. David did not know that she was paid at all. He thought Teacher was born on purpose to read and tell him things and answer his questions, just as his mother existed to cook his favorite soup and patch his trousers. So he brought his pet book from the library, and when the last pupil was gone, he took it from his desk, and laid it on Miss Ralston's, without a word; and Miss Ralston read, and they were both happy. When a little Jewish boy from Russia goes to school in America, all sorts of things are likely to happen that the School Board does not provide for. It might be amusing to figure out the reasons.

David's reserve slowly melted in the glowing intimacy of these happy half-hours; still he seldom made any comment on the reading at the time; he basked mutely in the warmth of his teacher's sympathy. But what he did not say orally he was very likely to say on paper. That also was one of Miss Ralston's discoveries. When she gave out the theme, "What I Mean to Do When I Grow Up," David wrote that he was going to be an American citizen, and always vote for honest candidates, and belong to a society for arresting illegal voters. You see David was only a greenhorn, and an excitable one. He thought it a very great matter to be a citizen, perhaps because such a thing was not allowed in the country he came from.

1. A poem by George Lippard (1822–1854), published in the *Saturday Currier* (1847), which originated the popular belief that the Liberty Bell was rung upon the signing of the Declaration of Independence. "Paul Revere's Ride": a famous patriotic poem by Henry Wadsworth Longfellow (1807–1882) that recounts the legend of the Revolutionary War hero who warned the Massachusetts colonial rebels that the British were approaching.

Miss Ralston probably knew how it was with him, or she guessed. She was great at guessing, as all her children knew. At any rate, she did not smile as she read of David's patriotic ambitions. She put his paper aside until their next quiet hour, and then she used it so as to get a great deal out of him that he would not have had the courage to tell if he had not believed that it was an exercise in composition.

This Miss Ralston was a crafty person. She learned from David about a Jewish restaurant where his father sometimes took him, a place where a group of ardent young Russians discussed politics over their inexpensive dinner. She heard about a mass meeting of Russian Jews to celebrate the death of Alexander III, "because he was a cruel tyrant, and was very bad to Jewish people." She even tracked some astonishing phrases in David's vocabulary to their origin in the Sunday orations he had heard on the Common, in his father's company.

Impressed by these and other signs of paternal interest in her pupil's education, Miss Ralston was not unprepared for the visit which David's father paid her soon after these revelations. It was a very cold day, and Mr. Rudinsky shivered in his thin, shabby overcoat; but his face glowed with inner warmth as he discovered David's undersized figure in one of the front seats.

"I don't know how to say it what I feel to see my boy sitting and learning like this," he said, with a vibration in his voice that told more than his words. "Do you know, ma'am, if I didn't have to make a living, I'd like to stay here all day and see my David get educated. I'm forty years old, and I've had much in my life, but it's worth nothing so much as this. The day I brought my children to school, it was the best day in my life. Perhaps you won't believe me, ma'am, but when I hear that David is a good boy and learns good in school, I wouldn't change places with Vanderbilt the millionaire."[2]

He looked at Miss Ralston with the eyes of David listening to "Paul Revere's Ride."

"What do you think, ma'am," he asked, as he got up to leave, "my David will be a good American, no?"

"He ought to be," said Miss Ralston, warmly, "with such a father."

Mr. Rudinsky did not try to hide his gratification.

"I am a citizen," he said, unconsciously straightening. "I took out citizen papers as soon as I came to America, four years ago."

So they came to the middle of February, when preparations for Washington's Birthday were well along. One day the class was singing "America,"[3] when Miss Ralston noticed that David stopped and stared absently at the blackboard in front of him. He did not wake out of his reverie till the singing was over, and then he raised his hand.

"Teacher," he asked, when he had permission to speak, "what does it mean, 'Land where my fathers died'?"

Miss Ralston explained, wondering how many of her pupils cared to analyze the familiar words as David did.

A few days later, the national hymn was sung again. Miss Ralston watched

2. A member of one of America's wealthiest and most prominent families who made its fortune in transportation and finance. This probably refers to New York philanthropist William Kissam Vanderbilt (1849–1920), who supported the arts and music.

3. A popular patriotic hymn, first published in 1832, with lyrics by clergyman and poet Samuel F. Smith (1808–1895).

David. His lips formed the words "Land where my fathers died," and then they stopped, set in the pout of childish trouble. His eyes fixed themselves on the teacher's, but her smile of encouragement failed to dispel his evident perplexity.

Anxious to help him over his unaccountable difficulty, Miss Ralston detained him after school.

"David," she asked him, when they were alone, "do you understand 'America' now?"

"Yes, ma'am."

"Do you understand 'Land where my fathers died'?"

"Yes, ma'am."

"You didn't sing with the others."

"No, ma'am."

Miss Ralston thought of a question that would rouse him.

"Don't you like 'America,' David?"

The boy almost jumped in his place.

"Oh, yes, ma'am, I do! I like 'America.' It's—fine."

He pressed his fist nervously to his mouth, a trick he had when excited.

"Then tell me, David, why you don't sing it."

David's eyes fixed themselves in a look of hopeless longing. He answered in a whisper, his pale face slowly reddening.

"*My* fathers didn't die here. How can I sing such a lie?"

Miss Ralston's impulse was to hug the child, but she was afraid to startle him. The attention she had lavished on the boy was rewarded at this moment, when her understanding of his nature inspired the answer to his troubled question. She saw how his mind worked. She realized, what a less sympathetic witness might have failed to realize, that behind the moral scruple expressed in his words, there was a sense of irreparable loss derived from the knowledge that he had no share in the national past. The other children could shout the American hymn in all the pride of proprietorship, but to him the words did not apply. It was a flaw in his citizenship, which he was so jealous to establish.

The teacher's words were the very essence of tact and sympathy. In her voice were mingled the yearning of a mother and the faith of a comrade.

"David Rudinsky, you have as much a right to those words as I or anybody else in America. Your ancestors did not die on our battlefields, but they would have if they'd had a chance. You used to spend all your time reading the Hebrew books, in Russia. Don't you know how your people—your ancestors, perhaps!—fought the Roman tyrants? Don't you remember the Maccabean brothers, and Bar Kochba,[4] and—oh, you know about them more than I! I'm ashamed to tell you that I haven't read much Jewish history, but I'm sure if we begin to look it up, we'll find that people of your race—people like your father, David—took a part in the fight for freedom, wherever they were allowed. And even in this country—David, I'm going to find out for you how many Jews there were in the armies of the Revolution. We don't think about

4. Leader of the widespread revolt in Judea against Rome and the emperor Hadrian in 135–132 B.C.E. "Maccabean brothers": Judah Maccabee and his brothers, sons of Mattathias, led a revolt of Jews against the Syrian tyrant Antiochus in 168 B.C.E. Their story is the basis for the festival of Hanukkah.

it here, you see, because we don't ask what a man's religion is, as long as he is brave and good."

David's eyes slowly lost their look of distress as his teacher talked. His tense little face, upturned to hers, reminded her of a withered blossom that revives in the rain. She went on with increasing earnestness, herself interested in the discoveries she was making, in her need.

"I tell you the truth, David, I never thought of these things before, but I do believe that the Pilgrim Fathers didn't all come here before the Revolution. Isn't your father just like them? Think of it, dear, how he left his home, and came to a strange land, where he couldn't even speak the language. That was a great trouble, you know; something like the fear of the Indians in the old days. And didn't he come looking for the very same things? He wanted freedom for himself and his family, and a chance for his children to grow up wise and brave. You know your father cares more for such things than he does for money or anything. It's the same story over again. Every ship that brings your people from Russia and other countries where they are ill-treated is a *Mayflower*. If I were a Jewish child like you, I would sing 'America' louder than anybody else!"

David's adoring eyes gave her the thanks which his tongue would not venture to utter. Never since that moment, soon after his arrival from Russia, when his father showed him his citizenship papers, saying, "Look, my son, this makes you an American," had he felt so secure in his place in the world.

Miss Ralston studied his face in silence while she gathered up some papers on her desk, preparatory to leaving. In the back of her mind she asked herself to how many of the native children in her class the Fourth of July meant anything besides fire-crackers.

"Get your things, David," she said presently, as she locked her desk. "It's time we were going. Think if we should get locked up in the building!"

David smiled absently. In his ears rang the familiar line, "Land where my fathers died—my fathers died—fathers died."

"It's something like the Psalms!" he said suddenly, himself surprised at the discovery.

"What is like the Psalms, dear?"

He hesitated. Now that he had to explain, he was not sure any more. Miss Ralston helped him out.

"You mean 'America,' sounds like the Psalms to you?"

David nodded. His teacher beamed her understanding. How did she guess wherein the similarity lay? David had in mind such moments as this when he said of Miss Ralston, "Teacher talks with her eyes."

Miss Ralston went to get her coat and hat from the closet.

"Get your things, David," she repeated. "The janitor will come to chase us out in a minute."

He was struggling with the torn lining of a coat-sleeve in the children's dressing-room, when he heard Miss Ralston exclaim,—

"Oh, David! I had almost forgotten. You must try this on. This is what you're going to wear when you speak the dialogue with Annie and Raymond. We used it in a play a few years ago. I thought it would do for you."

She held up a blue-and-buff jacket with tarnished epaulets. David hurried to put it on. He was to take the part of George Washington in the dialogue. At sight of the costume, his heart started off on a gallop.

Alas for his gallant aspirations! Nothing of David was visible outside the jacket except two big eyes above and two blunt boot-toes below. The collar reached to his ears; the cuffs dangled below his knees. He resembled a scarecrow in the cornfield more than the Father of his Country.

Miss Ralston suppressed her desire to laugh.

"It's a little big, isn't it?" she said cheerily, holding up the shoulders of the heroic garment. "I wonder how we can make it fit. Don't you think your mother would know how to take up the sleeves and do something to the back?"

She turned the boy around, more hopeless than she would let him see. Miss Ralston understood more about little boys' hearts than about their coats.

"How old are you, David?" she asked, absently, wondering for the hundredth time at his diminutive stature. "I thought the boy for whom this was made was about your age."

David's face showed that he felt reproved. "I'm twelve," he said, apologetically.

Miss Ralston reproached herself for her tactlessness, and proceeded to make amends.

"Twelve?" she repeated, patting the blue shoulders. "You speak the lines like a much older boy. I'm sure your mother can make the coat fit, and I'll bring the wig—a powdered wig—and the sword, David! You'll look just like George Washington!"

Her gay voice echoed in the empty room. Her friendly eyes challenged his. She expected to see him kindle, as he did so readily in these days of patriotic excitement. But David failed to respond. He remained motionless in his place, his eyes blank and staring. Miss Ralston had the feeling that behind his dead front his soul was running away from her.

This is just what was happening. David was running away from her, and from himself, and from the image of George Washington, conjured up by the scene with the military coat. Somewhere in the jungle of his consciousness a monster was stirring, and his soul fled in terror of its clutch. What was it—what was it that came tearing through the wilderness of his memories of two worlds? In vain he tried not to understand. The ghosts of forgotten impressions cackled in the wake of the pursuing monster, the breath of whose nostrils spread an odor of evil sophistries grafted on his boyish thoughts in a chimerical past.

His mind reeled in a whirlwind of recollection. Miss Ralston could not have understood some of the things David reviewed, even if he had tried to tell her. In that other life of his, in Russia, had been monstrous things, things that seemed unbelievable to David himself, after his short experience of America. He had suffered many wrongs,—yes, even as a little boy,—but he was not thinking of past grievances as he stood before Miss Ralston, seeing her as one sees a light through a fog. He was thinking of things harder to forget than injuries received from others. It was a sudden sense of his own sins that frightened David, and of one sin in particular, the origin of which was buried somewhere in the slime of the evil past. David was caught in the meshes of a complex inheritance; contradictory impulses tore at his heart. Fearfully he dived to the bottom of his consciousness, and brought up a bitter conviction: David Rudinsky, who called himself an American, who worshiped the names of the heroes, suddenly knew that he had sinned, sinned against his best friend, sinned even as he was planning to impersonate George Washington, the pattern of honor.

His white forehead glistened with the sweat of anguish. His eyes sickened. Miss Ralston caught him as he wavered and put him in the nearest seat.

"Why, David! what's the matter? Are you ill? Let me take this off—it's so heavy. There, that's better. Just rest your head on me, so."

This roused him. He wriggled away from her support, and put out a hand to keep her off.

"Why, David! what *is* the matter? Your hands are so cold—"

David's head felt heavy and wobbly, but he stood up and began to put on his coat again, which he had pulled off in order to try on the uniform. To Miss Ralston's anxious questions he answered not a syllable, neither did he look at her once. His teacher, thoroughly alarmed, hurriedly put on her street things, intending to take him home. They walked in silence through the empty corridors, down the stairs, and across the school yard. The teacher noticed with relief that the boy grew steadier with every step. She smiled at him encouragingly when he opened the gate for her, as she had taught him, but he did not meet her look.

At the corner where they usually parted David paused, steeling himself to take his teacher's hand; but to his surprise she kept right on, taking *his* crossing.

It was now that he spoke, and Miss Ralston was astonished at the alarm in his voice.

"Miss Ralston, where are you going? You don't go this way."

"I'm going to see you home, David," she replied firmly. "I can't let you go alone—like this."

"Oh, Teacher! don't, please don't. I'm all right—I'm not sick,—it's not far—Don't, Miss Ralston, *please*."

In the February dusk, Miss Ralston saw the tears rise to his eyes. Whatever was wrong with him, it was plain that her presence only made him suffer the more. Accordingly she yielded to his entreaty.

"I hope you'll be all right, David," she said, in a tone she might have used to a full-grown man. "Good-bye." And she turned the corner.

II

All the way home Miss Ralston debated the wisdom of allowing him to go alone, but as she recalled his look and his entreating voice she felt anew the compulsion that had made her yield. She attributed his sudden breakdown entirely to overwrought nerves, and remorsefully resolved not to subject him in the future to the strain of extra hours after school.

Her misgiving were revived the next morning, when David failed to appear with the ringing of the first gong, as was his habit. But before the children had taken their seats, David's younger brother, Bennie, brought her news of the missing boy.

"David's sick in bed," he announced in accents of extreme importance. "He didn't come home till awful late last night, and he was so frozen, his teeth knocked together. My mother says he burned like a fire all night, and she had to take little Harry in her bed, with her and papa, so's David could sleep all alone. We all went downstairs in our bare feet this morning, and dressed ourselves in the kitchen, so David could sleep."

"What is the matter with him? Did you have the doctor?"

"No ma'am, not yet. The dispensary don't open till nine o'clock."

Miss Ralston begged him to report again in the afternoon, which he did, standing before her, cap in hand, his sense of importance still dominating over brotherly concern.

"He's sick, all right," Bennie reported. "He don't eat at all—just drinks and drinks. My mother says he cried the whole morning, when he woke up and found out he'd missed school. My mother says he tried to get up and dress himself, but he couldn't anyhow. Too sick."

"Did you have the doctor?" interrupted Miss Ralston, suppressing her impatience.

"No, ma'am, not yet. My father went to the dispensary, but the doctor said he can't come till noon, but he didn't. Then I went to the dispensary, dinner time, but the doctor didn't yet come when we went back to school. My mother says you can die ten times before the dispensary doctor comes."

"What does your mother think it is?"

"Oh, she says it's a bad cold, but David isn't strong, you know, so she's scared. I guess if he gets worse I'll have to stay home from school to run for the medicines."

"I hope not, Bennie. Now you'd better run along, or you'll be late."

"Yes, ma'am. Good-bye."

"Will you come again in the morning and tell me about your brother?"

"Yes, ma'am. Good-bye.—Teacher."

"Yes, Bennie?"

"Do you think you can do something—something—about his *record?* David feels dreadful because he's broke his record. He never missed school before, you know. It's—it's too bad to see him cry. He's always so quiet, you know, kind of like grown people. He don't fight or tease or anything. Do you think you can, Teacher?"

Miss Ralston was touched by this tribute to her pupil, but she could not promise to mend the broken record.

"Tell David not to worry. He has the best record in the school, for attendance and everything. Tell him I said he must hurry and get well, as we must rehearse our pieces for Washington's Birthday."

The next morning Bennie reeled off a longer story than ever. He described the doctor's visit in great detail, and Miss Ralston was relieved to gather that David's ailment was nothing worse than grippe;[5] unless, as the doctor warned, his run-down condition caused complications. He would be in bed a week or more, in any case, "and he ought to sleep most of the time, the doctor said."

"I guess the doctor don't know our David!" Bennie scoffed. "He never wants at all to go to sleep. He reads and reads when everybody goes to bed. One time he was reading all night, and the lamp went out, and he was afraid to go downstairs for oil, because he'd wake somebody, so he lighted matches and read little bits. There was a heap of burned matches in the morning."

5. A heavy cold or the flu.

"Dear me!" exclaimed Miss Ralston. "He ought not to do that. Your father ought not— Does your father allow him to stay up nights?"

"Sure. My father's proud because he's going to be a great man; a doctor, maybe." He shrugged his shoulders, as if to say, "What may not a David become?"

"David is funny, don't you think, Teacher?" the boy went on. "He asks such funny questions. What do you think he said to the doctor?"

"I can't imagine."

"Well, he pulled him by the sleeve when he took out the—the thing he puts in your mouth, and said kind of hoarse, 'Doctor, did you ever tell a lie?' Wasn't that funny?"

Miss Ralston did not answer. She was thinking that David must have been turning over some problem in his mind, to say so much to a stranger.

"Did you give him my message?" she asked finally.

"Yes'm! I told him about rehearsing his piece for Washington's Birthday." Bennie paused.

"Well?"

"He acted so funny. He turned over to the wall, and cried and cried without any noise."

"The poor boy! He'll be dreadfully disappointed not to take his part in the exercises."

Bennie shook his head.

"That isn't for what he cries," he said oracularly.

Miss Ralston's attentive silence invited further revelations.

"He's *worrying* about something," Bennie brought out, rolling his head ominously.

"Why? How do you know?"

"The doctor said so. He told my father downstairs. He said, 'Make him tell, if you can, it may help to pull him off'—no, 'pull him up.' That's what the doctor said."

Miss Ralston's thoughts flew back to her last interview with David, two days before, when he had broken down so suddenly. Was there a mystery there? She was certain the boy was overwrought, and physically run down. Apparently, also, he had been exposed to the weather during the evening when he was taken ill; Bennie's chatter indicated that David had wandered in the streets for hours. These things would account for the grippe, and for the abnormal fever of which Bennie boasted. But what was David worrying about? She resolved to go and see the boy in a day or two, when he was reported to be more comfortable.

On his next visit Bennie brought a message from the patient himself.

"He said to give you this, Teacher," handing Miss Ralston a journal. "It's yours. It has the pieces in it for Washington's Birthday. He said you might need it, and the doctor didn't say when he could go again to school."

Miss Ralston laid the journal carelessly on a pile of other papers. Bennie balanced himself on one foot, looking as if his mission were not yet ended.

"Well, Bennie?" Miss Ralston encouraged him. She was beginning to understand his mysterious airs.

"David was awful careful about that book," the messenger said impressively. "He said over and over not to lose it, and not to give it to nobody only you."

III

It was not till the end of the day that Miss Ralston took up the journal Bennie had brought. She turned the leaves absently, thinking of David. He would be so disappointed to miss the exercises! And to whom should she give the part of George Washington in the dialogue? She found the piece in the journal. A scrap of paper marked the place. A folded paper. Folded several times. Miss Ralston opened out the paper and found some writing.

> Dear Teacher Miss Ralston:
> I can't be George Washington any more because I have lied to you. I must not tell you about what, because you would blame somebody who didn't do wrong.
>
> Your friend,
> David Rudinsky.

Again and again Miss Ralston read the note, unable to understand it. David, her David, whose soul was a mirror for every noble idea, had lied to her! What could he mean? What had impelled him? *Somebody who didn't do wrong*. So it was not David alone; there was some complication with another person. She studied the note word for word, and her eyes slowly filled with tears. If the boy had really lied—if the whole thing were not a chimera of his fevered nights—then what must he have suffered of remorse and shame! Her heart went out to him even while her brain was busy with the mystery.

She made a swift resolution. She would go to David at once. She was sure he would tell her more than he had written, and it would relieve his mind. She did not dread the possible disclosures. Her knowledge of the boy made her certain that she would find nothing ignoble at the bottom of his mystery. He was only a child, after all—an overwrought, sensitive child. No doubt he exaggerated his sin, if sin there were. It was her duty to go and put him at rest.

She knew that David's father kept a candy shop in the basement of his tenement, and she had no trouble in finding the place. Half the children in the neighborhood escorted her to the door, attracted by the phenomenon of a Teacher loose on their streets.

The tinkle of the shop bell brought Mr. Rudinsky from the little kitchen in the rear.

"Well, well!" he exclaimed, shaking hands heartily. "This is a great honor—a great honor." He sounded the initial *h*. "I wish I had a palace for you to come in, ma'am. I don't think there was such company in this house since it was built."

His tone was one of genuine gratification. Ushering her into the kitchen, he set a chair for her, and himself sat down at a respectful distance.

"I'm sorry," he began, with a wave of his hand around the room. "Such company ought not to sit in the kitchen, but you see—"

He was interrupted by Bennie, who had clattered in at the visitor's heels, panting for recognition.

"Never mind, Teacher," the youngster spoke up, "we got a parlor upstairs, with a mantelpiece and everything, but David sleeps up there—the doctor said it's the most air—and you dassn't wake him up till he wakes himself."

Bennie's father frowned, but the visitor smiled a cordial smile.

"I like a friendly kitchen like this," she said quietly. "My mother did not keep any help when I was a little girl and I was a great deal in the kitchen."

Her host showed his appreciation of her tact by dropping the subject.

"I'm sure you came about David," he said.

"I did. How is he?"

"Pretty sick, ma'am. The doctor says it's not the sickness so much, but David is so weak and small. He says David studies too much altogether. Maybe he's right. What do you think, ma'am?"

Miss Ralston answered remorsefully.

"I agree with the doctor. I think we are all to blame. We push him too much when we ought to hold him back."

Here Bennie made another raid on the conversation.

"He's going to be a great man, a doctor maybe. My mother says—"

Mr. Rudinsky did not let him finish. He thought it time to insure the peace of so important an interview.

"Bennie," said he, "you will go mind the store, and keep the kitchen door shut."

Bennie's discomfiture was evident in his face. He obeyed, but not without a murmur.

"Let us make a covenant to take better care of David in the future."

Miss Ralston was speaking when Mrs. Rudinsky appeared in the doorway. She was flushed from the exertions of a hasty toilet,[6] for which she had fled upstairs at the approach of "company." She came forward timidly, holding out a hand on which the scrubbing brush and the paring knife had left their respective marks.

"How do you do, ma'am?" she said, cordially, but shyly. "I'm glad to see you. I wish I can speak English better, I'd like to say how proud I am to see David's teacher in my haus."[7]

"Why, you speak wonderfully!" Miss Ralston exclaimed, with genuine enthusiasm. "I don't understand how you pick up the language in such a short time. I couldn't learn Russian so fast, I'm sure."

"My husband makes us speak English all the time," Mrs. Rudinsky replied. "From the fust day he said to speak English. He scolds the children if he hears they speak Jewish."[8]

"Sure," put in her husband, "I don't want my family to be greenhorns."

Miss Ralston turned a glowing face to him.

"Mr. Rudinsky, I think you've done wonders for your family. If all immigrants were like you, we wouldn't need any restriction laws." She threw all possible emphasis into her cordial voice. "Why, you're a better American than some natives I know!"

Mrs. Rudinsky sent her husband a look of loving pride.

"He wants to be a Yankee," she said.

Her husband took up the cue in earnest.

"Yes, ma'am," he said. "That's my ambition. When I was a young man, in the old country, I wanted to be a scholar. But a Jew has no chance in the old country; perhaps you know how it is. It wasn't the Hebrew books I wanted. I wanted to learn what the rest of the world learned, but a poor Jew

6. An archaism for washing and dressing quickly.
7. House—Antin's German transliteration of the Yiddish word *hoyz*.
8. Colloquial for Yiddish.

had no chance in Russia. When I got to America, it was too late for me to go to school. It took me all my time and strength to make a living—I've never been much good in business, ma'am—and when I got my family over, I saw that it was the children would go to school for me. I'm glad to be a plain citizen, if my children will be educated Americans."

People with eyes and hands like Mr. Rudinsky's can say a great deal in a few words. Miss Ralston felt as if she had known him all his life, and followed his striving in two worlds.

"I'm glad to know you, Mr. Rudinsky," she said in a low voice. "I wish more of my pupils had fathers like David's."

Her host changed the subject very neatly.

"And I wish the school children had more teachers like you. David likes you so much."

"Oh, he liked you!" the wife confirmed. "Please stay till he veks up.[9] He'll be sorry to missed your vis*it*."

While his wife moved quietly around the stove, making tea, Mr. Rudinsky entertained their guest with anecdotes of David's Hebrew-school days, and of his vain efforts to get at secular books.

"He was just like me," he said. "He wanted to learn everything. I couldn't afford a private teacher, and they wouldn't take him in the public school. He learned Russian all alone,[1] and if he got a book from somewhere—a history or anything—he wouldn't eat or drink till he read it all."

Mrs. Rudinsky often glanced at David's teacher, to see how her husband's stories were impressing her. She was too shy with her English to say more than was required of her as hostess, but her face, aglow with motherly pride, showed how she participated in her husband's enthusiasm.

"You see yourself, ma'am, what he is," said David's father, "but what could I make of him in Russia? I was happy when he got here, only it was a little late. I wished he started in school younger."

"He has time enough," said Miss Ralston. "He'll get through grammar school before he's fourteen. He's twelve now, isn't he?"

"Yes, ma'am—no, ma'am! He's really fourteen now, but I made him out younger on purpose."

Miss Ralston looked puzzled. Mr. Rudinsky explained.

"You see, ma'am, he was twelve years when he came, and I wanted he should go to school as long as possible, so when I made his school certificate, I said he was only ten. I have seven children, and David is the oldest one, and I was afraid he'd have to go to work, if business was bad, or if I was sick. The state is a good father to the children in America, if the real fathers don't mix in. Why should my David lose his chance to get educated and be somebody, because I am a poor business man, and have too many children? So I made out that he had to go to school two years more."

He narrated this anecdote in the same simple manner in which he had told a dozen others. He seemed pleased to rehearse the little plot whereby he had insured his boy's education. As Miss Ralston did not make any comment immediately, he went on, as if sure of her sympathy.

"I told you I got my citizen papers right away when I came to America. I

9. A transliteration of the Yiddish pronunciation for "wakes up."

1. In Russia, the Rudinsky family spoke Yiddish at home, while Russian was the language of the surrounding area.

worked hard before I could bring my family—it took me four years to save the money—and they found a very poor home when they got here, but they were citizens right away. But it wouldn't do them much good, if they didn't get educated. I found out all about the compulsory education, and I said to myself that's the policeman that will keep me from robbing my David if I fail in business."

He did not overestimate his visitor's sympathy. Miss Ralston followed his story with quick appreciation of his ideals and motives, but in her ingenuous American mind one fact separated itself from the others: namely, that Mr. Rudinsky had falsified his boy's age, and had recorded the falsehood in a public document. Her recognition of the fact carried with it no criticism. She realized that Mr. Rudinsky's conscience was the product of an environment vastly different from hers. It was merely that to her mind the element of deceit was something to be accounted for, be it ever so charitably, whereas in Mr. Rudinsky's mind it evidently had no existence at all.

"So David is really fourteen years old?" she repeated incredulously. "Why, he seems too little even for twelve! Does he know?—Of course he would know! I wonder that he consented—"

She broke off, struck by a sudden thought. "Consented to tell a lie" she had meant to say, but the unspoken words diverted her mind from the conversation. It came upon her in a flash that she had found the key to David's mystery. His note was in her pocketbook, but she knew every word of it, and now everything was plain to her. The lie was this lie about his age, and the person he wanted to shield was his father. And for that he was suffering so!

She began to ask questions eagerly.

"Has David said anything about—about a little trouble he had in school the day he became ill?"

Both parents showed concern.

"Trouble? what trouble?"

"Oh, it was hardly trouble—at least, I couldn't tell myself."

"David is so hard to understand sometimes," his father said.

"Oh, I don't think so!" the teacher cried. "Not when you make friends with him. He doesn't say much, it's true, but his heart is like a crystal."

"He's too still," the mother insisted, shaking her head. "All the time he's sick, he don't say anything, only when we ask him something. The doctor thinks he's worrying about something, but he don't tell."

The mother sighed, but Miss Ralston cut short her reflections.

"Mrs. Rudinsky—Mr. Rudinsky," she began eagerly, "*I* can tell you what David's troubled about."

And she told them the story of her last talk with David, and finally read them his note.

"And this lie," she ended, "you know what it is, don't you? You've just told me yourself, Mr. Rudinsky."

She looked pleadingly at him, longing to have him understand David's mind as she understood it. But Mr. Rudinsky was very slow to grasp the point.

"You mean—about the certificate? Because I made out that he was younger?"

Miss Ralston nodded.

"You know David has such a sense of honor," she explained, speaking slowly, embarrassed by the effort of following Mr. Rudinsky's train of thought and her own at the same time. "You know how he questions everything—sooner or later he makes everything clear to himself—and something must have started him thinking of this old matter lately— Why, of course! I remember I asked him his age that day, when he tried on the costume, and he answered as usual, and then, I suppose, he suddenly *realized* what he was saying. I don't believe he ever *thought* about it since—since you arranged it so, and now, all of a sudden—"

She did not finish, because she saw that her listeners did not follow her. Both their faces expressed pain and perplexity. After a long silence, David's father spoke.

"And what do *you* think, ma'am?"

Miss Ralston was touched by the undertone of submission in his voice. Her swift sympathy had taken her far into his thoughts. She recognized in his story one of those ethical paradoxes which the helpless Jews of the Pale, in their search for a weapon that their oppressors could not confiscate, have evolved for their self-defense. She knew that to many honest Jewish minds a lie was not a lie when told to an official; and she divined that no ghost of a scruple had disturbed Mr. Rudinsky in his sense of triumph over circumstances, when he invented the lie that was to insure the education of his gifted child. With David, of course, the same philosophy had been valid. His father's plan for the protection of his future, hinging on a too familiar sophistry, had dropped innocuous into his consciousness; until, in a moment of spiritual sensitiveness, it took on the visage of sin.

"And what do *you* think, ma'am?"

David's father did not have to wait a moment for her answer, so readily did her insight come to his defense. In a few eager sentences she made him feel that she understood him perfectly, and understood David perfectly.

"I respect you the more for that lie, Mr. Rudinsky. It was—a *noble* lie!" There was the least tremor in her voice. "And I love David for the way *he* sees it."

Mr. Rudinsky got up and paced slowly across the room. Then he stopped before Miss Ralston.

"You are very kind to talk like that, Miss Ralston," he said, with peculiar dignity. "You see the whole thing. In the old country we had to do such things so many times that we—got used to them. Here—here we don't have to." His voice took on a musing quality. "But we don't see it right away when we get here. I meant nothing, only just to keep my boy in school. It was not to cheat anybody. The state is willing to educate the children. I said to myself I will tie my own hands, so that I can't pull my child after me if I drown. I did want my David should have the best chance in America."

Miss Ralston was thrilled by the suppressed passion in his voice. She held out her hand to him, saying again, in the low tones that come from the heart, "I am glad I know you, Mr. Rudinsky."

There was unconscious chivalry in Mr. Rudinsky's next words. Stepping to his wife's side, he laid a gentle hand on her shoulder, and said quietly, "My wife had been my helper in everything."

Miss Ralston, as we know, was given to seeing things. She saw now, not a poor immigrant couple in the first stage of American respectability, which was all there was in the room to see, but a phantom procession of men with the faces of prophets, muffled in striped praying-shawls, and women radiant in the light of many candles, and youths and maidens with smoldering depths in their eyes, and silent children who pushed away joyous things for—for—

Dreams don't use up much time. Mr. Rudinsky was not aware that there had been a pause before he spoke again.

"You understand so well, Miss Ralston. But David"—he hesitated a moment, then finished quickly. "How can he respect me if he feels like that?"

His wife spoke tremulously from her corner.

"That's what I think."

"Oh, don't think that!" Miss Ralston cried. "He does respect you—he understands. Don't you see what he says: *I can't tell you—because you would blame somebody who didn't do wrong.* He doesn't blame you. He only blames himself. He's afraid to tell me because he thinks *I* can't understand."

The teacher laughed a happy little laugh. In her eagerness to comfort David's parents, she said just the right things, and every word summed up an instantaneous discovery. One of her useful gifts was the ability to find out truths just when she desperately needed them. There are people like that, and some of them are school-teachers hired by the year. When David's father cried, "How can he respect me?" Miss Ralston's heart was frightened while it beat one beat. Only one. Then she knew all David's thoughts between the terrible, "I have lied," and the generous, "But my father did no wrong." She guessed what the struggle had cost to reconcile the contradictions; she imagined his bewilderment as he tried to rule himself by his new-found standards, while seeking excuses for his father in the one he cast away from him as unworthy of an American. Problems like David's are not very common, but then Miss Ralston was good at guessing.

"Don't worry, Mr. Rudinsky," she said, looking out of her glad eyes. "And you, Mrs. Rudinsky, don't think for a moment that David doesn't understand. He's had a bad time, the poor boy, but I know—Oh, I must speak to him! Will he wake soon, do you think?"

Mr. Rudinsky left the room without a word.

"It's all right," said David's mother, in reply to an anxious look from Miss Ralston. "He sleeps already the whole afternoon."

It had grown almost dark while they talked. Mrs. Rudinsky now lighted the lamps, apologizing to her guest for not having done so sooner, and then she released Bennie from his prolonged attendance in the store.

Bennie came into the kitchen chewing his reward, some very gummy confection. He was obliged to look the pent-up things he wanted to say, until such time as he could clear his clogged talking-gear.

"Teacher," he began, before he had finished swallowing, "What for did you say—"

"Bennie!" his mother reproved him, "You must shame yourself to listen by the door."

"Well, there wasn't any trade, ma," he defended himself, "only Bessie Katz, and she brought back the peppermints she bought this morning, to change them for taffy, but I didn't because they were all dirty, and one was broken—"

Bennie never had a chance to bring his speeches to a voluntary stop. Somebody always interrupted. This time it was his father, who came down the stairs, looking so grave that even Bennie was impressed.

"He's awake," said Mr. Rudinsky. "I lighted the lamp. Will you please come up, ma'am?"

He showed her to the room where David lay, and closed the door on them both. It was not he, but Miss Ralston, the American teacher, that his boy needed. He went softly down to the kitchen, where his wife smiled at him through unnecessary tears.

Miss Ralston never forgot the next hour, and David never forgot. The woman always remembered how the boy's eyes burned through the dusk of the shadowed corner where he lay. The boy remembered how his teacher's voice palpitated in his heart, how her cool hands rested on his, how the lamplight made a halo out of her hair. To each of them the dim room with its scant furnishings became a spiritual rendezvous.

What did the woman say, that drew the sting of remorse from the child's heart, without robbing him of the bloom of his idealism? What did she tell him that transmuted the offense of ages into the marrow and blood of persecuted virtue? How did she weld in the boy's consciousness the scraps of his mixed inheritance, so that he saw his whole experience as an unbroken thing at last? There was nobody to report how it was done. The woman did not know, nor the child. It was a secret born of the boy's need and the woman's longing to serve him; just as in nature every want creates its satisfaction.

When she was ready to leave him, Miss Ralston knelt for a moment at David's bedside, and once more took his small, hot hands in hers.

"And I have made a discovery, David," she said, smiling in a way of her own. "Talking with your parents downstairs I saw why it was that the Russian Jews are so soon at home here in our dear country. In the hearts of men like your father, dear, is the true America."

1913

HORACE M. KALLEN
1882–1974

Horace Meyer Kallen was born in Silesia, Prussia, the son of a rabbi who was forced by the government to emigrate because he was "an alien Jew." Kallen was brought to America by his parents in 1887. His father became the rabbi of a German-language Orthodox synagogue in Boston, the city in which he grew up. He chafed at and rebelled against his father's religious orthodoxy, and when, as a high-school student, he discovered the writings of Spinoza, he felt liberated by its rationalism and universalism. He entered Harvard in 1900, earning an A.B. degree in 1903 and a Ph.D. in philosophy in 1908.

At Harvard, the teachers who had the greatest impact upon his development and thought were Barrett Wendell, a literary historian who taught the importance of the Old Testament upon America's foundational Puritan heritage, and the philosophers William James and Josiah Royce. James's most significant works, *The Varieties of Religious Experience* (1902) and *Pragmatism* (1907), appeared while Kallen was a student. He also did work at the Sorbonne with Henri Bergson and spent a year at Oxford.

While at Oxford, he was the classmate of another Harvard contemporary, African American poet and a father of the Harlem Renaissance of the 1920s Alain Locke. Both were made aware in various ways of their minority-group status, although there is evidence that Kallen was not himself free of racist attitudes. Nevertheless, that experience and the deep impression made by James's pluralistic philosophy and Royce's support of a kind of "particularism" laid the groundwork for Kallen's own later philosophical contributions.

Most notably, Kallen invented the term "cultural pluralism" in a book called *Culture and Democracy in the United States: Studies in the Group Psychology of the American People* (1924). His struggle to acknowledge and define his Jewishness had led him as early as 1906 to cofound the first Menorah Society, at Harvard, and to help launch its publication, the *Menorah Journal*. For many years, that was to be one of the most important publishing outlets for notable Jewish intellectuals and academics concerned with these questions. In 1915, in two installments of the *Nation,* he published *Democracy versus the Melting-Pot: A Study in American Nationality,* the most vital statement of his continuing effort to define the relationship between ethnic or group identity and national and even universal identity. Part Two of the article, which appears in this anthology, contains some of its best-known sections—on the inability to choose one's grandfather, and on America's future as "a federation . . . of nationalities." The logic and implications of these views have been seriously questioned, but their polemical vigor is unquestionable.

Kallen's article appeared during a serious controversy about the virtues and dangers of unlimited immigration to the United States. Most of the huge number of immigrants that arrived yearly until the outbreak of World War I came from nations, regions, and ethnic groups (including, very prominently, Eastern European Jews) that were thought by "restrictionists" to be unassimilable, even dangerous to American life and its values. Kallen argued that "melting" away ethnic traits was not only not desirable, but America's cultural heritage and its future promise lay precisely in its divergent nationalities. The "American Idea" of freedom and democracy, he argued, required variety and pluralism. In other words, "In order to be an American one had to be an ethnic."

Kallen went on to become a Zionist, believing in the compatibility and, indeed, the necessity of such a commitment if one were to be a good American. His arguments ultimately influenced Supreme Court judge Louis D. Brandeis along these same lines.

Throughout his long career, Kallen was a teacher of philosophy and the author of many books. He was one of the founders in 1919 of the New School for Social Research in New York and a member of its faculty until his formal retirement in 1952. He remained affiliated as an emeritus professor until 1970.

From Democracy versus the Melting-Pot

Part Two

V

The array of forces for and against that like-mindedness which is the stuff and essence of nationality aligns itself as follows: For it make social imitation of the upper by the lower classes, the facility of communications, the national pastimes of baseball and motion-picture, the mobility of population, the cheapness of printing, and the public schools. Against it make the primary ethnic differences with which the population starts, its stratification over an enormous extent of country, its industrial and economic stratification. We are an English-speaking country, but in no intimate and inevitable way, as is New Zealand or Australia, or even Canada. English is to us what Latin was to the Roman provinces and to the middle ages—the language of the upper and dominant class, the vehicle and symbol of culture: for the mass of our population it is a sort of Esperanto or Ido, a *lingua franca*[1] necessary less in the spiritual than the economic contacts of the daily life. This mass is composed of elementals, peasants—Mr. Ross[2] speaks of their menacing American life with "peasantism"—the proletarian foundation material of all forms of civilization. Their self-consciousness as groups is comparatively weak. This is a factor which favors their "assimilation," for the more cultivated a group is, the more it is aware of its individuality, and the less willing it is to surrender that individuality. One need think only of the Puritans themselves, leaving Holland for fear of absorption into the Dutch population; of the Creoles and Pennsylvania Germans of this country, or of the Jews, anywhere. In his judgment of the assimilability of various stocks Mr. Ross neglects this important point altogether, probably because his attention is fixed on existing contrasts rather than potential similarities. Peasants, however, having nothing much to surrender in taking over a new culture, feel no necessary break, and find the transition easy. It is the shock of confrontation with other ethnic groups and the feeling of aliency that generates in them an intenser self-consciousness, which then militates against Americanization in spirit by reinforcing the two factors to which the spiritual expression of the proletarian has been largely confined. These factors are language and religion. Religion is, of course, no more a "universal" than language. The history of Christianity makes evident enough how religion is modified, even inverted, by race, place, and time. It becomes a principle of separation, often the sole repository of the national spirit, almost always the conservator of the national language and of the tradition that is passed on with the language to succeeding generations. Among immigrants, hence, religion and language tend to be coordinate: a single expression of the spontaneous and instinctive mental life of the masses, and the primary inward factors making against assimilation. Mr. Ross, I note, tends to grow shrill over the competition of the parochial school with the public school, at the same time that he belittles the fact "that on Sundays Norwegian is preached in more churches in America than in Norway."

And Mr. Ross's anxiety would, I think, be more than justified were it not that religion in these cases always does more than it intends. For it conserves the inward aspect of nationality rather than mere religion, and tends to become the center of exfoliation of a higher type of personality among the peasants in the natural terms of their own *natio*. This *natio*, reaching consciousness first in a reaction against America, then as an effect of the competition with Americanization, assumes spiritual forms other than religious: the parochial school, to hold its own with the public school, gets secularized

1. Literally, a common language (Italian); a language that enables different language groups to communicate with one another, as French and Latin once were in Europe or that English is in India and some African countries. Esperanto, a universal language consisting of vocabulary from major European languages, was invented in 1887 by Russian scholar L. L. Zamenhof (1859–1917) using the pseudonym Dr. Esperanto. Ido was another artificial language, based on Esperanto, invented ca. 1907.

2. Edward Alsworth Ross (1866–1951), whose book *The Old World in the New* (1914) is the occasion for Kallen's two-part essay in the *Nation*.

while remaining national. *Natio* is what underlies the vehemence of the "Americanized" and the spiritual and political unrest of the Americans. It is the fundamental fact of American life to-day, and in the light of it Mr. Wilson's[3] resentment of the "hyphenated" American[4] is both righteous and pathetic. But a hyphen attaches, in things of the spirit, also to the 'pure' English American. His cultural mastery tends to be retrospective rather than prospective. At the present time there is no dominant American mind. Our spirit is inarticulate, not a voice, but a chorus of many voices each singing a rather different tune. How to get order out of this cacophony is the question for all those who are concerned about those things which alone justify wealth and power, concerned about justice, the arts, literature, philosophy, science. What must, what *shall* this cacophony become—a unison or a harmony?

For decidedly the older America, whose voice and whose spirit was New England, is gone beyond recall. Americans still are the artists and thinkers of the land, but they work, each for himself, without common vision or ideals. The older tradition has passed from a life into a memory, and the newer one, so far as it has an Anglo-Saxon base, is holding its own beside more and more formidable rivals, the expression in appropriate form of the national inheritances of the various populations concentrated in the various States of the Union, populations of whom their national self-consciousness is perhaps the chief spiritual asset. Think of the Creoles in the South and the French-Canadians in the North, clinging to French for so many generations and maintaining, however weakly, spiritual and social contacts with the mother-country; of the Germans, with their *Deutschthum*, their *Männerchöre, Turnvereine*, and *Schützenfeste*; of the universally separate Jews; of the intensely nationalistic Irish; of the Pennsylvania Germans; of the indomitable Poles, and even more indomitable Bohemians; of the 30,000 Belgians in Wisconsin, with their "Belgian" language, a mixture of Walloon and Flemish[5] welded by reaction to a strange social environment. Except in such cases as the town of Lead, South Dakota, the great ethnic groups of proletarians, thrown upon themselves in a new environment, generate from among themselves the other social classes which Mr. Ross misses so sadly among them: their shopkeepers, their physicians, their attorneys, their journalists, and their national and political leaders, who form the links between them and the greater American society. They develop their own literature, or become conscious of that of the mother-country. As they grow more prosperous and "Americanized," as they become freed from the stigma of "foreigner," they develop group self-respect: the "wop" changes into a proud Italian, the "hunky" into an intensely nationalist Slav. They learn, or they recall, the spiritual heritage of their nationality. Their cultural abjectness gives way to cultural pride and the public schools, the libraries, and the clubs become beset with demands for texts in the national language and literature.

The Poles are an instance worth dwelling upon. Mr. Ross's summary of

3. Woodrow Wilson (1856–1924), president of the United States (1913–21). "*Natio*": root of the word *nation*, from the Latin for "birth," "a race," "people"; derived from the past participle of *nasci*, "to be born."

4. A way to describe the national origins of American immigrants—e.g., Italian-Americans, German-Americans—that implies they had dual identities or loyalties and were not fully acceptable as "Americans." This perception was especially *en vogue* before and during World War I.

5. The languages of the two parts of Belgium, one of which is close to Dutch, the other to French. "Their *Deutschthum*, their *Männerchöre, Turnvereine*, and *Schützenfeste*": traditional German clubs organized for Germanhood, Men's Choruses, Gymnastics, and Marksmanship.

them is as striking as it is premonitory. There are over a million of them in the country, a backward people, prolific, brutal, priest-ridden—a menace to American institutions. Yet the urge that carries them in such numbers to America is not unlike that which carried the Pilgrim Fathers. Next to the Jews, whom their brethren in their Polish home are hounding to death, the unhappiest people in Europe, exploited by both their own upper classes and the Russian conqueror, they have resisted extinction at a great cost. They have clung to their religion because it was a mark of difference between them and their conquerors; because they love liberty, they have made their language of literary importance in Europe. Their aspiration, impersonal, disinterested, as it must be in America, to free Poland, to conserve the Polish spirit, is the most hopeful and American thing about them—the one thing that stands actually between them and brutalization through complete economic degradation. It lifts them higher than anything that, in fact, America offers them. The same thing is true for the Bohemians, 17,000 of them, workingmen in Chicago, paying a proportion of their wage to maintain schools in the Bohemian tongue and free thought; the same thing is true of many other groups.

How true it is may be observed from a comparison of the vernacular dailies and weeklies with the yellow American press[6] which is concocted expressly for the great American masses. The content of the former, when the local news is deducted, is a mass of information, political, social, scientific; often translations into the vernacular of standard English writing, often original work of high literary quality. The latter, when the news is deducted, consists of the sporting page and the editorial page. Both pander rather than awaken, so that it is no wonder that in fact the intellectual and spiritual pabulum of the great masses consists of the vernacular papers in the national tongue. With them go also the vernacular drama, and the thousand and one other phenomena which make a distinctive culture, the outward expression of that fundamental like-mindedness wherein men are truly "free and equal." This, beginning for the dumb peasant masses in language and religion, emerges in the other forms of life and art and tends to make smaller or larger ethnic groups autonomous, self-sufficient, and reacting as spiritual units to the residuum of America.

What is the cultural outcome likely to be, under these conditions? Surely not the melting-pot.[7] Rather something that has become more and more distinct in the changing State and city life of the last two decades, and which is most articulate and apparent among just those peoples whom Mr. Ross praises most—the Scandinavians, the Germans, the Irish, the Jews.

It is in the area where Scandinavians are most concentrated that Norwegian is preached on Sunday in more churches than in Norway. That area is Minnesota, not unlike Scandinavia in climate and character. There, if the newspapers are to be trusted, the "foreign language" taught in an increasingly larger number of high schools is Scandinavian. The Constitution of the State resembles in many respects the famous Norwegian Constitution of 1813.

6. A reference to yellow journalism, or the sensationalizing of news stories, a phenomenon that developed at the turn of the century. The name perhaps derives from the yellow color of one of the then-popular comic strips *The Yellow Kid*.

7. From the title of a 1908 play popular in New York by Israel Zangwill (1864–1926), a Jewish English writer. It supports the idea that in America various nationalities have their distinctive qualities "melted away," or melted together, to become something new and American.

The largest city has been chosen as the "spiritual capital," if I may say so, the seat of the Scandinavian "house of life," which the Scandinavian Society in America is reported to be planning to build as a center from which there is to spread through the land Scandinavian culture and ideals.

The eastern neighbor of Minnesota is Wisconsin, a region of great concentration of Germans. Is it merely a political accident that the centralization of State authority and control has been possible there to a degree heretofore unknown in this country? That the Socialist organization is the most powerful in the land, able under ordinary conditions to have elected the Mayor of a large city and a Congressman, and kept out of power only by coalition of the other parties? That German is the overwhelmingly predominant "foreign language" in the public schools and in the university? Or that the fragrance of *Deutschthum* pervades the life of the whole State? The earliest German immigrants to America were group conscious to a high degree. They brought with them a cultural tradition and political aspiration. They wanted to found a State. If a State is to be regarded as a mode of life of the mind, they have succeeded. Their language is the predominant "foreign" one throughout the Middle West. The teaching of it is required by law in many places, southern Ohio and Indianapolis, for example. Their national institutions, even to cooking, are as widespread as they are. They are organized into a great national society, the German-American Alliance, which is dedicated to the advancement of German culture and ideals. They encourage and make possible a close and more intimate contact with the fatherland. They endow Germanic museums, they encourage and provide for exchange professorships, erect monuments to German heroes, and disseminate translations of the German classics. And there are, of course, the very excellent German vernacular press, the German theater, the German club, the German organization of life.

Similar are the Irish, living in strength in Massachusetts and New York. When they began to come to this country they were far less well off and far more passionately self-conscious than the Germans. For numbers of them America was and has remained just a center from which to plot for the freedom of Ireland. For most it was an opportunity to escape both exploitation and starvation. The way they made was made against both race and religious prejudice: in the course of it they lost much that was attractive as well as much that was unpleasant. But Americanization brought the mass of them also spiritual self-respect, and their growing prosperity both here and in Ireland is what lies behind the more inward phases of Irish Nationalism—the Gaelic movement, the Irish theater, the Irish Art Society. I omit consideration of such organized bodies as the Ancient Order of Hibernians.[8] All these movements alike indicate the conversion of the negative nationalism of the hatred of England to the positive nationalism of the loving care and development of the cultural values of the Celtic spirit. A significant phase of it is the voting of Irish history into the curriculum of the high schools of Boston. In sum, once the Irish body had been fed and erected, the Irish mind demanded and generated its own peculiar form of self-realization and satisfaction.

8. An American-based lodge of people of Irish descent. "Gaelic movement": a movement to keep Gaelic, the ancient Irish language, alive.

And, finally, the Jews. Their attitude towards America is different in a fundamental respect from that of other immigrant nationalities. They do not come to the United States from truly native lands, lands of their proper natio and culture. They come from lands of sojourn, where they have been for ages treated as foreigners, at most as semi-citizens, subject to disabilities and persecutions. They come with no political aspirations against the peace of other states such as move the Irish, the Poles, the Bohemians. They come with the intention to be completely incorporated into the body-politic of the state. They alone, as Mr. H. G. Wells[9] notes, of all the immigrant peoples have made spontaneously conscious and organized efforts to prepare themselves and their brethren for the responsibilities of American citizenship. There is hardly a considerable municipality in the land, where Jews inhabit, that has not its Hebrew Institute, or its Educational Alliance, or its Young Men's Hebrew Association, or its Community House, especially dedicated to this task. They show the highest percentage of naturalization, according to Mr. Ross's tables, and he concedes that they have benefited politics. Yet of all self-conscious peoples they are the most self-conscious. Of all immigrants they have the oldest civilized tradition, they are longest accustomed to living under law, and are at the outset the most eager and the most successful in eliminating the external differences between themselves and their social environment. Even their religion is flexible and accommodating, as that of the Christian sectaries is not for change involves no change in doctrine, only in mode of life.

Yet, once the wolf is driven from the door and the Jewish immigrant takes his place in our society a free man and an American, he tends to become all the more a Jew. The cultural unity of his race, history, and background is only continued by the new life under the new conditions. Mr. H. G. Wells calls the Jewish quarter in New York a city within a city, and with more justice than other quarters because, although it is far more in tune with Americanism than the other quarters, it is also far more autonomous in spirit and self-conscious in culture. It has its sectaries, its radicals, its artists, its literati; its press, its literature, its theater, its Yiddish and its Hebrew, its Talmudical colleges and its Hebrew schools, its charities and its vanities, and its coordinating organization, the Kehilla,[1] all more or less duplicated wherever Jews congregate in mass. Here not religion alone, but the whole world of radical thinking, carries the mother-tongue and the father-tongue, with all that they imply. Unlike the parochial schools, their separate schools, being national, do not displace the public schools; they supplement the public schools. The Jewish ardor for pure learning is notorious. And, again, as was the case with the Scandinavians, the Germans, the Irish, democracy applied to education has given the Jews their will that Hebrew shall be coordinate with French and German in the regent's examination.[2] On a national scale of organization there is the American Jewish Committee, the Jewish Historical Society, the Jewish Publication Society. Rurally, there is the model Association of Jewish Farmers, with their cooperative organization for agri-

9. H[erbert] G[eorge] Wells (1866–1946), a popular English author, sociologist, and historian.
1. A once common and active Jewish organization, established for the control and regulation of community affairs. It no longer exists.
2. In New York State, these examinations, administered through a Board of Regents, are given in almost all subjects to high-school students. Note that Yiddish, the vernacular, is excluded.

culture and for agricultural education. In sum, the most eagerly American of the immigrant groups are also the most autonomous and self-conscious in spirit and culture.

VI

Immigrants appear to pass through four phases in the course of being Americanized. In the first phase they exhibit economic eagerness, the greed of the unfed. Since external differences are a handicap in the economic struggle, they "assimilate," seeking thus to facilitate the attainment of economic independence. Once the proletarian level of such independence is reached, the process of assimilation slows down and tends to come to a stop. The immigrant group is still a national group, modified, sometimes improved, by environmental influences, but otherwise a solitary spiritual unit, which is seeking to find its way out on its own social level. This search brings to light permanent group distinctions, and the immigrant, like the Anglo-Saxon American, is thrown back upon himself and his ancestry. Then a process of dissimilation begins. The arts, life, and ideals of the nationality become central and paramount: ethnic and national differences change in status from disadvantages to distinctions. All the while the immigrant has been using the English language and behaving like an American in matters economic and political, and continues to do so. The institutions of the Republic have become the liberating cause and the background for the rise of the cultural consciousness and social autonomy of the immigrant Irishman, German, Scandinavian, Jew, Pole, or Bohemian. On the whole, Americanization has not repressed nationality. Americanization has liberated nationality.

Hence, what troubles Mr. Ross and so many other Anglo-Saxon Americans is not really inequality; what troubles them is *difference*. Only things that are alike in fact and not abstractly, and only men that are alike in origin and in spirit and not abstractly, can be truly "equal" and maintain that inward unanimity of action and outlook which make a national life. The writers of the Declaration of Independence and of the Constitution were not confronted by the practical fact of ethnic dissimilarity among the whites of the country. Their descendants are confronted by it. Its existence, acceptance, and development provide one of the inevitable consequences of the democratic principle on which our theory of government is based, and the result at the present writing is to many worthies very unpleasant. Democratism and the Federal principle have worked together with economic greed and ethnic snobbishness to people the land with all the nationalities of Europe, and to convert the early American nation into the present American state. For in effect we are in the process of becoming a true federal state, such a state as men hope for as the outcome of the European war, a great republic consisting of a federation or commonwealth of nationalities.

Given, in the economic order, the principle of *laissez-faire*[3] applied to a capitalistic society, in contrast with the manorial and guild systems of the past and the Socialist utopias of the future, the economic consequences are the same, whether in America, full of all Europe, or in England, full of the

3. Literally, let people do as they choose (French). In economics, it means little or no government or other regulation over business or industry.

English, Scotch, and Welsh. Given, in the political order, the principle that all men are equal and that each, consequently, under the law at least, shall have the opportunity to make the most of himself, the control of the machinery of government by the plutocracy[4] is a foregone conclusion. *Laissez-faire* and unprecedentedly bountiful natural resources have turned the mind of the state to wealth alone, and in the haste to accumulate wealth considerations of human quality have been neglected and forgotten, the action of government has been remedial rather than constructive, and Mr. Ross's "peasantism," i.e., the growth of an expropriated, degraded industrial class, dependent on the factory rather than on land, has been rapid and vexatious.

The problems which these conditions give rise to are important, but not primarily important. Although they have occupied the minds of all our political theorists, they are problems of means, of instruments, not of ends. They concern the conditions of life, not the *kind of life*, and there appears to have been a general assumption that only one kind of human life is possible in America. But the same democracy which underlies the evils of the economic order underlies also the evils—and the promise—of the ethnic order. Because no individual is merely an individual, the political autonomy of the individual has meant and is beginning to realize in these United States the spiritual autonomy of his group. The process is as yet far from fruition. We are, in fact, at the parting of the ways. A genuine social alternative is before us, either of which parts we may realize if we will. In social construction the will is father is to the fact, for the fact is nothing more than the concord or conflict of wills. What do we will to make of the United States—a unison, singing the old Anglo-Saxon theme "America," the America of the New England school, or a harmony, in which that theme shall be dominant, perhaps, among others, but one among many, not the only one?

The mind reverts helplessly to the historic attempts at unison in Europe—the heroic failure of the pan-Hellenists,[5] of the Romans, the disintegration and the diversification of the Christian Church, for a time the most successful unison in history; the present-day failures of Germany and of Russia. Here, however, the whole social situation is favorable, as it has never been at any time elsewhere—everything is favorable but the basic law of America itself, and the spirit of American institutions. To achieve unison—it can be achieved—would be to violate these. For the end determines the means, and this end would involve no other means than those used by Germany in Poland, in Schleswig-Holstein, and Alsace-Lorraine; by Russia in the Pale, in Poland, in Finland.[6] Fundamentally it would require the complete nationalization of education, the abolition of every form of parochial and private school, the abolition of instruction in other tongues than English and the concentration of the teaching of history and literature upon the English tradition. The other institutions of society would require treatment analogous to that administered by Germany to her European acquisitions. And all

4. Control of government by a small wealthy class.

5. Alexander the Great, king of Macedon (356–323 B.C.E.), saw himself as the "spreader of pan-Hellenic ideals." That is, due to Alexander's military conquests, Greek culture, ideals, and civilization were spread throughout most of the Mediterranean world as well as the vast Persian Empire in Asia. In 1855–60, a movement advocating the union of all Greeks into one political body also took this designation of itself.

6. Russia seized parts of Poland in the 18th and 19th centuries, forced Jews to live in restricted areas (the Pale) of regions they controlled, and took land from Finland along their shared border. Schleswig-Holstein and Alsace-Lorraine were provinces of Denmark and France, respectively, which Germany annexed after wars with each country in 1866 and 1870–71.

of this, even if meeting with no resistance, would not completely guarantee the survival as a unison of the older Americanism. For the program would be applied to diverse ethnic types, and the reconstruction that, with the best will, they might spontaneously make of the tradition would more likely than not be a far cry from the original. It is, already.

The notion that the program might be realized by radical and even enforced miscegenation, by the creation of the melting-pot by law, and thus by the development of the new "American race," is, as Mr. Ross points out, as mystically optimistic as it is ignorant. In historic times, so far as we know, no new ethnic types have originated, and what we know of breeding gives us no assurance of the disappearance of the old types in favor of the new, only the addition of a new type, if it succeeds in surviving, to the already existing older ones. Biologically, life does not unify; biologically, life diversifies; and it is sheer ignorance to apply social analogies to biological processes. In any event, we know what the qualities and capacities of existing types are; we know how by education to do something towards the repression of what is evil in them and the conservation of what is good. The "American race" is a totally unknown thing; to presume that it will be better because (if we like to persist in the illusion that it is coming) it will be later, is no different from imagining that, because contemporary, Russia is better than ancient Greece. There is nothing more to be said to the pious stupidity that identifies recency with goodness. The unison to be achieved cannot be a unison of ethnic types. It must be, if it is to be at all, a unison of social and historic interests, established by the complete cutting-off of the ancestral memories of our populations, the enforced, exclusive use of the English language and English and American history in the schools and in the daily life.

The attainment of the other alternative, a harmony, also requires concerted public action. But the action would do no violence to our fundamental law and the spirit of our institutions, nor to the qualities of men. It would seek simply to eliminate the waste and the stupidity of our social organization, by way of freeing and strengthening the strong forces actually in operation. Starting with our existing ethnic and cultural groups, it would seek to provide conditions under which each may attain the perfection that is proper to its kind. The provision of such conditions is the primary intent of our fundamental law and the function of our institutions. And the various nationalities which compose our commonwealth must learn first of all this fact, which is perhaps, to most minds, the outstanding ideal content of "Americanism"—that democracy means self-realization through self-control, self-government, and that one is impossible without the other. For the application of this principle, which is realized in a harmony of societies, there are European analogies also. I omit Austria and Turkey, for the union of nationalities is there based more on inadequate force than on consent, and the form of their organization is alien to ours. I think of England and of Switzerland. England is a state of four nationalities—the English, Welsh, Scotch, and Irish (if one considers the Empire, of many more), and while English history is not unmarred by attempts at unison, both the home policy and the imperial policy have, since the Boer War,[7] been realized more and

7. A savage war (1899–1902) waged between Great Britain and the Boers (a name given by the English to the original Dutch settlers of South Africa) that gave Great Britain control of South Africa.

more in the application of the principle of harmony: the strength of the kingdom and the empire have been posited more and more upon the voluntary and autonomous cooperation of the component nationalities. Switzerland is a state of three nationalities, a republic as the United States is, far more democratically governed, concentrated in an area not much different in size, I suspect, from New York City, with a population not far from it in total. Yet Switzerland has the most loyal citizens in Europe. Their language, literary and spiritual traditions are on the one side German, on another Italian, on a third side French. And in terms of social organization, of economic prosperity, of public education, of the general level of culture, Switzerland is the most successful democracy in the world. It conserves and encourages individuality.

The reason lies, I think, in the fact that in Switzerland the the conception of "natural right" operates, consciously or unconsciously, as a generalization from the unalterable data of human nature. What is inalienable in the life of mankind is its intrinsic positive quality—its psychophysical inheritance. Men may change their clothes, their politics, their wives, their religions, their philosophies, to a greater or lesser extent: they cannot change their grandfathers. Jews or Poles or Anglo-Saxons, in order to cease being Jews or Poles or Anglo-Saxons, would have to cease to be. The selfhood which is inalienable in them, and for the realization of which they require "inalienable" liberty, is ancestrally determined, and the happiness which they pursue has its form implied in ancestral endowment. This is what, actually, democracy in operation assumes. There are human capacities which it is the function of the state to liberate and to protect; and the failure of the state as a government means its abolition. Government, the state, under the democratic conception, is merely an instrument, not an end. That it is often an abused instrument, that it is often seized by the powers that prey, that it makes frequent mistakes and considers only secondary ends, surface needs, which vary from moment to moment, is, of course, obvious: hence our social and political chaos. But that it is an instrument, flexibly adjustable to changing life, changing opinion, and needs, our whole electoral organization and party system declare. And as intelligence and wisdom prevail over "politics" and special interests, as the steady and continuous pressure of the inalienable qualities and purposes of human groups more and more dominate the confusion of our common life, the outlines of a possible great and truly democratic commonwealth become discernible.

Its form is that of the Federal republic; its substance a democracy of nationalities, cooperating voluntarily and autonomously in the enterprise of self-realization through the perfection of men according to their kind. The common language of the commonwealth, the language of its great political tradition, is English, but each nationality expresses its emotional and voluntary life in its own language, in its own inevitable aesthetic and intellectual forms. The common life of the commonwealth is politico-economic, and serves as the foundation and background for the realization of the distinctive individuality of each natio that composes it. Thus "American civilization," may come to mean the perfection of the cooperative harmonies of "European civilization," the waste, the squalor, and the distress of Europe being eliminated—a multiplicity in a unity, an orchestration of mankind. As in an orchestra, every type of instrument has its specific timbre and tonality, founded in its substance and form; as every type has its appropriate theme and melody in the whole symphony, so in society each ethnic group is the natural instrument, its spirit and culture are its theme and melody and the harmony and dissonances and discords of them all make the symphony of civilization, with this difference: a musical symphony is written before it is played; in the symphony of civilization the playing is the writing, so that there is nothing so fixed and inevitable about its progressions as in music, so that within the limits set by nature they may vary at will, and the range and variety of the harmonies may become wider and richer and more beautiful.

But the question is, do the dominant classes in America want such a society?

1915

MANI LEYB
1883–1953

His sense of the musicality of Yiddish made Mani Leyb the central poet of the Yunge aesthetics. He purified the language of his poems, eliminating political bombast, and contributed to the modernist project of creating a Yiddish literary tradition based in folk poetry by translating Scottish ballads and by adapting the rhythms of folk genres for his lyric poems.

Mani Leyb Brahinsky was one of six brothers and two sisters born to a poor family in the small city of Nizhyn in the Ukraine, famous for its lycée, where the Russian writer Gogol studied, and for its pickles. His father made a meager living selling animal pelts, horses, and cows at regional fairs, while his mother, the family breadwinner, sold hens, geese, and eggs in the town market. In an autobiographical sketch *A mayse vegn zikh* (A Tale about Myself), Mani Leyb describes his father's storytelling at the table on Sabbath afternoons and his mother's spontaneous rhymes, proverbs, and epigrams. These were the basis of his poetic education, for Mani Leyb's heder education ended at the age of eleven. He was apprenticed to a bootmaker whose son, a high-school student, encouraged him to write down the poems he was composing. Involved in strikes and revolutionary activities in his teens, Mani Leyb was arrested twice. On his way to America, he spent a year in London.

He arrived in New York in 1906, where he soon began publishing poems in the *Forverts* and *Fraye arbeter shtime*, dropped his surname, and worked in a shoe factory. He married a young woman from Nizhyn and had five children. The marriage was not a happy one, and in 1917 he began a relationship with the poet Rochelle Weprinski, which lasted throughout their lives. His friendships with David Ignatoff, Reuven Iceland, Zishe Landau, Joseph Rolnik, and other poets who were writing innovative poetry in a romantic strain encouraged Mani Leyb to write daring poetry himself. His poems, experimenting with musicality, a precious, symbolic aestheticism, and a sense of isolation, provoked controversy as well as parody from Moyshe-Leyb Halpern in 1910; Halpern, it is argued, became Mani Leyb's nemesis.

In 1914, Mani Leyb published *Shtiler, shtiler*, which we include here as *Hush*, a poem that admonishes its readers not to shout in the bombastic tones of the Labor poets but rather to seek redemption in the quiet of age-old Jewish messianic hopes.

He began to use the rhythms of folksongs and ballads in his work and brought the diction and cadences of the spoken language into his poems, which appeared in Yunge anthologies and miscellanies such as *Shriftn* (Writings). Like many of his peers, he translated poetry into Yiddish and was hired by Abraham Cahan to publish weekly in the *Forverts* a poem or a translation from Russian poetry and to help edit the advice column, *A bintl briv*. In 1918, he published three volumes of poetry—*Lider* (Poems), *Yidishe un slavishe motivn* (Jewish and Slavic Motifs), and *Baladn* (Ballads)—books that made him famous for his ability to convey with the directness of speech and the simplicity of a folk narrator the poetry of everyday incidents. The most famous of his ballads was *Yingl tsingl khvat*, a narrative about a boy who, stuck in the shtetl mud, persuades a nobleman to give him the magic ring and flying horse that allow him to escape and bring beauty—a snowstorm—to the world. That same year, Mani Leyb edited a collection of New York Yiddish poets.

In 1919, Mani Leyb contracted tuberculosis, which was not diagnosed for many years. In the 1920s, he translated into Yiddish many Russian poets—Pushkin, Kubrin, Lermontov, Tolstoy, Sologub, and Mandelstam, among others—and engaged in polemics with H. Leyvik, who attacked the Yunge poets (no longer young now) for remaining apolitical in a time of political controversy and confrontation between Zionism and socialism that penetrated all Jewish cultural life. He also began to write and publish poems for children, many of which were set to music and became very popular. He quit the *Forverts*, published briefly in the communist paper *Frayhayt* (Freedom), and then stopped writing for five years. He began to write again while he was in the Deborah Sanatorium in New Jersey, where he stayed from November 1932 through the spring of 1934. This is when he wrote his famous self-portrait *Ikh bin . . .* (I Am . . .), which sets his vocation as a shoemaker against his avocation as a poet. He also wrote a play, *Justice*, in 1933 and began to compose sonnets.

After leaving the sanatorium, Mani Leyb fell on hard times. It was the depression, he and Rochelle Weprinski were poor and lacked a stable home, and he continued to support his wife and five children. He began to do publicity work for the Bakers Union and to write for the *Forverts* again. His readers and friends bought him a small house in Far Rockaway, and he returned the generosity by publishing his friend Joseph Rolnik and publicly hosting other poets like Chaim Grade and Itsik Manger, newly arrived from Europe after the war.

Aside from the three volumes published in 1918, Mani Leyb never managed to collect his own poems. He continued to write the sonnets he had begun in the sanatorium—we include six of them here. According to scholar Ruth R. Wisse, he revised and reordered them during a hospitalization in 1953, the year he died of lung cancer, and published some of them individually. But they appeared together as a group only posthumously, in his collected poems, *Lider un balade* (1955). These sonnets are, perhaps, his best works, mature and nuanced and dark, reflecting the individual through his signature lyricism.

Hush[1]

Hush and hush—no sound be heard.
Bow in grief but say no word.
Black as pain and white as death,
Hush and hush and hold your breath.

1. Translated by Marie Syrkin. The poem is dedicated to the Yunge poet Zishe Landau.

Heard by none and seen by none
Out of the dark night will he,
Riding on a snow-white steed,
To our house come quietly.[2]

From the radiance of his face,
From his dress of shining white
Joy will shimmer and enfold;
Over us will fall his light.

Quieter—no sound be heard!
Bow in grief but say no word.
Black as pain and white as death,
Hush and hush and hold your breath.

If we have been mocked by them,
If we have been fooled again
And the long and weary night
We have waited all in vain,[3]

We will bend down very low
To the hard floor, and then will
Stand more quiet than before,
Stiller, stiller and more still.

1914

I Am . . . [1]

I am Mani Leyb, whose name is sung—
In Brownsville, Yehupets,[2] and farther, they know it:
Among cobblers, a splendid cobbler; among
Poetical circles, a splendid poet.

A boy straining over the cobbler's last
On moonlit nights . . . like a command,
Some hymn struck at my heart, and fast
The awl fell from my trembling hand.

Gracious, the first Muse came to meet
The cobbler with a kiss, and, young,
I tasted the Word that comes in a sweet
Shuddering first to the speechless tongue.

2. A reference to the Messiah, who will appear riding on a white horse or donkey (Zechariah 9.9).
3. Reiterates the continued Jewish hope for the Messiah, despite false claims throughout the centuries. This poem states its messianic hope in terms that are deliberately neither religious nor political.

1. Translated by John Hollander.
2. The fictional name given by Sholem Aleichem to the Ukrainian city of Kiev. "Brownsville": part of Brooklyn, New York, where many Jewish immigrants worked in shoe factories [adapted from Irving Howe, Ruth R. Wisse, Khone Shmeruk's note].

And my tongue flowed like a limpid stream,
My song rose as from some other place;
My world's doors opened onto dream;
My labor, my bread, were sweet with grace.

And all of the others, the shoemaker boys,
Thought that my singing was simply grand:
For their bitter hearts, my poems were joys.
Their source? They could never understand.

For despair in their working day's vacuity
They mocked me, spat at me a good deal,
And gave me the title, in perpetuity,
Of Purple Patchmaker, Poet and Heel.

Farewell then, brothers, I must depart:
Your cobbler's bench is not for me.
With songs in my breast, the Muse in my heart,
I went among poets, a poet to be.

When I came, then, among their company,
Newly fledged from out my shell,
They lauded and they laureled me,
Making me one of their number as well.

O Poets, inspired and pale, and free
As all the winged singers of the air,
We sang of beauties wild to see
Like happy beggars at a fair.

We sang, and the echoing world resounded.
From pole to pole chained hearts were hurled,
While we gagged on hunger, our sick chests pounded:
More than one of us left this world.

And God, who feedeth even the worm—
Was not quite lavish with his grace,
So I crept back, threadbare and infirm,
To sweat for bread at my working place.

But blessed be, Muse, for your bounties still,
Though your granaries will yield no bread—
At my bench, with a pure and lasting will,
I'll serve you solely until I am dead.

In Brownsville, Yehupets, beyond them, even,
My name shall ever be known, O Muse.
And I'm not a cobbler who writes, thank heaven,
But a poet who makes shoes.

1932

They . . . [1]

There had been multitudes, yea, multitudes, O God—
So many lively ones, and so many gallant,
So stately and so bearded, and so crowned with talent—
Whose language was astonishing, and nobly odd.

From under every rooftop with its gabled slopes
Such curious songs, and such haughty ones they'd sing,
Of the splendid peacock and Elimelekh the King,
With biblical cymbals, and the appropriate tropes.[2]

But high above their heads, only the sun could see
The raw attack, the cold knife of the murderer
As he descended on them in a violent stir,
And what a lot there was of savage butchery. . . .

Now they are melted, they are what violence can remember,
Two or three trees left standing amid the fallen timber.

ca. 1945–1953 1955

A Plum[1]

In the cool evening, the good provider plucked
From off a tree a fully ripened plum,
Still with its leaf on, and bit into some
Of its dewy, blue skin. From there, unlocked,

The long-slumbering juice came leaping up,
Foaming and cool. In order to make use
Of every single drop of all that juice,
Slowly, as one walks bearing a full cup

Of wine, he brought a double handful of plum
To his wife, and gently raised it to her mouth,
Whereupon she could lovingly begin—

1. Translated by John Hollander. This is one of a pair of sonnets that Mani Leyb wrote about the Nazi destruction of the Jews in Europe. They are part of his sequence of sonnets composed between the mid-1930s and 1953.
2. The melodies to which the reader chants the weekly Torah portion in synagogue. "Splendid peacock": a Yiddish folk song about cultural rebirth. "Elimelekh the King": Moyshe Nadir's modern Yiddish adaptation of the English nursery rhyme *Old King Cole* parodies a traditional Hasidic song that lauded a rebbe and his court. "Biblical cymbals": the instruments of the Jews, mentioned in the Bible and associated with King David and others (e.g., 2 Samuel 6.5) [adapted from Irving Howe, Ruth R. Wisse, and Khone Shmeruk's note].
1. Translated by John Hollander. Another of the sonnet series, reminiscent of but not derived from William Carlos Williams's famous free-verse poem of 1934 *This Is Just to Say.*

"Thanks," she said—to gnaw the plum from out
Of his hands, until those hands held only skin,
And pit, and flecks of overbrimming foam.

1933–1953 1955

Strangers[2]

Like a child, down onto her heart he fell there,
Wan-eyed, and in great lonely sorrow nursed
With all of his blood hungrily athirst
On her awakened springs, a golden pair,

Her taste of milk, then moved in like a knife
To open her sweet body up, to stay
Inside, die in cool damp, then fall away
Up in her Deep, back in her stuff of life.

They sat at evening with stars overhead
At table. And they both ate of the bread.
Between them on the table the knife stayed.

Their eyes like strangers', each other's eyes evaded,
As though their knot had been cut, and they were divided,
Like two ends of the table, by the blade.

ca. 1933–1953 1955

Odors[1]

Such pungent odors the old synagogues dispel:
Like those a cemetery's cleansing-shed will hold—
The basin, the copper of the pitcher,[2] reek of mold;
Of fine dust and the moth, the ark's silk curtains smell;

The books, of altars, sacrificial celebrations,
Old candles, and the sweet wine of the word of God;
To this the niches of the candelabra add
The stench of salt from tears of ancient lamentations.[3]

But from the tables caked with dirt there has arisen
A sweet, delicious odor now of something such
That your beard is quite damp, your mouth waters so much—

2. Translated by John Hollander.
1. Translated by John Hollander.
2. Jews wash their hands ritually upon leaving a cemetery by pouring water over each hand from a pitcher to cleanse them of contact with the dead, as prescribed in Leviticus 22.4–6.
3. The poem shifts in lines 4 through 8 from the cemetery to the synagogue. The poet loads the lines with Hebraic words for both the specific elements of ritual—*parokhes* (ark curtains), *karbones* (sacrifices), and *mizbeykhes* (altars)—and for common things, such as *yayin* instead of the Germanic *vayn* (wine) and the specific *kheylev-likht* (tallow candles).

This is the smell of cake and brandy passed at a circumcision
After prayers, by free-handed celebrants, to all
From where the poor sit to the high-toned eastern wall.[4]

ca. 1933–1953 1955

To the Gentile Poet[1]

Heir of Shakespeare, shepherds and cavaliers,
Bard of the gentiles, lucky you are indeed!
The earth is yours: it gives your fat hog feed
Where e'er it walks,[2] your Muse grazes on hers.

You've sat, a throstle in your tree, and trilled
Still answered by all the far-flung elsewheres,
By fullness of fields, by wide city squares,
By sated hearts' serenity fulfilled.

But I, a poet of the Jews—who needs it!—
A folk of wild grass grown on foreign earth,
Dust-bearded nomads, grandfathers of dearth—
The dust of fairs and texts is all that feeds it;

I chant, amid the alien corn, the tears[3]
Of desert wanderers under alien stars.

ca. 1933–1953 1955

Inscribed on a Tombstone[1]

Here lies Hersh Itsi's son: on his unseeing
Eyes are shards; in his shroud, like a good Jew.[2]
He walked into this world of ours as to
A yearly fair, from that far town Nonbeing

To peddle wind. On a scale he weighed out
All that he owned to a wheeler-dealer friend,

4. In Eastern European synagogues, the wealthy men would sit nearest the eastern wall, close to the Holy Ark.

1. Translated by John Hollander. In keeping with the poem's thematic connection to Shakespeare and British verse, the translator has changed the form from Mani Leyb's Petrarchan to the Shakespearean sonnet stanza, ending with a rhymed couplet.

2. "Where e'er it walks" echoes the first line of the well-known aria *Where'er you walk* from the oratorio *Semele* (1743) by George Frideric Handel (1685–1759), libretto by English dramatist William Congreve (1670–1729).

3. The translator echoes John Keats's (1795–1821) *Ode to a Nightingale,* lines 65–67: "Perhaps the selfsame song that found a path / Through the sad heart of Ruth, when, sick for home, / She stood in tears amid the alien corn." The Yiddish line, however, does not employ the metaphor of "corn": "*Un zingen zing ikh af a fremder velt di trern*" (And I sing in a foreign world the tears).

1. Translated by John Hollander.

2. Hersh Itsi was the name of the poet's father. Jews were traditionally buried in white shrouds, and shards were placed over their eyes as a symbol of their return to earth [Irving Howe, Ruth R. Wisse, Khone Shmeruk's note].

Got back home to light candles, tired at the end
When the first Sabbath stars had just about

Curtained his town's sky above all the Jews.
Now here he lies. His grave stands, mossed in green,
Between him and the gray week, as between
Sabbath delights and the fair's noisy stews.

Great blasts of wind that could outlast him still
Were left to all the children in his will.

ca. 1933–1953 1955

I. J. SCHWARTZ
1885–1971

Modeling it in part on *Leaves of Grass*, I. J. Schwartz, Walt Whitman's first Yiddish translator, wrote the quintessentially American Yiddish epic, *Kentucky*. Born in 1885 in a shtetl near Kovno, Lithuania, Yisroel-Yankev Shvarts (Israel Jacob Schwartz) was the second son of the town's rabbi. His father educated his son at home and then sent him to a yeshiva in Kovno, where he studied until age sixteen. There Schwartz encountered the Jewish Enlightenment and began to read secular literature in Hebrew, Russian, and Polish. This literature impelled him to begin translating poetry into Yiddish and writing his own lyrics.

Schwartz arrived in New York in 1906, where, at age twenty-one, he attended public high school and learned enough English to read and translate British and American literature into Yiddish, including Milton, Whitman, and Shakespeare.

His Hebrew education shaped Schwartz's work as a Yiddish writer. He taught Hebrew for a while in New York. But, more importantly, his first publications, in 1906 and 1907, included translations of poems by Ḥayim Naḥman Bialik, the early modern Hebrew nationalist poet. Throughout his career in Yiddish literature, Schwartz continued translating Hebrew poetry, publishing collections of his elegant translations of the modern Hebrew poets Bialik and Sha'ul Tshernikhovski, and the medieval Spanish Hebrew poets Solomon Ibn Gabirol, Moses Ibn Ezra, Judah Halevi. He also compiled and translated anthologies of rabbinic sources on specific themes, such as on the Sabbath and on Moses.

Soon after he arrived in New York, Schwartz met the Yunge poets and throughout the 1910s published in *Shriftn*, Opatoshu's breakaway collection *Di naye heym*, and other literary journals. In 1918, he, his wife, and his daughter moved to Lexington, Kentucky, where his sister had settled in 1904. There the Schwartzes started what became a successful clothing business. Soon after settling in Lexington, Schwartz began to write *Kentucky*, the book-length poem in Yiddish blank verse, which was composed between 1918 and 1922, and initially published in chapters in the journal *Tsukunft* (Future) before it appeared in book form in 1925. *Kentucky* narrates the story of Joshua, a Jew who immigrates to New York, makes his way as a peddler to Kentucky, and becomes a successful businessman, and of his progeny, who acculturate and assimilate. Like Abraham Cahan (*The Rise of David Levinsky*, 1917), Schwartz adapts the American success story, modeled on those by Horatio Alger and William Dean Howells, into a Jewish story. But unlike Cahan, Schwartz's *Kentucky* does not typify the treacheries of Americanization for the Jewish immigrant culture of New York City. Rather, Schwartz explores the ways that Jews complicated the society and history of blacks and whites in the American South. Cahan's novel focuses on the rise and fall of the main character while Schwartz presents a panoply of characters and their stories, introducing to Yiddish readers the various types of Americans that immigrants on the Lower East Side would not normally encounter: town dwellers and country folk, white and black Christians.

As Gertrude W. Dubrovsky, the English translator of *Kentucky*, argues, Whitman and Longfellow were Schwartz's models in the conception of *Kentucky* as an American poem that celebrates the American landscape, history, and people. Yet, that Schwartz chose to write *Kentucky* in unrhymed iambic pentameter—a new form in Yiddish—shows, too, how his translations of Shakespeare and Milton influenced him.

The excerpts included here are examples of Schwartz's descriptive writing. *Blue Grass*, a personal poem, opens *Kentucky* with the poet's evocation of the natural landscape. In the nineteen lines from *Litvaks* and in *Again Litvaks*, Schwartz prepares to introduce his protagonist, Joshua, by describing the arrival in the South of Jewish immigrants from Lithuania.

From Kentucky

Blue Grass[1]

The broad fields of Kentucky—
Even now I feel the tender breezes;
The same sun casts its light on me,
And the trees shelter me.
And I, child of the wandering Jew,
Who first sensed God's world in Lithuania
With its lonesome forests
And blue, delightful rivers,
Found myself, on the threshold of my youth,
In the maelstrom of New York,
On the shore of the yellow Hudson
Where streams converge
From the whole wide world.
And I learned to love
The great, wild restlessness.
I was a spray from its waves,
A flash among lightning flashes,
Until the city became dear to me
With its victors and vanquished,
Its fortunes and misfortunes,
Its wealth and poverty,
Its surpressed groans and gaiety.
I love the ruddy autumn,
Parks poured from copper and bronze,

1. Translated by Gertrude W. Dubrovsky.

And the warm-blue sky.
I love the sea shore of New Jersey
Where the waves pound forever,
Spilling over from green
Into light blue and dark blue,
Edged with white lace.
Now, as my hair starts to gray,
I stand here in Kentucky
Seeing the soft blue sky
And broad, unbounded expanse.
Fresh, bright mornings,
Green tobacco fields,
And meadows of blue-green grass.
In the night, with stars close overhead,
Sounds reach me, here on my porch:
Horses whinnying, and
The soft tender rhythm of mandolins
Which are interrupted
By the resounding laughter of black children.

1925

Litvaks[1]

The last to show up were
The lively, dynamic Litvaks,
Underfed, undernourished, faces green,
Bellies sunken like greyhounds,
Eyes sad and hungry.
They spoke only with hands and eyes.
With them they brought small sewing machines,
Milliners' frames and blocks,
Shoemakers' round, hollowed benches.
Awls and hammers.
This society of craftsmen from the old country,
Settled near the canals,
On Vine Street, Water Street, Clay Street[2]—
The streets which cut across
The gleaming train tracks,
And where convivial blacks congregate
For a glass of beer and whiskey.
The Litvaks settled in shacks
With small, dusty, broken windows.

* * *

1. Translated by Gertrude W. Dubrovsky. Jews from Lithuania are called Litvaks. Non-Jews are Lithuanians [Dubrovsky's note].
2. Poor streets in downtown Lexington, Kentucky.

Thus, shriveled, pale Lithuania
Moved in and spread out
In the rich and blessed South.

* * *

1925

Again Litvaks[1]

The trees bent under the burden of cool shining red apples
And transparent pink apricots.
The forest was still a forest: braided,
Branched, knotted, clustered, twisted.
And the density smelled of decay,
With wet mushrooms, wild raspberry bushes,
Centuries-old layers of wood growth,
Where one plant choked another
And grew out of the other's belly.
In the sharp bright moonlight
Lines of deer
With forest-like, thick branched horns
Still filed to the silvery waters.
Caravans of strong wild turkeys
Their powerful wings spotted with color,
And gray legs hard as stone,
Fled into the forest to observe the night,
Settled themselves in strong black branches,
And, at the least rustle, gobbled in their sleep.
At noon-hour, the air was full
With the smell of rich, heavy,
Liquid honey, like pure gold,
And the buzzing of fat, golden bees.
The distant plain still retained
The virgin fertility of young earth
Which ejaculated and implanted seed.
The grass was rich and heavy and sprouting,
And herds of fat oxen with enormous
Broad backs and horns moved around.
Cows dragged their heavy
Filled udders of milk in the rich grass.
Innumerable flocks of white sheep,
Like white mobile spots,
Rolled in the living green,
Like white waves in a green sea.
The farmer brought his rich surplus
From field and garden into the city:
Blood-red juicy beets,
Heavy white potatoes like stones,
Green and tightly curled heads of cabbage,

1. Translated by Gertrude W. Dubrovsky.

He didn't measure the produce by the bushel,
But distributed it in bags for small change.
A fat hen was sold in quarters,
And roosters were added to the bargain.

Lithuania[2] fell into this plenty,
In the land which flowed with milk and honey.[3]
When she learned how to eat,
She sat down in the dust of the stores
And started sending regards
To the languishing, hungry little towns.[4]
The letters told how well off they were:
There is meat to spare, even in the middle of the week,
And what meat at that: chickens, geese, and ducks.
They eat bread made of fine wheat flour.
Large red, sweet watermelons,
Which spurt honey-sweet juice,
Are lying around in the street.
The skinny, shriveled relatives
Who fed on black bread
And watery potatoes in the skins,
Hungrily started to dream
Of distant seas and of the rich land,
From which came pretty pictures
Of daughters with smooth faces and sons
Dressed up in shining top hats,
Thick, heavy chains on their stomachs.
And with round grandchildren, like bulldogs.
But when the thin greenhorn woman
Had stuffed the bulldogs
Of the pretty pictures to the gills
With chunks of bread and honey,
She began longing for herring.
She took it out on her husband
And gave Columbus a piece of her mind:
His bread is no bread, his meat is no meat,
Here, a chicken is not a chicken, and, for that matter,
A brother is not a brother—and that's it.

The husbands, meanwhile,
Conscientiously carried on their business:
They trudged over road and route
With heavy backbreaking packs.
The man on the road made do with bread,
With a baked potato, with an egg,
Which the farmer granted him.
They slaved day and night in the store,

2. Here Schwartz uses "Lithuania" to refer collectively to the Lithuanian Jews who settled in Kentucky. The subsequent lines personify the collective as "she."

3. Originally refers to the land to which God promises Moses he will deliver the Israelites after their escape from slavery in Egypt and wandering in the desert (Exodus 3.8, 3.17). From the 1880s on, Eastern European Jews used the phrase to refer to the United States. Here, it refers to Kentucky in particular.

4. I.e., the *shtetlekh* (shtetls) in Lithuania.

Roasting by the burning iron,
Clattering on the old sewing machine,
Talking their hearts out to the black.
And it was remarkable: how soon
The people without a common language understood—
Or more clearly stated—smelled, felt,
The naked nature of the strange,
Exotic and distant race. They recognized
Every twist, move, and nuance,
The sincere innocent laughter
And the newly acquired sadness.
They felt the spirit, and the rich tropic flavor.
It was natural that the black,
On his side, also immediately sensed that these
People were somehow closer to him,
Belonging, indeed, to the white race,
But a white race of another kind.

The German brothers[5] turned up their noses
At the skinny Jews
And called them "green beggars,"
Making fun of their customs.
Just twice a year, in the awesome days
Of *Rosh Hashana* and *Yom Kippur*, the abyss,
The brotherly abyss, closed.
They came together to pray in a *minyen*.[6]
After that they wished each other a good year
And parted until the next year.
The only one who, in a way,
Breached that gap was
The tall thin "*shokhet*"[7] with his knife.
But in the cemetery encircled by alien crosses
When a thin, sickly Lithuanian or German child
Could no longer endure the dust
Of his parent's business
And pined away into a better world,
They were laid like brothers together
In the small graves of the Jewish cemetery.
Because the first to be initiated into the cemetery
Were the wan frail children.
Small hills arose
With thin white boards for headstones,
And on the boards in the fine grass
The Southern sun revealed
The strange script—four cornered and new.[8]

1925

5. German Jews who had arrived in the United States in the mid-19th century and were well assimilated when the Eastern European Jews immigrated.
6. The quorum of ten men needed for traditional Jewish communal prayer. "*Rosh Hashana*": the Jewish New Year. "*Yom Kippur*": the Day of Atonement. Both holidays are in the autumn.
7. Emphasizes a pronunciation [of the Hebrew word] by German Jews [Dubrovsky's note]. The *shokhet* (in Yiddish, *shoykhet*) ritually slaughters kosher animals for food.
8. Refers to the Hebrew letters on the gravestones, new to Kentucky.

MOYSHE NADIR
1885–1943

Most famous for his wordplay and renewal of the Yiddish language, the satirist Moyshe Nadir left this epithet for himself: "Incidentally, Moyshe Nadir himself splintered, scattered, and spilled, like a ray of light that cannot be caught, like a sea that cannot be restrained." Moyshe Nadir, a comic pseudonym meaning "the lowest point" or "here, take," was born Isaac Reiss (Rayz) in Narayov, eastern Galicia, in 1885. His father, originally from Złoczew, the hometown of Moyshe-Leyb Halpern, who later became Nadir's closest friend and collaborator, was at first a wheat and honey merchant but later taught German to property owners. Nadir attended heder until the age of twelve and studied German with his father. In 1898, he, his siblings, and their mother joined his father, who had immigrated earlier, on the Lower East Side of New York City. Although Nadir apparently attended school and learned English, by age fourteen he had worked in a sweatshop and then as a window washer and an insurance-company agent. He seemed always to have been interested in having the Yiddish language and culture take their place as entities in the world at large.

Nadir's first publications—light poems, sketches, and articles—appeared in the newspaper *Teglikher herald* (Daily Herald) around 1902. Associated with the writers of the Yunge, he published in their journals and miscellanies; yet, as he developed his gifts as a satirist, Nadir parodied their aestheticism. When the Yiddish satirical and humorous periodical the *Groyser kundes* (Big Joker) began publication, Nadir became coeditor. In 1910, he and Jacob Adler edited a short-lived biweekly humor journal, the *Yidisher gazlon* (Jewish Bandit), and over the next decade, he contributed to other publications of the same type, such as the *Kibetser* (Kibitzer) and the miscellany *Humor un satire* (Humor and Satire).

Moyshe Nadir's first book, *Vilde royzn* (Wild Roses), appeared under his pseudonym in 1915, and its erotic miniatures made a splash on the literary scene. He continued to contribute to the Yunge monthly *Literatur un lebn*, edited by Kolye Teper and Zishe Landau. He and Moyshe-Leyb Halpern coedited the miscellany *Fun mentsh tsu mentsh* (From Person to Person) in 1916; later he took that title for his column in the newspaper the *Tog* (Day). He wrote another popular column of feuilletons under the title *Fun nekhtn biz morgn* (From Yesterday until Tomorrow) for the communist paper *Frayhayt* (Freedom). In 1919 with Halpern, Nadir coauthored a drama (never performed), *Unter der last fun tseylem* (Under the Burden of the Cross). He went on to write humorous plays for the Yiddish stage, including works for Maurice Schwartz's famous Yiddish Art Theater, the Yiddish marionette theater Modyakot, his own theater at his summer art colony in Loch Sheldrake, New York, and Artef, the avant-garde theater group. His most-often-produced play was the verse comedy *Rivington Street*.

Nadir wrote and translated in Yiddish and also published in English in such journals as the obscure *Smart Set* and the renowned *American Hebrew*. He even translated a play by Sholem Aleichem but complained that writing in English was like wearing "heavy spectacles." For a short while, he was proprietor of a café in New York, Nakinka's (Nadir's Artists' Cafe). During these years, he made a striking figure as an "aristocratic bohemian"—tall, thin, dark-complected, often wearing a cape and a colorful scarf.

In 1926, Nadir returned to Europe for the second time, visiting Paris, Warsaw, Vilna, and the Soviet Union, where, although embracing Soviet support for Yiddish culture and institutions, he did not in the end join the Communist party. Nadir renounced his communist sympathies only after the Hitler-Stalin Pact of 1939. On June 8, 1943, Nadir died of a heart attack at age fifty-eight in Woodstock, New York.

After his death, his widow published Nadir's last book, *Moyde-ani: lider un proze,*

1936–1943 (I Confess: Poems and Prose, 1936–1943), which includes a foreword by the poet L. Faynberg and an autobiographical introduction by Nadir himself. His work was translated into German, French, Russian, Polish, and Hebrew.

The sketch included here in its classic translation by Irving Howe, *The Man Who Slept through the End of the World*, was first published in Yiddish in 1924. This tale of a modern-day immigrant Rip Van Winkle echoes and parodies the classic Yiddish tales. Whereas Washington Irving's character awakens to find the world changed, Nadir's nameless protagonist awakens to find the world gone. Unlike I. L. Peretz's famous Polish Jewish victim Bontshe the Silent, who is so cowed by life that when God offers him all of paradise, he asks only for a buttered roll for breakfast, Nadir's American "alrightnik" tries to go on with his life—searching for his watch, his malted, his paycheck, his movies, and his wife. While complaining and protesting to God like Sholem Aleichem's Tevye the Milkman, Nadir's hero sputters absurdly into the vanished world. What can he do but enact the Yiddish expression *shlogn kop in vant*, beating his head against not the wall, but the void? Yet the void sustains him, and, despite himself, he survives in order, absurdly, to tell the story.

The Man Who Slept through the End of the World[1]

He was always sleepy. And always ready to sleep. Everywhere. At the biggest mass meetings, at all the concerts, at every important convention, he could be seen sitting asleep.

And he slept in every conceivable and inconceivable pose. He slept with his elbows in the air and his hands behind his head. He slept standing up, leaning against himself so that he shouldn't fall down. He slept in the theater, in the streets, in the synagogue. Wherever he went, his eyes would drip with sleep.

Neighbors used to say that he had already slept through seven big fires, and once, at a really big fire, he was carried out of his bed, still asleep, and put down on the sidewalk. In this way he slept for several hours until a patrol wagon came along and took him away.

It was said that when he was standing under the wedding canopy and reciting the vows, "Thou are to me . . ." he fell asleep at the word "sanctified," and they had to beat him over the head with brass pestles for several hours to wake him up. And then he slowly said the next word and again fell asleep.

We mention all this so that you may believe the following story about our hero.

Once, when he went to sleep, he slept and slept and slept; but in his sleep it seemed to him that he heard thunder in the streets and his bed was shaking somewhat; so he thought in his sleep that it was raining outside, and as a result his sleep became still more delicious. He wrapped himself up in his quilt and in his warmth.

When he awoke he saw a strange void: his wife was no longer there, his bed was no longer there, his quilt was no longer there. He wanted to look through the window, but there was no window through which to look. He wanted to run down the three flights and yell, "Help!" but there were no stairs on which to run and no air in which to yell. And when he wanted merely to go out of doors, he saw that there was no out of doors. Evaporated!

1. Translated by Irving Howe.

For a while he stood there in confusion, unable to comprehend what had happened. But afterward he bethought himself: I'll go to sleep. He saw, however, that there was no longer any earth on which to sleep. Only then did he raise two fingers to his forehead and reflect: Apparently I've slept through the end of the world. Isn't that a fine how-do-you-do?

He became depressed. No more world, he thought. What will I do without a world? Where will I go to work, how will I make a living, especially now that the cost of living is so high and a dozen eggs cost a dollar twenty and who knows if they're even fresh, and besides, what will happen to the five dollars the gas company owes me? And where has my wife gone off to? Is it possible that she too has disappeared with the world, and with the thirty dollars' pay I had in my pockets? And she isn't by nature the kind that disappears, he thought to himself.

And what will I do if I want to sleep? On what will I stretch out if there isn't any world? And maybe my back will ache? And who'll finish the bundle of work in the shop? And suppose I want a glass of malted, where will I get it?

Eh, he thought, have you ever seen anything like it? A man should fall asleep with the world under his head and wake up without it!

As our hero stood there in his underwear, wondering what to do, a thought occurred to him: To hell with it! So there isn't any world! Who needs it anyway? Disappeared is disappeared: I might as well go to the movies and kill some time. But to his astonishment he saw that, together with the world, the movies had also disappeared.

A pretty mess I've made here, thought our hero and began smoothing his mustache. A pretty mess I've made here, falling asleep! If I hadn't slept so soundly, he taunted himself, I would have disappeared along with everything else. This way I'm unfortunate, and where will I get a malted? I love a glass in the morning. And my wife? Who knows with whom she's disappeared? If it's with that presser from the top floor, I'll murder her, so help me God.

Who knows how late it is?

With these words our hero wanted to look at his watch but couldn't find it. He searched with both hands in the left and right pockets of the infinite emptiness but could find nothing to touch.

I just paid two dollars for a watch and here it's already disappeared, he thought to himself. All right. If the world went under, it went under. That I don't care about. It isn't my world. But the watch! Why should my watch go under? A new watch. Two dollars. It wasn't even wound.

And where will I find a glass of malted?

There's nothing better in the morning than a glass of malted. And who knows if my wife . . . I've slept through such a terrible catastrophe, I deserve the worst. Help, help, hee—lp! Where were my brains? Why didn't I keep an eye on the world and my wife? Why did I let them disappear when they were still so young?

And our hero began to beat his head against the void,[2] but since the void was a very soft one it didn't hurt him and he remained alive to tell this story.

1924, 1959

2. A play on the Yiddish idiom *shlogn kop in vant*, "to beat one's head against the wall," an expression of frustration.

ANZIA YEZIERSKA
ca. 1885–1970

Called during her few years of fame "Cinderella of the Sweatshops," Anzia Yezierska developed a prose style inflected with Yiddish to give the mark of authenticity to her impassioned fiction about the struggles of Jewish immigrant women. Yezierska, the youngest of nine children, was born in the shtetl Plinsk, near Warsaw, around 1885. Before 1898, the fifteen-year-old Anzia, her father, mother, and siblings came to New York, joining her eldest brother, Meyer, who had arrived several years before. Meyer's name had been changed by immigration officials to Max Mayer, and the entire family assumed the new last name as well, Yezierska taking the first name Harriet or Hattie. She reclaimed her own name only when she was in her late twenties. According to her daughter, Louise Levitas Henriksen, Yezierska herself was never certain of her birth date and, during her period of fame, recast her life repeatedly, changing the dates to make herself seem younger than she was.

Yezierska's family lived in a tenement apartment on the Lower East Side, where her father studied the sacred texts while her mother, working as a menial, supported the family. In contrast to her brothers, whom her parents encouraged to pursue higher education, Yezierska had only two years of elementary school before she went to work in sweatshops and factories and as a domestic. Her sisters married early, but conflicts with her father, whose traditional values and ways she scorned, led Yezierska to move into the Clara de Hirsch Home for Working Girls, a residential trade school for young immigrant Jews founded in 1897 by well-meaning "uptown" German Jews. There Yezierska found a way to continue her education, according to her daughter, for at age eighteen or nineteen she won a four-year scholarship to Columbia University, inventing a high-school diploma she did not possess and promising her patrons at the East Side settlement house that she would study domestic science to benefit the Jews. Despite her official concentration at Columbia's Teachers College (1901–05), she read poetry and philosophy, and honed her English to a refined elegance by memorizing nineteenth-century Romantic poetry. From 1908 to 1913, she taught elementary school and briefly attended the Academy of Dramatic Arts.

Yezierska married in 1910 but immediately annulled the marriage. In 1911, she married again—a schoolteacher and textbook writer. In 1912, their daughter was born. During a marital crisis in 1913, Yezierska wrote her first short story, *The Free Vacation House,* an angry work about how charity imprisons its recipients; it was published in 1915. She left her husband and moved to San Francisco with their daughter in 1916, divorcing him that same year. Their daughter eventually lived with her father. After doing social work, Yezierska returned to New York to teach again and met John Dewey, a world-famous authority on education and a professor at Columbia. During 1917 and 1918, the immigrant Jew and the Yankee developed a passionate but unconsummated relationship, and he encouraged her to write and publish, Dewey himself writing letters and poems to her. In *All I Could Never Be* (1932) and *Red Ribbon on a White Horse* (1950), Yezierska fictionalized their love as an ideal joining of two cultures that proves disillusioning. This story of the Gentile mentor and suitor became a prototype that recurred throughout her works as Yezierska examined the transformation of creative immigrant women from greenhorns to Americans.

When, after repeated rejections, her short story *The Fat of the Land* was accepted for publication and named the best short story of 1919 by noted editor Edward O'Brien, Yezierska became famous. Houghton Mifflin published her first collection of short stories, *Hungry Hearts,* in 1920, of which Samuel Goldwyn took note. The film mogul brought Yezierska to Hollywood as a screenwriter and produced a silent movie, *Hungry Hearts*, in 1922. Although Goldwyn offered her a $100,000 contract to write screenplays, she felt stymied in Hollywood and returned to New York.

Yezierska subsequently published another collection of short stories, *Children of Loneliness*, as well as her first novel, *Salome of the Tenements*, in 1923. A silent film based on this novel was directed by Sidney Alcott in 1925, the same year that she published *Bread Givers*, which, decades later, became her most famous novel. *Arrogant Beggar* came out in 1927 and *All I Could Never Be* in 1932.

During the depression, the Works Progress Administration's Writers Project gave Yezierska the trivializing task of cataloguing the trees in Central Park. For the next two decades, she published articles, essays, and book reviews, but only in 1950 did she publish another book, *Red Ribbon on a White Horse*, an autobiography that her daughter calls fiction. Although she had fallen into obscurity, Yezierska continued to write—powerful stories about the vicissitudes of old age. She died in 1970 in California. With the advent of the women's movement in the United States, feminist scholars and others have revived interest in Yezierska's works, and all of her books have been reissued.

We have included here Yezierska's short story *Children of Loneliness,* first published in her 1923 collection of the same title and reprinted in *The Open Cage* in 1979. It tells of the generational clash between Rachel, the college graduate, and her parents, still living in the squalor of the Lower East Side tenements and immersed in their traditional ways. Rejecting her parents and all they stand for, Rachel vainly seeks redemption from the pain in Frank Baker, her Gentile American college beau. Hers becomes the signature dilemma for the assimilating children of Jewish immigrants.

Children of Loneliness

I

"Oh, Mother, can't you use a fork?" exclaimed Rachel as Mrs. Ravinsky took the shell of the baked potato in her fingers and raised it to her watering mouth.

"Here, *Teacherin* mine,[1] you want to learn me in my old age how to put the bite in my mouth?" The mother dropped the potato back into her plate, too wounded to eat. Wiping her hands on her blue-checked apron, she turned her glance to her husband, at the opposite side of the table.

"Yankev," she said bitterly, "stick your bone on a fork. Our *teacherin* said you dassn't touch no eatings with the hands."

"All my teachers died already in the old country," retorted the old man. "I ain't going to learn nothing new no more from my American daughter." He continued to suck the marrow out of the bone with that noisy relish that was so exasperating to Rachel.

"It's no use," stormed the girl, jumping up from the table in disgust; "I'll never be able to stand it here with you people."

" 'You people?' What do you mean by 'you people?' " shouted the old man, lashed into fury by his daughter's words. "You think you got a different skin from us because you went to college?"

1. My (female) teacher (Yiddish). Note the Yiddish syntax transposed here and in the rest of the sentence of the mother's speech.

"It drives me wild to hear you crunching bones like savages. If you people won't change, I shall have to move and live by myself."

Yankev Ravinsky threw the half-gnawed bone upon the table with such vehemence that a plate broke into fragments.

"You witch you!" he cried in a hoarse voice tense with rage. "Move by yourself! We lived without you while you was away in college, and we can get on without you further. God ain't going to turn his nose on us because we ain't got table manners from America. A hell she made from this house since she got home."

"*Shah!* Yankev *leben*,"[2] pleaded the mother, "the neighbors are opening the windows to listen to our hollering. Let us have a little quiet for a while till the eating is over."

But the accumulated hurts and insults that the old man had borne in the one week since his daughter's return from college had reached the breaking-point. His face was convulsed, his eyes flashed, and his lips were flecked with froth as he burst out in a volley of scorn:

"You think you can put our necks in a chain and learn us new tricks? You think you can make us over for Americans? We got through till fifty years of our lives eating in our own old way—"

"Woe is me, Yankev *leben!*" entreated his wife. "Why can't we choke ourselves with our troubles? Why must the whole world know how we are tearing ourselves by the heads? In all Essex Street,[3] in all New York, there ain't such fights like by us."

Her pleadings were in vain. There was no stopping Yankev Ravinsky once his wrath was roused. His daughter's insistence upon the use of a knife and fork spelled apostasy, anti-Semitism, and the aping of the Gentiles.

Like a prophet of old condemning unrighteousness, he ran the gamut of denunciation, rising to heights of fury that were sublime and godlike, and sinking from sheer exhaustion to abusive bitterness.

"*Pfui* on all your American colleges! *Pfui* on the morals of America! No respect for old age. No feat for God. Stepping with your feet on all the laws of the holy Torah. A fire should burn out the whole new generation. They should sink into the earth, like Korah."[4]

"Look at him cursing and burning! Just because *I* insist on their changing their terrible table manners. One would think I was killing them."

"Do you got to use a gun to kill?" cried the old man, little red threads darting out of the whites of his eyes.

"Who is doing the killing? Aren't you choking the life out of me? Aren't you dragging me by the hair to the darkness of past ages every minute of the day? I'd die of shame if one of my college friends should open the door while you people are eating."

"You—you—"

The old man was on the point of striking his daughter when his wife seized the hand he raised.

"*Mincha!*[5] Yankev, you forgot *Mincha!*"

2. Literally, "life"; here, a term of endearment (Yiddish). "*Shah!*": Shush, be quiet (Yiddish).
3. An impoverished street of tenements on the Lower East Side of New York City.
4. Central figure in the story of the revolt against the authority of Moses during the wanderings in the wilderness. When Korah complained about the religious authority of Moses, he and the other rebels were swallowed up by the earth (Numbers 16).
5. Afternoon prayer service (Hebrew).

This reminder was a flash of inspiration on Mrs. Ravinsky's part, the only thing that could have ended the quarreling instantly. *Mincha* was the prayer just before sunset of the orthodox Jews. This religious rite was so automatic with the old man that at his wife's mention of *Mincha* everything was immediately shut out, and Yankev Ravinsky rushed off to a corner of the room to pray.

"Ashrai Yoishwai Waisahuh!"[6]

"Happy are they who dwell in Thy house. Ever shall I praise Thee. *Selah!*[7] Great is the Lord, and exceedingly to be praised; and His greatness is unsearchable. On the majesty and glory of Thy splendor, and on Thy marvelous deeds, will I mediate."

The shelter from the storms of life that the artist finds in his art, Yankev Ravinsky found in his prescribed communion with God. All the despair caused by his daughter's apostasy, the insults and disappointments he suffered, were in his sobbing voice. But as he entered into the spirit of his prayer, he felt the man of flesh drop away in the outflow of God around him. His voice mellowed, the rigid wrinkles of his face softened, the hard glitter of anger and condemnation in his eyes was transmuted into the light of love as he went on:

"The Lord is gracious and merciful; slow to anger and of great loving-kindness. To all that call upon Him in truth He will hear their cry and save them."

Oblivious to the passing and repassing of his wife as she warmed anew the unfinished dinner, he continued:

"Put not your trust in princes, in the son of man in whom there is no help." Here Reb[8] Ravinsky paused long enough to make a silent confession for the sin of having placed his hope on his daughter instead of on God. His whole body bowed with the sense of guilt. Then in a moment his humility was transfigured into exaltation. Sorrow for sin dissolved in joy as he became more deeply aware of God's unfailing protection.

"Happy is he who hath the God of Jacob for his help, whose hope is in the Lord his God. He healeth the broken in heart, and bindeth up their wounds."

A healing balm filled his soul as he returned to the table, where the steaming hot food awaited him. Rachel sat near the window pretending to read a book. Her mother did not urge her to join them at the table, fearing another outbreak, and the meal continued in silence.

The girl's thoughts surged hotly as she glanced from her father to her mother. A chasm of four centuries could not have separated her more completely from them than her four years at Cornell.

"To think that I was born of these creatures! It's an insult to my soul. What kinship have I with these two lumps of ignorance and superstition? They're ugly and gross and stupid. I'm all sensitive nerves. They want to wallow in dirt."

She closed her eyes to shut out the sight of her parents as they silently ate together, unmindful of the dirt and confusion.

"How is it possible that I lived with them and like them only four years

6. Ashkenazic pronunciation of the Hebrew *Ashrei yoshvei beitecha*, "What happiness to sit in Your house," the opening words of the first prayer of Mincha.

7. Pause, silence, interlude; the concluding word in some Psalms and in liturgy (Hebrew).

8. Mister (Yiddish).

ago? What is it in me that so quickly gets accustomed to the best? Beauty and cleanliness are as natural to me as if I'd been born on Fifth Avenue[9] instead of the dirt of Essex Street."

A vision of Frank Baker passed before her. Her last long talk with him out under the trees in college still lingered in her heart. She felt that she had only to be with him again to carry forward the beautiful friendship that had sprung up between them. He had promised to come shortly to New York. How could she possibly introduce such a born and bred American to her low, ignorant, dirty parents?

"I might as well tear the thought of Frank Baker out of my heart," she told herself. "If he just once sees the pigsty of a home I come from, if he just sees the table manners of my father and mother, he'll fly through the ceiling."

Timidly, Mrs. Ravinsky turned to her daughter.

"Ain't you going to give a taste the eating?"

No answer.

"I fried the *lotkes*[1] special' for you—"

"I can't stand your fried, greasy stuff."

"Ain't even my cooking good no more either?" Her gnarled, hard-worked hands clutched at her breast. "God from the world, for what do I need yet any more my life? Nothing I do for my child is no use no more."

Her head sank; her whole body seemed to shrivel and grow old with the sense of her own futility.

"How I was hurrying to run by the butcher before everybody else, so as to pick out the grandest, fattest piece of *brust!*"[2] she wailed, tears streaming down her face. "And I put my hand away from my heart and put a whole fresh egg into the *lotkes*, and I stuffed the stove full of coal like a millionaire so as to get the *lotkes* fried so nice and brown; and now you give a kick on everything I done—"

"Fool woman," shouted her husband, "stop laying yourself on the ground for your daughter to step on you! What more can you expect from a child raised up in America? What more can you expect but that she should spit in your face and make dirt from you?" His eyes, hot and dry under their lids, flashed from his wife to his daughter. "The old Jewish eating is poison to her; she must have *trefa*[3] ham—only forbidden food."

Bitter laughter shook him.

"Woman, how you patted yourself with pride before all the neighbors, boasting of our great American daughter coming home from college! This is our daughter, our pride, our hope, our pillow for our old age that we were dreaming about! This is our American *teacherin!* A Jew-hater, an anti-Semite we brought into the world, a betrayer of our race who hates her own father and mother like the Russian Czar once hated a Jew. She makes herself so refined, she can't stand it when we use the knife or fork the wrong way; but her heart is that of a brutal Cossack, and she spills her own father's and mother's blood like water."

Every word he uttered seared Rachel's soul like burning acid. She felt herself becoming a witch, a she-devil, under the spell of his accusations.

"You want me to love you yet?" She turned upon her father like an avenging

9. Elegant, expensive residential Manhattan avenue.

1. Potato pancakes (Yiddish).

2. Breast; here, breast of veal or lamb (Yiddish).

3. I.e., *treyf*, nonkosher (Yiddish, from the Hebrew *treif*).

fury. "If there's any evil hatred in my soul, you have roused it with your cursed preaching."

"*Oi-i-i*! Highest One! pity Yourself on us!" Mrs. Ravinsky wrung her hands. "Rachel, Yankev, let there be an end to this knife-stabbing! *Gottuniu!*[4] my flesh is torn to pieces!"

Unheeding her mother's pleading, Rachel rushed to the closet where she kept her things.

"I was a crazy idiot to think that I could live with you people under one roof." She flung on her hat and coat and bolted for the door.

Mrs. Ravinsky seized Rachel's arm in passionate entreaty.

"My child, my heart, my life, what do you mean? Where are you going?"

"I mean to get out of this hell of a home this very minute," she said, tearing loose from her mother's clutching hands.

"Woe is me! My child! We'll be to shame and to laughter by the whole world. What will people say?"

"Let them say! My life is my own; I'll live as I please." She slammed the door in her mother's face.

"They want me to love them yet," ran the mad thoughts in Rachel's brain as she hurried through the streets, not knowing where she was going, not caring. "Vampires, bloodsuckers fastened on my flesh! Black shadow blighting every ray of light that ever came my way! Other parents scheme and plan and wear themselves out to give their child a chance, but they put dead stones in front of every chance I made for myself."

With the cruelty of youth to everything not youth, Rachel reasoned:

"They have no rights, no claims over me like other parents who do things for their children. It was my own brains, my own courage, my own iron will that forced my way out of the sweatshop to my present position in the public schools. I owe them nothing, nothing, nothing."

II

Two weeks already away from home. Rachel looked about her room. It was spotlessly clean. She had often said to herself while at home with her parents: "All I want is an empty room, with a bed, a table, and a chair. As long as it is clean and away from them, I'll be happy." But was she happy?

A distant door closed, followed by the retreating sound of descending footsteps. Then all was still, the stifling stillness of a rooming-house. The white, empty walls pressed in upon her, suffocated her. She listened acutely for any stir of life, but the continued silence was unbroken save for the insistent ticking of her watch.

"I ran away from home burning for life," she mused, "and all I've found is the loneliness that's death." A wave of self-pity weakened her almost to the point of tears. "I'm alone! I'm alone!" she moaned, crumpling into a heap.

"Must it always be with me like this," her soul cried in terror, "either to live among those who drag me down or in the awful isolation of a hall bedroom? Oh, I'll die of loneliness among these frozen, each-shut-in-himself Americans! It's one thing to break away, but, oh, the strength to go on alone!

4. Dear God (Yiddish).

How can I ever do it? The love instinct is so strong in me; I can not live without love, without people."

The thought of a letter from Frank Baker suddenly lightened her spirits. That very evening she was to meet him for dinner. Here was hope—more than hope. Just seeing him again would surely bring the certainty.

This new rush of light upon her dark horizon so softened her heart that she could almost tolerate her superfluous parents.

"If I could only have love and my own life, I could almost forgive them for bringing me into the world. I don't really hate them; I only hate them when they stand between me and the new America that I'm to conquer."

Answering her impulse, her feet led her to the familiar Ghetto streets. On the corner of the block where her parents lived she paused, torn between the desire to see her people and the fear of their nagging reproaches. The old Jewish proverb came to her mind: "The wolf is not afraid of the dog, but he hates his bark." "I'm not afraid of their black curses for sin. It's nothing to me if they accuse me of being an anti-Semite or a murderer, and yet why does it hurt me so?"

Rachel had prepared herself to face the usual hailstorm of reproaches and accusations, but as she entered the dark hallway of the tenement, she heard her father's voice chanting the old familiar Hebrew psalm of "The Race of Sorrows":

"Hear my prayer, O Lord, and let me cry come unto Thee.

For my days are consumed like smoke, and my bones are burned as an hearth.

I am like a pelican of the wilderness.

I am like an owl of the desert.

I have eaten ashes like bread and mingled my drink with weeping."[5]

A faintness came over her. The sobbing strains of the lyric song melted into her veins like a magic sap, making her warm and human again. All her strength seemed to flow out of her in pity for her people. She longed to throw herself on the dirty, ill-smelling tenement stairs and weep: "Nothing is real but love—love. Nothing so false as ambition."

Since her early childhood she remembered often waking up in the middle of the night and hearing her father chant this age-old song of woe. There flashed before her a vivid picture of him, huddled in the corner beside the table piled high with Hebrew books, swaying to the rhythm of his Jeremiad,[6] the sputtering light of the candle stuck in a bottle throwing uncanny shadows over his gaunt face. The skull-cap, the side-locks, and the long gray beard made him seem like some mystic stranger from a far-off world and not a father. The father of the daylight who ate with a knife, spat on the floor, and who was forever denouncing America and Americans was different from this mystic spirit stranger who could thrill with such impassioned rapture.

Thousands of years of exile, thousands of years of hunger, loneliness, and want swept over her as she listened to her father's voice. Something seemed

5. Psalm 102.1–9. In the middle of what seems to be a personal lament, the psalmist entreats God to rebuild Zion as a power among the nations, thus making clear that the sorrows are those of the Jewish people in defeat or exile—in Yezierska's phrase, "The Race of Sorrows."

6. Moralizing sermon in the style of the prophet Jeremiah.

to be crying out to her to run in and seize her father and mother in her arms and hold them close.

"Love, love—nothing is true between us but love," she thought.

But why couldn't she do what she longed to do? Why, with all her passionate sympathy for them, should any actual contact with her people seem so impossible? No, she couldn't go in just yet. Instead, she ran up on the roof, where she could be alone. She stationed herself at the air-shaft opposite their kitchen window, where for the first time since she had left in a rage she could see her old home.

Ach! what sickening disorder! In the sink were the dirty dishes stacked high, untouched, it looked, for days. The table still held the remains of the last meal. Clothes were strewn about the chairs. The bureau drawers were open, and their contents brimmed over in mad confusion.

"I couldn't endure it, this terrible dirt!" Her nails dug into her palms, shaking with the futility of her visit. "It would be worse than death to go back to them. It would mean giving up order, cleanliness, sanity, everything that I've striven all these years to attain. It would mean giving up the hope of my new world—the hope of Frank Baker."

The sound of the creaking door reached her where she crouched against the air-shaft. She looked again into the murky depths of the room. Her mother had entered. With arms full of paper bags of provisions, the old woman paused on the threshold, her eyes dwelling on the dim figure of her husband. A look of pathetic tenderness illumined her wrinkled features.

"I'll make something good to eat for you, yes?"

Reb Ravinsky only dropped his head on his breast. His eyes were red and dry, sandy with sorrow that could find no release in tears. Good God! Never had Rachel seen such profound despair. For the first time she noticed the grooved tracings of withering age knotted on his face and the growing hump on her mother's back.

"Already the shadow of death hangs over them," she thought as she watched them. "They're already with one foot in the grave. Why can't I be human to them before they're dead? Why can't I?"

Rachel blotted away the picture of the sordid room with both hands over her eyes.

"To death with my soul! I wish I were a plain human being with a heart instead of a monster of selfishness with a soul."

But the pity she felt for her parents began now to be swept away in a wave of pity for herself.

"How every step in advance costs me my heart's blood! My greatest tragedy in life is that I always see the two opposite sides at the same time. What seems to me right one day seems all wrong the next. Not only that, but many things seem right and wrong at the same time. I feel I have a right to my own life, and yet I feel just as strongly that I owe my father and mother something. Even if I don't love them, I have no right to step over them. I'm drawn to them by something more compelling than love. It is the cry of their dumb, wasted lives."

Again Rachel looked into the dimly lighted room below. Her mother placed food upon the table. With a self-effacing stoop of humility, she entreated, "Eat only while it is hot yet."

With his eyes fixed almost unknowingly, Reb Ravinsky sat down. Her mother took the chair opposite him, but she only pretended to eat the slender portion of the food she had given herself.

Rachel's heart swelled. Yes, it had always been like that. Her mother had taken the smallest portion of everything for herself. Complaints, reproaches, upbraidings, abuse, yes, all these had been heaped by her upon her mother; but always the juiciest piece of meat was placed on her plate, the thickest slice of bread; the warmest covering was given to her, while her mother shivered through the night.

"Ah, I don't want to abandon them!" she thought; "I only want to get to the place where I belong. I only want to get to the mountaintops and view the world from the heights, and then I'll give them everything I've achieved."

Her thoughts were sharply broken in upon by the loud sound of her father's eating. Bent over the table, he chewed with noisy gulps a piece of herring, his temples working to the motion of his jaws. With each audible swallow and smacking of the lips, Rachel's heart tightened with loathing.

"Their dirty ways turn all my pity into hate." She felt her toes and her fingers curl inward with disgust. "I'll never amount to anything if I'm not strong enough to break away from them once and for all." Hypnotizing herself into her line of self-defense, her thoughts raced on: "I'm only cruel to be kind. If I went back to them now, it would not be out of love, but because of weakness—because of doubt and unfaith in myself."

Rachel bluntly turned her back. Her head lifted. There was iron will in her jaws.

"If I haven't the strength to tear free from the old, I can never conquer the new. Every new step a man makes is a tearing away from those clinging to him. I must get tight and hard as rock inside of me if I'm ever to do the things I set out to do. I must learn to suffer and suffer, walk through blood and fire, and not bend from my course."

For the last time she looked at her parents. The terrible loneliness of their abandoned old age, their sorrowful eyes, the wrung-dry weariness on their faces, the whole black picture of her ruined, desolate home, burned into her flesh. She knew all the pain of one unjustly condemned, and the guilt of one with the spilt blood of helpless lives upon his hands. Then came tears, blinding, wrenching tears that tore at her heart until it seemed that they would rend her body into shreds.

"God! God!" she sobbed as she turned her head away from them, "if all this suffering were at least for something worth while, for something outside myself. But to have to break them and crush them merely because I have a fastidious soul that can't stomach their table manners, merely because I can't strangle my aching ambitions to rise in the world!"

She could no longer sustain the conflict which raged within her higher and higher at every moment. With a sudden tension of all her nerves she pulled herself together and stumbled blindly downstairs and out of the house. And she felt as if she had torn away from the flesh and blood of her own body.

III

Out in the street she struggled to get hold of herself again. Despite the tumult and upheaval that racked her soul, an intoxicating lure still held her up—the hope of seeing Frank Baker that evening. She was indeed a storm-racked ship, but within sight of shore. She need but throw out the signal, and help was nigh. She need but confide to Frank Baker of her break with her people, and all the dormant sympathy between them would surge up. His understanding would widen and deepen because of her great need for his understanding. He would love her the more because of her great need for his love.

Forcing back her tears, stepping over her heartbreak, she hurried to the hotel where she was to meet him. Her father's impassioned rapture when he chanted the Psalms of David lit up the visionary face of the young Jewess.

"After all, love is the beginning of the real life," she thought as Frank Baker's dark, handsome face flashed before her. "With him to hold on to, I'll begin my new world."

Borne higher and higher by the intoxicating illusion of her great destiny, she cried:

"A person all alone is but a futile cry in an unheeding wilderness. One alone is but a shadow, an echo of reality. It takes two together to create reality. Two together can pioneer a new world."

With a vision of herself and Frank Baker marching side by side to the conquest of her heart's desire, she added:

"No wonder a man's love means so little to the American woman. They belong to the world in which they are born. They belong to their fathers and mothers; they belong to their relatives and friends. They are human even without a man's love. I don't belong; I'm not human. Only a man's love can save me and make me human again."

It was the busy dinner-hour at the fashionable restaurant. Pausing at the doorway with searching eyes and lips eagerly parted, Rachel's swift glance circled the lobby. Those seated in the dining-room beyond who were not too absorbed in one another, noticed a slim, vivid figure of ardent youth, but with dark, age-old eyes that told of the restless seeking of her homeless race.

With nervous little movements of anxiety, Rachel sat down, got up, then started across the lobby. Halfway, she stopped, and her breath caught.

"Mr. Baker," she murmured, her hands fluttering toward him with famished eagerness. His smooth, athletic figure had a cock-sureness that to the girl's worshipping gaze seemed the perfection of male strength.

"You must be doing wonderful things," came from her admiringly, "you look so happy, so shining with life."

"Yes,"—he shook her hand vigorously,—"I've been living for the first time since I was a kid. I'm full of such interesting experiences. I'm actually working in an East Side settlement."

Dazed by his glamorous success, Rachel stammered soft phrases of congratulations as he led her to a table. But seated opposite him, the face of this untried youth, flushed with the health and happiness of another world than that of the poverty-crushed Ghetto, struck her almost as an insincerity.

"You in an East Side settlement?" she interrupted sharply. "What reality can there be in that work for you?"

"Oh," he cried, his shoulders squaring with the assurance of his master's degree in sociology, "it's great to get under the surface and see how the other half lives. It's so picturesque! My conception of these people has greatly changed since I've been visiting their homes." He launched into a glowing account of the East Side as seen by a twenty-five-year-old college graduate.

"I thought them mostly immersed in hard labor, digging subways or slaving in sweatshops," he went on. "But think of the poetry which the immigrant is daily living!"

"But they're so sunk in the dirt of poverty, what poetry do you see there?"

"It's their beautiful home life, the poetic devotion between parents and children, the sacrifices they make for one another—"

"Beautiful home life? Sacrifices? Why, all I know of is the battle to the knife between parents and children. It's black tragedy that boils there, not the pretty sentiments that you imagine."

"My dear child,"—he waved aside her objection,—"you're too close to judge dispassionately. This very afternoon, on one of my friendly visits, I came upon a dear old man who peered up at me through horn-rimmed glasses behind his pile of Hebrew books. He was hardly able to speak English, but I found him a great scholar."

"Yes, a lazy old do-nothing, a bloodsucker on his wife and children."

Too shocked for remonstrance, Frank Baker stared at her.

"How else could he have time in the middle of the afternoon to pore over his books?" Rachel's voice was hard with bitterness. "Did you see his wife? I'll bet she was slaving for him in the kitchen. And his children slaving for him in the sweat-shop."

"Even so, think of the fine devotion that the women and children show in making the lives of your Hebrew scholars possible. It's a fine contribution to America, where our tendency is to forget idealism."

"Give me better a plain American man who supports his wife and children and I'll give you all those dreamers of the Talmud."

He smiled tolerantly at her vehemence.

"Nevertheless," he insisted, "I've found wonderful material for my new book in all this. I think I've got a new angle on the social types of your East Side."

An icy band tightened about her heart. "Social types," her lips formed. How could she possibly confide to this man of the terrible tragedy that she had been through that very day? Instead of the understanding and sympathy that she had hoped to find, there were only smooth platitudes, the sightseer's surface interest in curious "social types."

Frank Baker talked on. Rachel seemed to be listening, but her eyes had a far-off, abstracted look. She was quiet as a spinning-top is quiet, her thoughts and emotions revolving within her at high speed.

"That man in love with me? Why, he doesn't see me or feel me. I don't exist to him. He's only stuck on himself, blowing his own horn. Will he never stop with his 'I,' 'I,' 'I,'? Why, I was a crazy lunatic to think that just because we took the same courses in college, he would understand me out in the real world."

All the fire suddenly went out of her eyes. She looked a thousand years old as she sank back wearily in her chair.

"Oh, but I'm boring you with all my heavy talk on sociology." Frank Baker's words seemed to come to her from afar. "I have tickets for a fine musical comedy that will cheer you up, Miss Ravinsky—"

"Thanks, thanks," she cut in hurriedly. Spend a whole evening sitting beside him in a theater when her heart was breaking? No. All she wanted was to get away—away where she could be alone. "I have work to do," she heard herself say. "I've got to get home."

Frank Baker murmured words of polite disappointment and escorted her back to her door. She watched the sure swing of his athletic figure as he strode away down the street, then she rushed upstairs.

Back in her little room, stunned, bewildered, blinded with her disillusion, she sat staring at her four empty walls.

Hours passed, but she made no move, she uttered no sound. Doubled fists thrust between her knees, she sat there, staring blindly at her empty walls.

"I can't live with the old world, and I'm yet too green for the new. I don't belong to those who gave me birth or to those with whom I was educated."

Was this to be the end of all her struggles to rise in America, she asked herself, this crushing daze of loneliness? Her driving thirst for an education, her desperate battle for a little cleanliness, for a breath of beauty, the tearing away from her own flesh and blood to free herself from the yoke of her parents—what was it all worth now? Where did it lead to? Was loneliness to be the fruit of it all?

Night was melting away like a fog; through the open window the first lights of dawn were appearing. Rachel felt the sudden touch of the sun upon her face, which was bathed in tears. Overcome by her sorrow, she shuddered and put her hand over her eyes as though to shut out the unwelcome contact. But the light shone through her fingers.

Despite her weariness, the renewing breath of the fresh morning entered her heart like a sunbeam. A mad longing for life filled her veins.

"I want to live," her youth cried. "I want to live, even at the worst."

Live how? Live for what? She did not know. She only felt she must struggle against her loneliness and weariness as she had once struggled against dirt, against the squalor and ugliness of her Ghetto home.

Turning from the window, she concentrated her mind, her poor tired mind, on one idea.

"I have broken away from the old world; I'm through with it. It's already behind me. I must face this loneliness till I get to the new world. Frank Baker can't help me; I must hope for no help from the outside. I'm alone; I'm alone till I get there.

"But am I really alone in my seeking? I'm one of the millions of immigrant children, children of loneliness, wandering between worlds that are at once too old and too new to live in."

1923, 1979

MOYSHE-LEYB HALPERN
1886–1932

Rebellious and ironic, Moyshe-Leyb Halpern, the most original of the modern Yiddish poets in America, lived the life of an artist. Born in the town of Złoczew in eastern Galicia into an enlightened Jewish home, Halpern attended heder and studied in the secular Polish-language schools. In 1898, his father, a dry-goods merchant, took his twelve-year-old son to Vienna to study commercial art. Halpern returned to Złoczew in 1907 and emigrated to America in 1908, stopping on the way to attend the Czernowitz Yiddish Conference.

In New York, Halpern soon became part of the literary circles of the Yunge poets although he was too much of a rebel to accept their aesthetic strictures. He became widely known in the Yiddish world with the publication of his first book of poems in 1919, *In nyu york* (In New York). His second book, *Di goldene pave* (The Golden Peacock), appeared in 1924.

Halpern married in 1919, had a son in 1923, and lived with his family in New York City until 1924 and from 1929 until his death. Between 1924 and 1929, he stayed in Detroit, Cleveland, Los Angeles, and Boston sometimes with and sometimes without his family. He earned an unpredictable living as a journalist and peripatetic writer and artist, and died of a heart attack in 1932, at the age of forty-six.

In 1934, Yiddish poet and critic Eliezer Greenberg edited two posthumous volumes of Halpern's previously uncollected poems. The first of these volumes collects poems originally published in the New York Yiddish papers, and the second gathers previously unpublished poems. In 1954, *In nyu york* and *Di goldene pave* were reissued.

Halpern's significance lies in the sharp individuality of his voice, one that tempers a sweet, quasi-sentimental romantic lyricism with the irony of social criticism turned inward. Halpern, although associated with the Yunge poets, wrote for satirical magazines and the Communist daily newspaper *Frayhayt* (Freedom). The play between the lyric and the satiric, between the romantic individualist and the communal chastiser, characterizes Halpern's poetry. In fact, the distinctive quality of his poems depends upon Halpern's constant undercutting of poetic convention and the reader's expectation.

In his first book, *In nyu york*, the poems embody Halpern's struggle between the Jewish poet's traditional obligation to his people and the modern poet's individual sensibility and vision. The poem *In the Golden Land* reveals with Halpern's typical irony the alienation experienced by immigrants in America. *Isaac Leybush Peretz* elegizes the great Warsaw Yiddish writer in an anti-Kaddish. *Memento Mori*, which we present in two contrasting translations, encapsulates the dilemma of the modernist Yiddish poet at odds with his audience.

In his second collection of poems, *Di goldene pave*, Halpern develops his technique of subverting conventions in his art ballads, which parody the coherent dialogue between singer and community found in authentic folk ballads. The poem *Zlochov, My Home* ironically reverses the hackneyed nostalgia of the immigrant for the Old Country and invents a shocking counternarrative.

Among the poems in the two posthumous volumes are dramatic monologues, such as *My Only Son*, spoken by a persona or to a character who deflects the subjectivity of the poem. These characters are either illusorily "realistic" people, or they are fable figures that give ironic leverage to the poems. Halpern's brilliance comes forth in the inspired, manic colloquialisms with which these personae speak.

Halpern's importance to his contemporaries can be measured in part by the more than 50 poems and 400 articles written in Yiddish as a tribute to him from 1932 to 1954 by such diverse poets as Jacob Glatstein, Mani Leyb, Kadya Molodowsky, and Itzik Manger, and by such critics as Shmuel Niger, Eliezer Greenberg, and Moyshe

Nadir. The number of translations and scholarly assessments of his work that has been published just in English from the 1960s onward attests to Halpern's continuing appeal to an American poetic and scholarly audience. Ultimately a lone figure, Halpern wrote poetry that boldly joined the solipsistic modern self to those larger forces influencing the lives of Eastern European Jews in America.

Memento Mori[1]

And if Moyshe-Leyb, the poet, tells
That he saw Death on the high waves—
Just as he sees himself in a mirror,
And it was in the morning, around ten—
Will they believe Moyshe-Leyb?[2]

And if Moyshe-Leyb greeted Death from afar
With a wave of his hand, and asked how things are?
Just when thousands of people were
In the water, madly enjoying life—
Will they believe Moyshe-Leyb?

And if Moyshe-Leyb, tears in his eyes,
Swears that he was drawn to Death,
As a man is drawn at dusk in desire
To the window of a woman he adores—
Will they believe Moyshe-Leyb?

And if Moyshe-Leyb paints Death for them
Not gray and not dark, but dazzling and colorful,
As he appeared, around ten in the morning,
Far away, between sky and waves—
Will they believe Moyshe-Leyb?

1919

Memento Mori[1]

And if Moyshe-Leyb, Poet, recounted how
He's glimpsed Death in the breaking waves, the way
You catch that sight of yourself in the mirror
At about 10 A.M. on some actual day,
Who would be able to believe Moyshe-Leybl?[2]

And if Moyshe-Leyb greeted Death from afar,
With a wave of his hand, asking, "Things all right?"

1. Translated by Kathryn Hellerstein and Benjamin Harshav. "Memento Mori": "Remember, you must die" (Latin). The Latin title is Halpern's original title for the poem.
2. In the original Yiddish, the refrain is structured according to the internal rhyme of *gleybn* (to believe) and *moyshe-leybn* (the poet's name, inflected grammatically as the object of the verb).

1. Translated by John Hollander.
2. John Hollander's translation reflects the internal rhymes of the Yiddish refrain.

At the moment when many a thousand people
Lived there in the water, wild with delight,
Who would be able to believe Moyshe-Leybl?

And if Moyshe-Leyb were to swear
That he was drawn to Death in the way
An exiled lover is to the casement
Of his worshipped one, at the end of the day,
Who would be able to believe Moyshe-Leybl?

And if Moyshe-Leyb were to paint them Death
Not gray, dark, but color-drenched, as it shone
At around 10 A.M. there, distantly,
Between the sky and the breakers, alone,
Who would be able to believe Moyshe-Leybl?

1919

Memento Mori

(Yiddish and transliteration)

און אַז משה-לייב, דער פּאָעט, וועט דערציילן,
אַז ער האָט דעם טויט אויף די כוואַליעס געזען,
אַזוי ווי מען זעט זיך אַליין אין אַ שפּיגל,
און דאָס אין דער פרי גאָר, אַזוי אַרום צען —
צי וועט מען דאָס גלייבן משה-לייבן?

און אַז משה-לייב האָט דעם טויט פֿון דער ווײַטן
באַגריסט מיט אַ האַנט און געפֿרעגט ווי עס גייט?
און דווקא בעת ס׳האָבן מענטשן פֿיל טויזנט
אין וואַסער זיך ווילד מיט דעם לעבן געפרייט —
צי וועט מען דאָס גלייבן משה-לייבן?

און אַז משה-לייב וועט מיט טרערן זיך שווערן,
אַז ס׳האָט צו דעם טויט אים געצויגן אַזוי,
אַזוי ווי עס ציט אַ פֿאַרבענקטן אין אָוונט
צום פֿענצטער פֿון זײַנס אַ פֿאַרהייליקטער פרוי —
צי וועט מען דאָס גלייבן משה-לייבן?

און אַז משה-לייב וועט דעם טויט פֿאַר זיי מאָלן
ניט גרוי און ניט פֿינצטער, נאָר פאַרבן-רײַך כיין,
אַזוי ווי ער האָט אַרום צען זיך באַוויזן
דאָרט ווײַט צווישן הימל און כוואַליעס אַליין —
צי וועט מען דאָס גלייבן משה-לייבן?

1919

Un az moyshe-leyb, der poet, vet dertseyln,
As er hot dem toyt af di khvalyes gezen,
Azoy vi men zet zikh aleyn in a shpigl,
Un dos in der fri gor, azoy arum tsen—
Tsi vet men dos gleybn moyshe-leybn?

Un az moyshe-leyb hot dem toyt fun der vaytn
Bagrist mit a hant un gefregt vi es geyt?
Un davke bes s'hobn mentshn fil toyznt
In vaser zikh vild mit dem lebn gefreyt—
Tsi vet men dos gleybn moyshe-leybn?

Un az moyshe-leyb vet mit trern zikh shvern,
Az s'hot tsu dem toyt im getsoygn azoy,
Azoy vi es tsit a farbenktn in ovnt
Tsum fentster fun zayns a farheylikter froy—
Tsi vet men dos gleybn moyshe-leybn?

Un az moyshe-leyb vet dem toyt far zey moln
Nit groy un nit fintster, nor farbn-raykh sheyn,
Azoy vi er hot arum tsen zikh bavizn
Dort vayt tsvishn himl un khvalyes aleyn—
Tsi vet men dos gleybn moyshe-leybn?

1919

In the Golden Land[1]

Would you, mama, believe if I told
That everything here is changed into gold,
That gold is made from iron and blood,
Day and night, from iron and blood?

—My son, from a mother you cannot hide—
A mother can see, mother is at your side.
I can feel from here, you have not enough bread—
In the Golden Land you aren't properly fed.

—Mama, oh mama, can you not see
That here they throw bread in the sea,
Because, when too bountiful is the earth,
It begins to lose its golden worth?

—I don't know, my son, but my heart cries:
Your face looks dark as the night's skies,
Your eyelids close, your head on your chest,
Like the eyes of a man dying for rest.

—Mama, oh mama, haven't you heard
Of trains racing under the earth,
That drag us from bed at break of dawn
And late at night bring us back home.

—I don't know, my son, but my heart is wrung:
I sent you away healthy and young—
It seems it was just yesterday!
And I want to see you like that today.

—Why do you, mama, sap the blood of my heart?
Can you not feel how it pulls me apart?
Why are you crying? Do you see at all
What I see here—a high and dark wall?

—Why shouldn't I cry, my son? You see:
You've forgotten God and forgotten me.
Now your own life is a wall that will stand
Blocking your way in the Golden Land.

—Mama, you're right. We're divided in pain.
A golden chain[2] . . . and an iron chain . . .
A golden throne—in heaven for thee,
In the Golden Land—a gallows for me.

1919

1. Translated by Kathryn Hellerstein and Benjamin Harshav. "Golden" in Yiddish means "endearing, warm, good" as well as "wealthy, valuable, or promising," as in the phrase used by immigrants to America who expected the streets to be paved with gold [adaptation of Benjamin Harshav and Barbara Harshav's note].

2. Yiddish symbol for Jewish tradition that joins one generation to the next, made famous by I. L. Peretz's play *The Golden Chain* (1909).

Isaac Leybush Peretz[1]

And you are dead. The earth has not yet covered you,
And through a thousand distant streets like racing hooves
The news spreads. Headlines, quick as telegrams,
Cry out at us that your heart doesn't beat.
And, like a garish advertisement, your gray head
Is framed in black. And we, the bigshots who should now be dumb
And prostrate, circle around your spirit
Like lusty girls in a saloon around a rich old drunk.
And we have tears and speech like round smooth pearls,
Like big gold coins. And everyone who has a tongue
Drums out a rhythmic dirge like a cobbler boy
Pounding a thick nail in an old shoe's heel.
And every sound is full of filth and sweat,
Like a slave's skin, and everything is merchandise—
We deal in all that can be bought and sold—
Torahs and hog-bristles, men and devil's dirt.
It's amazing that we haven't cheated Death
Of his death-tools with copper coins and schnapps!
We are the flesh and blood of that great hero, Jacob,
Who bought his brother's birthright for a pot of lentils;[2]
And one of us, a great god, so it's said,
Sold the world for thirty shekels pay;[3]
And if all this is fact, why shouldn't we
Deal in you today? You, dust of our pride,
What, then, were you to us? A last charred log at night
Smoldering on the steppe in a gypsy camp;
A ship's sail struggling with the wind and sea;
The last tree in an enchanted, mazy wood
Where lightning cut down at the roots
Oak giants,[4] thousands of years old. What are you now?
A man on the cold earth, as still as if carved from
Marble in the shine of a death candle. A beginning-end;[5]
An image—a moment's vision of that long sleep
Depriving us of day and night, that bit of life
Containing all the beauty of the world. Can this be peace?
Is this the hope of our dark way?
Why, then, does man stoop deeply at the thought of death?
Why does he wail like a small child alone in the dark night?
Who guides the world? Who calls the spring to blossom and depart?
Who drives the wind through waste and wood in autumn days?

1. Translated by Kathryn Hellerstein. Isaac Leybush Peretz (1852–1915) was a major Yiddish writer and literary figure in Warsaw who encouraged and published younger writers. This poem of mourning, written upon Peretz's death, challenges the reader's notions of the mourner's Kaddish. Unlike the Kaddish, a prayer praising God, one form of which is recited by mourners on the anniversary of a death, this poem condemns the Jews for their behavior and predicts not resurrection, but universal death.

2. Genesis 25.27–34.

3. This garbled version of Matthew 26.14 collapses the stories of Jesus and Judas ironically; here Jesus becomes the mercantile betrayer, not the savior of mankind.

4. Alludes to Isaiah 6.13. "But while a tenth part yet remains in it, it shall repent. It shall be ravaged like the terebinth and the oak, of which stumps are left even when they are felled: its stump shall be a holy seed."

5. Alludes ironically to Jesus' words to John in Revelation 22.12–13, where Jesus announces his second coming and the messianic age.

And when the eagle fails in flight and falls,
Why must the raven gouge its eyes?
Why must a hand stretch out fearlessly
To the dead lion? Doesn't the lion's soul cry out
From its flayed hide—the kingly soul from the carcass?
Forgive me for my asking. Pardon me. Forgive.[6]
But what else can I do? I, too, love life,
And I have eyes, open eyes, and I am blind.
But I am just a common merchant's child.
And like the thirsty earth that longs for coming rain,
I tried to purify my life within your light.
And like the poor man's hand that trembles after bread,
Vainly I hope to see your spirit, which has turned away.
But I see only night in you and death in you,
And desolation, which without you is barrenness in me.
He who believes in an afterworld is blessed.
He has some solace. I have nothing, nothing at all.
I'll have only a candle lost in smoke.
I'll have a gravestone sinking in the earth.
And then I'll see the riddle that is death.
Its sickle glitters near me like red fire,
Like red fire,
Like gold,
Like blood.

1915 1915, 1919

Zlochov, My Home[1]

Oh, Zlochov, you my home, my town[2]
With the church spires, synagogue and bath,
Your women sitting in the market place,
Your little Jews, breaking loose
Like dogs at a peasant coming down
With a basket of eggs from the Sassov mountain—
Like life in spring awakens in me
My poor bit of longing for you—
My home, my Zlochov.

But when, steeped in longing, I recall
The rich man Rappeport, how he walks
With his big belly to the synagogue,
And Shaye Hillel's, the pious Jew,
Who could sell like a pig in a sack[3]

6. The litany of questions echoes Job 3.11–12, 16, 20–23, and the imagery of lions and ravens, Job 38.39–41.

1. Translated by Benjamin Harshav and Barbara Harshav. "Zlochov": also known as Złoczew, the shtetl in Galicia where Halpern was born. It was, at that time, under Austrian rule.

2. The poet breaks up the compound word "hometown" (*heymshtot*) to heighten the irony.

3. Like a pig in a poke—Jews are not supposed to deal with pigs; the sack covers up for it. The Yiddish idiom alluded to here is: "to sell a cat in a sack" [Benjamin Harshav and Barbara Harshav's note].

Even the sun with all its glowing—
Then it's enough to extinguish in me
Like a candle, my longing for you—
My home, my Zlochov.

How goes the story about that dandy:
Once in an evening he watched for so long
The angels roaming about the sun,
Till a drunken peasant with an axe
Cut him down under his dress-coat,
Poor man: he almost died from that—
The peasant with the axe is my hatred in me
For my grandfather,[4] and through him—for you—
My home, my Zlochov.

Your earth may witness, I'm not making it up.
When my grandfather called in the police
To chase my mother from his house,
My grandmother, her legs spread wide,
Smiled almost as honey-sweet
As a girl standing between two soldiers—
Cursed be my hatred inside me
Which reminds me of her and of you—
My home, my Zlochov.

Like a bunch of naked Jews in a bath
Surrounding a man who'd been scalded,
They nodded their heads and stroked their beards
Around the evicted packs and junk,
Thrown-out pillows-and-blankets in sacks,
And around the bit of broken bed—
To this day my mother is crying in me,
As then, under your sky, in you—
My home, my Zlochov.

But our world is full of wonders.
A horse and a cart over the fields
Will carry you out to a railway train,
Which flies like a demon over the fields
Till it brings you to a ship with a lower deck,
Which takes you away to Newyorkdowntown—
And this, indeed, is my only consolation
That they will not bury me in you—
My home, my Zlochov.

1924

4. A fictional grandfather. The reader should beware of inferring autobiographical facts from these poems.

My Only Son[1]

And if I talk nicely to my son—what good does it do?
When he looks at me, he stops just short
Of saying aloud: How about that!
My father the cow
Has opened his mouth again . . .

I tell him: Son,
Nowadays even a prince
Has to learn how to do something.
And you—touch wood—you're already a year-and-a-half
And what will become of you?
I admit: there are no annual fairs
Here in the big city;
But must it be only eggs or chickens one steals?
Why not money?
Why not silk and velvet from the big warehouses?
Why not gold and diamonds from those people
Who sneak around among poor Negroes
And swindle? The devil take them!

But when I see that my son
Doesn't have the slightest respect—
He stands across from me
With a paw to his ear, like a grown-up
Who pretends to be deaf—
Then I can see with my own eyes
That nothing will come of him,
And I have to shout.

I say: Listen, you son of the dark!
This very day go and light a fire,
No matter where,
But burn—I say—it must!
Wait—I say—I'll make you into a president,
With hands sticky as glue,
And if the holy fatherland
Goes to war,
You'd better be responsible for every drop of blood
From our heroes.
Remember—I say to him—
Blood of our heroes is not water.
Such blood is money, money and again money.
And if a guy has money,
The nicest women of the land
Fly into his hands like birds.
And then—I say—you'll have nothing to worry about . . .
Such birds—I say—just smear

1. Translated by Kathryn Hellerstein and Benjamin Harshav. *Mayn eyntsiker zunele*, a parody of Morris Rosenfeld's popular poem *Mayn yingele* (My Little Son).

Their faces with brick-color, their noses with flour,
And—giddy-up, kids!
Never mind if it's from shame—as long as you make a living.
If you have some extra change—you have everything, that's how it is, my son.

But even if I shout and jump out of my skin
My son looks at my words
As I look at the scum
The sea throws up every day.
And when I try to threaten him and show my fist,
He stands there, touches it, and makes a face
As if he were the only one in the Land of Tsimtsidrim,[2]
The fist-hero Dirty Dog McCarthy[3]—
What a zero he is!
I would really like to ask him
If he'll recite the Kaddish when I die.[4]

—"Waddya mean kadesh?
De old kike from stinkin' Polan' dragged wit' 'im
Some yaysh-may-rabberry—
To hel vit it—dats right."[5]

1934

2. A derogatory nonsense word [Benjamin Harshav and Barbara Harshav's note].
3. A fictional boxer's name.
4. Traditionally, only a son may recite the mourner's Kaddish upon the anniversary of a parent's death.
5. Halpern's Yiddish stanza presents these "Yinglish" lines transliterated into the Yiddish alphabet. "Kike": perjorative word for *Jew*. "Yaysh-may-rabberry": a distortion of the words of the Kaddish, making it close to *raspberry* [Benjamin Harshav and Barbara Harshav's note].

JOSEPH OPATOSHU
1886–1954

One of the most vigorous of the modernist Yiddish writers in New York, Opatoshu wrote short stories and novels in an understated, sensuous style that stripped both sentimentality and sensationalism from his depictions of the Jewish underworld in Poland, of ordinary Jewish life in New York, and of key episodes in Jewish history in nineteenth-century Poland, medieval Germany, and ancient Israel. Yosef Meyer Opatovski was born in the Stupsker Forest near the town of Mława, Poland. His father, a wood merchant who traced his lineage to an old Polish Hasidic family and to the famous sixteenth-century rabbi Yom-Tov Lipman Heller, was one of the earliest proponents of the Jewish Enlightenment; he published a book on the Kabbalah and wrote poems in Hebrew, which Opatoshu later incorporated into his fiction. His mother's family had lived in the forests for generations.

Opatoshu received a secular education in the local Russian school, from which he graduated at age twelve. His father tutored him and his two older brothers in the Hebrew language, the Bible, and the Talmud. He studied business in Warsaw and engineering in Nancy, France. When, in 1906, his funds ran out, Opatoshu returned to Mława. He began to write short stories and came under the influence of literary great I. L. Peretz.

Joining his father in New York in 1907, Opatoshu worked at menial jobs and then taught Hebrew to children. In 1914, he earned a degree in civil engineering from Cooper Union, a profession that he practiced only briefly.

As Opatoshu continued to write, he associated with the Yunge, a group of poets and writers whose aestheticism challenged the political purposefulness of Yiddish poetry and who had, in 1908, begun to publish their own magazines and miscellanies. Opatoshu's first publication, the short story *On the Other Side of the Bridge*, appeared in 1910; in 1912, *Romance of a Horse Thief* was published in the Yunge miscellany *Shriftn* (Writings), which Opatoshu had helped found and fund: and the 1913 issue of *Shriftn* included *Morris and His Son Philip*, a harsh narrative of the New York underworld. Opatoshu's interest in the subjects and style of naturalism led him to found a rival publication in 1914, *Di naye heym* (The New Home), where he published his novella *From the New York Ghetto*. He also began to publish short stories in the newspaper *Tog* (Day). In 1918, he published *Alone: Romance of a Forest-Girl*; in 1919, *Hebrew*, which satirized the plight of a Hebrew teacher in America; in 1921, his famous historical novel about a Polish Hasidic dynasty, *In Polish Woods*; and in 1926, *1863*, about the Polish uprising in that year. Other works included *The Dancer* and *A Day in Regensburg*, about Jewish German life in the sixteenth century.

Opatoshu returned to Poland twice—in 1922 and 1929—where he met Vilna publisher B. Kletskin, who, in 1928, began to publish his collected works in fourteen volumes. He continued to publish weekly short stories and translations under the pseudonym of A. Pen. From 1922 onward, he contributed to Yiddish papers in Warsaw, New York, and Buenos Aires as well as Tel Aviv.

Opatoshu visited Palestine and the Soviet Union in 1934 and in 1936 founded, with H. Leyvik, an influential journal, *Zamlbikher*, a proponent of communism. He later published a travelogue about his journey to Palestine, *Between Seas and Lands*. He toured South America in 1951 and Israel again in 1952. Opatoshu's final novel, *The Last Revolt*, appeared in two parts, the first volume in 1949 and the second posthumously, in 1955.

Brothers, the short story included here, is translated for the first time from a volume that appeared in 1928. Depicting Jewish characters in an American setting, it plays out the conflict between a union leader and a rabbi upon the death of their father. This story exemplifies Opatoshu's fine style as he focuses on concrete details that reveal the psychological and experiential reality of his characters.

Brothers[1]

At three in the morning, Rabbi Sholem Tuvim[2] returned home from visiting his sick father. His father was in great need of comfort, and he, Reb Sholem, would have stayed by him the entire night if the sick man had not abruptly insisted that his younger son be sent for—Fishl, who years ago had gone crazy.

For the rabbi, it was as shock. Ten years earlier, his father had driven Fishl off. He had not been able to bear to hear his name mentioned, and now, when Fishl was so distant that nothing bound him to the Jews, now, at this

1. Translated by Kathryn Hellerstein.
2. Rabbi Sholem Tuvim's name means "Peace Goodness" (Hebrew/Yiddish).

very moment, when their father was in need of comfort, he decided to summon Fishl.

Not wanting to encounter his brother, the rabbi went home.

Night filled the house. From the open rooms, sleep drifted, bringing with it words from another world.

Quietly the rabbi entered the room where he held court[3] and sat down near the open window. The moon, stuck somewhere behind the houses, left a residue of congealed flames. In the grayness, stars flickered and went out, covering the world with shadows.

Two milk wagons drove by, stopped before a house. The milkmen traded talk from wagon to wagon, and in the gray light, it sounded like a husband and wife conversing before dawn.[4]

The synagogue with its marble hearth-plates, with its iron gate graying opposite the rabbi's window, stood there, locked up, dead.

The rabbi looked at the building and thought about how Judaism was declining in America. Weeks went by without anyone coming to him with a question of Jewish law.[5]

Leah, the rabbi's wife, came downstairs, barefoot, in her nightgown. She snuggled up to her husband, rubbed her sleepy eyes, and asked him anxiously, "How's your father, Sholem? Better? Go lie down. You didn't sleep last night, either."

"I can't sleep, Leah. See how the synagogue across the way stands vacant?"

"What are you thinking of? It's night! What do you want? For people to come sit in the synagogue at night? It's enough that the dead are there!"[6]

"And who comes to synagogue during the day? The dead, too. God's house stands vacant, and I, the high priest, guard an empty Holy Ark. Don't you know I can barely pull together a minyan of old men, and not even every day? And that when my brother, Fishl, the offender against Israel, speaks in Madison Square, twenty thousand workers come to hear him? Let all the rabbis in New York try to call together even ten thousand Jews. . . . I think that Jews should hear Torah, it's Torah that they should hear. . . . No one will come, Leah!"

"Judaism isn't dying yet, not even in America," Leah put her face against her husband's beard, "and who is obligated to solve all the world's problems? Believe me, Sholem, somehow we'll manage to get through our remaining few years honorably."

At the first ring of the telephone, the rabbi grabbed the receiver in his hand and held it for a while. He was afraid to bring it to his ear. When he placed it there, his hands began to shake.

"What, Sholem?"

"It's all over."

Leah's shoulders writhed under the thick nightgown. She began to weep quietly and keenly. Tears fell on the rabbi's beard, on his hands. He did not comfort his wife, did not soothe her, but lightly unwound himself from her

3. *Beys-din-shtub* (Yiddish). Orthodox rabbis hear cases of Jewish law and can convene a court of rabbis and witnesses to decide on these cases.

4. *In der driter ashmore*: at the third watch (Yiddish, from the Hebrew). An *ashmore* is one of the four periods into which the night was divided, in the time of the Temple, for the priests to tend the holy fires; the third watch would be around 4:00 A.M. The rabbi thinks in the language of the Bible.

5. *Shayle* (Yiddish, from the Hebrew): a question regarding ritual purity.

6. Folklore holds that the spirits of the dead inhabit synagogues at night.

arms, took up his stick with the silver head, and walked slowly out of the house.

Behind the window, the crying grew quieter, keener, jabbing at the night like a needle and thread mending a cut body.

The rabbi walked through the dark, empty streets, step by step. He did not think about the fact that his father was dead. He could not free himself from his brother, who now must be sitting by the corpse, and whom he, Sholem, had not seen for the past ten years. Recently, Fishl had gone completely mad. It was rumored that he had not circumcised his youngest child, and instead of naming him Israel, after his grandfather, he named the child Lenin.[7] All this gossip didn't make sense to him—he had doubts. In the end, in spite of it all, Fishl had not been baptized.

For the rabbi, Lenin was as *treyf* as Titus.[8] Titus had obliterated the land of Israel, and the Great Russian Lenin wanted to destroy the entire world. Life around the rabbi divided in two. He, Rabbi Sholem, represented one half, and his brother, Fishl the other. After today he would tell this to Fishl, he would swear on the bones of their father, that as long as Fishl refused to repent, there could be no peace between them. Fishl was not the first villain the Jews had encountered. They would survive him, too.

These thoughts gave the rabbi courage. He began to walk faster, set the stick down before him, and heard the iron knob of the stick resound across the sidewalk, repeating his words.

He absolutely could not make peace as long as his brother, Fishl, was such a . . . was entirely outside, outside . . . he, Sholem, never attempted to say even a word to Fishl . . . If . . . what does the Gemara say: Even a sinful Jew is not equal to a Gentile prophet. Who was it who wanted to convert to Judaism? Yes, Onkeles, Titus's cousin, wanted to convert to Judaism. With magic, he summoned Titus, asked his uncle for advice. His uncle not only dissuaded him, he ordered him to persecute the Jews. Balaam, the same thing. So when Onkeles summoned Jesus, Jesus said that there was no better "nation and tongue" than the Jews.[9]

The rabbi entered the corridor. A nauseating smell wiped across his face, reminding him that his father was dead. He grew softer, yielding. Now there was pressure on his heart. His eyes overflowed with the heat. He couldn't see where he was going.

In the house, strangers were wandering about. Two candles in holders covered with drippings burned at the head of the corpse. The flames drew toward the open window. Fishl sat on an overturned box,[1] holding his face in his hands and barely moving. As the rabbi entered, he did not take his hands from his face.

7. Ashkenazic Jews traditionally name their children after deceased ancestors. Lenin (1870–1924) founded the Russian Communist party (the Bolsheviks), inspired and led the Bolshevik Revolution of 1917, and became the first head of the Soviet state (1917–24).

8. Titus Flavius Vespasianus (39–81), the Roman emperor who conquered and destroyed Jerusalem and the Second Temple in 70 C.E. "*Treyf*": non-kosher, forbidden by Jewish dietary laws (Yiddish); here, illegitimate, non-Jewish.

9. Onkeles (probably a corruption of Aquilas), a relative of Titus, converts to Judaism and then translates the Bible into Greek. Balaam is the Gentile prophet in Numbers 22–24 who sets out to curse the Jews but ends up blessing them. Jesus, before Onkeles, does the same thing that Balaam does—he praises the Jews. "Gemara": one part of the Talmud that comments on the other part of the Talmud—i.e., the Mishnah.

1. Traditionally during the shivah, the seven-day mourning period, Jews observe such customs as not wearing leather shoes, covering mirrors and pictures, and sitting on low stools or, here, boxes rather than in comfortable chairs to mark themselves as mourners.

The rabbi set his stick aside. He took a volume of *Mishnayes*[2] from the shelf of holy books, shuffled, leafed through it, set it back on the shelf, and reasoned with his brother wordlessly.

His hands, his face, above all, his eyes, spoke, complained, could not untangle themselves from Titus, who had destroyed the Temple, Jerusalem, a nation, but left a people. Now that this people has been destroyed, a corpse lay on the earth, listen, Fishl, on the ground lies a corpse over which we must weep, over which we must recite Lamentations. Is this not also a destruction?

Fishl raised his head. His weeping eyes recognized his brother, and he stood up: "Sholem."

The rabbi blinked rapidly, took his beard into his mouth, stuffed it in like a handful of straw to keep his shout from bursting forth, and through clenched lips began to recite the Psalms.

He leaned his hands against the wall, his head on his arms, and roared. His shoulders curved, sharpened, grew. His hands dropped down of their own accord. His nose became pale, longer, and the rabbi began to shake, squinting in one eye.

Fishl caught him, set him down on the bed, rubbed his hands, his temples, and when the rabbi came to, he wept.

Through the window, the morning intruded, playing with the little flames, pleating the black bedsheet around the corpse's stiff feet. The brothers noticed how the sheet stirred and then ripped itself off the bed. Immediately they realized it was the wind, and remained sitting across from each other, forgetting their hatred. Fear was written in their eyes: Maybe Father is still alive, maybe he is still alive.

1928

2. Verses of the Mishnah, the oral law, part of the Talmud.

CELIA DROPKIN
1887–1956

The explicitly sexual imagery and themes of Celia Dropkin's poems redefined the ways modern Yiddish poetry could depict relationships between women and men. Beautifully crafted lyrics, Dropkin's poems undo the poetic conventions implicit in their very forms and, with their anger and passion, call into question societal assumptions about love. These poems, written in the 1920s and 1930s, open up a woman's psyche in a voice that sounds contemporary. Even her poems about depression, mother love, and nature are infused with erotic energy. Although she is best known for her poetry, Dropkin also published short stories and was an accomplished fine artist.

Celia (Zipporah) Levine Dropkin was born in Bobruisk, White Russia, on December 5, 1887. Her father, a lumber merchant, died of tuberculosis when Celia was a young child; her mother, from a distinguished family, raised and educated Celia and her younger sister, Sima.

Until the age of eight, Dropkin studied traditional Jewish subjects with a *rebbetsin* (rabbi's wife). She also received a secular education from her artistic mother and attended a Russian school in Bobruisk as well as the high school (gymnasium) in the neighboring city of Novosybko. Upon graduating from high school, Dropkin taught in Warsaw and tutored privately. She wrote poetry in Russian as early as age ten. When she was seventeen, she went to Kiev to continue her studies and, in 1906, met the famous Hebrew writer Uri Nissan Gnessin (1881–1913), who encouraged her to continue to write. Dropkin formed a passionate friendship with Gnessin, but because he had tuberculosis, he prevented it from becoming a romance. Unbeknownst to Dropkin at the time, his translation into Hebrew of her poem *The Kiss* was included—without acknowledgment—in a posthumously published novel.

With Gnessin, Dropkin traveled to Warsaw, living there for several months. In January 1908, she returned to Bobruisk and, in 1909, married a Bund activist who, in 1910, fled from the czarist authorities for the United States. In 1912, Celia and their son, who had been born just before his father left Russia, joined him in New York, where she bore five more children.

Although she began to meet Yiddish writers in New York, Dropkin continued to write poetry in Russian. In 1917, she translated some of her poems into Yiddish, including *The Kiss*; they were published in 1919 and 1920, her first Yiddish publications. Throughout the 1920s and 1930s, Dropkin's poems appeared in the publications of the Yunge and the introspectivists. Her poems of sex, love, and death shocked and seduced her contemporaries, who acclaimed her as a leading woman poet. She also received encouragement from more established Yiddish writers such as Abraham Liessin, editor of *Tsukunft*, who published her short stories as well as her poems.

Despite her acclaim, only one book of Dropkin's poems was published in her lifetime: *In heysn vint* (In the Hot Wind) in 1935. After her husband died in 1943, Dropkin wrote his biography, which was never published. In her last years, she painted and took art courses.

Celia Dropkin died on August 17, 1956. Three years after her death, Dropkin's children sponsored the publication of a new and expanded edition of her poetry, short stories, and paintings, also entitled *In heysn vint* (1959), which includes the poems from the 1935 edition as well as later uncollected poems and previously unpublished poems. Much later, one poem for which there seems to be no written text, *Shvere gedanken* (Black Thoughts), was discovered on a tape recording that Dropkin had made; the transcription of this poem was published in *Yidishe kultur* (1990).

We have included seven of Dropkin's poems here, all newly translated from the original 1935 collection of her poems, as well as one of her short stories. The poems present the complexities of a woman's erotic life, *Adam* especially offering a radical reinterpretation of the creation story in Genesis, while the short story places a woman's erotic fantasies into a particularly American urban setting.

I Am Drowning[1]

I am a woman drowning
In a deep well.
My eyes still see your blue eye overhead
Seeking me, wanting to save me,
Or is it really
A bit of blue sky

1. Translated by Kathryn Hellerstein.

Like your blue eye
Gazing into the well?

The well's walls are slippery with mold,
And my hands lose their power
To keep hold of them.
You no longer see me.
You take your blue eye from the well.

ca. 1920–1930 1935

You Plowed My Fertile Soil[2]

You plowed my fertile soil
And sowed it.
Tall stalks grew out, love-stalks,
Their roots deep in the soil
And golden heads to the sky.
Above your sheaves, a red poppy
Burst into gorgeous bloom.
You stood, suspicious,
And thought: Who sowed that poppy?
As a breeze passed through,
You leaned back
To make way for it.
As a bird flew by,
You accompanied it with your eyes.

ca. 1920–1930 1935

My Mother[1]

Twenty-two years old,
A widow with two small children,
My mother modestly decided
Not to be anyone's wife again.
Her days and years continued quietly,
As if lit by a meager wax candle.
My mother became wife to no one,
But all the daily,
Yearly, nightly sighs
Of her young and affectionate being,
Of her longing blood
Seeped into me.
I knew them with my child's heart.

2. Translated by Kathryn Hellerstein.

1. Translated by Kathryn Hellerstein.

And like an underground spring,
My mother's seething, concealed longing
Flowed freely into me.
Now out of me, into the open
Spurts my mother's seething, holy,
Deeply hidden lust.

ca. 1920–1930 1935

The Circus Lady[2]

I am a circus lady
And dance among the daggers
Set in the arena
With their points erect.
My swaying, lissome body
Avoids a death-by-falling,
Touching, barely touching the dagger blades.

Holding their breaths, people are staring at my dancing,
And someone sends a prayer to God for me.
Before my eyes, the points gleam
Fiery, in a circle,
And no one knows how the falling calls to me.

I grow tired, dancing among you,
Daggers of cold steel.
I want my blood to heat you through and through.
You, unsheathed points,
I want to fall on you.

ca. 1920–1930 1935

Adam[1]

I

Spoiled,
Stroked by many women's hands,
You were the one I met on my way,
Young Adam.
And before I had placed my lips on you,
You begged me
With a face more pale and tender
Than the tenderest lily:

2. Translated by Kathryn Hellerstein.
1. Translated by Kathryn Hellerstein. "Adam": the Yiddish word *odem* (from the Hebrew *adam*) denotes both the name of the first man (Genesis 1.26 and Genesis 2.7) as well as the more generalized "man," "fellow." The Hebrew *adam*, "man," derives from *adamah*, "earth." The speaker is not Eve.

—Don't bite me, don't bite me.
I saw that your body
Was entirely covered with teeth marks,
So tremblingly, I bit into you.[2]

2

Above me, you flared
Your narrow nostrils,
And drew nearer to me,
Like a hot horizon to the field.[3]

3

HE: When shall I come to you again?
SHE: When you are longing.
HE: And you? Won't you be longing?
SHE: Don't worry about me,
I am used to living with images,
You will always be alive to me,
And even if you never open my door,
You will not hide from me.

ca. 1920–1930 1935

[You didn't sow a child in me—][1]

You didn't sow a child in me—
You sowed yourself.
Every day, now, you grow in me,
Ever clearer, ever larger.
There is no longer any room for myself,
And my soul lies at your feet like a dog
Becoming weaker and weaker.
But dying through you,
I sing to you, serenading, as ever.

ca. 1920–1930 1935

[I have not yet seen you][2]

I have not yet seen you
Asleep,
I wish I could see
How you sleep,
When you lose your power

2. Genesis 3.6–7.
3. Contrast this sexual union with Genesis 1.28, where God blesses the male and female he has just created and commands them, "Be fertile, and increase."
1. Translated by Kathryn Hellerstein.
2. Translated by Kathryn Hellerstein.

Over you, over me.
I wish I could see you
Helpless, weak, mute,
I wish I could see you, eyes
Closed, without breath,
I wish I could see you
Dead.

ca. 1920–1930 1935

Sonya's Room[1]

Sonya loves Gershon.

But Gershon loves Sonya's friend Soshe. Lately, Soshe has stopped coming to visit Sonya.

"Busy with Gershon," Sonya thinks bitterly.

But once, coming home from work, Sonya finds Soshe in her room.

The friends hug.

"How do you like that?" Soshe says. "My landlady told me to move out. She needs my room for herself."

"Do you have another room yet?"

"No, but I have an idea. You have a double bed, and your rent is too much for you alone. Maybe we can live together?"

Sonya reddens.

Right away it strikes her: Gershon will come! He'll be here every free moment!

She will see him as much as her heart desires, and with that thought, Sonya begins to feel warm and good.

Her lips answer, as if by themselves, "Good, Soshe! When can you move in?"

"Right away," Soshe answers happily. "As soon as Gershon comes home from work, he will help me bring my things here. Good-bye, I'm going home to meet Gershon." And Soshe runs out of the room.

Within the next hour, Gershon arrives with Soshe's bundles, smiling and more friendly than he was when he used to come to Sonya's. And Soshe flies in after him. The pair of chairs, the bed fill up with dresses, socks, ribbons, and underwear.

Sonya makes room everywhere for Soshe. Under the soft gaze of Gershon's eyes, Sonya makes sure that Soshe has the most space in the drawer and in the clothes closet. Done with settling in, Soshe looks at Gershon.

Gershon answers her with a long look. Sonya senses that she is superfluous. She suddenly remembers, "I have to go to my aunt's house today. She invited me." And Sonya leaves.

In the street, she realizes that she has been driven from her room and becomes angry at herself because she has let Soshe move in with her. She

1. Translated by Kathryn Hellerstein.

doesn't know what to do with herself. She blunders through the streets and enters a movie theater.

The next day, Soshe does not come straight home from work. Sonya waits for her impatiently, listening for her steps, watching the door: Soon she'll arrive with Gershon!

Her heart beats rapidly. Finally, at eleven o'clock, Soshe comes in without Gershon. "Where is Gershon?" Sonya wants to ask, but she doesn't ask and looks disappointedly at Soshe. Soshe walks over to her:

"Do you think I don't know that you invented that story about your aunt yesterday? Please, Sonya, don't fuss over us and don't leave the house when you don't need to, and we will do the same."

By "we," she means Gershon and herself.

Sonya is overcome with joy at Soshe's words. Tears in her eyes, she throws herself on Soshe's neck and kisses her.

Hugging and kissing Soshe, Sonya senses that she is squeezing too tight, that she wants to absorb the part of Gershon he's left with Soshe.

Embarrassed, Sonya quickly releases Soshe.

The two friends embrace each other in their sleep, and a sweet contentment flows through Sonya's limbs.

Gradually Gershon and Soshe begin to feel as if no one will disturb them.

Lips press against lips, arms braid around neck and waist.

Sighs of passion are restrained by a corset of "Thou Shalt Not."

Sonya lies in a corner of the bed with a book in front of her eyes, mostly with her back to them.

From time to time she leafs through the book, but she only pretends to read. In truth, she doesn't read even one line further.

With her entire being she absorbs this strange, other love.

And it becomes her own love. She feels Gershon's hands on her when he embraces Soshe, and every kiss this enamored couple exchanges makes her lips tremble with pleasure.

At last she stops covering her face with the book. Pale, she lies face up on the bed, and it seems that she lives in dreams.

Her eyes are covered by a haze, her lips half open, in oblivion. Often moisture appears on them, as if she is tasting something that makes her mouth wet.

Gershon is hers, hers as much as Soshe's.

She has given half the room to Soshe, and Soshe is sharing Gershon with her, perhaps not the actual Gershon, but the wonderful lover who is constantly in her dreams and constantly revealing to her his love for a woman. She feels she is that woman he is kissing and stroking.

And she becomes aroused, transported a thousand times more than Soshe.

Neither Gershon nor Soshe knows of Sonya's love. They never guess what kind of feelings they have ignited in Sonya.

In their eyes, Sonya seems sunken in sweet dreams of an imagined world. They nickname her "The Dreamer."

Day by day, Sonya grows paler, loses weight, and tires very quickly at work.

As Soshe blossoms, Sonya deteriorates.

An inner fire seems to devour her, but her eyes are radiant.

One fine morning, Sonya can not get out of bed.

At dusk, Gershon and Soshe both sit near her. This time, they do not kiss or stroke or embrace.

Soon Soshe goes out to buy something for Sonya.

Sonya lies there, transparent, white, and in her eyes is a triumphant smile of a love stronger than death, without boundaries, without an end. Conquered by that smile, Gershon bends down and kisses her.

Her languid lips open lightly for his manly kiss. This kiss awakens Sonya out of her dreams.

Like a gray day, reality spreads over her. In fact, she does not want to die. Reality is not actually gray.

The real kiss awakens in her a thirst for life. "Please," she murmurs, "tell Soshe it would be better if she rented her own room."

Gershon promises her this earnestly.

And his earnestness is that of someone who has understood.

ca. 1930s–1940s 1959

ANNA MARGOLIN
1887–1952

Perhaps the best known of the women poets, Anna Margolin (pseudonym for Rosa Lebensboym) was born in the Belorussian city of Brest Litovsk, in the province of Grodno, in 1887 and died in New York City in 1952. Her father, early in life a Hasid, later adhered to the thinking of the Enlightenment and Zionism. She was educated in a gymnasium or Jewish high school in Odessa. Lebensboym came to America in 1906 and soon embraced the philosophy of Dr. Chaim Zhitlovsky, eventually becoming his secretary. She began to publish in the Yiddish press and quickly became the secretary for the Yiddish anarchist newspaper *Fraye arbeter shtime* (Free Voice of Labor), publishing short stories there under the pseudonym Khava Gros.

From 1910 to 1911, she lived in London, Paris, and Warsaw. Lebensboym married, but the marriage was short-lived. After she gave birth to a son, she left her husband and returned first to Warsaw and then, in 1914, to New York. She became a writer and editor for a new Yiddish newspaper *Tog* (Day), wrote a weekly column called *In der froyenvelt* (In the Women's World) under her own name, and also wrote about women's issues under the pseudonym Clara Levin. With her distinctive style, Lebensboym distinguished herself as a journalist.

In 1919, she married the Yiddish poet Reuven Iceland and began to write poems under the pseudonym Anna Margolin in 1921, publishing them in prominent Yiddish papers and literary journals. She published a single volume of her own poems, *Lider* (Poems, 1929), and edited the anthology *Dos yidishe lid in amerike* (The Yiddish Poem in America, 1923). Her poems received the warmest acclaim from contemporary Yiddish critics. Both then and now, Margolin has been perceived as the quintessential modernist poet who "transcends" her sex, comparable, perhaps, to Marianne Moore.

I Was Once a Boy[1]

I was once a boy, a stripling,
Listening in Socrates' portico,
My bosom-buddy, my sweet darling,
Had Athens' most stunning torso.[2]

Was Caesar.[3] And from marble constructed
A glistening world, I the last there,
And for my own wife selected
My stately sister.

Rose-garlanded, drinking wine all night
In high spirits, heard tell the news
About the weakling from Nazareth
And wild tales about Jews.[4]

1928, 1929

I Was Once a Boy

(Yiddish and transliteration)

איך בין געווען אַ מאָל אַ ייִנגלינג,	ikh bin geven amol a yingling,
געהערט אין פּאָרטיקאָס סאָקראָטן,	gehert in portikos sokratn,
עס האָט מײַן בוזעם-פֿרײַנד, מײַן ליבלינג,	es hot mayn buzem-fraynt, mayn libling,
געהאַט דעם שענסטן טאָרס אין אַטען.	gehat dem shenstn tors in athen.
געוועזן צעזאַר. און אַ העלע וועלט	gevezn tsezar. un a hele velt
געבויט פֿון מאַרמאָר, איך דער לעצטער,	geboyt fun marmor, ikh der letster,
און פֿאַר אַ ווײַב מיר אויסדערוויילט	un far a vayb mir oysderveylt
מײַן שטאָלצע שוועסטער.	mayn shtoltse shvester.
אין רויזנקראַנץ בײַם ווײַן ביז שפּעט	in royznkrants baym vayn biz shpet
געהערט אין הויכמוטיקן פֿרידן	gehert in hoykhmutikn fridn
וועגן שוואַכלינג פֿון נאַזאַרעט	vegn shvabling fun nazaret
און ווילדע מעשׂיות וועגן ייִדן.	un vilde mayses vegn yidn.

1928, 1929

1. Translated by Kathryn Hellerstein. "Boy": the Yiddish word *yingling* is an unusual form of the noun *yingl*, "boy," translated as "stripling" in the first line.
2. Margolin deliberately imports many words from the Greek that are unusual in Yiddish: *sokratn* (Socrates), *portikos* (porticoes), *atn* (Athens), *tors* (torso). "Socrates": an ancient Greek philosopher (ca. 470–399 B.C.E.) whose teachings were recorded and refined by his students Plato and Xenophon. He was condemned to death.
3. Emperor (Latin). This is probably a reference to Claudius I (Tiberius Claudius Drusus Nero Germanicus, 10 B.C.E.–54 C.E.), who extended Roman rule in North Africa and annexed Judea after Herod's death. He executed his adulterous third wife in 48 C.E. and married his niece Agrippina (line 8), an act contrary to Roman law, which he then changed. Agrippina poisoned him to death.
4. The Yiddish word *mayses* (tales) is the only Hebraic word in the poem, emphasizing the marginality of Jewish culture for the speaker. "Weakling from Nazareth": Jesus.

Mother Earth[5]

Mother earth, much trampled, sun-washed,
Dark slave and mistress
Am I, beloved.
You grow—a mighty trunk—
Out of me, lowly and sad.
And like the eternal stars and like the flame of the sun
I circulate in long and blind silence
Through your roots, through your branches,
And half waking, and half drowsing
I seek the heavens through you.

1921, 1925, 1929

Forgotten Gods[1]

When Zeus, and Phoebus, and Pan,
And Kyprid,[2] silver-footed mistress,
World-intoxicateress, world-protectress,
Were veiled in silence
Down from Olympus,[3]
They in their long and lucid going
Through flaming and slow self-extinguishing generations
Ignited torches and built temples
In the hearts of the solitary,
Who still bring sacrifices and smoking incense.[4]
The world is deep and bright,
The old winds rustle eternally through the young leaves.
With fear I hear in my soul
The heavy treading of forgotten gods.

1920, 1929

My Ancestors Speak[1]

My ancestors:
Men in satin and velvet
Long gentle pale faces   silk
Fainting, glowing lips,
Thin hands caress the yellowed books,
Deep in the night they speak with God.

5. Translated by Kathryn Hellerstein.
1. Translated by Kathryn Hellerstein.
2. The Cyprian name for Aphrodite, Greek goddess of love, beauty, and fertility. "Zeus": chief deity of the Greek pantheon. "Phoebus": i.e., Apollo, Greek god of the sun, prophecy, music, and poetry. "Pan": Greek god of pastures, flocks, and shepherds. He is represented as having the horns, ears, and legs of a goat and playing the pipes.
3. The mountain home of the Greek gods.
4. *Doyres, korbones, ketores* (generations, sacrifices, incense): the poet chose these Yiddish words for their Hebraic roots and their denotations of the Jewish rituals associated with the ancient Temple on Mount Zion in Jerusalem.
1. Translated by Adrienne Cooper.

And merchants from Leipzig and Danzig[2]
Clean cuffs   the smoke of fine cigars
Gemora jokes   German manners[3]
Their gaze is wise and opaque
Wise and sated.
Don Juans, merchants and seekers after God.
A drunkard,
A couple of converts in Kiev.[4]

My ancestors:
Women like idols draped in diamonds,
Darkened red in Turkish shawls,
Heavy folds of Lyon[5] satin.
But their bodies are weeping willows
and their fingers withered flowers
and in their faded veiled eyes
is dead desire.

And grand ladies in calico and linen,
Big boned and strong and agile
with snide little smiles
with quiet talk and strange silences
In the evenings they show themselves
at the window of the poor house
like statues
and in the dimming eyes
cruel desire.

And a couple
Of whom I am ashamed.
They are all my ancestors
Blood of my blood
And flame of my flame
Dead and living come together
Sorrowful grotesque and big
They go through me as through a darkened house
Go with prayers and curses and moans,
Shake my heart like a copper bell
My tongue beats in my mouth
I don't know my own voice
My ancestors speak.

1922, 1929

2. Gdańsk, a port city in northern Poland. "Leipzig": a city in the eastern part of Germany.
3. I.e., the refined manners and dress of assimilated, "Germanized" Jews. "Gemora jokes": technical, legalistic witticisms of religious Jewish students of the Talmud.
4. A Ukrainian city with a large Jewish population. "Don Juans": profligate, flirtatious men; playboys.
5. A French city that served as a center of the silk industry.

A City by the Sea[1]

When did it all happen? I can't remember.
It hangs in the air like a ghostly song:
a seaside town, nocturnes of Chopin,[2]
iron lilies of balconies.

Night. Two sisters dreamily touching
with their slender fingers the dim stream
of memories in an old-fashioned album.
Slowly the old photographs grow young.

Through the half-open door, among the ferns,
trancelike, intoxicated figures fold
in a last waltz. O dead youth!
The dancers swim and fade like shadows.

It was—it was—I can't remember.

1928, 1929

Dear Monsters[1]

Dear monsters, be patient.
It's sober day, and the world
overflows with light and sound
to its farthest sunny shores.
I go among the crowds, on friendly roads,
grateful, miraculously
freed of you.

You are distant
as the thud of armies in the streets
heard from within a still, dreamy house;
as silhouettes in remote alleys
glimpsed through a golden haze of lamplight.
Yet something in the gesture, the stride,
reminds me that in some strange way
these things are familiar.
Dear monsters, be patient.

Because night is coming, and the heart,
sick from an old guilt,
defenseless, alone,
hears the approach of footsteps,
hears and waits, without resisting.
Now you are here! The room dissolves,

1. Translated by Adrienne Rich.
2. Frederic Chopin (1810–1849), Polish composer and pianist.
1. Translated by Marcia Falk.

as I sink, an untrained swimmer,
about to be trampled and broken.

You are terrible, yet vague.
You loom up around me like mountains,
howl blindly at my sides like giant hounds,
and murmur with me dully and madly
the tales of an old, old guilt.

And the heart, a stray sheep,
cries itself to sickly sleep.

ca. 1927 1928, 1929

Epitaph[1]

Say that she couldn't forgive
herself for her dark moods,
so she went through life
with apologetic steps.

Say that until her death
she guarded with bare hands
the fire entrusted to her
in which she finally burned.

And say how in spirited hours
she struggled hard with God,
and how her blood sang deep
and small men ruined her.

1927 1928, 1929

1. Translated by Marcia Falk. Margolin wrote two versions of her epitaph, one published, the other inscribed on her tombstone.

EDNA FERBER
1887–1968

Born in Kalamazoo, Michigan, Edna Ferber grew up in small midwestern towns and cities. Her mother's family were Chicago Jews, her father a Hungarian Jewish immigrant. He ran a general store in Ottumwa, Iowa, for a while, where Ferber was subjected to virulent anti-Semitism. The family moved to Appleton, Wisconsin, where she went to high school and helped in the family store after her father's death. Then Ferber became the first woman to be hired as a reporter on the local Appleton newspaper. She moved on from that to the *Milwaukee Journal*. In 1909, Ferber suffered a mild breakdown and took up writing as a way to occupy her mind. The following year, she published her first story and a year later her first novel, *Dawn O'Hara, the Girl Who Laughed* (1911). Urged by her publisher, she moved to New York City in 1912, which became her home. In the 1920s, she was a member of the Algonquin circle of wits; by the end of that decade and thereafter, as an enormously popular and successful writer she was lionized in social circles.

The selection of a chapter from *Fanny Herself* (1917), one of her early novels, is based on her own life, although, unlike the situation in the book in which Fanny takes over at her mother's death, her mother was actually alive and running the store. It is the only intensely Jewish work among her many stories, plays, and novels. In other works, Ferber does, however, focus on mother-daughter relationships and writes often about strong, moral, and interesting women. In this novel, Fanny goes off to Chicago, walks about sketching city scenes, ultimately becomes an artist—and meets and marries a nice high-school classmate.

Ferber's later novels became almost iconic in their use of sites like the Mississippi River, Chicago, Oklahoma, Texas, Alaska as settings for lusty stories on an epic scale. Many of her works became classics of stage and screen—*Show Boat* (1926), for instance, for which she also collaborated on the popular stage musical; *Saratoga Trunk* (1941), a "big" film vehicle for Ingrid Bergman; and especially the huge Texas story *Giant* (1952) because of the movie starring the legendary James Dean. Ferber also collaborated on five stage plays with George S. Kaufman and received the Pulitzer prize for her very first "best-seller," one of the first by a Jewish writer, *So Big* (1924).

Despite the limited part Jews play in her work overall, Ferber said she never forgot her Jewish past; and although anti-Zionist (after a trip to Israel, she thought it was just "a Jewish Texas"), she was always a fierce opponent of anti-Semitism, reputedly never letting an instance of it go unanswered. In her first autobiography, *A Peculiar Treasure* (1939), she wrote, "All my life I have been inordinately proud of being a Jew. But I have felt that one should definitely not brag about it." In that same book, she gave being Jewish an indelible, if only third, place in her definition of herself as an "American, a writer, and a Jew."

From Fanny Herself

Chapter Three

By spring Mrs. Brandeis had the farmer women coming to her for their threshing dishes and kitchenware, and the West End Culture Club for their whist[1] prizes. She seemed to realize that the days of the general store were numbered, and she set about making hers a novelty store. There was something terrible about the earnestness with which she stuck to business. She was not more than thirty-eight at this time, intelligent, healthy, fun-loving. But she stayed at it all day. She listened and chatted to every one, and learned much. There was about her that human quality that invites confidence.

She made friends by the hundreds, and friends are a business asset. Those blithe, dressy, and smooth-spoken gentlemen known as traveling men used to tell her their troubles, perched on a stool near the stove, and show her the picture of their girl in the back of their watch, and asked her to dinner at the Haley House. She listened to their tale of woe, and advised them; she admired the picture of the girl, and gave some wholesome counsel on the

1. A card game, related to bridge, invented in England in the 17th century.

subject of traveling men's lonely wives; but she never went to dinner at the Haley House.

It had not taken these debonair young men long to learn that there was a woman buyer who bought quickly, decisively, and intelligently, and that she always demanded a duplicate slip. Even the most unscrupulous could not stuff[2] an order of hers, and when it came to dating she gave no quarter. Though they wore clothes that were two leaps ahead of the styles worn by the Winnebago young men—their straw sailors[3] were likely to be saw-edged when the local edges were smooth, and their coats were more flaring, or their trousers wider than the coats and trousers of the Winnebago boys—they were not, for the most part, the gay dogs that Winnebago's fancy painted them. Many of them were very lonely married men who missed their wives and babies, and loathed the cuspidored discomfort of the small-town hotel lobby. They appreciated Mrs. Brandeis' good-natured sympathy, and gave her the long end of a deal when they could. It was Sam Kiser who had begged her to listen to his advice to put in Battenberg[4] patterns and braid, long before the Battenberg epidemic had become widespread and virulent.

"Now listen to me, Mrs. Brandeis," he begged, almost tearfully. "You're a smart woman. Don't let this get by you. You know that I know that a salesman would have as much chance to sell you a gold brick as to sell old John D. Rockefeller[5] a gallon of oil."

Mrs. Brandeis eyed his samples coldly. "But it looks so unattractive. And the average person has no imagination. A bolt of white braid and a handful of buttons—they wouldn't get a mental picture of the completed piece. Now, embroidery silk——"

"Then give 'em a real picture!" interrupted Sam. "Work up one of these water-lily pattern table covers. Use No. 100 braid and the smallest buttons. Stick it in the window and they'll tear their hair to get patterns."

She did it, taking turns with Pearl and Sadie at weaving the great, lacy square during dull moments. When it was finished they placed it in the window, where it lay like frosted lace, exquisitely graceful and delicate, with its tracery of curling petals and feathery fern sprays. Winnebago gazed and was bitten by the Battenberg bug. It wound itself up in a network of Battenberg braid, in all the numbers. It bought buttons of every size; it stitched away at Battenberg covers, doilies, bedspreads, blouses, curtains. Battenberg tumbled, foamed, cascaded over Winnebago's front porches all that summer. Listening to Sam Kiser had done it.

She listened to the farmer women too, and to the mill girls, and to the scant and precious pearls that dropped from the lips of the East End society section. There was something about her brown eyes and her straight, sensible nose that reassured them so that few suspected the mischievous in her. For she was mischievous. If she had not been I think she could not have stood the drudgery, and the heartbreaks, and the struggle, and the terrific manual labor.

She used to guy[6] people, gently, and they never guessed it. Mrs. G. Man-

2. Falsify (slang).
3. Men's straw hats with stiff brims, usually worn in the summertime. "Winnebago": a town in Wisconsin.
4. A kind of cutwork embroidery named after the German village where it originated. "Gay dogs" (slang): licentious males. "Cuspidored": equipped with spittoons.
5. Rockefeller (1839–1937) was an American oil magnate.
6. Make fun of, ridicule.

ville Smith, for example, never dreamed of the joy that her patronage brought Molly Brandeis, who waited on her so demurely. Mrs. G. Manville Smith (née Finnegan) scorned the Winnebago shops, and was said to send to Chicago for her hairpins. It was known that her household was run on the most niggardly basis, however, and she short-rationed her two maids outrageously. It was said that she could serve less real food on more real lace doilies than any other housekeeper in Winnebago. Now, Mrs. Brandeis sold Scourine two cents cheaper than the grocery stores, using it as an advertisement to attract housewives, and making no profit on the article itself. Mrs. G. Manville Smith always patronized Brandeis' Bazaar for Scourine alone, and thus represented pure loss. Also she my-good-womaned Mrs. Brandeis. That lady, seeing her enter one day with her comic, undulating gait, double-actioned like a giraffe's, and her plumes that would have shamed a Knight of Pythias,[7] decided to put a stop to these unprofitable visits.

She waited on Mrs. G. Manville Smith, a dangerous gleam in her eye.

"Scourine," spake Mrs. G. Manville Smith.

"How many?"

"A dozen."

"Anything else?"

"No. Send them."

Mrs. Brandeis, scribbling in her sales book, stopped, pencil poised. "We cannot send Scourine unless with a purchase of other goods amounting to a dollar or more."

Mrs. G. Manville Smith's plumes tossed and soared agitatedly. "But my good woman, I don't want anything else!"

"Then you'll have to carry the Scourine."

"Certainly not! I'll send for it."

"The sale closes at five." It was then 4:57.

"I never heard of such a thing! You can't expect me to carry them."

Now, Mrs. G. Manville Smith had been a dining-room girl at the old Haley House before she married George Smith, and long before he made his money in lumber.

"You won't find them so heavy," Molly Brandeis said smoothly.

"I certainly would! Perhaps you would not. You're used to that sort of thing. Rough work, and all that."

Aloysius, doubled up behind the lamps, knew what was coming, from the gleam in his boss's eye.

"There may be something in that," Molly Brandeis returned sweetly. "That's why I thought you might not mind taking them. They're really not much heavier than a laden tray."

"Oh!" exclaimed the outraged Mrs. G. Manville Smith. And took her plumes and her patronage out of Brandeis' Bazaar forever.

That was as malicious as Molly Brandeis ever could be. And it was forgivable malice.

Most families must be described against the background of their homes, but the Brandeis family life was bounded and controlled by the store. Their meals and sleeping hours and amusements were regulated by it. It taught

7. A member of a secret fraternal order, charitable and social, founded in 1864 and named after a mythological character noted for devotion to his friend, Damon. "Scourine": a brand of cleansing agent.

them much, and brought them much, and lost them much. Fanny Brandeis always said she hated it, but it made her wise, and tolerant, and, in the end, famous. I don't know what more one could ask of any institution. It brought her in contact with men and women, taught her how to deal with them. After school she used often to run down to the store to see her mother, while Theodore went home to practice. Perched on a high stool in some corner she heard, and saw, and absorbed. It was a great school for the sensitive, highly-organized, dramatic little Jewish girl, for, to paraphrase a well-known stage line, there are just as many kinds of people in Winnebago as there are in Washington.

It was about this time that Fanny Brandeis began to realize, actively, that she was different. Of course, other little Winnebago girls' mothers did not work like a man, in a store. And she and Bella Weinberg were the only two in her room at school who stayed out on the Day of Atonement, and on New Year,[8] and the lesser Jewish holidays. Also, she went to temple on Friday night and Saturday morning, when the other girls she knew went to church on Sunday. These things set her apart in the little Middle Western town; but it was not these that constituted the real difference. She played, and slept, and ate, and studied like the other healthy little animals of her age. The real difference was temperamental, or emotional, or dramatic, or historic, or all four. They would be playing tag, perhaps, in one of the cool, green ravines that were the beauty spots of the little Wisconsin town.

They nestled like exquisite emeralds in the embrace of the hills, those ravines, and Winnebago's civic surge had not yet swept them away in a deluge of old tin cans, ashes, dirt and refuse, to be sold later for building lots. The Indians had camped and hunted in them. The one under the Court Street bridge, near the Catholic church and monastery, was the favorite for play. It lay, a lovely, gracious thing, below the hot little town, all green, and lush, and cool, a tiny stream dimpling through it. The plump Capuchin Fathers,[9] in their coarse brown robes, knotted about the waist with a cord, their bare feet thrust into sandals, would come out and sun themselves on the stone bench at the side of the monastery on the hill, or would potter about the garden. And suddenly Fanny would stop quite still in the midst of her tag game, struck with the beauty of the picture it called from the past.

Little Oriental[1] that she was, she was able to combine the dry text of her history book with the green of the trees, the gray of the church, and the brown of the monk's robes, and evolve a thrilling mental picture therefrom. The tag game and her noisy little companions vanished. She was peopling the place with stealthy Indians. Stealthy, cunning, yet savagely brave. They bore no relation to the abject, contemptible, and rather smelly Oneidas who came to the back door on summer mornings, in calico, and ragged overalls, with baskets of huckleberries on their arm, their pride gone, a broken and conquered people. She saw them wild, free, sovereign, and there were no greasy, berry-peddling Oneidas among them. They were Sioux, and Pottawatomies (that last had the real Indian sound), and Winnebagos, and Men-

8. Yom Kippur and Rosh Hashanah, respectively (Hebrew); the High Holy Days (Leviticus 23.24–27). They fall in the seventh month of the Jewish year in autumn; the ten days between them are known as the Days of Awe.

9. A Catholic order of friars, a branch of the Franciscans.

1. A person from the East, a non-European.

omonees, and Outagamis.[2] She made them taciturn, and beady-eyed, and lithe, and fleet, and every other adjectival thing her imagination and history book could supply. The fat and placid Capuchin Fathers on the hill became Jesuits, sinister, silent, powerful, with France and the Church of Rome[3] behind them. From the shelter of that big oak would step Nicolet, the brave, first among Wisconsin explorers, and last to receive the credit for his hardihood. Jean Nicolet! She loved the sound of it. And with him was La Salle, straight, and slim, and elegant, and surely wearing ruffles and plumes and sword even in a canoe. And Tonty,[4] his Italian friend and fellow adventurer—Tonty of the satins and velvets, graceful, tactful, poised, a shadowy figure; his menacing iron hand, so feared by the ignorant savages, encased always in a glove. Surely a perfumed g—— Slap! A rude shove that jerked her head back sharply and sent her forward, stumbling, and jarred her like a fall.

"Ya-a-a! Tag! You're it! Fanny's it!"

Indians, priests, cavaliers, *coureurs de bois*,[5] all vanished. Fanny would stand a moment, blinking stupidly. The next moment she was running as fleetly as the best of the boys in savage pursuit of one of her companions in the tag game.

She was a strange mixture of tomboy and bookworm, which was a mercifully kind arrangement for both body and mind. The spiritual side of her was groping and staggering and feeling its way about as does that of any little girl whose mind is exceptionally active, and whose mother is unusually busy. It was on the Day of Atonement, known in the Hebrew as Yom Kippur, in the year following her father's death that that side of her performed a rather interesting handspring.

Fanny Brandeis had never been allowed to fast on this, the greatest and most solemn of Jewish holy days. Molly Brandeis' modern side refused to countenance the practice of withholding food from any child for twenty-four hours. So it was in the face of disapproval that Fanny, making deep inroads into the steak and fried sweet potatoes at supper on the eve of the Day of Atonement, announced her intention of fasting from that meal to supper on the following evening. She had just passed her plate for a third helping of potatoes. Theodore, one lap behind her in the race, had entered his objection.

"Well, for the land's sakes!" he protested. "I guess you're not the only one who likes sweet potatoes."

Fanny applied a generous dab of butter to an already buttery morsel, and chewed it with an air of conscious virtue.[6]

"I've got to eat a lot. This is the last bite I'll have until to-morrow night."

"What's that?" exclaimed Mrs. Brandeis, sharply.

"Yes, it is!" hooted Theodore.

Fanny went on conscientiously eating as she explained.

"Bella Weinberg and I are going to fast all day. We just want to see if we can."

2. These are all names of Native American tribes or peoples from the central and upper Midwest.
3. I.e., the Roman Catholic Church. "Jesuits": members of the Society of Jesus, founded 1534 in Spain for missionary and educational work. "France": a Catholic country.
4. Henry de Tonti (1650–1704), an Italian-born explorer and companion of La Salle (1643–1687) and Nicolet (1598–1642), French explorers in North America.
5. A woodsman who lives by hunting and trapping.
6. Note that since they are consuming butter and steak in the same meal, the Brandeis family does not keep kosher.

"Betcha can't," Theodore said.

Mrs. Brandeis regarded her small daughter with a thoughtful gaze. "But that isn't the object in fasting, Fanny—just to see if you can. If you're going to think of food all through the Yom Kippur services——"

"I sha'n't?" protested Fanny passionately. "Theodore would, but I won't."

"Wouldn't any such thing," denied Theodore. "But if I'm going to play a violin solo during the memorial service I guess I've got to eat my regular meals."

Theodore sometimes played at temple, on special occasions.[7] The little congregation, listening to the throbbing rise and fall of this fifteen-year-old boy's violin playing, realized, vaguely, that here was something disturbingly, harrowingly beautiful. They did not know that they were listening to genius.

Molly Brandeis, in her second best dress, walked to temple Yom Kippur eve, her son at her right side, her daughter at her left. She had made up her mind that she would not let this next day, with its poignantly beautiful service, move her too deeply. It was the first since her husband's death, and Rabbi Thalmann rather prided himself on his rendition of the memorial service that came at three in the afternoon.

A man of learning, of sweetness, and of gentle wit was Rabbi Thalmann, and unappreciated by his congregation. He stuck to the Scriptures for his texts, finding Moses a greater leader than Roosevelt, and the miracle of the Burning Bush[8] more wonderful than the marvels of twentieth-century wizardry in electricity. A little man, Rabbi Thalmann, with hands and feet as small and delicate as those of a woman. Fanny found him fascinating to look on, in his rabbinical black broadcloth and his two pairs of glasses perched, in reading, upon his small hooked nose. He stood very straight in the pulpit, but on the street you saw that his back was bent just the least bit in the world—or perhaps it was only his student stoop, as he walked along with his eyes on the ground, smoking those slender, dapper, pale brown cigars that looked as if they had been expressly cut and rolled to fit him.

The evening service was at seven. The congregation, rustling in silks, was approaching the little temple from all directions. Inside, there, was a low-toned buzz of conversation. The Brandeis' seat was well toward the rear, as befitted a less prosperous member of the rich little congregation. This enabled them to get a complete picture of the room in its holiday splendor. Fanny drank it in eagerly, her dark eyes soft and luminous. The bare, yellow-varnished wooden pews glowed with the reflection from the chandeliers. The seven-branched candlesticks on either side of the pulpit were entwined with smilax. The red plush curtain that hung in front of the Ark[9] on ordinary days, and the red plush pulpit cover too, were replaced by gleaming white satin edged with gold fringe and finished at the corners with heavy gold tassels. How the rich white satin glistened in the light of the electric candles! Fanny Brandeis loved the lights, and the gleam, and the music, so majestic, and solemn, and the sight of the little rabbi, sitting so straight and serious in his

7. The violin in the temple suggests that this is a Reform congregation.

8. God spoke to Moses from a miraculously burning bush (Exodus 3.2–4). "Roosevelt": Theodore Roosevelt (1858–1919), the twenty-sixth president of the United States, who served from 1901 to 1909.

9. The receptacle in which the scrolls of the Torah are kept. "Seven-branched candlesticks": symbols of Judaism, constructed as described in the Bible (Exodus 25.31–37). "Smilax": a vine with glossy leaves.

high-backed chair, or standing to read from the great Bible. There came to this emotional little Jewess a thrill that was not born of religious fervor at all, I am afraid.

The sheer drama of the thing got her. In fact, the thing she had set herself to do to-day had in it very little of religion. Mrs. Brandeis had been right about that. It was a test of endurance, as planned. Fanny had never fasted in all her healthy life. She would come home from school to eat formidable stacks of bread and butter, enhanced by brown sugar or grape jelly, and topped off with three or four apples from the barrel in the cellar. Two hours later she would attack a supper of fried potatoes, and liver, and tea, and peach preserve, and more stacks of bread and butter. Then there were the cherry trees in the back yard, and the berry bushes, not to speak of sundry bags of small, hard candies of the jelly-bean variety, fitted for quick and secret munching during school. She liked good things to eat, this sturdy little girl, as did her friend, that blonde and creamy person, Bella Weinberg.

The two girls exchanged meaningful glances during the evening service. The Weinbergs, as befitted their station, sat in the third row at the right, and Bella had to turn around to convey her silent messages to Fanny. The evening service was brief, even to the sermon. Rabbi Thalmann and his congregation would need their strength for to-morrow's trial.

The Brandeises walked home through the soft September night, and the children had to use all their Yom Kippur dignity to keep from scuffling through the piled-up drifts of crackling autumn leaves. Theodore went to the cellar and got an apple, which he ate with what Fanny considered an unnecessary amount of scrunching. It was a firm, juicy apple, and it gave forth a cracking sound when his teeth met in its white meat. Fanny, after regarding him with gloomy superiority, went to bed.

She had willed to sleep late, for gastronomic reasons, but the mental command disobeyed itself, and she woke early, with a heavy feeling. Early as it was, Molly Brandeis had tiptoed in still earlier to look at her strange little daughter. She sometimes did that on Saturday mornings when she left early for the store and Fanny slept late. This morning Fanny's black hair was spread over the pillow as she lay on her back, one arm outflung, the other at her breast. She made a rather startlingly black and white and scarlet picture as she lay there asleep. Fanny did things very much in that way, too, with broad, vivid, unmistakable splashes of color. Mrs. Brandeis, looking at the black-haired, red-lipped child sleeping there, wondered just how much determination lay back of the broad white brow. She had said little to Fanny about this feat of fasting, and she told herself that she disapproved of it. But in her heart she wanted the girl to see it through, once attempted.

Fanny awoke at half past seven, and her nostrils dilated to that most exquisite, tantalizing and fragrant of smells—the aroma of simmering coffee. It permeated the house. It tickled the senses. It carried with it visions of hot, brown breakfast rolls, and eggs, and butter. Fanny loved her breakfast. She turned over now, and decided to go to sleep again. But she could not. She got up and dressed slowly and carefully. There was no one to hurry her this morning with the call from the foot of the stairs of, "Fanny! Your egg'll get cold!"

She put on clean, crisp underwear, and did her hair expertly. She slipped an all-enveloping pinafore over her head, that the new silk dress might not be crushed before church time. She thought that Theodore would surely have finished his breakfast by this time. But when she came down-stairs he was at the table. Not only that, he had just begun his breakfast. An egg, all golden, and white, and crisply brown at the frilly edges, lay on his plate. Theodore always ate his egg in a mathematical sort of way. He swallowed the white hastily first, because he disliked it, and Mrs. Brandeis insisted that he eat it. Then he would brood a moment over the yolk that lay, unmarred and complete, like an amber jewel in the center of his plate. Then he would suddenly plunge his fork into the very heart of the jewel, and it would flow over his plate, mingling with the butter, and he would catch it deftly with little mops of warm, crisp, buttery roll.

Fanny passed the breakfast table just as Theodore plunged his fork into the egg yolk. She caught her breath sharply, and closed her eyes. Then she turned and fled to the front porch and breathed deeply and windily of the heady September Wisconsin morning air. As she stood there, with her stiff, short black curls still damp and glistening, in her best shoes and stockings, with the all-enveloping apron covering her sturdy little figure, the light of struggle and renunciation in her face, she typified something at once fine and earthy.

But the real struggle was to come later. They went to temple at ten, Theodore with his beloved violin tucked carefully under his arm. Bella Weinberg was waiting at the steps.

"Did you?" she asked eagerly.

"Of course not," replied Fanny disdainfully. "Do you think I'd eat old breakfast when I said I was going to fast all day?" Then, with sudden suspicion, "Did you?"

"No!" stoutly.

And they entered, and took their seats. It was fascinating to watch the other members of the congregation come in, the women rustling, the men subdued in the unaccustomed dignity of black on a week day. One glance at the yellow pews was like reading a complete social and financial register. The seating arrangement of the temple was the Almanach de Gotha of Congregation Emanu-el.[1] Old Ben Reitman, patriarch among the Jewish settlers of Winnebago, who had come over an immigrant youth, and who now owned hundreds of rich farm acres, besides houses, mills and banks, kinged it from the front seat of the center section. He was a magnificent old man, with a ruddy face, and a fine head with a shock of heavy iron-gray hair, keen eyes, undimmed by years, and a startling and unexpected dimple in one cheek that gave him a mischievous and boyish look.

Behind this dignitary sat his sons, and their wives, and his daughters and their husbands, and their children, and so on, back to the Brandeis pew, third from the last, behind which sat only a few obscure families branded as Russians, as only the German-born Jew can brand those whose misfortune it is to be born in that region known as hinter-Berlin.[2]

The morning flew by, with its music, its responses, its sermon in German, full of four- and five-syllable German words like *Barmherzigkeit* and *Eigen-*

1. Literally, "God is with us" (Hebrew). "Almanach de Gotha": the family records of Europe's aristocratic and royal lines, first published in Gotha, Germany, in 1763.
2. In back of, behind, or past Berlin (German).

tümlichkeit.[3] All during the sermon Fanny sat and dreamed and watched the shadow on the window of the pine tree that stood close to the temple, and was vastly amused at the jaundiced look that the square of yellow window glass cast upon the face of the vain and overdressed Mrs. Nathan Pereles. From time to time Bella would turn to bestow upon her a look intended to convey intense suffering and a resolute though dying condition. Fanny stonily ignored these mute messages. They offended something in her, though she could not tell what.

At the noon intermission she did not go home to the tempting dinner smells, but wandered off through the little city park and down to the river, where she sat on the bank and felt very virtuous, and spiritual, and hollow. She was back in her seat when the afternoon service was begun. Some of the more devout members had remained to pray all through the midday. The congregation came straggling in by twos and threes. Many of the women had exchanged the severely corseted discomfort of the morning's splendor for the comparative ease of second-best silks. Mrs. Brandeis, absent from her business throughout this holy day, came hurrying in at two, to look with a rather anxious eye upon her pale and resolute little daughter.

The memorial service was to begin shortly after three, and lasted almost two hours. At quarter to three Bella slipped out through the side aisle, beckoning mysteriously and alluringly to Fanny as she went. Fanny looked at her mother.

"Run along," said Mrs. Brandeis. "The air will be good for you. Come back before the memorial service begins."

Fanny and Bella met, giggling, in the vestibule.

"Come on over to my house for a minute," Bella suggested. "I want to show you something." The Weinberg house, a great, comfortable, well-built home, with encircling veranda, and a well-cared-for lawn, was just a scant block away. They skipped across the street, down the block, and in at the back door. The big sunny kitchen was deserted. The house seemed very quiet and hushed. Over it hung the delicious fragrance of freshly-baked pastry. Bella, a rather baleful look in her eyes, led the way to the butler's pantry that was as large as the average kitchen. And there, ranged on platters, and baking boards, and on snowy-white napkins, was that which made Tantalus's feast[4] seem a dry and barren snack. The Weinberg's had baked.

It is the custom in the household of Atonement Day fasters of the old school to begin the evening meal, after the twenty-four hours of abstainment, with coffee and freshly-baked coffee cake of every variety. It was a lead-pipe blow at one's digestion, but delicious beyond imagining. Bella's mother was a famous cook, and her two maids followed in the ways of their mistress. There were to be sisters and brothers and out-of-town relations as guests at the evening meal, and Mrs. Weinberg had outdone herself.

"Oh!" exclaimed Fanny in a sort of agony and delight.

"Take some," said Bella, the temptress.

The pantry was fragrant as a garden with spices, and fruit scents, and the melting, delectable perfume of brown, freshly-baked dough, sugar-coated. There was one giant platter devoted wholly to round, plump cakes, with puffy

3. Individuality. "*Barmherzigkeit*": compassion, charity.
4. According to Greek mythology, the thirsty and hungry Tantalus, king of Lydia, was condemned to have water and fruit always present but just out of reach.

edges, in the center of each a sunken pool that was all plum, bearing on its bosom a snowy sifting of powdered sugar. There were others whose centers were apricot, pure molten gold in the sunlight. There were speckled expanses of cheese *kuchen*,[5] the golden-brown surface showing rich cracks through which one caught glimpses of the lemon-yellow cheese beneath—cottage cheese that had been beaten up with eggs, and spices, and sugar, and lemon. Flaky crust rose, jaggedly, above this plateau. There were cakes with jelly, and cinnamon *kuchen*, and cunning cakes with almond slices nestling side by side. And there was freshly-baked bread—twisted loaf, with poppy seed freckling its braid, and its sides glistening with the butter that had been liberally swabbed on it before it had been thrust into the oven.

Fanny Brandeis gazed, hypnotized. As she gazed Bella selected a plum tart and bit into it—bit generously, so that her white little teeth met in the very middle of the oozing red-brown juice and one heard a little squirt as they closed on the luscious fruit. At the sound Fanny quivered all through her plump and starved little body.

"Have one," said Bella generously. "Go on. Nobody'll ever know. Anyway, we've fasted long enough for our age. I could fast till supper time if I wanted to, but I don't want to." She swallowed the last morsel of the plum tart, and selected another—apricot, this time, and opened her moist red lips. But just before she bit into it (the Inquisition[6] could have used Bella's talents) she selected its counterpart and held it out to Fanny. Fanny shook her head slightly. Her hand came up involuntarily. Her eyes were fastened on Bella's face.

"Go on," urged Bella. "Take it. They're grand! M-m-m-m!" The first bite of apricot vanished between her rows of sharp white teeth. Fanny shut her eyes as if in pain. She was fighting the great fight of her life. She was to meet other temptations, and perhaps more glittering ones, in her lifetime, but to her dying day she never forgot that first battle between the flesh and the spirit, there in the sugar-scented pantry—and the spirit won. As Bella's lips closed upon the second bite of apricot tart, the while her eye roved over the almond cakes and her hand still held the sweet out to Fanny, that young lady turned sharply, like a soldier, and marched blindly out of the house, down the back steps, across the street, and so into the temple.

The evening lights had just been turned on. The little congregation, relaxed, weary, weak from hunger, many of them, sat rapt and still except at those times when the prayer book demanded spoken responses. The voice of the little rabbi, rather weak now, had in it a timbre that made it startlingly sweet and clear and resonant. Fanny slid very quietly into the seat beside Mrs. Brandeis, and slipped her moist and cold little hand into her mother's warm, work-roughened palm. The mother's brown eyes, very bright with unshed tears, left their perusal of the prayer book to dwell upon the white little face that was smiling rather wanly up at her. The pages of the prayer book lay two-thirds or more to the left.[7] Just as Fanny remarked this, there was a little moment of hush in the march of the day's long service. The memorial hour had begun.

5. Cakes made with sweet yeast dough (German).
6. The extremely severe Roman Catholic tribunal in Spain (1481–92) that tried, convicted, and punished lapsed converts from Judaism as well as other apostates and heretics.
7. Reading in the Reform prayer book, from left to right, the memorial service has just begun.

Little Doctor Thalmann cleared his throat. The congregation stirred a bit, changed its cramped position. Bella, the guilty, came stealing in, a pink-and-gold picture of angelic virtue. Fanny, looking at her, felt very aloof, and clean, and remote.

Molly Brandeis seemed to sense what had happened.

"But you didn't, did you?" she whispered softly.

Fanny shook her head.

Rabbi Thalmann was seated in his great carved chair. His eyes were closed. The wheezy little organ in the choir loft at the rear of the temple began the opening bars of Schumann's Traümerei.[8] And then, above the cracked voice of the organ, rose the clear, poignant wail of a violin. Theodore Brandeis had begun to play. You know the playing of the average boy of fifteen—that nerve-destroying, uninspired scraping. There was nothing of this in the sounds that this boy called forth from the little wooden box and the stick with its taut lines of catgut. Whatever it was—the length of the thin, sensitive fingers, the turn of the wrist, the articulation of the forearm, the something in the brain, or all these combined—Theodore Brandeis possessed that which makes for greatness. You realized that as he crouched over his violin to get his cello tones. As he played to-day the little congregation sat very still, and each was thinking of his ambitions and his failures; of the lover lost, of the duty left undone, of the hope deferred; of the wrong that was never righted; of the lost one whose memory spells remorse. It felt the salt taste on its lips. It put up a furtive, shamed hand to dab at its cheeks, and saw that the one who sat in the pew just ahead was doing likewise. This is what happened when this boy of fifteen wedded his bow to his violin. And he who makes us feel all this has that indefinable, magic, glorious thing known as Genius.

When it was over, there swept through the room that sigh following tension relieved. Rabbi Thalmann passed a hand over his tired eyes, like one returning from a far mental journey; then rose, and came forward to the pulpit. He began, in Hebrew, the opening words of the memorial service, and so on to the prayers in English, with their words of infinite humility and wisdom.

"Thou hast implanted in us the capacity for sin, but not sin itself!"

Fanny stirred. She had learned that a brief half hour ago. The service marched on, a moving and harrowing thing. The amens[9] rolled out with a new fervor from the listeners. There seemed nothing comic now in the way old Ben Reitman, with his slower eyes, always came out five words behind the rest who tumbled upon the responses and scurried briskly through them, so that his fine old voice, somewhat hoarse and quavering now, rolled out its "Amen!" in solitary majesty. They came to that gem of humility, the mourners' prayer; the ancient and ever-solemn Kaddish[1] prayer. There is nothing in the written language that, for sheer drama and magnificence, can equal it as it is chanted in the Hebrew.

As Rabbi Thalmann began to intone it in its monotonous repetition of praise, there arose certain black-robed figures from their places and stood with heads bowed over their prayer books. These were members of the con-

8. *Dreaming*, a perennially popular piece of music by German composer Robert Schumann (1810–1856).

9. *Amen* (Hebrew) means "So be it!"

1. Recited daily at public services during the first eleven months after a parent's death, in the memorial service on holidays, and on the anniversary of the death. The Kaddish is in Aramaic.

gregation from whom death had taken a toll during the past year. Fanny rose with her mother and Theodore, who had left the choir loft to join them. The little wheezy organ played very softly. The black-robed figures swayed. Here and there a half-stifled sob rose, and was crushed. Fanny felt a hot haze that blurred her vision. She winked it away, and another burned in its place. Her shoulders shook with a sob. She felt her mother's hand close over her own that held one side of the book. The prayer, that was not of mourning but of praise, ended with a final crescendo from the organ. The silent black-robed figures were seated.

Over the little, spent congregation hung a glorious atmosphere of detachment. These Jews, listening to the words that had come from the lips of the prophets in Israel, had been, on this day, thrown back thousands of years, to the time when the destruction of the temple was as real as the shattered spires and dome of the cathedral at Rheims.[2] Old Ben Reitman, faint with fasting, was far removed from his everyday thoughts of his horses, his lumber mills, his farms, his mortgages. Even Mrs. Nathan Pereles, in her black satin and bugles and jets, her cold, hard face usually unlighted by sympathy or love, seemed to feel something of this emotional wave. Fanny Brandeis was shaken by it. Her head ached (that was hunger) and her hands were icy. The little Russian girl in the seat just behind them had ceased to wriggle and squirm, and slept against her mother's side. Rabbi Thalmann, there on the platform, seemed somehow very far away and vague. The scent of clove apples and ammonia salts[3] filled the air. The atmosphere seemed strangely wavering and luminous. The white satin of the Ark curtain gleamed and shifted.

The long service swept on to its close. Suddenly organ and choir burst into a pæon.[4] Little Doctor Thalmann raised his arms. The congregation swept to its feet with a mighty surge. Fanny rose with them, her face very white in its frame of black curls, her eyes luminous. She raised her face for the words of the ancient benediction that rolled, in its simplicity and grandeur, from the lips of the rabbi:

"May the blessing of the Lord our God rest upon you all. God bless thee and keep thee. May God cause His countenance to shine upon thee and gracious unto thee. May God lift up His countenance unto thee, and grant thee peace."

The Day of Atonement had come to an end. It was a very quiet, subdued and spent little flock that dispersed to their homes. Fanny walked out with scarcely a thought of Bella. She felt, vaguely, that she and this school friend were formed of different stuff. She knew that the bond between them had been the grubby, physical one of childhood, and that they never would come together in the finer relation of the spirit, though she could not have put this new knowledge into words.

Molly Brandeis put a hand on her daughter's shoulder.

"Tired, Fanchen?"[5]

"A little."

2. A great Gothic church built in the 13th century in the Champagne region of France. It was heavily damaged in World War I. "Destruction of the temple": in 70 C.E., the Romans destroyed the Temple, leaving only the Wailing Wall standing.

3. I.e., smelling salts. "Clove apples": cloves, a spice, stuck into apples were thought to stimulate the senses, thus combating drowsiness.

4. A hymn of praise.

5. Little Fanny (German).

"Bet you're hungry!" from Theodore.

"I was, but I'm not now."

"M-m-m—wait! Noodle soup. And chicken!"

She had intended to tell of the trial in the Weinberg's pantry. But now something within her—something fine, born of this day—kept her from it. But Molly Brandeis, to whom two and two often made five, guessed something of what had happened. She had felt a great surge of pride, had Molly Brandeis, when her son had swayed the congregation with the magic of his music. She had kissed him good night with infinite tenderness and love. But she came into her daughter's tiny room after Fanny had gone to bed, and leaned over, and put a cool hand on the hot forehead.

"Do you feel all right, my darling?"

"Umhmph," replied Fanny drowsily.

"Fanchen, doesn't it make you feel happy and clean to know that you were able to do the thing you started out to do?"

"Umhmph."

"Only," Molly Brandeis was thinking aloud now, quite forgetting that she was talking to a very little girl, "only, life seems to take such special delight in offering temptation to those who are able to withstand it. I don't know why that's true, but it is. I hope—oh, my little girl, my baby—I hope——"

But Fanny never knew whether her mother finished that sentence or not. She remembered waiting for the end of it, to learn what it was her mother hoped. And she had felt a sudden, scalding drop on her hand where her mother bent over her. And the next thing she knew it was morning, with mellow September sunshine.

1917, 1936

H. LEYVIK
ca. 1888–1962

Considered internationally the greatest Yiddish poet of the mid-twentieth century as well as a symbol of redemptive suffering in his life and work, H. Leyvik wrote poetry and verse dramas with ethical rather than aesthetic aims. Leyvik (originally Leyvick Halpern) was born into poverty around 1888 in Ihumen, a small town in Belorussia. His father, whom the poet characterized as an angry and abusive man, counted rabbis among his ancestors yet earned his living by teaching girls how to read and write Yiddish; his mother was a baker. Leyvik attended heder and then a yeshiva, where he studied both Talmud and Hebrew grammar (an Enlightenment subject), and read secular books in Hebrew. He joined the underground Jewish Socialist party, the Bund, during the 1905 revolution and began, under its influence, to write poetry in Yiddish.

His political involvement led to his arrest by czarist police in 1906. They imprisoned him in Minsk for two years, where he wrote his first verse drama, and, in 1908, sentenced him to four years of forced labor and to exile for life in Siberia. In 1912, he was marched to his place of exile, Vittim, a village on the River Lena. However, with the aid of political friends in America, he escaped. Leyvik traveled 1,000 miles down frozen rivers and across the steppes in a horse and sledge that he managed to buy, making his way across European Russia and Germany, where he boarded a ship for the United States. Arriving there in 1913, he earned his living as a wallpaper hanger.

Writing lyric poems and initially connecting with the Yunge poets, Leyvik soon revealed how his literary aims differed from their individualist aestheticism. His poetry and verse dramas were infused with messianism, mysticism, and symbolism that drew on Jewish legends and texts yet advocated social revolution and were shaped by a sensibility reminiscent of Dostoyevsky. His first book of poetry, *Lider*, came out in 1919 and contained poems about his Siberian exile. He wrote visionary poems about the pogroms following World War I. And his symbolist verse dramas—especially *Der goylem* (The Golem, 1921), based on the legend of the sixteenth-century Prague rabbi who brings a clay man to life to save the Jews—galvanized the Yiddish literary world, raising debate about Jewish redemption versus the socialist ideas of world revolution. *The Golem* was first performed in 1924 in Moscow by the Hebrew theater group Habimah. He also wrote plays in a realist style as well as verse dramas about biblical figures.

Leyvik was diagnosed with tuberculosis and spent 1932 to 1936 in Spivak Sanatorium in Denver, Colorado, where he wrote one cycle of lyric poems, *Lider fun ganeydn* (Poems from Paradise), and another about Spinoza. A poem from each cycle is included here. In 1936, he became very famous and traveled internationally. That same year, he joined the staff of the newspaper the *Tog* (Day) and began to coedit, with Joseph Opatoshu, series of literary anthologies, eight of which appeared between 1936 and 1952. His poems reflect his social concerns about America, Palestine (which he visited in 1937), and Europe. During and after World War II, he wrote poems and verse dramas reflecting his anguish over the Holocaust.

Leyvik was paralyzed for the last four years of his life and could not speak. But since he had acquired the stature of a figure as great in Yiddish literature as I. L. Peretz, many made the pilgrimage to be near him before he died.

The poems included here show Leyvik's lyric power and the range of his thematic concerns.

Clouds behind the Forest[1]

Clouds behind the forest come close to the tops of the trees,
Are impaled on them, like bellies on sharpened spears.
Red fills the sky and the Creator himself descends,
His body torn open, his entrails hanging out.
He smells of salty heat and the scream of his wound is searing.
—Creator, I say, your blood is running out. Are you dying, Creator?
But I do not see on His face an expression of twisted pain,
I see soft and quiet goodness. Instead of answering—
He lowers Himself to the very earth.
I leap to Him, I want to grasp Him by His fingertips—
—Creator, I say, you are covering me with blood—am I dying, Creator?
And again, instead of answering, He stretches over me,
His face covers my face, like a woman,
And his lips begin to move over my whole body,
And I feel the hot breath, like a licking tongue, over my body,

1. Translated by Benjamin Harshav and Barbara Harshav. Last passage of a long poem of the same title (1930) [Benjamin Harshav and Barbara Harshav's note].

The tongue moves and laps up the blood, like a mother animal,
Like a woman after childbirth lapping up the blood of her new-born infant.

I open my eyes, I see: the sun left a while ago, and the forest
Has moved closer to me, like a guard, and shouts with winged voices.—
The odor of God's torn-open body steams from me and from the earth around,
Odor of womb, of birth.—Here, in the middle of the world
At the shore of a forest, you created me once again, Creator,
For a second time—a second time you bore me,
Bore me and left me lying with traces of blood on my face.— —
—Creator—Creator—

1930 1940

Sanatorium[1]

Gate, open;
doorsill, creep near.
Room, I'm here;
back to the cell.

Fire in my flesh,
snow on my skull.
My shoulder heaves
a sack of grief.

Good-bye. Good-bye.
Hand. Eye.
Burning lip
charred by good-bye.

Parted from whom?
From whom fled?
Let the riddle slip
unsaid.

The circling plain
is fire and flame:
fiery snow
on the hills.

Look—this open door
and gate. Guess.
Hospital? Prison?
some monkish place?

1. Translated by Cynthia Ozick. From the series *Songs from Paradise,* written during Leyvik's four years in a sanatorium in Denver, Colorado.

Colorado! I throw
my sack of despair
on your fiery floor
of snow.

1932–1936 1940

How Did He Get Here? (Spinoza Cycle, No. 2)[2]

How did he get into this sickroom,
the philosopher from Amsterdam?

I look at him—there's no uncertainty.
It's he, it's he.

The full lips. The long nose.
The whole head as though under glass.

His sick chest heaves, straining,
racked, racked, by fits of coughing.

Three hundred years—as though one minute.
A drop of blood dots his lip.

Three hundred years of moonlight fall
on his head and pillow. Fall.

Holy one, I touch your sleeve.
Wake up. Rise up. Recognize me.

1932–1936 1940

Song of the Yellow Patch[1]

How does it look, the yellow patch
With a red or black Star-of-David
On the arm of a Jew in Naziland—
Against the white ground of a December snow?

2. Translated by Ruth Whitman. While in a sanatorium in Denver, Colorado, Leyvik wrote a cycle of poems about Baruch Spinoza (1632–1677), the Dutch Sephardic philosopher whose theological skepticism caused him to be excommunicated in 1656. Spinoza, considered a hero by secular Yiddish intellectuals, died of tuberculosis.

1. Translated by Benjamin Harshav and Barbara Harshav. First poem of a cycle, *Poems of the Yellow Patch*. The refrain, in parentheses, echoes Leyvik's first poem, *Somewhere Far Away* [Benjamin Harshav and Barbara Harshav's note]. "Yellow patch": Jews throughout medieval Europe were forced to wear yellow patches, often in the shape of a circle or a wheel with a red bull's-eye in the center, to distinguish them from the Christian population, a practice that was suspended in the 18th century. In October 1939, the Nazis revived this symbol to mark Jews off from the rest of the populace in occupied Poland and then throughout Nazi-occupied Europe. The Nazi version of the yellow patch often had a black or red Star of David or the word *Jude* (German for "Jew") in the center.

How would it look, a yellow patch
With a red or black Star-of-David
On the arms of my wife and my sons,
On my own arm—
On the white ground of a New York snow?
Truly—
The question gnaws like a gnat in my brain,
The question eats at my heart like a worm.

And why should we escape with mere words?
Why not share in full unity
And wear on our own arms
The destined yellow patch with the Star-of-David
Openly, in New York as in Berlin,
In Paris, in London, in Moscow as in Vienna?
Truly—
The question gnaws like a gnat in my brain,
The question eats at my heart like a worm.

Today the first snow descended.,
Children are gliding on sleds in the park,
The air is filled with clamor of joy.—
Like the children, I love the white snow,
And I have a special love for the month of December.[2]

(Somewhere far, somewhere far away
lies a prisoner, lies alone.)

O dear God, God of Abraham, of Isaac and of Jacob,
Scold me not for this love of mine—
Scold me for something else—
Scold me for not kneading
This wonderful snow of New York into a Moses,
For not building a Mount Sinai of snow.
As I used to in my childhood.—

(Somewhere wanders a man,
Deeply covered in snow.)

Scold me for not really wearing
The six-towered Star-of-David
And the infinite circle of the yellow patch—
To hearten the sons of Israel in Hangman's-Land
And to praise and raise our arm
With the pride of our ancestral emblem
In all the lands of the wide world.
Truly—
The question gnaws like a gnat in my brain,
The question eats at my heart like a worm.

2. Leyvik's Yiddish gives the Jewish month in a Hebraic phrase: *dem khoydesh kislev,* "the month of Kislev," which connotes Hanukkah, the festival marking the Maccabean revolt against the Assyrian tyrant's desecration of the Temple.

(Somewhere far, somewhere far away
Lies the land, the forbidden land.)

1940

To America[1]

For forty-one years I have lived in your borders, America,
Carrying within me the bounty of your freedom—that freedom,
Sanctified and blessed by the blood of Lincoln's sacrifice
And in the hymns of Walt Whitman. See, how strange it is: to this day
I seek an answer to the contradictions, to the unrest of my life,
I wonder, why haven't I sung you, to this day,
With joy, with praise, with pure admiration—
To match your vast expanses, your cities, your roads,
Your prairies, your mountains and valleys. Even more:
For my own small world—in Brownsville, or on Clinton Street,
In Borough Park, in the Bronx, or on the Heights,
And above all: for all my walks on East Broadway[2]—
That East-Broadway which fills me even now with stirring vitality,
With intimate hominess, as soon as I set foot in her streets.

For forty-one years I have lived under your skies,
For over thirty years I have been your citizen,
And until now I have not found in me the word, the mode
For painting my arrival and my rise on your earth
With strokes as broad and revealing as you are yourself, America.
As soon as speech would shift toward you, I would curb
My words, rein them in with austere restraint,
Bind them in knots of understatement. My whole world and my whole life
I held under secret locks, far from your wide open breadth.
I shall disclose it now: when I got off the ship
Forty-one years ago, and touched your earth—I wanted to
Fall prostrate upon it, kiss it with my lips. Yes, yes, I wanted to, should have,
And—I didn't . . . And later, on your blessed earth
I wrote, in memory of my father's image, songs of guilt and longing.
And I said to that image: accept, though late, the kisses
That I wanted to give—should have given—as a child
And ever was ashamed to give you . . . In all your greatness,
America, you surely will not bring yourself to say
That you are more, that you are privileged above my father.

And maybe you will say: I am not more, but am I less?—
Indeed, I would have liked to hear you say that.
Had I heard this, it would have been a balm to my heart;

1. Translated by Benjamin Harshav and Barbara Harshav.
2. A street on the Lower East Side of Manhattan. "Brownsville": a section of Brooklyn. "Clinton Street": on the Lower East Side. "Borough Park": a section of Brooklyn. "The Bronx": one of the five boroughs of New York City. "The Heights": i.e., Washington Heights, in northern Manhattan.

Even at the sunset of my life, I could have opened for you.
The still sealed confessions about you, America.
I say again—I tried to do it in hundreds of hints
In verse and rhyme, in the tempests of tragic dialogues,
In raised and fallen curtains. Often I sought a way
To tear down the curtain covering my own heart,
To be open, intimate with you, America, at least half
As intimate as I am with the little cemetery in small Ihumen,[3]
Where my father-mother rest, passed away in those far-off days,
In those far-off days of World War One, before the flood;
As I am intimate with the glowing snows in the village Vittim[4]
On the God-forsaken Irkutsk-Yakutsk[5] expanses of Siberia;
As I am intimate with Isaac's walk to Mount Moriah and with mother
   Rachel's grave,[6]
With David's prayers and with the bright prophecy of Isaiah,[7]
With Lekert's rise upon the gallows and with the dance-of-dawn in Eyn-
   Harod.[8]—

I tried,—and it is clear: the fault is mine, not yours,
That thirty years ago I mourned under your skies
Deep inside me, lamented that I carry my Yiddish song
In fear, through your streets and through your squares,
Clenched in my teeth, as a forsaken cat might carry
Her kittens, in search of a cellar, a place of rest;—
That when I think of my brothers—Yiddish poets—their destiny
Embraces me like a clamp, I want to pray for them,
For their lot—and then all words grow mute.
Certainly, it is my fault, not yours, when even now
After thirty years have passed my heart mourns again,
An elegy on how, now more than ever, the evil lot
Has scattered all Yiddish poets over New-Siberias,
And chased our trembling poets' ship into an abyss of storms,
Into an abyss of storms on your waters too, America,
In death-danger; and in that death-danger I search for the brave song
Of the brave captain.[9] The brave captain shall not betray
His song-of-destiny today.— — —
You see—I am cruel to myself when I say: It is *certainly* my fault,
If instead of "certainly" I could say "maybe," or "perhaps."
I am trying not to cast part of the blame on you, America.
And may God in Heaven witness that you are not yet worthy
To feel free of guilt, as white as snow—

3. Leyvik's tiny hometown in Byelorussia [Benjamin Harshav and Barbara Harshav's note].
4. The place of Leyvik's exile in Siberia, between 1912 and his escape in 1913 [adapted from Benjamin Harshav and Barbara Harshav's note].
5. Areas in Siberia.
6. The Matriarch Rachel was buried in Bethlehem on the road to Ephrath, separately from the other Patriarchs and Matriarchs (Genesis 35.19 and 48.7). "Isaac's walk to Mount Moriah": with his father, Abraham, on the way to being bound for sacrifice (Genesis 22.1–19).
7. A reference to the biblical prophet Isaiah. "David's prayers": the Psalms of King David.
8. The first kibbutz in the swamps of the Jezreel Valley, famous for its pioneering spirit and collective dances into the night. "Lekert's rise upon the gallows": Hirsh Lekert (1879–1902), a shoemaker and Bund activist in Vilna who organized an armed attack to liberate political prisoners. He assassinated the Russian governor of Vilna for flogging Socialists after a May Day demonstration and was hanged. Lekert became a hero of the Jewish labor movement and self-defense [Benjamin Harshav and Barbara Harshav's notes].
9. An allusion to Walt Whitman's "O, Captain, My Captain" [Benjamin Harshav and Barbara Harshav's note].

You see—you yourself should have come to my aid right now,
To ease my task of finding proper words
Expressing intimacy and fusion and farewell.
Fusion with your beauty and your expansive breath;
Farewell?—the stronger the fusion, the closer I can see
The moment of farewell. It may occur within your boundaries,
And it may happen far away, beyond your borders:
It may uplift me and carry me to those wonder-places,
Where as a boy I walked with Father Abraham near
Beer-Sheba, and with David[1] around the gates of Jerusalem,
It may bring me, too, to today's climbing road to New Jerusalem.[2]

You too, America, walked close with them,
You too, have absorbed in your heart God's commandment and blessing:
To be a land flowing with milk and honey,
To be numerous as the sands of the sea and the stars in the sky,
To be prophetic and free, as your Founders dreamed you.—
O, let the dream of Lincoln and Walt Whitman be your dream today!

In days of old age, when I stand in the bright vision
Of one or another shining farewell, I recall again
The moment, forty-one years ago, when I reached
Your shore, America, and I wanted to and should have
Fallen prostrate to your earth and touched it with my lips,
And in confused embarrassment I did not do it,—
Let me do it now—as I stand here truthfully,
Embracing the glare of intimacy and farewell, America.

September 12, 1954 1955

Sacrifice[1]

Bound[2] hand and foot he lies
on the hard altar stone
and waits.

Eyes half shut, he looks
on his father standing there
and waits.

His father sees his eyes
and strokes his son's brow
and waits.

1. I.e., King David. "Father Abraham near Beer-Sheba": Abraham made a covenant with Abimelech at Beer-Sheba (Genesis 21.22–34); he lived in Beer-Sheba after the binding of Isaac (Genesis 22.19).
2. In the modern State of Israel, the main highway from Tel Aviv ascends the mountains of Jerusalem.
1. Translated by Robert Friend. The Yiddish title, *Akeyda*, from the Hebrew, literally means "binding" and is the word Jews use to refer to Abraham's binding of his son Isaac (Genesis 22.9) on Mount Moriah at God's command. Leyvik retells this story from a different point of view.
2. "Bound" translates literally the Yiddish word here, *gebundn*.

With old and trembling hands
the father picks up the knife
and waits.

A Voice from above cries, "Stop!"
The hand freezes in air
and waits.

The veined throat suddenly throbs
with the miracle of the test
and waits.

The father gathers up the son.
The altar is bare
and waits.

Ensnared in thorns a lamb
looks at the hand with a knife
and waits.

1955

FRADL SHTOK
1890–ca. 1930

Although influenced by the Yunge's concept of *reyner dikhtung* (pure poetry), Fradl Shtok was a literary innovator who began her work in Yiddish with a sense of high culture. She was among the first of the Yiddish poets to write sonnets and the first to compose a sonnet cycle of fifteen formally linked poems. Her poems subvert musicality with violent eroticism; her understated fiction depicts the tensions of young women coming of age in Galician shtetls.

Fradl Shtok was born in Skale, Galicia, in 1890. Her mother died when she was two, and her father, said to possess extraordinary strength and who was imprisoned for his involvement in a murder, died when Shtok was ten years old. Raised by an aunt, Shtok was known for her beauty and her excellence as a student who played the violin, and could recite Goethe and Schiller in German. She arrived in New York in 1907, at the age of seventeen.

Her taut, elegant poems began to appear in publications of the Yunge in 1910, her short stories soon thereafter. She published in Abraham Reyzen's *Dos naye land* in 1911–12, in the miscellanies of the Yunge poets—*Di naye heym* in 1914, *Inzl*, and Halpern and Nadir's collection *Fun mentsh tsu mentsh* in 1916—in *Tsukunft*, and in *Fraye arbeter shtime*.

When her book of thirty-eight short stories, *Gezamlte ertseylungen* (Collected Stories) appeared in 1919 (dedicated to her father), harsh reviews by Leyeles in the *Tog* and by Moissaye Olgin in the socialist *Naye velt* are thought to have made her stop writing in Yiddish. Even the appreciative reviews praised her work in patronizing terms, failing to note how original and innovative were these terse stories and their treatment of the erotic desires and frustrations of women rebelling against the strictures of traditional Judaism. Shtok published a novel in English, *Musicians Only* (1927), which was ignored by both the English and the Yiddish literary worlds. It is believed that she spent her last years in a mental hospital and died there sometime around 1930. Her poems were never collected, and only a very few of the poems and the stories have appeared in English translation. The fact that such a significant writer as Shtok could die without record, her works remaining, until recently, forgotten, indicates how tenuous were the places that women writers occupied in Yiddish literature.

Shtok's short story *The Shorn Head* exemplifies the problems of Jewish women entering the modern world. The nineteen-year-old protagonist of this story, set in Galicia before the First World War, is a widow of an unconsummated marriage whose beloved parents have also recently died. The story evolves from Sheyndl's dilemma as her braids, shorn according to tradition for marriage, grow back, and she develops a sense of her identity that bucks the expectations and tolerance of the shtetl society in which she lives.

The three poems included here—*Sonnet, A Winter Echo,* and *Dusks*—reveal Shtok as a modernist, subversively employing literary convention and remaining alert to the risks of writing poetry. In particular, the sonnet, from the first sonnet cycle written in Yiddish, shows how Shtok imports the formal and thematic traditions of this European verse form while she distorts conventions with a female persona whose love is encased in resentment and with eros embodied as rage.

The Shorn Head[1]

(A gift for my Aunt Tsipora)

Her mother braided her hair till she was eighteen years old. And how it grew—God protect her!—by leaps and bounds. Black and thick and long—down, down past her waist.

Even when she was still very small, Sheyndl was already a wonderful little homemaker. Her dress carried her scent and seemed to grow right along with her. Her darning, her embroidery were passed around, miracles to behold. Was there anything she couldn't do? She could imitate a bird as it flew.

Her pious mother hadn't allowed her to go to school on account of Nekhe, who would never have written little love notes to the inspector if she hadn't learned to write.[2]

But what Sheyndl understood with her own common sense her mother could not take away from her. And Sheyndl had common sense. Ah, that at nineteen they had married her off to a sick widower and three months later he died—that was a piece of luck. The misfortune was that in that very same year both her father and mother died too—her devoted mother. And Sheyndl was set adrift.

Sheyndl cried and cried. She herself didn't know what made her cry more, her shorn braids—which always reminded her of her bound head[3]—or her

1. Translated by Irena Klepfisz.
2. The girl Nekhe is understood to be Jewish; the inspector, Gentile. *Sheyndl* means "beautiful" (Yiddish).
3. Traditional Jewish custom in Eastern Europe and among the Orthodox today holds that a woman, once married, must cover her hair for the sake of modesty. In many communities, the practice was to shave the bride's head immediately after the wedding night to ensure that no one would accidentally see her hair. The wife would then wear a kerchief, hat, and/or wig (*shaytl*) on her naked scalp.

devoted mother. All that remained for her now was the little room, her inheritance. The little tiny room with not even a piece of bread.

Sheyndl had nothing to eat. Her brothers were poor folk themselves and claimed it was nice enough of them to let her live in the apartment.

When her mother was alive, Sheyndl would buy a *graytser's*[4] worth of pumpkin seeds, wash them down with a drink of cold water and feel revived. But now, when she didn't even have a *graytser* she couldn't indulge herself.

Hungry, she'd run to the cemetery and undam a river of tears. And if it hadn't been for Esther, God only knows what would have become of her by now.

Esther was, in fact, a respectable child. But since people have mouths, they dreamed up that she liked to talk with the *klezmer* boy.[5] Sheyndl knew there was nothing to it. If only everyone had Esther's character—the way she sat and worked at the machine and contributed at home.

Esther wanted Sheyndl for a friend because Sheyndl had a reputation as a virtuous girl. And Sheyndl latched on to her. She knew Esther was smart and decent, despite what people said about her. But she never told Esther she was hungry. She was ashamed. It seemed to her it was a great crime that she was hungry. But how was she to blame?

Gradually Sheyndl learned to sew, and after that she earned a *manger*[6] a day, a whole *manger*, a *graytser* and a half. And so she wasn't so aimless anymore.

And when gradually she began to sew on her own and suddenly saw a whole *ranish*[7] before her eyes, she felt she was becoming prosperous. Soon a red satin apron came into being, a pair of gold slippers with little ornaments, and a bordeaux peasant blouse trimmed with lambskin. And the blouse had a scent.

People said: Sheyndl is right as the world. And so decent.

But she: inside her heart cried. Every time she looked at her *shaytele*[8] with the bangs in front, her heart would twinge . . . her head was already bound.

At night she would stroke her shorn head, back and forth, back and forth and her hair actually grew quickly, beautifully. Yet it seemed to her that her two braids would never grow back. But when they finally did? Wouldn't she have to cut them off? Cut them off again? No! No? A Jewish woman—a wife? Woe is me! My poor heart! But no! God forbid! Who says she has to walk around with her hair exposed. Let it stay under the *shaytl*—like that. Her head is already bound. And for what reason? And for how long, *gotenyu?*[9] She hadn't even known her husband, and he'd already been sick before he married her. And her own hair? God protect her! What kind of sin was it? A terrible, an enormous sin.

But if only her braids would grow back, she'd feel easier for a little while. She won't cut them till they've grown as long as they used to be.

Her little house sparkled with cleanliness. During the day, she would sit and work, and at night clean the little house till it sparkled.

4. I.e. kreuzer, a small coin formerly used in Galicia (Yiddish).
5. An often-itinerant Jewish musician who played at weddings and other religious celebrations.
6. A local coin worth one and a half *graytser* (Yiddish).
7. A coin worth more than a *manger* (Yiddish).
8. Diminutive of *shaytl* (wig); a metaphor for married women (Yiddish).
9. "My God!" (Yiddish).

But she was miserable and cried about her misery. Esther was indeed a friend, but a friend is not as deeply rooted in one's heart as one's misery, as one's grief. More than once her heart became more embittered as she looked at Esther's head of hair; more than once she wished herself an old maid, wished the town were gossiping about her, wished her head were not still bound.

Her brothers turned themselves inside out trying to convince her to remarry, especially when they saw how well she conducted herself. They'd wander over to their sister's house, sip a glass of warm tea, and by the by drop a few words: How will all this end? And how long can someone be alone? A person is obliged to marry—that's the way of the world. The oldest brother, the pious one, claimed a person is obliged to bequeath another generation . . .

Sheyndl would remember her growing hair and feel as if they were after her life, that they resented that her hair had grown back.

So she would concentrate on her sewing and not answer.

Only when she was left alone did she feel the depth of her unhappiness and cry and think: Oh, if only one could recapture those years . . . those young years . . . Old age brings a person troubles. Troubles make a person—make her old and gray before her time. Already little by little and thirty years old. So what good is it when you can't get those years back? And to be like you once were, as if this time had never even passed, is also impossible.

But things could be different. Perhaps even better? Better. Not for the sake of others, but for your own sake. Inside you feel quiet, peaceful, joyful; you don't eat yourself up. And so you yourself want to become more and more decent. And as you become more decent, you feel as if you were always dressed in a clean, new garment.

In the sparkling little house there was a large mirror and Sheyndl polished it with her golden hands, always polished it so the mirror was clear as water. There in the mirror she saw another sparkling little house, with another proper wife who polished another mirror. And the wife looks at her *shaytele* and her heart aches because her head was bound when she was so young and her years cut short.

The glassware stood on the polished table; two Majolica plates were in a green rack; and a blue vessel sparkled on the wall. A Turkish spread already covered the bed and an expensive dress sewn by Moyshe the Tailor hung in the closet.

When they got longer, Sheyndl began to steal a few of her own hairs and to mingle and entwine them in the *shaytl*. And when she stepped out on the street for the first time, her heart pounded for fear someone might see. The next week she snuck out more hair and her heart pounded again. In this way, little by little, she smuggled out more and more hair, and with her heart pounding, trembling, she waited to see if she'd be discovered. After each time she exposed herself in this way, dared, a new joy grew inside her and she hoped that things would become better, even better.

Once after *pesakh*,[1] the sun shone into the sparkling house with such devotion that tears of joy welled up in her. She looked out of the clear win-

1. Passover (Yiddish, from the Hebrew).

dowpanes and rejoiced without reason. On that day, she took all her hair from the front of her head and covered the *shaytele*.

With a joyous heart she went to Esther's. On the way, she met Itshe-Mayer's wife who took one look and clapped her hands:

—Oh my God! You're out with your own hair?

Sheyndl stood still and didn't know what to say. But her heart beat like a criminal's. And seeing how frightened Sheyndl had become, Itshe-Mayer's wife intensified her wrath.

—What can this mean! A Jewish woman—and with such pious mother!

And she went on and on thundering at her.

Sheyndl wept on her way home. The day was bright and this caused her even more pain.

Yiddish, 1919

Sonnet[1]

My friend, my terrible friend, how you are evil,
And proudly chaste as any saintly John
Who made the nights of the king's daughter sleepless.[2]
And as she hated him, I hate you now.

Your face is not as pale and cool as ivory,
Your hair does not curl, writhing like young snakes,
Your youth's heart is not as pure as any other's—
So why am I engulfed by burning hate?

I hate you. I reiterate it now:
And as I dance the sinful dance once more,
I gesture at the bidding of the devil.

And for my dance he'll show his gratitude
With pay well-worthy of a sinful heart:
He'll give me what I crave—your lilac tongue.

ca. 1910–1919, 1928

A Winter Echo[1]

A little sleigh in the white snow,
A trotting horse so small,
A young, sweet couple in the sleigh,
Voices chiming like a bell.

1. Translated by Kathryn Hellerstein.
2. The story of Herod, who violated religious law by marrying his brother's wife, Herodias, and was reprimanded by John the Baptist. Her daughter, Salome, danced before King Herod and, prompted by her mother, asked as a reward for the head of John the Baptist on a platter (Matthew 14.6–12, Mark 6.21–28).
1. Translated by Kathryn Hellerstein.

He takes the whip in his darling hand
And cracks it in the air,
He takes a look at his dear girl,
Her cheeks are flaming there.

Burning kisses now are born
Within his heart for his chosen—
And landing on red little lips
Immediately are frozen.

Then a frisky little horse
Overturns the sleigh—
A snowy, stony canopy
Buries their wedding-day.

ca. 1910–1919, 1928

Dusks[1]

1

In the quiet evening breeze
The branches gently sway,
A listless bird is flying through
The orchard, silently.

On the leaves, the larvae inch
Toward fruits, to putrefy—
And loneliness consumes me so,
I'm lonely enough to die.

2

Fly about in the sunset, you bee,
Your body of golden rings
Is shimmering into my eyes,
Is luring me to sing.

You fly in rings around me, too,
Intolerably tiresome,
Bringing no honey, for I know
You want to leave me venom.

ca. 1910–1919, 1928

1. Translated by Kathryn Hellerstein.

THE YANKEE TALMUD
1892, 1893

The Talmud is *the* classic literary work of Jewish tradition. Edited in Babylonia in the fifth century C.E., it is a massive encyclopedia of the law and lore of the rabbis who lived during the first five centuries of the common era. Written mainly in Aramaic—a Semitic language closely related to Hebrew and written in Hebrew characters, and the lingua franca of Jews in the ancient world—the Talmud consists of two parts: the Mishnah and the Gemara. The Mishnah, which is the basis of the Talmud, is an early rabbinic law code that was edited around 220 C.E. The Gemara, literally "study," presents itself as a commentary on the Mishnah, although it typically moves far beyond the parameters of a conventional commentary. With its endless debates and exchanges between rabbis and disciples, the Gemara actually reads like an unedited transcript of a study session in a Babylonian Talmudic academy in all its argumentative cacophony and disciplined energy.

Virtually since the time it was edited, the Talmud has been the central object of study in the traditional Jewish curriculum. And since the Middle Ages, it has also been the favorite subject of parodies by Talmudists and other respected Jewish scholars. It can, therefore, be seen as a true mark of the coming of age of American Jewish literary culture when Jews in the New World began to write their own parodies of the Talmud—or, more accurately, parodic treatments of American Jewish life as seen through Talmudic eyes. The two selections translated here are taken from the best-known American Talmudic parodies.

The first of these, *The Tractate "America,"* is perhaps the most famous American Talmudic parody. Its author, Gershon Rosenzweig (1861–1914), was born in Russian Poland and emigrated to America in 1888. A prominent figure in the American Hebraic and Yiddish literary world, he edited several important Hebrew periodicals but was most famous for his parodies in which he objected to the low standards of education among American Jews, to their low moral state (as attested by the prevalence of gambling among Jews), and to Reform rabbis, for whom he had a special distaste.

Abraham Kotlier, the author of the second selection, was born near Kovno and immigrated to America in 1880. He spent his years in the New World in Cleveland, where he was a well-known Jewish bookseller for more than fifty years. After retiring, he moved to Palestine, where he died.

From The Tractate "America"[1]

Gershon Rosenzweig

Dedicated to my uncle, Rabbi Samuel the Prince, also known as Uncle Sam.[2]

Mishnah: The single difference between America and other countries is that, in America, Jews are not enslaved to other peoples; this is the opinion of Rabbi Greener.[3] The sages disagree: America is just like every other country in every respect.

1. Translated, annotated, and introduced by David Stern.
2. A note for readers in other countries: Uncle Sam is an epithet often used as a synonym for the United States because they share the same first letters . . . [Rosenzweig's note]. "Samuel the Prince": a great 11th-century Jewish courtier/prince in Spain—a general and a court figure as well as a great poet. Rosenzweig is ridiculing the traditional figure—the great-grandfather of all Jewish politicians and power brokers—by conflating him with Uncle Sam, America personified.
3. *Yarka* (Hebrew), probably meaning a greenhorn here.

Gemara: The rabbis taught: America was created only in order to be a land of refuge. For when Columbus discovered America, the three other continents came before the Holy One, blessed be He, and complained: Master of the Universe! You wrote in Your Scriptures,[4] ". . . You shall divide into three parts the territory of the country" (Deuteronomy 19.3). The Holy One, blessed be He, replied, "[It will be a place to which] any manslayer may have a place to flee to" (Deuteronomy 19.3).[5]

Rabbi Scribener said: Through the astrological arts Columbus foresaw that America was destined to be a land of refuge for every scoundrel and empty-headed rake in the world, and he therefore asked mercy from God and prayed that the land not be called after him. And so, instead, they called it America—*ama reikah,* land of empty-headed rakes.[6]

1892

From The Tractate "The Ways of the New Land"[1]

Abraham Kotlier

Mishnah: At what time do people begin to come to America?[2] The elderly—when they become infirm. The barons and noblemen—when they grow bald; the treasurers—when they abscond; the heads of the community—when they forge the papers; the horse thieves—when they're shot; the soldiers—when they're taken captive; the bridegrooms—when they're disappointed with their dowries; the brides—when they become jealous; the old maids—when their hair turns white; the young virgins—when they get pregnant; the bankers—when they go bankrupt; the hypocrites—when they're humiliated; and everyone else—when they've gone broke.

Gemara: The rabbis taught: A visitor to the New Country—he is a greenhorn. One doesn't eat with him from the same bowl; one doesn't sleep in the same bed for that reason . . . and for another reason. And one makes fun of what he says. Even if he is as wise as King Solomon, you don't take him seriously.

Mar[3] said: One doesn't sleep in the same bed for that reason. What does "that reason" refer to? This is its meaning—the third plague that smote the Egyptians (namely, lice). And what is "another reason"? The sixth plague, the boils.

It is taught: If a person is genuinely poor, even if he or she has been in America for several years, s/he is always a greenhorn.

1893

4. The verse quoted deals with the law of "the city of refuge" and how such cities were planned from the time that the land of Canaan was reapportioned after Joshua reconquered the entire land. Note that the second verse, God's reply, is the continuation and conclusion of the same verse.

5. The three continents cite part of the verse from Deuteronomy as proof to God that there is only room for three continents in the world—i.e., that there is no room for America—to which God replies with the other half of the verse from Deuteronomy that America is simply a refuge for murderers, and not really a continent at all.

6. This is a phonetic pun between the Aramaic phrase and the word *America.*

1. Translated, annotated, and introduced by David Stern.

2. This first line parodies the very beginning of the tractate Berakhot, which begins, "At what time can people begin to say the evening Shema" (a prayer beginning with Deuteronomy 6.4: "Hear, O Israel! The Lord is our God, the Lord is One").

3. A famous 4th-century Babylonian sage.

A BINTL BRIV (A BUNDLE OF LETTERS) 1906–1923

"*Tayerer redaktor*," "Dear Editor," began the letters to the most popular feature in the Yiddish daily *Forverts* (Forward). *A bintl briv* (A Bundle of Letters), the immigrant working-class precursor of middle-American advice columns such as *Dear Abby* and *Ann Landers*, began to appear in the *Forverts* on January 20, 1906. The brainchild of *Forverts* founder and editor Abraham Cahan, who wanted to keep his readers from defecting to a rival newspaper, this column invited the *Forverts*'s audience to seek help with their problems. The letters came flooding in, and for the first few years Cahan answered them himself, although his staff writers frequently improved upon the semiliterate Yiddish of the impoverished and beleaguered supplicants.

As Cahan himself wrote in his 1929 memoirs: "People often need the opportunity to be able to pour out their heavy-laden hearts. Among our immigrant masses this need was very marked. Hundreds of thousands of people, torn from their homes and their dear ones, were lonely souls who thirsted for expression, who wanted to hear an opinion, who wanted advice in solving their weighty problems. The 'Bintel Brief' created just this opportunity for them."

The column was published well into the latter half of the twentieth century. Isaac Metzker, who compiled, translated, and edited the volume from which we draw our selections, notes that at the start, the letters were written by recent immigrants, many of them young. As the years went by and the letter writers aged and settled into American life, the concerns they wrote about changed from cultural and moral issues to matters of family life.

We have not included the vulgar, comic, or sentimental letters—although *A bintl briv* had its share, and they are often revealing. Rather, we have chosen letters that provide a sobering window into the lives and historical moment of individual Jews living in the United States in the first part of the twentieth century. You will notice that the editor's responses have been shortened, condensed, or summarized by Isaac Metzker.

[From a "Greenhorn"]

Esteemed Editor,

I hope that you will advise me in my present difficulty.

I am a "greenhorn," only five weeks in the country, and a jeweler by trade. I come from Russia, where I left a blind father and a stepmother. Before I left, my father asked me not to forget him. I promised that I would send him the first money I earned in America.

When I arrived in New York I walked around for two weeks looking for a job, and the bosses told me it was after the season. In the third week I was lucky, and found a job at which I earn eight dollars a week. I worked, I paid my landlady board, I bought a few things to wear, and I have a few dollars in my pocket.

Now I want you to advise me what to do. Shall I send my father a few dollars for Passover, or should I keep the little money for myself? In this place the work will end soon and I may be left without a job. The question is how to deal with the situation. I will do as you tell me.

Your thankful reader,
I. M.

ANSWER:
The answer to this young man is that he should send his father the few dollars for Passover because, since he is young, he will find it easier to earn a living than would his blind father in Russia.

1906

[Anti-Semitism on the Job]

Worthy Editor,

I am eighteen years old and a machinist by trade. During the past year I suffered a great deal, just because I am a Jew.

It is common knowledge that my trade is run mainly by the Gentiles and, working among the Gentiles, I have seen things that cast a dark shadow on the American labor scene. Just listen:

I worked in a shop in a small town in New Jersey, with twenty Gentiles. There was one other Jew besides me, and both of us endured the greatest hardships. That we were insulted goes without saying. At times we were even beaten up. We work in an area where there are many factories, and once, when we were leaving the shop, a group of workers fell on us like hoodlums and beat us. To top it off, we and one of our attackers were arrested. The hoodlum was let out on bail, but we, beaten and bleeding, had to stay in jail. At the trial, they fined the hoodlum eight dollars and let him go free.

After that I went to work on a job in Brooklyn.[1] As soon as they found out that I was a Jew they began to torment me so that I had to leave the place. I have already worked at many places, and I either have to leave, voluntarily, or they fire me because I am a Jew.

Till now, I was alone and didn't care. At this trade you can make good wages, and I had enough. But now I've brought my parents over, and of course I have to support them.

Lately I've been working on one job for three months and I would be satisfied, but the worm of anti-Semitism is beginning to eat at my bones again. I go to work in the morning as to Gehenna,[2] and I run away at night as from a fire. It's impossible to talk to them because they are common boors, so-called "American sports." I have already tried in various ways, but the only way to deal with them is with a strong fist. But I am too weak and they are too many.

Perhaps you can help me in this matter. I know it is not an easy problem.

Your reader,
E. H.

1. One of the five boroughs of New York City.

2. Hell (Hebrew).

ANSWER:
In the answer, the Jewish machinist is advised to appeal to the United Hebrew Trades[3] and and ask them to intercede for him and bring up charges before the Machinists Union about this persecution. His attention is also drawn to the fact that there are Gentile factories where Jews and Gentiles work together and get along well with each other.

Finally it is noted that people will have to work long and hard before this senseless racial hatred can be completely uprooted.

1907

[To Study or to Work?]

Worthy Editor,

Allow me a little space in your newspaper and, I beg you, give me some advice as to what to do.

There are seven people in our family—parents and five children. I am the oldest child, a fourteen-year-old girl. We have been in the country two years and my father, who is a frail man, is the only one working to support the whole family.

I go to school, where I do very well. But since times are hard now and my father earned only five dollars this week, I began to talk about giving up my studies and going to work in order to help my father as much as possible. But my mother didn't even want to hear of it. She wants me to continue my education. She even went out and spent ten dollars on winter clothes for me. But I didn't enjoy the clothes, because I think I am doing the wrong thing. Instead of bringing something into the house, my parents have to spend money on me.

I have a lot of compassion for my parents. My mother is now pregnant, but she still has to take care of the three boarders we have in the house. Mother and Father work very hard and they want to keep me in school.

I am writing to you without their knowledge, and I beg you to tell me how to act. Hoping you can advise me, I remain,

Your reader,
S.

ANSWER:
The advice to the girl is that she should obey her parents and further her education, because in that way she will be able to give them greater satisfaction than if she went out to work.

1907

3. The central body or federation of the Jewish unions, organized in New York City in 1888.

[Sexual Harassment in the Workplace]

Dear Editor,

I am one of those unfortunate girls thrown by fate into a dark and dismal shop,[1] and I need your counsel.

Along with my parents, sisters and brothers, I came from Russian Poland where I had been well educated. But because of the terrible things going on in Russia we were forced to emigrate to America. I am now seventeen years old, but I look younger and they say I am attractive.

A relative talked us into moving to Vineland, New Jersey, and here in this small town I went to work in a shop. In this shop there is a foreman who is an exploiter, and he sets prices on the work. He figures it out so that the wages are very low, he insults and reviles the workers, he fires them and then takes them back. And worse than all of this, in spite of the fact that he has a wife and several children, he often allows himself to "have fun" with some of the working girls. It was my bad luck to be one of the girls that he tried to make advances to. And woe to any girl who doesn't willingly accept them.

Though my few hard-earned dollars mean a lot to my family of eight souls, I didn't want to accept the foreman's vulgar advances. He started to pick on me, said my work was no good, and when I proved to him he was wrong, he started to shout at me in the vilest language. He insulted me in Yiddish and then in English, so the American workers could understand too. Then, as if the Devil were after me, I ran home.

I am left without a job. Can you image my circumstances and that of my parents who depend on my earnings? The girls in the shop were very upset over the foreman's vulgarity but they don't want him to throw them out, so they are afraid to be witnesses against him. What can be done about this? I beg you to answer me.

Respectfully,
A Shopgirl

ANSWER:
Such a scoundrel should be taught a lesson that could be an example to others. The girl is advised to bring out into the open the whole story about the foreman, because there in the small town it shouldn't be difficult to have him thrown out of the shop and for her to get her job back.

1907

1. Sweatshop, factory.

[Socialist Freethinking and Jewish Tradition]

Worthy Mr. Editor,

Please help us decide who is right in the debate between friends, whether a Socialist and freethinker should observe *yohrzeit*?[1]

Among the disputants there is a Socialist, a freethinker, who observes his mother's *yohrzeit* in the following manner: He pays a pious man to say the *kaddish* prayer for the dead, and burns a *yohrzeit* candle in his home.[2] He himself doesn't say *kaddish*, because he doesn't believe in religion. But his desire to respect the memory of his mother is so strong that it does not prevent him from performing this religious ceremony.

Among the debaters there are those who do not want to know of such an emotion as honoring the dead. But if one does desire to do so, one should say *kaddish* himself, even if he does not believe in it.

Therefore, our first question is: Can we recognize the beautiful human emotion of honoring the dead, especially when it concerns one so near as a mother? The second question: If so, should the expression of honor be in keeping with the desires of the honored? Third: Would it be more conscientious and righteous if the freethinker said *kaddish* himself, or if he hired a pious man to do it for him?

Being convinced that this matter interests a great number of people, we hope you, Mr. Editor, will answer us soon.

With regards,
The Debating Group

ANSWER:
Honoring a departed one who was cherished and loved is a gracious sentiment and a requisite for the living. And everyone wants to be remembered after his death. Socialists and freethinkers observe the anniversaries of their great leaders—just recently they commemorated the twenty-fifth anniversary of the death of Karl Marx.

Saying *kaddish* is certainly a religious rite, and to pay someone to say *kaddish* is not the act of a freethinker. But we can understand the psychology of a freethinker who feels that hiring someone else is not as much against his own convictions as to say *kaddish* himself.

1908

1. *Yortsayt* (Yiddish), the anniversary of a parent's death.
2. Traditional Jews mark the anniversary of a parent's death by going to synagogue to recite the mourners' Kaddish, a prayer that praises God, and, at home, lighting a candle that burns for the twenty-four hours of the *yortsayt*.

[White Slavery]

Dear Editor,

Please print my letter and give me an answer. You might possibly save my life with it. I have no peace, neither day nor night, and I am afraid I will go mad because of my dreams.

I came to America three years ago from a small town in Lithuania, and I was twenty years old at that time. Besides me, my parents had five more unmarried daughters. My father was a Hebrew teacher. We used to help out by plucking chickens, making cigarettes, washing clothes for people, and we lived in poverty. The house was like a Gehenna. There was always yelling, cursing, and even beating of each other. It was bitter for me till a cousin of mine took pity on me. He sent a steamship ticket and money. He wrote that I should come to America and he would marry me.

I didn't know him, because he was a little boy when he left our town, but my delight knew no bounds. When I came to him, I found he was a sick man, and a few weeks later he died.

Then I began to work on ladies' waists.[1] The "pleasant" life of a girl in the dreary shop must certainly be familiar to you. I toiled, and like all shopgirls, I hoped and waited for deliverance through a good match.

Landsleit[2] and matchmakers were busy. I met plenty of prospective bridegrooms, but though I was attractive and well built, no one grabbed me. Thus a year passed. Then I met a woman who told me she was a matchmaker and had many suitors "in stock." I spilled out all my heartaches to her. First she talked me out of marrying a work-worn operator with whom I would have to live in poverty, then she told me that pretty girls could wallow in pleasure if they made the right friends. She made such a connection for me. But I had not imagined what that meant.

What I lived through afterwards is impossible for me to describe. The woman handed me over to bandits, and when I wanted to run away from them they locked me in a room without windows and beat me savagely.

Time passed and I got used to the horrible life. Later I even had an opportunity to escape, because they used to send me out on the streets, but life had become meaningless for me anyway, and nothing mattered any more. I lived this way for six months, degraded and dejected, until I got sick and they drove me out of that house.

I appealed for admission into several hospitals, but they didn't want to take me in. I had no money, because the rogues had taken everything from me. I tried to appeal to *landsleit* for help, but since they already knew all about me, they chased me away. I had decided to throw myself into the river, but wandering around on the streets, I met a richly dressed man who was quite drunk. I took over six hundred dollars from him and spent the money on doctors, who cured me.

Then I got a job as a maid for fine people who knew nothing about my past, and I have been working for them for quite a while. I am devoted and diligent, they like me, and everything is fine.

1. A garment that covers the body from the neck to the waist.
2. *Landslayt* (Yiddish): landsmen, Jewish immigrants who came from the same town or region in Eastern Europe.

A short time ago the woman of the house died, but I continued to work there. In time, her husband proposed that I marry him. The children, who are not yet grown up, also want me to be their "mother." I know it would be good for them and for me to remain there. The man is honest and good; but my heart won't allow me to deceive him and conceal my past. What shall I do now?

Miserable

ANSWER:
Such letters from victims of "white slavery" come to our attention quite often, but we do not publish them. We are disgusted by this plague on society, and dislike bringing it to the attention of our readers. But as we read this letter we felt we dare not discard it, because it can serve as a warning for other girls. They must, in their dreary lives, attempt to withstand these temptations and guard themselves from going astray.

This letter writer, who comes to us with her bitter and earnest tears, asking advice, has sufficient reason to fear that if the man finds out about her past he will send her away. But it is hard to conceal something that many people know. Such a thing cannot be kept secret forever. When the man finds out about it from someone else, he would feel that she had betrayed him and it would be worse.

Therefore, "Honesty is the best policy." She should tell him the truth, and whatever will be, will be.

1909

[From a Union Scab]

Dear Editor,

I am an operator on ladies' waists for the past four years and I earn good wages. I work steady but haven't saved money, because I have a sick wife. I had to put her in the hospital where she lay for four weeks, and then I had to bring her home.

Just after I brought her home, the General Strike[1] began and I could see that I was in trouble. I had to go to the union to beg them not to let me down in my situation. I just asked for some money to have a little soup for my sick wife, but they answered that there wasn't any money. I struggled along with my wife for four weeks, and when I saw that I might lose her I had to go back to work at the shop where we were striking. Now my conscience bothers me because I am a scab.[2]

I am working now, I bring home fifteen, sometimes sixteen dollars a week. But I am not happy, because I was a scab and left the union. I want to state here that I was always a good union man.

1. A widespread strike declared on November 22, 1909, by the mostly female shirtwaist makers' union of the ILGWU (International Ladies' Garment Workers' Union), which lasted into February 1910, followed by the huge cloakmakers' union strike, July 7–September 3, 1910.
2. Strikebreaker.

Dear Editor, how can I now go back in the union and salve my conscience? I am ready to swear that I will remain a loyal union man forever.

Your reader,
F. H.

ANSWER:
Neither the operator nor the union is guilty. During the strike, thousands upon thousands of workers complained that they were in need, but at the beginning of the strike there really was no money.

It is now the duty of the union to investigate the case, and if it is shown that circumstances were as the operator describes, they will certainly forgive him and he can again become a good union man.

1910

[Staying in School]

Dear Editor,

I am a newsboy, fourteen years old, and I sell the *Forverts*[1] in the streets till late into the night. I come to you to ask your advice.

I was born in Russia and was twelve years old when I came to America with my dear mother. My sister, who was in the country before us, brought us over.

My sister worked and supported us. She didn't allow me to go to work but sent me to school. I went to school for two years and didn't miss a day, but then came the terrible fire at the Triangle shop,[2] where she worked, and I lost my dear sister. My mother and I suffer terribly from the misfortune. I had to help my mother and after school hours I go out and sell newspapers.

I have to go to school three more years, and after that I want to go to college. But my mother doesn't want me to go to school because she thinks I should go to work. I tell her I will work days and study at night but she won't hear of it.

Since I read the *Forverts* to my mother every night and read your answers in the "Bintel Brief," I beg you to answer me and say a few words to her.

Your Reader,
The Newsboy

ANSWER:
The answer to this letter is directed to the boy's mother, whose daughter was one of the shopworkers who perished in the Triangle fire. The unfortunate woman is comforted in the answer, and she is told that she must not hinder her son's nighttime studies but must help him reach his goal. And an appeal

1. The *Jewish Daily Forward*, the largest Yiddish daily newspaper in the United States, founded and edited by Abraham Cahan in 1897, where the *Bintl briv* column was published.

2. In the spring of 1911, a fire broke out in the Triangle Shirtwaist Company, one of New York's largest garment factories, located on the Lower East Side, and 146 workers were burned to death.

is made to good people who are in a position to do something for the boy to come forward and help him further his education.

1911

[Fighting for the Kaiser]

Worthy Mr. Editor,

I, an old woman of seventy, write you this letter with my heart's blood, because I am distressed.

In Galicia,[1] I was a respected housewife and my husband was a well-known businessman. God blessed us with three daughters and three sons and we raised them properly. When they grew up, one by one they left home, like birds leaving their nest. Our daughters got married, and later left for America with their husbands. Our oldest son also married but a month after his wedding a misfortune befell us—he went swimming and was drowned.

This tragedy had such a bad effect on my husband that he neglected his business, began to ail, and died. The two younger sons both went to America after that, and I was left alone. I longed for the children and wrote to them that I wanted to come to America, to be with them and the grandchildren. But from the first they wrote me that America was not for me, that they do not keep *kosher* and that I would be better off staying at home.

But I didn't let them convince me, and I went to America. All of my children came to meet me at the boat, and I will never forget that moment when they and my grandchildren hugged me and kissed me. Is there any greater happiness for a mother?

But now a new trouble has fallen on me. A few weeks ago when Austria declared war and we heard that Russia was fighting against Austria, my two sons, who are ardent patriots of Kaiser Franz Josef,[2] announced that they were sailing home to help him in the war. When I heard this, I began to cry and begged them not to rush into the fire because they would be shortening my life. But so far they have not given up the idea of going to fight for the Kaiser.

Worthy Editor, I hope you will voice your opinion on this serious matter. Maybe you can have influence on them to give up the idea of leaving this country and their old mother, and going to war.

Your reader,
The Suffering Mother

ANSWER:

In the answer it says that the woman's two sons should thank God that they are in America, where they are free and can't be forced to shed their blood for the Austrian Kaiser.

1914

1. A region in Austria where many Jews lived.

2. The outbreak of World War I.

[Returning to Russia]

Dear Editor,

Four years ago, because of my activity in the revolutionary movement in Russia, I was forced to leave the country and come to America. I had no trade, because I was brought up in a wealthy home, so I struggled terribly at first. Thanks to my education and my ability to adjust, I am now a manager of a large wholesale firm and earn good wages. In time I fell in love with an intelligent, pretty American girl and married her.

America was my new home, and my wife and I tried to live in a way that would be most interesting and pleasant. From time to time, however, I had the desire to visit Russia to see what was going on there. But in America one is always busy and there is no time to be sentimental so I never went.

But now everything is changed. The Russian freedom movement, in which I took part, has conquered Czarism.[1] The ideal for which I fought has become a reality, and my heart draws me there more than ever now. I began to talk about it to my wife, but her answer is that she hasn't the least desire to go to Russia. My revolutionary fire has cooled down here in the practical America, but it is not altogether extinguished, and I'm ready to go home now.

The latest events in Russia do not let me rest, and my mind is not on my job. But my wife and her parents tell me it would be foolish to leave such a good job and ruin everything. My wife doesn't want to go, and she holds me back. I can't leave my wife, whom I love very much, but it's hard to turn my back on my beloved homeland. I don't know how to act and I beg you to advise me what to do.

I will be very thankful for this.

Respectfully,
A.

ANSWER:

Many of those who took part in the freedom struggle are drawn to take a look at liberated Russia. But not everyone can do so. This is also the position of the writer, who has obligations to his wife. She is an American, she has her family here, so how can she leave her home and go to a strange country? The writer must take this into consideration. Besides, while the terrible battles are still raging, there can be no discussion about visiting Russia.

1917

[From a Rape Victim]

Worthy Mr. Editor,

I was born in a small town in Russia and my mother brought me up alone, because I had lost my father when I was a child. My dear mother used all her energies to give me a proper education.

1. The revolution of 1905 failed but convinced Czar Nicholas II to change the Russian government from an autocracy to a constitutional monarchy. The Russian Revolution of March 1917 overthrew Nicholas's government, and the October Revolution of 1917 placed the Bolsheviks in power.

A pogrom broke out and my mother was the first victim of the blood bath. They spared no one, and no one was left for me. But that wasn't enough for the murderers, they robbed me of my honor. I begged them to kill me instead, but they let me live to suffer and grieve.

After that there were long days and nights of loneliness and grief. I was alone, despondent and homeless, until relatives in America brought me over. But my wounded heart found no cure here either. Here I am lonely, too, and no one cares. I am dejected, without a ray of hope, because all my former dreams for the future are shattered.

A few months ago, however, I met a young man, a refined and decent man. It didn't take long before we fell in love. He has already proposed marriage and he is now waiting for my answer.

I want to marry this man, but I keep putting off giving him an answer because I can't tell him the secret that weighs on my heart and bothers my conscience. I have no rest and am almost going out of my mind. When my friend comes to hear my answer, I want to tell him everything. Let him know all; I've bottled up the pain inside me long enough. Let him hear all and then decide. But I have no words and can tell him nothing.

I hope you will answer and advise me what I can do.

I thank you,
A Reader

ANSWER:

In the pogroms, in the great Jewish disasters, this misfortune befell many Jewish girls like you. But you must not feel guilty and not be so dejected, because you are innocent. A man who can understand and sympathize can be told everything. If your friend is one of these people and he really loves you, he will cherish you even after he learns your secret.

Since we do not know your friend, it is hard for us to advise you whether to tell him everything now, or not. In this matter you must take more responsibility on yourself. You know the man, and you must know, more or less, if he will be able to understand.

1923

Jewish Humor

> Why the people of Israel adhered to their God all the more devotedly the worse they were treated by Him, that is a question we must leave open.
>
> —Sigmund Freud

Henry James commented in the 1870s on the many things absent from American life that a serious novelist could profitably use: no ancient schools like Harrow or Eton, no great manor houses and aristocracy, no Ascot, and the like. He noted, however, that the country had one great resource—its private joke, as it were—and that was its native humor and humorists. Similarly, deprived for centuries of the trappings that James ironically lists, Jews have possessed that last resource in abundance—especially over the past two centuries—in the many lands in which they have resided. Humor has been a way of coping with the challenges of modern life, of dealing with vulnerability in oppressive situations, of self-criticizing and self-affirming, of expressing and sharing pleasures as well as discomforts, of defusing fears.

There have been many efforts to explain the scope, persistence, and character of Jewish humor. Among the best-known theorists of the sources of humor generally have been French philosopher Henri Bergson (1859–1941) and Sigmund Freud (1856–1939), both Jews. Bergson theorizes that laughter can temporarily resolve the conflict involved in two opposing conceptions that define what it is to be human. The sight of a haughty, pompous, rigid person slipping on a banana peel can elicit laughter (serious accident or death, of course, is no laughing matter). It reveals that a human being is a vulnerable creature, sharing characteristics with others of the species—even with animals—no matter what or how high his/her socially defined role or status may be. The enduring appeal of the pratfall. The revelation can have a tragic as well as humanizing dimension, as when Shakespeare's King Lear recognizes that in the end he is, like all of us, a "bare forked animal."

Freud relates much humor to the same kind of mental activity that goes on in dreams. He interprets dreams as dealing often with forbidden actions or desires that the dreamer wishes, on an unconscious level, to be fulfilled or that, alternatively (sometimes even simultaneously), could produce anxiety. The apparent or manifest content of a dream might appear to be absurd, illogical, highly condensed and inverted (time sequences, for example, could be reversed, altered, conflated), surreal. Much of the same patterns and techniques, as well as the latent fears and wishes, could be seen in the jokes and witticisms that Freud analyzed and interpreted.

Freud was a great admirer of Jewish jokes and humor, judging from the liberal sprinkling and analysis of such jokes in his major treatise, *Jokes and Their Relation to the Unconscious.* He could often sound disrespectful or condescending, especially to *Ostjuden* (Eastern European Jews). For instance, he uses a joke based on the stereotype of such Jews as dirty: Two Jews meet in front of the bathhouse. One sighs and says to the other, "A year goes by so fast." An American version of this enduring stereotype is set in a Lower East Side café in the 1920s: Two customers order glasses of tea with lemon. One urges the waiter to be sure the glass is clean. The waiter returns to the table with the tea and asks, "Which one of you ordered the clean glass?" Freud processes many schnorrer (beggar) jokes as well in which he frequently admires the schnorrer's insufferable self-assurance and sense of entitlement. Though they be beggars, the ancient and continuing Jewish commitment to charity makes them indispensable—as good as the givers, who may be Rothschilds. A story repeated and admired by scholar and translator Robert Alter displays this quality: A schnorrer finally gets in to see Rothschild personally, whereupon he asks Rothschild for alms. Impatiently Rothschild asks, "If that's all you wanted, couldn't you see my secretary?"

"Look here, Mr. Rothschild," replies the schnorrer, "You may be very competent in your field, but don't tell me how to run my business."

Freud also repeats many *shadchen* (matchmaker) jokes. These provide him with the opportunity to attack an institution that frequently dehumanized people—usually women—by considering them mere property. Yet Freud clearly enjoys the quick wit in many of the jokes, even when they seem sophistical. One such has the *shadchen* chiding a potential groom for noting that a prospective bride has a humpback, a wen on her neck, one leg shorter than the other, and is loudmouthed and stupid besides. "Did you expect perfection?" he asks.

Freud also admired the sheer mental complexity of some jokes. One such, a classic (not used by Freud), tells of two Jewish merchants who meet at the railroad station. One asks the other where he is going. The second replies, "To Kraków to buy cloth." The first says, "You say Kraków to buy cloth, but you want me to think you are going to Lvov to buy seed. I know you really are going to Kraków, so why do you lie to me?"

A more famous story, in one of its versions, concerns a rabbi returning from Budapest to his provincial town in Hungary. He occupies the same train compartment as a well-dressed man who had purchased a ticket for the same town. He wonders who this fine gentleman can be and why the man would want to travel to his small village. He then proceeds through a tortuous (and brillant) process of Talmudic deduction, elimination, and logic to conclude that the man is a successful dentist, who had left the village thirty years earlier, changed his name from Jacob Cohen to a more Hungarian one, and is now returning to treat his brother Feivel, who the rabbi knew recently had trouble with his teeth. The rabbi smiles and addresses his traveling companion. "Doctor John Kovac, I believe. Permit me to introduce myself. I am Rabbi Scharf." Taken aback, the stranger asks incredulously, "How did you know I was Doctor Kovac?" The rabbi leans back, at ease, "It was obvious."

Freud discusses the various dynamics at work in jokes and humor: as displaced aggression and rebellion, the desire to reveal the forbidden, an expression of skepticism, cynicism, or self-criticism, or simply as the desire to give and participate in pleasure. His most cogent statement about Jewish humor is:

> The occurrence of self-criticism as a determinant may explain how it is that a number of the most apt jokes (of which we have given plenty of

> instances) have grown upon the soil of Jewish popular life. They are stories created by Jews and directed against Jewish characteristics. . . .
>
> The jokes made about Jews by foreigners are for the most part brutal comic stories . . . Jews are regarded by foreigners as comic figures. The Jewish jokes which originate from Jews admit this too, but they know their real faults as well as the connection between them and their good qualities, and the share which the subject has in the person found fault with. . . . Incidentally, I do not know whether there are many other instances of a people making fun to such a degree of its own character.

We may take issue with Freud on several points—probably on what he regards as the Jewish "character"—but there is certainly sympathy and an understanding here that will help us grasp the long life and salient, often irreverent, characteristics of Jewish humor.

Jewish jokes and humorous stories flourish when traditions are changing or being undermined, when life is precarious (as when isn't it, in Jewish history?), or when the spectacle of human folly or vanity unfolds daily to the perceptive observer. The sharpening of Jewish wits and powers of perception have taken place over centuries of Talmud study and *pilpul* (the method of sharp questioning and answering, of spinning out logic and close analysis of language). There is also the gift of awareness that comes from being in the minority—the kind of double consciousness that W. E. B. Du Bois defined as the condition of African Americans. Every Jew in Christendom knows there are at least two answers to every question. The overarching irony, at times a tragic joke, of Jewish existence has been the status of Jews as a people with "their feet in the mud and their brows touching heaven"—that is, the great discrepancy between a proud chosen people and their endured centuries of contempt, poverty, and persecution in much of Christian Europe.

A great deal of Jewish humor really dates only from the nineteenth and twentieth centuries, when the great break from traditional life, with its deeply embedded religious and cultural values, and the challenge of modernism occurred. The Yiddish literature that developed after the Enlightenment reached Eastern European regions was ripe with satire, often self-critical—as in the work of Mendele Moykhr Sforim (Mendele the Bookseller), the nom de plume of the writer considered the first of the great classical masters of Yiddish literature—and with humor that focused on the dualities of Jewish life—as in Sholem Aleichem's Tevye the Milkman stories. There was a folk tradition of humor as well, exemplified by the many Chelm jokes, Chelm being a legendary town inhabited by fools. One such is of their building a tower at the edge of town from which it would be easier to see the approach of the Messiah. The watchman employed to keep the vigil, the town beggar, was asked what he was being paid. "Not very much," he answers, "but it's steady work." There were also many jokes about Hasidim and wonder-working rabbis, even about the ambiguities or wisdom of rabbinic advice in general. A cautionary joke that displays Jewish skepticism and wisdom applicable in many situations familiar to Jews and non-Jews alike concerns the search for a new rabbi. The members of the search committee for a small Eastern European shul write to their colleagues in another shtetl for their help. These worthies reply that in fact their own rabbi has been looking for another position and that he combines the qualities of Moses,

Socrates, and Einstein. The searchers are enthralled and hire this apparent paragon at once. Within a short time it becomes obvious to them that he is terrible as a rabbi, a dud in every way. They write indignantly to the other shul's committee and ask how they could be so flagrantly untruthful in their dealing with fellow Jews? It is a scandal and a shame to designate this flop as a Moses, Socrates, and Einstein. "Not at all," the offending group replies. "We told the truth. Like Moses, he cannot speak; like Socrates, he knows no Hebrew; like Einstein, he's an athiest!"

At Jewish weddings, the institution of the *badkhen* was developed. The *badkhen* was a poet employed to compose spontaneously and in witty fashion rhymes about the couple and related matters. Comic traditions were part of the Yiddish theater that was begun in Romania in the 1880s and brought to America by Abraham Goldfaden. The Yiddish theater that flourished in New York City through the 1930s featured much comedy and music as well as serious drama and tragedy (the latter produced chiefly in the Yiddish Art Theatre of Maurice Schwartz). It helped develop the careers of many comic writers and actors—among the best known being Molly Picon and Menasha Skulnik—and the taste of a large audience. That audience was the foundation for the rapid increase of Jewish comedians performing in English for Jewish audiences and ultimately the wider general American public.

Even as a not particularly endangered minority in a usually tolerant American society, Jews often display the double awareness—and humor—that can be ironic, bleak, skeptical, and critical. Frequently, its subjects are the lure and threat of assimilation. There is the generic joke about the old mother from the Lower East Side invited to her son's fancy new dwelling on fashionable Riverside Drive. He has, of course, in his upward climb changed his name. Waiting impatiently for her arrival, he finally goes down to the lobby, where he finds her sitting on a bench, hours after her expected arrival. "Why didn't you come up when you got here?" he asks. "To tell you the truth," she replies, "when the elevator operator asked me who I was going to see, I forgot your name." Or the sense of ethnic otherness, as in Harry Golden's story of the two Jews who meet at a convention. "Where are you from?" one asks. "Charlotte, North Carolina [Golden's home city]," the other replies. "How many Jews in Charlotte?" is the next question. "About three thousand." Then, "And how many Gentiles are there?" "Gentiles we have plenty; about two hundred and fifty thousand." The final response, "You need that many?"

There are numerous jokes about intermarriage—reflecting a perennial concern—and some about conversion. One tells of the Jew who converts to Christian Science. On his way out of the house to attend a meeting in the Science reading room, he puts on his yarmulke (skullcap) and carries his tallis (prayer shawl) bag. "What are you doing with those things now?" his wife asks incredulously. "Oy," he says, smacking his brow, "I forgot! That's my *goyishe kop!*" (literally, "my Gentile head," but colloquially, "my Gentile stupidity" as opposed to a *Yiddishe kop*, or "Jewish intelligence").

The lure and risks of the marketplace are also a favorite subject, especially in hard times. There's the lawyer during the depression boasting of the good week he has had, with a $5 case, a $3 one, "and two small ones." Or the merchant bragging about his $200,000 order from Sears Roebuck: "If you don't believe me, I'll show you the cancellation." Such crises or tensions, flirting with the potentially damaging or tragic outcomes of real life, could be eased with humor.

As in the blues, humor can confront the painful elements of life, not offer any easy anodyne, but give relief and pleasure in the style and manner of presentation. The part played by Jewish comedians in American popular culture has been enormous. Until the 1960s, however, most of them, except when working before largely Jewish audiences—as in the Catskill Mountain resorts, the so-called Borscht Belt—were at pains to "de-ethnicize" themselves. Names were often changed to less "Jewish sounding" ones. David Kaminsky became Danny Kaye; Joseph Levitch, Jerry Lewis—a routine procedure in Hollywood for its many Jewish actors, actresses, and screenwriters as well. Jack Benny, born Benny Kubelsky, enormously popular in radio and later in the movies, is a prime example. He distanced himself from Jewishness further by creating on his radio show two subsidiary characters, Shlepperman and Mr. Kitzel, replete with stereotypical names and dialects, which he could make fun of. The great Marx Brothers' comedy, honed in the period between the wars, is anarchic, wild, subversive, and appeals to all ages right to the present but seems scarcely Jewish (except when Captain Spaulding, "the African explorer," played by the inimitable Groucho, sings, "Don't no one call me Schnorrer!"). Groucho's intelligence and irreverent wit can be clearly appreciated in his letter to the Warner Brothers (Hollywood moguls among those prone to de-ethnicize themselves and those they controlled) that appears here, at the end of this essay. There were also Ed Wynn, "the perfect fool" of the Ziegfeld Follies, who was a radio pioneer, as was Eddie Cantor in film; the great "funny girl" of vaudeville and the Follies, Fanny Brice; and Milton Berle, Sid Caesar, and Phil Silvers (Sergeant Bilko), all of whom were on early television. None, with the exception of Brice in her early routines, emphasized Jewishness. But who could doubt that Jewish life and its traditions sharpened their comedic talents?

Jewish writers for the stage and screen created humorous skits, sketches, and scripts prolifically but rarely evoked specifically identifiable Jewish themes. Besides name changes, there were often half disguises as in the use of initials to cover over "Jewish" names like Sidney, Sam, or Abe (as in the cases of humorist S. J. Perelman, playwright S. N. Behrman, and journalist A. J. Liebling). Ira Gershwin wrote brilliant lyrics for his brother George's songs, for the scathing political satire in *Of Thee I Sing* (1931), the first musical to win a Pulitzer Prize, and for the first authentic American folk opera, *Porgy and Bess*, based on black life in the South, with its witty commentary on biblical stories in the song *It Ain't Necessarily So*. Arthur Kober's comedy about Catskill resorts, "*Having Wonderful Time*," replete with stereotypes, as were his "Dear Bella" letters in the *New Yorker*, was popular in the 1930s, as was Garson Kanin's *Born Yesterday* with Judy Holliday in the 1940s. Neil Simon is probably the most successful and prolific playwright of the century—and among the funniest; he only began to use the material of his own Jewish American life and upbringing markedly after the 1960s. Wendy Wasserstein, of a younger generation, has always used such material. Mike Nichols and Elaine May, popular for their early 1960s humor, were crossover figures who bridged the world of comic improvisation and the "serious" stage and screen (where they occasionally still do comedies). S. J. Perelman, whose parody of Odets's *Waiting for Lefty* and his manic description of his brother-in-law Nathanael West (né Nathan Weinstein) are anthologized here, was also a writer of many humorous books, scripts for plays and movies, and witty pieces for the sophisticated audience of the *New Yorker*.

In literature of the 1920s, there was the raw comedy and satire of Ben Hecht's *A Jew in Love*, who is best known, however, for his coauthorship with Charles MacArthur of the decidedly non-Jewish *The Front Page*. There is also Samuel Ornitz's *Haunch, Paunch and Jowl*, about a Jewish arriviste who anticipates Jerome Weidman's *I Can Get It for You Wholesale* of the 1930s and Budd Schulberg's *What Makes Sammy Run?* of the 1940s. In that period, as noted earlier, we have the mordant humor and satire of Nathanael West. From the 1950s onward, the era of the Jewish "breakthrough" in American letters, there has been a flood of significant Jewish American writers of fiction in whose work humor is prominent. Among the most notable included in this anthology are Bernard Malamud, Grace Paley, Bruce Jay Friedman, and Philip Roth. Forty years after his *Portnoy's Complaint* changed Jewish American and American literature forever, Roth is as powerful, controversial, and funny as ever. Others one can name who should be read and enjoyed include Nora Ephron, Joanna Kaplan, Fran Liebowitz, Susan Fromberg Schaeffer, Wallace Markfield, Stanley Elkin.

It is in the field of stand-up comedy that Jews have been a most substantial influence upon American popular culture. First there was vaudeville and various painful but funny dialect acts, such as Dr. Kronkheit. One routine opens with a man deciding he's feeling so sick he'll go to see the doctor—for the first time in his life. In Dr. Kronkheit's office, he sees a sign that reads, "First visit $10; second visit $5." When the doctor enters the office, the "erstwhile" patient extends his hand and says, "Good to see you again, Doctor!" After the examination, the man pays his $5 and asks, "Well, what is the diagnosis?" "Oh," says Dr. Kronkheit, "the same as last time!" Not bad.

But vaudeville spawned talents that went on to better things. Willy Howard came on stage in the ideological 1930s with a soapbox, exclaiming to his single, lonely straight man, "Hey, you! Come here—make a circle!" He begins to orate: "Comes the revolution, you'll eat strawberries and cream!" "But I don't like strawberries and cream" is the response. "Goddamnit!" he yells, "you'll eat it!" Jewish women—"unkosher comediennes" in Sarah Blacher Cohen's phrase—made unique contributions, from the "red-hot momma" Sophie Tucker, with her ribald and sexually emancipating routines and songs such as *When Am I Getting the Mink, Mr. Fink*, through the "funny girl" Fanny Brice, to the inimitable Dorothy Parker, Joan Rivers, and scores of others.

Sophie Tucker was born on the road, as it were, while her mother was fleeing Russia in 1884 (or perhaps 1887) to join her husband in America. Tucker was an anomaly as well as a ground-breaking headliner for several decades in American cabarets, nightclubs, stages. She was a large woman who sang and joked about her size and sexuality with an unabashed view of women's desire and power, challenging stereotypes of the day. It was said of her when she started out that she dressed like a hooker (which she was not, although sympathetic to women in the trade) and, in her glory days, like a madam. One of her songs, sung in 1906–7, when she worked a club in New York's red-light district, was *There's Company in the Parlor, Girls, Come on Down*. She claimed to make such songs funny, not salacious. The same might be said of her jokes, which she interspersed as patter between songs. One such goes: "I got a call the other night from my old boyfriend, Ernie. 'Soph,' he said, 'when I celebrate my eightieth birthday, in honor of the occasion I am gonna marry myself a twenty-year-old girl. What do you think of that, Soph?' 'Ernie,' says I, 'when I am eighty years old, I shall marry myself a twenty-year-old boy. And let me tell you something, Ernie, twenty goes into eighty a hell of a lot more than eighty goes into twenty.' " Her "hot" (sexy) songs were done with humor and a sense of her own power. She sang: "I'm the last of the red-hot mamas, they've all cooled down but me—Flapper vamps, say, what do they know? Come get your hot stuff from this volcano! I'm the last of the red-hot mamas, I'm gettin' hotter all the time!" And her signature song, *Some of These Days* (written by African American songwriter Shelton Brooks) ends with the refrain "You're gonna miss your mama, your big fat mama, some of these days." This was no shrinking violet, passive victim of masculine desire and control. Among her many songs, one of her most popular, cited by Sarah Blacher Cohen, should be noted for, among other things, its bilingual appeal to a Yiddishly aware audience:

> Mistah Siegel, you'd better make it legal, Mistah Siegel
> *Mazel Tov:*[1]
> Something happened, accidently.
> Consequently, we should marry.
> No, no, it isn't a mistake.
> I'm swearing I should live so.
> It wasn't Sam or Jake.
> *A klug tzu Columbus,*[2] what you made from me.
> My mamma told me yesterday I'm gaining weight.
> It's not from something I ate.
> You said, "Come'on make whoopy, come'on, just one little kiss."
> *Ich hob moira far da chupah*[3]
> *Vet dos zein bei uns a bris.*[4]
> Mistah Siegel, Mister Siegel, in my *boich is schoen a kiegel.*[5]
> Mistah Siegel, make it legal for me.

Roughly contemporaneous with Tucker and, like her, from an impoverished immigrant background, Fanny Brice (1891–1951) was a great star of vaudeville, musical comedy, and several Ziegfeld Follies before, at the end of her career in the 1930s and 1940s, she became a radio star with her portrayal of a de-ethnicized, precocious, bratty toddler—Baby Snooks. Prior to that, as Barbara Grossman has shown in her expert biography, *Funny Woman* (1991), her chief shtick, done with great facial and physical mobility, was to portray an awkward, klutzy girl with a whiny Lower East Side, Yiddish-inflected voice attempting to rise above or out of her obvious immigrant cultural status. Brice's efforts at ballet dancing, for example, apparently laid audiences in the aisle.

A female wit at the other end of the cultural scale from Brice or Tucker, Dorothy Parker (1893–1967) was born Dorothy Rothschild in New York City

1. Literally, "Good luck" (Yiddish).
2. "A curse on Columbus" (Yiddish).
3. "I fear the wedding canopy" (Yiddish).
4. "We'll have a circumcision ceremony instead" (Yiddish).
5. "I already have a noodle pudding in my belly" (Yiddish).

to affluent parents, whom she cordially disliked along with a good many other things. She was renowned for her acerbic wit and, in the 1920s and early 1930s, for being the sole female member of the Algonquin Round Table (which also included, among others, Robert Benchley and Alexander Woollcott). She did not display notable interest in Jewish subjects, although she could be fiercely abrasive in denouncing social hypocrisies and injustices. Her mordant humor can be seen in her 1926 inspired doggerel verse on the subject of suicide, called *Résumé*: "Razors pain you; / Rivers are damp; / Acids stain you; / And drugs cause cramp. / Guns aren't lawful; / Nooses give; / Gas smells awful; / You might as well live."

Finally, to bring things up to the present, there are now scores of Jewish women comics, among them Bette Midler, Fran Drescher, and especially Joan Rivers, the queen of chutzpah, who made her reputation on television as a stand-up comedian when the field was largely male-dominated. Still performing, she carries on a tradition of sexual frankness but, unlike Tucker, ruefully, as in her comment on Jewish porn in a supposedly sexually liberated era: one minute of sex and six minutes of guilt.

One of the richest veins of Jewish humor in America centered on the garment industry, predominently Jewish and New York–located. This is especially true of the work of Myron Cohen. One of his stories has a manufacturer telling another: "Jack jumped from the window of his shop last week." "Really," the other responds, "poor Jack—business was so bad he had to commit suicide!" "He didn't get killed," the first explains. "He fell on a bundle of returns." When things get really bad, Jack eludes the arms of his partner and leaps again from the window. As he is falling, he passes the windows of the loft below, in which he sees 200 sewing machines busily whirring. He calls up to his startled partner, "Morris, cut velvet!" These jokes slayed them in Sha-Wan-Ga Lodge and other Catskill resorts in the 1940s.

There were gentle comedians like Sam Levenson, a former high-school Spanish teacher in Brooklyn. Warm and folksy, he told of his grandfather stuffing his kishke (intestines) with kishke (stuffed derma, a Jewish "delicacy" made by stuffing beef intestines with flour, seasonings, and fat, and then cooking it) which produced a heartburn that kept him warm throughout the Russian winters. Like this joke, much of Jewish humor makes a virtue of necessity. The line of comedians extends through Shelly Berman and Mort Sahl in the 1960s heyday of Jewish comics, along with Lenny Bruce and Woody Allen, through to the present popularity of ("I don't get no respect!") Rodney Dangerfield (formerly, Jack Roy, né Jacob Cohen), Jackie Mason, Mel Brooks and Carl Reiner and their 2,000-year-old-man routines, and Jerry Seinfeld, among others. Billy Crystal's film *Mr. Saturday Night* is an affectionate tribute to this tradition, as is the opening sequence of Woody Allen's *Broadway Danny Rose,* in which four comedians, including Jackie Mason and Morty Gunty, sit at a table in the Carnegie Delicatessen in New York, reminiscing about the late, affable agent, Danny Rose (a fictional character played by Allen).

All of these commented, often acerbically, on the foibles of their times and their contemporaries, giving pleasure in the process. From the almost innocent humor of their forebears in Second Avenue cafés to the challenging, corrosive, seemingly nihilistic wit of Bruce and Allen, they have made their indelible mark on our culture. One of the old stories: Two rival Yiddish poets meet at the Café Royale on Second Avenue after a long absence. After ordering their tea with lemon, one boasts to the other, "Since we last met, I have twice as many readers!" *"Mazel tov! Mazel tov!"* the other replies, shaking his hand vigorously, "I didn't know you got married." Compared with the world of that joke, Lenny Bruce and Woody Allen (born Allen Stewart Konigsberg) are difficult cases.

Bruce challenged his era with his general irreverence and sharp questioning of hypocrisies in American life. In his routines, which can still be heard on records, he attacks racism, the prurience that often lies under puritanical attitudes, and shibboleths regarding language uses. Most famously, he was arrested for uttering "lewd" and forbidden words in the course of his act. Most of these words, if not commonplace, have become accepted and widely used in film, television, and popular culture generally. A clip from today's MTV or a rap hit would make Bruce in his prime—the 1960s, when he helped Jewish humor enter mainstream America—seem relatively tame. His use of drugs, from which he may have died in 1966, made him seem like a moral outlaw. His challenge extends to Jews as well, some of whom may be alarmed when evil or stupidity is confronted so uncompromisingly and in a way that might be misunderstood.

We include Woody Allen's take on the tribulations of Job and his retelling of the Abraham–Isaac story, the *Akedah,* one of the most important and commented-upon in the Bible. They are in the great Jewish tradition of commentaries, albeit Allen's is full of irreverence, chutzpah, and a contemporary secular perspective. His films, for which he is best known, display these characteristics as well. Lines and situations from them have become minor classics, repeated often by the Jewish middle class, intellectuals, intellectual wannabes, and professionals or near-professionals who are often at the center of his humor as subjects and targets. They usually live in a New York City (Manhattan, specifically) that is remarkably clean as well as Jewish. It is romantically evoked in such landmarks as Central Park, the old Thalia cinema, where the people line up to see *The Sorrow and the Pity* (the brilliant four-and-a-half-hour documentary by Marcel Ophuls about the German occupation of France during World War II), the Museum of Modern Art, and the Hayden Planetarium. In *Annie Hall,* there is the unforgettable line about the beloved journals of the New York Jewish intellegentsia, *Dissent* and *Commentary,* merging in a new journal to be called *Dysentery.* Or in *Play It Again, Sam,* the scene in front of a Jackson Pollock painting is memorable. The Woody Allen character, as usual a nervous, neurotic nebbish looking for a date, always sexually driven and fearful of rebuffs, sidles up to a young woman and asks: "What does it say to you?" She: "It restates the negativeness of the universe. The hideous lonely emptiness of existence. Nothingness. The predicament of Man forced to live in a barren, Godless eternity like a tiny flame flickering in an immense void with nothing but waste, horror and degradation, forming a useless bleak straightjacket in a bleak absurd chaos." He (after a short pause): "What're you doing on Saturday night?" She: "Committing suicide." He: "What about Friday night?"

Along with his often exaggerated vulnerability and sensitivity as a *kleine mensh* type of Jew (the "little person," so central to the image he projects, as it was to much of Yiddish literature as a foil to the arrogance and brutality of Power), this undercutting of philosophical pretentiousness seemed to fit the mood of Allen's time. That mood—and, perhaps even more fittingly, that of the postmodern era—was expressed well by the playwright Eugène Ionesco when he said: "God is dead. Marx is dead. And I don't feel so well myself."

Now *that's* Jewish humor. At least Lenny Bruce might have said so in the routine in which he identified people and things as Jewish (even if they weren't) by their cultural baggage, *tam* or tone (rye bread is Jewish, white bread is "goyish"; if you live in Montana, you are goyish, even if you're Jewish; and if you live in New York, you're Jewish, even if you are not). Although Ionesco was not Jewish (or was he?), his formulation has the Jewish *knaitch* (twist or turn) that enables one to face the worst, smile ruefully, shrug, and go on living as best one can.

GROUCHO MARX
1890–1977

Groucho Marx was born Julius Henry Marx in New York City, the third of five sons of Samuel and Minna Palmer (Schoenberg) Marx. Chico and Harpo were older, Gummo and Zeppo younger. His father had come from Alsace and was an impecunious tailor; his mother was the sister of Al Shean of the popular—supposedly Irish—comedy team of Gallagher and Shean. The uncle's success inspired the brothers, encouraged by their mother, to try their fortunes on the vaudeville stage. They enjoyed meager success, however, touring the various circuits until they hit, almost by chance, upon the comedic possibilities in their by-now-familiar roles: Chico's immigrant Italian status, Harpo's wild mute antics, and the ad-libbing of an irrepressible Groucho (plus his greasepaint mustache, thick glasses, leer). One of the Marx Brothers' earliest Broadway hits in the 1920s was *The Cocoanuts*, a lampoon of the Florida land boom of the period, which became their first film in 1929. They were induced to come to Hollywood upon the advent of sound because their humor relied often on speech and language and delivery more than on the visual and miming humor of the silent screen. A series of popular films followed: *Animal Crackers* (1930); *Horse Feathers* (1932); *Duck Soup* (1933); and, in 1935, under the tutelage of Irving Thalberg, Hollywood's legendary young producer, their most successful film and the one Groucho liked best, *A Night at the Opera*. Other films followed, with the brothers and some with Groucho alone, but these early films are the classic ones. Their attacks upon conventional attitudes, anarchic at times, and Groucho's witty wisecracks and puns (a grammar-school dropout, he had a rich sense of language) have made their films popular ever since with young and old, ordinary and elite audiences.

In 1947, Groucho was the star of a radio quiz program called *You Bet Your Life*, which in the 1950s became a very successful show on television. Again, it was a format that allowed Groucho to display his ad-lib witticisms to advantage. In 1972, three thousand people filled Carnegie Hall in New York City to enjoy for two hours *An Evening with Groucho* (which is still available on record). He is the author as well of delightful memoirs, *Groucho and Me* (1959) and *Memoirs of a Mangy Lover* (1963), and his letters, including some to President Harry S. Truman, poet T. S. Eliot, and the great comic writer and cartoonist James Thurber, were acquired by the Library of Congress, much to Groucho's pleasure. The letter below was read, along with letters by Thomas Jefferson and Abraham Lincoln, at the library's bicentennial celebration in 1997 and later published in the *New York Times*. It was written in response to the attempt by Warner Brothers to prevent the use of the title *A Night in Casablanca* proposed for the next Marx Brothers' film.

[We Were Brothers before You Were]

Apparently there is more than one way of conquering a city and holding it as your own. For example, up to the time that we contemplated making a picture, I had no idea that the city of Casablanca belonged to Warner Brothers.

However, it was only a few days after our announcement appeared that we received a long, ominous legal document warning us not to use the name "Casablanca."

It seems that in 1471, Ferdinand Balboa Warner, the great-great grandfather of Harry and Jack, while looking for a shortcut to the city of Burbank, had stumbled on the shores of Africa and, raising his alpenstock, which he later turned in for a hundred shares of the common, he named it Casablanca.

I just can't understand your attitude. Even if they plan on re-releasing the picture, I am sure that the average movie fan could learn to distinguish between Ingrid Bergman and Harpo. I don't know whether I could, but I certainly would like to try.

You claim you own Casablanca and that no one else can use the name without their permission. What about Warner Brothers—do you own that, too? You probably have the right to use the name Warner, but what about Brothers? Professionally, we were brothers long before you were.

Even before us, there had been other brothers—the Smith Brothers, the Brothers Karamazov; Dan Brouthers, an outfielder with Detroit, and "Brother, can you spare a dime?" This was originally, "Brothers, can you spare a dime," but this was spreading a dime pretty thin.

The younger Warner Brother calls himself Jack. Does he claim that, too? It's not an original name—it was used long before he was born. Offhand, I can think of two Jacks—there was Jack of "Jack and the Beanstalk" and Jack the Ripper, who cut quite a figure in his day.

As for Harry, offhand, I can think of two Harrys that preceded him. There was Lighthorse Harry of Revolutionary fame and a Harry Appelbaum, who lived on the corner of 93d Street and Lexington Avenue.

This all seems to add up to a pretty bitter tirade but I don't mean to. I love Warners—some of my best friends are Warner Brothers. I have a hunch that this attempt to prevent us from using the title is the scheme of some ferret-faced shyster serving an apprenticeship in their legal department. I know the type—hot out of law school, hungry for success and too ambitious to follow the natural laws of promotion, this bar sinister probably needled Warners' attorneys, most of whom are fine fellows with curly black hair, double-breasted suits etc. in attempting to enjoin us.

Well, he won't get away with it! We'll fight him to the highest court! No pasty-faced legal adventurer is going to cause bad blood between the Warners and the Marxes. We are all brothers under the skin and we'll remain friends till the last reel of "A Night in Casablanca" goes tumbling over the spool.

1946 1997

WOODY ALLEN
b. 1935

Born Allen Stewart Konigsberg in Brooklyn in 1935, Woody Allen attended Midwood High School there and very briefly went to New York University and City College night school. At nineteen, he began writing jokes for comics and television shows. In his early twenties, he was a high-priced writer for many such clients, along with becoming the youngest member of the legendary writing group that included Mel Brooks and Carl Reiner for Sid Caesar's *Your Show of Shows.* He soon became a stand-up comic himself. Among his influences, he claimed Mort Sahl and Bob Hope (for his timing). His lifelong admiration, however, was reserved for the Marx Brothers, whose zany, anarchic exuberance seems to suggest that while life may be meaningless, it is worth living—a theme that was to emerge in many of Allen's later films.

In 1969, with *Take the Money and Run,* Allen began directing and occasionally acting in films. Movies became his chief artistic endeavor: he has written, directed, acted in over twenty films that have won a devoted following, although none has been, in Hollywood terms, a big money-maker. In fact, according to Joanna E. Rapf, his 1977 prize-winning *Annie Hall* "was one of the lowest grossing films ever to win an Academy Award for Best Picture."

In 1969, he also began publishing essays, parodies, and short stories in the *New Yorker, Playboy, Esquire,* and elsewhere. One of them, *The Kugelmass Episode,* in which famous fictional characters (like Emma Bovary) step out of their books and provide a commentary on the dreariness of "real life," won the O. Henry Award for 1977. These pieces have been collected in three volumes, in one of which, *Without Feathers* (1975), *The Scrolls* is included.

The Scrolls[1]

Scholars will recall that several years ago a shepherd, wandering in the Gulf of Aqaba, stumbled upon a cave containing several large clay jars and also two tickets to the ice show. Inside the jars were discovered six parchment scrolls with ancient incomprehensible writing which the shepherd, in his ignorance, sold to the museum for $750,000 apiece. Two years later the jars turned up in a pawnshop in Philadelphia. One year later the shepherd turned up in a pawnshop in Philadelphia and neither was claimed.

Archaeologists originally set the date of the scrolls at 4000 B.C., or just after the massacre of the Israelites by their benefactors. The writing is a mixture of Sumerian, Aramaic, and Babylonian and seems to have been done by either one man over a long period of time, or several men who shared the same suit. The authenticity of the scrolls is currently in great doubt, particularly since the word "Oldsmobile" appears several times in the text, and the few fragments that have finally been translated deal with familiar religious themes in a more than dubious way. Still, excavationist A. H. Bauer has noted that even though the fragments seem totally fraudulent, this is probably the greatest archeological find in history with the exception of the recovery of

1. Documents in the form of scrolls, discovered in a cave at Qumran, Israel, near the Dead Sea in 1947, which are records of a monastic sect called Essenes, who lived in the region from about the second century B.C.E. to 66–67 C.E., when it was overrun by the Romans. Allen pretends that what follows is a translated fragment of the Dead Sea Scrolls.

his cuff links from a tomb in Jerusalem. The following are the translated fragments.

One . . . And the Lord made an bet with Satan to test Job's loyalty and the Lord, for no apparent reason to Job, smote him on the head and again on the ear and pushed him into an thick sauce so as to make Job sticky and vile and then He slew a tenth part of Job's kine and Job calleth out: "Why doth thou slay my kine? Kine are hard to come by. Now I am short kine and I'm not even sure what kine are." And the Lord produced two stone tablets and snapped them closed on Job's nose. And when Job's wife saw this she wept and the Lord sent an angel of mercy who anointed her head with a polo mallet and of the ten plagues, the Lord sent one through six, inclusive, and Job was sore and his wife angry and she rent her garment and then raised the rent but refused to paint.

And soon Job's pastures dried up and his tongue cleaved to the roof of his mouth so he could not pronounce the word "frankincense" without getting big laughs.

And once the Lord, while wreaking havoc upon his faithful servant, came too close and Job grabbed him around the neck and said. "Aha! Now I got you! Why are thou giving Job a hard time, eh? Eh? Speak up!"

And the Lord said, "Er, look—that's my neck you have . . . Could you let me go?"

But Job showed no mercy and said, "I was doing very well till you came along. I had myrrh and fig trees in abundance and a coat of many colors with two pairs of pants of many colors. Now look."

And the Lord spake and his voice thundered: "Must I who created heaven and earth explain my ways to thee? What hath thou created that thou doth dare question me?"

"That's no answer," Job said. "And for someone who's supposed to be omnipotent, let me tell you, 'tabernacle' has only one *l*." Then Job fell to his knees and cried to the Lord, "Thine is the kingdom and the power and glory. Thou hast a good job. Don't blow it."

Two . . . And Abraham awoke in the middle of the night and said to his only son, Isaac,[2] "I have had an dream where the voice of the Lord sayeth that I must sacrifice my only son, so put your pants on." And Isaac trembled and said, "So what did you say? I mean when He brought this whole thing up?"

"What am I going to say?" Abraham said. "I'm standing there at two A.M. in my underwear with the Creator of the Universe. Should I argue?"

"Well, did he say why he wants me sacrificed?" Isaac asked his father.

But Abraham said, "The faithful do not question. Now let's go because I have a heavy day tomorrow."

And Sarah[3] who heard Abraham's plan grew vexed and said, "How doth thou know it was the Lord and not, say, thy friend who loveth practical jokes, for the Lord hateth practical jokes and whosoever shall pull one shall be delivered into the hands of his enemies whether they can pay the delivery

2. The story of Abraham's near-sacrifice of Isaac is one of the most commented-upon stories in the Bible (Genesis 22.12).

3. Sarah, Abraham's wife, does not appear in the Genesis account.

charge or not." And Abraham answered, "Because I know it was the Lord. It was a deep, resonant voice, well modulated, and nobody in the desert can get a rumble in it like that."

And Sarah said, "And thou art willing to carry out this senseless act?" But Abraham told her, "Frankly yes, for to question the Lord's word is one of the worst things a person can do, particularly with the economy in the state it's in."

And so he took Isaac to a certain place and prepared to sacrifice him but at the last minute the Lord stayed Abraham's hand and said, "How could thou doest such a thing?"

And Abraham said, "But thou said—"

"Never mind what I said," the Lord spake. "Doth thou listen to every crazy idea that comes thy way?" And Abraham grew ashamed. "Er—not really . . . no."

"I jokingly suggest thou sacrifice Isaac and thou immediately runs out to do it."

And Abraham fell to his knees, "See, I never know when you're kidding."

And the Lord thundered, "No sense of humor. I can't believe it."

"But doth this not prove I love thee, that I was willing to donate mine only son on thy whim?"

And the Lord said, "It proves that some men will follow any order no matter how asinine as long as it comes from a resonant, well-modulated voice."

And with that, the Lord bid Abraham get some rest and check with him tomorrow.

Three . . . And it came to pass that a man who sold shirts was smitten by hard times. Neither did any of his merchandise move nor did he prosper. And he prayed and said, "Lord, why hast thou left me to suffer thus? All mine enemies sell their goods except I. And it's the height of the season. My shirts are good shirts. Take a look at this rayon. I got button-downs, flare collars, nothing sells. Yet I have kept thy commandments. Why can I not earn a living when mine younger brother cleans up in children's ready-to-wear?"

And the Lord heard the man and said, "About thy shirts . . ."

"Yes, Lord," the man said, falling to his knees.

"Put an alligator over the pocket."

"Pardon me, Lord?"

"Just do what I'm telling you. You won't be sorry."

And the man sewed on to all his shirts a small alligator symbol and lo and behold, suddenly his merchandise moved like gangbusters, and there was much rejoicing while amongst his enemies there was wailing and gnashing of teeth, and one said, "The Lord is merciful. He maketh me to lie down in green pastures. The problem is, I can't get up."

Laws and Proverbs

Doing abominations is against the law, particularly if the abominations are done while wearing a lobster bib.

The lion and the calf shall lie down together but the calf won't get much sleep.

Whosoever shall not fall by the sword or by famine, shall fall by pestilence so why bother shaving?

The wicked at heart probably know something.

Whosoever loveth wisdom is righteous but he that keepeth company with fowl is weird.

My Lord, my Lord! What hast Thou done, lately?

1975

A SCATTERING OF CONTEMPORARY AND PERENNIAL JEWISH JOKES

A Jewish man calls his mother and says, "Mom, I'm bringing home a wonderful woman that I want to marry. She is a Native American and her name is Shooting Star."

"How nice," says his mother.

"I have an Indian name, too—it's Running River. You have to call me that from now on."

"How nice," says his mother.

"You have to have an Indian name, too, Mom."

"I do," says the mother. "Just call me Sitting Shiva."

Two Jewish men are sitting in a deli frequented by Jews. A Chinese waiter comes up and asks in fluent Yiddish can he get them something. The Jewish men are dumbfounded. "Where did he learn such perfect Yiddish?" they ask the deli owner.

The owner whispers to them, "Shhhh, he thinks we're teaching him English."

A Jewish boy comes home from school and tells his mother he has been given a part in the school play. "Wonderful," says the mother. "What part is it?"

The boy says, "I play the part of a Jewish husband."

The mother frowns and says, "Go back and tell the teacher you want a speaking part!"

A Hebrew teacher stood in front of his classroom and said, "The Jewish people have observed their 5,759th year as a people. Consider that the Chinese, for example, have only observed their 4,692nd year as a people. What does that mean to you?" After a moment of silence, one student raised his hand. "Yes, David," the teacher said. "What does it mean?"

"It means that the Jews had to wait 1,067 years for Chinese food."

An elderly Jewish woman is leaving the garment district to go home from work. Suddenly a man who has been walking toward her stands in front of her, blocks her path, opens up his raincoat, and flashes her. Unruffled, she takes a look and remarks, "This you call a lining?"

There is a big controversy these days about when life begins. In Jewish tradition, the fetus is not considered a viable human being until after graduation from medical school.

The first Jewish president calls his mother in Queens and invites her for Purim. "I'd like to," she says, "but it's so much trouble. First, I have to get a cab to the airport, and I hate waiting on Queens Boulevard. . . ."

"Mom," he tells her, "I'm the president. You won't need a cab. I'll send a limo."

"That would be nice, but I'll still have to get my ticket at the airport and get a seat. I hate sitting in the middle."

"Mom I'm the president of the United States! I'll send Air Force One!"

"Yes, well, when we land, I'll still have to get my luggage, find a cab, and you know what holiday crowds are like."

"Mom! I'll have a helicopter pick you up! You'll go straight from the plane to my front lawn!"

"But I'll still have to get a hotel room. And hotels are so expensive. And they're not what they once were."

"Ma! You'll stay at the White House!"

"Well, all right, I'll come," she finally agrees. Later that day her neighbor asks her what she will be doing for the holiday. "Oh," she says, "my son invited me to come and celebrate with him."

"Oh," says the neighbor, "your son the doctor?"

"No," she replies, "the other one."

Just before Rosh Hashanah, a team of terrorists invades the shul and takes the rabbi, cantor, and shul president hostage. Hours later, the governor hangs tough and won't give them the million dollars they asked for, nor a getaway car or jumbo jet. The terrorists gather the three hostages in a corner and inform them that things look bad, and they're going to have to shoot them. But to show they're not really a bad bunch, they'll grant each hostage one wish. "Please," says the rabbi, "for the last two months I have been working on my Rosh Hashanah sermon. What a waste to die now without having presented it before an audience. I'll go happily if you let me recite my sermon. It's an hour—maybe ninety minutes long, tops." They promise to grant him his wish.

"Please," says the cantor, "after fifty years I've finally got the *Hineni* prayer just right. What a waste to die and not sing it to an audience. It's only about forty-five minutes long—then I'll go happily." The terrorists promise to grant his wish, too, and they turn to the shul president.

"Please," says the president with tears in his eyes, "shoot me first!"

During a service at an old synagogue in Eastern Europe when the Shema prayer was said, half the congregants stood up and half remained sitting. The half that was seated started yelling at those standing to sit down, and the ones standing yelled at the ones sitting to stand up. The rabbi, learned as he was in the law and commentaries, didn't know what to do. His congregation suggested that he consult a housebound ninety-eight-year-old man, who was one of the original founders of their shul. The rabbi hoped the elderly man would be able to tell him what the actual temple tradition was, so he went to the nursing home with a representative of each faction of the congregation. The one whose followers stood during Shema said to the old man, "Is the tradition to stand during the prayer?"

The old man answered, "No, that is not the tradition."

"Then the tradition is to sit during the Shema!"

The old man answered, "No, that is not the tradition."

Then the rabbi said to the old man, "But the congregants fight all the time, yelling at each other about whether they should sit or stand. . . . "

The old man interrupted, exclaiming, "*That* is the tradition!"

A shipwrecked Jewish Robinson Crusoe was finally rescued after twenty years alone on his island. The rescuers were astonished to see a magnificent three-story construction of stone, palm, driftwood next to Robinson's humble hut. "What is that?" they asked.

"My shul," he proudly replied. The sailors were impressed. Rounding the island with him aboard they were surprised to see an identical three-story construction on the other side of the island.

"What in the world is that?" asked the ship's captain.

"That," said the rescued man, "that is the shul I don't go to."

From Margin to Mainstream in Difficult Times, 1924–1945

From the end of the First World War to the end of the Second was a volatile period for Americans generally and for Jewish Americans particularly; more and more they felt the growing threat of Nazism abroad and persistent and growing anti-Semitism at home. Nevertheless, during this period Jews advanced socially and economically—despite the setbacks that affected everyone during the Great Depression of the 1930s—and the literary and cultural contributions of American Jews increasing markedly in quality and influence. The world that the mass of Eastern European Jews (and their second- and third-generation descendants) found and were remaking with their own institutions and personalities became more assured, a secure launching pad for the great leap forward in all areas of American life that was to take place in the expansive post–World War II era.

FROM THE ROARING TWENTIES TO THE DEPRESSION

Fundamentally, the 1920s were a time of optimism in which Jews, like other Americans, dealt with Prohibition (and drank homemade or bootleg spirits), enjoyed an expanding economy, sought new careers, speculated in real estate and the stock market. They danced to the music of the Jazz Age and worried about the supposed decline of the morals of their children. They went to the movies (often instead of to shul on Saturdays) and exulted as Al Jolson portrayed a cantor's-son-become-pop-music-celebrity (but one who beautifully sings the great Yom Kipper prayer Kol Nidre, asking for God's absolution of incurred debts) in the first major sound film, *The Jazz Singer* (1927). But even before the 1929 crash and the resulting depression of the 1930s, Jews were anxious and concerned about the promise of American life.

Religious groupings shifted with the rise of the three major branches of Reform, Conservative, and Orthodox Judaism—even as religious attendance and observance dropped throughout the community. There was an inevitable loosening of family ties as the younger generation grew more Americanized, which increasingly meant the perceptible dropping of Yiddish for English. The role of women changed as they entered the workplace and became more educated in ever greater numbers, often achieving prominence in labor and in educational and political organizations. The nation at large during the 1920s saw an increased nativism and xenophobia, manifest in fear and hostility toward immigrants and ethnic "others." Some Ivy League and professional schools of law and medicine created quotas to keep down the number of Jews when they believed this group was disproportionately represented. Racial and religious prejudices were frequently promoted by bigoted groups in America.

Jews were often the main, but not the only, target of such attitudes and actions. The Ku Klux Klan (KKK), which reemerged in 1922, claimed a membership by 1924 of 4 million (the numbers were probably less) and ranted against and attacked Catholics and, especially, blacks. There was a growth of Sunday blue laws—an effort to enforce Sunday as the Sabbath—which was seen by many Jews (who fought against the movement) as an effort to reinforce the claim that America was essentially a Christian nation. The immigrant restriction acts of 1921 and 1924 (the Johnson Act) effectively curbed immigration from southern and eastern Europe, with far-reaching consequences for Jewish life in America (ending the continuing influx of Yiddish-speaking Jews) and subsequently for the many thousands of Jews caught in the Nazi trap who were unable to escape and enter the United States.

Henry Ford contributed to the persistence of anti-Semitism during the 1920s by serially publishing from 1922 onward in his newspaper, the *Dearborn Independent*, and widely distributing the whole of the false and pernicious *Protocols of the Meeting of the Learned Elders of Zion*, a forgery by the czarist police that first appeared in 1905 and that is still distributed by anti-Semitic groups. Based on an invention in a minor nineteenth-century French novel, the *Protocols* were purportedly the plans for world domination outlined at a meeting of Jews in a Prague cemetery. Ford only stopped and apologized for the anti-Jewish content of his paper in 1927, after much Jewish protest. Some literature in periodicals and books, such as Henry Pratt Fairchild's *The Melting-Pot Mistake*, spread the anti-immigrant message while other literature was specifically anti-Jewish, such as Burton J. Hendrick's *The Jews in America* (1924). The usual charge was that these people were unassimilable to American life and a serious danger to its best values. The literature of even our most esteemed writers was not entirely free of this virus, as in the portraits of Robert Cohn in Hemingway's *The Sun Also Rises* and of Meyer Wolfsheim in Fitzgerald's *The Great Gatsby*. Of course, Jewish—and non-Jewish—writers often countered such images, as in the work of Ludwig Lewisohn, the bohemian views of Ben Hecht (*A Jew in Love*) or Maxwell Bodenheim. In popular culture, the long-running play *Abie's Irish Rose* (1922) put a benign spin on stereotypes as Hollywood and Tin Pan Alley intermittently tried to do.

Some of the animus against immigrants and "foreign" or "alien" elements in American life at this time can be traced to America's involvement in World War I. To mainstream Americans, many so-called "hyphenate" Americans seemed more interested in the fate of their European homelands than in American interests. Then the Russian Revolution burst upon the world scene. It exacerbated an American propensity to associate foreigners with radicalism, insurrection, and immorality. Such attitudes can be traced back to the early Alien and Sedition Acts of the 1790s, a reaction to the presumed threat of the French Revolution, or to the nineteenth-century sloganeering against "Rum, Romanism and Rebellion," which is how the Democratic party was characterized by a Presbyterian clergyman at a Republican rally during the presidential campaign of 1884, thus estranging Irish Catholic voters and assuring the victory of Grover Cleveland. The Palmer Raids of 1919, illegal seizure by the U.S. attorney general's office of hundreds of aliens suspected of radicalism who were then unceremoniously deported, illustrated dramatically this pervasive fear and hostility. The canard that Jews were villainously leading both the international banking and financial worlds *and* international bolshevism grew in this period—an absurd contradiction that is treated satirically here in Nathanael West's *A Cool Million* in this section of the anthology.

Many industries and professions were hostile toward having Jews in their ranks. We have mentioned the efforts of the legal and medical professions to stop the growth of Jewish members in these professions; it was rare for Jews to become engineers in the 1920s; and major industries (iron, coal, rubber, auto, energy, finance) rarely had Jews in management or even at entry-level jobs. Major colleges and universities (especially the elite ones) had quotas—sometimes disguised, as at Harvard, as a desired "geographical distribution"—aimed at keeping down the number of Jews attending or seeking admittance. There were housing restrictions in certain neighborhoods and suburbs, and restrictions in club memberships. Most Jews knew not to apply to certain places for work or admittance. Many changed their names—among writers represented here, Edwin Rolfe was born Solomon Fishman, Nathanael West was Nathan Weinstein—"Americanizing" obviously Jewish-sounding names.

Despite these obstructions and restrictions, Jews managed to strengthen their hold upon American life, although it may be true for many, as Samuel Ornitz observed of himself and others in his satire about a Jewish arriviste in *Haunch, Paunch and Jowl* (1923), that "there was not yet an American identity." They were, however, becoming more highly educated (outstripping other immigrant and ethnic groups), breaking into and prospering in many fields that were risky but open to them (junk, clothing, fashion, commerce, entertainment, real estate), buying more of their own homes. In short, they were developing their confidence and assurance as Jews and as Americans.

DEPRESSION POLITICS AND LITERARY CURRENTS

Jewish Americans would need these positive achievements because the depression of the 1930s threatened the viability of the whole of American society. In his classic three-volume biography of Franklin Delano Roosevelt, historian Arthur M. Schlesinger, Jr. draws an alarming picture of the state of that society when Roosevelt took office in 1933. Schlesinger begins his first volume with a harrowing description of native fascist and some "red" movements that were coming to the fore when the entire system seemed to be crumbling. The picture may be overdrawn, highlighting the historian's belief that Roosevelt and his New Deal saved America from the possibility of extreme "solutions." But it is significant that in the 1932 presidential election, an impressive array of American writers and intellectuals—including Theodore Dreiser and John Dos Passos—supported the Communist party ticket of William Z. Foster and James W. Ford. The 1930s also saw the creation of more than one hundred fascist and totalitarian organizations, many drawing their support and inspiration from the regnant fascist and Nazi regimes in Italy and Germany.

These fascistically oriented groups were outspokenly bigoted racially and religiously; and while most were marginal, some, like the Silver Shirts of William Dudley Pelley or Fritz Kuhn's largely New York–based German-American Bund, were stridently visible and effective hate groups. Significantly, the weekly radio broadcasts of a viciously anti-Jewish priest, Father Charles Coughlin, from 1937 until 1940 (when he was silenced by the Roman Catholic Church) claimed to reach an audience of 25 million. Of course, many Jewish antifascist and defense organizations such as the Anti-Defamation League of B'nai B'rith took strong stands against such activities, strengthening themselves and giving coherence in the process to disparate Jewish voices and interests as well. The entrance of the United States into World War II at the close of 1941 brought an end to these anti-Semitic groups, though some of their propaganda lived on covertly during the war years. Only after the war, especially after the horrible revelations of the Nürnberg Trials (1945–46), did the tide turn decisively against anti-Semitism and toward the full and open acceptance of Jews at all levels of American society.

Economically, Jews by and large shared the fate of other Americans. During this period, unemployment reached 25 percent, and its threat as well as reduced workloads bedeviled Jews and their families. Most Jews were working class, and they and the middle class eked out a precarious living. The play by Clifford Odets, *Awake and Sing!* (1934), is a graphic portrayal of the effects of the depression upon a lower-middle-class family and its efforts to cope. Many works on stage and screen dealt with similar themes—John Howard Lawson's (born Levy) *Johnny Johnson* (1931), Sidney Kingsley's *Dead End*, the *Living Newspapers* of the Works Progress Administration's (WPA's) Federal Theatre Project among them—and writers generally moved leftward. The economic crisis, as Edmund Wilson had observed in 1929, when Michael Gold (born Itzok, later Irwin, Granich), author of the significantly titled *Jews without Money* (1930), a model for the so-called "proletarian literature" that remained popular until 1935, attacked Thornton Wilder and his apparently "escapist" aesthetics, was to be accompanied by a literary one. The dominant literary style of the 1930s was realism, a reaction to the literary modernism of the 1920s in which complexity, allusiveness, and difficulty were valued by critics. The 1930s crisis seemed to demand straightforward and accurate accounts of what was happening and, among those who became "social realists," what was to be done about it. The 1920s completed the rout of "the genteel tradition" in American letters that had been under attack since the beginning of the century. The demand for a more sophisticated literature, free to discuss sex, money and its acquisition, the social realities of American life, had actually been met, and even in the socially conscious 1930s, its effects were evident. Henry Roth's *Call It Sleep*, a masterful 1934 novel about a Jewish immigrant family, told through the sensibility of a seven year old, owes a great debt to James Joyce's *Ulysses* (1922), one of the foundational texts of literary modernism; and many of the 1930s poets represented in this anthology owe much to that other foundational text and author, *The Waste Land* (1922) of T. S. Eliot. Tess Slesinger, a member of the elite intellectual circle at the *Menorah Journal*, bridges the two decades in her 1932 story *Missis Flinders,* about the psychological effect of an abortion, the first such story to be published in a "respectable journal." By the 1940s and with the writing about World War II, realism and literary modernism can be said to be comfortably conjoined, as the poetry of Karl Shapiro, Delmore Schwartz, Stanley Kunitz, and Muriel Rukeyser will show.

A significant number of Jewish writers during the 1930s identified with one or another liberal movement or with those on the Left—New Dealers, socialists, Stalinist and anti-Stalinist communists, and a range of sympathizers and fellow travelers. In all of this, a prophetic tendency became evident, rather than signaling alienation from America and its culture. Many writers called upon America to live up to its best potential and hoped for broader democratization in American life. Because of the depression and its shared hardships, previously marginal writers we now call "ethnics" moved from the periphery of American literary life toward its center. Not only the popularity of a playwright like Clifford Odets, but the phenomenal reception and popularity of books by the Italian American Pietro di Donato, the Irish American James T. Farrell, the Armenian American William Saroyan, the African American Richard Wright evidenced this trend. The paradox to be grasped is that in the crisis, ethnic identities could be affirmed and celebrated (or at least written about) when it was "politically correct" to show that all groups shared similar class-based fates. That paradox can be seen in a specifically Jewish American context: in the general precariousness of the 1930s, the commitment to America of Jewish Americans grew stronger.

Many factors contributed to this situation. First, the cutting off of Yiddish-speaking immigration, as has been mentioned, increased within the generation of the 1920s and 1930s the influence of English-language media, workplace, schools. Then, too—and most significantly—the general economic collapse spawned, in the New Deal and its agencies, as well as in the nation's churches, fraternal organizations, and grassroots politics, a strong impulse to build upon what was solid, democratic, and enduring in America. A celebration of regional values and of a national sharing in the country's fate and history, a growth in ideas of brotherhood and sisterhood, and mutual support took place, much of it chronicled in various movements of the time. The federally sponsored relief programs for artists, writers, and theater people—for example, those projects under the aegis of the WPA—launched undertakings such as the gathering of urban and rural folktales, chronicles by surviving African American former slaves, historic pageants, the multivolume guidebooks to the history and geography of all the states that are a national treasure trove of information preserved. Finally, one must not minimize the belief—encouraged dramatically by the until then unparalleled use of radio addresses by President Roosevelt, who was gifted with a charismatic voice and manner and great speech writers—that all shared in the national calamity and that only by a united effort would the situation be improved. Although, as he said in his second inaugural address, "I see one third of a nation ill-housed, ill-fed and ill-clad," FDR conveyed unforgettably that America *was* one nation. And Jews supported Roosevelt more faithfully and overwhelmingly than any other group in America.

This variety and double sidedness of the interwar period is reflected both in literature and in popular culture, which is alternately critical and hopeful about the failed promise of the American dream, of equality and brotherhood. So we can read Lewisohn's account of his traumatic response to academic anti-Semitism, or Odets's and Gold's leftist view of poverty, or Rolfe's and Rukeyser's antifascist poems. There are also great hope and creative originality in the work of those literary "sports" Dahlberg and West. Their humor is occasionally bleak, but one cannot miss or fail to enjoy their spirit. That élan abounds in the modernism of Gertrude Stein and in the work of many poets represented here who often attempted to combine the modernist aesthetics of T. S. Eliot with their own socially conscious vision. They all share in and influence—as in the case of Delmore Schwartz and Isaac Rosenfeld—the major literary currents of their time. The calm professionalism of Hortense Calisher, Arthur Miller, Irwin Shaw, ineluctably mainstream, shines even as they display their Jewish background and commitment. Some, like Meyer Levin, were laying the groundwork for a firm commitment to Zionism and the creation and defense of the State of Israel. That was not a notable strain among the English-language Jewish writers of the period—they were usually more concerned with solidifying their claim to America—but the echo and shadow of the ancient Jewish dream crops up in surprising places. Edwin Rolfe, a dedicated fighter along with, it is estimated, nine hundred other American Jews in the 2,900-member Abraham Lincoln Battalion in Spain, writes: "Madrid, if I ever forget you, may my right hand lose its human cunning," substituting Madrid for Jerusalem in the ancient prayer (Psalm 137.5). Still, the dominant commitment in almost all the work of the period, however critical at times—in the spirit of Jewish prophecy—was to America, conceived of in its most promising potential.

WORLD WAR II AND THE HOLOCAUST

This commitment and the general incipient American nationalism promoted by all that has been previously noted met its great test in the Second World War. True to their history, most Americans, despite news reports of the dangers of fascism in Europe, were reluctant to get involved. Roosevelt had to tread carefully even as he saw the danger, grown exponentially by 1941 with the conquest of most of Europe by Nazi Germany. By then, the threat to Great Britain and, beyond that, to America was palpable. In a speech at Chautauqua, New York, in the summer of 1940, before his election to a third term, Roosevelt promised he would not send American troops to fight overseas. But in gradual steps, from proclaiming the United States "an arsenal of democracy," through a lend-lease program geared to providing England with desperately needed munitions (including a transfer of fifty destroyers) and later to helping the Soviet Union when it was attacked by Germany in June 1941, to defending convoys in the North Atlantic, FDR, assured that the United States was largely unified and ready to participate wholeheartedly in the struggle after Japan attacked Pearl Harbor, announced in December 1941 that America would enter the war.

Jews, of course, had been quite sensitive to the Nazi threat from the time of Hitler's rise to power in 1933. Their alarm and concern grew as Germany launched its war against the half-million German Jews and, later, Austrian and Czech Jews. When German forces conquered much of Eastern Europe and large parts of European Russia in 1941 and 1942, they came into control of millions of Jews who lived in those regions. The Nazis began then to put into operation the plans for their infamous *Endlösung* (the Final Solution, as they called it), formulated at the Wannsee Conference in Berlin in 1942. The horror of the Shoah/Holocaust began, eventually consuming the lives of 5 million to 6 million European Jews.

The question of whether and how much American Jews knew about the Holocaust has been often debated: by now scholars have made it clear that people who were paying attention were quite aware of the mortal danger to Europe's Jews. No one could divine the full scale of horror until the war ended, although Ben Hecht wrote a pageant, presented in New York's Madison Square Garden in 1943, that called attention to the slaughter of millions of Jews. Jewish groups and high-placed individuals like Secretary of the Treasury Henry Morgenthau tried to get America and the Allied powers to take more active steps to stop the slaughter—bombing the gas chambers and crematoria of Auschwitz, for instance—and to accept more refugees. They largely failed in these efforts. That failure has led to much reflection—and some guilt—as to how or if they could have been more effective. It has since become clear that, in the face of this crisis, the Jewish American community and its network of communal organizations did not "speak with one voice" to power; it remains a question whether, if they had, they would have been heard. The Roosevelt administration argued that the best way to save Jewish lives was to win and end the war as soon as possible and to aim for the conquest of the enemy armies by our forces without diversion to other actions. A certain logic and plausibility adhered to this argument, and it prevailed. Unfortunately, by the time the Allied armies were victorious in May 1945, European Jewry, for the most part, had been annihilated. During the war, one of the reasons given for FDR's and his government's caution in coming directly to the aid of the trapped Jews in Europe was the fear that the war would be seen as being fought "for the Jews." In hindsight, we can see the bitter irony of that position.

Despite this overarching tragedy, the Second World War consolidated American Jewry's fervent Americanization. Over 550,000 Jews served in the armed forces (representing 8 percent more than their proportion of the total population); over 61,000 received medals and awards for gallantry; they suffered more than 40,000 casualties, including over 8,000 killed in action. They worked in defense industries; in governmental bureaus aiding the war effort; in film, journalism, and other media; in raising money in bond drives. The war was also a springboard for unparalleled growth for America in general.

The United States emerged from World War II as the greatest military and economic power on earth. Its factories and productive capacities, which had never been destroyed or captured in a hostile occupation, had expanded enormously. The country neither lost nor gained colonies; it emerged as the world's sole atomic power. The socioeconomic status of Jews changed as well, after the war becoming increasingly middle class and professional. Jews moved out of city slums and ghettolike neighborhoods to more affluent areas and suburbs. Young Jews, both veterans (aided by tuition money provided by the GI bill) and nonveterans, energetically and ambitiously embraced higher education. The Jewish contribution to American culture in the arts and sciences widened and deepened. In the post-war period, the success and position of Jews as an ethnic group was ultimately to equal that of WASPs.

What had begun with the uncertainty and mixed currents of the 1920s and continued in the 1930s with the double threat of economic collapse at home and fascist menace abroad ended in 1945, as the radio writer Norman Corwin put it, "on a note of triumph." That sense of triumph required something akin to amnesia by Jewish American writers of English in putting aside or repressing the reality of the Holocaust and the impossible quest to fathom its deepest meaning. Only in coming decades would the issue be confronted and the quest resumed by some of the writers represented in this section and by younger writers. Yiddish writers, here and abroad, could never forget it or fail to feel its devastating effect. But that is another chapter.

GERTRUDE STEIN
1874–1946

Massive, solid, and looking, as some of her friends thought, like a "great Jewish Buddha" in the portrait of her painted by her friend Pablo Picasso in 1906, Gertrude Stein was an important presence in the world of modernist art and literature during the first half of the twentieth century. Her apartment in Paris, which she first occupied with her brother, Leo, in 1902, was covered from floor to ceiling with paintings by modern masters. From 1907 onward, she lived there with her lifelong companion, Alice B. Toklas. Their apartment, at 27, rue de Fleurus, was a literary salon, visited by many acclaimed writers of the international avant-garde, most famously by the young Ernest Hemingway (F. Scott Fitzgerald and Sherwood Anderson also paid homage to Stein), who changed American prose style under her influence.

Stein was born in Allegheny, Pennsylvania; when she was two, the family moved to Vienna and Paris for a few years, where she learned, she said, to "prattle" in German and French. In 1879, the family moved to Oakland, California, where they lived until the parents' death in the late 1880s. Since Stein's father, son of German Jewish émigrés of the 1840s, had been a successful clothier, the family was well enough off so that the orphaned children, sent to live with warm and loving relatives in Baltimore, were amply provided for.

Stein attended Radcliffe College and studied with poet and philosopher George Santayana as well as William James, psychologist and a founder of pragmatism, who encouraged her to go to medical school as a basis for a career in psychology. She attended the Johns Hopkins Medical School in Baltimore for two years but dropped out. Leo had been writing to her about his growing excitement with the new art of Picasso, Cézanne, Matisse, and others, and she went off to join him in Paris. Besides acquiring art, she began her experimental writing.

Her first published work was *Three Lives* (1909), the story of three working-class women, followed by more obscure and experimental pieces like *Tender Buttons* (1914). During the First World War, she and Toklas volunteered for ambulance duty, after which they reestablished their home as a salon for intellectuals and artists. The interwar period saw her greatest productivity and success. Famous for enigmatic, amusing repetitions of words and rhythms—"Rose is a rose is a rose" and "Pigeons in the grass alas" are lines long identified with her—she began to write plays and operas. *Four Saints in Three Acts* (1927) was made into an opera by Virgil Thomson in 1934, to be followed by a successful lecture tour of England and America. Even though she was famous, the only work of hers widely read was her autobiography, composed as *The Autobiography of Alice B. Toklas* in 1933. The excerpt published here is part of Chapter I of *The Making of Americans*, which she began writing in 1906–08 but which was only published in 1925 in its 1,000-page version. It is based on the life of her own family, which she intended to serve as a model for the Americanization of all immigrants.

During the Second World War, Stein and Toklas left Paris for a small village in as-yet-unoccupied France, where they had a summer house. Inexplicably, they were left alone by the Germans and the Vichy French. After the Liberation and their return to Paris, their apartment became a much-visited site for American GIs, who were warmly welcomed. Her last opera, completed in 1946, was *The Mother of Us All*, based on the life of American reformer Susan B. Anthony.

From The Making of Americans: Being a History of a Family's Progress

From *Chapter I*

THE DEHNINGS AND THE HERSLANDS

Once an angry man dragged his father along the ground through his own orchard. "Stop!" cried the groaning old man at last, "Stop! I did not drag my father beyond this tree."

It is hard living down the tempers we are born with. We all begin well, for in our youth there is nothing we are more intolerant of than our own sins writ large in others and we fight them fiercely in ourselves; but we grow old and we see that these our sins are of all sins the really harmless ones to own, nay that they give a charm to any character, and so our struggle with them dies away.

It has always seemed to me a rare privilege, this, of being an American, a real American, one whose tradition it has taken scarcely sixty years to create. We need only realize our parents, remember our grandparents and know ourselves and our history is complete.

The old people in a new world, the new people made out of the old, that is the story that I mean to tell, for that is what really is and what I really know.

Some of the fathers we must realize so that we can tell our story really, were little boys then, and they came across the water with their parents, the grandparents we need only just remember. Some of these our fathers and our mothers, were not even made then, and the women, the young mothers, our grandmothers we perhaps just have seen once, carried these our fathers and our mothers into the new world inside them, those women of the old world strong to bear them. Some looked very weak and little women, but even these so weak and little, were strong always, to bear many children.

These certain men and women, our grandfathers and grandmothers, with their children born and unborn with them, some whose children were gone ahead to prepare a home to give them; all countries were full of women who brought with them many children; but only certain men and women and the children they had in them, to make many generations for them, will fill up this history for us of a family and its progress.

Many kinds of all these women were strong to bear many children.

One was very strong to bear them and then always she was very strong to lead them.

One was strong to bear them and then always she was strong to suffer with them.

One, a little gentle weary woman was strong to bear many children, and then always after she would sadly suffer for them, weeping for the sadness of all sinning, wearying for the rest she knew her death would bring them.

And then there was one sweet good woman, strong just to bear many children, and then she died away and left them, for that was all she knew then to do for them.

And these four women and the husbands they had with them and the children born and unborn in them will make up the history for us of a family and its progress.

Other kinds of men and women and the children they had with them, came at different times to know them; some, poor things, who never found how they could make a living, some who dreamed while others fought a way to help them, some whose children went to pieces with them, some who thought and thought and then their children rose to greatness through them, and some of all these kinds of men and women and the children they had in them will help to make the history for us of this family and its progress.

These first four women, the grandmothers we need only just remember, mostly never saw each other. It was their children and grandchildren who, later, wandering over the new land, where they were seeking first, just to make a living, and then later, either to grow rich or to gain wisdom, met with one another and were married, and so together they made a family whose progress we are now soon to be watching.

We, living now, are always to ourselves young men and women. When we, living always in such feeling, think back to them who make for us a beginning, it is always as grown and old men and women or as little children that we feel them, these whose lives we have just been thinking. We sometimes talk it long, but really, it is only very little time we feel ourselves ever to have being as old men and women or as children. Such parts of our living are little ever really there to us as present in our feeling. Yes; we, who are always all our lives, to ourselves grown young men and women, when we think back to them who make for us a beginning, it is always as grown old men and women or as little children that we feel them, such as them whose lives we have just been thinking.

Yes it is easy to think ourselves and our friends, all our lives as young grown men and women, indeed it is hard for us to feel even when we talk it long, that we are old like old men and women or little as a baby or as children. Such parts of our living are never really there to us as present, to our feeling.

Yes we are very little children when we first begin to be to ourselves grown men and women. We say then, yes we are children, but we know then, way inside us, we are not to ourselves real as children, we are grown to ourselves, as young grown men and women. Nay we never know ourselves as other than young and grown men and women. When we know we are no longer to ourselves as children. Very little things we are then and very full of such feeling. No, to be feeling ourselves to be as children is like the state between when we are asleep and when we are just waking, it is never really there to us as present to our feeling.

And so it is to be really old to ourselves in our feeling; we are weary and are old, and we know it in our working and our thinking, and we talk it long, and we can see it just by looking, and yet we are a very little time really old to ourselves in our feeling, old as old men and old women once were and still are to our feeling. No, no one can be old like that to himself in his feeling. No it must be always as grown and young men and women that we know ourselves and our friends in our feeling. We know it is not so, by our saying, but it must be so always to our feeling. To be old to ourselves in our feeling is a losing of ourselves like just dropping off into sleeping. To be awake, we must have it that we are to ourselves young and grown men and women.

To be ourself like an old man or an old woman to our feeling must be a horrid losing-self sense to be having. It must be a horrid feeling, like the hard leaving of our sense when we are forced into sleeping or the coming to it when we are just waking. It must be a horrid feeling to have such a strong sense of losing, such a feeling as being to ourselves like children or like grown old men and women. Perhaps to some it is a gentle sense of losing some who like themselves to be without a self sense feeling, but certainly it must be always a sense of self losing in each one who finds himself really having a very young or very old self feeling.

Our mothers, fathers, grandmothers and grandfathers, in the histories, and the stories, all the others, they all are always little babies grown old men and women or as children for us. No, old generations and past ages never have grown young men and women in them. So long ago they were, why they must be old grown men and women or as babies or as children. No, them we never can feel as young grown men and women. Such only are ourselves and our friends with whom we have been living.

And so since there is no other way to do with our kind of thinking we will make our elders to be for us the grown old men and women in our stories, or the babies or the children. We will be always, in ourselves, the young grown men and women.

And so now we begin, and with such men and women as we have old or as very little, in us, to our thinking.

One of these four women, the grandmothers old always to us the generation of grandchildren, was a sweet good woman, strong just to bear many children and then she died away and left them for that was all she knew then to do for them.

Like all good older women she had all her life born many children and she had made herself a faithful working woman to her husband who was a good enough ordinary older man.

Her husband lived some years after his wife had died away and left him.

He was just a decent well-meaning faithful good-enough ordinary man. He was honest, and he left that very strongly to his children and he worked hard, but he never came to very much with all his faithful working.

He was just a decent honest good-enough man to do ordinary working. He always was good to his wife and always liked her to be with him, and to have good children, and to help him with her working. He always liked all of his children and he always did all that he could to help them, but they were all soon strong enough to leave him, and now that his wife had died away and left him, he was not really needed much by the world or by his children.

They were good daughters and sons to him, but his sayings and his old ordinary ways of doing had not much importance for them. They were strong, all of them, in their work and in their new way of feeling and full always of their new ways of living. It was alright, he always said it to them, and he thought it so really in him, but it was all too new, it could never be any comfort to him. He had been left out of all life while he was still living. It was all too new for his feeling and his wife was no longer there to stay beside him. He felt it always in him and he sighed and at last he just slowly left off living. "Yes," he would say of his son Henry who was the one who took most care and trouble for him, "Yes, Henry, he is a good man and he knows how to make a living. Yes he is a good boy to me always but he never does anything like I tell him. It aint wrong in him, never I don't say so like that ever for him, only I don't need it any more just to go on like I was living. My wife she did always like I told her, she never knew any way to do it different, and now she is gone peace be with her, and it is all now like it was all over, and I, I got no right now to say do so to my children. I don't ever say it now ever no more to them. What have I got to do with living? I've got no place to go on now like I was really living. I got nobody now always by me to do things like I tell them. I got nothing to say now anymore to my children. I got all done with what I got to say to them. Well young folks always knows things different, and they got it right not to listen, I got nothing now really to do with their new kinds of ways of living. Anyhow Henry, he knows good how to make a living. He makes money such a way I got no right to say it different to him. He makes money and I never can see how his way he can make it and he is honest and a good man always, with all his making such a good living. And he has got right always to do like he wants it, and he is good to me always, I can't ever say it any different. He always is good to me, and the others, they come to see me always only now it is all different. My wife she stayed right by me always and the children they always got some new place where they got to go and do it different." And then the old man sighed and then soon too he died away and left them.

Henry Dehning was a grown man and for his day a rich one when his father died away and left them. Truly he had made everything for himself very different; but it is not as a young man making himself rich that we are now to feel him, he is for us an old grown man telling it all over to his children.

And it is strange how all forget when they have once made things for themselves to be very different. A man like Dehning never can feel it real to himself, things as they were in his early manhood, now that he has made his life and habits and his feelings all so different. He says it often, as we all do childhood and old age and pain and sleeping, but it can never anymore be really present to his feeling.

Now the common needs in his life are very different. No, not he, nor they all who have made it for themselves to be so different, can remember meekness, nor poor ways, nor self attendance, nor no comforts, all such things are to all of them as indifferent as if they in their own life time themselves had not made it different. It is not their not wanting to remember, these things that were so different. Nay they love to remember, and to tell it over, and most often to their children, what they have been and what they have done and how they themselves have made it all to be so different and how well it is for these children that they have had a strong father who knew how to do it so that youngsters could so have it.

Yes, they say it long and often and yet it is never real to them while they are thus talking. No it is not as really present to their thinking as it is to the young ones who never really had the feeling. These have it through their fear, which makes it for them a really present feeling. The old ones have not such a fear and they have it all only like a dim beginning, like the being as babies or as children or as grown old men and women.

And this father Dehning was always very full of such talking. He had made everything for himself and for his children. He was a good and honest man was Henry Dehning. He was strong and rich and good tempered and respected and he showed it in his look, that look that makes young people think older ones are very aged, and he loved to tell it over to his children, how he had made it all for them so they could have it and not have to work to make it different.

This father was proud of his children and yet, too, very reproachful in his feeling toward them. His wife from perhaps more than equal living with him never much regarded such a feeling in him, but to the young ones it was new for them however often it came to them, for it always meant a new fighting for the right to their kind of power that they felt strongly inside them.

But always there was a little of the dread in them that comes to even grown young men and women from an old man's sharp looking, for deep down is the fear, perhaps he really knows, his look is so outward from him, he certainly has used it all up the things inside him at which young ones are still always looking. And then comes the strong feeling, no he never has had it inside him the way that gives it a real meaning, and so the young ones are firm to go on with their fighting. And always they stay with their father and listen to him.

His wife from her more than equal living, as it sometimes is in women, has not such a dread of his really knowing when it comes to their ways of living, and then it is really only talking with him for now it is completely his own only way of living, and so she never listens to him, is deaf to him or goes away when he begins this kind of talking. But his children always stay and listen to him. They are ready very strongly to explain their new ways to him. But he does not listen to them, he goes on telling what he has done and what he thinks of them.

The young Dehnings had all been born and brought up in the town of Bridgepoint. Their mother too had been born in Bridgepoint. It was there that they had first landed, her father, a harsh man, hard to his wife and to his children but not very good with all his fierceness at knowing how to make a living, and her mother a good gentle wife who never left him, though surely he was not worthy to have her so faithful to him, and she was a good woman who with all her woe was strong to bear many children and always after she was strong to do her best for them and always strong to suffer with them.

And this harsh hard man and his good gentle little wife had many children, and one daughter had long ago married Henry Dehning. It was a happy marriage enough for both of them, their faults and the good things they each had in them made of them a man and wife to very well content all who had to do with them.

All the Dehnings were very fond of Bridgepoint. They had their city and their country house like all the people who were well to do in Bridgepoint.

Yes the Dehnings in the country were simple pleasant people. There they were a contented joyous household. All day the young ones played and bathed and rode and then the family altogether would sail and fish. Yes the Dehnings in the country were simple pleasant people. The Dehning country house was very pleasant too for all young men and boys, the uncles and the cousins of the Dehning family, who all delighted in the friendly freedom of this country home, rare in those days among this kind of people, and so the Dehning house was always full of youth and kindly ways and sport and all altogether there they all always lead a pleasant family life.

The Dehning family itself was made up of the parents and three children. They made a group very satisfying to the eye, prosperous and handsome.

Mrs. Dehning was the quintessence of loud-voiced good-looking prosperity. She was a fair heavy woman, well-looking and firmly compacted and hitting the ground as she walked with the same hard jerk with which she rebuked her husband for his sins. Yes Mrs. Dehning was a woman whose rasping insensibility to gentle courtesy deserved the prejudice one cherished against her, but she was a woman, to do her justice generous and honest, one whom one might like better the more one saw her less.

* * *

The Dehning family was made of this father and mother and three children. Mr. Dehning was very proud of his children and proud of all the things he knew that they could teach him. There were two daughters and a son of them.

Julia Dehning was named after her grandmother, but, as her father often told her, she never looked the least bit like her and yet there was a little in her that made the old world not all lost to her, a little that made one always remember that her grandmother and her father had had always a worn old world to remember.

Yes Julia looked much like her mother. That fair good-looking prosperous woman had stamped her image on each one of her children, and with her eldest, Julia, the stamp went deep, far deeper than just for the fair good-looking exterior.

Julia Dehning was now just eighteen and she showed in all its vigor, the self-satisfied crude domineering American girlhood that was strong inside her. Perhaps she was born too near to the old world to ever attain quite altogether that crude virginity that makes the American girl safe in all her liberty. Yes the American girl is a crude virgin and she is safe in her freedom.

And now, so thought her mother, and Julia was quite of the same opinion, the time had come for Julia to have a husband and to begin her real important living.

Under Julia's very American face, body, clothes and manner and her vigor of the domineering and crude virgin, there were now and then flashes of passion that lit up an older well hidden tradition. Yes in Julia Dehning the prosperous, good-looking, domineering woman was a very attractive being. Julia irradiated energy and brilliant enjoying, she was vigorous, and like her mother, fair and firmly compacted, and she was full of bright hopes, and strong in the spirit of success that she felt always in her. Julia was much given to hearty joyous laughing and to an ardent honest feeling, and she hit the ground as she walked with the same hard jerking with which her mother Mrs. Dehning always rebuked her husband's sinning. Yes Julia Dehning was bright and full of vigor, and with something always a little harsh in her, making underneath her young bright vigorous ardent honest feeling a little of the sense of rasping that was just now in her mother's talking.

And so those who read much in story books surely now can tell what to expect of her, and yet, please reader, remember that this is perhaps not the whole of our story either, neither her father for her, nor the living down her mother who is in her, for I am not ready yet to take away the character from our Julia, for truly she may work out as the story books would have her or we may find all different kinds of things for her, and so reader, please remember, the future is not yet certain for her, and be you well warned reader, from the vain-glory of being sudden in your judgment of her.

After Julia came the boy George and he was not named after his grandfather. And so it was right that in his name he should not sound as if he were the son of his father, so at least his mother decided for him, and the father, he laughed and let her do the way she liked it. And so the boy was named George and the other was there but hidden as an initial to be only used for signing.

The boy George bade fair to do credit to his christening. George Dehning now about fourteen was strong in sport and washing. He was not foreign in his washing. Oh, no, he was really an american.

It's a great question this question of washing. One never can find any one who can be satisfied with anybody else's washing. I knew a man once who never as far as any one could see ever did any washing, and yet he described another with contempt, why he is a dirty hog sir, he never does any washing. The French tell me it's the Italians who never do any washing, the French and the Italians both find the Spanish a little short in their washing, the English find all the world lax in this business of washing, and the East finds all the West a pig, which never is clean with just the little cold water washing. And so it goes.

Yes it has been said that even a flea has other little fleas to bite him, and so it is with this washing, everybody can find some one to condemn for his lack of washing. Even the man who, when he wants to take a little hut in the country to live in, and they said to him, but there is no water to have there, and he said, what does that matter, in this country one can always have wine for his drinking, he too has others who for him don't think enough about their washing; and then there is the man who takes the bath-tub out of his house because he don't believe in promiscuous bathing; and there is the plumber who says, yes I have always got to be fixing bath-tubs for other people to get clean in, and I, I haven't got time enough to wash my hands even; and then there are the French bohemians, now one never would think of them as extravagantly cleanly beings, and yet in a village in Spain they were an astonishment to all the natives, why do you do so much washing, they all demanded of them, when your skin is so white and clean even when you first begin to clean them; and then there is the dubious smelly negro woman who tells you about another woman who is as dirty as a dog and as ragged as a spring chicken, and yet some dogs certainly do sometimes do some washing and this woman had certainly not much sign of ever having had such a thing happening; and then there is the virtuous poor woman who brings her child to the dispensary for a treatment and the doctor says to her, no I won't touch her now anymore until you clean her, and the woman cries out in her indignation, what you think I am poor like a beggar, I got money enough to pay for a doctor, I show you I can hire a real doctor, and she slams the door and rushes out with her daughter. Yes it certainly is very queer in her. All this washing business is certainly most peculiar. Surely it is true that even little fleas have always littler ones to bite them.

* * *

For us now as well as for the mother the important matter in the history of the Dehning family is the marrying of Julia. I have said that a strong family likeness bound all the three children firmly to their mother. That fair good-looking prosperous woman had stamped her image on each one of her children, but with only the eldest Julia was the stamp deep, deeper than for the fair good-looking exterior.

* * *

Julia as a little girl had had the usual experiences of governess guarded children. She was first the confidant, then the advisor, and last the arranger of the love affairs of her established guardians. Then at her finishing school she became acquainted with that dubious character, the adventuress, the type to be found always in all kinds of places, a character eternally attractive in its mystery and daring, and always able to attach unto itself the most intelligent and honest of its comrades and introduce them to queer vices.

And so Julia Dehning, like all other young girls, learnt many kinds of lessons, and she saw many of the kinds of ways that lead to wisdom, and always her life was healthy vigorous and active. She learnt very well all the things young girls of her class were taught then and she learnt too, in all kinds of ways, all the things girls always can learn, somehow, to be wise in. And so Julia was well prepared now to be a woman. She had singing and piano-playing and sport and all regular school learning, she had good looks, honesty, and brilliant courage, and in her young way a certain kind of wisdom.

Always Julia was a passionate young woman and she had too a heroical kind of sweetness in her way of winning. She was a passionate young woman in the sense that always she was all alive and always all the emotions she had in her being were as intense and present to her feeling as a sensation like a pain is to others who are less alive in their living. And all this time too,

Julia Dehning was busily arranging and directing the life and aspirations of her family, for she was strong always in her good right to lead them.

In Julia Dehning all experience had gone to make her wise now in a desire for a master in the art of life, and it came to pass that in Alfred Hersland brought by a cousin to visit at the house she found a man who embodied her ideal in a way to make her heart beat with surprise.

* * *

Brother Singulars, we are misplaced in a generation that knows not Joseph.[1] We flee before the disapproval of our cousins, the courageous condescension of our friends who gallantly sometimes agree to walk the streets with us, from all them who never any way can understand why such ways and not the others are so dear to us, we fly to the kindly comfort of an older world accustomed to take all manner of strange forms into its bosom and we leave our noble order to be known under such forms as Alfred Hersland, a poor thing, and even hardly then our own.

The Herslands were a Western family. David Hersland, the father, had gone out to a Western state to make his money. His wife had been born and brought up in the town of Bridgepoint. Later Mr. Hersland had sent his son Alfred back there to go to college and then to stay on and to study to become a lawyer. Now it was some years later and Alfred Hersland had come again to Bridgepoint, to settle down there to practice law there, and to make for himself his own money.

The Hersland family had not had their money any longer than the others of this community, but they had taken to culture and to ideas quicker.

Alfred Hersland was well put together to impress a courageous crude young woman, who had an ambition for both passion and position and who needed too to have a strain of romance with them.

Not many months from this first meeting, Julia gave her answer. "Yes, I do care for you," she said, "and you and I will live our lives together, always learning things and doing things, good things they will be for us whatever other people may think or say."

* * *

1925

1. Reference to the biblical story of Joseph and his brothers (Genesis 42.8).

LUDWIG LEWISOHN
1882–1955

Ludwig Lewisohn, born in Berlin, immigrated with his parents to South Carolina in 1890. He grew up and attended school in Charleston, distinguishing himself in its high school and at the College of Charleston. He graduated at the age of nineteen with a B.A. and M.A. in literature with honors—the college awarded him an honorary doctorate in 1914. The family had been culturally assimilated in Germany; in America, they became Christians, despite his mother's having been the daughter of a rabbi. Lewisohn was an active Methodist for ten years but was nevertheless refused a position at a church-affiliated school because of his Jewish background. This event was to be replicated later in New York at Columbia University, as the excerpt from his autobiographical *Up Stream* (1922) graphically relates.

When Lewisohn entered the doctoral program at Columbia in 1902, he joined New York's literary and academic scene as well. Nevertheless, warned by his advisers that no Jew could hope for a position teaching English literature in an American university, he withdrew in 1904 before completing his doctorate. Thus began a long process of a growing commitment to Jewishness and, in the 1920s, to Zionism.

Returning to Charleston, Lewisohn embarked on a disastrous marriage in which he was sexually dissatisfied and in which divorce, which his wife steadfastly refused, was impossible to obtain—a situation that he attributed to American puritanical attitudes. He began to write stories and poems, completed a novel, and returned to New York. With the help of Theodore Dreiser, the novel was published in 1908 as *The Broken Snare*. Daring in its time, it dealt with a young woman's growing acceptance of her inner desires—including the sexual, a subject that was to occupy Lewisohn for the rest of his life. His other great theme became the pursuit of his Jewish identity and then its celebration.

After leaving Columbia, he taught German literature for a year at the University of Wisconsin and then, from 1913 to 1917, at Ohio State University. Because of his sympathy for German culture and his general lack of support for uncritical American nationalism, he was asked to leave when the United States entered the war. He returned to New York and made his way successfully as a man of letters. From 1919 to 1924, he was drama and fiction editor of the *Nation*. He was ultimately the author of acclaimed works on Goethe and other German writers as well as significant studies of American and French literature and European drama. Two additional volumes of his autobiography were *Mid-Channel* (1929) and *Haven* (1940).

Lewisohn was a formidable presence in the intellectual life of his time. In the 1920s, his novel about the devastation wrought by sexual repressiveness in marriage, *The Case of Mr. Crump* (1926), received high praise from Sigmund Freud and Thomas Mann (with whom Lewisohn carried on a long and mutually admiring literary friendship). Two years later, he published *The Island Within* (1928), a novel dealing explicitly with Jewish Americans' need to return to a strong identification with the Jewish people.

By 1920, he had become a Zionist, in 1924 undertaking a secret mission at Chaim Weizmann's urging to find out about Jewish life in Eastern Europe and Palestine. His passport was confiscated by the State Department when it learned that the woman he was traveling with, Thelma Spears, and with whom he was to live for fifteen years, was not his wife, as he had claimed. He had to remain in Europe for a decade before being allowed to return to the United States in 1954.

His relation to Zionism was stormy. The movement, wary of scandal, repudiated him when he left Thelma Spears for a third woman. Nevertheless, his strong anti-Nazi stand early on and, later, his polemics against the British for their refusal to allow refugees into Palestine returned him to favor. In 1944, Lewisohn became editor of *New Palestine*, an official organ of the Zionist Organization of America.

He became, in 1948, one of the first faculty members of the newly founded Brandeis University. He taught there until his death, often embroiled in controversy because he thought there was insufficient contact with Jewish life at Brandeis. Controversy and contention were never strangers to Lewisohn.

Lewisohn's was always a passionate voice, and *Up Stream* depicts a crucial, paradigmatic moment for many Jewish Americans in the often-inhospitable interwar years. Denied entry into the mainstream culture and institutions, often after willingly suppressing their Jewish identity, they were forced to confront that identity and frequently became, as Lewisohn did, strongly nationalistic.

From Up Stream: An American Chronicle

From *Chapter V*

THE AMERICAN DISCOVERS EXILE

I

In those days the steamers from the South landed at piers on the North River.[1] I was too deeply preoccupied with that first, tremendous, lonely plunge into the world to watch the harbor or the sky-line of New York. I stood on deck, grasping my valise tightly, holding my hat. The sharp wind was full of scurries of rain. It was almost dark when we passengers trickled across the plank into the appalling mud of the streets. The lower West side is, I still think, the dismalist part of the city. On that day, coming from the bland and familiar South and from a life that touched reality so feebly, it seemed brutal, ferocious, stark. . . . An indifferent acquaintance met me and hustled me to the nearest station of the Ninth Avenue "L."[2] We climbed the iron staircase, scrambled for tickets and were jammed into a car. It was the evening rush hour and we had barely standing room. The train rattled on its way to Harlem.[3] At one Hundred and Sixteenth Street we slid down in the elevator to the street, frantically dodged people and vehicles across Eighth Avenue, turned south and west and stood presently before one of a row of three story houses wedged in between huge, dark buildings. My guide introduced me to the boarding-house keeper, a hard-featured, heavily rouged woman who seemed in pain and in a hurry. They led me to a hall bedroom on the third floor, lit a whirring gas-jet and, in another minute, were gone. I put down my valise and took off my overcoat and stood still, quite still, between the bed and the chiffonier. I could touch one with either hand. I was in New York. I was alone.

At such moments one's intentions to conquer the world avail little. Especially if one is twenty. I heard the far away roar of New York like the roar of a sinister and soulless machine that drags men in and crunches them between its implacable wheels. It seemed to me that I would never be able to face it. I huddled in that small, cold room in an old traveling robe of my father's and bit my lips. But I had the manhood not to write home in that mood. Indeed my old stoicism had not deserted me and my parents never learned of the grinding misery of my first weeks in New York.

In the morning the October sun shone. At breakfast the landlady seemed not nearly so menacing. I may add at once that she was an intelligent and courageous woman who had suffered much and undeservedly and that we became great friends. She gave me on that first day what simple directions I needed. I left the house, walked to the corner and turned my face toward the west. Morningside Heights[4] with its many poplars rose sheer against a

1. Another name for the part of the Hudson River on the west side of Manhattan.
2. An elevated train.
3. A section of northern Manhattan.
4. An area of the Upper West Side of Manhattan, where Columbia University is located.

sparkling autumn sky. The beauty of it seemed much colder to me that day than it does now. But it was beauty—something to dwell with, to calm and to console the mind. I took heart at once and climbed the heights and presently came upon the approach to the University library. The river shone still farther to the west, with the russet palisades[5] beyond. But I hastened across the quadrangle, eager for some human contact in this new world full of cold power and forbidding brilliance.

Professor Brent of the department of English, with whom I had had some correspondence, received me with a winning kindliness. We had a talk the other day and I observed him and remembered the old days. He has grown greyer. Otherwise he is the same—the lank, unathletic but not graceless form, the oblong head lengthened by a pointed beard, the pleasant, humorous but powerful glance, the easy pose, tilted back in his chair, the eternal cigarette between his long, bony, sensitive fingers. A scholarly and poetic figure, languid enough, but capable of a steady tenacity at the urge of some noble passion of the mind. That he was a trenchant and intrepid thinker I always knew. How magnificently he would stand the ultimate intellectual test of this, or perhaps, any age, I was to learn much later. . . . He introduced me to Brewer, secretary of the department, a pale, hesitant, chill-eyed New Englander with a thin strain of rhetorical skill and literary taste.

German was to be my second "minor," largely because it would be easy and would give me more time for my English studies. And so I went to present myself to Professor Richard who had also written me a pleasant letter. I found him tall, erect, frugal and incisive of speech, a spirit of great rectitude, of a purity almost too intense to grasp the concrete forces and passions of the fevered world; clear, high-souled, a little passionless, but all that without effort or priggishness. His intellectual and artistic sympathies were, of course, limited. But within its limits his was an admirable and a manly mind.

The qualities of Brent and Richard did not, of course, reveal themselves to me at once. Nor, indeed, for long thereafter and then in private interviews and at club-meetings. The lectures of these excellent professors were dull and dispiriting to me. I found in them no living sustenance of any sort. For years I sought to grasp the reasons for this fact. I do not think I grasped them wholly until I myself began to lecture to graduate students and to have such students in my own seminar. I came to the university with the reading I have described. I knew all the books that one was required to know in the various lecture courses. What I wanted was ideas, interpretative, critical, aesthetic, philosophical, with which to vivify, to organize, to deepen my knowledge, on which to nourish and develop my intellectual self. And my friends, the professors, ladled out information. Poor men, how could they help it? I thought in those days that all graduate students knew what I and a small group of my friends knew. I am aware now of the literally incredible ignorance of the average bachelors of our colleges. . . . I cannot, of course, absolve the professors entirely, though only the rigorous veracity that gives its meaning to this narrative can force me to admit even so much of friends who have stood by me so long and so wholeheartedly as Brent and Richard. They did not give themselves enough, nor freely enough. They did not realize that, the elementary tools of knowledge once gained, there is but one thing

5. The cliffs on the New Jersey shore of the Hudson River, visible from Manhattan.

that can teach men and that is the play of a large and an incisive personality. In a word, I was an ardent disciple and I found no master. So I drifted and occasionally "cut" lectures and wrote my reports and passed creditable examinations without doing a page of the required reading. I had done it all! I read for myself in entirely new directions—books that changed the whole tenor of my inner life—and struggled to make a living and wrote verses and walked and talked and sat in bar-rooms and cheap eating-houses with my friend Ellard—my friend of friends, whom I found at this time and who is still *animae dimidium meae*.[6]

II

It was on a grey, windy November forenoon that we first talked on the steps of Fayerwether Hall. He was tall and lank and thin to emaciation. An almost ragged overcoat fluttered behind him, a shapeless, discolored hat tilted a little on his head. His delicate nostrils seemed always about to quiver, his lips to be set in a half-petulant, half-scornful determination. From under the hat shone two of the most eloquent eyes—fiery and penetrating, gloomy and full of laughter in turn—that were ever set in a human head. He spoke with large, loose, expressive gestures and with a strange, abrupt way of ending his sentences. I felt drawn to him at once. Freedom and nobility seemed to clothe him and a stoic wildness. A young eagle with plumage ruffled by the storm. . . . ! I asked him, I don't know why, whether he wrote verse. And when he said that he did I knew instinctively that his verses were better than mine, far better, and curiously enough I was not sorry but glad, and, in a way, elated. I cannot tell at this distance of time how rapidly our friendship ripened, but I know that we soon saw a great deal of each other.

He lived in a small, crowded room up four flights of stairs. A large kerosene lamp stood on his study table. A sharp, triangular shadow lay steadily across bed and wall. He was tormented by poverty and love and by the intellectual bleakness that was all about us. For two years he had been at Bonn and though by blood a New England Brahmin[7] of the purest strain, the sunny comradeship and spiritual freedom of the Rhineland city had entered into his very being. I see him standing there in the blue cloud of our cigarette smoke chanting me his verses. I had never met a poet before and poetry meant everything to me in those days. A lovely or a noble line, a sonorous or a troubling turn of rhythm could enchant me for days. So that I was wholly carried away by my friend and his poems. And we both felt ourselves to be in some sort exiles and wandered the streets as the fall deepened into winter, engaged in infinite talk. We watched as evening came the bursting of the fiery blooms of light over the city and again, late at night, met in some eating house or bar-room on Amsterdam Avenue where the belated, frozen car men watched us with heavy curiosity. We found ourselves then, as we have found ourselves ever since, in complete harmony as to the deeper things in life. That that harmony has become, if anything, more entire during the past seven crucial years of the world's history,[8] I account as one of the few sus-

6. I.e., a person (or friend) one values most (Latin, a quotation from Horace).

7. Brahmins were the highest caste in India. The term "New England Brahmin" denotes people of superior intellectual ability, often from upper-class old New England families. "Bonn": there is an old German university in the town of Bonn.

8. A reference to the years of World War I (1914–18) and its aftermath—the Versailles Treaty, the League of Nations, the Russian Revolution (1917),

taining factors in my life and to it I attach, not foolishly I think, an almost mystical significance. . . .

* * *

Other friendships there were for me at the university, pleasant enough at that time, but all impermanent save one more. I still count George Fredericks, sober-minded, virile, generous, among my chosen comrades. And I still think, with much kindness, of G., now a college professor in the East, a fine, pure spirit, a New Englander like Ellard, but unlike him striving quite in vain to transcend the moral and intellectual parochialism of his section and his blood. But, indeed, I sought no companionship, taking only such as came my way. For mean anxieties soon beset me as my slender borrowings came to an end and I tramped the streets in search of tutoring. A crowd of queer and colorful and comic scenes—sorrowful and humiliating enough at that time—floats into my mind. In a gorgeous palace near Central Park[9] the footman eyed me contemptuously and an elderly woman tried to hire me to conduct her evidently rowdy boys to and from school. I refused curtly to do a nurse-maid's work. But walking across the rich carpet to the door I heard my torn shoes make a squdgy sound and almost repented. In another elaborate establishment I gave, in a very ready-made Louis XV room[1] a single lesson to the young daughter of the house. Next day a note came dispensing with my services. I wasn't surprised. The girl was pretty and I was hungry for charm and love and she had evidently not disliked me. . . . At last I got a couple of boys to tutor (one a deaf-mute) and lessons in scientific German to give to the staff of one of the city institutions. Two evenings a week I was ferried across Hellgate[2] in the icy wind to give this instruction. It was a bleak and tiresome business, but it paid room and board and tobacco and an occasional glass of beer.

* * *

V

The various experiences which I have set down so briefly extended over two years. At the end of the first year I duly took my master's degree and applied for a fellowship. Among the group of students to which I belonged it was taken for granted that, since Ellard had completed his studies for the doctorate, I would undoubtedly be chosen. I record this, heaven knows, not from motives of vanity but as part of the subtler purpose of this story. The faculty elected my friend G. I went, with a heavy heart, to interview Professor Brewer, not to push my claims to anything, but because I was at my wits' end. I dreaded another year of tutoring and of living wretchedly from hand to mouth, without proper clothes, without books. Brewer leaned back in his chair, pipe in hand, with a cool and kindly smile. "It seemed to us," he stuttered, "that the university hasn't had its full influence on you." He suggested their disappointment in me and, by the subtlest of stresses, their sorrow over this disappointment. I said that I had been struggling for a live-

among other important events. "Frozen car men": streetcar operators and conductors working during the cold winter.
9. A large park in the center of Manhattan.

1. Designed in the style made popular during the reign of the French king Louis XV (1710–1774).
2. A waterway separating Manhattan and the Bronx.

lihood and that, nevertheless, my examinations had uniformly received high grades and my papers, quite as uniformly, the public approval of Brent and himself. He avoided a direct answer by explaining that the department had recommended me for a scholarship for the following year. The truth is, I think, that Brewer, excessively mediocre as he was, had a very keen tribal instinct of the self-protective sort and felt in me—what I was hardly yet consciously—the implacable foe of the New England dominance over our national life. I wasn't unaware of his hostility, but I had no way of provoking a franker explanation.

I forgot my troubles in three beautiful months at home—three months seemed so long then—or, rather, I crowded these troubles from my field of consciousness. I wouldn't even permit the fact that I wasn't elected to a scholarship to depress me. Brewer wrote a letter of regret and encouragement that was very kindly in tone. The pleasant implication of that letter was, of course, a spiritual falsehood of the crassest. He knew then precisely what he knew and finally told me ten months later. But his kind has a dread of the bleak weather of the world of truth, and approaches it gingerly, gradually, with a mincing gait. He, poor man, was probably unconscious of all that. In him, as in all like him, the corruption of the mental life is such that the boundaries between the true and the false are wholly obliterated.

In the passionate crises of the second year I often walked as in a dream. And I was encouraged by the fact that the department arranged a loan for my tuition. In truth, I was deeply touched by so unusual a kindness and I feel sure that the suggestion came from Brent. If so, Brewer again did me a fatal injury by not preventing that kindness. For he had then, I must emphasize, the knowledge he communicated to me later—the knowledge that held the grim upshot of my university career.

Spring came and with it the scramble for jobs among the second year men. My friends were called in to conferences with Brewer; I was not. They discussed vacancies, chances here and there. It wasn't the chagrin that hurt so; it wasn't any fear for myself. After all I was only twenty-two and I was careless of material things. I thought of my father and my mother in the cruel sunshine of Queenshaven. Their hope and dream and consolation were at stake. I could see them, not only by day, but in the evening, beside their solitary lamps, looking up from their quiet books, thinking of me and of the future. . . . I remembered how my father had believed in certain implications of American democracy. I remembered . . . I was but a lad, after all. I couldn't face Brewer's cool and careless smile. I wrote him a letter—a letter which, in its very earnestness and passionate veracity must have struck like a discord upon the careful arrangements of his safe and proper nature. For in it I spoke of grave things gravely, not jestingly, as one should to be a new England gentleman: I spoke of need and aspiration and justice. His answer lies before me now and I copy that astonishingly smooth and chilly document verbatim: "It is very sensible of you to look so carefully into your plans at this juncture, because I do not at all believe in the wisdom of your scheme. A recent experience has shown me how terribly hard it is for a man of Jewish birth to get a good position. I had always suspected that it was a matter worth considering, but I had not known how widespread and strong it was. While we shall be glad to do anything we can for you, therefore, I cannot help feeling that the chances are going to be greatly against you."

I sat in my boarding-house room playing with this letter. I seemed to have no feeling at all for the moment. By the light of a sunbeam that fell in I saw that the picture of my parents on the mantelpiece was very dusty. I got up and wiped the dust off carefully. Gradually an eerie, lost feeling came over me. I took my hat and walked out and up Amsterdam Avenue, farther and farther to High Bridge and stood on the bridge and watched the swift, tiny tandems on the Speedway below and the skiffs gliding up and down the Harlem River. A numbness held my soul and mutely I watched life, like a dream pageant, float by me. . . . I ate nothing till evening when I went into a bakery and, catching sight of myself in a mirror, noted with dull objectivity my dark hair, my melancholy eyes, my unmistakably Semitic nose. . . . An outcast. . . . A sentence arose in my mind which I have remembered and used ever since. So long as there is discrimination, there is exile. And for the first time in my life my heart turned with grief and remorse to the thought of my brethren in exile all over the world. . . .

VI

The subconscious self has a tough instinct of self-preservation. It thrusts from the field of vision, as Freud[3] has shown, the painful and the hostile things of life. Thus I had forgotten, except at moments of searching reflection, the social fate of my father and mother, my failure to be elected to the fraternity at college, and other subtler hints and warnings. I had believed the assertion and made it myself that equality of opportunity was implicit in the very spiritual foundations of the Republic. This is what I wanted to believe, what I needed to believe in order to go about the business of my life at all. I had listened with a correct American scorn to stories of how some distant kinsman in Germany, many years ago, had had to receive Christian baptism in order to enter the consular service of his country. At one blow now all these delusions were swept away and the facts stood out in the sharp light of my dismay. Discrimination there was everywhere. But a definite and public discrimination, is at least, an enemy in the open. In pre-war Germany, for instance, no Jew could be prevented from entering the academic profession. Unless he was very brilliant and productive his promotion was less rapid than that of his Gentile colleagues. He knew that and reckoned with it. He knew, too, for instance, that he could not become senior professor of German at Berlin (only associate professor like the late R. M. Meyer), nor Kultusminister,[4] but he could become a full professor of Latin or philosophy, and, of course, of all the sciences. I am not defending these restrictions and I think the argument for them—that the German state was based upon an ethnic homogeneity which corresponds to a spiritual oneness—quite specious. I am contrasting these conditions with our own. We boast our equality and freedom and call it Americanism and speak of other countries with disdain. And so one is unwarned, encouraged and flung into the street. With exquisite courtesy, I admit. And the consciousness of that personal courtesy soothes the minds of our Gentile friends. . . . It will be replied that there are a num-

3. Sigmund Freud (1856–1939), a Viennese Jew, was a physician and the founder of psychoanalysis.

4. Minister of Public Worship and Education (German).

ber of Jewish scholars in American colleges and universities. There are. The older men got in because nativistic anti-Semitism was not nearly as strong twenty-five years ago as it is to-day. Faint remnants of the ideals of the early Republic still lingered in American life. But in regard to the younger men I dare to assert that in each case they were appointed through personal friendship, family or financial prestige or some other abnormal relenting of the iron prejudice which is the rule. But that prejudice has not, to my knowledge, relented in a single instance in regard to the teaching of English. So that our guardianship of the native tongue is far fiercer than it is in an, after all, racially homogeneous state like Germany. Presidents, deans and departmental heads deny this fact or gloss it over in public. Among themselves it is admitted as a matter of course.

* * *

I do not wish to speak bitterly or flippantly. I am approaching the analysis of thoughts and events beside which my personal fate is less than nothing. And I need but think of my Queenshaven youth or of some passage of Milton or Arnold,[5] or of those tried friendships that are so large a part of the unalterable good of life, or of the bright hair and grey English eyes of my own wife, to know that I can never speak as an enemy of the Anglo-Saxon race.[6] But unless that race abandons its duality of conscience, unless it learns to honor and practice a stricter spiritual veracity, it will either destroy civilization through disasters yet unheard of or sink into a memory and into the shadow of a name.

1922

5. Matthew Arnold (1822–1888) and John Milton (1608–1674), major English writers.
6. The name originally applied to the Germanic people who colonized southern England in the 5th century C.E. and dominated the region until the Norman Conquest (1066 C.E.). It came to mean, from the late 19th century onward, white Gentiles of English-speaking lands or of British descent.

A. LEYELES (AARON GLANZ)
1889–1966

A. Leyeles, pseudonym for Aaron Glanz, was the chief theorist for introspectivism, the modernist literary movement in American Yiddish that he, Jacob Glatstein, and N. B. Minkov established in 1919.

Born in Włocławek, Poland, into a family descended from famous rabbis, Glanz grew up in Łódź, where his father taught in a Jewish school and occasionally wrote for the Hebrew press. He attended his father's school until age twelve and then the local Russian school. From 1905 until 1908, he studied at the University of London and became active in the Socialist-Zionist party. He immigrated to the United States in 1909 and, becoming involved in the Socialist-Territorialist party, traveled throughout the United States and Canada as its emissary. He also studied literature at Columbia University between 1910 and 1913.

An activist for Yiddish culture in the United States, Glanz helped establish Yiddish schools in Toronto, Winnipeg, Rochester (New York), Chicago, and Sioux City, and taught at the first Yiddish school in New York. He remained involved in the territorial movement, exploring the possibility of a Jewish immigrant settlement in Alaska. A cofounder of the Workmen's Circle schools, Leyeles, throughout his life, took leadership roles in the major Yiddish cultural and literary organizations in the United States, such as the YIVO Institute, the Yiddish Pen Club, the World Congress for Jewish Culture, and the Central Yiddish Culture Organization.

Glanz started publishing in the New York and Vilna Yiddish presses while living in London in 1906. Upon the publication of several poems in 1914, he began to use the pseudonym A. Leyeles, under which he published his most serious poetry throughout his career, although he was known publicly as A. Glanz-Leyeles. At this time, he joined the staff of the Yiddish daily the *Tog*, where for more than fifty years he served as a political and literary editor and wrote a weekly column on world literature and culture.

Although his first book was a treatise on territorialism, published in German in 1913, Leyeles wrote poetry in Yiddish. His first collection of poems, *Labirint* (Labyrinth), came out in New York in 1918 and his second, *Yungharbst* (Young Autumn), in 1922. These two books rejected traditional verse form and exemplified the poetic and aesthetic theories that Leyeles, Glatstein, and Minkov put forth in their anthology *In Zikh* (1920). Around the journal *Inzikh*, published from 1920 through 1940, a group of poets formed who called themselves the *inzikhistn*, or introspectivists.

The principles put forth by Leyeles, Glatstein, and Minkov in their manifesto of 1919 included an emphasis on the integrity of poetry as the product and process of the individual psyche, which filters and mirrors all reality—aesthetic, personal, political, social—through the emotions, senses, and intellect. The introspectivists advanced a theory of the kaleidoscopic: the chaos of fragmented perception characteristic of the modern world, which the poem makes whole through juxtaposition, layering, and association. Emphasizing the individuality of rhythm and free verse, the introspectivists wrote with exquisite control of poetic form as well as with an unparalleled awareness of the Yiddish language as a complex poetic instrument.

The poems of Leyeles's third full-length book, *Rondeaux and Other Poems* (1926), celebrate the city, with its artificial constructions of urban culture and architecture, and experiment with verse forms that range from the classical strophes of the rondeau, villanelle, and sonnet to free verse. *Fabius Lind* (1937) presents the spiritual autobiography of an urban modernist in verse; it is prefaced by an essay restating the poet's credo. *A yid oyfn yam* (A Jew at Sea) (1947) is a prize-winning collection of Holocaust poems. *Baym fus fun barg* (At the Foot of the Mountain) (1957) advocates a poetry of ideas joined with emotions, a poetry of feeling infused with the intellect. In his 1963 book, *Amerike un ikh* (America and I), Leyeles celebrates American ideals.

Leyeles published four verse dramas, two of which, *Shlomo Molkho* (1926) and *Asher Lemlen* (1928), center on conflicting ideas of Jewish peoplehood and survival. *Shlomo Molkho*, from which we include a poem here, presents the conflict between two historical figures, David Reuveni, who advocated Jewish militarism as a means of returning to the ancestral land, and his student Solomon Molcho, a sixteenth-century Marrano who wanted the Jews to redeem all humankind through their sufferings in the Diaspora yet who was, in the end, martyred by the Inquisition. This play was performed in the Vilna ghetto in 1941. *Asher Lemlen*, set in Germany just before the Lutheran Reformation, showed how Jewish messianic longing was defeated by the harsh realities of politics and society.

Leyeles collected the best of his essays from his column in the *Tog* in *Velt un vort* (World and Word) (1958). He translated many English, Russian, and Polish works into Yiddish, wrote poems for children, contributed to literary journals, and edited a series of miscellanies with Joseph Opatoshu. Two years before his death, Leyeles's visit to Israel inspired him to write biblical poems, infused with the poetic skill and music of his earlier work.

Fabius Lind's Days[1]

Fabius Lind's days are running out in blood.
Red serpents of failures empty his veins.
In his head—white muddy stains. Confusion.
And a heavy load in on his heart.
He could have . . .
He could have . . .
Gray spiderwebs of melancholy
Cover his mind, veil his eyes
And a strange taut bow
Aims at the tip of his nose.
Fabius Lind, sunk in contemplation,
In talking, in reading, tightens—
Out of sheer being lost—
The noose around his neck.

Why can't Fabius Lind hold on to
The coattails of these times
And stride in the rows of all the marchers?
Why can't he swing back to his childhood playground
And bring his flutes to play
The song of calm?
Why is he so indifferent at funerals,
So nervous at a birth?
Why can't he grab the two whores—
death and life
And let himself go in a holy-foolish dance?

Whom does he ask?
No one. Just himself.
If he could brain-out an answer,
He would not have asked.

In these days of straight rails, Fabius Lind
Is not awake.
He strays for hours, for days,
And dreams of pure isn'ts.
A time that isn't,
A land that isn't,
People that aren't,
A Fabius Lind who doesn't exist.
He could have . . .
He could have . . .
Yes, yes, he could have!

1. Translated by Benjamin Harshav and Barbara Harshav. "Fabius Lind": the central fictional character in Leyeles's 1937 book *Fabius Lind*.

The desire, the thought, flies away on an uninvited wind
And comes back in a ball of smoke.
The calculating mind has never served Fabius Lind.

1937

Shlomo Molkho Sings on the Eve of His Burning[1]

Night, metamorphoser of forms,
You who pile up doubts in your darknesses,
Who weaken a weak and weary soul—
Be now the witness of my truth.
Night, awakener of hidden fears,
You who magnify dangers,
Who extort unwanted confessions from split lives—
Now, put your black seal
On the joyful, liberated will
Of my confession.

Soon it will be here—my most truthful hour,
Ash and nothingness will remain of my proud fame.
Soon the fire will strip me
Of the false plight that deluded me with sweetness.
Soon the great silence will be here.

Oh, sweeter than all lusts of the body
Was the belief of the crowds:
Redeemer! Leader!
I clung to them with passion,
Each throb of blood in me rejoiced:
Redeemer. Leader. I.

In sinful clandestine silence
I sang a song of my I.
And while, like multitudes of sand,
My faithful gathered around me,
While I selected words to match their heavy anguish,
I built a sparkling throne
For myself.
Frivolously, my arrogance embraced my faith.
Their belief grew, and with it
My haughty head.
And my loneliness too, and the fear—
Of myself.
I saw their faith become a heart with no eyes,

1. Translated by Benjamin Harshav and Barbara Harshav. "Shlomo Molkho": Or Molcho, Solomon. Born Diego Pires in 1500 in Portugal of Marrano parents. Announced the coming of the Messiah, obtained the protection of the Pope and aroused the expectations of European Jews. In 1532, was burned at the stake by the Inquisition in Mantua [Benjamin Harshav and Barbara Harshav's note].

I saw their blind pain spread
Like a carpet
Before the treading, fondled feet
Of the redeemer;
And like stairs—
For the climbing, insolent steps
Of the leader.
Appalled, I saw
A forest of wills, tall as cedars,
Fall under the axe of falsehood:
The hewer sinks in indignity,
And the great bright goal—
The estranged wonder-bird—
Flies back, abashed,
To his distant, hidden nest.

Now Shlomo Molkho is humble and silent with joy.
He sensed in time the redeemer's poison
And exchanged it
For the good, free, pure breath
Of the flame.

1947

The God of Israel[1]

The God of Israel is not rich.
I saw the Sistine Chapel,
Notre-Dame, the Cathedral of Cologne[2]—
You can feast your eyes on them, you can enjoy.

The God of Israel is stingy.
He won't fill his museum with statues,
Paintings, altars, thrones,
Purple gowns, three-tiered crowns,
He does not wish to live in a Palais.[3]
The Jewish museum has a modest display.
A Chanukah-lamp, a curtain, a scroll,
A spice-box, tefillin, a pointing Hand,
A menorah, a Torah Crown, tools for circumcision,
And an old, ancient manuscript.[4]

1. Translated by Benjamin Harshav and Barbara Harshav.
2. The largest Gothic church in northern Europe, it was built from the 13th through the 19th centuries and is filled with relics and art treasures. "Sistine Chapel": the papal chapel in the Vatican Palace in Rome, built 1473–81 and famous for its ceiling frescoes painted by Michelangelo. "Notre-Dame": i.e., Paris Cathedral, one of the earliest and most famous of the Gothic cathedrals of the Middle Ages; noted for its architecture, sculptures, and stained glass.
3. Palace (French).
4. Objects used in Jewish religious rituals. "Chanukah-lamp": a nine-branched candelabrum used to celebrate Chanukah. "Curtain": i.e., an embroidered curtain that covers the opening of the Holy Ark, which holds the Torah scrolls. "Scroll": i.e., a Torah scroll. "Spice-box": a container of fragrant spices used in the Havdalah service, which marks the end of the Sabbath. "Tefillin": phylacteries, small leather boxes containing parchment on which biblical verses are written, that a Jewish man binds with leather straps to his forehead and left arm during morning prayer. "Pointing Hand": a *yad*, a small pointer often in the shape of a hand,

And another manuscript and another manuscript,
Entangled, bound, locked together.
Letters in love with letters.

What does the God of Israel ask?
What does the God of Israel demand?
The God of Israel is a just demander.
The God of Israel is a strict demander.
The God of Israel is a stingy demander:
Search by yourself, research by yourself, suffer yourself—
For your own and for my honor.

In a gray-gray once-upon-a-time,
From a mountain-top into a valley,
He dropped two handfuls of letters,
Scattered them over the roads of the earth.
They sparkled with speech, blazed with sayings,[5]
And since then—
For thousands of years we seek them,
For thousands of years we save them,
For thousands of years we explain them,
And there is no solution on earth
For the letters, the sayings, the words.

Another manuscript, and another manuscript,
Entangled, bound, locked together—
Letters in love with letters.

1947

New York[1]

Metal. Granite. Uproar. Racket. Clatter.
Automobile. Bus. Subway. El.
Burlesque. Grotesque. Café. Movie-theater.
Electric light in screeching maze. A spell.

In eyes—a pending verdict, faces—strangers:
No smile, no Bless-you, no nod, no gentle word.
And straying, rambling, imminent danger.
And jungle, crush, upheaval, wild absurd.

1918 — 1918, 1956

used to keep one's place while reading from the Torah scroll. "Menorah": a seven-branched candelabrum used in the synagogue. In America, *menorah* also denotes a Chanukah lamp. "Torah Crown": a decorative crown made of precious metal that is placed on top of the Torah scroll. "Tools for circumcision": special knives and clamps used in circumcising eight-day-old baby boys.

5. Leyeles retells and revises a legend from the *Zohar* (Book of Splendor—the collection of works central to Jewish mysticism): before the creation of the world, the letters of the Hebrew alphabet descended from God's crown, where they had been written with a pen of flames, and each letter requested that God create the world through it.

1. Translated by Benjamin Harshav and Barbara Harshav.

MICHAEL GOLD
1893–1967

Born in extreme poverty as Itzok (later Irwin) Granich on New York's Lower East Side, Michael Gold took his pen name in 1921, probably to avoid the attention of Attorney General A. Mitchell Palmer's raids upon radicals and their organizations. Gold had become radicalized in 1914, contributing until 1917 to publications like the socialist *New York Call* and *Masses*. He wrote socially conscious one-act plays for the Provincetown Players and in 1918 fled to Mexico to avoid the draft. In the 1920s, he edited *Liberator* and began a long career as editor of the *New Masses*, an organ of the Communist party. Gold was a party activist and a regular columnist for the *Daily Worker* and the *People's World* until the end of his life, despite the Moscow Trials, the Nazi-Soviet Pact, and the murder of Jewish intellectuals in Stalin's Soviet Union.

Gold wrote many tendentious plays and stories in his early years and much bitter criticism later, but only his account of impoverished Jewish life on the Lower East Side at the turn of the century, *Jews without Money* (1930), promises to endure. Based on an idealized version of his own life and family—a hard-working father disappointed in the promise of America; a noble, loving, and strong mother holding the family and much of the neighborhood together; a young boy growing to manhood in the midst of grinding poverty and demeaning work, redeemed only, in an early version of the book, by his conversion at the very end to the promise of a workers' revolution—it has gone through numerous translations and editions. *Fifty Cents a Night* is the opening chapter of the novel, showing the widespread prostitution and its attendant evils that for some Jews were the reality of the failed American dream.

From Jews without Money

Fifty Cents a Night

1

I can never forget the East Side[1] street where I lived as a boy.

It was a block from the notorious Bowery, a tenement canyon hung with fire-escapes,[2] bed-clothing, and faces.

Always these faces at the tenement windows. The street never failed them. It was an immense excitement. It never slept. It roared like a sea. It exploded like fireworks.

People pushed and wrangled in the street. There were armies of howling pushcart peddlers. Women screamed, dogs barked and copulated. Babies cried.

A parrot cursed. Ragged kids played under truck-horses. Fat housewives fought from stoop to stoop. A beggar sang.

At the livery stable coach drivers lounged on a bench. They hee-hawed with laughter, they guzzled cans of beer.

Pimps, gamblers and red-nosed bums; peanut politicians, pugilists in

1. Below Fourteenth Street, the East Side of Manhattan was home to many immigrants from Eastern Europe.
2. A street of saloons and drunks. "Tenement": an apartment house that meets minimum standards for health and safety but provides cheap housing for the urban poor.

sweaters; tinhorn sports[3] and tall longshoremen in overalls. An endless pageant of East Side life passed through the wicker doors of Jake Wolf's saloon.

The saloon goat lay on the sidewalk, and dreamily consumed a *Police Gazette*.

East Side mothers with heroic bosoms pushed their baby carriages, gossiping. Horse cars jingled by. A tinker hammered at brass. Junkbells clanged.[4]

Whirlwinds of dust and newspaper. The prostitutes laughed shrilly. A prophet passed, an old-clothes Jew with a white beard. Kids were dancing around the hurdy-gurdy. Two bums slugged each other.

Excitement, dirt, fighting, chaos! The sound of my street lifted like the blast of a great carnival or catastrophe. The noise was always in my ears. Even in sleep I could hear it; I can hear it now.

2

The East Side of New York was then the city's red light district, a vast 606 playground under the business management of Tammany Hall.[5]

The Jews had fled from the European pogroms; with prayer, thanksgiving and solemn faith from a new Egypt into a new Promised Land.

They found awaiting them the sweatshops,[6] the bawdy houses and Tammany Hall.

There were hundreds of prostitutes on my street. They occupied vacant stores, they crowded into flats and apartments in all the tenements. The pious Jews hated the traffic. But they were pauper strangers here; they could do nothing. They shrugged their shoulders, and murmured: "This is America." They tried to live.

They tried to shut their eyes. We children did not shut our eyes. We saw and knew.

On sunshiny days the whores sat on chairs along the sidewalks. They sprawled indolently, their legs taking up half the pavements. People stumbled over a gauntlet of whores' meaty legs.

The girls gossiped and chirped like a jungle of parrots. Some knitted shawls and stockings. Others hummed. Others chewed Russian sunflower seeds and monotonously spat out the shells.

The girls winked and jeered, made lascivious gestures at passing males. They pulled at coat-tails and cajoled men with fake honeyed words. They called their wares like pushcart peddlers. At five years I knew what it was they sold.

The girls were naked under flowery kimonos. Chunks of breast and belly occasionally flashed. Slippers hung from their feet; they were always ready for "business."

3. Cheats and braggarts, gamblers, who run dice games. The tinhorn was the cup in which the dice were shaken. "Livery stable": a place where cab horses were quartered.

4. Bells rung by dealers collecting cast-off household goods. "*Police Gazette*": a weekly paper published from the 1840s through the 1870s that was concerned with boxing, horse racing, other sports, betting, and crime. "Horse cars": streetcars drawn by horses. "Tinker": an itinerant mender of household utensils.

5. Headquarters of the political organization that controlled New York City from 1865 to 1871; more generally, a corrupt organization that exercises political control over a municipality. "606": salvorsan, a remedy for syphilis.

6. Small factories in which workers work in unsanitary conditions for long hours at low pay. "Pogroms": violent attacks against Jews in Russia between 1881 and the Russian Revolution in 1917. Pogroms also occurred in Germany and Poland under Hitler. "Promised Land": the Jews were promised entry into a land of "milk and honey" when they escaped from slavery in Egypt (Exodus 3.17).

Earth's trees, grass, flowers could not grow on my street; but the rose of syphilis bloomed by night and by day.

3

It was a spring morning. I had joined, as on other mornings, my gang of little Yids gathered on the sidewalk. There were six or seven of us.

Spring excited us. The sky was blue over our ghetto.[7] The sidewalks sparkled, the air was fresh. Everything seemed hopeful. In winter the streets were vacant, now people sprang up by magic.

Parades of Jews had appeared in these first soft days, to walk, to talk. To curse, to bargain, to smoke pipes, to sniff like hibernating bears at the spring.

Pushcarts appeared. Pale bearded peddlers crawled from their winter cellars, again shouted in the street. Oranges blazed on the carts; calico was for sale, clocks, sweet potatoes, herrings, potted geraniums and goloshes. Spring ushered in a huge, ragged fair.

We spun tops on the sidewalks. We chased street cars and trucks and stole dangerous rides. Nigger,[8] our leader, taught us how to steal apples from a pushcart. We threw a dead cat into the store of the Chinese laundryman. He came out, a yellow madman, a hot flat-iron in his hand. We ran away.

Nigger then suggested a new game: that we tease the prostitutes.

We began with Rosie. She lounged in a tenement hallway, a homely little woman in a red shawl. Ready, go. We spurted before her in short dashes, our hearts beating with danger and joy.

We screamed at her, making obscene gestures:

"Fifty cents a night! That's what you charge; fifty cents a night! Yah, yah, yah!"

Rosie started. A look came into her sleepy eyes. But she made no answer. She drew her shawl about her. We were disappointed. We had hoped she would rave and curse.

"Fifty cents a night! Fifty cents a night!"

Rosie bit her lip. Spots appeared on her sallow face. That was all; she wouldn't talk. The game didn't work. We tried again. This time she turned on her heel and walked into the gloomy hallway. We looked for another victim.

4

A fat, haughty prostitute sat on a chair two tenements away. She wore a red kimono decorated with Japanese cherry trees, mountains, waterfalls and old philosophers. Her black hair was fastened by a diamond brooch. At least a million dollars' worth of paste diamonds glittered from her fat fingers.

She was eating an apple. She munched it slowly with the dignity of a whole Chamber of Commerce at its annual banquet. Her lap spread before her like a table.

We scampered around her in a monkey gang. We yelled those words whose terrible meaning we could not fully guess:

7. That part of a city where, formerly, Jews had been forced to live separate from the dominant Christians. Ghettos were reinstituted in Poland and Germany during World War II.

8. At the time, a nickname for a person of dark complexion. It was—and is—an extremely offensive term when applied to an African American.

"Fifty cents a night!"

Aha. This time the plans of our leader worked. The game was a good one. The fat prostitute purpled with rage. Her eyes bulged with loathing. Sweat appeared on her painted cheeks. She flung her apple at us, and screamed: "Thieves! American bummers! Loafers! Let me catch you! I'll rip you in half!"

She spat like a poisoned cat. She shook her fist. It was fun. The whole street was amused.

"Fifty cents a night! Yah, yah, yah!"

Then I heard my mother's voice calling me from the tenement window. I hated to leave the fun, just when it was good. But my mother called me again and again. So up I went.

I entered blinking from the sunlight. I was surprised to find Rosie sitting in our kitchen. She was crying. My mother pounced upon me and slapped my face.

"Murderer!" she said, "why did you make Rosie cry?"

"Did I make her cry?" I asked stupidly.

My mother grabbed me, and laid me across her knee. She beat me with the cat-o'-nine-tails.[9] I howled and wriggled, but she gave me a good licking. Rosie stood there pleading for me. The poor girl was sorry she had gotten me this licking. My mother was in a rage.

"This will teach you not to play with that Nigger! This will teach you not to learn all those bad, nasty things in the street!"

Vain beating; the East Side street could not be banished with a leather strap. It was my world; it was my mother's world, too. We *had* to live in it, and learn what it chose to teach us.

5

I will always remember that licking, not because it humiliated me, or taught me anything, but because the next day was my fifth birthday.

My father was young then. He loved good times. He took the day off from work and insisted that I be given a birthday party. He bought me a velvet suit with lace collar and cuffs, and patent leather shoes. In the morning he insisted that we all go to be photographed. He made my mother wear her black plush[1] gown. He made her dress my sister in the Scotch plaid. Himself he arrayed in his black suit that made him look like a lawyer.

My mother groaned as we walked through the street. She hated new shoes, new clothes, all fuss or feathers. I was miserable, too. My gang saw me, and snickered at my velvet suit.

But my father was happy, and so was my sister, Esther. They chattered like two children.

It was solemn at the photographer's. My father sat stiffly in a dark carved throne. My mother stood upright beside him, with one hand on his shoulder, to show her wedding ring. My sister rested against my father's knee. I stood on the other side of the throne, holding a basket of artificial flowers.

The bald, eager little photographer disappeared behind a curtain. He snapped his fingers before us, and said, "Watch the birdie." I watched, my

9. A whip made of nine knotted cords fastened to a handle.

1. A fabric with a high pile, less dense than velvet.

neck hurting me because of the clamp.[2] Something clicked; the picture was taken. We went home, exhausted but triumphant.

In the evening the birthday party was held. Many tenement neighbors came with their children. Brandy was drunk, sponge cake and herring eaten, songs were sung. Every one pinched my cheek and praised me. They prophesied I would be a "great man."

Then there was talk. Reb Samuel the umbrella maker was a pious and learned Jew. Whenever he was in a group the talk turned to holy things.

"I have read in the paper," said my father, "that a Dybbuk[3] has entered a girl on Hester Street. But I don't believe it. Are there Dybbuks in America, too?"

"Of course," said Reb Samuel quietly.

Mendel Bum laughed a raucous brandy laugh. He had eaten of everything; the sponge cake, the herring, the quince jam, the apples, *kraut knishes*, fried fish and cheese *blintzes*. He had drunk from every bottle, the fiery Polish *slivovitz*, the *wishniak*,[4] the plum brandy, the Roumanian wine. Now his true nature appeared.

"I don't believe in Dybbuks!" he laughed. "It is all a grandmother story!"

My father banged on the table and leaped to his feet. "Silence, atheist!" he shouted, "in my house we want no wisdom from you!"

Mendel shrugged his shoulders.

"Well," said Reb Samuel quietly, "in the synagogue at Korbin,[5] a girl was once brought. Her lips did not move. From her belly came shrieks and groans of a Dybbuk. He had entered her body while she was in the forest. She was dying with agony.

"The Rabbi studied the matter. Then he instructed two men to take her in a wagon back into that forest. They were told to nail her hair to a tree, drive away with her, and cut off her hair with a scissors.

"This they did. They whipped the horses, and drove and drove. The girl screamed, she raved of fire and water. But when they reached home she was cured. The Dybbuk had left her. All this, my friends, I saw myself."

"Once," said my mother shyly, "I myself saw a Dybbuk that had entered a dog. It was in Hungary. The dog lay under the table and talked in a human voice. Then he gave a long howl and died. So it must be true about the Dybbuks."

6

Some one broke into song. Others marked time with feet and chairs, or beat glasses on the table. When the chorus came, there was a glorious volume of sound. Every one sang, from the venerable Reb Samuel to the smallest child.

My father, that marvelous story-teller, told about a Roumanian ne'er-do-well, who married a grave-digger's daughter that he might succeed to her father's job, and bury all the people who had despised him.

2. A metal device to hold the person's head still while he or she is being photographed.
3. An evil spirit or wandering soul that can enter and control a living person (Hebrew and Yiddish).
4. Russian brandy. *"Kraut knishes"*: portions of dough filled with cabbage and then baked (Yiddish). *"Blintzes"*: filled and rolled-up pancakes (Yiddish). *"Slivovitz"*: a brandy made of plums (Slavic origin).
5. Perhaps a reference to Kobrin on the then Polish-Russian border, now Belarus.

Mottke the vest-maker attacked Jews who changed their names in this country.

"If his name is Garlic in the old country, here he thinks it refined to call himself Mr. Onions," said Mottke.

The mothers talked about their babies. A shy little banana peddler described a Russian pogrom.

"It started at both bazaars, just before the Passover,"[6] he said. "Some one gave vodka to the peasants, and told them we Jews had killed some Christian children to use the blood. Ach, friends, what one saw then; the yelling, the murder, the flames! I myself saw a peasant cut off my uncle's head with an ax."

At the other end of the table Fyfka the Miser was gobbling all the roast chicken he could grab, and drinking glass after glass of beer. It was a free meal, so he was stuffing himself.

Some one told of a pregnant mother in Russia who had been frightened by a Cossack,[7] and had borne a child with a pig's head.

Leichner the housepainter drank some wine. He told of a Jew in his native village who had been troubled by devils. They were colored red and green and blue. They rattled at the windows every night until the man could get no sleep. He went to a Rabbi and bought six magic words which he repeated until the devils retreated.

The hum of talk, tinkle of glasses, all the hot, happy excitement of the crowded room made me sleepy. I climbed on my mother's lap and began to fall asleep.

"What, too tired even for your own party?" said my mother affectionately.

I heard Reb Samuel talking again in his slow kind voice.

Bang, bang! Two pistol shots rang out in the backyard! I jumped to my feet, with the others. We rushed to the windows. We saw two men with pistols standing in the moonlit yard. Bang, bang! They fired again at each other. One man fell.

The other ran through the hall. A girl screamed in the bawdy house. The clothesline pole creaked. In the moonlight a cat crawled on its belly. It sniffed at the sudden corpse.

"Two gamblers fighting, maybe," said my father.

"Ach, America," Reb Samuel sighed.

All of us left the windows and went back to the singing, and story-telling. It was commonplace, this shooting. The American police would take care of it. It was discussed for some minutes, then forgotten by the birthday party.

But I have never forgotten it, for it burned into my mind the memory of my fifth birthday.

1930

6. A holiday in spring during which the Jews celebrate their exodus out of slavery in Egypt. The name refers to the sparing from death of the Jewish firstborn children.

7. A member of a military caste and mounted guard in czarist Russia, frequently employed in pogroms.

CHARLES REZNIKOFF
1894–1976

Charles Reznikoff has been called "the dean of Jewish American poets"—as much for his wedding of a modernist sensibility attuned to concrete images with a focus upon the specifics of an urban landscape as for his lifelong concern with Jewish themes and a Jewish fate. He was the author of more than fifteen volumes of verse, in addition to plays, novels, and historical works. Only with *By the Waters of Manhattan: Selected Verse* in 1962, the title as well of his 1930 novel, did he emerge from relative obscurity. That work received wide recognition, winning the Jewish Book Council of America Award for English Poetry.

Reznikoff was born in Brooklyn, his parents immigrants from Russia and hat manufacturers. He depicted their lifetime of toil, in Europe and America, with Dreiserian intensity in *Family Chronicle* (1963). He studied law at New York University and was admitted to the New York Bar in 1916 but never seriously practiced. He preferred to take various odd jobs over the years because, as he said, "I wanted to use whatever mental energy I had for my writing."

Reznikoff is known for his collaboration with the poets George Oppen and Louis Zukofsky in the creation of a 1930s movement called objectivism. Socially conscious but influenced by Ezra Pound's imagism, they established the Objectivist Press to self-publish their works. The essential point of the movement for Reznikoff was to produce verse whose images were clear, with "meaning not stated but suggested by the objective details and the music of the verse; words pithy and plain; without the artifice of regular metres; themes chiefly Jewish, American, urban."

Building Boom[1]

The avenue of willows leads nowhere:
it begins at the blank wall of a new apartment house
and ends in the middle of a lot for sale.
Papers and cans are thrown about the trees.
The disorder does not touch the flowing branches;
but the trees have become small among the new houses,
and will be cut down;
their beauty cannot save them.

How difficult for me is Hebrew:
even the Hebrew for *mother*, for *bread*, for *sun*
is foreign. How far have I been exiled, Zion.

I have learnt the Hebrew blessing before eating bread;[2]
is there no blessing before reading Hebrew?

My thoughts have become like the ancient Hebrew
in two tenses only, past and future—
I was and I shall be with you.

1. From *Poems 1918–1975* (1989).
2. I.e., the blessing praising God as "the one who brings forth bread from the earth." "Zion": the hill in the center of Jerusalem where King David's palace stood.

God saw Adam in a town
without flowers and trees and fields to look upon,
and so gave him Eve[3]
to be all these.
There is no furniture for a room
like a beautiful woman.

The sun shone into the bare, wet tree;
it became a pyramid of criss-cross lights,
and in each corner the light nested.

After I had worked all day at what I earn my living,
I was tired. Now my own work has lost another day,
I thought, but began slowly,
and slowly my strength came back to me.
Surely, the tide comes in twice a day.

ca. 1922–1926 1927

Russia: *Anno* 1905[1]

A Young Jew. The weed of their hatred
which has grown so tall
now turns towards us
many heads,
many pointed petals and leaves;
what did they whisper to each other before the ikons,
and smile at over the glasses of vodka,
the spies and gendarmes, Cossacks and police,
that a crowd of ragged strangers burst into the street
leaving crooked shields of David[2] in every pane of glass
and a Jew here and there in the gutter
clubbed to death for his coat like an animal for its skin,
the open mouth toothless, the beard stiffened with blood—
away, Jew, away!
obey the ancient summons, hurry out of this land!

Republic,
garrisoned by the waves;
every man welcome if distressed by lord or king;
and learning free to all as the streets and highways,
free as the light of street lamps,
piped into every house as the sweet water;
nation whose founders were not leaders of legions or regiments,
or masters of the long ships of war, of bowmen or artillery,
but farmers, who spoke of liberty and justice for all

3. The first woman, made for the first man, Adam (Genesis 2–3).
1. From *Poems 1918–1975* (1989). The year 1905 was the date of a failed revolution in Russia.
2. The six-pointed star, Magen David (Hebrew), is one of the traditional emblems of Judaism. "Ikons": sacred images of the saints, the Virgin, Christ, and so forth that are traditional in the Eastern Church. "Gendarmes": police officers. "Cossacks": the czar's mounted troops.

and planted these abstractions in the soil
to send their seed
by every current of wind and water
to the despotisms of the earth;
your name
is like the cool wind
in a summer day
under the tyranny of the sun;
like a warm room
when, against the tyranny of the wind,
one has come a long way
on frozen ruts and clods;
the oblongs of your buildings in the west—
smooth brightness of electric light
on the white stone
and the motorcars gliding along your crowded streets—
are as the triangles of Egypt were,
and the semicircles of the arches of Rome;
how great you have become, United States!

Or to the land of rock and sand, mountain and marsh,
where the sun still woos Delilah
and the night entraps Samson,
Palestine[3]—
and your speech shall be Hebrew;
what the mother has spun,
the daughter shall weave;
where the father has cleared away the stones,
the son shall sow and reap;
and lives will not burn singly
in single candlesticks—
how much better to live
where his fathers have lived,
than to be going about from land to land—
wasting one's life in beginnings;
how pleasant it is
for the body to sweat in the sun,
to be cool in the wind,
from dawn until twilight,
starlight to starlight;
how much better to live in the tip of the flame,
the blue blaze of sunshine,
than creep about in corners,
safe in cracks—
dribble away your days in pennies.
In that air
salty with the deeds of heroes and the speech of prophets,
as when one has left the streets and come to the
plunging and orderly sea, the green water

3. The name of the State of Israel before 1948. Samson was a Hebrew hero, a strong warrior, betrayed to the Philistines by Delilah during their love affair (Judges 13–16).

tumbling into yellow sand and rushing foam,
and rising in incessant waves—
upon your hills, Judah,
in your streets and narrow places
upon your cobblestones, Jerusalem![4]

Yet like the worm in horseradish
for whom there is no sweeter root,
should I, setting my wits against this icy circumstance,
make, like the Eskimo, my home of it?
The dust of this Russia,
breathed these many years,
is stored in my bones,
stains the skull and cortex of my brain—
the chameleon in us
that willy-nilly
takes the color where we lie.
Should I, like Abraham become the Hebrew,
leave Ur of the Chaldees,[5] the accident of place,
and go to other pastures, from well to well;
or, the Jew, stay,
others buzzing on the windowpanes of heaven,
flatten myself
against the ground
at the sound of a boot;
as others choose the thistle or the edelweiss,[6]
take the reed, knowing that the grey hairs of murderers
sometimes go bloody to the grave,
that the wicked die even as the good.
Or, a Russian,
the heat by day, the same frost at night,
the same enemies in microbes and in stars,
say,
These are my people,
Russian and Ukrainian, Cossack and Tartar, my brothers—
even Ishmael and Esau;[7]
know myself a stitch, a nail, a word
printed in its place, a bulb screwed in its socket,
alight by the same current as the others
in the letters of this sign—*Russia*.
Or better still,
there is no Russia;
there is no peoples, only man!

Stay or go;
be still the shining piston
moving heavy wheels;

4. The ancient holy city for Jews, Christians, and Muslims; capital of present-day Israel. Judah is a name for southern Palestine.
5. An ancient Sumerian city where Abraham, the progenitor of the Jewish people, was born.
6. An alpine plant with a white flower.
7. The older son of Isaac and Rebecca who sold his birthright to his younger brother, Jacob (Genesis 25). "Tartar": a Mongolian people in Central Asia. "Ishmael": the cast-out son of Abraham and Hagar, traditionally considered the progenitor of the Arab peoples (Genesis 21).

the propeller
before whom ocean and the heavens divide:
the steamer seen from the land
moves slowly
but leaves a tide
that washes shore and banks;
the airplane from the ground—
an insect crawling
but filling all the heavens with its drone;
a small cloud
raining its sound
from the wide sky.

1933 1934

From A Short History of Israel, Notes and Glosses[1]

XI

A hundred generations, yes, a hundred and twenty-five,
had the strength each day
not to eat this and that (unclean!)
not to say this and that,
not to do this and that (unjust!),
and with all this and all that
to go about
as men and Jews
among their enemies
(these are the Pharisees[2] you mocked at, Jesus).
Whatever my grandfathers did or said
for all of their brief lives
still was theirs,
as all of its drops at a moment make the fountain
and all of its leaves a palm.
Each word they spoke and every thought
was heard, each step and every gesture seen,
by God;
their past was still the present and the present
a dread future's.
But I am private as an animal.

I have eaten whatever I liked,
I have slept as long as I wished,
I have left the highway like a dog
to run into every alley;
now I must learn to fast and to watch.
I shall walk better in these heavy boots
than barefoot.

1. From *Poems 1937–1975* (1989). This is the final section.
2. A Jewish sect originating in the 3d century B.C.E. who were strict observers of the law. "Unclean": not kosher, food forbidden by Jewish law.

I will fast for you, Judah,
and be silent for you
and wake in the night because of you;
I will speak for you
in psalms,
and feast because of you
on unleavened bread and herbs.[3]

1936–1940 1941

Te Deum[1]

Not because of victories
I sing,
having none,
but for the common sunshine,
the breeze,
the largess of the spring.

Not for victory
but for the day's work done
as well as I was able;
not for a seat upon the dais[2]
but at the common table.

1944–1956 1956

From Early History of a Writer[1]

15

I went to my grandfather's to say good-bye:
I was going away to a school out West.[2]
As I came in,
my grandfather turned from the window at which he sat
(sick, skin yellow, eyes bleary—
but his hair still dark,
for my grandfather had hardly any grey hair in his beard or on his head—
he would sit at the window, reading a Hebrew[3] book).
He rose with difficulty—
he had been expecting me, it seemed—
stretched out his hands and blessed me in a loud voice:
in Hebrew, of course,

3. The foods eaten at Passover to remind the Jews of their exile in Egypt and their escape out of slavery from there. "Judah": the southern Kingdom of Israel. "Psalms": sacred songs.

1. From *Poems 1918–1975* (1989). "Te deum": a hymn in praise of God (Latin).

2. A raised platform for the table occupied by those of high rank or, in this case, the table itself.

1. From *Poems 1918–1975* (1989).

2. Reznikoff attended the University of Missouri from 1910 to 1911.

3. The language of Jewish learning, of the Bible and sacred books.

and I did not know what he was saying.
When he had blessed me,
my grandfather turned aside and burst into tears.
"It is only for a little while, Grandpa," I said
in my broken Yiddish.[4] "I'll be back in June."
(By June my grandfather was dead.)
He did not answer.
Perhaps my grandfather was in tears for other reasons:
perhaps, because, in spite of all the learning I had acquired in high school,
I knew not a word of the sacred text of the Torah[5]
and was going out into the world
with none of the accumulated wisdom of my people to guide me,
with no prayers with which to talk to the God of my people,
a soul—
for it is not easy to be a Jew or, perhaps, a man—
doomed by his ignorance to stumble and blunder.

1959–1969 1969

[The invitation read: not to mourn][1]

The invitation read: not to mourn
but to rejoice in a good life.
The widower, his false teeth showing in a wide smile,
entered
and, turning from side to side,
greeted us.
He began by reading a long essay on his dead wife.
And as he read, we heard those who were washing dishes in the rear of the hotel's restaurant
joking and laughing about some matter of their own.
At the end, we were asked to stand
while the widower recited the ancient prayer of mourning[2]—
used at first at all religious gatherings of Jews only to glorify God—
and yet, even as he read,
he began to cry.

1969–1973 1973

4. The Germanic language spoken by Eastern European Jews.
5. Jewish Scripture.
1. From *Poems 1918–1975* (1989).
2. I.e., Kaddish, which is said every day during the year of mourning. The prayer blesses, glorifies, praises, and exalts the name of God.

JACOB GLATSTEIN (YANKEV GLATSHTEYN)
1896–1971

The master of free verse in Yiddish and an architect of Yiddish modernism, Jacob Glatstein (Yankev Glatshteyn) combined elements of James Joyce, T. S. Eliot, and Sigmund Freud with the literary use of spoken Yiddish established by Sholem Aleichem.

Born in Lublin, Poland, in 1896 into a rabbinical family on his mother's side and, on his father's, a family of cantors and composers, Glatstein received a traditional religious education along with tutoring in secular subjects, including the classic Yiddish writers I. L. Peretz, Sholem Aleichem, and Avrom Reyzen. He began to write stories in Yiddish and, at age thirteen, went to Warsaw to show his writing to Peretz. In 1914, his parents sent him to New York to join his brother, where he published his first short story in the *Fraye arbeter shtime* (Free Voice of Labor). In 1918, after working in sweatshops and factories, Glatstein began his law studies at New York University, where he met N. B. Minkov, who soon, along with A. Leyeles, joined him to form the modernist group *inzikhistn*, or introspectivists. In 1919, he published three experimental Yiddish poems in the journal *Poezye* (Poetry), the first of which, *1919,* is included here. That same year, Glatstein, Minkov, and Leyeles wrote a literary manifesto that outlined the principles of their new kind of poetry; they published it in 1920 in the anthology *In Zikh*. They also published a journal containing poetry, criticism, theory, and polemics from 1920 through 1940. The journal, *Inzikh* (Introspectivism), became the mouthpiece of Yiddish modernism, publishing one hundred avant-garde Yiddish poets and critics, including some still living in Europe.

In 1921, Glatstein published his first book of poems, *Yankev Glatshteyn*. Having failed his law-school exams and needing to earn a living to support his wife and child, Glatstein, in 1925, began to write for the Yiddish press, where his columns and short stories appeared regularly until his death in 1971. His second book of poems, *Fraye ferzn* (Free Verses), came out in 1926 and his third, *Kredos* (Credos), in 1929; we have included one poem—*Autobiography*—from *Kredos*. Glatstein's first three books of poetry were characterized by the experimental poetics of free verse, word play, and the kaleidoscopic juxtaposition of fragments of language and sensory experience.

When, in 1934, he returned to Lublin to see his dying mother, Glatstein gained an awareness of the impending tragedy that would lead to the destruction of Jewish European culture, a quality that infuses the two autobiographical novels he wrote about that journey as well as his subsequent poetry. *Yidishtaytshn* (Yiddishmeanings or Exegyddish), published in 1937, exhibits this new concern, its poems darkened by an awareness of the world, as in *We the Wordproletariat*, included here.

The poems that he collected in *Gedenklider* (Memorypoems), published in 1943, of which we include *Good Night, World*, directly express Glatstein's premonitions and fears about the fate of the Jews in Europe just before and during World War II. With these poems and those in subsequent volumes, Glatstein became known as a poet of collective Jewish grief, grappling with the anger, despair, and isolation of both those who were murdered in and those who survived the *Khurbm* (Destruction), as in the 1946 poems *Without Jews* and *Resistance in the Ghetto*.

His last three books of poems, as well as an anthology of Holocaust poems that he edited, exhibit less of the experimental energy of his earlier work. Because these poems communicated the poet's sense of communal endeavor in more accessible language, they were Glatstein's best-known works among his general readership.

1919[1]

Lately, there's no trace left
Of Yankl, son of Yitskhok,[2]
But for a tiny round dot[3]
That rolls crazily through the streets
With hooked-on, clumsy limbs.
The lord-above surrounded
The whole world with heaven-blue
And there is no escape.
Everywhere "Extras!" fall from above
And squash my watery head.
And someone's long tongue
Has stained my glasses for good with a smear of red,
And red, red, red.
You see:
One of these days something will explode in my head,
Ignite there with a dull crash
And leave behind a heap of dirty ashes.
And I,
The tiny dot,
Will spin in ether for eternities,
Wrapped in red veils.

1919 1921

Autobiography[1]

Yesterday I dumped on my son the following story:
That my father was a cyclops[2] and, of course, had one eye,
That my fifteen brothers wanted to devour me,
So, I barely got myself out of their clutches
And started rolling all over the world.
Rolling, I grew up in two days,
But I wouldn't go back to my father's house.
So, I went to Tsefania and learned *sprechen* Jewish,[3]
I got myself circumcised and became a Yid.[4]

1. Translated by Kathryn Hellerstein and Benjamin Harshav. "1919": The political events of 1919 included [President Woodrow] Wilson's attempts to create a lasting world peace, the fresh impressions of the Russian Revolution and Civil War, the Red Scare in America, and the wave of massive pogroms in the Ukraine [Benjamin Harshav and Barbara Harshav's note].

2. A familiarizing form of the biblical Jacob, son of Isaac, using, however, the real names of the poet and his father [Benjamin Harshav and Barbara Harshav's note]. "Yankl" also connotes the American word *Yankee*.

3. An allusion to the Yiddish phrase *dos pintele Yid,* the tiny dot of Jewishness or the Jewish essence within a person. This also refers to *dos pintele yud,* the vowel mark for the short *i* sound beneath the Yiddish letter *yud* (*y*), which is the first letter in the words *Yid* (Jew), several of the names for God, Yankl, and Yitskhok. Glatstein strips the idiom of its Jewish connotations here, just as he strips the political connotations from the color red [adaptation of Benjamin Harshav and Barbara Harshav's note].

1. Translated by Benjamin Harshav and Barbara Harshav.

2. A one-eyed monster in Homer's *Odyssey*.

3. I.e., the Yiddish language (ironic). "Tsefania": an imaginary place. "*Sprechen*": to speak (German).

4. Jew (in Yiddish, a neutral or positive term; in English, derogatory).

So, I started selling flax, wax, esrogs with bitten-off tips,[5]
And earned water for kasha.[6]
Till I met an old princess
Who willed me an estate and died.
So, I became a landowner
And began guzzling and gorging.
And when I saw I was getting fat,
I made up my mind and got married.
After the marriage, my estate burned down.
So, I became a poor newspaper writer.

To my father, the cyclops, I sometimes write a letter,
But to my fifteen brothers—the finger.[7]

1929

We the Wordproletariat[1]

Night. In the darkest places sparkle traces
Of words. Loaded ships with ideo-glyphs[2]
Sail away. And you, armored in silence and wisdom,
Unwrap word from sense.

Mementos—rain-veiled horizon,
Flickering return, barely recalled:
A book, a face, a smile, a yawn.

The cursed night has got into your bones.

Soften up, cover up, forget.
Don't make a miracle of a trouser button.

Wordproletarian. Airplanes leave land
Full of understands.[3]
And you in your vest of Sesames and Ali-Babas.[4]
Don't you hear how yokes sigh?
Iron girders lie on your words.
Gnash them, curse them with disaster.
Where are your laughters, where are your groans?

The cursed night has got into your bones.

5. The Yiddish pronunciation of the Hebrew *ethrog* or *etrog;* a citron, the lemonlike fruit used in rituals for the holiday of Sukkot, which is kosher only if its tip is unbroken [adaptation of Benjamin Harshav and Barbara Harshav's note].

6. Buckwheat groats. This Yiddish idiom refers to making a meager living [adaptation of Benjamin Harshav and Barbara Harshav's note].

7. The translator has Americanized Glatshteyn's Yiddish phrase *a sasye,* which denotes a rude gesture not known among American readers.

1. Translated by Benjamin Harshav and Barbara Harshav. "Wordproletariat": Glatstein's compound neologism linking those who work with words to the working class, playing against the Labor poets' literal expressions of class solidarity.

2. Literally, "images of ideas," the translators' inventive translation of the Yiddish *bagrifn.*

3. This is a creative translation of the Yiddish *farshtanen* ("understandings"), a formation that is both noun and verb.

4. In the *Arabian Nights* tale, Ali-Baba says the magic words "Open Sesame" to unseal the cave of the forty thieves.

Your palm dates under your windows.
A stone and Here-Lies.
The in-between times have brought you to the absolute.
Graves of individuals, masses, Jews, races—
Archives.
Now whole collectives sing,
Stratospheres, stars, even buildings, stones.

The cursed night has got into your bones.

The sky, the blue hazard, went out.
You still sit and seek the shadows of a word
And scrape the mold off meanings.
Words take on sadder and purer tones.

The cursed night has got into your bones.

1937

Good Night, World[1]

Good night, wide world.
Big, stinking world.
Not you, but I, slam the gate.
In my long robe,[2]
With my flaming, yellow patch,[3]
With my proud gait,
At my own command—
I return to the ghetto.
Wipe out, stamp out all the alien traces.
I grovel in your dirt,
Hail, hail, hail,
Humpbacked Jewish life.
A ban, world, on your unclean cultures.
Though all is desolate,
I roll in your dust,
Gloomy Jewish life.

Piggish German, hostile Polack,
Sly Amalek,[4] land of guzzling and gorging.
Flabby democracy, with your cold

1. Translated by Benjamin Harshav and Barbara Harshav.
2. The traditional black overcoat of religious Jews [Benjamin Harshav and Barbara Harshav's note].
3. Jews throughout medieval Europe were forced to wear yellow patches to distinguish them from the Christian population, a practice that was suspended in the eighteenth century. In October 1939, one and a half years after Glatstein wrote this poem, the Nazis revived this practice to separate the Jews from the rest of the populace in occupied Poland. Glatstein may have seen the German Zionist Organization periodical *Die Welt,* which, to protest the Nazi rise to power, placed a yellow badge on the cover of its April 4, 1933, issue with the motto "Wear it with pride, this yellow badge."
4. A perjorative list of anti-Semites, both contemporary (the German Nazis and Poles) and traditional (the Amaleks, a people who, upon slaughtering many of the children of Israel after the latter left Egypt, were annihilated by God [Exodus 17.14]) [adaptation of Benjamin Harshav and Barbara Harshav's note].

Compresses of sympathy.
Good night, world of electrical insolence.
Back to my kerosene, tallowy shadow,
Eternal October, wee little stars,
To my crooked alleys, hunchbacked street-lamp,
My stray pages, my Twenty-Four-Books,[5]
My Talmud, to the puzzling
Questions, to the bright Hebrew-Yiddish,[6]
To Law, to deep meaning, to duty, to right.
World, I stride with joy to the quiet ghetto-light.

Good night. I grant you, world,
All my liberators.
Take the Jesusmarxes,[7] choke on their courage.
Drop dead on a drop of our baptized blood.
And I believe that even though he tarries,[8]
Day after day rises my waiting.
Surely, green leaves will rustle
On our withered tree.
I do not need consolation.
I go back to my four walls,
From Wagner's pagan music—to tune, to humming.[9]
I kiss you, tangled Jewish life.
It cries in me, the joy of coming.

April 1938

1943

Without Jews[1]

Without Jews there will be no Jewish God.
If we go away from the world,
The light will go out in your poor tent.
For ever since Abraham saw you in a cloud[2]
Your fire has been on all Jewish faces,
Your radiance in all Jewish eyes,

5. I.e., the Bible (in Yiddish, *svarbe*, which is a contraction of the Hebrew *esrim-ve-arbe*, or "twenty-four"). "Stray pages": of torn holy books, preserved in the synagogue in a *geniza*, a special repository for anything with the name of God written on it, which Jews are forbidden to discard or destroy.

6. I.e., *Ivritaytsh*, or traditional translations of the Hebrew Bible into old-fashioned Yiddish. "Talmud": the comprehensive, multivolumed basic book of Jewish law comprised of rabbinic discussions, legends, commentaries, and interpretations of the Hebrew Bible. "Puzzling Questions": hard questions that arise in the study of Jewish law [adaptation and expansion of Benjamin Harshav and Barbara Harshav's notes].

7. Perjorative combination of the names of the key figures in Christianity (Jesus) and socialism (Karl Marx). Glatstein rejects all religions and ideologies of the world that drew many modern Jews away from their religious traditions.

8. An allusion to the [Jewish] credo *Ani Maamim* ("I believe" [Hebrew]), the affirmation of faith in the coming of the Messiah [Benjamin and Barbara Harshav's note].

9. The Yiddish *nign* (in Hebrew, *nigun*) is a traditional tune that, when hummed, serves as a form of wordless prayer. "Wagner's pagan music": Richard Wagner (1813–1883) was a German composer whose operas based on Germanic legends were much admired by Hitler and were, thus, anathema to many Jews.

1. Translated by Benjamin Harshav and Barbara Harshav.

2. Perhaps a midrash on Genesis 12.7, where God appears to Abraham and promises him and his offspring the land of Canaan, invoking the first statement of the Covenant.

We have shaped you in our own image.
In every country, in every town,
A stranger lived with us,
The Jewish God.
And every shattered Jewish head
Is God's disgraced, broken bowl,
For we were your vessel of light,[3]
The living sign of your palpable wonder.
Now our dead heads
Are counted in millions.[4]
The stars around you flicker out.
The memory of you is dimmed.
Your kingdom will soon fade away.
All the Jewish sowing and planting
Is burned.
On dead grass cries the dew.
The Jewish dream and the Jewish reality are ravaged,
They die together.
Whole tribes asleep—
Babies, women,
Young and old.
Even your Pillars, the Rocks,
The Thirty-Six Just,[5]
Sleep their dead, eternal sleep.

Who will dream you?
Who will remember?
Who will deny you,
Who will long for you then?
Who will go to you, on a nostalgic bridge,
Away from you, to return again?[6]

The night is eternal for a dead people.
Sky and earth wiped out.
The light goes out in your poor tent.
The last Jewish hour flickers.
Jewish God, soon you are no more.

1946

3. An image from the Kabbalah, especially the teachings of the Jewish mystic Isaac Luria (1543–1572) [adaptation and expansion of Benjamin Harshav and Barbara Harshav's note].
4. A reference to the 6 million Jews who perished in the Holocaust.
5. The legendary thirty-six righteous Jews (*tsadikim*) who wander the world in disguise and ensure the world's continued existence through their good deeds. "Your Pillars, the Rocks": biblical epithets applied to great sages [Benjamin Harshav and Barbara Harshav's notes].
6. An allusion to a personal, religious poem by the Spanish Hebrew classical poet Ibn Gabirol, talking to God of fleeing "from You to You" [Benjamin Harshav and Barbara Harshav's note].

Resistance in the Ghetto[1]

We were starving,
Trampled, feeble Jews.
We did not cry, we did not raise our voices.
The earth bore us quietly.
Now we are beautiful, proud,
Radiant Jews.
We are dead Jews.

We intertwined, as brother
To brother, branched out, became
A forest of black trees.
The watchman lashed lightning over us.
But the forest burned without fear,
The fire climbed up to the skies,
The branches sang.

We were little, timid daddies,
Sickly mommies,
Stooped grandpas,
Dead babies.
We said nothing,
We were tongueless.
Suddenly we took on
A fearful and mighty voice.
We shouted louder and louder,
All together, we became
One divine anonymous.

They came racing,
Flying, driving over our bodies,
They poured hot oil on us.
Our homes, like little graves, disappeared.
They encircled us with fire.
But we were transformed in the flame.
The little daddies became
Forest choirs,
And we sang:
    We are the forest—
    A burning chorus—
    And God walks with us
    In the burning forest.

We crawled, we walked,
We rose up to the last stand.
Our own awesome scream
Put us on our feet.

1. Translated by Benjamin Harshav and Barbara Harshav. "Ghetto": a reference to the Warsaw ghetto uprising, on Passover Eve, April 19, 1943, when Jews in the Warsaw ghetto fought back against the Nazis who had imprisoned and starved them, and were deporting them to the Treblinka concentration camp.

We shot, we killed.
We slaughtered and wrung.
We saw their blood,
We saw it with our living eyes.

Sparks flew up like pieces of the sun.
How beautifully the forest burned.
And we aimed and shot,
We saw their blood running,
Their blood flowing.

We no longer crawled, we ran,
We aimed, we shot, we hit.[2]
We saw their dead heads,
We died with their death
In our eyes.
We intertwined, branched inward,
We, the mute, shouted like victorious fighters,
Shouted with one voice—
We, the divine anonymous.

We didn't win.
The forest burned out.
But in the divine darkness
We stroll: little daddies,
Sickly mommies,
Stooped grandpas,
Dead babies.
We saw their blood
And we rejoice.
We are beautiful, proud,
Radiant Jews.

1946

The Joy of the Yiddish Word[1]

Oh, let me through to the joy of the Yiddish word.
Give me whole, full days.
Tie me to it, weave me in,
Strip me of all vanities.
Send crows to feed me, bestow crumbs on me,
A leaking roof and a hard bed.
But give me whole, full days,
Let me not forget for a moment
The Yiddish word.

2. A line from a song by Shmerke Katcherjinsky in Vilna Ghetto about Vitka Kovner who blew up a German military train in 1941 [Benjamin Harshav and Barbara Harshav's note].

1. Translated by Benjamin Harshav and Barbara Harshav. This is part of a longer poem of the same name [Benjamin Harshav and Barbara Harshav's note].

I become stern and commanding
Like the hand of my livelihood.
The capons and the champagne
Undigest my time.
The Yiddish word lies in a granary,
The key rusts in my hand.
My sober day robs my reason.

Oh, sing, sing yourself down to the bare bones.
The world gets fat on your couch.
Soon there will be no room for the two of you.
The Yiddish word waits for you, faithful and dumb.
And you sigh in your ignited dream:
I come, I come.

1961

EDWARD DAHLBERG
1900–1977

Boston-born Edward Dahlberg has been called a "sport"—that is, an oddity—of American literature. As if being reared by a single mother who was an itinerant "lady barber" and then moving through a string of midwestern towns and cities until the 1920s were not enough, his literary career was unusual. He began as an acknowledged forerunner of the naturalistic literature of the 1930s but later went on to amaze and dazzle critics and readers with his elegant high style and densely allusive mythic imagination.

Bottom Dogs (1929), his first book, appeared with an appreciative introduction by D. H. Lawrence. It tells the story of his life in fictionalized form. When he is not in the Jewish Orphan Asylum in Cleveland (only referred to as the J.O.A. in the book) he lives with his barber mother, Lizzie, in a series of small towns, settling in Kansas City, Missouri, in 1905. He drifts through the lower reaches of society, wondering who his father might be, searching for knowledge in alleys, box cars, reading. The language is earthy and slangy, its vernacular and "bottom dogs" concerns in the year of the stock-market crash and the beginning of the Great Depression harbingers of the coming vogue of the "proletarian" novel. His second book, *From Flushing to Calvary* (1932), carries the story forward, ending with a moving evocation of Lizzie's death on Long Island.

Unlike his early fictional self, Dahlberg did manage two years at UCLA in the 1920s and in 1925 completed his degree at Columbia University. He was part of the socially conscious but modernist avant-garde in the first years of the 1930s, publishing in the magazine *Pagany* with, among others, Louis Zukofsky, Charles Reznikoff, Kenneth Rexroth, William Carlos Williams. In 1934, he wrote an anti-Nazi play and was close to the Communists, but soon broke with them on aesthetic as well as political grounds. He married several times, traveled a great deal, lived abroad on Majorca and elsewhere, taught briefly after World War II at the University of Missouri, Columbia, and at Boston University. He was also a pioneer in the study and literary use of pre-Columbian civilizations.

In his later years, Dahlberg developed an orphic, often epigrammatic, style, his sentences thick with arcane myths, classical and religious references. Among his many books in this period were *The Confessions of Edward Dahlberg* (1971), in which he reworks in his mature style the material concerning his mother and their relationship. The selection included here is part of that book, although it appeared originally in the *Massachusetts Review*, whose editor suggested the title. It comes from a speech of Hamlet's, in which the prince replies to King Claudius's request that he say farewell to Claudius as well as to his mother by saying: "My mother. Father and mother is man and wife, man and wife is one flesh, and so my mother" (*Hamlet* 4.3.53–54). Dahlberg thought the quotation most appropriate to his piece.

From The Confessions of Edward Dahlberg

From *Chapter IX*

AND SO . . . MY MOTHER. . . .
—HAMLET[1]

Before going to New York, I returned to Kansas City, the burial ground of all my memories, and where my mother was still the proprietor of the Star Lady Barbershop. She was fifty years old now, with scrawny, nervous hair colored with a cheap henna dye. Ever since Popkin, her second husband, had taken all her savings, she had lost her bloom, though she was still vigorous. Her strength shone through her clouts.

My mother's appearance humiliated me. When I regarded the loose, dangling throat and the skin of her face that was beginning to yellow, or looked at a straggling shoelace, I thought no other son was so unfortunate as I. How I once envied Marion Moneysmith, whose mother had been a pretty woman with such a tidy figure. The young are savage and do not realize that after a short while they too will be dry, crumpled leaves. But wrinkles and rough guts in the skin are symptoms of compassion—that were not seen in the same man when his complexion was radiant but his features blank.

My mother continued to prate over her respectability, mentioning how noble she was, though there was always some man hanging around her. Still a very passionate woman, she once told me, as we sat on the front porch at the 8th Street flat on an August evening, that Captain Henry Smith had been all played out by the time she met him. How many regal and delicious women, who ache to eat of the tree of knowledge because the fruit is a delight, have tolerated impotent men.

When I considered my mother's privy sheets and illicit pillowcases I abhorred them, though I myself was weaker than grass. If I saw a milkwhite rump, my body became a seminal song. My flesh cried: let me smell her sandals or clap my nose upon her navel, for I hunger, itch, piss, eat and die. In spite of my own incontinent blood, I refused to see that a grim angel had warped my mother's luck, and that she was deprived of one constant man who would cherish her paps.

That she was a drudge in a barbershop and spent the pennies she earned on a son more useless than a gnat did not occur to me. Nor did I realize that she was far more honest than Society, which had rejected her. Was she not an angelic pariah? Little wonder that I myself would roam through the earth,

1. Shakespeare's passage also quotes Genesis 2.23 and the marriage rite of the Christian Book of Common Prayer.

and that wherever I was a wild forest would spring up around me. However, by the time I had come to have a moiety of my mother's good sense, I was more afraid of virtue than of vice.

For a while Lizzie saw an old-time railroader named Circlear who had previously been a steady customer. He was a fancy tipper in the old days and after having a massage, haircut and tonic, Circlear would get up from the chair in his sporting braces and, bantering me, he would say, "If you'll cover your Jew nose with your hand, I'll give you a dollar." The girls believed this was a tremendous piece of wit, but I never thought about anything except the dollar, though I was sometimes chased by neighborhood boys and called a Sheeney.[2]

Although my mother had stopped investing in imaginary oil wells, or in Coca-Cola when shares were offered for sale to the public, she was now speculating in something far wilder—the man business.

Circlear was no longer a sport nor connected with the Burlington Railroad. Formerly, he revealed, he had been a vice-president of that railway company and had had a private Pullman car for his office. He confided to my mother that during the War[3] his Chinese cook, since deceased, had buried a million dollars for him and that when the time was ripe he would take the fortune from its hiding place and share it with her.

The imperial offices of the Burlington Railroad were on Walnut Street, no more than a few blocks from the 8th Street viaduct, but my mother was too timorous to enquire whether his tale were true. She cringed when she thought of asking a high Burlington official whether he knew Circlear; she was sure that a prince of such a realm would exclaim: "Madam, will you leave these premises at once, or must I call the police!" She had an infernal fear of rich people; the invisible grace of money that is represented in the visible grace of the law was never questioned by her.

Circlear washed clothes for Lizzie at the flat, swept up the hair from the floor before the shop was closed, counted the dirty barber towels, mopped the linoleum, cleaned out the spittoons and carried home her basket filled with grapes, St. John's bread, Winesaps,[4] jars of orange marmalade and marinated herring. But after a time he drifted away.

Then Lizzie complained of a flaccid, dropping belly. She had gone under the knife three times; her new surgeon, in whom she had the utmost confidence, was a Doctor Joy, who had a medical diploma from the College of Hippocrates,[5] which was somewhere in a Mississippi bog. Whenever she had the blues, she thought of having an operation. However, if she saw a marriage opportunity she became quite spirited again.

On the first evening that a new beau came to call, she would primp, daub her seamy neck and face with several kinds of creams and dust her breast with talcum powder; then she put on the gold-embroidered linen dress that Popkin had brought back from Jerusalem and pinned her watch to her bosom. Tokay grapes hung over the rim of the cut-glass bowl, and the settee was polished and placed near the sofa, so that they could talk to each other

2. A derogatory term for a Jew.
3. I.e., World War I (1914–18). America entered the war in 1917.
4. A variety of apple. "St. John's bread": the fruit of the carob tree (sometimes called a locust bean). John the Baptist was supposed to have subsisted on honey and locusts while in the desert, which may account for the association.
5. Greek physician (ca. 460–ca. 377 B.C.E.); called "the father of medicine."

and be close but still refined. She had no intention of hurrying into the flabby arms of a short, stale miser.

There was not much variety to the sort of beaus who came into Lizzie's parlor; they were stubby, with round, parsimonious necks, and wore blue serge suits and vests with a pocket for a watch that was as large as a silver dollar. If the evening courtship were not going well, or her guest took out his Hamilton railroad timepiece[6] from his vest pocket earlier than he should have, Lizzie hopped to her feet at once. She would help him into his coat with a flurry of haste and show him to the door with more passion than she had anticipated.

Usually when she had a visitor she would walk very slowly toward the upright piano, almost swaying as she tiptoed, and after wiping the yellow keys with a chamois cloth—which she had already done before he had arrived—she would run over her scales for several minutes. She then played a few notes from *Cavalleria Rusticana*[7] before turning to her favorite semi-classic: "I was jealous and hurt when your lips kissed a rose, or your eyes from my own chanced to stray."

She had a thin treble, quite soft and courteous, and sometimes she removed her pince-nez glasses after she had turned one of the pages of the sheet music to give her recital a professional touch. She was extremely proud that she could read the score and did not have to play by ear like some of the common 12th Street trash.

Following her performance, she would set a saucer and napkin near her guest on the oval-shaped mahogany table so that he could put the grape skins on the dish and politely wipe his chin with the napkin. She nibbled a few grapes—so that she could part her lips just enough to show what kind of a family she had come from; delicately spitting out the seeds, she heaped them into a cultured, neat pile on her saucer. The embroidered napkins smelled of moth balls, since she never used them except for such occasions.

Lizzie was the most finished listener for the first night or two. She wanted to find out whether she had a four-flusher on her hands; she felt sure she could recognize an old two-timer or a shrewd windbag the moment she smelled him. If her bladder troubled her, she did not make shift or put herself out, and often she grew tired of the game before she could believe in it. Otherwise, she did her best to give herself the right sort of advice, and I often heard her speak aloud to herself without knowing it, saying that one had to take a chance with a two-faced schemer just as one did with any other risky business proposition. Had she not learned that much from those low chippies?[8] Give a man his way, but just so far, until he lost his footing. Well, a piece of he nonsense was a big gamble, but she would come out all right.

She showed the visitor every civility, bowing now and then to words whose sense only came later to her mind, but her thoughts were of Captain Henry Smith. What a dandy, rosy future they would have had together; he was a stingy one, but jolly, and what company over a solid rib steak or a plate of stewed oysters, with a bottle of Bock beer.[9]

In her mind she could still see the Captain with his hair peeled off like

6. A large pocket watch made by the firm Hamilton.
7. An opera (1890) by Pietro Mascagni (1863–1945), usually translated as "Rustic Chivalry" (Italian).
8. Slang for "loose women."
9. Dark beer.

the gilt of a picture frame. He had often been grumpy and he belched, broke wind and sometimes smelled sour, but how she used to enjoy washing out his drawers and smelly socks! He was a pot-like man, a big, sweaty laugher, small where he should have been long—but you can't have everything in this world. The steamboat trade was finished; the Missouri River was dead, but it was so much better to have a man fill the rooms. Pshaw, you can have all the clean white linen there is, but if there isn't some man-dirt on the sheets what good is it? Then he had run off with that rotten little piece from St. Louis; his sister, Clara, had written her that she was a good fifty-seven—an old hen, you could be sure of that.

Kansas City remained still half rural; the elms and maples lining the streets gave health to the heart and the lungs. Yet there were those long periods of dryness in her, followed by that gentlest rain in the spirit, hope. Yes, it was still a wooden rather than an iron town, and the rocky hills, and the clothes hanging on the lines and flagging in the breeze eased her.

But when my mother asked herself what could she do with her life, God was as deaf as the adder. The Lord chastises those whom he loves, but why had He placed a heavy rod upon her neck? For what reason must she drink the bitter waters?

The tears that spring from the flood of Noah and which cover our nights ran down Lizzie's loose cheeks. What was left of her mouth? My God, where do the swelling hips go? And the skin dries on the wrist and hand, and the leg shrinks. Her bosom once could make a man forget that he was in the dumps; and her calves—the skirt-chasers would turn their necks around to look. But that was past, and so much of her had disappeared. Good Lord, we die all day long and every hour; each minute we age somewhere in our bones. She examined her hands and half shut her eyes so as not to see too plainly the coarse, tortoise-shelled veins. How much she had accomplished with her fingers! But how hard they had grown; you can't handle steel scissors and a hair clipper all day long and have a smooth, lady's hands. How honest can you be when you have nothing in this world except a pair of hands—and with a son to take care of, too? Poor Emma Moneysmith used to say it was fine to have principles—if you were rich enough to afford them. Not even Cromwell, that good old soul, who was an alderman, could swear that all the dollars in his safe were legal. Oh, sing the song of money, the psalm of deceit! Who isn't a cheat? And who has a sock on his foot, a shirt button or a corset that is not ill-gotten and whore-rotten?

Should she not be rewarded in some way? Had she not held her head high? What had she gotten for twenty-seven years of drudging, cutting hair and shaving the tough, gray whiskers of switchmen, railroaders, deadbeats and bluffers, and of massaging old rounders? And oh how she ached when night came. . . . O God, do not forsake me; I have nothing between me and the gutter except my pair of scissors, my razor and hone and hair clipper. Let me live long enough to hear the grass coming up in Northmoor, and to bend over my plump, red tomatoes. Give me, for I am alone, another fifty summers and Aprils, and fifty more hopes; it's so little to ask. Do not go away, O God, lest I die. Die? What is that? Can that be? Is it possible to disappear? Look, I am a womb, a belly where I had my son, Edward, two hands and a pair of stout feet. Do you, O Lord, really kill people? The Holy Living God is no thief that comes in the night and breaks into your soul and carries it away.

This cannot be. I know it; for as I breathe, I will never die; would not my body, my lungs, heart and bowels tell me! . . .

Lizzie, on a sudden, awakened from her reverie. Her small, wrinkled brown eyes were slyly peering over her glasses at the man in the parlor; the skins of the grapes were slobbered over his meaty, nether lip. His loose buttocks spread morosely over the chintz cover on the settee. How could she take a worm-eaten crank like that into her polite bed? He told her of the ketchup factory he owned in the West Bottoms, and the thousands of shares he had in the brand-new $50,000,000 Union Station out at 15th and Main Streets. Nearsighted, she was positive his vest was frayed; she could not keep her eyes off the grape pulp that slopped about his mouth, though she endeavored to show the strictest attention to what he was saying. Wasn't he wearing a secondhand blue serge suit? But then every bachelor was a born miser. Yet one had to have some confidence in the public; there was, she had to admit, a kind of pleasant odor of high-tone money about him.

He now assured her that he would lend her a thousand dollars at six per cent interest, or if she wished she could give him a second mortgage on the cottage Captain Henry Smith had built in Northmoor. Lizzie had spoken of her desire to invest a small sum in property or land in that country village. Before another suitor had come up the steps, she had earnestly made a vow to herself that she would be patient, wait and let him slip a little into the net—and when she had caught him, she would make a real bargain for herself. Let him propose first, and then she could make him a plain speech: "Sir, I know you have a noble heart, and I regard your offer of marriage as true blue; but don't you think it would only be respectable for you to set aside so many thousands of dollars in my name? God forbid that anything should happen to you . . . well, let's not look at the dark side of things." Her original elocution was far more eloquent than this, but after all why should she take such pains and be so careful with a short slob? He must certainly be past his seventieth year. Look at his old stomach, and rumbling all evening, so that she could hardly hear what she had been saying to herself. What was there in it for her, except a marriage license, if he refused to cough up some of his fortune?

As usual she was too nervous to wait, and her blood was so heady that no matter what a miserable prospect a man appeared to be, she had to go on with her intrigue, just to discover how it would turn out, though she had not the least intention of marrying this sort of man. She was mighty particular about her brass bed in the alcove. If he thought he could get under the blankets without first putting everything down on paper in black and white, he was too stupid for her.

Accustomed to grasping the meaning of what others said some time after it was uttered, she leaped up abruptly when she caught the words *lend* and *second mortgage*, which had reached the bottom of her nature and by now were coming back in a great tidal wave. She rose at once to her feet to show that cheap skate out of her courteous parlor.

Then when she remembered that he had called without even bringing her a box of Lowney's chocolates or a bouquet of roses, or so much as said, "Here is a sack of fruit," she went into the kitchen and watered the geraniums and afterwards made a broken prayer, half in Hebrew and the rest in midwestern

American: *"Baruch atah Adonai Elohenu . . ."*[1] Deploring her situation, she sobbed, "I'm the most unlucky woman on the earth; my eyes are so strained from cutting hair I can hardly see straight, and my bladder has dropped, Doctor Joy told me. . . ."

After the curmudgeon had left she closed the mahogany piano, picked up the one good rug, which was the meal of the moth, and put it away in the clothes closet. Then she took off her parlor dress, removed her one pair of patent leather shoes and put on a smeary kitchen apron. She shuffled aimlessly from the sitting room to the alcove, while the pince-nez, fastened to one ear by a thin gold wire, kept falling onto her breast.

She dusted the postcards in the parlor, then stumbled back to the kitchen to light the gas range and heat the pot of soup she had made the day before. Suddenly she became frantic because she could not find her glasses. Sitting in a straight, oak chair next to the table, and staring at the mouldy crumbs, flies and chunks of sodden bread she was in the habit of tearing out of the loaf, she moaned, "I'm blind; I cannot see, O God." Her hands fumbled over her heart, and she felt the pince-nez against her apron; with a sigh of gratitude, she went on with her orison[2]—perhaps God would not forsake her after all.

The next morning she got up and took her cold bath, which she believed would keep the seams out of her complexion and would invigorate her lungs and heart. She shook out her blanket on the latticed back porch which was strewn with sun, and when the air was upon her bare neck and cheeks she revived. A very deep sleeper, she had awakened earlier than usual this morning; she had to open up the shop herself; that acid hypocrite Harney was in bed, either with the drummer who sold Rogers' silverware or because of her troublesome appendix, and wouldn't be at her chair that day.

For a short while Lizzie sat on the rear steps that were four stories up, putting cold cream on her face, neck and arms; it was the latest vanishing cream for wrinkles. She wished she could sell the Star Lady Barbershop and be rid of those chippies; they were always tramping from one bed to another or chasing a rancher or a sucker from Oklahoma City. No wonder she stole their checks—they were no good anyway. And why not? Business was business.

When she walked along 8th Street to open the shop, her feet were so slow and she had a miserable, heavy feeling; what she needed was an operation. Then she remembered her son who still lay sleeping in one of the bedrooms at the flat, and she cried, "O son of my bowels, and of all my troubles, you whom I carried in my arms from Dallas to Memphis, to Louisville, to New Orleans, to Denver, to Kansas City. What a skinny one you are, and still so green around a woman. You ought to fill out a little. Why don't you run about with a hussy or two, like Stedna's son? O Edward, my son, son of all my hopes!"

My life was a heavy affliction to me at this time; the chasm between my mother and me had widened. I blamed her for everything; whom else could I find fault with except my sole protector? Why had she not provided me

1. "Blessed art Thou O Lord, our God" (Hebrew), the phrase that begins all the blessings.

2. Prayer.

with a family? Could the bastard issue of a lady barber with dyed, frizzled hair amount to anything? Why had not my mother given up that common trade? Was I to stumble in the winds, too? No matter how we begin our lives it is a misfortune. One has to overcome the best as well as the worst of circumstances. But thinking this did not help me; my grievous childhood stuck in my gizzard, and I recalled how Captain Henry Smith had persuaded my mother to send me to an orphanage.

Now the sight of a suitor in loose, acid pants and slept-in suspenders made me prudish. How could my mother stomach such men? How immoral was her sensual hymn of flesh and sweat to me. It is everybody's folly to judge others; did we not do so there would be no morals at all. Lizzie always tried to keep me from seeing what went on between herself and her admirers. They were of use, though swill to her imagination. Nor could I bear any longer that cranny at 16 East 8th Street; when I saw the cuspidors bespattered with tobacco juice and watched one of the barber girls step away from her chair to cast her phlegm into one of them, I ran out of the shop.

I had acquired airs and prejudices that I believed were natural. How much difference is there between the educated and the commoner sort except in the way they spit and rasp their throats? It takes no more than a single adage from Lord Chesterfield[3] to make a debonair fop: "Do not look into your handkerchief after you blow your nose."

Who is my father? was my continual liturgy. Was I got upon the knop of a little hillock, like Gargantua?[4] It did not matter. Not where or how, but who? Has not the pismire a sire? Eber was born unto Shem, and Cush begat Nimrod,[5] but who begot me? In an old midrash[6] it is told that birds are fashioned out of marshy ground saturated with water. Was my origin similar, or did I come out of the loins of the maggot? We live in an unfilial age, and though the son curse the father, he ranges the whole earth looking for the Cave of Machpelah,[7] where lie Abraham, Isaac and Jacob.

Had I no progenitor? Christ can revivify mouldy Lazarus,[8] but who can raise the living from the grave? I wanted to feel, but had no emotions, and I sighed for thoughts and had no conceptions. My sleep spoke to me, but it was slack and shoaly, and it came up only as far as my ankles, and I could not drink it. I was a dark root of nothing, and my own emptiness groaned. An hour would come when morning, like a cerecloth,[9] would be wrapped around me, and I would say, "I never had a mother; she neither was nor is." I heard the pangs of this phantom, but she was invisible. She was next to her son, and she was not. There were myriads of galled and palsied phantoms who gnawed themselves, and yet were starved, for they ate their ribs that did not exist and supped upon a vacant chin or neck. They wailed all night and at daybreak, when the cock crowed, they fled. What ailed them most was the cold; for unless they could warm themselves in some other wraith's pulses or find a covert in a coat pocket or crawl through a hole in an imaginary

3. English nobleman and writer (1694–1773) whose letters to his son (1774) include the line quoted here.
4. A mythic giant, the subject of a 1534 work of that name by the French humorist and satirist François Rabelais (ca. 1494–1553).
5. A lineage of descent found in Genesis.
6. A rabbinic interpretation of a biblical text.
7. A cave in Israel that Abraham purchased for the burial of his wife, Sarah, and where he and the other fathers of the Jewish people were buried (Genesis 25.9–10).
8. A dead man who was resurrected by Jesus (John 11.43–44).
9. A winding sheet for a corpse's burial.

gloved hand, they could not be seen. Sometimes they hung upon a neck that had been kissed and embraced, and were perched there like some great pensive bird or cherub, and though terrible winds blew upon them from the Void, they would not leave this nesting place.

We are nothing, we know, though God has feigned we are something. We have been deceived, O First Cause[1] and Mocker—you who told us we were created. What is there betwixt our coming and our dying but the fumes rising up out of Nowhere? The fool licks the fat and scum of this non-existence until he is gouty and swollen.

How long is misery? I cried; how much space is there between Nazareth and Capernaum, those apocryphal, pneumatic towns that lie in the gullet of the paraclete?[2]

I said, "Let there be darkness, for I cannot see in the light; and my sepulchre laughed at Him who pretended that on the fourth day He had made the moon, the stars, fish, birds, mice and the dream, and who thought He had created Adam on the sixth day."[3] But I spurned Him and said, "When Thou gavest man dreams, he knew that Thou hadst lied to him, even to Thyself, for Thou hast created nothing." And I bellowed, "Take away Thy follies and images and Thy six days of Void, for all that I require is the DREAM. Why didst Thou plague Adam with a conscience, for what need has man of it when his visions of the night judge him?" Wrinkled and old, I lifted up my voice and wept, "Thou knowest well there are no days, and that time is only the noise of the wings of the seraphim.[4] Away with Thy sun; are not ashes wiser than the flame, and does not the moon know more than the sun? Thou nihilist, does a phantasm require anything which is nothing, except the dream, for if a man perceives as he sleeps, what has he but a trance when he awakens?"

Meanwhile Sirach[5] sat in my ear, which was stuffed with the adage: "And forget not thy mother who bare thee in pangs." She sat in the parlor on the oak rocker, hiding behind the *Kansas City Star*. She knew what was in my mind. Was I not her belly, hand and feet, and did she not comprehend her own flesh? On a sanitary inspection tour of the rooms, I glanced about the kitchen; what a babel of greasy dishes, bent, charred saucepans and pots. Flies hovered over the crumbs and smutty cups and dishes on the oilcloth. Another pile of plates, slimy with yesterday's food, stood in the sink. There was an aluminum casserole filled with a withered scum of soup and suet. I opened the door to the oven of the gas range and saw a copy of Fielding's *Tom Jones*[6] inside. It was stained with butter, and pieces of bread and orange peelings lay on top of it. My mother had resolved to be educated.

A few days before, in one of our easy, jocular moments, when we were playing pinochle, she had asked me whether such dirty words as Fielding used were literature, and her eyes were rinsed with tears of mirth. While she was relating that the picaresque language of Fielding was no different from the everyday words of chippies, I caught her cheating. My cheeks burned

1. God.
2. An advocate. "Nazareth and Capernaum": cities in which Jesus spent his childhood and his adulthood, respectively.
3. Genesis 1.14–31.
4. An order of angels.
5. From the Apocrypha, a spirit.
6. Henry Fielding (1707–1754), English novelist and author of *A History of Tom Jones, a Foundling* and other works.

with fever and I said that she had no principles. We had the fewest of agreeable moments with one another.

Carrying the soiled volume of *Tom Jones* into the parlor, I upbraided my mother; why had she put Fielding into the bake oven? But she made no answer. I stared at the copious brass bed in the alcove where my mother had lain with Harry Cohen, who had burnt his team of horses to collect money from the insurance company. I heard that he now had a pair of upstairs rooms in Independence Avenue where he lived with a decayed whore. Harry Cohen was a parcel of my boyhood, and I yearned to look upon his face. What is foul feeds the eyes also; besides, I was so alone and had nobody to speak to but my own tomb. And so I visited him, but when he turned to his bony prostitute who called him "Daddy," I went away undone.

Moving around listlessly in our sitting room, I looked at my childhood. All my kin were in this room: there was my aunt, the mahogany oval-shaped table; the cut-glass bowl in the center of the table was my sister; in the corner of the parlor was an avuncular oak table, and the settee, which was for company, was my cousin. What an orphan I would have been without this familied room. My fingers would have been waifs in the world, and my hands no part of my body, if my mother moved away from the 8th Street flat. I had been begotten in Boston, but this was my borning-room; here I had hoped and dwindled and now I died every hour.

I had forgotten that my mother was in the parlor with me. Then I looked at that woman, less than five feet of relentless will. Oh God, her stockings were sick and raveled again. Could I have come out of such wild rags? She was still sitting in the rocker, the upper part of her torso covered by the newspaper. My neck was hard. She rocked slow and sly, peering at me, I knew. How could I wrest from her the knowledge of my beginnings?

When I turned toward her, all my interred bones groaned: "I am a man, and there are ghosts of trees and a ravine howling within me, and at the root of a mountain sits a man. Who is he? You have always talked to me about your father, sisters and brothers, but I never saw one of them. What relations have I ever had or touched or smelled? In what city are my father's footprints? Does he walk, does he breathe, and is he suckled by the winds? See, I am a shade emptied of ancestors; I am twenty-three years old and grown into full sorrow."

The rocker was mute, and I stood there filled with a fatherless emptiness. Stepping backward, I slipped on a tattered, woolly rug and I shouted, "O heaven, these rags, all our hopes have been moth-eaten rags."

Then I caught sight of the rusty tin rack of stale postcards on the wall. What paternal finger had grazed that faded brown wallpaper? For a moment I stood bowed in front of these holy relics: there were three scenic views of Swope Park, one of Fairmount Park, one of Cliff Drive, another of Swift's packing house. There was the Grand Opera House where Chauncey Alcott had sung so many times, and the Willis Woods Theater where I had seen Anna Held[7] when I was eight. There were the photographs of the old-timers; Lizzie never threw anything away, not even a reminder of her most wretched experiences.

7. Anna Held (ca. 1865–1918) was a French-born musical-comedy star, often seen in Florenz Ziegfeld's *Follies*. "Chauncey Alcott": a popular singer.

I studied a card that showed Lizzie when her hair was still brown and tender and her face had a meditative contour. Next, the U.S. Major, bald, with a stylish military mustache, and in uniform, stared at me—but he had been too pallid for my mother's bed. I passed him to glance at skinny Birdie, then Gladys from Tulsa, and Blanche Beasley, for whose stupendous buttocks a cashier for the M-K-T had stolen ten thousand dollars. What a victual was Ruby du Parr, but destined for the public stews, and there was the dear, fetching figure of Emma Moneysmith. Such a big-trousered man was Hagen. Popkin had a spruce, carroty mustache, with tidy fringes of hair around his ears and neck, but he looked so quick and tailored. And old Cromwell, wearing spectacles, who was now in his grave; he would never let anyone give him a chin-scrape except Lizzie.

My origins were still unriddled. The rocker was creaking; the newspaper lay on my mother's crumpled kitchen apron. When I contemplated her untied shoelaces, I moaned, "You sent me to an orphanage because Henry was fat and I leaned on him; before that I was in a Catholic home, and then in a parochial school where the boys beat me every day because I was a Jew."

The woman, so distant from my anguish and the bitterness of my days, now replied, "My son, when I went under the knife, what could I do? I sent you to the Jewish home in Cleveland[8] because I could not manage you. You were in the streets all day, and sick and puking, and I had the scissors and comb in my hands. I could not give you regular meals or control you. What could I accomplish with a widow's ten fingers, and who was there to help me? Do you think I could find money in the gutter? I wanted you to be high-tone; you have the aristocratic face, my son, of my brother Ignatz, may he rest in peace."

"Don't mention a brother or sister to me; even a worm has a parent, but nobody begat me. I am nothing, and I came out of nowhere," and I was filled with gall, and layers of grief lay over it. I heard Job on his muckheap: "The ox knoweth his owner, and the ass his master's crib."[9]

I crossed the front room, returning to the tin rack of postcards, for these sepulchral memories bound my mother and me together. On a sudden, I was gazing at a hand-tinted picture of a man with the curls of a dandy; he wore the dude's chestnut-colored vest with the usual fob, gold chain and watch. He was showing the teeth of the fox that spoils the vines.[1] It was Saul! Whenever business was slow or her bladder gave her that desponding, dragging feeling, Lizzie would often exclaim, "May Saul burn in hell," and then breaking off into German, she would let out a blasphemy: *"Verdammter Saul!"*[2]

I pulled the tintype out of the rack and leaning against the cemetery of postcards, I roared, "It is Saul! Who else could my father be? I know it is Saul. My blood is ruined; a thousand lusts boil in his skin and his tumored brain. But where is he? You must know. He is my father. Tell me, I must know . . . or live and die unborn . . . for I will wail all the hours of my flesh if I am unfilled by a father!"

She sat immovable. No grave was more silent than she, and no matter what words and sounds I made, she did not move. I stared at her helplessly,

8. The Jewish Orphan Asylum, referred to only as "the J.O.A." in Dahlberg's 1929 version of this story in *Bottom Dogs*.

9. A reference to the Book of Job.

1. Song of Songs 2.15.

2. "Damned Saul" (German).

for she was a terrible headstone without an epitaph, from which no secret could be wrung.

* * *

With the money she had given me I purchased an old house on Cape Cod and a secondhand car, and one night my wife and I sat in the car outside the flat saying good-bye to my mother. Then I watched this shamble of loneliness, less than five feet of it, covered with a begrimed and nibbled coat, walk away from me.

For the next two years letters came from her twice a week, always beginning with "My beloved Son." Once as my eyes crawled down to the bottom of the last page, overrun with her strong, gothic script, I read: "You know, my dearest one on earth to me, what a good future we have. . . ." I took the *future* and cast it violently to the ground, and pressed my heel against it until it hissed and crept away. Had not Jehovah made enough tragic sport of her life? Now I sank beneath all her hopes and even her endearments crushed me.

On the 15th of February, 1946, I lay in my bed, going to and fro in it and unable to seal the wandering scenes that passed through my head. Again a river arose and a cruse of water and a loaf of bread grew out of it, but stare as hard as I could, there was nothing else, and when I awakened, I shrieked, "Mother, your wicked, fallen son will come to your side; you will not die alone." Shaking the sleep from me, I prodded my wife, saying, "Let us go to my mother before she dies." Her face was a stranger to me and she gave me no answer.

On the 18th of February there came another letter from my mother, but I would not open it. Had I had a hammer, I could not have broken this envelope made of black basalt. On that night in the month known as Shebat in Hebrew, which is a time of tears and lamentations, she died. She was alone, and her body lay on the cot for five days before a neighbor found her.

It is hideous and coarse to assume that we can do something for others—and it is vile not to endeavor to do it. I had not the strength to handle her tragedy, for my will has failed me every hour of each day. It is said that a wise man falls down seven times a day and rises; I have fallen and never gotten up.

My mother was born unfortunate, and she was pursued until her end by that evil genius, ill luck. The Psalmist says, "No one can keep his own soul alive"—nor anybody else's either. We despair because we are no better and are not consoled that we can be no worse. A life is a single folly, but two lives would be countless ones, for nobody profits by his mistakes.

I do not go to her grave because it would do her no good. Though everything in the earth has feeling—the granite mourns, the turf sleeps and has fitful nights, and the syenite chants as melodiously as Orpheus and Musaeus[3]—it would be idle to say that Lizzie Dalberg, whose bones still have sentience, is what she was. She is and she is not, and that is the difference between the trance we call being and the other immense experience we name death.

3. Orpheus and Musaeus are figures from Greek mythology. Orpheus is a poet and musician, favorite of the Muses, who symbolizes the spirit of music; Musaeus is his son. "Syenite": a variety of granite quarried in ancient times in Syene (now Aswan) in Upper Egypt.

Who was Lizzie Dalberg? I wish to God I knew, but it is my infamy that I do not. How often had she pleaded with heaven to lead her out of the peopleless desert of Beersheba, but to what avail? She only questioned God in anger once: "Why am I miserable, while others who are pitiless and contemptible are so fortunate?"

But she never received an answer. Not God, but gibing Pilate came to her and asked, "What is Truth?"[4]

And I knew not why until I had heard her quiet reply: "My life."

When the image of her comes up on a sudden—just as my bad demons do—and I see again her dyed henna hair, the eyes dwarfed by the electric lights in the Star Lady Barbershop, and the dear, broken wing of her mouth, and when I regard her wild tatters, I know that not even Solomon in his lilied raiment[5] was so glorious as my mother in her rags. *Selah*.[6]

1962 1971

4. Pontius Pilate was the Roman governor of Jerusalem when Christ was crucified. For not defending Jesus against his accusers, Pilate is often seen as "gibing" or jesting, a relativist and skeptic evading his responsibility.

5. King Solomon (d. 933 B.C.E.), ruler of Israel, wore gorgeous clothes but was famed mostly for his wisdom.

6. The traditional ending of a psalm (Hebrew).

KENNETH FEARING
1902–1961

Kenneth Fearing, poet and novelist, also wrote for pulp magazines and worked as an editor in Chicago and New York. Born in Oak Park, Illinois, he attended the University of Wisconsin. He was noticeable—and noticed—as a young writer of irregular habits and is remembered in the *Wisconsin Alumnus* of 1967, along with fellow poet and student Carl Rakosi, as one of a "circle," himself marked by a "great shock of uncut, unkempt hair, which was the talk of the campus." Rakosi reports that Fearing "seldom left his room . . . laundry lay piled up on the floor . . . he was already a heavy drinker and did his writing at night . . . skipping classes. . . . He had admirers . . . who hung around him, basking in his bohemian boldness and waiting for his next bon mot."

Fearing graduated in 1924 and moved to New York City, where, in the radical milieu of the 1930s, he established himself as a proletarian poet and novelist. He was no dogmatist, however, but basically skeptical, iconoclastic, and sharply satirical. His mordant wit and boisterously sardonic renderings of the platitudes of the American way of life/business have not often been equaled. Influenced by W. H. Auden and C. Day-Lewis as well as by Carl Sandburg's long lines, Fearing's poems would sometimes be regarded as light verse, comparable to those of Ogden Nash and Dorothy Parker in the *New Yorker*, where he also published. He won Guggenheim fellowships in 1936 and 1939, and ultimately published seven volumes of verse and eight novels.

In the 1940s, Fearing wrote scripts for several outstanding Hollywood psychothrillers, and one of his novels, *The Big Clock* (1946), became a Paramount film in 1947. This novel has become a classic in its field, and a new film version of it, *No Way Out*, was made in 1987.

Fearing lived in New York in the post–World War II years, and his work (with that of Horace Gregory and Muriel Rukeyser) became the subject of a Columbia dissertation, *Chief Poets of the American Depression*, by M. L. Rosenthal, who also became a friend. Rosenthal sees these poets as "survivors of the literary and political battle of the thirties . . . increasingly neglected . . . though at the height of their powers."

The poems included here were published in *Poems* (1935) and *Afternoon of a Pawnbroker* (1943).

Dirge[1]

1-2-3 was the number he played but today the number came 3-2-1;
Bought his Carbide at 30 and it went to 29; had the favorite at Bowie[2] but the track was slow—

O executive type, would you like to drive a floating-power, knee-action, silk-upholstered six? Wed a Hollywood star? Shoot the course in 58? Draw to the ace, king, jack?[3]
O fellow with a will who won't take no, watch out for three cigarettes on the same, single match;[4] O democratic voter born in August under Mars, beware of liquidated rails—

Denouement to denouement, he took a personal pride in the certain, certain way he lived his own, private life,
But nevertheless, they shut off his gas; nevertheless, the bank foreclosed; nevertheless, the landlord called; nevertheless, the radio broke,

And twelve o'clock arrived just once too often,
Just the same he wore one gray tweed suit, bought one straw hat, drank one straight Scotch, walked one short step, took one long look, drew one deep breath,
Just one too many,

And wow he died as wow he lived,
Going whop to the office and blooie home to sleep and biff got married and bam had children and oof got fired,
Zowie did he live and zowie did he die,

With who the hell are you at the corner of his casket, and where the hell're we going on the right-hand silver knob, and who the hell cares walking second from the end with an American Beauty[5] wreath from why the hell not,

Very much missed by the circulation staff of the New York Evening Post; deeply, deeply mourned by the B.M.T.[6]

1. From *Complete Poems* (1994). "Dirge": a funeral hymn.
2. A racetrack in Washington, D.C. "Number": refers to the number that is picked to wager on in a lottery. "Carbide": stock in a metal company.
3. In poker, starting with a weak hand and getting a good one.
4. In World War I, soldiers believed that three men lighting their cigarettes from one match would give the enemy time and illumination enough to shoot them; it later was seen as an act that brought on bad luck. "Mars": a planet named for the Roman god of war.
5. A popular long-stemmed rose.
6. I.e., Brooklyn Manhattan Transit, part of New York's public transit system. "New York Evening Post": a daily newspaper.

Wham, Mr. Roosevelt; pow, Sears Roebuck;[7] awk, big dipper; bop, summer rain;
Bong, Mr., bong, Mr., bong, Mr., bong.

1934

Beware[1]

Someone, somewhere, is always starting trouble,
Either a relative, or a drunken friend, or a foreign state.
Trouble it is, trouble it was, trouble it will always be.
Nobody ever leaves well enough alone.

It begins, as a rule, with an innocent face and a trivial remark:
"There are two sides to every question," or "Sign right here, on the dotted line,"
But it always ends with a crash of glass and a terrible shout—
No one, no one lets sleeping dragons sleep.[2]

And it never happens, when the doorbell rings, that you find a troupe of houris[3] standing on your stoop.
Just the reverse.
So beware of doorbells. (And beware, beware of houris, too)
And you never receive a letter that says: "We enclose, herewith, our check for a million."
You know what the letter always says, instead.
So beware of letters. (And anyway, they say, beware of great wealth)

Be careful of doorbells, be cautious of telephones, watch out for genial strangers, and for ancient friends;
Beware of dotted lines, and mellow cocktails; don't touch letters sent specifically to you;
Beware, especially, of innocent remarks;
Beware of everything,
Damn near anything leads to trouble,
Someone is always, always stepping out of line.

1943

Afternoon of a Pawnbroker[1]

Still they bring me diamonds, diamonds, always diamonds,
Why don't they pledge something else for a change, if they must have loans, other than those diamond clasps and diamond rings,
Rubies, sapphires, emeralds, pearls,

7. A mail-order house, started in 1880s, famous for its all-inclusive catalogues of household goods. "Mr. Roosevelt": Franklin Delano Roosevelt (1882–1945) served as president from 1933 until his death. He led the United States out of the depression and through World War II.

1. From *Afternoon of a Pawnbroker* (1943).

2. Cf. "let sleeping dogs lie" (English proverb).

3. The beautiful virgins said to be provided for faithful Muslims in paradise.

1. From *Afternoon of a Pawnbroker* (1943).

Ermine wraps, silks and satins, solid gold watches and silver plate and violins two hundred years old,
And then again diamonds, diamonds, the neighborhood diamonds I have seen so many times before, and shall see so many times again?

Still I remember the strange afternoon (it was a season of extraordinary days and nights) when the first of the strange customers appeared.
And he waited, politely, while Mrs. Nunzio redeemed her furs, then he stepped to the counter and he laid down a thing that looked like a trumpet,
In fact, it was a trumpet, not mounted with diamonds, not plated with gold or even silver, and I started to say: "We can't use trumpets—"
But a light was in his eyes,
And after he was gone, I had the trumpet. And I stored it away. And the name on my books was Gabriel.[2]

It should be made clear my accounts are always open to the police, I have nothing to conceal.
I belong, myself, to the Sounder Business Principles League,
Have two married daughters, one of them in Brooklyn, the other in Cleveland,
And nothing like this had ever happened before.
How can I account for my lapse of mind?
All I can say is, it did not seem strange. Not at the time. Not in that neighborhood. And not in that year.

And the next to appear was a man with a soft, persuasive voice,
And a kindly face, and the most honest eyes I have ever seen, and ears like arrows, and a pointed beard,[3]
And what he said, after Mrs. Case had pledged her diamond ring and gone, I cannot now entirely recall,
But when he went away I found I had an apple. An apple, just an apple.
"It's been bitten," I remember that I tried to argue. But he smiled, and said in his quiet voice: "Yes, but only once."[4]
And the strangest thing is, it did not seem strange. Not strange at all.

And still those names are on my books.
And still I see listed, side by side, those incongruous, and not very sound securities:
(1) Aladdin's lamp (I must have been mad), (1) Pandora's box, (1) Magic carpet,
(1)Fountain of youth (in good condition), (1) Holy Grail,[5] (1)Invisible man

2. One of the archangels, usually a divine messenger (Daniel 8.16, 9.21; Luke 1.19, 1.26). He is also associated with the trumpet that tradition says will be blown to announce the End of Days (see the African American spirituals *Blow Your Trumpet, Gabriel* and *Blow, Gabriel*).
3. Satanic characteristic.
4. A reference to the apple from the tree of the knowledge of good and evil from which Eve took a bite.
5. A cup with regenerative powers supposedly used at the Last Supper and sought by medieval knights. "Aladdin's lamp": in the *Arabian Nights' Entertainments*, the lamp contains a genie who must do the owner's bidding when called. "Pandora's box": in Greek mythology, Pandora opened a closed box containing all the evils that could befall human beings. "Magic carpet": in the *Arabian Nights' Entertainments*, a carpet that transports its owner instantly to anywhere. "Fountain of youth": a mythical spring whose waters could restore health and youth; it was sought out in Florida and the Bahamas by explorers.

(the only article never redeemed, and I cannot locate him), and others, others, many others,
And still I recall how my storage vaults hummed and crackled from time to time, or sounded with music, or shot forth flame,
And I wonder, still, that the season did not seem one of unusual wonder, not even different—not at the time.

And still I think, at intervals, why didn't I, when the chance was mine, drink just once from that Fountain of youth?
Why didn't I open that box of Pandora?
And what if Mr. Gabriel, who redeemed his pledge and went away, should some day decide to blow on his trumpet?
Just one short blast, in the middle of some busy afternoon.

But here comes Mr. Barrington, to pawn his Stradivarius.[6]
And here comes Mrs. Case, to redeem her diamond ring.

1943

6. A violin made by the Italian Antonio Stradivari (1644–1737). It is the yardstick against which other violins are measured.

NATHANAEL WEST
1903–1940

Nathanael West, born Nathan Weinstein in New York City of parents who prospered in and much admired America and its mores, lived raffishly in his younger years. He wrote four slim novels that were admired only by a small group of readers when they appeared but that have become much treasured since. Two of them, *Miss Lonelyhearts* (1933) and *The Day of the Locust* (1939), are generally regarded to be minor classics. West died tragically young in a car crash when returning to his Hollywood home from a hunting trip with his recent bride, Eileen McKenney (who was the model for Ruth McKenney's novel and film *My Sister Eileen*).

West's youth was privileged. The family lived in what West's friend, the novelist John Sanford (born Julian Shapiro), called "the Gilded Ghetto" of Central Park West. West rebelled by dropping out of DeWitt Clinton High School and then forging his records in order to get into Tufts University. He was dropped after a year of carousing and a little study, whereupon he submitted the transcript of another and more successful student, also named Nathan Weinstein, and was admitted to Brown University. He buckled down to serious work, preparing himself for a literary career, although he was also known as something of a dandy. He graduated successfully.

He spent a few months in Paris; then, from 1927 to 1931, he was a night clerk in hotels near Greenwich Village, getting to know many would-be and successful writers, including William Faulkner, a coterie of leftists that included Michael Gold, Edward Dahlberg, Dashiell Hammett, and his future brother-in-law, S. J. Perelman. He also met John Dos Passos and Edmund Wilson at the *New Republic*.

While at Brown, West had begun a satiric tale about a flea, St. Puce, who lived in Christ's armpit. He enlarged upon this irreverent conceit in his first novel, completed in 1930, called *The Dream Life of Balso Snell*. Snell is a mediocre boob who dreams of entering the Trojan Horse through its anus and, in its innards, meets a variety of types (including St. Puce), composes songs, a play, diatribes against pseudosophisticates (based on West's own experiences and aversions) and religious beliefs in the art, literary, and intellectual worlds. A young man's book, meant to shock and even disgust, it had difficulty finding a publisher until William Carlos Williams recommended it to Contact Editions. It sold very poorly, although Williams asked West to coedit *Contact*, his magazine in which sections of *Miss Lonelyhearts* first appeared.

Miss Lonelyhearts is about a newspaperman given the assignment of writing a column of advice to the lovelorn and other needy souls. The misery and hopelessness he is daily exposed to in the letters he receives and the undercutting of all remedies by his cynical editor drive him mad. He assumes a Christlike posture, finally being shot accidentally by a hapless handicapped man he is offering to embrace. A mordant tale, it is also a satiric and unforgettable gem about an age in which love and compassion are seen as essentially futile gestures.

A Cool Million (1934), from which the selection printed here is taken, was West's next novel, originally called *America, America*. The satire gleefully exposes the Horatio Alger myth. The central character, Lemuel Pitkin, is an all-American farm boy from Vermont who believes in the American dream of opportunity and success through hard work and a pure heart. But he is thwarted at every turn: as he proceeds on his picaresque path, he is literally dismantled (the subtitle of the book is *The Dismantling of Lemuel Pitkin*), losing an eye, a leg, his scalp. He is finally shot and killed at a rally of American fascists led by his mentor, an ex-president named Shagpoke Whipple, and becomes the movement's martyr and symbol.

West was by this time a man of the Left, deeply affected by the Great Depression of the 1930s, though he had work as a Hollywood screenwriter from 1933 onward. His concern about the shoddiness of America's mass commercial culture and his alarm at the presence of American fascist organizations were based on reality. Over one hundred anti-Semitic groups were formed in the 1930s—"the worst decade of anti-Semitism in American history," according to historian Gerald Sorin. Much of this movement drew support and sustenance from the fascist regime in Italy and the Nazis in Germany.

West took aim at these groups' hollow rhetoric and their violent, irrational notions. In our excerpt, the irrationality is satirized in the claim that "the Jews" were at the same time the leaders both of international banking (and capitalism) as well as of international bolshevism. This absurd contradiction was not merely an aberrant belief among right-wing groups. Henry Ford had been publishing such matter in his newspaper, the *Dearborn Independent*, throughout most of the 1920s, and from 1937 to 1940 a priest named Father Charles Coughlin preached similarly on the radio weekly to an estimated audience of 25 million listeners. His publication, *Social Justice*, was finally stopped during the war, in 1942, by the Catholic Church.

The potential for apocalyptic violence anticipated in these early works reached its fruition in *The Day of the Locust*, considered by many the finest Hollywood novel ever. In it, West focuses primarily on the seamy side of the movie capital—bit players, phony cowboys and stuntmen, aspiring amoral starlets, cockfights, brothels, dwarfs, and various misfits—chiefly on Homer Simpson, a displaced and pathetic Midwesterner. All of these people are encountered by the central character, Todd Hackett, an artist working as a designer, who is painting a large canvas called *The Burning of Los Angeles*. The painting turns out to be prophetic at the explosive end of the novel, when a huge crowd of "middle Americans" who had moved to California in pursuit of movie-inspired dreams are driven to riot and murderous violence by their frustrations.

The sketch of West by his brother-in-law, the humorist S. J. Perelman, that is included in this section displays both the comic ebullience of Perelman and the affection in which West was held by those close to him.

From A Cool Million

INTERNATIONAL JEWISH BANKERS AND BOLSHEVIKS

One wintry morning, several weeks after the incident in the park, Lem was dismissed from the hospital minus his right eye. It had been so severely damaged that the physicians had thought best to remove it.

He had no money, for, as we have recounted, Snodgrasse's henchmen had robbed him. Even the teeth that Warden Purdy had given him were gone. They had been taken from him by the hospital authorities, who claimed that they did not fit properly and were therefore a menace to his health.

The poor lad was standing on a windy corner, not knowing which way to turn, when he saw a man in a coonskin hat. This remarkable headgear made Lem stare, and the more he looked the more the man seemed to resemble Shagpoke Whipple.

It was Mr. Whipple. Lem hastened to call out to him, and the ex-President stopped to shake hands with his young friend.

"About those inventions," Shagpoke said immediately after they had finished greeting each other. "It was too bad that you left the penitentiary before I could hand them over to you. Not knowing your whereabouts, I perfected them myself.

"But let us repair to a coffee place," he added, changing the subject, "where we can talk over your prospects together. I am still very much interested in your career. In fact, my young friend, America has never had a greater need for her youth than in these parlous times."

After our hero had thanked him for his interest and good wishes, Mr. Whipple continued to talk. "Speaking of coffee," he said, "did you know that the fate of our country was decided in the coffee shops of Boston during the hectic days preceding the late rebellion?"

As they paused at the door of a restaurant, Mr. Whipple asked Lem still another question. "By the way," he said, "I am temporarily without funds. Are you able to meet the obligation we will incur in this place?"

"No," replied Lem, sadly, "I am penniless."

"That's different," said Mr. Whipple with a profound sigh. "In that case we will go where I have credit."

Lem was conducted by his fellow townsman to an extremely poor section of the city. After standing on line for several hours, they each received a doughnut and a cup of coffee from the Salvation Army lassie in charge. They then sat down on the curb to eat their little snack.

"You are perhaps wondering," Shagpoke began, "how it is that I stand on line with these homeless vagrants to obtain bad coffee and soggy doughnuts. Be assured that I do it of my own free will and for the good of the state."

Here he paused long enough to skillfully "shoot a snipe"[1] that was still burning. He puffed contentedly on his catch.

"When I left jail, it was my intention to run for office again. But I discovered to my great amazement and utter horror that my party, the Democratic Party, carried not a single plank in its platform that I could honestly endorse.

1. To pick up a cigarette butt.

Rank socialism was and is rampant. How could I, Shagpoke Whipple, ever bring myself to accept a program which promised to take from American citizens their inalienable birthright; the right to sell their labor and their children's labor without restrictions as to either price or hours?

"The time for a new party with the old American principles was, I realized, overripe. I decided to form it; and so the National Revolutionary Party, popularly known as the 'Leather Shirts,' was born. The uniform of our 'Storm Troops'[2] is a coonskin cap like the one I am wearing, a deerskin shirt and a pair of moccasins. Our weapon is the squirrel rifle."

He pointed to the long queue of unemployed who stood waiting before the Salvation Army canteen. "These men," he said, "are the material from which I must fill the ranks of my party."

With all the formality of a priest, Shagpoke turned to our hero and laid his hand on his shoulder.

"My boy," he said, and his voice broke under the load of emotion it was forced to bear, "my boy, will you join me?"

"Certainly, sir," said Lem, a little unsurely.

"Excellent!" exclaimed Mr. Whipple. "Excellent! I herewith appoint you a commander attached to my general staff."

He drew himself up and saluted Lem, who was startled by the gesture.

"Commander Pitkin," he ordered briskly, "I desire to address these people. Please obtain a soapbox."

Our hero went on the errand required of him, and soon returned with a large box, which Mr. Whipple immediately mounted. He then set about attracting the attention of the vagrants collected about the Salvation Army canteen by shouting:

"Remember the River Raisin!

"Remember the Alamo!

"Remember the Maine!"[3] and many other famous slogans.

When a large group had gathered, Shagpoke began his harangue.

"I'm a simple man," he said with great simplicity, "and I want to talk to you about simple things. You'll get no highfalutin talk from me.

"First of all, you people want jobs. Isn't that so?"

An ominous rumble of assent came from the throats of the poorly dressed gathering.

"Well, that's the only and prime purpose of the National Revolutionary Party—to get jobs for everyone. There was enough work to go around in 1927, why isn't there enough now? I'll tell you; because of the Jewish international bankers and the Bolshevik labor unions, that's why. It was those two agents that did the most to hinder American business and to destroy its glorious expansion. The former because of their hatred of America and love

2. The corps of bullies Adolf Hitler used to intimidate and beat people in his drive to bring the National Socialist German Workers' party (the Nazis) to power in Germany in 1933. They wore brown shirts; later, the SS, an elite corps of his killers, wore black shirts. Many fascist groups in 1930s America emulated them, wearing and calling themselves "Silver Shirts" and the like.

3. A U.S. battleship blown up in obscure circumstances in Havana harbor. The incident provided the occasion for America to declare war on Spain (which ruled Cuba then) in 1898. "River Raisin": the scene of a massacre in 1813 following an American defeat at the hands of the British during the War of 1812. "Alamo": a mission house and fort in San Antonio, Texas, occupied in 1836 by Americans who wanted to make Texas independent of Mexico. They were besieged and overrun by Mexican troops led by General Santa Anna and were killed. The event became a rallying cry later in the U.S. war with Mexico (1846–48) that led to American seizure of much territory from Mexico.

for Europe and the latter because of their greed for higher and still higher wages.

"What is the role of the labor union today? It is a privileged club which controls all the best jobs for its members. When one of you applies for a job, even if the man who owns the plant wants to hire you, do you get it? Not if you haven't got a union card. Can any tyranny be greater? Has Liberty ever been more brazenly despised?"

These statements were received with cheers by his audience.

"Citizens, Americans," Mr. Whipple continued, when the noise had subsided, "we of the middle class are being crushed between two gigantic millstones. Capital is the upper stone and Labor the lower, and between them we suffer and die, ground out of existence.

"Capital is international; its home is in London and in Amsterdam. Labor is international; its home is in Moscow. We alone are American; and when we die, America dies.

"When I say that, I make no idle boast, for history bears me out. Who but the middle class left aristocratic Europe to settle on these shores? Who but the middle class, the small farmers and storekeepers, the clerks and petty officials, fought for freedom and died that America might escape from British tyranny?

"This is our country and we must fight to keep it so. If America is ever again to be great, it can only be through the triumph of the revolutionary middle class.

"We must drive the Jewish international bankers out of Wall Street! We must destroy the Bolshevik labor unions! We must purge our country of all the alien elements and ideas that now infest her!

"America for Americans! Back to the principles of Andy Jackson and Abe Lincoln!"

Here Shagpoke paused to let the cheers die down, then called for volunteers to join his "Storm Battalions."

A number of men came forward. In their lead was a very dark individual, who had extra-long black hair of an extremely coarse quality, and on whose head was a derby hat many sizes too small for him.

"Me American mans," he announced proudly. "Me got heap coon hat, two maybe six. By, by catchum plenty more coon maybe." With this he grinned from ear to ear.

But Shagpoke was a little suspicious of his complexion, and looked at him with disfavor. In the South, where he expected to get considerable support for his movement, they would not stand for Negroes.

The good-natured stranger seemed to sense what was wrong, for he said, "Me Injun, mister, me chief along my people. Gotum gold mine, oil well. Name of Jake Raven. Ugh!"

Shagpoke grew cordial at once. "Chief Jake Raven," he said, holding out his hand, "I am happy to welcome you into our organization. We 'Leather Shirts' can learn much from your people, fortitude, courage and relentless purpose among other things."

After taking down his name, Shagpoke gave the Indian a card which read as follows:

EZRA SILVERBLATT
Official Tailor
to the
NATIONAL REVOLUTIONARY PARTY

Coonskin hats with extra long tails, deerskin shirts with or without fringes, blue jeans, moccasins, squirrel rifles, everything for the American Fascist at rock bottom prices. 30% off for Cash.

But let us leave Mr. Whipple and Lem busy with their recruiting to observe the actions of a certain member of the crowd.

The individual in question would have been remarkable in any gathering, and among the starved, ragged men that surrounded Shagpoke, he stuck out like the proverbial sore thumb. For one thing he was fat, enormously fat. There were other fat men present to be sure, but they were yellow, unhealthy, while this man's fat was pink and shone with health.

On his head was a magnificent bowler hat. It was a beautiful jet in color, and must have cost more than twelve dollars. He was snugly encased in a tight-fitting Chesterfield overcoat with a black velvet collar. His stiff-bosomed shirt had light gray bars, and his tie was of some rich but sober material in black and white pin-checks. Spats, rattan stick and yellow gloves completed his outfit.

This elaborate fat man tiptoed out of the crowd and made his way to a telephone booth in a nearby drug store, where he called two numbers.

His conversation with the person answering his first call, a Wall Street exchange, went something like this:

"Operative 6384XM, working out of the Bourse, Paris, France. Middle-class organizers functioning on unemployed front, corner of Houston and Bleecker Streets."[4]

"Thank you, 6384XM, what is your estimate?"

"Twenty men and a fire hose."

"At once, 6384XM, at once."

His second call was to an office near Union Square.[5]

"Comrade R, please. . . . Comrade R?"

"Yes."

"Comrade R, this is Comrade Z speaking. Gay Pay Oo,[6] Moscow, Russia. Middle-class organizers recruiting on the corner of Houston and Bleecker Streets."

"Your estimate, comrade, for liquidation of said activities?"

"Ten men with lead pipes and brass knuckles to cooperate with Wall Street office of the I.J.B."[7]

"No bombs required?"

"No, comrade."

"Der Tag!"[8]

"Der Tag!"

4. Streets in Greenwich Village in Manhattan.
5. A spot where radicals orated at open-air meetings. Its southern boundary is at Fourteenth Street and Broadway in Manhattan.
6. GPU were initials of the Soviet intelligence agency.
7. I.e., International Jewish Bankers.
8. "To the day!" (when they gain control of the whole world) (German).

Mr. Whipple had just enrolled his twenty-seventh recruit, when the forces of both the international Jewish bankers and the Communists converged on his meeting. They arrived in high-powered black limousines and deployed through the streets with a skill which showed long and careful training in that type of work. In fact their officers were all West Point graduates.

Mr. Whipple saw them coming, but like a good general his first thoughts were for his men.

"The National Revolutionary Party will now go underground!" he shouted.

Lem, made wary by his past experiences with the police, immediately took to his heels, followed by Chief Raven. Shagpoke, however, was late in getting started. He still had one foot on the soapbox when he was hit a terrific blow on the head with a piece of lead pipe.

1934

S. J. PERELMAN
1904–1979

Sidney Joseph Perelman was born in Brooklyn, New York, the son of Joseph and Sophia Perelman. The family soon moved to Rhode Island, where they ran a chicken farm, and Perelman grew up in Providence. He attended Brown University from 1921 to 1925 but took no degree. Shortly thereafter he collaborated on an early comic novel with Quentin Reynolds, a writer and Brown alumnus, as was Nathanael West, whose sister Perelman married in 1929. He is probably best known as a comic writer of short essays and pieces, 500 of them, 278 of which appeared in the *New Yorker* from the early 1930s until shortly before his death. Many of these were collected in a series of popular books, among them *Dawn Ginsbergh's Revenge* (1929), *Westward Ha! or Around the World in Eighty Clichés* (1948), *The Swiss Family Perelman* (1950). He specialized in literary parodies and burlesques as well as the comic travel genre, all executed in a tone of witty urbanity. His work is said to have influenced writers as various as Paul Theroux, John Updike, and Woody Allen.

Perelman also wrote a great deal for the movies. Most enduringly, he collaborated on the screenplays of two early Marx Brothers' films: *Monkey Business* (1931) and *Horse Feathers* (1932). He shared an Oscar for best screenplay for *Around the World in Eighty Days* (1956). His greatest love, however, was writing for the stage, where his only real success was his book for *One Touch of Venus* in 1943. That long-running play had music by Kurt Weill, lyrics by Ogden Nash, and starred a young Mary Martin in her first success.

Although Perelman was a political liberal himself, the perfect ear and antic mockery of his *Waiting for Santy* is a deft deflation of the rhetoric and style of Clifford Odets's *Waiting for Lefty*, one of the more popular agitprop plays of the 1930s. It also lampoons much of the politically correct literature of the period. His send-up of the literary "portrait" in his short Nathanael West piece speaks for itself.

Waiting for Santy: A Christmas Playlet by S. J. Perelman (with a bow to Mr. Clifford Odets)[1]

SCENE: *The sweatshop*[2] *of S. Claus, a manufacturer of children's toys, on North Pole Street. Time: The night before Christmas.*[3]

At rise, seven gnomes, Rankin, Panken, Rivkin, Riskin, Ruskin, Briskin, and Praskin, are discovered working furiously to fill orders piling up at stage right. The whir of lathes, the hum of motors, and the hiss of drying lacquer are so deafening that at times the dialogue cannot be heard, which is very vexing if you vex easily. (Note: The parts of Rankin, Panken, Rivkin, Riskin, Ruskin, Briskin, and Praskin are interchangeable, and may be secured directly from your dealer or the factory.)

RISKIN [*filing a Meccano*[4] *girder, bitterly*]: —A parasite, a leech, a bloodsucker—altogether a five-star nogoodnick! Starvation wages we get so he can ride around in a red team with reindeers!

RUSKIN [*jeering*]: —Hey, Karl Marx, whyn'tcha hire a hall?

RISKIN [*sneering*]: —Scab! Stool pigeon! Company spy![5] [*They tangle and rain blows on each other. While waiting for these to dry, each returns to his respective task.*]

BRISKIN [*sadly, to Panken*]: —All day long I'm painting "Snow Queen" on these Flexible Flyers[6] and my little Irving lays in a cold tenement with the gout.

PANKEN: —You said before it was the mumps.

BRISKIN [*with a fatalistic shrug*]: —The mumps—the gout—go argue with City Hall.

PANKEN [*kindly, passing him a bowl*]: —Here, take a piece fruit.

BRISKIN [*chewing*]: —It ain't bad, for wax fruit.

PANKEN [*with pride*]: —I painted it myself.

BRISKIN [*rejecting the fruit*]: —Ptoo! Slave psychology!

RIVKIN [*suddenly, half to himself, half to the Party*]: —I got a belly full of stars, baby. You make me feel like I swallowed a Roman candle.

PRASKIN [*curiously*]: —What's wrong with the kid?

RISKIN: —What's wrong with all of us? The system! Two years he and Claus's daughter's been making googoo eyes behind the old man's back.

PRASKIN: —So what?

RISKIN [*scornfully*]: —So what? Economic determinism! What do you think the kid's name is—J. Pierpont Rivkin? He ain't even got for a bottle Dr. Brown's Celery Tonic.[7] I tell you, it's like gall in my mouth two young people shouldn't have a room where they could make great music.

RANKIN [*warningly*]: —Shhh! Here she comes now! [*Stella Claus enters, carrying a portable phonograph. She and Rivkin embrace, place a record*

1. The author of *Waiting for Lefty* (1935) and *Awake and Sing!* (1935) as well as many other plays.

2. A small factory employing exploited or "sweated" workers, often immigrants.

3. Part of the first line of the popular poem by Clement Moore (1779–1863), actually entitled *A Visit from St. Nicholas* (1823).

4. The trade name of a building toy.

5. Terms used to describe antiunion workers unwilling to organize and / or go on strike. "Karl Marx" (1818–1883): German philosopher, economist, and revolutionary; author of *The Communist Manifesto* (1848) and *Das Kapital* (1867).

6. Trade name of sleds with movable steering bars. "Snow Queen": an 1845 story by the Danish writer of fairy tales Hans Christian Andersen (1805–1875).

7. A bottled soft drink. "J. Pierpont": the first two names of American banker and financier J. P. Morgan (1837–1913).

on the turntable, and begin a very slow waltz, unmindful that the phonograph is playing "Cohen on the Telephone."][8]

STELLA [*dreamily*]: —Love me, sugar?

RIVKIN: —I can't sleep, I can't eat, that's how I love you. You're a double malted with two scoops of whipped cream; you're the moon rising over Mosholu Parkway; you're a two weeks' vacation at Camp Nitgedaiget! I'd pull down the Chrysler Building[9] to make a bobbie pin for your hair!

STELLA: —I've got a stomach full of anguish. Oh, Rivvy, what'll we do?

PANKEN [*sympathetically*]: —Here, try a piece fruit.

RIVKIN [*fiercely*]: —Wax fruit—that's been my whole life! Imitations! Substitutes! Well, I'm through! Stella, tonight I'm telling your old man. He can't play mumblety-peg[1] with two human beings! [*The tinkle of sleigh bells is heard offstage, followed by a voice shouting, "Whoa, Dasher! Whoa, Dancer!" A moment later S. Claus enters in a gust of mock snow. He is a pompous bourgeois of sixty-five who affects a white beard and a false air of benevolence. But tonight the ruddy color is missing from his cheeks, his step falters, and he moves heavily. The gnomes hastily replace the marzipan they have been filching.*]

STELLA [*anxiously*]: —Papa! What did the specialist say to you?

CLAUS [*brokenly*]: —The biggest professor in the country . . . the best cardiac man that money could buy. . . . I tell you I was like a wild man.

STELLA: —Pull yourself together, Sam!

CLAUS: —It's no use. Adhesions, diabetes, sleeping sickness, decalcomania—oh, my God! I got to cut out climbing in chimneys, he says—me, Sanford Claus, the biggest toy concern in the world!

STELLA [*soothingly*]: —After all, it's only one man's opinion.

CLAUS: —No, no, he cooked my goose. I'm like a broken uke[2] after a Yosian picnic. Rivkin!

RIVKIN: —Yes, Sam.

CLAUS: —My boy, I had my eye on you for a long time. You and Stella thought you were too foxy for an old man, didn't you? Well, let bygones be bygones. Stella, do you love this gnome?

STELLA [*simply*]: —He's the whole stage show at the Music Hall, Papa; he's Toscanini conducting Beethoven's Fifth;[3] he's—

CLAUS [*curtly*]: —Enough already. Take him. From now on he's a partner in the firm. [*As all exclaim, Claus holds up his hand for silence.*] And tonight he can take my route and make the deliveries. It's the least I could do for my own flesh and blood. [*As the happy couple kiss, Claus wipes away a suspicious moisture and turns to the other gnomes.*] Boys, do you know what day tomorrow is?

GNOMES [*crowding around expectantly*]: —Christmas!

CLAUS: —Correct. When you look in your envelopes tonight, you'll find a little present from me—a forty-percent pay cut. And the first one who

8. A short sound film made in 1929, in which Jewish immigrant speech is the source of humor.
9. The tallest building in the United States from 1926 to 1929; located in Manhattan. "Mosholu Parkway": a highway in the Bronx. "Camp Nitgedaiget": Camp Blighted (Yiddish).
1. A game played with a pocketknife.
2. Abbreviation for *ukulele,* a four-stringed Hawaiian guitar.
3. A symphony by Ludwig van Beethoven (1770–1827). "Music Hall": i.e., Radio City Music Hall, a large movie palace in New York City famous for its elaborate stage shows; now used for concerts, special events, and holiday extravaganzas. "Toscanini": Arturo Toscanini (1867–1957) was an Italian conductor of symphony orchestras who was famous for his interpretations of Beethoven.

opens his trap—gets this. [*As he holds up a tear-gas bomb and beams at them, the gnomes utter cries of joy, join hands, and dance around him shouting exultantly. All except Riskin and Briskin, that is, who exchange a quick glance and go underground.*]

CURTAIN

1936

Nathanael West: A Portrait[1]

"Picture to yourself a ruddy-cheeked, stocky sort of chap, dressed in loose tweeds, a stubby briar[2] in his teeth, with a firm yet humorous mouth, generous to a fault, everready for a flagon of nut-brown ale with his cronies, possessing the courage of a lion and the tenderness of a woman, an intellectual vagabond, a connoisseur of first editions, fine wines, and beautiful women, well above six feet in height and distinguished for his pallor, a dweller in the world of books, his keen grey eyes belying the sensual lip, equally at home browsing through the bookstalls along the Paris quais and rubbing elbows in the smart literary salons of the Faubourg St. Honore,[3] a rigid abstainer and non-smoker, living entirely on dehydrated fruits, cereals, and nuts, rarely leaving his monastic cell, an intimate of Cocteau, Picasso, Joyce and Lincoln Kirstein,[4] a dead shot, a past master of the foils, dictating his novels, plays, poems, short stories, epigrams, aphorisms, and sayings to a corps of secretaries at lightning speed, an expert judge of horseflesh, the owner of a model farm equipped with the latest dairy devices—a man as sharp as a razor, as dull as a hoe, as clean as a whistle, as tough as nails, as white as snow, as black as the raven's wing, and as poor as Job. A man kind and captious, sweet and sour, fat and thin, tall and short, racked with fever, plagued by the locust, beset by witches, hag-ridden, cross-grained, a fun-loving, serious-minded dreamer, visionary and slippered pantaloon.[5] Picture to yourself such a man, I say, and you won't have the faintest idea of Nathanael West.

"To begin with, the author of *Miss Lonelyhearts*[6] is only eighteen inches high. He is very sensitive about his stature and only goes out after dark, and then armed with a tiny umbrella with which he beats off cats who try to attack him. Being unable to climb into his bed, which is at least two feet taller than himself, he has been forced to sleep in the lower drawer of a bureau since childhood, and is somewhat savage in consequence. He is

1. From *Contempo* (1933); reprinted in 1965 in the *Massachusetts Review*.
2. A pipe carved from the root of the brier.
3. A section of Paris (French). "Quais": walkways edging the river Seine (French).
4. Kirstein (1907–1999), an American writer and dance enthusiast, was cofounder with George Balanchine of the American Ballet Company. Jean Cocteau (1889–1963) was a French author and film maker. The Spanish artist Pablo Picasso (1881–1973) worked in France; he was a creator of cubism. James Joyce (1882–1941), Irish novelist and author of *Ulysses*, was a major 20th-century writer in English.
5. Short, loose trousers. "Epigrams": short, polished sayings, usually in verse. "Aphorisms": maxims or principles expressed in a few words. "Job": in the Bible, a good and faithful man whom God tests with great suffering and losses. "Locust": in the Bible, one of the plagues God visited on the Egyptians to force them to let the Jews go free.
6. A novel by Nathanael West (1933).

meticulously dressed, however, and never goes abroad without his green cloth gloves and neat nankeen breeches. His age is a matter of speculation. He claims to remember the Battle of the Boyne[7] and on a fine night his piping voice may be heard in the glen lifted in the strains of 'For She's my Molly-O.' Of one thing we can be sure; he was seen by unimpeachable witnesses at Austerlitz, Jena, and Wagram,[8] where he made personal appearances through the courtesy of Milton Fink of Fink & Biesemyer, his agents. What I like about him most is his mouth, a jagged scarlet wound etched against the unforgettable blankness of his face. I love his sudden impish smile, the twinkle of those alert green eyes, and the print of his cloven foot in the shrubbery. I love the curly brown locks cascading down his receding forehead; I love the wind in the willows, the boy in the bush, and the seven against Thebes.[9] I love coffee, I love tea, I love the girls and the girls love me. And I'm going to be a civil engineer when I grow up, no matter WHAT Mamma says."

1933 — 1965

7. A reference to an important battle (1690) fought on the banks of Ireland's Boyne River in which King William III's forces defeated those under James II. "Nankeen": a rough cotton made in China.

8. The site of a battle in 1808 in which the forces of Napoleon I defeated Austria. At Austerlitz in 1805, Napoleon defeated Russia and Austria. At Jena in 1806, he defeated Prussia.

9. A Greek myth in which seven heroes try to conquer Thebes. "Cloven foot": the mark of the devil. *The Wind in the Willows* (1908) is the title of a children's book by Kenneth Grahame (1859–1932).

LOUIS ZUKOFSKY
1904–1978

Louis Zukofsky's background and early years seem paradigmatic for an intellectual Jewish American boy of his generation. He was the youngest child of uneducated working-class parents both born in the same village in Lithuania, then under Russian rule. Three older children had been born before the father left for New York to earn the money to send for his family. Louis, born on Manhattan's Lower East Side, grew up close to his mother; his orthodox father worked long hours as a presser in a factory. The son would move away from religious observance as he became independent.

The parents' language remained Yiddish, and Zukofsky learned English only when he went to school. His earliest experience of literature was the Yiddish stage: between the ages of four and nine he had seen Yiddish Shakespeare and Aeschylus, Yiddish Ibsen and Strindberg and Tolstoy. At age eleven, he read all of Shakespeare's plays in English to win a school prize. The poems he was writing then were exercises in language acquisition, but when he entered Columbia College at not quite sixteen, he was ready to contribute verse to undergraduate publications. Mark Van Doren and John Erskine, well-known literary figures, taught him English literature; he admired John Dewey as a teacher. Whittaker Chambers, then a poet and soon a Communist party member, was a close friend.

After earning a master's degree, Zukofsky taught at the University of Wisconsin; he returned to New York to edit trade manuals and, as the depression deepened, to work on WPA projects. In 1947, Zukofsky began to teach at the Polytechnic Institute of Brooklyn, where Edward Dahlberg became a friend and colleague. He retired in

1966. He had married Celia Thaew, a musician, in 1939; their son Paul would become a violinist and composer.

It pleased Zukofsky to note that the year of his birth on Christie Street coincided with Henry James's visit to the Lower East Side, where, James observed, the inhabitants seemed each to display an "individual share of the whole hard glitter of Israel." By the time Zukofsky reached his mid-twenties, his poetry glittered with literary technique and talent enough to attract the interest of influential American poets. Ezra Pound and William Carlos Williams became his friends, and Pound—in spite of his anti-Semitism and fascist sympathies—remained a life-long hero. Zukofsky's *Poem beginning "The,"* which he considered a direct reply to T. S. Eliot's *The Waste Land*, had been accepted for publication by Pound in 1927. Zukofsky visited Pound in Italy, and Pound persuaded Harriet Monroe to devote an issue of *Poetry* magazine to Zukofsky and the objectivist group—a loose coalition of poets that then included Williams, Basil Bunting, George Oppen, Charles Reznikoff, Kenneth Rexroth, and others. Pound used Zukofsky's work in *Active Anthology* in 1932, and Zukofsky brought out *An "Objectivists" Anthology* a year later.

Zukofsky's objectivism has been discussed by the critic Marjorie Perloff, who suggests that his poetry, characterized by artifice, abstraction, parody, and breaks in tone, found an approach to writing between the dominant modes of modernism and social realism. Like the more recent postmodernists, the objectivists questioned the assumption that language needed to be thematic and representational. Among the poets who have testified to Zukofsky's innovative importance are Robert Creeley, Robert Duncan, Hugh Seidman, and Charles Tomlinson.

Zukofsky had begun to make plans for his major work in the years 1927–28, but its composition was not completed until 1974. *A* would become a book of more than 800 pages in 24 movements, the final one a 5-part musical score. Critic Barry Ahearn calls it a purposefully constructed collage; it is also a work in which each movement modifies and acts with and against all the others in the manner of music. For example, *A–8* uses the writings of the American Adams family, Karl Marx, Veblen, interwoven with still others, in the manner of a fugue to consider American history, decline, and rejuvenation; the Zukofsky family's place in that history; and the nature of music and art. Often revised and modified, sections of the poem had appeared in the 1930s; *A1–12*, printed by Cid Corman's Origin Press in Japan in 1959, was reissued under different imprints during the 1960s; later sections were also brought out separately. *"A": The Complete Poem* was published in its entirety the year of Zukofsky's death.

From Poem beginning "The"

FIFTH MOVEMENT: AUTOBIOGRAPHY[1]

Speaking about epics,[2] mother,
How long ago is it since you gathered mushrooms,
Gathered mushrooms while you mayed.[3]
Is it your mate, my father, boating.
A stove burns like a full moon in a desert night.

1. In *The Complete Short Poetry* (1991). *Poem beginning "The"* is a sequence in six movements in which the lines, from 1 through 330, are numbered consecutively.

2. Long poems, written in an elevated style, that recount the achievements of heroes (for example, *Odyssey, Iliad, Paradise Lost*). The writing of an epic poem has been thought to be a poet's major task to gain a place in history. "Symbol of our Relatively Most Permanent Self, Origin and Destiny—Wherever the reference is to the word Mother . . ." [Zukofsky's note].

3. Robert Herrick—187, 188 [Zukofsky's note]. A punning reference to the first line of Herrick's (1591–1674) English lyric *To Virgins to Make Much of Time*: "Gather ye rosebuds while ye may."

Un in hoyze is kalt.[4] You think of a new grave,
In the fields, flowers.
Night on the bladed grass, bayonets dewed.
Is it your mate, my father, boating.
Speaking about epics, mother,—
Down here among the gastanks, ruts, cemetery-tenements—
It is your Russia[5] that is free.
And I here, can I say only—
    "So then an egoist can never embrace a party
    Or take up with a party?
    Oh, yes, only he cannot let himself
    Be embraced or taken up by the party.'[6]
It is your Russia that is free, mother.
Tell me, mother.

Winged wild geese, where lies the passage,
In far away lands lies the passage.
Winged wild geese, who knows the pathway?
Of the winds, asking, we shall say:
Wind of the South and wind of the North
Where has our sun gone forth?
Naked, twisted, scraggly branches,
And dark, gray patches through the branches,
Ducks with puffed-up, fluttering feathers
On a cobalt stream.
And faded grass that's slowly swaying.
A barefoot shepherd boy
Striding in the mire:
Swishing indifferently a peeled branch
On jaded sheep.
An old horse strewn with yellow leaves
By the edge of the meadow
Draws weakly with humid nostrils
The moisture of the clouds.[7]
Horses that pass through inappreciable woodland,
Leaves in their manes tangled, mist, autumn green,
Lord, why not give these bright brutes—your good land—
Turf for their feet always, years for their mien.
See how each peer lifts his head, others follow,
Mate paired with mate, flanks coming full they crowd,
Reared in your sun, Lord, escaping each hollow
Where life-struck we stand, utter their praise aloud.
Very much Chance, Lord, as when you first made us,
You might forget them, Lord, preferring what
Being less lovely where sadly we fuss?

4. Jewish Folk Song—191 [Zukofsky's note]. "And it's cold in the house" (Yiddish).
5. Zukofsky's mother was born in 1862 and spent her youth in Lithuania when it belonged to czarist Russia. The poem was written when Russia was part of the Union of Soviet Socialist Republics.
6. Max Stirner—199–202 [Zukofsky's note]. Pseudonym of German philosopher Johann Kaspar Schmidt (1806–1856). The quotation is from his book *The Ego and His Own*, translated into English in 1905.
7. Yehoash . . . 205–223 [Zukofsky's note]. The pen name of Yehoash-Solomon Bloomgarden, Yiddish poet (1872–1927). These lines translate a song, *Cheshvan* (October), by Yehoash.

Weed out these horses as tho they were not?
Never alive in brute delicate trembling
Song to your sun, against autumn assembling.[8]

If horses could but sing Bach, mother,—
Remember how I wished it once—
Now I kiss you who could never sing Bach, never read Shakespeare.[9]

In Manhattan here the Chinamen[1] are yellow in the face, mother,
Up and down, up and down our streets they go yellow in the face,
And why is it the representatives of your, my, race are always hankering for
  food, mother?
We, on the other hand, eat so little.
Dawn't you think Trawtsky rawthaw a darrling,
I ask our immigrant cousin querulously.
Naw! I think hay is awlmawst a Tchekoff.[2]
But she has more color in her cheeks than the Angles[3]—Angels—mother,—
They have enough, though. We should get some more color, mother.
If I am like them in the rest, I should resemble them in that, mother,
Assimilation is not hard,
And once the Faith's askew
I might as well look Shagetz[4] just as much as Jew.
I'll read their Donne as mine,
And leopard in their spots
I'll do what says their Coleridge,[5]
Twist red hot pokers into knots.
The villainy they teach me I will execute
And it shall go hard with them,
For I'll better the instruction,
Having learned, so to speak, in their colleges.
    It is engendered in the eyes
    With gazing fed, and fancy dies
    In the cradle where it lies
    In the cradle where it lies[6]
I, Senora, am the Son of the Respected Rabbi,
Israel of Saragossa,[7]

8. Horses—224–237 [Zukofsky's note]. Horses are a favorite image in Zukofsky's work. In *A*, he indexes the term over one hundred times.

9. William Shakespeare (1564–1616), English poet and dramatist. Johann Sebastian Bach (1685–1750), German organist and composer.

1. The Yellow Menace—241–242 [Zukofsky's note]. The Yellow Menace or Yellow Peril alludes to the supposed dangers to the United States' population from Chinese and Japanese immigrants. From 1882 through the 1920s, nativist fears worked to limit such immigration.

2. Max Beerbohm—245 [Zukofsky's note]. English author, caricaturist, essayist, and parodist (1872–1956). His novel *Zuleika Dobson* (1911) parodied undergraduate life at Oxford. "Tchekoff": i.e., Anton Chekhov (1860–1904), Russian short story writer and dramatist. "Trawtsky": i.e., Leon Trotsky (1879–1940), Russian revolutionary and writer.

3. "Bede's Ecclesiastical History"—248 [Zukofsky's note]. The Angles (Anglos) were said to look like angels because they were so fair in color.

4. A non-Jewish male (Yiddish).

5. I.e., Samuel Taylor Coleridge (1772–1834), English poet, critic, and philosopher. John Donne (1572–1631) was an English poet and clergyman.

6. *The Merchant of Venice*—250–265 [Zukofsky's note]. This play (1597), sometimes known as *The Jew of Venice*, is by William Shakespeare. The reference is to the second stanza of the song *Tell me where is fancy bred* from *The Merchant of Venice* 3.2.67–69.

7. Heinrich Heine—266, 267, 269 . . . [Zukofsky's note]. German/Jewish lyric and satirical poet, journalist, critic (1797–1856). In these lines, the rabbi's son reveals himself as a Jew at the end of Heine's satiric poem *Donna Clara*.

Not that the Rabbis give a damn,
Keine Kadish wird man sagen.[8]

1926 1927

From A–8

[ARRIVED MOSTLY WITH BEDDING IN A SHEET]

Arrived mostly with bedding in a sheet
Samovar,[1] with tall pitcher of pink glass,
With copper mugs, with a beard,
Without shaving mug—
To America's land of the pilgrim Jews?
To buy, after 20 years in a railroad flat,[2]
A living room suite of varnished
Mahogany framed chairs and
Blue leather upholstery,
To be like everybody, with what
is about us.
And the youngest being born
here (in New York)
Always regretted having as a kid
Hit his brother's head with a shoe
In bed one bright Sunday morning.
Just like THAT, while his older brother
was still sleeping.
For no reason at all.

* * *

1935–1937 1959

From A–12

[IN HEBREW "IN THE BEGINNING"]

In Hebrew "In the beginning"
Means literally *from the head?*
A source creating
The heaven and the earth
And every plant in the field
Before it was in the earth.[1]
Sweet shapes from a head
Whose thought must live forever—

8. "No prayer for the dead will be said" (German).
1. A metal urn used in Russia for making tea.
2. A flat laid out with the rooms coming one after the other in a straight line. "Pilgrim": a wayfarer and stranger; also, one who visits a holy place or shrine.
1. A reference to the creation (Genesis 1.10–11).

Be the immortelle—
Before it is thought
A prayer to the East.[2]
Before light—the sun later—
To get over even its chaos early.
"You should not forget Him after crossing the sea, Pinchos"[3]

Maishe Afroim[4] to Pinchos—
Paul, after he had crossed it,
To those who could not say Pinchos.

Naming little Paul for him
Almost ninety—
I knew Pinchos would not mind
Their "English" names being the same.
He might have said to reprove me:
Jews remember the dead in time
Are in no hurry to flatter the living.
He never reproved me.
"Let it be Paul—I know
Ivanovich named for Ivan,
Before he is born.
Still, our Hebrew names are not the same.
Bless him, may he live
120 years."[5]
And the end is the same:
Bach remembers his own name.
Had he asked me to say Kadish
I believe I would have said it for him.
How fathom his will
Who had taught himself to be simple.
Everything should be as simple as it *can* be,
Says Einstein,[6]
But not simpler.

* * *

A Michtam[7] of David,
So many times on his lips:
You have said to Him
My goodness does not extend to you,
The pious in the earth and the excellent
Are all of my delight.
These lines are pleasant to me
That I have inherited.
My heart teaches me at night.
You are before me,
You strengthen my right hand

2. Jews face the East to say Kaddish. "Immortelle": the flower of the plant everlasting, which can be dried without the loss of color or shape.
3. The given name of Zukofsky's father.
4. The given names of Zukofsky's grandfather.
5. A traditional Yiddish blessing.
6. German-born (1879–1955), Jewish American theoretical physicist who formulated the theory of relativity.
7. A technical term of uncertain meaning used in Psalm titles (Hebrew).

That my breath rejoices.
You will not let me see death.
You lead me to life
Its pleasures, with your hand
Forever.[8]

* * *

1950–1951 1959

8. A reference to the King James version of Psalm 16, which Zukofsky has reworked and compressed.

BERISH VAYNSHTEYN (BERISH WEINSTEIN) 1905–1967

Called by critics "the most American" of the Yiddish poets, Berish Vaynshteyn wrote in long, free-verse lines reminiscent of Walt Whitman and Carl Sandburg that present, through the accumulation of detail, people in the grip of nature and society.

Vanyshteyn was born in Rzeszów (Reyshe, in Yiddish), Galicia, a center of Hasidic learning. His experiences as a refugee during World War I and the during the pogroms in Poland made him especially sensitive to the effects of prejudice, hatred, and brutality, themes that recur throughout his poems. He came to the United States in 1925 and began publishing poems in 1927. His first book, *Brukhvarg* (Broken Pieces), was published in 1936. Although this was not his most famous work during his lifetime, critics and translators rediscovered its rough, sensual poems in the 1980s. Vaynshteyn was better known for his autobiographical verse trilogy—*Reyshe* (1947), *Amerike* (1955), and *In dovid ha-melekhs giter* (In King David's Domains) (1960)—a series of book-length poems, written after World War II, that first evokes the hero's life in his now-destroyed shtetl, then describes his experience of immigration and Americanization, and finally depicts him in Israel. *Lider un poemes* (Poems and Long Poems, 1949) collected Vaynshteyn's poems from 1929 through 1949, and *Basherte lider* (Destined Poems, 1965), those written after 1949. In 1964, he published *Homeriade*, an imitation of Homer's Greek epics.

The poems we have included are from Vaynshteyn's first book, *Brukhvarg*. They convey the feeling of the depression years using, in translator Benjamin Harshav's terms, "rich, naturalistic American details in a surrealist composition." *On the Docks* and *Lynching* show the poet's vision of urban America, where the objects surrounding people characterize the human condition. Generalized portraits of people as types rather than as individuals come to life through the things they use. Vaynshteyn depicts with naturalistic detail specific neighborhoods and streets in New York—Harlem, Sheepshead Bay, Mangin Street, Division Street—and portrays workers and their environment—sailors and longshoremen on the docks, workers in the slaughterhouses—as well as the underworld—gangsters, prostitutes, drunks, homeless men "who talk to themselves." He observes and identifies with the hardships of African Americans in New York. In *Lynching*, a list of three places joins the victimization of African Americans in the South with that of Jews suffering under Hitler in Germany and Austria. *Earth*, set in the Galician countryside, shows Vaynshteyn in a pastoral, sensuous mood.

Earth[1]

Deep straw roofs dawn in gold, facing the sun.
There's the smell of stables, of raw wind and plowed earth.
Sweating peasants sound whips over the plow's pace.

When the sun is high, the earth lies tired, folded, and fertile.
Barefoot peasant women lie heavily with bosoms on the crumbled field
And cool their breasts in the plowed earth.
The dew still dampens their hair with daybreak droplets,
And on their laps their skirts fold, warm and transparent.

Horses. Hooves peel muddily, hides shudder at dung-covered flies;
And hay rustles wildly between their teeth;
Bridles run with sated foam from their tongues.

Midday sucks up the mist from the fields, the earth is mild, yielding.
Bent-over girls with seeds in their fingers tease the abundance,
And the earth rises monthly in heavy, swaying stalks.
The striving for harvest ripens, sheaves blaze beneath the sunset,
And kernels fall willingly under the thresher.

Rain. The earth renews its innards and refreshes the blossoms,
Buds open softly toward light, peasant women in the rain pluck wild grass,
And from soaked-through blouses their backs steam with young scent.
Herbs swell up wounded, from each leaflet falls rainy grace.
Prayerfully, village windows flare and shine like evening cliffs.
Horses run easily across twilit meadows. Witnessing—the earth darkens.
Behind the wood—dull church bells, mealtime behind bright panes.

1936

On the Docks[2]

On stone floors lie heavy ropes with steel anchors,
Crates, bales and high piles of bulging sacks.
Chests with rich, brass locks lie scattered about,
Oil barrels and hooped wooden casks filled with reinforced concrete,
And the walls give off a cool smell of goods from foreign lands.

Wide cargo-ships pull in from Cherbourg and Le Havre
With dark French faces of young sailors,
Agile and light for climbing on high ropes.
Their endless voyages have taught them to read signs of clouds and storms
  and rains,
They know how to call their signals out at night in the winds of the sea.

1. Translated by Kathryn Hellerstein.
2. Translated by Kathryn Hellerstein and Benjamin Harshav.

Poles, Negroes, Italians, and sturdy Jews load merchandise;
Their shoulders carry sharp hooks, on their waists hang bundles of food,
Their clothes: leather aprons, rough burlap shirts.
The strongest have tense bellies, powerful hands with thick fingers,
Their skin, torn by ropes and nailed crates,
Is yellow and coarse, cracking like the hooves of horses.

Ships from foreign places anchor at the docks, thrust the waters into the wind.
Immigrant faces disembark, Germans and Jews with frightened children,
On their clothes hang pinned-on names of a relative, of a street;
The faces are mute behind iron spikes, behind the heavy cold of bars,
Bars of disciplined fear before uniforms and rigid calendar-destiny.[3]

On stone floors lie heavy ropes with steel anchors,
Familiar baskets with scattered seals of borders and countries.
At the docks the pavement is shining, eroded by footsteps and cargo-carts.
From the harbor looms the dark mist of a railway station, panes grow heavy with evening,
And the walls give off a cool smell of goods from foreign lands.

1936

Lynching[1]

White wild hands snare you with a stray rope,
And a July tree crucifies your Negro neck,
In its heavy ripeness, in its full bloom.
In the thick of green leaves the branch is more pliant,
It does not break with the weight of a noose.
Your neck with marks of the hangman's fingers—blots in the sun.
Leaves break out in dew and sway gently as ever
And don't feel that they are shaken by the wind of a hanged man.

You hang black in flayed clothes.
Your drooping shame dies open and young.
The extinguished lips sag thickly
And the dazzle of your strong teeth—a mute challenge to all eyes.

Your singing prayer wept so mournfully to God,
But he won't appear to you, his legs burst, his nailed hands,
He cannot even open an eye with a tear for you
Or accept your last word as a confession—He's crucified Himself.

Negro!
Your body blossoms on a summer day though you hang, though you no longer see the sun,

3. A literal translation of the Yiddish *shtrengn kalender-goyrl*, a compound neologism that joins the Germanic and connotatively worldly *kalendar* (calendar) with the Hebraic and connotatively divine *goyrl* (destiny).

1. Translated by Benjamin Harshav and Barbara Harshav.

Your wife making her evening bed on a back doorstep in a street
Or your father, counting pieces of suet in the morning on a meat wagon.

Negro, the fate of destruction fell not only on you.
Many, many die like you. Such a death is now in fashion,
Like this they now die everywhere— — —
In Wedding, in Leopoldstadt and in Carolina.[2]

1936

2. A reference to North or South Carolina. "Wedding": a district of Berlin where the working-class populace expressed strong anti-Nazi sentiments. "Leopoldstadt": District II of Vienna, Austria, where Jews lived from 1622 until 1938, when Hitler annexed Austria to Germany.

HENRY ROTH
1905–1995

When Henry Roth published *Call It Sleep* in 1934, his first and for many years his only novel, he was praised by respected reviewers for his brilliance, realism, honesty, great sincerity, and profound artistry. He was compared favorably to James Joyce and Theodore Dreiser—although one obtuse review in *New Masses* sneered at a novel about the imaginings of a seven-year-old Proust (referring to the novel's central character). Yet the novel was all but forgotten for more than twenty years and only reprinted again to great success in 1960. During those intervening years, Roth published several unmemorable short stories and a few parables, as he called them, in the *New Yorker* and *Commentary*. In 1987, the Jewish Publication Society published a collection of his short works and interviews with the book's Italian editor, Mario Materassi. Finally, in 1994, sixty years after *Call It Sleep*, he published the first of a four-volume novel called *Mercy of a Rude Stream*, the last two volumes appearing posthumously.

The history of his first novel's reception, rescued from obscurity to its current high regard as perhaps the finest Jewish American novel of the century and a modernist masterpiece, is an extraordinary story and the stuff of publishing legend—as is the possible reason (or reasons) for Roth's long "writer's block." In the late 1930s, he had all but disappeared from view of the literary world. During World War II, he moved to New England and worked at various jobs, moved to Maine and became a psychiatric aide and then a duck and goose farmer. He and his wife, whom he had married in 1939, raised their two sons, and he apparently did very little writing. Then in 1956, Alfred Kazin and Leslie Fiedler cited *Call It Sleep* in a symposium on unjustly neglected books of the past twenty-five years. Walter Rideout in that same year called it one of the best of the 1930s novels in his book on the radical novel. So the book was reissued in hardback; it did not sell well. Then in 1960, Irving Howe gave its new paperback edition an unprecedented front-page review in the *New York Times Book Review* (the *Times* otherwise never reviewed paperbacks), and the book went on to sell 1 million copies. The novel's critical stature—as well as interest in its author—has grown ever since.

Roth was born in Galicia (then part of Austria) and brought to America by his parents when he was eighteen months old. They lived first in Brownsville, a section of Brooklyn, then on the Lower East Side, and, when he was eight, in Harlem. This last relocation was upsetting to the youngster, moving from a supportive Jewish community and family connections to a largely Gentile and predominantly Irish neighborhood. It seems to have begun a long alienation from Jewishness—odd in an author of such a Jewish book as *Call It Sleep*—which ended only with the Six Day War of June 1967, when Roth identified with the Israeli Jews, still advocating the assimilation of America's Jews. He changed his position in his old age, when he found himself moving toward his Jewishness again. In Manhattan, he attended DeWitt Clinton High School and then entered City College in New York in 1924. He published his first story, *Impressions of a Plumber* (about a summer job), in the college literary journal. Through another literary friend, he met Eda Lou Walton, a poet from New Mexico and a professor of English at New York University, who encouraged his writing. Twelve years his senior, not Jewish, she introduced him to the heady Greenwich Village world of her intellectual and literary friends. In 1928, he moved in with her, remaining with her until 1938, when he met Muriel Parker at an artists' colony and a year later married her.

In 1930, he accompanied Walton to the writers' colony at Yaddo, where she was in residence, and began to write his novel in examination blue books she left in the hotel room he occupied while she was at the colony. Supported by Walton during all the years he worked on the book—he dedicated it to her—which also coincided with the onset of the Great Depression, he undoubtedly felt guilty and in 1933 joined the Communist party. Radical herself though no party member, she felt that this was a mistake on his part, injurious to him as a writer.

At times, Roth seems to have thought so, too. He tried to write robustly proletarian fiction after *Call It Sleep* but failed at it, discarding manuscripts and finally falling silent. Roth probably did not leave the Communist party until 1956, the year of Khrushchev's revelations about the crimes of Stalin and the year he suffered a debilitating depression. He thought Marxism had shunted his career, as it had other writers of his generation. But he also felt that there were more personal reasons for his failure to write, including his incestuous relationship with his younger sister, Rose, during their early adolescence. His inability or unwillingness to admit or deal with that and its implications until the end of his life, along with the strong Oedipal dynamics of the family relationship in *Call It Sleep* (never fully resolved, according to many critical assessments), may be among the most credible or significant factors explaining his long block.

From Call It Sleep

From *Book I. The Cellar*

[The cellar of the tenement in which the family of David Schearl lives is a site of darkness, dirt, terror to the young protagonist, and it is related as well to the darkness of a closet in which, to his horror, he is induced to "play dirty" with a lame neighbor girl. This chapter begins with David's efforts to avoid meeting her on his way home from school.]

IX

The three o'clock bell sounded at last. Dismissed, he hurried through the milling crowd of noisy children. He had seen neither Yussie nor Annie, and now, as at lunch time, he darted ahead of the other children for fear of being overtaken by either.

It had stopped snowing, and although clouds still dulled the light, the air was warmer than it had been in the morning. Beside the curb, snow-forts squatted, half built during the lunch recess, waiting completion. A long sliding-pond stretched like a black ribbon in the gutter. Where the snow had been swept from the sidewalks, treacherous grey patches of ice tenaciously clung.

He went as swiftly as he could, picking his way. From time to time, he glanced hastily over his shoulder. No, they weren't there. He had outstripped them. He turned a corner, stopped in midstride, staring at the strange sight before him; cautiously he drew near.

A line of black carriages listed away from the snowbanked curb. He had seen such carriages before. But what was that in front of the house, that curious one, square and black with windows in its sides? Black plumes on the horses. Why those small groups of people beside the doorway whispering so quietly and craning their necks to look inside the hallway? Above the street, in all the nearby houses, windows were open, men and women were leaning out. In one of these a woman gesticulated to some one behind her. A man came forward, furtively grinning, patted her jutting hips and wedged into the space beside her. What were they all staring at. What was coming out of that house? Suddenly he remembered. The flowers had been there! Yes he knew the doorway. White, flattened pillars. Flowers! What? He looked about for someone to ask, but he could see no one his own age. Near one of the carriages, stood a small group of men, all dressed alike in long black coats and tall hats. The drivers. They alone seemed unperturbed, yet even they spoke quietly. Perhaps he could hear what they said. He sidled over, straining his ears.

"An' wattayuh t'ink he had de crust to tell me?" A man with a raw, weathered face was speaking, smoke from his cigarette unwreathing his words. "He siz, wadjuh stop fer? Now wouldn' dat give yuh de shits?"

He stared at the others for affirmation. They nodded agreement with their eyes.

Vindicated, the man continued, but more slowly and with greater emphasis. "His pole smacks into my hack,[1] and he squawks wadjuh stop fer? I coulda spit in his mug, de donkey!"

"At's twiset now, ain' it?" asked another.

"Twiset, my pudd'n," retorted the first in wrathful contempt. "It's de toid time. Wuzn't Jeff de foist one he rammed, an' wuzn't Toiner de secon'? An' yestiddy me!"

"Hey!" Another man nudged his neighbor abruptly. "Dere goes de rowboat!"[2]

Hastily throwing their cigarettes away, they scattered, and each one swung himself up to his box on the carriage.

More confused now than before, David drew near the doorway. A man in a tall black hat had just come out and was standing on the step looking solicitously into the hallway. A hush fell on the crowd; they huddled together as if for protection. Terror seemed to emanate from the hallway. At a sign from the man in the tall hat, the doors in back of the strange carriage were thrown open. Inside the gloomy interior metal glimmered, tassled curtains

1. A hackney is a four-wheel, six-seat, two-horse carriage let out to hire. "Pole": the tongue to which the horses are fastened.
2. I.e., the coffin.

shut out the light. Suddenly out of the hallway, a scraping sound and slow shuffling of feet. A soft moan came from the crowd.

"He's coming!" someone whispered, craning her neck.

A sense of desolation. A fear.

Two men came out, laboring under the front-end of a huge black box, then two more at the other end. Redfaced, they trod carefully down the steps, advanced toward the carriage, rested one end of the box on the carriage floor.

That was—! Yes! That was! He suddenly understood. Mama said—Inside! Yes! Man! Inside! His flesh went cold with terror.

"Easy," cautioned the man in the black hat.

They shoved the box in, lunging after it. It squealed softly, sliding in without effort as if on ways or wheels. The man who had opened the doors, shot a large silvered pin into a hole behind the box, then in one skillful motion shut the doors. At a nod from the man in the black hat, the carriage rolled on a little distance, then stopped. Another carriage drew up before the house.

Supported by a man on either side of her, a woman in black, all bowed and veiled, came sobbing out of the house. The crowd murmured, a woman whimpered. David had never seen a handkerchief with a black border. Hers seemed white as snow.

Voices of children. He looked around.

Annie and Yussie were there, staring at the woman as she entered the carriage. He shuddered, contracting, crept behind the crowd and broke into a run.

At the doorway of his house he stopped, peered in, stepped back. What was he going to do now? At lunch time, as he neared the house, he had seen Mrs. Nerrick, the landlady, climb up the stoop.[3] By running frantically, he had caught up to her, had raced past the cellar, before she shut her door. But now there was no one in sight. At any moment Annie and Yussie might come round the corner. He must—before they saw—but the darkness, the door, the darkness. The man in the box in the carriage. Alone. He must.

Make a noise. Noise . . . He advanced. What? Noise. Any.

"Aaaaah! Ooooh!" he quavered, "My country 'tis of dee!" He began running. The cellar door. Louder. "Sweet land of liberty," he shrilled, and whirled toward the stairs. "Of dee I sing." His voice rose in a shriek. His feet pounded on the stair. At his back, the monstrous horde of fear. "Land where our fodders died!" The landing; he dove for the door, flinging himself upon it—Threw it open, slammed it shut, and stood there panting in terror.

His mother was standing, staring at him in wide-eyed amazement. "Was that you?"

Close to tears, he lowered his head.

"What is it?"

"I don't know," he whimpered.

She laughed hopelessly and sat down. "Come here, you strange child. Come here. You're white!"

David went over and sank against her breast.

"You're trembling," she stroked his hair.

"I'm afraid," he murmured against her throat.

3. The front steps of tenements or apartment houses; originally a Dutch word, familiar to and used by New Yorkers.

"Still afraid?" she said soothingly. "Still the dream pursuing you?"

"Yes," a dry sob shook him. "And something else."

"What else?" She pressed him toward her with an encircling arm. In the other hand, she took both of his. "What?" she murmured. Her lips' soft pressure against his temples seemed to sink inward, downward, radiating a calm and a sweetness that only his body could grasp. "What else?"

"I saw a—a man who was in a box. You told me once."

"What? Oh!" her puzzled face cleared. "A funeral. God grant us life. Where was it?"

"Around the corner."

"And that frightened you?"

"Yes. And the hall was dark."

"I understand."

"Will you wait in the hall if I call you next time?"

"Yes. I'll wait as often as you like."

David heaved a quivering sigh of relief and kissed her cheek in gratitude.

"If I didn't," she laughed, "Mrs. Nerrick, the landlady, would dispossess us. I never heard such a thunder of feet!" When she had unbuttoned his leggings she rose and set him in a chair. "Sit there, darling. It's Friday, I have so much to do."[4]

For a while, David sat still and watched her, feeling his heart grow quiet again, then turned and looked out of the window. A fine rain had begun to fall, serrying the windows with aimless ranks. In the yard the snow under the rain was beginning to turn from white to grey. Blue smoke beat down, strove upward, was gone. Now and then, the old house creaked when the wind elbowed in and out the alley. Borne through mist and rain from some remote river, a boat horn boomed, set up strange reverberations in the heart . . .

Friday. Rain. The end of school. He could stay home now, stay home and do nothing, stay near his mother the whole afternoon. He turned from the window and regarded her. She was seated before the table paring beets. The first cut into a beet was like lifting a lid from a tiny stove. Sudden purple under the peel; her hands were stained with it. Above her blue and white checkered apron her face bent down, intent upon her work, her lips pressed gravely together. He loved her. He was happy again.

His eyes roamed about the kitchen: the confusion of Friday afternoons. Pots on the stove, parings in the sink, flour smeared on the rolling pin, the board. The air was warm, twined with many odors. His mother rose, washed the beets, drained them, set them aside.

"There!" she said. "I can begin cleaning again."

She cleared the table, washed what dishes were soiled, emptied out the peelings that cluttered the sink into the garbage can. Then she got down on all fours and began to mop the floor. With knees drawn up, David watched her wipe the linoleum beneath his chair. The shadow between her breasts, how deep! How far it—No! No! Luter![5] When he looked! That night! Mustn't! Mustn't! Look away! Quick! Look at—look at the linoleum there, how it glistened under a thin film of water.

4. I.e., cleaning the apartment and cooking before the Sabbath, which begins at sundown.

5. The man who works with his father, whom David believes is trying to seduce his mother.

"Now you'll have to sit there till it dries," she cautioned him, straightening up and brushing back the few wisps of hair that had fallen over her cheek. "It will only be a few minutes." She stooped, walked backward to the steps, trailing the mop over her footprints, then went into the frontroom.

Left alone, he became despondent again. His thoughts returned to Luter. He would come again this evening. Why? Why didn't he go away. Would they have to run away every Thursday? Go to Yussie's house? Would he have to play with Annie again? He didn't want to. He never wanted to see her again. And he would have to. The way he did this afternoon beside the carriages. The black carriage with the window. Scared. The long box. Scared. The cellar. No! No!

"Mama!" he called out.

"What is it, my son?"

"Are you going to—to sleep inside?"

"Oh, no. Of course not! I'm just straightening my hair a little."

"Are you coming in here soon?"

"Why yes. Is there anything you want?"

"Yes."

"In just a moment."

He waited impatiently for her to appear. In a little while she came out. She had changed her dress and combed her hair. She spread a frayed clean towel out on the parlor steps and sat down.

"I can't come over unless I have to," she smiled. "You're on an island. What is it you want?"

"I forgot," he said lamely.

"Oh, you're a goose!"

"It has to dry," he explained. "And I have to watch it."

"And so I do too, is that it? My, what a tyrant you'll make when you're married!"

David really didn't care what she thought of him just as long as she sat there. Beside he did have something to ask her, only he couldn't make up his mind to venture it. It might be too unpleasant. Still no matter what her answer would be, no matter what he found out, he was always safe near her.

"Mama, did you ever see anyone dead?"

"You're very cheerful to-day!"

"Then tell me." Now that he had launched himself on this perilous sea, he was resolved to cross it. "Tell me," he insisted.

"Well," she said thoughtfully, "The twins who died when I was a little girl I don't remember. My grandmother though, she was the first I really saw and remember. I was sixteen then."

"Why did she die?"

"I don't know. No one seemed to know."

"Then why did she die?"

"What a dogged questioner you are! I'm sure she had a reason. But do you want to know what I think?"

"Yes!" eagerly.

His mother took a deep breath, lifted a finger to arouse an already fervent attention. "She was very small, my grandmother, very frail and delicate. The light came through her hands like the light through a fan. What has that to do with it? Nothing. But while my grandfather was very pious, she only pretended to be—just as I pretend, may God forgive us both. Now long ago, she had a little garden before her house. It was full of sweet flowers in the summertime, and she tended it all by herself. My grandfather, stately Jew, could never understand why she should spend a whole spring morning watering the flowers and plucking off the dead leaves, and snipping here and patting there, when she had so many servants to do it for her. You would hardly believe how cheap servants were in those days—my grandfather had five of them. Yes, he would fret when he saw her working in the garden and say it was almost irreligious for a Jewess of her rank—she was rich then remember—the forests hadn't been cut"—

"What forests?"

"I've told you about them—the great forests and the lumber camps. We were rich while the forests were there. But after they were cut and the lumber camps moved away, we grew poor. Do you understand? And so my grandfather would fret when he saw her go dirtying her hands in the soil like any peasant's wife. But my grandmother would only smile at him—I can still see her bent over and smiling up at him—and say that since she had no beautiful beard like his to stroke, what harm could there be in getting a little dirt on her hands. My grandfather had a beard that turned white early; he was very proud of it. And once she told him that she was sure the good Lord would not be angry at her if she did steal a little from Esau's heritage—the earth and the fields are Esau's heritage—since Esau himself, she said, was stealing from Isaac on every side—she meant all the new stores that were being opened by the other gentiles[6] in our town. What could my grandfather do? He would laugh and call her a serpent. Now wait! Wait! I'm coming to it." She smiled at his impatience.

"As she grew older, she grew very strange. Shall I tell you what she used do? When autumn came and everything had died—"

"Died? Everything?" David interrupted her.

"Not everything, little goose. The flowers. When they died she didn't want to leave the house. Wasn't that strange? She stayed for days and days in her large living room—it had crystal chandeliers. You wouldn't believe how quietly she would sit—not seeing the servants, hardly hearing what was said—and her hands folded in her lap—So. Nor could my grandfather, though he begged her to come out, ever make her. He even went to ask a great Rabbi about it—it was no use. Not till the first snow fall, did she willingly leave the house again."

"Why?"

"Here is the answer. See if you can find it. When I came to visit her once on a day in late autumn, I found her sitting very quietly, as usual, in her large arm-chair. But when I was about to take my coat off, she said, keep it on, Genya, darling, there is mine on the chair in the corner. Will you get it for me, child?

"Well, I stood still staring at her in surprise. Her coat? I thought. Was

6. A reference to Genesis 25.20–27, in which the Patriarch Isaac, being tricked by Jacob and his mother, gives his son Jacob his blessing instead of giving it to the older brother, Esau, who is condemned thereafter to a life of hunting and working in the fields—the prototype of the Gentile or non-Jew. This reversal by the grandmother suggests that Esau has gotten some of his own back by opening stores—in effect, going into Jewish occupations.

she really of her own accord going out and in Autumn? And then for the first time I noticed that she was dressed in her prettiest Sabbath clothes—a dark, shimmering satin—very costly. I can see her yet. And on her head—she had never let them cut her hair—she had set a broad round comb with rows of pearls in it—the first present my grandfather had ever given her. It was like a pale crown. And so I fetched her coat and helped her put it on. Where are you going, grandmother? I asked. I was puzzled. In the garden, she said, in the garden. Well, an old woman must have her way, and into the garden we went. The day was very grey and full of winds, whirling, strong winds that could hold the trees down like a hand. Even us it almost blew about and it was cold. And I said to her, Grandmother, isn't it too cold out here? Isn't the wind too strong? No, her coat was warm, so she said. And then she said a very strange thing. Do you remember Petrush Kolonov? I wasn't sure. A goy,[7] she said, a clod. He worked for your grandfather many years. He had a neck like a tree once, but he grew old and crooked at last. And when he grew so old he couldn't lift a faggot, he would sit on a stone and look at the mountains. This was my grandmother talking, you understand?"

David couldn't quite follow these threads within threads, but nodded. "Why did he sit?" he asked, afraid that she might stop talking.

She laughed lightly. "That same question has been asked by three generations. You. Myself. My grandmother. He had been a good drudge this Petrush, a good ox. And when my grandmother asked him, Petrush, why do you sit like a keg and stare at the mountains, his only answer was, my teeth are all gone. And that's the story my grandmother told me while we walked. You look puzzled," she laughed again.

He was indeed, but she didn't explain.

"And so we walked and the leaves were blowing. Shew-w-w! How they lifted, and one blew against her coat, and while the wind held it there, you know, like a finger, she lifted it off and crumbled it. And then she said suddenly, come let us turn back. And just as we were about to go in she sighed so that she shivered—deep—the way one sighs just before sleep—and she dropped the bits of leaves she was holding and she said, it is wrong being the way I am. Even a leaf grows dull and old together! Together! You understand? Oh, she was wise! And we went inside."

His mother stopped, touched the floor to see if it was dry. Then she rose and went to the stove to push the seething beet soup from where it had been over the heat of the coals to the cooler end of the stove.

"And now the floor is dry," she smiled, "I'm liberated."

But David felt cheated, even resentful. "You—you haven't told me anything!" he protested. "You haven't even told me what happened?"

"Haven't I?" She laughed. "There's hardly anything more to tell? She died the winter of that same year, before the snow fell." She stared at the rain beating against the window. Her face sobered. The last wink of her eyelids before she spoke was the slowest. "She looked so frail in death, in her shroud[8]—how shall I tell you, my son? Like early winter snow. And I thought to myself even then, let me look deeply into her face for surely she

7. A non-Jew (Hebrew and Yiddish).
8. Traditionally, Jews would be buried wrapped in a simple shroud or sheet. Some men were buried with or even wrapped in their prayer shawls.

will melt before my eyes." She smiled again. "Have I told you enough now?"

He nodded. Without knowing why, her last words stirred him. What he had failed to grasp as thought, her last gesture, the last supple huskiness of her voice conveyed. Was it in his heart this dreamlike fugitive sadness dwelled, or did it steep the feathery air of the kitchen? He could not tell. But if only the air were always this way, and he always here alone with his mother. He was near her now. He was part of her. The rain outside the window set continual seals upon their isolation, upon their intimacy, their identity. When she lifted the stove lid, the rosy glow that stained her wide brow warmed his own body as well. He was near her. He was part of her. Oh, it was good being here. He watched her every movement hungrily.

She threw a new white table cloth over the table. It hovered like a cloud in air and settled slowly. Then she took down from the shelf three brass candlesticks and placed them in the center of whiteness, then planted candles into each brass cup.

"Mama?"

"Yes?"

"What do they do when they die?"

"What?" she repeated. "They are cold; they are still. They shut their eyes in sleep eternal years."

Eternal years. The words echoed in his mind. Raptly, he turned them over and over as though they had a lustre and shape of their own. *Eternal years.*

His mother set the table. Knives ringing faintly, forks, spoons, side by side. The salt shaker, secret little vessel of dull silver, the pepper, greyish-brown eye in the shallow glass, the enameled sugar bowl, headless shoulders of silver tongs leaning above the rim.

"Mama, what are eternal years?"

His mother sighed somewhat desperately, lifted her eyes a moment then dropped them to the table, her gaze wandered thoughtfully over the dishes and silverware. Then her eyes brightened. Reaching toward the sugar bowl she lifted out the tongs, carefully pinched a cube of sugar, and held it up before his eyes.

"This is how wide my brain can stretch," she said banteringly. "You see? No wider. Would you ask me to pick up a frozen sea with these narrow things? Not even the ice-man[9] could do it." She dropped the tongs back into the bowl. "The sea to this—"

"But—" David interrupted, horrified and bewildered. "But when do they wake up, mama?"

She opened her two palms in a gesture of emptiness. "There is nothing left to waken."

"But sometime, mama," he urged.

She shook her head.

"But sometime."

"Not here, if anywhere. They say there is a heaven and in heaven they waken. But I myself do not believe it. May God forgive me for telling you

9. The person who delivered the ice that went into iceboxes before the days of refrigerators.

this. But it's all I know. I know only that they are buried in the dark earth and their names last a few more lifetimes on their gravestones."

The dark. In the dark earth. Eternal years. It was a terrible revelation. He stared at her fixedly. Picking up a cloth that lay on the washtub, she went to the oven, flipped the door open, drew out a pan. The warmth and odor of new bread entered his being as through a rigid haze of vision. She spread out a napkin near the candlesticks, lifted the bread out of the pan and placed it on the square of linen.

"I still have the candles to light," she murmured sitting down, "and my work is done. I don't know why they made Friday so difficult a day for women."

—Dark. In the grave. Eternal years . . .

Rain in brief gusts seething at the window . . . The clock ticked too briskly. No, never. It wasn't sometime . . . In the dark.

Slowly the last belated light raveled into dusk. Across the short space of the kitchen, his mother's face trembled as if under sea, grew blurred. Flecks, intricate as foam, swirled in the churning dark—

—Like popcorn blowing in that big window in that big candystore. Blowing and settling. That day. Long ago.

His gaze followed the aimless flux of light that whirled and flickered in the room, troubling the outline of door and table.

—Snow it was, grey snow. Tiny bits of paper, floating from the window, that day. Confetti, a boy said. Confetti, he said. They threw it down on those two who were going to be married. The man in the tall, black shiny hat, hurrying. The lady in white laughing, leaning against him, dodging the confetti, winking it out of her eyes. Carriages waiting. Confetti on the step, on the horses. Funny. Then they got inside, both laughing. Confetti. Carriages.

—Carriages!

—The same!

—This afternoon! When the box came out! Carriages.

—Same!

—Carriages—!

"Dear God!" exclaimed his mother. "You startled me! What makes you leap that way in your chair? This is the second time today!"

"They were the same," he said in a voice of awe. It was solved now. He saw it clearly. Everything belonged to the same dark. Confetti and coffins.

"What were the same?"

"The carriages!"

"Oh, child!" she cried with amused desperation. "God alone knows what you're dreaming about now!" She rose from her chair, went over to the wall where the match-box hung, "I had better light these candles before you see an angel."

The match rasped on the sandpaper, flared up, making David aware of how dark it had become.

One by one she lit the candles. The flame crept tipsily up the wick, steadied, mellowed the steadfast brass below, glowed on each knot of the crisp golden braid of the bread on the napkin. Twilight vanished, the kitchen gleamed. Day that had begun in labor and disquiet, blossomed now in candlelight and sabbath.

With a little, deprecating laugh, his mother stood before the candles, and bowing her head before them, murmured through the hands she spread before her face the ancient prayer for the Sabbath[1] . . .

The hushed hour, the hour of tawny beatitude . . .

1934

1. One of the functions of the mother in the Jewish family.

TESS SLESINGER
1905–1945

Born in New York City, where she grew up in a Hungarian and Russian family, Tess Slesinger was educated at the Ethical Culture Society and at Swarthmore College, and received a degree from the Columbia School of Journalism. Like Isaac Rosenfeld a star that shone brightly but too briefly, greatly admired by her fellow New York intellectuals, Tess Slesinger published only two books before she died of cancer at the age of thirty-nine. Lionel Trilling compared her to Mary McCarthy for "vivacity and wit" (though her satire was gentler), saying she was "born to be a novelist."

Her only novel, *The Unpossessed*, about the group around Elliot Cohen and his *Menorah Journal* (her first husband, Herbert Solow, was an assistant editor of the journal), appeared in 1934 to high critical praise and enjoyed decent commercial success. Shortly thereafter, she went to Hollywood with her second husband, a producer and screenwriter, where she spent the rest of her life. She had two children and wrote screenplays that included *A Tree Grows in Brooklyn* and *The Good Earth*. She also published a few stories in *Vanity Fair,* the *New Yorker*, and elsewhere.

Missis Flinders had appeared in *Story* magazine in 1932, perhaps the first abortion story in an aboveground publication. Slesinger then included it as a section of her novel and again in a collection of stories called *Time: The Present* (1935), which was reprinted in 1971 as *On Being Told That Her Second Husband Has Taken His First Lover.*

Missis Flinders

"Home you go!" Miss Kane, nodding, in her white nurse's dress, stood for a moment—she would catch a breath of air—in the hospital door; "and thank you again for the stockings, you needn't have bothered"—drew a sharp breath and turning, dismissed Missis Flinders from the hospital, smiling, dismissed her forever from her mind.

So Margaret Flinders stood next to her basket of fruit on the hospital steps; both of them waiting, a little shame-faced in the sudden sunshine, and in no hurry to leave the hospital—no hurry at all. It would be nicer to be alone, Margaret thought, glancing at the basket of fruit which stood respectable and a little silly on the stone step (the candy-bright apples were blushing caricatures of Miles: Miles' comfort, not hers). Flowers she could have left behind (for the nurses, in the room across the hall where they made tea at night); books she could have slipped into her suit-case; but fruit—Miles' gift, Miles' guilt, man's tribute to the Missis in the hospital—must be eaten; a half-eaten basket of fruit (she had tried to leave it: Missis Butter won't you . . . Missis Wiggam wouldn't you like . . . But Missis Butter had aplenty of her own thank you, and Missis Wiggam said she couldn't hold acids after a baby)—a half-eaten basket of fruit, in times like these, cannot be left to rot.

Down the street Miles was running, running, after a taxi. He was going after the taxi for her; it was for her sake he ran; yet this minute that his back was turned he stole for his relief and spent in running away, his shoulders crying guilt. And don't hurry, don't hurry, she said to them; I too am better off alone.

The street stretched in a long white line very finally away from the hospital, the hospital where Margaret Flinders (called there so solemnly Missis) had been lucky enough to spend only three nights. It would be four days before Missis Wiggam would be going home to Mister Wiggam with a baby; and ten possibly—the doctors were uncertain, Miss Kane prevaricated—before Missis Butter would be going home to Mister Butter without one. Zig-zagging the street went the children; their cries and the sudden grinding of their skates she had listened to upstairs beside Missis Butter for three days. Some such child had she been—for the styles in children had not changed—a lean child gliding solemnly on skates and grinding them viciously at the nervous feet of grown-ups. Smile at these children she would not or could not; yet she felt on her face that smile fixed, painful and frozen that she had put there, on waking from ether three days back, to greet Miles. The smile spoke to the retreating shoulders of Miles: I don't need you; the smile spoke formally to life: thanks, I'm not having any. Not so the child putting the heels of his skates together Charlie Chaplin-wise[1] and describing a scornful circle on the widest part of the sidewalk. Not so a certain little girl (twenty years back) skating past the wheels of autos, pursuing life in the form of a ball so red! so gay! better death than to turn one's back and smile over one's shoulder at life!

Upstairs Missis Butter must still be writhing with her poor caked breasts. The bed that had been hers beside Missis Butter's was empty now; Miss Kane would be stripping it and Joe would come in bringing fresh sheets. Whom would they put in beside Missis Butter, to whom would she moan and boast all night about the milk in her breasts that was turning, she said, into cheese?

Now Miles was coming back, jogging sheepishly on the running-board of a taxi, he had run away to the end of his rope and now was returning penitent, his eyes doglike searching her out where she stood on the hospital steps (did they rest with complacence on the basket of fruit, his gift?), pleading with her, Didn't I get the taxi fast? like an anxious little boy. She stood with that smile on her face that hurt like too much ice-cream. Smile and smile; for she felt like a fool, she had walked open-eyed smiling into the trap (*Don't wriggle, Missis, I might injure you for life, Miss Kane had said cheerfully*) and felt the spring only when it was too late, when she waked from ether and knew like the thrust of a knife what she had ignored before. *Whatever did*

1. The film comedian Charlie Chaplin, in his role as the Tramp, walked with his heels together and his toes spread widely to the left and the right.

you do it for, Missis Flinders Missis Butter was always saying; if there's nothing the matter with your insides—doesn't your husband . . . and Won't you have some fruit, Missis Butter, her calm reply: meaning, My husband gave me this fruit so what right have you to doubt that my husband . . . Her husband who now stumbled up the steps to meet her; his eyes he had sent ahead, but something in him wanted not to come, tripped his foot as he hurried up the steps.

"Take my arm, Margaret," he said. "Walk slowly," he said. The bitter pill of taking help, of feeling weakly grateful stuck in her throat. Miles' face behind his glasses was tense like the face of an amateur actor in the rôle of a strike-leader. That he was inadequate for the part he seemed to know. And if he felt shame, shame in his own eyes, she could forgive him; but if it was only guilt felt man-like in her presence, a guilt which he could drop off like a damp shirt, if he was putting it all off on her for being a woman! "The fruit, Miles!" she said; "you've forgotten the fruit." "The fruit can wait," he said bitterly.

He handed her into the taxi as though she were a package marked glass—something, she thought, not merely troublesomely womanly, but ladylike. "Put your legs up on the seat," he said. "I don't want to, Miles." *Goodbye Missis Butter* Put your legs up on the seat. I don't want to—*better luck next time Missis Butter* Put your legs *I can't make out our window, Missis Butter* Put your "All right, it will be nice and uncomfortable." (She put her legs up on the seat.) *Goodbye Missis But* . . . "Nothing I say is right," he said. "It's good with the legs up," she said brightly.

Then he was up the steps agile and sure after the fruit. And down again, the basket swinging with affected carelessness, arming him, till he relinquished it modestly to her outstretched hands. Then he seated himself on the little seat, the better to watch his woman and his woman's fruit; and screwing his head round on his neck said irritably to the man who had been all his life on the wrong side of the glass pane: "Charles street!"[2]

"Hadn't you better ask him to please drive slowly?" Margaret said.

"I was just going to," he said bitterly.

"And drive slowly," he shouted over his shoulder.

The driver's name was Carl C. Strite. She could see Carl Strite glance cannily back at the hospital; Greenway Maternity Home; pull his lever with extreme delicacy as though he were stroking the neck of a horse. There was a small roar—and the hospital glided backward: its windows ran together like the windows of a moving train; a spurt—watch out for those children on skates!—and the car was fairly started down the street.

Goodbye Missis Butter I hope you get a nice roommate in my place, I hope you won't find that Mister B let the ice-pan[3] *flow over again—and give my love to the babies when Miss Kane stops them in the door for you to wave at—goodbye Missis Butter, really goodbye.*

Carl Strite (was he thinking maybe of his mother, an immigrant German woman she would have been, come over with a shawl on her head and worked herself to skin and bone so the kids could go to school and turn out good Americans—and what had it come to, here he was a taxi-driver, and what

2. A street in Manhattan's Greenwich Village once favored by artists, bohemians, and intellectuals.
3. A pan placed below the ice in iceboxes (forerunners of refrigerators) that caught the water as the ice melted and that had to be periodically emptied before it overflowed.

taxi-drivers didn't know! what in the course of their lackeys' lives they didn't put up with, fall in with! well, there was one decent thing left in Carl Strite, he knew how to carry a woman home from a maternity hospital) drove softly along the curb . . . and the eyes of his honest puzzled gangster's snout photographed as "Your Driver" looked dimmed as though the glory of woman were too much for them, in a moment the weak cruel baby's mouth might blubber. Awful to lean forward and tell Mr. Strite he was laboring under a mistake. *Missis Wiggam's freckled face when she heard that Missis Butter's roommate . . . maybe Missis Butter's baby had been born dead but anyway she had had a baby . . . whatever did you do it for Missis Flind . . .*

"Well, patient," Miles began, tentative, nervous (bored? perturbed? behind his glasses?).

"How does it feel, Maggie?" he said in a new, small voice.

Hurt and hurt this man, a feeling told her. He is a man, he could have made you a woman. "What's a D and C[4] between friends?" she said. "Nobody at the hospital gave a damn about my little illegality."

"Well, but I do," he protested like a short man trying to be tall.

She turned on her smile; the bright silly smile that was eating up her face.

Missis Butter would be alone now with no one to boast to about her pains except Joe who cleaned the corridors and emptied bed-pans—and thought Missis Butter was better than an angel because although she had incredible golden hair she could wise-crack like any brunette. Later in the day the eight-day mothers wobbling down the corridors for their pre-nursing constitutional would look in and talk to her; for wasn't Missis Butter their symbol and their pride, the one who had given up her baby that they might have theirs (for a little superstition is inevitable in new mothers, and it was generally felt that there must be one dead baby in a week's batch at any decent hospital) for whom they demanded homage from their visiting husbands? for whose health they asked the nurses each morning second only to asking for their own babies? That roommate of yours was a funny one, Missis Wiggam would say. Missis Wiggam was the woman who said big breasts weren't any good: here she was with a seven-pound baby and not a drop for it (here she would open the negligée Mister Wiggam had given her not to shame them before the nurses, and poke contemptuously at the floppy parts of herself within) while there was Missis Butter with no baby but a dead baby and her small breasts caking because there was so much milk in them for nothing but a . . . Yes, that Missis Flinders was sure a funny one, Missis Butter would agree.

"Funny ones," she and Miles, riding home with numb faces and a basket of fruit between them—past a park, past a museum, past elevated pillars—intellectuals they were, bastards, changelings . . . giving up a baby for economic freedom which meant that two of them would work in offices instead of one of them only, giving up a baby for intellectual freedom which meant that they smoked their cigarettes bitterly and looked out of the windows of a taxi onto streets and people and stores and hated them all. "We'd go soft," Miles had finally said, slamming the door of the Middleton party; "we'd go bourgeois." Yes, with diapers drying on the radiators, bottles wrapped in

4. I.e., dilation and curettage: the dilation of the cervix and scraping of the endometrium, procedures followed in abortions.

flannel, Mr. Papenmeyer getting to know one too well—yes, they would go soft, they might slump and start liking people, they might weaken and forgive stupidity, they might yawn and forget to hate. "Funny ones," class-straddlers, intellectuals, tightrope-walking somewhere in the middle (how long could they hang on without falling to one side or the other? one more war? one more depression?); intellectuals, as Bruno[5] said, with habits generated from the right and tastes inclined to the left. Afraid to perpetuate themselves, were they? Afraid of anything that might loom so large in their personal lives as to outweigh other considerations? Afraid, maybe, of a personal life?

"Oh give me another cigarette," she said.

And still the taxi, with its burden of intellectuals and their inarticulate fruit-basket, its motherly, gangsterly, inarticulate driver, its license plates and its photographs all so very official, jogged on; past Harlem now; past fire-escapes loaded with flower-pots and flapping clothes; dingy windows opening to the soot-laden air blown in by the elevated roaring down its tracks. Past Harlem and through 125th street: stores and wise-cracks, Painless Dentists, cheap florists: Eight Avenue, boarded and plastered, concealing the subway that was reaching its laborious birth beneath. But Eighth Avenue was too jouncy for Mr. Strite's precious burden of womanhood (who was reaching passionately for a cigarette); he cut through the park, and they drove past quiet walks on which the sun had brought out babies as the fall rains give birth to worms.

"But ought you to smoke so much, so soon after—so soon?" Miles said, not liking to say so soon after what. His hand held the cigarettes out to her, back from her.

"They do say smoking's bad for child-birth," she said calmly, and with her finger-tips drew a cigarette from his reluctant hand.

And tapping down the tobacco on the handle of the fruit-basket she said, "But we've got the joke on them there, we have." (Hurt and hurt this man, her feeling told her; he is a man and could have made you a woman.)

"It was your own decision too," he said harshly, striking and striking at the box with his match.

"This damn taxi's shaking you too much," he said suddenly, bitter and contrite.

But Mr. Strite was driving like an angel. He handled his car as though it were a baby-carriage. Did he think maybe it had turned out with her the way it had with Missis Butter? I could have stood it better, Missis Butter said, if they hadn't told me it was a boy. And me with my fourth little girl, Missis Wiggam had groaned (but proudly, proudly); why I didn't even want to see it when they told me. But Missis Butter stood it very well, and so did Missis Wiggam. They were a couple of good bitches; and what if Missis Butter had produced nothing but a dead baby this year, and what if Missis Wiggam would bring nothing to Mister Wiggam but a fourth little girl this year—why there was next year and the year after, there was the certain little world from grocery-store to kitchen, there were still Mister Butter and Mister Wiggam who were both (Missis Wiggam and Missis Butter vied with each other) just *crazy* about babies. Well, Mister Flinders is different, she had lain there

5. Middleton, Papenmeyer, and Bruno are characters in the novel *The Unpossessed* who do not appear in the original 1932 short story.

thinking (he cares as much for his unborn gods as I for my unborn babies); and wished she could have the firm assurance they had in "husbands," coming as they did year after year away from them for a couple of weeks, just long enough to bear them babies either dead-ones or girl-ones . . . good bitches they were: there was something lustful besides smug in their pride in being "Missis." Let Missis Flinders so much as let out a groan because a sudden pain grew too big for her groins, let her so much as murmur because the sheets were hot beneath her—and Missis Butter and Missis Wiggam in the security of their maternity-fraternity exchanged glances of amusement: SHE don't know what pain is, look at what's talking about PAIN. . . .

"Mr. Strite flatters us," she whispered, her eyes smiling straight and hard at Miles. (Hurt and hurt . . .)

"And why does that give you so much pleasure?" He dragged the words as though he were pounding them out with two fingers on the typewriter.

The name without the pain—she thought to say; and did not say. All at once she lost her desire to punish him; she no more wanted to "hurt this man" for he was no more man than she was woman. She would not do him the honor of hurting him. She must reduce him as she felt herself reduced. She must cut out from him what made him a man, as she had let be cut out from her what would have made her a woman. He was no man: he was a dried-up intellectual husk; he was sterile; empty and hollow as she was.

Missis Butter lying up on her pillow would count over to Missis Wiggam the fine points of her tragedy: how she had waited two days to be delivered of a dead baby; how it wouldn't have been so bad if the doctor hadn't said it was a beautiful baby with platinum-blond hair exactly like hers (and hers bleached unbelievably, but never mind, Missis Wiggam had come to believe in it like Joe and Mister Butter, another day and Missis Flinders herself, intellectual skeptic though she was, might have been convinced); and how they would pay the last installment on—what a baby-carriage, Missis Wiggam, you'd never believe me!—and sell it second-hand for half its worth. I know when I was caught with my first, Missis Wiggam would take up the story her mouth had been open for. And that Missis Flinders was sure a funny one. . . .

But I am not such a funny one, Margaret wanted, beneath her bright and silly smile, behind her cloud of cigarette smoke (for Miles had given in; the whole package sat gloomily on Margaret's lap) to say to them; even though in my "crowd" the girls keep the names they were born with, even though some of us sleep for a little variety with one another's husbands, even though I forget as often as Miles—Mister Flinders to you—to empty the pan under the ice-box. Still I too have known my breasts to swell and harden, I too have been unable to sleep on them for their tenderness to weight and touch, I too have known what it is to undress slowly and imagine myself growing night to night. . . . I knew this for two months, my dear Missis Wiggam; I had this strange joy for two months, my dear Missis Butter. But there was a night last week, my good ladies, on coming home from a party, which Mister Flinders and I spent in talk—and damn fine talk, if you want to know, talk of which I am proud, and talk not one word of which you, with your grocery-and-baby minds, could have understood; in a régime like this, Miles said, it is a terrible thing to have a baby—it means the end of independent thought and the turning of everything into a scheme for making money; and there must be institutions such as there are in Russia,[6] I said, for taking care of the babies and their mothers; why in a time like this, we both said, to have a baby would be suicide—goodbye to our plans, goodbye to our working out schemes for each other and the world—our courage would die, our hopes concentrate on the sordid business of keeping three people alive, one of whom would be a burden and an expense for twenty years. . . . And then we grew drunk for a minute making up the silliest names that we could call it if we had it, we would call it Daniel if it were a boy, call it for my mother if it were a girl—and what a tough little thing it is, I said, look, look, how it hangs on in spite of its loving mother jumping off tables and broiling herself in hot water . . . until Miles, frightened at himself, washed his hands of it: we mustn't waste any more time, the sooner these things are done the better. And I as though the ether cap had already been clapped to my nose, agreed offhandedly. That night I did not pass my hands contentedly over my hard breasts; that night I gave no thought to the nipples grown suddenly brown and competent; I packed, instead, my suit-case: I filled it with all the white clothes I own. Why are you taking white clothes to the hospital, Miles said to me. I laughed. Why did I? White, for a bride; white, for a corpse; white for a woman who refuses to be a woman. . . .

"Are you all right, Margaret?" (They were out now, safely out on Fifth Avenue, driving placidly past the Plaza[7] where ancient coachmen dozed on the high seats of the last hansoms left in New York.)

"Yes, dear," she said mechanically, and forgot to turn on her smile. Pity for him sitting there in stolid New England inadequacy filled her. He was a man, and he could have made her a woman. She was a woman, and could have made him a man. He was not a man; she was not a woman. In each of them the life-stream flowed to a dead-end.

And all this time that the blood, which Missis Wiggam and Missis Butter stored up preciously in themselves every year to make a baby for their husbands, was flowing freely and wastefully out of Missis Flinders—toward what? would it pile up some day and bear a Magazine? would it congeal within her and make a crazy woman?—all this time Mr. Strite, remembering, with his pudgy face, his mother, drove his taxi softly along the curb; no weaving in and out of traffic for Mr. Strite, no spurting at the corners and cheating the side-street traffic, no fine heedless rounding of rival cars for Mr. Strite; he kept his car going at a slow and steady roll, its nose poked blunt ahead, following the straight and narrow—Mr. Strite knew what it was to carry a woman home from the hospital.

But what in their past had warranted this? She could remember a small girl going from dolls to books, from books with colored pictures to books with frequent conversations; from such books to the books at last that one borrowed from libraries, books built up of solemn text from which you took notes; books which were gray to begin with, but which opened out to your eyes subtle layers of gently shaded colors. (And where in these texts did it say that one should turn one's back on life? Had the coolness of the stone library at college made one afraid? Had the ivy nodding in at the open dor-

6. The belief held by many 1930s radicals that Soviet Russia had created more humane institutions—for child care and maternal help, for instance—than existed in capitalist America.

7. The square at the entrance to Central Park at Fifth Avenue and Fifty-ninth Street, where the Plaza Hotel is located.

mitory windows taught one too much to curl and squat looking out?) And Miles? What book, what professor, what strange idea, had taught him to hunch his shoulders and stay indoors, had taught him to hide behind his glasses? Whence the fear that made him put, in cold block letters, implacably above his desk the sign announcing him "Not at Home" to life?

Missis Flinders, my husband scaled the hospital wall at four o'clock in the morning, frantic I tell you . . . But I just don't understand you, Missis Flinders (if there's really nothing the matter with your insides), do you understand her, Missis Wiggam, would your husband . . . ? Why goodness, no, Mister Wiggam would sooner . . . ! And there he was, and they asked him, Shall we try an operation, Mister Butter? scaled the wall . . . shall we try an operation? (Well, you see, we are making some sort of a protest, my husband and I; sometimes, she thought, recalling Norah, I forget just what.) If there's any risk to Shirley, he said, there mustn't be any risk to Shirley . . . Missis Wiggam's petulant, childish face, with its sly contentment veiled by what she must have thought a grown-up expression: Mister Wiggam bought me this negligée new, surprised me with it, you know—and generally a saving man, Mister Wiggam, not tight, but with three children—four now! Hetty, he says, I'm not going to have you disgracing us at the hospital this year, he says. Why the nurses will all remember that flannel thing you had Mabel and Suzy and Antoinette in, they'll talk about us behind our backs. (It wasn't that I couldn't make the flannel do again, Missis Butter, it wasn't that at all.) But he says, Hetty, you'll just have a new one this year, he says, and maybe it'll bring us luck, he says—you know, he was thinking maybe this time we'd have a boy. . . . Well, I just have to laugh at you, Missis Flinders, not *wanting* one, why my sister went to doctors for five years and spent her good money just *trying* to have one. . . . Well, poor Mister Wiggam, so the negligée didn't work, I brought him another little girl—but he didn't say boo to me, though I could see he was disappointed. Hetty, he says, we'll just have another try! oh I thought I'd die, with Miss Kane standing right there you know (though they do say these nurses . . .); but that's Mister Wiggam all over, he wouldn't stop a joke for a policeman. . . . No, I just can't get over you, Missis Flinders, if Gawd was willing to let you have a baby—and there really isn't anything wrong with your insides?

Miles' basket of fruit standing on the bed-table, trying its level inadequate best, poor pathetic inarticulate intellectual basket of fruits, to comfort, to bloom, to take the place of Miles himself who would come in later with Sam Butter for visiting hour. Miles' too-big basket of fruit standing there, embarrassed. Won't you have a peach, Missis Wiggam (I'm sure they have less acid)? Just try an apple, Missis Butter? Weigh Miles' basket of fruit against Mister Wiggam's negligée for luck, against Mister Butter scaling the wall at four in the morning for the mother of his dead baby. *Please* have a pear, Miss Kane; a banana, Joe? How they spat the seeds from Miles' fruit! How it hurt her when, unknowing, Missis Butter cut away the brown bruised cheek of Miles' bright-eyed, weeping apple! Miles! they scorn me, these ladies. They laugh at me, dear, almost as though I had no "husband," as though I were a "fallen woman." Miles, would you buy me a new negligée if I bore you three daughters? Miles, would you scale the wall if I bore you a dead baby? . . . Miles, I have an inferiority complex because I am an intellectual. . . . But a peach, Missis Wiggam! can't I possibly tempt you?

To be driving like this at mid-day through New York; with Miles bobbing like an empty ghost (for she could see he was unhappy, as miserable as she, he too had had an abortion) on the side-seat; with a taxi-driver, solicitous, respectful to an ideal, in front; was this the logical end of that little girl she remembered, of that girl swinging hatless across a campus as though that campus were the top of the earth? And was this all they could give birth to, she and Miles, who had closed up their books one day and kissed each other on the lips and decided to marry?

And now Mr. Strite, with his hand out, was making a gentle righthand turn. Back to Fifth Avenue they would go, gently rolling, in Mr. Strite's considerate charge. Down Fourteenth Street[8] they would go, past the stores unlike any stores in the world: packed to the windows with imitation gold and imitation embroidery, with imitation men and women coming to stand in the doorways and beckon with imitation smiles; while on the sidewalks streamed the people unlike any other people in the world, drawn from every country, from every stratum, carrying babies (the real thing, with pinched anemic faces) and parcels (imitation finery priced low in the glittering stores). There goes a woman, with a flat fat face, will produce five others just like herself, to dine off one-fifth the inadequate quantity her Mister earns today. These are the people not afraid to perpetuate themselves (forbidden to stop, indeed) and they will go on and on until the bottom of the world is filled with them; and suddenly there will be enough of them to combine their wild-eyed notions and take over the world to suit themselves. While I, while I and my Miles, with our good clear heads will one day go spinning out of the world and leave nothing behind . . . only diplomas crumbling in the museums. . . .

The mad street ended with Fifth Avenue; was left behind.

They were nearing home. Mr. Strite, who had never seen them before (who would never again, in all likelihood, for his territory was far uptown) was seeing them politely to the door. As they came near home all of Margaret's fear and pain gathered in a knot in her stomach. There would be nothing new in their house; there was nothing to expect; yet she wanted to find something there that she knew she could not find, and surely the house (once so gay, with copies of old paintings, with books which lined the walls from floor to ceiling, with papers and cushions and typewriters) would be suddenly empty and dead, suddenly, for the first time, a group of rooms unalive as rooms with "For Rent" still pasted on the windows. And Miles? did he know he was coming home to a place which had suffered no change, but which would be different forever afterward? Miles had taken off his glasses; passed his hand tiredly across his eyes; was sucking now as though he expected relief, some answer, on the tortoise-shell curve which wound around his ear.

Mr. Strite would not allow his cab to cease motion with a jerk. Mr. Strite allowed his cab to slow down even at the corner (where was the delicatessen that sold the only loose ripe olives in the Village), so they rolled softly past No. 14; on past the tenement which would eventually be razed to give place to modern three-room apartments with In-a-Dor beds;[9] and then slowly, so

8. A street in Manhattan that had department and bargain stores that catered to the general public.

9. Trade name for a Murphy bed, which folds up or swings into a closet or cabinet when it is not in use. It was invented by W. L. Murphy around 1900.

slowly that Mr. Strite must surely be an artist as well as a man who had had a mother, drew up and slid to a full stop before No. 60, where two people named Mister and Missis Flinders rented themselves a place to hide from life (both life of the Fifth Avenue variety, and life of the common, or Fourteenth Street, variety: in short, life).

So Miles, with his glasses on his nose once more, descended; held out his hand; Mr. Strite held the door open and his face most modestly averted; and Margaret Flinders painfully and carefully swung her legs down again from the seat and alighted, step by step, with care and confusion. The house was before them; it must be entered. Into the house they must go, say farewell to the streets, to Mr. Strite who had guided them through a tour of the city, to life itself; into the house they must go and hide. It was a fact that Mister Flinders (was he reluctant to come home?) had forgotten his key; that Missis Flinders must delve under the white clothes in her suit-case and find hers; that Mr. Strite, not yet satisfied that his charges were safe, sat watchful and waiting in the front seat of his cab. Then the door gave. Then Miles, bracing it with his foot, held out his hand to Margaret. Then Mr. Strite came rushing up the steps (something had told him his help would be needed again!), rushing up the steps with the basket of fruit hanging on his arm, held out from his body as though what was the likes of him doing holding a woman's basket just home from the hospital. "You've forgot your fruit, Missis!"

Weakly they glared at the fruit come to pursue them; come to follow them up the stairs to their empty rooms; but that was not fair: come, after all, to comfort them. "You must have a peach," Margaret said.

No, Mr. Strite had never cared for peaches; the skin got in his teeth.

"You must have an apple," Margaret said.

Well, no, he must be getting on uptown. A cigarette (he waved it, deprecated the smoke it blew in the lady's face) was good enough for him.

"But a pear, just a pear," said Margaret passionately.

Mr. Strite wavered, standing on one foot. "Maybe he doesn't want any fruit," said Miles harshly.

"Not want any *fruit!*" cried Margaret gayly, indignantly. Not want any fruit?—ridiculous! Not want the fruit my poor Miles bought for his wife in the hospital? Three days I spent in the hospital, in a Maternity Home, and I produced, with the help of my husband, one basket of fruit (tied with ribbon, pink—for boys). Not want any of our fruit? I couldn't bear it, I couldn't bear it. . . .

Mr. Strite leaned over; put out a hand and gingerly selected a pear—"For luck," he said, managing an excellent American smile. They watched him trot down the steps to his cab, all the time holding his pear as though it were something he would put in a memory book. And still they stayed, because Margaret said foolishly, "Let's see him off"; because she was ashamed, suddenly, before Miles; as though she had cut her hair unbecomingly, as though she had wounded herself in some unsightly way—as though (summing up her thoughts as precisely, as decisively as though it had been done on an adding-machine) she had stripped and revealed herself not as a woman at all, but as a creature who would not be a woman and could not be a man. And then they turned (for there was nothing else to stay for, and on the street and in the sun before Missis Salvemini's fluttering window-curtains they were ashamed as though they had been naked or dead)—and went in the door and heard it swing to, pause on its rubbery hinge, and finally click behind them.

1932 1934

STANLEY KUNITZ
b. 1905

The son of immigrants from Lithuania, Stanley Kunitz was born in Worcester, Massachusetts. He grew up without knowing his father, who had killed himself six weeks before his child was born. Since his mother subsequently did not allow his father to be mentioned, the poems *Father and Son* and *Quinnapoxet* take on particular poignancy, although the autobiographical element cannot exhaust their mythic and historical reverberations or account wholly for the son's strained feelings toward his heritage.

Kunitz grew up knowing the countryside of central Massachusetts as well as the museums and libraries of Worcester, and graduated summa cum laude from Harvard, where he received an M.A. in 1927. By his own account, he was denied a teaching assistantship there on the grounds that "Anglo Saxons would resent being instructed in English by a Jew."

In his twenties, Kunitz began to publish in such journals as *Poetry*, the *Dial*, and the *Nation* while working as an editor in New York. At the H. W. Wilson publishing company, he was responsible for starting the reference series on twentieth-century authors. Meanwhile, he was invited to spend time at the writer's colony, Yaddo, soon after its inception; his first book of poems, *Intellectual Things*, was published in 1930. During the depression, Kunitz left New York to farm, first in Connecticut, then in Pennsylvania. He mentions that he found "consolation . . . [for a failing marriage] in the ritual of ploughing the fields with a yoke of white oxen." He served in the army during World War II and published *Passport to the War* in 1944.

Kunitz launched a distinguished career as a teacher of poetry (at Bennington, Columbia, Brandeis) without settling down at any one institution and, in 1957, began to spend his summers in Provincetown, Massachusetts, where his third wife, the painter Elise Asher, had her studio. (He was married to Helen Pearce in 1930, whom he divorced in 1937, and then to Eleanor Evans in 1939, with whom he had a child, Gretchen, and whom he divorced in 1958.) When his *Selected Poems, 1928–1958* (1958) won the Pulitzer Prize, this was only the beginning. Honors and prizes would continue: Harvard's Centennial Medal, the National Book Award, the Bollingen Prize, the National Medal of the Arts, and many others. At the same time, Kunitz furthered generously the work of many younger American poets as he edited the Yale Younger Poets series and founded poetry centers in Provincetown and New York that he intended to be "idealistic, openhearted, and free."

The publication of Kunitz's 1995 National Book Award–winning *Passing Through: The Later Poems, New and Selected* coincided with his ninetieth birthday. He continues to cherish the English poets—Hopkins, the Metaphysicals, Blake—whose language forms his own earliest poetic idiom. He has, however, said of his latest work that he wished to write poems "natural, luminous, deep, spare, 'so transparent that one can look through and see the world.' "

Father and Son[1]

Now in the suburbs and the falling light
I followed him, and now down sandy road
Whiter than bone-dust, through the sweet
Curdle of fields, where the plums
Dropped with their load of ripeness, one by one.[2]
Mile after mile I followed, with skimming feet,
After the secret master of my blood,
Him, steeped in the odor of ponds,[3] whose indomitable love
Kept me in chains. Strode years; stretched into bird;
Raced through the sleeping country where I was young,
The silence unrolling before me as I came,
The night nailed like an orange to my brow.

How should I tell him my fable[4] and the fears,
How bridge the chasm in a casual tone,
Saying, "The house, the stucco one you built,
We lost. Sister married and went from home,
And nothing comes back, it's strange, from where she goes.
I lived on a hill that had too many rooms:[5]
Light we could make, but not enough of warmth,
And when the light failed, I climbed under the hill.[6]
The papers are delivered every day;
I am alone and never shed a tear."

At the water's edge, where the smothering ferns lifted
Their arms, "Father!" I cried, "Return! You know
The way. I'll wipe the mudstains from your clothes;
No trace, I promise, will remain. Instruct
Your son, whirling between two wars,
In the Gemara[7] of your gentleness,
For I would be a child to those who mourn
And brother to the foundlings of the field
And friend of innocence and all bright eyes.
O teach me how to work and keep me kind."

Among the turtles and the lilies he turned to me
The white ignorant hollow of his face.

1942

1. From *The Poems of Stanley Kunitz, 1928–1978* (1979). Comments on the poem by Kunitz and others appear in *The Contemporary Poet as Artist and Critic*, edited by Anthony Ostroff (1964), and in Kunitz's *A Kind of Order, a Kind of Folly* (1975).
2. Kunitz notes that these lines refer to the rural environs of Worcester, Massachusetts, as they were in his youth.
3. The body of a boy drowned in a pond of unplumbed depth had never been recovered.
4. The story, or connected series of events, that make up an epic poem or a drama. One archetypal fable is that of a son seeking a lost father.
5. Kunitz notes that this line was suggested by "in my father's house are many mansions" (John 14.2). "The house, the stucco one you built": the family had lived in a stucco house in Worcester. "Sister": one sister had died.
6. Kunitz gives a source: "Tho' thou art worshipped by the Names Divine of Jesus and Jehovah, thou art still The Son of Morn in weary Night's decline, The lost Traveller's Dream under the hill," from William Blake's (1757–1827) *To the Accuser Who is the God of This World* and *For the Sexes: The Gates of Paradise*.
7. The Gemara is the section of commentary in the Talmud on the oral law of the Jews [Kunitz's note].

Foreign Affairs[1]

We are two countries girded for the war,
Whisking our scouts across the pricked frontier
To ravage in each other's fields, cut lines
Along the lacework of strategic nerves,
Loot stores; while here and there,
In ambushes that trace a valley's curves,
Stark witness to the dangerous charge we bear,
A house ignites, a train's derailed, a bridge
Blows up sky-high, and water floods the mines.
Who first attacked? Who turned the other cheek?[2]
Aggression perpetrated is as soon
Denied, and insult rubbed into the injury
By cunning agents trained in these affairs,
With whom it's touch-and-go, don't-tread-on-me,
I-dare-you-to, keep-off, and kiss-my-hand.
Tempers could sharpen knives, and do; we live
In states provocative
Where frowning headlines scare the coffee cream
And doomsday[3] is the eighth day of the week.

Our exit through the slammed and final door
Is twenty times rehearsed, but when we face
The imminence of cataclysmic rupture,
A lesser pride goes down upon its knees.
Two countries separated by desire!—
Whose diplomats speed back and forth by plane,
Portmanteaus stuffed with fresh apologies
Outdated by events before they land.
Negotiations wear them out: they're driven mad
Between the protocols of tears and rapture.

Locked in our fated and contiguous selves,
These worlds that too much agitate each other,
Interdependencies from hip to head,
Twin principalities both slave and free,
We coexist, proclaiming Peace together.
Tell me no lies! We are divided nations
With malcontents by thousands in our streets,
These thousands torn by inbred revolutions.
A triumph is demanded, not moral victories
Deduced from small advances, small retreats.
Are the gods of our fathers not still daemonic?
On the steps of the Capitol
The outraged lion[4] of our years roars panic,
And we suffer the guilty cowardice of the will,

1. From *The Poems of Stanley Kunitz, 1928–1978* (1979).
2. See Matthew 5.39.
3. The Day of Judgment, marking the end of the world. "Touch-and-go": a running and chasing game. "Don't-tread-on-me": the motto on a number of flags, picturing a rattlesnake, designed for the American Revolution.
4. The king of beasts; also a constellation and a sign of the Zodiac. In Aesop's fable of the lion

Gathering its bankrupt slogans up for flight
Like gold from ruined treasuries.
And yet, and yet, although the murmur rises,
We are what we are, and only life surprises.

1958

Quinnapoxet[1]

I was fishing in the abandoned reservoir
back in Quinnapoxet,[2]
where the snapping turtles cruised
and the bullheads swayed
in their bower of tree-stumps,
sleek as eels and pigeon-fat.
One of them gashed my thumb
with a flick of his razor fin
when I yanked the barb
out of his gullet.
The sun hung its terrible coals
over Buteau's farm: I saw
the treetops seething.

They came suddenly into view
on the Indian road,
evenly stepping
past the apple orchard,
commingling with the dust[3]
they raised, their cloud of being,
against the dripping light
looming larger and bolder.
She was wearing a mourning bonnet
and a wrap of shining taffeta.
"Why don't you write?" she cried
from the folds of her veil.

"We never hear from you."
I had nothing to say to her.
But for him who walked behind her

hunting in company with smaller animals, the lion appropriates all the prey. "Gods of our fathers": a reference to the biblical address, probably made most famous by Rudyard Kipling (1865–1936) in his end-of-the-British-Empire poem *Recessional*, which begins "God of our fathers" and has been set to music as a hymn. "Capitol": the Roman temple of Jupiter where the Senate met, as well as the building in Washington, D.C., where the U.S. Senate meets.

1. From *The Poems of Stanley Kunitz, 1928–1978* (1979).

2. From the Indian word meaning "little long pond" or "place of the little long pond." Quinnapoxet is the name of a river, town, and reservoir in central Massachusetts. "Also sometimes spelled with one n . . . a backwater village outside Worcester, Massachusetts, where I spent my childhood summers as a boarder on the Buteau farm. The village no longer exists, and its place-name is all but forgotten" [Kunitz's note].

3. It is said of Adam (Genesis 3.19): "For you are, and to dust you shall return." "Indian road": used by the Nipmuc, who were the original inhabitants of the region. They had been driven out or confined to special villages, their numbers decimated by the end of the eighteenth century. "Apple orchard": a reference to the tree of knowledge in the Garden of Eden, the fruit of which is traditionally pictured as an apple (Genesis 2.9).

in his dark worsted suit,
with his face averted
as if to hide a scald,
deep in his other life,
I touched my forehead
with my swollen thumb
and splayed my fingers out—
in deaf-mute country
the sign[4] for father.

1979

4. In American Sign Language, a hand gesture that expresses a concept or a letter of the alphabet.

MEYER LEVIN
1905–1981

Born in Chicago of parents from Eastern Europe, Meyer Levin graduated from the University of Chicago in 1924 and worked as a reporter for the *Chicago Daily News.* A crucial trip in the 1920s to Europe—where he met his wife—and Palestine started him on a lifelong search for and celebration of his Jewish roots. He joined a kibbutz in 1929 but returned to the United States in pursuit of a literary career. Over the next thirty years, he made many trips between Palestine/Israel and the United States, finally settling permanently in Israel in 1958. He is one of the few Jewish American writers in English to have been so actively partisan to Israel and its creation as a State, and to have written early on about the Holocaust.

Of the fourteen novels he composed between 1929 and 1981, only *Compulsion* (1956) achieved wide public appeal. A fictionalization of the sensational 1924 Leopold and Loeb murder of young Bobby Franks in Chicago, it was made into a successful Hollywood film. Deeply involved in the great events of his time, Levin covered the Spanish Civil War in 1938 as a reporter on the Loyalist side. During World War II, he worked for the Office of War Information and the Psychological Warfare Division, accompanying U.S. troops as they liberated the concentration camps.

Levin was instrumental in bringing Anne Frank and her diary to American attention. His wife discovered a French edition of Frank's diary that he arranged to have published in the United States. He prepared a draft of a dramatization, which was at first accepted and then rejected by the Broadway producer Cheryl Crawford, who later supported the Albert Hackett/Frances Goodrich version that became a long-running success. Levin sued the producers and Anne Frank's father for having, according to him, appropriated much of his original material. The long litigation that followed and the small victory he ultimately achieved embittered him for years, a story he tells in his aptly named account of these events, *The Obsession* (1973).

The Old Bunch (1937), from which the selections that follow are taken, tells the interlocked stories of a dozen Jewish boys and girls, their families, their relationships and varied careers in Chicago between 1921 and 1934. The style is reportorial, owing much to that of John Dos Passos's then-influential *U.S.A.* trilogy, focusing on the protagonists' efforts to come to terms with their Jewishness and their Americanness—an important, almost inescapable, theme for many in the interwar generation of Jewish Americans. Set mostly in Chicago, *The Old Bunch* contains scenes in France and

Palestine, reflecting Levin's own experiences, including his membership in a kibbutz in the 1920s. *The Old Bunch* is not only an important document sociologically, it is also one of Levin's most engaging books. In the cumulative power of its detailed accounting of the characters' lives as most of them succumb to the forces of assimilation (which he decries), it invites favorable comparison with the contemporaneous *Studs Lonigan*, by Chicagoan James T. Farrell.

From The Old Bunch

WHAT'S IN A NAME

Rose Heller got Aline Freedman off into the bedroom, clutched her hand, and gasped: "Oh, kid! He wants to take me home!"

Aline stared into her eyes with a look that said: Kiddo, I know how it begins. "Oh, Rose! That's scrumptious!" she squeaked.

"But he came here with Thelma. She'll have a fit!"

"Well, let her! Anyway they all came together in a bunch."

Rose couldn't give up this chance of getting a fellow tall enough for her. He was at least six feet tall with a long face and slick brilliantined hair. His name was Manny Kassell and he was a dentist. Not as good as a lawyer or a doctor, but he was already graduated and practicing. He had a sense of humor too and he was answering everything with the statement: Yes, we have no bananas.[1] When Aline asked him would he like a piece of cake he answered solemnly: Yes, we have no banaan', and when Rose asked him if he had seen the Moscow Art Theatre[2] he said: Yes, we have no bananinsky! That line got to be a scream.

There were hardly any Jewish fellows that tall; and if a girl didn't grab what she could she'd be out of luck.

He took her home on the bus.

"I see where they gave that prize for naming that new magazine," he remarked. "Twenty thousand smackers for a name!" and whistled.

"What did they name it?"

"Liberty. A Magazine for Everybody. Imagine! Twenty thousand berries!"

"They must have got in a million names."

"It was more than a million. I even took a shot at it."

"Yah? What was yours? I bet it was good."

He flipped out a pencil and pulled a scrap of paper from his pocket. "You have to see this to appreciate it." He printed: U S.

"Get it? US. A Magazine for Americans."

"Say, that's cute," she appreciated. "You know a friend of mine just had a baby. I wonder what they'll name it. . . . Sam Eisen, do you know him?"

"Eisen? Is he a short fellow?"

"Yah. He's kind of heavy-set."

"Brown hair?"

"Yah, that's the one."

"Then I don't know him!" he guffawed.

1. "Yes, We Have No Bananas," a popular song of the time.

2. A world-famous theater company, home to the great director and teacher of acting, Konstantin Stanislavsky. Anton Chekhov's plays, among others, were given powerful productions here.

"An aunt of mine just had a kid and they named him Isidore," Rose confided. "Isn't that terrible? Izzy! Imagine what a kid has to go through with a name like that!"

"Know a name I always liked? Vincent. That's a nice name."

"Mygod, the names some people give their kids! I was to a *briss*[3] downstairs of us and they're old-fashioned Jews and they named the kid Mattashmayas or Shmatenyuh or some Bible name, it certainly sounded terrible. I don't see why people should persist in giving their children Jewish names. After all, we're Americans."

"Well, you know the old folks came from the old country and didn't know any better. You know what my Jewish name is?" he confessed, "Manasheh." He snickered.

"Ich!" she squealed. "Bet you'll never guess mine?"

"Rochel?" Manny Kassell submitted. "Rifka?"

She shook her head. Her eyes popped with laughter. "Chayah-Shaynah!" Rose exploded.

"A rose by any other name is just as sweet," he said.

"When I started to school I changed it to Rose. Once I changed it to Rosalind but everybody kept on calling me Rose."

"Some of those Jewish names aren't so bad," he said. "But imagine being called Yankel or Shmool or some of those terrible Bible names like Mordecai!"

"Say, I'll bet that used to be Mort Abramson's name. You know what Sylvia Abramson's name was? Shulamith!" They roared. "And Aline Freedman's name used to be Lena. Her mother still persists in calling her that. Honest! Aline has a fit, every time."

"That's nothing. I got a kid sister named Ethel, and my mother calls her Gittel!"

"Some people just have no consideration," Rose said. "If I ever have a kid, I'll give him a decent name."

"What would you call him?" He dropped his arm around her.

"I like a name like Ronald. That's a nice name. Or Peter."

"Y' know a name I like? Clarence," he said.

"Me too." It was thrilling, the way they agreed on things! "Clarence is a doggy name."

Lil's folks wanted them to call the kid Jacob, after Mrs. Klein's dead father, Yankel Silverman.

"Let's humor them," Lil said. "After, we can change it to James."

Alone at home, Sam thought of looking in the Bible to refresh his mind about Jacob, after whom he was naming his son. He found the Bible that he had swiped out of a Y.M.C.A. that time when the crazy old coot who made speeches trying to convert the Jews on Roosevelt Road had got him curious about the New Testament.

And as he read the story of Jacob, Sam thought: What a clever rascal, what a crook! No, not really a crook! Everything Jacob did was within the law. Sure, he knew people like Jacob. Lou Margolis, and his own father-in-law, Marcus Klein.

3. A rite in which a Jewish male child, eight days after he is born, is circumcised (Yiddish).

See, Jacob doesn't steal his brother's birthright, he buys it with a mess of pottage. And is it Jacob who fools his father with the hairy goatskin? No, he lets the old woman be responsible for the scheme. And later, what of the flocks that he steals from his father-in-law? Does he paint them with rings and spots? Oh, no, technically he is innocent. He merely breeds them that way, and lets nature load the dice for him.

A smart Jew, Sam thought, and a physical coward too, hiding behind the skirts of his wives when he met the brother he had wronged.

And yet, even as he saw the narrow, slippery qualities of this patriarch, Sam could not feel that it would be a shame to name his son after Jacob. For Jacob was only using his cleverness to strike back at fate for making him a second son, at Laban for giving him cow-eyed Leah instead of the girl he loved, and for whom he had slaved seven years.

It was as though some cord of Sam's own body and mind grew way back into those times, reaching Jacob, and Sam remembered, and understood the faking and lying that a Jew sometimes had to do, against his own best conscience, to make his way in the world. This imperfect creature, this Jacob, now stood to Sam as a kind of archetype of the Jew, embracing all the good and bad qualities of the race, and lovable because he was so humanly and truly the father of all the stanch and slippery, lying, idealistic, smart, bragging, cowardly, boot-licking, and swaggering little gleamy-eyed Jews who now inhabited the earth. He could call his son Jacob. That was what Jews came from, and that was what Jews were like.

Sitting alone, reading, Sam sensed himself at last an adult who could judge his own elders; he was a man who had come upon an old family record, for the first time seeing his ancestors as humans and sometimes rascals, instead of as the mythically perfect beings presented to him in childhood.

He read on, of Joseph, the son of that wily old Jacob, and here he saw the cleverness of the father skillfully used to good ends, benefiting whole peoples, Egyptians as well as the Jews; and in Joseph, Sam recognized the wish of himself. He too must rise from nothing to be a power in the land, showing people how to conserve and divide their wealth; and wasn't America, after all, a kind of Egypt to the Jews?

Look, he had made his own son into Jacob, and himself into Joseph, the son of his own son.

Was he afraid to have his son a better man than himself?

Or, was this the way in which the Jewish strain eternally renewed itself, going back and forth from Isaac to Jacob to Joseph, mixing their qualities of loyalty and cunning and subtlety.

Sam sat there, smiling with himself.

And Sam Eisen did all right for himself. There was this year when the warm wet baby smell continuously filled the flat, and diapers hung on all the chairs, and Lil was a mother, and Sam felt himself driving, driving, like a throbbing power eating up the law, pushing toward the top.

In mock court was where he shone. He had something the other boys didn't have. It wasn't oratory, it wasn't superior knowledge of the law. He had a powerful sense of conviction. There was something almost hypnotic about Sam when he quoted a case, questioned a witness. He was positive.

Where the other fellows mumbled their citations he shot them out like bombs.

Lou Margolis stopped in once and listened to Sam. "He's good," another kid near the doorway said. Lou shrugged and made a wise face. "He'll antagonize the judges," Lou said.

* * *

COMPARATIVE RELIGIONS

* * *

Up above Safed, they said, there was marble to be found. A New York Jew had even tried to open a quarry there, oh, it was fine stone, better than Italian marble! But the expense of hauling to Haifa defeated the business. The stone lay way up almost to the Syrian border; it was even a little beyond Cfar Giladi, the last outpost of the *chalutz*[4] communes. A mountainous region, gray, and yellow, spotted with the deep green of olive groves.

Joe was in shorts, brown-legged, and brown deep below his throat. He carried a knapsack containing a few clothes and his carving tools. Coming up toward Giladi, he saw a young Jew with a shepherd's crook tending the commune's flocks. Sheep, and black, silken-haired goats.

In this land, biblical phrases were as native and as fresh as the songs of Walt Whitman to America.

"Behold, thou art fair, my love . . . thy hair is as a flock of goats, that appear from Mount Gilead . . ."[5]

Even at this moment Mitch Wilner's letter burned in Joe's mind. "I sat down and had a good laugh. To think that we should ever quarrel over a girl . . ." Was that the fellow Sylvia loved, and was going to marry? "I've seen plenty of fellows, especially in my profession, wreck their careers because of a wife hanging around their necks. That's one thing I'm not going to do. I'll get married when I'm good and ready, Joeboy, no matter how impatient it makes you . . ." Only one sentence in Mitch Wilner's letter stopped him from turning back to America. After joshing for pages, Mitch said: "But one thing is certain, Sylvia and I will end our days together."

Joe had formed the habit of imagining that Sylvia was with him, especially in moments on this voyage when the high, emotional beauty of the country quickened him, made him feel as though he were living within a prophecy that was coming toward fulfillment.

Surely Sylvia must see with him the mountain-grown quality of this group of stone houses, must share his fearful sense of coming home among the settlers here.

They were stony, silent, tall, as if in harmony with these wild surroundings. Their faces were strong, stubborn, sudden. They rode horses like bedouin;[6] their moods of laughter and of anger were sudden and fierce and childlike,

4. Pioneer (Hebrew; plural, *chalutzim*). "Safed": a sacred Jewish city, site of the creation of modern Kabbalah (esoteric and mystic interpretation of the Bible) by Rabbi Isaac Luria in the 16th century. "Cfar Giladi": Kfar Giladi, a kibbutz in the north of the country and the site of a major battle in the 1920s against Arab marauders in which the kibbutz leader Trumpeldor was killed. It gave Jews a stake in northern Galillee.

5. The Song of Songs 4.1.

6. A nomadic people living in Palestine and surrounding countries.

like the Arabs'. These were like an old tribe of Hebrew people, Habirim[7] out of the wilderness.

During Joe's first days among them, he was contemptuously left to himself; none asked questions about his world, for unlike the valley *chalutzim*, these were incurious. They had their place. Let the American see what he wanted, and go away.

It was a walk of two hours up a further hill, to the abandoned marble quarry. There, too, Joe exulted with the emotion of discovery. "Look, Syl, look what we have found!" The stone was even-grained, silky, and reddish tan in color. There was a rudimentary chute, for getting it down to the cutting-shack. Crude machinery for blocking the marble was still intact.

Joe clambered around the slope. He saw where the last break had been made, and outlined a great stone that could be loosed; if he could get it down! Eight foot of it!

In the courtyard of the commune was a smithy's shed; Joe prowled excitedly through a pile of scrap iron, and found a long iron bar. Shlomo, the smith, fixed a chisel edge on the bar. Then Joe asked Chayim Ben Yehuda, one of the leaders: "Could I get a man to help me for a day? I want to bring down a stone."

Shlomo went with him the next day. When they went to work quarrying the stone, Joe noticed Shlomo's huge hands, red hair sprouting from the knuckles.

Now they were changed toward him, treating him as one of themselves, a worker, who knew his own craft.

Coming back from the quarry, Shlomo took him by the small cemetery on a hillock, perhaps half a mile from the commune. Three graves were together in a center mound.

"You know who died here?" Shlomo asked.

Joe knew the legend of the three graves.

Years back, in the first flush of Zionist immigration, when this commune had been founded, there had been trouble here. A sheikh, known and thought to be friendly to the settlers, had galloped up to the gate of this isolated, lonely colony. He had declared himself to be hunting a personal enemy, who might have taken refuge here. They had opened the gates to him, let him search for his enemy.

The sheikh and his followers had gone into the barn. A moment later, shots were heard.

In that barn, the leader of the commune, Trumpeldor, a one-armed veteran, had held off the band of attacking Arabs. Trumpeldor and two young women had lost their lives.

Who knew why the Arabs had begun to shoot? The Arab is a creature of dark motives, of sudden fury; know him, and he is treacherous too.

Through the years, this incident had grown into legend, as typical of all the dangers and hardships of settlement, of the treachery of Arabs, of the struggle against isolation, disease, malaria, homesickness; all were included in the memory of the hero, Trumpeldor, who had fought in the barn, single-handed, wounded, against the whole party of attacking Arabs, and held them until the colonists could gather and save their settlement.

7. Comrades, in a kibbutz-commune context.

"Why don't you make a stone to his memory?" Shlomo said.

Why not? Already Joe felt in his blood something of the wild deep hatred of the enemy, call him Arab, call him some universal adversary: all that was against Jewish settlement in this land. You had to be here to know it, to feel this primitive stubborn urge, born in these stones. He had already schemed the rugged figure of a man, a monument to the settlers of these hills; now he saw him as a hero, too; as Trumpeldor, the national hero.

A crew of men turned out; with a tractor and a sledge they brought the stone and set it up where it would be a monument. There, Joe went to work.

He remembered the gaping crowd that had watched the stone-carvers on the Straus Building on Michigan and Jackson, until the artisans had to be screened from the curious watchers. He remembered the flocks of awed and timid visitors who had been shepherded periodically through the Midway studios,[8] remembered their inane remarks.

Here, he worked in the sun. Occasionally, the comrades[9] came by and spoke with him. He was one of themselves, a man who toiled. He used mallet and chisels, sweated at his labor, and was skilled.

On Sabbath, the comrades would stroll about the farm, and many of them made the cemetery the goal of their walk. Chayim Ben Yehuda and his wife, Shulamith, came by. She was a girl born in Palestine, the first Joe had known. She was a purely Semitic type, far different from the short-legged, short-necked women of Russian-Jewish stock who filled the communes. Had there, then, been Jews in Palestine before this Zionist movement? Ah, but what kind of Jews! Huddled together in settlements in the ancient holy cities—Jerusalem, Safed, Hebron—entire communities of mothy alms-eaters. Colonies of orthodox prayer-sayers, thin sap of generations of talmudists,[1] who busied themselves these hundreds of years in writing begging letters to the Jews scattered throughout the world, for were they not performing a mission for the entire race by the mere fact of living in the holy land? Generation after generation, they had compiled and guarded the addresses of Jews throughout the world who might respond to a begging letter sent out around Yom Kippur or Passover. The entire community lived on the proceeds of these letters. Cooped in their holy ghettos, they loathed the influx of young settlers, godless, beardless, who smoked on Sabbath and worked for a living. But among their own sons and daughters, a few stuck out their heads, whiffed the new life, and abandoned the orthodox slums for labor in the colonies. Shulamith had been one of these, and in a *chalutz* commune she had met her husband, Chayim Ben Yehuda.

Here she is, Ann, with her doe's eyes, olive skin, and her two black crinkly braids; should I seek out her sister, and remain here, breeding native Jews?

Shulamith walked around the forming monument. "Trumpeldor was a cripple, with only one arm," she said, "but it is good you are giving him two.

8. A main thoroughfare in South Chicago, running through the University of Chicago. It was a site for the Chicago World's Columbian Exposition of 1893. "Straus Building": built in 1923–24, it was named originally for the investment firm of S. W. Straus & Co., which for a time had an elegant banking floor in its innovative building. During the depression, the firm went into receivership, and in the 1940s the building was more than half empty.

9. Members of the left-wing Labor Zionist commune.

1. Students of the vast commentaries (the Talmud) on the Bible. "Hebron": the sacred city in which Abraham and Sarah are buried.

It is not necessary that this should be the image of the man, but it must be in his memory, the image of a hero, a pioneer."

Could you say it better, at the Select, Ann?

Joe smoked his pipe. Tobacco grown in the colony.[2]

The figure was emerging, a wiry and powerful Hebrew, with large hands, and a hawklike dreamy Semitic face. Here, more than at any time before, except for those few months in Chicago when he thought he was getting ready to marry Sylvia, Joe felt he was working well.

The trouble came vaguely, first a rumor to be treated lightly, of riots at the Wailing Wall.[3] Who cares for the Wailing Wall where the dying graybeards mumble and spit, in that passageway damp with the piss of Arab donkeys! The *chalutzim* have other things in mind, in Palestine, than crying at a stinking old wall!

And yet, haven't Jews been praying there since the time of Solomon?[4] If the graybeards want to pray there, they have a right to pray.

Then came a swift visit by two authoritative comrades in an auto. They held a sudden council with Ben Yehuda and the other leaders, left a small box, and were gone. In the evening, a general meeting of the commune. Comrades, how many have pistols? And then the order: Wear dark clothes only, white shines at night.

Shulamith saw Joe in his white shirt. "Have you no other? I'll lend you one of Chayim's." In the morning: "Comrade, better not go up the hill to work, it's dangerous for you to be there alone." Joe hung around the yard. At noon, another general meeting, and then each man was assigned his post, in case of trouble. The women and children were to go to the barn. That night, doubled guards. Every hour, a rider clattered into the yard. "All quiet."

None knew how the news came. The commune was cut off, without telephone, the roads were closed: several Arab villages lay between Giladi and the next Jewish settlement. Yet all over the yard there was whispering of the massacre at Hebron. Many American students in the Yeshiva[5] there had been butchered, too.

Here in the clear mountain air, the rumor of insane strife seemed unreal to Joe. He was clumsy when Chayim showed him how to put a magazine of cartridges into an automatic, and remembered wryly how he had walked out on military drill at Illinois. There was no pistol for him anyway. "Arm yourself as best you can, comrade." Joe picked up the immense crowbar he had used in the quarry. His post, if trouble came, was at the door of the dairy.

"But why should they attack us? Why? We have been on good terms with the Arabs. What is all this about Arab nationalism?"

"Nationalism!" Chayim snorted. "What does the Arab fellah[6] know about nationalism! He sees a chance to raid and steal our livestock. The bedouin will drive the horses and cattle over the border and sell them in Syria. Even

2. Some tobacco was grown in Palestine. "Colony" may be a mistranslation of *Moshavah* (Hebrew for "settlement"). "Select": a Paris café. "Ann": a woman in Paris Joe had been attached to, part of the 1920s American expatriate scene he had begun to find meaningless.

3. The last remaining section of the Temple destroyed by the Romans in 70 C.E.

4. The ruler of Jews in the 9th century B.C.E. who first united Israel. He was renowned for his wisdom.

5. An institution for higher religious studies.

6. Peasant (Arabic).

Sheikh Salich, our friend from the village down the road, might take an opportunity such as this."

That night Joe stood a turn on watch. For this hour he had been given a pistol. Chayim, who seemed endlessly on duty, was mounted and wore an Arab abayeh.[7] At a suspicion of movement, he would dash down the road, leaving Joe alone, sitting on the doorstep of the *cheder ochel*.[8] It would seem hours before his return.

Once, while Chayim was gone, Joe thought he heard a distant shot. He stood trembling, wondering—to wake the others? It might have been a rock, falling. He stood, waiting, and in that space of time the thought came to him that perhaps he was near death. It would be so strange to meet it here on a lonely mountainside in Israel, Joe Freedman from Chicago. Would Sylvia come to his grave, up there next to Trumpledor's? And Sylvia's name was Shulamith; Shulamith must be her true Hebrew name.

Behold, thou art fair, my love, thou art fair, thou hast doves' eyes, thy hair is as a flock of goats, that appear from Mount Gilead.

Surely, wherever she was, she knew he was standing here alone, and needed, at last.

And if he should die now, what would his young life have been but a failure? He had failed with Sylvia, he had failed with his work, only here perhaps the thing he had made, rugged and as yet roughly finished, could stand.

How strange that the thought of death was in no way alarming; something cool, like this night, and vaguely elating, like this whole mountain region. Perhaps the saddest thing about his life was that he had found nothing so far to which he felt he had to cling; all of his life had been a severing, trying to rid himself of the fixation on Sylvia, trying to rid himself of his background of the West Side of Chicago, of the ugliness of his father's flophouse; and death would be the final, the perfect riddance. The most tragic thing of all, Joe thought, was that at this moment, scarcely having lived, he felt ready and willing to die, for no cause, with no heroism as these others might die, but through having little will to live.

Then laughingly, like a sudden breeze against his cheeks, he realized that he had no need to rid himself of anything. He could possess, embrace, be big! Why so mournful! He wanted to end, when he was just beginning.

There were hoofbeats. Joe waited, the whistle at his lips. Now he made out the rider.

Chayim slid off the horse. "They tried to pull me down, there, on the mountain. There are bedouin."

As if by intuition men had begun to emerge from the cottages; then women came.

—What? What is it? An attack?

—No, nothing, be still, hush. Only, to be safe, let the outpost men go to their places.

Eight men crept off, radiating toward different corners of the farm. Little groups gathered, whispering.

—The English have a warship at Haifa, it will soon be quiet now.

7. Cloak (Arabic).

8. The dining hall of the kibbutz (Hebrew).

—Bedouin have attacked Tul Kerem.[9] Two comrades are dead.

Joe handed his pistol over to Shlomo, took his crowbar again, and went to his post. With him was Ben Maimon, a comrade whom he scarcely knew.

"Women, go back to sleep," Chayim said. Still they prowled nervously around the yard. "Better go into the barn then." The children, as a precaution, had already been taken to sleep there.

Awaited, and yet unbelievably, there came a rapid succession of shots from above, on the mountainside.

—Theirs, or ours?

The women fell absolutely silent.

Five horsemen burst across the yard, riding toward the shooting. Several men began to run in the same direction.

Chayim halted his horse, wheeled. "Wait here! Shmarya, you are in charge. Wait till you are called. All others keep to your posts."

There were more shots. Joe stood still, his hands clamped around the bar of iron, chill as the night. What use would it be? If bedouin rode into the courtyard, shooting and cutting, could he swing at them, strike them from their horses? He had heard tales, too, of what they did to men. Cut off the genitals, and stuck them in the mouth.

From a distance, a wild war scream, ludicrously like a yodel, spiraled into the night. He had heard Arab horsemen yelling like that as they rode around immense fires on distant hills, in their games called *fantasia*.

The women closed around Shulamith. How is it? Are they many? The vermin. . . .

And now, completely, Joe felt what they felt. It was an inexpressible hatred. The word, the thought, of Arab aroused in him only the wish to kill, to see them fall, dead; he had not dreamed that it was within himself to wish to gloat on killing.

The firing began again, and endured. From two sides.

Shulamith cried: "They must need ammunition!" Then, incredibly, Joe saw her run out, and toward the battle. She was carrying the box. He started after her, took hold of one handle. It was mad. If the men had need, they would have sent a message. But with the panic of intuition, the girl ran.

Voices called them back, but they ran.

The firing had died again. A crack, and then an answering shot.

They ran together, over the stones, sure-footed, toward the olive grove blotting the hill. They had reached the first trees, and could make out the forms of white Arab horses, turning, clambering up the hill, fleeing.

They ran harder, feeling the power of triumph.

Just then, Shulamith was struck. She stopped, waited as if to know, then folded to the ground.

In the commune they sensed that the skirmish was over, and rushed forward to meet the defenders.

One of the men had a flesh wound in the shoulder; not serious, the comrade nurse could take care of him. But further, a group formed out of the darkness, carrying Shulamith.

9. A Jewish settlement in Palestine.

In the morning her fever was 103. Utter quiet lay upon the commune. The people seemed to Joe to have become like some mute creatures of the mountains, moving silently, silently breathing the air. Small groups collected, with their faces toward each other, but didn't speak. They were like melancholy cattle gathered under a tree.

The doubled sentries went out to the edges of the farm, those they relieved came in, sat in the kitchen drinking tea. None could sleep.

At last Joe saw the mechanic, Maishe Levin, binding down the canvas sides of the farm truck. Then he filled the body of the truck deep with straw.

Chayim Ben Yehuda came out of the barn where his wife lay, and approached Joe.

"Listen, Yosef," he said. "Lower down, the road is already closed by the English. They may not let us pass. Someone will have to talk English to them."

"Will you take me along?" Joe said.

"Good."

Two comrades carried the girl out of the barn and placed her on the bed of straw. Her husband climbed into the truck; her eyes were open; she reached out her hand and clasped his tightly. Joe sat with the driver.

The comrades followed the truck to the gate.

The road was narrow, steep, and wound insanely around blind corners. They would have to pass two Arab villages.

As they neared the first, they saw a few Arabs with donkeys coming towards them. Joe looked back into the truck; the girl had her lover's hand close against her cheek. Maishe Levin stepped on the gas. The truck hit the bumps wildly, and slewed past the group of Arabs.

Two shots followed, in a shower of stones.

"We should not have come in daylight," Maishe said.

It was only when they were well past, spun around a curve, the first village out of sight, that Joe realized: he had been shot at. Last night had not seemed personal, but this was aimed at himself. Why? Why this? Coupled to his abhorrence of violence was an idealistic feeling that plain people, the real people of earth, were not bloodthirsty, but peaceable. Why had the Arabs risen, gone berserk, hacking to pieces the talmudists of Hebron, besieging the isolated colonies?

Were the Jews harming the Arabs?

Maishe Levin pointed his chin toward two bedouin tents, black upon the gray mountain rubble.

What can Jews take away from them?

Outside of Palestine, Joe knew, there was much talk about Arab fellahin being forced off their ancestral lands by the hordes of incoming Jews. But the attack last night had not been that of vengeful natives, driving out an invader. It had only been a furtive, sneaking raid, an attempt to steal the stock of an isolated farm.

And he had seen these fellahin. What had they to lose by the Jewish immigration? Treading out their meager harvest of grain under the hooves of camels, giving a third and a half over to their feudal sheikh, to whom they were perpetually in debt for seed. It would take the wild imagination of a political economist living in London to prove that the Jews had deprived them of their ancestral land, for, on the spot, anybody could see that the Jews had bought and developed waste lands, marshes, and land left idle by absentee owners, fat sheikhs who lived in Syria. Then why were the fellahin slaughtering Jews, who had brought them no harm, but a raised price for labor? What had let loose the bloodlust of this submerged people?

Riding beside him, Maishe Levin seemed to divine his perplexity.

"They have been told that the Mosque in Jerusalem has been sold to the Jews," he said, simply.

For a moment Joe couldn't grasp his meaning. The Mosque? But how could anyone believe such a story? And to slaughter human beings on the strength of it!

"They believe it," Maishe said. "In each village, there is a mukhtar,[1] who reads them this news out of the Arab papers. What has happened in Hebron, and in the old city of Jerusalem—these were holy wars."

"But why should these mukhtars spread such lies?"

The truck, progressing slowly with the wounded girl, made a turn, and below them, with jewel-cut clarity, lay the valley; the olive trees of distant orchards stood leaf-clear, as in primitive painting. Everything was believable here; Joe felt that he knew why religions had arisen here.

"Why should they spread such lies?" the driver repeated, and answered: "To raise the price of the land."

"Who?"

Maishe looked at him, wondering at the simple-mindedness of the American. "Who? The sheikhs. The Arab landowners. They caused this thing to be printed in the Arab newspapers, to be spread by the mukhtars in the villages—that a great council of Jews, meeting in Europe, had bought the Mosque of Jerusalem. That is why the talmudists were the first to be attacked."

"But how will this raise the price of land? I should think it would lower it."

Maishe smiled wryly. "We Jews are a stubborn people, and this the Arabs know. Trouble only makes the Jews more anxious to buy up land, to bring their villages close together. And, as the Jews are anxious to buy, the sheikhs are reluctant to sell."

Maishe Levin concluded sadly. "You see, it is all a question of property, of money. But they who kill, don't know."

And yet, out of the confused pressure of these multiple forces, it seemed to Joe that some truth must come. It was in the tender beauty of this strange country, in the intimate mystery of this land. This trouble was like the seething of the world at its center. And his imagination, quickened in this stress, pictured this trouble between the Arabs and Jews as the intimation, the first small thematic sound, of a world turbulence, out of which peace and truth might finally prevail. For wasn't the world in tension again, for the final struggle between east and west, between a spiritual and a material approach to life? When the next war came, it would be the uprising of all the oppressed peoples of Africa and Asia, and Palestine would be the bridge between Europe and her possessions, here again would be the center of conflict, and the Jews would play their prophetic and historic role.

The buildings of Salich's village were plainly visible now; a group of squat,

1. A village headman (Arabic; of Turkish origin).

muddy hovels groveling under the sheikh's two-story house. Ordinarily this was a friendly village; the sheikh had built his new house with Jewish money. But now they saw Arabs drifting toward the road.

The truck, making a hairpin turn, was confronted with a blockade.

A swarm of Arabs, on foot, on donkeys, gesticulated and screamed.

Maishe Levin drew his gun. Chayim scrambled to the cab of the truck, his face between them.

Now it would happen. Joe, too, held a gun. It felt meaningless against his palm.

"Dash through," Chayim muttered.

Impossible. They had placed rocks in the road. "I'll try to talk to them," Maishe murmured, at the final moment, applying the brake.

Chayim laughed bitterly.

It was at this instant, when they had reached the impasse, that a car appeared from below.

It isn't true, Joe said to himself. Things don't happen like this!

Yet their rescue was before them; the immense touring car halted not ten feet away, and half a dozen British marines, carrying bayoneted rifles, piled out.

The Arabs spread to the side of the road, muttering.

The marines were kids, none looked over seventeen, all were stunted by wartime childhood, all with a sadly vicious air of indifference, of hatred for the bloody Arabs and the bloody Jews.

A sergeant got out of the car. "Road's shut off!" he yelled at Maishe Levin. And then, with the irritated speed of a man who knows his language isn't being understood, swore: "The bloody fuckn goddamn Jew bastards! Stick their bloody fuckn heads out, and then they squeal bloody murder 'cause they don't get protection! Get back to your holes!" he shouted, waving at the truck. "Turn around, man! Back! *Yalla!*[2]" He dropped his voice, and spoke to a civilian who had remained in the car. "How the devil does a man make these Jews understand. I say, you talk their Chinese Hebrew, don't you? Come on, tell these fat-headed blighters to go home!"

A civilian, stoutish, bald-headed, emerged from the tonneau. At once Joe knew he had seen the man before.

"Our beloved benefactors, the British," said the civilian, "have closed the road, and this military genius is angry with you for venturing forth. He orders you to turn back."

"We have a wounded woman here, we're taking her to a hospital," Joe said to the sergeant.

For a moment, hearing English spoken, the sergeant seemed appeased. Then he snarled: "Sick woman, is it? Now what's the game? You ain't out hunting a few Arabs by any chance?"

"Look for yourself."

The British closed around the truck. The Arabs crowded in from the road-edges, angry, gesticulating, yet afraid of the half-dozen tin-helmeted lads with rifles, who remained utterly contemptuous of the danger of their position.

2. "Hurry up!" or "Get going!" (Arabic).

The sergeant hoisted himself up onto the truck. "How do I know she's sick? What's under that straw?"

"She's very sick! She's running a high fever! We were attacked last night and she was wounded!" Joe screamed. "I'm an American citizen . . ."

He realized Bialystoker had recognized him, too.

"Trust these bloody fuckn Americans to make a mess!" the sergeant swore. "Now, you, fellow, I'll take no responsibility for you! You're a Jew same as the rest of these, and your bloody American passport won't do you any fuckn good when a couple of Arabs pulls out what's in your breeches."

"This woman has to be taken to a hospital at once. What possible reason could we have for risking our necks if this wasn't true!" Joe persisted.

Shulamith had closed her eyes. The sergeant climbed down from the truck. Bialystoker spoke to him quietly.

"Come ahead," the officer said to his men. "We'll have to escort these blasted Hebrews to town." He turned on the Arabs and shouted angrily: "Go on! Scatter! Vamoose!"

Bialystoker climbed onto the truck. "Yes, we have met before," he said, putting out his hand to Joe.

"In Chicago, at the Abramsons'?"

"Yes. Several years ago." Bialystoker chuckled. "What am I doing here? I am now a correspondent for the *Wiener Zeitung*.[3] So. I was here to write articles of Palestine, when the trouble happened."

That seemed simple enough. A coincidence. The British had allowed the journalist to accompany the patrol. But why was it always happening, so? As though she still had some meaning in his life.

"I have seen your friend in Vienna, only last month," Bialystoker said.

"Who?"

"But my niece, Miss Abramson. She is traveling in Europe."

"Oh. Oh, yes." Joe pretended to have known.

"She spoke also of visiting Palestine, but now, with this trouble, I imagine she will not come."

"No. Probably not. It would be foolish."

Safed was hushed, the streets deserted. The car drove up to a house that had been taken over as the Hadassah Hospital.[4] A nurse, an American girl, perhaps visiting Palestine to see what all the Hadassah bridge parties had accomplished, spoke to them in the doorway. "I don't know where we'll put her, we can't possibly take care of her," she murmured distractedly. Seeing Joe, an American, she seized onto him, at last to talk her heart out. "We haven't the room, we haven't the funds—oh, what do they expect of us!"

Maishe Levin and Chayim were carrying Shulamith up the stairs, and as the American girl saw the wounded Palestinian, she shuddered, with fear, hysteria. Joe thought of his sister and her friends, Rose Heller, Thelma, and even of Sylvia—dutifully arranging their annual dances for Hadassah, and the millions like them all over America, the turmoil and the fuss they made.

3. The newspaper the *Vienna Times* (German).

4. Hadassah (the Hebrew name of biblical queen Esther) was founded in 1912 by Henrietta Szold (1860–1945) as an organization of Jewish women in America whose purpose was to bring modern health care to Palestine and to foster Zionism in America.

Well, after all, they were here in the emergency; without them there might have been nothing.

"Do you want to see? I can show you," Bialystoker said, with his narrow smile.

They went into a room crowded with wounded. Mostly bearded Jews from the old city, synagogue Jews, alms-livers of Safed. They had not been able to defend themselves, as had the new breed of settler. There had been a massacre in the ancient part of Safed. Joe walked among these wounded, Jews with orthodox ear-curls limp against their yellowish cheeks.

There was one younger man, whose bandaged stump lay upon the sheet. His hand had been hacked off.

In all the room, in the faces of the nurses, in the faces of the visitors, and of the wounded, was an unearthly despair. The riots had reminded them: this land was not theirs.

For the first time, Joe really felt the ominous message of the pogrom.[5] He had not been like those other comrades, given over permanently to this homeland, to Eretz Yisrael.[6] During the last month, love of the homeland had been growing within him, and he had glimpsed the possibility of a clear, unified, purposeful life in remaining here.

Now it was a twig nipped off. Nothing would grow there any more. And for these others, a whole flowering had been cut down.

1937

5. An organized massacre of Jews.

6. Literally "the land of Israel" (Hebrew).

CLIFFORD ODETS
1906–1963

The shining light of the left-wing theater of the 1930s, Clifford Odets went to Hollywood in 1940 as a highly paid scriptwriter, where he remained, more or less, until his death in 1963 of cancer. He wrote some excellent screenplays, such as *Humoresque* (1946) and *None but the Lonely Heart* (1943), as well as several interesting plays—for instance, *The Big Knife* (1949), about Hollywood's corrosive effect upon artistic integrity; *The Country Girl* (1950), about marriage to an alcoholic actor; and *The Flowering Peach* (1954), a retelling of the Noah story as a Broadway vehicle for the great Yiddish actor Menasha Skulnik. But none of these had the impact of his work for the Group Theatre in the 1930s. His first produced play, *Waiting for Lefty* (1935), was inspired agitprop that brought the audience to its feet with its call to "Strike! Strike!" at the end; and *Awake and Sing!* (1935), which followed that same year although it had actually been written earlier, was less strident but moving in its acerbic but loving depiction of a middle-class Jewish family in the Bronx caught in the moil of the Great Depression. His later work inspired the witty but perhaps unfair bon mot by Dorothy Parker (who was also in Hollywood in the 1940s), "Odets, where is thy sting?"

Clifford Odets was born in Philadelphia of poor parents who later prospered and moved to the Bronx in New York when he was six years old. He dropped out of high school and decided to become an actor. In 1931, he became a charter member of the

Group Theatre, one of the most influential companies in American theater history. Socially conscious, its guiding spirit based largely on the teachings of Stanislavsky (domesticated and Americanized), it nurtured during the decade of its existence such important talents as Elia Kazan, Lee J. Cobb, John Garfield, Morris Carnovsky, Lee Strasberg, Luther Adler, and Sylvia Sidney. Its story is well told in *The Fervent Years* (1975) by Harold Clurman, one of its founders and the director of most of Odets's plays in the 1930s. Clurman's introduction to *Six Plays by Clifford Odets* (1939) is cogent and sensitive to Odets's essential qualities.

In addition to *Waiting for Lefty* (who never comes) and *Awake and Sing!*, his plays for the Group were *Paradise Lost* (1935–36); *Golden Boy* (1937), which Odets himself directed, the play of Odets's that has been most produced, on stage and in film, here and abroad; *Rocket to the Moon* (1938–39); and *Night Music* (1940). The failure of *Night Music* was a great disappointment to Odets, well documented in his journal of the year, called *The Time Is Ripe* (1988), and the occasion for his final move to Hollywood.

Awake and Sing!, despite its moments of leftist rhetoric by the grandfather and Ralph at the end as well as hyperbolic utterance ("a toilet like a monument"), is essentially a warm and intimate portrait of a recognizable Jewish family of the time. The mother, Bessie, may be limited in her insight and values, but she is basically trying to keep the family afloat in hard times—a complex and not wholly unsympathetic character. Odets's great gift was his use of vernacular experience and language in fresh and surprising ways, best exemplified in this play in the speech of Moe Axelrod. As a writer, therefore, he can be seen as a necessary forerunner of Saul Bellow and Philip Roth whose easy combination of vernacular and high style created a new tone in American writing of the 1950s and beyond.

Awake and Sing!

Awake and Sing was presented by the Group Theatre at the Belasco Theatre on the evening of February 19th, 1935, with the following members of the Group Theatre Acting Company:[1]

	Played by
MYRON BERGER	ART SMITH
BESSIE BERGER	STELLA ADLER
JACOB	MORRIS CARNOVSKY
HENNIE BERGER	PHOEBE BRAND
RALPH BERGER	JULES GARFIELD
SCHLOSSER	ROMAN BOHNEN
MOE AXELROD	LUTHER ADLER
UNCLE MORTY	J. E. BROMBERG
SAM FEINSCHREIBER	SANFORD MEISNER

The entire action takes place in an apartment in the Bronx,[2] *New York City*

The production was directed by HAROLD CLURMAN
The setting was designed by BORIS ARONSON

1. Founded in 1931 by Harold Clurman (1901–1980), Lee Strasberg, and Cheryl Crawford, the Group Theatre lasted until 1941 as one of the most important and influential acting companies in the United States. Clurman was its managing director; *Awake and Sing!* was the first play he directed for the company after Strasberg had rejected it. He went on to direct four more plays by Odets for the Group and had a distinguished career as director and theater critic. The actors formed a relatively permanent ensemble and Americanized the Konstantin Stanislavsky (1863–1938) method of acting and teaching, many becoming major Hollywood and Broadway stars.
2. One of the five boroughs comprising New York City.

THE CHARACTERS OF THE PLAY

All of the characters in Awake and Sing! *share a fundamental activity: a struggle for life amidst petty conditions.*

BESSIE BERGER, *as she herself states, is not only the mother in this home but also the father. She is constantly arranging and taking care of her family. She loves life, likes to laugh, has great resourcefulness and enjoys living from day to day. A high degree of energy accounts for her quick exasperation at ineptitude. She is a shrewd judge of realistic qualities in people in the sense of being able to gauge quickly their effectiveness. In her eyes all of the people in the house are equal. She is naïve and quick in emotional response. She is afraid of utter poverty. She is proper according to her own standards, which are fairly close to those of most middle-class families. She knows that when one lives in the jungle one must look out for the wild life.*

MYRON, *her husband, is a born follower. He would like to be a leader. He would like to make a million dollars. He is not sad or ever depressed. Life is an even sweet event to him, but the "old days" were sweeter yet. He has a dignified sense of himself. He likes people. He likes everything. But he is heartbroken without being aware of it.*

HENNIE *is a girl who has had few friends, male or female. She is proud of her body. She won't ask favors. She travels alone. She is fatalistic about being trapped, but will escape if possible. She is self-reliant in the best sense. Till the day she dies she will be faithful to a loved man. She inherits her mother's sense of humor and energy.*

RALPH *is a boy with a clean spirit. He wants to know, wants to learn. He is ardent, he is romantic, he is sensitive. He is naïve too. He is trying to find why so much dirt must be cleared away before it is possible to "get to first base."*

JACOB, *too, is trying to find a right path for himself and the others. He is aware of justice, of dignity. He is an observer of the others, compares their activities with his real and ideal sense of life. This produces a reflective nature. In this home he is a constant boarder. He is a sentimental idealist with no power to turn ideal to action.*

With physical facts—such as housework—he putters. But as a barber he demonstrates the flair of an artist. He is an old Jew with living eyes in his tired face.

UNCLE MORTY *is a successful American business man with five good senses. Something sinister comes out of the fact that the lives of others seldom touch him deeply. He holds to his own line of life. When he is generous he wants others to be aware of it. He is pleased by attention—a rich relative to the* BERGER *family. He is a shrewd judge of material values. He will die unmarried. Two and two make four, never five with him. He can blink in the sun for hours, a fat tomcat. Tickle him, he laughs. He lives in a penthouse with a real Japanese butler to serve him. He sleeps with dress models, but not from his own showrooms. He plays cards for hours on end. He smokes expensive cigars. He sees every Mickey Mouse cartoon that appears. He is a 32-degree Mason.*[3] *He is really deeply intolerant finally.*

MOE AXELROD *lost a leg in the war.*[4] *He seldom forgets that fact. He has killed*

3. The Free and Accepted Masons (sometimes known as Free Masonry) is an international fraternal and charitable organization with secret rites and signs; members of the lodges of Masons ascend in degrees of importance in the organization by passing certain tests and initiations. It has roots in the Middle Ages, though modern Masonry began in the 18th century. The first American lodge was founded in 1730.

4. I.e., World War I (1914–18). America entered the war in 1917.

two men in extra-martial activity. He is mordant, bitter. Life has taught him a disbelief in everything, but he will fight his way through. He seldom shows his feelings: fights against his own sensitivity. He has been everywhere and seen everything. All he wants is HENNIE. *He is very proud. He scorns the inability of others to make their way in life, but he likes people for whatever good qualities they possess. His passionate outbursts come from a strong but contained emotional mechanism.*

SAM FEINSCHREIBER *wants to find a home. He is a lonely man, a foreigner in a strange land, hypersensitive about this fact, conditioned by the humiliation of not making his way alone. He has a sense of others laughing at him. At night he gets up and sits alone in the dark. He hears acutely all the small sounds of life. He might have been a poet in another time and place. He approaches his wife as if he were always offering her a delicate flower. Life is a high chill wind weaving itself around his head.*

SCHLOSSER, *the janitor, is an overworked German whose wife ran away with another man and left him with a young daughter who in turn ran away and joined a burlesque show as chorus girl. The man suffers rheumatic pains. He has lost his identity twenty years before.*

THE SCENE

Exposed on the stage are the dining room and adjoining front room of the BERGER *apartment. These two rooms are typically furnished. There is a curtain between them. A small door off the front room leads to* JACOB'S *room. When his door is open one sees a picture of* SACCO *and* VANZETTI[5] *on the wall and several shelves of books. Stage left of this door presents the entrance to the foyer hall of the apartment. The two other bedrooms of the apartment are off this hall, but not necessarily shown.*

Stage left of the dining room presents a swinging door which opens on the kitchen.

Awake and sing, ye that dwell in dust:
ISAIAH—26:19

Act One

Time: The present; the family finishing supper.
Place: An apartment in the Bronx, New York City.

RALPH: Where's advancement down the place? Work like crazy! Think they see it? You'd drop dead first.

MYRON: Never mind, son, merit never goes unrewarded. Teddy Roosevelt[6] used to say——

HENNIE: It rewarded you—thirty years a haberdashery clerk!
[JACOB *laughs.*]

RALPH: All I want's a chance to get to first base!

HENNIE: That's all?

RALPH: Stuck down in that joint on Fourth Avenue—a stock clerk in a

5. These two Italian immigrants, self-described as "a shoemaker and a poor fish-peddler," were anarchists who were accused of committing a payroll robbery and killing the payroll master and his guard in 1920, in Braintree, Massachusetts. After many appeals and worldwide protest against an apparent gross miscarriage of justice, they were electrocuted in Boston in 1927.

6. Theodore Roosevelt (1858–1919), the twenty-sixth president of the United States (1901–08).

silk house! Just look at Eddie. I'm as good as he is—pulling in two-fifty a week for forty-eight minutes a day. A headliner, his name in all the papers.

JACOB: That's what you want, Ralphie? Your name in the paper?

RALPH: I wanna make up my own mind about things . . . be something! Didn't I want to take up tap dancing, too?

BESSIE: So take lessons. Who stopped you?

RALPH: On what?

BESSIE: On what? Save money.

RALPH: Sure, five dollars a week for expenses and the rest in the house. I can't save even for shoe laces.

BESSIE: You mean we shouldn't have food in the house, but you'll make a jig on the street corner?

RALPH: I mean something.

BESSIE: You also mean something when you studied on the drum, Mr. Smartie!

RALPH: I don't know. . . . Every other day to sit around with the blues and mud in your mouth.

MYRON: That's how it is—life is like that—a cake-walk.[7]

RALPH: What's it get you?

HENNIE: A four-car funeral.

RALPH: What's it for?

JACOB: What's it for? If this life leads to a revolution it's a good life. Otherwise it's for nothing.

BESSIE: Never mind, Pop! Pass me the salt.

RALPH: It's crazy—all my life I want a pair of black and white shoes and can't get them. It's crazy!

BESSIE: In a minute I'll get up from the table. I can't take a bite in my mouth no more.

MYRON [*restraining her*]: Now, Momma, just don't excite yourself——

BESSIE: I'm so nervous I can't hold a knife in my hand.

MYRON: Is that a way to talk, Ralphie? Don't Momma work hard enough all day? [BESSIE *allows herself to be reseated.*]

BESSIE: On my feet twenty-four hours?

MYRON: On her feet——

RALPH [*jumps up*]: What do I do—go to night-clubs with Greta Garbo?[8] Then when I come home can't even have my own room? Sleep on a day-bed in the front room! [*Choked, he exits to front room.*]

BESSIE: He's starting up that stuff again. [*Shouts to him*]: When Hennie here marries you'll have her room—I should only live to see the day.

HENNIE: Me, too. [*They settle down to serious eating.*]

MYRON: This morning the sink was full of ants. Where they come from I just don't know. I thought it was coffee grounds . . . and then they began moving.

BESSIE: You gave the dog eat?

JACOB: I gave the dog eat. [HENNIE *drops a knife and picks it up again.*]

7. Originating as a black American entertainment for which a cake was awarded as a prize to the best performance, it consisted of stylized walking and, later, dance steps.

8. A Swedish movie actress (1895–1990) who became a great Hollywood star from the 1920s until the 1940s. She was famous for her beauty.

BESSIE: You got dropsy tonight.
HENNIE: Company's coming.
MYRON: You can buy a ticket for fifty cents and win fortunes. A man came in the store—it's the Irish Sweepstakes.[9]
BESSIE: What?
MYRON: Like a raffle, only different. A man came in——
BESSIE: Who spends fifty-cent pieces for Irish raffles? They threw out a family on Dawson Street today. All the furniture on the sidewalk. A fine old woman with gray hair.
JACOB: Come eat, Ralph.
MYRON: A butcher on Beck Street won eighty thousand dollars
BESSIE: Eighty thousand dollars! You'll excuse my expression you're bughouse!
MYRON: I seen it in the paper—on one ticket—765 Beck Street.
BESSIE: Impossible!
MYRON: He did . . . yes he did. He says he'll take his old mother to Europe . . . an Austrian——
HENNIE: Europe . . .
MYRON: Six per cent on eighty thousand—forty-eight hundred a year.
BESSIE: I'll give you money. Buy a ticket in Hennie's name. Say, you can't tell—lightning never struck us yet. If they win on Beck Street we could win on Longwood Avenue.
JACOB [*ironically*]: If it rained pearls—who would work?
BESSIE: Another county heard from. [RALPH *enters and silently seats himself.*]
MYRON: I forgot, Beauty—Sam Feinschreiber sent you a present. Since I brought him for supper he just can't stop talking about you.
HENNIE: What's that "mockie"[1] bothering about? Who needs him?
MYRON: He's a very lonely boy.
HENNIE: So I'll sit down and bust out crying " 'cause he's lonely."
BESSIE [*opening candy*]: He'd marry you one two three.
HENNIE: Too bad about him.
BESSIE [*naïvely delighted*]: Chocolate peanuts.
HENNIE: Loft's[2] week-end special, two for thirty-nine.
BESSIE: You could think about it. It wouldn't hurt.
HENNIE [*laughing*]: To quote Moe Axelrod, "Don't make me laugh."
BESSIE: Never mind laughing. It's time you already had in your head a serious thought. A girl twenty-six don't grow younger. When I was your age it was already a big family with responsibilities.
HENNIE [*laughing*]: Maybe that's what ails you, Mom.
BESSIE: Don't you feel well?
HENNIE: 'Cause I'm laughing? I feel fine. It's just funny—that poor guy sending me presents 'cause he loves me.
BESSIE: I think it's very, very nice.
HENNIE: Sure . . . swell!
BESSIE: Mrs. Marcus' Rose is engaged to a Brooklyn boy, a dentist. He

9. An annual horse race in Ireland for which tickets backing individual horses are sold to bettors worldwide.
1. A derogatory term for a Jew, especially an immigrant with an accent.
2. The name of a candy manufacturer, especially of chocolate, with a chain of stores in New York and elsewhere.

came in his car today. A little dope should get such a boy. [*Finished with the meal,* BESSIE, MYRON *and* JACOB *rise. Both* HENNIE *and* RALPH *sit silently at the table, he eating. Suddenly she rises.*]

HENNIE: Tell you what, Mom. I saved for a new dress, but I'll take you and Pop to the Franklin. Don't need a dress. From now on I'm planning to stay in nights. Hold everything!

BESSIE: What's the matter—a bedbug bit you suddenly?

HENNIE: It's a good bill—Belle Baker. Maybe she'll sing "Eli, Eli."[3]

BESSIE: We was going to a movie.

HENNIE: Forget it. Let's go.

MYRON: I see in the papers [*as he picks his teeth*] Sophie Tucker[4] took off twenty-six pounds. Fearful business with Japan.

HENNIE: Write a book, Pop! Come on, we'll go early for good seats.

MYRON: Moe said you had a date with him for tonight.

BESSIE: Axelrod?

HENNIE: I told him no, but he don't believe it. I'll tell him no for the next hundred years, too.

MYRON: Don't break appointments, Beauty, and hurt people's feelings. [BESSIE *exits.*]

HENNIE: His hands got free wheeling. [*She exits.*]

MYRON: I don't know . . . people ain't the same. N-O- The whole world's changing right under our eyes. Presto! No manners. Like the great Italian lover in the movies. What was his name? The Sheik.[5] . . . No one remembers? [*Exits, shaking his head.*]

RALPH [*unmoving at the table*]: Jake . . .

JACOB: Noo?

RALPH: I can't stand it.

JACOB: There's an expression—"strong as iron you must be."

RALPH: It's a cock-eyed world.

JACOB: Boys like you could fix it some day. Look on the world, not on yourself so much. Every country with starving millions, no? In Germany and Poland a Jew couldn't walk in the street. Everybody hates, nobody loves.

RALPH: I don't get all that.

JACOB: For years, I watched you grow up. Wait! You'll graduate from my university. [*The others enter, dressed.*]

MYRON [*lighting*]: Good cigars now for a nickel.

BESSIE [*to* JACOB]: After take Tootsie on the roof. [*to* RALPH]: What'll you do?

RALPH: Don't know.

BESSIE: You'll see the boys around the block?

RALPH: I'll stay home every night!

MYRON: Momma don't mean for you——

3. Belle Baker, a musical-comedy and dramatic actress (1894–1957) active from the 1920s to the 1940s in the United States and the United Kingdom, was well known for her rendition of Jacob K. Sandler's (1860–1931) *Eli, Eli* (My God, My God [Aramaic]), first published in 1907 and thereafter the most published Yiddish song.

4. The legendary singer and entertainer (1884–1966), often called "the last of the red hot mommas."

5. A reference to silent-film star Rudolph Valentino (1895–1926), in the title role of his second film. It had women fainting in the aisles of movie theaters.

RALPH: I'm flying to Hollywood by plane, that's what I'm doing. [*Doorbell rings.* MYRON *answers it.*]

BESSIE: I don't like my boy to be seen with those tramps on the corner.

MYRON [*without*]: Schlosser's here, Momma, with the garbage can.

BESSIE: Come in here, Schlosser. [*Sotto voce*][6] Wait, I'll give him a piece of my mind. [MYRON *ushers in* SCHLOSSER *who carries a garbage can in each hand.*] What's the matter the dumbwaiter's[7] broken again?

SCHLOSSER: Mr. Wimmer sends new ropes next week. I got a sore arm.

BESSIE: He should live so long your Mr. Wimmer. For seven years already he's sending new ropes. No dumbwaiter, no hot water, no steam—— In a respectable house, they don't allow such conditions.

SCHLOSSER: In a decent house dogs are not running to make dirty the hallway.

BESSIE: Tootsie's making dirty? Our Tootsie's making dirty in the hall?

SCHLOSSER [*to* JACOB]: I tell you yesterday again. You must not leave her——

BESSIE [*indignantly*]: Excuse me! Please don't yell on an old man. He's got more brains in his finger than you got—I don't know where. Did you ever see—he should talk to you an old man?

MYRON: Awful.

BESSIE: From now on we don't walk up the stairs no more. You keep it so clean we'll fly in the windows.

SCHLOSSER: I speak to Mr. Wimmer.

BESSIE: Speak! Speak. Tootsie walks behind me like a lady any time, any place. So good-bye . . . good-bye, Mr. Schlosser.

SCHLOSSER: I tell you dot—I verk verry hard here. My arms is. . . . [*Exits in confusion.*]

BESSIE: Tootsie should lay all day in the kitchen maybe. Give him back if he yells on you. What's funny?

JACOB [*laughing*]: Nothing.

BESSIE: Come. [*Exits.*]

JACOB: Hennie, take care. . . .

HENNIE: Sure.

JACOB: Bye-bye. [HENNIE *exits.* MYRON *pops head back in door.*]

MYRON: Valentino! That's the one! [*He exits.*]

RALPH: I never in my life even had a birthday party. Every time I went and cried in the toilet when my birthday came.

JACOB [*seeing* RALPH *remove his tie*]: You're going to bed?

RALPH: No, I'm putting on a clean shirt.

JACOB: Why?

RALPH: I got a girl. . . . Don't laugh!

JACOB: Who laughs? Since when?

RALPH: Three weeks. She lives in Yorkville[8] with an aunt and uncle. A bunch of relatives, but no parents.

JACOB: An orphan girl—tch, tch.

RALPH: But she's got me! Boy, I'm telling you I could sing! Jake, she's like

6. Very softly (Italian).

7. An small elevator used for lowering garbage to the basement, where it was disposed of.

8. A district on the Upper East Side of Manhattan in New York City.

stars. She's so beautiful you look at her and cry! She's like French words! We went to the park the other night. Heard the last band concert.

JACOB: Music. . . .

RALPH [*stuffing shirt in trousers*]: It got cold and I gave her my coat to wear. We just walked along like that, see, without a word, see. I never was so happy in all my life. It got late . . . we just sat there. She looked at me—you know what I mean, how a girl looks at you—right in the eyes? "I love you," she says, "Ralph." I took her home. . . . I wanted to cry. That's how I felt!

JACOB: It's a beautiful feeling.

RALPH: You said a mouthful!

JACOB: Her name is——

RALPH: Blanche.

JACOB: A fine name. Bring her sometimes here.

RALPH: She's scared to meet Mom.

JACOB: Why?

RALPH: You know Mom's not letting my sixteen bucks out of the house if she can help it. She'd take one look at Blanche and insult her in a minute—a kid who's got nothing.

JACOB: Boychick![9]

RALPH: What's the diff?

JACOB: It's no difference—a plain bourgeois prejudice—but when they find out a poor girl—it ain't so kosher.[1]

RALPH: They don't have to know I've got a girl.

JACOB: What's in the end?

RALPH: Out I go! I don't mean maybe!

JACOB: And then what?

RALPH: Life begins.

JACOB: What life?

RALPH: Life with my girl. Boy, I could sing when I think about it! Her and me together—that's a new life!

JACOB: Don't make a mistake! A new death!

RALPH: What's the idea?

JACOB: Me, I'm the idea! Once I had in *my* heart a dream, a vision, but came marriage and then you forget. Children come and you forget because——

RALPH: Don't worry, Jake.

JACOB: Remember, a woman insults a man's soul like no other thing in the whole world!

RALPH: Why get so excited? No one——

JACOB: Boychick, wake up! Be something! Make your life something good. For the love of an old man who sees in your young days his new life, for such love take the world in your two hands and make it like new. Go out and fight so life shouldn't be printed on dollar bills. A woman waits.

RALPH: Say, I'm no fool!

JACOB: From my heart I hope not. In the meantime—— [*Bell rings.*]

9. Little boy (Yiddish); an affectionate diminutive.
1. Literally, acceptable under Jewish dietary laws; figuratively, acceptable or okay.

RALPH: See who it is, will you? [*Stands off.*] Don't want Mom to catch me with a clean shirt.

JACOB [*calls*]: Come in. [*Sotto voce.*] Moe Axelrod. [MOE *enters.*]

MOE: Hello girls, how's your whiskers? [*To* RALPH]: All dolled up. What's it, the weekly visit to the cat house?[2]

RALPH: Please mind your business.

MOE: Okay, sweetheart.

RALPH [*taking a hidden dollar from a book*]: If Mom asks where I went——

JACOB: I know. Enjoy yourself.

RALPH: Bye-bye. [*He exits.*]

JACOB: Bye-bye.

MOE: Who's home?

JACOB: Me.

MOE: Good. I'll stick around a few minutes. Where's Hennie?

JACOB: She went with Bessie and Myron to a show.

MOE: She what?!

JACOB: You had a date?

MOE [*hiding his feelings*]: Here—I brought you some halavah.[3]

JACOB: Halavah? Thanks. I'll eat a piece after.

MOE: So Ralph's got a dame? Hot stuff—a kid can't even play a card game.

JACOB: Moe, you're a no-good, a bum of the first water.[4] To your dying day you won't change.

MOE: Where'd you get that stuff, a no-good?

JACOB: But I like you.

MOE: Didn't I go fight in France for democracy? Didn't I get my goddam leg shot off in that war the day before the armistice? Uncle Sam give me the Order of the Purple Heart,[5] didn't he? What'd you mean, a no-good?

JACOB: Excuse me.

MOE: If you got an orange I'll eat an orange.

JACOB: No orange. An apple.

MOE: No oranges, huh?—what a dump!

JACOB: Bessie hears you once talking like this she'll knock your head off.

MOE: Hennie went with, huh? She wantsa see me squirm, only I don't squirm for dames.

JACOB: You came to see her?

MOE: What for? I got a present for our boy friend, Myron. He'll drop dead when I tell him his gentle horse galloped in fifteen to one. He'll die.

JACOB: It really won? The first time I remember.

MOE: Where'd they go?

JACOB: A vaudeville by the Franklin.

MOE: What's special tonight?

JACOB: Someone tells a few jokes . . . and they forget the street is filled with starving beggars.

MOE: What'll they do—start a war?

JACOB: I don't know.

MOE: You oughta know. What the hell you got all the books for?

2. Brothel.
3. A confection of Turkish origin, popular among Jews, made with crushed sesame seeds bound with honey or a sugar syrup.
4. A phrase used in the diamond trade to describe a diamond of unusual purity and luster; here used ironically to indicate that Moe is a real bum, a pure bum.
5. A medal awarded to American servicemen for wounds incurred in combat.

JACOB: It needs a new world.

MOE: That's why they had the big war—to make a new world, they said—safe for democracy. Sure every big general laying up in a Paris hotel with a half dozen broads pinned on his mustache. Democracy! I learned a lesson.

JACOB: An imperial war. You know what this means?

MOE: Sure, I know everything!

JACOB: By money men the interests must be protected. Who gave you such a rotten haircut? Please [*fishing in his vest pocket*], give me for a cent a cigarette. I didn't have since yesterday——

MOE [*giving one*]: Don't make me laugh. [*A cent passes back and forth between them,* MOE *finally throwing it over his shoulder.*] Don't look so tired all the time. You're a wow—always sore about something.

JACOB: And you?

MOE: You got one thing—you can play pinochle. I'll take you over in a game. Then you'll have something to be sore on.

JACOB: Who'll wash dishes? [MOE *takes deck from buffet drawer.*]

MOE: Do 'em after. Ten cents a deal.

JACOB: Who's got ten cents?

MOE: I got ten cents. I'll lend it to you.

JACOB: Commence.

MOE [*shaking cards*]: The first time I had my hands on a pack in two days. Lemme shake up these cards. I'll make 'em talk. [JACOB *goes to his room where he puts on a Caruso*[6] *record.*]

JACOB: You should live so long.

MOE: Ever see oranges grow? I know a certain place—— One summer I laid under a tree and let them fall right in my mouth.

JACOB [*off, the music is playing; the card game begins*]: From "L'Africana"[7] . . . a big explorer comes on a new land—"O Paradiso." From act four this piece. Caruso stands on the ship and looks on a Utopia. You hear? "Oh paradise! Oh paradise on earth! Oh blue sky, oh fragrant air——"

MOE: Ask him does he see any oranges? [BESSIE, MYRON *and* HENNIE *enter.*]

JACOB: You came back so soon?

BESSIE: Hennie got sick on the way.

MYRON: Hello, Moe. . . . [MOE *puts cards back in pocket.*]

BESSIE: Take off the phonograph, Pop. [*To* HENNIE]: Lay down . . . I'll call the doctor. You should see how she got sick on Prospect Avenue. Two weeks already she don't feel right.

MYRON: Moe . . . ?

BESSIE: Go to bed, Hennie.

HENNIE: I'll sit here.

BESSIE: Such a girl I never saw! Now you'll be stubborn?

MYRON: It's for your own good, Beauty. Influenza——

6. Enrico Caruso (1873–1921), a world-famous Italian tenor who sang at New York's Metropolitan Opera House from 1903 until shortly before his death. His last appearance was in Halevy's *La Juive* (1920).

7. Jacob refers to *L'Africaine*, an opera by Giacomo Meyerbeer (1791–1864), among the most important composers of French opera in the 19th century.

HENNIE: I'll sit here.

BESSIE: You ever seen a girl should say no to everything. She can't stand on her feet, so——

HENNIE: Don't yell in my ears. I hear. Nothing's wrong. I ate tuna fish for lunch.

MYRON: Canned goods. . . .

BESSIE: Last week you also ate tuna fish?

HENNIE: Yeah, I'm funny for tuna fish. Go to the show—have a good time.

BESSIE: I don't understand what I did to God He blessed me with such children. From the whole world——

MOE [*coming to aid of* HENNIE]: For Chris' sake, don't kibitz[8] so much!

BESSIE: You don't like it?

MOE [*aping*]: No, I don't like it.

BESSIE: That's too bad, Axelrod. Maybe it's better by your cigar-store friends. Here we're different people.

MOE: Don't gimme that cigar store line, Bessie. I walked up five flights——

BESSIE: To take out Hennie. But my daughter ain't in your class. Axelrod.

MOE: To see Myron.

MYRON: Did he, did he, Moe?

MOE: Did he what?

MYRON: "Sky Rocket"?

BESSIE: You bet on a horse!

MOE: Paid twelve and a half to one.

MYRON: There! You hear that, Momma? Our horse came in. You see, it happens, and twelve and a half to one. Just look at that!

MOE: What the hell, a sure thing. I told you.

BESSIE: If Moe said a sure thing, you couldn't bet a few dollars instead of fifty cents?

JACOB [*laughs*]: "Aie, aie, aie."

MOE [*at his wallet*] I'm carrying six hundred "plunks" in big denominations.

BESSIE: A banker!

MOE: Uncle Sam sends me ninety a month.

BESSIE: So you save it?

MOE: Run it up, Run-it-up-Axelrod, that's me.

BESSIE: The police should know how.

MOE [*shutting her up*]: All right, all right—— Change twenty, sweetheart.

MYRON: Can you make change?

BESSIE: Don't be crazy.

MOE: I'll meet a guy in Goldman's restaurant. I'll meet 'im and come back with change.

MYRON [*figuring on paper*]: You can give it to me tomorrow in the store.

BESSIE [*acquisitive*]: He'll come back, he'll come back!

MOE: Lucky I bet some bucks myself. [*In derision to* HENNIE]: Let's step out tomorrow night, Par-a-dise. [*Thumbs his nose at her, laughs mordantly and exits.*]

MYRON: Oh, that's big percentage. If I picked a winner every day. . . .

8. Stand on the sidelines and offer opinions or advice, whether desired or not.

BESSIE: Poppa, did you take Tootsie on the roof?

JACOB: All right.

MYRON: Just look at that—a cake walk. We can make——

BESSIE: It's enough talk. I got a splitting headache. Hennie, go in bed. I'll call Dr. Cantor.

HENNIE: I'll sit here . . . and don't call that old Ignatz 'cause I won't see him.

MYRON: If you get sick Momma can't nurse you. You don't want to go to a hospital.

JACOB: She don't look sick, Bessie, it's a fact.

BESSIE: She's got fever. I see in her eyes, so he tells me no. Myron, call Dr. Cantor. [MYRON *picks up phone, but* HENNIE *grabs it from him.*]

HENNIE: I don't want any doctor. I ain't sick. Leave me alone.

MYRON: Beauty, it's for your own sake.

HENNIE: Day in and day out pestering. Why are you always right and no one else can say a word?

BESSIE: When you have your own children——

HENNIE: I'm not sick! Hear what I say? I'm not sick! Nothing's the matter with me! I don't want a doctor. [BESSIE *is watching her with slow progressive understanding.*]

BESSIE: What's the matter?

HENNIE: Nothing, I told you!

BESSIE: You told me, but—— [*A long pause of examination follows.*]

HENNIE: See much?

BESSIE: Myron, put down the . . . the. . . . [*He slowly puts the phone down.*] Tell me what happened. . . .

HENNIE: Brooklyn Bridge fell down.

BESSIE [*approaching*]: I'm asking a question. . . .

MYRON: What's happened, Momma?

BESSIE: Listen to me!

HENNIE: What the hell are you talking?

BESSIE: Poppa—take Tootsie on the roof.

HENNIE [*holding* JACOB *back*]: If he wants he can stay here.

MYRON: What's wrong, Momma?

BESSIE [*her voice quivering slightly*]: Myron, your fine Beauty's in trouble. Our society lady. . . .

MYRON: Trouble? I don't under—is it——?

BESSIE: Look in her face. [*He looks, understands and slowly sits in a chair, utterly crushed.*] Who's the man?

HENNIE: The Prince of Wales.

BESSIE: My gall is busting in me. In two seconds——

HENNIE [*in a violent outburst*]: Shut up! Shut up! I'll jump out the window in a minute! Shut up! [*Finally she gains control of herself, says in a low, hard voice*]: You don't know him.

JACOB: Bessie. . . .

BESSIE: He's a Bronx boy?

HENNIE: From out of town.

BESSIE: What do you mean?

HENNIE: From out of town!!

BESSIE: A long time you know him? You were sleeping by a girl from the office Saturday nights? You slept good, my lovely lady. You'll go to him . . . he'll marry you.

HENNIE: That's what you say.

BESSIE: That's what I say! He'll do it, take MY word he'll do it!

HENNIE: Where? [*To* JACOB]: Give her the letter. [JACOB *does so.*]

BESSIE: What? [*Reads.*] "Dear sir: In reply to your request of the 14th inst., we can state that no Mr. Ben Grossman has ever been connected with our organization . . ." You don't know where he is?

HENNIE: No.

BESSIE [*walks back and forth*]: Stop crying like a baby, Myron.

MYRON: It's like a play on the stage. . . .

BESSIE: To a mother you couldn't say something before. I'm old-fashioned—like your friends I'm not smart—I don't eat chop suey and run around Coney Island[9] with tramps. [*She walks reflectively to buffet, picks up a box of candy, puts it down, says to* MYRON]: Tomorrow night bring Sam Feinschreiber for supper.

HENNIE: I won't do it.

BESSIE: You'll do it, my fine beauty, you'll do it!

HENNIE: I'm not marrying a poor foreigner like him. Can't even speak an English word. Not me! I'll go to my grave without a husband.

BESSIE: You don't say! We'll find for you somewhere a millionaire with a pleasure boat. He's going to night school, Sam. For a boy only three years in the country he speaks very nice. In three years he put enough in the bank, a good living.

JACOB: This is serious?

BESSIE: What then? I'm talking for my health? He'll come tomorrow night for supper. By Saturday they're engaged.

JACOB: Such a thing you can't do.

BESSIE: Who asked your advice?

JACOB: Such a thing——

BESSIE: Never mind!

JACOB: The lowest from the low!

BESSIE: Don't talk! I'm warning you! A man who don't believe in God—with crazy ideas——

JACOB: So bad I never imagined you could be.

BESSIE: Maybe if you didn't talk so much it wouldn't happen like this. You with your ideas—I'm a mother. I raise a family they should have respect.

JACOB: Respect? [*Spits.*] Respect! For the neighbors' opinion! You insult me, Bessie!

BESSIE: Go in your room, Papa. Every job he ever had he lost because he's got a big mouth. He opens his mouth and the whole Bronx could fall in. Everybody said it——

MYRON: Momma, they'll hear you down the dumbwaiter.

BESSIE: A good barber not to hold a job a week. Maybe you never heard charity starts at home. You never heard it, Pop?

JACOB: All you know, I heard, and more yet. But Ralph you don't make

9. A Brooklyn, New York, seaside beach and recreation area with many amusement parks and sideshows.

like you. Before you do it, I'll die first. He'll find a girl. He'll go in a fresh world with her. This is a house? Marx[1] said it—abolish such families.

BESSIE: Go in your room, Papa.

JACOB: Ralph you don't make like you!

BESSIE: Go lay in your room with Caruso and the books together.

JACOB: All right!

BESSIE: Go in the room!

JACOB: Some day I'll come out I'll—— [*Unable to continue, he turns, looks at* HENNIE, *goes to his door and there says with an attempt at humor*]: Bessie, some day you'll talk to me so fresh . . . I'll leave the house for good! [*He exits.*]

BESSIE [*crying*]: You ever in your life seen it? He should dare! He should just dare say in the house another word. Your gall could bust from such a man. [*Bell rings,* MYRON *goes.*] Go to sleep now. It won't hurt.

HENNIE: Yeah? [MOE *enters, a box in his hand.* MYRON *follows and sits down.*]

MOE [*looks around first—putting box on table*]: Cake. [*About to give* MYRON *the money, he turns instead to* BESSIE]: Six fifty, four bits change . . . come on, hand over half a buck. [*She does so. Of* MYRON]: Who bit him?

BESSIE: We're soon losing our Hennie, Moe.

MOE: Why? What's the matter?

BESSIE: She made her engagement.

MOE: Zat so?

BESSIE: Today it happened . . . he asked her.

MOE: Did he? Who? Who's the corpse?

BESSIE: It's a secret.

MOE: In the bag, huh?

HENNIE: Yeah. . . .

BESSIE: When a mother gives away an only daughter it's no joke. Wait, when you'll get married you'll know. . . .

MOE [*bitterly*]: Don't make me laugh—when I get married! What I think a women? Take 'em all, cut 'em in little pieces like a herring in Greek salad. A guy in France had the right idea—dropped his wife in a bathtub fulla acid. [*Whistles.*] Sss, down the pipe! Pfft—not even a corset button left!

MYRON: Corsets don't have buttons.

MOE [*to* HENNIE]: What's the great idea? Gone big time, Paradise? Christ, it's suicide! Sure, kids you'll have, gold teeth, get fat, big in the tangerines——

HENNIE: Shut your face!

MOE: Who's it—some dope pullin' down twenty bucks a week? Cut your throat, sweetheart. Save time.

BESSIE: Never mind your two cents, Axelrod.

MOE: I say what I think—that's me!

HENNIE: That's you—a lousy fourflusher[2] who'd steal the glasses off a blind man.

1. Karl Marx (1818–1883), author of *The Communist Manifesto* (1848) and *Das Kapital* (1867), was a major influence on social and revolutionary anticapitalist thought and movements.

2. Originally, a poker term meaning a person who bluffs; by extension, someone not to be trusted or who does not fulfill promises or obligations.

MOE: Get hot!

HENNIE: My God, do I need it—to listen to this mutt shoot his mouth off?

MYRON: Please. . . .

MOE: Now wait a minute, sweetheart, wait a minute. I don't have to take that from you.

BESSIE: Don't yell at her!

HENNIE: For two cents I'd spit in your eye.

MOE [*throwing coin to table*]: Here's two bits. [HENNIE *looks at him and then starts across the room.*]

BESSIE: Where are you going?

HENNIE [*crying*]: For my beauty nap, Mussolini.[3] Wake me up when it's apple blossom time in Normandy.[4] [*Exits.*]

MOE: Pretty, pretty—a sweet gal, your Hennie. See the look in her eyes?

BESSIE: She don't feel well. . . .

MYRON: Canned goods. . . .

BESSIE: So don't start with her.

MOE: Like a battleship she's got it. Not like other dames—shove 'em and they lay. Not her. I got a yen for her and I don't mean a Chinee coin.

BESSIE: Listen, Axelrod, in my house you don't talk this way. Either have respect or get out.

MOE: When I think about it . . . maybe I'd marry her myself.

BESSIE [*suddenly aware of* MOE]: You could—— What do you mean, Moe?

MOE: You ain't sunburnt—you heard me.

BESSIE: Why don't you, Moe? An old friend of the family like you. It would be a blessing on all of us.

MOE: You said she's engaged.

BESSIE: But maybe she don't know her own mind. Say, it's——

MOE: I need a wife like a hole in the head. . . . What's to know about women, I know. Even if I asked her. She won't do it! A guy with one leg—it gives her the heebie-jeebies. I know what she's looking for. An arrow-collar[5] guy, a hero, but with a wad of jack. Only the two don't go together. But I got what it takes . . . plenty, and more where it comes from. . . . [*Breaks off, snorts and rubs his knee. A pause. In his room* JACOB *puts on Caruso singing the lament from "The Pearl Fishers."*][6]

BESSIE: It's right—she wants a millionaire with a mansion on Riverside Drive.[7] So go fight City Hall. Cake?

MOE: Cake.

BESSIE: I'll make tea. But one thing—she's got a fine boy with a business brain. Caruso! [*Exits into the front room and stands in the dark, at the window.*]

MOE: No wet smack . . . a fine girl. . . . She'll burn that guy out in a month. [MOE *retrieves the quarter and spins it on the table.*]

3. Benito Mussolini (1883–1945), founder of Italian fascism, seized power in Italy in 1922 and, in 1940, led the country into World War II on the side of the Axis powers.

4. The name of a popular song.

5. The Arrow company manufactured conservative dress shirts.

6. A French opera (1863) by Georges Bizet (1838–1875).

7. A fashionable avenue on the Upper West Side of Manhattan.

MYRON: I remember that song . . . beautiful. Nora Bayes[8] sang it at the old Proctor's Twenty-third Street—"When It's Apple Blossom Time in Normandy." . . .

MOE: She wantsa see me crawl—my head on a plate she wants! A snowball in hell's got a better chance. [*Out of sheer fury he spins the quarter in his fingers.*]

MYRON [*as his eyes slowly fill with tears*]: Beautiful . . .

MOE: Match you for a quarter. Match you for any goddam thing you got. [*Spins the coin viciously.*] What the hell kind of house is this it ain't got an orange!!

SLOW CURTAIN

Act Two

SCENE I

One year later, a Sunday afternoon. The front room. JACOB *is giving his son* MORDECAI (UNCLE MORTY) *a haircut, newspapers spread around the base of the chair.* MOE *is reading a newspaper, leg propped on a chair.* RALPH, *in another chair, is spasmodically reading a paper.* UNCLE MORTY *reads colored jokes.*[9] *Silence, then* BESSIE *enters.*

BESSIE: Dinner's in half an hour, Morty.

MORTY [*still reading jokes*]: I got time.

BESSIE: A duck. Don't get hair on the rug, Pop. [*Goes to window and pulls down shade.*] What's the matter the shade's up to the ceiling?

JACOB [*pulling it up again*]: Since when do I give a haircut in the dark? [*He mimics her tone.*]

BESSIE: When you're finished, pull it down. I like my house to look respectable. Ralphie, bring up two bottles seltzer from Weiss.

RALPH: I'm reading the paper.

BESSIE: Uncle Morty likes a little seltzer.

RALPH: I'm expecting a phone call.

BESSIE: Noo, if it comes you'll be back. What's the matter? [*Gives him money from apron pocket.*] Take down the old bottles.

RALPH [*to* JACOB]: Get that call if it comes. Say I'll be right back. [JACOB *nods assent.*]

MORTY [*giving change from vest*]: Get grandpa some cigarettes.

RALPH: Okay. [*Exits.*]

JACOB: What's new in the paper, Moe?

MOE: Still jumping off the high buildings like flies—the big shots who lost all their cocoanuts. Pfft!

JACOB: Suicides?

MOE: Plenty can't take it—good in the break, but can't take the whip in the stretch.[1]

MORTY [*without looking up*]: I saw it happen Monday in my building. My

8. A singer and composer of popular songs (1880–1928).

9. Comic strips, invariably colored in those Sunday newspapers that carried the comics, or "funnies," as they were sometimes called.

1. In horse races, the final part of the race to the finish line.

hair stood up how they shoveled him together—like a pancake—a bankrupt manufacturer.

MOE: No brains.

MORTY: Enough . . . all over the sidewalk.

JACOB: If someone said five-ten years ago I couldn't make for myself a living, I wouldn't believe——

MORTY: Duck for dinner?

BESSIE: The best Long Island duck.

MORTY: I like goose.

BESSIE: A duck is just like a goose, only better.

MORTY: I like a goose.

BESSIE: The next time you'll be for Sunday dinner I'll make a goose.

MORTY [*sniffs deeply*]: Smells good. I'm a great boy for smells.

BESSIE: Ain't you ashamed? Once in a blue moon he should come to an only sister's house.

MORTY: Bessie, leave me live.

BESSIE: You should be ashamed!

MORTY: Quack quack!

BESSIE: No, better to lay around Mecca Temple[2] playing cards with the Masons.

MORTY [*with good nature*]: Bessie, don't you see Pop's giving me a haircut?

BESSIE: You don't need no haircut. Look, two hairs he took off.

MORTY: Pop likes to give me a haircut. If I said no he don't forget for a year, do you, Pop? An old man's like that.

JACOB: I still do an A-1 job.

MORTY [*winking*]: Pop cuts hair to fit the face, don't you, Pop?

JACOB: For sure, Morty. To each face a different haircut. Custom built, no ready made. A round face needs special——

BESSIE [*cutting him short*]: A graduate from the B.M.T.[3] [*going*]: Don't forget the shade. [*The phone rings. She beats* JACOB *to it.*] Hello? Who is it, please? . . . Who is it please? . . . Miss Hirsch? No, he ain't here. . . . No, I couldn't say when. [*Hangs up sharply.*]

JACOB: For Ralph?

BESSIE: A wrong number. [JACOB *looks at her and goes back to his job.*]

JACOB: Excuse me!

BESSIE [*to* MORTY]: Ralphie took another cut down the place yesterday.

MORTY: Business is bad. I saw his boss Harry Glicksman Thursday. I bought some velvets . . . they're coming in again.

BESSIE: Do something for Ralphie down there.

MORTY: What can I do? I mentioned it to Glicksman. He told me they squeezed out half the people. . . . [MYRON *enters dressed in apron.*]

BESSIE: What's gonna be the end? Myron's working only three days a week now.

MYRON: It's conditions.

BESSIE: Hennie's married with a baby . . . money just don't come in. I never saw conditions should be so bad.

MORTY: Times'll change.

2. The name of a Masonic lodge building in New York.

3. The abbreviation for Brooklyn Manhattan Transit, part of New York City's subway system.

MOE: The only thing'll change is my underwear.

MORTY: These last few years I got my share of gray hairs. [*Still reading jokes without having looked up once.*] Ha, ha, ha—Popeye the sailor ate spinach and knocked out four bums.

MYRON: I'll tell you the way I see it. The country needs a great man now—a regular Teddy Roosevelt.

MOE: What this country needs is a good five-cent earthquake.

JACOB: So long labor lives it should increase private gain——

BESSIE [*to* JACOB]: Listen, Poppa, go talk on the street corner. The government'll give you free board the rest of your life.

MORTY: I'm surprised. Don't I send a five-dollar check for Pop every week?

BESSIE: You could afford a couple more and not miss it.

MORTY: Tell me jokes. Business is so rotten I could just as soon lay all day in the Turkish bath.[4]

MYRON: Why'd I come in here? [*Puzzled, he exits.*]

MORTY [*to* MOE]: I hear the bootleggers[5] still do business, Moe.

MOE: Wake up! I kissed bootlegging bye-bye two years back.

MORTY: For a fact? What kind of racket is it now?

MOE: If I told you, you'd know something. [HENNIE *comes from bedroom.*]

HENNIE: Where's Sam?

BESSIE: Sam? In the kitchen.

HENNIE [*calls*]: Sam. Come take the diaper.

MORTY: How's the Mickey Louse? Ha, ha, ha. . . .

HENNIE: Sleeping.

MORTY: Ah, that's life to a baby. He sleeps—gets it in the mouth—sleeps some more. To raise a family nowadays you must be a damn fool.

BESSIE: Never mind, never mind, a woman who don't raise a family—a girl—should jump overboard. What's she good for? [*To* MOE*—to change the subject*]: Your leg bothers you bad?

MOE: It's okay, sweetheart.

BESSIE [*to* MORTY]: It hurts him every time it's cold out. He's got four legs in the closet.

MORTY: Four wooden legs?

MOE: Three.

MORTY: What's the big idea?

MOE: Why not? Uncle Sam gives them out free.

MORTY: Say, maybe if Uncle Sam gave out less legs we could balance the budget.

JACOB: Or not have a war so they wouldn't have to give out legs.

MORTY: Shame on you, Pop. Everybody knows war is necessary.

MOE: Don't make me laugh. Ask me—the first time you pick up a dead one in the trench—then you learn war ain't so damn necessary.

MORTY: Say, you should kick. The rest of your life Uncle Sam pays you ninety a month. Look, not a worry in the world.

MOE: Don't make me laugh. Uncle Sam can take his *seventy* bucks and—— [*Finishes with a gesture.*] Nothing good hurts. [*He rubs his stump.*]

4. Featuring wet and dry steam rooms, massages, and rubdowns. Popular at the time in many Jewish neighborhoods.

5. Distributors and occasional producers of illegal liquor during Prohibition (1920–33).

HENNIE: Use a crutch, Axelrod. Give the stump a rest.

MOE: Mind your business, Feinschreiber.

BESSIE: It's a sensible idea.

MOE: Who asked you?

BESSIE: Look, he's ashamed.

MOE: So's your Aunt Fanny.

BESSIE [*naïvely*]: Who's got an Aunt Fanny? [*She cleans a rubber plant's leaves with her apron.*]

MORTY: It's a joke!

MOE: I don't want my paper creased before I read it. I want it fresh. Fifty times I said that.

BESSIE: Don't get so excited for a five-cent paper—our star boarder.

MOE: And I don't want no one using my razor either. Get it straight. I'm not buying ten blades a week for the Berger family. [*Furious, he limps out.*]

BESSIE: Maybe I'm using his razor too.

HENNIE: Proud!

BESSIE: You need luck with plants. I didn't clean off the leaves in a month.

MORTY: You keep the house like a pin and I like your cooking. Any time Myron fires you, come to me, Bessie. I'll let the butler go and you'll be my housekeeper. I don't like Japs so much—sneaky.

BESSIE: Say, you can't tell. Maybe any day I'm coming to stay. [HENNIE *exits.*]

JACOB: Finished.

MORTY: How much, Ed. Pinaud?[6] [*Disengages self from chair.*]

JACOB: Five cents.

MORTY: Still five cents for a haircut to fit the face?

JACOB: Prices don't change by me. [*Takes a dollar.*] I can't change——

MORTY: Keep it. Buy yourself a Packard.[7] Ha, ha, ha.

JACOB [*taking large envelope from pocket*]: Please, you'll keep this for me. Put it away.

MORTY: What is it?

JACOB: My insurance policy. I don't like it should lay around where something could happen.

MORTY: What could happen?

JACOB: Who knows, robbers, fire . . . they took next door. Fifty dollars from O'Reilly.

MORTY: Say, lucky a Berger didn't lose it.

JACOB: Put it downtown in the safe. Bessie don't have to know.

MORTY: It's made out to Bessie?

JACOB: No, to Ralph.

MORTY: To Ralph.

JACOB: He don't know. Some day he'll get three thousand.

MORTY: You got good years ahead.

JACOB: Behind. [RALPH *enters.*]

RALPH: Cigarettes. Did a call come?

JACOB: A few minutes. She don't let me answer it.

6. A manufacturer of lotions and other barber supplies.

7. An expensive automobile made by the Packard motor company, now defunct.

RALPH: Did Mom say I was coming back?

JACOB: No. [MORTY *is back at new jokes.*]

RALPH: She starting that stuff again? [BESSIE *enters.*] A call come for me?

BESSIE [*waters pot from milk bottle*]: A wrong number.

JACOB: Don't say a lie, Bessie.

RALPH: Blanche said she'd call me at two—was it her?

BESSIE: I said a wrong number.

RALPH: Please, Mom, if it was her tell me.

BESSIE: You call me a liar next. You got no shame—to start a scene in front of Uncle Morty. Once in a blue moon he comes——

RALPH: What's the shame? If my girl calls I wanna know it.

BESSIE: You made enough mish mosh[8] with her until now.

MORTY: I'm surprised, Bessie. For the love of Mike tell him yes or no.

BESSIE: I didn't tell him? No!

MORTY [*to* RALPH]: No! [RALPH *goes to a window and looks out.*]

BESSIE: Morty, I didn't say before—he runs around steady with a girl.

MORTY: Terrible. Should he run around with a foxie-woxie?

BESSIE: A girl with no parents.

MORTY: An orphan?

BESSIE: I could die from shame. A year already he runs around with her. He brought her once for supper. Believe me, she didn't come again, no!

RALPH: Don't think I didn't ask her.

BESSIE: You hear? You raise them and what's in the end for all your trouble?

JACOB: When you'll lay in a grave, no more trouble. [*Exits.*]

MORTY: Quack quack!

BESSIE: A girl like that he wants to marry. A skinny consumptive-looking . . . six months already she's not working—taking charity from an aunt. You should see her. In a year she's dead on his hands.

RALPH: You'd cut her throat if you could.

BESSIE: That's right! Before she'd ruin a nice boy's life I would first go to prison. Miss Nobody should step in the picture and I'll stand by with my mouth shut.

RALPH: Miss Nobody! Who am I? Al Jolson?[9]

BESSIE: Fix your tie!

RALPH: I'll take care of my own life.

BESSIE: You'll take care? Excuse my expression, you can't even wipe your nose yet! He'll take care!

MORTY [*to* BESSIE]: I'm surprised. Don't worry so much, Bessie. When it's time to settle down he won't marry a poor girl, will you? In the long run common sense is thicker than love. I'm a great boy for live and let live.

BESSIE: Sure, it's easy to say. In the meantime he eats out my heart. You know I'm not strong.

MORTY: I know . . . a pussy cat . . . ha, ha, ha.

BESSIE: You got money and money talks. But without the dollar who sleeps at night?

RALPH: I been working for years, bringing in money here—putting it in

8. A jumble, a confusion (Yiddish).

9. A popular entertainer and star of the first major talking film, *The Jazz Singer* (1927), in which he plays a cantor's son who becomes a stage star and a singer of jazz and popular songs.

your hand like a kid. All right, I can't get my teeth fixed. All right, that a new suit's like trying to buy the Chrysler Building.[1] You never in your life bought me a pair of skates even—things I died for when I was a kid. I don't care about that stuff, see. Only just remember I pay some of the bills around here, just a few . . . and if my girl calls me on the phone I'll talk to her any time I please. [*He exits.* HENNIE *applauds.*]

BESSIE: Don't be so smart, Miss America! [*To* MORTY]: He didn't have skates! But when he got sick, a twelve-year-old boy, who called a big specialist for the last $25 in the house? Skates!

JACOB [*just in. Adjusts window shade*]: It looks like snow today.

MORTY: It's about time—winter.

BESSIE: Poppa here could talk like Samuel Webster,[2] too, but it's just talk. He should try to buy a two-cent pickle in the Burland Market without money.

MORTY: I'm getting an appetite.

BESSIE: Right away we'll eat. I made chopped liver for you.

MORTY: My specialty!

BESSIE: Ralph should only be a success like you, Morty. I should only live to see the day when he rides up to the door in a big car with a chauffeur and a radio. I could die happy, believe me.

MORTY: Success she says. She should see how we spend thousands of dollars making up a winter line and winter don't come—summer in January. Can you beat it?

JACOB: Don't live, just make success.

MORTY: Chopped liver—ha!

JACOB: Ha! [*Exits.*]

MORTY: When they start arguing, I don't hear. Suddenly I'm deaf. I'm a great boy for the practical side. [*He looks over to* HENNIE *who sits rubbing her hands with lotion.*]

HENNIE: Hands like a raw potato.

MORTY: What's the matter? You don't look so well . . . no pep.

HENNIE: I'm swell.

MORTY: You used to be such a pretty girl.

HENNIE: Maybe I got the blues. You can't tell.

MORTY: You could stand a new dress.

HENNIE: That's not all I could stand.

MORTY: Come down to the place tomorrow and pick out a couple from the "eleven-eighty" line. Only don't sing me the blues.

HENNIE: Thanks. I need some new clothes.

MORTY: I got two thousand pieces of merchandise waiting in the stock room for winter.

HENNIE: I never had anything from life. Sam don't help.

MORTY: He's crazy about the kid.

HENNIE: Crazy is right. Twenty-one a week he brings in—a nigger don't have it so hard. I wore my fingers off on an Underwood[3] for six years. For what? Now I wash baby diapers. Sure, I'm crazy about the kid too.

1. A landmark Art Deco skyscraper that helps define New York's skyline. It was completed in 1926 and, at that time, was the highest building in the United States.

2. She means Daniel Webster, the great U.S. senator and orator (1782–1852).

3. A typewriter produced by the firm of that name.

But half the night the kid's up. Try to sleep. You don't know how it is, Uncle Morty.

MORTY: No, I don't know. I was born yesterday. Ha, ha, ha. Some day I'll leave you a little nest egg. You like eggs? Ha?

HENNIE: When? When I'm dead and buried?

MORTY: No, when *I'm* dead and buried. Ha, ha, ha.

HENNIE: You should know what I'm thinking.

MORTY: Ha, ha, ha, I know. [MYRON *enters.*]

MYRON: I never take a drink. I'm just surprised at myself, I——

MORTY: I got a pain. Maybe I'm hungry.

MYRON: Come inside, Morty. Bessie's got some schnapps.[4]

MORTY: I'll take a drink. Yesterday I missed the Turkish bath.

MYRON: I get so bitter when I take a drink, it just surprises me.

MORTY: Look how fat. Say, you live once. . . . Quack, quack.

[*Both exit.* MOE *stands silently in the doorway.*]

SAM [*entering*]: I'll make Leon's bottle now!

HENNIE: No, let him sleep, Sam. Take away the diaper. [*He does. Exits.*]

MOE [*advancing into the room*]: That your husband?

HENNIE: Don't you know?

MOE: Maybe he's a nurse you hired for the kid—it looks it—how he tends it. A guy comes howling to your old lady every time you look cock-eyed. Does he sleep with you?

HENNIE: Don't be so wise!

MOE [*indicating newspaper*]: Here's a dame strangled her hubby with wire. Claimed she didn't like him. Why don't you brain Sam with an axe some night?

HENNIE: Why don't you lay an egg, Axelrod?

MOE: I laid a few in my day, Feinschreiber. Hard-boiled ones too.

HENNIE: Yeah?

MOE: Yeah. You wanna know what I see when I look in your eyes?

HENNIE: No.

MOE: Ted Lewis[5] playing the clarinet—some of those high crazy notes! Christ, you coulda had a guy with some guts instead of a cluck stands around boilin' baby nipples.

HENNIE: Meaning you?

MOE: Meaning me, sweetheart.

HENNIE: Think you're pretty good.

MOE: You'd know if I slept with you again.

HENNIE: I'll smack your face in a minute.

MOE: You do and I'll break your arm. [*Holds up paper.*] Take a look. [*Reads*]: "Ten-day luxury cruise to Havana." That's the stuff you coulda had. Put up at ritzy hotels, frenchie soap, champagne. Now you're tied down to "Snake-Eye" here. What for? What's it get you? . . . a 2 × 4 flat on 108th Street . . . a pain in the bustle it gets you.

HENNIE: What's it to you?

MOE: I know you from the old days. How you like to spend it! What I mean! Lizard-skin shoes, perfume behind the ears. . . . You're in a mess,

4. Any of several liquors (German and Yiddish).

5. A popular entertainer (1892–1971) known for his clarinet playing, his songs—the best known of which was *Me and My Shadow*—and his saying at all his performances "Is everybody happy?"

Paradise! Paradise—that's a hot one—yah, crazy to eat a knish[6] at your own wedding.

HENNIE: I get it—you're jealous. You can't get me.

MOE: Don't make me laugh.

HENNIE: Kid Jailbird's been trying to make me for years. You'd give your other leg. I'm hooked? Maybe, but you're in the same boat. Only it's worse for you. I don't give a damn no more, but you gotta yen makes you——

MOE: Don't make me laugh.

HENNIE: Compared to you I'm sittin' on top of the world.

MOE: You're losing your looks. A dame don't stay young forever.

HENNIE: You're a liar. I'm only twenty-four.

MOE: When you comin' home to stay?

HENNIE: Wouldn't you like to know?

MOE: I'll get you again.

HENNIE: Think so?

MOE: Sure, whatever goes up comes down. You're easy—you remember—two for a nickel—a pushover! [*Suddenly she slaps him. They both seem stunned.*] What's the idea?

HENNIE: Go on . . . break my arm.

MOE [*as if saying "I love you"*]: Listen, lousy.

HENNIE: Go on, do something!

MOE: Listen——

HENNIE: You're so damn tough!

MOE: You like me. [*He takes her.*]

HENNIE: Take your hand off! [*Pushes him away.*] Come around when it's a flood again and they put you in the ark with the animals. Not even then—if you was the last man!

MOE: Baby, if you had a dog I'd love the dog.

HENNIE: Gorilla! [*Exits.* RALPH *enters.*]

RALPH: Were you here before?

MOE [*sits*]: What?

RALPH: When the call came for me?

MOE: What?

RALPH: The call came. [JACOB *enters.*]

MOE [*rubbing his leg*]: No.

JACOB: Don't worry, Ralphie, she'll call back.

RALPH: Maybe not. I think somethin's the matter.

JACOB: What?

RALPH: I don't know. I took her home from the movie last night. She asked me what I'd think if she went away.

JACOB: Don't worry, she'll call again.

RALPH: Maybe not, if Mom insulted her. She gets it on both ends, the poor kid. Lived in an orphan asylum most of her life. They shove her around like an empty freight train.

JACOB: After dinner go see her.

RALPH: Twice they kicked me down the stairs.

JACOB: Life should have some dignity.

6. A piece of dough that is stuffed with a filling and then baked or fried.

RALPH: Every time I go near the place I get heart failure. The uncle drives a bus. You oughta see him—like Babe Ruth.[7]

MOE: Use your brains. Stop acting like a kid who still wets the bed. Hire a room somewhere—a club room for two members.

RALPH: Not that kind of proposition, Moe.

MOE: Don't be a bush leaguer[8] all your life.

RALPH: Cut it out!

MOE [*on a sudden upsurge of emotion*]: Ever sleep with one? Look at 'im blush.

RALPH: You don't know her.

MOE: I seen her—the kind no one sees undressed till the undertaker works on her.

RALPH: Why give me the needles all the time? What'd I ever do to you?

MOE: Not a thing. You're a nice kid. But grow up! In life there's two kinds—the men that's sure of themselves and the ones who ain't! It's time you quit being a selling-plater[9] and got in the first class.

JACOB: And you, Axelrod?

MOE [*to* JACOB]: Scratch your whiskers! [*To* RALPH]: Get independent. Get what-it-takes and be yourself. Do what you like.

RALPH: Got a suggestion? [MORTY *enters, eating.*]

MOE: Sure, pick out a racket. Shake down the cocoanuts. See what that does.

MORTY: We know what it does—puts a pudding on your nose! Sing Sing![1] Easy money's against the law. Against the law don't win. A racket is illegitimate, no?

MOE: It's all a racket—from horse racing down. Marriage, politics, big business—everybody plays cops and robbers. You, you're a racketeer yourself.

MORTY: Who? Me? Personally I manufacture dresses.

MOE: Horse feathers!

MORTY [*seriously*]: Don't make such remarks to me without proof. I'm a great one for proof. That's why I made a success in business. Proof—put up or shut up, like a game of cards. I heard this remark before—a rich man's a crook who steals from the poor. Personally, I don't like it. It's a big lie!

MOE: If you don't like it, buy yourself a fife and drum—and go fight your own war.

MORTY: Sweatshop talk. Every Jew and Wop[2] in the shop eats my bread and behind my back says, "a sonofabitch." I started from a poor boy who worked on an ice wagon for two dollars a week. Pop's right here—he'll tell you. I made it honest. In the whole industry nobody's got a better name.

JACOB: It's an exception, such success.

7. I.e., popular baseball player George Herman Ruth (1895–1948), the "Sultan of Swat," noted for his home runs and hitting the ball out of the ballpark. Since for most of his career he was a New York Yankee, Yankee Stadium in the Bronx, the team's home field, is often called "the House that Ruth Built."

8. Baseball slang for a Minor Leaguer. When applied to non–baseball players, it means inferior, unworthy, not good enough to make it to the highest levels.

9. In horse racing, a term for a horse who can't win and should be sold.

1. A state penitentiary in Ossining, New York.

2. A derogatory term for an Italian.

MORTY: Ralph can't do the same thing?

JACOB: No, Morty, I don't think. In a house like this he don't realize even the possibilities of life. Economics comes down like a ton of coal on the head.

MOE: Red rover, red rover, let Jacob come over![3]

JACOB: In my day the propaganda was for God. Now it's for success. A boy don't turn around without having shoved in him he should make success.

MORTY: Pop, you're a comedian, a regular Charlie Chaplin.[4]

JACOB: He dreams all night of fortunes. Why not? Don't it say in the movies he should have a personal steamship, pyjamas for fifty dollars a pair and a toilet like a monument? But in the morning he wakes up and for ten dollars he can't fix the teeth. And millions more worse off in the mills of the South—starvation wages. The blood from the worker's heart. [MORTY *laughs loud and long.*] Laugh, laugh . . . tomorrow not.

MORTY: A real, a real Boob McNutt[5] you're getting to be.

JACOB: Laugh, my son. . . .

MORTY: Here is the North, Pop.

JACOB: North, south, it's one country.

MORTY: The country's all right. A duck quacks in every pot![6]

JACOB: You never heard how they shoot down men and women which ask a better wage? Kentucky 1932?[7]

MORTY: That's a pile of chopped liver, Pop. [BESSIE *and others enter.*]

JACOB: Pittsburgh, Passaic, Illinois[8]—slavery—it begins where success begins in a competitive system. [MORTY *howls with delight.*]

MORTY: Oh Pop, what are you bothering? Why? Tell me why? Ha ha ha. I bought you a phonograph . . . stick to Caruso.

BESSIE: He's starting up again.

MORTY: Don't bother with Kentucky. It's full of moonshiners.[9]

JACOB: Sure, sure——

MORTY: You don't know practical affairs. Stay home and cut hair to fit the face.

JACOB: It says in the Bible how the Red Sea opened and the Egyptians went in and the sea rolled over them.[1] [*Quotes two lines of Hebrew.*] In this boy's life a Red Sea will happen again. I see it!

MORTY: I'm getting sore, Pop, with all this sweatshop talk.

BESSIE: He don't stop a minute. The whole day, like a phonograph.

MORTY: I'm surprised. Without a rich man you don't have a roof over your head. You don't know it?

MYRON: Now you can't bite the hand that feeds you.

RALPH: Let him alone—he's right!

BESSIE: Another county heard from.

RALPH: It's the truth. It's——

3. A song in a children's game.
4. The great comic actor (1889–1977), world-famous for his many films featuring his "Tramp" persona.
5. A made-up name for a foolish person.
6. Echoing Herbert Hoover's 1928 campaign promise that there would be a chicken in every American pot if he were elected president.
7. Site of bitter labor dispute as coal miners attempted to organize a union.
8. Sites of major strikes and labor unrest: Pittsburgh, 1919; Passaic, New Jersey, 1926; Chicago, 1919.
9. Those who make liquor and spirits illegally. The term usually refers to mountain people in the South.
1. Exodus 14.21–29.

MORTY: Keep quiet, snotnose!

JACOB: For sure, charity, a bone for an old dog. But in Russia an old man don't take charity so his eyes turn black in his head. In Russia they got Marx.

MORTY [*scoffingly*]: Who's Marx?

MOE: An outfielder for the Yanks.[2] [MORTY *howls with delight.*]

MORTY: Ha ha ha, it's better than the jokes. I'm telling you. This is Uncle Sam's country. Put it in your pipe and smoke it.

BESSIE: Russia, he says! Read the papers.

SAM: Here is opportunity.

MYRON: People can't believe in God in Russia. The papers tell the truth, they do.

JACOB: So you believe in God . . . you got something for it? You! You worked for all the capitalists. You harvested the fruit from your labor? You got God! But the past comforts you? The present smiles on you, yes? It promises you the future something? Did you found a piece of earth where you could live like a human being and die with the sun on your face? Tell me, yes, tell me. I would like to know myself. But on these questions, on this theme—the struggle for existence—you can't make an answer. The answer I see in your face . . . the answer is your mouth can't talk. In this dark corner you sit and you die. But abolish private property!

BESSIE [*settling the issue*]: Noo, go fight City Hall!

MORTY: He's drunk!

JACOB: I'm studying from books a whole lifetime.

MORTY: That's what it is—he's drunk. What the hell does all that mean?

JACOB: If you don't know, why should I tell you.

MORTY [*triumphant at last*]: You see? Hear him? Like all those nuts, don't know what they're saying.

JACOB: I know, I know.

MORTY: Like Boob McNutt you know! Don't go in the park, Pop—the squirrels'll get you. Ha, ha, ha. . . .

BESSIE: Save your appetite, Morty. [*To* MYRON]: Don't drop the duck.

MYRON: We're ready to eat, Momma.

MORTY [*to* JACOB]: Shame on you. It's your second childhood. [*Now they file out.* MYRON *first with the duck, the others behind him.*]

BESSIE: Come eat. We had enough for one day. [*Exits.*]

MORTY: Ha, ha, ha. Quack, quack. [*Exits.*]

[JACOB *sits there trembling and deeply humiliated.* MOE *approaches him and thumbs the old man's nose in the direction of the dining room.*]

MOE: Give 'em five. [*Takes his hand away.*] They got you pasted on the wall like a picture, Jake. [*He limps out to seat himself at the table in the next room.*]

JACOB: Go eat, boychick. [RALPH *comes to him.*] He gives me eat, so I'll climb in a needle. One time I saw an old horse in summer . . . he wore a straw hat . . . the ears stuck out on top. An old horse for hire. Give me back my young days . . . give me fresh blood . . . arms . . . give me—— [*The telephone rings. Quickly* RALPH *goes to it.* JACOB *pulls the curtains and stands there, a sentry on guard.*]

2. I.e., the New York Yankees baseball team.

RALPH: Hello? . . . Yeah, I went to the store and came right back, right after you called. [*Looks at* JACOB.]

JACOB: Speak, speak. Don't be afraid they'll hear.

RALPH: I'm sorry if Mom said something. You know how excitable Mom is . . . Sure! What? . . . Sure, I'm listening. . . . Put on the radio, Jake. [JACOB *does so. Music comes in and up, a tango, grating with an insistent nostalgic pulse. Under the cover of the music* RALPH *speaks more freely.*] Yes . . . yes . . . What's the matter? Why're you crying? What happened? [*To* JACOB]: She's putting her uncle on. Yes? . . . Listen, Mr. Hirsch, what're you trying to do? What's the big idea? Honest to God. I'm in no mood for joking! Lemme talk to her! Gimme Blanche! [*Waits.*] Blanche? What's this? Is this a joke? Is that true? I'm coming right down! I know, but—— You wanna do that? . . . I know, but—— I'm coming down . . . tonight! Nine o'clock . . . sure . . . sure . . . sure. . . . [*Hangs up.*]

JACOB: What happened?

MORTY [*enters*]: Listen, Pop. I'm surprised you didn't—— [*He howls, shakes his head in mock despair, exits.*]

JACOB: Boychick, what?

RALPH: I don't get it straight. [*To* JACOB]: She's leaving . . .

JACOB: Where?

RALPH: Out West—— To Cleveland.

JACOB: Cleveland?

RALPH: . . . In a week or two. Can you picture it? It's a put-up job. But they can't get away with that.

JACOB: We'll find something.

RALPH: Sure, the angels of heaven'll come down on her uncle's cab and whisper in his ear.

JACOB: Come eat. . . . We'll find something.

RALPH: I'm meeting her tonight, but I know—— [BESSIE *throws open the curtain between the two rooms and enters.*]

BESSIE: Maybe we'll serve for you a special blue plate supper in the garden?

JACOB: All right, all right. [BESSIE *goes over to the window, levels the shade and on her way out, clicks off the radio.*]

MORTY [*within*]: Leave the music, Bessie. [*She clicks it on again, looks at them, exits.*]

RALPH: I know . . .

JACOB: Don't cry, boychick. [*Goes over to* RALPH.] Why should you make like this? Tell me why you should cry, just tell me. . . . [JACOB *takes* RALPH *in his arms and both, trying to keep back the tears, trying fearfully not to be heard by the others in the dining room, begin crying.*] You mustn't cry. . . .

[*The tango twists on. Inside the clatter of dishes and the clash of cutlery sound.* MORTY *begins to howl with laughter.*]

CURTAIN

SCENE II

That night. The dark dining room.

At rise JACOB *is heard in his lighted room, reading from a sheet, declaiming aloud as if to an audience.*

JACOB: They are there to remind us of the horrors—under those crosses lie hundreds of thousands of workers and farmers who murdered each other in uniform for the greater glory of capitalism. [*Comes out of his room.*] The new imperialist war will send millions to their death, will bring prosperity to the pockets of the capitalist—aie, Morty—and will bring only greater hunger and misery to the masses of workers and farmers. The memories of the last world slaughter are still vivid in our minds. [*Hearing a noise he quickly retreats to his room.* RALPH *comes in from the street. He sits with hat and coat on.* JACOB *tentatively opens door and asks*]: Ralphie?

RALPH: It's getting pretty cold out.

JACOB [*enters room fully, cleaning hair clippers*]: We should have steam till twelve instead of ten. Go complain to the Board of Health.

RALPH: It might snow.

JACOB: It don't hurt . . . extra work for men.

RALPH: When I was a kid I laid awake at nights and heard the sounds of trains . . . far-away lonesome sounds . . . boats going up and down the river. I used to think of all kinds of things I wanted to do. What was it, Jake? Just a bunch of noise in my head?

JACOB [*waiting for news of the girl*]: You wanted to make for yourself a certain kind of world.

RALPH: I guess I didn't. I'm feeling pretty, pretty low.

JACOB: You're a young boy and for you life is all in front like a big mountain. You got feet to climb.

RALPH: I don't know how.

JACOB: So you'll find out. Never a young man had such opportunity like today. He could make history.

RALPH: Ten P.M. and all is well. Where's everybody?

JACOB: They went.

RALPH: Uncle Morty too?

JACOB: Hennie and Sam he drove down.

RALPH: I saw her.

JACOB [*alert and eager*]: Yes, yes, tell me.

RALPH: I waited in Mount Morris Park till she came out. So cold I did a buck'n wing[3] to keep warm. She's scared to death.

JACOB: They made her?

RALPH: Sure. She wants to go. They keep yelling at her—they want her to marry a millionaire, too.

JACOB: You told her you love her?

RALPH: Sure. "Marry me," I said. "Marry me tomorrow." On sixteen bucks a week. On top of that I had to admit Mom'd have Uncle Morty get me fired in a second. . . . Two can starve as cheap as one!

JACOB: So what happened?

3. A fast, complicated tap dance.

RALPH: I made her promise to meet me tomorrow.

JACOB: Now she'll go in the West?

RALPH: I'd fight the whole goddam world with her, but not her. No guts. The hell with her. If she wantsa go—all right—I'll get along.

JACOB: For sure, there's more important things than girls. . . .

RALPH: You said a mouthful . . . and maybe I don't see it. She'll see what I can do. No one stops me when I get going. . . . [*Near to tears, he has to stop.* JACOB *examines his clippers very closely.*]

JACOB: Electric clippers never do a job like by hand.

RALPH: Why won't Mom let us live here?

JACOB: Why? Why? Because in a society like this today people don't love. Hate!

RALPH: Gee, I'm no bum who hangs around pool parlors. I got the stuff to go ahead. I don't know what to do.

JACOB: Look on me and learn what to do, boychick. Here sits an old man polishing tools. You think maybe I'll use them again! Look on this failure and see for seventy years he talked with good ideas, but only in the head. It's enough for me now I should see your happiness. This is why I tell you—DO! Do what is in your heart and you carry in yourself a revolution. But you should act. Not like me. A man who had golden opportunities but drank instead a glass tea. No . . . [*A pause of silence.*]

RALPH [*listening*]: Hear it? The Boston air mail plane. Ten minutes late. I get a kick the way it cuts across the Bronx every night. [*The bell rings:* SAM, *excited, disheveled, enters.*]

JACOB: You came back so soon?

SAM: Where's Mom?

JACOB: Mom? Look on the chandelier.

SAM: Nobody's home?

JACOB: Sit down. Right away they're coming. You went in the street without a tie?

SAM: Maybe it's a crime.

JACOB: Excuse me.

RALPH: You had a fight with Hennie again?

SAM: She'll fight once . . . some day. . . . [*Lapses into silence.*]

JACOB: In my day the daughter came home. Now comes the son-in-law.

SAM: Once too often she'll fight with me, Hennie. I mean it. I mean it like anything. I'm a person with a bad heart. I sit quiet, but inside I got a——

RALPH: What happened?

SAM: I'll talk to Mom. I'll see Mom.

JACOB: Take an apple.

SAM: Please . . . he tells me apples.

RALPH: Why hop around like a billiard ball?

SAM: Even in a joke she should dare say it.

JACOB: My grandchild said something?

SAM: To my father in the old country they did a joke . . . I'll tell you: One day in Odessa he talked to another Jew on the street. They didn't like it, they jumped on him like a wild wolf.

RALPH: Who?

SAM: Cossacks.[4] They cut off his beard. A Jew without a beard! He came home—I remember like yesterday how he came home and went in bed for two days. He put like this the cover on his face. No one should see. The third morning he died.

RALPH: From what?

SAM: From a broken heart. . . . Some people are like this. Me too. I could die like this from shame.

JACOB: Hennie told you something?

SAM: Straight out she said it—like a lightning from the sky. The baby ain't mine. She said it.

RALPH: Don't be a dope.

JACOB: For sure, a joke.

RALPH: She's kidding you.

SAM: She should kid a policeman, not Sam Feinschreiber. Please . . . you don't know her like me. I wake up in the nighttime and she sits watching me like I don't know what. I make a nice living from the store. But it's no use—she looks for a star in the sky. I'm afraid like anything. You could go crazy from less even. What I shall do I'll ask Mom.

JACOB: "Go home and sleep," she'll say. "It's a bad dream."

SAM: It don't satisfy me more, such remarks, when Hennie could kill in the bed. [JACOB *laughs.*] Don't laugh. I'm so nervous—look, two times I weighed myself on the subway station.[5] [*Throws small cards to table.*]

JACOB [*examining one*]: One hundred and thirty-eight—also a fortune. [*Turns it and reads*]: "You are inclined to deep thinking, and have a high admiration for intellectual excellence and inclined to be very exclusive in the selection of friends." Correct! I think maybe you got mixed up in the wrong family, Sam. [MYRON *and* BESSIE *now enter.*]

BESSIE: Look, a guest! What's the matter? Something wrong with the baby? [*Waits.*]

SAM: No.

BESSIE: Noo?

SAM [*in a burst*]: I wash my hands from everything.

BESSIE: Take off your coat and hat. Have a seat. Excitement don't help. Myron, make tea. You'll have a glass tea. We'll talk like civilized people. [MYRON *goes.*] What is it, Ralph, you're all dressed up for a party? [*He looks at her silently and exits. To* SAM]: We saw a very good movie, with Wallace Beery.[6] He acts like life, very good.

MYRON [*within*]: Polly Moran too.

BESSIE: Polly Moran too—a woman with a nose from here to Hunts Point,[7] but a fine player. Poppa, take away the tools and the books.

JACOB: All right. [*Exits to his room.*]

BESSIE: Noo, Sam, why do you look like a funeral?

SAM: I can't stand it. . . .

BESSIE: Wait. [*Yells*]: You took up Tootsie on the roof.

JACOB [*within*]: In a minute.

4. Fierce horsemen or cavalry from the Ukraine and the Don River area in what was Russia, they were often involved in pogroms—massacres of Jews.

5. New York City subways had machines installed on their platforms on which you could stand, deposit a coin, and receive your weight and a fortune printed on a small card.

6. A movie actor with a gruff voice and manner (1885–1949).

7. A major meat and produce market in the Bronx. "Polly Moran": movie actress (1883–1952).

BESSIE: What can't you stand?
SAM: She said I'm a second fiddle in my own house.
BESSIE: Who?
SAM: Hennie. In the second place, it ain't my baby, she said.
BESSIE: What? What are you talking? [MYRON *enters with dishes.*]
SAM: From her own mouth. It went like a knife in my heart.
BESSIE: Sam, what're you saying?
SAM: Please, I'm making a story? I fell in the chair like a dead.
BESSIE: Such a story you believe?
SAM: I don't know.
BESSIE: How you don't know?
SAM: She told me even the man.
BESSIE: Impossible!
SAM: I can't believe myself. But she said it. I'm a second fiddle, she said. She made such a yell everybody heard for ten miles.
BESSIE: Such a thing Hennie should say—impossible!
SAM: What should I do? With my bad heart such a remark kills.
MYRON: Hennie don't feel well, Sam. You see, she——
BESSIE: What then?—a sick girl. Believe me, a mother knows. Nerves. Our Hennie's got a bad temper. You'll let her she says anything. She takes after me—nervous. [*To* MYRON]: You ever heard such a remark in all your life? She should make such a statement! Bughouse.
MYRON: The little one's been sick all these months. Hennie needs a rest. No doubt.
BESSIE: Sam don't think she means it——
MYRON: Oh, I know he don't, of course——
BESSIE: I'll say the truth, Sam. We didn't half the time understand her ourselves. A girl with her own mind. When she makes it up, wild horses wouldn't change her.
SAM: She don't love me.
BESSIE: This is sensible, Sam?
SAM: Not for a nickel.
BESSIE: What do you think? She married you for your money? For your looks? You ain't no John Barrymore,[8] Sam. No, she liked you.
SAM: Please, not for a nickel. [JACOB *stands in the doorway.*]
BESSIE: We stood right here the first time she said it. "Sam Feinschreiber's a nice boy," she said it, "a boy he's got good common sense, with a business head." Right here she said it, in this room. You sent her two boxes of candy together, you remember?
MYRON: Loft's candy.
BESSIE: This is when she said it. What do you think?
MYRON: You were just the only boy she cared for.
BESSIE: So she married you. Such a world . . . plenty of boy friends she had, believe me!
JACOB: A popular girl. . . .
MYRON: Y-e-s.
BESSIE: I'll say it plain out—Moe Axelrod offered her plenty—a servant, a house . . . she don't have to pick up a hand.

8. An actor renowned for his handsome profile (1882–1942).

MYRON: Oh, Moe? Just wild about her. . . .

SAM: Moe Axelrod? He wanted to——

BESSIE: But she didn't care. A girl like Hennie you don't buy. I should never live to see another day if I'm telling a lie.

SAM: She was kidding me.

BESSIE: What then? You shouldn't be foolish.

SAM: The baby looks like my family. He's got Feinschreiber eyes.

BESSIE: A blind man could see it.

JACOB: Sure . . . sure. . . .

SAM: The baby looks like me. Yes. . . .

BESSIE: You could believe me.

JACOB: Any day. . . .

SAM: But she tells me the man. She made up his name too?

BESSIE: Sam, Sam, look in the phone book—a million names.

MYRON: Tom, Dick and Harry. [JACOB *laughs quietly, soberly*.]

BESSIE: Don't stand around, Poppa. Take Tootsie on the roof. And you don't let her go under the water tank.

JACOB: Schmah Yisroeal.[9] Behold! [*Quietly laughing he goes back into his room, closing the door behind him*.]

SAM: I won't stand he should make insults. A man eats out his——

BESSIE: No, no, he's an old man—a second childhood. Myron, bring in the tea. Open a jar of raspberry jelly. [MYRON *exits*.]

SAM: Mom, you think——?

BESSIE: I'll talk to Hennie. It's all right.

SAM: Tomorrow, I'll take her by the doctor. [RALPH *enters*.]

BESSIE: Stay for a little tea.

SAM: No, I'll go home. I'm tired. Already I caught a cold in such weather. [*Blows his nose*.]

MYRON [*entering with stuffs*]: Going home?

SAM: I'll go in bed. I caught a cold.

MYRON: Teddy Roosevelt used to say, "When you have a problem, sleep on it."

BESSIE: My Sam is no problem.

MYRON: I don't mean . . . I mean he said——

BESSIE: Call me tomorrow, Sam.

SAM: I'll phone supper time. Sometimes I think there's something funny about me. [MYRON *sees him out. In the following pause Caruso is heard singing within*.]

BESSIE: A bargain! Second fiddle. By me he don't even play in the orchestra—a man like a mouse. Maybe she'll lay down and die 'cause he makes a living?

RALPH: Can I talk to you about something?

BESSIE: What's the matter—I'm biting you?

RALPH: It's something about Blanche.

BESSIE: Don't tell me.

RALPH: Listen now——

BESSIE: I don't wanna know.

9. "Hear O Israel" (Hebrew), the first words of the most famous prayer in the Jewish religion: "Hear O Israel, the Lord Thy God, the Lord is One."

RALPH: She's got no place to go.

BESSIE: I don't want to know.

RALPH: Mom, I love this girl. . . .

BESSIE: So go knock your head against the wall.

RALPH: I want her to come here. Listen, Mom, I want you to let her live here for a while.

BESSIE: You got funny ideas, my son.

RALPH: I'm as good as anyone else. Don't I have some rights in the world? Listen, Mom, if I don't do something, she's going away. Why don't you do it? Why don't you let her stay here for a few weeks? Things'll pick up. Then we can——

BESSIE: Sure, sure. I'll keep her fresh on ice for a wedding day. That's what you want?

RALPH: No, I mean you should——

BESSIE: Or maybe you'll sleep here in the same bed without marriage. [JACOB *stands in his doorway, dressed.*]

RALPH: Don't say that, Mom. I only mean. . . .

BESSIE: What you mean, I know . . . and what I mean I also know. Make up your mind. For your own good, Ralphie. If she dropped in the ocean I don't lift a finger.

RALPH: That's all, I suppose.

BESSIE: With me it's one thing—a boy should have respect for his own future. Go to sleep, you look tired. In the morning you'll forget.

JACOB: "Awake and sing, ye that dwell in dust, and the earth shall cast out the dead."[1] It's cold out?

MYRON: Oh, yes.

JACOB: I'll take up Tootsie now.

MYRON [*eating bread and jam*]: He come on us like the wild man of Borneo,[2] Sam. I don't think Hennie was fool enough to tell him the truth like that.

BESSIE: Myron! [*A deep pause.*]

RALPH: What did he say?

BESSIE: Never mind.

RALPH: I heard him. I heard him. You don't needa tell me.

BESSIE: Never mind.

RALPH: You trapped that guy.

BESSIE: Don't say another word.

RALPH: Just have respect? That's the idea?

BESSIE: Don't say another word. I'm boiling over ten times inside.

RALPH: You won't let Blanche here, huh. I'm not sure I want her. You put one over on that little shrimp. The cat's whiskers, Mom?

BESSIE: I'm telling you something!

RALPH: I got the whole idea. I get it so quick my head's swimming. Boy, what a laugh! I suppose you know about this, Jake?

JACOB: Yes.

RALPH: Why didn't you do something?

JACOB: I'm an old man.

1. Isaiah 26.19.
2. A stereotypical attraction in sideshows and carnivals of a ferocious man advertised as "the wild man of Borneo" (which he wasn't).

RALPH: What's that got to do with the price of bonds? Sits around and lets a thing like that happen! You make me sick too.

MYRON [*after a pause*]: Let me say something, son.

RALPH: Take your hand away! Sit in a corner and wag your tail. Keep on boasting you went to law school for two years.

MYRON: I want to tell you——

RALPH: You never in your life had a thing to tell me.

BESSIE [*bitterly*]: Don't say a word. Let him, let him run and tell Sam. Publish in the papers, give a broadcast on the radio. To him it don't matter nothing his family sits with tears pouring from the eyes. [*To* JACOB]: What are you waiting for? I didn't tell you twice already about the dog? You'll stand around with Caruso and make a bughouse. It ain't enough all day long. Fifty times I told you I'll break every record in the house. [*She brushes past him, breaks the records, comes out.*] The next time I say something you'll maybe believe it. Now maybe you learned a lesson. [*Pause.*]

JACOB [*quietly*]: Bessie, new lessons . . . not for an old dog. [MOE *enters.*]

MYRON: You didn't have to do it, Momma.

BESSIE: Talk better to your son, Mr. Berger! Me, I don't lay down and die for him and Poppa no more. I'll work like a nigger? For what? Wait, the day comes when you'll be punished. When it's too late you'll remember how you sucked away a mother's life. Talk to him, tell him how I don't sleep at night. [*Bursts into tears and exits.*]

MOE [*sings*]: "Good-by to all your sorrows. You never hear them talk about the war, in the land of Yama Yama. . . ."[3]

MYRON: Yes, Momma's a sick woman, Ralphie.

RALPH: Yeah?

MOE: We'll be out of the trenches by Christmas. Putt, putt, putt . . . here, stinker . . . [*Picks up Tootsie, a small, white poodle that just then enters from the hall.*] If there's reincarnation in the next life I wanna be a dog and lay in a fat lady's lap. Barrage over? How 'bout a little pinochle, Pop?

JACOB: Nnno.

RALPH [*taking dog*]: I'll take her up. [*Conciliatory.*]

JACOB: No, I'll do it. [*Takes dog.*]

RALPH [*ashamed*]: It's cold out.

JACOB: I was cold before in my life. A man sixty-seven. . . . [*Strokes the dog.*] Tootsie is my favorite lady in the house. [*He slowly passes across the room and exits. A settling pause.*]

MYRON: She cried all last night—Tootsie—I heard her in the kitchen like a young girl.

MOE: Tonight I could do something. I got a yen . . . I don't know.

MYRON [*rubbing his head*]: My scalp is impoverished.

RALPH: Mom bust all his records.

MYRON: She didn't have to do it.

MOE: Tough tit! Now I can sleep in the morning. Who the hell wantsa hear a wop air his tonsils all day long!

RALPH [*handling the fragment of a record*]: "O Paradiso!"

MOE [*gets cards*]: It's snowing out, girls.

3. Lines from a popular song.

MYRON: There's no more big snows like in the old days. I think the whole world's changing. I see it, right under our very eyes. No one hardly remembers any more when we used to have gaslight and all the dishes had little fishes on them.

MOE: It's the system, girls.

MYRON: I was a little boy when it happened—the Great Blizzard.[4] It snowed three days without a stop that time. Yes, and the horse cars stopped. A silence of death was on the city and little babies got no milk . . . they say a lot of people died that year.

MOE [*singing as he deals himself cards*]:

"Lights are blinking while you're drinking,
That's the place where the good fellows go.
Good-by to all your sorrows,
You never hear them talk about the war,
In the land of Yama Yama
Funicalee, funicala, funicalo. . . ."

MYRON: What can I say to you, Big Boy?

RALPH: Not a damn word.

MOE [*goes "ta ra ta ra" throughout.*]

MYRON: I know how you feel about all those things, I know.

RALPH: Forget it.

MYRON: And your girl. . . .

RALPH: Don't soft soap me all of a sudden.

MYRON: I'm not foreign born. I'm an American, and yet I never got close to you. It's an American father's duty to be his son's friend.

RALPH: Who said that—Teddy R.?

MOE [*dealing cards*]: You're breaking his heart, "Litvak."[5]

MYRON: It just happened the other day. The moment I began losing my hair I just knew I was destined to be a failure in life . . . and when I grew bald I was. Now isn't that funny, Big Boy?

MOE: It's a pisscutter!

MYRON: I believe in Destiny.

MOE: You get what-it-takes. Then they don't catch you with your pants down. [*Sings out*]: Eight of clubs. . . .

MYRON: I really don't know. I sold jewelry on the road before I married. It's one thing to—— Now here's a thing the druggist gave me. [*Reads*]: "The Marvel Cosmetic Girl of Hollywood is going on the air. Give this charming little radio singer a name and win five thousand dollars. If you will send——"

MOE: Your old man still believes in Santy Claus.

MYRON: Someone's got to win. The government isn't gonna allow everything to be a fake.

MOE: It's a fake. There ain't no prizes. It's a fake.

MYRON: It says——

RALPH [*snatching it*]: For Christ's sake, Pop, forget it. Grow up. Jake's right—everybody's crazy. It's like a zoo in this house. I'm going to bed.

4. A reference to the record blizzard that hit New York City in 1888.

5. A Jew from the Lithuanian region of Eastern Europe.

MOE: In the land of Yama Yama. . . . [*Goes on with ta ra.*]

MYRON: Don't think life's easy with Momma. No, but she means for your good all the time. I tell you she does, she——

RALPH: Maybe, but I'm going to bed. [*Downstairs doorbell rings violently.*]

MOE [*ring*]: Enemy barrage begins on sector eight seventy-five.

RALPH: That's downstairs.

MYRON: We ain't expecting anyone this hour of the night.

MOE: "Lights are blinking while you're drinking, that's the place where the good fellows go. Good-by to ta ra tara ra," etc.

RALPH: I better see who it is.

MYRON: I'll tick the button. [*As he starts, the apartment doorbell begins ringing, followed by large knocking.* MYRON *goes out.*]

RALPH: Who's ever ringing means it. [*A loud excited voice outside.*]

MOE: "In the land of Yama Yama, Funicalee, funicalo, funic——"

[MYRON *enters followed by* SCHLOSSER *the janitor.* BESSIE *cuts in from the other side.*]

BESSIE: Who's ringing like a lunatic?

RALPH: What's the matter?

MYRON: Momma. . . .

BESSIE: Noo, what's the matter? [*Downstairs bell continues.*]

RALPH: What's the matter?

BESSIE: Well, well . . . ?

MYRON: Poppa. . . .

BESSIE: What happened?

SCHLOSSER: He shlipped maybe in de snow.

RALPH: Who?

SCHLOSSER [*to* BESSIE]: Your fadder fall off de roof. . . . Ja. [*A dead pause.* RALPH *then runs out.*]

BESSIE [*dazed*]: Myron . . . Call Morty on the phone . . . call him. [MYRON *starts for phone.*] No. I'll do it myself. I'll . . . do it. [MYRON *exits.*]

SCHLOSSER [*standing stupidly*]: Since I was in dis country . . . I was pudding out de ash can . . . The snow is vet. . . .

MOE [*to* SCHLOSSER]: Scram. [SCHLOSSER *exits.*]

[BESSIE *goes blindly to the phone, fumbles and gets it.* MOE *sits quietly, slowly turning cards over, but watching her.*]

BESSIE: He slipped. . . .

MOE [*deeply moved*]: Slipped?

BESSIE: I can't see the numbers. Make it, Moe, make it. . . .

MOE: Make it yourself. [*He looks at her and slowly goes back to his game of cards with shaking hands.*]

BESSIE: Riverside 7— . . . [*Unable to talk she dials slowly. The dial whizzes on.*]

MOE: Don't . . . make me laugh. . . . [*He turns over cards.*]

CURTAIN

Act Three

A week later in the dining room. MORTY, BESSIE *and* MYRON *eating. Sitting in the front room is* MOE *marking a "dope sheet,"*[6] but really listening to the others.

BESSIE: You're sure he'll come tonight—the insurance man?

MORTY: Why not? I shtupped[7] him a ten-dollar bill. Everything's hot delicatessen.

BESSIE: Why must he come so soon?

MORTY: Because you had a big expense. You'll settle once and for all. I'm a great boy for making hay while the sun shines.

BESSIE: Stay till he'll come, Morty. . . .

MORTY: No, I got a strike downtown. Business don't stop for personal life. Two times already in the past week those bastards threw stink bombs in the showroom. Wait! We'll give them strikes—in the kishkas[8] we'll give them. . . .

BESSIE: I'm a woman. I don't know about policies. Stay till he comes.

MORTY: Bessie—sweetheart, leave me live.

BESSIE: I'm afraid, Morty.

MORTY: Be practical. They made an investigation. Everybody knows Pop had an accident. Now we'll collect.

MYRON: Ralphie don't know Papa left the insurance in his name

MORTY: It's not his business. And I'll tell him.

BESSIE: The way he feels. [*Enter* RALPH *into front room.*] He'll do something crazy. He thinks Poppa jumped off the roof.

MORTY: Be practical, Bessie. Ralphie will sign when I tell him. Everything is peaches and cream.

BESSIE: Wait for a few minutes. . . .

MORTY: Look, I'll show you in black on white what the policy says. *For God's sake, leave me live!* [*Angrily exits to kitchen. In parlor,* MOE *speaks to* RALPH *who is reading a letter.*]

MOE: What's the letter say?

RALPH: Blanche won't see me no more, she says. I couldn't care very much, she says. If I didn't come like I said. . . . She'll phone before she leaves.

MOE: She don't know about Pop?

RALPH: She won't ever forget me she says. Look what she sends me . . . a little locket on a chain . . . if she calls I'm out.

MOE: You mean it?

RALPH: For a week I'm trying to go in his room. I guess he'd like me to have it, but I can't. . . .

MOE: Wait a minute! [*Crosses over.*] They're trying to rook you—a freeze-out.

RALPH: Who?

MOE: That bunch stuffin' their gut with hot pastrami. Morty in particular. Jake left the insurance—three thousand dollars—for you.

RALPH: For me?

6. A printed sheet or section of a newspaper read by bettors that contains past performances of horses and jockeys, and their potential for the day's races.

7. Pushed (Yiddish); figuratively, slipped him some money.

8. Intestines or guts (Yiddish).

MOE: Now you got wings, kid. Pop figured you could use it. That's why. . . .
RALPH: That's why what?
MOE: It ain't the only reason he done it.
RALPH: He done it?
MOE: You think a breeze blew him off? [HENNIE *enters and sits.*]
RALPH: I'm not sure what I think.
MOE: The insurance guy's coming tonight. Morty "shtupped" him.
RALPH: Yeah?
MOE: I'll back you up. You're dead on your feet. Grab a sleep for yourself.
RALPH: No!
MOE: Go on! [*Pushes boy into room.*]
SAM [*whom* MORTY *has sent in for the paper*]: Morty wants the paper.
HENNIE: So?
SAM: You're sitting on it. [*Gets paper.*] We could go home now, Hennie! Leon is alone by Mrs. Strasberg a whole day.
HENNIE: Go on home if you're so anxious. A full tub of diapers is waiting.
SAM: Why should you act this way?
HENNIE: 'Cause there's no bones in ice cream. Don't touch me.
SAM: Please, what's the matter. . . .
MOE: She don't like you. Plain as the face on your nose. . . .
SAM: To me, my friend, you talk a foreign language.
MOE: A quarter you're lousy. [SAM *exits.*] Gimme a buck, I'll run it up to ten.
HENNIE: Don't do me no favors.
MOE: Take a chance. [*Stopping her as she crosses to doorway.*]
HENNIE: I'm a pushover.
MOE: I say lotsa things. You don't know me.
HENNIE: I know you—when you knock 'em down you're through.
MOE [*sadly*]: You still don't know me.
HENNIE: I know what goes in your wise-guy head.
MOE: Don't run away. . . . I ain't got hydrophobia. Wait. I want to tell you. . . . I'm leaving.
HENNIE: Leaving?
MOE: Tonight. Already packed.
HENNIE: Where?
MORTY [*as he enters followed by the others.*]: My car goes through snow like a dose of salts.
BESSIE: Hennie, go eat. . . .
MORTY: Where's Ralphie?
MOE: In his new room. [*Moves into dining room.*]
MORTY: I didn't have a piece of hot pastrami in my mouth for years.
BESSIE: Take a sandwich, Hennie. You didn't eat all day. . . . [*At window.*]: A whole week it rained cats and dogs.
MYRON: Rain, rain, go away. Come again some other day. [*Puts shawl on her.*]
MORTY: Where's my gloves?
SAM [*sits on stool*]: I'm sorry the old man lays in the rain.
MORTY: Personally, Pop was a fine man. But I'm a great boy for an honest opinion. He had enough crazy ideas for a regiment.
MYRON: Poppa never had a doctor in his whole life. . . . [*Enter* RALPH.]

MORTY: He had Caruso. Who's got more from life?

BESSIE: Who's got more? . . .

MYRON: And Marx he had.

[MYRON *and* BESSIE *sit on sofa.*]

MORTY: Marx! Some say Marx is the new God today. Maybe I'm wrong. Ha ha ha. . . . Personally I counted my ten million last night . . . I'm sixteen cents short. So tomorrow I'll go to Union Square[9] and yell no equality in the country! Ah, it's a new generation.

RALPH: You said it!

MORTY: What's the matter, Ralphie? What are you looking funny?

RALPH: I hear I'm left insurance and the man's coming tonight.

MORTY: Poppa didn't leave no insurance for you.

RALPH: What?

MORTY: In your name he left it—but not for you.

RALPH: It's my name on the paper.

MORTY: Who said so?

RALPH [*to his mother*]: The insurance man's coming tonight?

MORTY: What's the matter?

RALPH: I'm not talking to you. [*To his mother*]: Why?

BESSIE: I don't know why.

RALPH: He don't come in this house tonight.

MORTY: That's what *you* say.

RALPH: I'm not talking to you, Uncle Morty, but I'll tell you, too, he don't come here tonight when there's still mud on a grave. [*To his mother*]: Couldn't you give the house a chance to cool off?

MORTY: Is this a way to talk to your mother?

RALPH: Was that a way to talk to your father?

MORTY: Don't be so smart with me, Mr. Ralph Berger!

RALPH: Don't be so smart with *me*.

MORTY: What'll you do? I say he's coming tonight. Who says no?

MOE [*suddenly, from the background*]: Me.

MORTY: Take a back seat, Axelrod. When you're in the family——

MOE: I got a little document here. [*Produces paper.*] I found it under his pillow that night. A guy who slips off a roof don't leave a note before he does it.

MORTY [*starting for* MOE *after a horrified silence*]: Let me see this note.

BESSIE: Morty, don't touch it!

MOE: Not if you crawled.

MORTY: It's a fake. Poppa wouldn't——

MOE: Get the insurance guy here and we'll see how—— [*The bell rings.*] Speak of the devil . . . Answer it, see what happens. [MORTY *starts for the ticker.*]

BESSIE: Morty, don't!

MORTY [*stopping*]: Be practical, Bessie.

MOE: Sometimes you don't collect on suicides if they know about it.

MORTY: You should let. . . . You should let him. . . . [*A pause in which* ALL *seem dazed. Bell rings insistently.*]

9. A square at the intersection of Fourteenth Street and Broadway in New York City, a popular site at one time for people to gather to hear political orators, usually radical, and to argue politics.

MOE: Well, we're waiting.

MORTY: Give me the note.

MOE: I'll give you the head off your shoulders.

MORTY: Bessie, you'll stand for this? [*Points to* RALPH.] Pull down his pants and give him with a strap.

RALPH [*as bell rings again*]: How about it?

BESSIE: Don't be crazy. It's not my fault. Morty said he should come tonight. It's not nice so soon. I didn't——

MORTY: I said it? Me?

BESSIE: Who then?

MORTY: You didn't sing a song in my ear a whole week to settle quick?

BESSIE: I'm surprised. Morty, you're a big liar.

MYRON: Momma's telling the truth, she is!

MORTY: Lissen. In two shakes of a lamb's tail, we'll start a real fight and then nobody won't like nobody. Where's my fur gloves? I'm going downtown. [*To* SAM]: You coming? I'll drive you down.

HENNIE [*to* SAM, *who looks questioningly at her*]: Don't look at me. Go home if you want.

SAM: If you're coming soon, I'll wait.

HENNIE: Don't do me any favors. Night and day he pesters me.

MORTY: You made a cushion——sleep!

SAM: I'll go home. I know . . . to my worst enemy I don't wish such a life——

HENNIE: Sam, keep quiet.

SAM [*quietly; sadly*]: No more free speech in America? [*Gets his hat and coat.*] I'm a lonely person. Nobody likes me.

MYRON: I like you, Sam.

HENNIE [*going to him gently; sensing the end*]: Please go home, Sam. I'll sleep here. . . . I'm, tired and nervous. Tomorrow I'll come home. I love you. . . . I mean it. [*She kisses him with real feeling.*]

SAM: I would die for you. . . . [SAM *looks at her. Tries to say something, but his voice chokes up with a mingled feeling. He turns and leaves the room.*]

MORTY: A bird in the hand is worth two in the bush. Remember I said it. Good night. [*Exits after* SAM.] [HENNIE *sits depressed.* BESSIE *goes up and looks at the picture calendar again.* MYRON *finally breaks the silence.*]

MYRON: Yesterday a man wanted to sell me a saxophone with pearl buttons. But I——

BESSIE: It's a beautiful picture. In this land, nobody works. . . . Nobody worries. . . . Come to bed, Myron. [*Stops at the door, and says to* RALPH]: Please don't have foolish ideas about the money.

RALPH: Let's call it a day.

BESSIE: It belongs for the whole family. You'll get your teeth fixed——

RALPH: And a pair of black and white shoes?

BESSIE: Hennie needs a vacation. She'll take two weeks in the mountains and I'll mind the baby.

RALPH: I'll take care of my own affairs.

BESSIE: A family needs for a rainy day. Times is getting worse. Prospect Avenue, Dawson, Beck Street—every day furniture's on the sidewalk.

RALPH: Forget it, Mom.

BESSIE: Ralphie, I worked too hard all my years to be treated like dirt. It's no law we should be stuck together like Siamese twins. Summer shoes you didn't have, skates you never had, but I bought a new dress every week. A lover I kept—Mr. Gigolo! Did I ever play a game of cards like Mrs. Marcus? Or was Bessie Berger's children always the cleanest on the block?! Here I'm not only the mother, but also the father. The first two years I worked in a stocking factory for six dollars while Myron Berger went to law school. If I didn't worry about the family who would? On the calendar it's a different place, but here without a dollar you don't look the world in the eye. Talk from now to next year—this is life in America.

RALPH: Then it's wrong. It don't make sense. If life made you this way, then it's wrong!

BESSIE: Maybe you wanted me to give up twenty years ago. Where would you be now? You'll excuse my expression—bum in the park!

RALPH: I'm not blaming you, Mom. Sink or swim—I see it. But it can't stay like this.

BESSIE: My foolish boy. . . .

RALPH: No, I see every house lousy with lies and hate. He said it, Grandpa— Brooklyn hates the Bronx. Smacked on the nose twice a day. But boys and girls can get ahead like that, Mom. We don't want life printed on dollar bills, Mom!

BESSIE: So go out and change the world if you don't like it.

RALPH: I will! And why? 'Cause life's different in my head. Gimme the earth in two hands. I'm strong. There . . . hear him? The air mail off to Boston. Day or night, he flies away, a job to do. That's us and it's no time to die. [*The airplane sound fades off as* MYRON *gives alarm clock to* BESSIE *which she begins to wind.*]

BESSIE: "Mom, what does she know? She's old-fashioned!" But I'll tell you a big secret: My whole life I wanted to go away too, but with children a woman stays home. A fire burned in *my* heart too, but now it's too late. I'm no spring chicken. The clock goes and Bessie goes. Only my machinery can't be fixed. [*She lifts a button: the alarm rings on the clock; she stops it, says "Good night" and exits.*]

MYRON: I guess I'm no prize bag. . . .

BESSIE [*from within*]: Come to bed, Myron.

MYRON [*tears page off calendar*]: Hmmm. . . . [*Exits to her.*]

RALPH: Look at him, draggin' after her like an old shoe.

MOE: Punch drunk. [*Phone rings.*] That's for me. [*At phone.*] Yeah? . . . Just a minute. [*To* RALPH]: Your girl . . .

RALPH: Jeez, I don't know what to say to her.

MOE: Hang up? [RALPH *slowly takes phone.*]

RALPH: Hello. . . . Blanche, I wish. . . . I don't know what to say. . . . Yes . . . Hello? . . . [*Puts phone down.*] She hung up on me . . .

MOE: Sorry?

RALPH: No girl means anything to me until. . . .

MOE: Till when?

RALPH: Till I can take care of her. Till we don't look out on an airshaft. Till we can take the world in two hands and polish off the dirt.

MOE: That's a big order.

RALPH: Once upon a time I thought I'd drown to death in bolts of silk and velour. But I grew up these last few weeks. Jake said a lot.

MOE: Your memory's okay?

RALPH: But take a look at this. [*Brings armful of books from* JACOB'S *room—dumps them on table.*] His books, I got them too—the pages ain't cut in half of them.

MOE: Perfect.

RALPH: Does it prove something? Damn tootin'! A ten-cent nailfile cuts them. Uptown, downtown, I'll read them on the way. Get a big lamp over the bed. [*Picks up one.*] My eyes are good. [*Puts book in pocket.*] Sure, inventory tomorrow. Coletti to Driscoll to Berger—that's how we work. It's a team down the warehouse. Driscoll's a show-off, a wiseguy, and Joe talks pigeons day and night. But they're like me, looking for a chance to get to first base too. Joe razzed me about my girl. But he don't know why. I'll tell him. Hell, he might tell me something I don't know. Get teams together all over. Spit on your hands and get to work. And with enough teams together maybe we'll get steam in the warehouse so our fingers don't freeze off. Maybe we'll fix it so life won't be printed on dollar bills.

MOE: Graduation Day.

RALPH [*starts for door of his room, stops*]: Can I have . . . Grandpa's note?

MOE: Sure you want it?

RALPH: Please— [MOE *gives it.*] It's blank!

MOE [*taking note back and tearing it up*]: That's right.

RALPH: Thanks! [*Exits.*]

MOE: The kid's a fighter! [*To* HENNIE]: Why are you crying?

HENNIE: I never cried in my life. [*She is now.*]

MOE [*starts for door. Stops*]: You told Sam you love him. . . .

HENNIE: If I'm sore on life, why take it out on him?

MOE: You won't forget me to your dyin' day—I was the first guy. Part of your insides. You won't forget. I wrote my name on you—indelible ink!

HENNIE: One thing I won't forget—how you left me crying on the bed like I was two for a cent!

MOE: Listen, do you think——

HENNIE: Sure. Waits till the family goes to the open air movie. He brings me perfume. . . . He grabs my arms——

MOE: You won't forget me!

HENNIE: How you left the next week?

MOE: So I made a mistake. For Chris' sake, don't act like the Queen of Roumania!

HENNIE: Don't make me laugh!

MOE: What the hell do you want, my head on a plate?! Was my life so happy? Chris', my old man was a bum. I supported the whole damn family—five kids and Mom. When they grew up they beat it the hell away like rabbits. Mom died. I went to the war; got clapped down like a bedbug; woke up in a room without a leg. What the hell do you think, anyone's got it better than you? I never had a home either. I'm lookin' too!

HENNIE: So what?!

MOE: So you're it—you're home for me, a place to live! That's the whole parade, sickness, eating out your heart! Sometimes you meet a girl—she stops it—that's love. . . . So take a chance! Be with me, Paradise. What's to lose?

HENNIE: My pride!

MOE [*grabbing her*]: What do you want? Say the word—I'll tango on a dime. Don't gimme ice when your heart's on fire!

HENNIE: Let me go! [*He stops her.*]

MOE: WHERE?!!

HENNIE: What do you want, Moe, what do you want?

MOE: You!

HENNIE: You'll be sorry you ever started——

MOE: You!

HENNIE: Moe, lemme go—— [*Trying to leave*]: I'm getting up early—lemme go.

MOE: No! . . . I got enough fever to blow the whole damn town to hell. [*He suddenly releases her and half stumbles backwards. Forces himself to quiet down.*] You wanna go back to him? Say the word. I'll know what to do. . . .

HENNIE [*helplessly*]: Moe, I don't know what to say.

MOE: Listen to me.

HENNIE: What?

MOE: Come away. A certain place where it's moonlight and roses. We'll lay down, count stars. Hear the big ocean making noise. You lay under the trees. Champagne flows like—— [*Phone rings.* MOE *finally answers the telephone*]: Hello? . . . Just a minute. [*Looks at* HENNIE.]

HENNIE: Who is it?

MOE: Sam.

HENNIE [*starts for phone, but changes her mind*]: I'm sleeping . . .

MOE [*in phone*]: She's sleeping. . . . [*Hangs up. Watches* HENNIE *who slowly sits.*] He wants you to know he got home O.K. . . . What's on your mind?

HENNIE: Nothing.

MOE: Sam?

HENNIE: They say it's a palace on those Havana boats.

MOE: What's on your mind?

HENNIE [*trying to escape*]: Moe, I don't care for Sam—I never loved him——

MOE: But your kid—?

HENNIE: All my life I waited for this minute.

MOE [*holding her*]: Me too. Made believe I was talkin' just bedroom golf, but you and me forever was what I meant! Christ, baby, there's one life to live! Live it!

HENNIE: Leave the baby?

MOE: Yeah!

HENNIE: I can't. . . .

MOE: You can!

HENNIE: No. . . .

MOE: But you're not sure!

HENNIE: I don't know.

MOE: Make a break or spend the rest of your life in a coffin.

HENNIE: Oh God, I don't know where I stand.

MOE: Don't look up there. Paradise, you're on a big boat headed south. No more pins and needles in your heart, no snake juice squirted in your arm. The whole world's green grass and when you cry it's because you're happy.

HENNIE: Moe, I don't know. . . .

MOE: Nobody knows, but you do it and find out. When you're scared the answer's zero.

HENNIE: You're hurting my arm.

MOE: The doctor said it—cut off your leg to save your life! And they done it—one thing to get another. [*Enter* RALPH.]

RALPH: I didn't hear a word, but do it, Hennie, do it!

MOE: Mom can mind the kid. She'll go on forever, Mom. We'll send money back, and Easter eggs.

RALPH: I'll be here.

MOE: Get your coat . . . get it.

HENNIE: Moe!

MOE: I know . . . but get your coat and hat and kiss the house good-by.

HENNIE: The man I love. . . . [MYRON *entering.*] I left my coat in Mom's room. [*Exits.*]

MYRON: Don't wake her up, Beauty. Momma fell asleep as soon as her head hit the pillow. I can't sleep. It was a long day. Hmmm. [*Examines his tongue in buffet mirror*]: I was reading the other day a person with a thick tongue is feebleminded. I can do anything with my tongue. Make it thick, flat. No fruit in the house lately. Just a lone apple. [*He gets apple and paring knife and starts paring.*] Must be something wrong with me—I say I won't eat but I eat. [HENNIE *enters dressed to go out.*] Where you going, little Red Riding Hood?

HENNIE: Nobody knows, Peter Rabbit.

MYRON: You're looking very pretty tonight. You were a beautiful baby too. 1910, that was the year you was born. The same year Teddy Roosevelt come back from Africa.

HENNIE: Gee, Pop; you're such a funny guy.

MYRON: He was a boisterous man, Teddy. Good night. [*He exits, paring apple.*]

RALPH: When I look at him, I'm sad. Let me die like a dog, if I can't get more from life.

HENNIE: Where?

RALPH: Right here in the house! My days won't be for nothing. Let Mom have the dough. I'm twenty-two and kickin'! I'll get along. Did Jake die for us to fight about nickels? No! "Awake and sing," he said. Right here he stood and said it. The night he died, I saw it like a thunderbolt! I saw he was dead and I was born! I swear to God, I'm one week old! I want the whole city to hear it—fresh blood, arms. We got 'em. We're glad we're living.

MOE: I wouldn't trade you for two pitchers and an outfielder. Hold the fort!

RALPH: So long.

MOE: So long.

[They go and RALPH *stands full and strong in the doorway seeing them off as the curtain slowly falls.*]

CURTAIN

1933 1935

LEO ROSTEN
1908–1997

Highly educated and accomplished in a variety of fields, Leo Rosten, whose full name was Leonard Calvin Ross and who occasionally used the pseudonym Leonard Q. Ross, had an extraordinary career. He is perhaps best known for his Hyman Kaplan stories, published in two books, and for his very popular and influential *The Joys of Yiddish* (1968). Born in Lodz, Poland, he was brought by his parents at the age of three to Chicago, where he grew up and attended the public schools. He studied at the University of Chicago, earning a Ph.D. degree in 1930 while also teaching English to immigrant adults in evening school—a fertile experience for his later stories. Rosten traveled abroad a good deal, studying from 1934 at the London School of Economics and Political Science, earning a Ph.D. in those subjects in 1937. During World War II, he served as a high-level economist, administrator, and consultant in government and defense industries. In the late 1930s, he worked as well in Hollywood, as a screenwriter for at least ten films. By 1941, he had published three books of sociological interest about that experience.

*The Education of H*Y*M*A*N K*A*P*L*A*N* (1937) began as sketches for the *New Yorker*, written, Rosten claimed, to earn money to pay bills incurred by his wife's illness. He had recently married, in 1935. His wife died a few years later, leaving three children, and Rosten remarried in 1960. The comic inventiveness of the Hyman Kaplan stories brings to life a cast of characters representing many aspiring immigrants who came over between the wars. Chief among them is the irrepressible Kaplan, who expresses his devotion to America—and his own high self-regard—by placing stars after the letters in his name. His classmates are nicely individualized but are characterized, for the most part, as an appreciative audience or as disdained opponents for the limelight. Kaplan flaunts his fractured English pronunciation and spelling, and a blandly idiosyncratic, but usually warmly human, view of language, literature, and history. The teacher of the class, Mr. Parkhill, is a proper WASP, pedantic but beloved and in an entirely different, bemused world from his students. He is a perfect innocent and foil who learns, ultimately, to let his star pupil go his own way.

From The Education of H*Y*M*A*N K*A*P*L*A*N

MR. K*A*P*L*A*N AND SHAKESPEARE

It was Miss Higby's idea in the first place. She had suggested to Mr. Parkhill that the students came to her class unaware of the *finer* side of English, of its beauty and, as she put it, "the glorious heritage of our literature." She suggested that perhaps poetry might be worked into the exercises of Mr. Parkhill's class. The beginners' grade had, after all, been subjected to almost a year of English and might be presumed to have achieved some linguistic sophistication. Poetry would make the students conscious of precise enunciation; it would make them read with greater care and an ear for sounds. Miss Higby, who had once begun a master's thesis on Coventry Patmore,[1] *loved* poetry. And, it should be said in all justice, she argued her cause with considerable logic. Poetry *would* be excellent for the enunciation of the students, thought Mr. Parkhill.

So it was that when he faced the class the following Tuesday night, Mr. Parkhill had a volume of Shakespeare on his desk, and an eager, almost an expectant, look in his eye. The love that Miss Higby bore for poetry in general was as nothing compared to the love that Mr. Parkhill bore for Shakespeare in particular. To Mr. Parkhill, poetry meant Shakespeare. Many years ago he had played Polonius[2] in his senior class play.

"Tonight, class," said Mr. Parkhill, "I am going to try an experiment."

The class looked up dutifully. They had come to regard Mr. Parkhill's pedagogical innovations as part of the natural order.

"I am going to introduce you to poetry—great poetry. You see—" Mr. Parkhill delivered a modest lecture on the beauty of poetry, its expression of the loftier thoughts of men, its economy of statement. He hoped it would be a relief from spelling and composition exercises to use poetry as the subject matter of the regular Recitation and Speech period. "I shall write a passage on the board and read it for you. Then, for Recitation and Speech, you will give short addresses, using the passage as the general topic, telling us what it has brought to your minds, what thoughts and ideas."

The class seemed quite pleased by the announcement. Miss Mitnick blushed happily. (This blush was different from most of Miss Mitnick's blushes; there was aspiration and idealism in it.) Mr. Norman Bloom sighed with a business-like air: you could tell that for him poetry was merely another assignment, like a speech on "What I Like to Eat Best" or a composition on "A Day at a Picnic." Mrs. Moskowitz, to whom any public performance was unpleasant, tried to look enthusiastic, without much success. And Mr. Hyman Kaplan, the heroic smile on his face as indelibly as ever, looked at Mr. Parkhill with admiration and whispered to himself: "Poyetry! Now is poyetry! My! Mus' be progriss ve makink awreddy!"

"The passage will be from Shakespeare," Mr. Parkhill announced, opening the volume.

An excited buzz ran through the class as the magic of that name fell upon them.

"Imachine!" murmured Mr. Kaplan. "Jakesbeer!"

"*Shake*speare, Mr. Kaplan!"

Mr. Parkhill took a piece of chalk and, with care and evident love, wrote the following passage on the board in large, clear letters:

Tomorrow, and tomorrow, and tomorrow
Creeps in this petty pace from day to day,

1. English poet (1823–1896).
2. A character in Shakespeare's tragedy *Hamlet* (1600).

To the last syllable of recorded time;
And all our yesterdays have lighted fools
The way to dusty death. Out, out, brief candle!
Life's but a walking shadow, a poor player
That struts and frets his hour upon the stage,
And then is heard no more; it is a tale
Told by an idiot, full of sound and fury,
Signifying nothing.[3]

A reverent hush filled the classroom, as eyes gazed with wonder on this passage from the Bard.[4] Mr. Parkhill was pleased at this.

"I shall read the passage first," he said. "Listen carefully to my enunciation—and—er—let Shakespeare's thoughts sink into your minds."

Mr. Parkhill read: " 'Tomorrow, and tomorrow, and tomorrow . . . ' " Mr. Parkhill read very well and this night, as if some special fire burned in him, he read with rare eloquence. "Out, out, brief candle!" In Miss Mitnick's eyes there was inspiration and wonder. "Life's but a walking shadow . . ." Mrs. Moskowitz sat with a heavy frown, indicating cerebration. "It is a tale told by an idiot . . ." Mr. Kaplan's smile had taken on something luminous; but his eyes were closed: it was not clear whether Mr. Kaplan had surrendered to the spell of the Immortal Bard or to that of Morpheus.[5]

"I shall—er—read the passage again," said Mr. Parkhill, clearing his throat vociferously until he saw Mr. Kaplan's eyes open. " 'Tomorrow, and tomorrow, and tomorrow. . . . ' "

When Mr. Parkhill had read the passage for the second time, he said: "That should be quite clear now. Are there any questions?"

There were a few questions. Mr. Scymzak wanted to know whether "frets" was "a little kind excitement." Miss Schneiderman asked about "struts." Mr. Kaplan wasn't sure about "cripps." Mr. Parkhill explained the words carefully, with several illustrative uses of each word. "No more questions? Well, I shall allow a few minutes for you all to—er—think over the meaning of the passage. Then we shall begin Recitation and Speech."

Mr. Kaplan promptly closed his eyes again, his smile beatific. The students sank into that revery miscalled thought, searching their souls for the symbols evoked by Shakespeare's immortal words.

"Miss Caravello, will you begin?" asked Mr. Parkhill at last.

Miss Caravello went to the front of the room. "Da poem isa gooda," she said slowly. "Itsa have—"

"It *has*."

"It hasa beautiful wordsa. Itsa lak Dante,[6] Italian poet—"

"Ha!" cried Mr. Kaplan scornfully. "Shaksbeer you metchink mit Tante? *Shaksbeer*? Mein Gott!"[7]

It was obvious that Mr. Kaplan had identified himself with Shakespeare and would tolerate no disparagement of his *alter ego*.[8]

"Miss Caravello is merely expressing her own ideas," said Mr. Parkhill pacifically. (Actually, he felt completely sympathetic to Mr. Kaplan's point of view.)

3. From Shakespeare's *Macbeth*, 5.5. 18–27.
4. Literally, the Poet, an epithet often applied to Shakespeare.
5. The Greek god of dreams.
6. Dante Alighieri (1265–1321), great Italian poet, author of *The Divine Comedy*.
7. My God (German).
8. A second self (Latin).

"Hau Kay," agreed Mr. Kaplan, with a generous wave of the hand. "But to me is no comparink a high-cless man like Shaksbeer mit a Tante, dat's all."

Miss Caravello, her poise shattered, said a few more words and sat down.

Mrs. Yampolsky's contribution was brief. "This is full deep meanings," she said, her eyes on the floor. "Is hard for a person not so good in English to unnistand. But I like."

" '*Like*!' " cried Mr. Kaplan with a fine impatience. " '*Like?*' Batter *love*, Yampolsky. Mit Shaksbeer mus' be *love!*"

Mr. Parkhill had to suggest that Mr. Kaplan control his aesthetic passions. He did understand how Mr. Kaplan felt, however, and sensed a new bond between them. Mrs. Yampolsky staggered through several more nervous comments and retired.

Mr. Bloom was next. He gave a long declamation, ending: "So is passimistic ideas in the poem, and I am optimist. Life should be happy—so we should remember this is only a poem. Maybe is Shakespeare too passimistic."

"You wronk, Bloom!" cried Mr. Kaplan with prompt indignation. "Shaksbeer is passimist because is de *life* passimist also!"

Mr. Parkhill, impressed by this philosophical stroke, realized that Mr. Kaplan, afire with the glory of the Swan of Avon,[9] could not be suppressed. Mr. Kaplan was the kind of man who brooked no criticism of his gods. The only solution was to call on Mr. Kaplan for his recitation at once. Mr. Parkhill was, indeed, curious about what fresh thoughts Mr. Kaplan would utter after his passionate defences of the Bard. When Mr. Parkhill had corrected certain parts of Mr. Bloom's speech, emphasizing Mr. Bloom's failure to use the indefinite article, he said: "Mr. Kaplan, will *you* speak next?"

Mr. Kaplan's face broke into a glow; his smile was like a rainbow. "Soitinly," he said, walking to the front of the room. Never had he seemed so dignified, so eager, so conscious of a great destiny.

"Er—Mr. Kaplan," added Mr. Parkhill, suddenly aware of the possibilities which the situation (Kaplan on Shakespeare) involved: "Speak *carefully*."

"*Spacially* careful vill I be," Mr. Kaplan reassured him. He cleared his throat, adjusted his tie, and began: "Ladies an' gantleman, you hoid all kinds minninks abot dis piece poyetry, an'—"

"*Po*etry."

"—abot dis piece *po*etry. But to me is a difference minnink altogadder. Ve mus' tink abot Julius Scissor[1] an' how *he* falt!"

Mr. Parkhill moved nervously, puzzled.

"In dese exact voids is Julius Scissor sayink—"

"Er—Mr. Kaplan," said Mr. Parkhill once he grasped the full import of Mr. Kaplan's error. "The passage is from 'Macbeth.' "

Mr. Kaplan looked at Mr. Parkhill with injured surprise. "*Not* fromm 'Julius Scissor'?" There was pain in his voice.

"No. And it's—er—'Julius *Cae*sar.' "

Mr. Kaplan waited until the last echo of the name had permeated his soul. "Podden me, Mr. Pockheel. Isn't '*see*zor' vat you cottink somting op mit?"

"That," said Mr. Parkhill quickly, "is 'scissor.' You have used 'Caesar' for 'scissor' and 'scissor' for 'Caesar.' "

9. An epithet applied to Shakespeare, who was born at Stratford-upon-Avon; the Avon is a river.

1. I.e., *Julius Caesar*, a tragedy by Shakespeare.

Mr. Kaplan nodded, marvelling at his own virtuosity.

"But go on with your speech, please." Mr. Parkhill, to tell the truth, felt a little guilty that he had not announced at the very beginning that the passage was from "Macbeth." "Tell us *why* you thought the lines were from 'Julius Caesar.' "

"Vell," said Mr. Kaplan to the class, his smile assuming its normal serenity. "I vas positif, becawss I can *see* de whole ting." He paused, debating how to explain this cryptic remark. Then his eyes filled with a strange enchantment. "I see de whole scinn. It's in a tant, on de night bafore dey makink Julius de Kink fromm Rome. So he is axcited an' ken't slip. He is layink in bad, tinking: 'Tomorrow an' tomorrow an' tomorrow. How slow dey movink! Almost cripps! Soch a pity de pace!' "

Before Mr. Parkhill could explain that "petty pace" did not mean "Soch a pity de pace!" Mr. Kaplan had soared on.

"De days go slow, fromm day to day, like leetle tsyllables on phonograph racords fromm time."

Anxiety and bewilderment invaded Mr. Parkhill's eyes.

" 'An' vat abot yestidday?' tinks Julius Scissor. Ha! 'All our yestiddays are only makink a good light for fools to die in de dost!' "

" 'Dusty death' doesn't mean—" There was no interrupting Mr. Kaplan.

"An' Julius Scissor is so tired, an' he vants to fallink aslip. So he hollers, mit fillink, 'Go ot! Go ot! Short candle!' So it goes ot."

Mr. Kaplan's voice dropped to a whisper. "But he ken't slip. Now is bodderink him de idea fromm life. 'Vat is de life altogadder?' tinks Julius Scissor. An' he gives enswer, de pot I like de bast. 'Life is like a bum actor, strottink an' hollerink arond de stage for only vun hour bafore he's kicked ot. Life is a tale told by idjots, dat's all, full of fonny sonds an' phooey!' "

Mr. Parkhill could be silent no longer. " 'Full of sound and fury!' " he cried desperately. But inspiration, like an irresistible force, swept Mr. Kaplan on.

" 'Life is monkey business! It don' minn a ting. It signifies nottink!' An' den Julius Scissor closes his ice fest—" Mr. Kaplan demonstrated the Consul's exact ocular process in closing his "ice"—"—an' falls dad!"

The class was hushed as Mr. Kaplan stopped. In the silence, a tribute to the fertility of Mr. Kaplan's imagination and the power of his oratory, Mr. Kaplan went to his seat. But just before he sat down, as if adding a postscript, he sighed: "Dat vas mine idea. But ufcawss is all wronk, becawss Mr. Pockheel said de voids ain't abot Julius Scissor altogadder. It's all abot an Irishman by de name Macbat."

Then Mr. Kaplan sat down.

It was some time before Mr. Parkhill could bring himself to criticize Mr. Kaplan's pronunciation, enunciation, diction, grammar, idiom, and sentence structure. For Mr. Parkhill discovered that he could not easily return to the world of reality. He was still trying to tear himself away from that tent outside Rome, where "Julius Scissor," cursed with insomnia, had thought of time and life—and philosophized himself to a strange and sudden death.

Mr. Parkhill was distinctly annoyed with Miss Higby.

1937

DANIEL FUCHS
1909–1993

The author of the only full-length study of Daniel Fuchs's work asserts that Fuchs enjoys "a place in the first rank of American Jewish writers." Yet his work is not nearly as well known as that of Henry Roth (a near contemporary), Saul Bellow, Bernard Malamud, and many others.

Daniel Fuchs was born on the Lower East Side of Manhattan, the son of Jewish immigrants from Russia and Poland. The family moved to the Williamsburg section of Brooklyn when he was five years old. He attended Eastern District High School there and then New York's City College. He edited the college literary magazine, graduating in 1930. He taught in New York City high schools, but after receiving encouragement from Malcolm Cowley, literary editor of the *New Republic*—who published his first piece, about his Brooklyn boyhood—he began to write full time, publishing his first novel in 1934.

Fuchs was a prolific writer in a variety of modes, best known, probably, for his early and occasionally grim so-called "Williamsburg Trilogy": *Summer in Williamsburg* (1934), *Homage to Blenholt* (1936), *Low Company* (1937). The first of these represents immigrant and tenement life naturalistically, the second is more comic in its exposure of the sordid contradictions in the life of the central character (based on an actual local political figure), while the last is a bleak portrayal of the milieu seen without illusion. All three were reissued as *Three Novels by Daniel Fuchs* (1961) and received respectful attention, although they did not have the same impact as Henry Roth's *Call It Sleep*, reissued the year before.

In the 1940s and 1950s, Fuchs enjoyed a career as a writer of stories for the *New Yorker* and, from 1940 onward, as a Hollywood screenwriter. Among his better-known screenplays are *Criss Cross* (1949) and *Panic in the Streets* (1950). He adapted *Low Company* as *The Gangster* (1947).

The Apathetic Bookie Joint (1979), the collection of stories in which *A Hollywood Diary* appears, received a very good reception from major critics. The story shows Fuchs as the consummate satirist—drily ironic.

A Hollywood Diary[1]

April 26—For ten days I have been sitting around in my two-room office, waiting for some producer on the lot to call me up and put me to work on a script. Every morning I walk the distance from my apartment on Orchid Avenue and appear at the studio promptly at nine. The other writers pass my window an hour or so later, see me ready for work in my shirt sleeves and suspenders, and yell jovially "Scab!"[2] But I don't want to miss that phone call.

I sent my secretary back to the stenographic department and told her I'd call her when I needed her. It was embarrassing with the two of us just sitting there and waiting.

Naturally, I can't expect an organization of this size to stop everything until I'm properly placed, but they pay me two hundred dollars a week and I do

1. From *The Apathetic Bookie Joint* (1979).
2. A worker who accepts employment during a strike or replaces a striking union worker.

nothing to earn it. Himmer, my agent, tells me I'm getting "beans" and have no reason to think of the waste of money.

The main thing is not to grow demoralized and cynical.

A letter from home: "Hollywood must be different and exciting. Which actress are you bringing east for a wife?"

In the evening I walk down Hollywood Boulevard with all the other tourists, hoping for a glimpse of Carole Lombard and Adolphe Menjou.[3] And after I get tired of walking I drop into a drugstore, where, with the lonely ladies from Iowa, I secretly drink a thick strawberry soda.

APRIL 27—The telephone rang today but it was only the parking-lot attendant across the street. He wanted to know why I hadn't been using the parking space the studio assigned to me. I explained I had no car, which left him bewildered.

The truth is I can't buy one. When I left New York I owned a five-dollar bill and had to borrow six hundred dollars from my agent to pay my debts and get out here respectably.

My agent is collecting his six hundred dollars in weekly installments of fifty dollars. Also taking nips out of my check are his twenty-dollar weekly commission, the California unemployment tax, the federal old-age relief tax, and the Motion Picture Relief Fund, so that what actually comes to me isn't two hundred dollars at all, and it would take some time to get enough money together for a car.

With all these cuts I'm still making more money than I ever earned per week. Just the same, I'm kicking. The trouble is, I suppose, that it's misleading to think of salary in weekly figures when you work for the movies. Hardly anyone works fifty-two weeks a year; my own contract lasts thirteen weeks.

Still no telephone call from any producer.

APRIL 28—Himmer, my agent, dropped in. He doesn't seem worried by my inactivity. "The check comes every week, doesn't it?" he asks. "It's good money, isn't it?"

APRIL 29—I was put to work this morning. Mara, a sad-looking man who produces B pictures for the studio, asked me to do a "treatment"[4] of a story called *No Bread to Butter*. This is an "original"—a twenty-page synopsis of a picture for which the studio paid fifteen hundred dollars. Mara had put some other writers to work on treatments, but hadn't liked what they'd done any better than he liked the original. I didn't understand at all. Why had he bought *No Bread to Butter* if it was no good, I asked him. Mara smoked his cigar patiently for a while. "Listen," he said, "do I ask you personal questions?"

He wouldn't tell me what was wrong with the original or what he wanted. "The whole intention in the matter is to bring on a writer with a fresh approach. If I talk, you'll go to work with preconceived notions in your head. Tell the story as you see it and we'll see what comes out."

I went back to my office. *No Bread to Butter* seems to be a baldly manufactured story, but I'm anxious to see what I can do with it. I feel good, a regular writer now, with an assignment. It appears to worry the other writers

3. A leading man in early films; later, a character actor (1890–1963). "Hollywood Boulevard": the street on which many tourist attractions and film-industry sights are concentrated. "Carole Lombard": a comedienne and leading lady in films (1909–1942).

4. A tentative first draft for a movie script based on another text.

that I have found something to do at last. They seemed fonder of me when I was just hanging around.

I phoned Himmer to tell him the good news. "See?" he said. "Didn't I tell you I'd take care of it? You let me handle everything and don't worry." He talked with no great enthusiasm.

May 5—The boys tell me I'm a fool to hand in my treatment so soon. Two or three weeks are the minimum time, they say, but I was anxious to get the work done to show Mara what I could do. Mara's secretary said I should hear from him in the morning.

May 6—Mara did not phone.

May 10—No phone.

May 11—No phone.

May 12—Mr. Barry phoned. He's assistant to the vice-president in charge of production and represents the front office. He called me at my apartment last night, after work. "Listen here, kid," he said, "I've been trying to reach you at your home all day. You've been out on the Coast[5] a month now. Don't you think it's time you showed up at the lot?"

I protested, almost tearfully.

Seems that the administration building checked up on the absences of writers by the report sent in by the parking-lot attendant. Since I had no car, I hadn't been checked in. I explained, but Barry hung up, sounding unconvinced.

May 13—Nothing.

The malted milks in this town are made with three full scoops of ice cream. Opulence.

May 14—Mara finally called me in today, rubbed his nose for a few minutes, and then told me my treatment was altogether too good. "You come in with a script," he explained. "It's fine, it's subtle and serious. It's perfect—for Gary Cooper,[6] not for my kind of talent."

I tried to get Mara to make a stab at the script anyhow, but nothing doing. Naturally, I'm not especially depressed.

May 17—Barry, front-office man, called me up again, this time at my office. He told me Mara had sent in an enthusiastic report on me. I was a fine writer—"serious"—and fit only for the A producers. Barry, who is taking "personal charge" of me, told me to see St. John, one of the company's best producers.

St. John's secretary made an appointment for me for the morning. She seemed to know who I was.

May 18—St. John gave me a cordial welcome and told me he's been wanting to do a historical frontier picture but has been held up because he can't find the right character. He's been hunting for three years now and asked me to get to work on the research.

I told him frankly I didn't imagine I'd be very successful with this, but he brushed my objections aside.

I'm back at the office and don't know exactly what to do. I don't want to spend time on anything as flimsy as this assignment. Nevertheless, I phoned the research department and asked them to send me everything they had on

5. A film-industry term for southern California and Hollywood.

6. A movie actor noted for playing strong, quiet heroes (1901–1961).

the early West. This turns out to be several very old books on Texas. I go through them with no great interest.

MAY 19—Still Texas. Sometimes, when I stop to see myself sitting in a room and reading books on Texas, I get a weird, dreamlike feeling.

Frank Coleman, one of the writers I've come to know, dropped in and asked me to play a little casino[7] with him, five cents a hand. We played for about a half hour.

MAY 21—Interoffice memo from St. John: "The front office tells me their program for the year is full and they have no room for an expensive frontier picture. Sorry."

I was struck again with the dreamlike quality of my work here.

Frank Coleman, who dropped in for some casino, explained St. John's note. When a writer goes to work for a producer, the writer's salary is immediately attached to the producer's budget. St. John simply didn't want to be responsible for my salary.

At any rate I'm glad to be free of the Texas research.

MAY 24—Barry, front-office man, sent me to another producer, Marc Wilde, who gave me the full shooting script of *Dark Island,* which was made in 1926 as a silent picture. "My thought," said Wilde, "is to shoot the story in a talking version. However, before I put you to work on it, I want to find out what you think of it, whether you care to work on it, et cetera. So read it."

MAY 25—I didn't like *Dark Island* at all, but I didn't want to antagonize Wilde by being too outspoken. I asked him what *he* thought of it. "Me?" Wilde asked. "Why ask me? I haven't read the script."

Coleman and I play casino every afternoon now.

MAY 26—I've been coming to work at nine-thirty lately and today I walked in at ten. All the boys seem to like me now, and it is well-intentioned friendship, too. They pick me up at twelve for lunch at the commissary, where we all eat at the "round table." That is, the lesser writers ($100–$500) eat at a large round table. The intermediates ($500–$750) eat privately or off the lot. The big shots eat at the executives' table along with topflight stars and producers. They shoot crap[8] with their meals.

We're at lunch from twelve to two. Afterward we tour the lot for an hour or so in the sunshine, just walking around and looking at the sets in the different barns. Then it takes us a half hour to break up at the doorway to the writers' building. When we finally go to our separate offices the boys generally take a nap. I took one, too, today. Coleman comes in at four for a half hour's play at the cards and then we meet the other boys again at the commissary for afternoon tea, which amounts to a carbonated drink called 7 Up. This leaves me a few minutes for these notes; I put on my hat and go home.

MAY 28—My fingernails seem to grow very rapidly. It may be the climate or simply because I have more time to notice them.

JUNE 1—Very lazy. I read picture magazines from 10:30 until 12. After that the day goes fast enough.

JUNE 3—The story editor called me up today and said Kolb wants to see me. Kolb is second- or third-ranking producer on the lot; when I mentioned

7. A card game.

8. A dice-throwing game (slang).

the news to the boys, they all grew silent and ill at ease with me. No casino, no tour, no tea.

Appointment with Kolb in the morning. Himmer, who dropped in, seemed impressed. "Kid," he said, "this is your big chance."

JUNE 4—Kolb strikes me as a man who knows what he wants and how to get it. He is a short man, conscious of his shortness. He stands on his toes when he talks, for the sake of the height, and punches out his words.

It seems I have to take a special course of instruction with him before he will put me to work. We spent an hour today in friendly conversation, mainly an autobiographical sketch of Kolb, together with lessons drawn therefrom for my own advantage. I'm to return to his office after the weekend.

Coleman passed me and didn't speak.

JUNE 6—Today Kolb described his system to me. You start off with a premise.

"Just for the sake of example," he said, "you take a girl who always screams when she sees a milkman. See, she's got a grudge against the milkman because a dearly beloved pet dog was once run over by a milk truck." Something like that—good comedy situation. Only, you must first invent a springboard. This is the scene which starts the picture, and Kolb wants it intriguing, even mystifying. "I'm not afraid of any man, big or small," he said, "but I shake in my boots when that skinny little guy in the movie theater begins to reach under his seat for his hat." The function of the springboard is to hold the skinny man in his seat. "For example, purely for example, suppose we show the boy when the picture opens. See, he's walking into the Automat.[9] He goes to the cake slot. He puts in two nickels or three nickels, as the case may be. The slot opens and out comes—the girl! Is that interesting? Will the skinny guy take his hat? No, he wants to know how that girl got there and what's going to happen now."

Kolb started to continue with the complications his springboard made possible, but was still fascinated by the Automat girl. He considered for a while and then said, "What the hell. It's nuts!" Then he seemed to lose interest in the lesson. "Listen," he finally said, "the best way to know what I want is to see the actual products. You go down and see the stuff I've made." He told his secretary to make arrangements.

JUNE 7—Kolb's secretary sent me to a projection room, where I was shown three of his pictures. I understand what Kolb means by springboards. His pictures all begin very well, sometimes with shock, but the rest of the plot is a mess because it has to justify the outrageous beginning.

JUNE 8—Kolb's secretary phoned and told me I was to see three more Kolb *opera*.[1] I sit all by myself in a projection room, thinking of Ludwig of Bavaria[2] in his exclusive theater, and feeling grand too.

What impresses me is the extent to which these pictures duplicate themselves, not only in the essential material, but in many details of character, gags, plot, etc.

JUNE 9—Three more pictures today.

9. A now-defunct chain of inexpensive New York City restaurants in which customers served themselves by inserting coins in mechanical display cases in order to withdraw food.

1. Works (Latin).

2. A king of Bavaria (1845–1886) and patron of the composer Richard Wagner.

JUNE 10—More Kolb masterpieces. He has been in movies for twenty years and must have made a hundred pictures.

JUNE 14—Today I was rescued from the projection room and was put to work. Kolb really shone with enthusiasm for the assignment he was giving me.

His idea was to rewrite a picture he did two years ago called *Dreams at Twilight*. If it pulled them in once, he said, then it would pull them in again. *Dreams at Twilight* involved a dashing, lighthearted hero who was constantly being chased by a flippant-minded girl. The hero deeply loved the girl, but avoided her because he was prejudiced against matrimony. "Sweet premise," Kolb said. "It's got charm, see what I mean?"

In addition to outwitting the heroine, the hero is fully occupied in the course of the picture: He is a detective and has a murder to solve.

"Now," Kolb said, "we remake the picture. *But*—instead of having the dashing boy detective, we make it a dashing girl this time. In other words, we make the picture in reverse. How's that for a new twist?"

He stood back in triumph and regarded my face for shock.

"Know why I'm changing the roles?" He whispered. His whole manner suddenly became wickedly secretive. "This picture is for Francine Waldron!"

I began to tremble gently, not because Waldron was one of the three most important actresses in Hollywood but because Kolb's mood was contagious and I had to respond as a matter of common politeness. When he saw the flush of excitement deepen on my face, he sent me off to work. He told his secretary to put me on his budget.

JUNE 15—I finished a rough outline of the Waldron script, working hard on it—nine to five, and no drifting about the lot. It's a bare sketch but I'd like to get Kolb's reaction to it before going ahead. His secretary, however, told me Mr. Kolb was all tied up at the moment.

I'm going ahead, filling in the outline rather than waste the time.

JUNE 18—Phoned Kolb's secretary, but he's still busy.

That peculiar feeling of dreamy suspension is very strong with me lately.

JUNE 20—*Hollywood Reporter*[3] notes that Kolb has bought a property called *Nothing for a Dime*. It is described as a story in which a girl plays the part of a debonair detective, usually assigned to a man.

What's going on?

JUNE 21—Finished a forty-page treatment of the Waldron script and asked Kolb's secretary to show this to him, since he couldn't see me. She said he would get it immediately, and would let me know very shortly.

JUNE 22—Begins nothing again.

JUNE 23—Nothing.

JUNE 24—Frank Coleman dropped in for casino—a depressing sign.

JUNE 25—Barry, of the front office, called me in for a long personal interview. He told me that I was respected as a fine, serious writer, held in high regard. Was everything—office accommodations—suitable in every way? Then he said that the studio was putting me entirely on my own, allowing me to work without restrictions or supervision. The point was, I was an artist and could work without shackles.

3. A newspaper that, like *Variety*, concentrates on aspects of the entertainment industry.

At this point I interrupted and told him about the script I had written for Kolb.

"Kolb?" Barry asked. "Who says you're working for Kolb? He hasn't got you listed as one of his writers. You've been marked 'available' for twenty-four days now."

Nevertheless, I insisted that the story editor had sent me to Kolb, I had worked for him, and was waiting to see what he thought of my story. Barry didn't understand it. "Okay," he said uncertainly. "I'll see Kolb at once and clear this all up."

More and more confusing. What impresses me, though, is that I don't feel bewildered or affected in any way. It's as though I'm not the one who's concerned here. Other days, other places, I should have been, to put it mildly, raving. However, I did phone Himmer, my agent. He heard me out and said he would scout around and that I was not to worry.

JUNE 29—Barry phoned. He had seen Kolb and Kolb didn't like my script. Would I please get to work on my unrestricted, unsupervised assignment?

I didn't know quite how to begin on a thing like that and so I decided to make a beginning after the weekend. Went to the commissary for a soda and bumped into Kolb himself, coming out. He beamed kindly at me. "Kid, I know what it is to wait around," he said. "I'm awfully busy at the moment but sooner or later I'll get around to reading your script." He patted my shoulder and left.

JUNE 30—Himmer dropped in. "About that Kolb," he said. "I picked up the inside story. See, what it was was this: When Kolb came to put you on his budget he called up to find out what your salary was. That's how he found out you get two hundred."

"So?"

"So. Kolb figures he deserves the best writers on the lot. He told them he wouldn't put up with any two-hundred-dollar trash. It's a natural reaction."

We both sat there a while, passing time and talking about the administration in Washington.

"By the way," Himmer asked, "what kind of story did Kolb have you work on?"

"A business for Francine Waldron."

Himmer laughed genially. "Waldron has no commitments on this lot. She doesn't work here, you know."

We both laughed pleasantly at the strange mind Kolb had and what went on in it.

JULY 1—Nothing worth noting.

JULY 12—I asked Coleman over casino how the front office told you that you were fired. "They don't tell you," Coleman said. "They're supposed to pick up options two weeks before the contract expires. If they don't, they don't. That's all."

The two-week period with me began some days ago.

JULY 14—I keep coming to work although I understand this isn't really necessary. But it's pleasant to see the boys, who are touching in their solicitude for me.

JULY 15—I came to work at ten-thirty this morning and found a genial, eager chap sitting at my desk in his shirt sleeves. "There must be some mistake," he stammered. "I'm new here. They told me to take this office."

I assured him there was no mistake. He seemed to be a fine fellow, sincere and impatient to start work. We sat around and chatted for an hour or so. While I cleaned up my desk, he had the embarrassed tact to leave me alone.

1979

EDWIN ROLFE
1909–1954

Edwin Rolfe, born in New York City as Solomon Fishman, was the son of Russian immigrants. Since his father was a socialist and a union official, his mother a member of the Communist party, the family scene was rife with political discussion and argument. Like many radicals of the period, Rolfe changed his name ostensibly to something more "American"-sounding so that he could be more effective in working with and organizing his fellow Americans.

Rolfe joined the Communist party in 1925 at the age of fifteen and quit in 1929 when he attended the University of Wisconsin. He later rejoined the party in New York and worked full time for its newspaper, the *Daily Worker*. He is the author of three published books and of unpublished, uncollected poems. According to scholar Cary Nelson, he is the writer whom "Americans who fought in the Spanish Civil War regard as their poet laureate." His book of poems about that war is *First Love and Other Poems* (1951); an earlier volume is *To My Contemporaries* (1936) and is about the depression; a later one is *Permit Me Refuge* (1955), about the McCarthy era.

His poem *Epitaph* was written on July 30, 1938, three days after Arnold Reid, a political commissar in the Abraham Lincoln Battalion whom he had known at the University of Wisconsin, was killed in Spain. Rolfe wrote the elegy on the spot where Reid was killed but never mentions his birth name, Arnold Reisky, or that Reid, like Rolfe and about nine hundred other volunteers in the 2,900-man battalion, was a Jew. *Elegia* was much admired by Rolfe's friend Ernest Hemingway. It contains an echo of the ancient Jewish lament and reverence for a lost Jerusalem. In Rolfe's poem, Madrid is the holy city because of the fierce struggle put up in its defense against Franco, and may his right arm wither if he forgets it! Surely, the ancient Jewish passion for justice and, in the 1930s, the heightened Jewish awareness of the menace of fascism contributed to his dedication to the cause of the Spanish Republic—and to a political party that was to prove unworthy of his and others' passion and sacrifices.

Epitaph

FOR ARNOLD REID[1]
D. JULY 27, 1938
AT VILLALBA DE LOS ARCOS

Deep in this earth,
deeper than grave was dug
ever, or body of man ever lowered,

1. A friend of Rolfe's from college, killed in Spain as a volunteer in the Abraham Lincoln Battalion.

runs my friend's blood,
spilled here. We buried him
here where he fell,
here where the sniper's eye
pinned him, and everything
in a simple moment's
quick explosion of pain was over.

Seven feet by three
measured the trench we dug,
ample for body of man ever murdered.
Now in this earth his blood
spreads through far crevices,
limitless, nourishing vineyards for miles around,
olive groves slanted on hillocks, trees
green with young almonds, purple with ripe figs,
and fields no enemy's boots
can ever desecrate.

This is no grave,
no, nor a resting place.
This is the plot where the self-growing seed
sends its fresh fingers to turn soil aside,
over and under earth ceaselessly growing,
over and under earth endlessly growing.

July 30, 1938
Villalba de los Arcos 1951

Elegia

Madrid Madrid Madrid Madrid
I call your name endlessly, savor it like a lover.
Ten irretrievable years have exploded like bombs
since last I saw you, since last I slept
in your arms of tenderness and wounded granite.
Ten years since I touched your face in the sun,
ten years since the homeless Guadarrama[1] winds
moaned like shivering orphans through your veins
and I moaned with them.
When I think of you, Madrid,
locked in the bordello of the Universal Pimp,[2]
the blood that rushes to my heart and head
blinds me, and I could strangle your blood-bespattered jailors,
choke them with these two hands which once embraced you.
When I think of your breathing body of vibrancy and sun,
silently I weep, in my own native land
which I love no less because I love you more.

1. A mountain range north of Madrid, beyond which was Fascist-controlled territory, the scene of much fighting during the Spanish Civil War.

2. I.e., General Francisco Franco (1892–1975), leader of the rebel forces; after the war, dictator of Spain until his death.

Yet I know, in the heart of my heart, that until your liberation
rings through the world of free men near and far
I must wander like an alien everywhere.

Madrid, in these days of our planet's anguish,
forged by the men whose mock morality
begins and ends with the tape of the stock exchanges,
I too sometimes despair. I weep with your dead young poet.
Like him I curse our age and cite the endless wars,
the exiles, dangers, fears, our weariness
of blood, and blind survival, when so many
homes, wives, even memories, are lost.

Yes, I weep with Garcilaso.[3] I remember
your grave face and your subtle smile
and the heart-leaping beauty of your daughters and even
the tattered elegance of your poorest sons.
I remember the gaiety of your *milicianos*[4]—
my comrades-in-arms. What other city
in history ever raised a battalion of barbers
or reared its own young shirt-sleeved generals?
And I recall them all. If I ever forget you,
Madrid, Madrid, may my right hand lose its cunning.[5]

I speak to you, Madrid, as lover, husband, son.
Accept this human trinity of passion.
I love you, therefore I am faithful to you
and because to forget you would be to forget
everything I love and value in the world.
Who is not true to you is false to every man[6]
and he to whom your name means nothing never loved
and they who would use your flesh and blood again
as a whore for their wars and their wise investments,
may they be doubly damned! the double murderers
of you and their professed but fictional honor,
of everything untarnished in our time.

Wandering, bitter, in this bitter age,
I dream of your broad avenues like brooks in summer
with your loveliest children alive in them like trout.
In my memory I walk the Calle de Velasquez
to the green Retiro and its green gardens.
Sometimes when I pace the streets of my own city
I am transported to the flowing Alcalá
and my footsteps quicken, I hasten to the spot
where all your living streams meet the Gateway to the Sun.
Sometimes I brood in the shadowed Plaza Mayor[7]

3. I.e., Garcilaso de la Vega (1503–1536), a poet and soldier.
4. A militia made up of Spanish volunteers fighting for the government (loyalist) side.
5. An echo of Psalms 137.5. The poet substitutes Madrid for Jerusalem.
6. An echo of Polonius's speech in *Hamlet* 1.3.78–80.
7. The main square in the city. It is very old and was once the site of public executions and of bullfights but is now filled with pleasant shops and cafés. "Calle de Velasquez" a main street in the

with the ghosts of old Kings and Inquisitors
agitating the balconies with their idiot stares
(which Goya[8] later knew) and under whose stone arches,
those somber rooms beneath the colonnades,
the old watchmaker dreams of tiny, intricate minutes,
the old woman sells pencils and gaudy amber combs,
dreaming of the days when her own body was young,
and the rheumatic peasant with fingers gnarled as grapevines
eagerly displays his muscat raisins;
and the intense boys of ten, with smouldering aged eyes,
kneel, and gravely, quixotically,
polish the rawhide boots of the soldiers in for an hour
from the mined trenches of the Casa de Campo,
from their posts, buzzing with death, within the skeleton
of University City.[9]
And the girls stroll by,
the young ones, conscious of their womanhood,
and I hear in my undying heart called Madrid
the soldiers boldly calling to them: Oye, guapa, oye![1]

I remember your bookshops, the windows always crowded
with new editions of the Gypsy Ballads,
with *Poetas en la España Leal*
and *Romanceros de los Soldados en las Trincheras.*[2]
There was never enough food, but always poetry.
Ah the flood of song that gushed with your blood
into the world during your three years of glory!

And I think: it is a fine thing to be a man
only when man has dignity and manhood.
It is a fine thing to be proud and fearless
only when pride and courage have direction, meaning.
And in our world no prouder words were spoken
in those three agonized years than *I am from Madrid.*

Now ten years have passed with small explosions of hope,
yet you remain, Madrid, the conscience of our lives.
So long as you endure, in chains, in sorrow,
I am not free, no one of us is free.
Any man in the world who does not love Madrid
as he loves a woman, as she values his sex,
that man is less than a man and dangerous,
and so long as he directs the affairs of our world
I must be his undying enemy.

most elegant part of Madrid. "Retiro": a park within the city's gates, this one leading to the town of Alcalá. "Gateway to the Sun": Puerta del Sol in Spanish, a square in the center of the city near the Plaza Mayor.

8. I.e., Francisco de Goya y Lucientes (1746–1828), a great Spanish artist who produced, among many works, a series of prints, *The Disasters of War*, decrying the inhumanity of war.

9. The site of severe fighting in the Civil War. It is at the northwestern edge of Madrid and is the campus of the oldest university in the city. "Casa de Campo": literally, "countryside house" (Spanish), a park at the outskirts of Madrid.

1. Hey, beautiful, hey! (Spanish).

2. *Poets in Loyal Spain* and *Songs of the Soldiers in the Trenches* (Spanish).

Madrid Madrid Madrid Madrid
Waking and sleeping, your name sings in my heart
and your need fills all my thoughts and acts
(which are gentle but have also been intimate with rifles).
Forgive me, I cannot love you properly from afar—
no distant thing is ever truly loved—
but this, in the wrathful impotence of distance,
I promise: Madrid, if I ever forget you,
may my right hand lose its human cunning,
may my arm and legs wither in their sockets,
may my body be drained of its juices and my brain
go soft and senseless as an imbecile's.
And if I die before I can return to you,
or you, in fullest freedom, are restored to us,
my sons will love you as their father did
Madrid Madrid Madrid

November 6, 1948 1951

HORTENSE CALISHER
b. 1911

Hortense Calisher was born in New York City. Her father was from an old Virginia Jewish family, her mother a more recent German Jewish immigrant. Educated at Hunter College High School and Barnard College, Calisher worked as a social worker for the Department of Welfare and also, briefly, as a model. She married and had two children before establishing herself as a writer.

Calisher was the firstborn child of a man already approaching sixty; her family history goes back to before the Civil War through her father: his father had been "recorded 'elder' of the earliest Richmond synagogue in 1832." In *Kissing Cousins* (1988), a moving memoir, Calisher discusses the two important strands of her linguistic and cultural heritage, the southern and the Jewish—both American—and seems to exclude her mother's more recently arrived German Jewishness. About her own Jewishness, however, she has written: "That was satisfyingly in all of me, no more to be questioned than the body I walked around in." She attributes some of her sensitivity to the multifaceted nature of human speech, and her interest in distinguishing among its many kinds, to her early awareness of the differing ways in which people said, or suggested, what they meant: "Southern Jews . . . had . . . a double expressiveness . . . one could never be sure which end was up, Jehova or Jefferson Davis," and "It seemed to me that Southerners, like Jews, had a special talent for telling stories but, unlike Northerners, knew very well when not to believe them."

Calisher, who published the first of many *New Yorker* stories in 1948, turned to writing late, apparently plotting and planning her first published story in the midst of maternal duties: while walking her children to and from school. Her attitude toward feminist commitments in writing has been cool, not unlike that of some other women writers (Gertrude Stein, Katherine Anne Porter, Elizabeth Bishop) who rejected the suggestion of gender categorization and any hint of special pleading. In her own words: "I was never to be a conventional feminist, conventional thought is not for writers. . . . But I had always wanted to do a novel from within the female feelings I did have from youth, through motherhood and the wish for other creation." Thus, she wrote sympathetically, and in depth, about women's lives and concerns, and gave those themes their full value. Two novels, *False Entry* (1961) and *The New Yorkers* (1969), deal with the fall from fortune of a well-to-do New York Jewish family. In a reversal of the classic patriarchal pattern, daughter slays mother in the tragic 1969 fable.

Calisher has published some twenty books, held several Guggenheim fellowships, been nominated for three National Book Awards, and won the O. Henry Prize for short stories four times; in 1981, she edited (with Shannon Ravenel) *The Best American Short Stories*. She has taught at many colleges and universities, been president of PEN and of the American Academy of Arts and Letters. Her work includes short stories, novels, novellas, and science fiction written in a wide range of voices and manners. It has been highly valued by writers like Anne Tyler, Cynthia Ozick, and Joyce Carol Oates.

The Rabbi's Daughter

They all came along with Eleanor and her baby in the cab to Grand Central,[1] her father and mother on either side of her, her father holding the wicker bassinet on his carefully creased trousers. Rosalie and Helene, her cousins, smart in their fall ensembles, just right for the tingling October dusk, sat in the two little seats opposite them. Aunt Ruth, Dr. Ruth Brinn, her father's sister and no kin to the elegant distaff cousins, had insisted on sitting in front with the cabman. Eleanor could see her now, through the glass, in animated talk, her hat tilted piratically on her iron-gray braids.

Leaning forward, Eleanor studied the dim, above-eye-level picture of the driver. A sullen-faced young man, with a lock of black hair belligerent over his familiar nondescript face: "Manny Kaufman." What did Manny Kaufman think of Dr. Brinn? In ten minutes she would drag his life history from him, answering his unwilling statements with the snapping glance, the terse nods which showed that she got it all, at once, understood him down to the bone. At the end of her cross-questioning she would be quite capable of saying, "Young man, you are too pale! Get another job!"

"I certainly don't know why you wanted to wear that get-up," said Eleanor's mother, as the cab turned off the Drive[2] toward Broadway. "On a train. And with the baby to handle, all alone." She brushed imaginary dust from her lap, scattering disapproval with it. She had never had to handle her babies alone.

Eleanor bent over the basket before she answered. She was a thin fair girl whom motherhood had hollowed, rather than enhanced. Tucking the bottle-bag further in, feeling the wad of diapers at the bottom, she envied the baby blinking solemnly up at her, safe in its surely serviced world.

"Oh, I don't know," she said. "It just felt gala. New Yorkish. Some people dress down for a trip. Others dress up—like me." Staring at her own lap, though, at the bronze velveteen which had been her wedding dress, sensing the fur blob of hat insecure on her unprofessionally waved hair, shifting the

1. A large railroad terminal in midtown Manhattan in New York City.

2. Riverside Drive is a fashionable residential street on the Upper West Side of Manhattan.

shoes, faintly scuffed, which had been serving her for best for two years, she felt the sickening qualm, the frightful inner blush of the inappropriately dressed.

In front of her, half-turned toward her, the two cousins swayed neatly in unison, two high-nostriled gazelles, one in black, one in brown, both in pearls, wearing their propriety, their utter rightness, like skin. She had known her own excess when she had dressed for the trip yesterday morning, in the bare rooms, after the van had left, but her suits were worn, stretched with wearing during pregnancy, and nothing went with anything any more. Tired of house dresses, of the spotted habiliments of maternity, depressed with her three months' solitude in the country waiting out the lease after Dan went on to the new job, she had reached for the wedding clothes, seeing herself cleansed and queenly once more, mysterious traveler whose appearance might signify anything, approaching the pyrrhic towers of New York, its effervescent terminals, with her old brilliance, her old style.

Her father sighed. "Wish that boy could find a job nearer New York."

"You know an engineer has to go where the plants are," she said, weary of the old argument. "It's not like you—with your own business and everything. Don't you think I'd like . . . ?" She stopped, under Rosalie's bright, tallying stare.

"I know, I know." He leaned over the baby, doting.

"What's your new house like?" said Rosalie.

"You know," she said gaily, "after all Dan's letters, I'm not just sure, except that it's part of a two-family. They divide houses every which way in those towns. He's written about 'Bostons,' and 'flats,' and 'duplexes.' All I really know is it has automatic heat, thank goodness, and room for the piano." She clamped her lips suddenly on the hectic, chattering voice. Why had she had to mention the piano, especially since they were just passing Fifty-seventh Street, past Carnegie[3] with all its clustering satellites—the Pharmacy, the Playhouse, the Russian restaurant—and in the distance, the brindled windows of the galleries, the little chiffoned store fronts, spitting garnet and saffron light? All her old life smoked out toward her from these buildings, from this parrot-gay, music-scored street.

"Have you been able to keep up with your piano?" Helene's head cocked, her eyes screened.

"Not—not recently. But I'm planning a schedule. After we're settled." In the baby's nap time, she thought. When I'm not boiling formulas or wash. In the evenings, while Dan reads, if I'm only—just not too tired. With a constriction, almost of fear, she realized that she and Dan had not even discussed whether the family on the other side of the house would mind the practicing. That's how far I've come away from it, she thought, sickened.

"All that time spent." Her father stroked his chin with a scraping sound and shook his head, then moved his hand down to brace the basket as the cab swung forward on the green light.

My time, she thought, my life—your money, knowing her unfairness in the same moment, knowing it was only his devotion, wanting the best for her, which she deplored. Or, like her mother, did he mourn too the preening

3. Carnegie Hall is one of New York's premier concert halls.

pride in the accomplished daughter, the long build-up, Juilliard,[4] the feverish, relative-ridden Sunday afternoon recitals in Stengel's studio, the program at Town Hall,[5] finally, with her name, no longer Eleanor Goldman, but Elly Gold, truncated hopefully, euphoniously for the professional life to come, that had already begun to be, thereafter, in the first small jobs, warm notices?

As the cab rounded the corner of Fifth, she saw two ballerinas walking together, unmistakable with their dark Psyche knots over their fichus,[6] their sandaled feet angled outwards, the peculiar compensating tilt of their little strutting behinds. In that moment it was as if she had taken them all in at once, seen deep into their lives. There was a studio of them around the hall from Stengel's, and under the superficial differences the atmosphere in the two studios had been much the same: two tight, concentric worlds whose *aficionados*[7] bickered and endlessly discussed in their separate argots, whose students, glowing with the serious work of creation, were like trajectories meeting at the burning curve of interest.

She looked at the cousins with a dislike close to envy, because they neither burned nor were consumed.[8] They would never throw down the fixed cards. Conformity would protect them. They would marry for love if they could; if not, they would pick, prudently, a candidate who would never remove them from the life to which they were accustomed. Mentally they would never even leave Eighty-sixth Street, and their homes would be like their mothers', like her mother's, *bibelots*[9] suave on the coffee tables, bonbon dishes full, but babies postponed until they could afford to have them born at Doctors Hospital. "After all the money Uncle Harry spent on her, too," they would say later in mutually confirming gossip. For to them she would simply have missed out on the putative glory of the prima donna; that it was the work she missed would be out of their ken.

The cab swung into the line of cars at the side entrance to Grand Central. Eleanor bent over the basket and took out the baby. "You take the basket, Dad." Then, as if forced by the motion of the cab, she reached over and thrust the bundle of baby onto Helene's narrow brown crepe lap, and held it there until Helene grasped it diffidently with her suede gloves.

"She isn't—she won't wet, will she?" said Helene.

A porter opened the door. Eleanor followed her mother and father out and then reached back into the cab. "I'll take her now." She stood there hugging the bundle, feeling it close, a round comforting cyst of love and possession.

Making her way through the snarled mess of traffic on the curb, Aunt Ruth came and stood beside her. "Remember what I told you!" she called to the departing driver, wagging her finger at him.

"What did you tell him?" said Eleanor.

"Huh! What I told him!" Her aunt shrugged, the blunt Russian shrug of inevitability, her shrewd eyes ruminant over the outthrust chin, the spread

4. The Juilliard School of Music, located in New York City, is one of the nation's best.
5. A concert and lecture hall located in midtown Manhattan.
6. Triangular shaped shawls draped over the shoulders (French). "Psyche knots": a way of knotting the hair, after illustrations of Psyche from Greek mythology.
7. Fans, devotees, or experts of a sport, art, or profession (Spanish).
8. A reference to the burning bush in the Bible, which God causes to burn but not be consumed.
9. Small decorative objects (French).

hands. "Can I fix life? Life in Brooklyn on sixty dollars a week? I'm only a medical doctor!" She pushed her hat forward on her braids. "Here! Give me that baby!" She whipped the baby from Eleanor's grasp and held it with authority, looking speculatively at Eleanor. "Go on! Walk ahead with them!" She grinned. "Don't I make a fine nurse? Expensive, too!"

Down at the train, Eleanor stood at the door of the roomette while the other women, jammed inside, divided their ardor for the miniature between the baby and the telescoped comforts of the cubicle. At the end of the corridor, money and a pantomime of cordiality passed between her father and the car porter. Her father came back down the aisle, solid gray man, refuge of childhood, grown shorter than she. She stared down at his shoulder, rigid, her eyes unfocused, restraining herself from laying her head upon it.

"All taken care of," he said. "He's got the formula in the icebox and he'll take care of getting you off in the morning. Wish you could have stayed longer, darling." He pressed an envelope into her hand. "Buy yourself something. Or the baby." He patted her shoulder. "No . . . now never mind now. This is between you and me."

"Guess we better say good-bye, dear," said her mother, emerging from the roomette with the others. Doors slammed, passengers swirled around them. They kissed in a circle, nibbling and diffident.

Aunt Ruth did not kiss her, but took Eleanor's hands and looked at her, holding on to them. She felt her aunt's hands moving softly on her own. The cousins watched brightly.

"What's this, what's this?" said her aunt. She raised Eleanor's hands, first one, then the other, as if weighing them in a scale, rubbed her own strong, diagnostic thumb back and forth over Eleanor's right hand, looking down at it. They all looked down at it. It was noticeably more spatulate, coarser-skinned than the left, and the middle knuckles were thickened.

"So . . . ," said her aunt. "So-o . . . ," and her enveloping stare had in it that warmth, tinged with resignation, which she offered indiscriminately to cabmen, to nieces, to life. "So . . . , the 'rabbi's daughter'[1] is washing dishes!" And she nodded, in requiem.

"Prescription?" said Eleanor, smiling wryly back.

"No prescription!" said her aunt. "In my office I see hundreds of girls like you. And there is no little pink pill to fit." She shrugged, and then whirled on the others. "Come. Come on." They were gone, in a last-minute flurry of ejaculations. As the train began to wheel past the platform, Eleanor caught a blurred glimpse of their faces, her parents and aunt in anxious trio, the two cousins neatly together.

People were still passing by the door of the roomette, and a woman in one group paused to admire the baby, frilly in the delicately lined basket, "Ah, look!" she cooed. "Sweet! How old is she?"

"Three months."

"It *is* a she?"

Eleanor nodded.

"Sweet!" the woman said again, shaking her head admiringly, and went on down the aisle. Now the picture was madonna-perfect, Eleanor knew—the

1. In folk tradition, a rabbi's daughter is privileged in not having to get her hands worn by the toil common to other women.

harsh, tintype lighting centraled down on her and the child, glowing in the viscous paneling that was grained to look like wood, highlighted in the absurd plush-cum-metal fixtures of this sedulously planned manger. She shut the door.

The baby began to whimper. She made it comfortable for the night, diapering it quickly, clipping the pins in the square folds, raising the joined ankles in a routine that was like a jigging ballet of the fingers. Only after she had made herself ready for the night, hanging the dress quickly behind a curtain, after she had slipped the last prewarmed bottle out of its case and was holding the baby close as it fed, watching the three-cornered pulse of the soft spot winking in and out on the downy head—only then did she let herself look closely at her two hands.

The difference between them was not enough to attract casual notice, but enough, when once pointed out, for anyone to see. She remembered Stengel's strictures on practicing with the less able left one. "Don't think you can gloss over, Miss. It shows!" But that the scrubbing hand, the working hand, would really "show" was her first intimation that the daily makeshift could become cumulative, could leave its imprint on the flesh with a crude symbolism as dully real, as conventionally laughable, as the first wrinkle, the first gray hair.

She turned out the light and stared into the rushing dark. The physical change was nothing, she told herself, was easily repaired; what she feared almost to phrase was the death by postponement, the slow uneventful death of impulse. "Hundreds of girls like you," she thought, fearing for the first time the compromises that could arrive upon one unaware, not in the heroic renunciations, but erosive, gradual, in the slow chip-chipping of circumstance. Outside the window the hills of the Hudson Valley loomed and receded, rose up, piled, and slunk again into foothills. For a long time before she fell asleep she probed the dark for their withdrawing shapes, as if drama and purpose receded with them.

In the morning the porter roused her at six, returning an iced bottle of formula, and one warmed and made ready. She rose with a granular sense of return to the real, which lightened as she attended to the baby and dressed. Energized, she saw herself conquering whatever niche Dan had found for them, revitalizing the unknown house as she had other houses, with all the artifices of her New York chic, squeezing ragouts from the tiny salary spent cagily at the A & P,[2] enjoying the baby instead of seeing her in the groggy focus of a thousand tasks. She saw herself caught up at odd hours in the old exaltation of practice, even if they had to hire a mute piano, line a room with cork. Nothing was impossible to the young, bogey-dispersing morning.

The station ran past the window, such a long one, sliding through the greasy lemon-colored lights, that she was almost afraid they were not going to stop, or that it was the wrong one, until she saw Dan's instantly known contour, jointed, thin, and his face, raised anxiously to the train windows with the vulnerability of people who do not know they are observed. She saw him for a minute as other passengers, brushing their teeth hastily in the

2. Abbreviation for the Great Atlantic and Pacific Tea Company, which has a chain of grocery stores in major American cities known as A & Ps.

washrooms, might look out and see him, a young man, interesting because he was alone on the platform, a nice young man in a thick jacket and heavy work pants, with a face full of willingness and anticipation. Who would get off for him?

As she waited in the jumble of baggage at the car's end, she warned herself that emotion was forever contriving toward moments which, when achieved, were not single and high as they ought to have been, but often splintered slowly—just walked away on the little centrifugal feet of detail. She remembered how she had mulled before their wedding night, how she had been unable to see beyond the single devouring picture of their two figures turning, turning toward one another. It had all happened, it had all been there, but memory could not recall it so, retaining instead, with the pedantic fidelity of some poet whose interminable listings recorded obliquely the face of the beloved but never invoked it, a whole rosary of irrelevancies, in the telling of which the two figures merged and were lost. Again she had the sense of life pushing her on by minute, imperceptible steps whose trend would not be discerned until it was too late, as the tide might encroach upon the late swimmer, making a sea of the sand he left behind.

"Dan!" she called. "Dan!"

He ran toward her. She wanted to run too, to leap out of the hemming baggage and fall against him, rejoined. Instead, she and the bags and the basket were jockeyed off the platform by the obsequious porter, and she found herself on the gray boards of the station, her feet still rocking with the leftover rhythm of the train, holding the basket clumsily between her and Dan, while the train washed off hoarsely behind them. He took the basket from her, set it down, and they clung and kissed, but in all that ragged movement, the moment subdivided and dispersed.

"Good Lord, how big she is!" he said, poking at the baby with a shy, awkward hand.

"Mmm. Tremendous!" They laughed together, looking down.

"Your shoes—what on earth?" she said. They were huge, laced to the ankle, the square tips inches high, like blocks of wood on the narrow clerkly feet she remembered.

"Safety shoes. You have to wear them around a foundry. Pretty handy if a casting drops on your toe."

"Very swagger." She smiled up at him, her throat full of all there was to tell—how, in the country, she had spoken to no one but the groceryman for so long that she had begun to monologue to the baby; how she had built up the first furnace fire piece by piece, crouching before it in awe and a sort of pride, hoping, as she shifted the damper chains, that she was pulling the right one; how the boy who was to mow the lawn had never come, and how at last she had taken a scythe to the knee-deep, insistent grass and then grimly, jaggedly, had mown. But now, seeing his face dented with fatigue, she saw too his grilling neophyte's day at the foundry, the evenings when he must have dragged hopefully through ads and houses, subjecting his worn wallet and male ingenuousness to the soiled witcheries of how many landlords, of how many narrow-faced householders tipping back in their porch chairs, patting tenderly at their bellies, who would suck at their teeth and look him over. "You permanent here, mister?" Ashamed of her city-bred heroisms, she said nothing.

"You look wonderful," he said. "Wonderful."

"Oh." She looked down. "A far cry from."

"I borrowed a car from one of the men, so we can go over in style." He swung the basket gaily under one arm. "Let's have breakfast first, though."

"Yes, let's." She was not eager to get to the house.

They breakfasted in a quick-lunch place on the pallid, smudged street where the car was parked, and she waited, drinking a second cup of coffee from a grainy white mug while Dan went back to the station to get the trunk. The mug had an indistinct blue V on it in the middle of a faded blue line running around the rim; it had probably come secondhand from somewhere else. The fork she had used had a faint brassiness showing through its nickel-colored tines and was marked "Hotel Ten Eyck, Albany," although this was not Albany. Even the restaurant, on whose white, baked look the people made gray transient blurs which slid and departed, had the familiar melancholy which pervaded such places because they were composed everywhere, in a hundred towns, of the same elements, but were never lingered in or personally known. This town would be like that too; one would be able to stand in the whirling center of the five-and-dime[3] and fancy oneself in a score of other places where the streets had angled perhaps a little differently and the bank had been not opposite the post office, but a block down. There would not even be a need for fancy because, irretrievably here, one was still in all the resembling towns, and going along these streets one would catch oneself nodding to faces known surely, plumbed at a glance, since these were overtones of faces in all the other towns that had been and were to be.

They drove through the streets, which raised an expectation she knew to be doomed, but cherished until it should be dampened by knowledge. Small houses succeeded one another, gray, coffee-colored, a few white ones, many with two doors and two sets of steps.

"Marlborough Road," she said. "My God."

"Ours is Ravenswood Avenue."

"No!"

"Slicker!" he said. "Ah, darling, I can't believe you're here." His free arm tightened and she slid down on his shoulder. The car made a few more turns, stopped in the middle of a block, and was still.

The house, one of the white ones, had two close-set doors, but the two flights of steps were set at opposite ends of the ledge of porch, as if some craving for a privacy but doubtfully maintained within had leaked outside. Hereabouts, in houses with the cramped deadness of diagrams, was the special ugliness created by people who would keep themselves a toehold above the slums by the exercise of a terrible, ardent neatness which had erupted into the foolish or the grotesque—the two niggling paths in the common driveway, the large trellis arching pompously over nothing. On Sundays they would emerge, the fathers and mothers, dressed soberly, even threadbare, but dragging children outfitted like angelic visitants from the country of the rich, in poke bonnets and suitees of pink and mauve, larded triumphantly with fur.

3. A retail store that sells a variety of inexpensive items.

As Dan bent over the lock of one of the doors, he seemed to her like a man warding off a blow.

"Is the gas on?" she said hurriedly. "I've got one more bottle."

He nodded. "It heats with gas, you know. That's why I took it. They have cheap natural gas up here." He pushed the door open, and the alien, anti-people smell of an empty house came out toward them.

"I know. You said. Wait till I tell you about me and the furnace in the other place." Her voice died away as, finally, they were inside.

He put the basket on the floor beside him. "Well," he said, "this am it."

"Why, there's the sofa!" she said. "It's so funny to see everything—just two days ago in Erie, and now here." Her hand delayed on the familiar pillows, as if on the shoulder of a friend. Then, although a glance had told her that no festoonings of the imagination were going to change this place, there was nothing to do but look.

The door-cluttered box in which they stood predicated a three-piece "suite" and no more. In the center of its mustard woodwork and a wallpaper like cold cereal, two contorted pedestals supported less the ceiling than the status of the room. Wedged in without hope of rearrangement, her own furniture had an air of outrage, like social workers who had come to rescue a hovel and had been confronted, instead, with the proud glare of mediocrity.

She returned the room's stare with an enmity of her own. Soon I will get to know you the way a woman gets to know a house—where the baseboards are roughest, and in which corners the dust drifts—the way a person knows the blemishes of his own skin. But just now I am still free of you—still a visitor.

"Best I could do." The heavy shoes clumped, shifting.

"It'll be all right," she said. "You wait and see." She put her palms on his shoulders. "It just looked queer for a minute, with windows only on one side." She heard her own failing voice with dislike, quirked it up for him. "Half chick. That's what it is. Half-chick house!"

"Crazy!" But some of the strain left his face.

"Uh-huh, *Das Ewig Weibliche*,[4] that's me!" She half pirouetted. "Dan!" she said. "Dan, where's the piano?"

"Back of you. We had to put it in the dinette. I thought we could eat in the living room anyway."

She opened the door. There it was, filling the box room, one corner jutting into the entry to the kitchenette. Tinny light, whitening down from a meager casement, was recorded feebly on its lustrous flanks. Morning and evening she would edge past it, with the gummy dishes and the clean. Immobile, in its cage, it faced her, a great dark harp lying on its side.

"Play something, for luck." Dan came up behind her, the baby bobbing on his shoulder.

She shook her head.

"Ah, come on." His free arm cinched the three of them in a circle, so that the baby participated in their kiss. The baby began to cry.

"See," she said. "We better feed her."

"I'll warm the bottle. Have to brush up on being a father." He nudged his

4. The eternally feminine (German). Johann Wolfgang von Goethe (1749–1832) uses the phrase in *Faust* 2.5 as that which draws us upward and onward.

way through the opening. She heard him rummaging in a carton, then the clinking of a pot.

She opened the lid of the piano and struck the A, waiting until the tone had died away inside her, then struck a few more notes. The middle register had flattened first, as it always did. Sitting down on the stool, she looked into her lap as if it belonged to someone else. What was the piano doing here, this opulent shape of sound, five hundred miles from where it was the day before yesterday; what was she doing here, sitting in the lopped-off house, in the dress that had been her wedding dress, listening to the tinkle of a bottle against a pan? What was the mystery of distance—that it was not only geographical but clove through the map, into the heart?

She began to play, barely flexing her fingers, hearing the nails she had let grow slip and click on the keys. Then, thinking of the entities on the other side of the wall, she began to play softly, placating, as if she would woo them, the town, providence. She played a Beethoven andante with variations, then an adagio, seeing the Von Bülow footnotes[5] before her: ". . . the ascending diminished fifth may be phrased, as it were, like a question, to which the succeeding bass figure may be regarded as the answer."

The movement finished but she did not go on to the scherzo.[6] Closing the lid, she put her head down on her crossed arms. Often, on the fringes of concerts, there were little haunting crones of women who ran up afterward to horn in on the congratulatory shoptalk of the players. She could see one of them now, batting her stiff claws together among her fluttering draperies, nodding eagerly for notice: "I studied . . . I played too, you know . . . years ago . . . with De Pachmann!"[7]

So many variants of the same theme, she thought, so many of them—the shriveled, talented women. Distance has nothing to do with it; be honest—they are everywhere. Fifty-seventh Street is full of them. The women who were once "at the League,"[8] who cannot keep themselves from hanging the paintings, the promising *juvenilia*,[9] on their walls, but who flinch, deprecating, when one notices. The quondam writers, chary of ridicule, who sometimes, over wine, let themselves be persuaded into bringing out a faded typescript, and to whom there is never anything to say, because it is so surprisingly good, so fragmentary, and was written—how long ago? She could still hear the light insistent note of the A, thrumming unresolved, for herself, and for all the other girls. A man, she thought jealously, can be reasonably certain it was his talent which failed him, but the women, for whom there are still so many excuses, can never be so sure.

"You're tired." Dan returned, stood behind her.

She shook her head, staring into the shining case of the piano, wishing that she could retreat into it somehow and stay there huddled over its strings, like those recalcitrant nymphs whom legend immured in their native wood or water, but saved.

5. Hans von Bülow (1830–1894) was a German pianist and conductor who edited the works of Beethoven.
6. Literally, "joke" (Italian); a sprightly, humorous musical composition or movement.
7. Vladimir de Pachman (1848–1933) was a Russian pianist famous as a performer of Chopin.
8. I.e., Art Students League.
9. Works produced in one's youth (Latin).

"I have to be back at the plant at eleven." He was smiling uncertainly, balancing the baby and the bottle.

She put a finger against his cheek, traced the hollows under his eyes. "I'll soon fatten you up," she murmured, and held out her arms to receive the baby and the long, coping day.

"Won't you crush your dress? I can wait till you change."

"No." She heard her own voice, sugared viciously with wistfulness. "Once I change I'll be settled. As long as I keep it on . . . I'm still a visitor."

Silenced, he passed her the baby and the bottle.

This will have to stop, she thought. Or will the denied half of me persist, venomously arranging for the ruin of the other? She wanted to warn him standing there, trusting, in the devious shadow of her resentment.

The baby began to pedal its feet and cry, a long nagging ululation. She sprinkled a few warm drops of milk from the bottle on the back of her own hand. It was just right, the milk, but she sat on, holding the baby in her lap, while the drops cooled. Flexing the hand, she suddenly held it out gracefully, airily, regarding it.

"This one is still 'the rabbi's daughter,' " she said. Dan looked down at her, puzzled. She shook her head, smiling back at him, quizzical and false, and bending, pushed the nipple in the baby's mouth. At once it began to suck greedily, gazing back at her with the intent, agate eyes of satisfaction.

1953

PAUL GOODMAN
1911–1972

The author of some forty books, including six novels, four collections of short stories, several volumes of poetry, and eighteen plays, Paul Goodman made his greatest impact with two nonliterary works in the early 1960s: *Growing Up Absurd: Problems of Youth in the Organized System* (1960) and *Compulsory Mis-Education* (1964). Sections of these books critical of the repressive aspects of American society from Goodman's philosophically anarchist and sexually permissive position were published in *Commentary* (as well as in the *Partisan Review*)—the high-water mark of that journal's once liberal position. The ideas (and Goodman) were taken up in the surge of the 1960s youth rebellion against the Vietnam War and many aspects of the bourgeois state, family, and institutions. Despite his short-lived notoriety, Goodman always considered himself an outsider—in a state of perpetual "exile" more extreme than was usual, even among the other New York intellectuals of his generation.

Born in New York City's Greenwich Village to immigrant parents from Eastern Europe, Goodman grew up poor; his father abandoned the family when Paul was an infant. He received a Hebrew school education, was first in his class at the elite Townsend Harris High School, attended the City College of New York (graduating in 1931 with highest honors).

At CCNY, he had been influenced by the philosopher Morris Raphael Cohen and went on to earn a Ph.D. in philosophy at the University of Chicago (after a brief stay at Columbia). He wrote an Aristotelian dissertation, later published, on the structures of literature. Besides Aristotle and his Chicago professors, another key influence on him was the anarchist thinker Pyotr Alekseyevich Kropotkin, especially the Russian's belief in decentralized nonauthoritarian social forms as the basis for a humane and liberated life. Goodman always refused to be intellectually pigeonholed, writing on a variety of subjects—he collaborated with his brother, professor of architecture Percival Goodman, on *Communitas* and with Fritz Perls and others in a pioneering study, *Gestalt Psychology*.

Goodman was openly bisexual, although married twice and the father of three children. The death of his son Matthew in a mountain-climbing accident in his beloved New Hampshire retreat was a blow late in his life from which he never recovered. His sexual proclivities led to several scandals and dismissals from teaching positions at Chicago, Black Mountain College, and elsewhere. In later years, he was a popular teacher and lecturer at Columbia, Sarah Lawrence College, the University of Wisconsin, Smith College, and many other schools.

Goodman's major fictional work is the four-part novel *The Empire City* (1959), which features the adventures of an improbable hero named Horatio Alger and his equally unlikely family and acquaintances as they make their way through New York and America of the 1940s and 1950s. The first part appeared in 1942, the last in 1957. The whole is a surreal compound of lectures, dialogues, theories of education and sexual development, the search for community, and the need for Gestalt therapy (he was also a therapist), dance, music, play, and much else. There is a wonderful section in the first book on how Horatio learns geography, math, and related subjects by negotiating the New York subway system.

For several years, Goodman was a Jewish summer-camp counselor—the background of his collection *The Break-Up of Our Camp and Other Stories* (1949), in which *A Memorial Synagogue* appears. The narrator of these stories returns to New York from the camp in Vermont, determined, despite his nonreligious radicalism, to advertise the opening of a synagogue memorializing the disasters of the Jews and all other people. The background is the Second World War, in which Goodman was a conscientious objector, and the Holocaust, whose full dimensions were scarcely known at the time of the story's composition. When urged to advocate a purely Jewish memorial, the narrator, Matthew, quotes Rabbi Hillel's "*Im ani l'otzmi, ma ani?*" (If I am only for myself, what am I?). Nevertheless, the solemnity and the people's tears at the end of the story, as architect, sculptor, and artist discuss the shape of the building, is as powerful and moving as anything Goodman ever wrote.

A Memorial Synagogue

> It is not incumbent on you to complete the work; but neither are you free to withdraw from it.
>
> —RABBI TARFON[1]

> We willingly commit some folly, just to live on a little.
>
> —GOETHE[2]

1

We three came to the city where, despite much busyness, there was little useful work; despite much art and entertainment, little joy; despite many

1. Important figure in early (late 1st–early 2d century C.E.) rabbinic Judaism. He established procedures for making legal decisions regarding the performance of religious obligations and emphasized the importance of deeds and actions over intention or subjective thought.
2. Johann Wolfgang von Goethe (1749–1832), a major German poet, dramatist, and essayist.

physical comforts, almost no sexual happiness; where among thousands of thousands there was almost not one person exercising most of his human powers, but every one pursued with earnest concentration some object not really to his advantage and which, perhaps fortunately for himself and us, he could not achieve. Yet such as it was! so I remembered my city from early childhood and I shared its ways; and Lord! I was glad to come back to it, as each time I come back.

Yet for conversation, we three exchanged only sighs. There were many fine things here and many distractions, but as it turned out, it was not possible for us to turn our minds to anything but recent disasters, unfinished disasters, wreck of our happiness both by our own stupidity and by compulsion, inextricably involved, both by commission and omission, with the many disasters of other people. The suggestion of any distraction decayed on our lips, but heaving each his own sighs we communicated with each other—the Canadian and Ostoric and I.

2

Also we—and I think many many others at this time—were simply *floundering*. (One cannot help saying that the young persons of the end of the first half of the century, those who have intellectual energy, are floundering.) Floundering: that is, willing to give ourselves, and *giving* ourselves, to what we *know* to be unlikely. It is not even a matter of faith, or of misplaced faith. But what would *you* do—just to live on a little?

3

We came to a crowded part of the city and at once began distributing our handbills.

The proposal of these bills was neither daring nor modest, but in the middle; it was what seemed appropriate to us in the circumstance that we could not succeed in turning our minds from the recent disasters.[3] The fact is that one *cannot* do nothing but sigh, without a more athletic and social exercise. But if the reader's response to our proposal is just to heave a tired sigh, that is not inappropriate.—

A PROJECTION,
IN HEAVY MATERIALS,
OF OUR GRIEF

The Jews ought to make, of heavy materials, of medium size, embellished by great artists, a synagogue dedicated to Grief for their own recent disasters and the disasters of all peoples

On corners of a busy intersection, we stood giving out these bills.

3. In 1935, when Goodman began the story, the Nazis had taken over Germany and were persecuting the Jews, stripping them step by step of their rights. By 1947, when the story was completed, the full horror of the Holocaust was known.

4

There are some persons who, when offered a free handbill, harden their jaws and stare stonily ahead, and will not take it. Sometimes they jam their hands defensively in their pockets, for the hand is naturally apt to give and take. The reasons for this behavior are obvious: those that spring from fear are contemptible, but those that spring from wounded dignity are not (in our city) contemptible. But what is disheartening is to see a young person behave in this way.

Other persons accept the bill by an absent-minded reflex or out of courtesy, but they at once repent and angrily throw the offending paper into the mud.

Now still others courteously put the paper in their pocket, unread, perhaps carefully folding it. This delaying behavior creates a relation of complicity, almost of conspiracy. The moment will come—one may imagine in what dramatic circumstances! a man after the fourth ineffectual drink gives in to the distraction of emptying his pocket, to escape from the personal problem he is faced with across the table—and *out* of his pocket emerges this forgotten message, that he holds up unbelievingly to the light.

The man who has stonily declined a bill on the other corner stoops in the gutter to pick up the bill thrown away, now he is no longer face to face.

There are those who read and laugh nervously or snarl—for most handbills contain unpleasant matter; or who stand stock still, screw up their faces and seem to be spelling out the letters; or who, the experts in the kind of matters treated in free political handbills, give a cursory glance and at once engage you in argument.

5

Before long fellows of mine (I am an anarchist) came by. They gave the bill a cursory glance.

"What's this!" they cried. "Have you taken leave of your senses? War-memorials! Do you think that war-memorials stop wars?"

"No, I don't," I said.

"Why the Jews? And *why* a synagogue? Have you suddenly become religious?"

"No, I haven't. But the city is full of Jews."

"The city is full of *people*," they corrected me.

"Look, Matt," one of them said, troubled. "What's the use of grieving and making Yom Kippur?[4] The thing to do is to prevent a recurrence."

"You're right, you're right," I said wearily. "There's no use crying over spilled milk; the thing to do is to make a change for the better. But when I try to do it, the *fact* is that when I try to do it, it comes to nothing but sighing."

My friends respected me enough not to greet this remark with a hoot. But, a small knot of people having gathered around us, they at once began to harangue them about more hair-raising immediate and long-range action than we were proposing.

"I think," said a little old woman to me, "that the idea of a war-memorial

4. The Day of Atonement, the holiest day in the Jewish religion, given over to fasting, prayers, meditation, and hopes of forgiveness for past sins and a year of life to follow.

is beautiful; there should be a great war-memorial. But it ought to be something useful, not statues. Many people are proposing that we build a great community-center, with social activities and sports for boys and girls."

"No no," I said stubbornly, "it has to be something heavy, of hard materials like stone and bronze, because there is a heavy place in my breast that I want to get rid of, out there."

6

A man who had been listening to the harangue cried out, "The speaker is right! But he's too god-damned reasonable. We don't need so much sweetness and light; we need more anger."

I touched him on the sleeve. "Not anger. Not just now. Let me tell you something I remember. I remember when the war was just breaking out in Europe, that Toscanini gave a concert, they were playing the *Eroica* symphony;[5] and in the performance, in the performance by Toscanini, there was an edge of anger—even in the last movement—of anger. What do you think?"

Another man read the leaflet carefully. "You boys are floundering," he said.

A policeman dispersed the crowd.

7

"You Jews ought to grieve for yourselves," said a woman. "You had enough trouble without grieving for other people's trouble too."

"That's just what the Canadian said!" I cried, "—my friend on the other corner. But he was wrong. Because we have a saying: *Im ein ani li, mi li? Aval im ani l'otzmi, ma ani?* It means: *If I'm not for myself, who is for me? But if I'm only for myself, what am I?*—"

I stopped short.

The saying had a third part. But when the third part came to my tongue, I stopped short and the tears flooded my eyes. *V'im lo achshav*, is the third part, *eimatai?*—

> *And if not now,* WHEN?[6]

When this third question, this crucial question, came to my tongue, my tongue stuck to the roof of my mouth and I stopped short.

Next moment I burst into heavy sobs and stood on the corner with the tears streaming down my face, not even handing out the bills.

Hereupon (such is our city), whereas previously a knot of people had gathered, now they gave me a wide berth and a space opened around me.

8

> *The oxen that drew the Ark brought it, without a guide, to Beth-Shemesh, singing.*[7]

5. Ludwig van Beethoven (1770–1827) composed his Symphony no. 3, the *Eroica* or *Heroic Symphony,* in honor of Napoleon in 1804. Arturo Toscanini: the Italian-born (1867–1957) conductor and the director, for many years, of the NBC Symphony Orchestra. He was famous for his dramatic interpretations of Beethoven.

6. One of the best-known quotations of Rabbi Hillel, in the *Pirke Avot* (Ethics of the Fathers [Hebrew]), written two generations before the common era.

7. Samuel 6.12.

The sculptor who had chosen himself to embellish the building (as we had all chosen ourselves, for so comes into being the project that people only potentially want: it is forced upon them)—the sculptor said:

"The chief object of embellishment must be the Ark, the box where the scrolls of the Law are kept, because this is the chief center of attention.

"Now for the right and left sides of the Ark I have designed two Cherubim,[8] and they are these: Violence and Nature. But—but—"

He began to stammer, and then he began to weep.

"What's the matter, sculptor?"

"When I look at my designs," he said, "I can no longer remember, I can no longer distinguish, which is Nature and which is Violence.

"Once it was clear to me—if indeed it ever was.

"See, this one. His wings are spread across the top of the box, his hair is streaming: he is going aloft, from it, or with it—

"Ach! if I meant him to be an *ideal* motion, then he's Violence; ideas are *violence* to the nature of things: raising, raping, tearing by the roots, it's all one. But maybe I meant him to be soaring and spreading wide, like growing Nature.

"Well, the other Angel has his feet firmly planted, that's clear. He's standing in the live rock, and that's how we'll build it, too! But isn't he dragging the structure down, like a terrible wrestler? Good!—between us, I don't believe in that Law.

"I see that the two are fighting for the box—I didn't consciously mean this—the raised wings are trying to cover it, the wrestler is wresting it away. Maybe they aren't Nature and Violence at all. No matter!" he cried.

"Don't worry, sculptor; these are only designs. When you come to the execution and can think with your hands again, it will come back to you which is Nature and which is Violence."

"They aren't fighting at all. They're trying to embrace each other. But the box is in the way. Ha! I can fix that."

His face had a crafty look.

"I have planned the box as a movable furniture, according to the ancient way. It's a box of books in a dead language.[9] If I—remove out this box—a bit—or *push* it back out of the way! won't they fall into each other's arms?"

"What! will they move?"

"Certainly they'll move!" said the sculptor arrogantly. "When my dolls move, you'll cry out, and the musician will blow the horn!"

He laughed raucously. "They're a pair of brawny movingmen," he said contemptuously, "tugging that little box as tho it were as heavy as a safe."

9

The Painter had a different personality. A tiny Polish Jew, he was famous as a creator of wonderful whimsical animals. He said:

"For my part I wanted to use stained glass. But the architect says we must have white light for reading. Why must they read so much when they can look at my pictures? O.K. I can tell the story on the walls."

8. Angels, their positioning here prescribed in Exodus 25.18–20.

9. The biblical Sacred Scrolls in Hebrew—the Torah—are kept in an ark, a kind of box, in front of the congregation.

"What story?"

"A fable I heard in the old country, unless it came to me in a dream. It goes like this:

"God said to Noah, 'Build the ark, three stories high; then the animals, two of each kind, will go up in it and be saved from the flood.' This was the arrangement and Noah set to work and did his part. But when the animals heard about it they called a world Congress. (Maybe some of the finest animals didn't even come to the Congress.) They chattered and jabbered; finally it came down to two factions. The first faction was superstitious and they thought they'd better do as they were told. But the other faction was indignant and didn't trust the arrangement at all.

" 'Since when,' said they, 'have these men been so good to us that now we should put our trust in them and, to be quite frank, walk like boobies into a trap. I for my part have a lively memory of Nimrod, that mighty hunter.[1] Ha! you turn pale. So.

" 'And what do you think of the accommodations? We go by twos; but Noah! he doesn't go alone with his wife, but he also takes with him those three fat boys, of whom I need say no further. *And* their wives. Include us out.'

"The others only said, 'We'd better go.'

"So the day came and Noah blew on his shofar[2] a loud blast—"

"Excuse me," said Armand, "what's a shofar?"

"A shofar—is a shofar."

"Yes, but what is it? Noah blew a blast on his shofar; what's a shofar?"

"A shofar is a shofar, dummy," said the painter angrily.

"What is it, a kind of bugle?"

"Yes, it's a bugle. Noah blew a blast on his bugle!"

"What's to get angry about? How should I know? Why didn't you say it was a bugle in the first place?"

"Please—" the painter screwed up his face in pain and turned to us appealingly, "*is* a shofar a bugle?"

"—He blew a blast and some of the animals came, and then came the rain and the flood. But the others *didn't* come, and they *drowned*. *Ach!*—So perished from the earth the wonderful snodorgus and the kafooziopus, and klippy, and Petya, and the marmape, and Sadie—"

It was impossible to believe one's eyes and ears, for suddenly the little man began to bawl in strange little sobs at the top of his chest, for his fantastic animals whose names he was making up as he went along.

"So died," he screamed, "the loveliest and the shrewdest. Petya! And my sister's little girls, and my brothers, and long ago my friend Apollinaire,[3] who had the alivest voice.

"But I shall paint these beauties into existence again, on every wall in the world!"

1. In Genesis a descendant of Ham who was known for his hunting prowess.
2. A ram's horn that, when blown into at the narrow end, emits a piercing sound on Rosh Hashanah and Yom Kippur—the High Holidays—to alert the Jews and to welcome the new year.
3. I.e., Guillaume Apollinaire (1880–1918), the French poet who was killed in World War 1.

10

The architect said:

"In a building of this kind the chief thing to communicate is the sense of the Congregation. The sense of itself *by* the Congregation. Therefore we must be careful about the sight-lines."

He hesitated. "The sight-lines. I arrange the seats in two banks, facing each other across a plain. The Ark is at the eastern end of the plain. See, the sight-lines: everybody is in full view."

He hesitated and began to draw lines on the tracing-paper.

"They flash across the space! Sometimes they get tangled in mid-air. What does *that* mean? It means that a man gets the impression he is being stared at.

"Don't misunderstand me," he apologized. "I'm not saying that it's embarrassing to be looked at; if that were so it would be the end of architecture; but—not just now.

"Strictly speaking there is nothing else to see in the Jewish service except the Congregation itself. There is no sacrificial act.

"A few men are called up to bless the passage; that's all the service consists of. That's what we have to keep in full view. Here they open the scroll to read it, and quidam[4] is called on to bless the passage. Ach! *everybody* is suddenly looking at him, a fine representative figure of a man!

"Suppose with an angry flush on his face, he turns and stares at *you!*

"Maybe the visible Congregation is not such a good idea after all and something is to be said for the stained glass.

"The old men cover their heads with their prayer-shawls, but you could never get the young ones to do it. They are ashamed to be ashamed."

He began to slash the paper with heavy lines, as if the sight-lines were clashing in the space like knives.

He hesitated. The hesitation endured, but there was no moment at which you could say he fell silent.

Finally some one prompted him. "What about the sight-lines? What do they see?"

"The people are crying," he said.

He heaved a sigh of relief. "That solves the problem!" he said more cheerfully. "Each one is hiding behind a shiny wall of tears; they can't see each other anyway."

New York City 1935–1947 1949

4. Somebody or one unknown (Latin).

J. L. TELLER
1912–1972

A prolific political author and journalist in English, J. L. Teller was not a visible figure on the Yiddish literary scene. Nonetheless, he was, in the words of his translator,

Benjamin Harshav, a "remarkable Yiddish poet" whose work intersected with the poetry of the American objectivists and the Yiddish introspectivist-modernists.

Yehuda-Leyb Teller was born in Ternopol in eastern Galicia in 1912. His father had emigrated to America before World War I, and the young Teller, with his brother and mother, endured great hardship until they were able to leave for the United States in 1921. In New York, this brilliant young boy wrote poems, stories, and essays in both Yiddish and Hebrew. He attended Hebrew day schools, including the Herzeliya High School and Teachers College, the forerunner of Yeshiva University, and earned a B.A. from the City College of New York and a doctorate in psychology from Columbia University. In 1937, he traveled to Poland and then, in 1938, visited Germany and Palestine illegally. He was the editor in chief of the Jewish English press syndicate the Independent Jewish Press Service and served as political secretary of the World Zionist Organization.

In 1926, Teller published his first poems in *Dos yidishe likht* (The Yiddish Light), one of New York's little magazines. Soon he was contributing poems, essays, and articles to a number of Yiddish literary journals and anthologies in the United States, Poland, and Mexico, including, in New York, Leyvik's *Tsukunft* (Future), Glatstein and Leyeles's *Inzikh*, and the newspapers *Di fraye arbeter shtime* (Free Voice of Labor) and *Morgen-zshurnal* (Morning Journal).

Before the age of thirty, he had published three books of poetry: *Simboln* (Symbols, 1930), *Miniaturn* (Miniatures, 1934), and *Lider fun der tsayt* (Poems of the Age, 1940). He then began to write for the American Jewish press under the name Judd L. Teller in such magazines as *Commentary, Congress Weekly, Reconstructionism, New Comment, Jewish Frontier, Journal American,* and *New Currents.* His articles on literature, culture, and politics were often polemical and stirred up heated debates, as did at least one of his many books in English on politics and society: *Scapegoat of Revolution.* Others were *Strangers and Natives: The Evolution of the American Jew from 1921 to the Present* and *The Kremlin, the Jews, and the Middle East.* In 1959, he resumed publishing poems in Yiddish journals. A posthumous volume of his collected poems, *Durkh yidishn gemit* (In a Jewish Mood), was published in Tel Aviv in 1975.

We include here two poems from Teller's *Lider fun der tsayt* and one from his posthumous collection. *Sigmund Freud at the Age of Eighty-Two*, from the sequence *Psychoanalysis*, is narrated by a person whom Teller based on Jud' Süss Oppenheimer (1698–1738), a Jewish financier who oversaw the treasury of the duke of Württemberg. As the wealth of the duke increased, so did his sexual extravagance and his harsh policies. When the duke died, Jud' Süss was executed. *Of Immigration* is the ninth poem in an autobiographical cycle, *Invasion,* which depicts Teller's memories of his childhood during World War I in his Galician hometowns of Ternopol and Zbarazh, and his departure with his mother for America. *New York in a Jewish Mood* is from the 1975 posthumous book of poems *In a Jewish Mood.*

Sigmund Freud at the Age of Eighty-Two[1]

Birds scream with mama's voice.
Papa throws himself under the wheels.
A frog creeps out of the boy's hair.
Do you remember the dream of little Sigmund?

1. Translated by Benjamin Harshav and Barbara Harshav. "Sigmund Freud": Jewish Austrian neurologist and founder of psychoanalysis (1856–1939).

Now, at the age of eighty-two,
His night is dry and clear
And squeaks with silence.
Sleep is elucidated.
The complexes smoked out.
Every fear, chained in.
Every fright, bolted up.

Only in the drainpipes of nightly rest
Clatters the fear of death.
Like birds in flight, like wind in trees
Everyone has grasped it:
Patriarchs, warriors, saints.
The blind Isaac didn't even trust Rebecca,[2]
The old Jacob spoke wisely,
Tearful with age,
Wishing to enliven an old thigh
With Joseph's young hand.[3]

It's not death. To follow death boldly
He had long since
Fastened with copper
The locks of his knees.
It's something else, and just as old.
By day, he looked out the window,
Saw the arms in salute.
The Swastika. He smelled with his clever nose
The old evil blood
In young Aryan *shkotsim*.[4]
Shkotsim. Those whose name he carries
Have chewed the word in Hebrew-Joodisch-Yiddish,[5]
Chewed it like matzo, kneaded it like challah,
Braided it like *Havdolah*-candles[6]—
Orel. Esau. Goy.[7]

As Adam named all animals, he named all evils.
He wrote his own Rashi[8]
On Cain-Abel and Isaac's sacrifice.[9]

2. Rebecca counsels her younger son, Jacob, to trick his blind father, Isaac, into believing that Jacob is actually the older son, Esau, thereby gaining Esau's inheritance and blessing (Genesis 27.5–13).
3. The elderly Jacob, about to die, makes his second youngest son, Joseph, promise by placing his hand under his father's thigh, not to bury him in Egypt, where the family has taken refuge during the famine, but to return his body to the cave of Machpelah, the ancestral burial place in the Promised Land (Genesis 47.29) [adaptation of Benjamin Harshav and Barbara Harshav's note].
4. Young Gentile men (Yiddish) [Benjamin Harshav and Barbara Harshav's note].
5. The central term in Teller's ironic compound name for the Jewish languages, *Ivris-Yodish-Yidish*, combines *Jude*, German for "Jew," with the suffix *-isch*.
6. The braided candle lit in the Havdolah ceremony to mark the end of the Sabbath. "Matzo": unleavened bread eaten during the week of Passover to commemorate the Exodus from Egypt. "Challah": a braided, yeast-risen loaf of egg bread eaten on the Sabbath.
7. Various epithets for non-Jews [Benjamin Harshav and Barbara Harshav's note].
8. Acronym of Rabbi Shlomo Yitzkhak . . . of Troyes (1040–1105), the most famous, lucid, and systematic commentator on the Hebrew Bible and the Talmud. His commentary became a mainstay of Jewish education, and the word *Rashi* became synonymous with commentary, explanation [Benjamin Harshav and Barbara Harshav's note and glossary entry].
9. Abraham bound his son Isaac to prepare him for sacrifice in accordance with God's orders, which God rescinded at the last moment and for

Yet, as the Patriarch savored his son's fresh game,
He savors now the smell of simple Hebrew-Yiddish:[1]
Orel. Esau. Goy.

The drainpipes of nightly rest clatter with rain.
The trees murmur with dawn.
Fear? What is fear?
One Egyptian kills another and covers him in sand.[2]
Only Akiva's[3] courage, ripe as orchards in late summer,
Masters itself,
The pyre and the gallows
And ties the whole being
To the wings of a Jewish letter.

To overcome oneself is more
Than Charcot's[4] hypnosis.

Sigmund Freud at eighty-two
Climbs out of the Swastikas,
Recites:
Haman.[5] *Orel. Esau. Goy.*

1938, 1940

Of Immigration[1]

My mother leads me through streets
Of a big city.
A scorching summer afternoon
Teases with lemonade, pears,
And ice cream.
Suddenly—like lightning,
Dark—like a tree in a storm,
A Negro rises—
The first one in my life.

---

which obedience God reiterated the Covenant (Genesis 22.1–19). "Cain-Abel": a reference to Cain's murder of his brother, Abel, out of jealousy for Abel's favor in God's eyes (Genesis 4.3–8).

1. Here, the language of the traditional Yiddish translations of the Hebrew Bible.

2. Refers to Exodus 2.11–12, the story of the young Moses, raised as an Egyptian prince in pharaoh's palace, who, upon witnessing an Egyptian beating a Jewish slave, kills the Egyptian and buries him in the sand [adaptation of Benjamin Harshav and Barbara Harshav's note].

3. Akiva ben Joseph (50–135 C.E.), Rabbi Akiva, the most important rabbinic scholar of his time who systematized the Jewish law. He was a great teacher as well as a patriot and a martyr who enthusiastically supported Bar Kokhba's revolt in 132 C.E. against the Roman emperor's decree forbidding the practice and teaching of Judaism. Imprisoned by the Romans for disobeying this decree, Rabbi Akiva was executed by torture. Jewish legend tells that he was the only one of four men who went into the "orchard" of divine secrets and returned [adaptation of Benjamin Harshav and Barbara Harshav's note].

4. Jean-Martin Charcot (1825–1893), a French neurologist and pathologist whose study of hysteria and hypnosis led Freud, one of his students, to investigate the psychological rather than physiological causes of neurosis.

5. This powerful adviser to the Persian king Ahasuerus, angry at Mordecai the Jew for not bowing down to him, persuaded the king to order the murder of all the Jews but was exposed and defeated by Mordecai's niece, Queen Esther (Book of Esther). "Sigmund Freud": having escaped the Nazis in Vienna, Freud died in London in 1939.

1. Translated by Benjamin Harshav and Barbara Harshav.

Children roll big thin hoops.
Behind the palings
Arbors rustle and darken.

Mother hurries and holds me
By the hand.
Piano sounds hover
Like a thin fragrance
Among curtains and branches.
Tram clatter
And elegant horses
On all corners.

We go through banks, postoffices,
For foreign stamps,
For father's money.
My mother's face in all visa bureaus.
At strict desks and angry bald heads
She pushes me forward,
As a beggar would his lameness.

Men sign,
Seal forever,
Like God,
Like fate.

At twilight,
When color-voices flood the city,
In a chilly, distant street—
My mother with swollen legs,
My hand in hers,
Is tired

How many years ago?

Every summer reminds me anew
Of the anguish-joys
Of a little Jew.

1940

New York in a Jewish Mood[1]

Big-city streets
Gaping solemnly
Like homes waiting
For men's
Return from holiday prayers.[2]

1. Translated by Benjamin Harshav and Barbara Harshav.
2. Literally, "return from holiday evening prayers." Typically, on the eve of a holiday, the men would go to synagogue to pray, while the women stayed home.

Winds nag
Like a cantor's liturgy.
Skyscrapers aflame
Like pagan worship
Against a sun
Of scoured Jewish brass.
Evening awe
Descends on me
Like a tallis[3]
And I sense the meaning of my days
Like clear square letters
Under the pointing hand
Of a Reader.[4]

1975

3. Prayer shawl (Yiddish, from the Hebrew *tallit*).
4. The person who chants aloud from the Torah scroll during the synagogue service. "Clear square letters": the Hebrew letters carefully handwritten in the Torah scroll. "Pointing hand": the *yad*, or hand-shaped pointer, that helps the reader keep place while chanting from the Torah.

MURIEL RUKEYSER
1913–1980

Born of affluent parents in New York City, Muriel Rukeyser attended the Fieldston School, Vassar College, and Columbia University. At Vassar, rebellious and independent in her social and literary views, she joined fellow classmates Mary McCarthy and Elizabeth Bishop to start a literary magazine in opposition to the established *Vassar Review*. Rukeyser wrote social-protest poetry in the 1930s, but, influenced by T. S. Eliot and W. H. Auden and other modernists, her work was more sophisticated technically and stylistically than was usual in the politically engaged verse of the time. *Boy with His Hair Cut Short* shows this in its oblique but unmistakable portrait of a brother and sister's fears and forlorn hope among the unemployed of the depression.

Rukeyser was always committed to radical causes and the plight of the persecuted and oppressed. She left Vassar in 1933, going to Alabama to report on the Scottsboro case—nine young African American men unjustly convicted of raping two white women, a conviction later overturned by the Supreme Court. Her first volume of verse, *Theory of Flight* (1935), which was selected for the Yale Younger Poets series, contains the line in *Poem Out of Childhood*, "Not Sappho, Sacco," referring to the Sacco-Vanzetti case in the 1920s in which two Italian immigrant anarchists were put to death, despite worldwide protest, for their dubious complicity in the killing of a payroll master and his guard. The next year she was in Spain as a journalist, an ardent supporter of the Spanish Republic against General Franco's fascist effort to overturn it. Volumes of poetry followed quickly: *U.S. 1* (1938), *A Turning Wind* (1939), *The Soul and Body of John Brown* (1940), and a biography of the scientist Willard Gibbs (1942). During World War II, her horror at its carnage was reflected in *Beast in View* (1944), in which she also asserted her deep feelings as a Jew in the poem *To Be a Jew in the Twentieth Century*, published in this and many other anthologies.

A witness to and participant in many of the significant social issues and causes that wracked her lifetime, she displayed a prescient awareness of the connections between public and private life. She was aware of the many-sidedness of a fully human life and the need to see and live things whole. In a 1944 symposium, she observed that the "themes and the use I have made of them have depended on my life as a poet, as a woman, as an American, and as a Jew."

She had a marriage annulled after two months, had a son by another man, and remained a single mother for the rest of her life. Occupied with child rearing, she did not publish in the 1950s, but published in the 1960s several works that reflected the impact of giving birth. In the 1970s and thereafter, with the growth of feminism and the women's movement, she became a very influential teacher—at Vassar, the California Labor School, and, for many years, at Sarah Lawrence College—and a role model for a newer generation of women writers. Having shared platforms with Rukeyser at readings and demonstrations against the Vietnam War, Adrienne Rich has beautifully described the sense of female power Rukeyser brought with her, despite a stroke that she was overcoming at the time: she carried "her large body and strongly molded head with enormous pride." The poet Anne Sexton wrote of her in this period as "Muriel, mother of everyone."

Boy with His Hair Cut Short

Sunday shuts down on this twentieth-century evening.
The El[1] passes. Twilight and bulb define
the brown room, the overstuffed plum sofa,
the boy, and the girl's thin hands above his head.
A neighbor radio sings stocks, news, serenade.

He sits at the table, head down, the young clear neck exposed,
watching the drugstore sign from the tail of his eye;
tattoo, neon, until the eye blears, while his
solicitous tall sister, simple in blue, bending
behind him, cuts his hair with her cheap shears.

The arrow's electric red always reaches its mark,
successful neon! He coughs, impressed by that precision.
His child's forehead, forever protected by his cap,
is bleached against the lamplight as he turns head
and steadies to let the snippets drop.

Erasing the failure of weeks with level fingers,
she sleeks the fine hair, combing: "You'll look fine tomorrow!
You'll surely find something, they can't keep turning you down;
the finest gentleman's not so trim as you!" Smiling, he raises
the adolescent forehead wrinkling ironic now.

He sees his decent suit laid out, new-pressed,
his carfare on the shelf. He lets his head fall, meeting
her earnest hopeless look, seeing the sharp blades splitting,

1. One of several elevated trains that ran above Second, Third, Sixth, and Ninth avenues in Manhattan as well as in parts of Brooklyn and the Bronx from the 1890s until 1955.

the darkened room, the impersonal sign, her motion,
the blue vein, bright on her temple, pitifully beating.

1935

More of a Corpse Than a Woman

Give them my regards when you go to the school reunion;
and at the marriage-supper, say that I'm thinking about them.
They'll remember my name; I went to the movies with that one,
feeling the weight of their death where she sat at my elbow;
she never said a word,
but all of them were heard.

All of them alike, expensive girls, the leaden friends:
one used to play the piano, one of them once wrote a sonnet,[2]
one even seemed awakened enough to photograph wheatfields—
the dull girls with the educated minds and technical passions—
pure love was their employment,
they tried it for enjoyment.

Meet them at the boat: they've brought the souvenirs of boredom,
a seashell from the faltering monarchy;
the nose of a marble saint; and from the battlefield,
an empty shell divulged from a flower-bed.
The lady's wealthy breath
perfumes the air with death.

The leaden lady faces the fine, voluptuous woman,
faces a rising world bearing its gifts in its hands.
Kisses her casual dreams upon the lips she kisses,
risen, she moves away; takes others; moves away.
Inadequate to love,
supposes she's enough.

Give my regards to the well-protected woman,
I knew the ice-cream girl, we went to school together.
There's something to bury, people, when you begin to bury.
When your women are ready and rich in their wish for the world,
destroy the leaden heart,
we've a new race to start.

1936

Paper Anniversary[1]

The concert-hall was crowded the night of the Crash[2]
but the wives were away; many mothers gone sick to their beds

2. An English verse form of fourteen lines, linked in a variety of ways.

1. The first wedding anniversary is traditionally celebrated with gifts made of paper.

2. The stock market began its collapse on October 29, 1929, known as Black Thursday. In the following days, thousands of people lost huge sums of money, and banks and businesses began to fold. Some men, demoralized by the crash, jumped out of buildings.

or waiting at home for late extras[3] and latest telephone calls
had sent their sons and daughters to hear music instead.

I came late with my father; and as the car flowed stop
I heard the Mozart[4] developing through the door
where the latecomers listened; water-leap, season of coolness,
talisman of relief; but they worried, they did not hear.

Into the hall of formal rows and the straight-sitting seats
(they took out pencils, they muttered at the program's margins)
began the double concerto, Brahms'[5] season of fruit
but they could not meet it with love; they were lost with their fortunes.

In that hall was no love where love was often felt
reaching for music, or for the listener beside:
orchids and violins—precision dances of pencils
rode down the paper as the music rode.

Intermission with its spill of lights found heavy
breathing and failure pushing up the aisles,
or the daughters of failure greeting each other under
the eyes of an old man who has gone mad and fails.

And this to end the cars, the trips abroad, the summer
countries of palmtrees, toy moneys, curt affairs,
ending all music for the evening-dress audience.
Fainting in telephone booth, the broker[6] swears.

"I was cleaned out at Forty—" "No golf tomorrow" "Father!"
but fathers there were none, only a rout of men
stampeded in a flaming circle; and they return
from the telephones and run down the velvet lane

as the lights go down and the Stravinsky[7] explodes
spasms of rockets to levels near delight,
and the lawyer thinks of his ostrich-feather wife
lying alone, and knows it is getting late.

He journeys up the aisle, and as Debussy[8] begins,
drowning the concert-hall, many swim up and out,
distortions of water carry their bodies through
the deformed image of a crippled heart.

The age of the sleepless and the sealed arrives.
The music spent. Hard-breathing, they descend,

3. Special editions of newspapers.
4. Wolfgang Amadeus Mozart (1756–1791), Austrian Classical composer.
5. Johannes Brahms (1833–1897), German Romantic composer. "Double concerto" : written in 1887, it is for violin and cello. "Margins": in finance, moneys or securities deposited with a broker as a provision against loss.
6. An agent who negotiates sales in return for a fee.
7. Igor Stravinsky (1882–1971), a Russian-born composer particularly renowned for his ballets and operas.
8. Claude Debussy (1862–1918), French Impressionist composer. Among his best-known orchestral works are *Prelude to "The Afternoon of a Faun," The Sea*, and *Nocturnes and Images*.

wait at the door or at the telephone.
While from the river streams a flaw of wind,

washing our sight; while all the fathers lie
heavy upon their graves, the line of cars progresses
toward the blue park, and the lobby darkens, and we
go home again to the insane governess.

The night is joy, and the music was joy alive,
alive is joy, but it will never be
upon this scene upon these fathers these cars
for the windows already hold photography

of the drowned faces the fat the unemployed—
pressed faces lie upon the million glass
and the sons and daughters turn their startled faces
and see that startled face.

1939

From Letter to the Front

7. [TO BE A JEW IN THE TWENTIETH CENTURY]

To be a Jew in the twentieth century
Is to be offered a gift. If you refuse,
Wishing to be invisible, you choose
Death of the spirit, the stone insanity.
Accepting, take full life. Full agonies:
Your evening deep in labyrinthine blood
Of those who resist, fail, and resist; and God
Reduced to a hostage among hostages.

The gift is torment. Not alone the still
Torture, isolation; or torture of the flesh.
That may come also. But the accepting wish,
The whole and fertile spirit as guarantee
For every human freedom, suffering to be free,
Daring to live for the impossible.

1944

DELMORE SCHWARTZ
1913–1966

Born in Brooklyn of immigrant parents from Romania, Delmore Schwartz, a brilliant student of philosopher Sidney Hook and others, obtained a bachelor's degree from

NYU in philosophy in 1935. He did graduate work at Harvard but left abruptly in 1937 when he failed to get a fellowship. He returned to New York, eager to pursue a literary career, which received an auspicious start that year when he published the story *In Dreams Begin Responsibilities* and became famous.

Although he published some ten collections of poems, stories, verse dramas, and critical essays from the 1950s onward, Schwartz suffered increasingly from insomnia, paranoia, and withdrawal. His second wife left him in 1955, and he spent short periods in Bellevue and the Payne Whitney Clinic. In the 1940s, he was an editor of *Partisan Review* and, for a brief time, poetry editor of the *New Republic*. He taught composition at Harvard from 1940 to 1947 and for a year at Princeton, frustrated in his attempt to get a permanent position. In his final four years, he taught at Syracuse University, his erratic behavior causing him to leave suddenly in 1966. Schwartz went to live in isolation in New York City midtown hotels. In July, he suffered a heart attack in one of their elevators and died on the way to the hospital. His body lay unclaimed for two days; but two hundred people attended his funeral, with eulogies delivered by cultural luminaries of the day.

Schwartz had been influenced by and wrote on the great literary modernists—Yeats, Auden, Eliot, Stevens—and, in turn, was an influence upon John Berryman and Robert Lowell. His enduring interest may depend upon, besides the lyricism and high intelligence of many of his poems, his acute and occasionally acerbic accounts of New York's Jewish intellectuals, in which he chronicles as well the strains of the Jewish American experience generally.

The imaginative achievement of *In Dreams Begin Responsibilities* was acknowledged immediately. The narrator dreams of a balmy June day in Brooklyn, during which he attends a movie in which he imagines the film is showing the courtship of his parents. He breaks down and weeps, shouting out to the actors on screen not to go through with it—their union will be an unhappy one (which it was), their children "monstrous." Unable to control himself, he is escorted out of the theater, awakening to snow and his twenty-first birthday.

Critic and scholar Irving Howe recalled that he and other youthful readers of *Partisan Review* were "stunned" by the story and felt a not-to-be-forgotten "shock of recognition." Likewise, the poetry that Schwartz published in various journals and combined with his prose to make his first book was met by unusually strong approbation.

Influential southern poet Allen Tate wrote to publisher James Laughlin that "Schwartz's poetic style is the only genuine innovation since Pound and Eliot . . . there is a whole new feeling for language and in the regular versification a new metrical system of great subtlety and originality." The magisterial T. S. Eliot himself responded to an article by Schwartz with the words "You are certainly a critic, but I want to see more poetry from you; I was much impressed by *In Dreams Begin Responsibilities*." His first book, which contained the stunning title story, brought the twenty-five-year-old writer professional validation and success: first, the approval of the mainly Jewish New York intellectuals, represented by the editors of the Trotskyist-leaning *Partisan Review*, who had chosen to give his story pride of place; second, the approval of the conservative new-critical and Catholic-tending arbiters of taste in poetry. Holding on to approval from such divergent quarters of the literary world while earning a living would not be easy. Schwartz's *Summer Knowledge*, his "new and selected . . . 1938–1959" collection, would show the doubleness of potentially contradictory commitments. He dedicated it jointly to John Crowe Ransom, the dean of conservative southern editors and poets, and to Dwight MacDonald, a longtime radical *Partisan* friend and associate.

The memorable *The Heavy Bear Who Goes with Me*, which some readers have called Schwartz's best poem, may provide a paradigm for the poet's awareness of contradiction and split, of irreconcilable doubleness and oppositions. The figure of the grotesque, lumbering, dark circus animal that represents the physical body and its desires joined to "the scrimmage of appetite everywhere" is split from the "me." The bear is the "other" that ironically holds the purer, better self captive. The poem is one of self-alienation and alienation from the world.

Themes of alienation, doubt, and separation are repeated throughout the poems, stories, and plays, although at its best the lyrical language can lift the heart. In 1960, at a time when his mental and emotional condition was worsening rapidly, Schwartz was awarded the Bollingen Prize in Poetry.

In Dreams Begin Responsibilities[1]

I

I think it is the year 1909. I feel as if I were in a motion picture theatre, the long arm of light crossing the darkness and spinning, my eyes fixed on the screen. This is a silent picture as if an old Biograph[2] one, in which the actors are dressed in ridiculously old-fashioned clothes, and one flash succeeds another with sudden jumps. The actors too seem to jump about and walk too fast. The shots themselves are full of dots and rays, as if it were raining when the picture was photographed. The light is bad.

It is Sunday afternoon, June 12th, 1909, and my father is walking down the quiet streets of Brooklyn on his way to visit my mother. His clothes are newly pressed and his tie is too tight in his high collar. He jingles the coins in his pockets, thinking of the witty things he will say. I feel as if I had by now relaxed entirely in the soft darkness of the theatre; the organist peals out the obvious and approximate emotions on which the audience rocks unknowingly. I am anonymous, and I have forgotten myself. It is always so when one goes to the movies, it is, as they say, a drug.

My father walks from street to street of trees, lawns and houses, once in a while coming to an avenue on which a street-car skates and gnaws, slowly progressing. The conductor, who has a handle-bar mustache helps a young lady wearing a hat like a bowl with feathers on to the car. She lifts her long skirts slightly as she mounts the steps. He leisurely makes change and rings his bell. It is obviously Sunday, for everyone is wearing Sunday clothes, and the street-car's noises emphasize the quiet of the holiday. Is not Brooklyn the City of Churches? The shops are closed and their shades drawn, but for an occasional stationery store or drug-store with great green balls in the window.

My father has chosen to take this long walk because he likes to walk and think. He thinks about himself in the future and so arrives at the place he is to visit in a state of mild exaltation. He pays no attention to the houses he is passing, in which the Sunday dinner is being eaten, nor to the many trees which patrol each street, now coming to their full leafage and the time when they will room the whole street in cool shadow. An occasional carriage passes, the horse's hooves falling like stones in the quiet afternoon, and once

1. The title story in the volume *In Dreams Begin Responsibilities* (1944, 1978). The phrase was used as an epigraph by W. B. Yeats for his book of poems *Responsibilities* (1914).

2. One of the first motion-picture production companies in the United States. D. W. Griffith (1875–1948) and Mack Sennett (1880–1960) were important directors of Biograph's silent films.

in a while an automobile, looking like an enormous upholstered sofa, puffs and passes.

My father thinks of my mother, of how nice it will be to introduce her to his family. But he is not yet sure that he wants to marry her, and once in a while he becomes panicky about the bond already established. He reassures himself by thinking of the big men he admires who are married: William Randolph Hearst, and William Howard Taft,[3] who has just become President of the United States.

My father arrives at my mother's house. He has come too early and so is suddenly embarrassed. My aunt, my mother's sister, answers the loud bell with her napkin in her hand, for the family is still at dinner. As my father enters, my grandfather rises from the table and shakes hands with him. My mother has run upstairs to tidy herself. My grandmother asks my father if he has had dinner, and tells him that Rose will be downstairs soon. My grandfather opens the conversation by remarking on the mild June weather. My father sits uncomfortably near the table, holding his hat in his hand. My grandmother tells my aunt to take my father's hat. My uncle, twelve years old, runs into the house, his hair touseled. He shouts a greeting to my father, who has often given him a nickel, and then runs upstairs. It is evident that the respect in which my father is held in this household is tempered by a good deal of mirth. He is impressive, yet he is very awkward.

II

Finally my mother comes downstairs, all dressed up, and my father being engaged in conversation with my grandfather becomes uneasy, not knowing whether to greet my mother or continue the conversation. He gets up from the chair clumsily and says "hello" gruffly. My grandfather watches, examining their congruence, such as it is, with a critical eye, and meanwhile rubbing his bearded cheek roughly, as he always does when he reflects. He is worried; he is afraid that my father will not make a good husband for his oldest daughter. At this point something happens to the film, just as my father is saying something funny to my mother; I am awakened to myself and my unhappiness just as my interest was rising. The audience begins to clap impatiently. Then the trouble is cared for but the film has been returned to a portion just shown, and once more I see my grandfather rubbing his bearded cheek and pondering my father's character. It is difficult to get back into the picture once more and forget myself, but as my mother giggles at my father's words, the darkness drowns me.

My father and mother depart from the house, my father shaking hands with my mother once more, out of some unknown uneasiness. I stir uneasily also, slouched in the hard chair of the theatre. Where is the older uncle, my mother's older brother? He is studying in his bedroom upstairs, studying for his final examination at the College of the City of New York, having been dead of rapid pneumonia for the last twenty-one years. My mother and father walk down the same quiet streets once more. My mother is holding my father's arm and telling him of the novel which she has been reading; and

3. The twenty-seventh president of the United States, (1857–1930); served from 1909 to 1913. "William Randolph Hearst": founder of the newspaper and publishing empire still named for him (1863–1951).

my father utters judgments of the characters as the plot is made clear to him. This is a habit which he very much enjoys, for he feels the utmost superiority and confidence when he approves and condemns the behavior of other people. At times he feels moved to utter a brief "Ugh,"—whenever the story becomes what he would call sugary. This tribute is paid to his manliness. My mother feels satisfied by the interest which she has awakened; she is showing my father how intelligent she is, and how interesting.

They reach the avenue, and the street-car leisurely arrives. They are going to Coney Island[4] this afternoon, although my mother considers that such pleasures are inferior. She has made up her mind to indulge only in a walk on the boardwalk and a pleasant dinner, avoiding the riotous amusements as being beneath the dignity of so dignified a couple.

My father tells my mother how much money he has made in the past week, exaggerating an amount which need not have been exaggerated. But my father has always felt that actualities somehow fall short. Suddenly I begin to weep. The determined old lady who sits next to me in the theatre is annoyed and looks at me with an angry face, and being intimidated, I stop. I drag out my handkerchief and dry my face, licking the drop which has fallen near my lips. Meanwhile I have missed something, for here are my mother and father alighting at the last stop, Coney Island.

III

They walk toward the boardwalk, and my father commands my mother to inhale the pungent air from the sea. They both breathe in deeply, both of them laughing as they do so. They have in common a great interest in health, although my father is strong and husky, my mother frail. Their minds are full of theories of what is good to eat and not good to eat, and sometimes they engage in heated discussions of the subject, the whole matter ending in my father's announcement, made with a scornful bluster, that you have to die sooner or later anyway. On the boardwalk's flagpole, the American flag is pulsing in an intermittent wind from the sea.

My father and mother go to the rail of the boardwalk and look down on the beach where a good many bathers are casually walking about. A few are in the surf. A peanut whistle pierces the air with its pleasant and active whine, and my father goes to buy peanuts. My mother remains at the rail and stares at the ocean. The ocean seems merry to her; it pointedly sparkles and again and again the pony waves are released. She notices the children digging in the wet sand, and the bathing costumes of the girls who are her own age. My father returns with the peanuts. Overhead the sun's lightning strikes and strikes, but neither of them are at all aware of it. The boardwalk is full of people dressed in their Sunday clothes and idly strolling. The tide does not reach as far as the boardwalk, and the strollers would feel no danger if it did. My mother and father lean on the rail of the boardwalk and absently stare at the ocean. The ocean is becoming rough; the waves come in slowly, tugging strength from far back. The moment before they somersault, the moment when they arch their backs so beautifully, showing green and white veins amid the black, that moment is intolerable. They finally crack, dashing

4. An amusement park and beach on Brooklyn, New York's, southern perimeter.

fiercely upon the sand, actually driving, full force downward, against the sand, bouncing upward and forward, and at last petering out into a small stream which races up the beach and then is recalled. My parents gaze absentmindedly at the ocean, scarcely interested in its harshness. The sun overhead does not disturb them. But I stare at the terrible sun which breaks up sight, and the fatal, merciless, passionate ocean, I forget my parents. I stare fascinated and finally, shocked by the indifference of my father and mother, I burst out weeping once more. The old lady next to me pats me on the shoulder and says "There, there, all of this is only a movie, young man, only a movie," but I look up once more at the terrifying sun and the terrifying ocean, and being unable to control my tears, I get up and go to the men's room, stumbling over the feet of the other people seated in my row.

IV

When I return, feeling as if I had awakened in the morning sick for lack of sleep, several hours have apparently passed and my parents are riding on the merry-go-round. My father is on a black horse, my mother on a white one, and they seem to be making an eternal circuit for the single purpose of snatching the nickel rings which are attached to the arm of one of the posts. A hand-organ is playing; it is one with the ceaseless circling of the merry-go-round.

For a moment it seems that they will never get off the merry-go-round because it will never stop. I feel like one who looks down on the avenue from the 50th story of a building. But at length they do get off; even the music of the hand-organ has ceased for a moment. My father has acquired ten rings, my mother only two, although it was my mother who really wanted them.

They walk on along the boardwalk as the afternoon descends by imperceptible degrees into the incredible violet of dusk. Everything fades into a relaxed glow, even the ceaseless murmuring from the beach, and the revolutions of the merry-go-round. They look for a place to have dinner. My father suggests the best one on the boardwalk and my mother demurs, in accordance with her principles.

However they do go to the best place, asking for a table near the window, so that they can look out on the boardwalk and the mobile ocean. My father feels omnipotent as he places a quarter in the waiter's hand as he asks for a table. The place is crowded and here too there is music, this time from a kind of string trio. My father orders dinner with a fine confidence.

As the dinner is eaten, my father tells of his plans for the future, and my mother shows with expressive face how interested she is, and how impressed. My father becomes exultant. He is lifted up by the waltz that is being played, and his own future begins to intoxicate him. My father tells my mother that he is going to expand his business, for there is a great deal of money to be made. He wants to settle down. After all, he is twenty-nine, he has lived by himself since he was thirteen, he is making more and more money, and he is envious of his married friends when he visits them in the cozy security of their homes, surrounded, it seems, by the calm domestic pleasures, and by delightful children, and then, as the waltz reaches the moment when all the dancers swing madly, then, then with awful daring, then he asks my mother to marry him, although awkwardly enough and puzzled, even in his excitement, at how he had arrived at the proposal, and she, to make the whole business worse, begins to cry, and my father looks nervously about, not knowing at all what to do now, and my mother says: "It's all I've wanted from the moment I saw you," sobbing, and he finds all of this very difficult, scarcely to his taste, scarcely as he had thought it would be, on his long walks over Brooklyn Bridge[5] in the revery of a fine cigar, and it was then that I stood up in the theatre and shouted: "Don't do it. It's not too late to change your minds, both of you. Nothing good will come of it, only remorse, hatred, scandal, and two children whose characters are monstrous." The whole audience turned to look at me, annoyed, the usher came hurrying down the aisle flashing his searchlight, and the old lady next to me tugged me down into my seat, saying: "Be quiet. You'll be put out, and you paid thirty-five cents to come in." And so I shut my eyes because I could not bear to see what was happening. I sat there quietly.

V

But after awhile I began to take brief glimpses, and at length I watch again with thirsty interest, like a child who wants to maintain his sulk although offered the bribe of candy. My parents are now having their picture taken in a photographer's booth along the boardwalk. The place is shadowed in the mauve light which is apparently necessary. The camera is set to the side on its tripod and looks like a Martian man. The photographer is instructing my parents in how to pose. My father has his arm over my mother's shoulder, and both of them smile emphatically. The photographer brings my mother a bouquet of flowers to hold in her hand but she holds it at the wrong angle. Then the photographer covers himself with the black cloth which drapes the camera and all that one sees of him is one protruding arm and his hand which clutches the rubber ball which he will squeeze when the picture is finally taken. But he is not satisfied with their appearance. He feels with certainty that somehow there is something wrong in their pose. Again and again he issues from his hidden place with new directions. Each suggestion merely makes matters worse. My father is becoming impatient. They try a seated pose. The photographer explains that he has pride, he is not interested in all of this for the money, he wants to make beautiful pictures. My father says: "Hurry up, will you? We haven't got all night." But the photographer only scurries about apologetically, and issues new directions. The photographer charms me. I approve of him with all my heart, for I know just how he feels, and as he criticizes each revised pose according to some unknown idea of rightness, I become quite hopeful. But then my father says angrily: "Come on, you've had enough time, we're not going to wait any longer." And the photographer, sighing unhappily, goes back under his black covering, holds out his hand, says: "One, two, three, Now!", and the picture is taken, with my father's smile turned to a grimace and my mother's bright and false. It takes a few minutes for the picture to be developed and as my parents sit in the curious light they become quite depressed.

5. Designed by John A. Roebling (1806–1869) in 1867 and opened in 1883, it crosses the East River, connecting Brooklyn and Manhattan.

VI

They have passed a fortune-teller's booth, and my mother wishes to go in, but my father does not. They begin to argue about it. My mother becomes quite stubborn, my father once more impatient, and then they begin to quarrel, and what my father would like to do is walk off and leave my mother there, but he knows that that would never do. My mother refuses to budge. She is near to tears, but she feels an uncontrollable desire to hear what the palm-reader will say. My father consents angrily, and they both go into a booth which is in a way like the photographer's, since it is draped in black cloth and its light is shadowed. The place is too warm, and my father keeps saying this is all nonsense, pointing to the crystal ball on the table. The fortune-teller, a fat, short woman, garbed in what is supposed to be Oriental robes, comes into the room from the back and greets them, speaking with an accent. But suddenly my father feels that the whole thing is intolerable; he tugs at my mother's arm, but my mother refuses to budge. And then, in terrible anger, my father lets go of my mother's arm and strides out, leaving my mother stunned. She moves to go after my father, but the fortune-teller holds her arm tightly and begs her not to do so, and I in my seat am shocked more than can ever be said, for I feel as if I were walking a tight-rope a hundred feet over a circus-audience and suddenly the rope is showing signs of breaking, and I get up from my seat and begin to shout once more the first words I can think of to communicate my terrible fear and once more the usher comes hurrying down the aisle flashing his searchlight, and the old lady pleads with me, and the shocked audience has turned to stare at me, and I keep shouting: "What are they doing? Don't they know what they are doing? Why doesn't my mother go after my father? If she does not do that, what will she do? Doesn't my father know what he is doing?"—But the usher has seized my arm and is dragging me away, and as he does so, he says: "What are *you* doing? Don't you know that you can't do whatever you want to do? Why should a young man like you, with your whole life before you, get hysterical like this? Why don't you *think* of what you're doing? You can't act like this even if other people aren't around! You will be sorry if you do not do what you should do, you can't carry on like this, it is not right, you will find that out soon enough, everything you do matters too much," and he said that dragging me through the lobby of the theatre into the cold light, and I woke up into the bleak winter morning of my 21st birthday, the windowsill shining with its lip of snow, and the morning already begun.

1937, 1944, 1978

The Ballet of the Fifth Year[1]

Where the sea gulls sleep or indeed where they fly
Is a place of different traffic. Although I
Consider the fishing bay (where I see them dip and curve
And purely glide) a place that weakens the nerve

1. From *Summer Knowledge* (1959).

Of will, and closes my eyes, as they should not be
(They should burn like the street-light all night quietly,
So that whatever is present will be known to me),
Nevertheless the gulls and the imagination
Of where they sleep, which comes to creation
In strict shape and color, from their dallying
Their wings slowly, and suddenly rallying
Over, up, down the arabesque of descent,
Is an old act enacted, my fabulous intent
When I skated, afraid of policemen, five years old,
In the winter sunset, sorrowful and cold,
Hardly attained to thought, but old enough to know
Such grace, so self-contained, was the best escape to know.

1938

The Heavy Bear Who Goes with Me[1]

"the withness of the body"[2]

The heavy bear who goes with me,
A manifold honey to smear his face,
Clumsy and lumbering here and there,
The central ton of every place,
The hungry beating brutish one
In love with candy, anger, and sleep,
Crazy factotum,[3] dishevelling all,
Climbs the building, kicks the football,
Boxes his brother in the hate-ridden city.

Breathing at my side, that heavy animal,
That heavy bear who sleeps with me,
Howls in his sleep for a world of sugar,
A sweetness intimate as the water's clasp,
Howls in his sleep because the tight-rope
Trembles and shows the darkness beneath.
—The strutting show-off is terrified,
Dressed in his dress-suit, bulging his pants,
Trembles to think that his quivering meat
Must finally wince to nothing at all.

That inescapable animal walks with me,
Has followed me since the black womb held,
Moves where I move, distorting my gesture,
A caricature, a swollen shadow,
A stupid clown of the spirit's motive,
Perplexes and affronts with his own darkness,
The secret life of belly and bone,

1. From *Summer Knowledge* (1959).
2. In earlier versions, this was attributed to Alfred North Whitehead, professor of philosophy at Harvard.
3. Someone employed to do every kind of work (Latin).

Opaque, too near, my private, yet unknown,
Stretches to embrace the very dear
With whom I would walk without him near,
Touches her grossly, although a word
Would bare my heart and make me clear,
Stumbles, flounders, and strives to be fed
Dragging me with him in his mouthing care,
Amid the hundred million of his kind,
The scrimmage of appetite everywhere.

1938

Summer Knowledge[1]

Summer knowledge is not the winter's truth, the truth of fall,
the autumn's fruition, vision, and recognition:
It is not May knowledge, little and leafing and growing green,
blooming out and blossoming white,
It is not the knowing and the knowledge of the gold fall and
the ripened darkening vineyard,
Nor the black tormented, drenched and rainy knowledge of birth,
April, and travail,
The knowledge of the womb's convulsions, and the coiled cord's
ravelled artery, severed and cut open,
as the root forces its way up from the dark loam:
The agony of the first knowledge of pain is worse than death,
or worse than the thought of death:
No poppy, no preparation, no initiation, no illusion, only
the beginning, so distant from all knowledge
and all conclusion, all indecision and all illusion.
Summer knowledge is green knowledge, country knowledge,
the knowledge of growing and the supple recognition
of the fullness and the fatness and the roundness of ripeness.
It is bird knowledge and the knowing that trees possess when
The sap ascends to the leaf and the flower and the fruit,
Which the root never sees and the root believes in the darkness
and the ignorance of winter knowledge
—The knowledge of the fruit is not the knowledge possessed
by the root in its indomitable darkness of ambition
Which is the condition of belief beyond conception of
experience or the gratification of fruition.
Summer knowledge is not picture knowledge, nor is it the
knowledge of lore and learning.
It is not the knowledge known from the mountain's height, it
is not the garden's view of the distant mountains of hidden fountains;
It is not the still vision in a gold frame, it is not the
measured and treasured sentences of sentiments;
It is cat knowledge, deer knowledge, the knowledge of the

1. From *Summer Knowledge* (1959).

full-grown foliage, of the snowy blossom and the rounding fruit.
It is the phoenix[2] knowledge of the vine and the grape near
summer's end, when the grape swells and the apple reddens:
It is the knowledge of the ripening apple when it moves to the
fullness of the time of falling to rottenness and death.
For summer knowledge is the knowledge of death as birth,
Of death as the soil of all abounding flowering flaring rebirth.
It is the knowledge of the truth of love and the truth of growing:
it is the knowledge before and after knowledge:
For, in a way, summer knowledge is not knowledge at all: it is
second nature, first nature fulfilled, a new birth
and a new death for rebirth, soaring and rising out
of the flames of turning October, burning November,
the towering and falling fires, growing more and
more vivid and tall
In the consummation and the annihilation of the blaze of fall.

1959

2. A legendary bird that, at age five hundred, burned itself and arose as a new bird from its own ashes.

IRWIN SHAW
1913–1984

In an introduction to *Irwin Shaw Short Stories: Five Decades* (1978), a collection of sixty-three of his stories, Shaw wrote:

> I am a product of my times. I remember the end of World War I, the bells and whistles and cheering, and as an adolescent I profited briefly from the boom years. I suffered the Depression; exulted at the election of Franklin D. Roosevelt; drank my first glass of legal 3.2 beer the day Prohibition ended; mourned over Spain; listened to the Communist sirens; sensed the coming of World War II; went to that war; was shamed by the McCarthy era; saw the rebirth of Europe; marveled at the new generation of students; admired Kennedy; mourned over Vietnam. I have been praised and blamed, and all the while living my private life the best way I could.

As Alfred Kazin said in a preface to that volume, Irwin Shaw "got with exceptional vividness the feel of a time"—the eventful periods in which he lived his life and about which he wrote prolifically.

Born poor in Brooklyn as Irwin Gilbert Shamforoff, he was variously a truck driver, factory worker, semipro football player, and, in 1934, a graduate of Brooklyn College when it had no campus, merely space in some downtown office buildings. In 1936, he became well known for a strong antiwar play, *Bury the Dead*, followed shortly by *The Gentle People*, an antifascist play. Several short stories also made his reputation—chiefly, *Sailor off the Bremen* (anti-Nazi), *The Eighty Yard Run* (later a TV drama), and *The Girls in Their Summer Dresses* (President Kennedy's favorite story, it is said).

He published often in the *New Yorker* before World War II, afterward in more "middlebrow" magazines like *Collier's*, *Redbook*, *Mademoiselle*. The author of nine novels, his best-known and most enduring work is his book about World War II, *The*

Young Lions (1948), which was often compared to Norman Mailer's *The Naked and the Dead* (1948) and James Jones's *From Here to Eternity* (1951). Shaw's novel is multifaceted, dealing with a Jewish soldier named Noah Ackerman as he faces anti-Semitism in the American army and combat in Europe, as well as a German junior officer fighting his way through the war's major battles. Ackerman ultimately kills the German and is himself killed. It was made into a film in 1958 in which Marlon Brando played the German officer.

Shaw's Jewish stories and themes are not many considering his voluminous overall production, but they are noteworthy. He saw the concentration camps and wrote on refugees; he covered the Eichmann trial in Jerusalem; and, with noted film director Jules Dassin, he collaborated on a documentary on the Six Day War. *The Lament of Madame Rechevsky* was published in a collection of stories called *Welcome to the City* (1942) and displays Shaw's finely attuned ear for New York and for class and ethnic speech rhythms and idioms, as well as his knowledge of the vanishing world of Yiddish theater.

The Lament of Madame Rechevsky

The telephone rang and rang through the silken room, tumbled with sleep, lit here and there by the morning sunlight that broke through the hangings in little bright patches. Helen sighed and wriggled in the bed, and, still with her eyes closed, reached out and picked up the phone. The ringing stopped and Helen sighed in relief and wearily put the phone to her ear.

The sound of weeping, deep and bitter, welled along the wires.

"Hello, Momma," Helen said, still with her eyes closed.

"Helen," Madam Rechevsky said. "How are you, Helen?"

"Fine, Momma." Helen stretched desperately under the covers. "What time is it?"

"Nine o'clock." Helen winced, closed her eyes more tightly. "Momma, darling," she said gently, "why must you call so early?"

"When I was your age," Madam Rechevsky said, weeping, "I was up at six in the morning. Working my fingers to the bone. A woman thirty-eight shouldn't spend her whole life sleeping."

"Why do you always say thirty-eight?" Helen protested. "Thirty-six. Why can't you remember—thirty-six!"

"On this subject, Helen, darling," Madam Rechevsky said coldly, through her tears, "I am absolutely definite."

Helen finally opened her eyes, slowly, with effort, looked wearily up at the sun-streaked ceiling. "Why're you crying, Momma?"

There was a pause over the wires, then the weeping started afresh, on a new high pitch, deep, despairing, full of sorrow.

"Tell me, Momma," Helen said.

"I must go to Poppa's grave. You must come right downtown and take me to Poppa's grave."

Helen sighed. "Momma, I have three different places I have to be today."

"My own child!" Madam Rechevsky whispered. "My own daughter! Refuses to take her mother to the grave of her own father."

"Tomorrow," Helen pleaded. "Can't you make it tomorrow?"

"Today!" Madam Rechevsky's voice reached across Manhattan high and tragic, as in the old days, when she strode on the stage and discovered that her stepmother was wearing her dead mother's jewels. "I woke up this morning and a voice spoke to me. 'Go to Abraham's grave! Immediately! Go to the grave of your husband!' "

"Momma," Helen said gently. "Poppa's been dead fifteen years. How much difference can one day make to him?"

"Never mind," Madam Rechevsky said, with magnificent, resounding resignation. "Forgive me if I have troubled you on this trifling matter. Go. Go to your appointments. Go to the beauty parlor. Go to the cocktail parties. I will take the subway to your dead father's grave."

Helen closed her eyes. "I'll pick you up in an hour, Momma."

"Yes," said Madam Rechevsky decisively. "And please don't wear that red hat. For your father's sake."

"I won't wear the red hat." Helen lay back and wearily put the phone back on its pedestal.

"This is a fine car to be going to a cemetery in," Madam Rechevsky was saying as they drove out through Brooklyn. She sat up straight as a little girl in school, savagely denying her seventy-three years with every line of her smart seal coat, every expert touch of rouge, every move of her silken legs. She looked around her contemptuously at the red leather and chromium of Helen's roadster. "A sport model. A great man lies buried, his relatives come to visit him in a cream-colored convertible automobile."

"It's the only car I have, Momma." Helen delicately twisted the wheel in her eloquent, finely gloved hands. "And I'm lucky they haven't taken it away from me by now."

"I told you that was the wrong man for you, in the first place, didn't I?" Madam Rechevsky peered coldly at her daughter, her deep gray eyes flashing and brilliant, rimmed beautifully in mascara, with a touch of purple. "Many years ago I warned you against him, didn't I?"

"Yes, Momma."

"And now—now you are lucky when you collect alimony six months out of twelve." Madam Rechevsky laughed bitterly. "Nobody ever listened to me, not my own children. Now they suffer."

"Yes, Momma."

"And the theater." Madam Rechevsky waved her hands fiercely. "Why aren't you on the stage this season?"

Helen shrugged. "The right part hasn't come along this season."

"The right part!" Madam Rechevsky laughed coldly. "In my day we did seven plays a year, right part or no right part."

"Momma, darling . . ." Helen shook her head. "It's different now. This isn't the Yiddish Theater and this isn't 1900."

"That was a better theater," Madam Rechevsky said loudly. "And that was a better time."

"Yes, Momma."

"Work!" Madam Rechevsky hit her thighs emphatically with her two hands. "We worked! The actor acted, the writer wrote, the audience came! Now—movies! Pah!"

"Yes, Momma."

"Even so, you're lazy." Madam Rechevsky looked at herself in her handbag mirror to make sure that the violence of her opinions had not disarranged her face. "You sit back and wait for alimony and even so it doesn't come. Also . . ." She examined her daughter critically. "The way you dress is very extreme." She squinted to sharpen the image. "But you make a striking impression, I won't deny that. Every one of my daughters makes a striking impression." Madam Rechevsky shook her head. "But nothing like me, when I was a little younger . . ." She sat back and rode in silence. "Nothing like me . . ." she murmured. "Nothing like me, at all. . . ."

Helen walked briskly beside her mother through the marble-crowded cemetery, their feet making a busy scuffle along the well-kept gravel walks. Madam Rechevsky clutched a dozen yellow chrysanthemums in her hands and on her face was a look of anticipation, almost pleasure, as they approached the grave.

"Perhaps . . ." A bearded old man in holy black, all very clean and pink-faced, came up to them and touched Madam Rechevsky's arm. "Perhaps you would like me to make a prayer for the dead, lady?"

"Go away!" Madam Rechevsky pulled her arm away impatiently. "Abraham Rechevsky does not need professional prayers!"

The old man bowed gently, spoke softly, "For Abraham Rechevsky I will pray for nothing."

Madam Rechevsky stopped, looked at the man for a moment. Her cold gray eyes smiled a little. "Give the old man a dollar, Helen," she said and touched the man's arm with royal condescension.

Helen dug in her bag and produced a dollar and the old man bowed gravely again.

Helen hurried after her mother.

"See," Madam Rechevsky was muttering as she charged along. "See. Dead fifteen years and still he is famous, all over the world. I bet that old man hasn't offered to pray for anyone free for twenty-five years." She turned on Helen. "And yet you didn't want to come!" She strode on, muttering, "All over the world."

"Don't walk so fast, Momma," Helen protested. "Your heart . . ."

"Don't worry about my heart." Madam Rechevsky stopped, put her arm out sharply to stop her daughter. "We are in sight. You stay here. I want to go to the grave alone." She spoke without looking at Helen, her eyes on the massive gray granite tombstone thirty yards away, with her husband's name on it and underneath his, space for her own. She spoke very softly. "Turn around, Helen, darling. I want this to be private. I'll call you when I'm ready for you."

She walked slowly toward the tombstone, holding the chrysanthemums before her like a gigantic bride's bouquet. Helen sat on a marble bench near the grave of a man named Axelrod, and turned her head.

Madam Rechevsky approached her husband's grave. Her face was composed, the lips set, the chin high, out of the smart seal collar. She knelt gracefully, placed the chrysanthemums in a compact spray of yellow on the cold earth against the granite. She patted the flowers lightly with one hand to make a pattern more pleasing to the eye, and stood up. She stood without speaking, looking at the even, dead, winter-brown grass that spread across the grave.

Slowly, still looking at the faded grass, she took off first one glove, then the other, and absently stuffed them into a pocket, leaving her white and brilliantly manicured hands bare.

Then she spoke.

"Abraham!" she cried, her voice ringing and imperious and fiercely intimate. "Abraham!" the proud, useful voice echoed and re-echoed among the marble on the small rolling hills of the cemetery. "Abraham, listen to me!"

She took a deep breath, and disregarding the formal stone, spoke directly to the earth beneath her. "You've got to help me, Abraham. Trouble, trouble . . . I'm old and I'm poor and you've left me alone for fifteen years." The resonance and volume had gone from her voice, and she spoke quietly, with the little touch of impatience that comes to women's voices when they are complaining to their husbands. "Money. All your life you never made less than fifteen hundred dollars a week and now they bother me for rent." Her lips curled contemptuously as she thought of the miserable men who came to her door on the first of each month. "You rode in carriages, Abraham. You always owned at least four horses. Wherever you went everybody always said, 'There goes Abraham Rechevsky!' When you sat down to eat, fifty people always sat down with you. You drank wine with breakfast, dinner and supper, and fifty people always drank it with you. You had five daughters by me and God knows how many by other women and every one of them was dressed from Paris from the day she could walk. You had six sons and each one of them had a private tutor from Harvard College. You ate in the best restaurants in New York, London, Paris, Budapest, Vienna, Berlin, Warsaw, Rio de Janeiro. You ate more good food than any other man that ever lived. You had two overcoats at one time lined with mink. You gave diamonds and rubies and strings of pearls to enough women to make up three ballet companies! Sometimes you were paying railroad fare for five women at one time crossing the country after you, on tour. You ate and you drank and you always had a baby daughter in your lap till the day you died, and you lived like a king of the earth, in all respects." Madam Rechevsky shook her head at the grave. "And I? Your wife? Where is the rent?"

Madam Rechevsky paced deliberately to the foot of the grave and addressed herself even more directly to her husband. "A king, to the day you died, with a specialist from Vienna and three trained nurses and four consulting doctors for an old man, seventy-seven, who had exhausted himself completely with eating and drinking and making love. Buried . . . buried like a king. Three blocks long. The line behind your coffin was three blocks long on Second Avenue[1] at the funeral, thousands of grown men and women crying into their handkerchiefs in broad daylight. And I? Your wife? Forgotten! Money spent, theater gone, husband dead, no insurance . . . Only one thing left—children."

Madam Rechevsky smiled coldly at her husband. "And the children—like their father. Selfish. Thinking of themselves. Silly. Doing crazy things. Getting mixed up with ridiculous people. Disastrous. The whole world is disastrous, and your children have led disastrous lives. Alimony, movies, trouble with girls, never any money, never . . . Relatives are dying in Germany. Five hundred dollars would have saved them. No five hundred dollars. And I am

1. From the turn of the century until the 1940s, many Yiddish theaters were located on Second Avenue below Fourteenth Street.

getting older day by day and the ones that can help won't, and the ones that want to help, can't. Three times a week the dressmaker calls me with old bills. Disastrous! Why should it happen to me?"

Once more, for a moment, Madam Rechevsky's voice went high and clear and echoed among the small graveyard hills. "Why should it happen to me? I worked for you like a slave. I got up at five o'clock in the morning. I sewed the costumes. I rented the theaters. I fought with the authors about the plays. I picked the parts for you. I taught you how to act, Abraham. The Great Actor, they said, the Hamlet of the Yiddish Theater, people knew your name from South Africa to San Francisco, the women tore off their gowns in your dressing room. You were an amateur before I taught you; on every line you tried to blow down the back of the theater. I worked on you like a sculptor on a statue. I made you an artist. And in between . . ." Madam Rechevsky shrugged ironically. "In between I took care of the books, I hired the ushers, I played opposite you better than any leading lady you ever had, I gave you a child every two years and fed all the others other women gave you the rest of the time. With my own hands I polished the apples they sold during intermission!"

Madam Rechevsky slumped a little inside her fashionable seal coat, her voice sank to a whisper. "I loved you better than you deserved and you left me alone for fifteen years and I'm getting older and now they bother me for rent. . . ." She sat down on the cold earth, on the dead winter grass covering the grave. "Abraham," she whispered, "you've got to help me. Please help me. One thing . . . One thing I can say for you—whenever I was in trouble, I could turn to you. Always. Help me, Abraham."

She was silent a moment, her bare hands outspread on the grass. Then she shrugged, stood up, her face more relaxed, confident, at peace, than it had been in months. She turned away from the grave and called.

"Helen, darling," she called. "You can come here now."

Helen left the marble bench on the plot of the man named Axelrod and walked slowly toward her father's grave.

1942, 1978

KARL SHAPIRO
1913–2000

Karl Shapiro, poet, editor, and critic, was born in Baltimore. He was the second son in a moderately observant Jewish family of fluctuating fortunes. He attended various local colleges and universities, among them Johns Hopkins. During a semester at the University of Virginia, he felt ostracized as an Eastern European Jew and would later observe that Jews and poets alike were "outsiders," that Jewishness enveloped one in "an atmosphere of mysterious pride and sensitivity" in which even the highest achievement, however, "was touched by a sense of the comic." Shapiro decided early that he was a poet, publishing his first book privately at age twenty-two. He worked for some time in his father's business but was attending library school when he was drafted to serve in the Pacific in World War II. While a soldier, he produced a surprising volume of work—four books of poems between 1941 and 1945, one published in Melbourne, Australia. During the war, his poems appeared in *Good Housekeeping* as well as in *Poetry* and other journals; a Shapiro poem was included in the prestigious *Five Young American Poets*. One of his wartime books, *V-Letter and Other Poems* (1944), would win the Pulitzer prize.

Shapiro married his literary agent in 1945; two years later he was appointed poetry consultant at the Library of Congress. After two years as an associate professor at Johns Hopkins, he became editor of *Poetry*, the magazine that, since its 1912 founding, had more than any other influenced the course of American poetry. In the years of his editorship (1950–55), the magazine flourished, printing interesting new American and British poets, publishing controversial reviews, and introducing issues devoted to the poetry of other countries. After *Poetry*, he edited *Prairie Schooner* at the University of Nebraska, where he would remain and teach for ten years. He also taught at the Universities of Chicago and California, and shared the Bollingen Prize with John Berryman in 1969.

Shapiro's work was variously influenced by the works of W. H. Auden, Walt Whitman, and William Carlos Williams. His career was marked by his often-courageous stands against other literary powers. Taking a strong position against T. S. Eliot, Allen Tate, Robert Lowell, and ten others, he voted against awarding the first Bollingen Prize to Ezra Pound for *The Pisan Cantos,* which contain highly anti-Semitic passages. He fought against the conservatism of Eliot and the academicism of the New Critics, while being ironically aware of his own embourgeoisement, which he attacked in *The Bourgeois Poet*. Several of the poems that appear here are from *Poems of a Jew*. In 1958, that title was still a provocation.

My Grandmother[1]

My grandmother moves to my mind in context of sorrow
And, as if apprehensive of near death, in black;
Whether erect in chair, her dry and corded throat harangued by grief,
Or at ragged book bent in Hebrew prayer,
Or gentle, submissive, and in tears to strangers;
Whether in sunny parlor or back of drawn blinds.

Though time and tongue made any love disparate,
On daguerreotype[2] with classic perspective
Beauty I sigh and soften at is hers.
I pity her life of deaths, the agony of her own,
But most that history moved her through
Stranger lands and many houses,
Taking her exile for granted, confusing
The tongues and tasks of her children's children.

1942 — 1942, 1978

1. From *Person, Place and Thing* (1942); *Collected Poems 1940–1978* (1978).
2. An early kind of photograph produced on a silverplate made sensitive by iodine. The process was invented in France by Louis Daguerre (1789–1851).

Lord, I Have Seen Too Much[1]

Lord, I have seen too much for one who sat
In quiet at his window's luminous eye
And puzzled over house and street and sky,
Safe only in the narrowest habitat;
Who studied peace as if the world were flat,
The edge of nature linear and dry,
But faltered at each brilliant entity
Drawn like a prize from some magician's hat.

Too suddenly this lightning is disclosed:
Lord, in a day the vacuum of Hell,
The mouth of blood, the ocean's ragged jaw,
More than embittered Adam ever saw
When driven from Eden to the East[2] to dwell,
The lust of godhead hideously exposed!

1943 1944, 1978

Sunday: New Guinea[1]

The bugle sounds the measured call to prayers,
The band starts bravely with a clarion hymn,
From every side, singly, in groups, in pairs,
Each to his kind of service comes to worship Him.

Our faces washed, our hearts in the right place,
We kneel or stand or listen from our tents;
Half-naked natives with their kind of grace
Move down the road with balanced staffs like mendicants.[2]

And over the hill the guns bang like a door
And planes repeat their mission in the heights.
The jungle outmaneuvers creeping war
And crawls within the circle of our sacred rites.

I long for our disheveled Sundays home,
Breakfast, the comics, news of latest crimes,
Talk without reference, and palindromes,
Sleep and the Philharmonic and the ponderous *Times*.[3]

I long for lounging in the afternoons
Of clean intelligent warmth, my brother's mind,

1. *From V-Letter and Other Poems* (1944); *Collected Poems 1940–1978* (1978).
2. God sent Adam and Eve to the east when he expelled them from paradise and set a flaming sword at the eastern side of the Garden of Eden to prevent their return (Genesis 3.24). "Hell": the place of the dead (*scheol* [Hebrew]) and the place of punishment after death.

1. *From V-Letter and Other Poems* (1944); *Collected Poems 1940–1978* (1978).
2. Members of religious communities required to support themselves by begging for alms.
3. The Sunday newspaper. "Palindromes": words, sentences, or rhymes that read the same both forward and backward—for instance "Madam I'm Adam." "Philharmonic": a symphony orchestra.

Books and thin plates and flowers and shining spoons,
And your love's presence, snowy, beautiful, and kind.

1943 1944, 1978

Israel[1]

When I think of the liberation of Palestine,
When my eye conceives the great black English[2] line
Spanning the world news of two thousand years,
My heart leaps forward like a hungry dog,
My heart is thrown back on its tangled chain,
My soul is hangdog in a Western[3] chair.

When I think of the battle for Zion[4] I hear
The drop of chains, the starting forth of feet,
And I remain chained in a Western chair.
My blood beats like a bird against a wall,
I feel the weight of prisons in my skull
Falling away; my forebears stare through stone.

When I see the name of Israel[5] high in print
The fences crumble in my flesh; I sink
Deep in a Western chair and rest my soul.
I look the stranger clear to the blue depths
Of his unclouded eye. I say my name
Aloud for the first time unconsciously.

Speak of the tillage of a million heads
No more. Speak of the evil myth no more
Of one who harried Jesus on his way
Saying, *Go faster*. Speak no more
Of the yellow badge, *secta nefaria*.[6]
Speak the name only of the living land.

1948 1958, 1978

1. From *Poems of a Jew* (1958); *Collected Poems 1940–1978* (1978).
2. After World War I, the League of Nations gave the English a mandate over Palestine. In 1948, Palestine became the State of Israel.
3. Occidental.
4. A hill in Jerusalem, the royal residence of King David and his successors; figuratively, the Jewish homeland.
5. Jacob, the son of Isaac, is chosen by God to inherit the land and pass it on to his descendants. When God chooses him, God changes his name to Israel (Genesis 35.10–12).
6. Evil cult (Latin). "Tillage": preparing land for cultivation. "Yellow badge": European Jews wore yellow badges from the thirteenth to the fifteenth centuries in accord with papal decree and, in Nazi Germany, wore similar star-shaped badges from 1942 until the end of World War II.

The Alphabet[1]

The letters of the Jews[2] as strict as flames
Or little terrible flowers lean
Stubbornly upwards through the perfect ages,
Singing through solid stone the sacred names.
The letters of the Jews are black and clean
And lie in chain-line over Christian pages.
The chosen letters bristle like barbed wire
That hedge the flesh of man,
Twisting and tightening the book that warns.
These words, this burning bush, this flickering pyre
Unsacrifices the bled son of man
Yet plaits his crown of thorns.[3]

Where go the tipsy idols of the Roman
Past synagogues of patient time,
Where go the sisters of the Gothic rose,
Where go the blue eyes of the Polish women
Past the almost natural crime,
Past the still speaking embers of ghettos,[4]
There rise the tinder flowers of the Jews.
The letters of the Jews are dancing knives
That carve the heart of darkness seven ways.
These are the letters that all men refuse
And will refuse until the king arrives
And will refuse until the death of time
And all is rolled back in the book of days.[5]

1954 — 1958, 1978

1. From *Poems of a Jew* (1958); *Collected Poems 1940–1978* (1978).
2. I.e., the Hebrew alphabet.
3. Jesus was crowned with thorns by the Roman soldiers who crucified him (Matthew 27.29). "Burning bush": appeared to Moses in the wilderness, from which the voice of God spoke (Exodus 3.2, Acts 7.30). "Son of man": a phrase often used in the Bible to mean "human being" (Job 25.6).
4. In Europe, limited enclosures within Christian territory where Jews were enjoined to live until Napoleon I (1769–1821) abolished them. Ghettos were reinstituted in Germany and Poland by the Nazis during World War II. "The Roman": Roman forces destroyed the Temple in Jerusalem and ruled the Jews in 70 C.E. "Gothic": a style of architecture, popular in the Middle Ages, characterized by pointed arches, vaulting, and great height. "Rose": a reference to rose windows, which are of stained glass, are circular, and often appear above the doorway of a cathedral. "Polish": Auschwitz, the most infamous of the death camps set up by the Nazis, was in Poland. Many Poles aided the Nazis in their implementation of the Final Solution—exterminating (at Auschwitz, this meant gassing and cremating) the Jews.
5. God's record book, which determines who will live or die, prosper or come to evil in the coming year, is sealed on Yom Kippur. "Heart of darkness": the title of Joseph Conrad's 1902 novel. "Seven": a significant number in the Bible—for instance, in the story of the creation (Genesis 1), the story of Noah and the Flood (Genesis 7), the story of Jacob and his wives (Genesis 29), the story of Joseph and the dreams of the pharaoh (Genesis 41). "Until the king arrives": a reference to the Messiah, who ends evil, brings exiles home, and ushers in the world to come.

ARTHUR MILLER
b. 1915

Arthur Miller is one of the preeminent playwrights of the twentieth century and one of America's most distinguished men of letters. For more than six decades, his plays, fiction, screenplays, television scripts, and essays have been unremittingly concerned with the claims of the individual conscience and the need for moral and social responsibility, all couched in language that is rooted in reality while reaching toward poetry.

Miller, one of three children, was born in Manhattan into a solidly middle-class family. His mother was born in the United States, his father, a manufacturer of women's coats, in pre–World War I Austria-Hungary. During the depression of the 1930s, his father's business suffered, and the family moved to Brooklyn, where Miller attended Abraham Lincoln High School. Since his family was unable to afford to send him to college, he went to work as a clerk in a warehouse, saving enough to attend the University of Michigan from 1934 to 1938. At Michigan, he began to write plays and twice won its prestigious Avery Hopwood Award for student writers. After graduation, he worked for a time for the Federal Theatre Project in Manhattan, while living and continuing to write on Long Island. His first production in New York was *The Man Who Had All the Luck* (1944), which closed after four performances. But his career was launched. He had become known and was solicited for more work, including the play *All My Sons* (1947), which won the New York Drama Critics Award and established his reputation.

He was married in 1940 to Mary Slattery, a social worker, with whom he had two children. They were divorced in 1956, the year in which he married Marilyn Monroe. The disaster of that marriage, which ended in divorce in 1960, is part of the fabric of his play *After the Fall* (1964) and of Monroe's last film, *The Misfits* (1961). Miller married Inge Morath, an Austrian-born photographer, in 1962, with whom he has had a daughter and with whom he has collaborated on several projects, notably a record in prose and photographs of their trip to the Soviet Union, *In Russia* (1969).

Miller is perhaps best known and honored for three of his early plays, which helped define their epochs. *All My Sons*, the one play he said he "tried to do in completely realistic Ibsen-like form," marked his real debut in the theater. It concerns Joe Keller, an aircraft manufacturer who, presumably to help his family maintain their status, delivers defective equipment that may have been the cause of death to many United States pilots, including his own son, in World War II. He is denounced by his disillusioned surviving son and kills himself.

In *Death of a Salesman* (1949), the central character, Willy Loman, is similarly denounced by a disillusioned son for the hollowness of the myths and the faulty values he lives by and that he tries uncritically to transmit to his sons. Miller attempts to impart a tragic dimension to this ordinary man—a "low" man rather than one of high station, familiar to classical tragedy. Loman's failure and fall, in which he sacrifices himself for his family, is given an almost heroic aspect. The play was awarded a Pulitzer prize and has been translated and produced all over the world as well as successfully revived in fine productions right up to the present time. Miller experimented with form and style in this play, creating a fluid, often dreamlike sequence of events, with past and present interpenetrating and with language that is more poetic than naturalistic. His subsequent work usually represents similar departures from excessive realism (with the exception of *A Memory of Two Mondays*, 1955) yet is frequently and erroneously considered under that rubric. He has written: "I prize the poetic above all else in the theater." His play *A View from the Bridge* (1955), which he has characterized as his most "operatic," was, indeed, made into a most successful opera in 1999.

The Crucible (1953) has been his most often-produced play in this country and throughout the world. The play deals with the Salem witch trials of the late seventeenth century but is invariably seen to have contemporary relevance. Miller had been led to its subject of mass hysteria, guilt by association, and demand for public confession by the events of the McCarthy era of the early 1950s. Senator Joseph McCarthy conducted and inspired often groundless investigations and persecution of people for their beliefs—in that period, of those suspected of being "subversive" or Communists. The parallels are compelling, but Miller also shows that the hero John Proctor's honorable refusal to respond to the hysteria is based not only on his being true to himself, but also on a recognition of his own fallibility. This complexity of theme heightens one's admiration for Miller's own refusal to respond to the House Un-American Activities Committee's request in 1956 that he become an informer and "name names" of those people he had known whom he suspected of being Communists. He was indicted for contempt, sentenced to prison, but the sentence was overturned upon appeal to the Supreme Court.

Miller's politics have always been liberal, inclining him toward social engagement. He has taken part in various Democratic National Conventions, and in 1965 he was elected to the first of his two terms as president of International PEN (Poets, Playwrights, Editors, Essayists and Novelists). In that role, he did notable work promoting international understanding and freedom for writers everywhere.

His work often includes characters whose speech rhythms (Miller was fluent in Yiddish) and family and social values could be considered Jewish, even when not specifically so identified. He may have consciously de-ethnicized, as it were, *Death of a Salesman* and other early works not so much out of a desire to "universalize" his themes perhaps—as critics have often observed—but because he did not want to provide fuel for anti-Semites who might seize upon some unsavory aspect of his characters. According to scholar Louis Harap, Miller was sensitive to such a possibility after the publication of his novel *Focus* (1945), which attacked middle-class anti-Semitism, when "a torrent of anti-semitic venom" descended upon him. Nevertheless, Miller often does deal with Jews and Jewish concerns. Among other works, he wrote explicitly about Jews and against Nazi ideology in *Incident at Vichy* (1964) and in a strong television play, *Playing for Time* (1985), the account of a French survivor of Auschwitz. Most recently, *Broken Glass* (1994) (the title refers to the Nazis' 1938 Kristallnacht—Crystal Night—pogrom against German Jews, so called because of all the broken glass from windows of Jewish-owned shops) is a play set in the 1930s about a Brooklyn woman's paralysis, revealed to be related to her husband's fear and rejection of his Jewishness. The play was first produced at the Long Wharf Theatre in New Haven, then to great success in London (he has always been much admired in England), where it was awarded England's Olivier Award for Best Play of 1995. It returned to America as a drama on public television.

Monte Sant' Angelo, his story about the survival of Jewishness in the most unlikely circumstances and its vivifying effect upon the central character, was originally published in *Harper's* magazine in March 1951 and was included in that year's *O. Henry Prize Stories*.

Monte Sant' Angelo[1]

The driver, who had been sitting up ahead in perfect silence for nearly an hour as they crossed the monotonous green plain of Foggia, now said something. Appello quickly leaned forward in the back seat and asked him what he had said. "That is Monte Sant' Angelo[2] before you." Appello lowered his

1. From *I Don't Need You Anymore* (1967).

2. The name of both a town and a mountain in

head to see through the windshield of the rattling little Fiat.[3] Then he nudged Bernstein, who awoke resentfully, as though his friend had intruded. "That's the town up there," Appello said. Bernstein's annoyance vanished, and he bent forward. They both sat that way for several minutes, watching the approach of what seemed to them a comically situated town, even more comic than any they had seen in the four weeks they had spent moving from place to place in the country. It was like a tiny old lady living on a high roof for fear of thieves.

The plain remained as flat as a table for a quarter of a mile ahead. Then out of it, like a pillar, rose the butte; squarely and rigidly skyward it towered, only narrowing as it reached its very top. And there, barely visible now, the town crouched, momentarily obscured by white clouds, then appearing again tiny and safe, like a mountain port looming at the end of the sea. From their distance they could make out no road, no approach at all up the side of the pillar.

"Whoever built that was awfully frightened of something," Bernstein said, pulling his coat closer around him. "How do they get up there? Or do they?"

Appello, in Italian, asked the driver about the town. The driver, who had been there only once before in his life and knew no other who had made the trip—despite his being a resident of Lucera, which was not far away—told Appello with some amusement that they would soon see how rarely anyone goes up or comes down Monte Sant' Angelo. "The donkeys will kick and run away as we ascend, and when we come into the town everyone will come out to see. They are very far from everything. They all look like brothers up there. They don't know very much either." He laughed.

"What does the Princeton chap say?" Bernstein asked.

The driver had a crew haircut, a turned-up nose, and a red round face with blue eyes. He owned the car, and although he spoke like any Italian when his feet were on the ground, behind his wheel with two Americans riding behind him he had only the most amused and superior attitude toward everything outside the windshield. Appello, having translated for Bernstein, asked him how long it would take to ascend. "Perhaps three quarters of an hour—as long as the mountain is," he amended.

Bernstein and Appello settled back and watched the butte's approach. Now they could see that its sides were crumbled white stone. At this closer vantage it seemed as though it had been struck a terrible blow by some monstrous hammer that had split its structure into millions of seams. They were beginning to climb now, on a road of sharp broken rocks.

"The road is Roman," the driver remarked. He knew how much Americans made of anything Roman. Then he added, "The car, however, is from Milan." He and Appello laughed.

And now the white chalk began drifting into the car. At their elbows the altitude began to seem threatening. There was no railing on the road, and it turned back on itself every two hundred yards in order to climb again. The Fiat's doors were wavering in their frames; the seat on which they sat kept inching forward onto the floor. A fine film of white talc settled onto their clothing and covered their eyebrows. Both together began to cough. When

---

the southern province of Puglia in Italy. "Foggia": an area east-southeast of Rome whose center is the great Puglia plain, which meets Monte Sant' Angelo.

3. An automobile made by an Italian company.

they were finished Bernstein said, "Just so I understand it clearly and without prejudice, will you explain again in words of one syllable why the hell we are climbing this lump of dust, old man?"

Appello laughed and mocked a punch at him.

"No kidding," Bernstein said, trying to smile.

"I want to see this aunt of mine, that's all." Appello began taking it seriously.

"You're crazy, you know that? You've got some kind of ancestor complex. All we've done in this country is look for your relatives."

"Well, Jesus, I'm finally in the country, I want to see all the places I came from. You realize that two of my relatives are buried in a crypt in the church up there? In eleven hundred something."

"Oh, is this where the monks came from?"

"Sure, the two Appello brothers. They helped build that church. It's very famous, that church. Supposed to be Saint Michael[4] appeared in a vision or something."

"I never thought I'd know anybody with monks in his family. But I still think you're cracked on the whole subject."

"Well, don't you have any feeling about your ancestors? Wouldn't you like to go back to Austria[5] or wherever you came from and see where the old folks lived? Maybe find a family that belongs to your line, or something like that?"

Bernstein did not answer for a moment. He did not know quite what he felt and wondered dimly whether he kept ragging his friend a little because of envy. When they had been in the country courthouse where Appello's grandfather's portrait and his great-grandfather's hung—both renowned provincial magistrates; when they had spent the night in Lucera where the name Appello meant something distinctly honorable, and where his friend Vinny was taken in hand and greeted in that intimate way because he was an Appello—in all these moments Bernstein had felt left out and somehow deficient. At first he had taken the attitude that all the fuss was childish, and yet as incident after incident, landmark after old landmark, turned up echoing the name Appello, he gradually began to feel his friend combining with this history, and it seemed to him that it made Vinny stronger, somehow less dead when the time would come for him to die.

"I have no relatives that I know of in Europe," he said to Vinny. "And if I had they'd have all been wiped out by now."

"Is that why you don't like my visiting this way?"

"I don't say I don't like it," Bernstein said and smiled by will. He wished he could open himself as Vinny could; it would give him ease and strength, he felt. They stared down at the plain below and spoke little.

The chalk dust had lightened Appello's black eyebrows. For a fleeting moment it occurred to Appello that they resembled each other. Both were over six feet tall, both broad-shouldered and dark men. Bernstein was thinner, quite gaunt and long-armed. Appello was stronger in his arms and stooped a little, as though he had not wanted to be tall. But their eyes were

4. An archangel, who was supposed to have appeared here ca. 490 C.E. The sanctuary is a destination for pilgrims. Michael has been considered the special protector of the Jewish people (Daniel 10.13). "Crypt": a vault under a church that is used for burials or as a chapel.

5. One of the countries to which Russian and Polish Jews fled between ca. 1888 and 1914.

not the same. Appello seemed a little Chinese around the eyes, and they glistened black, direct, and, for women, passionately. Bernstein gazed rather than looked; for him the eyes were dangerous when they could be fathomed, and so he turned them away often, or downward, and there seemed to be something defensively cruel and yet gentle there.

They liked each other not for reasons so much as for possibilities; it was as though they both had sensed they were opposites. And they were lured to each other's failings. With Bernstein around him Appello felt diverted from his irresponsible sensuality, and on this trip Bernstein often had the pleasure and pain of resolving to deny himself no more.

The car turned a hairpin curve with a cloud below on the right, when suddenly the main street of the town arched up before them. There was no one about. It had been true, what the driver had predicted—in the few handkerchiefs of grass that they had passed on the way up the donkeys had bolted, and they had seen shepherds with hard mustaches and black shakos[6] and long black cloaks who had regarded them with the silent inspection of those who live far away. But here in the town there was no one. The car climbed onto the main street, which flattened now, and all at once they were being surrounded by people who were coming out of their doors, putting on their jackets and caps. They did look strangely related, and more Irish than Italian.

The two got out of the Fiat and inspected the baggage strapped to the car's roof, while the driver kept edging protectively around and around the car. Appello talked laughingly with the people, who kept asking why he had come so far, what he had to sell, what he wanted to buy, until he at last made it clear that he was looking only for his aunt. When he said the name the men (the women remained at home, watching from the windows) looked blank, until an old man wearing rope sandals and a knitted skating cap came forward and said that he remembered such a woman. He then turned, and Appello and Bernstein followed up the main street with what was now perhaps a hundred men behind them.

"How come nobody knows her?" Bernstein asked.

"She's a widow. I guess she stays home most of the time. The men in the line died out here twenty years ago. Her husband was the last Appello up here. They don't go much by women; I bet this old guy remembered the name because he knew her husband by it, not her."

The wind, steady and hard, blew through the town, washing it, laving its stones white. The sun was cool as a lemon, the sky purely blue, and the clouds so close their keels seemed to be sailing through the next street. The two Americans began to walk with the joy of it in their long strides. They came to a two-story stone house and went up a dark corridor and knocked. The guide remained respectfully on the sidewalk.

There was no sound within for a few moments. Then there was—short scrapes, like a mouse that started, stopped, looked about, started again. Appello knocked once more. The doorknob turned, and the door opened a foot. A pale little woman, not very old at all, held the door wide enough for her face to be seen. She seemed very worried.

"Ha?" she asked.

"I am Vincent Georgio."

6. High fur hats.

"Ha?" she repeated.

"Vicenzo Giorgio Appello."

Her hand slid off the knob, and she stepped back. Appello, smiling in his friendly way, entered, with Bernstein behind him closing the door. A window let the sun flood the room, which was nevertheless stone cold. The woman's mouth was open, her hands were pressed together as in prayer, and the tips of her fingers were pointing at Vinny. She seemed crouched, as though about to kneel, and she could not speak.

Vinny went over to her and touched her bony shoulder and pressed her into a chair. He and Bernstein sat down too. He told her their relationship, saying names of men and women, some of whom were dead, others whom she had only heard of and never met in this sky place. She spoke at last, and Appello could not understand what she said. She ran out of the room suddenly.

"I think she thinks I'm a ghost or something. My uncle said she hadn't seen any of the family in twenty or twenty-five years. I bet she doesn't think there are any left."

She returned with a bottle that had an inch of wine at the bottom of it. She ignored Bernstein and gave Appello the bottle. He drank. It was vinegar. Then she started to whimper and kept wiping the tears out of her eyes in order to see Appello. She never finished a sentence, and Appello kept asking her what she meant. She kept running from one corner of the room to another. The rhythm of her departures and returns to the chair was getting so wild that Appello raised his voice and commanded her to sit.

"I'm not a ghost, Aunty. I came here from America—" He stopped. It was clear from the look in her bewildered, frightened eyes that she had not thought him a ghost at all, but what was just as bad—if nobody had ever come to see her from Lucera, how could anybody have so much as thought of her in America, a place that did exist, she knew, just as heaven existed and in exactly the same way. There was no way to hold a conversation with her.

They finally made their exit, and she had not said a coherent word except a blessing, which was her way of expressing her relief that Appello was leaving, for despite the unutterable joy at having seen with her own eyes another of her husband's blood, the sight was itself too terrible in its associations, and in the responsibility it laid upon her to welcome him and make him comfortable.

They walked toward the church now. Bernstein had not been able to say anything. The woman's emotion, so pure and violent and wild, had scared him. And yet, glancing at Appello, he was amazed to see that his friend had drawn nothing but a calm sort of satisfaction from it, as though his aunt had only behaved correctly. Dimly he remembered himself as a boy visiting an aunt of his in the Bronx,[7] a woman who had not been in touch with the family and had never seen him. He remembered how forcefully she had fed him, pinched his cheeks, and smiled and smiled every time he looked up at her, but he knew that there was nothing of this blood in that encounter; nor could there be for him now if on the next corner he should meet a woman who said she was of his family. If anything, he would want to get away from

7. A borough of New York City.

her, even though he had always gotten along with his people and hadn't even the usual snobbery about them. As they entered the church he said to himself that some part of him was not plugged in, but why he should be disturbed about it mystified him and even made him irritated with Appello, who now was asking the priest where the tombs of the Appellos were.

They descended into the vault of the church, where the stone floor was partly covered with water. Along the walls, and down twisting corridors running out of a central arched hall, were tombs so old no candle could illuminate most of the worn inscriptions. The priest vaguely remembered an Appello vault but had no idea where it was. Vinny moved from one crypt to another with the candle[8] he had bought from the priest. Bernstein waited at the opening of the corridor, his neck bent to avoid touching the roof with his hat. Appello, stooped even more than usual, looked like a monk himself, an antiquary, a gradually disappearing figure squinting down the long darkness of the ages for his name on a stone. He could not find it. Their feet were getting soaked. After half an hour they left the church and outside fought off shivering small boys selling grimy religious postcards, which the wind kept taking from their fists.

"I'm sure it's there," Appello said with fascinated excitement. "But you wouldn't want to stick out a search, would you?" he asked hopefully.

"This is no place for me to get pneumonia," Bernstein said.

They had come to the end of a side street. They had passed shops in front of which pink lambs hung head down with their legs stiffly jutting out over the sidewalk. Bernstein shook hands with one and imagined for Vinny a scene for Chaplin[9] in which a monsignor would meet him here, reach out to shake his hand, and find the cold lamb's foot in his grip, and Chaplin would be mortified. At the street's end they scanned the endless sky and looked over the precipice upon Italy.

"They might even have ridden horseback down there, in armor—Appellos." Vinny spoke raptly.

"Yeah, they probably did," Bernstein said. The vision of Appello in armor wiped away any desire to kid his friend. He felt alone, desolate as the dried-out chalk sides of this broken pillar he stood upon. Certainly there had been no knights in his family.

He remembered his father's telling of his town in Europe, a common barrel of water, a town idiot, a baron[1] nearby. That was all he had of it, and no pride, no pride in it at all. Then I am an American, he said to himself. And yet in that there was not the power of Appello's narrow passion. He looked at Appello's profile and felt the warmth of that gaze upon Italy and wondered if any American had ever really felt like this in the States. He had never in his life sensed so strongly that the past could be so peopled, so vivid with generations, as it had been with Vinny's aunt an hour ago. A common water barrel, a town idiot, a baron who lived nearby. . . . It had nothing to do with *him*. And standing there he sensed a broken part of himself and wondered with a slight amusement if this was what a child felt on discovering that the

8. Commonly sold at the entrance to a Catholic sanctuary. Candles are lit before shrines as an offering that supports prayers.
9. Charlie Chaplin (1889–1977), British-born internationally beloved film actor, comedian, and director, most famous for creating the "Tramp" character in silent films.
1. A nobleman and landowner.

parents who brought him up were not his own and that he entered his house not from warmth but from the street, from a public and disordered place. . . .

They sought and found a restaurant for lunch. It was at the other edge of the town and overhung the precipice. Inside, it was one immense room with fifteen or twenty tables; the front wall was lined with windows overlooking the plain below. They sat at a table and waited for someone to appear. The restaurant was cold. They could hear the wind surging against the window-panes, and yet the clouds at eye level moved serenely and slow. A young girl, the daughter of the family, came out of the kitchen, and Appello was questioning her about food when the door to the street opened and a man came in.

For Bernstein there was an abrupt impression of familiarity with the man, although he could not fathom the reason for his feeling. The man's face looked Sicilian, round, dark as earth, high cheekbones, broad jaw. He almost laughed aloud as it instantly occurred to him that he could converse with this man in Italian. When the waitress had gone, he told this to Vinny, who now joined in watching the man.

Sensing their stares, the man looked at them with a merry flicker of his cheeks and said, "*Buon giorno*."[2]

"*Buon giorno*," Bernstein replied across the four tables between them, and then to Vinny, "Why do I feel that about him?"

"I'll be damned if I know," Vinny said, glad now that he could join his friend in a mutually interesting occupation.

They watched the man, who obviously ate here often. He had already set a large package down on another table and now put his hat on a chair, his jacket on another chair, and his vest on a third. It was as though he were making companions of his clothing. He was in the prime of middle age and very rugged. And to the Americans there was something mixed up about his clothing. His jacket might have been worn by a local man; it was tight and black and wrinkled and chalkdust-covered. His trousers were dark brown and very thick, like a peasant's, and his shoes were snubbed up at the ends and of heavy leather. But he wore a black hat, which was unusual up here where all had caps, and he had a tie. He wiped his hands before loosening the knot; it was a striped tie, yellow and blue, of silk, and no tie to be bought in this part of the world, or worn by these people. And there was a look in his eyes that was not a peasant's inward stare; nor did it have the innocence of the other men who had looked at them on the streets here.

The waitress came with two dishes of lamb for the Americans. The man was interested and looked across his table at the meat and at the strangers. Bernstein glanced at the barely cooked flesh and said, "There's hair on it."

Vinny called the girl back just as she was going to the newcomer and pointed at the hair.

"But it's lamb's hair," she explained simply.

They said, "Oh," and pretended to begin to cut into the faintly pink flesh.

"You ought to know better, signor, than to order meat today."

The man looked amused, and yet it was unclear whether he might not be a trifle offended.

"Why not?" Vinny asked.

2. "Good morning" (Italian).

"It's Friday,[3] signor," and he smiled sympathetically.

"That's right!" Vinny said although he had known all along.

"Give me fish," the man said to the girl and asked with intimacy about her mother, who was ill these days.

Bernstein had not been able to turn his eyes from the man. He could not eat the meat and sat chewing bread and feeling a rising urge to go over to the man, to speak to him. It struck him as being insane. The whole place—the town, the clouds in the streets, the thin air—was turning into a hallucination. He knew this man. He was sure he knew him. Quite clearly that was impossible. Still, there was a thing beyond the impossibility of which he was drunkenly sure, and it was that if he dared he could start speaking Italian fluently with this man. This was the first moment since leaving America that he had not felt the ill-ease of traveling and of being a traveler. He felt as comfortable as Vinny now, it seemed to him. In his mind's eye he could envisage the inside of the kitchen; he had a startlingly clear image of what the cook's face must look like, and he knew where a certain kind of soiled apron was hung.

"What's the matter with you?" Appello asked.

"Why?"

"The way you're looking at him."

"I want to talk to him."

"Well, talk to him." Vinny smiled.

"I can't speak Italian, you know that."

"Well, I'll ask him. What do you want to say?"

"Vinny—" Bernstein started to speak and stopped.

"What?" Appello asked, leaning his head closer and looking down at the tablecloth.

"Get him to talk. Anything. Go ahead."

Vinny, enjoying his friend's strange emotionalism, looked across at the man, who now was eating with careful but immense satisfaction. "*Scusi*, signor."[4]

The man looked up.

"I am a son of Italy from America. I would like to talk to you. We're strange here."

The man, chewing deliciously, nodded with his amiable and amused smile and adjusted the hang of his jacket on the nearby chair.

"Do you come from around here?"

"Not very far."

"How is everything here?"

"Poor. It is always poor."

"What do you work at, if I may ask?"

The man had now finished his food. He took a last long drag of his wine and got up and proceeded to dress and pull his tie up tightly. When he walked it was with a slow, wide sway, as though each step had to be conserved.

"I sell cloth here to the people and the stores, such as they are," he said. And he walked over to the bundle and set it carefully on a table and began untying it.

3. A day of abstinence from meat, traditionally observed by Roman Catholics to memorialize Christ's suffering and dying on a Friday.

4. "Excuse me, Sir" (Italian).

"He sells cloth," Vinny said to Bernstein.

Bernstein's cheeks began to redden. From where he sat he could see the man's broad back, ever so slightly bent over the bundle. He could see the man's hands working at the knot and just a corner of the man's left eye. Now the man was laying the paper away from the two bolts of cloth, carefully pressing the wrinkles flat against the table. It was as though the brown paper were valuable leather that must not be cracked or rudely bent. The waitress came out of the kitchen with a tremendous round loaf of bread at least two feet in diameter. She gave it to him, and he placed it flat on top of the cloth, and the faintest feather of a smile curled up on Bernstein's lips. Now the man folded the paper back and brought the string around the bundle and tied the knot, and Bernstein uttered a little laugh, a laugh of relief.

Vinny looked at him, already smiling, ready to join the laughter, but mystified. "What's the matter?" he asked.

Bernstein took a breath. There was something a little triumphant, a new air of confidence and superiority in his face and voice. "He's Jewish, Vinny," he said.

Vinny turned to look at the man. "Why?"

"The way he works that bundle. It's exactly the way my father used to tie a bundle—and my grandfather. The whole history is packing bundles and getting away. Nobody else can be as tender and delicate with bundles. That's a Jewish man tying a bundle. Ask him his name."

Vinny was delighted. "Signor," he called with that warmth reserved in his nature for members of families, any families.

The man, tucking the end of the string into the edge of the paper, turned to them with his kind smile.

"May I ask your name, signor?"

"My name? Mauro di Benedetto."

"Mauro di Benedetto. Sure!" Vinny laughed, looking at Bernstein. "That's Morris of the Blessed. Moses."

"Tell him I'm Jewish," Bernstein said, a driving eagerness charging his eyes.

"My friend is Jewish," Vinny said to the man, who now was hoisting the bundle onto his shoulder.

"Heh?" the man asked, confused by their sudden vivacity. As though wondering if there were some sophisticated American point he should have understood, he stood there smiling blankly, politely, ready to join in this mood.

"*Judeo*, my friend."

"*Judeo?*" he asked, the willingness to get the joke still holding the smile on his face.

Vinny hesitated before this steady gaze of incomprehension. "*Judeo*. The people of the Bible," he said.

"Oh, yes, yes!" The man nodded now, relieved that he was not to be caught in ignorance. "*Ebreo*,"[5] he corrected. And he nodded affably to Bernstein and seemed a little at a loss for what they expected him to do next.

"Does he know what you mean?" Bernstein asked.

"Yeah, he said, 'Hebrew,' but it doesn't seem to connect. Signor," he

5. *Ebreo* is the more common term (Italian).

addressed the man, "why don't you have a glass of wine with us? Come, sit down."

"Thank you, signor," he replied appreciatively, "but I must be home by sundown and I'm already a little late."

Vinny translated, and Bernstein told him to ask why he had to be home by sundown.

The man apparently had never considered the question before. He shrugged and laughed and said, "I don't know. All my life I get home for dinner on Friday night, and I like to come into the house before sundown. I suppose it's a habit; my father—you see, I have a route I walk, which is this route. I first did it with my father, and he did it with his father. We are known here for many generations past. And my father always got home on Friday night before sundown. It's a manner of the family I guess."

"*Shabbas*[6] begins at sundown on Friday night," Bernstein said when Vinny had translated. "He's even taking home the fresh bread for the Sabbath. The man is a Jew, I tell you. Ask him, will you?"

"*Scusi*, signor." Vinny smiled. "My friend is curious to know whether you are Jewish."

The man raised his thick eyebrows not only in surprise but as though he felt somewhat honored by being identified with something exotic. "Me?" he asked.

"I don't mean American," Vinny said, believing he had caught the meaning of the man's glance at Bernstein. *"Ebreo,"* he repeated.

The man shook his head, seeming a little sorry he could not oblige Vinny. "No," he said. He was ready to go but wanted to pursue what obviously was his most interesting conversation in weeks. "Are they Catholics? The Hebrews?"

"He's asking me if Jews are Catholics," Vinny said.

Bernstein sat back in his chair, a knotted look of wonder in his eyes. Vinny replied to the man, who looked once again at Bernstein as though wanting to investigate this strangeness further, but his mission drew him up and he wished them good fortune and said good-by. He walked to the kitchen door and called thanks to the girl inside, saying the loaf would warm his back all the way down the mountain, and he opened the door and went out into the wind of the street and the sunshine, waving to them as he walked away.

They kept repeating their amazement on the way back to the car, and Bernstein told again how his father wrapped bundles. "Maybe he doesn't know he's a Jew, but how could he not know what Jews are?" he said.

"Well, remember my aunt in Lucera?" Vinny asked. "She's a schoolteacher, and she asked me if you believed in Christ. She didn't know the first thing about it. I think the ones in these small towns who ever heard of Jews think they're a Christian sect of some kind. I knew an old Italian once who thought all Negroes were Jews and white Jews were only converts."

"But his name . . ."

" 'Benedetto' is an Italian name too. I never heard of 'Mauro' though. 'Mauro' is strictly from the old sod."

"But if he had a name like that, wouldn't it lead him to wonder if . . . ?"

"I don't think so. In New York the name 'Salvatore' is turned into 'Sam.'

6. Sabbath (Yiddish).

Italians are great for nicknames; the first name never means much. 'Vicenzo' is 'Enzo,' or 'Vinny' or even 'Chico.' Nobody would think twice about 'Mauro' or damn near any other first name. He's obviously a Jew, but I'm sure he doesn't know it. You could tell, couldn't you? He was baffled."

"But, my God, bringing home a bread for *Shabbas!*" Bernstein laughed, wide-eyed.

They reached the car, and Bernstein had his hand on the door but stopped before opening it and turned to Vinny. He looked heated; his eyelids seemed puffed. "It's early—if you still want to I'll go back to the church with you. You can look for the boys."

Vinny began to smile, and then they both laughed together, and Vinny slapped him on the back and gripped his shoulder as though to hug him. "Goddam, now you're starting to enjoy this trip!"

As they walked briskly toward the church the conversation returned always to the same point, when Bernstein would say, "I don't know why, but it gets me. He's not only acting like a Jew, but an Orthodox Jew.[7] And doesn't even know—I mean it's strange as hell to me."

"You look different, you know that?" Vinny said.

"Why?"

"You do."

"You know a funny thing?" Bernstein said quietly as they entered the church and descended into the vault beneath it. "I feel like—at home in this place. I can't describe it."

Beneath the church, they picked their way through the shallower puddles on the stone floor, looking into vestibules, opening doors, searching for the priest. He appeared at last—they could not imagine from where—and Appello bought another candle from him and was gone in the shadows of the corridors where the vaults were.

Bernstein stood—everything was wet, dripping. Behind him, flat and wide, rose the stairway of stones bent with the tread of millions. Vapor steamed from his nostrils. There was nothing to look at but shadow. It was dank and black and low, an entrance to hell. Now and then in the very far distance he could hear a step echoing, another, then silence. He did not move, seeking the root of an ecstasy he had not dreamed was part of his nature; he saw the amiable man trudging down the mountains, across the plains, on routes marked out for him by generations of men, a nameless traveler carrying home a warm bread on Friday night—and kneeling in church on Sunday. There was an irony in it he could not name. And yet pride was running through him. Of what he should be proud he had no clear idea; perhaps it was only that beneath the brainless crush of history a Jew had secretly survived, shorn of his consciousness but forever caught by that final impudence of a Saturday Sabbath in a Catholic country; so that his very unawareness was proof, a proof as mute as stones, that a past lived. A past for me, Bernstein thought, astounded by its importance for him, when in fact he had never had a religion or even, he realized now, a history.

He could see Vinny's form approaching in the narrow corridor of crypts, the candle flame flattening in the cold draft. He felt he would look differently

7. The most traditional of the three main branches of the Jewish religion (Orthodox, Conservative, and Reform).

into Vinny's eyes; his condescension had gone and with it a certain embarrassment. He felt loose, somehow the equal of his friend—and how odd that was when, if anything, he had thought of himself as superior. Suddenly, with Vinny a yard away, he saw that his life had been covered with an unrecognized shame.

"I found it! It's back there!" Vinny was laughing like a young boy, pointing back toward the dark corridor.

"That's great, Vinny," Bernstein said. "I'm glad."

They were both stooping slightly under the low, wet ceiling, their voices fleeing from their mouths in echoed whispers. Vinny held still for an instant, catching Bernstein's respectful happiness, and saw there that his search was not worthless sentiment. He raised the candle to see Bernstein's face better, and then he laughed and gripped Bernstein's wrist and led the way toward the flight of steps that rose to the surface. Bernstein had never liked anyone grasping him, but from this touch of a hand in the darkness, strangely, there was no implication of a hateful weakness.

They walked side by side down the steep street away from the church. The town was empty again. The air smelled of burning charcoal and olive oil. A few pale stars had come out. The shops were all shut. Bernstein thought of Mauro di Benedetto going down the winding, rocky road, hurrying against the setting of the sun.

1951

ISAAC ROSENFELD
1918–1956

Like a bright comet, Isaac Rosenfeld passed through and illuminated the 1940s and 1950s for Jewish intellectuals. He and his work were affectionately admired by all who knew him, especially by his long-time friend Saul Bellow. He died tragically young of a heart attack in Chicago, leaving a wife and two children. He left as well a small body of significant work: one novel, *Passage from Home* (1946), and two posthumous books: *An Age of Enormity* (1962), a collection of his essays, and *Alpha and Omega* (1966), a collection of stories.

Born and educated in Chicago, where he earned an M.A. in philosophy at the University of Chicago, he married and moved to New York City in pursuit of a Ph.D. at New York University. He was to claim later that reading *Moby-Dick* turned him away from logical positivism and toward literature. For a while during the war years, he became a barge skipper on the East River, then a regular contributor to and an editor of the *New Republic*, and a prized writer for *Partisan Review, Commentary*, the *New Leader*, and the *Nation*. In his reviews, he favored realist and naturalist fiction, while his own stories often approached the surreal. His novel, *Passage from Home*, was quasi-autobiographical, recounting an unsatisfactory relationship with his father (his mother died when he was two years old) and his search for "home." A Jew bereft of religion, community, family, the central character does respond to a Hasidic rabbi's enthusiastic spirit. Rosenfeld's persistent theme was alienation and loneliness, which he sees as the center of both the Jewish and the

American experience. Despite that, he gravitated toward Jewish life and themes, and even wrote four stories in Yiddish.

His Yiddish was exemplary, he and Bellow often collaborating on translating T. S. Eliot and others. Bellow admired his sense of fun and irreverent mimicking, writing, "He [Rosenfeld] invented Yiddish proletarian poets, he did a translation of Eliot's *Prufrock*, a startling x-ray of those hallowed bones which bring Anglo-Saxons and Jews together in a surrealistic unity, a masterpiece of irreverence."

By the end of the 1940s, Rosenfeld felt blocked as a writer, a situation he sometimes attributed to the sexual repressions and inhibitions of his Jewish American life. He attempted to get back to a healthy, free, instinctual life with a commitment of several years to the theories of Austrian psychologist Wilhelm Reich (1897–1957). Reich had begun as a disciple of Sigmund Freud but was expelled from the international psychoanalytical movement, having taken to extremes the emphasis upon sexuality and its repression as the wellspring of character and behavior. Reich believed he had discovered an element called "orgone," which was a primal source of energy in the universe. Orgone energy could be drawn upon or "accumulated" in a box designed for this purpose, in which one sat in order to increase and potentially free one's sexual energy. As Rosenfeld admitted, perhaps exaggeratedly, to a colleague at the University of Minnesota, where he taught from 1951 to 1953, his flirtation with Reichian theory may have been just one more effort to energize his language. Since Yiddish was his first language, he said, English always seemed "flat" to him, and he came to see that his early Trotskyism (with which he became bored), his use of jazz and idioms from popular culture (in which he was a pioneer), his use of Yiddishisms in his criticism (now a commonplace among writers) were all efforts to enliven his prose. Most readers would agree that he succeeded, and his penetrating intellect and humane orientation can still please and enlighten.

The Situation of the Jewish Writer[1]

All discussions pertaining to the Jews must begin with some very gloomy observations. The Jews are, everywhere, a minority group, and it is a particular misfortune these days to be a minority group in the United States. A conscious member of such a group is necessarily overconscious: he is distracted by race and religion, distressed by differences which in a healthy society would be considered healthful. The very simple state of being a Jew—and it should occupy no more of a man's attention than any ordinary fact of his history—has created traumas, fears of violence, defenses against aggression.[2] These are about the worst conditions under which an artist could seek to carry on his work. An artist should first of all have the security of a dignified neutrality. He should be able to consider himself a *mensch mit alle menschen gleich*[3]—that is, an equal, a man among men, a representative even if extraordinary individual. But a Jewish writer unconsciously feels that he may at any time be called to account not for his art, nor even for his life, but for his Jewishness. Only a brave man can be a brave artist, let alone a good one, in a hostile world. It is therefore clear to me that whatever con-

1. From *Under Forty: A Symposium of American Literature and the Younger Generation of American Jews* (1944).
2. Anti-Semitism in the United States began to decline only after the revelations of the Nazi death camps in Eastern Europe in 1945 and the Nürnberg Trials in 1947.
3. "A person equal to all other people" (Yiddish).

tribution Jewish writers may make to American literature will depend on matters beyond their control as writers.

But the position of Jewish writers—artists and intellectuals in general—is not entirely an unfortunate one. For the most part the young Jewish writers of today are the children of immigrants, and as such—not completely integrated in society and yet not wholly foreign to it—they enjoy a critical advantage over the life that surrounds them. They are bound to observe much that is hidden to the more accustomed native eye.

The insight available to most Jewish writers is a natural result of their position in American life and culture. Jews are marginal men. As marginal men, living in cities and coming from the middle classes they are open to more influences than perhaps any other group. I vaguely recall a Yiddish proverb to the effect that bad luck always knows where to find a Jew; and as a barometer of political calamity the Jews in this country are second only to the Negroes. But even gentler influences, short of fatality, know where to find Jews—in the middle, in the overlapping area where events converge. And the middle position has its cultural correlate, that of being centrally exposed to all movements in art and in thought. This position of cultural exposure gives the Jewish writer the advantage of access. (There is much more to be said about this point—more than I have the space or the knowledge to disclose. But, generally speaking, the position of Jewish writers illustrates one of the strangest phenomena of modern life. Since modern life is so complex that no man can possess it in its entirety, the outsider often finds himself the perfect insider.)

Close as they are to the main developments in America, some Jewish writers may retain more than a little of European culture. Either through their position in the Jewish community, their childhood, or the influence of their immigrant parents, they may possess a sense of reference to an earlier community. I don't know how widespread this old world feeling is among Jewish writers. But if it is at all common, I should say it is a valuable thing. Jews in America have relatively little contact with country life, with small town folk and farmers. But through cultural retention, through a subliminal orientation to more primitive surroundings, they may still find in themselves access to rural life, understanding of its character and traditions.

But it is one thing to consider the Jewish writer's social equipment, and quite another to regard his actual position in society. As a member of an internationally insecure group he has grown personally acquainted with some of the fundamental themes of insecurity that run through modern literature. He is a specialist in alienation (the one international banking system the Jews actually control). Alienation puts him in touch with his own past traditions, the history of the Diaspora;[4] with the present predicament of almost all intellectuals and, for all one knows, with the future conditions of civilized humanity. Today nearly all sensibility—thought, creation, perception—is in exile, alienated from the society in which it barely managed to stay alive.

But alienation from society, like the paradox of the outsider, may function as a condition of entrance into society. Surely it is not a condition for the

4. Historically, the exile of the Jews from Israel to Babylonia in the sixth century B.C.E.; now a reference to all Jews who have been dispersed to non-Jewish lands.

Jew's re-entrance into the world that has rejected him. But persecution may lead him, as it has in the past, to a further effort to envisage the good society. No man suffers injustice without learning, vaguely but surely, what justice is. The desire for justice, once it passes beyond revenge, becomes the deepest motive for social change. Out of their recent sufferings one may expect Jewish writers to make certain inevitable moral discoveries. These discoveries, enough to indict the world, may also be crucial to its salvation.

I do not want to make too much of alienation. It is the only possible condition, the theme we have to work with, but it is undesirable, for it falls short of the full human range. Besides, in every society, in every group, there are what Saul Bellow[5] has called "colonies of the spirit." Artists create their colonies. Some day these may become empires.

1944 1944

5. A Jewish American novelist who won the Nobel prize in 1976 (b.1915).

Achievement and Ambivalence, 1945–1973

Sometime after World War II, a certain Passover joke could be heard in Jewish American circles. It seems that Queen Elizabeth is inspecting her knights, walking with an officer up and down the ranks of her loyal troops, their helmets and breastplates shining. Each man she addresses is as fine as the last, until she stops in front of a real loser, a nebbish, his helmet askew, chain mail tarnished, gauntlets dented. Turning to her officer, the queen inquires: *Mah nishtanah halaila hazeh mikol haleylot?* Or, "Why is this (k)night different from all other (k)nights?"

Difference—for three millennia, the Jews' identifying mark, both resolute and fateful—took on a fresh questionableness in postwar America. During the war, Jews in the armed forces served (and died) alongside other Americans without much regard for race or religion. Thus, movie audiences became familiar with the typical infantry-squad order: "Listen up! I want four volunteers for the next patrol. OK: Houlihan, Jones, Goldberg, Grabowski—front and center!" Hitler had to be defeated not because he was destroying European Jewry, but because he threatened democracy. Meanwhile, stateside Jews backed the war effort like everyone else, growing victory gardens, saving aluminum foil and newsprint, volunteering as neighborhood air-raid wardens. And they went on trusting FDR—President Franklin Delano Roosevelt—who assured them that the way to save Europe's Jews was to defeat the Axis.

That assurance would not come in for much scrutiny until almost a generation later. After the European war ended on May 8, 1945, and atomic bombs had been dropped on Hiroshima and Nagasaki on August 6 and 9, relief and rejoicing prevailed. Difficult as it may be to realize, knowing what we know now, Nazi-ridden Europe's recent horror and mass murder did not leave American Jewry traumatized. "No news reached Woodenton?" a survivor in 1948 asks an assimilated Jew in Philip Roth's *Eli, the Fanatic*. A protective numbing, combined with belated reports and the slow straggle of survivors, let American Jews resume life as usual—or better than usual. Nativism, xenophobia, virulent 1930s anti-Semitism, and the tagging of Roosevelt's New Deal as a "Jew Deal" mainly subsided, although the Senate did pass a 1948 law discriminating against Jewish immigration. The peacetime economy began to flourish.

Yet Jewish students, for instance, could still feel the tail end of prewar prejudice. A small-town midwestern Jew who graduated from Yale in 1920,

Alexander Lowenthal, recalled that back then he'd gone to football games and "rushed to daily chapel together" with classmates Henry Luce (later founder of *Time, Life, Fortune*) and Thornton Wilder (author of *Our Town*). But he definitely could not join most fraternities or take part in other Gentile socializing. And in 1918, the college dean disliked where all the scholarships were going: "We must put a ban on the Jews." A generation later, things hadn't fully improved. In 1944, a Yale alumnus, Leonard Shiman, questioned the college president about quotas. Because a "larger than ever" percentage of applicants came from Jewish homes, Shiman was told, Yale was being selective "to preserve . . . balance." In 1945, they admitted the smallest proportion of Jews since 1922. The director of admissions identified Yale's "Jewish problem": Jews are too pushy, bookish, competitive; the number of those scholastically qualified "remains too large for comfort." Such stereotyping and discrimination persisted into the 1950s. And it was not until the 1960s that Jews started rising into faculty ranks in expectable numbers.

Nagging, subjacent perceptions of difference tainted the literary world, too. Henry Adams and Henry James were gone, with their distaste for the teeming Jews in New York City. But literary anti-Semitism still hung in the air à la Ezra Pound, T. S. Eliot, Thomas Wolfe, E. E. Cummings, John Dos Passos, even William Carlos Williams. Poets such as Stanley Kunitz and Karl Shapiro had early on been informed that merely their names would prevent their commanding an audience. Kirby Allbee, in Saul Bellow's *The Victim* (1947), accosts the protagonist, Asa Leventhal: "Last week I saw a book about Thoreau and Emerson by a man named Lipschitz. . . . People of such background simply couldn't understand." And when Herbert Gold's first story was accepted in 1946, the magazine editor offered some "friendly advice" on his name: to slip a *u* between the *o* and the *l* and launch his career as Herbert Gould. At first, he agreed, then after a sleepless night called back: "*Gold*. My father's name. Without the 'u,' please." The story appeared "back among the lingerie advertisements, in very small type, and it was unlisted in the table of contents." Even from the Jewish standpoint, difference was not always something to be sought after. Arthur Miller's novel *Focus* (1945) and Laura Hobson's *Gentleman's Agreement* (1947) condemned anti-Semitism on the basis that Jews simply wanted to be no different from their fellow American WASPs.

One fairly evident giveaway of difference had been Zionism and the specter of "dual loyalty." Since before the 1776 Revolution, American Jews supported the indigent community in Palestine. Puritans, Mormons, and some Protestant sects were oriented to Zion, and George Eliot's *Daniel Deronda* (1876) spurred Zionist feelings. But it was not until Europe's First Zionist Congress in 1897 that decisive organizing occurred in the United States; even then it remained sporadic and factional. Reform rabbis and long-settled German Jews opposed the movement: "Political Zionism and true Americanism have always seemed mutually exclusive," one rabbi said in 1931. "No man can be a member of two nationalities, Jewish and American."

This wariness of dual loyalty on the part of both Jews and non-Jews intensified when the Nazis came to power in 1933, began persecuting German Jews, and in 1938 threatened Czechoslovak and Austrian Jews. The Balfour Declaration had been signed in 1917, promising a Jewish national homeland in Palestine. Yet in 1939, only months before Hitler invaded Poland, Britain issued a white paper to appease the Arabs, stopping the flow of Jewish immigration to Palestine. This galvanized the American Zionist cause. But such "special pleading" fell by the wayside when Japan bombed Pearl Harbor on December 7, 1941, and Roosevelt rallied the whole country behind a just war. Despite feverish Zionist efforts, the president's ambivalence and an anti-Semitic State Department made it exceedingly difficult to rescue Jews from the midst of a war-torn Europe. Even afterward, with the Axis defeated and survivors adrift throughout Europe, Britain still held the mandate for Palestine. And America, with the world's largest Jewish population, nonetheless kept on restricting the immigration of displaced European Jews, thus aggravating their losses.

In November 1947, Jews and others throughout the world used every means to effect the United Nations' partition plan for Palestine, and President Harry Truman helped swing the vote. Then in May 1948, guided by leading Jews and with an election upcoming, he promptly recognized the new State of Israel. Although Jewish Americans rushed to help defend Israel against the Arab invasions that ensued, few settled there. Too much held them at home.

The matter of Jewish at-homeness versus difference in America is complex, bearing inevitably on every area of life—family, community, work, education, religion—as well as on literature. How people define themselves hinges also on where and when they live; their identity changes over generations and from one historical period to another. After Hitler's attempted genocide made a homeland their most compelling need, Jews realized more acutely than ever their perilous difference, their tenuous, albeit tenacious, identity. Yet while the genocidal slaughter demonstrated that Jews needed a nation like every other nation, Jews in the major remaining diaspora after World War II felt that they deserved to be American like every other American. The turn-of-the-century immigrant generation, like Henry Roth's Albert and Genya in *Call It Sleep* and Tillie Olsen's Eva and David in *Tell Me a Riddle*, had struggled to find their footing on streets not paved with gold after all. Then their children wanted the staple American liberties, the unalienable rights that had been postponed through depression and world war. Alfred Kazin wrote his first work on modern American literature, confidently entitling it *On Native Grounds* (1942), and the book was immediately reprinted as a pocket book for U.S. troops overseas. In Bernard Malamud's story *The Lady of the Lake*, Henry Levin decides that his Jewish past is parochial, expendable, and he travels to postwar Europe, calling himself Henry R. Freeman.

POPULAR CULTURE

The 1920s and 1930s had seen a host of patently Jewish entertainers on stage, in the movies, in print. By 1944 or so and in the immediate postwar years, that rich comic scene largely faded. In literature, too, Jewish presence and particularism were muted. Arthur Miller explained this in 1947, saying that "even an innocent allusion to individual wrong-doing of an individual Jew" might be used as fuel for bigotry. (Philip Roth would later come under attack for ignoring this precaution.) Thus, Miller's greatly successful play

Death of a Salesman (1949), though deriving from his own family experience, shows no explicit Jewish traces.

Another, related reason for the muting of Jewish identity was a slightly uneasy sense, among non-Orthodox Jews, that the task of acculturation remained unfinished. Parents at home might share with their children the delicious linguistic travails in *The Education of H*Y*M*A*N K*A*P*L*A*N* (1937) by Leonard Q. Ross (Leo Rosten) or even Milt Gross's wildly word-mangling immigrants. But for the world at large those parents made sure their children spoke proper English. Indeed, beneath this book's ebullient humor, the parents may have cherished Hyman Kaplan precisely because they felt grateful at living beyond his immigrant tribulations. A kindred humor arose in ritual family gatherings around the radio—Sunday evening at seven—to hear comedian Jack Benny's show, which ran until 1954. The younger members of his audience had no idea he was Jewish, born Benny Kubelsky. On the show, Jack's penny-pinching and his squeaking violin, however Jewishly self-parodic, were offset by his dealings with Mr. Kitzel, whose nasal, Yiddish-flavored speech gave Benny (and his listeners) a sympathetic amusement while distancing them from "Meester Keetzel."

A mixed mind-set also drew many Jews, particularly from the urban Northeast, to two very different entertainers. *The Goldbergs*, listened to religiously for over two decades until 1949 and then, through 1955, watched as one of television's first popular sitcoms, starred Gertrude Berg as Molly, a Bronx matriarch who was a good deal more ethnic and observant than her creator (Berg) or her audience. Her warm Yiddish lilt and sane motherliness fed the nostalgia of her listeners without any threateningly regressive greenhorn vulgarity. "I like to keep things average," Gertrude Berg said. In contrast, there was nothing average or inoffensive about Milton Berle (or Sid Caesar, for that matter). Uncle Miltie's wild, if coarse, verbality and slapstick on TV (1948–56) afforded a cathartic hilarity to acculturated Jews whose own unrefined past was not that deeply out of mind.

In a more pronounced way than anything else, the American fate of Anne Frank's diary furnished a litmus test for postwar sensibilities, though very few people recognized this at the time. For the 1947 Dutch edition, Otto Frank cut out his daughter's remarks on her budding sexuality, plus skeptical asides on her mother and family friends. Meyer Levin, a former war correspondent, responded strongly to the diary's French translation and offered to secure its American publication. Ten publishers rejected it, among them the German Jewish firm of Schocken Books, and the German Jewish philosopher Hannah Arendt disapproved of the diary as sentimental. Eventually, Doubleday brought it out in 1952, introduced by no less a figure than Eleanor Roosevelt, who, instead of specifying Anne's Jewishness, honored her "ultimate shining nobility." (Incidentally, a high point for Jewish communities in those years after her husband's death would be a visit from Eleanor Roosevelt, graciously, equably dining at the rabbi's or temple president's home and then speaking at services.)

Meyer Levin's eulogistic review for the *New York Times* helped start the diary's sensational American career, and Otto Frank agreed to let Levin write a stage adaptation. But Levin's version proved too Jewish for Broadway, too particularist. A scriptwriting couple, then working for MGM, took over and fashioned what was wanted by Otto Frank and the play's producer, Kermit

Bloomgarden, along with his consultant, playwright Lillian Hellman: namely, a drama minimizing Anne's acute Jewish consciousness, making her into a universal voice of martyrdom, a good-hearted, optimistic, and thus consoling icon. As the play's director, Garson Kanin, put it: Anne's thoughts on perennial Jewish persecution were "incidental" and "an embarrassing piece of special pleading." Of course, the Frank family, fleeing Germany in 1933, reveals that ruinous illusion of Jewish universalism and its fellow illusion, the vain hope for German Jewish symbiosis. In any case, the play was a huge success in 1955 (see Philip Roth's *The Ghost Writer*), as was the equally sentimental, sanitized movie (1959).

Such was American Jewry's relatively unobtrusive or nonproblematic presence in the decade following World War II that Senator Joseph McCarthy's crusade against Communists in government (1950–54) did not provoke an anti-Semitic backlash, even though a disproportionate number of the people he investigated were Jews, as were his unsavory lawyer Roy Cohn and aide Gerard David Schine. Nor did the 1951 espionage trial of Julius and Ethel Rosenberg, convicted of giving atomic bomb secrets to the Russians and executed in 1953 (note that the judge and the prosecutor were also Jewish). A generation later, poet Adrienne Rich would write: "She sank however into my soul . . . / Ethel Greenglass Rosenberg Would you / have . . . / collected signatures / for battered women who kill."

INTO THE LITERARY MAINSTREAM

Restrictions against Jews still existed in many social clubs during the 1950s, and few Jews headed major banks or corporations. But they were already prominent in medicine, psychoanalysis, science, law, music, and entertainment, and before long Jews entered the literary mainstream.

A sign of the times can be seen in the *Paris Review* interviews with prominent writers, an ably conducted and widely circulated series. The first collection, stemming from the early to mid-1950s, included two practically invisible Jews, Dorothy Parker and Nelson Algren. In the next, from 1960 to 1961, were two more recognizable but hardly mainstream Jews, Boris Pasternak and S. J. Perelman. But the third set of interviews, from 1962 to 1966, featured Saul Bellow, Norman Mailer, Arthur Miller, Allen Ginsberg, Lillian Hellman, and was introduced by Alfred Kazin. By this time, people "of the Mosaic persuasion," as was said not all that long before, were epitomizing American fiction—so much so that the critic Leslie Fiedler could speak of "Zion as Main Street." Jewish authors have become "representative Americans," he said, while "the American is becoming an imaginary Jew." And what makes these authors representative? Their wisdom "that home itself is exile, that it is the nature of man to feel himself everywhere alienated." Not only Bellow's "dangling man" and Malamud's and Roth's misfits tapped an American vein, but even Miller's Willy Loman in *Death of a Salesman* (1949), J. D. Salinger's Holden Caulfield in *The Catcher in the Rye* (1951), and Mailer's *White Negro* (1957)—none of these outwardly Jewish. Mailer even published some commentaries making existentialist parables out of Martin Buber's Hasidic tales (1962–63). Otherhood joined brotherhood as a Jewish attribute. The question is what wisdom otherhood really engenders.

In an often-cited 1944 symposium held by the predecessor of *Commentary* magazine, Kazin had not felt himself "a part of any meaningful Jewish life or culture," and for Lionel Trilling, the Jewish community could "give no sustenance to the American artist or intellectual who is born a Jew." Of course, this was before the full damage of Hitlerism had shown American Jews how precarious and precious their predicament was. But in that same 1944 symposium, Muriel Rukeyser declared herself "as a poet, woman, American, and Jew." A few years later, she wrote: "To be a Jew in the twentieth century / Is to be offered a gift"—the "agonies" together with "The whole and fertile spirit as guarantee / For every human freedom." And also in 1944, Isaac Rosenfeld said: "Out of their recent sufferings one may expect Jewish writers to make certain inevitable moral discoveries"; "alienation from society . . . may function as a condition of entrance into society."

As the Eisenhower fifties wore on, Jewish writers were "quick to show the lunacy and hollowness of so many present symbols of authority," as Kazin puts it. Certainly, they touched a nerve. The National Book Award was given to Bellow in 1954, Malamud in 1958, Roth in 1959, and those three were so often spoken of in one breath, they might have been playing shortstop, second base, and first in a champion double-play combo. The Pulitzer prize went to Miller in 1957, Kunitz in 1959. And though Allen Ginsberg certainly got no prizes, his prophetlike *Howl* (1956) and *Kaddish* (1961) gave the Beat Generation a Judaic jump start. A Jewish ethos surged to the fore, almost regional in its accent—urban, ironic, richly wordy—much as William Faulkner had made the South strangely exemplary. That ethos involved an ambiguous chosenness in the aftermath of the European Jewish catastrophe, as brilliantly caught in Malamud's *The Last Mohican* (1958) and Roth's *Eli, the Fanatic* (1959). This exchange (from *The Last Mohican*) between a New Yorker and a survivor quite literally makes the Jewish question common parlance: "Am I responsible for you then, Susskind?" "Who else?" By 1960 or so, Edward Field could imagine two famous authors bathing at Coney Island: "They tell me you are called the Yiddish Mark Twain." / "Nu? The way I heard it you are the American Sholem Aleichem." Together they end up "splashing about in the sea like crazy monks."

Why I Choose to Be a Jew, Arthur A. Cohen's 1959 essay, announces that "in the United States today, it is at last possible to choose *not* to remain a Jew." From the Middle Ages through the reigns of communism and Nazism, Jews had no such choice. But now, says Cohen, with acculturation, affluence, and educational achievement, with fear of anti-Semitism and hope for Israel's restoration mainly resolved, Jews can, if they wish, relax or repudiate their Jewishness. Cohen made his choice on religious grounds, for the God of Abraham, Isaac, and Jacob and for the Law of Moses. Most Jews then, as social Judaism proliferated in new suburban synagogues and temples, schools, and community centers, probably fell between Cohen's doctrinal affirmation and Malamud's Henry Levin, alias Henry R. Freeman.

Unlike Jews, black Americans at the turn of the decade enjoyed no such choice. The civil rights movement gaining force then deeply involved many Jewish activists and organizations, as it had for decades. Theologian Abraham Joshua Heschel locked arms with the Reverend Martin Luther King, Jr. in Selma, Alabama; rabbis marched with ministers and priests; Jewish youth flocked south in the summers to work against segregation. In Philadelphia,

Mississippi, in 1964, racists brutally murdered a young black man along with his two Jewish coworkers. Later in the decade, interracial relations became strained. "Black power" and separatism rather than integration, plus the radicalized Black Panthers and Black Muslims, made whites less welcome in the movement. "The Jewish community," sociologist Nathan Glazer says, "which had seen much of its reason for being in its liberal political and social attitudes, began to question the value of these attitudes." Still it remains true that the American Jewish 1960s, like the women's movement a little later, owe in part to the evolution of ethnic self-awareness among black Americans.

Already by 1965, an astute critic such as Robert Alter could observe that the American Jewish literary "renaissance" was playing itself out. Sentimentality was setting in, marked by "garbled Yiddish, misconstrued folklore" from writers "only peripherally or vestigially Jewish," lacking any nutritive cultural matrix. The mid-1960s were not exactly a time when Jewish writers could, like James Joyce's Stephen Dedalus, "forge in the smithy of my soul the uncreated conscience of my race." They were, after all, as Leslie Fiedler notes, dealing in alienation and the fading of deep-dyed Judaic practice. Many novels then were indeed getting a comic lift out of American Jewish life, and Neil Simon's *The Odd Couple* (1965) flourished on Broadway. So did *Fiddler on the Roof* (1964), based on Sholem Aleichem's Tevye tales, though a captivated public may too readily have taken its bittersweet cheer as the truth of shtetl existence.

Meanwhile, two superbly serious novels appeared to great acclaim in 1964: Bellow's *Herzog*, which won the National Book Award, and Henry Roth's *Call It Sleep*, which first came out in 1934 and was rediscovered a generation later, gripping readers not only with its rich Joycean narrative, but because it summoned the poignant hardships of immigrant existence. Chaim Potok's *The Chosen* (1967) takes place later, during the war, genocide, and struggle for Israel. It presents two Orthodox boys, one Hasidic and the other modern, who draw toward each other under differing fatherly constraints. Despite its pointedly Judaic conflicts, the general public greeted this book fervently. As they did a wildly different book, Philip Roth's *Portnoy's Complaint* (1969), whose protagonist shooting off his mouth (and more) might well have gotten his go-ahead from Milton Berle. "Brash Jews" are what Roth wanted in order to dislodge the restraining stereotype—"unaccommodating Jews, full of anger, insult, argument, impudence."

During the 1960s, a "New Left" emerged chiefly on college campuses, spurring and spurred on by an older cadre, including many Jews (among others), and by younger ones such as Abbie Hoffman, Jerry Rubin, and Mark Rudd. Possibly the young were fueled in part by a sense that their parents' generation had not stopped the genocide of a previous war. Protest against the Vietnam War overlapped with the civil rights struggle; Dr. King was assassinated in April 1968, and in June a Palestinian, disturbed by Bobby Kennedy's stance on Israel, shot him to death. Anti-Vietnam protesters disrupting the August 1968 Democratic convention in Chicago were violently put down (and later tried by a judge named Julius Hoffman). That summer's race riots again claimed incidental victims, small Jewish merchants and landlords left in the inner cities after most Jews had moved to the suburbs. The literary reverberations of black-Jewish interaction show up with gusto in Mailer's *The White Negro* (1957), which eagerly fuses hip onto existential daring; with skepticism in Bellow's *Mr. Sammler's Planet* (1970); and with humane anguish in Malamud's *The Tenants* (1971).

Two other events cut shockingly into American consciousness, Jewish and otherwise, during the 1960s. In May 1960, Israeli agents in Argentina seized Adolf Eichmann, the executor of Nazi Germany's so-called "Final Solution to the Jewish Problem." At his 1961 trial in Jerusalem, he claimed to have been a mere functionary obeying orders—though several years earlier he'd told a journalist: "Had we killed all of them, the 10.3 million, I would be happy and say, 'All right, we managed to destroy an enemy.' " Beyond Eichmann's own zeal, hundreds of witnesses and thousands of documents exposed the entire history, effecting a worldwide education. Eichmann was executed in May 1962. Reporting for the *New Yorker*, Hannah Arendt was rebuked for holding European Jewish leadership plus the victims themselves partially responsible for their fate, while Eichmann, she said, exemplified "the banality of evil." And Denise Levertov wrote of his bullet-proof glass "cage, where we may view / ourselves."

But primary sources of understanding were becoming available, translated into English: Elie Wiesel's memoir *Night* (September 1960), André Schwarz-Bart's *The Last of the Just* (1960), Primo Levi's *Survival in Auschwitz (If This Is a Man*, 1961), Piotr Rawicz's *Blood from the Sky* (1964), Jorge Semprún's *The Long Voyage* (1964), Jerzy Kosinski's *The Painted Bird* (1965), Jakov Lind's *Soul of Wood* (1966). In addition, even though detailed accounts of the genocide had surfaced in America as early as 1943, in *The Black Book of Polish Jewry*, along with diaries and memoirs from the 1940s onward, it was not until 1961 that studies such as Raul Hilberg's *The Destruction of the European Jews* and Gerald Reitlinger's *The Final Solution* reached a wide audience.

Naturally, some American novelists felt compelled to respond to the terrible, albeit belated, news brought by the Eichmann trial, but they did not attempt to depict the catastrophe directly. Edward Wallant's *The Pawnbroker* (1961) concerns a survivor in New York's Harlem beset by memories, and Malamud's *The Fixer* (1966) recreates a 1911 anti-Semitic Russian blood libel—the anti-Semitic fantasy that Jews kill Christians to use their blood in making Passover matzo—as a way of gazing peripherally at what happened in Eastern Europe thirty years later. Both these novels were made into striking movies. Norma Rosen's *Touching Evil* (1969) also refracts the horror, by registering the Eichmann trial through American non-Jews who witness it on TV. Finally, it is worth remembering that over twenty years passed before Americans began inquiring into what was known when, from 1941 to 1944, and why the United States did not do more to stop the slaughter and rescue the Jews. David Wyman's *Paper Walls* (1968) is subtitled *America and the Refugee Crisis*, and Arthur Morse's *While Six Million Died* (1968), *A Chronicle of American Apathy*.

One other event touched a nerve among American Jews during the years between John F. Kennedy's assassination in 1963 and the turbulence of 1968—namely, the June 1967 Six Day War. Earlier, in the Sinai campaign of 1956, Israel responded to Egyptian aggression by taking the Gaza Strip and the Sinai Peninsula, only to evacuate them under U.S. and Soviet pressure. This crisis had relatively little impact on American Jews. In May 1967, the major Arab states surrounding Israel—Syria, Egypt, Iraq, Jordan—

threatened (with lavish Soviet support) the country's economy and very existence. Given the traumatic history exposed in the Eichmann trial, American Jews abruptly realized how tied they were by fear and pride to the young state's aloneness and vulnerability. Even those shaped by the Vietnam era to oppose imperialist and military power were thrilled when Israeli air and ground forces broke the Arab armies in a matter of hours and days, occupying Sinai, Gaza, the West Bank of the Jordan, the Golan Heights, and reunifying Jerusalem. At a huge New Politics convention that September, black Americans demanded and got a resolution condemning Israel's "imperialist Zionist war." Some Jews on the Left were troubled because the Six Day War felt necessary—more authentic than Leon Uris's *Exodus* (1958), for example, whose movie version (1960), with the young Paul Newman, goldenly championed Israeli freedom fighters.

Understandably enough, Diaspora writers have not much attempted to evoke Israeli reality from outside. Meyer Levin wrote two novels—on kibbutz life (1931) and on a Polish boy escaping to Palestine (1947)—plus later works. Charles Reznikoff's *Jerusalem the Golden* (1934) and many other poems offer a recuperative memorial vision. Ben Hecht's play *A Flag Is Born* is defiantly Zionist. In 1965, Hugh Nissenson published *A Pile of Stones*, with two stories on Israel, and later he treated the Six Day War. A convincing perspective on Israel comes from Shirley Kaufman. Her first book, *The Floor Keeps Turning* (1970), sets poems in Tiberias, in Jerusalem, and at the Western Wall, whose prayer slips "fall / from every hollow, every crack, / fall in the small pores of my skin, / and I am huge with prayers I cannot hold." Her next books develop a sensitive stance and nuanced voice for an American in Israel—for instance, watching her rebellious daughter at Eilat on the Red Sea: "You wade in it / as far as you can go." Kaufman moved to Jerusalem in 1973 and, while still writing for American ears, has tightened her bond by translating Abba Kovner, Amir Gilboa, and other Israelis.

JEWISH AMERICAN POETRY

The Sorrows of American Jewish Poetry, Harold Bloom put it in a 1972 essay, or *The Question of American Jewish Poetry* in John Hollander's 1988 title: it is a vexed matter, more so than with fiction. What of Emily Dickinson's *kvetchen zikh mit Got*, a constant quarreling with the Bible, as in her stanzas on Jacob and the angel: "And the astonished wrestler found / That he had worsted God." Isn't this more Jewish, or at least Hebraic, than Emma Lazarus's verses before the 1881 Russian pogroms stirred her to compose *Songs of a Semite* (1882)? Were Zukofsky, Kunitz, Schwartz, Rukeyser, Ignatow, Nemerov, and others writing Jewishly only in their few biblical or historical or ethnic poems fit for anthologies such as the present one? Do Halpern's Yiddish and Preil's Hebrew poems ipso facto qualify, even when their subject is a bird or a sunset?

Does "subject" or "content" identify Jewish poetry or possibly something less overt: angst, irony, self-doubt, nostalgia, parental ligature, ethical passion, apostasy? Or is it, more likely, a restless, wrestling reverence for the text, for the word, a reverence more chary and spare than lavish?—though Ginsberg's breath and Levertov's inspiration seem never to give out. At bottom, maybe the question of Jewish American poetry resides in the question itself, the questioning spirit ingrained through centuries of marginalized, exilic chosenness. This would account for a lot: Ginsberg giving Walt Whitman's prophetic line a new Hebraic torque to elegize his wretched mother, Naomi; George Oppen dumbfounded when his young daughter asks about *b'nei Yisrael*, "the children of Israel" in Exodus: "Where were the adults?"; Shirley Kaufman opening her first book's opening poem, on Lot's wife: "But it was right that she / looked back."

John Hollander's essay focuses on a phrase the German-speaking survivor-poet Paul Celan took from Marina Tsvetayeva: "All poets are Jews"—or, more accurately, "All poets are Yids." Every true poet lives "a kind of diaspora in his own langauge," says Hollander, and thus "all poetry is in some way or another unofficial midrash," a searching and revising, even of one's own language. In that sense, a Jewish American poet cannot "write Jewish poetry without thereby writing American poetry." Witness the pared verse of *The Niche Narrows* (2000) by Samuel Menashe, as in his *Promised Land*:

I know Exile
Is always
Green with hope—
The river
We cannot cross
Flows forever.

And the ever-inceptive lines of Gustaf Sobin, as in *Odèss* (where his father was born):

nowhere's too far, you'd
written, if the fingers a-
light amongst letters, and the letters,
bearing the weight of their own impression, still
smoulder with must

"Must"—that is, frenzy, new wine, and necessity. Or take, in translation, Celan's *Psalm*, which is already translating sacred Scripture under the sign of the Shoah:

Blessèd art thou, No One.
In thy sight would
we bloom.
In thy
spite.

Celan's unappeasable honesty, his charged language darkening language, has become a touchstone, and not only for Jewish poets in America. An anthology of world Jewish poetry, *Voices within the Ark* (1980), took its title from Celan's line *Stimmen im Innern der Arche*, "Voices in the innards [or bowels] of the ark."

On the question of identity, we keep coming back to the title, as it were, of this anthology. Our authors—are they Jewish Americans (with the memory of a demeaning hyphen, like Irish-American, Polish-American), or are they

American Jews, Jews living as such in America? During the immigrant surge, Jews and others were considered "unassimilable." As if to disprove that suspicion, the musical sons of New York City immigrants had the chutzpah to newly conceive of American life, even American hinterland—George Gershwin's *Porgy and Bess* (1935), Richard Rodgers and Oscar Hammerstein's *Oklahoma!* (1943), Aaron Copland's *Rodeo* (1942) and *Appalachian Spring* (1944), Leonard Bernstein's *West Side Story* (1957)—and these works swept the country. What gave their composers such native surety? Hammerstein's Oklahoma corn farmers were not singing for themselves only: "We know we belong to the land, and the land we belong to is grand."

Jewish second-generation children grew up hearing (or intuitively knowing) that they were to have what their parents did not—the American birthright: equal entry into college, society, culture, business, professions. Many of them did achieve life, liberty, and the pursuit of happiness. But eventually, in the 1970s, with *Holocaust* and *Israel* becoming quasi watchwords of the faith, a kind of dialectic kicked in. Those children began wanting for *their* children what they themselves had not had: namely, rooted Jewish affiliation, particularist if not parochial. No longer deemed unassimilable or a minority group, Jews might well feel the difficulty of *not* assimilating. Call this, after Freud's *Civilization and Its Discontents*, "Assimilation and Its Discontents."

On September 16, 1919, smarting from the Versailles Treaty's "stab in the back" of German nationalism, Adolf Hitler complained in a letter: "It's the Jew who never calls himself a Jewish German, Jewish Pole, or Jewish American, but always a German, Polish, or American Jew." To be an American Jew might mean (de)nominating oneself nounwise, kin to Russian and Iranian Jews as well as to Canadian and English, while making one's national bond adjectival, circumstantial. A few writers seem to have done that, such as Cynthia Ozick and Shirley Kaufman (and, being European-born, Isaac Bashevis Singer and Elie Wiesel). Most other writers have not. Of course, if "all men are Jews" (Malamud) in suffering or "all poets are Yids" (Celan) in alienation, then Jewish difference gets either universalized or effaced, depending on your vantage point: the more Jewish, the more human, and/or vice versa. Now arrogance, even a pariah's arrogance, arrogating radical humanness primarily to Jews, will not do. It was Franz Kafka, after all, who wrote in his diary in 1914: "What have I in common with Jews? I have scarcely anything in common with myself." Was he, then, being quintessentially Jewish or merely, starkly, human? Kafka also wrote this in his notebook one day: "Writing as a form of prayer."

What form and what future belong to Jewish American literature? One view has it that the cultural community such writing must draw from and speak to was vanishing in the 1970s. Irving Howe, fresh from his masterly *World of Our Fathers* (1976), declared that Jewish American writing had "passed its peak." Admittedly, the immigrant years, becoming the memory of a memory for people born after 1930, could no longer yield the vital stuff of storytelling. Nor could "the historic, moral and religious weight of Judaism," Ruth Wisse said. It's true, the Jewish American community has had no great scribe like Ezra bringing it out of exile, rebuilding the Temple, reading aloud from *Sefer haTorah* so that "all the people were weeping as they listened to the words of the Teaching" (Nehemiah 8.9). Nor a Vilna partisan-poet such as the Israeli Abba Kovner: "When I write I am like a man praying . . . with the community."

In 1973, Charles Leibman's *The Ambivalent American Jew* asserted: "If the Jewish community is to survive, it must become more explicit and conscious about the incompatibility of integration and survival." (Later, a misguided analogy arose: the "Holocaust" brought about by American Jewish intermarriage and assimilation.) Yet in 1973, even as the Yom Kippur assault in September again threatened Israel's survival, most American Jews, like others in the once-vaunted "melting pot," did not sense a clear and present need to choose between integration and survival.

Then, as always, it was probably premature to announce the exhaustion of Jewish content in literature. And, anyway, how can such content be measured or identified? Can you pick up a poem and turn it around the way you do a package in the grocery store, to read a label with its content itemized? Total fat (or let us say schmaltz) 49%, sodium 50%, protein 1%. And what would be the minimum daily requirement of Jewish content? In the foreseeable future, there will probably always be someone looking up from a moment of hard justice in the Bible and saying, with Carl Rakosi,

> I have stumbled
> on the ancient voice
> of honesty
> and tremble
> at the voice
> of my people.

Or, as Cynthia Ozick ventured in 1970: "If we blow into the narrow end of the *shofar*, we will be heard far. But if we choose to be Mankind rather than Jewish and blow into the wider part, we will not be heard at all; for us America will have been in vain."

EPHRAIM E. LISITZKY
1885–1962

One of the central group of Hebrew poets in America, Ephraim E. Lisitzky, in the words of Israeli scholar Gershon Shaked, broke "through the limitations of place and generation" in his innovative dealing with the subjects and themes of the American Indian and the black American. Whether or not Lisitzky knew the poetry on these subjects by his Yiddish contemporaries I. J. Schwartz and Berish Vaynshteyn, this congruence between Hebrew and Yiddish poetry shows how literature in these two Jewish languages became American.

Born in Minsk, Lisitzky was essentially orphaned as a boy. His mother died when he was seven, and his father, a water carrier facing conscription into the czarist army, fled to New York six months later. Living with his stepmother in poverty near his grandfather, a coachman, in Slutzk, Lisitzky studied in several famous local yeshivas, where he proved to be a brilliant student and sought rabbinical ordination. In 1900, he and his stepmother joined his father, now a rag and bottle peddler and part-time bar mitzvah tutor, in Boston.

After obtaining certification in New York to become a *shohet*, or kosher ritual slaughterer, Lisitzky took a job in Auburn, a city in upstate New York. There, he was introduced to Hebrew *Haskalah* writings by a fellow boarder and to socialism and the Yiddish Labor poets by his landlady's son-in-law, and lost his religious faith.

He spent the next decade and a half moving among a variety of jobs in Boston, upstate New York, central Canada, and Milwaukee until he finally settled in New Orleans as the principal of the Hebrew school. During these years, he became known for his poetry and fiction in Hebrew, most of which has never been translated into English. His 1922 narrative poem *Keteko'a shofar* (When the Shofar Sounds) contrasts the spiritual emptiness of small-town American Jews with the religiosity of Eastern European Jews. His 1934 dramatic poem *Naftulei elohim* (The Contests of God) explores the doctrines of Judaism, Christianity, Islam, and Buddhism. In 1937, he published *Medurot do'akhot* (Dying Bonfires), a verse narrative written in the meter of Henry Wadsworth Longfellow's *Hiawatha*, which draws upon Indian legends and evokes the American landscape to tell a story of two American Indian tribes. In 1953, his long poem *Be-oholei kush* (In the Tents of Cush) utilizes spirituals, folklore, and sermons to tell a story of African Americans. His 1960 *Bi-ymei sho'ah u-misho'ah* (In the Days of the Holocaust and Out of the Holocaust) depicts the Nazi destruction of European Jewry. Articles and essays on literature and education published in the Hebrew press were collected in the 1961 *Bi'shevilei hayyim ve-sifrut* (On the Paths of Life and Literature). He also translated into Hebrew two plays by Shakespeare: *The Tempest* (1941) and *Julius Caesar* (1960).

Perhaps Lisitzky's best-known work is his autobiography, *Eleh toledot adam* (These Are the Generations of Mankind), first published in Hebrew in 1949 and, in 1959, as *In the Grip of Cross-Currents*, an English translation by Moshe Kohn, Jacob Sloan, and Gershon Gelbart. The autobiography focuses on specific periods in Lisitzky's early life that illuminate his later work as a poet and teacher of Hebrew. It is both the story of this writer's evolution from a yeshiva student to an American Hebraist and poet, and, by Lisitzky's own account, a universal story for Jews in the modern world.

From In the Grip of Cross-Currents

From *Part IV*[1]

CHAPTER VIII. [THE URGE TO WRITE]

The old urge to write, buried for some time by practical preoccupations, returned to me during this idle period.[2] Only now I began to write poetry instead of scholarly essays. The poetic muse transmitted her poetic spirit to me through an organ grinder.

One evening I was walking home from the park through one of Boston's better neighborhoods, when a raggedy man came toward me pulling an organ. He was middle-aged and thin, with a bent back, a gaunt face where the cheekbones protruded, and skin the color of old parchment. But his features were delicate: his eyes were enormous, dreamy, deep blue.

The organ grinder parked the organ at the curb and ground out a melancholy tune. He shut his eyes, his head sank to his chest, his whole body

1. This part is translated by Moshe Kohn, Jacob Sloan, and Gershon Gelbart.

2. Lisitzky returned to Boston after losing his job as a *shohet* in Auburn, New York.

trembled, as though the organ handle were connected to a musical machine inside *him*, and he were producing the music, rather than the organ. When the tune was done, he took his hat off and held it up, waiting for a window of mercy to open on him. His eyes wandered up and down the stories of the house, but it did no good. The windows of mercy remained shut. No one threw him a coin. He moved the organ and set it opposite another house. His next tune was even sadder than the first—like a prayer of a poor man in his distress to the noblemen of the world: "Turn from your luxurious chambers—heed the cry of a breadless pauper! I do not begrudge you what you have, all I ask of you is: toss me a few crumbs from your rich table!" Again there was no response. He walked down the length of the street, stopping before each house, but everywhere it was the same—no one opened a window, no one threw a coin into his upraised hat.

Finally, the organ grinder parked his organ at the street corner, leaned his elbows on it and cupped his head dejectedly in his hands, his dusk-lit face expressing soul-dejection.

My heart filled with pity for him and hidden strings quivered sadly in my soul as if the grinding organ of that poor man were playing within me, protesting his humiliating misery and asking mercy for him. I hurried to him, drew my pennies from my pocket and placed them on the organ—a gift from one pauper to another—and went my way. I went—but his figure hovered before me and a sad melody filled my soul. I fled to the bank of the Charles River,[3] sat down on a nearby bench and gazed at the beautiful sunset in its resplendent revelation in this glorious landscape to dispel my sorrow—but in vain. The figure of that poor man hovered before my eyes and I saw in him a symbolization of the image of the world. The sorrow of a poor man and the sorrow of a poor world combined in my soul into a melody as sad as the melody of that organ.

I took out a notebook that I carried around in my pocket to jot down notes on my reading, and wrote a poem spontaneously, of a man and a world both poor, forsaken, forgotten, vainly asking for mercy, and of a poor poet who answered their cry and protested their humiliating misery.

A hand touched my shoulder. I looked up, startled. It was Rose.[4] The sadness in her eyes was too much for me to face—I averted my eyes. She sat down next to me, her arm touching mine.

"I have a complaint," she reproached me. "Why do you stay away from our house? We've begun to miss you."

"I haven't just begun to miss you. I've missed you from the first day I stopped coming. But I did it for your sake—believe me, Rose. Rose, I can't marry you—I have no job and no prospects. Take that lucky fellow my uncle is trying to match you with. He can offer you money and position, and I can't. I don't want to stand in your way. I want to leave before it's too late."

An ironic smile creased the corner of Rose's mouth. She nodded: "But it's too late already."

3. A river that separates Boston from Cambridge, Massachusetts.
4. The elder daughter of Lisitzky's uncle's landsman. Lisitzky fell in love with her but broke it off when his uncle matched Rose with his boss.

CHAPTER IX. [MEETING DOLITZKY]

Word got about in Hebrew circles in Boston that Menachem Mendel Dolitzky was coming to town. It was decided to give a public reception in honor of the poet whom J. L. Gordon, then the king of Hebrew poets, had named his heir apparent.[1] True, Dolitzky was coming to Boston to sell some Yiddish novels he had published, and at first the radical young Boston Hebraists boycotted the preparations for the reception. They viewed Dolitzky's penchant for writing trashy Yiddish romances as disgraceful for a Hebrew poet—and they didn't think much of his poetry, either. It was definitely outmoded. But finally, the youngsters decided to forgive Dolitzky because of his past importance, and joined the preparations. I was a member of the planning committee, and was singled out to deliver a formal address of welcome to the guest of honor and present him with an inscribed gold fountain pen.

When I was a yeshiva student I thought there was nothing grander than an author. I saw the square letters of the Hebrew book as godly letters, which were handed down from Sinai, and its author as a sublime, almost divine, superhuman being. The only Hebrew author I had ever met was the Ridbaz,[2] author of a commentary on the Jerusalem Talmud; I imagined every other author would be a man of God, like the Ridbaz. Even after I had given up my religious studies, books and authors remained sacred to me.

I had never even hoped to see a Hebrew writer in person, and here I was to greet a poet! A poet was something of a prophet, I had learned from *Ha-Igron*,[3] the Hebrew-writing primer. Like the prophet, the poet received his inspiration in nightly visions, in meditations, amid fear and trembling and perception of still voices. And the author of this book is none other than Dolitzky, the poet, who had certainly experienced the poetic inspiration he describes, as I had myself, in small measure, at dusk along the banks of the Charles River. In those days I was enthusiastic over the newer Hebrew literature. Still, I remained true to the Haskalah writers, principally J. L. Gordon. It was enough for me that Gordon approved of Dolitzky.

The reception turned out to be a dismal affair. Entering the hall I felt the melancholy that had settled everywhere—on the sooty walls, the dim gaslights, the chandeliers and globes, covered with cobwebs and fly offal. The same melancholy sat on the faces of the Maskilim[4] who comprised the audience. They were gloomy because the occasion reminded them of vanished dreams and days and climes of long ago, when they were young, from which they were banished. The universal black mood was only intensified by the appearance of the guest of honor. I looked at Dolitzky, and felt personally

1. J. L. Gordon (1831–1892) was a major early Hebrew poet, writer, and critic, and an important proponent of the Jewish Enlightenment in Russia. He wrote a poem proclaiming Dolitzky as his successor when Dolitzky was expelled from Moscow. Hebrew poet and Yiddish popular fiction writer Menachem Dolitzky (1856–1931) wrote Hebrew verse satires and short stories about the sufferings of Jews in Russia. He was expelled from Moscow and immigrated to the United States in 1892, where, after failing to make a living from his Hebrew poetry, he wrote serialized novels for the daily Yiddish press for pay.

2. An acronym for Rabbi Jacob David, son of Zev, the rabbi of Slutzk, a famous Talmudic scholar and author of *Commentary and Addenda of the Ridbaz*. An advocate of the harshly moralistic, ascetic Musar movement (the 19th-century reaction against the *Haskalah*'s enlightening influence; its yeshivas educated students in strict ethical behavior) and founder of a *musar* yeshiva, he was one of Lisitzky's teachers.

3. A book by Dolitzky.

4. Proponents of the nineteenth-century *Haskalah,* the Jewish Enlightenment; here, as opposed to the newer writers in Hebrew.

affronted. Indeed, this was no superman at all! Why, he looked nothing like the Ridbaz!

Dolitzky's fat, fleshy body was bloated with a kind of huge flabbiness. His head, broader than it was high, lay heavily, helplessly, between his shoulders. His dirty gray hair was stiff and bristling. There were deep furrows in his heavy-muscled face, which wore an expression of utter pessimism. His dead eyes were cold, fixed, resigned. He mounted the platform to recite some poems; his voice had a leaden clang. He read with no emotion at all: even the poems, which were affecting when read silently, became clichés in rhythm as their author recited them. I sat there funereally all evening. When I went up to the platform to present Dolitzky with the fountain pen, my welcoming speech was like a dirge. It was eminently fitting that the evening should end as it did: a lame pale boy leaning on crutches sang Dolitzky's elegiac "On Zion's Ruins." . . .

CHAPTER X. [THE HEBREW WRITER IN PERSON]

Dolitzky had agreed to see me in his hotel the next evening. It was a dilapidated building, in one of the narrow streets in the Jewish West Side of Boston neighborhood. I found him sprawled out on a threadbare couch, tired and depressed after a day spent going from house to house soliciting subscribers for his Yiddish book. He looked grim. It had been a hot summer day; towards evening the air was stifling and humid. Dolitzky lay there sweating and panting. Outside, the heat rose from the pavement in waves, streetcars clattered back and forth over the iron tracks, and wagons and coaches rattled across the cobblestones. Dolitzky's books lay on a bench in the corner opposite the couch next to an open valise; the gilded letters of his name on the bindings stared at the exhausted poet.

While I struggled to overcome my shyness and hand him the poem I had written on the banks of the Charles River, for his opinion of its merits, he smiled sarcastically:

"Have you read Mendle Mocher Sefarim's *The Book of the Paupers*?[1] You remember the pauper—author, that is to say—who canvasses the rich people in Odessa trying to sell subscriptions to the book he carries around with him in manuscript form—and how Fishke, the pauper, joins up with the author, and the big-hearted people give Fishke more money as a handout than they give the author for a subscription? I'm that author. Fishke was right: 'author' is just a new-fangled way for saying *schnorrer*, beggar. Then why do I write novels? I have a stomach to fill.

"You can't reproach a poet for giving up the Muse when he has a wife and children who don't appreciate his heavenly flights when they're hungry. A poet may be willing to sacrifice himself—but he can't allow his family to have empty bellies on his account. Hell is preferable to that."

His harsh voice softened. Dolitzky was silent a moment, then asked: "You told me last night you wanted to talk to me. What about?"

I handed him the poem and asked him to read it and give me his opinion of it.

1. A famous satirical book of fiction by Mendele Moykhr Sforim (Mendele the Bookseller), a pseudonym for S. Abramovitsh (1835–1917), the founding figure of both modern Yiddish and modern Hebrew literature in Eastern Europe.

I studied Dolitzky's face intently as he read, to get his reaction. My heart was pounding. He looked at me, the same sarcastic smile as before creasing the corners of his mouth.

"Stop it," he said bitterly. "There's no glory in it. The devil with poetry! Don't be a fool poetaster! You know what happens to Hebrew poets in this country: First stage—Hebrew poet. Second stage—Hebrew teacher—or rather cattle herder, with the children in the role of unwilling cattle. Third stage—you write trashy novels for servant maids and teamsters. You're young, you can get into the university here. Learn an honorable profession that will give you a decent living. Do anything, be anything—peddle candles and matches—sell windbags and bubbles, if you must. Be a tailor, a shoemaker, a cobbler—anything but a Hebrew poet in America!"

The street lights outside sifted pallidly through the drawn window shades into the room. Dolitzky did not get up to turn on the gas lamp. He was in the mood to talk and preferred the dark.

"I came to America. I couldn't endure Russia any more. Pogroms, persecution, oppression, restrictions, humiliation—living in Russia was like living in a snake pit for the Jews. It took me a long time to decide to come here. It's very hard leaving a country where you've been born and raised, have studied, have gotten some reputation, and are at home, among your own—the largest and finest Jewish community in the world. Gordon helped me make up my mind. Change your place, change your luck, he thought. He told me I'd have more scope in a free country. The American Jewish community was young; I would sing new songs there.

"So I took his advice. He wrote me across the ocean: 'Go forth to life and to do battle. . . . for the dreams I have dreamt and you shall yet dream.'

" 'Do battle'? With whom? Against whom? What for? In Russia there were people one could fight—respectable enemies. We fought the battle of the Enlightenment and Zionism against our Orthodox brethren; but even the most fanatical of them were men of stature. We may have thought their opinions damaging, but we knew they were solid, stable. They had a tradition to fight for, and you had to respect them for fighting.

"But here in America? If we only had some of those fanatics and reactionaries from the Old Country here! They at least were loyal and devout Jews. Here we have a pack of boors, ignoramuses, whose only thought is to 'make a living,' with nothing spiritual about them. You can despise or pity people like that—you can't fight them. And then there's no one to fight *with* you. The Jewish intellectuals? Heretic Socialists, heroes of Yom Kippur and Tisha B'Av balls;[2] or else professional careerists, uninterested in their own people. The few immigrant Maskilim are like those lean stalks of corn in Pharaoh's dream.[3] The harvest of their enlightenment is meager: a little pedantic grammar, Hebraic crossword puzzles, the elucidation of obscure allusions in Ibn Ezra's commentary on the Bible,[4] and similar trivialities.

2. To express their ideological disregard for religious practices, some Jewish socialists in the United States held dances and feasts on the two most solemn fast days of the Jewish calendar – Yom Kippur, the day of Atonement, and Tisha B'Av, the ninth of Av, commemorating the destruction of both the First and Second Temples in Jerusalem in 586 B.C.E. and 70 C.E, respectively.

3. Joseph interpreted the corn in the pharaoh's dream as symbolizing the seven years of famine that Egypt was destined to suffer (Genesis 41.1–33).

4. Abraham Ibn Ezra (1089–1164), poet, grammarian, biblical commentator, philosopher, astronomer, physician, was born in Toledo, Spain. After 1140, he traveled to Rome, where he wrote commentaries on the Pentateuch, Isaiah, and so forth. Folk tradition calls him a man of few needs

"Then, there's nothing to fight *for*. The Enlightenment and Zionism are disembodied spirits floating in chaos in this country—in the Old Country they were concrete ideas directly related to Jewish life and tradition. So there you are: in America, the Hebrew poet has no one to fight against, no one to fight with, and nothing to fight for. There's no place for him here—he's pushed aside into a corner."

Dolitzky stopped, the words choking in his throat. Silence filled the room, except for the pendulum of the old clock on the wall. Finally, he controlled his emotions and resumed.

"There was one fight I couldn't avoid: making a living. What was a man like me to do in America? Become a door-to-door peddler? A Hebrew poet with a reputation? I tried all kinds of jobs. There was only one that wasn't dishonorable—Hebrew teaching.

"There are two kinds of Hebrew teaching in this country. There's the private kind and there's the public kind. A Jew rents a room, usually in a basement, hangs up a gilt sign reading, 'Expert Teacher, Alphabet, *Maftir*,[5] Bar Mitzvah'—and he's in business as a teacher. He doesn't make enough out of just teaching, so he takes on a few side lines, more or less related, either because of their sacred or their beneficial character and he puts on his sign an added inscription: 'Expert Mohel,[6] Expert Marriage Performer, Expert Matchmaker, Expert Evil-Eye Exorciser, Expert Hemorrhoid Remover,' et cetera.

"On the other hand, if you know how and when to pull the right strings, and grease the right wheels, you can get a job teaching in a proper Hebrew school and have your salary paid by the public charity funds. I gave up private teaching and became a public school teacher. But if you think the magic name 'Dolitzky' opened all doors for me and got me a decent job in a good school, you're very much mistaken.

"I was looking for a Hebrew school job once in the middle of the semester, when they were particularly hard to come by. I looked through the 'Religious Help Wanted' section of the Yiddish newspapers. One day I saw something that looked promising, and rushed to the address listed. I found several people already there before me. They were sitting on a bench in the hall waiting to be called into the office to be interviewed by the so-called 'Chairman of the Education Committee.' I took a seat. As I sat there waiting for my turn in this contest I remembered another contest, in the Old Country, where I had won the literary prize given by the B'nai Zion[7] Association in Moscow for my poem 'On Zion's Hills.' . . .

"I looked around at my competitors: bearded and smooth-faced, lean and fat, they all had one thing in common—they didn't sound like, or look like, men of learning. My fellow contestants!

"Finally, it was my turn. I walked into the office shamefaced. The Chairman of the Education Committee was sitting at the head of the table—a man with a coarse face, pointed beard, a wily look in his eyes.

" 'What's your name, friend?'

---

who laughed at his own poverty and used his wisdom to help others.

5. The "additional service" following the Torah reading in synagogue on Mondays, Thursdays, and the Sabbath.

6. One who performs the Jewish ritual of circumcision on eight-day old Jewish boys (Hebrew).

7. Sons of Zion (Hebrew), an early Zionist organization.

" 'Menachem Mendel Dolitzky.'

" 'Russian or Galician?'

" 'Russian.'

" 'Have you ever taught children before?'

" 'Yes.'

" 'Can you read Hebrew?'

" 'They say I can even read the small print.'

" 'They say? Who's *they*? In America *they say* doesn't mean a thing. I have ears, thank God. Let *me* hear you read the small print in this prayer book. . . . '

"Finally, I got disgusted with Hebrew teaching and became a Yiddish writer, scribbling fantastic romances for the rabble. It's hack work, but it requires talent, imagination, insight into human nature, a little art and a lot of work. There are devotees of the Yiddish novel—they're the ones that pay me generally. But in hard times I have to throw my books into a valise, and go out soliciting handouts for them from door to door, among people who won't or can't read them. You want to write novels? That's the third stage for the Hebrew poet in America."

A knock on the door interrupted Dolitzky's long speech. He got up, turned on the gaslight, and opened the door. The hotel owner had brought a bundle of just-arrived books—volumes of Dolitzky's collected poetry for distribution among the Boston Maskilim. He gave me a copy in appreciation of my speech of the night before. Then he continued, somewhat more mildly.

"But don't you listen to me! Write, young man, write! Your poem shows promise. Who knows, maybe there is still hope, we may have fresh young Hebrew poets in this country. Maybe I'm exaggerating American Jewry's defects. Maybe I'm accusing myself, under disguise, when I accuse them. They came to America, oppressed, crushed, impoverished, rootless. They found themselves strangers, everything foreign to them—land, language, way of life. They struggled hard to overcome many obstacles, and that age-old will to live gave them the strength to succeed. It's amazing how they established themselves here: beginning small in petty business, ending up big, everywhere in the economy—factories, trades, professions. It's unbelievable!

"True, there are many things wrong with American Jewish life. But still, its very survival is a feat serving to be commemorated. When the marranos built a synagogue in Amsterdam they put a phoenix there, as an emblem of their resurrection.[8] The phoenix is the immortal bird that arises from its own ashes. The phoenix should be our emblem in America, too. And this material success of ours is certain to precede a victorious conquest of the spirit. That's the way it was with every Jewish settlement—Babylon, Persia, France, Germany, Poland, and Russia—they all began the way American Jewry did, and we'll achieve a spiritual renaissance such as they achieved."

The tears came to his eyes.

"We were the first. We came too early to America, when the material conquests of the American Jews were still in a progressive stage and could not divert their minds and efforts to matters of spirit. And we came too late in life, in middle age, lacking youthful enthusiasm and vigor and faith in

8. The Marranos were the "Hidden Jews" of Spain who survived the Inquisition by converting to Christianity while maintaining their Jewish practice and faith in secret. Many fled Spain for Amsterdam, where they were allowed to resume their Judaism openly.

victory. We gave up with the excuse that there was nothing to fight against, with or for. We isolated ourselves in a Maskilic unworldly corner we procured. However, it was a sacred corner. We preserved in it the sacred Hebrew banner we had brought from the Old Country. This sacred banner we now commit to you, the youth, to your keeping. J. L. Gordon's charge is now addressed to you: 'You who go into life—go and make battle!' You will win no easy victory—a difficult struggle lies ahead—and when you are triumphant, do not forget us—the guardians of the Hebrew banner—and do not despise us—the forerunners—do not despise us or deprecate the sorrow of our solitude and the humiliation of our defeat! A little understanding—understanding—and forgiveness."

From *Part VI*[1]

CHAPTER IV. [THE HEBREW TEACHER]

Now that the cup of poison is broken, there is no way out but to drink the cup of sorrows. . . .

My affirmation of life demanded that I should dedicate all the powers of my mind and body to one supreme life goal. This goal was not merely something to provide me with a *raison d'être*,[2] but rather to fill my life with a spiritual content that would render it worth while in my eyes. To attain this goal, I must first drain the cup of sorrows. . . .

All my life I have been given to fits of weeping. The wellspring of my tears has always been gushing and free-flowing, inexhaustible. Even so, never had I been so flooded with tears as while draining this cup of sorrows. . . .

Much laborious effort and deep probing went into the search for a suitable life goal, but at last I found it—the vocation of a Hebrew teacher in America.

Actually, I did not have to look for it. It was nothing new, for I was engaged in Hebrew teaching all along. This, however, had been until now in the nature of a temporary occupation, a job to work at while training for a profession that would be free from the insecurity and degradation that marked Hebrew teaching in America. My pharmacist's training now provided me with a comfortable and respectable means of livelihood. More than that, it was now possible for me to realize my heart's desire which had prompted me to choose this profession in the first place—my dream of settling in Erets Yisrael.[3]

The more I read and the more I heard about Erets Yisrael, that new land resurrected from its ruins, the more it rose in my imagination, an ever-present vision of peerless splendor and majesty, by day and by night. And it filled me with a passionate yearning through and through.

Many years were to elapse before I was granted the privilege of making a pilgrimage to the new land of Israel and to behold it with my own eyes. I saw it then in its stark reality, unretouched by the brush of the imagination, in the disenchanting light of reality. But when I left, I felt as if I were departing

1. This part is translated by Moshe Kohn and Jacob Sloan.
2. A reason for existence (French). "Cup of poison": the author had been about to commit suicide by drinking poison when the vision of his first memory—a Minsk sunset—and of his mother caused him to drop the vial of poison.
3. The land of Israel (Hebrew); the traditional Jewish way to refer to Palestine, from the Middle Ages until the 1948 establishment of the State of Israel.

from the Garden of Eden, to go back to a living hell, doomed once more to its tortures.

And yet, notwithstanding the prospect it offered of settling in Erets Yisrael, I gave up pharmacy in favor of Hebrew teaching in America.

I did this not because Hebrew teaching had prospered and gained in prestige, in the meantime. No change for the better had occurred in its lowly condition. I did so only because it promised to provide me with an ultimate goal in life.

In the years I have lived in America, I have witnessed the continuing growth of a flourishing Jewish community, a community destined to exert a decisive influence on the rest of the Jewish Diaspora. No less substantial is bound to be its share in the upbuilding of Erets Yisrael through the contributions of its wealth and energy.

True, this amazing growth has been mainly in the material sense. Yet material growth is not unrealated to spiritual growth. Those same vital forces, so creative in the material sphere, are equally effective in the realm of the spirit, and to foster this creative process is the great mission of Jewish education in this country. A great and difficult task indeed, but wholly within the bounds of possibility.

Whatever the reason for the failure of Jewish education in America, in no way is the Jewish child himself to blame for it. I had ample opportunity to get to know this child well during my years of teaching. He is excellent human material, free from the dross which ghetto life used to deposit in his counterpart across the ocean. What is more, through the public school he comes into possession of an American culture which, potentially, is a blessing for Jewish education, for he is thus better prepared to absorb the best and the highest that Jewish culture has to offer. The great enemy, then, of Jewish education in America is not the make-up of the Jewish child but the utter contempt in which it is held by unworthy parents and teachers. What it needs is inspired and enthusiastic teachers, and above all, a spirit of dedicated pioneering, of *halutsiut*.[4] *Halutsiut*—that is the essential dimension of Hebrew teaching in this country, not unlike the bold vanguard pioneering carried on in Erets Yisrael. Here you might call it rearguard pioneering. I took upon myself this pioneering task, and along with it, its inescapable burdens.

I had not the slightest doubt about my qualification for this type of *halutsiut*, neither on the score of the tenacity nor the power of endurance which it required. These qualities had served me well in my heavy ordeals throughout life. I could not have kept going without them.

If, at first, I did question my qualifications it was on account of my deficiency in another resource which, to my mind, was a *sine qua non*.[5] This resource is spiritual wholeness and a harmonious conception of Judaism.

My mind was broken up into too many separate sovereignties, mutually contradictory and at odds with one another, each claiming exclusive obedience. This multiplicity of sovereignty prevailed also in my conception of Judaism. As a result, my Jewish outlook, too, became subject to conflicts and contradictions.

4. Pioneering spirit (Hebrew); a term usually referring to the Jewish settlers in the land of Israel from the late 19th century until 1948.

5. Something essential or indispensable (literally, "without which not") (Latin).

This is the way I saw it. The basic objective of any teacher is to help his pupils to acquire a spiritual wholeness. A Hebrew teacher must strive to impart, in addition to this spiritual wholeness, a Jewish outlook that is integrated and harmonious. How to go about imparting these two qualities to my pupils when I lacked them myself? Can a teacher inculcate in his pupils something he doesn't have himself? I grappled at length with this doubt as to my qualifications for being a Hebrew teacher. It lingered awhile, but finally it left me.

CHAPTER V. [A TEACHER'S MISSION]

That doubt left me, having been displaced by another doubt, as soon as its negative proof was established. I first became skeptical about the very possibility of spiritual wholeness in a man of independent spirit, as well as about the possibility of an absolutely integrated conception, at least on the level of a cosmic philosophy. My skeptism soon turned to a firm certainty.

A Hasidic rabbi once put it very well by interpreting this biblical passage: "Why sayest thou, O Jacob, and speakest, O Israel, My path is hid from the Lord?" There should be a pause between "is hid" and "from the Lord," meaning that all the contradictions derive from the Lord Himself.[1]

God made the universe and man the subjects of conflicts and contradictions, and man has presumed to seek various devices to resolve and reconcile them. But all these calculations are fundamentally erroneous and false. For the very concept of "being" implies contradictions, while "not being" means harmony. Reality signifies conflicts; only in nothingness there is unity.

The very act of creation consisted of the creation of conflicts out of harmony, of contradictions out of unity. Man's soul is but one atom among many in the total mass of created beings, and this soul far more than the rest, is invested with a totality of those atoms. In it, as in a mirror, are reflected the individual conflicts and contradictions of all those untold myriads of beings. These then are added to its own, to form its own special amalgam.

To be sure, these conflicts and contradictions are susceptible of harmonious integration. But this integrated whole, inclusive as it is of all the conflicts and contradictions, encompasses their tragic nature as well, the tragedy of an irreparable fundamental split. It is from this tragic element that the *Weltschmerz*[2] is distilled, and the sense of universal beauty flowing from it.

It is not, then, the teacher's mission to impart a spiritual wholeness, nor is it the Jewish teacher's task to impart, along with this spiritual wholeness, an integrated conception of Judaism. The task consists of imparting a sense of that harmonious totality, along with the *Weltschmerz* and the sense of universal beauty—the distillation of conflicts and contradictions.

In choosing Hebrew teaching as my supreme life goal, I decided to combine with it the writing of Hebrew poetry on American soil.

The first steps in my poetic career were hesitant and exploratory, but in the end I hit upon its proper course.

American Hebrew poetry may be compared to a trailing branch of a creep-

1. In this Hebrew passage from Isaiah 40.27, the word, *nisterah*, "is hid," can also mean "was contradicted" [adapted from Kohn and Sloan's note].

2. Sentimental sadness; depression or apathy caused by comparing actual with ideal worlds (literally, "world pain") (German).

ing plant which, as it runs along the ground, puts down its own roots. As a limb it remains attached to the trunk, the trunk's roots supplying it with its main nourishment. But at the same time it draws nourishment from its own roots as well, blending both elements within it. Thus, in fact, the trunk and the branch nurture each other.

American soil is one vast battleground. A new life is being forged on it, out of a clash of elements violently torn from their context and matrix and wrenched from their ordered categories and equations, so that they might be recreated in a new organic form.

There is something sublime in this drama of the struggle of the titans, at once sublime and tragic. One people—the Indians—being extirpated from American soil, its ancient homeland. Another—the Negroes—trampled, pushed around, cast down. And a third—the Jews—struggling to preserve something of its own character in the midst of this new existence. This drama, with its aspect of the sublime and the tragic, holds great promise for American Hebrew poetry and, indeed, for Hebrew poetry in general.

Like Hebrew teaching, Hebrew poetry in America, too, partakes of the nature of pioneering.

I felt myself equally qualified for this kind of pioneering as well. I had come to feel at home in America, gaining an intimate knowledge of the country through the study of its literature and, even more, through the various types of people, Jews and gentiles alike, with whom my rovings brought me together.

Poetic inspiration may come in the midst of an abundance of happiness, yet it is more apt to come amid an abundance of sorrow. As for me, surely mine has been a superabundance of sorrow.

When a heart is broken, strings stretch across its fractures playing a melody notated within that broken heart in fiery musical notes.

I am a man that hath seen pain and affliction, and his heart is broken.[3]

New Orleans, Louisiana

Hebrew, 1949
English, 1959

3. Compare the Book of Lamentations 3.1: "I am the man that hath seen affliction by the rod of his wrath" (King James version).

MALKA HEIFETZ TUSSMAN
1893–1987

Although she declared the natural rhythms of speech and breath her poetic credo, at the peak of her powers Malka Heifetz Tussman introduced into Yiddish one of the most rigid verse forms, the triolet, and mastered another, the sonnet corona. A teacher of Yiddish language and literature in the Midwest and West, Tussman published her books of poetry relatively late in life. She was awarded the Itsik Manger Prize for Yiddish poetry in Tel Aviv in 1981.

Born around the holiday of Shavuoth, Tussman herself disputed the exact year, stating it variously as 1893, 1895, or 1896. She considered May 15 her American birthday. Her father was the third generation of the Hasidic Heifetz family to manage an estate in the village of her birth, Khaytshe or Bol'shaya Chaitcha, in the Ukrainian province of Volhynia.

The second of eight children, Tussman and her siblings were educated in Hebrew, Yiddish, Russian, and English initially by private tutors and later in the Russian schools in the nearby towns of Norinsk and Korosten. As a young child, Tussman began to write poems in Russian about the poverty of the neighboring peasants.

She came to America in 1912 and joined family members in Chicago. Her first Yiddish short story appeared in 1918, her first poem in 1919. In 1914, she also wrote in English for the Chicago anarchist publication *Alarm*.

After her marriage at age eighteen to cantor Shloyme Tussman and the birth of her two sons (in 1914 and 1918), the family lived in Milwaukee, Wisconsin. In 1924, Tussman began to teach in a Yiddish secular school, while studying at the University of Wisconsin. She also studied briefly at the University of California, Berkeley. In 1941 or 1942, the family moved to Los Angeles, where Tussman taught Yiddish elementary and high-school students at the Workmen's Circle School in Boyle Heights. She became an instructor of Yiddish language and literature at the University of Judaism in 1949. After her husband's death in 1971, she lived for a year in Israel. Upon her return, she moved to Berkeley, where she resided until her death.

Although she lived far from the centers of Yiddish letters, Tussman's poems, short stories, and essays appeared in the leading Yiddish newspapers and journals from 1918 onward: the New York papers *Fraye arbeter shtime* and *Vokh* as well as the journals *Oyfkum*, *Inzikh*, *Yidisher kemfer*, *Svive*, *Kinder zshurnal*, and *Tsukunft*; the Warsaw weekly *Literarishe bleter*; the Toronto literary magazine *Tint un feder*; the Tel Aviv quarterly *Goldene keyt*. Her poems were represented in collections of Yiddish poetry such as *Antologye—mitvest–mayrev* (Anthology—From Midwest to North Pacific, 1933) and *Amerike in yidishn vort* (America in Yiddish Literature, 1955). She published six volumes of poetry between 1949 and 1977. Until her death, Tussman continued to work on a seventh volume, *Un ikh shmeykhl* (And I Smile), which has not been published.

Throughout her career as a poet, Tussman sustained literary friendships and extensive correspondences with Yiddish writers in the United States, Canada, Poland, France, and Israel, including the poets Kalman Marmor, Jacob Glatstein, H. Leyvik, Rokhl Korn, Kadya Molodowsky, Melekh Ravitsh, and Avraham Sutzkever. She read poetry of many languages, modern and ancient, and exercised her poetic voice by translating into Yiddish poems by writers as various as Yeats, Rossetti, Auden, and Tagore. By maintaining a ferocious poetic independence from any school or movement, Tussman achieved a compressed lyrical style noted by critic M. Litvine for its elliptical syntax and free-verse rhythms that render the strophe inconspicuous but dense. Sutzkever praised her poetry for asserting an ever more flexible, youthful voice the older the poet herself grew.

Tussman is significant as a woman poet in Yiddish. Although she did not believe that poetry should be read or written in terms of gender, her poems are fueled by an explicitly female sensuality. Denying any feminist orientation, she nonetheless acknowledged the difficulties that women writing poetry in Yiddish had—even in the heyday of Yiddish poetry in America—in getting their poems published in periodicals or finding sponsors for their books. In an interview, she once expressed her sense that women who excelled in writing poems for children, such as Kadya Molodowsky, were often categorized by the Yiddish literary establishment as "merely children's poets," so that their other work remained unacknowledged. In her later years, she taught informally and befriended a number of younger poets, many American-born and writing in English, who helped disseminate her poetry through their translations, including Eli Katz, Marcia Falk, Kathryn Hellerstein, and Daniel Marlin. She also served as a mentor for some younger Yiddish poets, of whom an Israeli recipient of the Manger Prize, the late Rukhl Fishman, was the best known. Tussman thus served as a bridge between the generations of Yiddish poets who emigrated from Eastern Europe and those American-born Jewish poets who have taken up the task of making Yiddish poetry accessible to a readership that knows little Yiddish.

With Teeth in the Earth[1]

My cheek upon the earth
and I know mercy.

With lips to the earth
I know love.

My nose in the earth
and I know thievery.

With teeth in the earth
I know murder.

And I know why those
who dig their teeth into the earth

and why those
who tear themselves away from the earth

must always weep over themselves.

1949

Water without Sound[2]

The sea
tore a rib from its side[3]
and said:
Go! Lie down there, be
a sign that I
am great and mighty.
Go
be a sign.

The canal
lies at my window,
speechless.

1. Translated by Marcia Falk.
2. Translated by Marcia Falk. The Yiddish title, *Vaser on loshn*, means, literally, "Water without language."
3. An allusion to God's creation of Eve from Adam's rib (Genesis 2.21–23).

What can be sadder
than water
without sound?

1965

Thunder My Brother[1]

Thunder my brother,
My powerful brother,
Stones rolling on stones—your voice.
Like a forest, forceful, your voice.
What pleasure you take in making mountains rattle,
How happy you feel
When you bewilder creeping creatures in the valley.

Once
Long ago
The storm—my father—
Rode on a dark cloud,
And stared at the other side of the Order-of-the-Universe,
Across to the chaos.[2]
I, too,
Have a voice—
A voice of fearsome roaring
In the grip of my muteness.

And there are commandments
Forbidding me:
"Thou shalt not,
Thou shalt not"[3]
O thunder,
My wild unbridled brother.

ca. 1970s 1972

Sweet Father[1]

And I call Him
Sweet Father
Although I don't remember my father.
But I do remember
A thorn,
A fire,

1. Translated by Kathryn Hellerstein.
2. The Yiddish employs the Hebraic phrases *seder-haoylem* (the order of the universe) and *toyevoye* (chaos; literally, unformed and void), the first of which sounds biblical, the second of which quotes Genesis 1.2.
3. Nine of the Ten Commandments incorporate the phrase "Thou shalt not" (Deuteronomy 5.7–21).

1. Translated by Kathryn Hellerstein.

A thunder,
A mountain
And something of a voice.[2]
When I think
I hear His voice
I shout at once
Here I am![3]
Here I am, Sweet Father!
When a father abandons
He is still a father,
And I will not stop longing
And calling
"Here I am"
Until He hears me,
Until He remembers me
And calls my name
And talks to me
Through fire.

1977

Forgotten[1]

Master of the world!
Creator,
I stand before You with bared head,
With eyes uncovered,[2]
Stubbornly
Facing Your light.
Not a single hair
Trembles on my brow
Before Your greatness.
I place my Sabbath candles
In candlesticks
Tall and straight as a ruler
So they may flicker toward You
Without a drop of humbleness.[3]
I rise to You
Without the slightest fear.
For a long time I've sharpened my daring

2. "Thorn," "fire," "thunder," "mountain," "voice" allude to several biblical stories: Moses and the burning bush (Exodus 3.2–4); the binding of Isaac (Genesis 22.1–19); the boy Samuel's first calling by God (1 Samuel 3.1–21); Elijah's revelation (1 Kings 19.11–12).

3. The Yiddish phrase *do bin ikh* is a translation of the Hebrew *hinnaini*, the response that biblical figures give when they hear God's voice calling them, such as Abraham in the binding of Isaac (Genesis 22.1–19), Moses when God calls him from the burning bush (Exodus 3,4), and Samuel (1 Samuel 3.1–21).

1. Translated by Kathryn Hellerstein.

2. Jewish law gives women three positive commandments: to light the Sabbath candles, to throw a small piece of dough from a loaf they are baking into the fire, and to keep the laws of family purity. Custom holds that a married woman cover her hair for modesty. When she blesses the Sabbath candles, she covers her eyes with her hands so as not to enjoy the light before she has recited the blessing.

3. Some women follow the custom of tilting the candles slightly in their holders to express humbleness before God.

To stand before You
Face to face, Creator,
And to let my just complaints
Open out before You
From my mouth.

Woe is me: I've forgotten!
I can't remember
What I came to demand.[4]
I've forgotten.
Woe is me.

1977

In Spite[1]

You say:
"You are a Jew and a poet
And you've written no poems
On the destruction.[2]
How can a Yiddish poet not,
When the destruction is enormous,
So enormous?"

Simple:
In spite of the destroyers,
To spite them I will not cry openly,
I will not write down my sorrow
On paper.
(A degradation to write
"Sorrow" on paper.)
To spite them
I'll walk the world
As if the world were mine.
Of course it's mine!
If they hindered me,
Fenced in my roads,
The world would still be mine.

To spite them I will not wail
Even if (God forbid) my world becomes
As big as where my sole stands—
The world will still be mine!

To spite them
I'll marry off my children

4. Wordplay connects the Yiddish word *dermonen* (remember) with *monen* (demand).
1. Translated by Kathryn Hellerstein.
2. In Yiddish, the Holocaust in known as the *Khurbm* (Destruction), a word that originally denotes the destruction of the First and Second Temples in ancient Jerusalem in 586 B.C.E. and 70 C.E, respectively.

That they shall have children—
To spite the villains who breed
In my world
And make it narrow
For me.

1977

KADYA MOLODOWSKY
1894–1975

One of the few women Yiddish poets able to sustain and develop her writing in several genres throughout her life, Kadya Molodowsky's works reflect the vast cultural and historical crises for Jews in the twentieth century.

Born in the shtetl Bereza Kartuska, White Russia, Molodowsky was the second of four children. Her father, a learned man who taught Hebrew and Gemara to young boys in heder, was also an adherent of the Enlightenment and an early Zionist. Her mother ran a dry-goods shop and later opened a factory for the distillation of rye kvass, a lightly alcoholic beverage made from fermented cereal.

Molodowsky was taught to read Yiddish by her paternal grandmother. Her father instructed her in the study of the Pentateuch and also hired various Russian tutors to teach her the Russian language, geography, philosophy, and world history. Such an education, especially instruction in Hebrew, was not typical for a shtetl girl, and Kadya was better educated than either of her sisters.

From the age of seventeen, when she graduated from high school, until her marriage to a young scholar and teacher in 1921, Molodowsky taught and worked at a variety of day-home jobs for displaced Jewish children in Bereza, Warsaw, Odessa, and Kiev, and trained to teach Hebrew to children in the new Zionist and Bundist schools. In 1920, having survived the Kiev pogrom, she published her first poem, and, living in Warsaw in 1927, her first book of poetry, *Kheshvndike nekht* (Nights of Heshvan). The book's narrator, a woman in her thirties, moves through the landscape of Jewish Eastern Europe. Molodowsky contrasts the narrator's modernity with the roles decreed by Jewish tradition for women, according to law, custom, or history. *Nights of Heshvan* received approximately twenty reviews in the Yiddish press, nearly all of them laudatory.

As a teacher, Molodowsky was deeply aware of the poverty in which many of her students lived and wrote poems for and about them. Her second book, *Mayselekh* (Tales, 1930), was awarded a prize by the Warsaw Jewish Community and the Yiddish Pen Club. Her third book of poems, *Dzshike gas* (Dzshike Street, 1933), was reviewed negatively on the political grounds of being too "aesthetic." And her fourth book, *Freydke* (1935), features a sixteen-part narrative poem about a heroic, Jewish working-class woman.

Molodowsky emigrated to the United States in 1935, settling in New York City, where her husband joined her in 1937 or 1938. Her fifth book, *In land fun mayn gebeyn* (In the Country of My Bones, 1937), contains fragmented poems that represent an internalization of exile.

Molodowsky's literary endeavors then branched out in several directions. In 1938, a new edition of her children's poems, *Afn barg* (On the Mountain), was released; in 1942, she published *Fun lublin biz nyu-york: togbukh fun Rivke Zilberg* (From Lublin to New York: Diary of Rivke Zilberg), a novel about a young immigrant woman. At this time, Molodowsky also wrote a series of columns, "Great Jewish Women," for the Yiddish daily *Forverts*, using "Rivke Zilberg," the name of the novel's protagonist, as her pseudonym.

Fearful for her brother and other family members still in Poland in 1944, Molodowsky put aside her editorship of the literary journal *Svive* (Surroundings), which she had cofounded in 1943, and began to write the poems of *Der melekh dovid aleyn iz geblibn* (Only King David Remained, 1946). *Only King David Remained* contains many *khurbm-lider* (destruction poems), which draw upon traditional Jewish literary responses to catastrophe.

In 1945, another edition of her children's poems *Yidishe kinder* (Jewish Children) was published in New York. That same year, a book of her children's poems in Hebrew translations by Lea Goldberg, Natan Alterman, Fanya Bergshteyn, Avraham Levinson, and Yaakov Faykhman appeared in Tel Aviv. She published a long poem, *Donna Gracia Mendes*; two plays—*Nokhn got fun midbar* (After the God of the Desert, 1949), which was produced in Chicago and Israel, and *A hoyz af grand strit* (A House on Grand Street, 1953), which was produced in New York; a chapbook of poems, *In yerushalayim kumen malokhim* (In Jerusalem Angels Come, 1952); a book of essays, *Af di vegn fun tsion* (On the Roads of Zion, 1957); and a collection of short stories, *A shtub mit zibn fentster* (A House with Seven Windows, 1957). She also edited the anthology *Lider fun khurbm* (Poems of the Holocaust, 1962). In the 1950s, she revived the literary journal *Svive*.

From 1950 through 1952, Molodowsky and her husband lived in Tel Aviv. There, she edited *Heym* (Home), a journal for the Pioneer Women Organization that portrayed life in Israel. She also started a novel, *Baym toyer: roman fun dem lebn in yisroel* (At the Gate: Novel about Life in Israel, 1967), and began her autobiography, *Mayn elter-zeydns yerushe* (My Great-Grandfather's Inheritance), which appeared serially in *Svive* between March 1965 and April 1974.

Published in Buenos Aires in 1965, Molodowsky's last book of poems, *Likht fun dornboym* (Lights of the Thorn Bush), includes dramatic monologues in the voices of legendary personae from Jewish and non-Jewish traditions as well as contemporary characters. The book concludes with a section of poems on Israel from the 1950s, which, like the ending of her autobiography, expresses her Zionism.

In Tel Aviv, in 1971, Molodowsky received the Itzik Manger Prize, the most prestigious award in the world of Yiddish letters, for her achievement in poetry. She died in Philadelphia on March 23, 1975.

All of Molodowsky's poems included here were written in America. *Alphabet Letters*, from *In the Country of My Bones*, makes literal the immigrant's confrontation with the new language, English. *Letters from the Ghetto* and *God of Mercy* reflect the poet's fears and anger as she encountered the destruction of Europe's Jews during the Second World War. *The Lost Shabes,* a short story written in the early 1950s, portrays the losses of Jewish culture and identity in America that Molodowsky feared.

Alphabet Letters[1]

In the Bronx, in Brooklyn and in New York City,
My cousins all have stores.
Seven cousins with seven stores, like commandments.
Business people with long lists of going bankrupt.

1. Translated by Kathryn Hellerstein.

And my family name stares at me from their signs
With a gaze that's wild and foreign.
The flaming *mem* (of Moses and of Marx)
Skips on one green foot.
The *alef* winks glossily at the street below.
The *lamed* loops a knot like a gallows.[2]
And the alphabet shrieks in the city's iron uproar:
—Bankrupt, bankrupt and bankrupt some more.
But beneath the sign, my Uncle Mikhl and Aunt Sore
Have gotten fat—evil eye, stay away—*keyn ayen hore.*[3]
She—a blue silk barrel,
And he—a gray steel spring.
And their children—Julie, Beatrice, Max and Carolyn—
Proudly wear letters like stars on short sleeves and long,
For the card clubs and Boy Scout troops to which they belong.[4]

1937

Letters from the Ghetto[1]

Your brief letters—
Three lines on a card, nothing more.
As if every mile added a stone—
That is how heavy they are.

A line about everybody's health,
Each one mentioned by name,
There is no need to worry,
And the white blankness pleads for mercy on the paper,
Thus, probably, is the script of tears.

These brief letters—
They all lie gathered to me,
They will remain until the end of generations.
I see the trembling hand that writes them now,
I know the fiery hand
That will inscribe the blankness with mercy.

1941 1946

2. These Yiddish letters correspond to *M, A* (or, in this case, *O*), and *L*, the first three letters in Molodowsky's name.
3. Literally, "no evil eye" (Yiddish); an expression to ensure good luck.
4. Molodowsky transliterates the English words "Boy Scouts" and the children's names in her Yiddish lines to emphasize the American quality of the poem.
1. Translated by Kathryn Hellerstein.

God of Mercy[1]

O God of Mercy
Choose—
another people.[2]
We are tired of death, tired of corpses,
We have no more prayers.
Choose—
another people.
We have run out of blood
For victims,
Our houses have been turned into desert,
The earth lacks space for tombstones,
There are no more lamentations
Nor songs of woe
In the ancient texts.

God of Mercy
Sanctify another land,
Another Sinai.
We have covered every field and stone
With ashes and holiness.
With our crones
With our young
With our infants
We have paid for each letter in your Commandments.

God of Mercy
Lift up your fiery brow,
Look on the peoples of the world,
Let them have the prophecies and Holy Days
Who mumble your words in every tongue.
Teach them the Deeds
And the ways of temptation.

God of Mercy
To us give rough clothing
Of shepherds who tend sheep
Of blacksmiths at the hammer
Of washerwomen, cattle slaughterers
And lower still.
And O God of Mercy
Grant us one more blessing—
Take back the divine glory of our genius.

1945 1946

1. Translated by Irving Howe. "God of Mercy": *Eyl-khanun* (Hebrew) is the God of Mercy, in contrast to the God of Justice, whom Jews address in the Yom Kippur liturgy.
2. From a recorded reading by the poet, it is clear that Molodowsky intended the Yiddish word to be the verb *derveyl*, "choose, elect," and not the adverb *dervayl*, "meanwhile" or "for the time being," as Howe rendered it in a famous earlier version of his translation.

The Lost Shabes[1]

Mrs. Haynes drops in on her neighbor Sore Shapiro at least twice a day. She does it out of the goodness of her heart. She is teaching Sore Shapiro, who is all of two years in the country (dragged herself through Siberia, Japan, and finally reached New York)[2]—she is teaching her how to be a homemaker in America while keeping in mind the role of *vaytaminz*.[3] She sticks her head in the door (she is wearing the red bow which she never removes from her hair) and without any preliminaries begins talking about *vaytaminz*. She speaks with gusto, with heart, as if she were keeping Sore Shapiro alive.

The little red bow in Mrs. Haynes' hair looks alive as if it had swallowed all the vitamins at one time and had become fiery hot.

Mrs. Haynes comes in with her six-year-old daughter Teresa Filipine. While her mother is busy with the theory of vitamins, Teresa Filipine hangs around the kitchen testing the faucets to see if water pours out when they are turned. Every so often Mrs. Haynes calls the child to her.

—Teresa Filipine!—And seeing the child is wet, adds—You good-for-nothing.

—Why call such a small child by such a long name, Mrs. Haynes?

—What's to be done? My mother's name was Toybe Faygl. And it's forbidden to give only half a name. If you do, they say the ghost is disappointed.

Sore Shapiro calls the child by her Yiddish name Toybe Faygele,[4] gives her a prune to eat and teaches her a rhyme:

—Toybe Faygl a girl like a bagel.

The little one repeats the rhyme, nibbles on the prune and laughs.

Teresa Filipine's grandfather calls her Toybe Faygele. He visits them every Friday night and brings her a lollipop, and Teresa Filipine understands that her grandfather and the neighbor Mrs. Shapiro have some connection to Friday night and to her Yiddish name Toybe Faygele.

Sometimes the little one drops in on Mrs. Shapiro by herself without her mother. She knocks on her door, and before anyone asks who's there, she gives her Yiddish name: Toybe Faygele. Sore Shapiro gives her a piece of bread with butter and talks to her in Yiddish, just like her grandfather:

—Eat, Toybe Faygele! Eat! A trifle, all they feed her constantly are *vaytaminz*.

Teresa Filipine sits on a stool and eats simply and with great pleasure. The piece of bread with butter which she eats at Mrs. Shapiro's has also something to do with her Yiddish name, with her grandfather and with Friday nights when her grandfather brings her a lollipop. Teresa Filipine eats obediently and seriously with childlike self-importance.

When her mother looks around and sees that the child has disappeared, she calls out through the open window down into the street:

—Teresa Filipine! *Kam hir*![5] Where are you, you good-for-nothing?

Teresa Filipine hears "good-for-nothing" and knows that her mother is

1. Translated by Irena Klepfisz. "Shabes": Sabbath (Yiddish).

2. Some Jews escaped the Nazis by spending the war years in the Soviet Union and then making their way to the United States via the Far East.

3. Vitamins (Yiddish pronunciation of the American word). Because Molodowsky transliterates these English words in her Yiddish text, Klepfisz has rendered them this way in her English translation.

4. Diminutive of the Yiddish name Toybe Foygl (literally, "Dove Bird"); pronounced *Feygl*.

5. The Yiddish-accented pronunciation of "Come here."

angry. With a sly smile, she places the piece of bread with butter on the table, stops being Toybe Faygele and immediately begins speaking English:

—*Am hir*![6]—and her small steps click rapidly through the stone corridor.

Mrs. Haynes asks Sore Shapiro with a friendly reproach:

—*Pliz*, don't give Teresa Filipine bread and butter. What does she get from it? A little bit of *startsh*?[7] The child needs protein.

But Teresa Filipine doesn't know what she needs. When her mother leaves her neighbor's house, the little one slips inside, in an instant reverts to being Toybe Faygele again and finishes eating the piece of bread and butter which she had left on the table. She eats with obedient earnestness down to the very last crumb, as if she were finishing praying.

Friday night Teresa Filipine's mother lights four candles. She puts on velvet slacks, sticks a red handkerchief in the pocket of her white blouse; in the light of the candles the red bow in her hair becomes a flaming yellow. Teresa Filipine stands, looks at her mother's fingers as she lights the candles. Soon her grandfather will come, will give her a lollipop, will call her Toybe Faygele—and that's *shabes*.

One Friday evening after her mother put on her velvet slacks and lit the candles, she told Teresa Filipine that her grandfather was not coming. He is sick and is in the hospital. Teresa Filipine became lonely: without her grandfather, without her grandfather's lollipop, and without her Yiddish name Toybe Faygele, she was left with half a *shabes*. She remembered their neighbor Mrs. Shapiro. She left and knocked on her door looking for the second half of *shabes*.

—Toybe Faygele—she announced even before anyone asked who was knocking.

There were no candles on Mrs. Shapiro's table. She herself was dressed in a housecoat and not in velvet pants: it was like any other day.

—Oh, Toybe Faygele! Come in, Toybe Faygele!

Teresa Filipine stood in the middle of the room and looked around. She walked slowly into the kitchen, took a look at the table, turned around, and feeling dejected, walked towards the door.

What are you looking for, Toybe Faygele?—the neighbor asked her and followed her.

—*Nottink*[8]—Teresa Filipine answered in English.

—So why did you come?

The child didn't answer, moved slowly closer to the exit.

From the other apartment Mrs. Haynes' voice echoed in the summer air:

—Teresa Filipine! *Ver ar u*?[9]—and angrily threw the words good-for-nothing.

It was all like any other weekday.

This time Teresa Filipine did not run to her mother. Her small steps clicked slowly on the stone floor of the corridor. She went down to the floor below, sat down on a stone step and cried.

1957

6. The Yiddish-accented pronunciation of "I'm here."

7. Starch. "*Pliz*": please. These are Yiddish-accented pronunciations of English words.

8. The Yiddish accented-pronunciation of "Nothing."

9. The Yiddish-accented pronunciation of "Where are you?"

CARL RAKOSI
b. 1903

"How strange to meet myself here, Mr. Rakosi, the pre-Adamite." Carl Rakosi sees himself in "pre-historic man contemplating a rock," seeking out "the mysterious spirit behind all things in nature." This is not to call his poetry mystical, supernatural, abstract, immaterial—it is just the opposite. Asked once about his own favorite work, he named "my meditative poems," which open his *Collected Poems* with the title *Lord, What Is Man?* (borrowing from Psalms), as well as "my simplest, personal poems . . . in the section called 'L'Chayim' " (Hebrew for "To Life"). In the so-called "objectivists" issue of *Poetry* magazine (1931), sponsored by Ezra Pound, Rakosi was grouped with Louis Zukofsky, Charles Reznikoff, and George Oppen. Though all four were Jews, their writing did not show it.

Rakosi himself aimed to "present objects in their most essential reality and to make of each poem an object" rather than something vague, solipsistic, sentimental. "I mean to penetrate the particular / the way an owl waits / for a kangaroo rat," he says in a credolike poem. So are you "an American Jewish poet?" he has been asked. "I am, of course, a Jew and an American, but any poem that's worth its salt, no matter what its subject matter, expresses human experience, and human experience is not ethnic or racial." Yet he remembers asking Zukofsky what being Jewish meant to him as a poet: "He said, 'Nothing.' That didn't seem believable, so I said, 'Come on, it must mean something.' " To Rakosi, it may mean no more and no less than these lines of his: "Praised be thou / as the Jews say, / who have engraved clarity."

Carl Rakosi was born on November 6, 1903, in Berlin to Hungarian parents. He recounts that his Orthodox grandfather, a traveling grain merchant, was called "father Abraham" by the peasants and that his father was transformed into an "idealistic Socialist" by once hearing Karl Liebknecht and Rosa Luxemburg. Rakosi, coming to America in 1910 when he was six, retains a "clear image of Ellis Island . . . and seeing the Statue of Liberty." Kids in school at first made fun of his accent, but in Kenosha, Wisconsin, he discovered a public library—"That was like heaven." At the University of Chicago, he began writing poetry, influenced at first by the elegant language of Wallace Stevens, later by William Carlos Williams, and then by his own dictates alone. He had a long career in social work, eventually directing the Jewish Family and Children's Service of Minneapolis. This work was his "way of listening," as poetry was his "way of seeing."

But Rakosi's career and parenthood, along with a sense of poetry's irrelevance after the depression and world war, forced him to stop writing for twenty-seven years—"Terrible. I thought I was going to die." In 1967, he resumed. Those decades in a helping profession made this later phase of writing, from which *Israel* and *Services* are drawn, more personal and humane, though also detached and often witty, ironic. With an "ancient voice of honesty," Carl Rakosi moves between "the earth / which expands my thought / . . . and the musing of my heart," as in his *Meditation* after the medieval Hebrew poet Ibn Gabirol.

Meditation

After Solomon Ibn Gabirol[1]

Three things remind me of You,
the heavens
who are a witness to Your name
the earth
which expands my thought
and is the thing on which I stand
and the musing of my heart
when I look within.

1971–1975

Meditation

After Moses Ibn Ezra[2]

Men are children of this world
yet God has set eternity in my heart.

All my life I have been in the desert
but the world is a fresh stream.

I drink from it. How potent this water is!
How deeply I crave it!

An ocean rushes into my throat
but my thirst remains unquenched.

1971–1975

Song

After Jehudah Halevi[3]

On the wind
in the cool of the evening
I send greetings to my friend.

I ask him only to remember the day
of our parting when we made a covenant
of love by an apple tree.

1971–1975

1. Ibn Gabirol (ca. 1020–ca. 1057), Sephardic poet and philosopher, one of the great figures of the Jewish golden age in Spain.
2. Ibn Ezra (ca. 1055–1135), Sephardic poet and philosopher, was one of the first Jewish poets to write secular verse.
3. The Sephardic Halevy (ca. 1075–1141), Hebrew poet and philosopher, was known for poems celebrating Jerusalem and Zion.

Israel

I hear the voice
of David and Bathsheba[1]
and the judgment
on the continual
backslidings
of the Kings of Israel.

I have stumbled
on the ancient voice
of honesty
and tremble
at the voice
of my people.

1975

Services

There was a man in the land of Ur.[1]

Who's that at my coattails?
A pale cocksman.

Hush!
The rabbi walks in thought
as in an ordained measure
to the Ark[2]
and slowly opens its great doors.
The congregation rises
and faces the six torahs
and the covenant
and all beyond.
The Ark glows.
Hear, O Israel![3]

The rabbi stands before the light
inside, alone, and prays.
It is a modest prayer
for the responsibilities of his office.
The congregation is silent.

I too pray:
Let Leah my wife be recompensed for her sweet smile

1. King David, seeing Bathsheba bathing, took her and had her husband slain. She bore him Solomon (2 Samuel 11, 12).

1. An ancient Middle Eastern city, whence came Abraham.

2. The chest containing the stone tablets with the Ten Commandments; also, the cabinet holding the Torah scrolls in a synagogue.

3. *Shema Yisrael* (Hebrew), the opening of the watchword of Judaism (Deuteronomy 6.4).

and our many years of companionship
and not stick me when she cuts my hair.
And let her stay at my side at large gatherings.
And let my son George and his wife Leanna
and my daughter Barbara be close,
and let their children, Jennifer, Julie and Joanna
be my sheep
                    and I their old shepherd.
Let them remain as they are.

And let not my white hair frighten me.

The tiger leaps,
the baboon cries,
Pity, pity.
The rabbi prays.

There was a man in the land of Ur.

I, son of Leopold and Flora,
also pray:
I pray for meaning.
I pray for the physical,
for my soul needs no suppliant.
I pray for man.

And may a special providence look out
for those who feel deeply.

1975

ISAAC BASHEVIS SINGER
1904–1991

"I am happy to call myself a Jewish writer, a Yiddish writer, an American writer." In 1974, Isaac Bashevis Singer closed his acceptance speech for the National Book Award by acknowledging his people, his mother tongue, his country of refuge. The order of those identities points up a complex fate that had taken the writer some years to name with equanimity.

In April 1943, just as the Warsaw ghetto's Jewish Fighting Organization was revolting against German military forces, a recent émigré from Warsaw published a kind of manifesto, *Problems of Yiddish Prose in America,* in a small New York magazine. "Life here is so rich and varied that probably no one could name in Yiddish everything that his eyes perceive or his heart conceives," Singer said, noting that "the better Yiddish prose writers avoid, consciously or unconsciously, writing about American Jewish life. . . . Through his language, the Yiddish writer is bound to the past . . . any attempt to push our language into the future is in vain."

The acute irony of declaring Yiddish obsolete for American Jews just as the mother tongue was being obliterated in several million European Jewish mouths cannot have escaped Singer. He insists that American Yiddish writers must find their proper subject in the vital, variegated, centuries-long diaspora of Polish, Lithuanian, Russian, and Romanian Jews, although "this way of life is vanishing, if it has not already vanished without a trace."

Surprisingly enough, Isaac Bashevis Singer's own career from 1943 on, more than any other writer's, helped sustain Yiddish into whatever American future it may have—even though much of his work appeared in English translation before the Yiddish original. And surely no modern writer has employed so many translators: twenty-two (plus Singer himself) in the *Collected Stories* alone (in this connection, compare Cynthia Ozick's story *Envy; or, Yiddish in America*). What's more, the prewar Eastern European Jewish way of life that did "vanish" between 1939 and 1945 can at least be traced in some form within Singer's fiction and autobiographical writing.

Born on July 14, 1904, in Leoncin, near Warsaw, Isaac Singer came from an Orthodox family: his father was an unofficial rabbi, his mother a rabbi's daughter. In 1908, the family moved to Warsaw, where Isaac's father held a rabbinical court, visited for advice and judgment by a colorful mix of the neighborhood's Jews (Singer's *In My Father's Court* [1966] recalls that milieu). Then, in 1917, when the Germans occupied Warsaw, the family fled to Biłgoraj (not far from Frampol, where *Gimpel the Fool* is set). Biłgoraj later served as model for the the shtetls, the Jewish towns in Singer's fiction. "In this world of old Jewishness I found a spiritual treasure trove. I had a chance to see our past as it really was. Time seemed to flow backwards. I lived Jewish history."

Besides absorbing the piety, the lore, and a firsthand sense of the Jewish past, Singer began attending a rabbinical seminary. Yet he joined a progressive Zionist youth movement and also felt the bracing shock of secular Jewish Enlightenment. He was reading Dostoyevsky, Tolstoy, Turgenev, Chekhov, Maupassant, Strindberg, and Poe, and became deeply influenced by Spinoza's challenge to Judaic Orthodoxy. After beginning in Hebrew, he turned in 1925 to writing Yiddish stories. Because his older brother, Israel Joshua Singer, already had a name as a writer, Isaac took the pseudonym, Bashevis, from his mother's name Bathsheba. I. J. Singer, who died in 1944, was for a long time the more famous of the two, especially for his superb saga *The Brothers Ashkenazi*. Singer's older sister, Hinde Esther, was also a writer.

Singer's first novel, *Satan in Goray*, depicted the demonic and erotic streaks of a false messianism in seventeenth-century Poland. When it appeared in 1935, Polish anti-Semitism was worsening. Singer immigrated to America and worked for the New York Yiddish daily *Forward*. After a period of disorientation, he began writing stories again in 1943; *Gimpel tam* (Gimpel the Simpleton) was written in 1944, at the nadir of Polish Jewish existence, and a historical novel, *The Family Moskat*, in 1945. When Saul Bellow's translation of *Gimpel the Fool* came out in *Partisan Review* in 1953, Singer's career in the United States took hold. He went on to publish numerous novels with historical and contemporary settings, which were usually serialized first in the *Forward*; several memoirs about his life in Poland and early days in the United States; and many children's books, such as *Zlateh the Goat, When Shlemiel Went to Warsaw, Naftali the Storyteller*. In 1978, he received the Nobel prize for literature—the only Yiddish writer so honored. Isaac Bashevis Singer died on July 24, 1991.

Singer's novels and stories reveal an unsettled imagination, faring constantly between the European past and the American present. Certainly, the conflicts and skepticism in his writing resisted the stereotype of a naïve, impish folklorist chronicling a simple, colorful, bygone era.

Singer is most characteristic and striking in his several hundred short stories. Unlike the novels, which are mainly composed in a realistic mode, his stories, especially those set in Eastern Europe, present the fantastic, fabulous side of life—"demons, dybbuks, and imps of two hundred years ago," as Singer put it. We may be at once perturbed and enthralled by the seemingly remote, exotic nature of Singer's stories, their "range of demonic, apocalyptic, and perversely sacred moments of *shtetl* life," in Irving Howe's words. But there has been no doubt about Singer's stylistic richness: the tactile detail threaded into a no less palpable presence of the invisible, the supernatural, the divine. Singer struck a note in postwar America that will go on drawing readers, thanks (as Howe says) to "a mind that reveres and delights in religious customs and emotions, yet is simultaneously drenched in modern psychological skepticism."

A traditional, sometimes mystical Judaic faith jostles startlingly with earthiness and disruptive sexuality in Singer's world. *Gimpel the Fool,* in the person of a saintly schlemiel, carries us beyond familiar calculations of justice, and even in *The Séance,* love and "pure truth" have their say.

Gimpel the Fool[1]

I

I am Gimpel the fool. I don't think myself a fool. On the contrary. But that's what folks call me. They gave me the name while I was still in school. I had seven names in all: imbecile, donkey, flax-head, dope, glump, ninny, and fool. The last name stuck. What did my foolishness consist of? I was easy to take in. They said, "Gimpel, you know the rabbi's wife has been brought to childbed?" So I skipped school. Well, it turned out to be a lie. How was I supposed to know? She hadn't had a big belly. But I never looked at her belly. Was that really so foolish? The gang laughed and hee-hawed, stomped and danced and chanted a good-night prayer. And instead of the raisins they give when a woman's lying in, they stuffed my hand full of goat turds. I was no weakling. If I slapped someone he'd see all the way to Cracow. But I'm really not a slugger by nature. I think to myself: Let it pass. So they take advantage of me.

I was coming home from school and heard a dog barking. I'm not afraid of dogs, but of course I never want to start up with them. One of them may be mad, and if he bites there's not a Tartar[2] in the world who can help you. So I made tracks. Then I looked around and saw the whole market place wild with laughter. It was no dog at all but Wolf-Leib the thief. How was I supposed to know it was he? It sounded like a howling bitch.

When the pranksters and leg-pullers found that I was easy to fool, every one of them tried his luck with me. "Gimpel, the czar is coming to Frampol; Gimpel, the moon fell down in Turbeen; Gimpel, little Hodel Furpiece found a treasure behind the bathhouse." And I like a golem[3] believed everyone. In the first place, everything is possible, as it is written in *The Wisdom of the Fathers,*[4] I've forgotten just how. Second, I had to believe when the whole town came down on me! If I ever dared to say, "Ah, you're kidding!" there was trouble. People got angry. "What do you mean! You want to call everyone a liar?" What was I to do? I believed them, and I hope at least that did them some good.

1. Translated by Saul Bellow.
2. A Mongolian people; a person of ferocious temper.
3. In Jewish lore, a zombie-like creature, a dummy, or an automaton. "Frampol" and "Turbeen": Polish towns south of Lublin.
4. *Pirke Avot* (Hebrew), a popular collection of Jewish moral sayings.

I was an orphan. My grandfather who brought me up was already bent toward the grave. So they turned me over to a baker, and what a time they gave me there! Every woman or girl who came to bake a batch of noodles had to fool me at least once. "Gimpel, there's a fair in Heaven; Gimpel, the rabbi gave birth to a calf in the seventh month; Gimpel, a cow flew over the roof and laid brass eggs." A student from the yeshiva came once to buy a roll, and he said, "You, Gimpel, while you stand here scraping with your baker's shovel the Messiah has come. The dead have arisen." "What do you mean?" I said. "I heard no one blowing the ram's horn!" He said, "Are you deaf?" And all began to cry, "We heard it, we heard!" Then in came Rietze the candle-dipper and called out in her hoarse voice, "Gimpel, your father and mother have stood up from the grave. They're looking for you."

To tell the truth, I knew very well that nothing of the sort had happened, but all the same, as folks were talking, I threw on my wool vest and went out. Maybe something had happened. What did I stand to lose by looking? Well, what a cat music went up! And then I took a vow to believe nothing more. But that was no go either. They confused me so that I didn't know the big end from the small.

I went to the rabbi to get some advice. He said, "It is written, better to be a fool all your days than for one hour to be evil. You are not a fool. They are the fools. For he who causes his neighbor to feel shame loses Paradise himself." Nevertheless, the rabbi's daughter took me in. As I left the rabbinical court she said, "Have you kissed the wall yet?" I said, "No; what for?" She answered, "It's the law; you've got to do it after every visit." Well, there didn't seem to be any harm in it. And she burst out laughing. It was a fine trick. She put one over on me, all right.

I wanted to go off to another town, but then everyone got busy matchmaking, and they were after me so they nearly tore my coat tails off. They talked at me and talked until I got water on the ear. She was no chaste maiden, but they told me she was virgin pure. She had a limp, and they said it was deliberate, from coyness. She had a bastard, and they told me the child was her little brother. I cried, "You're wasting your time. I'll never marry that whore." But they said indignantly, "What a way to talk! Aren't you ashamed of yourself? We can take you to the rabbi and have you fined for giving her a bad name." I saw then that I wouldn't escape them so easily and I thought: They're set on making me their butt. But when you're married the husband's the master, and if that's all right with her it's agreeable to me too. Besides, you can't pass through life unscathed, nor expect to.

I went to her clay house, which was built on the sand, and the whole gang, hollering and chorusing, came after me. They acted like bear-baiters. When we came to the well they stopped all the same. They were afraid to start anything with Elka. Her mouth would open as if it were on a hinge, and she had a fierce tongue. I entered the house. Lines were strung from wall to wall and clothes were drying. Barefoot she stood by the tub, doing the wash. She was dressed in a worn hand-me-down gown of plush. She had her hair put up in braids and pinned across her head. It took my breath away, almost, the reek of it all.

Evidently she knew who I was. She took a look at me and said, "Look who's here! He's come, the drip. Grab a seat."

I told her all; I denied nothing. "Tell me the truth," I said, "are you really a virgin, and is that mischievous Yechiel actually your little brother? Don't be deceitful with me, for I'm an orphan."

"I'm an orphan myself," she answered, "and whoever tries to twist you up, may the end of his nose take a twist. But don't let them think they can take advantage of me. I want a dowry of fifty guilders, and let them take up a collection besides. Otherwise they can kiss my you-know-what." She was very plainspoken. I said, "It's the bride and not the groom who gives a dowry." Then she said, "Don't bargain with me. Either a flat yes or a flat no. Go back where you came from."

I thought: No bread will ever be baked from *this* dough. But ours is not a poor town. They consented to everything and proceeded with the wedding. It so happened that there was a dysentery epidemic at the time. The ceremony was held at the cemetery gates, near the little corpse-washing hut. The fellows got drunk. While the marriage contract was being drawn up I heard the most pious high rabbi ask, "Is the bride a widow or a divorced woman?" And the sexton's wife answered for her, "Both a widow and divorced." It was a black moment for me. But what was I to do, run away from under the marriage canopy?

There was singing and dancing. An old granny danced opposite me, hugging a braided white hallah.[5] The master of revels made a "God 'a mercy" in memory of the bride's parents. The schoolboys threw burrs, as on Tishe b'Av[6] fast day. There were a lot of gifts after the sermon: a noodle board, a kneading trough, a bucket, brooms, ladles, household articles galore. Then I took a look and saw two strapping young men carrying a crib. "What do we need this for?" I asked. So they said, "Don't rack your brains about it. It's all right, it'll come in handy." I realized I was going to be rooked. Take it another way though, what did I stand to lose? I reflected: I'll see what comes of it. A whole town can't go altogether crazy.

II

At night I came where my wife lay, but she wouldn't let me in. "Say, look here, is this what they married us for?" I said. And she said, "My monthly has come." "But yesterday they took you to the ritual bath, and that's afterwards, isn't it supposed to be?" "Today isn't yesterday," said she, "and yesterday's not today. You can beat it if you don't like it." In short, I waited.

Not four months later, she was in childbed. The townsfolk hid their laughter with their knuckles. But what could I do? She suffered intolerable pains and clawed at the walls. "Gimpel," she cried, "I'm going. Forgive me!" The house filled with women. They were boiling pans of water. The screams rose to the welkin.

The thing to do was to go to the house of prayer to repeat psalms, and that was what I did.

The townsfolk liked that, all right. I stood in a corner saying psalms and prayers, and they shook their heads at me. "Pray, pray!" they told me. "Prayer

5. A braided loaf of bread for the Sabbath.
6. The ninth day of the month of Av, set aside to mourn the destruction of Solomon's Temple in 586 B.C.E. and of the Second Temple in 70 C.E.

never made any woman pregnant." One of the congregation put a straw to my mouth and said, "Hay for the cows." There was something to that too, by God!

She gave birth to a boy. Friday at the synagogue the sexton stood up before the Ark, pounded on the reading table, and announced, "The wealthy Reb Gimpel invites the congregation to a feast in honor of the birth of a son." The whole house of prayer rang with laughter. My face was flaming. But there was nothing I could do. After all, I *was* the one responsible for the circumcision honors and rituals.

Half the town came running. You couldn't wedge another soul in. Women brought peppered chick-peas, and there was a keg of beer from the tavern. I ate and drank as much as anyone, and they all congratulated me. Then there was a circumcision, and I named the boy after my father, may he rest in peace. When all were gone and I was left with my wife alone, she thrust her head through the bed-curtain and called me to her.

"Gimpel," said she, "why are you silent? Has your ship gone and sunk?"

"What shall I say?" I answered. "A fine thing you've done to me! If my mother had known of it she'd have died a second time."

She said, "Are you crazy, or what?"

"How can you make such a fool," I said, "of one who should be the lord and master?"

"What's the matter with you?" she said. "What have you taken it into your head to imagine?"

I saw that I must speak bluntly and openly. "Do you think this is the way to use an orphan?" I said. "You have borne a bastard."

She answered, "Drive this foolishness out of your head. The child is yours."

"How can he be mine?" I argued. "He was born seventeen weeks after the wedding."

She told me then that he was premature. I said, "Isn't he a little too premature?" She said, she had had a grandmother who carried just as short a time and she resembled this grandmother of hers as one drop of water does another. She swore to it with such oaths that you would have believed a peasant at the fair if he had used them. To tell the plain truth, I didn't believe her; but when I talked it over next day with the schoolmaster, he told me that the very same thing had happened to Adam and Eve. Two they went up to bed, and four they descended.

"There isn't a woman in the world who is not the granddaughter of Eve," he said.

That was how it was; they argued me dumb. But then, who really knows how such things are?

I began to forget my sorrow. I loved the child madly, and he loved me too. As soon as he saw me he'd wave his little hands and want me to pick him up, and when he was colicky I was the only one who could pacify him. I bought him a little bone teething ring and a little gilded cap. He was forever catching the evil eye from someone, and then I had to run to get one of those abracadabras for him that would get him out of it. I worked like an ox. You know how expenses go up when there's an infant in the house. I don't want to lie about it; I didn't dislike Elka either, for that matter. She swore at me and cursed, and I couldn't get enough of her. What strength she had! One of her looks could rob you of the power of speech. And her orations! Pitch and sulphur, that's what they were full of, and yet somehow also full of charm. I adored her every word. She gave me bloody wounds though.

In the evening I brought her a white loaf as well as a dark one, and also poppyseed rolls I baked myself. I thieved because of her and swiped everything I could lay hands on: macaroons, raisins, almonds, cakes. I hope I may be forgiven for stealing from the Saturday pots the women left to warm in the baker's oven. I would take out scraps of meat, a chunk of pudding, a chicken leg or head, a piece of tripe, whatever I could nip quickly. She ate and became fat and handsome.

I had to sleep away from home all during the week, at the bakery. On Friday nights when I got home she always made an excuse of some sort. Either she had heartburn, or a stitch in the side, or hiccups, or headaches. You know what women's excuses are. I had a bitter time of it. It was rough. To add to it, this little brother of hers, the bastard, was growing bigger. He'd put lumps on me, and when I wanted to hit back she'd open her mouth and curse so powerfully I saw a green haze floating before my eyes. Ten times a day she threatened to divorce me. Another man in my place would have taken French leave[7] and disappeared. But I'm the type that bears it and says nothing. What's one to do? Shoulders are from God, and burdens too.

One night there was a calamity in the bakery; the oven burst, and we almost had a fire. There was nothing to do but go home, so I went home. Let me, I thought, also taste the joy of sleeping in bed in midweek. I didn't want to wake the sleeping mite and tiptoed into the house. Coming in, it seemed to me that I heard not the snoring of one but, as it were, a double snore, one a thin enough snore and the other like the snoring of a slaughtered ox. Oh, I didn't like that! I didn't like it at all. I went up to the bed, and things suddenly turned black. Next to Elka lay a man's form. Another in my place would have made an uproar, and enough noise to rouse the whole town, but the thought occurred to me that I might wake the child. A little thing like that—why frighten a little swallow, I thought. All right then, I went back to the bakery and stretched out on a sack of flour and till morning I never shut an eye. I shivered as if I had had malaria. "Enough of being a donkey," I said to myself. "Gimpel isn't going to be a sucker all his life. There's a limit even to the foolishness of a fool like Gimpel."

In the morning I went to the rabbi to get advice, and it made a great commotion in the town. They sent the beadle[8] for Elka right away. She came, carrying the child. And what do you think she did? She denied it, denied everything, bone and stone! "He's out of his head," she said. "I know nothing of dreams or divinations." They yelled at her, warned her, hammered on the table, but she stuck to her guns: it was a false accusation, she said.

The butchers and the horse-traders took her part. One of the lads from the slaughterhouse came by and said to me, "We've got our eye on you, you're a marked man." Meanwhile, the child started to bear down and soiled itself. In the rabbinical court there was an Ark of the Covenant,[9] and they couldn't allow that, so they sent Elka away.

I said to the rabbi, "What shall I do?"

7. A hasty departure, one made without saying good-bye or paying debts.
8. The caretaker of a synagogue.
9. In Biblical times, the ornate chest housing the two tablets of the law given to Moses; in modern times, a cabinet holding the Torah scroll with the five books of Moses.

"You must divorce her at once," said he.

"And what if she refuses?" I asked.

He said, "You must serve the divorce. That's all you'll have to do."

I said, "Well, all right, Rabbi. Let me think about it."

"There's nothing to think about," said he. "You mustn't remain under the same roof with her."

"And if I want to see the child?" I asked.

"Let her go, the harlot," said he, "and her brood of bastards with her."

The verdict he gave was that I mustn't even cross her threshold—never again, as long as I should live.

During the day it didn't bother me so much. I thought: It was bound to happen, the abscess had to burst. But at night when I stretched out upon the sacks I felt it all very bitterly. A longing took me, for her and for the child. I wanted to be angry, but that's my misfortune exactly, I don't have it in me to be really angry. In the first place—this was how my thoughts went—there's bound to be a slip sometimes. You can't live without errors. Probably that lad who was with her led her on and gave her presents and what not, and women are often long on hair and short on sense, and so he got around her. And then since she denies it so, maybe I was only seeing things? Hallucinations do happen. You see a figure or a mannikin or something, but when you come up closer it's nothing, there's not a thing there. And if that's so, I'm doing her an injustice. And when I got so far in my thoughts I started to weep. I sobbed so that I wet the flour where I lay. In the morning I went to the rabbi and told him that I had made a mistake. The rabbi wrote on with his quill, and he said that if that were so he would have to reconsider the whole case. Until he had finished I wasn't to go near my wife, but I might send her bread and money by messenger.

III

Nine months passed before all the rabbis could come to an agreement. Letters went back and forth. I hadn't realized that there could be so much erudition about a matter like this.

Meanwhile, Elka gave birth to still another child, a girl this time. On the Sabbath I went to the synagogue and invoked a blessing on her. They called me up to the Torah, and I named the child for my mother-in-law—may she rest in peace. The louts and loudmouths of the town who came into the bakery gave me a going over. All Frampol refreshed its spirits because of my trouble and grief. However, I resolved that I would always believe what I was told. What's the good of *not* believing? Today it's your wife you don't believe; tomorrow it's God Himself you won't take stock in.

By an apprentice who was her neighbor I sent her daily a corn or a wheat loaf, or a piece of pastry, rolls or bagels, or, when I got the chance, a slab of pudding, a slice of honeycake, or wedding strudel—whatever came my way. The apprentice was a goodhearted lad, and more than once he added something on his own. He had formerly annoyed me a lot, plucking my nose and digging me in the ribs, but when he started to be a visitor to my house he became kind and friendly. "Hey, you, Gimpel," he said to me, "you have a very decent little wife and two fine kids. You don't deserve them."

"But the things people say about her," I said.

"Well, they have long tongues," he said, "and nothing to do with them but babble. Ignore it as you ignore the cold of last winter."

One day the rabbi sent for me and said, "Are you certain, Gimpel, that you were wrong about your wife?"

I said, "I'm certain."

"Why, but look here! You yourself saw it."

"It must have been a shadow," I said.

"The shadow of what?"

"Just of one of the beams, I think."

"You can go home then. You owe thanks to the Yanover rabbi. He found an obscure reference in Maimonides[1] that favored you."

I seized the rabbi's hand and kissed it.

I wanted to run home immediately. It's no small thing to be separated for so long a time from wife and child. Then I reflected: I'd better go back to work now, and go home in the evening. I said nothing to anyone, although as far as my heart was concerned it was like one of the Holy Days.[2] The women teased and twitted me as they did every day, but my thought was: Go on, with your loose talk. The truth is out, like the oil upon the water. Maimonides says it's right, and therefore it is right!

At night, when I had covered the dough to let it rise, I took my share of bread and a little sack of flour and started homeward. The moon was full and the stars were glistening, something to terrify the soul. I hurried onward, and before me darted a long shadow. It was winter, and a fresh snow had fallen. I had a mind to sing, but it was growing late and I didn't want to wake the householders. Then I felt like whistling, but I remembered that you don't whistle at night because it brings the demons out. So I was silent and walked as fast as I could.

Dogs in the Christian yards barked at me when I passed, but I thought: Bark your teeth out! What are you but mere dogs? Whereas I am a man, the husband of a fine wife, the father of promising children.

As I approached the house my heart started to pound as though it were the heart of a criminal. I felt no fear, but my heart went thump! thump! Well, no drawing back. I quietly lifted the latch and went in. Elka was asleep. I looked at the infant's cradle. The shutter was closed, but the moon forced its way through the cracks. I saw the newborn child's face and loved it as soon as I saw it—immediately—each tiny bone.

Then I came nearer to the bed. And what did I see but the apprentice lying there beside Elka. The moon went out all at once. It was utterly black, and I trembled. My teeth chattered. The bread fell from my hands, and my wife waked and said, "Who is that, ah?"

I muttered, "It's me."

"Gimpel?" she asked. "How come you're here? I thought it was forbidden."

"The rabbi said," I answered and shook as with a fever.

"Listen to me, Gimpel," she said, "go out to the shed and see if the goat's all right. It seems she's been sick." I have forgotten to say that we had a goat. When I heard she was unwell I went into the yard. The nannygoat was a good little creature. I had a nearly human feeling for her.

1. Moses ben Maimon (1135–1204), Spanish Jewish philosopher.

2. A reference to the holidays of Rosh Hashanah (New Year) and Yom Kippur (Day of Atonement).

With hesitant steps I went up to the shed and opened the door. The goat stood there on her four feet. I felt her everywhere, drew her by the horns, examined her udders, and found nothing wrong. She had probably eaten too much bark. "Good night, little goat," I said. "Keep well." And the little beast answered with a "Maa" as though to thank me for the good will.

I went back. The apprentice had vanished.

"Where," I asked, "is the lad?"

"What lad?" my wife answered.

"What do you mean?" I said. "The apprentice. You were sleeping with him."

"The things I have dreamed this night and the night before," she said, "may they come true and lay you low, body and soul! An evil spirit has taken root in you and dazzles your sight." She screamed out, "You hateful creature! You moon calf! You spook! You uncouth man! Get out, or I'll scream all Frampol out of bed!"

Before I could move, her brother sprang out from behind the oven and struck me a blow on the back of the head. I thought he had broken my neck. I felt that something about me was deeply wrong, and I said, "Don't make a scandal. All that's needed now is that people should accuse me of raising spooks and dybbuks."[3] For that was what she had meant. "No one will touch bread of my baking."

In short, I somehow calmed her.

"Well," she said, "that's enough. Lie down, and be shattered by wheels."

Next morning I called the apprentice aside. "Listen here, brother!" I said. And so on and so forth. "What do you say?" He stared at me as though I had dropped from the roof or something.

"I swear," he said, "you'd better go to an herb doctor or some healer. I'm afraid you have a screw loose, but I'll hush it up for you." And that's how the thing stood.

To make a long story short, I lived twenty years with my wife. She bore me six children, four daughters and two sons. All kinds of things happened, but I neither saw nor heard. I believed, and that's all. The rabbi recently said to me, "Belief in itself is beneficial. It is written that a good man lives by his faith."

Suddenly my wife took sick. It began with a trifle, a little growth upon the breast. But she evidently was not destined to live long; she had no years. I spent a fortune on her. I have forgotten to say that by this time I had a bakery of my own and in Frampol was considered to be something of a rich man. Daily the healer came, and every witch doctor in the neighborhood was brought. They decided to use leeches, and after that to try cupping. They even called a doctor from Lublin, but it was too late. Before she died she called me to her bed and said, "Forgive me, Gimpel."

I said, "What is there to forgive? You have been a good and faithful wife."

"Woe, Gimpel!" she said. "It was ugly how I deceived you all these years. I want to go clean to my Maker, and so I have to tell you that the children are not yours."

If I had been clouted on the head with a piece of wood it couldn't have bewildered me more.

"Whose are they?" I asked.

3. Condemned spirits who inhabit the bodies of living persons and control their actions.

"I don't know," she said. "There were a lot . . . but they're not yours." And as she spoke she tossed her head to the side, her eyes turned glassy, and it was all up with Elka. On her whitened lips there remained a smile.

I imagined that, dead as she was, she was saying, "I deceived Gimpel. That was the meaning of my brief life."

IV

One night, when the period of mourning was done, as I lay dreaming on the flour sacks, there came the Spirit of Evil himself and said to me, "Gimpel, why do you sleep?"

I said, "What should I be doing? Eating kreplech?"[4]

"The whole world deceives you," he said, "and you ought to deceive the world in your turn."

"How can I deceive all the world?" I asked him.

He answered, "You might accumulate a bucket of urine every day and at night pour it into the dough. Let the sages of Frampol eat filth."

"What about the judgment in the world to come?" I said.

"There is no world to come," he said. "They've sold you a bill of goods and talked you into believing you carried a cat in your belly. What nonsense!"

"Well then," I said, "and is there a God?"

He answered, "There is no God either."

"What," I said, "*is* there, then?"

"A thick mire."

He stood before my eyes with a goatish beard and horn, long-toothed, and with a tail. Hearing such words, I wanted to snatch him by the tail, but I tumbled from the flour sacks and nearly broke a rib. Then it happened that I had to answer the call of nature, and, passing, I saw the risen dough, which seemed to say to me, "Do it!" In brief, I let myself be persuaded.

At dawn the apprentice came. We kneaded the bread, scattered caraway seeds on it, and set it to bake. Then the apprentice went away, and I was left sitting in the little trench by the oven, on a pile of rags. Well, Gimpel, I thought, you've revenged yourself on them for all the shame they've put on you. Outside the frost glittered, but it was warm beside the oven. The flames heated my face. I bent my head and fell into a doze.

I saw in a dream, at once, Elka in her shroud. She called to me, "What have you done, Gimpel?"

I said to her, "It's all your fault," and started to cry.

"You fool!" she said. "You fool! Because I was false is everything false too? I never deceived anyone but myself. I'm paying for it all, Gimpel. They spare you nothing here."

I looked at her face. It was black; I was startled and waked, and remained sitting dumb. I sensed that everything hung in the balance. A false step now and I'd lose eternal life. But God gave me His help. I seized the long shovel and took out the loaves, carried them into the yard, and started to dig a hole in the frozen earth.

My apprentice came back as I was doing it. "What are you doing boss?" he said, and grew pale as a corpse.

4. Triangular pockets of noodle dough filled with chopped meat or cheese, boiled and eaten in soup or as a side dish.

"I know what I'm doing," I said, and I buried it all before his very eyes.

Then I went home, took my hoard from its hiding place, and divided it among the children. "I saw your mother tonight," I said. "She's turning black, poor thing."

They were so astounded they couldn't speak a word.

"Be well," I said, "and forget that such a one as Gimpel ever existed." I put on my short coat, a pair of boots, took the bag that held my prayer shawl in one hand, my stock in the other, and kissed the mezuzah.[5] When people saw me in the street they were greatly surprised.

"Where are you going?" they said.

I answered, "Into the world." And so I departed from Frampol.

I wandered over the land, and good people did not neglect me. After many years I became old and white; I heard a great deal, many lies and falsehoods, but the longer I lived the more I understood that there were really no lies. Whatever doesn't really happen is dreamed at night. It happens to one if it doesn't happen to another, tomorrow if not today, or a century hence if not next year. What difference can it make? Often I heard tales of which I said, "Now this is a thing that cannot happen." But before a year had elapsed I heard that it actually had come to pass somewhere.

Going from place to place, eating at strange tables, it often happens that I spin yarns—improbable things that could never have happened—about devils, magicians, windmills, and the like. The children run after me, calling, "Grandfather, tell us a story." Sometimes they ask for particular stories, and I try to please them. A fat young boy once said to me, "Grandfather, it's the same story you told us before." The little rogue, he was right.

So it is with dreams too. It is many years since I left Frampol, but as soon as I shut my eyes I am there again. And whom do you think I see? Elka. She is standing by the washtub, as at our first encounter, but her face is shining and her eyes are as radiant as the eyes of a saint, and she speaks outlandish words to me, strange things. When I wake I have forgotten it all. But while the dream lasts I am comforted. She answers all my queries, and what comes out is that all is right. I weep and implore, "Let me be with you." And she consoles me and tells me to be patient. The time is nearer than it is far. Sometimes she strokes and kisses me and weeps upon my face. When I awaken I feel her lips and taste the salt of her tears.

No doubt the world is entirely an imaginary world, but it is only once removed from the true world. At the door of the hovel where I lie, there stands the plank on which the dead are taken away. The grave-digger Jew has his spade ready. The grave waits and the worms are hungry; the shrouds are prepared—I carry them in my beggar's sack. Another *shnorrer*[6] is waiting to inherit my bed of straw. When the time comes I will go joyfully. Whatever may be there, it will be real, without complication, without ridicule, without deception. God be praised: there even Gimpel cannot be deceived.

1944

Magazine, 1953
Book, 1954

5. A small piece of parchment inscribed with a passage from Deuteronomy (6.1–12), rolled up in a scroll, placed in a case or tube, and affixed to the doorpost of Jewish homes as a sign of faith in God.

6. A beggar who shows wit and resourcefulness in getting money from others as though it were his right.

The Séance[1]

I

It was during the summer of 1946, in the living room of Mrs. Kopitzky on Central Park West. A single red bulb burned behind a shade adorned with one of Mrs. Kopitzky's automatic drawings[2]—circles with eyes, flowers with mouths, goblets with fingers. The walls were all hung with Lotte Kopitzky's paintings, which she did in a state of trance and at the direction of her control[3]—Bhaghavar Krishna, a Hindu sage supposed to have lived in the fourth century. It was he, Bhaghavar Krishna, who had painted the peacock with the golden tail, in the middle of which appeared the image of Buddha; the otherworldly trees hung with elflocks and fantastic fruits; the young women of the planet Venus with their branch-like arms and their ears from which stretched silver nets—organs of telepathy. Over the pictures, the old furniture, the shelves with books, there hovered reddish shadows. The windows were covered with heavy drapes.

At the round table on which lay a Ouija board,[4] a trumpet, and a withered rose, sat Dr. Zorach Kalisher, small, broad-shouldered, bald in front and with sparse tufts of hair in the back, half yellow, half gray. From behind his yellow bushy brows peered a pair of small, piercing eyes. Dr. Kalisher had almost no neck—his head sat directly on his broad shoulders, making him look like a primitive African statue. His nose was crooked, flat at the top, the tip split in two. On his chin sprouted a tiny growth. It was hard to tell whether this was a remnant of a beard or just a hairy wart. The face was wrinkled, badly shaven, and grimy. He wore a black corduroy jacket, a white shirt covered with ash and coffee stains, and a crooked bow tie.

When conversing with Mrs. Kopitzky, he spoke an odd mixture of Yiddish and German. "What's keeping our friend Bhaghavar Krishna? Did he lose his way in the spheres of Heaven?"

"Dr. Kalisher, don't rush me," Mrs. Kopitzky answered. "We cannot give them orders . . . They have their motives and their moods. Have a little patience."

"Well, if one must, one must."

Dr. Kalisher drummed his fingers on the table. From each finger sprouted a little red beard. Mrs. Kopitzky leaned her head on the back of the upholstered chair and prepared to fall into a trance. Against the dark glow of the red bulb, one could discern her freshly dyed hair, black without luster, waved into tiny ringlets; her rouged face, the broad nose, high cheekbones, and eyes spread far apart and heavily lined with mascara. Dr. Kalisher often joked that she looked like a painted bulldog. Her husband, Leon Kopitzky, a dentist, had died eighteen years before, leaving no children. The widow supported herself on an annuity from an insurance company. In 1929 she had lost her fortune in the Wall Street crash, but had recently begun to buy securities again on the advice of her Ouija board, planchette, and crystal ball. Mrs. Kopitzky even asked Bhaghavar Krishna for tips on the races. In a few cases, he had divulged in dreams the names of winning horses.

1. Translated by Roger H. Klein and Cecil Hemley.
2. Drawings conveyed through a "medium," who claims to communicate with spirits of the dead.
3. The particular spirit communicating with a medium.
4. A board with the alphabet and other signs on it that, when touched with the fingers, is thought to spell out spiritual or telepathic messages.

Dr. Kalisher bowed his head and covered his eyes with his hands, muttering to himself as solitary people often do. "Well, I've played the fool enough. This is the last night. Even from kreplech one has enough."

"Did you say something, Doctor?"

"What? Nothing."

"When you rush me, I can't fall into the trance."

"Trance-shmance," Dr. Kalisher grumbled to himself. "The ghost is late, that's all. Who does she think she's fooling? Just crazy—meshugga."

Aloud, he said: "I'm not rushing you, I've plenty of time. If what the Americans say about time is right, I'm a second Rockefeller."

As Mrs. Kopitzky opened her mouth to answer, her double chin, with all its warts, trembled, revealing a set of huge false teeth. Suddenly she threw back her head and sighed. She closed her eyes, and snorted once. Dr. Kalisher gaped at her questioningly, sadly. He had not yet heard the sound of the outside door opening, but Mrs. Kopitzky, who probably had the acute hearing of an animal, might have. Dr. Kalisher began to rub his temples and his nose, and then clutched at his tiny beard.

There was a time when he had tried to understand all things through his reason, but that period of rationalism had long passed. Since then, he had constructed an anti-rationalistic philosophy, a kind of extreme hedonism which saw in eroticism the *Ding an sich*,[5] and in reason the very lowest stage of being, the entropy which led to absolute death. His position had been a curious compound of Hartmann's[6] idea of the Unconscious with the Cabala[7] of Rabbi Isaac Luria,[8] according to which all things, from the smallest grain of sand to the very Godhead itself, are Copulation and Union. It was because of this system that Dr. Kalisher had come from Paris to New York in 1939, leaving behind in Poland his father, a rabbi, a wife who refused to divorce him, and a lover, Nella, with whom he had lived for years in Berlin and later in Paris. It so happened that when Dr. Kalisher left for America, Nella went to visit her parents in Warsaw. He had planned to bring her over to the United States as soon as he found a translator, a publisher, and a chair at one of the American universities.

In those days Dr. Kalisher had still been hopeful. He had been offered a cathedra[9] in the Hebrew University in Jerusalem; a publisher in Palestine was about to issue one of his books; his essays had been printed in Zurich and Paris. But with the outbreak of the Second World War, his life began to deteriorate. His literary agent suddenly died, his translator was inept and, to make matters worse, absconded with a good part of the manuscript, of which there was no copy. In the Yiddish press, for some strange reason, the reviewers turned hostile and hinted that he was a charlatan. The Jewish organizations which arranged lectures for him canceled his tour. According to his own philosophy, he had believed that all suffering was nothing more than negative expressions of universal eroticism: Hitler, Stalin, the Nazis who sang the Horst Wessel song and made the Jews wear yellow armbands,[1] were

5. Thing in itself (German).
6. I.e., Karl Hartmann (1842–1906), German philosopher.
7. Jewish mystical teachings originating in 12th-century Europe.
8. Luria (1534–1572) was a cabalist in Egypt and Safed, Palestine.
9. Literally, a bishop's throne; in this context, a professorial "chair."
1. European Jews were traditionally forced to wear yellow patches or armbands to set them apart. "Horst Wessel song": inspirational anti-Semitic song of the Nazi party.

actually searching for new forms and variations of sexual salvation. But Dr. Kalisher began to doubt his own system and fell into despair. He had to leave his hotel and move into a cheap furnished room. He wandered about in shabby clothes, sat all day in cafeterias, drank endless cups of coffee, smoked bad cigars, and barely managed to survive on the few dollars that a relief organization gave him each month. The refugees whom he met spread all sorts of rumors about visas for those left behind in Europe, packages of food and medicines that could be sent them through various agencies, ways of bringing over relatives from Poland through Honduras, Cuba, Brazil. But he, Zorach Kalisher, could save no one from the Nazis. He had received only a single letter from Nella.

Only in New York had Dr. Kalisher realized how attached he was to his mistress. Without her, he became impotent.

II

Everything was exactly as it had been yesterday and the day before. Bhaghavar Krishna began to speak in English with his foreign voice that was half male and half female, duplicating Mrs. Kopitzky's errors in pronunciation and grammar. Lotte Kopitzky came from a village in the Carpathian Mountains. Dr. Kalisher could never discover her nationality—Hungarian, Rumanian, Galician? She knew no Polish or German, and little English; even her Yiddish had been corrupted through her long years in America. Actually she had been left languageless and Bhaghavar Krishna spoke her various jargons. At first Dr. Kalisher had asked Bhaghavar Krishna the details of his earthly existence but had been told by Bhaghavar Krishna that he had forgotten everything in the heavenly mansions in which he dwelt. All he could recall was that he had lived in the suburbs of Madras. Bhaghavar Krishna did not even know that in that part of India Tamil was spoken. When Dr. Kalisher tried to converse with him about Sanskrit, the Mahabharata, the Ramayana, the Sakuntala,[2] Bhaghavar Krishna replied that he was no longer interested in terrestrial literature. Bhaghavar Krishna knew nothing but a few theosophic and spiritualistic brochures and magazines which Mrs. Kopitzky subscribed to.

For Dr. Kalisher it was all one big joke; but if one lived in a bug-ridden room and had a stomach spoiled by cafeteria food, if one was in one's sixties and completely without family, one became tolerant of all kinds of crackpots. He had been introduced to Mrs. Kopitzky in 1942, took part in scores of her séances, read her automatic writings, admired her automatic paintings, listened to her automatic symphonies. A few times he had borrowed money from her which he had been unable to return. He ate at her house—vegetarian suppers, since Mrs. Kopitzky touched neither meat, fish, milk, nor eggs, but only fruit and vegetables which mother earth produces. She specialized in preparing salads with nuts, almonds, pomegranates, avocados.

In the beginning, Lotte Kopitzky had wanted to draw him into a romance. The spirits were all of the opinion that Lotte Kopitzky and Zorach Kalisher derived from the same spiritual origin: *The Great White Lodge*. Even Bhag-

2. A 5th-century Indian theater piece by Kalidasa. "Sanskrit": ancient language of Hindus in India. "Mahabharata" and "Ramayana": Sanskrit epics of the 5th–4th centuries B.C.E.

havar Krishna had a taste for matchmaking. Lotte Kopitzky constantly conveyed to Dr. Kalisher regards from the Masters, who had connections with Tibet, Atlantis,[3] the Heavenly Hierarchy, the Shambala, the Fourth Kingdom of Nature and the Council of Sanat Kumara. In Heaven as on the earth, in the early forties, all kinds of crises were brewing. The Powers having realigned themselves, the members of the Ashrams[4] were preparing a war on Cosmic Evil. The Hierarchy sent out projectors to light up the planet Earth, and to find esoteric men and women to serve special purposes. Mrs. Kopitzky assured Dr. Kalisher that he was ordained to play a huge part in the Universal Rebirth. But he had neglected his mission, disappointed the Masters. He had promised to telephone, but didn't. He spent months in Philadelphia without dropping her a postcard. He returned without informing her. Mrs. Kopitzky ran into him in an automat[5] on Sixth Avenue and found him in a torn coat, a dirty shirt, and shoes worn so thin they no longer had heels. He had not even applied for United States citizenship, though refugees were entitled to citizenship without going abroad to get a visa.

Now, in 1946, everything that Lotte Kopitzky had prophesied had come true. All had passed over to the other side—his father, his brothers, his sisters, Nella. Bhaghavar Krishna brought messages from them. The Masters still remembered Dr. Kalisher, and still had plans for him in connection with the Centennial Conference of the Hierarchy. Even the fact that his family had perished in Treblinka, Maidanek, Stutthof[6] was closely connected with the Powers of Light, the Development of Karma, the New Cycle after Lemuria, and with the aim of leading humanity to a new ascent in Love and a new Aquatic Epoch.

During the last few weeks, Mrs. Kopitzky had become dissatisfied with summoning Nella's spirit in the usual way. Dr. Kalisher was given the rare opportunity of coming into contact with Nella's materialized form. It happened in this way: Bhaghavar Krishna would give a sign to Dr. Kalisher that he should walk down the dark corridor to Mrs. Kopitzky's bedroom. There in the darkness, near Mrs. Kopitzky's bureau, an apparition hovered which was supposed to be Nella. She murmured to Dr. Kalisher in Polish, spoke caressing words into his ear, brought him messages from friends and relatives. Bhaghavar Krishna had admonished Dr. Kalisher time and again not to try to touch the phantom, because contact could cause severe injury to both, to him and Mrs. Kopitzky. The few times that he sought to approach her, she deftly eluded him. But confused though Dr. Kalisher was by these episodes, he was aware that they were contrived. This was not Nella, neither her voice nor her manner. The messages he received proved nothing. He had mentioned all these names to Mrs. Kopitzky and had been questioned by her. But Dr. Kalisher remained curious: Who was the apparition? Why did she act the part? Probably for money. But the fact that Lotte Kopitzky was capable of hiring a ghost proved that she was not only a self-deceiver but a swindler of others as well. Every time Dr. Kalisher walked down the dark corridor, he murmured, "Crazy, meshugga, a ridiculous woman."

Tonight Dr. Kalisher could hardly wait for Bhaghavar Krishna's signal. He

3. A legendary island in the Atlantic that sank beneath the sea.
4. Hindu religious retreats.
5. A self-service cafeteria with coin-operated compartments for individual dishes.
6. Nazi concentration and death camps in Poland and Germany.

was tired of these absurdities. For years he had suffered from a prostate condition and now had to urinate every half hour. A Warsaw doctor who was not allowed to practice in America, but did so clandestinely nonetheless, had warned Dr. Kalisher not to postpone an operation, because complications might arise. But Kalisher had neither the money for the hospital nor the will to go there. He sought to cure himself with baths, hot-water bottles, and with pills he had brought with him from France. He even tried to massage his prostate gland himself. As a rule, he went to the bathroom the moment he arrived at Mrs. Kopitzky's, but this evening he had neglected to do so. He felt a pressure on his bladder. The raw vegetables which Mrs. Kopitzky had given him to eat made his intestines twist. "Well, I'm too old for such pleasures," he murmured. As Bhaghavar Krishna spoke, Dr. Kalisher could scarcely listen. "What is she babbling, the idiot? She's not even a decent ventriloquist."

The instant Bhaghavar Krishna gave his usual sign, Dr. Kalisher got up. His legs had been troubling him greatly but had never been as shaky as tonight. "Well, I'll go to the bathroom first," he decided. To reach the bathroom in the dark was not easy. Dr. Kalisher walked hesitantly, his hands outstretched, trying to feel his way. When he had reached the bathroom and opened the door, someone inside pulled the knob back. It is she, the girl, Dr. Kalisher realized. So shaken was he that he forgot why he was there. "She most probably came here to undress." He was embarrassed both for himself and for Mrs. Kopitzky. "What does she need it for, for whom is she playing this comedy?" His eyes had become accustomed to the dark. He had seen the girl's silhouette. The bathroom had a window giving on to the street, and the shimmer of the street lamp had fallen on to it. She was small, broadish, with a high bosom. She appeared to have been in her underwear. Dr. Kalisher stood there hypnotized. He wanted to cry out, "Enough, it's all so obvious," but his tongue was numb. His heart pounded and he could hear his own breathing.

After a while he began to retrace his steps, but he was dazed with blindness. He bumped into a clothes tree and hit a wall, striking his head. He stepped backwards. Something fell and broke. Perhaps one of Mrs. Kopitzky's otherworldly sculptures! At that moment the telephone began to ring, the sound unusually loud and menacing. Dr. Kalisher shivered. He suddenly felt a warmth in his underwear. He had wet himself like a child.

IV

"Well, I've reached the bottom," Dr. Kalisher muttered to himself. "I'm ready for the junkyard." He walked toward the bedroom. Not only his underwear, his pants also had become wet. He expected Mrs. Kopitzky to answer the telephone; it happened more than once that she awakened from her trance to discuss stocks, bonds, and dividends. But the telephone kept on ringing. Only now he realized what he had done—he had closed the living-room door, shutting out the red glow which helped him find his way. "I'm going home," he resolved. He turned toward the street door but found he had lost all sense of direction in that labyrinth of an apartment. He touched a knob and turned it. He heard a muffled scream. He had wandered into the bathroom again. There seemed to be no hook or chain inside. Again he saw the woman in a corset, but this time with her face half in the light. In that split second he knew she was middle-aged.

"Forgive, please." And he moved back.

The telephone stopped ringing, then began anew. Suddenly Dr. Kalisher glimpsed a shaft of red light and heard Mrs. Kopitzky walking toward the telephone. He stopped and said, half statement, half question: "Mrs. Kopitzky!"

Mrs. Kopitzky started. "Already finished?"

"I'm not well, I must go home."

"Not well? Where do you want to go? What's the matter? Your heart?"

"Everything."

"Wait a second."

Mrs. Kopitzky, having approached him, took his arm and led him back to the living room. The telephone continued to ring and then finally fell silent. "Did you get a pressure in your heart, huh?" Mrs. Kopitzky asked. "Lie down on the sofa, I'll get a doctor."

"No, no, not necessary."

"I'll massage you."

"My bladder is not in order, my prostate gland."

"What? I'll put on the light."

He wanted to ask her not to do so, but she had already turned on a number of lamps. The light glared in his eyes. She stood looking at him and at his wet pants. Her head shook from side to side. Then she said, "This is what comes from living alone."

"Really, I'm ashamed of myself."

"What's the shame? We all get older. Nobody gets younger. Were you in the bathroom?"

Dr. Kalisher didn't answer.

"Wait a moment, I still have *his* clothes. I had a premonition I would need them someday."

Mrs. Kopitzky left the room. Dr. Kalisher sat down on the edge of a chair, placing his handkerchief beneath him. He sat there stiff, wet, childishly guilty and helpless, and yet with that inner quiet that comes from illness. For years he had been afraid of doctors, hospitals, and especially nurses, who deny their feminine shyness and treat grownup men like babies. Now he was prepared for the last degradations of the body. "Well, I'm finished, *kaput*." He made a swift summation of his existence. "Philosophy? what philosophy? Eroticism? whose eroticism?" He had played with phrases for years, had come to no conclusions. What had happened to him, in him, all that had taken place in Poland, in Russia, on the planets, on the faraway galaxies, could not be reduced either to Schopenhauer's blind will or to his, Kalisher's, eroticism. It was explained neither by Spinoza's substance, Leibniz's monads, Hegel's dialectic, or Heckel's monism.[7] "They all just juggle words like Mrs. Kopitzky. It's better that I didn't publish all that scribbling of mine. What's the good of all these preposterous hypotheses? They don't help at all . . ." He looked up at Mrs. Kopitzky's pictures on the wall, and in the blazing light they resembled the smearings of school children. From the street came the

7. Theories of famous philosophers: Arthur Schopenhauer (1788–1860), Baruch Spinoza (1632–1677), Gottfried Wilhelm Leibniz (1646–1716), Georg Wilhelm Friedrich Hegel (1770–1831), and Ernst Haeckel (1834–1919).

honking of cars, the screams of boys, the thundering echo of the subway as a train passed. The door opened and Mrs. Kopitzky entered with a bundle of clothes: a jacket, pants, and shirt, and underwear. The clothes smelled of mothballs and dust. She said to him, "Have you been in the bedroom?"

"What? No."

"Nella didn't materialize?"

"No, she didn't materialize."

"Well, change your clothes. Don't let me embarrass you."

She put the bundle on the sofa and bent over Dr. Kalisher with the devotion of a relative. She said, "You'll stay here. Tomorrow I'll send for your things."

"No, that's senseless."

"I knew that this would happen the moment we were introduced on Second Avenue."

"How so? Well, it's all the same."

"*They* tell me things in advance. I look at someone, and I know what will happen to him."

"So? When am I going to go?"

"You still have to live many years. You're needed here. You have to finish your work."

"My work has the same value as your ghosts."

"There *are* ghosts, there are! Don't be so cynical. They watch over us from above, they lead us by the hand, they measure our steps. We are much more important to the Cyclic Revival of the Universe than you imagine."

He wanted to ask her: "Why then, did you have to hire a woman to deceive me?" but he remained silent. Mrs. Kopitzky went out again. Dr. Kalisher took off his pants and underwear and dried himself with his handkerchief. For a while he stood with his upper part fully dressed and his pants off like some mad jester. Then he stepped into a pair of loose drawers that were as cool as shrouds. He pulled on a pair of striped pants that were too wide and too long for him. He had to draw the pants up until the hem reached his knees. He gasped and snorted, had to stop every few seconds to rest. Suddenly he remembered! This was exactly how as a boy he had dressed himself in his father's clothes when his father napped after the Sabbath pudding: the old man's white trousers, his satin robe, his fringed garment, his fur hat. Now his father had become a pile of ashes somewhere in Poland, and he, Zorach, put on the musty clothes of a dentist. He walked to the mirror and looked at himself, even stuck out his tongue like a child. Then he lay down on the sofa. The telephone rang again, and Mrs. Kopitzky apparently answered it, because this time the ringing stopped immediately. Dr. Kalisher closed his eyes and lay quietly. He had nothing to hope for. There was not even anything to think about.

He dozed off and found himself in the cafeteria on Forty-second Street, near the Public Library. He was breaking off pieces of an egg cookie. A refugee was telling him how to save relatives in Poland by dressing them up in Nazi uniforms. Later they would be led by ship to the North Pole, the South Pole, and across the Pacific. Agents were prepared to take charge of them in Tierra del Fuego, in Honolulu and Yokohama . . . How strange, but that smuggling had something to do with his, Zorach Kalisher's, philosophic system, not with his former version but with a new one, which blended eroticism with memory. While he was combining all these images, he asked himself in astonishment: "What kind of relationship can there be between sex, memory, and the redemption of the ego? And how will it work in infinite time? It's nothing but casuistry, casuistry. It's a way of explaining my own impotence. And how can I bring over Nella when she has already perished? Unless death itself is nothing but a sexual amnesia." He awoke and saw Mrs. Kopitzky bending over him with a pillow which she was about to put behind his head.

"How do you feel?"

"Has Nella left?" he asked, amazed at his own words. He must still be half asleep.

Mrs. Kopitzky winced. Her double chin shook and trembled. Her dark eyes were filled with motherly reproach.

"You're laughing, huh? There is no death, there isn't any. We live forever, and we love forever. This is the pure truth."

1968

LIONEL TRILLING
1905–1975

"The stories of *Red Cavalry* have as their principle of coherence what I have called the anomaly, or the joke of a Jew who is a member of a Cossack regiment—Babel was a supply officer under General Budenny in the campaign of 1920." So writes Lionel Trilling in his 1955 recollection of first reading, when he was twenty-four, the Russian Jewish storyteller Isaac Babel (1894–1941). Because the Jewish ethos is "intellectual, pacific, humane," Babel's involvement in Russia's postrevolutionary civil war "disturbed me in a way I can still remember." Yet Trilling sees that Cossack violence itself did not draw Babel, rather "what the violence goes along with, the boldness, the passionateness, the simplicity and directness—and the grace." For Trilling, the spectacle of Babel's Jewish psyche jostling with its Cossack opposite connects with Freud uncovering "the truth of the body, the truth of full sexuality, the truth of open aggressiveness. . . . the 'discontent' of civilization which Freud describes is our self-recrimination at having surrendered too much." The Cossack "in his savagery [has] some quality that might raise strange questions in a Jewish mind"—in Babel's and in the young Trilling's.

Lionel Trilling was born on July 4, 1905, in New York City. After attending Columbia, he began teaching there and in 1929 married Diana Rubin, a writer and critic. "When I decided to go into academic life, my friends thought me naive to the point of absurdity, nor were they wholly wrong—my appointment to an instructorship in Columbia College was pretty openly regarded as an experiment, and for some time my career in the college was complicated by my being Jewish." In 1939, Trilling became the first Jew appointed as professor in Columbia's English Department. He had written some stories (1925–28) for *Menorah Journal*, a secular magazine dedicated to "Jewish humanism." These showed him divided, rather squeamish, about raw Jewishness. The "great fact for American Jews," Trilling felt, was being excluded from the general life and, in response, transcending anti-Semitism. Alfred Kazin had his own sense of the situation: "For Trilling I would always be 'too Jewish,' too full of my lower-class experience. He would always defend himself from the things he had left behind." For this "extraordinarily accomplished son of an immigrant tailor," the requisite was "manners" and "modulation."

Trilling never did develop anything like Kazin's elegiac grasp of the Jewish past, nor was it particularly Manhattan's Jewish present that he thrived in. "I do not think of myself as a 'Jewish writer.' . . . I should resent it if a critic of my work were to discover in it either faults or virtues which he called Jewish," Trilling wrote in 1944 (refining his point by the British "should," the subjunctive, the lucid, balanced phrasing). And he added: "As the Jewish community now exists, it can give no sustenance to the American artist or intellectual who is born a Jew." At the same time, it is worth noting that many such people, whatever their varied sustenance, were Trilling's students at Columbia and became significant literary figures: Allen Ginsberg, John Hollander, Norman Podhoretz, Jason Epstein, Steven Marcus, Richard Howard, Robert Gottlieb.

More to the point, the demanding critical stance articulated in Trilling's fine books on Matthew Arnold (1939) and E. M. Forster (1943), the moral and imaginative tensions explored in *The Liberal Imagination* (1950) and *Beyond Culture* (1965), may have deeper springs than are easily evident. They may owe something to those early complications of "my being Jewish" that he experienced at Columbia. What's more, the Isaac Babel whom Trilling discerned half-hankering after Cossack bodiliness, sexuality, and aggressiveness finds some echo in Philip Roth's novels. And Trilling's insistence on the life of the individual mind, his displacement of "simple humanitarian optimism" with the Freudian search into man's pain, terror, death, "a kind of hell within him," and, ultimately, love—all this helps open a terrain for Saul Bellow's *Herzog*, Ginsberg's *Howl*, and much else.

When Lionel Trilling died, on November 5, 1975, Irving Howe wrote that Trilling had "believed passionately—and taught a whole generation also to believe—in the power of literature, its power to transform, elevate and damage."

From The Liberal Imagination

From *Freud*[1] *and Literature*

IV

If, then, we can accept neither Freud's conception of the place of art in life nor his application of the analytical method, what is it that he contributes to our understanding of art or to its practice? In my opinion, what he contributes outweighs his errors; it is of the greatest importance, and it lies in no specific statement that he makes about art but is, rather, implicit in his whole conception of the mind.

For, of all mental systems, the Freudian psychology is the one which makes poetry indigenous to the very constitution of the mind. Indeed, the mind, as Freud sees it, is in the greater part of its tendency exactly a poetry-making organ. This puts the case too strongly, no doubt, for it seems to make the working of the unconscious mind equivalent to poetry itself, forgetting that between the unconscious mind and the finished poem there supervene the social intention and the formal control of the conscious mind. Yet the statement has at least the virtue of counterbalancing the belief, so commonly

1. Sigmund Freud (1856–1939), an Austrian neurologist and founder of psychoanalysis.

expressed or implied, that the very opposite is true, and that poetry is a kind of beneficent aberration of the mind's right course.

Freud has not merely naturalized poetry; he has discovered its status as a pioneer settler, and he sees it as a method of thought. Often enough he tries to show how, as a method of thought, it is unreliable and ineffective for conquering reality; yet he himself is forced to use it in the very shaping of his own science, as when he speaks of the topography of the mind and tells us what a kind of defiant apology that the metaphors of space relationship which he is using are really most inexact since the mind is not a thing of space at all, but that there is no other way of conceiving the difficult idea except by metaphor.[2] In the eighteenth century Vico[3] spoke of the metaphorical, imagistic language of the early stages of culture; it was left to Freud to discover how, in a scientific age, we still feel and think in figurative formations, and to create, what psychoanalysis is, a science of tropes, of metaphor and its variants, synecdoche and metonymy.[4]

Freud showed, too, how the mind, in one of its parts, could work without logic, yet not without that directing purpose, that control of intent from which, perhaps it might be said, logic springs. For the unconscious mind works without the syntactical conjunctions which are logic's essence. It recognizes no *because*, no *therefore*, no *but*; such ideas as similarity, agreement, and community are expressed in dreams imagistically by compressing the elements into a unity. The unconscious mind in its struggle with the conscious always turns from the general to the concrete and finds the tangible trifle more congenial than the large abstraction. Freud discovered in the very organization of the mind those mechanisms by which art makes its effects, such devices as the condensations of meanings and the displacement of accent.

All this is perhaps obvious enough and, though I should like to develop it in proportion both to its importance and to the space I have given to disagreement with Freud, I will not press it further. For there are two other elements in Freud's thought which, in conclusion, I should like to introduce as of great weight in their bearing on art.

Of these, one is a specific idea which, in the middle of his career (1920), Freud put forward in his essay *Beyond the Pleasure Principle*. The essay itself is a speculative attempt to solve a perplexing problem in clinical analysis, but its relevance to literature is inescapable, as Freud sees well enough, even though his perception of its critical importance is not sufficiently strong to make him revise his earlier views of the nature and function of art. The idea is one which stands besides Aristotle's notion of the catharsis,[5] in part to supplement, in part to modify it.

Freud has come upon certain facts which are not to be reconciled with his earlier theory of the dream. According to this theory, all dreams, even the unpleasant ones, could be understood upon analysis to have the intention of fulfilling the dreamer's wishes. They are in the service of what Freud calls

2. Figurative language in which a word or phrase is substituted for another to suggest an analogy between them.
3. Giambattista Vico (1668–1744), an Italian philosopher of cultural history and law who laid the foundation for the study of cultural anthropology. He influenced James Joyce's *Finnegans Wake*.
4. The use of the name of one thing as a substitute for another of which it is an attribute. "Tropes": figures of speech. "Synecdoche": the use of a part to designate the whole.
5. This 4th-century-B.C.E. philosopher wrote that drama and art enable catharsis, the venting of strong emotion or tension.

the pleasure principle, which is opposed to the reality principle. It is, of course, this explanation of the dream which had so largely conditioned Freud's theory of art. But now there is thrust upon him the necessity for reconsidering the theory of the dream, for it was found that in cases of war neurosis—what we once called shellshock—the patient, with the utmost anguish, recurred in his dreams to the very situation, distressing as it was, which had precipitated his neurosis. It seemed impossible to interpret these dreams by any assumption of a hedonistic intent. Nor did there seem to be the usual amount of distortion in them: the patient recurred to the terrible initiatory situation with great literalness. And the same pattern of psychic behavior could be observed in the play of children; there were some games which, far from fulfilling wishes, seemed to concentrate upon the representation of those aspects of the child's life which were most unpleasant and threatening to his happiness.

To explain such mental activities Freud evolved a theory for which he at first refused to claim much but to which, with the years, he attached an increasing importance. He first makes the assumption that there is indeed in the psychic life a repetition-compulsion[6] which goes beyond the pleasure principle. Such a compulsion cannot be meaningless, it must have an intent. And that intent, Freud comes to believe, is exactly and literally the developing of fear. "These dreams," he says, "are attempts at restoring control of the stimuli by developing apprehension, the pretermission[7] of which caused the traumatic neurosis." The dream, that is, is the effort to reconstruct the bad situation in order that the failure to meet it may be recouped; in these dreams there is no obscured intent to evade but only an attempt to meet the situation, to make a new effort of control. And in the play of children it seems to be that "the child repeats even the unpleasant experiences because through his own activity he gains a far more thorough mastery of the strong impression than was possible by mere passive experience."

Freud, at this point, can scarcely help being put in mind of tragic drama; nevertheless, he does not wish to believe that this effort to come to mental grips with a situation is involved in the attraction of tragedy. He is, we might say, under the influence of the Aristotelian tragic theory which emphasizes a qualified hedonism through suffering. But the pleasure involved in tragedy is perhaps an ambiguous one; and sometimes we must feel that the famous sense of cathartic resolution is perhaps the result of glossing over terror with beautiful language rather than an evacuation of it. And sometimes the terror even bursts through the language to stand stark and isolated from the play, as does Oedipus's's[8] sightless and bleeding face. At any rate, the Aristotelian theory does not deny another function for tragedy (and for comedy, too) which is suggested by Freud's theory of the traumatic neurosis—what might be called the mithridatic[9] function, by which tragedy is used as the homeopathic administration of pain to inure ourselves to the greater pain which life will force upon us. There is in the cathartic theory of tragedy, as it is usually understood, a conception of tragedy's function which is too negative

6. A compulsion to keep evoking traumatic experiences from one's past.
7. Omission, interruption.
8. In Greek mythology, a tragic hero who, after unwittingly murdering his father and marrying his mother, blinds himself.
9. From King Mithridates; tolerant of a poison through gradually increased exposure to it.

and which inadequately suggests the sense of active mastery which tragedy can give.

In the same essay in which he sets forth the conception of the mind embracing its own pain for some vital purpose, Freud also expresses a provisional assent to the idea (earlier stated, as he reminds us, by Schopenhauer)[1] that there is perhaps a human drive which makes of death the final and desired goal. The death instinct is a conception that is rejected by many of even the most thoroughgoing Freudian theorists (as, in his last book, Freud mildly noted); the late Otto Fenichel[2] in his authoritative work on the neurosis argues cogently against it. Yet even if we reject the theory as not fitting the facts in any operatively useful way, we still cannot miss its grandeur, its ultimate tragic courage in acquiescence to fate. The idea of the reality principle and the idea of the death instinct form the crown of Freud's broader speculation on the life of man. Their quality of grim poetry is characteristic of Freud's system and the ideas it generates for him.

And as much as anything else that Freud gives to literature, this quality of his thought is important. Although the artist is never finally determined in his work by the intellectual systems about him, he cannot avoid their influence; and it can be said of various competing systems that some hold more promise for the artist than others. When, for example, we think of the simple humanitarian optimism which, for two decades, has been so pervasive, we must see that not only has it been politically and philosophically inadequate, but also that it implies, by the smallness of its view of the varieties of human possibility, a kind of check on the creative faculties. In Freud's view of life no such limitation is implied. To be sure, certain elements of his system seem hostile to the usual notions of man's dignity. Like every great critic of human nature—and Freud is that—he finds in human pride the ultimate cause of human wretchedness, and he takes pleasure in knowing that his ideas stand with those of Copernicus and Darwin[3] in making pride more difficult to maintain. Yet the Freudian man is, I venture to think, a creature of far more dignity and far more interest than the man which any other modern system has been able to conceive. Despite popular belief to the contrary, man, as Freud conceives him, is not to be understood by any simple formula (such as sex) but is rather an inextricable tangle of culture and biology. And not being simple, he is not simply good; he has, as Freud says somewhere, a kind of hell within him from which rise everlastingly the impulses which threaten his civilization. He has the faculty of imagining for himself more in the way of pleasure and satisfaction than he can possibly achieve. Everything that he gains he pays for in more than equal coin; compromise and the compounding with defeat constitute his best way of getting through the world. His best qualities are the result of a struggle whose outcome is tragic. Yet he is a creature of love; it is Freud's sharpest criticism of the Adlerian psychology[4] that to aggression it gives everything and to love nothing at all.

One is always aware in reading Freud how little cynicism there is in his

1. Arthur Schopenhauer (1788–1860), German philosopher of pessimism and human will.
2. Austrian psychoanalyst (1897–1946).
3. Nicolaus Copernicus (1473–1543) and Charles Darwin (1809–1882) were scientists who revolutionized the fields of astronomy and natural history, respectively.
4. A reference to Alfred Adler (1870–1937), the Austrian psychologist who believed that individuals compensate for feelings of inferiority by aggressive behavior.

thought. His desire for man is only that he should be human, and to this end his science is devoted. No view of life to which the artist responds can insure the quality of his work, but the poetic qualities of Freud's own principles, which are so clearly in the line of the classic tragic realism, suggest that this is a view which does not narrow and simplify the human world for the artist but on the contrary opens and complicates it.

1950

From Isaac Babel[1]

* * *

There was anomaly at the very heart of the book, for the Red cavalry of the title were Cossack regiments, and why were Cossack fighting for the Revolution, they who were the instrument and symbol of Tsarist repression? The author, who represented himself in the stories, was a Jew; and a Jew in a Cossack regiment was more than an anomaly, it was a joke, for between Cossack and Jew there existed not merely hatred but a polar opposition. Yet here was a Jew riding as a Cossack and trying to come to terms with the Cossack ethos. At that first reading it seemed to me—although it does not now—that the stories were touched with cruelty. They were about violence of the most extreme kind, yet they were composed with a striking elegance and precision of objectivity, and also with a kind of lyric *joy*, so that one could not at once know just how the author was responding to the brutality he recorded, whether he thought it good or bad, justified or not justified. Nor was this the only thing to be in doubt about. It was not really clear how the author felt about, say, Jews; or about religion; or about the goodness of man. He had—or perhaps, for the sake of some artistic effect, he pretended to have—a secret. This alienated and disturbed me. It was impossible not to be overcome by admiration for *Red Cavalry*, but it was not at all the sort of book that I had wanted the culture of the Revolution to give me.

* * *

Babel was not a political man except as every man of intelligence was political at the time of the Revolution. Except, too, as every man of talent or genius is political who makes his heart a battleground for conflicting tendencies of culture. In Babel's heart there was a kind of fighting—he was captivated by the vision of two ways of being, the way of violence and the way of peace, and he was torn between them. The conflict between the two ways of being was an essential element of his mode of thought. And when Soviet culture was brought under full discipline, the fighting in Babel's heart could not be permitted to endure. It was a subversion of discipline. It implied that there was more than one way of being. It

1. Isaac Babel (1894–1941) was a Russian Jewish author who perished in Stalin's purges. His stories in *Red Cavalry* (1926; English translation, 1929) concern the civil war of 1918–20 between bolshevik Reds and anticommunist Whites after the revolution against czarist rule. Cossacks fought on both sides.

hinted that one might live in doubt, that one might live by means of a question.

It is with some surprise that we become aware of the centrality of the cultural, the moral, the *personal* issue in Babel's work, for what strikes us first is the intensity of his specifically aesthetic preoccupation. In his school-days Babel was passionate in his study of French literature; for several years he wrote his youthful stories in French, his chief masters being Flaubert and Maupassant.[2] When, in an autobiographical sketch, he means to tell us that he began his mature work in 1923, he puts it that in that year he began to express his thoughts "clearly, and not at great length." This delight in brevity became his peculiar mark. When Eisenstein[3] spoke of what it was that literature might teach the cinema, he said that "Isaac Babel will speak of the extreme laconicism of literature's expressive means—Babel, who, perhaps, knows in practice better than anyone else that great secret, 'that there is no iron that can enter the human heart with such stupefying effect, as a period placed at just the right moment.' " Babel's love of the laconic implies certain other elements of his aesthetic, his commitment (it is sometimes excessive) to *le mot juste*,[4] to the search for the word or phrase that will do its work with a ruthless speed, and his remarkable powers of significant distortion, the rapid foreshortening, the striking displacement of interest and shift of emphasis—in general his pulling all awry the arrangement of things as they appear in the "certified true copy."

Babel's preoccupation with form, with the aesthetic surface, is, we soon see, entirely at the service of his moral concern. James Joyce[5] has taught us the word *epiphany,* a showing forth—Joyce had the "theory" that suddenly, almost miraculously, by a phrase or a gesture, a life would thrust itself through the veil of things and for an instant show itself forth, startling us by its existence. In itself the conception of the epiphany makes a large statement about the nature of human life; it suggests that the human fact does not dominate the scene of our existence—for something to "show forth" it must first be hidden, and the human fact is submerged in and subordinated to a world of circumstance, the world of things; it is known only in glimpses, emerging from the danger or the sordidness in which it is implicated. Those writers who by their practice subscribe to the theory of the epiphany are drawn to a particular aesthetic. In the stories of Maupassant, as in those of Stephen Crane, and Hemingway,[6] and the Joyce of *Dubliners,* as in those of Babel himself, we perceive the writer's intention to create a form which shall in itself be shapely and autonomous and at the same time unusually responsible to the truth of external reality, the truth of things and events. To this end he concerns himself with the given moment, and, seeming almost hostile to the continuity of time, he presents the past only as it can be figured in the present. In his commitment to event he affects to be indifferent to "meanings" and "values"; he seems to be saying that although he can tell us with unusual accuracy what is going on, he does not presume to interpret it, scarcely to understand it, certainly not to judge it.

2. Gustave Flaubert (1821–1880) and Guy de Maupassant (1850–1893) were French realist authors.
3. Sergei Eisenstein (1898–1948) was a Russian film director.
4. The right word (French); associated with Flaubert.
5. Irish writer (1882–1941), author of *Ulysses* (1922).
6. Ernest Hemingway (1899–1961), American author. "Stephen Crane": American author (1871–1900).

* * *

The stories of *Red Cavalry* have as their principle of coherence what I have called the anomaly, or the joke of a Jew who is a member of a Cossack regiment—Babel was a supply officer under General Budenny in the campaign of 1920. Traditionally the Cossack was the feared and hated enemy of the Jew. But he was more than that. The principle of his existence stood in total antithesis to the principle of the Jew's existence. The Jew conceived his own ideal character to consist in his being intellectual, pacific, humane. The Cossack was physical, violent, without mind or manners. When a Jew of Eastern Europe wanted to say what we mean by "a bull in a china shop," he said "a Cossack in a *succah*"—in, that is, one of the fragile decorated booths or tabernacles in which the meals of the harvest festival of *Succoth* are eaten: he intended an image of animal violence, of aimless destructiveness. And if the Jew was political, if he thought beyond his own ethnic and religious group, he knew that the Cossack was the enemy not only of the Jew—although that in special—but the enemy also of all men who thought of liberty; he was the natural and appropriate instrument of ruthless oppression.

There was, of course, another possible view of the Cossack, one that had its appeal for many Russian intellectuals, although it was not likely to win the assent of the Jew. Tolstoy[7] had represented the Cossack as having a primitive energy, passion, and virtue. He was the man as yet untrammeled by civilization, direct, immediate, fierce. He was the man of enviable simplicity, the man of the body—and of the horse, the man who moved with speed and grace. We have devised an image of our lost freedom which we mock in the very phrase by which we name it: the noble savage. No doubt the mockery is justified, yet our fantasy of the noble savage represents a reality of our existence, it stands for our sense of something unhappily surrendered, the truth of the body, the truth of full sexuality, the truth of open aggressiveness. Something, we know, must inevitably be surrendered for the sake of civilization; but the "discontent"[8] of civilization which Freud describes is our self-recrimination at having surrendered too much. Babel's view of the Cossack was more consonant with that of Tolstoy than with the traditional view of his own people. For him the Cossack was indeed the noble savage, all too savage, not often noble, yet having in his savagery some quality that might raise strange questions in a Jewish mind.

* * *

We can only marvel over the vagary of the military mind by which Isaac Babel came to be assigned as a supply officer to a Cossack regiment. He was a Jew of the ghetto. As a boy—so he tells us in his autobiographical stories—he had been of stunted growth, physically inept, subject to nervous disorders. He was an intellectual, a writer—a man, as he puts it in striking phrase, with spectacles on his nose and autumn in his heart. The orders that sent him to General Budenny's command were drawn either by a conscious and ironical Destiny with a literary bent—or at his own personal request. For the reasons that made it bizarre that he should have been attached to a Cossack regiment

7. Leo Tolstoy (1828–1910) was a Russian novelist and reformer.

8. A reference to Sigmund Freud's *Civilization and Its Discontents* (1920).

are the reasons why he was there. He was there to be submitted to a test, he was there to be initiated. He was there because of the dreams of his boyhood. Babel's talent, like that of many modern writers, is rooted in the memory of boyhood, and Babel's boyhood was more than usually dominated by the idea of the test and the initiation. We might put it that Babel rode with a Cossack regiment because, when he was nine years old, he had seen his father kneeling before a Cossack captain who wore lemon-colored chamois gloves and looked ahead with the gaze of one who rides through a mountain pass.

Isaac Babel was born in Odessa, in 1894. The years following the accession of Nicholas II were dark years indeed for the Jews of Russia. It was the time of the bitterest official anti-Semitism, of the Pale, of the Beilis trial, of the Black Hundreds and the planned pogroms.[9] And yet in Odessa the Jewish community may be said to have flourished. Odessa was the great port of the Black Sea, an eastern Marseille or Naples, and in such cities the transient, heterogeneous population dilutes the force of law and tradition, for good as well as for bad. The Jews of Odessa were in some degree free to take part in the general life of the city. They were, to be sure, debarred from the schools, with but few exceptions. And they were sufficiently isolate when the passions of a pogrom swept the city. Yet all classes of the Jewish community seem to have been marked by a singular robustness and vitality, by a sense of the world, and of themselves in the world. The upper classes lived in affluence, sometimes in luxury, and it was possible for them to make their way into a Gentile society in which prejudice had been attenuated by cosmopolitanism. The intellectual life was of a particular energy, producing writers, scholars and journalists of very notable gifts; it is in Odessa that modern Hebrew poetry takes its rise with Bialyk[1] and Tchernokovsky.[2] As for the lower classes, Babel himself represents them as living freely and heartily. In their ghetto, the Moldavanka, they were far more conditioned by their economic circumstances than by their religious ties; they were not at all like the poor Jews of the *shtetln*,[3] the little towns of Poland, whom Babel was later to see. He represents them as characters of a Breughel[4]-like bulk and brawn; they have large, coarse, elaborate nicknames; they are draymen and dairy-farmers; they are gangsters—the Jewish gangs of the Moldavanka were famous; they made upon the young Babel an ineradicable impression and to them he devoted a remarkable group of comic stories.

It was not Odessa, then, it was not even Odessa's ghetto, that forced upon Babel the image of the Jew as a man not in the actual world, a man of no body, a man of intellect, or wits, passive before his secular fate. Not even his image of the Jewish intellectual was substantiated by the Odessa actuality—Bialyk and Tchernokovsky were anything but men with spectacles on their noses and autumn in their hearts, and no one who ever encountered in America the striking figure of Dr. Chaim Tchernowitz, the great scholar of

9. Violent attacks on Jewish communities. "The Pale": the Russian Pale of Settlement, regions within which Jews were permitted to live. "Beilis": Mendel Beilis was a Kiev Jew who was an innocent victim of 1911 blood libel (he was charged with murdering a Christian to get blood for Passover matzos). "Black Hundreds": antirevolutionary and anti-Semitic groups that appeared after the 1905 revolution.

1. Chaim Nachman Bialik (1873–1934), the first modern Hebrew poet; his *In the City of Slaughter* was inspired by the 1903 Kishinev pogrom.

2. Saul Tchernichowsky (1875–1943) was a Russian-born Hebrew poet.

3. Small Jewish towns and villages in Eastern Europe.

4. Pieter Breughel the Elder (ca. 1525–1569) was a Flemish painter who was well known for his vigorous scenes of peasant life.

the Talmud[5] and formerly the Chief Rabbi of Odessa, a man of Jovian port and large, free mind, would be inclined to conclude that there was but a single season of the heart available to a Jew of Odessa.

But Babel had seen his father on his knees before a Cossack captain on a horse, who said, "At your service," and touched his fur cap with his yellow-gloved hand and politely paid no heed to the mob looting the Babel store. Such an experience, or even a far milder analogue of it, is determinative in the life of a boy. Freud speaks of the effect upon him when, at twelve, his father told of having accepted in a pacific way the insult of having his new fur cap knocked into the mud by a Gentile who shouted at him, "Jew, get off the pavement." It is clear that Babel's relation with his father defined his relation to his Jewishness. Benya Krik, the greatest of the gangsters, he who was called King, was a Jew of Odessa, but he did not wear glasses and he did not have autumn in his heart—it is in writing about Benya that Babel uses the phrase that sets so far apart the intellectual and the man of action. The exploration of Benya's pre-eminence among gangsters does indeed take account of his personal endowment—Benya was a "lion," a "tiger," a "cat"; he "could spend the night with a Russian woman and satisfy her." But what really made his fate was his having had Mendel Krik, the drayman, for his father. "What does such a father think about? He thinks about drinking a good glass of vodka, of smashing somebody in the face, of his horses—and nothing more. You want to live and he makes you die twenty times a day. What would you have done in Benya Krik's place? You would have done nothing. But *he* did something. . . ." But Babel's father did not think about vodka, and smashing somebody in the face, and horses; he thought about large and serious things, among them respectability and fame. He was a shopkeeper, not well to do, a serious man, a failure. The sons of such men have much to prove, much to test themselves for, and, if they are Jewish, their Jewishness is ineluctably involved in the test.

Babel, in the brief autobiographical sketch to which I have referred, speaks with bitterness of the terrible discipline of his Jewish education. He thought of the Talmud Torah as a prison shutting him off from all desirable life, from reality itself. One of the stories he tells—conceivably the incident was invented to stand for his feelings about his Jewish schooling—is about his father's having fallen prey to the Messianic delusion which beset the Jewish families of Odessa, the belief that any one of them might produce a prodigy of the violin, a little genius who could be sent to be processed by Professor Auer[6] in Petersburg, who would play before crowned heads in a velvet suit, and support his family in honor and comfort. Such miracles had occurred in Odessa, whence had come Elman, Zimbalist, Gabrilowitsch, and Heifetz.[7] Babel's father hoped for wealth, but he would have forgone wealth if he could have been sure, at a minimum, of fame. Being small, the young Babel at fourteen might pass for eight and a prodigy. In point of fact, Babel had not even talent, and certainly no vocation. He was repelled by the idea of becoming a musical "dwarf," one of the "big-headed freckled children with necks

5. The compilation of Jewish law and interpretation.
6. Leopold Auer (1845–1930) was a Hungarian violinist and teacher.
7. Mischa Elman (1891–1967), Efrem Zimbalist (1890–1985), and Jascha Heifetz (1901–1987) were Russian Jewish violinists, all students of Leopold Auer; Ossip Gabrilowitsch (1878–1936) was a Russian pianist.

as thin as flower stalks and an epileptic flush on their cheeks." This was a Jewish fate and he fled from it, escaping to the port and the beaches of Odessa. Here he tried to learn to swim and could not: "the hydrophobia of my ancestors—Spanish rabbis and Frankfurt money-changers—dragged me to the bottom." But a kindly proofreader, an elderly man who loved nature and children, took pity on him. "How d'you mean, the water won't hold you? Why shouldn't it hold you?"—his specific gravity was no different from anybody else's and the good Yefim Nikitich Smolich taught him to swim. "I came to love that man," Babel says in one of the very few of his sentences over which no slightest irony plays, "with the love that only a boy suffering from hysteria and headaches can feel for a real man."

* * *

We can scarcely fail to see that when in the stories of *Red Cavalry* Babel submits the ethos of the intellectual to the criticism of the Cossack ethos, he intends a criticism of his own ethos not merely as an intellectual but as a Jew. It is always as an intellectual, never as a Jew, that he is denounced by his Cossack comrades, but we know that he has either suppressed, for political reasons, the denunciations of him as a Jew that were actually made, or, if none were actually made, that he has in his heart supposed that they were made. These criticisms of the Jewish ethos, as he embodies it, Babel believes to have no small weight. When he implores fate to grant him the simplest of proficiencies, the ability to kill his fellow-man, we are likely to take this as nothing but an irony, and as an ironic assertion of the superiority of his moral instincts. But it is only in part an irony. There comes a moment when he should kill a fellow-man. In "The Death of Dolgushov," a comrade lies propped against a tree; he cannot be moved, inevitably he must die, for his entrails are hanging out; he must be left behind and he asks for a bullet in his head so that the Poles will not "play their dirty tricks" on him. It is the narrator whom he asks for the *coup de grâce*,[8] but the narrator flees and sends a friend, who, when he has done what had to be done, turns on the "sensitive" man in a fury of rage and disgust: "You bastards in spectacles have about as much pity for us as a cat has for a mouse." Or again, the narrator has incurred the enmity of a comrade through no actual fault—no moral fault—of his own, merely through having been assigned a mount that the other man passionately loved, and riding it badly so that it developed saddle galls. Now the horse has been returned, but the man does not forgive him, and the narrator asks a superior officer to compound the quarrel. He is rebuffed. "You're trying to live without enemies," he is told. That's all you think about, not having enemies." It comes at us with momentous force. This time we are not misled into supposing that Babel intends irony and a covert praise of his pacific soul; we know that in this epiphany of his refusal to accept enmity he means to speak adversely of himself in his Jewish character.

But his Jewish character is not the same as the Jewish character of the Jews of Poland. To these Jews he comes with all the presuppositions of an acculturated Jew of Russia, which were not much different from the suppositions of an acculturated Jew of Germany. He is repelled by the conditions

8. Literally, stroke of mercy (French); a death blow.

of their life; he sees them as physically uncouth and warped; many of them seem to him to move "monkey-fashion." Sometimes he affects a wondering alienation from them, as when he speaks of "the occult crockery that the Jews use only once a year at Eastertime."[9] His complexity and irony being what they are, the Jews of Poland are made to justify the rejection of the Jews among whom he was reared and the wealthy assimilated Jews of Petersburg. "The image of the stout and jovial Jews of the South, bubbling like cheap wine, takes shape in my memory, in sharp contrast to the bitter scorn inherent in these long bony backs, these tragic yellow beards." Yet the Jews of Poland are more than a stick with which Babel beats his own Jewish past. They come to exist for him as a spiritual fact of consummate value.

Almost in the degree that Babel is concerned with violence in the stories of *Red Cavalry*, he is concerned with spirituality. It is not only Jewish spirituality that draws him. A considerable number of the stories have to do with churches, and although they do indeed often express the anticlerical feeling expectable in the revolutionary circumstances, the play of Babel's irony permits him to respond in a positive way to the aura of religion. "The breath of an invisible order of things," he says in one story, "glimmers beneath the crumbling ruin of the priest's house, and its soothing seduction unmanned me." He is captivated by the ecclesiastical painter Pan Apolek, he who created ecclesiastical scandals by using the publicans and sinners of the little towns as the models for his saints and virgins. Yet it is chiefly the Jews who speak to him of the life beyond violence, and even Pan Apolek's "heretical and intoxicating brush" had achieved its masterpiece in his Christ of the Berestechko church, "the most extraordinary image of God I had ever seen in my life," a curly-headed Jew, a bearded figure in a Polish great-coat of orange, barefooted with torn and bleeding mouth, running from an angry mob with a hand raised to ward off a blow.

* * *

If Babel's experience with the Cossacks may be understood as having reference to the boy's relation to his father, his experience of the Jews of Poland has, we cannot but feel, a maternal reference. To the one Babel responds as a boy, to the other as a child. In the story "Gedali" he speaks with open sentimentality of his melancholy on the eve of Sabbaths—"On those evenings my child's heart was rocked like a little ship upon enchanted waves. O the rotted Talmuds of my childhood! O the dense melancholy of memories." And when he has found a Jew, it is one who speaks to him in this fashion: ". . . All is mortal. Only the mother is destined to immortality. And when the mother is no longer living, she leaves a memory which none yet has dared to sully. The memory of the mother nourishes in us a compassion that is like the ocean, and the measureless ocean feeds the rivers that dissect the universe."

He has sought Gehali in his gutted curiosity-shop. ("Where was your kindly shade that evening, Dickens?") to ask for "a Jewish glass of tea, and a little of that pensioned-off God in a glass of tea." He does not, that evening, get what he asks for; what he does get is a discourse on revolution, on the

9. Trilling's remark is based on a mistranslation; Babel actually refers to Passover, not Easter.

impossibility of a revolution made in blood, on the International[1] that is never to be realized, the International of the good.

It was no doubt the easier for Babel to respond to the spiritual life of the Jews of Poland because it was a life coming to its end and having about it the terrible strong pathos of its death. He makes no pretense that it could ever claim him for its own. But it established itself in his heart as an image, beside the image of the other life that also could not claim him, the Cossack life. The opposition of these two images made his art—but it was not a dialectic that his Russia could permit.

1955

1. Socialist or communist organization to unite workers of all lands.

GEORGE OPPEN
1908–1984

"yes, I will say, yes, I am yes (I am)." This is George Oppen (à la Molly Bloom's throbbing "yes I said yes I will Yes" at the end of *Ulysses*) responding to someone who'd written asking him, "Are you Jewish?" Of course, it was not all that simple in his writing or his life, if only because what mattered most to Oppen was the clarity, sincerity, honesty, faith, awe, joy (he used these words) of wakening to the truth of things through poetry—through prosody, in fact.

On the everyday surface, Oppen neither regretted nor flaunted his tenuous attachment to Judaism. "He had warm, open feelings about his Jewishness," Carl Rakosi reports and tells how sitting in New York City's Washington Square one day, Oppen cheerfully agreed to be bar mitzvahed by some seminary students. And Oppen recounts sailing into Castine, Maine, and being invited to visit Robert Lowell, whom he found among "the official representatives of the New England virtues. They were drinking cocktails And there we stood in our dripping oil-skins in their pretty living-room. HEAR, O ISRAEL! (Shema Israel, or something like that Wish I could remember the spelling) A great fisherman's cry."

Deeper than everyday, Oppen felt an insistent tug from the Jewish condition, as in his poem *Exodus,* where father and daughter dream open-endedly to each other of the "children of Israel":

The brilliant children   Miracle

Of their brilliance   Miracle
of

And in *Disasters,* written after his 1975 visit to Jerusalem:

I see
myself   Sarah   Sarah   I see the tent
in the desert my life
narrows . . .

Having read Shirley Kaufman's translation of the Vilna partisan and survivor Abba Kovner's poetry, Oppen wrote to her: "There is nothing, nothing at all I value so much" as the Hebraic ground beneath Kovner's story. "Indeed it is deep in my blood, and I know it."

George Oppen, of German Jewish ancestry, was born on April 24, 1908, in New Rochelle, New York, to George August Oppenheimer and Elsie Rothfeld—"born of a couple of rather millionaire lines," he said, "something on the order of the International Set, etc. . . . Disastrous, of course." His mother took her own life when he was four, and when his father remarried, the family moved to San Francisco in 1918. Escaping his stepmother and father's life style, Oppen entered Oregon State University in 1926; there he heard Carl Sandburg read, discovered modern poetry, and met his wife, Mary Colby. Hitchhiking to New York, they encountered Louis Zukofsky and Charles Reznikoff, and the February 1931 issue of *Poetry* magazine featured Zukofsky, Reznikoff, Rakosi, and Oppen as "objectivists." Between the too-little of imagist observation and the too-much of symbolist appropriation, the objectivist aim was to see, to realize, the concrete object as object. Oppen also stresses the need to achieve poetic form, to make the poem a crafted object. The Objectivist Press published William Carlos Williams, Reznikoff, and Oppen's first book, *Discrete Series* (1934).

George and Mary Oppen joined the Communist party in 1935, working as political organizers, and for over two decades he wrote no poetry: "Fifteen million families . . . were faced with the threat of immediate starvation. . . . for some people it was impossible not to do something." Unlike, say, Denise Levertov, Oppen says he "didn't believe in political poetry or poetry as being politically efficacious." As an infantry soldier, he saw action in Europe, fought in the Battle of the Bulge, and, in April 1945, was badly wounded, trapped in a foxhole for ten hours with dead companions: "Wyatt's little poem—'they flee from me . . . ,' and poem after poem of [Reznikoff's] ran through my mind over and over, these poems seemed to fill all the space around me and I wept and wept." A later poem juxtaposes images of battle—

> Fought
> No man but the fragments of metal
> Burying my dogtag with H
> For Hebrew in the rubble of Alsace

—with his rage at Ezra Pound, who broadcast anti-Semitic diatribes during the war.

Threatened by the McCarthy committee and the FBI, the Oppens went to Mexico in 1950, returning only eight years later to New York. Oppen helped Reznikoff prepare a poetry collection, *By the Waters of Manhattan* (1962), and he himself finally began writing again. *The Materials* (1962) bears an epigraph from Jacques Maritain: "We awake in the same moment to ourselves and to things." Its closing poem, *Leviathan,* may recall the Lord challenging Job's place in creation (Job 40.25): "Can you draw out Leviathan by a fishhook?" For this poem begins:

> Truth also is the pursuit of it:
> Like happiness, and it will not stand.

This in Which appeared in 1965, and a year later the Oppens moved to San Francisco. *Of Being Numerous* (1968) won the Pulitzer prize, at which point Oppen, in his sixties, came into some fame and currency. There followed *Seascape: Needle's Eye* (1972) and his last book, *Primitive* (1978). By this time, he was suffering from Alzheimer's disease. George Oppen died on July 7, 1984, and his ashes were scattered on Tomales Bay, north of San Francisco, where he used to sail.

Psalm, one of Oppen's most favored poems, calls on the Hebrew Bible in its title and Saint Thomas Aquinas in its epigraph (of which Oppen omits the last two words): *Veritas sequitur esse rerum* ("Truth follows the existence of things"). This reach embodies his tacit assumption that poetry forms the better part of religion and philosophy. In interviews, as in *Psalm,* he uses the term "faith" for his "sense of awe, simply to feel that the thing is there and that it's quite something to see. It's . . . a lyric reaction to the world." George Oppen prized "the small nouns / Crying faith" not simply in the things of this world, but in our awareness of them. Only a poem's wording can discover that "paradise of the real" he speaks of elsewhere. After all, "the wild deer / Startle, and stare out" only just at the moment the poem, the "psalm," has had its say. For that moment they do stand—like truth, and happiness.

Psalm

Veritas sequitur . . .

In the small beauty of the forest
The wild deer bedding down—
That they are there!

Their eyes
Effortless, the soft lips
Nuzzle and the alien small teeth
Tear at the grass

The roots of it
Dangle from their mouths
Scattering earth in the strange woods.
They who are there.

Their paths
Nibbled thru the fields, the leaves that shade them
Hang in the distances
Of sun

The small nouns
Crying faith
In this in which the wild deer
Startle, and stare out.

1965

Exodus[1]

Miracle of the children[2]   the brilliant
Children   the word
Liquid as woodlands   Children?

When she was a child I read Exodus
To my daughter   'The children of Israel . . . '

1. Cf. Exodus 13.21: "The Lord went before them in a pillar of cloud by day, . . . and in a pillar of fire by night."

2. *B'nei Yisrael* (Hebrew); biblically, the people of Israel.

Pillar of fire
Pillar of cloud

We stared at the end
Into each other's eyes   Where
She said hushed

Were the adults   We dreamed to each other
Miracle of the children
The brilliant children   Miracle

Of their brilliance   Miracle
of

1972

Disasters

of wars o western
wind and storm

of politics I am sick with a poet's
vanity   legislators

of the unacknowledged

world *it is   dreary*
to descend

and be a stranger how
shall we descend

who have become strangers in this wind that

rises like a gift
in the disorder   the gales

of a poet's vanity if our story shall end
untold to whom and

to what are we ancestral *we wanted to know*

if we were any good

out there   the song
changes the wind has blown the sand about
and we are alone the sea dawns
in the sunrise verse with its rough

beach-light crystal extreme

sands dazzling under the near
and not less brutal feet journey
in light

and wind
and fire and water and air *the five*

bright elements
the marvel

of the obvious and the marvel
of the hidden is there

in fact a distinction dance

of the wasp wings dance as
of the mother-tongues can they

with all their meanings

        dance?   O

O I see my love I see her go

over the ice alone I see

myself   Sarah   Sarah   I see the tent
in the desert my life

narrows my life
is another I see
him in the desert I watch
him he is clumsy
and alone my young
brother he is my lost
sister her small

voice among the people the salt

and terrible hills whose armies

have marched and the caves
of the hidden
people.

1978

If It All Went Up in Smoke

that smoke
would remain

the forever
savage country poem's light borrowed

light of the landscape and one's footprints praise

from distance
in the close
crowd all

that is strange the sources

the wells the poem begins

neither in word
nor meaning but the small
selves haunting

us in the stones and is less

always than that help me I am
of that people the grass

blades touch

and touch in their small

distances the poem
begins

1978

CHAIM GRADE
1910–1982

"I wear your Yiddish like a drowned man's shirt, / wearing out the hurt," says Chaim Grade (translated by Cynthia Ozick) in his elegy for the Soviet Yiddish writers executed under Stalinism in August 1952. No less strongly, no less steadfastly than Isaac Bashevis Singer, Grade served as a custodian of Yiddish after the catastrophe that eradicated that language in the mouths of millions. Alongside *loshn koydesh,* the Hebrew holy tongue, he called Yiddish *loshn koydushim*, the martyrs' tongue. Yet his inspiration was not solely elegiac. Grade's prose fiction reconstitutes prewar yeshiva life in Europe and the ethical, dialectical genius of Talmudic thinking, even after the war.

Chaim Grade was born in 1910 in Vilna, Lithuania. We can enter intimately into the first half of his life through a memoir he published in 1955, *Der mames shabosim* (My Mother's Sabbath Days, 1986). His father, a religious teacher, was a champion of Jewish Enlightenment against Orthodoxy and was an early Zionist but died when Chaim was young, and his mother peddled fruit at a market stand to give him an education. He attended traditional yeshivas and was drawn to the Musar movement, which stressed strict ethical behavior and self-examination, with an ascetic devotion to halakah, Judaic legal dogma.

During the early 1930s, Grade began publishing lyric poetry and became a leader of Young Vilna, a progressive literary movement. Though he had broken from Orthodoxy, he married a woman from that tradition. In June 1941, when the Germans seized Soviet-occupied Vilna, he fled into the interior of Russia and wandered for years, as far as the Tadzhik Soviet Socialist Republic in Central Asia. Meanwhile, his mother and wife perished. On returning to Vilna, Grade found devastation—"spider-webs," "ruined synagogues," as he calls the closing chapters of *My Mother's Sabbath Days*.

Grade went to Paris, where he worked to revivify Yiddish culture, and in 1948 he settled in the United States, writing verse and prose fiction and contributing Sunday pieces to the Yiddish daily *Forward* as late as the 1970s.

In *My Quarrel with Hersh Rasseyner,* Chaim Grade is at his strongest, both in delineating character and in animating the spiritual struggle of Eastern European Jews after the Holocaust. Because he never ceased to love the zealously devout world he broke from, this dialogue between a freethinking writer and a Musarist teacher gives dramatic emotional form to moral philosophy—witness the effective film, *The Quarrel* (1992), directed by Eli Cohen, made from it. The scholar Ruth Wisse calls the debate a draw.

While Isaac Bashevis Singer's earthy yet fabulous storytelling has found a larger audience, Grade's concentration on the very experience of Jewish morality forces us, as Irving Howe remarks, "to share his rages of thought." Chaim Grade died in New York City in 1982.

My Quarrel with Hersh Rasseyner[1]

1.

In 1937 I returned to Bialystok,[2] seven years after I had been a student in the Novaredok Yeshiva of the Mussarists,[3] a movement that gives special importance to ethical and ascetic elements in Judaism. When I came back I found many of my old schoolmates still there. A few even came to my lecture one evening. Others visited me secretly; they did not want the head of the yeshiva to find out. I could see that their poverty had brought them suffering and that the fire of their youthful zeal had slowly burned itself out. They continued to observe all the laws and usages meticulously, but the weariness of spiritual wrestlings lay upon them. For years they had tried to tear the desire for pleasure out of their hearts, and now they realized they had lost the war with themselves. They had not overcome the evil urge.

There was one I kept looking for and could not find, my former schoolmate

1. Translated by Milton Himmelfarb.
2. A city in Grodno province, in White Russia, the Pale of Settlement.
3. Followers of the Musar (or Mussar) ethics movement in the second half of the 19th century. It was founded by Israel Salanter in Lithuania, who, through study of moralistic treatises and harsh self-criticism, fought the dilution of traditional piety by the Jewish Enlightenment and worldliness.

Hersh Rasseyner. He was a dark young man with bright, downcast eyes. I did not meet him, but heard that he kept to his garret in solitude and did not even come to the yeshiva.

Then we met unexpectedly in the street. He was walking with his eyes lowered, as is the custom with the Mussarists; they do not wish to be "eye to eye" with the world. But he saw me anyway. He put his arms behind him, thrusting his hands into his sleeves, so that he would not have to shake hands. The closer he came, the higher rose his head. When we finally stood face to face, he looked at me intently. He was so moved his nostrils seemed to quiver—but he kept silent.

Among the Mussarists, when you ask, "How are you?" the question means, What is the state of your religious life? Have you risen in spirituality? But I had forgotten and asked quite simply, "Hersh Rasseyner, how are you?"

Hersh moved back a little, looked me over from head to toe, saw that I was modishly dressed, and shrugged. "And how are you, Chaim Vilner? My question, you see, is more important."

My lips trembled and I answered hotly, "Your question, Hersh Rasseyner, is no question at all. I do what I have to."

Right there, in the middle of the street, he cried out, "Do you think, Chaim Vilner, that by running away from the yeshiva you have saved yourself? You know the saying among us: Whoever has learned Mussar can have no enjoyment in his life. You will always be deformed, Chaim Vilner. You will remain a cripple the rest of your life. You write godless verses and they reward you by patting you on the cheek. Now they're stuffing you with applause as they stuff a goose with grain. But later you'll see, when you've begun to go to their school, oh, won't the worldly ones beat you! Which of you isn't hurt by criticism? Is there one of you really so self-confident that he doesn't go around begging for some authority's approval? Is there one of you who's prepared to publish his book anonymously? The big thing with you people is that your name should be seen and known. You have given up our tranquillity of spirit for what? For passions you will never be able to satisfy and for doubts you will never be able to answer, no matter how much you suffer."

When he had spoken his fill, Hersh Rasseyner began to walk away with a quick, energetic stride. But I had once been a Mussarist too, so I ran after him.

"Hersh, listen to me now. No one knows better than I how torn you are. You're proud of yourself because you don't care if the whole street laughs at you for wearing a prayer vest down to your ankles. You've talked yourself into believing that the cloth with the woolen fringes is a partition between you and the world. You despise yourself because you're afraid you may find favor in the eyes of the world, the world that is to you like Potiphar's wife.[4] You fear you won't have the strength to tear yourself away as the righteous Joseph did. So you flee from temptation and think the world will run after you. But when you see that the world doesn't run after you, you become angry and cry out: Nobody enjoys life. You want to console yourself with that idea. You live in solitude in your garret because you would rather have nothing at all

4. The wife of Potiphar, Joseph's master in Egypt, tried to seduce Joseph and, upon his refusal, accused him falsely of attempted rape and had him imprisoned (Genesis 39.7–20).

than take the crumb that life throws you. Your modesty is pride, not self-denial.

"And who told you that I seek pleasure? I seek a truth you don't have. For that matter, I didn't run away, I simply returned to my own street—to Yatkev Street in Vilna.[5] I love the porters with their backs broken from carrying their burdens; the artisans sweating at their workbenches; the market women who would cut off a finger to give a poor man a crust of bread. But you scold the hungry for being sinners, and all you can tell them is to repent. You laugh at people who work because you say they don't trust in God. But you live on what others have made. Women exhausted with work bring you something to eat, and in return you promise them the world to come. Hersh Rasseyner, you have long since sold your share of the world to come to those poor women."[6]

Hersh Rasseyner gave a start and disappeared. I returned to Vilna with a burden removed from my conscience. In the disputation with the Mussarist I myself began to understand why I had left them. If at the time, I said to myself, I didn't know why and where I was going, someone else thought it out for me, someone stronger than I. That someone else was—my generation and my environment.

2.

Two years passed. War broke out between Germany and Poland.[7] The western Ukraine and western White Russia were taken over by the Red Army. After they had been in Vilna a few weeks, the Russians announced that they were giving the city back to the Lithuanians. To Vilna there began to come refugees who did not want to remain under Soviet rule. The Novaredok Yeshiva came also. Meanwhile the Soviets remained. Hunger raged in the city. Every face was clouded with fear of the arrests carried out at night by NKVD agents.[8] My heart was heavy. Once, standing in line for a ration of bread, I suddenly saw Hersh Rasseyner.

I had heard that he had married. His face was framed by a little black beard, his gait was more restrained, his clothing more presentable. I was so glad to see him that I left my place in the line, pushed through the crowd, and came up to him.

He said little and was very cautious. I understood why. He did not trust me and was afraid of trouble. I could see that he was trying to make up his mind whether to speak to me. But when he saw how despondent I was, he hid his mouth with his hand, as though to conceal his twisted smile, and a gleam of derision came into his eyes. With his head he motioned toward the bridge, on which were parked a few tanks with Red Army soldiers.

"Well, Chaim," Hersh said to me quietly, "are you satisfied now? Is this what you wanted?"

I tried to smile and answered just as quietly, "Hersh, I bear no more responsibility for all that than you do for me."

He shook himself and pronounced a few sharp, cutting words, seeming to

5. Vilnius (Yiddish), Chaim Vilner's home town (his name means "from Vilna"); the capital of Lithuania and a major center of Jewish culture in Eastern Europe.
6. Chaim Vilner has been lecturing in Białystok as a socialist activist, in sympathy with the working classes.
7. The year is 1939, the beginning of World War II.
8. The Soviet secret police or intelligence.

forget his fear. "You're wrong, Chaim. I do bear responsibility for you." He retreated a few steps and motioned with his eyes to the Red Army soldiers, as though to say, "And you for them."

3.

Nine more years passed, years of war and destruction, during which I wandered across Russia, Poland, and Western Europe. In 1948, on a summer afternoon, I was riding in the Paris Métro.[9] Couples stood close together. Short Frenchwomen, as though fainting, hung by the sides of their black-haired lovers.

I saw a familiar face. Until then it had been concealed by someone's shoulder, and only when the couples had to move a little did that corner of the car open up. My heart began to pound. Could he really be alive? Hadn't he been in Vilna under the German occupation? When I returned to the ruins of my home in 1945 I did not see him or hear of him. Still, those were the same eyes, the same obstinately upturned nose; only the broad black beard had begun to turn gray. It was astonishing to me that he could look at the couples so calmly, and that a good-natured smile lit up his melancholy glance. That was not like him. But after a moment I noticed that there was a faraway look in his eyes. He really did not see the people on the train. He was dressed neatly, in a long cloak and a clean white shirt buttoned at the throat, without a necktie. I thought to myself, He never wore ties. This more than anything else convinced me that it was he.

I pushed my way to him through the passengers and blurted out, "Excuse me, aren't you Reb Hersh Rasseyner?"

He looked at me, wrinkled his forehead, and smiled. "Ah, Chaim, Chaim, is that you? *Sholom aleichem!* How are you?"

I could tell that this time when Hersh Rasseyner asked, "How are you?" he did not mean what he had meant eleven years before. Then his question was angry and derisive. Now he asked the question quietly, simply. It came from his heart and it showed concern, as for an old friend.

We got into a corner and he told me briefly that he had been in a camp[1] in Latvia. Now he was in Germany, at the head of a yeshiva in Salzheim.

"The head of a yeshiva in Germany? And who are your students, Reb Hersh?"

He smiled. "Do you think that the Holy One is an orphan? We still have lads, praise be to the Almighty, who study Torah."

He told me that he had been in the camp with about ten pupils. He had drawn them close to him and taught them Jewishness. Because they were still only children and very weak he helped them in their work. At night they used to gather about his cot and all would recite Psalms together. There was a doctor in the camp who used to say that he would give half his life to be able to recite Psalms too. But he couldn't. He lacked faith, poor man.

I was happy to meet my old friend and I preferred to avoid a debate, so I merely asked, "And what brings you here so often? Are you in business?"

"Of course we're in business." He stroked his beard with satisfaction. "Big

9. The subway.

1. I.e., a concentration camp.

business. We bring yeshiva people here and send them off to Israel and America. We take books back from here. With the help of the Almighty, I have even flown twice to Morocco."

"Morocco? What did you do there, Reb Hersh?"

"Brought back students from among the Moroccan Jews, spoke in their synagogue."

"And how did you talk to them? You don't know Arabic or French."

"The Almighty helps. What difference does it make how you speak? The main thing is *what* you speak."

Unexpectedly he began to talk about me. "How will it be with you, Chaim? It's time for you to start thinking about repentance. We're nearer rather than farther."

"What do you mean?"

"I mean," he said, drawing out his words in a chant, "that we have both lived out more than half our lives. What will become of Reb Chaim?" He strongly accented the word Reb. "Where are you voyaging? Together with them, perhaps?" His eyes laughed at the young couples. "Will you get off where they do? Or do you still believe in this merciless world?"

"And you, Reb Hersh," I asked in sudden irritation, "do you still believe in particular providence?[2] You say that the Holy One is not, as it were, an orphan. But we are orphans. A miracle happened to you, Reb Hersh, and you were saved. But how about the rest? Can you still believe?"

"Of course I believe," said Hersh Rasseyner, separating his hands in innocent wonder. "You can touch particular providence, it's so palpable. But perhaps you're thinking of the kind of man who has faith that the Almighty is to be found only in the pleasant places of this world but is not to be found, God forbid, in the desert and wasteland? You know the rule: Just as a man must make a blessing over the good, so must he make a blessing over evil. We must fall before the greatness—"

"What do you want, Reb Hersh?" I interrupted. "Shall I see the greatness of God in the thought that only He could cause such destruction, not flesh and blood? You're outdoing the Psalms you recited on your bed in the concentration camp. The Psalmist sees the greatness of God in the fact that the sun comes out every day, but you see miracles in catastrophes."

"Without any doubt," Hersh Rasseyner answered calmly, "I see everywhere, in everything, at every moment, particular providence. I couldn't remain on earth for one minute without the thought of God. How could I stand it without Him in this murderous world?"

"But I won't say that His judgment is right. I can't!"

"You can," said Hersh Rasseyner, putting a friendly hand on my shoulder, "you can—gradually. First the repentant understands that the world can't be without a Guide. Then he understands that the Guide is the God of Israel and that there is no other power besides Him to help Him lead the world. At last he recognizes that the world is in Him, as we read: 'There is no place void of Him.' And if you understood that, Chaim, you would also understand how the Almighty reveals Himself in misfortune as well as in salvation."

Hersh Rasseyner spoke in a warm voice. He did not once take his hand

2. *Hashgahah l'pratit* (Hebrew): the belief that God pays attention to the deeds of individuals.

off my shoulder. I felt a great love for him and saw that he had become more pious than ever.

4.

We left the Métro near the Jewish quarter, at the rue de Rivoli, and we passed the old city hall, the Hôtel de Ville. In the niches of the walls of the Hôtel de Ville, between the windows, in three rows, stand stone figures, some with a sword, some with a book, some with brush and palette, and some with geometric instruments. Hersh Rasseyner saw me looking at the monuments. He glanced at them out of the corners of his eyes and asked, "Who are those idols?"

I explained to him that they were famous Frenchmen: statesmen, heroes, scholars, and artists.

"Reb Hersh," I pleaded with him, "look at those statues. Come closer and see the light streaming from their marble eyes. See how much goodness lies hidden in their stone faces. You call it idolatry, but I tell you that, quite literally, I could weep when I walk about Paris and see these sculptures. It's a miracle, after all. How could a human being breathe the breath of life into stone? When you see a living man, you see only one man. But when you see a man poured out in bronze, you see mankind itself. Do you understand me? That one there, for instance, is a poet famous all over the world. The great writer broadens our understanding and stirs our pity for our fellow men. He shows us the nature of the man who can't overcome his desires. He doesn't punish even the wicked man, but sees him according to his afflictions in the war he wages with himself and the rest of the world. You don't say he's right, but you understand that he can't help it. Why are you pulling at your beard so angrily, Reb Hersh?"

He stared at me with burning eyes and cried out, "For shame! How can you say such foolish things? So you could weep when you look at those painted lumps of matter? Why don't you weep over the charred remains of the Gaon of Vilna's[3] synagogue? Those artists of yours, those monument-choppers, those poets who sang about their emperors, those tumblers who danced and played before the rulers—did those masters of yours even bother to think that their patron would massacre a whole city and steal all it had, to buy them, your masters, with the gold? Did the prophets flatter kings? Did they take gifts of harlots' wages? And how merciful you are! The writer shows how the wicked man is the victim of his own bad qualities. I think that's what you said. It's really a pity about the arrogant rebel! He destroys others, and of course he's destroyed too. What a pity! Do you think it's easier to be a good man than an adulterer? But you particularly like to describe the lustful man. You know him better, there's something of him in you artists. If you make excuses for the man who exults in his wickedness, then as far as I'm concerned all your scribbling is unclean and unfit. Condemn the wicked man! Condemn the glutton and drunkard! Do you say he can't help it? He has to help it! You've sung a fine song of praise to the putrid idols, Chaim Vilner."

Hersh Rasseyner looked into my eyes with the sharp, threatening expres-

3. The Gaon of Vilna—literally, "the Genius of Vilna"—refers to Elijah ben Solomon (1720–1797), the leading rabbi of his time and a great Talmudist.

sion I had seen eleven years earlier, when we met in that Bialystok street. His voice had become hard and resounding. Passers-by stopped and stared at the bearded Jew who shook his finger at the sculptures of the Hôtel de Ville. Hersh did not so much as notice the passers-by. I felt embarrassed in the face of these Frenchmen, smiling and looking at us curiously.

"Don't shout so," I told him irritably. "You really think you have a monopoly on mercy and truth. You're starting where we left off eleven years ago. In Novaredok you always kept the windows closed, but it was still too light for you in the House of Study, so you ran off to your garret. From the garret you went down into a cellar. And from the cellar you burrowed down into a hole under the earth. That's where you could keep your commandment of solitude and that's where you persuaded yourself that a man's thoughts and feelings are like his hair; if he wants to, he can trim his hair and leave nothing but a beard and earlocks—holy thought and pious conduct. You think the world is what you imagine it, and you won't have anything to do with it. You think men are what you imagine them, but you tell them to be the opposite. But even the concentration camps couldn't make men different from what they are. Those who were evil became worse in the camps. They might have lived out their lives and not known themselves for what they were, but in the crisis men saw themselves and others undisguised. And when we were all freed, even the better ones among us weren't freed of the poison we had to drink behind the barbed wire. Now, if the concentration camp couldn't change men from top to bottom, how can you expect to change them?"

Hersh Rasseyner looked at me with astonishment. The anger that had flared in his eyes died down, though a last flicker seemed to remain.

"You don't know what you're talking about, Chaim," he said quietly and reluctantly. "Who ever told you that afflictions as such make people better? Take the day of a man's death, for instance. When a God-fearing man is reminded of death, he becomes even more God-fearing, as we read in Scripture: 'It is better to go to the house of mourning than to the house of feasting.'[4] But when a free thinker is reminded of death he becomes even wilder, as the prophet says about the thoughts of the wicked: 'Let us eat and drink, for tomorrow we shall die.'[5] It's quite clear that external causes can't drag people back to a Jewish life. A man's heart and mind have to be ready.

"If a man didn't come to the concentration camp with a thirst for a higher life, he certainly didn't elevate himself there. But the spiritual man knows that always and everywhere he must keep mounting higher or else he will fall lower. And as for the claim that a man can't change—that is a complete lie. 'In my flesh shall I see God!' The case of Hersh Rasseyner proves that a man can change. I won't tell you a long story about how many lusts I suffered from; how often the very veins in my head almost burst from the boiling of the blood; how many obstinacies I had to tear out of myself. But I knew that whoever denies himself affirms the Master of the World. I knew that the worst sentence that can be passed on a man is that he shall not be able to renounce his old nature. And because I truly wanted to conquer myself, the Almighty helped me."

"You are severe in your judgments," I answered. "You always were, Reb Hersh, if you'll pardon my saying so. You call these wise men putrid idols,

4. Ecclesiastes 7.2.

5. Isaiah 22.13.

but you refuse to see that they lifted mankind out of its bestial state. They weren't butchers of the soul and they didn't talk themselves into believing that human beings can tear their lower urges out of themselves and lop them off. They were very well aware of the hidden root of the human race. They wanted to illuminate men's minds with wisdom, so that men would be able to grow away from their untamed desires. You can't banish shadows with a broom, only with a lighted lamp. These great men—"

Hersh began to laugh so loud that I had to interrupt myself. He immediately stopped laughing and sighed. "I am very tired," he said. "I have been traveling the whole night. But somehow I don't want to leave you. After all, you were once a student at Novaredok; perhaps there is still a spark of the spirit left in you somewhere."

We walked to a bench in silence. On first meeting him I had thought that he had become milder. Now I realized regretfully that his demands upon me and his negation of the whole world had grown greater. I hoped, though, that the pause would ease the tension that had arisen between us, and I was in no hurry to be the first to talk again. Hersh, however, wrinkled his forehead as though he were collecting his thoughts, and when we were seated on the bench he returned to my last words.

5.

"Did you say they were great men? The Germans insist they produced all the great men. I don't know whether they produced the very greatest, but I don't suppose that you worldly people would deny that they did produce learned men. Well, did those philosophers influence their own nation to become better? And the real question is, were the philosophers themselves good men? I don't want you to think that I underestimate their knowledge. During my years in the concentration camp I heard a good deal. There were exceptionally learned men among us, because the Germans mixed us all together, and in our moments of leisure we used to talk. Later, when with the help of the Almighty I was saved, I myself looked into the books of you worldly people, because I was no longer afraid they would hurt me. And I was really very much impressed by their ideas. Occasionally I found in their writings as much talent and depth as in our own Holy Books, if the two may be mentioned in one breath. But they are satisfied with talk! And I want you to believe me when I say that I concede that their poets and scientists wanted to be good. Only—only they weren't able to. And if some did have good qualities, they were exceptions. The masses and even their wise men didn't go any farther than fine talk. As far as talking is concerned, they talk more beautifully than we do.

"Do you know why they weren't able to become better? Because they were consumed with a passion to enjoy life. And since pleasure is not something that can be had by itself, murder arose among them—the pleasure of murder. And that's why they talk such fine talk, because they want to use it for fooling themselves into doing fine deeds. Only it doesn't help. They're satisfied with rhetoric, and the reason is that they care most of all for systems. The nations of the world inherited from the Greeks the desire for order and for pretty systems.

"First of all, they do what they do in public. They have no pleasure from their lusts if they can't sin openly, publicly, so that the whole world will know. They say of us that we're only hypocrites, whereas they do what they want to do publicly. But they like to wage war, not only with others, but with themselves as well, argue with themselves (of course, not too vigorously), even suffer and repent. And when they come to do repentance, the whole world knows about that too. That is the kind of repentance that gives them an intense pleasure; their self-love is so extreme it borders on sickness. They even like their victims, because their victims afford them the pleasure of sinning and the sweet afflictions of regret."

Hersh Rasseyner had moved away from me to the other end of the bench and had begun to look at me as though it had occurred to him that by mistake he might be talking to a stranger. Then he lowered his head and muttered as though to himself, "Do you remember that time in Bialystok?" He was silent for a moment and pulled a hair out of his beard as though he were pulling memories with it. "Do you remember, Chaim, how you told me on that Bialystok street that we were running away from the world because we were afraid we wouldn't be able to resist temptation? A Mussarist can labor for a lifetime on improving his qualities, yet a single word of criticism will stick in him like a knife. Yes, it's true! All the days of my youth I kept my eyes on the earth, without looking at the world. Then came the German. He took me by my Jewish beard, yanked my head up, and told me to look him straight in the eyes. So I had to look into his evil eyes, and into the eyes of the whole world as well. And I saw, Chaim, I saw—you know what I saw. Now I can look at all the idols and read all the forbidden impurities and contemplate all the pleasures of life, and it won't tempt me any more because now I know the true face of the world. Oh, Reb Chaim, turn and repent! It's not too late. Remember what the prophet Isaiah said: 'For my people have committed two evils: they have forsaken me, the fountain of living waters, and hewed them out cisterns, broken cisterns, that can hold no water.' "[6]

Hersh had spoken like a broken man. Tears were dropping on his beard. He rubbed his eyes to hold the tears back, but they continued to flow down his cheeks.

I took his hand and said to him with emotion, "Reb Hersh, you say that I have forsaken a fountain of living waters for a broken cistern. I must tell you that you're wrong. I draw water from the same pure fountain as you, only I use a different vessel. But calm yourself, Reb Hersh.

"You yourself said that you believe that the nations of the world had men of wisdom and men of action who wanted to be good, but couldn't. I think I'm quoting you accurately. What I don't understand is this. It's a basic principle of Judaism that man has free will. The Novaredok people actually maintain that it's possible to attain such a state of perfection that we can do good deeds without the intervention of our physical bodies. Well then, if a man can actually peel the evil husks from himself, as he would peel an onion, how do you answer this question: Since the wise men among the gentiles wanted to be good, why couldn't they?"

I was unable to keep a mocking note of triumph out of my question. It

6. Hersh misidentifies as Isaiah his quotation from the prophet Jeremiah (2.13). He may be thinking of Isaiah 36.16, where the king of Assyria tempts the Jews, "Make your peace with me . . . and drink water from your cisterns."

stirred Hersh Rasseyner out of his mournful abstraction. With deliberation he straightened himself and answered gently, "Chaim, you seem to have forgotten what you learned at Novaredok, so I'll remind you. In His great love for mankind, the Almighty has endowed us with reason. If our sages of blessed memory tell us that we can learn from the animals, surely we can learn from reason as well. And we know that the elders of Athens erected systems of morality according to pure reason. They had many disciples, each with his own school.

"But the question hasn't changed. Did they really live as they taught, or did their system remain only a system? You must understand once and for all that when his reason is calm and pure, a man doesn't know what he's likely to do when his dark desire overtakes him. A man admires his own wisdom and is proud of his knowledge, but as soon as a little desire begins to stir in him he forgets everything else. Reason is like a dog on a leash who follows sedately in his master's footsteps—until he sees a bitch. With us it's a basic principle that false ideas come from bad qualities. Any man can rationalize whatever he wants to do. Is it true that only a little while ago he was saying the opposite of what he is now saying? He'll tell you he was wrong then. And if he lets you prove to him that he wasn't wrong then, he'll shrug and say, 'When I want to do something, I can't be an Aristotle.'[7] As soon as his desire is sated, his reason revives and he's sorry for what he did. As soon as he feels desire beginning to stir once more, he forgets his reason again. It's as though he were in a swamp; when he pulls one foot out, the other sinks in. There is delicacy in his character, he has a feeling for beauty, he expresses his exalted thoughts in measured words, and there is no flaw in him; then he sees a female ankle and his reason is swallowed up. If a man has no God, why should he listen to the philosopher who tells him to be good? The philosopher himself is cold and gloomy and empty. He is like a man who wants to celebrate a marriage with himself.

"The one way out is this. A man should choose between good and evil only as the Law chooses for him. The Law wants him to be happy. The Law is the only reality in life. Everything else is a dream. Even when a man understands rationally what he should do, he must never forget that before all else he should do it because the Law tells him to do it. That is how he can guard against the time when his reason will have no power to command him.

"Wait a moment, I'm not through yet. A man may tell himself, 'I don't live according to reason but according to the Law.' And he may feel certain that when temptation comes he'll look into the appropriate book to see what he should do, and he'll do it. He tells himself that he is free. Actually, the freedom of his choice goes no farther than his wish. Even a man who has a Law won't be able to withstand his temptation if he doesn't watch over himself day and night. He who knows all secrets knew that our father Abraham would stand ready to sacrifice Isaac; but only after the Binding did the angel say to Abraham, 'Now I know.'[8] Hence we learn that until a man has accomplished what he should, the Law does not trust him. A child has the capacity to grow, but we don't know how tall he'll grow. His father and mother may be as high as the trees, but he may favor a dwarf grandfather. Only by good

7. Greek philosopher (384–322 B.C.E.).
8. "Now I know that you fear God" (Genesis 22.12).

deeds can we drive out bad deeds. Therefore the Jews cried out at Sinai, 'We will do'—only do, always do; 'and we will obey'[9]—and now we want to know what the Law tells us to do. Without deeds all inquiry is vain.

"That is the outlook and the moral way of 'the old one,' Reb Joseph Yoizl,[1] may his merit be a shield for us, and thousands of students at Novaredok steeped themselves in it day and night. We labored to make ourselves better, each of us polished and filed his own soul, with examiners gathering evidence of improvement like pearls. But you laughed at us. Then came the German, may his name be blotted out, and murdered our sainted students. And now we're both face to face with the destruction of the Community of Israel. But you are faced with another destruction as well—the destruction of your faith in the world. That's what hurts you and torments you, so you ask me: Why weren't the wise men of the gentiles able to be good if they wanted to be good? And you find contradictions in what I said. But the real contradiction you find is not in what I said but in yourself. You thought the world was striving to become better, and you discovered it was striving for our blood.

"Even if they wanted to, the wise men of the gentiles couldn't have become good to the very roots of their being because they didn't have a Law and because they didn't labor to perfect their qualities all their lives long. Their ethics were worked out by human minds. They trusted their reasoned assumptions as men trust the ice of a frozen river in winter. Then came Hitler and put his weight on the wisdom of the wise men of the nations. The ice of their slippery reasoning burst, and all their goodness was drowned.

"And together with their goodness to others their own self-respect was drowned. Think of it! For a word they didn't like they used to fight with swords or shoot one another. To keep public opinion from sneering or a fool from calling them coward, though they trembled at the thought of dying, they went to their death. Generation after generation, their arrogance grew like a cancer, until it ended by eating their flesh and sucking their marrow. For centuries they speculated, they talked, and they wrote. Does duty to nation and family come first, or does the freedom of the individual come before his obligations to parents, wife, and children—or even to one's self? They considered the matter solemnly and concluded that there are no bonds that a nation is not free to break; that truth and reason are like the sun, which must rise; can the sun be covered by throwing clods of earth at it? So there came in the West a booted ruler with a little mustache, and in the East a booted ruler with a big mustache,[2] and both of them together struck the wise man to the ground, and he sank into the mud. I suppose you'll say that the wise men wanted to save their lives. I can understand that. But didn't they insist that freedom, truth, and reason were more precious to the philosopher than his life? Take that wise man whose statue is standing there, with his instruments for measuring the stars and planets. When everyone else argued, 'The sun revolves about the earth,' he said, 'Not so; do what you will to me, break me, draw and quarter me, the earth revolves about the sun!' What would he have said to his grandchildren today? If the spirit of life could return to him, he would crawl down from his niche in the wall, strike his stone head against the stone bridge, and recite Lamentations."

9. Exodus 19.8 and Joshua 24.24.
1. Probably Joseph Hurwitz, a leader of the Musar movement who, in 1896, founded a yeshiva in the Belarus city of Novaredok (Novogrudok).
2. A reference to Hitler and Stalin, respectively.

6.

Hersh Rasseyner had begun by speaking slowly, like the head of a yeshiva trying to explain a difficult passage to his pupil for the hundredth time, pausing briefly every now and then so that I could follow what he was saying. Gradually he grew animated. I was reminded of the discussions we used to have at Novaredok during the evenings after the Sabbath in the weeks before the Days of Awe.[3] He began to speak more quickly, there was more excitement in his voice, and he ended his sentences like a man hammering nails into a wall. He shouted at me as though I were a dark cellar and he was calling to someone hiding in me.

The square and the neighboring streets had grown quieter and the flow of people had thinned out. On the benches in the little park passers-by sat mutely, exhausted by the intense heat of the day and trying to get some relief from the cool evening breeze that had begun to blow in the blue twilight of Paris.

"Hear me out, Chaim," Hersh resumed. "I'll tell you a secret. I have to talk to you. I talked to you during all those years when I was in the ghetto and later in the camps. Don't wonder at it, because you were always dear to me, from the time you were a student in Bialystok. Even then I had the feeling that you stood with one foot outside our camp.[4] I prayed for you. I prayed that you would remain Jewish. But my prayers didn't help. You yourself didn't want to be pious. You left us, but I never forgot you. They used to talk about you in the yeshiva; your reputation reached us even there. And I suppose you remember the time we met in Bialystok. Later our yeshiva was in Vilna, under the Bolsheviks, and we met again, only then you were very downhearted. In the ghetto they said you had been killed while trying to escape. Afterward we heard from partisans in the forest that you were living in Russia. I used to imagine that if we were both saved, a miracle might happen. We would meet and I could talk to you. That's why you mustn't be surprised if I talk to you as fluently as though I were reciting the daily prayers. Believe me, I have had so many imaginary debates with you that I know my arguments as well as the first prayer of the morning."

"Reb Hersh," I said, "it's getting late. The time for afternoon prayers will be over soon."

"Don't worry about my afternoon prayers, Chaim!" He laughed. "I said them just after twelve o'clock. In the camp it became a habit with me not to delay carrying out any commandment. I reasoned that if any hour was to be my last, I didn't want to come to heaven naked.

"Do you have time and strength to go on listening to me? You do? Good. So far I've talked to you about the gentile wise men. But first we ought to be clear in our own minds about our relation to them and to the whole world. And one thing more: if anything I say strikes you as too harsh, don't take it amiss. Even though I'm talking to you, I don't mean you personally; I really mean secular Jews in general. So don't be angry."

3. The High Holy Days, Rosh Hashanah and Yom Kippur.

4. Here, used figuratively in the translation, meaning "outside of our religious and ideological group or position."

7.

"Your Enlighteners used to sing this tune: 'Be a Jew at home and a man in public.'[5] So you took off our traditional coat and shaved your beard and earlocks. Still, when you went out into the street, the Jew pursued you in your language, in your gestures, in every part of you. So you tried to get rid of the incubus. And the result was that the Jew left you, like an old father whose children don't treat him with respect; first he goes to the synagogue and then, because he has no choice, to the home for the aged. Now that you've seen what has happened to us, you've turned your slogan around. Now it's be a man at home and a Jew in public. You can't be pious at home because you're lacking in faith. Out of anger against the gentile and nostalgia for the father you abandoned, you want to parade your Jewishness in public. Only the man you try to be at home—I'm using your language—follows you out of your house. The parable of the Prince and the Nazirite[6] applies to you. A dog was invited to two weddings, one near and one far. He thought, I won't be too late for the nearer one. So he ran first to the farther wedding—and missed it. Out of breath he ran to the one nearer home, and came after the feast. When he tried to push through the door, all he got was the stick. The upshot was that he missed both. The moral may be coarse, but you remember from your Novaredok days that it was applied to those who wanted to have both the pleasures of this world and the Law.

"You cried in the public square, 'The nations of the world dislike us because we're different. Let us be like them!' And you were like them. Not only that, but you stood at the head of their civilization. Where there was a famous scientist, thinker, writer—there you found a Jew. And precisely for that reason they hated us all the more. They won't tolerate the idea of our being like them. In the Middle Ages the priests wanted to baptize us. They used to delight in the torments of a Jew who tried to separate himself from the Community of Israel—with his family mourning him as though he were dead and the entire congregation lamenting as though it were the fast of *Tishe b'Av*.[7] In our day, though, when they saw how easy it had become for a Jew to leap over into their camp, they stationed themselves at the outposts with axes in their hands, as though to fend off wild beasts. But you were hungry and blind, so you leaped—onto their axes.

"When you ran away from being Jewish, you disguised your flight with high-sounding names. An enlightened man would talk in the most elevated rhetoric about Enlightenment; but what he really had in mind was to become a druggist. He yearned for the fleshpots of Egypt. His ambition was to dig his hands into the pot with no one to look him in the eyes, like the miser who doesn't like anyone near him when he's eating. With the nations of the earth the great thing is the individual—his sovereignty, his pleasure, and his repose. But they understand that if they acted on the principle that might is right, one man would devour the other; so they have a government of individuals, and the rule is: Let me alone and I'll let you alone. With us Jews the individual doesn't exist; it's the community that counts. What's good for all

5. A saying attibuted to the leading thinker and writer of the German Jewish Enlightenment, Moses Mendelssohn (1729–1786).

6. A medieval Hebrew allegorical poem of the early 13th century by Abraham Ibn Hasdai of Barcelona.

7. The Ninth of Av, the fast day commemorating the destruction of the First and Second Temples in Jerusalem in 586 B.C.E. and 70 C.E., respectively.

must be good for each. Till your rebellion Jews lived as one—in prayer and in study, in joy and in sorrow. But you incited the tribes: 'Every man to your tents, O Israel!'[8] Let each of us follow his own law, like the nations of the world. What's more, not only did you want to live as individuals, you wanted to die as individuals too. To avoid being confused with the other dead on the day of your death, you spent your lives erecting monuments for yourselves—one by great deeds; another by imposing his dominion; a third by a great business enterprise; and you by writing books. You didn't violate the commandment against idolatry.[9] Of course not! You were your own gods. You prophesied, 'Man will be a god.' So naturally he became a devil.

"Why are you uneasy, Reb Chaim? Didn't we agree you wouldn't be angry? I don't mean you personally; I'm only speaking figuratively. But if you really feel I mean you, then I do! The wicked are as the unquiet sea. Every wave thinks it will leap over the shore, though it sees millions of others shattered before its eyes. Every man who lives for this world alone thinks that he will succeed in doing what no one else has ever been able to do. Well, you know now how far you got! But instead of looking for solace in the Master of the World and in the Community of Israel, you're still looking for the glass splinters of your shattered dreams. And little as you'll have the world to come, you have this world even less.

"Still, not all of you secularists wanted to overthrow the yoke of the Law altogether. Some grumbled that Judaism kept on getting heavier all the time: *Mishnah* on Bible; *Gemarah* on *Mishnah*; commentaries on *Gemarah*; codes; commentaries[1] on the codes; commentaries on the commentaries, and commentaries on them. Lighten the weight a little, they said, so what is left can be borne more easily. But the more they lightened the burden, the heavier the remainder seemed to them. I fast twice a week without difficulty, and they can hardly do it once a year. Furthermore, what the father rejected in part, the son rejected in its entirety. And the son was right! Rather nothing than so little. A half-truth is no truth at all. Every man, and particularly every young man, needs a faith that will command all of his intellect and ardor. The devout cover a boy's head with a cap when he's a year old, to accustom him to commandments; but when a worldly father suddenly asks his grown son to cover his head with a paper cap and say the prayer over the wine on a Friday evening, the young man rightly thinks the whole thing is absurd. If he doesn't believe in Creation, and if the Exodus from Egypt is not much of a miracle, and if the Song of Songs[2] is to him only the song of a shepherd and a shepherdess—God forbid!—and not the song of love between the Assembly of Israel and the Holy One, blessed be He, or between the supernal soul and the Almighty, why should he bless the Sabbath wine? Anyone who thinks he can hold on to basic principles and give up what he considers

8. 2 Chronicles 10.16.
9. The second of the Ten Commandments (Exodus 20.4).
1. Interpretations of biblical texts. "*Mishnah*": the basis of the Talmud; it is the classical code of early rabbinic law, edited by Judah the Prince in the early third century C.E. "*Gemarah*": literally, "study"; it is the second part of the Talmud that purports to be commentary or elaboration upon the Mishnah by later rabbis but is actually an encyclopedic work containing all the teachings of rabbinic Judaism from the third through the fifth centuries C.E. "Codes": of law.
2. Also known as the Song of Solomon; a book of the Hebrew Bible that is a love poem, often interpreted as an allegory of the love between God and Israel. "Creation": i.e., God's creation of the universe (Genesis 1.1–2.25). "Exodus from Egypt": with God's help and miracles, Moses led the Hebrews out of slavery in Egypt (Exodus 3.1–15.21).

secondary is like a man who chops down the trunk of a tree and expects the roots not to rot.

"I've already told you, Chaim, that we of the Mussar school are very mindful of criticism. Do you remember telling me, on a street in Bialystok, that we try to escape by withdrawal because we would rather have nothing in this world than only a little? That's true. We want a more onerous code, more commandments, more laws, more prohibitions. We know that all the pleasures of life are like salt water: the more a man drinks of it, the thirstier he becomes. That's why we want a Torah that will leave no room in us for anything else.

"Suppose the Master of the World were to come to me and say, 'Hersh, you're only flesh and blood. Six hundred and thirteen commandments[3] are too many for you, I will lighten your burden. You don't need to observe all of them. Don't be afraid, you won't be deprived of the resurrection of the dead!' Do you understand, Chaim, what it means to be at the resurrection of the dead and see life given again to all the Jews who fell before my eyes? If the Father of Mercy should ask less sacrifice of me, it would be very bitter for me. I would pray, 'Father of Mercy, I don't want my burden to be lightened, I want it to be made heavier.' As things are now, my burden is still too light. What point is there to the life of a fugitive, of a Jew saved from the crematorium, if he isn't always ready to sacrifice his bit of a rescued life for the Torah? But you, Chaim, are you as daring in your demands upon the world as I am in my demands upon the Master of the World? When you were studying with us, you were so strong and proud that you could be satisfied only by getting to the very bottom of the truth. And now do you think it right to crawl under the table of life, hoping for a bone from the feast of unclean pleasures, or a dry crumb of the joys of this world? Is that what's left to you of your pride and confidence in the warfare of life? I look at you and think, I'm still very far from being what I ought to be. If I had reached a higher stage, my heart would be torn with pity for you.

"The rebellious seducer rejected everything, while the one who halted between two opinions left something; but both of them, when they wanted to show their unfaltering good sense, first denounced the Community of Israel for allowing itself to be bound in the cobwebs of a profitless dialectic, living in a cemetery and listening to ghost stories, concerning itself with unrealities and thinking that the world ends at the ruined mill on the hilltop. The clever writer described it with great artistry, and the vulgar laughed. And the secularist reformers with their enlightened little beards justified themselves with a verse: 'Whom the Lord loveth He correcteth.'[4] In other words, only because they really loved us did they attack us. But they groveled before everything they saw elsewhere. They called us fawning lickspittles—but with their own souls, like rags, they wiped the gentry's boots. The overt rebel and the man who prayed secretly and sinned secretly—why antagonize either side?—were at one in this, that the thing they mocked us for most enthusiastically was our belief in being chosen. What's so special about us? they asked, laughing. And I say, you may not feel very special—but you have to be! You may not want it, but the Almighty does! Thousands of years ago the

3. According to Jewish law, the prescribed number of commandments that a traditional Jewish man must obey.
4. Proverbs 3.12.

God of Israel said through Ezekiel His prophet: 'And that which cometh into your mind shall not be at all; in that ye say: We will be as the nations, as the families of the countries, to serve wood and stone. As I live, saith the Lord God'—do you hear, Chaim? the Almighty swears by His own life—'As I live, saith the Lord God, surely with a mighty hand, and with an outstretched arm, and with fury poured out, will I be king over you.'[5] You're a writer; write it on your forehead. You don't seem very impressed. You don't consider a verse to be proof. But the German is a proof, isn't he? Today, because so many Jews have been cut down, you don't want to remember how you used to laugh at them. But tomorrow, when the destruction will be forgotten, you'll laugh again at the notion that God has chosen us. That's why I want to tell you something.

"You know that I was in a camp. I lay on the earth and was trampled by the German in his hobnailed boots. Well, suppose that an angel of God had come to me then, that he had bent down and whispered into my ear, 'Hersh, in the twinkling of an eye I will turn you into the German. I will put his coat on you and give you his murderous face; and he will be you. Say the word and the miracle will come to pass.' If the angel had asked me—do you hear, Chaim?—I would not have agreed at all. Not for one minute would I have consented to be the other, the German, my torturer. I want the justice of law! I want vengeance, not robbery! But I want it as a Jew. With the Almighty's help I could stand the German's boots on my throat, but if I had had to put on his mask, his murderous face, I would have been smothered as though I had been gassed. And when the German shouted at me, 'You are a slave of slaves,' I answered through my wounded lips, 'Thou hast chosen me.'

"I want to ask you only one question, no more. What happened is known to all Jews. 'Let the whole House of Israel bewail the burning which the Lord hath kindled.'[6] All Jews mourn the third of our people who died a martyr's death. But anyone with true feeling knows that it was not a third of the House of Israel that was destroyed, but a third of himself, of his body, his soul. And so we must make a reckoning—you as well as I. Anyone who doesn't make the reckoning must be as bestial as the beasts of the wood. Let's make the reckoning together. In justice and in mercy, may we forgive the murderers? No, we may not! To the end of all generations we may not forgive them. Forgiving the murderer is a fresh murder, only this time of brother by brother.

"Neither you nor I has the right to sleep at night. We have no right to flee the laments, the eyes, and the outstretched arms of the murdered; though we break under the anguish and affliction, we have no right to flee their outcry. What then? I know that the reckoning is not yet over; far from it. And I have never thought for one moment that anyone in the world besides the jealous and vengeful God would avenge the helpless little ones that the Gestapo stuffed into the trains for Treblinka,[7] treading on their delicate little bodies to get as many children as possible into the cars. That is why I don't have the slightest shadow of a doubt that the great and terrible day, behold

5. Ezekiel 20.32–34.
6. Moses' words regarding the sons of his brother, Aaron—Nadab and Abihu—who offered "strange fire" before God and were punished by being consumed in flames (Leviticus 10.6).
7. A Nazi death camp in Poland. "Gestapo": the Nazi military police.

it comes! When I hear people quibbling about politics and calculating the position of the powers, I know that there is another set of books, kept in fire and blood. There's no use asking me whether I want it that way or not; that's the way it has to be! And that's what sustains me as I try to go in tranquillity about the work of the Creator.

"But you, Chaim, how can you eat and sleep and laugh and dress so elegantly? Don't you have to make your reckoning too? How can you thrust yourself into the world when you know it consorts with the murderers of the members of your own house? And you thought the world was becoming better! Your world has fallen! As for me, I have greater faith than ever. If I had only as much faith as in the past, that would be an offense against the martyred saints. My answer is, more and more self-sacrifice for the Master of the World; to cry out until the spirit is exhausted: 'For Thy sake are we killed all the day';[8] to go about, until the soul departs, with a shattered heart and hands raised to heaven: 'Father, Father, only You are left to us!' But what has changed with you, Chaim? What is your answer?"

8.

Hersh Rasseyner's speech was like a dry flame, progressively taking fire from itself. I realized he was unburdening himself of much accumulated anger. Finally he grew quiet. His lips were pinched with the effort he had to make to obey himself and speak no more.

The blue of the evening sky was growing darker. The stone figures around the Hôtel de Ville had shrunk, as though frightened by what Hersh Rasseyner had said, and quietly burrowed deeper into the walls. The old building was now half in darkness. The street lamps brought out the flat green color of our surroundings. Black shining autos slid quietly over the asphalt. A thin little rain began to come down. Windows were lighting up. The people walking along on the other side of the street seemed to be moving with a silent, secret pace behind a thick silken curtain, woven of the summer rain.

From our little empty corner I glanced across the street. In the light of the electric lamps the raindrops looked like millions of fireflies joyously hastening down from the sky. I had an impulse to merge myself with the human stream flowing down the surrounding lighted streets. I stirred, and I felt little pricks of pain in my stiffened limbs. The light rain came to an end. Hersh sat near me, motionless and as though deaf, his shoulders sharp and angular and his head bowed and sunk in darkness. He was waiting for me to answer.

"Reb Hersh," I finally said, "as I sat here listening to you, I sometimes thought I was listening to myself. And since it's harder to lie to yourself than to someone else, I will answer you as though you were my own conscience, with no thought either of merely being polite or of trying to win a debate. I am under no greater obligation than you to know everything. I don't consider it a special virtue not to have doubts. I must tell you that just as the greatness of the faithful consists in their innocence and wholeness, so the heroism of thinkers consists in their being able to tolerate doubt and make their peace

8. Psalm 44.23.

with it. You didn't discover your truth; you received it ready-made. If anyone should ask you about something in your practice of which you yourself don't know the meaning, you answer, 'The work of my fathers is in my hands.' As a rule, a man is a rebel in his youth; in age he seeks tranquillity. You had tranquillity in your youth, while I don't have it even now; you once predicted it would be so with me. But is your tranquillity of soul a proof that the truth is with you? For all your readiness to suffer and make sacrifices, there is an element of self-satisfaction in you. You say of yourself that you were born in a coat of many colors.

"They used to call 'the old one,' the founder of Novaredok, the master of the holes. It was said that Reb Joseph Yoizl lived apart for many years in the woods in a hut that had two holes in the wall; through one they would hand him dairy foods and through the other meat foods. When he put his withdrawal behind him and came back into the world, his philosophy was either milk or meat, one extreme or the other, but nothing in between. His disciples, including you, took this teaching from him. His disciples want what they call wholeness too, and they have no use for compromises. What you said about our wanting a small Torah so that it would be easier for us was simply idle talk. On the contrary, we make it harder for ourselves, because we acknowledge a double responsibility—toward Jewish tradition and toward secular culture.

"You said that among Jews the important thing was always the community and not the individual, until we came along and spoiled it; we wanted to be like the gentiles, for whom the 'I' is more important than anything else. And in order to hurt me you tried to persuade me that what I want to do is to climb up the Hôtel de Ville and put myself there as a living monument to myself. You allow yourself to mock, because, after all, what you do is for the sake of heaven, isn't that so? I won't start now to tell you historical facts about leaders and rulers who made the community their footstool. As for what you say, that the principle among Jews was always the community until we came, I agree. We secularists want to free the individual.[9] You say a man should tear his individual desires out of himself. But for hundreds of years men have gone to torture and death so that the commonwealth shall consist of free and happy individuals. I could read you an all but endless list of our own boys and girls whose youth was spent in black dungeons because they would not be deterred from trying to make the world better. You yourself know about Jewish workers who fought against all oppressors and tyrants. The only thing is that you won't concede that free thinkers can sacrifice themselves too, so you complain that they left Jewish tradition only to enjoy forbidden pleasures. That is untrue. In my own quarter I knew as many 'seekers' as in Novaredok—and more. Because you denied the world, Reb Hersh, you withdrew into an attic. But these young people dearly loved the world, and they sacrificed themselves—to better it.

"What right then do you have to complain to us about the world? You yourself said that we dreamed about another, a better world—which nullifies your accusation. We carried into the world our own vision of what the world should be, as the Jews in the wilderness carried the Ark with the tablets of

9. One of the central issues for Jewish writers since the *Haskalah* (Jewish Enlightenment) has been the conflict between their moral and artistic responsibilities to the collective and to the individual.

the Covenant, so that they could enter the land of Canaan with their own Torah. You laugh; you say that we deceived ourselves. I'll ask you: Do you renounce Judaism because the Samaritans and the Karaites distorted the Law of Moses?[1]

"But I don't have to apologize to you. You lump me together with the murderers and demand an accounting of me for the world. I can be as harsh an accuser as you. I can cry out against you and demand an accounting of you. If we have abandoned Jewish tradition, it's your fault! You barricaded yourself, shut the gates, and let no one out into the open. If anyone put his head out, you tried to pull him back by his feet; and if you couldn't, you threw him out bodily and shut the doors behind him with a curse. Because he had no place to go back to he had to go farther away than he himself would have wished. From generation to generation you became more fanatical. Your hearts are cold and your ears deaf to all the sciences of the world. You laugh at them and say they are futile things. If you could, you would put people in the pillory again, as the Gaon of Vilna did to a follower of the Enlightenment who dared say that the old exegetes didn't know Hebrew grammar too well.[2] Even today, for the smallest transgression you would impose the gravest punishment, if you could. But because you can't, you shorten your memories. You pretend not to remember how you used to persecute anyone who was bold enough to say anything different from you without basing himself on the authority of the ancient sages of blessed memory, or even with their authority. All your life you studied *The Path of the Upright*.[3] Do you know how much its author was suspected and persecuted, how much anguish they caused him, how they hunted for heresy in his writings? Do you know that, at least? And you yourself, didn't you examine the contents of your students' trunks, looking for forbidden books? Even now, doesn't your voice have in it something of the trumpet of excommunication? Doesn't your eye burn like the black candle of excommunication? And do you really think that, with all your protestations, you love Jews more than the writers for whom it was so painful to write critically of the Jewish community? Didn't you bury them outside the wall, when you could, with no stones to mark their graves? Incidentally, Reb Hersh, I want you to know that this neighborhood we're in is old Paris. Here by the Hôtel de Ville, where we're sitting, is the Place de Grève—that is, Execution Square, where they used to torture and execute those who were condemned to death. It was right here, more than seven hundred years ago, that Maimonides' *Guide to the Perplexed* was burned, on a denunciation by eminent and zealous rabbis. Rabbi Jonah Gerondi had a hand in it.[4] Later, when the priests began to burn the Talmud too, Rabbi Jonah felt that it was a punishment from

1. The Samaritans are descendants of an ancient people living in the land of Israel who claim to be the true heirs of biblical Israel. The Karaites are members of a sect that split off from Babylonian Jewry in the 8th century and that rejects normative Judaism, claiming instead to follow the literal meaning of the Bible.
2. Hebrew grammar, the analytic systemization of the Hebrew language, was considered a modern, Enlightened desecration of the holy tongue by traditional Jews such as the Vilna Gaon.
3. *Mesillat Yesharim* (Hebrew); an ethical work by Moshe Hayyim Luzzatto of Padua (1707–1746).
4. Maimonides (Moses ben Maimon; acronym, Rambam, 1135–1204), the Jewish philosopher and legalist of Muslim Spain and Egypt, wrote his work of religious philosophy, *Guide [for] the Perplexed*, between 1185 and 1190. Rabbi Jonah ben Abraham Gerondi (ca. 1200–1263) was an opponent of Maimonides' philosophy and involved in the bitter Maimonidean controversies of 1230, which ended when, in 1232, the Roman Catholic Inquisition in France burned copies of Maimonides' works.

heaven for his warfare against Maimonides, and he repented. That was when he wrote his *Gates of Repentance.*[5] In Novaredok they used to read the *Gates of Repentance* with such outcries that their lungs were almost torn to shreds; but they never thought to learn its moral, which is not to be fanatical.

"How estranged you feel from all secular Jews can be seen in your constant repetition of 'we' and 'you.' You laugh at us poor secularists. You say that our suffering is pointless: we don't want to be Jews, but we can't help it. It would follow that the German made a mistake in taking us for Jews. But it's you who make that mistake. The enemies of Israel know very well that we're the same; they say it openly. And we're the same not only for the enemies of Israel, but for the Master of the World as well! In the other world your soul won't be wearing a cap or a beard or earlocks. Your soul will come there as naked as mine. You would have it that the real Community of Israel is a handful of Hersh Rasseyners. The others are quarter-Jews, tenth-Jews—or not even that. You say that being Jewish is indivisible, all or nothing. So you make us Jews a thousand times fewer than we already are.

"You were right when you said that it was not a third of our people who were murdered, but rather that a third was cut out of the flesh and soul of every Jew who survived. As far as you're concerned though, Reb Hersh, was it really a third person of our people who perished? The gist of what you say—again the same thing!—is that anyone who isn't your kind of Jew is not a Jew at all. Doesn't that mean that there were more bodies burned than Jews murdered? You see to what cruelty your religious fanaticism must lead.

"I want you to consider this and settle it with yourself. Those Jews who didn't worry night and day about the high destiny of man, who weren't among the thirty-six hidden righteous men who sustain the world, but who lived a life of poverty for themselves, their wives, and their children;[6] those Jews who got up in the morning without saying the proper morning prayers and ate their black bread without saying the blessing for bread; those Jews who labored on the Sabbath and didn't observe the last detail of the Law on Holy Days; those Jews who waited submissively and patiently at the table of this world for a crumb to fall their way—that's what you, Reb Hersh, the hermit of Novaredok, the man who lives apart, taunted them with; those Jews who lived together in neighborliness, in small quarrels and small reconciliations, and perished together in the same way—do you admit them to your Paradise or not? And where will they sit? At the east wall, together with the Mussarists, or at the door, with their feet outside? You will tell me that the simple man is saintly and pure, because he perished as a Jew. But if he survived, is he wicked and evil, because he doesn't follow in your way? Is that your mercy and love for the Community of Israel? And you dare to speak in their name and say you're the spokesman of the sainted dead! Why are you getting up? Do you want to run away? But you assured me you used to dream of meeting me and talking it out with me. Can you only talk and not listen? Novaredok Mussarist, sit down and hear me out!

5. Chaim Vilner states the legendary belief that Rabbi Jonah Gerondi wrote *Gates of Repentance* to recant his opposition to Maimonides. Modern scholarship disputes this as fact.

6. Jewish tradition tells that, in the disguise of poverty, there are thirty-six righteous men living in the world upon whose good deeds the continued existence of the world depends.

"If secular Jews are so alien to you, why should I be surprised at the blackness of your hatred against the whole non-Jewish world? But let's not quarrel any more, Reb Hersh; let's reckon our accounts quietly. May we hate the whole non-Jewish world? You know as well as I do that there were some who saved the lives of Jews. I won't enter into a discussion with you about the exact number of such people. It's enough for me that you know there were some.

"In nineteen forty-six, in Poland, I once attended a small gathering in honor of a Pole, a Christian who had hidden ten Jews. At that little party we all sat around a table. We didn't praise the doctor, we didn't talk about noble and exalted things, about humanity and heroism, or even about Jews and Poles. We simply asked him how it was that he wasn't afraid to hide ten Jews behind the wall of his office. The doctor was a small, gray-haired man. He kept on smiling, almost childishly, and he thanked us in embarrassment for the honor—a great honor!—that we were doing him. He answered our question in a low voice, almost tongue-tied: when he hid the Jews he felt sure that, since it was a good deed, nothing bad would happen to him.

"Here in Paris there's an old lady, a Lithuanian. I know her well. Everybody knows that in the Vilna ghetto she saved the lives of Jews, and also hid books. The Germans sentenced her to death, but she was spared by a miracle. She's an old revolutionist, an atheist; that is to say, she doesn't believe in God.

"Imagine that both of them, the old lady and the old man, the Lithuanian and the Pole, the revolutionist and the Christian, were sitting here listening to us! They don't say anything, they only listen. They are frightened by your accusations, but not angry, because they understand that your hatred grows out of sorrow. Neither do they regret having saved the lives of Jews; they feel only an ache in their hearts, a great pain. Why do you think they saved the lives of Jews? The devout Christian didn't try to convert anyone. The old revolutionist didn't try to make anyone an atheist; on the contrary, she hid our sacred books. They saved the lives of Jews not from pity alone, but for their own sakes as well. They wanted to prove to themselves—no one else could possibly have known—that the whole world does not consist only of criminals and those who are indifferent to the misfortunes of others. They wanted to save their own faith in human beings and the lives of Jews as well. Now you come along and repudiate everything in the world that isn't piously Jewish. I ask you: Is there room in your world for these two old people? Don't you see that you would drive them out into the night? Will you take them, the righteous of the nations of the world, out of the category of gentile and put them in a special category? They didn't risk their lives so that Reb Hersh Rasseyner, who hates everyone, everyone, could make an exception of them.

"But you ask me what has changed for me since the destruction. And what has changed for you, Reb Hersh? You answer that your faith has been strengthened. I tell you openly that your answer is a paltry, whining answer. I don't accept it at all. You must ask God the old question about the righteous man who fares ill and the evil man who fares well—only multiplied for a million murdered children. The fact that you know in advance that there will be no explanation from heaven doesn't relieve you of the responsibility of asking, Reb Hersh! If your faith is as strong as Job's, then you must have his courage to cry out to heaven: 'Though He slay me, yet will I trust in Him; but I will argue my ways before Him!'[7] If a man hasn't sinned, he isn't allowed to declare himself guilty. As for us, even if we were devils, we couldn't have sinned enough for our just punishment to be a million murdered children. That's why your answer that your faith has been strengthened is no answer at all, as long as you don't demand an accounting of heaven.

"Reb Hersh, we're both tired and burned out from a whole day of arguing. You ask what has changed for me. The change is that I want to make peace with you, because I love you deeply. I never hated you and I never searched for flaws in your character, but what I did see I didn't leave unsaid. When you became angry with me before I left, I became angry with you, but now I'm filled with love for you. I say to you as the Almighty said to the Jews assembled in Jerusalem on the feast days: I want to be with you one day more, it is hard for me to part from you. That's what has changed for me, and for all Jewish writers. Our love for Jews has become deeper and more sensitive. I don't renounce the world, but in all honesty I must tell you we want to incorporate into ourselves the hidden inheritance of our people's strength, so that we can continue to live. I plead with you, do not deny us a share in the inheritance. However loudly we call out to heaven and demand an accounting, our outcry conceals a quiet prayer for the Divine Presence, or for the countenance of those destroyed in the flames, to rest on the alienated Jews. The Jewish countenance of the burned still hangs in clouds of gas in the void. And our cry of impotent anger against heaven has a deeper meaning as well: because we absolutely refuse our assent to the infamous and enormous evil that has been visited on us, because we categorically deny its justice, no slavish or perverse acquiescence can take root in our hearts, no despairing belief that the world has no sense or meaning.

"Reb Hersh, we have been friends since the old days in the yeshiva. I remember that I once lost the little velvet bag in which I kept my phylacteries. You didn't eat breakfast and you spent half a day looking for it, but you couldn't find it. I got another bag to hold my phylacteries, but you're still looking for the old one.

"Remember, Reb Hersh, that the texts inscribed in my phylacteries are about the Community of Israel.[8] Don't think that it's easy for us Jewish writers. It's hard, very hard. The same misfortune befell us all, but you have a ready answer, while we have not silenced our doubts, and perhaps we never will be able to silence them. The only joy that's left to us is the joy of creation, and in all the travail of creation we try to draw near to our people.

"Reb Hersh, it's late, let us take leave of each other. Our paths are different, spiritually and practically. We are the remnant of those who were driven out. The wind that uprooted us is dispersing us to all the corners of the earth. Who knows whether we shall ever meet again? May we both have the merit of meeting again in the future and seeing how it is with us. And may I then be as Jewish as I am now. Reb Hersh, let us embrace each other."

1954

7. Job 13.15.
8. The phylacteries, two small leather boxes containing the Shema, the Ten Commandments, and other biblical verses, are bound to a man's forehead and left arm during morning prayer.

EMMA ADATTO SCHLESINGER
b. 1910

Born in Istanbul, Turkey, in 1910, Emma Adatto was brought to the United States by her parents in 1912, where they settled in Seattle, Washington, a city noted for its large Sephardic community. Adatto attended the University of Washington during the depression, encouraged to do so by her mother despite the family's economic hardships. She earned a B.A. in Spanish and, in 1938, an M.A. in Sephardic folklore.

Schlesinger is one of a number of contemporary Sephardic writers and poets in the United States whose works are anthologized in *Sephardic American Voices: Two Hundred Years of a Literary Legacy*, edited by Diane Matza (1997). Matza's anthology provides a corrective to the misapprehension that Jewish American literature stems exclusively from the Eastern European immigrants. We have included Schlesinger's autobiographical narrative "*La Tía Estambolía*" for its vivid depiction of an extraordinary woman, Madame Vida de Veisí, who, in the 1920s and 1930s, imparted to the young Schlesinger a wealth of Sephardic traditions, especially that of storytelling and the five-centuries-old tradition of the *Romancero*, Judeo-Spanish recitations of Spanish ballads. Schlesinger's narrative style incorporates words and phrases from the Sephardic languages, Hebrew, Judeo-Spanish or Ladino, and, here, Turkish (elsewhere, Arabic), which, along with details of food, clothing, and customs, expand the cultural range of Jewish American literature.

"La Tía Estambolía"[1]

We began calling Madame Vida de Veisí, "La Tía Estambolía," shortly after she came to Seattle from Constantinople at the end of World War I. Madame Veisí was a childless widow, a little over the age of 65, when she made that trip alone to Seattle, Washington, in 1920.

It was an unexpectedly early arrival at the King Street Station at night; instead of a depot full of relatives, she saw only an old janitor sweeping the floor. Clutching her valise, she walked outside the station, never doubting for a moment she would find someone to help her. Either her keen powers of observation or plain luck made her turn to a stranger who was waiting at the corner for a streetcar. She asked him in Ladino if he was a Jew. His response in the style of a 15th-century Spanish gentleman evoked her immediate confidence.

When he identified himself as Señor Chiprut of the Sephardic community of Seattle who knew her relatives, Madame Veisí boarded the Jackson Street streetcar and allowed him to guide her to the front door of the home of her nephew, Haim Benaltabet. She banged on the door, which opened after a few minutes to expose a houseful of relatives busily preparing a *pranso*, a feast for the morrow's welcome home party for her. Her niece Vitoria fainted; her nephew Haim wept openly; everyone was crying and shrieking as they divided their time between taking care of Vitoria and kissing and hugging Vida. While the emotional outburst was at its peak, it is reported that she asked for a glass of water with a teaspoon of sugar, a traditional remedy for

1. Literally, "the aunt from Estambol," the Sephardic name for Constantinople, Turkey.

shock, and a cigarette. Everyone rushed to serve her as she revealed her status and position.

There was little in her appearance that made an immediate impression. A rather short woman, she was neither fat nor thin, neither ugly nor pretty. Her gray hair was combed smoothly and ended in a small bun. She often wore a *toca*, a filmy scarf, which may have been a token hair covering in lieu of the wig worn by other Orthodox women. I can't remember the color of her eyes, they might have been green. Her features and the color of her skin were not unusual. Madame Veisí was always dressed in a well-made dress, carefully pressed with every hook and eye in its proper place. She wore the finest cotton stockings and shoes with Cuban heels. We never saw her without her diamond earrings dangling from her pierced ears. Sometimes she would wear a *colana*, a long gold chain, and on formal occasions she would wear her gold bracelets and diamond rings. Except on the Sabbath, she always held a cigarette between the yellowish thumb and forefinger of her left hand. On Saturdays, she carried a *tespil*, a string of amber beads used mostly by men, as a rosary by the Mohammedans and by the Greeks for comfort and solace. Because of her age, it was considered proper for a woman to play with the *tespil*.

I was about ten years old when she first visited our home and remember seeing my father rush to greet her and lead her to the honored place at the sofa. At a time when I was taught to serve the men first, it amazed me to watch him offer her a cigarette and light it for her with a flourish. My mother ordered me to prepare the Turkish coffee at once, but before it was to be served, I was to bring the *dulce*, the sweet that was offered as soon as a guest entered the house.

As the eldest daughter, I had been trained in my duties. I took out a large silver tray and placed a dish of sweets in the center. Usually it was strawberry preserves, but that day it was *cidra*, candied grapefruit rind, a delicacy served on special occasions. On one side of the *cidra*, I placed a crystal dish containing long-handled spoons made by the silversmiths of Constantinople, and on the other side, an empty glass dish on which the used spoons were to be placed. Then I placed glasses of fresh water on the tray before passing it to each guest, always beginning with the men. When my mother passed the tray, there was always a blessing in Hebrew, but when I did, there was an additional prayer, *novia*, may you marry.

As time went on and the Americanization process began to set in, the men began to tease about "ladies first" and the style was slowly accepted. If the rabbi was visiting, he was the first one served, then the older women and men, and finally the younger women. On the day that Madame Veisí came, my father took the tray from me and served her himself. She was quick to recognize the honor. After that I soon learned to serve her the demitasse with the thickest *kaymak*, the cream of foam that surfaced to the top of the cup when the Turkish coffee was carefully poured. Sometimes, if Madame Veisí had had a dairy dinner, we would put real cream in the cup for her. It was never done for anyone else.

Madame Veisí was a popular guest because of her wit and her charm. Her fame as a storyteller began to follow her wherever she went. In the days before television, when even radios were scarce, storytelling was live entertainment for those who could not speak English. Everyone loved the movies, where the piano music and the pantomime were an international language, but nothing could compare to a storyteller who had a repertoire of tales that could be altered to suit the mood of the narrator and the audience. Madame Veisí came to be called La Tía de Estambol, in keeping with her reputation as a Scherezade.[2] Older women were often referred to as *tías*, aunts, but she became so well-known that everyone recognized her as the Tía from Estambol, as Constantinople was then called by the Sephardim. It didn't take long for the ear and the tongue to elide it to La Tiastambolía. There were some who never did know that her real name was Vida de Veisí.

In spite of her witticisms, ranging from plays on words to stories with sexual overtones, La Tía Estambolía always maintained a dignified air, bordering on snobbishness. She was like a grand actress making sure the scene was properly set. One could never ask her to tell a story. After the sweets, the coffee, and the small talk, the host would begin with such blessings upon her as may she have a long life, may she live to see all her nieces and nephews married, and may she see Jerusalem. Then she—always addressed in the third person, never in the second person—would be begged to tell a tale. Immediately, someone would light her cigarette; she would puff for a while while everyone remained quite still. This ritualistic appeal was always repeated three times before she would tilt her head to one side and ask, "What story would you like to hear?"

Then she would begin, *avía de ser*, there was once. With these magic words, we heard about the clever orphan girl whose intelligence and beauty enabled her to marry a handsome, wealthy man who had been cuckolded; the man with the blue umbrella who played such an important role in the life of an abandoned wife and her seven daughters; the princess who was kept in a tower but flew on the back of a parrot to meet an enchanted prince; the king's son who was exiled by his father for his kindness to a fish and married a maiden out of whose mouth came snakes. The plots were most often of Greek, Turkish, or other origins, but all the characters, except for those in one tale, were distinctly Jewish: Avrams and Rajels who observed the traditions of marriages, circumcisions, Sabbaths, kindness to strangers and the needy. The fascination was as much with their way of life as with the development of the plot. To this day I remember the Sabbath feast described in one of the tales. Every detail was complete: the embroidered cloth, the silver candelabra, the fish baked in lemon sauce, the roasted chicken, the rice cooked with tomatoes sauteed in oil, the psalms sung by the man of the house.

La Tía's voice would rise and fall, growing louder or softer to fit the story. Aside from raising her eyebrows and shaking or turning her head, she used no other gestures. Occasionally, she would use her right hand to indicate height or to emphasize a facial expression. The words flowed like a mountain stream, rapidly, crisply, forcefully, unceasingly, until the end of the tale. Even if she stopped to sip some water, the story continued as if without interruption. Saturdays were a favorite storytelling day since no work could be done, not even making of *oyá*, lace, one of her pastimes. La Tía suffered

2. The narrator of the *Arabian Nights* and the king's wife who avoids death by telling the king suspenseful stories that she interrupts at a crucial moment and completes only the following night.

from *nervios* when she couldn't smoke and would calm herself a bit with the *tespil*. The clack of the amber beads, each one hitting the next as she pushed them along the string, sounded like tiny drums beating rhythmically with her words.

She was about eighty years old when my mother and I went to see her to beg her to allow me to write down some of her tales for a collection of folk material of the Seattle Sephardim for my Master's thesis at the University of Washington. We found La Tía seated at one end of the *minder*, the stiff sofa found in every Turquina's kitchen. The white gas and coal stove glistened, the linoleum floor was scrubbed, the starched white curtains were immaculate. Estreya, her niece, wiped the clean chairs for us to sit on.

"Estreya is so fussy, cleaning and scrubbing, scrubbing and cleaning," complained La Tía.

The slender Estreya just smiled and greeted us in Ladino, asking me in Spanish accented English, "How are you, Emma?"

We had our *dulce* and *cafe con leche*, coffee with milk, and *bizcochos*, cookies. My mother, La Tía, and Estreya were exchanging news when I nudged my mother.

"May you live long, Vida," began my mother, "would you please tell Amada [my name in Ladino] one of your stories for her to write down?"

"What do you want them for?" asked La Tía.

Before I could answer, Mama told her, "They will put you in the books of the university."

I thought it might be a waste of time to explain a university to a woman who had never had a formal education. La Tía must have read my thoughts, for she said instantly with pride, "Mademoiselle, in case you don't know, we have universities, museums, concerts and clothes from Paris in Estambol, better than there is here in Seattle."

I spluttered an apology for my unspoken thoughts and said, "You are the best storyteller in Seattle, and I would like to write the stories down exactly as you tell them."

La Tía seemed somewhat mollified. She looked at my mother and then at me and commanded, "Take out your pencil and paper."

And she began to recite one of her tales as I wrote down her words as fast as I could. She was very patient with me and would wait if I needed more time to write. Sometimes I would read back to her what I had written, and she would make a few corrections. Sometimes she didn't want to be bothered. Occasionally she would say, "I have no *kef*, I'm not in the mood."

I soon learned to defer to her moods even when it seemed to be a wasted afternoon. She reminded me now and then that she was doing this out of great affection for my mother. I never went to La Tía's without my mother since she constantly encouraged us and frequently saved me from making a *faux pas*.[3]

"Madame Anna, do you remember the story about the rabbi and his wife?" La Tía would ask my mother.

"Of course," my mother replied, "but only you know how it should be told."

My mother was a very good storyteller herself and had a phenomenal mem-

3. Social blunder (French).

ory, but the repetitions required to add a certain suspense to the tale would often bore her; she was more interested in getting to the point than in embroidery of the plot. Mother's stories were more often homilies than pure entertainment. La Tía would defer to her wisdom, and Mama would defer to La Tía's artistry. The women were sometimes identified by such titles as Rosa the rich one, Estreya the clean one, Anna the wise one and counselor, Zimbul the dumb one, Vida the storyteller. These titles were not spoken openly to avoid a breach of etiquette. Madame Veisí knew we called her La Tía Estambolía, but we never addressed her as anything but Madame Vida.

The afternoons continued, and my notebooks were being filled when Dr. George Umphrey, head of the Spanish Department at the University of Washington, told me that the University of Washington Broadcasting Studio would be available to us through the courtesy of the Departments of English and Anthropology. Since I was a teaching fellow in Spanish at the university, I was eligible to receive such a service. The folksongs and tales were to be recorded on aluminum discs for a permanent collection.

There were about nine women from four or five areas of Turkey and the Island of Rhodes who were invited to come. Dr. Melville Jacobs of the Anthropology Department made the arrangements not only for the recording sessions, he also chauffered the women to the studio. The women liked his black hair and dark eyes and his friendly, encouraging manner—he seemed like one of their sons. They put on their best dresses and sprinkled themselves with rosewater for this important occasion. Since only a few spoke English, I was the interpreter, and we managed very well except when some of the more personal remarks were too embarrassing for me to translate.

It was difficult for most of the women to sing the *romanzas*[4] in an alien environment without the inspiration of an occasion such as an engagement party, a holiday, an important visitor. As they became accustomed to the room and the equipment, they began to relax, and the singing became less strained as the ballads of King Tarquino, Turunja, the Three Sisters, the Little Moors, the Three Doves, and the King of France were sung in the slow deliberate style that had been taught from generation to generation since the expulsion from Spain 1492.

La Tía was totally unimpressed, but she behaved like a professional, waiting quietly for her turn. Her voice is recorded asking during an interruption if the light went out, referring to the electrical connection of the machine, and should she cut short her story; she continued the recitation without a break in the thread of the tale.

Once I asked La Tía where she had learned these stories. According to her, everyone learned from hearing them in childhood. Not everyone remembered them because they weren't as interested or had poor memories. At the coffee-houses frequented only by men, there were often merchants and mariners who told tales of wonder, and there was a natural exchange and exaggeration. So it was usually the men who were the storytellers, especially on the Sabbath when not only work was forbidden, but also smoking, writing,

4. Traditional Sephardic poems in the oral tradition, recited by women at family celebrations such as circumcisions, engagement parties, weddings.

and playing cards. The Sabbath was spent going to the *Kehillah*,[5] eating, napping, singing, and storytelling.

"May he be in Paradise," La Tía would say, referring to her deceased husband, "he used to take care of me as the eyes in his face. Wherever he went, he took me so that I often traveled to many places many women couldn't go. As he was a merchant he had many customers from France, Italy, Greece, Persia, and other places, who were invited to our home. Although I couldn't sit with the men, as I served the food with the help of my maid, I would hear much of what they were saying, and I learned a lot. They would talk about their countries, their customs, their tales. You can't imagine the marvels they would relate. There is nothing here that compares to the wonders of Europe and the East."

I pointed out the beauties of Mt. Rainier, Mt. Baker, the Cascades, the Olympics, Lake Washington, and Puget Sound, all surrounding Seattle.

"Very nice," she would say condescendingly, "but *crudo*[raw]. Where are the magnificent palaces and buildings, the intricately carved cornices and pillars, the exquisite rugs? Where are the cafes? Where are the beautifully dressed men and women? This is a new country but you still keep the old-fashioned customs that we have already forgotten in Estambol." She was referring to the display of the bride's trousseau for everyone to see, the inordinate amount of housecleaning and the many superstitions of Seattle's Sephardic women.

The last time I saw La Tía was on a Saturday, just before she left for Los Angeles to live with relatives who had moved there. Except for a more pronounced shaking of her head, she hadn't changed much. She was seated in her favorite corner of the *minder*. I could see her eyes glittering behind her glasses. There was little that escaped her attention. I was always grateful to her for not asking me why I was not married. She knew I was teaching Spanish in Olympia and asked me how my work was coming along.

Estreya and the other women were putting finishing touches to the big *desayuno*, what we now call a brunch. I think it was Succoth, but since it was raining we were in the kitchen instead of the *Succah*[6] in the backyard. We had to wait for the men to return from the *Kehillah*. The table was covered with a white linen cloth. On it were placed plates of salted raw fish, white cheeses, ripe olives, tomatoes, *fila* pastries filled with cheese, potatoes, spinach, eggplant, hard-boiled eggs, rolls covered with sesame seeds, cookies with a raki[7] flavor and a large *pan de españa*, sponge cake, a sweet reminder of a bitter experience.

The men entered saying, "*Shabbat shalom*," and kissed their fingers, then touched the *mezuzah*[8] on the door. We could see the white tassels of the prayer garment hanging below their jackets. After taking off their coats and putting aside the *taledes*[9] in their velvet cases, they washed their hands. They

5. The Jewish community (Hebrew); here, the synagogue, perhaps.

6. During the Jewish harvest festival of Sukkot, or the Festival of Booths, each family builds a *succah*, a temporary shelter or booth with a roof open to the stars, in which the family eats and traditionally sleeps for the holiday week.

7. Anise.

8. A small parchment scroll on which verses from Deuteronomy have been written; it is nailed to the doorposts of houses, and rooms within those houses, belonging to Jews, according to Jewish law (Deuteronomy 6.9 and 11.20). "*Shabbat shalom*": Good Sabbath (Hebrew).

9. Prayer shawls (Ladino for the Hebrew *tallitot*, plural of *tallit*).

didn't remove their hats since the men's heads had to be covered during the prayers and even while eating. Haim walked to the cupboard where the bottle of raki was kept. The white liquor was poured into tiny glasses for the first blessing; only the older women beginning with La Tía were given some also. After the first blessing, they said, "*Salud, beracha, buyurun*" in Spanish, Hebrew, and Turkish, meaning: please, sit down, and begin eating.

There was not much conversation during the meal except for complimenting the cooks, *bendichas manos*, blessed hands, or a teasing *te afitó el horno*, the oven was in good form. After the final blessings, the men sang *pizmonim* and told tales from the Midrash.[1] The women were busy with the serving of the meal and they listened more than they talked. La Tía remained seated in her favorite corner and took out her *tespil*. She knew her place and the conversation around her was concerned with tidbits of local gossip. The men would bring the news exchanged at the *Kehillah*, relating it with relish. The dishes were scraped as unobtrusively as possible since the actual dishwashing could be done only after dark, at the end of the Sabbath.

When it was time to leave, I thanked Tanti Estreya, as I called her and the other ladies who were close friends of my mother even though they were not my aunts. I kissed and embraced La Tía.

"My, my," said my mother, "we don't kiss the hand anymore, do we. We are living in modern times. There is not the same respect. Our grandchildren will never know how we lived. It will seem like fairy tales to them."

Everyone was quiet at this observation.

"Don't say that, Anna," said La Tía. "Didn't you tell us that our customs will be preserved by scholars and put in books? Isn't Amada doing all her work to keep these memories?"

I couldn't help but kiss her again for having understood and her faith in me.

"*Ya basta*, that's enough," she said softly, "*Aide, novia*, it is time for you to marry."

We lost touch with each other, and in 1940, the year after I was married, my mother wrote me the sad news that La Tía had died in California of pneumonia, following an accident.

I put aside my Sephardic studies for 30 years and when *la hora buena*, the right time came, I opened up my collection of folktales that were not included in my thesis. As I reread La Tía's tales, I had a most unusual experience. She had been tucked away in the cells of my memory, completely intact. She was as alive, as charming, as interesting, as I had left her in 1938.

1981, 1996

1. Collections of rabbinic interpretations of the Hebrew Bible. "*Pizmonim*": plural of *pizmon*, a genre of poem praising God and characterized by a refrain. Later, *pizmonim* designated poems or songs in general, especially those composed in

GABRIEL PREIL
1911–1993

Eyneni binyu-york, writes Gabriel Preil, "I am not in New York." Actually he *is* in New York, but persisting as a Hebrew poet there somehow locates him somewhere else—perhaps in a literary-spiritual homeland, perhaps everywhere and nowhere. Emigrants, exiles, and especially Jews, for millennia a people with no dwelling place of their own, have lived with language as the only homeland. This could be any diaspora language—think of Paul Celan in Paris with his Hapsburg German and, indeed, Edmond Jabès there with his Egyptian French. More likely, Yiddish would be the Jew's portable homeland. Preil must have observed with some interest the phenomenal success of Isaac Bashevis Singer (1904–1991), sustaining and sustained by Yiddish in America's golden land of promise for whoever adopted her ways. But there were so many Yiddish speakers in the *goldene medina*, and unlike Preil's unassuming lyrics, Singer's fiction found multiple translators for its enticing style and themes. Many other Yiddish authors also managed, at least during the immigrant first generation, but most Hebrew poets in America left for Israel. Before Preil, there was one who stayed: Ephraim Lisitzky (1885–1962), who came from Minsk at fifteen. "Do anything, be anything, peddle candles and matches—sell windbags and bubbles," a fellow poet urged him. "Be a tailor, a shoemaker, a cobbler—anything but a Hebrew poet in America."

Gabriel Preil was born on August 21, 1911, in Dorpat, Estonia, and was raised in Lithuania. "My grandfather was a Hebrew writer and a rabbi in a small town," says Preil, who at eight decided to publish a Hebrew periodical. Coming to the United States with his mother in 1922, he attended seminary and took various jobs. While avidly absorbing English and American literature, he began writing poetry in Yiddish, his mother tongue at home, influenced by Jacob Glatstein and the *In Zikh* movement. In the 1930s, he started making Hebrew versions of his Yiddish lyrics and later published some poems in both languages simultaneously. He also made Hebrew translations of Edwin Arlington Robinson, Carl Sandburg, Robert Frost, Robinson Jeffers, and Wallace Stevens.

Preil's lyrics respond to everyday or momentary things—events, landscapes, thoughts, memories—in conversational yet imagistic free verse. Although he did not visit Israel until 1967, he influenced younger Israeli poets, such as Natan Zach, in breaking away from the elevated, controlled verse of their founding fathers. "I work in isolation, rooted in Israeli literature, affected by English and American influences," Preil said. It is oddly refreshing, for instance, to hear Preil's Hebrew encounter "Food in Maine / a modest parade of potatoes . . . / the dazzle, the sudden flare of blueberries." Yet exile still obtains. Living in the Bronx, "I sink in mud . . . / I am not in New York." And an earlier poem opens tellingly with "My pen wandering / over this paper desert." Gabriel Preil died on June 5, 1993.

I Am Not in New York

I am enclosed in a town beyond the sea,
I sink in mud, drown in fancies,
a bachelor playing little games,
pursuing a romanticism far from Byronic,[1]
wooing dreams—soon fabricated, sooner crumbling—

1. A reference to George Gordon Lord Byron (1788–1824), a Romantic poet renowned as a "gloomy egoist."

among houses patched with the sadness
or renunciations.

My former geography
duplicates itself
in the mirror of this evening's sunset.
More and more it makes itself known to me.
In a little while I shall meet Gnessin[2] in a heavy rain.

I am not in New York.

English, 1985

Van Gogh. Williamsburg[1]

My pen wandering
over this paper desert
cannot, this time,
capture on its point
the pain flowing between endless shores,
the image glowing hot and dark.

Cool plaques of bronze
revive the memory
of a poet's distant afternoons,
but my time of afternoons
today
foams with a Van Gogh's
colors of despair,
and a thousand sunset drums
shiver the window-panes.

Tomorrow I shall slip away
to orchard skies of Torah.[2]
Maybe there in Williamsburg,
where a pacified, brute summer reigns,
they cork rich wines of ancient prayer.
And it may be
the mirror of my room
will no longer show
the desert face
of a Job-like Jew.[3]

Hebrew, 1968 English, 1985

2. Uri Gnessin (1881–1913), a Hebrew author who lived in Poland and Russia, except for a brief stay in Palestine in 1907.

1. A section of Brooklyn, New York, that is home to many Orthodox Jews. "Van Gogh": Dutch painter Vincent Van Gogh (1853–1890), famous for his broad, expressive brushwork and heightened colors depicting peasant, rural, and domestic life. He went mad and committed suicide.
2. The five books of Moses.
3. From the biblical book of Job, who is the prototype for staunch faith in the face of great suffering.

Moving

In my old neighborhood the finest Hasidim[1]
made bridges of the street.
Henry Miller,[2] on the other hand,
invented for himself a vagabond.
I, in that same place,
bore on my shoulder
birds of Hebrew song,
while ships departed for one sea or another.

Now my new, my seething neighborhood
seems glad to make me old,
even though Heine[3] blossoms here
from clouded marble,
and another poet[4] keeps saying
that only God makes trees.

Both are younger than a morning smile,
but even one as tired of banalities as I am
accepts unquestioningly that banal observation:
no one can make time green.

Hebrew, 1972 English, 1985

The Eternal Present

My mother's uncle was physician to the Persian Shah.
Before this, or later, he built bridges near the Caspian Sea.[1]
His greying photograph attests to his youth in 1888,
in Lithuania, close to the East Prussian border,
in the spring of a good wheat-year.

I don't know, however, the exact date of his sister's marriage,
but she gave birth to a daughter in the above-mentioned spring,
and she is, and has been for a long time now,
my mother—a baby-girl grown old.

And the summers and winters arrive in New York
year after year
and there is no then.
I am not a forgotten ring in a chain or a beloved heir.
I am a man engaged in talk this moment,
or biting into a pear, or drinking tea,
or listening behind the shutters
to the voice of the cantor on a Saturday night.

1. Pious Jews, members of a mystical sect originating in 18th-century Poland.
2. An American author (1891–1980) noted for his explicitly sexual work.
3. Heinrich Heine (1797–1856), a German Jewish poet and critic.
4. I.e., Joyce Kilmer (1886–1918), famous for his poem *Trees* (1913).
1. The world's largest inland lake (143, 550 square miles), extending north of Iran (Persia).

Here, of course, there is no mere historic documentary.
One present of dark and light exists.
There is no then.

Hebrew, 1976 English, 1985

KATE SIMON
1912–1990

Kate Simon was born Kaila Grobsmith, in a Warsaw, Poland, ghetto and came to America in 1917. The daughter of a shoe designer, sample maker, and corsetiere, Simon spent her childhood in a working-class neighborhood in the Bronx, New York. Simon was raised in a time and place where a girl's first priority should have been marriage, but she transgressed conventional mores in favor of the life her mother advised: college and a profession.

A graduate of Hunter College of the City University of New York, Simon cut her literary teeth in a genre rarely glorified for its aesthetic value—the travel guide. But in Simon's hands, the genre was transformed. Known for their "rare good taste and discernment," Simon's travel guides exhibited an "urbane and witty style" and earned her high artistic marks in a field where artistry is often, if anything, an afterthought. In this same sophisticated and informed style, Simon began to write novels and memoirs.

Bronx Primitive: Portraits of a Childhood (1982), from which this chapter is drawn, is the first of her three memoirs. Set in the Bronx of her childhood, *Bronx Primitive* is written in the same open, honest, witty manner as her guidebooks, but tells the story of her childhood spent in a poor immigrant neighborhood in the northernmost borough of New York, "where her Borghese Garden was Crotona Park, her cultural mecca the neighborhood library, and her Museum of Natural History the tenement hallways." The word "primitive" in Simon's title plays on a term from art history, such as "American primitive," for artists without formal training who render commonplace scenes or portraits. This memoir offers a first-generation tale of a young Jewish girl learning the ropes of dating, of societal pressures, and of the distance between her upbringing and that of "real" Americans.

The quality of Simon's prose and her uncompromising directness distinguish *Bronx Primitive* from similar stories. The *Los Angeles Times* praised the book, saying it "recalls the 1920s with piercing clarity, and while the ingredients are familiar, the results are often unexpected. There are unfiltered memories of the immigrant experience, with the grounds still settling and a slight sharp aftertaste."

Kate Simon is the author of three autobiographies (*Bronx Primitive, A Wider World* [1986], and *Etching in an Hourglass* [1990]) as well as many works of nonfiction, including *Fifth Avenue: A Very Social Story* (1978) and *A Renaissance Tapestry: The Gonzaga of Mantua* (1988).

From Bronx Primitive: Portraits of a Childhood

Five

THE MOVIES AND OTHER SCHOOLS

Life on Lafontaine offered several schools. School-school, P.S. 59, was sometimes nice, as when I was chosen to be Prosperity in the class play, blond, plump, dressed in a white pillow case banded with yellow and green crepe paper, for the colors of grasses and grain, and waving something like a sheaf of wheat. The cringing days were usually Fridays, when arithmetic flash cards, too fast, too many, blinded me and I couldn't add or subtract the simplest numbers. (For many years, into adulthood, I carried around a sack of churning entrails on Friday mornings.) The library, which made me my own absolutely special and private person with a card that belonged to no one but me, offered hundreds of books, all mine and no tests on them, a brighter, more generous school than P.S. 59. The brightest, most informative school was the movies. We learned how tennis was played and golf, what a swimming pool was and what to wear if you ever got to drive a car. We learned how tables were set, "How do you do? Pleased to meet you," how primped and starched little girls should be, how neat and straight boys should be, even when they were temporarily ragamuffins. We learned to look up soulfully and make our lips tremble to warn our mothers of a flood of tears, and though they didn't fall for it (they laughed), we kept practicing. We learned how regal mothers were and how stately fathers, and of course we learned about Love, a very foreign country like maybe China or Connecticut. It was smooth and slinky, it shone and rustled. It was petals with Lillian Gish, gay flags with Marion Davies, tiger stripes with Rudolph Valentino, dog's eyes with Charlie Ray.[1] From what I could see, and I searched, there was no Love on the block, nor even its fairy-tale end, Marriage. We had only Being Married, and that included the kids, a big crowded barrel with a family name stamped on it. Of course, there was Being Married in the movies, but except for the terrible cruel people in rags and scowls, it was as silky as Love. Fathers kissed their wives and children when they came home from work and spoke to them quietly and nobly, like kings, and never shouted or hit if the kids came in late or dirty. Mothers in crisp dresses stroked their children's heads tenderly as they presented them with the big ringletted doll and the football Grandma had sent, adding, "Run off and play, darlings." "Darling," "dear," were movie words, and we had few grandmothers, most of them dead or in shadowy conversation pieces reported from At Home, the Old Country. And "Run off and play" was so superbly refined, silken gauze to the rough wool of our hard-working mothers whose rules were to feed their children, see that they were warmly dressed in the wintertime, and run to the druggist on Third Avenue for advice when they were sick. Beyond that it was mostly "Get out of my way." Not all the mothers were so impatient. Miltie's mother helped him with his arithmetic homework; my mother often found us amus-

1. All were famous movie stars of the 1920s and 1930s. Lillian Gish (1893–1993) was considered the "first lady" of the silent screen. The career of silent-screen star Marion Davies (1897–1961) was relatively short, but she was newpaper and magazine publisher William Randolph Hearst's mistress for thirty-six years. Rudolph Valentino (1895–1926), famous as "the Sheik," became America's first great film lover and matinee idol. Actor, producer, director Charles Ray (1891–1943) was known primarily for his country-boy-in-the-big-city roles.

ing and laughed with and at us a lot. From other apartments, on rainy afternoons: Joey—"What'll I do, Maaa?" His Mother—*"Va te ne! Gherradi!"* (the Italian version of "Get out of here"); Lily—"What'll I do, Maaa?" Mrs. Stavicz—"Scratch your ass on a broken bottle." I sometimes wished my mother would say colorful, tough things like that but I wasn't sure I wouldn't break into tears if she did, which would make her call me a *"pianovi chasto"* (as I remember the Polish phrase), a delicate meringue cake that falls apart easily, which would make me cry more, which would make her more lightly contemptuous, and so on. Despite my occasional wish to see her as one of the big-mouth, storming women, I was willing to settle for her more modest distinction, a lady who won notebooks in her English class at the library and sang many tunes from "Polish operettas" that, with later enlightenment, I realized were *The Student Prince* and *The Merry Widow*.[2]

Being Married had as an important ingredient a nervous father. There must have been other kitchens, not only ours, in which at about seven o'clock, the fathers' coming-home time, children were warned, "Now remember, Papa is coming home soon. He's nervous from working in the factory all day and riding in the crowded El. Sit quiet at the table, don't laugh, don't talk." It was hard not to giggle at the table, when my brother and I, who played with keen concentration a game of mortal enemies at other times, became close conspirators at annoying Them by making faces at each other. The muffled giggles were stopped by a shout of "Respect!" and a long black look, fork poised like a sword in midair while no one breathed. After the silent meal, came the part we disliked most, the after-dinner lecture. There were two. The first was The Hard Life of the Jewish worker, the Jewish father, the deepest funereal sounds unstopped for the cost of electricity (a new and lovely toy but not as pretty as throbbing little mazda lamps)[3] for which he had to pay an immense sum each time we switched it on and off, like the wastrels we were. Did we think butter cost a penny a pound that we slathered it on bread as if it were Coney Island mud pies? Those good expensive shoes he bought us (he was an expert shoe worker, a maker of samples, and tortured us with embarrassment when he displayed his expertise to the salesman, so don't try to fool him), which were old and scuffed and dirty within a week, did we know how much bloody sweat was paid for them? The second lecture was the clever one whose proud, sententious repetitions I listened to with shame for him, wanting to put my head down not to see my handsome father turn into a vaudeville comic whose old monologues strained and fell. This lecture was usually inspired by my brother who, in spite of the "nervous" call, dashed at my father as soon as he heard the key in the lock with "Hello, Pa. Gimme a penny?" That led it off: "You say you want a penny, *only* a penny. I've got dimes and quarters and half-dollars in my pockets, you say, so what's a penny to me? Well, let's see. If you went to the El station and gave the man four cents, he wouldn't let you on the train, you'd need another penny. If Mama gave you two cents for a three-cent ice cream cone, would Mrs. Katz in the candy store give it to you? If Mama had only forty-eight cents for a forty-nine-cent chicken, would the butcher give it to her?" And on and on, a carefully rehearsed long slow aria, with dramatic runs of words

2. *The Student Prince* (1924), by Sigmund Romberg, and *The Merry Widow* (1905), by Franz Lehár, were popular operettas.

3. A type of decorative lamp, originating in Japan, that was a huge fad in the 1920s.

and significant questioning pauses. Once or twice I heard my mother mutter as she went out of the room, "That Victrola record again," but her usual policy was to say nothing. She was not afraid of my father, nor particularly in awe of him. (I heard him say frequently how fresh she was, but with a smile, not the way he said it to us.)

In none of my assiduous eavesdropping on the street did I ever hear any mention of unhappy marriage or happy marriage. Married was married. Although a Jewish divorce was a singularly easy matter except for the disgrace it carried, the Jewish women were as firmly imbedded in their marriages as the Catholic. A divorce was as unthinkable as adultery or lipstick. No matter what—beatings, infidelity, drunkenness, verbal abuse, outlandish demands—no woman could run the risk of making her children fatherless. Marriage and children were fate, like being skinny, like skeletal Mr. Roberts, or humpbacked, like the leering watchman at the hat factory. *"Es is mir beschert,"* "It is my fate," was a common sighing phrase, the Amen that closed hymns of woe.

My mother didn't accept her fate as a forever thing. She began to work during our school hours after her English classes had taught her as much as they could, and while I was still young, certainly no more than ten, I began to get her lecture on being a woman. It ended with extraordinary statements, shocking in view of the street mores. "Study. Learn. Go to college. Be a schoolteacher," then a respected, privileged breed, "and don't get married until you have a profession. With a profession you can have men friends and even children, if you want. You're free. But don't get married, at least not until you can support yourself and make a careful choice. Or don't get married at all, better still." This never got into "My mother said" conversations with my friends. I sensed it to be too outrageous. My mother was already tagged "The Princess" because she never went into the street unless fully, carefully dressed: no grease-stained housedress, no bent, melted felt slippers. Rarely, except when she was pregnant with my little sister, did she stop for conversations on the street. She was one of the few in the building who had gone to classes, the only mother who went out alone at night to join her mandolin group. She was sufficiently marked, and though I was proud of her difference, I didn't want to report her as altogether eccentric. In the community fabric, as heavy as the soups we ate and the dark, coarse "soldier's bread" we chomped on, as thick as the cotton on which we practiced our cross-stitch embroidery, was the conviction that girls were to marry as early as possible, the earlier the more triumphant. (Long after we moved from the area, my mother, on a visit to Lafontaine to see appealing, inept little Fannie Herman who had for many years been her charge and mine, met Mrs. Roth, who asked about me. When my mother said I was going to Hunter College, Mrs. Roth, looking both pleased and sympathetic, said, "*My* Helen married a man who makes a nice living, a laundry man. Don't worry, your Katie will find a husband soon." She knew that some of the boys of the block wound up in City College, but a girl in college? From a pretty, polite child, I must have turned into an ugly, bad-tempered shrew whom no one would have. Why else would my marrying years be spent in college?)

I never saw my mother and father kiss or stroke each other as people did in the movies. In company she addressed him, as did most of the Jewish women, by our family name, a mark of respectful distance. They inhabited two separate worlds, he adventuring among anti-Semites to reach a shadowy dungeon called "Factory," where he labored ceaselessly. In the evening he returned to her world for food, bed, children, and fighting. We were accustomed to fighting: the boys and, once in a while, fiery little girls tearing at each other in the street; bigger Italian boys punching and being punched by the Irish gangs that wandered in from Arthur Avenue; females fighting over clotheslines—whose sheets were blocking whose right to the sun—bounced around the courtyard constantly. The Genoese in the houses near 178th Street never spoke to the Sicilians near 179th Street except to complain that somebody's barbaric little southern slob had peed against a northern tree. To my entranced ears and eyes, the Sicilians seemed always to win, hotter, louder, faster with *"Fangu"*—the southern version of *"Fa' in culo"* (up yours)—than the aristocrats who retired before the Sicilians could hit them with *"Mortacci"*—the utterly insupportable insult. My brother and I fought over who grabbed the biggest apple, who hid the skate key, and where he put my baby picture, I lying on a white rug with my bare ass showing, a picture he threatened to pass among his friends and humiliate me beyond recovery. I would have to kill him.

These sorts of fighting were almost literally the spice of daily life, deliciously, lightly menacing, grotesque and entertaining. The fighting between my mother and father was something else entirely, at times so threatening that I still, decades later, cringe in paralyzed stupidity, as if I were being pelted with stones, when I hear a man shouting. The fights often concerned our conduct and my mother's permissiveness. My father had a rich vocabulary which he shaped into theatrical phrases spoken in a voice as black and dangerous as an open sewer. The opening shot was against my brother, who was six or seven when the attacks began. He was becoming a wilderness boy, no sense, no controls, dirty, disobedient, he did badly in school (not true: with a minimum of attention he managed mediocrity). There was no doubt that he would become a bum, then a thief, wind up alone in a prison cell full of rats, given one piece of bread a day and one cup of dirty water. He would come out a gangster and wind up in the electric chair.

When it was my turn, I was disobedient and careless; I didn't do my homework when I should, I didn't practice enough, my head was always in a book, I was always in the street running wild with the Italian and Polish beasts. I didn't take proper care of my brother, I climbed with boys, I ran with boys, I skated with them on far streets. Mr. Kaplan had seen me and told him. And how would this life, this playing with boys, end? I would surely become a street girl, a prostitute, and wind up being shipped to a filthy, diseased brothel crawling with hairy tropical bugs, in Buenos Aires. My mother's response was sharp and short: we acted like other children and played like other children; it was he who was at fault, asking more of us than he should. And enough about prisons and electric chairs and brothels. He went on shouting, entranced by his gorgeous words and visions, until she left the room to wash the dishes or scrub the kitchen floor. We, of course, had heard everything from our bedroom; the oratory was as much for us as for our mother. When the big rats in the windowless cell came to our ears, my brother began to shake with terror beyond crying. I tried to comfort him, as accustomed a role as trying to maim him. I didn't know what a street girl was, and I certainly didn't know what a brothel was, but I wasn't afraid—I was too angry. If our father hated us so, why didn't he go away? I didn't examine consequences, who would feed us and pay the rent. I just wanted him out, out, dead.

Other fights were about money, and that, too, involved us. How dare she, without consulting him, change from a fifty-cent-a-lesson piano teacher to another—and who knows how good *he* was?—who charged a dollar? What about the embroidered tablecloth and the stone bowl with the pigeons that she bought from the Arab peddler, that crook. Did she realize how hard he had to work to pay for our school supplies each fall? And add to that the nickel for candy to eat at the movies every Saturday, and the ten cents each for the movie and the three cents for ice-cream cones on Friday nights. And God only knew how much money she slipped us for the sweet garbage we chewed on, which would certainly rot our teeth, and where would he get the money for dentists? Maybe she thought she was still in her shop in Warsaw, dancing and singing and spilling money like a fool. And on and on it went. These tirades, too, were answered very briefly. Our lives were meager enough. Did he ever think of buying us even the cheapest toy, like the other fathers did, instead of stashing every spare penny in the bank and taking it out only for his relatives? The ignorant Italians he so despised, they had celebrations for their children. Where were our birthday presents?

Long silences followed these fights and we became messengers. "Tell your mother to take my shoes to the shoemaker." "Aw, Pa, I'm doing my homework. Later." "Tell your mother I have no clean shirts." "Aw, Pa, I'm just sitting down to practice. I'll tell her later." We used the operative words "homework" and "practice" mercilessly while he seethed at our delays. My mother heard all these instructions but it was her role neither to notice nor to obey. Those were great days and we exploited our roles fattily, with enormous vengeful pleasure.

One constant set of squabbles that didn't circle around us concerned her relaxed, almost loose judgments of other people. She showed no sympathy when he complained about the nigger sweeper in the factory who talked back to him, when he complained about the Italian who reeked of garlic and almost suffocated him in the train. Most loudly he complained about her availability, spoiling his sleep, letting his supper get cold, neglecting her own children, to run to any Italian idiot who didn't know to take care of her own baby. Let them take care of their own convulsions or get some Wop[4] neighbor to help. It was disgraceful that she sat on Mrs. Santini's porch in open daylight trying to teach her not to feed her infant from her own mouth. If the fat fool wanted to give it germs, let her. If it died, she'd, next year, have another; they bred like rabbits. Why didn't my mother mind her own business, what the hell did these people, these foreign ignoramuses, mean to her? The answer was short and always the same, *"Es is doch a mench,"* yet these are human beings, the only religious training we ever had, perhaps quite enough.

There were fights with no messengers, no messages, whispered fights when the door to our bedroom was shut tight and we heard nothing but hissing. The slow unfolding of time and sophistications indicated that these were fights about women, women my father saw some of those evenings when he

4. The derogatory term for a person of Italian descent.

said he was going to a Workmen's Circle[5] meeting. There was no more "Tell your mother," "Tell your father," and except for the crying of our baby, no more evening sounds. No Caruso, no Rosa Ponselle,[6] no mandolin practice, no lectures. My father busied himself with extra piecework, "skiving" it was called, cutting with breathtaking delicacy leaf and daisy designs into the surface of the sample shoes to be shown to buyers. She, during one such period, crocheted a beaded bag, tiny beads, tiny stitches. We watched, struck dumb by their skill, and because it was no time to open our mouths about anything, anything at all. The silence was dreadful, a creeping, dark thing, a night alley before the murderer appears. The furniture was waiting to be destroyed, the windows to be broken, by a terrible storm. We would all be swept away, my brother and I to a jungle where wild animals would eat us, my parents and the baby, separated, to starve and burn alone in a desert. School now offered the comforts of a church, the street its comforting familiarities, unchanging, predictable. We stayed out as long as we could, dashing up for a speedy supper, and down again. On rainy nights we read a lot, we went to bed early, anything to remove us from our private-faced parents, who made us feel unbearably shy.

One spring evening, invited to jump Double Dutch with a few experts, uncertain that I could leap between two ropes whipping in rapid alternation at precisely the exact moment, and continue to stay between them in small fast hops from side to side, I admitted a need, urgent for some time, to go to the toilet. I ran up the stairs to find our door locked, an extraordinary thing. Maybe they had run away. Maybe they had killed each other. Sick with panic, I kept trying the door, it wouldn't give. Then I heard the baby making squirmy, sucking baby noises. No matter what, my mother would never leave the baby, and anyway, maybe they were doing their whispering fighting again. Still uneasy, I knocked on the Hermans' door and asked to use their toilet. When I came out, I asked Fannie Herman if she knew whether my parents were at home. Yes, she said. Her door was wide open and she would have seen or heard them come out, but they hadn't. The Double Dutch on the street was finished when I got down so I joined the race, boys and girls, around the block, running hard, loving my pumping legs and my swinging arms and my open mouth swallowing the breeze. When most of the kids had gone home and it was time for us, too, I couldn't find my brother, who was hiding from me to destroy my power and maybe get me into trouble. I went up alone. The door had been unlocked, and as I walked uneasily through the long hallway of our railroad flat with wary steps, I heard sounds from the kitchen. My mother was sitting on a kitchen chair, her feet in a basin of water. My father was kneeling before her on spread newspaper. Her plump foot rested in his big hand while he cut her toenails, flashing his sharp work knife, dexterous, light, and swift. She was splashing him a little, playing the water with her free foot. They were making jokes, lilting, laughing. Something, another branch in the twisted tree that shaded our lives, was going to keep us safe for a while.

1982

5. A Jewish fraternal organization with strong prolabor and socialist affiliations.
6. Tenor Enrico Caruso (1873–1921) and coloratura soprano Rosa Ponselle (1897–1981) were popular opera singers; Caruso was Ponselle's mentor.

TILLIE OLSEN
b. 1913

"Time on the bus, even when I had to stand, was enough; the stolen moments at work, enough; the deep night hours for as long as I could stay awake, after the kids were in bed, after the household tasks were done, sometimes during. It is no accident that the first work I considered publishable began: 'I stand here ironing.' " Tillie Olsen's eloquent, idiosyncratic book *Silences* (1978) lets us know what has stilled or stifled many writers: class, sex, also race and age. For her, religion was a hindrance only in that immigrant Jewish families had such straitened circumstances, economically and educationally. Although her writing is not marked overtly by Jewishness as such, Olsen's radical background shapes her whole outlook. And *Yiddishkeit* permeates *Tell Me a Riddle,* her finest story, in both spirit and language.

Tillie Olsen was born in 1913 (or 1912) in Omaha (or Mead or Wahoo), Nebraska. Her parents took part in the 1905 Russian revolution. After her father escaped from a czarist prison, they fled to the United States and settled on a farm. Later he became secretary of the Nebraska Socialist party. From her mother, illiterate until her twenties, Olsen absorbed a capacity for humane resourcefulness and communal responsibility. She strongly remembers labor strife in the 1920s, reading revolutionary pamphlets, the oratory of William Jennings Bryan and Clarence Darrow as well as socialists such as Eugene Debs, and hearing Carl Sandburg read in Omaha. After eleventh grade, she left school to work, joined the Young Communist League, and was jailed for a month for passing out handbills to packinghouse workers.

In 1932, Olsen became pregnant and in the same month began writing a novel about the wear and tear on a working-class family. Then a daughter was born, Olsen was "terribly, terribly poor," and she moved to San Francisco in 1933. The next year, *Partisan Review* published a story drawn from her novel that was enthusiastically received, but she could not finish the writing. Motherhood and political work took over: she married Jack Olsen, a labor activist born in Kiev, had three more daughters, took various jobs, worked for the CIO and the PTA, and wrote when she could. After the war, both she and her husband were harassed by the House Un-American Activities Committee and the FBI.

Finally, as soon as her youngest child was in school, Olsen took a creative-writing class at San Francisco State, then in 1955 received a fellowship from Stanford University; "I made the mysterious turn and became a writing writer." She wrote the stories that appeared in *Tell Me a Riddle* (1961); her title story won the O. Henry award that year and has been read and revered ever since. While continuing to be politically and socially active, she taught as well as helped recover women's writing, especially Rebecca Harding Davis's 1861 *Life in the Iron Mills,* which the Feminist Press published in 1972. Then, forty years after beginning her working-class novel, Olsen came upon chapters and scraps of it and reworked them as *Yonnondio: From the Thirties* (1974), named after Walt Whitman's lament for American aborigines. She cites Whitman: "No picture, poem, statement, passing them to the future: / Yonnondio! Yonnondio!—unlimn'd they disappear . . . / Then blank and gone and still, and utterly lost."

Much the same sentiment of loss and writerly recovery holds good for the story *Tell Me a Riddle,* which Olsen says she wrote to "celebrate a generation of revolutionaries." Of course, it basically celebrates (if that's the word) the generation of her parents, limned as David and Eva in the story. After forty-seven years of quarrelsome yet bonded marriage, the mother is dying of cancer; her husband thinks they should move to the old Workmen's home, where there's "a reading circle. Chekhov they read that you like, and Peretz." But Eva wants "at last to live within, and not move to the rhythm of others." And "still the springs, the springs were in her seeking." Motherhood, which could swallow the springs of a writer's life, also forms the heart of Tillie Olsen's vision, her sense of generational richness and of a baby's infinite potential. "Yiddish in me," she says, "is inextricable from what is woman in me, from woman who is mother." At the same time, Eva repudiates traditional Judaism. She is "not for rabbis. . . . Tell them to write: Race, human; Religion, none." On the Sabbath blessings, her curse falls in age-old rhythms: "Candles bought instead of bread and stuck into a potato for a candlestick? Religion that stifled and said: in Paradise, woman, you will be the footstool of your husband, and in life—poor chosen Jew—ground under, despised, trembling in cellars. And cremated. And cremated." What heritage then? "To smash all ghettos that divide us—not to go back, not to go back—this to teach." That is, secular Jewish utopianism.

Tell Me a Riddle

1.

For forty-seven years they had been married. How deep back the stubborn, gnarled roots of the quarrel reached, no one could say—but only now, when tending to the needs of others no longer shackled them together, the roots swelled up visible, split the earth between them, and the tearing shook even to the children, long since grown.

Why now, why now? wailed Hannah.

As if when we grew up weren't enough, said Paul.

Poor Ma. Poor Dad. It hurts so for both of them, said Vivi. They never had very much; at least in old age they should be happy.

Knock their heads together, insisted Sammy; tell 'em: you're too old for this kind of thing; no reason not to get along now.

Lennie wrote to Clara: They've lived over so much together; what could possibly tear them apart?

Something tangible enough.

Arthritic hands, and such work as he got, occasional. Poverty all his life, and there was little breath left for the running. He could not, could not turn away from this desire: to have the troubling of responsibility, the fretting with money, over and done with; to be free, to be *care*free where success was not measured by accumulation, and there was use for the vitality still in him.

There was a way. They could sell the house, and with the money join his lodge's Haven, cooperative for the aged. Happy communal life, and was he not already an official; had he not helped organize it, raise funds, served as a trustee?

But she—would not consider it.

"What do we need all this for?" he would ask loudly, for her hearing aid was turned down and the vacuum was shrilling. "Five rooms" (pushing the sofa so she could get into the corner) "furniture" (smoothing down the rug) "floors and surfaces to make work. Tell me, why do we need it?" And he was glad he could ask in a scream.

"Because I'm use't."

"Because you're use't. This is a reason, Mrs. Word Miser? Used to can get unused!"

"Enough unused I have to get used to already . . . Not enough words?" turning off the vacuum a moment to hear herself answer. "Because soon enough we'll need only a little closet, no windows, no furniture, nothing to make work but for worms. Because now I want room . . . Screech and blow like you're doing, you'll need that closet even sooner . . . Ha, again!" for the vacuum bag wailed, puffed half up, hung stubbornly limp. "This time fix it so it stays; quick before the phone rings and you get too important-busy."

But while he struggled with the motor, it seethed in him. Why fix it? Why have to bother? And if it can't be fixed, have to wring the mind with how to pay the repair? At the Haven they come in with their own machines to clean your room or your cottage; you fish, or play cards, or make jokes in the sun, not with knotty fingers fight to mend vacuums.

Over the dishes, coaxingly: "For once in your life, to be free, to have everything done for you, like a queen."

"I never liked queens."

"No dishes, no garbage, no towel to sop, no worry what to buy, what to eat."

"And what else would I do with my empty hands? Better to eat at my own table when I want, and to cook and eat how I want."

"In the cottages they buy what you ask, and cook it how you like. *You* are the one who always used to say: better mankind born without mouths and stomachs than always to worry for money to buy, to shop, to fix, to cook, to wash, to clean."

"How cleverly you hid that you heard. I said it then because eighteen hours a day I ran. And you never scraped a carrot or knew a dish towel sops. Now—for you and me—who cares? A herring out of a jar is enough. But when *I* want, and nobody to bother." And she turned off her ear button, so she would not have to hear.

But as *he* had no peace, juggling and rejuggling the money to figure: how will I pay for this now?; prying out the storm windows (there they take care of this); jolting in the streetcar on errands (there I would not have to ride to take care of this or that); fending the patronizing of relatives just back from Florida (there it matters what one is, not what one can afford), he gave *her* no peace.

"Look! In their bulletin. A reading circle. Twice a week it meets."

"Haumm," her answer of not listening.

"A reading circle. Chekhov[1] they read that you like, and Peretz.[2] Cultured people at the Haven that you would enjoy."

"Enjoy!" She tasted the word. "Now, when it pleases you, you find a reading circle for me. And forty years ago when the children were morsels and there was a Circle,[3] did you stay home with them once so I could go? Even once? You trained me well. I do not need others to enjoy. Others!" Her voice trembled. "Because *you* want to be there with others. Already it makes me sick

1. Anton Chekhov (1860–1904), Russian playwright and master of the modern short story.
2. Isaac Leib Peretz (1852–1915), a leading writer of Yiddish poems, short stories, drama, humorous sketches, and satire.
3. I.e., Workmen's Circle (*Arbeiter Ring*), a Jewish Socialist organization.

to think of you always around others. Clown, grimacer, floormat, yesman, entertainer, whatever they want of you."

And now it was he who turned on the television loud so he need not hear.

Old scar tissue ruptured and the wounds festered anew. Chekhov indeed. She thought without softness of that young wife, who in the deep night hours while she nursed the current baby, and perhaps held another in her lap, would try to stay awake for the only time there was to read. She would feel again the weather of the outside on his cheek when, coming late from a meeting, he would find her so, and stimulated and ardent, sniffing her skin, coax: "I'll put the baby to bed, and you—put the book away, don't read, don't read."

That had been the most beguiling of all the "don't read, put your book away" her life had been. Chekhov indeed!

"Money?" She shrugged him off. "Could we get poorer than once we were? And in America, who starves?"

But as still he pressed:

"Let me alone about money. Was there ever enough? Seven little ones—for every penny I had to ask—and sometimes, remember, there was nothing. But always *I* had to manage. Now *you* manage. Rub your nose in it good."

But from those years she had had to manage, old humiliations and terrors rose up, lived again, and forced her to relive them. The children's needings; that grocer's face or this merchant's wife she had had to beg credit from when credit was a disgrace, the scenery of the long blocks walked around when she could not pay; school coming, and the desperate going over the old to see what could yet be remade; the soups of meat bones begged "for-the-dog" one winter . . .

Enough. Now they had no children. Let *him* wrack his head for how they would live. She would not exchange her solitude for anything. *Never again to be forced to move to the rhythms of others.*

For in this solitude she had won to a reconciled peace.

Tranquillity from having the empty house no longer an enemy, for it stayed clean—not as in the days when (by the perverse logic of exhausted housewifery) it was her family, the life in it, that had seemed the enemy: tracking, smudging, littering, dirtying, engaging her in endless defeating battle—and on whom her endless defeat had been spewed.

The few old books, memorized from rereading; the pictures to ponder (the magnifying glass superimposed on her heavy eyeglasses). Or if she wishes, when he is gone, the phonograph, that if she turns up very loud and strains, she can hear: the ordered sounds, and the struggling.

Out in the garden, growing things to nurture. Birds to be kept out of the pear tree, and when the pears are heavy and ripe, the old fury of work, for all must be canned, nothing wasted.

And her one social duty (for she will not go to luncheons or meetings) the boxes of old clothes left with her, as with a life-practiced eye for finding what is still wearable within the worn (again the magnifying glass superimposed on the heavy glasses) she scans and sorts—this for rag or rummage, that for mending and cleaning, and this for sending abroad.

Being able at last to live within, and not move to the rhythms of others, as life had helped her to: denying; removing; isolating; taking the children one by one; then deafening, half-blinding—and at last, presenting her solitude.

And in it she had won to a reconciled peace.

Now he was violating it with his constant campaigning: *Sell the house and move to the Haven.* (You sit, you sit—there too you could sit like a stone.) He was making of her a battleground where old grievances tore. (Turn on your ear button—I am talking.) And stubbornly she resisted—so that from wheedling, reasoning, manipulation, it was bitterness he now started with.

And it came to where every happening lashed up a quarrel.

"I will sell the house anyway," he flung at her one night. "I am putting it up for sale. There will be a way to make you sign."

The television blared, as always it did on the evenings he stayed home, and as always it reached her only as noise. She did not know if the tumult was in her or outside. Snap! she turned the sound off. "Shadows," she whispered to him, pointing to the screen, "look, it is only shadows." And in a scream: "Did you say that you will sell the house? Look at me, not at that. I am no shadow. You cannot sell without me."

"Leave on the television. I am watching."

"Like Paulie, like Jenny, a four-year-old. Staring at shadows. *You cannot sell the house.*"

"I will. We are going to the Haven. There you would not have the television when you do not want it. I could sit in the social room and watch. You could lock yourself up to smell your unpleasantness in a room by yourself—for who would want to come near you?"

"No, no selling." A whisper now.

"The television is shadows. Mrs. Enlightened! Mrs. Cultured! A world comes into your house—and it is shadows. People you would never meet in a thousand lifetimes. Wonders. When you were four years old, yes, like Paulie, like Jenny, did you know of Indian dances, alligators, how they use bamboo in Malaya? No, you scratched in your dirt with the chickens and thought Olshana[4] was the world. Yes, Mrs. Unpleasant, I will sell the house, for there better can we be rid of each other than here."

She did not know if the tumult was outside, or in her. Always a ravening inside, a pull to the bed, to lie down, to succumb.

"Have you thought maybe Ma should let a doctor have a look at her?" asked their son Paul after Sunday dinner, regarding his mother crumpled on the couch, instead of, as was her custom, busying herself in Nancy's kitchen.

"Why not the President too?"

"Seriously, Dad. This is the third Sunday she's lain down like that after dinner. Is she that way at home?"

"A regular love affair with the bed. Every time I start to talk to her."

Good protective reaction, observed Nancy to herself. The workings of hos-til-ity.

"Nancy could take her. I just don't like how she looks. Let's have Nancy arrange an appointment."

"You think she'll go?" regarding his wife gloomily. "All right, we have to

4. A small Russian town in the Ukraine.

have doctor bills, we have to have doctor bills." Loudly: "Something hurts you?"

She startled, looked to his lips. He repeated: "Mrs. Take It Easy, something hurts?"

"Nothing . . . Only you."

"A woman of honey. That's why you're lying down?"

"Soon I'll get up to do the dishes, Nancy."

"Leave them, Mother, I like it better this way."

"Mrs. Take It Easy, Paul says you should start ballet. You should go see a doctor and ask: how soon can you start ballet?"

"A doctor?" she begged. "Ballet?"

"We were talking, Ma," explained Paul, "you don't seem any too well. It would be a good idea for you to see a doctor for a checkup."

"I get up now to do the kitchen. Doctors are bills and foolishness, my son. I need no doctors."

"At the Haven," he could not resist pointing out, "a doctor is *not* bills. He lives beside you. You start to sneeze, he is there before you open up a Kleenex. You can be sick there for free, all you want."

"Diarrhea of the mouth, is there a doctor to make you dumb?"

"Ma. Promise me you'll go. Nancy will arrange it."

"It's all of a piece when you think of it," said Nancy, "the way she attacks my kitchen, scrubbing under every cup hook, doing the inside of the oven so I can't enjoy Sunday dinner, knowing that half-blind or not, she's going to find every speck of dirt . . ."

"Don't, Nancy, I've told you—it's the only way she knows to be useful. What did the *doctor* say?"

"A real fatherly lecture. Sixty-nine is young these days. Go out, enjoy life, find interests. Get a new hearing aid, this one is antiquated. Old age is sickness only if one makes it so. Geriatrics, Inc."

"So there was nothing physical."

"Of course there was. How can you live to yourself like she does without there being? Evidence of a kidney disorder, and her blood count is low. He gave her a diet, and she's to come back for follow-up and lab work . . . But he was clear enough: Number One prescription—start living like a human being. When I think of your dad, who could really play the invalid with that arthritis of his, as active as a teenager, and twice as much fun . . ."

"You didn't tell me the doctor says your sickness is in you, how you live." He pushed his advantage. "Life and enjoyments you need better than medicine. And this diet, how can you keep it? To weigh each morsel and scrape away the bits of fat to make this soup, that pudding. There, at the Haven, they have a dietician, they would do it for you."

She is silent.

"You would feel better there, I know it," he says gently. "There there is life and enjoyments all around."

"What is the matter, Mr. Importantbusy, you have no card game or meeting you can go to?"—turning her face to the pillow.

For a while he cut his meetings and going out, fussed over her diet, tried to wheedle her into leaving the house, brought in visitors:

"I should come to a fashion tea. I should sit and look at pretty babies in clothes I cannot buy. This is pleasure?"
"Always you are better than everyone else. The doctor said you should go out. Mrs. Brem comes to you with goodness and you turn her away."
"Because *you* asked her to, she asked me."

"They won't come back. People you need, the doctor said. Your own cousins I asked; they were willing to come and make peace as if nothing had happened . . ."
"No more crushers of people, pushers, hypocrites, around me. No more in *my* house. You go to them if you like."

"Kind he is to visit. And you, like ice."
"A babbler. All my life around babblers. Enough!"

"She's even worse, Dad? Then let her stew a while," advised Nancy. "You can't let it destroy you; it's a psychological thing, maybe too far gone for any of us to help."

So he let her stew. More and more she lay silent in bed, and sometimes did not even get up to make the meals. No longer was the tongue-lashing inevitable if he left the coffee cup where it did not belong, or forgot to take out the garbage or mislaid the broom. The birds grew bold that summer and for once pocked the pears, undisturbed.

A bellyful of bitterness, and every day the same quarrel in a new way and a different old grievance the quarrel forced her to enter and relive. And the new torment: I am not really sick, the doctor said it, then why do I feel so sick?

One night she asked him: "You have a meeting tonight? Do not go. Stay . . . with me."

He had planned to watch "This Is Your Life"[5] anyway, but half sick himself from the heavy heat, and sickening therefore the more after the brooks and woods of the Haven, with satisfaction he grated:

"Hah, Mrs. Live Alone And Like It wants company all of a sudden. It doesn't seem so good the time of solitary when she was a girl exile in Siberia. 'Do not go. Stay with me.' A new song for Mrs. Free As A Bird. Yes, I am going out, and while I am gone chew this aloneness good, and think how you keep us both from where if you want people you do not need to be alone."

"Go, go. All your life you have gone without me."

After him she sobbed curses he had not heard in years, old-country curses from their childhood: Grow, oh shall you grow like an onion, with your head in the ground. Like the hide of a drum shall you be, beaten in life, beaten in death. Oh shall you be like a chandelier, to hang, and to burn . . .

She was not in their bed when he came back. She lay on the cot on the sun porch. All week she did not speak or come near him; nor did he try to make peace or care for her.

5. A popular TV program in which individual guests were presented with significant persons from their past.

He slept badly, so used to her next to him. After all the years, old harmonies and dependencies deep in their bodies; she curled to him, or he coiled to her, each warmed, warming, turning as the other turned, the nights a long embrace.

It was not the empty bed or the storm that woke him, but a faint singing. *She* was singing. Shaking off the drops of rain, the lightning riving her lifted face, he saw her so; the cot covers on the floor.

"This is a private concert?" he asked. "Come in, you are wet."

"I can breathe now," she answered; "my lungs are rich." Though indeed the sound was hardly a breath.

"Come in, come in." Loosing the bamboo shades. "Look how wet you are." Half helping, half carrying her, still faint-breathing her song.

A Russian love song of fifty years ago.

He had found a buyer, but before he told her, he called together those children who were close enough to come. Paul, of course, Sammy from New Jersey, Hannah from Connecticut, Vivi from Ohio.

With a kindling of energy for her beloved visitors, she arrayed the house, cooked and baked. She was not prepared for the solemn after-dinner conclave, they too probing in and tearing. Her frightened eyes watched from mouth to mouth as each spoke.

His stories were eloquent and funny of her refusal to go back to the doctor; of the scorned invitations; of her stubborn silences or the bile "like a Niagara"; of her contrariness: "If I clean it's no good how I cleaned; if I don't clean, I'm still a master who thinks he has a slave."

("Vinegar he poured on me all his life; I am well marinated; how can I be honey now?")

Deftly he marched in the rightness for moving to the Haven; their money from social security free for visiting the children, not sucked into daily needs and into the house; the activities in the Haven for him; but mostly the Haven for *her*: her health, her need of care, distraction, amusement, friends who shared her interests.

"This does offer an outlet for Dad," said Paul; "he's always been an active person. And economic peace of mind isn't to be sneezed at, either. I could use a little of that myself."

But when they asked: "And you, Ma, how do you feel about it?" could only whisper:

"For him it is good. It is not for me. I can no longer live between people."

"You lived all your life *for* people," Vivi cried.

"Not with." Suffering doubly for the unhappiness on her children's faces.

"You have to find some compromise," Sammy insisted. "Maybe sell the house and buy a trailer. After forty-seven years there's surely some way you can find to live in peace."

"There is no help, my children. Different things we need."

"Then live alone!" He could control himself no longer. "I have a buyer for the house. Half the money for you, half for me. Either alone or with me to the Haven. You think I can live any longer as we are doing now?"

"Ma doesn't have to make a decision this minute, however you feel, Dad," Paul said quickly, "and you wouldn't want her to. Let's let it lay a few months, and then talk some more."

"I think I can work it out to take Mother home with me for a while," Hannah said. "You both look terrible, but especially you, Mother. I'm going to ask Phil to have a look at you."

"Sure," cracked Sammy. "What's the use of a doctor husband if you can't get free service out of him once in a while for the family? And absence might make the heart . . . you know."

"There was something after all," Paul told Nancy in a colorless voice. "That was Hannah's Phil calling. Her gall bladder . . . Surgery."

"Her *gall* bladder. If that isn't classic. 'Bitter as gall'—talk of psychosom—"

He stepped closer, put his hand over her mouth and said in the same colorless, plodding voice. "We have to get Dad. They operated at once. The cancer was everywhere, surrounding the liver, everywhere. They did what they could . . . at best she has a year. Dad . . . we have to tell him."

2.

Honest in his weakness when they told him, and that she was not to know. "I'm not an actor. She'll know right away by how I am. O that poor woman. I am old too, it will break me into pieces. O that poor woman. She will spit on me: 'So my sickness was how I live.' O Paulie, how she will be, that poor woman. Only she should not suffer . . . I can't stand sickness, Paulie, I can't go with you."

But went. And play-acted.

"A grand opening and you did not even wait for me . . . A good thing Hannah took you with her."

"Fashion teas I needed. They cut out what tore in me; just in my throat something hurts yet . . . Look! so many flowers, like a funeral. Vivi called, did Hannah tell you? And Lennie from San Francisco, and Clara; and Sammy is coming." Her gnome's face pressed happily into the flowers.

> It is impossible to predict in these cases, but once over the immediate effects of the operation, she should have several months of comparative well-being.
>
> *The money, where will come the money?*
>
> Travel with her, Dad. Don't take her home to the old associations. The other children will want to see her.
>
> *The money, where will I wring the money?*
>
> Whatever happens, she is not to know. No, you can't ask her to sign papers to sell the house; nothing to upset her. Borrow instead, then after . . .
>
> *I had wanted to leave you each a few dollars to make life easier, as other fathers do. There will be nothing left now. (Failure! you and your "business is exploitation." Why didn't you make it when it could be made?—Is that what you're thinking Sammy?*
>
> Sure she's unreasonable, Dad—but you have to stay with her; if there's to be any happiness in what's left of her life, it depends on you.
>
> *Prop me up children, think of me, too. Shuffled, chained with her, bitter woman. No Haven, and the little money going . . . How happy she looks, poor creature.*

The look of excitement. The straining to hear everything (the new hearing aid turned full). Why are you so happy, dying woman?

How the petals are, fold on fold, and the gladioli color. The autumn air.

Stranger grandsons, tall above the little gnome grandmother, the little spry grandfather. Paul in a frenzy of picture-taking before going.

She, wandering the great house. Feeling the books; laughing at the maple shoemaker's bench of a hundred years ago used as a table. The ear turned to music.

"Let us go home. See how good I walk now." "One step from the hospital," he answers, "and she wants to fly. Wait till Doctor Phil says."

"Look—the birds too are flying home. Very good Phil is and will not show it, but he is sick of sickness by the time he comes home."

"Mrs. Telepathy, to read minds," he answers; "read mine what it says: when the trunks of medicines become a suitcase, then we will go."

The grandboys, they do not know what to say to us . . . Hannah, she runs around here, there, when is there time for herself?

Let us go home. Let us go home.

Musing; gentleness—*but for the incidents of the rabbi in the hospital, and of the candles of benediction.*[6]

Of the rabbi in the hospital:

Now tell me what happened, Mother.

From the sleep I awoke, Hannah's Phil, and he stands there like a devil in a dream and calls me by name. I cannot hear. I think he prays. Go away please, I tell him, I am not a believer. Still he stands, while my heart knocks with fright.

You scared *him*, Mother. He thought you were delirious.

Who sent him? Why did he come to me?

It is a custom. The men of God come to visit those of their religion they might help. Jew, Protestant, Catholic, the hospital makes up the list for them, and you are on the Jewish list.

Not for rabbis. At once go and make them change. Tell them to write: Born, human; Religion, none.

And of the candles of benediction:

Look how you have upset yourself, Mrs. Excited Over Nothing. Pleasant memories you should leave.

Go in, go back to Hannah and the lights. Two weeks I saw the candles and said nothing. But she asked me.

So what was so terrible? She forgets you never did, she asks you to light the Friday candles and say the benediction like Phil's mother when she visits. If the candles give her pleasure, why shouldn't she have the pleasure?

Not for pleasure she does it. For emptiness. Because his family does. Because all around her do.

That is not a good reason too? But you did not hear her. For heritage, she told you. For the boys. from the past they should have tradition.

6. I.e., the candles that are lit on Friday evenings in Jewish homes and synagogues, and that usher in the Sabbath.

Superstition! From the savages, afraid of the dark, of themselves: mumbo words and magic lights to scare away ghosts.
She told you: how it started does not take away the goodness. For centuries, peace in the house it means.
Swindler! does she look back on the dark centuries? Candles bought instead of bread and stuck into a potato for a candlestick? Religion that stifled and said: in Paradise, woman, you will be the footstool of your husband, and in life—poor chosen Jew—ground under, despised, trembling in cellars. And cremated. And cremated.
This is religion's fault? You think you are still an orator of the 1905 revolution?[7] Where are the pills for quieting? Which are they?
Heritage. How have we come from the savages, how no longer to be savages—this to teach. To look back and learn what ennobles man—this to teach. To smash all ghettos that divide man—not to go back, not to go back—this to teach. Learned books in the house, will man live or die, and she gives to her boys—superstition.
Hannah that is so good to you. Take your pill, Mrs. Excited For Nothing, swallow.
Heritage! But when did I have time to teach? Of Hannah I asked only hands to help.
Swallow.

Otherwise—musing; gentleness.

Not to travel. To go home.

The children want to see you. We have to show them you are as thorny a flower as ever.

Not to travel.

Vivi wants you should see her new baby. She sent the tickets—airplane tickets—a Mrs. Roosevelt[8] she wants to make of you. To Vivi's we have to go.

A new baby. How many warm, seductive babies. She holds him stiffly, *away* from her, so that he wails. And a long shudder begins, and the sweat beads on her forehead.

"Hush, shush," croons the grandfather, lifting him back. "You should forgive your grandmamma, little prince, she has never held a baby before, only seen them in glass cases. Hush, shush."

"You're tired, Ma," says Vivi. "The travel and the noisy dinner. I'll take you to lie down."

(*A long travel from, to, what the feel of a baby evokes.*)

In the airplane, cunningly designed to encase from motion (no wind, no feel of flight), she had sat severely and still, her face turned to the sky through which they cleaved and left no scar.

So this was how it looked, the determining, the crucial sky, and this was

7. After the Russo-Japanese War (1904–05), diverse social groups demonstrated their discontent with the Russian social and political system.

8. Eleanor Roosevelt (1884–1962), political and social activist, humanitarian, and wife of President Franklin Delano Roosevelt.

how man moved through it, remote above the dwindled earth, the concealed human life. Vulnerable life, that could scar.

There was a steerage ship of memory that shook across a great, circular sea: clustered, ill human beings; and through the thick-stained air, tiny fretting waters in a window round like the airplane's—sun round, moon round. (The round thatched hut roofs of Olshana.) Eye round—like the smaller window that framed distance the solitary year of exile when only her eyes could travel, and no voice spoke. And the polar winds hurled themselves across snow trackless and endless and white—like the clouds which had closed together below and hidden the earth.

Now they put a baby in her lap. Do not ask me, she would have liked to beg. Enough the worn face of Vivi, the remembered grandchildren. I cannot, cannot . . .

Cannot what? Unnatural grandmother, not able to make herself embrace a baby.

She lay there in the bed of the two little girls, her new hearing aid turned full, listening to the sound of the children going to sleep, the baby's fretful crying and hushing, the clatter of dishes being washed and put away. They thought she slept. Still she rode on.

It was not that she had not loved her babies, her children. The love—the passion of tending—had risen with the need like a torrent; and like a torrent drowned and immolated all else. But when the need was done—o the power that was lost in the painful damming back and drying up of what still surged, but had nowhere to go. Only the thin pulsing left that could not quiet, suffering over lives one felt, but could no longer hold nor help.

On that torrent she had borne them to their own lives, and the riverbed was desert long years now. Not there would she dwell, a memoried wraith. Surely that was not all, surely there was more. Still the springs, the springs were in her seeking. Somewhere an older power that beat for life. Somewhere coherence, transport, meaning. If they would but leave her in the air now stilled of clamor, in the reconciled solitude, to journey to her self.

And they put a baby in her lap. Immediacy to embrace, and the breath of *that* past: warm flesh like this that had claims and nuzzled away all else and with lovely mouths devoured; hot-living like an animal—intensely and now; the turning maze; the long drunkenness; the drowning into needing and being needed. Severely she looked back—and the shudder seized her again, and the sweat. Not that way. Not there, not now could she, not yet . . .

And all that visit, she could not touch the baby.

"Daddy, is it the . . . sickness she's like that?" asked Vivi. "I was so glad to be having the baby—for her. I told Tim, it'll give her more happiness than anything, being around a baby again. And she hasn't played with him once."

He was not listening, "Aahh little seed of life, little charmer," he crooned, "Hollywood should see you. A heart of ice you would melt. Kick, kick. The future you'll have for a ball. In 2050 still kick. Kick for your granddaddy then."

Attentive with the older children; sat through their performances (command performance; we command you to be the audience); helped Ann sort autumn leaves to find the best for a school program; listened gravely to Richard tell about his rock collection, while her lips mutely formed the words to remember: *igneous, sedimentary, metamorphic*; looked for missing socks, books and bus tickets; watched the children whoop after their grandfather who knew how to tickle, chuck, lift, toss, do tricks, tell secrets, make jokes, match riddle for riddle. (Tell me a riddle, Grammy. I know no riddles, child.) Scrubbed sills and woodwork and furniture in every room; folded the laundry; straightened drawers; emptied the heaped baskets waiting for ironing (while he or Vivi or Tim nagged: You're supposed to rest here, you've been sick) but to none tended or gave food—and could not touch the baby.

After a week she said: "Let us go home. Today call about the tickets."

"You have important business, Mrs. Inahurry? The President waits to consult with you?" He shouted, for the fear of the future raced in him. "The clothes are still warm from the suitcase, your children cannot show enough how glad they are to see you, and you want home. There is plenty of time for home. We cannot be with the children at home."

"Blind to around you as always: the little ones sleep four in a room because we take their bed. We are two more people in a house with a new baby, and no help."

"Vivi is happy so. The children should have their grandparents a while, she told to me. I should have my mommy and daddy . . ."

"Babbler and blind. Do you look at her so tired? How she starts to talk and she cries? I am not strong enough yet to help. Let us go home."

(To reconciled solitude.)

For it seemed to her the crowded noisy house was listening to her, listening for her. She could feel it like a great ear pressed under her heart. And everything knocked: quick constant raps: let me in, let me in.

How far was it that soft reaching tendrils also became blows that knocked?

C'mon Grandma, I want to show you . . .

Tell me a riddle, Grandma. (*I know no riddles*)

Look Grammy, he's so dumb he can't even find his hands. (Dody and the baby on a blanket over the fermenting autumn mound)

I made it—for you. (Flat paper dolls with aprons that lifted on scalloped skirts that lifted on flowered pants; hair of yarn and great ringed questioning eyes) (Ann)

Watch me, Grandma. (Richard snaking up the tree, hanging exultant, free, with one hand at the top. Below Dody hunching over in pretend-cooking.) (Climb too, Dody, climb and look)

Be my nap bed, Grammy. (The "No!" too late.)

Morty's abandoned heaviness, while his fingers ladder up and down her hearing-aid cord to his drowsy chant: eentsiebeentsiespider. (*Children trust*)

It's to start off your own rock collection, Grandma. That's a trilobite fossil, 200 million years old (millions of years on a boy's mouth) and that one's obsidian, black glass.

Knocked and knocked.

Mother, I *told* you the teacher said we had to bring it back all filled out

this morning. Didn't you even ask Daddy? Then tell *me* which plan and I'll check it: evacuate or stay in the city or wait for you to come and take me away. (Seeing the look of straining to hear) It's for Disaster, Grandma. (*Children trust*)
Vivi in the maze of the long, the lovely drunkenness. The old old noises: baby sounds; screaming of a mother flayed to exasperation; children quarreling; children playing; singing; laughter.

And Vivi's tears and memories, spilling so fast, half the words not understood.

She had started remembering out loud deliberately, so her mother would know the past was cherished, still lived in her.

Nursing the baby: My friends marvel, and I tell them, oh it's easy to be such a cow. I remember how beautiful my mother seemed nursing my brother, and the milk just flows . . . Was that Davy? It must have been Davy . . .

Lowering a hem: How did you ever . . . when I think how you made everything we wore . . . Tim, just think, seven kids and Mommy sewed everything . . . do I remember you sang while you sewed? That white dress with the red apples on the skirt you fixed over for me, was it Hannah's or Clara's before it was mine?

Washing sweaters: Ma, I'll never forget, one of those days so nice you washed clothes outside; one of the first spring days it must have been. The bubbles just danced up and down while you scrubbed, and we chased after, and you stopped to show us how to blow our own bubbles with green onion stalks . . . you always . . .

"Strong onion, to still make you cry after so many years," her father said, to turn the tears into laughter.

While Richard bent over his homework: Where is it now, do we still have it, the Book of the Martyrs?[9] It always seemed so, well—exalted, when you'd put it on the round table and we'd all look at it together; there was even a halo from the lamp. The lamp with the beaded fringe you could move up and down; they're in style again, pulley lamps like that, but without the fringe. You know the book I'm talking about, Daddy, the Book of the Martyrs, the first picture was a bust of Socrates?[1] I wish there was something like that for the children, Mommy, to give them what you . . . (And the tears splashed again)

(What I intended and did not? Stop it, daughter, stop it, leave that time. And he, the hypocrite, sitting there with tears in his eyes too—it was nothing to you then, nothing.)

. . . The time you came to school and I almost died of shame because of your accent and because I knew you knew I was ashamed; how could I? . . . Sammy's harmonica and you danced to it once, yes you did, you and Davy squealing in your arms . . . That time you bundled us up and walked us down to the railroad station to stay the night 'cause it was heated and we didn't have any coal, that winter of the strike, you didn't think I remembered that, did you, Mommy? . . . How you'd call us out to see the sunsets . . .

9. An influential history (1563), by John Foxe (1516–1587), of Christian persecutions.
1. Greek philosopher Socrates (ca. 470–399 B.C.E.), who developed a method of inquiry and instruction, was falsely accused of impiety and corruption. He was condemned to death and took his own life.

Day after day, the spilling memories. Worse now, questions, too. Even the grandchildren: Grandma, in the olden days, when you were little . . .

It was the afternoons that saved.

While they thought she napped, she would leave the mosaic on the wall (of children's drawings, maps, calendars, pictures, Ann's cardboard dolls with their great ringed questioning eyes) and hunch in the girls' closet, on the low shelf where the shoes stood, and the girls' dresses covered.

For that while she would painfully sheathe against the listening house, the tendrils and noises that knocked, and Vivi's spilling memories. Sometimes it helped to braid and unbraid the sashes that dangled, or to trace the pattern on the hoop slips.

Today she had jacks and children under jet trails to forget. Last night, Ann and Dody silhouetted in the window against a sunset of flaming man-made clouds of jet trail, their jacks ball accenting the peaceful noise of dinner being made. Had she told them, yes she had told them of how they played jacks in her village though there was no ball, no jacks. Six stones, round and flat, toss them out, the seventh on the back of the hand, toss, catch and swoop up as many as possible, toss again . . .

Of stones (repeating Richard) there are three kinds: earth's fire jetting; rock of layered centuries; crucibled new out of the old. But there was that other—frozen to black glass, never to transform or hold the fossil memory . . . (let not my seed fall on stone). There was an ancient man who fought to heights a great rock that crashed back down eternally—eternal labor, freedom, labor . . .[2] (stone will perish, but the word remain). And you, David, who with a stone slew,[3] screaming: Lord, take my heart of stone and give me flesh

Who was screaming? Why was she back in the common room of the prison, the sun motes dancing in the shafts of light, and the informer being brought in, a prisoner now, like themselves. And Lisa leaping, yes, Lisa, the gentle and tender, biting at the betrayer's jugular. Screaming and screaming.

No, it is the children screaming. Another of Paul and Sammy's terrible fights?

In Vivi's house. Severely: you are in Vivi's house.

Blows, screams, a call: "Grandma!" For her? O please not for her. Hide, hunch behind the dresses deeper. But a trembling little body hurls itself beside her—surprised, smothered laughter, arms surround her neck, tears rub dry on her cheek, and words too soft to understand whisper into her ear (Is this where you hide too, Grammy? It's my secret place, we have a secret now).

And the sweat beads, and the long shudder seizes.

It seemed the great ear pressed inside now, and the knocking. "We have to go home," she told him, "I grow ill here."

"It is your own fault, Mrs. Bodybusy, you do not rest, you do too much." He raged, but the fear was in his eyes. "It was a serious operation, they told you to take care . . . All right, we will go to where you can rest."

2. In Greek mythology, Sisyphus, king of Corinth, was punished in Hades by having repeatedly to roll a huge stone up a hill only to have it roll down again as soon as he had brought it to the summit.
3. In 1 Samuel 17, David slays the Philistine giant Goliath with a single stone.

But where? Not home to death, not yet. He had thought to Lennie's, to Clara's; beautiful visits with each of the children. She would have to rest first, be stronger. If they could but go to Florida—it glittered before him, the never-realized promise of Florida. California: of course. (The money, the money dwindling!) Los Angeles first for sun and rest, then to Lennie's in San Francisco.

He told her the next day. "You saw what Nancy wrote: snow and wind back home, a terrible winter. And look at you—all bones and a swollen belly. I called Phil: he said: 'A prescription, Los Angeles sun and rest.' "

She watched the words on his lips. "You have sold the house," she cried, "that is why we do not go home. That is why you talk no more of the Haven. Why there is money for travel. After the children you will drag me to the Haven."

"The Haven! Who thinks of the Haven any more? Tell her, Vivi, tell Mrs. Suspicious: a prescription, sun and rest, to make you healthy . . . And how could I sell the house without *you*?"

At the place of farewells and greetings, of winds of coming and winds of going, they say their good-bys.

They look back at her with the eyes of others before them: Richard with her own blue blaze; Ann with the Nordic eyes of Tim; Morty's dreaming brown of a great-grandmother he will never know; Dody with the laughing eyes of him who had been her springtime love (who stands beside her now); Vivi's, all tears.

The baby's eyes are closed in sleep.

Good-by, my children.

3.

It is to the back of the great city he brought her, to the dwelling places of the cast-off old. Bounded by two lines of amusement piers to the north and to the south, and between a long straight paving rimmed with black benches facing the sand—sands so wide the ocean is only a far fluting.

In the brief vacation season, some of the boarded stores fronting the sands open, and families, young people and children, may be seen. A little tasseled tram shuttles between the piers, and the lights of roller coasters prink and tweak over those who come to have sensation made in them.

The rest of the year it is abandoned to the old, all else boarded up and still; seemingly empty, except the occasional days and hours when the sun, like a tide, sucks them out of the low rooming houses, casts them onto the benches and sandy rim of the walk—and sweeps them into decaying enclosures back again.

A few newer apartments glint among the low bleached squares. It is in one of these Lennie's Jeannie has arranged their rooms. "Only a few miles north and south people pay hundreds of dollars a month for just this gorgeous air, Granddaddy, just this ocean closeness."

She had been ill on the plane, lay ill for days in the unfamiliar room. Several times the doctor came by—left medicine she would not take. Several times Jeannie drove in the twenty miles from work, still in her Visiting Nurse uniform, the lightness and brightness of her like a healing.

"Who can believe it is winter?" he said one morning. "Beautiful it is outside like an ad. Come, Mrs. Invalid, come to taste it. You are well enough to sit in here, you are well enough to sit outside. The doctor said it too."

But the benches were encrusted with people, and the sands at the sidewalk's edge. Besides, she had seen the far ruffle of the sea: "there take me," and though she leaned against him, it was she who led.

Plodding and plodding, sitting often to rest, he grumbling. Patting the sand so warm. Once she scooped up a handful, cradling it close to her better eye; peered, and flung it back. And as they came almost to the brink and she could see the glistening wet, she sat down, pulled off her shoes and stockings, left him and began to run. "You'll catch cold," he screamed, but the sand in his shoes weighed him down—he who had always been the agile one—and already the white spray creamed her feet.

He pulled her back, took a handkerchief to wipe off the wet and the sand. "O no," she said, "the sun will dry," seized the square and smoothed it flat, dropped on it a mound of sand, knotted the kerchief corners and tied it to a bag—"to look at with the strong glass" (for the first time in years explaining an action of hers)—and lay down with the little bag against her cheek, looking toward the shore that nurtured life as it first crawled toward consciousness the millions of years ago.

He took her one Sunday in the evil-smelling bus, past flat miles of blister houses, to the home of relatives. O what is this? she cried as the light began to smoke and the houses to dim and recede. Smog, he said, everyone knows but you . . . Outside he kept his arms about her, but she walked with hands pushing the heavy air as if to open it, whispered: who has done this? sat down suddenly to vomit at the curb and for a long while refused to rise.

One's age as seen on the altered face of those known in youth. Is this they he has come to visit? This Max and Rose, smooth and pleasant, introducing them to polite children, disinterested grandchildren, "the whole family, once a month on Sundays. And why not? We have the room, the help, the food."

Talk of cars, of houses, of success: this son that, that daughter this. And *your* children? Hastily skimped over, the intermarriages, the obscure work—"my doctor son-in-law, Phil"—all he has to offer. She silent in a corner. (Carsick like a baby, he explains.) Years since he has taken her to visit anyone but the children, and old apprehensions prickle: "no incidents," he silently begs, "no incidents." He itched to tell them. "A very sick woman," significantly, indicating her with his eyes, "a very sick woman." Their restricted faces did not react. "Have you thought maybe she'd do better at Palm Springs?" Rose asked. "Or at least a nicer section of the beach, nicer people, a pool." Not to have to say "money" he said instead: "would she have sand to look at through a magnifying glass?" and went on, detail after detail, the old habit betraying of parading the queerness of her for laughter.

After dinner—the others into the living room in men- or women-clusters, or into the den to watch TV—the four of them alone. She sat close to him, and did not speak. Jokes, stories, people they had known, beginning of reminiscence, Russia fifty-sixty years ago. Strange words across the Duncan Phyfe[4] table: *hunger; secret meetings; human rights; spies; betrayals; prison;*

4. Phyfe (1768–1854) was a popular American furniture designer born in Scotland.

escape—interrupted by one of the grandchildren: "Commercial's on; any Coke left? Gee, you're missing a real hair-raiser." And then a granddaughter (Max proudly: "look at her, an American queen") drove them home on her way back to U.C.L.A.[5] No incident—except that there had been no incidents.

The first few mornings she had taken with her the magnifying glass, but he would sit only on the benches, so she rested at the foot, where slatted bench shadows fell, and unless she turned her hearing aid down, other voices invaded.

Now on the days when the sun shone and she felt well enough, he took her on the tram to where the benches ranged in oblongs, some with tables for checkers or cards. Again the blanket on the sand in the striped shadows, but she no longer brought the magnifying glass. He played cards, and she lay in the sun and looked toward the waters; or they walked—two blocks down to the scaling hotel, two blocks back—past chili-hamburger stands, open-doored bars, Next to New and Perpetual Rummage Sale stores.

Once, out of the aimless walkers, slow and shuffling like themselves, someone ran unevenly toward them, embraced, kissed, wept: "dear friends, old friends." A friend of *hers*, not his: Mrs. Mays who had lived next door to them in Denver when the children were small.

Thirty years are compressed into a dozen sentences; and the present, not even in three. All is told: the children scattered; the husband dead; she lives in a room two blocks up from the sing hall—and points to the domed auditorium jutting before the pier. The leg? phlebitis;[6] the heavy breathing? that, one does not ask. She too comes to the benches each nice day to sit. And tomorrow, tomorrow, are they going to the community sing? Of course he would have heard of it, everybody goes—the big doings they wait for all week. They have never been? She will come to them for dinner tomorrow and they will all go together.

So it is that she sits in the wind of the singing, among the thousand various faces of age.

She had turned off her hearing aid at once they came into the auditorium—as she would have wished to turn off sight.

One by one they streamed by and imprinted on her—and though the savage zest of their singing came voicelessly soft and distant, the faces still roared—the faces densened the air—chorded

children-chants, mother-croons, singing of the chained;
love serenades, Beethoven storms, mad Lucia's[7] scream;
drunken joy-songs, keens for the dead, work-singing

> *while from floor to balcony to dome a bare-footed sore-covered little girl threaded the sound-thronged tumult, danced her ecstasy of grimace to flutes that scratched at a crossroads village wedding*
>
> *Yes, faces became sound, and the sound became faces; and faces and sound became weight—pushed, pressed*

5. I.e., the University of California, Los Angeles.
6. Inflammation of a vein.
7. The heroine of Donizetti's opera *Lucia di Lammermoor*.

"Air"—her hand claws his.

"Whenever I enjoy myself . . ." Then he saw the gray sweat on her face. "Here. Up. Help me, Mrs. Mays," and they support her out to where she can gulp the air in sob after sob.

"A doctor, we should get for her a doctor."

"Tch, it's nothing," says Ellen Mays, "I get it all the time . . . You've missed the tram; come to my place . . . close . . . tea. My view. See, she *wants* to come. Steady now, that's how." Adding mysteriously: "Remember your advice, easy to keep your head above water, empty things float. Float."

The singing a fading march for them, tall woman with a swollen leg, weaving little man, and the swollen thinness they help between.

The stench in the hall: mildew? decay? "We sit and rest then climb. My gorgeous view. We help each other and here we are."

The stench along into the slab of room. A washstand for a sink, a box with oilcloth tacked around for a cupboard, a three-burner gas plate. Artificial flowers, colorless with dust. Everywhere pictures foaming: wedding, baby, party, vacation, graduation, family pictures. From the narrow couch under a slit of window, sure enough the view: lurching rooftops and a scallop of ocean heaving, preening, twitching under the moon.

"While the water heats. Excuse me . . . down the hall." Ellen Mays has gone.

"You'll live?" he asks mechanically, sat down to feel his fright; tried to pull her alongside.

She pushed him away. "For air," she said; stood clinging to the dresser. Then, in a terrible voice:

After a lifetime of room. Of many rooms.

Shhh.

You remember how she lived. Eight children. And now one room like a coffin. Shrinking the life of her into one room

She pays rent!

Like a coffin. Rooms and rooms like this. I lie on the quilt and hear them talk Once you went for coffee I walked I saw A Balzac[8] a Chekhov to write it Rummage Alone One scraps

Shhh, Mrs. Orator Without Breath. Better here old than in the old country.

And they sang like . . . like . . . Wondrous. *Man, one has to believe.* So strong. For what? To rot not grow?

Your poor lungs beg you: *Please*. They sob between each word.

Singing. Unused the life in them. She in this poor room with her pictures. Max You The children. Everywhere. And who has meaning? Century after century still all in man not to grow?

Coffins, rummage, plants: sick woman. O lay down. We will get for you the doctor.

"And when will it end. O, *the end*." That nightmare thought, and this time she writhed, crumpled beside him, seized his hand (for a moment again the weight, the soft distant roaring of humanity) and on the strangled-for breath, begged: "Man . . . will destroy ourselves?"

8. Honoré de Balzac (1799–1850), French author and founder of the realistic novel, was best known for *La Comédie humaine* (The Human Comedy).

And looking for answer—in the helpless pity and fear for her (for *her*) that distorted his face—she understood the last months, and knew that she was dying.

4.

"Let us go home," she said after several days.

"You are in training for a cross-country trip? That is why you do not even walk across the room? Here, like a prescription Phil said, till you are stronger from the operation. You want to break doctor's orders?"

She saw the fiction was necessary to him, was silent; then: "At home I will get better. If the doctor here says?"

"And winter? And the visits to Lennie and to Clara? All right," for he saw the tears in her eyes, "I will write Phil, and talk to the doctor."

Days passed. He reported nothing. Jeannie came and took her out for air, past the boarded concessions, the hooded and tented amusement rides, to the end of the pier. They watched the spent waves feeding the new, the gulls in the clouded sky; even up where they sat, the windblown sand stung.

She did not ask to go down the crooked steps to the sea.

Back in her bed, while he was gone to the store, she said: "Jeannie, this doctor, he is not one I can ask questions. Ask him for me, can I go home?"

Jeannie looked at her, said quickly: "Of course, poor Granny, you want your own things around you, don't you? I'll call him tonight . . . Look, I've something to show you," and from her purse unwrapped a large cookie, intricately shaped like a little girl. "Look at the curls—can you hear me well, Granny?—and the darling eyelashes. I just came from a house where they were baking them."

"The dimples," she marveled, "there in the knees," holding it to the better light, turning, studying, "like art. Each singly they cut, or a mold?"

"Singly," said Jeannie, "and if it is a child only the mother can make them. O Granny, it's the likeness of a real little girl who died yesterday—Rosita. She was three years old. *Pan del Muerto*, the Bread of the Dead. It was the custom in the part of Mexico they came from."

Still she turned and inspected. "Look, the hollow in the throat, the little cross necklace . . . I think for the mother it is a good thing to be busy with such bread. You know the family?"

Jeannie nodded. "On my rounds. I nursed . . . O Granny, it is like a party; they play songs she liked to dance to. The coffin is lined with pink velvet and she wears a white dress. There are candles . . ."

"In the house?" Surprised, "They keep her in the house?"

"Yes," said Jeannie, "and it is against the health law. I think she is . . . prepared there. The father said it will be sad to bury her in this country; in Mazatlán[9] they have a feast night with candles each year; everyone picnics on the graves of those they loved until dawn."

"Yes Jeannie, the living must comfort themselves." And closed her eyes.

"You want to sleep, Granny?"

"Yes, tired from the pleasure of you. I may keep the Rosita? There stand it, on the dresser, where I can see; something of my own around me."

9. Mexico's largest seaport on the Pacific coast.

In the kitchenette, helping her grandfather unpack the groceries, Jeannie said in her light voice:

"I'm resigning my job, Granddaddy."

"Ah, the lucky young man. Which one is he?"

"Too late. You're spoken for." She made a pyramid of cans, unstacked, and built again.

"Something is wrong with the job?"

"With me. I can't be"—she searched for the word—"professional enough. I let myself feel things. And tomorrow I have to report a family . . ." The cans clicked again. "It's not that, either. I just don't know what I want to do, maybe go back to school, maybe go to art school. I thought if you went to San Francisco I'd come along and talk it over with Mommy and Daddy. But I don't see how you can go. She wants to go home. She asked me to ask the doctor."

The doctor told her himself. "Next week you may travel, when you are a little stronger." But next week there was the fever of an infection, and by the time that was over, she could not leave the bed—a rented hospital bed that stood beside the double bed he slept in alone now.

Outwardly the days repeated themselves. Every other afternoon and evening he went out to his newfound cronies, to talk and play cards. Twice a week, Mrs. Mays came. And the rest of the time, Jeannie was there.

By the sickbed stood Jeannie's FM radio. Often into the room the shapes of music came. She would lie curled on her side, her knees drawn up, intense in listening (Jeannie sketched her so, coiled, convoluted like an ear), then thresh her hand out and abruptly snap the radio mute—still to lie in her attitude of listening, concealing tears.

Once Jeannie brought in a young Marine to visit, a friend from high-school days she had found wandering near the empty pier. Because Jeannie asked him to, gravely, without self-consciousness, he sat himself cross-legged on the floor and performed for them a dance of his native Samoa.[1]

Long after they left, a tiny thrumming sound could be heard where, in her bed, she strove to repeat the beckon, flight, surrender of his hands, the fluttering footbeats, and his low plaintive calls.

Hannah and Phil sent flowers. To deepen her pleasure, he placed one in her hair. "Like a girl," he said, and brought the hand mirror so she could see. She looked at the pulsing red flower, the yellow skull face; a desolate, excited laugh shuddered from her, and she pushed the mirror away—but let the flower burn.

The week Lennie and Helen came, the fever returned. With it the excited laugh, and incessant words. She, who in her life had spoken but seldom and then only when necessary (never having learned the easy, social uses of words), now in dying, spoke incessantly.

In a half-whisper: "Like Lisa she is, your Jeannie. Have I told you of Lisa, she who taught me to read? Of the highborn she was, but noble in herself. I was sixteen; they beat me; my father beat me so I would not go to her. It was forbidden, she was a Tolstoyan.[2] At night, past dogs that howled, terrible

1. A group of islands in the South Pacific.
2. Russian author Count Leo Tolstoy (1828–1910) was a renowned moral and religious reformer.

dogs, my son, in the snows of winter to the road, I to ride in her carriage like a lady, to books. To her, life was holy, knowledge was holy, and she taught me to read. They hung her. Everything that happens one must try to understand why. She killed one who betrayed many. Because of betrayal, betrayed all she lived and believed. In one minute she killed, before my eyes (there is so much blood in a human being, my son), in prison with me. All that happens, one must try to understand.

"The name?" Her lips would work. "The name that was their pole star; the doors of the death houses fixed to open on it; I read of it my year of penal servitude. Thuban!" very excited, "Thuban, in ancient Egypt the pole star. Can you see, look out to see it, Jeannie, if it swings around *our* pole star that seems to *us* not to move.

"Yes, Jeannie, at your age my mother and grandmother had already buried children . . . yes, Jeannie, it is more than oceans between Olshana and you . . . yes, Jeannie, they danced, and for all the bodies they had they might as well be chickens, and indeed, they scratched and flapped their arms and hopped.

"And Andrei Yefimitch, who for twenty years had never known of it and never wanted to know, said as if he wanted to cry: but why my dear friend this malicious laughter?" Telling to herself half-memorized phrases from her few books. "Pain I answer with tears and cries, baseness with indignation, meanness with repulsion . . . for life may be hated or wearied of, but never despised."

Delirious: "Tell me, my neighbor, Mrs. Mays, the pictures never lived, but what of the flowers? Tell them who ask: no rabbis, no ministers, no priests, no speeches, no ceremonies: ah, false—let the living please themselves. Tell Sammy's boy, he who flies, tell him to go to Stuttgart[3] and see where Davy has no grave. And what?" A conspirator's laugh. "And what? where millions have no graves."

In delirium or not, wanting the radio on; not seeming to listen, the words still jetting, wanting the music on. Once, silencing it abruptly as of old, she began to cry, unconcealed tears this time. "You have pain, Granny?" Jeannie asked.

"The music," she said, "still it is there and we do not hear; knocks, and our poor human ears too weak. What else, what else we do not hear?"

Once she knocked his hand aside as he gave her a pill, swept the bottles from her bedside table: "no pills, let me feel what I feel," and laughed as on his hands and knees he groped to pick them up.

Nighttimes her hand reached across the bed to hold his.

A constant retching began. Her breath was too faint for sustained speech now, but still the lips moved:

When no longer necessary   to injure others
Pick   pick pick   Blind chicken
As a human being   responsibility for

"David!" imperious, "Basin!" and she would vomit, rinse her mouth, the wasted throat working to swallow, and begin the chant again.

3. An industrial city in southwestern Germany.

She will be better off in the hospital now, the doctor said.

He sent the telegrams to the children, was packing her suitcase, when her hoarse voice startled. She had roused, was pulling herself to sitting.

"Where now?" she asked. "Where now do you drag me?"

"You do not even have to have a baby to go this time," he soothed, looking for the brush to pack. "Remember, after Davy you told me—worthy to have a baby for the pleasure of the hospital?"

"Where now? Not home yet?" Her voice mourned. "Where *is* my home?"

He rose to ease her back. "The doctor, the hospital," he started to explain, but deftly, like a snake, she had slithered out of bed and stood swaying, propped behind the night table.

"Coward," she hissed, "runner."

"You stand," he said senselessly.

"To take me there and run. Afraid of a little vomit."

He reached her as she fell. She struggled against him, half slipped from his arms, pulled herself up again.

"Weakling," she taunted, "to leave me there and run. Betrayer. All your life you have run."

He sobbed, telling Jeannie. "A Marilyn Monroe[4] to run for her virtue. Fifty-nine pounds she weighs, the doctor said, and she beats at me like a Dempsey.[5] Betrayer, she cries, and I running like a dog when she calls; day and night, running to her, her vomit, the bedpan. . . ."

"She wants you, Granddaddy," said Jeannie. "Isn't that what they call love? I'll see if she sleeps, and if she does, poor worn-out darling, we'll have a party, you and I; I brought us rum babas."[6]

They did not move her. By her bed now stood the tall hooked pillar that held the solutions—blood and dextrose—to feed her veins. Jeannie moved down the hall to take over the sickroom, her face so radiant, her grandfather asked her once: "you are in love?" (Shameful the joy, the pure overwhelming joy from being with her grandmother; the peace, the serenity that breathed.) "My darling escape," she answered incoherently, "my darling Granny"—as if that explained.

Now one by one the children came, those that were able. Hannah, Paul, Sammy. Too late to ask: and what did you learn with your living, Mother, and what do we need to know?

Clara, the eldest, clenched:

Pay me back, Mother, pay me back for all you took from me. Those others you crowded into your heart. The hands I needed to be for you, the heaviness, the responsibility.

Is this she? Noises the dying make, the crablike hands crawling over the covers. The ethereal singing.

She hears that music, that singing from childhood; forgotten sound—not heard since, since. . . . And the hardness breaks like a cry: Where did we lose each other, first mother, singing mother?

4. A Hollywood actress (1926–1962) who was world-famous as a "sex symbol."

5. American Jack Dempsey (1895–1983), the world heavyweight boxing champion from 1919 to 1926.

6. Also known as *babas au rhum* (French), these are rich raisin- or currant-studded yeast cakes that have been soaked in rum.

Annulled: the quarrels, the gibing, the harshness between; the fall into silence and the withdrawal.

I do not know you, Mother. Mother, I never knew you.

Lennie, suffering not alone for her who was dying, but for that in her which never lived (for that which in him might never live). From him too, unspoken words: *good-by mother who taught me to mother myself.*

Not Vivi, who must stay with her children; not Davy, but he is already here, having to die again with *her* this time, for the living take their dead with them when they die.

Light she grew, like a bird, and, like a bird, sound bubbled in her throat while the body fluttered in agony. Night and day, asleep or awake (though indeed there was no difference now) the songs and the phrases leaping.

And he, who had once dreaded a long dying (from fear of himself, from horror of the dwindling money) now desired her quick death profoundly, for *her* sake. He no longer went out, except when Jeannie forced him; no longer laughed, except when, in the bright kitchenette, Jeannie coaxed his laughter (and she, who seemed to hear nothing else, would laugh too, conspiratorial wisps of laughter).

Light, like a bird, the fluttering body, the little claw hands, the beaked shadow on her face; and the throat, bubbling, straining:

He tried not to listen, as he tried not to look on the face in which only the forehead remained familiar, but trapped with her the long nights in that little room, the sounds worked themselves into his consciousness, with their punctuation of death swallows, whimpers, gurglings.

Even in reality (swallow) *life's lack of it*

The bell   Summon   what ennobles

78,000 in one minute (whisper of a scream) *78,000 human beings   destroy ourselves?*

"Aah, Mrs. Miserable," he said, as if she could hear, "all your life working, and now in bed you lie, servants to tend, you do not even need to call to be tended, and still you work. Such hard work it is to die? Such hard work?"

The body threshed, her hand clung in his. A melody, ghost-thin, hovered on her lips, and like a guilty ghost, the vision of her bent in listening to it, silencing the record instantly he was near. Now, heedless of his presence, she floated the melody on and on.

"Hid it from me," he complained, "how many times you listened to remember it so?" And tried to think when she had first played it, or first begun to silence her few records when he came near—but could reconstruct nothing. There was only this room with its tall hooked pillar and its swarm of sounds.

An unexamined life   not worth

Strong   with the not yet   in the now

Dogma dead   war dead   one country

"It helps, Mrs. Philosopher, words from books? It helps?" And it seemed to him that for seventy years she had hidden a tape recorder, infinitely microscopic, within her, that it had coiled infinite mile on mile, trapping every song, every melody, every word read, heard and spoken—and that maliciously she was playing back only what said nothing of him, of the children, of their intimate life together.

"Left us indeed, Mrs. Babbler," he reproached, "you who called others babbler and cunningly saved your words. A lifetime you tended and loved, and now not a word of us, for us. Left us indeed? Left me."

And he took out his solitaire deck, shuffled the cards loudly, slapped them down.

Lift high   *banner of reason* (tatter of an orator's voice)   *justice*   *freedom and light*

Mankind   *life worthy*   *heroic capacities*

Seeks (blur of shudder) *belong*   *human being*

"Words, words," he accused, "and what human beings did *you* seek around you, Mrs. Live Alone, and what mankind think worthy?"

Though even as he spoke, he remembered she had not always been isolated, had not always wanted to be alone (as he knew there had been a voice before this gossamer one; before the hoarse voice that broke from silence to lash, make incidents, shame him—a girl's voice of eloquence that spoke their holiest dreams). But again he could reconstruct, image, nothing of what had been before, or when, or how, it had changed.

Ace, queen, jack. The pillar shadow fell, so, in two tracks; in the mirror depths glistened a moonlike blob, the empty solution bottle. And it worked in him: *of reason and justice and freedom. Dogma dead:* he remembered the quotation, laughed bitterly. "Hah, good you do not know what you say; good Victor Hugo[7] died and did not see it, his twentieth century."

Deuce, ten, five. Dauntlessly she began a song of their youth of belief:

These things shall be, a loftier race
than e'er the world hath known shall rise
with flame of freedom in their souls
and light of knowledge in their eyes

King, four, jack. "In the twentieth century, hah!"

They shall be gentle, brave and strong
to spill no drop of blood, but dare
all that may plant man's lordship firm
on earth and fire and sea and air

"To spill no drop of blood, hah! So, cadaver, and you too, cadaver Hugo, 'in the twentieth century ignorance will be dead, dogma will be dead, war will be dead, and for all mankind one country—of fulfillment.' Hah!"

And every life (long strangling cough) *shall*
      be a   *song*

The cards fell from his fingers. Without warning, the bereavement and betrayal he had sheltered—compounded through the years—hidden even from himself—revealed itself,

uncoiled,
released,
sprung

7. Hugo (1802–1885), Romantic French poet, novelist, and dramatist, was a spokesman for the poor and the author of *Les Misérables*.

and with it the monstrous shapes of what had actually happened in the century.

A ravening hunger or thirst seized him. He groped into the kitchenette, switched on all three lights, piled a tray—"you have finished your night snack, Mrs. Cadaver, now I will have mine." And he was shocked at the tears that splashed on the tray.

"Salt tears. For free. I forgot to shake on salt?"

Whispered: "Lost, how much I lost."

Escaped to the grandchildren whose childhoods were childish, who had never hungered, who lived unravaged by disease in warm houses of many rooms, had all the school for which they cared, could walk on any street, stood a head taller than their grandparents, towered above—beautiful skins, straight backs, clear straightforward eyes. "Yes, you in Olshana," he said to the town of sixty years ago, "they would be nobility to you."

And was this not the dream then, come true in ways undreamed? he asked.

And are there no other children in the world? he answered, as if in her harsh voice.

And the flame of freedom, the light of knowledge?

And the drop, the drop of blood?

And he thought that at six Jeannie would get up and it would be his turn to go to her room and sleep, that he could press the buzzer and she would come now; that in the afternoon Ellen Mays was coming, and this time they would play cards and he could marvel at how rouge can stand half an inch on the cheek; that in the evening the doctor would come, and he could beg him to be merciful, to stop the feeding solutions, to let her die.

To let her die, and with her their youth of belief out of which her bright, betrayed words foamed; stained words, that on her working lips came stainless.

Hours yet before Jeannie's turn. He could press the buzzer and wake her to come now; he could take a pill, and with it sleep; he could pour more brandy into his milk glass, though what he had poured was not yet touched.

Instead he went back, checked her pulse, gently tended with his knotty fingers as Jeannie had taught.

She was whimpering; her hand crawled across the covers for his. Compassionately he enfolded it, and with his free hand gathered up the cards again. Still was there thirst or hunger ravening in him.

That world of their youth—dark, ignorant, terrible with hate and disease—how was it that living in it, in the midst of corruption, filth, treachery, degradation, they had not mistrusted man nor themselves; had believed so beautifully, so . . . falsely?

"Aaah, children," he said out loud, "how we believed, how we belonged." And he yearned to package for each of the children, the grandchildren, for everyone, *that joyous certainty, that sense of mattering, of moving and being moved, of being one and indivisible with the great of the past, with all that freed, ennobled man.* Package it, stand on corners, in front of stadiums and on crowded beaches, knock on doors, give it as a fabled gift.

"And why not in cereal boxes, in soap packages?" he mocked himself. "Aah. You have taken my senses, cadaver."

Words foamed, died unsounded. Her body writhed; she made kissing motions with her mouth. (Her lips moving as she read, poring over the Book of the Martyrs, the magnifying glass superimposed over the heavy eyeglasses.) *Still she had believed?* "Eva!" he whispered. "Still you believed? You lived by it? These Things Shall Be?"[8]

"One pound soup meat," she answered distinctly, "one soup bone."

"My ears heard you. Ellen Mays was witness: 'Man . . . one has to believe.' " Imploringly: "Eva!"

"Bread, day-old." She was mumbling. "Please, in a wooden box . . . for kindling. The thread, hah, the thread breaks. Cheap thread"—and a gurgling, enormously loud, began in her throat.

"I ask for stone; she gives me bread—day-old."[9] He pulled his hand away, shouted: "Who wanted questions? Everything you have to wake?" Then dully, "Ah, let me help you turn, poor creature."

Words jumbled, cleared. In a voice of crowded terror:

"Paul, Sammy, don't fight.

"Hannah, have I ten hands?

"How can I give it, Clara, how can I give it if I don't have?"

"You lie," he said sturdily, "there was joy too." Bitterly: "Ah how cheap you speak of us at the last."

As if to rebuke him, as if her voice had no relationship with her flailing body, she sang clearly, beautifully, a school song the children had taught her when they were little; begged:

"Not look my hair where they cut . . ."

(The crown of braids shorn.) And instantly he left the mute old woman poring over the Book of the Martyrs; went past the mother treadling at the sewing machine, singing with the children; past the girl in her wrinkled prison dress, hiding her hair with scarred hands, lifting to him her awkward, shamed, imploring eyes of love; and took her in his arms, dear, personal, fleshed, in all the heavy passion he had loved to rouse from her.

"Eva!"

Her little claw hand beat the covers. How much, how much can a man stand? He took up the cards, put them down, circled the beds, walked to the dresser, opened, shut drawers, brushed his hair, moved his hand bit by bit over the mirror to see what of the reflection he could blot out with each move, and felt that at any moment he would die of what was unendurable. Went to press the buzzer to wake Jeannie, looked down, saw on Jeannie's sketch pad the hospital bed, with *her*; the double bed alongside, with him; the tall pillar feeding into her veins, and their hands, his and hers, clasped, feeding each other. And as if he had been instructed he went to his bed, lay down, holding the sketch as if it could shield against the monstrous shapes of loss, of betrayal, of death—and with his free hand took hers back into his.

So Jeannie found them in the morning.

That last day the agony was perpetual. Time after time it lifted her almost off the bed, so they had to fight to hold her down. He could not endure and left the room; wept as if there never would be tears enough.

Jeannie came to comfort him. In her light voice she said: Granddaddy,

8. A line from *Hymn*, by English writer J. A. Symonds (1840–1893).

9. Cf. Matthew 7.9: "Or what man is there of you, whom if his son ask bread, will he give him a stone?"

Granddaddy don't cry. She is not there, she promised me. On the last day, she said she would go back to when she first heard music, a little girl on the road of the village where she was born. She promised me. It is a wedding and they dance, while the flutes so joyous and vibrant tremble in the air. Leave her there, Granddaddy, it is all right. She promised me. Come back, come back and help her poor body to die.

For two of that generation
Seevya and Genya
Infinite, dauntless, incorruptible.

Death deepens the wonder

1961

DAVID IGNATOW
1914–1997

"The old man was living on a quarter a day!" David Ignatow recalls from the depression years. "But I absolutely had to be a writer. My old man had a little insight into these things. He came from Russia and loved Russian literature. . . . When he was younger he told me stories by Dostoevsky and others which I found fascinating. He had such a great *love* for these writers that I said: 'I must emulate them because I want that kind of love from my father!' " At eighteen, Ignatow wrote a short story to make his family rich, but the *Saturday Evening Post* rejected it. His father lost patience, and the son went to work for him. "Machine work. Or I had to push carts through the streets downtown, just above Canal Street [in New York City]." Drained of strength for writing, David would quit at 5:30 while his father worked late. "He'd come home at eight o'clock and say, 'Where is that bastard?! Where's that son-of-a-bitch!?' It really broke my heart . . . because I *knew* how much he loved me."

The wrenching father-son relationship signals Jewishness in Ignatow (as in many other writers), it's often said, and European Jewish sons would bear this out: Kafka, Freud, Buber, Osip Mandelstam, Paul Celan. But surely in America, the immigrant predicament itself, of whatever people, is enough to produce generational—and sometimes generative—conflict. Ignatow's *Europe and America* (1948) registers the conflict between a father's "emigrant bundle / of desperation" and the son "bedded upon soft green money" (not that he ever got rich on poetry). Then three decades later, a poem entitled *1905* (the year of Russian revolution and pogroms) imagines his father back in Kiev:

> . . . while he worked in a cellar bindery
> and slept on workbenches rats leapt over
> at night, Dostoevsky's *White Nights*
> and *Anna Karenina* were being read avidly
> . . . He walked, his work bundle under arm,
> from cellar to monastery, to bind holy books
> and volumes of the Russian classics,

and when they had enough of classics
and needed blood, he fled . . .

Here, with the empathy that imaginative recall can release, a Jewish ingredient of poverty and oppression does emerge.

David Ignatow was born on February 7, 1914, in Brooklyn to immigrant parents—his mother "was very stoic. . . . She kept the whole thing together." He attended Brooklyn College but did not graduate. In 1939, he married the painter Rose Graubart and adopted her son, David, who suffered from mental illness. *In Limbo* (under)states the pain of that father-son relationship, which ended with the son's death in 1985. Ignatow and his wife also had a daughter. For years, he was involved in his father's business and beset by the exigencies of living, while his poetry went largely unnoticed. Recognition came with *Say Pardon* (1961), and after his father's death Ignatow sold the business. He taught in many places and received the Bollingen Prize along with other awards.

Having drawn at first on the openness of Walt Whitman's verse, Ignatow came to find him "just a little too euphoric" and turned to William Carlos Williams's vernacular, anti-Romantic inspiration. Then Pablo Neruda and especially César Vallejo struck him: "the guts and the mind . . . how they get together and inform one another." At the same time, Ignatow decided that his poems had to avoid the "genteel tradition" and cleave to plain street talk, which (he says) met with "very strong resistance from men like [Harold] Bloom and [John] Hollander"—though Louis Simpson welcomed poems that "deal with ordinary life—the confined, sweating, hallucinatory life of a city." If David Ignatow is "a master, in the American grain," as Stanley Kunitz called him, then both urban pessimism and comic earthiness run together in that grain—the poet somersaulting down the street "like a bagel / and strangely happy with myself." He died on November 17, 1997.

Autumn Leaves

Children of the road, autumn leaves,
forced from once well-stocked homes,
what depression has shriveled their sources?
What supply and demand dropped them:
yellowed with ragged edges, mobs
over the whole land; mouldering
on streets, crumbling on windswirls?
Have they left their homes for good,
comrades to spring, frost's victims?

God stalks by stubble fields
in a shivering garment of brown, wrinkled leaves,
at the heels mud, on His face the weather,
and in His hand a bunch of unripened torn-up grain.
God, like a shriveled nut where plumpness
and the fruit have fed the worm,
lies sprawled beneath a tree,
gaunt in His giving.

1930s 1948

Europe and America

My father brought the emigrant bundle
of desperation and worn threads,
that in anxiety as he stumbles
tumble out distractedly;
while I am bedded upon soft green money
that grows like grass.
Thus, between my father
who lives on bed of anguish for his daily bread,
and I who tear money at leisure by the roots,
where I lie in sun or shade,
a vast continent of breezes, storms to him,
shadows, darkness to him, small lakes, rough channels
to him, and hills, mountains to him, lie between
us.

My father comes of a small hell
where bread and man have been kneaded and baked together.
You have heard the scream as the knife fell;
while I have slept
as guns pounded offshore.

1948

God Said

God said, Have you finished my thinking?
Now think yourself into stone
and I will lift you
and set you upon a mountain.

1961

In Limbo

I have a child in limbo
I must bring back.
My experience grows
but there is no wisdom
without a child in the house.

1961

The Bagel

I stopped to pick up the bagel
rolling away in the wind,

annoyed with myself
for having dropped it
as it were a portent.
Faster and faster it rolled,
with me running after it
bent low, gritting my teeth,
and I found myself doubled over
and rolling down the street
head over heels, one complete somersault
after another like a bagel
and strangely happy with myself.

1968

BERNARD MALAMUD
(1914–1986)

"Every man is a Jew though he may not know it," Bernard Malamud has said. For him, this notion of the Jew as Everyman comprises "the primal knowledge . . . that life is tragic, no matter how sweet or apparently full." Beginning with God's gift of "a spirituality that raises man to his highest being," the Jewish drama persists through betrayal of that gift, destruction, exile, and "an oftentimes agonizing defense" of moral selfhood, human responsibility, even occasional joy. As for the local version of this drama, Malamud sees the ethical ideal of compassion echoed in American democratic principle, and he sees Jewish historical experience—"a rich and tragic drama of the self-realization of a people"—akin to this country's own self-realization. Malamud (in 1966) thinks it "a lucky break to be a member of a minority group . . . in America." "Everyone has a heritage," he says, "but the Jews because of their everlasting struggle to maintain theirs, are especially conscious of it." However debatable Malamud's inclination to "see the Jew as universal man," it can justify and deepen his fiction.

Bernard Malamud was born in Brooklyn on April 26, 1914, to an immigrant grocer, Max Malamud, and his theatrically talented wife, Bertha Fidelman, who helped him in the store. The Jewish past "came to me . . . through the immigrant Jews of New York City, those who visited our house to sit and talk, or came to my father's place of business . . . and those whom I saw on the streets and in the trolley cars." These were hardworking shopkeepers or else *luftmenschen*, people with no discernible occupation, especially during the depression. Their concerns were money, health, citizenship—"How much of being a Jew did you give up to be an American?" Alfred Kazin recalls Malamud's "memories of his father's keeping a failing grocery in a hostile gentile neighborhood, his mother's death when he was fifteen, a younger brother's descent into schizophrenia," and notes the aloneness of Malamud's characters, with no connection to Jewish socialism of the period or to Jewish synagogal faith.

After earning a B.A. at City College of New York, Malamud wrote a Columbia master's thesis on Thomas Hardy's poetry while also teaching at his former high school and in Harlem. Later he taught at Oregon State and at Bennington College in Vermont. His first novel, *The Natural* (1952), has to do with the quintessential

American sport, baseball, and not at all with Jewish characters or milieus. In *The Assistant* (1957), however, an ailing, struggling Jewish grocer is robbed by a young Italian whom he then, unknowingly, takes on as "assistant." Frank Alpine falls in love with (and at one point rapes) Morris Bober's daughter but also studies him: " 'Tell me why is it that the Jews suffer so damn much, Morris? . . . What do you suffer for, Morris?' . . . 'I suffer for you,' Morris said calmly." Eventually, Morris dies and Frank takes over the store. The novel ends with his being circumcised: "For a couple of days he dragged himself around with a pain between his legs. The pain enraged and inspired him. After Passover he became a Jew." Despite the somewhat discordant image of Morris as a Christ figure, *The Assistant*, with its charged prose and human sympathy, is Malamud's best novel.

The Magic Barrel (1958), Malamud's first collection of stories and probably his finest, staked the terrain that still seems most his: urban, bleak, unforgiving, tenanted by luckless Jews, yet a world in which goodness and grace crop up sporadically. In *Take Pity,* a census taker enters a dim, sparsely furnished room and asks Rosen: " 'What's the matter you don't pull the shades up?' . . . 'Who needs light?' 'What then you need?' 'Light I don't need,' " replies Rosen. But in *Angel Levine,* a beneficent Negro angel recites the blessing for bread "in sonorous Hebrew." And in the book's title story, a betrothal occurs with Chagallesque élan: "Violins and lit candles revolved in the sky. Leo ran forward with flowers outthrust."

Several appealing elements mark Malamud's storytelling: a strong folkloric hint of fable or fairy tale or fantasy, as in *The Magic Barrel* and *The Last Mohican;* an affectionate ear for Yiddishly inflected speech, as in the rhythms and questions of *Take Pity;* and a wry comic bent. All of these combine in *The Jewbird,* from Malamud's second collection, *Idiots First* (1963), which begins in the kitchen of the Cohen family's top-floor apartment near New York's East River: "The window was open so the skinny bird flew in. Flappity-flap with its frazzled black wings. That's how it goes. It's open, you're in. Closed, you're out and that's your fate." The Jewbird, whose name happens to be Schwartz, is fleeing "Anti-Semeets"; he tutors the son of the family, but Cohen eventually throws him out. Here, too, what matters most is the moral Law (often capitalized in Malamud): "Connection, indebtedness, responsibility, these are his moral concerns," as Philip Roth put it.

Yet Malamud, Roth also says, does not really write about modern American Jews, their "anxieties and dilemmas and corruptions." Malamud's people "live in a timeless depression and a placeless Lower East Side." And the scholar Robert Alter notes the absence of Jewish milieus and communities in Malamud's work. We are faced again with the idea of the Jew as Everyman since Malamud digs for universal themes: failure, entrapment, isolation, gentleness, choice, compassion, redemption. Yet Malamud insists that the drama of "Jewish history—suffering, expiation, renewal"—inspires him. "I'm an American, I'm a Jew, and I write for all men. . . . I write about Jews, because they set my imagination going."

Malamud did once present an actual Jew in a Jewish plight, in *The Fixer* (1966), which won the National Book Award (like *The Magic Barrel*) and also the Pulitzer prize. This novel recreates the story of Mendel Beilis, a simple man in czarist Russia (1911) who suddenly finds himself accused of ritual murder, the age-old libel that Jews kill Christians to use their blood for Passover matzoth. Malamud paints a gripping portrait of anti-Semitism, imprisonment, degradation, torture, and human integrity. At the same time, *The Fixer* works as a semblance of the Holocaust, which Malamud otherwise dealt with only indirectly, as in *The Last Mohican.*

In that story, too, the ethical burden straddles humanness and Jewishness. Susskind, a European refugee, tries to cadge a warm suit off the American Fidelman. "Am I responsible for you then, Susskind?" "Who else?" Susskind replies and tells why: "Because you are a man. Because you are a Jew, aren't you?"

Bernard Malamud died on March 18, 1986, and is buried on a grassy slope in Mount Auburn Cemetery, Cambridge, Massachusetts.

The Last Mohican

Fidelman, a self-confessed failure as a painter, came to Italy to prepare a critical study of Giotto,[1] the opening chapter of which he had carried across the ocean in a new pigskin leather brief case, now gripped in his perspiring hand. Also new were his gum-soled oxblood shoes, a tweed suit he had on despite the late-September sun slanting hot in the Roman sky, although there was a lighter one in his bag; and a dacron[2] shirt and set of cotton-dacron underwear, good for quick and easy washing for the traveler. His suitcase, a bulky, two-strapped affair which embarrassed him slightly, he had borrowed from his sister Bessie. He planned, if he had any money left at the end of the year, to buy a new one in Florence. Although he had been in not much of a mood when he had left the U.S.A., Fidelman picked up in Naples, and at the moment, as he stood in front of the Rome railroad station, after twenty minutes still absorbed in his first sight of the Eternal City, he was conscious of a certain exaltation that devolved on him after he had discovered that directly across the many-vehicled piazza stood the remains of the Baths of Diocletian. Fidelman remembered having read that Michelangelo[3] had had a hand in converting the baths into a church and convent, the latter ultimately changed into the museum that presently was there. "Imagine," he muttered. "Imagine all that history."

In the midst of his imagining, Fidelman experienced the sensation of suddenly seeing himself as he was, to the pinpoint, outside and in, not without bittersweet pleasure; and as the well-known image of his face rose before him he was taken by the depth of pure feeling in his eyes, slightly magnified by glasses, and the sensitivity of his elongated nostrils and often tremulous lips, nose divided from lips by a mustache of recent vintage that looked, Fidelman thought, as if it had been sculptured there, adding to his dignified appearance although he was a little on the short side. But almost at the same moment, this unexpectedly intense sense of his being—it was more than appearance—faded, exaltation having gone where exaltation goes, and Fidelman became aware that there was an exterior source to the strange, almost tri-dimensional reflection of himself he had felt as well as seen. Behind him, a short distance to the right, he had noticed a stranger—give a skeleton a couple of pounds—loitering near a bronze statue on a stone pedestal of the heavy-dugged Etruscan wolf suckling the infant Romulus and Remus,[4] the man contemplating Fidelman already acquisitively so as to suggest to the traveler that he had been mirrored (lock, stock, barrel) in the other's gaze for some time, perhaps since he had stepped off the train. Casually studying him, though pretending no, Fidelman beheld a person of about his own height, oddly dressed in brown knickers and black, knee-length woolen socks drawn up over slightly bowed, broomstick legs, these grounded in small, porous, pointed shoes. His yellowed shirt was open at the gaunt throat, both sleeves rolled up over skinny, hairy arms. The stranger's high forehead was bronzed, his black hair thick behind small ears, the dark, close-shaven beard

1. Giotto di Bondone (1266–1337), a Florentine painter and architect whose lifelike, expressive figures changed the course of European art.
2. A synthetic polyester textile fiber.
3. Michelangelo Buonarroti (1475–1564), an Italian sculptor, painter, architect, and poet. "Diocletian": a Roman emperor (245–313).
4. Romulus, the legendary founder of Rome, and his twin brother, Remus, were said to have been suckled by a she-wolf.

tight on the face; his experienced nose was weighted at the tip, and the soft brown eyes, above all, *wanted*. Though his expression suggested humility, he all but licked his lips as he approached the ex-painter.

"Shalom," he greeted Fidelman.

"Shalom," the other hesitantly replied, uttering the word—so far as he recalled—for the first time in his life. My God, he thought, a handout for sure. My first hello in Rome and it has to be a schnorrer.[5]

The stranger extended a smiling hand. "Susskind," he said, "Shimon Susskind."

"Arthur Fidelman." Transferring his brief case to under his left arm while standing astride the big suitcase, he shook hands with Susskind. A blue-smocked porter came by, glanced at Fidelman's bag, looked at him, then walked away.

Whether he knew it or not Susskind was rubbing his palms contemplatively together.

"Parla italiano?"[6]

"Not with ease, although I read it fluently. You might say I need the practice."

"Yiddish?"

"I express myself best in English."

"Let it be English then." Susskind spoke with a slight British intonation. "I knew you were Jewish," he said, "the minute my eyes saw you."

Fidelman chose to ignore the remark. "Where did you pick up your knowledge of English?"

"In Israel."

Israel interested Fidelman. "You live there?"

"Once, not now," Susskind answered vaguely. He seemed suddenly bored.

"How so?"

Susskind twitched a shoulder. "Too much heavy labor for a man of my modest health. Also I couldn't stand the suspense."

Fidelman nodded.

"Furthermore, the desert air makes me constipated. In Rome I am light hearted."

"A Jewish refugee from Israel, no less," Fidelman said good humoredly.

"I'm always running," Susskind answered mirthlessly. If he was light hearted, he had yet to show it.

"Where else from, if I may ask?"

"Where else but Germany, Hungary, Poland? Where not?"

"Ah, that's so long ago." Fidelman then noticed the gray in the man's hair. "Well, I'd better be going," he said. He picked up his bag as two porters hovered uncertainly nearby.

But Susskind offered certain services. "You got a hotel?"

"All picked and reserved."

"How long are you staying?"

What business is it of his? However, Fidelman courteously replied, "Two weeks in Rome, the rest of the year in Florence, with a few side trips to Siena, Assisi, Padua and maybe also Venice."

"You wish a guide in Rome?"

5. A wily beggar or one with a beggarly disposition.

6. Do you speak Italian? (Italian).

"Are you a guide?"

"Why not?"

"No," said Fidelman. "I'll look as I go along to museums, libraries, et cetera."

This caught Susskind's attention. "What are you, a professor?"

Fidelman couldn't help blushing. "Not exactly, really just a student."

"From which institution?"

He coughed a little. "By that I mean a professional student, you might say. Call me Trofimov,[7] from Chekov. If there's something to learn I want to learn it."

"You have some kind of a project?" the other persisted. "A grant?"

"No grant. My money is hard earned. I worked and saved a long time to take a year in Italy. I made certain sacrifices. As for a project, I'm writing on the painter Giotto. He was one of the most important—"

"You don't have to tell me about Giotto," Susskind interrupted with a little smile.

"You've studied his work?"

"Who doesn't know Giotto?"

"That's interesting to me," said Fidelman, secretly irritated. "How do you happen to know him?"

"How do you?"

"I've given a good deal of time and study to his work."

"So I know him too."

I'd better get this over with before it begins to amount up to something, Fidelman thought. He set down his bag and fished with a finger in his leather coin purse. The two porters watched with interest, one taking a sandwich out of his pocket, unwrapping the newspaper and beginning to eat.

"This is for yourself," Fidelman said.

Susskind hardly glanced at the coin as he let it drop into his pants pocket. The porters then left.

The refugee had an odd way of standing motionless, like a cigar store Indian about to burst into flight. "In your luggage," he said vaguely, "would you maybe have a suit you can't use? I could use a suit."

At last he comes to the point. Fidelman, though annoyed, controlled himself. "All I have is a change from the one you now see me wearing. Don't get the wrong idea about me, Mr. Susskind. I'm not rich. In fact, I'm poor. Don't let a few new clothes deceive you. I owe my sister money for them."

Susskind glanced down at his shabby, baggy knickers. "I haven't had a suit for years. The one I was wearing when I ran away from Germany, fell apart. One day I was walking around naked."

"Isn't there a welfare organization that could help you out—some group in the Jewish community, interested in refugees?"

"The Jewish organizations wish to give me what they wish, not what I wish," Susskind replied bitterly. "The only thing they offer me is a ticket back to Israel."

"Why don't you take it?"

"I told you already, here I feel free."

7. A character in *The Cherry Orchard* by Anton Chekhov (1860–1904), Russian playwright and short-story writer.

"Freedom is a relative term."

"Don't tell me about freedom."

He knows all about that, too, Fidelman thought. "So you feel free," he said, "but how do you live?"

Susskind coughed, a brutal cough.

Fidelman was about to say something more on the subject of freedom but left it unsaid. Jesus, I'll be saddled with him all day if I don't watch out.

"I'd better be getting off to the hotel." He bent again for his bag.

Susskind touched him on the shoulder and when Fidelman exasperatedly straightened up, the half dollar he had given the man was staring him in the eye.

"On this we both lose money."

"How do you mean?"

"Today the lira sells six twenty-three on the dollar, but for specie they only give you five hundred."

"In that case, give it here and I'll let you have a dollar." From his billfold Fidelman quickly extracted a crisp bill and handed it to the refugee.

"Not more?" Susskind sighed.

"Not more," the student answered emphatically.

"Maybe you would like to see Diocletian's bath? There are some enjoyable Roman coffins inside. I will guide you for another dollar."

"No, thanks." Fidelman said goodbye, and lifting the suitcase, lugged it to the curb. A porter appeared and the student, after some hesitation, let him carry it toward the line of small dark-green taxis in the piazza. The porter offered to carry the brief case too, but Fidelman wouldn't part with it. He gave the cab driver the address of the hotel, and the taxi took off with a lurch. Fidelman at last relaxed. Susskind, he noticed, had disappeared. Gone with his breeze, he thought. But on the way to the hotel he had an uneasy feeling that the refugee, crouched low, might be clinging to the little tire on the back of the cab; however, he didn't look out to see.

Fidelman had reserved a room in an inexpensive hotel not far from the station, with its very convenient bus terminal. Then, as was his habit, he got himself quickly and tightly organized. He was always concerned with not wasting time, as if it were his only wealth—not true, of course, though Fidelman admitted he was an ambitious person—and he soon arranged a schedule that made the most of his working hours. Mornings he usually visited the Italian libraries, searching their catalogues and archives, read in poor light, and made profuse notes. He napped for an hour after lunch, then at four, when the churches and museums were re-opening, hurried off to them with lists of frescoes and paintings he must see. He was anxious to get to Florence, at the same time a little unhappy at all he would not have time to take in in Rome. Fidelman promised himself to return again if he could afford it, perhaps in the spring, and look at anything he pleased.

After dark he managed to unwind himself and relax. He ate as the Romans did, late, enjoyed a half litre of white wine and smoked a cigarette. Afterward he liked to wander—especially in the old sections near the Tiber. He had read that here, under his feet, were the ruins of Ancient Rome. It was an inspiring business, he, Arthur Fidelman, after all, born a Bronx boy, walking around in all this history. History was mysterious, the remembrance of things unknown, in a way burdensome, in a way a sensuous experience. It uplifted and depressed, why he did not know, except that it excited his thoughts more than he thought good for him. This kind of excitement was all right up to a point, perfect maybe for a creative artist, but less so for a critic. A critic, he thought, should live on beans. He walked for miles along the winding river, gazing at the star-strewn skies. Once, after a couple of days in the Vatican Museum, he saw flights of angels—gold, blue, white—intermingled in the sky. "My God, I got to stop using my eyes so much," Fidelman said to himself. But back in his room he sometimes wrote till morning.

Late one night, about a week after his arrival in Rome, as Fidelman was writing notes on the Byzantine style mosaics he had seen during the day, there was a knock on the door, and though the student, immersed in his work, was not conscious he had said "Avanti,"[8] he must have, for the door opened, and instead of an angel, in came Susskind in his shirt and baggy knickers.

Fidelman, who had all but forgotten the refugee, certainly never thought of him, half rose in astonishment. "Susskind," he exclaimed, "how did you get in here?"

Susskind for a moment stood motionless, then answered with a weary smile, "I'll tell you the truth, I know the desk clerk."

"But how did you know where I live?"

"I saw you walking in the street so I followed you."

"You mean you saw me accidentally?"

"How else? Did you leave me your address?"

Fidelman resumed his seat. "What can I do for you, Susskind?" He spoke grimly.

The refugee cleared his throat. "Professor, the days are warm but the nights are cold. You see how I go around naked." He held forth bluish arms, goosefleshed. "I came to ask you to reconsider about giving away your old suit."

"And who says it's an old suit?" Despite himself, Fidelman's voice thickened.

"One suit is new, so the other is old."

"Not precisely. I am afraid I have no suit for you, Susskind. The one I presently have hanging in the closet is a little more than a year old and I can't afford to give it away. Besides, it's gabardine, more like a summer suit."

"On me it will be for all seasons."

After a moment's reflection, Fidelman drew out his billfold and counted four single dollars. These he handed to Susskind.

"Buy yourself a warm sweater."

Susskind also counted the money. "If four," he said, "then why not five?"

Fidelman flushed. The man's warped nerve. "Because I happen to have four available," he answered. "That's twenty-five hundred lire. You should be able to buy a warm sweater and have something left over besides."

"I need a suit," Susskind said. "The days are warm but the nights are cold." He rubbed his arms. "What else I need I won't say."

"At least roll down your sleeves if you're so cold."

"That won't help me."

8. Come in (Italian).

"Listen, Susskind," Fidelman said gently, "I would gladly give you the suit if I could afford to, but I can't. I have barely enough money to squeeze out a year for myself here. I've already told you I am indebted to my sister. Why don't you try to get yourself a job somewhere, no matter how menial? I'm sure that in a short while you'll work yourself up into a decent position."

"A job, he says," Susskind muttered gloomily. "Do you know what it means to get a job in Italy? Who will give me a job?"

"Who gives anybody a job? They have to go out and look for it."

"You don't understand, professor. I am an Israeli citizen and this means I can only work for an Israeli company. How many Israeli companies are there here?—maybe two, El Al and Zim, and even if they had a job, they wouldn't give it to me because I have lost my passport. I would be better off now if I were stateless. A stateless person shows his laissez passer[9] and sometimes he can find a small job."

"But if you lost your passport why didn't you put in for a duplicate?"

"I did, but did they give it to me?"

"Why not?"

"Why not? They say I sold it."

"Had they reason to think that?"

"I swear to you somebody stole it from me."

"Under such circumstances," Fidelman asked, "how do you live?"

"How do I live?" He chomped with his teeth. "I eat air."

"Seriously?"

"Seriously, on air. I also peddle," he confessed, "but to peddle you need a license, and that the Italians won't give me. When they caught me peddling I was interned for six months in a work camp."

"Didn't they attempt to deport you?"

"They did, but I sold my mother's old wedding ring that I kept in my pocket so many years. The Italians are a humane people. They took the money and let me go but they told me not to peddle anymore."

"So what do you do now?"

"I peddle. What should I do, beg?—I peddle. But last spring I got sick and gave my little money away to the doctors. I still have a bad cough." He coughed fruitily. "Now I have no capital to buy stock with. Listen, professor, maybe we can go in partnership together? Lend me twenty thousand lire and I will buy ladies' nylon stockings. After I sell them I will return you your money."

"I have no funds to invest, Susskind."

"You will get it back, with interest."

"I honestly am sorry for you," Fidelman said, "but why don't you at least do something practical? Why don't you go to the Joint Distribution Committee, for instance, and ask them to assist you? That's their business."

"I already told you why. They wish me to go back, but I wish to stay here."

"I still think going back would be the best thing for you."

"No," cried Susskind angrily.

"If that's your decision, freely made, then why pick on me? Am I responsible for you then, Susskind?"

9. A permit or pass, usually for travel. "El Al and Zim": the first, Israel's national airline; the second, its merchant and (until 1970) passenger shipping company.

"Who else?" Susskind loudly replied.

"Lower your voice, please, people are sleeping around here," said Fidelman, beginning to perspire. "Why should I be?"

"You know what responsibility means?"

"I think so."

"Then you are responsible. Because you are a man. Because you are a Jew, aren't you?"

"Yes, goddamn it, but I'm not the only one in the whole wide world. Without prejudice, I refuse the obligation. I am a single individual and can't take on everybody's personal burden. I have the weight of my own to contend with."

He reached for his billfold and plucked out another dollar.

"This makes five. It's more than I can afford, but take it and after this please leave me alone. I have made my contribution."

Susskind stood there, oddly motionless, an impassioned statue, and for a moment Fidelman wondered if he would stay all night, but at last the refugee thrust forth a stiff arm, took the fifth dollar and departed.

Early the next morning Fidelman moved out of the hotel into another, less convenient for him, but far away from Shimon Susskind and his endless demands.

This was Tuesday. On Wednesday, after a busy morning in the library, Fidelman entered a nearby trattoria and ordered a plate of spaghetti with tomato sauce. He was reading his *Messaggero*,[1] anticipating the coming of the food, for he was unusually hungry, when he sensed a presence at the table. He looked up, expecting the waiter, but beheld instead Susskind standing there, alas, unchanged.

Is there no escape from him? thought Fidelman, severely vexed. Is this why I came to Rome?

"Shalom, professor," Susskind said, keeping his eyes off the table. "I was passing and saw you sitting here alone, so I came in to say shalom."

"Susskind," Fidelman said in anger, "have you been following me again?"

"How could I follow you?" asked the astonished Susskind. "Do I know where you live now?"

Though Fidelman blushed a little, he told himself he owed nobody an explanation. So he had found out he had moved—good.

"My feet are tired. Can I sit five minutes?"

"Sit."

Susskind drew out a chair. The spaghetti arrived, steaming hot. Fidelman sprinkled it with cheese and wound his fork into several tender strands. One of the strings of spaghetti seemed to stretch for miles, so he stopped at a certain point and swallowed the forkful. Having foolishly neglected to cut the long spaghetti string he was left sucking it, seemingly endlessly. This embarrassed him.

Susskind watched with rapt attention.

Fidelman at last reached the end of the long spaghetti, patted his mouth with a napkin, and paused in his eating.

"Would you care for a plateful?"

1. A Roman daily newspaper.

Susskind, eyes hungry, hesitated. "Thanks," he said.

"Thanks yes or thanks no?"

"Thanks no." The eyes looked away.

Fidelman resumed eating, carefully winding his fork; he had had not too much practice with this sort of thing and was soon involved in the same dilemma with the spaghetti. Seeing Susskind still watching him, he soon became tense.

"We are not Italians, professor," the refugee said. "Cut it in small pieces with your knife. Then you will swallow it easier."

"I'll handle it as I please," Fidelman responded testily. "This is my business. You attend to yours."

"My business," Susskind sighed, "don't exist. This morning I had to let a wonderful chance get away from me. I had a chance to buy ladies' stockings at three hundred lire if I had money to buy half a gross. I could easily sell them for five hundred a pair. We would have made a nice profit."

"The news doesn't interest me."

"So if not ladies' stockings, I can also get sweaters, scarves, men's socks, also cheap leather goods, ceramics—whatever would interest you."

"What interests me is what you did with the money I gave you for a sweater."

"It's getting cold, professor," Susskind said worriedly. "Soon comes the November rains, and in winter the tramontana.[2] I thought I ought to save your money to buy a couple of kilos of chestnuts and a bag of charcoal for my burner. If you sit all day on a busy street corner you can sometimes make a thousand lire. Italians like hot chestnuts. But if I do this I will need some warm clothes, maybe a suit."

"A suit," Fidelman remarked sarcastically, "why not an overcoat?"

"I have a coat, poor that it is, but now I need a suit. How can anybody come in company without a suit?"

Fidelman's hand trembled as he laid down his fork. "To my mind you are utterly irresponsible and I won't be saddled with you. I have the right to choose my own problems and the right to my privacy."

"Don't get excited, professor, it's bad for your digestion. Eat in peace." Susskind got up and left the trattoria.

Fidelman hadn't the appetite to finish his spaghetti. He paid the bill, waited ten minutes, then departed, glancing around from time to time to see if he were being followed. He headed down the sloping street to a small piazza where he saw a couple of cabs. Not that he could afford one, but he wanted to make sure Susskind didn't tail him back to his new hotel. He would warn the clerk at the desk never to allow anybody of the refugee's name or description even to make inquiries about him.

Susskind, however, stepped out from behind a plashing fountain at the center of the little piazza. Modestly addressing the speechless Fidelman, he said, "I don't wish to take only, professor. If I had something to give you, I would gladly give it to you."

"Thanks," snapped Fidelman, "just give me some peace of mind."

"That you have to find yourself," Susskind answered.

2. The north wind, from beyond the Alps.

In the taxi Fidelman decided to leave for Florence the next day, rather than at the end of the week, and once and for all be done with the pest.

That night, after returning to his room from an unpleasurable walk in the Trastevere[3]—he had a headache from too much wine at supper—Fidelman found his door ajar and at once recalled that he had forgotten to lock it, although he had as usual left the key with the desk clerk. He was at first frightened, but when he tried the armadio[4] in which he kept his clothes and suitcase, it was shut tight. Hastily unlocking it, he was relieved to see his blue gabardine suit—a one-button jacket affair, the trousers a little frayed on the cuffs, but all in good shape and usable for years to come—hanging amid some shirts the maid had pressed for him; and when he examined the contents of the suitcase he found nothing missing, including, thank God, his passport and travelers' checks. Gazing around the room, Fidelman saw all in place. Satisfied, he picked up a book and read ten pages before he thought of his brief case. He jumped to his feet and began to search everywhere, remembering distinctly that it had been on the night table as he had lain on the bed that afternoon, rereading his chapter. He searched under the bed and behind the night table, then again throughout the room, even on top of and behind the armadio. Fidelman hopelessly opened every drawer, no matter how small, but found neither the brief case, nor, what was worse, the chapter in it.

With a groan he sank down on the bed, insulting himself for not having made a copy of the manuscript, for he had more than once warned himself that something like this might happen to it. But he hadn't because there were some revisions he had contemplated making, and he had planned to retype the entire chapter before beginning the next. He thought now of complaining to the owner of the hotel, who lived on the floor below, but it was already past midnight and he realized nothing could be done until morning. Who could have taken it? The maid or hall porter? It seemed unlikely they would risk their jobs to steal a piece of leather goods that would bring them only a few thousand lire in a pawn shop. Possibly a sneak thief? He would ask tomorrow if other persons on the floor were missing something. He somehow doubted it. If a thief, he would then and there have ditched the chapter and stuffed the brief case with Fidelman's oxblood shoes, left by the bed, and the fifteen-dollar R. H. Macy sweater that lay in full view of the desk. But if not the maid or porter or a sneak thief, then who? Though Fidelman had not the slightest shred of evidence to support his suspicions he could think of only one person—Susskind. This thought stung him. But if Susskind, why? Out of pique, perhaps, that he had not been given the suit he had coveted, nor was able to pry it out of the armadio? Try as he would, Fidelman could think of no one else and no other reason. Somehow the peddler had followed him home (he suspected their meeting at the fountain) and had got into his room while he was out to supper.

Fidelman's sleep that night was wretched. He dreamed of pursuing the refugee in the Jewish catacombs under the ancient Appian Way,[5] threatening him a blow on the presumptuous head with a seven-flamed candelabrum he clutched in his hand; while Susskind, clever ghost, who knew the ins and

3. Literally, "Across the Tiber River" (Italian); a section of Rome originally inhabited by sailors and foreigners.

4. A wardrobe or large cupboard.

5. The first of the ancient Roman roads, running from Rome to southern Italy.

outs of all the crypts and alleys, eluded him at every turn. Then Fidelman's candles all blew out, leaving him sightless and alone in the cemeterial dark; but when the student arose in the morning and wearily drew up the blinds, the yellow Italian sun winked him cheerfully in both bleary eyes.

Fidelman postponed going to Florence. He reported his loss to the Questura, and though the police were polite and eager to help, they could do nothing for him. On the form on which the inspector noted the complaint, he listed the brief case as worth ten thousand lire, and for "valore del manuscritto"[6] he drew a line. Fidelman, after giving the matter a good deal of thought, did not report Susskind, first, because he had absolutely no proof, for the desk clerk swore he had seen no stranger around in knickers; second, because he was afraid of the consequences for the refugee if he were written down "suspected thief" as well as "unlicensed peddler" and inveterate refugee. He tried instead to rewrite the chapter, which he felt sure he knew by heart, but when he sat down at the desk, there were important thoughts, whole paragraphs, even pages, that went blank in the mind. He considered sending to America for his notes for the chapter but they were in a barrel in his sister's attic in Levittown,[7] among many notes for other projects. The thought of Bessie, a mother of five, poking around in his things, and the work entailed in sorting the cards, then getting them packaged and mailed to him across the ocean, wearied Fidelman unspeakably; he was certain she would send the wrong ones. He laid down his pen and went into the street, seeking Susskind. He searched for him in neighborhoods where he had seen him before, and though Fidelman spent hours looking, literally days, Susskind never appeared; or if he perhaps did, the sight of Fidelman caused him to vanish. And when the student inquired about him at the Israeli consulate, the clerk, a new man on the job, said he had no record of such a person or his lost passport; on the other hand, he was known at the Joint Distribution Committee, but by name and address only, an impossibility, Fidelman thought. They gave him a number to go to but the place had long since been torn down to make way for an apartment house.

Time went without work, without accomplishment. To put an end to this appalling waste Fidelman tried to force himself back into his routine of research and picture viewing. He moved out of the hotel, which he now could not stand for the harm it had done him (leaving a telephone number and urging he be called if the slightest clue turned up), and he took a room in a small pensione near the Stazione and here had breakfast and supper rather than go out. He was much concerned with expenditures and carefully recorded them in a notebook he had acquired for the purpose. Nights, instead of wandering in the city, feasting himself upon its beauty and mystery, he kept his eyes glued to paper, sitting steadfastly at his desk in an attempt to recreate his initial chapter, because he was lost without a beginning. He had tried writing the second chapter from notes in his possession but it had come to nothing. Always Fidelman needed something solid behind him before he could advance, some worthwhile accomplishment upon which to build another. He worked late, but his mood, or inspiration,

6. Value of the manuscript (Italian). "Questura": police headquarters (Italian).
7. A planned residential community on Long Island, New York, developed between 1946 and 1951 to provide low-cost homes and accompanying social institutions.

or whatever it was, had deserted him, leaving him with growing anxiety, almost disorientation; of not knowing—it seemed to him for the first time in months—what he must do next, a feeling that was torture. Therefore he again took up his search for the refugee. He thought now that once he had settled it, knew that the man had or hadn't stolen his chapter—whether he recovered it or not seemed at the moment immaterial—just the knowing of it would ease his mind and again he would *feel* like working, the crucial element.

Daily he combed the crowded streets, searching for Susskind wherever people peddled. On successive Sunday mornings he took the long ride to the Porta Portese market and hunted for hours among the piles of second-hand goods and junk lining the back streets, hoping his brief case would magically appear, though it never did. He visited the open market at Piazza Fontanella Borghese, and observed the ambulant vendors at Piazza Dante. He looked among fruit and vegetable stalls set up in the streets, whenever he chanced upon them, and dawdled on busy street corners after dark, among beggars and fly-by-night peddlers. After the first cold snap at the end of October, when the chestnust sellers appeared throughout the city, huddled over pails of glowing coals, he sought in their faces the missing Susskind. Where in all of modern and ancient Rome was he? The man lived in the open air—he had to appear somewhere. Sometimes when riding in a bus or tram, Fidelman thought he had glimpsed somebody in a crowd, dressed in the refugee's clothes, and he invariably got off to run after whoever it was—once a man standing in front of the Banco di Santo Spirito, gone when Fidelman breathlessly arrived; and another time he overtook a person in knickers, but this one wore a monocle. Sir Ian Susskind?

In November it rained. Fidelman wore a blue beret with his trench coat and a pair of black Italian shoes, smaller, despite their pointed toes, than his burly oxbloods which overheated his feet and whose color he detested. But instead of visiting museums he frequented movie houses sitting in the cheapest seats and regretting the cost. He was, at odd hours in certain streets, several times accosted by prostitutes, some heartbreakingly pretty, one a slender, unhappy-looking girl with bags under her eyes whom he desired mightily, but Fidelman feared for his health. He had got to know the face of Rome and spoke Italian fairly fluently, but his heart was burdened, and in his blood raged a murderous hatred of the bandy-legged refugee—although there were times when he bethought himself he might be wrong—so Fidelman more than once cursed him to perdition.

One Friday night, as the first star glowed over the Tiber, Fidelman, walking aimlessly along the left riverbank, came upon a synagogue and wandered in among a crowd of Sephardim[8] with Italianate faces. One by one they paused before a sink in an antechamber to dip their hands under a flowing faucet, then in the house of worship touched with loose fingers their brows, mouths, and breasts as they bowed to the Arc,[9] Fidelman doing likewise. Where in the world am I? Three rabbis rose from a bench and the service began, a long prayer, sometimes chanted, sometimes accompanied by invisible organ

8. The Jews, or their descendants, who lived in Spain and Portugal from the Middle Ages until their persecution and mass expulsion in the late 15th century.

9. I.e., the ark of the Covenant, the chest housing the Torah scrolls.

music, but no Susskind anywhere. Fidelman sat at a desk-like pew in the last row, where he could inspect the congregants yet keep an eye on the door. The synagogue was unheated and the cold rose like an exudation from the marble floor. The student's freezing nose burned like a lit candle. He got up to go, but the beadle,[1] a stout man in a high hat and short caftan, wearing a long thick silver chain around his neck, fixed the student with his powerful left eye.

"From New York?" he inquired, slowly approaching.

Half the congregation turned to see who.

"State, not city," answered Fidelman, nursing an active guilt for the attention he was attracting. Then, taking advantage of a pause, he whispered, "Do you happen to know a man named Susskind? He wears knickers."

"A relative?" The beadle gazed at him sadly.

"Not exactly."

"My own son—killed in the Ardeatine Caves."[2] Tears stood forth in his eyes.

"Ah, for that I'm sorry."

But the beadle had exhausted the subject. He wiped his wet lids with pudgy fingers and the curious Sephardim turned back to their prayer books.

"Which Susskind?" the beadle wanted to know.

"Shimon."

He scratched his ear. "Look in the ghetto."

"I looked."

"Look again."

The beadle walked slowly away and Fidelman sneaked out.

The ghetto lay behind the synagogue for several crooked, well-packed blocks, encompassing aristocratic palazzi ruined by age and unbearable numbers, their discolored facades strung with lines of withered wet wash, the fountains in the piazzas, dirt-laden, dry. And dark stone tenements, built partly on centuries-old ghetto walls, inclined towards one another across narrow, cobblestoned streets. In and among the impoverished houses were the wholesale establishments of wealthy Jews, dark holes ending in jeweled interiors, silks and silver of all colors. In the mazed streets wandered the present-day poor, Fidelman among them, oppressed by history, although, he joked to himself, it added years to his life.

A white moon shone upon the ghetto, lighting it like dark day. Once he thought he saw a ghost he knew by sight, and hastily followed him through a thick stone passage to a blank wall where shone in white letters under a tiny electric bulb: VIETATO URINARE.[3] Here was a smell but no Susskind.

For thirty lire the student bought a dwarfed, blackened banana from a street vendor (not S) on a bicycle, and stopped to eat. A crowd of ragazzi[4] gathered to watch.

"Anybody here know Susskind, a refugee wearing knickers?" Fidelman announced, stooping to point with the banana where the pants went beneath the knees. He also made his legs a trifle bowed but nobody noticed.

There was no response until he had finished his fruit, then a thin-faced

1. Sexton, custodian.
2. The site in Rome where the Nazis, led by Erich Priebke, massacred 335 hostages in 1944.
3. Urinating Forbidden (Italian).
4. Boys, urchins (Italian).

boy with brown liquescent eyes out of Murillo,[5] piped: "He sometimes works in the Cimitero Verano, the Jewish section."

There too? thought Fidelman. "Works in the cemetery?" he inquired. "With a shovel?"

"He prays for the dead," the boy answered, "for a small fee."

Fidelman bought him a quick banana and the others dispersed.

In the cemetery, deserted on the Sabbath—he should have come Sunday—Fidelman went among the graves, reading legends carved on tombstones, many topped with small brass candelabra, whilst withered yellow chrysanthemums lay on the stone tablets of other graves, dropped stealthily, Fidelman imagined, on All Souls Day[6]—a festival in another part of the cemetery—by renegade sons and daughters unable to bear the sight of their dead bereft of flowers, while the crypts of the goyim[7] were lit and in bloom. Many were burial places, he read on the stained stones, of those who, for one reason or another, had died in the late large war,[8] including an empty place, it said under a six-pointed star engraved upon a marble slab that lay on the ground, for "My beloved father/Betrayed by the damned Fascists/ Murdered at Auschwitz by the barbarous Nazis/ *O Crime Orribile*." But no Susskind.

Three months had gone by since Fidelman's arrival in Rome. Should he, he many times asked himself, leave the city and this foolish search? Why not off to Florence, and there, amid the art splendors of the world, be inspired to resume his work? But the loss of his first chapter was like a spell cast over him. There were times he scorned it as a man-made thing, like all such, replaceable; other times he feared it was not the chapter per se, but that his volatile curiosity had become somehow entangled with Susskind's strange personality—Had he repaid generosity by stealing a man's life work? Was he so distorted? To satisfy himself, to know man, Fidelman had to know, though at what a cost in precious time and effort. Sometimes he smiled wryly at all this; ridiculous, the chapter grieved him for itself only—the precious thing he had created then lost—especially when he got to thinking of the long diligent labor, how painstakingly he had built each idea, how cleverly mastered problems of order, form, how impressive the finished product, Giotto reborn! It broke the heart. What else, if after months he was here, still seeking?

And Fidelman was unchangingly convinced that Susskind had taken it, or why would he still be hiding? He sighed much and gained weight. Mulling over his frustrated career, on the backs of envelopes containing unanswered letters from his sister Bessie he aimlessly sketched little angels flying. Once, studying his minuscule drawings, it occurred to him that he might someday return to painting, but the thought was more painful than Fidelman could bear.

One bright morning in mid-December, after a good night's sleep, his first in weeks, he vowed he would have another look at the Navicella and then be off to Florence. Shortly before noon he visited the porch of St. Peter's, trying, from his remembrance of Giotto's sketch, to see the mosaic as it had

5. Bartolomé Esteban Murillo (1618–1682), Spanish painter chiefly of religious subjects.
6. A Catholic day of supplication for souls in Purgatory.
7. Non-Jews; literally, "nations" (Hebrew).
8. I.e., World War II.

been before its many restorations. He hazarded a note or two in shaky handwriting, then left the church and was walking down the sweeping flight of stairs, when he beheld at the bottom—his heart misgave him, was he still seeing pictures, a sneaky apostle added to the overloaded boatful?—ecco, Susskind! The refugee, in beret and long green G. I.[9] raincoat, from under whose skirts showed his black-stockinged, rooster's ankles—indicating knickers going on above though hidden—was selling black and white rosaries to all who would buy. He held several strands of beads in one hand, while in the palm of the other a few gilded medallions glinted in the winter sun. Despite his outer clothing, Susskind looked, it must be said, unchanged, not a pound more of meat or muscle, the face though aged, ageless. Gazing at him, the student ground his teeth in remembrance. He was tempted quickly to hide, and unobserved observe the thief; but his impatience, after the long unhappy search, was too much for him. With controlled trepidation he approached Susskind on his left as the refugee was busily engaged on the right, urging a sale of beads upon a woman drenched in black.

"Beads, rosaries, say your prayers with holy beads."

"Greetings, Susskind," Fidelman said, coming shakily down the stairs, dissembling the Unified Man, all peace and contentment. "One looks for you everywhere and finds you here. Wie gehts?"[1]

Susskind, though his eyes flickered, showed no surprise to speak of. For a moment his expression seemed to say he had no idea who was this, had forgotten Fidelman's existence, but then at last remembered—somebody long ago from another country, whom you smiled on, then forgot.

"Still here?" he perhaps ironically joked.

"Still," Fidelman was embarrassed at his voice slipping.

"Rome holds you?"

"Rome," faltered Fidelman, "—the air." He breathed deep and exhaled with emotion.

Noticing the refugee was not truly attentive, his eyes roving upon potential customers, Fidelman, girding himself, remarked, "By the way, Susskind, you didn't happen to notice—did you?—the brief case I was carrying with me around the time we met in September?"

"Brief case—what kind?" This he said absently, his eyes on the church doors.

"Pigskin. I had in it—" Here Fidelman's voice could be heard cracking, "—a chapter of a critical work on Giotto I was writing. You know, I'm sure, the Trecento[2] painter?"

"Who doesn't know Giotto?"

"Do you happen to recall whether you saw, if, that is—" He stopped, at a loss for words other than accusatory.

"Excuse me—business." Susskind broke away and bounced up the steps two at a time. A man he approached shied away. He had beads, didn't need others.

Fidelman had followed the refugee. "Reward," he muttered up close to his ear. "Fifteen thousand for the chapter, and who has it can keep the brand new brief case. That's his business, no questions asked. Fair enough?"

9. Government issue; refers to American enlisted military personnel. "Ecco": behold (Italian).
1. How goes it? (German).
2. Designates Italy's cultural and artistic movements in the 1300s.

Susskind spied a lady tourist, including camera and guide book. "Beads—holy beads." He held up both hands, but she was just a Lutheran, passing through.

"Slow today," Susskind complained as they walked down the stairs, "but maybe it's the items. Everybody has the same. If I had some big ceramics of the Holy Mother, they go like hot cakes—a good investment for somebody with a little cash."

"Use the reward for that," Fidelman cagily whispered, "buy Holy Mothers."

If he heard, Susskind gave no sign. At the sight of a family of nine emerging from the main portal above, the refugee, calling addio[3] over his shoulder, fairly flew up the steps. But Fidelman uttered no response. I'll get the rat yet. He went off to hide behind a high fountain in the square. But the flying spume raised by the wind wet him, so he retreated behind a massive column and peeked out at short intervals to keep the peddler in sight.

At two o'clock, when St. Peter's closed to visitors, Susskind dumped his goods into his raincoat pockets and locked up shop. Fidelman followed him all the way home, indeed the ghetto, although along a street he had not consciously been on before, which led into an alley where the refugee pulled open a left-handed door, and without transition, was "home." Fidelman, sneaking up close, caught a dim glimpse of an overgrown closet containing bed and table. He found no address on wall or door, nor, to his surprise, any door lock. This for a moment depressed him. It meant Susskind had nothing worth stealing. Of his own, that is. The student promised himself to return tomorrow, when the occupant was elsewhere.

Return he did, in the morning, while the entrepreneur was out selling religious articles, glanced around once and was quickly inside. He shivered—a pitch black freezing cave. Fidelman scratched up a thick match and confirmed bed and table, also a rickety chair, but no heat or light except a drippy candle stub in a saucer on the table. He lit the yellow candle and searched all over the place. In the table drawer a few eating implements plus safety razor, though where he shaved was a mystery, probably a public toilet. On a shelf above the thin-blanketed bed stood half a flask of red wine, part of a package of spaghetti, and a hard panino.[4] Also an unexpected little fish bowl with a bony gold fish swimming around in Arctic seas. The fish, reflecting the candle flame, gulped repeatedly, threshing its frigid tail as Fidelman watched. He loves pets, thought the student. Under the bed he found a chamber pot, but nowhere a brief case with a fine critical chapter in it. The place was not more than an ice-box someone probably had lent the refugee to come in out of the rain. Alas, Fidelman sighed. Back in the pensione, it took a hot water bottle two hours to thaw him out; but from the visit he never fully recovered.

In this latest dream of Fidelman's he was spending the day in a cemetery all crowded with tombstones, when up out of an empty grave rose this long-nosed brown shade, Virgilio[5] Susskind, beckoning.

Fidelman hurried over.

3. Farewell (Italian).
4. A roll (Italian).
5. A reference to Virgil (70–19 B.C.E.), classical Roman poet, who was Dante's guide through Hell and Purgatory in *The Divine Comedy* (ca. 1308–21).

"Have you read Tolstoy?"[6]

"Sparingly."

"Why is art?" asked the shade, drifting off.

Fidelman, willy nilly, followed, and the ghost, as it vanished, led him up steps going through the ghetto and into a marble synagogue.[7]

The student, left alone, for no reason he could think of lay down upon the stone floor, his shoulders keeping strangely warm as he stared at the sunlit vault above. The fresco therein revealed this saint in fading blue, the sky flowing from his head, handing an old knight in a thin red robe his gold cloak. Nearby stood a humble horse and two stone hills.

Giotto. San Francesco dona le vesti al cavaliere povero.[8]

Fidelman awoke running. He stuffed his blue gabardine into a paper bag, caught a bus, and knocked early on Susskind's heavy portal.

"Avanti." The refugee, already garbed in beret and raincoat (probably his pajamas), was standing at the table, lighting the candle with a flaming sheet of paper. To Fidelman the paper looked the underside of a typewritten page. Despite himself, the student recalled in letters of fire his entire chapter.

"Here, Susskind," he said in a trembling voice, offering the bundle, "I bring you my suit. Wear it in good health."

The refugee glanced at it without expression. "What do you wish for it?"

"Nothing at all." Fidelman laid the bag on the table, called goodbye and left.

He soon heard footsteps clattering after him across the cobblestones.

"Excuse me, I kept this under my mattress for you." Susskind thrust at him the pigskin brief case.

Fidelman savagely opened it, searching frenziedly in each compartment, but the bag was empty. The refugee was already in flight. With a bellow the student started after him. "You bastard, you burned my chapter!"

"Have mercy," cried Susskind, "I did you a favor."

"I'll do you one and cut your throat."

"The words were there but the spirit was missing."

In a towering rage, Fidelman forced a burst of speed, but the refugee, light as the wind in his marvelous knickers, his green coattails flying, rapidly gained ground.

The ghetto Jews framed in amazement in their medieval windows, stared at the wild pursuit. But in the middle of it, Fidelman, stout and short of breath, moved by all he had lately learned, had a triumphant insight.

"Susskind, come back," he shouted, half sobbing. "The suit is yours. All is forgiven."

He came to a dead halt but the refugee ran on. When last seen he was still running.

1958

6. Count Leo Tolstoy (1828–1910), Russian author and reformer, argued for the moral responsibility of the artist in his *What Is Art?*

7. Giotto's frescoes of Saint Francis are actually in a church in Assisi.

8. Saint Francis gives his clothes to the poor knight (Italian).

The Magic Barrel

Not long ago there lived in uptown New York, in a small, almost meager room, though crowded with books, Leo Finkle, a rabbinical student in the Yeshivah University. Finkle, after six years of study, was to be ordained in June and had been advised by an acquaintance that he might find it easier to win himself a congregation if he were married. Since he had no present prospects of marriage, after two tormented days of turning it over in his mind, he called in Pinye Salzman, a marriage broker whose two-line advertisement he had read in the *Forward*.[1]

The matchmaker appeared one night out of the dark fourth-floor hallway of the graystone rooming house where Finkle lived, grasping a black, strapped portfolio that had been worn thin with use. Salzman, who had been long in the business, was of slight but dignified build, wearing an old hat, and an overcoat too short and tight for him. He smelled frankly of fish, which he loved to eat, and although he was missing a few teeth, his presence was not displeasing, because of an amiable manner curiously contrasted with mournful eyes. His voice, his lips, his wisp of beard, his bony fingers were animated, but give him a moment of repose and his mild blue eyes revealed a depth of sadness, a characteristic that put Leo a little at ease although the situation, for him, was inherently tense.

He at once informed Salzman why he had asked him to come, explaining that his home was in Cleveland, and that but for his parents, who had married comparatively late in life, he was alone in the world. He had for six years devoted himself almost entirely to his studies, as a result of which, understandably, he had found himself without time for a social life and the company of young women. Therefore he thought it the better part of trial and error—of embarrassing fumbling—to call in an experienced person to advise him on these matters. He remarked in passing that the function of the marriage broker was ancient and honorable, highly approved in the Jewish community, because it made practical the necessary without hindering joy. Moreover, his own parents had been brought together by a matchmaker. They had made, if not a financially profitable marriage—since neither had possessed any worldly goods to speak of—at least a successful one in the sense of their everlasting devotion to each other. Salzman listened in embarrassed surprise, sensing a sort of apology. Later, however, he experienced a glow of pride in his work, an emotion that had left him years ago, and he heartily approved of Finkle.

The two went to their business. Leo had led Salzman to the only clear place in the room, a table near a window that overlooked the lamp-lit city. He seated himself at the matchmaker's side but facing him, attempting by an act of will to suppress the unpleasant tickle in his throat. Salzman eagerly unstrapped his portfolio and removed a loose rubber band from a thin packet of much-handled cards. As he flipped through them, a gesture and sound that physically hurt Leo, the student pretended not to see and gazed steadfastly out the window. Although it was still February, winter was on its last legs, signs of which he had for the first time in years begun to notice. He now observed the round white moon, moving high in the sky through a cloud

1. A New York Yiddish daily paper with strong pro-labor and socialist leanings.

menagerie, and watched with half-open mouth as it penetrated a huge hen, and dropped out of her like an egg laying itself. Salzman, though pretending through eyeglasses he had just slipped on, to be engaged in scanning the writing on the cards, stole occasional glances at the young man's distinguished face, noting with pleasure the long, severe scholar's nose, brown eyes heavy with learning, sensitive yet ascetic lips, and a certain, almost hollow quality of the dark cheeks. He gazed around at shelves upon shelves of books and let out a soft, contented sigh.

When Leo's eyes fell upon the cards, he counted six spread out in Salzman's hand.

"So few?" he asked in disappointment.

"You wouldn't believe me how much cards I got in my office," Salzman replied. "The drawers are already filled to the top, so I keep them now in a barrel, but is every girl good for a new rabbi?"

Leo blushed at this, regretting all he had revealed of himself in a curriculum vitae he had sent to Salzman. He had thought it best to acquaint him with his strict standards and specifications, but in having done so, felt he had told the marriage broker more than was absolutely necessary.

He hesitantly inquired, "Do you keep photographs of your clients on file?"

"First comes family, amount of dowry, also what kind promises," Salzman replied, unbuttoning his tight coat and settling himself in the chair. "After comes pictures, rabbi."

"Call me Mr. Finkle. I'm not yet a rabbi."

Salzman said he would, but instead called him doctor, which he changed to rabbi when Leo was not listening too attentively.

Salzman adjusted his horn-rimmed spectacles, gently cleared his throat and read in an eager voice the contents of the top card:

"Sophie P. Twenty four years. Widow one year. No children. Educated high school and two years college. Father promises eight thousand dollars. Has wonderful wholesale business. Also real estate. On the mother's side comes teachers, also one actor. Well known on Second Avenue."

Leo gazed up in surprise. "Did you say a widow?"

"A widow don't mean spoiled, rabbi. She lived with her husband maybe four months. He was a sick boy she made a mistake to marry him."

"Marrying a widow has never entered my mind."

"This is because you have no experience. A widow, especially if she is young and healthy like this girl, is a wonderful person to marry. She will be thankful to you the rest of her life. Believe me, if I was looking now for a bride, I would marry a widow."

Leo reflected, then shook his head.

Salzman hunched his shoulders in an almost imperceptible gesture of disappointment. He placed the card down on the wooden table and began to read another:

"Lily H. High school teacher. Regular. Not a substitute. Has savings and new Dodge car. Lived in Paris one year. Father is successful dentist thirty-five years. Interested in professional man. Well Americanized family. Wonderful opportunity."

"I knew her personally," said Salzman. "I wish you could see this girl. She is a doll. Also very intelligent. All day you could talk to her about books and theyater and what not. She also knows current events."

"I don't believe you mentioned her age?"

"Her age?" Salzman said, raising his brows. "Her age is thirty-two years."

Leo said after a while, "I'm afraid that seems a little too old."

Salzman let out a laugh. "So how old are you, rabbi?"

"Twenty-seven."

"So what is the difference, tell me, between twenty-seven and thirty-two? My own wife is seven years older than me. So what did I suffer?—Nothing. If Rothschild's[2] a daughter wants to marry you, would you say on account her age, no?"

"Yes," Leo said dryly.

Salzman shook off the no in the yes. "Five years don't mean a thing. I give you my word that when you will live with her for one week you will forget her age. What does it mean five years—that she lived more and knows more than somebody who is younger? On this girl, God bless her, years are not wasted. Each one that it comes makes better the bargain."

"What subject does she teach in high school?"

"Languages. If you heard the way she speaks French, you will think it is music. I am in the business twenty-five years, and I recommend her with my whole heart. Believe me, I know what I'm talking, rabbi."

"What's on the next card?" Leo said abruptly.

Salzman reluctantly turned up the third card:

"Ruth K. Nineteen years. Honor student. Father offers thirteen thousand cash to the right bridegroom. He is a medical doctor. Stomach specialist with marvelous practice. Brother in law owns own garment business. Particular people."

Salzman looked as if he had read his trump card.

"Did you say nineteen?" Leo asked with interest.

"On the dot."

"Is she attractive?" He blushed. "Pretty?"

Salzman kissed his finger tips. "A little doll. On this I give you my word. Let me call the father tonight and you will see what means pretty."

But Leo was troubled. "You're sure she's that young?"

"This I am positive. The father will show you the birth certificate."

"Are you positive there isn't something wrong with her?" Leo insisted.

"Who says there is wrong?"

"I don't understand why an American girl her age should go to a marriage broker."

A smile spread over Salzman's face.

"So for the same reason you went, she comes."

Leo flushed. "I am pressed for time."

Salzman, realizing he had been tactless, quickly explained. "The father came, not her. He wants she should have the best, so he looks around himself. When we will locate the right boy he will introduce him and encourage. This makes a better marriage than if a young girl without experience takes for herself. I don't have to tell you this."

"But don't you think this young girl believes in love?" Leo spoke uneasily.

2. A wealthy dynastic Jewish banking family that influenced European economic and political history for two hundred years.

Salzman was about to guffaw but caught himself and said soberly, "Love comes with the right person, not before."

Leo parted dry lips but did not speak. Noticing that Salzman had snatched a glance at the next card, he cleverly asked, "How is her health?"

"Perfect," Salzman said, breathing with difficulty. "Of course, she is a little lame on her right foot from an auto accident that it happened to her when she was twelve years, but nobody notices on account she is so brilliant and also beautiful."

Leo got up heavily and went to the window. He felt curiously bitter and upbraided himself for having called in the marriage broker. Finally, he shook his head.

"Why not?" Salzman persisted, the pitch of his voice rising.

"Because I detest stomach specialists."

"So what do you care what is his business? After you marry her do you need him? Who says he must come every Friday night in your house?"

Ashamed of the way the talk was going, Leo dismissed Salzman, who went home with heavy, melancholy eyes.

Though he had felt only relief at the marriage broker's departure, Leo was in low spirits the next day. He explained it as arising from Salzman's failure to produce a suitable bride for him. He did not care for his type of clientele. But when Leo found himself hesitating whether to seek out another matchmaker, one more polished than Pinye, he wondered if it could be—his protestations to the contrary, and although he honored his father and mother—that he did not, in essence, care for the matchmaking institution? This thought he quickly put out of mind yet found himself still upset. All day he ran around in the woods—missed an important appointment, forgot to give out his laundry, walked out of a Broadway cafeteria without paying and had to run back with the ticket in his hand; had even not recognized his landlady in the street when she passed with a friend and courteously called out, "A good evening to you, Doctor Finkle." By nightfall, however, he had regained sufficient calm to sink his nose into a book and there found peace from his thoughts.

Almost at once there came a knock on the door. Before Leo could say enter, Salzman, commercial cupid, was standing in the room. His face was gray and meager, his expression hungry, and he looked as if he would expire on his feet. Yet the marriage broker managed, by some trick of the muscles, to display a broad smile.

"So good evening. I am invited?"

Leo nodded, disturbed to see him again, yet unwilling to ask the man to leave.

Beaming still, Salzman laid his portfolio on the table. "Rabbi, I got for you tonight good news."

"I've asked you not to call me rabbi. I'm still a student."

"Your worries are finished. I have for you a first-class bride."

"Leave me in peace concerning this subject." Leo pretended lack of interest.

"The world will dance at your wedding."

"Please, Mr. Salzman, no more."

"But first must come back my strength," Salzman said weakly. He fumbled with the portfolio straps and took out of the leather case an oily paper bag, from which he extracted a hard, seeded roll and a small, smoked white fish. With a quick motion of his hand he stripped the fish out of its skin and began ravenously to chew. "All day in a rush," he muttered.

Leo watched him eat.

"A sliced tomato you have maybe?" Salzman hesitantly inquired.

"No."

The marriage broker shut his eyes and ate. When he had finished he carefully cleaned up the crumbs and rolled up the remains of the fish, in the paper bag. His spectacled eyes roamed the room until he discovered, amid some piles of books, a one-burner gas stove. Lifting his hat he humbly asked, "A glass tea you got, rabbi?"

Conscience-stricken, Leo rose and brewed the tea. He served it with a chunk of lemon and two cubes of lump sugar, delighting Salzman.

After he had drunk his tea, Salzman's strength and good spirits were restored.

"So tell me, rabbi," he said amiably, "you considered some more the three clients I mentioned yesterday?"

"There was no need to consider."

"Why not?"

"None of them suits me."

"What then suits you?"

Leo let it pass because he could give only a confused answer.

Without waiting for a reply, Salzman asked, "You remember this girl I talked to you—the high school teacher?"

"Age thirty-two?"

But, surprisingly, Salzman's face lit in a smile. "Age twenty-nine."

Leo shot him a look. "Reduced from thirty-two?"

"A mistake," Salzman avowed. "I talked today with the dentist. He took me to his safety deposit box and showed me the birth certificate. She was twenty-nine years last August. They made her a party in the mountains where she went for her vacation. When her father spoke to me the first time I forgot to write the age and I told you thirty-two, but now I remember this was a different client, a widow."

"The same one you told me about? I thought she was twenty-four?"

"A different. Am I responsible that the world is filled with widows?"

"No, but I'm not interested in them, nor for that matter, in school teachers."

Salzman pulled his clasped hands to his breast. Looking at the ceiling he devoutly exclaimed, "Yiddishe kinder,[3] what can I say to somebody that he is not interested in high school teachers? So what then you are interested?"

Leo flushed but controlled himself.

"In what else will you be interested," Salzman went on, "if you not interested in this fine girl that she speaks four languages and has personally in the bank ten thousand dollars? Also her father guarantees further twelve thousand. Also she has a new car, wonderful clothes, talks on all subjects, and she will give you a first-class home and children. How near do we come in our life to paradise?"

"If she's so wonderful, why wasn't she married ten years ago?"

3. Jewish children (Yiddish).

"Why?" said Salzman with a heavy laugh. "—Why? Because she is *partikiler*. This is why. She wants the *best*."

Leo was silent, amused at how he had entangled himself. But Salzman had aroused his interest in Lily H., and he began seriously to consider calling on her. When the marriage broker observed how intently Leo's mind was at work on the facts he had supplied, he felt certain they would soon come to an agreement.

Late Saturday afternoon, conscious of Salzman, Leo Finkle walked with Lily Hirschorn along Riverside Drive.[4] He walked briskly and erectly, wearing with distinction the black fedora he had that morning taken with trepidation out of the dusty hat box on his closet shelf, and the heavy black Saturday coat he had thoroughly whisked clean. Leo also owned a walking stick, a present from a distant relative, but quickly put temptation aside and did not use it. Lily, petite and not unpretty, had on something signifying the approach of spring. She was au courant,[5] animatedly, with all sorts of subjects, and he weighed her words and found her surprisingly sound—score another for Salzman, whom he uneasily sensed to be somewhere around, hiding perhaps high in a tree along the street, flashing the lady signals with a pocket mirror; or perhaps a cloven-hoofed Pan,[6] piping nuptial ditties as he danced his invisible way before them, strewing wild buds on the walk and purple grapes in their path, symbolizing fruit of a union, though there was of course still none.

Lily startled Leo by remarking, "I was thinking of Mr. Salzman, a curious figure, wouldn't you say?"

Not certain what to answer, he nodded.

She bravely went on, blushing, "I for one am grateful for his introducing us. Aren't you?"

He courteously replied, "I am."

"I mean," she said with a little laugh—and it was all in good taste, or at least gave the effect of being not in bad—"do you mind that we came together so?"

He was not displeased with her honesty, recognizing that she meant to set the relationship aright, and understanding that it took a certain amount of experience in life, and courage, to want to do it quite that way. One had to have some sort of past to make that kind of beginning.

He said that he did not mind. Salzman's function was traditional and honorable—valuable for what it might achieve, which, he pointed out, was frequently nothing.

Lily agreed with a sigh. They walked on for a while and she said after a long silence, again with a nervous laugh, "Would you mind if I asked you something a little bit personal? Frankly, I find the subject fascinating." Although Leo shrugged, she went on half embarrassedly, "How was it that you came to your calling? I mean was it a sudden passionate inspiration?"

Leo, after a time, slowly replied, "I was always interested in the Law."[7]

"You saw revealed in it the presence of the Highest?"

4. A fashionable residential street on Manhattan's Upper West Side.
5. Well informed on the newest things.
6. The Greek god of pastures, forests, flocks, and herds; also, the personification of deity displayed in creation. Pan is frequently depicted playing the pipes.
7. I.e., Jewish teachings, the Torah.

He nodded and changed the subject. "I understand that you spent a little time in Paris, Miss Hirschorn?"

"Oh, did Mr. Salzman tell you, Rabbi Finkle?" Leo winced but she went on, "It was ages ago and almost forgotten. I remember I had to return for my sister's wedding."

And Lily would not be put off. "When," she asked in a trembly voice, "did you become enamored of God?"

He stared at her. Then it came to him that she was talking not about Leo Finkle, but of a total stranger, some mystical figure, perhaps even passionate prophet that Salzman had dreamed up for her—no relation to the living or dead. Leo trembled with rage and weakness. The trickster had obviously sold her a bill of goods, just as he had him, who'd expected to become acquainted with a young lady of twenty-nine, only to behold, the moment he laid eyes upon her strained and anxious face, a woman past thirty-five and aging rapidly. Only his self control had kept him this long in her presence.

"I am not," he said gravely, "a talented religious person," and in seeking words to go on, found himself possessed by shame and fear. "I think," he said in a strained manner, "that I came to God not because I loved Him, but because I did not."

This confession he spoke harshly because its unexpectedness shook him.

Lily wilted. Leo saw a profusion of loaves of bread go flying like ducks high over his head, not unlike the winged loaves by which he had counted himself to sleep last night. Mercifully, then, it snowed, which he would not put past Salzman's machinations.

He was infuriated with the marriage broker and swore he would throw him out of the room the minute he reappeared. But Salzman did not come that night, and when Leo's anger had subsided, an unaccountable despair grew in its place. At first he thought this was caused by his disappointment in Lily, but before long it became evident that he had involved himself with Salzman without a true knowledge of his own intent. He gradually realized—with an emptiness that seized him with six hands—that he had called in the broker to find him a bride because he was incapable of doing it himself. This terrifying insight he had derived as a result of his meeting and conversation with Lily Hirschorn. Her probing questions had somehow irritated him into revealing—to himself more than her—the true nature of his relationship to God, and from that it had come upon him, with shocking force, that apart from his parents, he had never loved anyone. Or perhaps it went the other way, that he did not love God so well as he might, because he had not loved man. It seemed to Leo that his whole life stood starkly revealed and he saw himself for the first time as he truly was—unloved and loveless. This bitter but somehow not fully unexpected revelation brought him to a point of panic, controlled only by extraordinary effort. He covered his face with his hands and cried.

The week that followed was the worst of his life. He did not eat and lost weight. His beard darkened and grew ragged. He stopped attending seminars and almost never opened a book. He seriously considered leaving the Yeshivah, although he was deeply troubled at the thought of the loss of all his years of study—saw them like pages torn from a book, strewn over the city—and at the devastating effect of this decision upon his parents. But he had lived without knowledge of himself, and never in the Five Books and all the Commentaries[8]—mea culpa[9]—had the truth been revealed to him. He did not know where to turn, and in all this desolating loneliness there was no *to whom*, although he often thought of Lily but not once could bring himself to go downstairs and make the call. He became touchy and irritable, especially with his landlady, who asked him all manner of personal questions; on the other hand, sensing his own disagreeableness, he waylaid her on the stairs and apologized abjectly, until mortified, she ran from him. Out of this, however, he drew the consolation that he was a Jew and that a Jew suffered. But gradually, as the long and terrible week drew to a close, he regained his composure and some idea of purpose in life: to go on as planned. Although he was imperfect, the ideal was not. As for his quest of a bride, the thought of continuing afflicted him with anxiety and heartburn, yet perhaps with this new knowledge of himself he would be more successful than in the past. Perhaps love would now come to him and a bride to that love. And for this sanctified seeking who needed a Salzman?

The marriage broker, a skeleton with haunted eyes, returned that very night. He looked, withal, the picture of frustrated expectancy—as if he had steadfastly waited the week at Miss Lily Hirschorn's side for a telephone call that never came.

Casually coughing, Salzman came immediately to the point: "So how did you like her?"

Leo's anger rose and he could not refrain from chiding the matchmaker: "Why did you lie to me, Salzman?"

Salzman's pale face went dead white, the world had snowed on him.

"Did you not state that she was twenty-nine?" Leo insisted.

"I give you my word—"

"She was thirty-five, if a day. *At least* thirty-five."

"Of this don't be too sure. Her father told me—"

"Never mind. The worst of it was that you lied to her."

"How did I lie to her, tell me?"

"You told her things about me that weren't true. You made me out to be more, consequently less than I am. She had in mind a totally different person, a sort of semimystical Wonder Rabbi."

"All I said, you was a religious man."

"I can imagine."

Salzman sighed. "This is my weakness that I have," he confessed. "My wife says to me I shouldn't be a salesman, but when I have two fine people that they would be wonderful to be married, I am so happy that I talk too much." He smiled wanly. "This is why Salzman is a poor man."

Leo's anger left him. "Well, Salzman, I'm afraid that's all."

The marriage broker fastened hungry eyes on him.

"You don't want any more a bride?"

"I do," said Leo, "but I have decided to seek her in a different way. I am no longer interested in an arranged marriage. To be frank, I now admit the necessity of premarital love. That is, I want to be in love with the one I marry."

8. The Torah and Talmud.
9. Literally, "through my fault" (Latin); an acknowledgment of personal error.

"Love?" said Salzman, astounded. After a moment he remarked, "For us, our love is our life, not for the ladies. In the ghetto they—"

"I know, I know," said Leo. "I've thought of it often. Love, I have said to myself, should be a by-product of living and worship rather than its own end. Yet for myself I find it necessary to establish the level of my need and fulfill it."

Salzman shrugged but answered, "Listen, rabbi, if you want love, this I can find for you also. I have such beautiful clients that you will love them the minute your eyes will see them."

Leo smiled unhappily. "I'm afraid you don't understand."

But Salzman hastily unstrapped his portfolio and withdrew a manila packet from it.

"Pictures," he said, quickly laying the envelope on the table.

Leo called after him to take the pictures away, but as if on the wings of the wind, Salzman had disappeared.

March came. Leo had returned to his regular routine. Although he felt not quite himself yet—lacked energy—he was making plans for a more active social life. Of course it would cost something, but he was an expert in cutting corners; and when there were no corners left he would make circles rounder. All the while Salzman's pictures had lain on the table, gathering dust. Occasionally as Leo sat studying, or enjoying a cup of tea, his eyes fell on the manila envelope, but he never opened it.

The days went by and no social life to speak of developed with a member of the opposite sex—it was difficult, given the circumstances of his situation. One morning Leo toiled up the stairs to his room and stared out the window at the city. Although the day was bright his view of it was dark. For some time he watched the people in the street below hurrying along and then turned with a heavy heart to his little room. On the table was the packet. With a sudden relentless gesture he tore it open. For a half-hour he stood by the table in a state of excitement, examining the photographs of the ladies Salzman had included. Finally, with a deep sigh he put them down. There were six, of varying degrees of attractiveness, but look at them long enough and they all became Lily Hirschorn: all past their prime, all starved behind bright smiles, not a true personality in the lot. Life, despite their frantic yoohooings, had passed them by; they were pictures in a brief case that stank of fish. After a while, however, as Leo attempted to return the photographs into the envelope, he found in it another, a snapshot of the type taken by a machine for a quarter. He gazed at it a moment and let out a cry.

Her face deeply moved him. Why, he could at first not say. It gave him the impression of youth—spring flowers, yet age—a sense of having been used to the bone, wasted; this came from the eyes, which were hauntingly familiar, yet absolutely strange. He had a vivid impression that he had met her before, but try as he might he could not place her although he could almost recall her name, as if he had read it in her own handwriting. No, this couldn't be; he would have remembered her. It was not, he affirmed, that she had an extraordinary beauty—no, though her face was attractive enough; it was that *something* about her moved him. Feature for feature, even some of the ladies of the photographs could do better; but she leaped forth to his heart—had *lived*, or wanted to—more than just wanted, perhaps regretted how she had lived—had somehow deeply suffered: it could be seen in the depths of those reluctant eyes, and from the way the light enclosed and shone from her, and within her, opening realms of possibility: this was her own. Her he desired. His head ached and eyes narrowed with the intensity of his gazing, then as if an obscure fog had blown up in the mind, he experienced fear of her and was aware that he had received an impression, somehow, of evil. He shuddered, saying softly, it is thus with us all. Leo brewed some tea in a small pot and sat sipping it without sugar, to calm himself. But before he had finished drinking, again with excitement he examined the face and found it good: good for Leo Finkle. Only such a one could understand him and help him seek whatever he was seeking. She might, perhaps, love him. How she had happened to be among the discards in Salzman's barrel he could never guess, but he knew he must urgently go find her.

Leo rushed downstairs, grabbed up the Bronx[1] telephone book, and searched for Salzman's home address. He was not listed, nor was his office. Neither was he in the Manhattan book. But Leo remembered having written down the address on a slip of paper after he had read Salzman's advertisement in the "personals" column of the *Forward*. He ran up to his room and tore through his papers, without luck. It was exasperating. Just when he needed the matchmaker he was nowhere to be found. Fortunately Leo remembered to look in his wallet. There on a card he found his name written and a Bronx address. No phone number was listed, the reason—Leo now recalled—he had originally communicated with Salzman by letter. He got on his coat, put a hat on over his skull cap and hurried to the subway station. All the way to the far end of the Bronx he sat on the edge of his seat. He was more than once tempted to take out the picture and see if the girl's face was as he remembered it, but he refrained, allowing the snapshot to remain in his inside coat pocket, content to have her so close. When the train pulled into the station he was waiting at the door and bolted out. He quickly located the street Salzman had advertised.

The building he sought was less than a block from the subway, but it was not an office building, nor even a loft, nor a store in which one could rent office space. It was a very old tenement house. Leo found Salzman's name in pencil on a soiled tag under the bell and climbed three dark flights to his apartment. When he knocked, the door was opened by a thin, asthmatic, gray-haired woman, in felt slippers.

"Yes?" she said, expecting nothing. She listened without listening. He could have sworn he had seen her, too, before but knew it was an illusion.

"Salzman—does he live here? Pinye Salzman," he said, "the matchmaker?"

She stared at him a long minute. "Of course."

He felt embarrassed. "Is he in?"

"No." Her mouth, though left open, offered nothing more.

"The matter is urgent. Can you tell me where his office is?"

"In the air."[2] She pointed upward.

"You mean he has no office?" Leo asked.

"In his socks."

He peered into the apartment. It was sunless and dingy, one large room divided by a half-open curtain, beyond which he could see a sagging metal

1. One of the New York City's five boroughs.
2. An allusion to the Yiddish *luftmensch*, someone with no firm livelihood who seemingly lives on air.

bed. The near side of a room was crowded with rickety chairs, old bureaus, a three-legged table, racks of cooking utensils, and all the apparatus of a kitchen. But there was no sign of Salzman or his magic barrel, probably also a figment of the imagination. An odor of frying fish made Leo weak to the knees.

"Where is he?" he insisted. "I've got to see your husband."

At length she answered, "So who knows where he is? Every time he thinks a new thought he runs to a different place. Go home, he will find you."

"Tell him Leo Finkle."

She gave no sign she had heard.

He walked downstairs, depressed.

But Salzman, breathless, stood waiting at his door.

Leo was astounded and overjoyed. "How did you get here before me?"

"I rushed."

"Come inside."

They entered. Leo fixed tea, and a sardine sandwich for Salzman. As they were drinking he reached behind him for the packet of pictures and handed them to the marriage broker.

Salzman put down his glass and said expectantly, "You found somebody you like?"

"Not among these."

The marriage broker turned away.

"Here is the one I want." Leo held forth the snapshot.

Salzman slipped on his glasses and took the picture into his trembling hand. He turned ghastly and let out a groan.

"What's the matter?" cried Leo.

"Excuse me. Was an accident this picture. She isn't for you."

Salzman frantically shoved the manila packet into his portfolio. He thrust the snapshot into his pocket and fled down the stairs.

Leo, after momentary paralysis, gave chase and cornered the marriage broker in the vestibule. The landlady made hysterical outcries but neither of them listened.

"Give me back the picture, Salzman."

"No." The pain in his eyes was terrible.

"Tell me who she is then."

"This I can't tell you. Excuse me."

He made to depart, but Leo, forgetting himself, seized the matchmaker by his tight coat and shook him frenziedly.

"Please," sighed Salzman. *"Please."*

Leo ashamedly let him go. "Tell me who she is," he begged. "It's very important for me to know."

"She is not for you. She is a wild one—wild, without shame. This is not a bride for a rabbi."

"What do you mean wild?"

"Like an animal. Like a dog. For her to be poor was a sin. This is why to me she is dead now."

"In God's name, what do you mean?"

"Her I can't introduce to you," Salzman cried.

"Why are you so excited?"

"Why, he asks," Salzman said, bursting into tears. "This is my baby, my Stella, she should burn in hell."

Leo hurried up to bed and hid under the covers. Under the covers he thought his life through. Although he soon fell asleep he could not sleep her out of his mind. He woke, beating his breast. Though he prayed to be rid of her, his prayers went unanswered. Through days of torment he endlessly struggled not to love her; fearing success, he escaped it. He then concluded to convert her to goodness, himself to God. The idea alternately nauseated and exalted him.

He perhaps did not know that he had come to a final decision until he encountered Salzman in a Broadway cafeteria. He was sitting alone at a rear table, sucking the bony remains of a fish. The marriage broker appeared haggard, and transparent to the point of vanishing.

Salzman looked up at first without recognizing him. Leo had grown a pointed beard and his eyes were weighted with wisdom.

"Salzman," he said, "love has at last come to my heart."

"Who can love from a picture?" mocked the marriage broker.

"It is not impossible."

"If you can love her, then you can love anybody. Let me show you some new clients that they just sent me their photographs. One is a little doll."

"Just her I want," Leo murmured.

"Don't be a fool, doctor. Don't bother with her."

"Put me in touch with her, Salzman," Leo said humbly. "Perhaps I can be of service."

Salzman had stopped eating and Leo understood with emotion that it was now arranged.

Leaving the cafeteria, he was, however, afflicted by a tormenting suspicion that Salzman had planned it all to happen this way.

Leo was informed by letter that she would meet him on a certain corner, and she was there one spring night, waiting under a street lamp. He appeared, carrying a small bouquet of violets and rosebuds. Stella stood by the lamp post, smoking. She wore white with red shoes, which fitted his expectations, although in a troubled moment he had imagined the dress red, and only the shoes white. She waited uneasily and shyly. From afar he saw that her eyes—clearly her father's—were filled with desperate innocence. He pictured, in her, his own redemption. Violins and lit candles revolved in the sky. Leo ran forward with flowers outthrust.

Around the corner, Salzman, leaning against a wall, chanted prayers for the dead.

1954 1958

SAUL BELLOW
b. 1915

"This spare old man," as Saul Bellow recalls the Hebrew writer S. Y. Agnon in Jerusalem, "asked me if any of my books had been translated into Hebrew. If they had not been, I had better see to it immediately, because, he said, they would survive only in the Holy Tongue." But what about Heinrich Heine's imperishable German? "Ah," said Agnon, "we have him beautifully translated into Hebrew. He is safe." Bellow's account then turns to Isaac Babel, whose stories he calls "characteristically Jewish" though "written in Russian by a man who knew Yiddish well enough to have written them in that language." It's not that Bellow, in post-Holocaust America, had the option to write in a Jewish language, whether Hebrew or Yiddish. What's at issue is a vital, viable identity for Jewish fiction in the Diaspora.

Although the marks of this identity are too variegated, too dispersed, to be found fully in any single writer, Saul Bellow has often seemed to epitomize them. His heroes all suffer, Robert Alter points out, from "humanitis," as in Bellow's play *The Last Analysis* (1965): that is, "when the human condition gets to be too much for you." Yet they don't merely suffer, they act—or rather, they speak, like Moses Herzog (in Bellow's 1964 novel *Herzog*) "writing letters to everyone under the sun," including Nietzsche, Spinoza, Eisenhower, even God. They need to know what it is to be human. Philosophers do not know it, but a novelist can show us (in Herzog's words) "the strength of a man's virtue or spiritual capacity measured by his ordinary life." By this measure, Bellow rejects what he calls "Wasteland pessimism."

The often-comic irony of a craving mind in a failing body, or of spirit versus history—that is, the essential human condition—has sometimes seemed quintessentially Jewish: witness the half-Hebrew half-Yiddish proverb "Thou hast chosen us from among the nations—why did you have to pick on the Jews?" Saul Bellow's prose embodies this irony. "The dominant American Jewish style," as Irving Howe sees it, is "brought to a pitch by Saul Bellow": "a yoking of opposites, gutter vividness with . . . high-culture rhetoric"; "a strong infusion of Yiddish . . . through ironic twistings"; "a rapid, nervous, breathless tempo"; "a deliberate loosening of syntax, as if to mock those niceties of Correct English which Gore Vidal and other untainted Americans hold dear."

Saul Bellow was born in Lachine, Quebec, on June 10, 1915, soon after his parents emigrated from Russia. "My life in Canada was partly frontier, partly the Polish ghetto, partly the Middle Ages. . . . I was brought up in a polyglot community," with Hebrew, Yiddish, French, and English. When Bellow was nine, his family moved from Montreal to Chicago, where he went to the University of Chicago and graduated from Northwestern in sociology and anthropology. He spent most of his life in that city, was close friends with Isaac Rosenfeld and Delmore Schwartz, and became a permanent member of the University of Chicago's Committee on Social Thought. His early books *The Victim* (1947) and *Seize the Day* (1956) articulated a postwar existential malaise, at once thwarted and driven, far from the half-assimilating suburban Jews that Philip Roth satirized. These novels depict "the city man who feels that the sky is constantly coming down on him," as Alfred Kazin puts it, and who seeks above all to know "the reason of things."

Bellow is the only writer to have won the National Book Award three times: for *The Adventures of Augie March* (1953), *Herzog* (1964), and *Mr. Sammler's Planet* (1970). Probably his authorial genius emerges most compellingly over the span of a novel, yet his short stories can draw us in fully, too. *The Old System*, from *Mosby's Memoirs* (1968), stands alongside Tillie Olsen's *Tell Me a Riddle* (and also Faulkner's work) as a twentieth-century family saga. Told from the vantage point of immigrants and their offspring, these searching stories expose Jewish American families tangling in the bonds of love.

Bellow has resisted the label "Jewish American writer" as "intellectually vulgar, unnecessarily parochial." "I'm well aware of being Jewish and also of being American and of being a writer. But I'm also a hockey fan, a fact which nobody ever mentions." But if Babel's Red Cavalry tales are "characteristically Jewish," then Bellow's own stories are no less so. *Something to Remember Me By,* while not circumstantially Jewish, has the (ironically undercut) quality of a traditional Hebrew "Ethical Will." And it begins, we're told exactly, in February 1933, but we're not told that this is just days after Hitler's accession to power: here in Chicago, the innocent victim is only a sexual schlemiel. Like Kazin the schoolboy reading books even while pulling on his socks in the morning, Bellow's protagonist (age seventeen as Bellow himself was in February 1933) carries around pages torn from a book he's reading and regrets their loss more than anything else. When his father cuffs him at the end of the day, this gladdens the son: his mother, who was dying, must not yet have died.

One test of Bellow's Diaspora Jewishness took the form of a three-month Israeli sojourn in 1975, an effort few American authors have made. Whereas his own fictional characters almost flourish in the gap between the ideal and the real, Israeli reality, Bellow finds, abrades against the nation's spiritual aspiration. "I listen carefully, closely, more closely than I've ever listened in my life." Here, "you cannot take your right to live for granted"; he feels for Israel's writers, "continuously summoned to solidarity." Throughout, Bellow takes empathic, yet balanced, views and finds what's lacking in America: "Life in Israel is far from enviable, yet there is a clear purpose in it." He is "heartsick about leaving" but entitles his 1976 account of this journey, significantly, *To Jerusalem and Back*.

Something to Remember Me By

When there is too much going on, more than you can bear, you may choose to assume that nothing in particular is happening, that your life is going round and round like a turntable. Then one day you are aware that what you took to be a turntable, smooth, flat, and even, was in fact a whirlpool, a vortex. My first knowledge of the hidden work of uneventful days goes back to February 1933. The exact date won't matter much to you. I like to think, however, that you, my only child, will want to hear about this hidden work as it relates to me. When you were a small boy you were keen on family history. You will quickly understand that I couldn't tell a child what I am about to tell you now. You don't talk about deaths and vortices to a kid, not nowadays. In my time my parents didn't hesitate to speak of death and the dying. What they seldom mentioned was sex. We've got it the other way around.

My mother died when I was an adolescent. I've often told you that. What I didn't tell you was that I knew she was dying and didn't allow myself to think about it—there's your turntable.

The month was February, as I've said, adding that the exact date wouldn't matter to you. I should confess that I myself avoided fixing it.

Chicago in winter, armored in gray ice, the sky low, the going heavy.

I was a high school senior, an indifferent student, generally unpopular, a background figure in the school. It was only as a high jumper that I performed in public. I had no form at all; a curious last-minute spring or convulsion put me over the bar. But this was what the school turned out to see.

Unwilling to study, I was bookish nevertheless. I was secretive about my family life. The truth is that I didn't want to talk about my mother. Besides, I had no language as yet for the oddity of my peculiar interests.

But let me get on with that significant day in the early part of February.

It began like any other winter school day in Chicago—grimly ordinary. The temperature a few degrees above zero, botanical frost shapes on the windowpane, the snow swept up in heaps, the ice gritty and the streets, block after block, bound together by the iron of the sky. A breakfast of porridge, toast, and tea. Late as usual, I stopped for a moment to look into my mother's sickroom. I bent near and said, "It's Louie, going to school." She seemed to nod. Her eyelids were brown; the color of her face was much lighter. I hurried off with my books on a strap over my shoulder.

When I came to the boulevard on the edge of the park, two small men rushed out of a doorway with rifles, wheeled around aiming upward, and fired at pigeons near the rooftop. Several birds fell straight down, and the men scooped up the soft bodies and ran indoors, dark little guys in fluttering white shirts. Depression hunters and their city game. Moments before, the police car had loafed by at ten miles an hour. The men had waited it out.

This had nothing to do with me. I mention it merely because it happened. I stepped around the blood spots and crossed into the park.

To the right of the path, behind the wintry lilac twigs, the crust of the snow was broken. In the dead black night Stephanie and I had necked there, petted, my hands under her raccoon coat, under her sweater, under her skirt, adolescents kissing without restraint. Her coonskin cap had slipped to the back of her head. She opened the musky coat to me to have me closer.

Approaching the school building, I had to run to reach the doors before the last bell. I was on notice from the family—no trouble with teachers, no summons from the principal at a time like this. And I did observe the rules, although I despised classwork. But I spent all the money I could lay hands on at Hammersmark's Bookstore. I read *Manhattan Transfer, The Enormous Room*, and *A Portrait of the Artist.*[1] I belonged to the Cercle Français[2] and the Senior Discussion Club. The club's topic for this afternoon was Von Hindenburg's choice of Hitler to form a new government.[3] But I couldn't go to meetings now; I had an after-school job. My father had insisted that I find one.

After classes, on my way to work, I stopped at home to cut myself a slice of bread and a wedge of Wisconsin cheese, and to see whether my mother might be awake. During her last days she was heavily sedated and rarely said anything. The tall, square-shouldered bottle at her bedside was filled with clear red Nembutal.[4] The color of this fluid was always the same, as if it could tolerate no shadow. Now that she could no longer sit up to have it washed, my mother's hair was cut short. This made her face more slender,

1. Novels by John Dos Passos (1925), E. E. Cummings (1922), and James Joyce (1916), respectively.
2. French club (French).
3. On Jan. 30, 1933, President Paul Von Hindenburg appointed Hitler chancellor of Germany.
4. Trademark name for pentobarbitol, a sedative.

and her lips were sober. Her breathing was dry and hard, obstructed. The window shade was halfway up. It was scalloped at the bottom and had white fringes. The street ice was dark gray. Snow was piled against the trees. Their trunks had a mineral-black look. Waiting out the winter in their alligator armor, they gathered coal soot.

Even when she was awake, my mother couldn't find the breath to speak. She sometimes made signs. Except for the nurse, there was nobody in the house. My father was at business, my sister had a downtown job, my brothers hustled. The eldest, Albert, clerked for a lawyer in the Loop.[5] My brother Len had put me onto a job on the Northwestern commuter trains, and for a while I was a candy butcher, selling chocolate bars and evening papers. When my mother put a stop to this because it kept me too late, I had found other work. Just now I was delivering flowers for a shop on North Avenue and riding the streetcars carrying wreaths and bouquets to all parts of the city. Behrens the florist paid me fifty cents for an afternoon; with tips I could earn, as much as a dollar. That gave me time to prepare my trigonometry lesson and, very late at night, after I had seen Stephanie, to read my books. I sat in the kitchen when everyone was sleeping, in deep silence, snowdrifts under the windows, and below, the janitor's shovel rasping on the cement and clanging on the furnace door. I read banned books circulated by my classmates, political pamphlets, read "Prufrock" and "Mauberley."[6] I also studied arcane books, too far out to discuss with anyone.

I read on the streetcars (called trolleys elsewhere). Reading shut out the sights. In fact there *were* no sights—more of the same and then more of the same. Shop fronts, garages, warehouses, narrow brick bungalows.

The city was laid out on a colossal grid, eight blocks to the mile, every fourth street a car line. The days short, the streetlights weak, the soiled snowbanks toward evening became a source of light. I carried my carfare in my mitten, where the coins mixed with lint worn away from the lining. Today I was delivering lilies to an uptown address. They were wrapped and pinned in heavy paper. Behrens, spelling out my errand for me, was pale, a narrow-faced man who wore nose glasses. Amid the flowers, he alone had no color—something like the price he paid for being human. He wasted no words: "This delivery will take an hour each way in this traffic, so it'll be your only one. I carry these people on the books, but make sure you get a signature on the bill."

I couldn't say why it was such a relief to get out of the shop, the damp, warm-earth smell, the dense mosses, the prickling cactuses, the glass ice-boxes with orchids, gardenias, and sickbed roses. I preferred the brick boredom of the street, the paving stones and steel rails. I drew down the three peaks of my racing-skater's cap and hauled the clumsy package to Robey Street. When the car came panting up there was room for me on the long seat next to the door. Passengers didn't undo their buttons. They were chilled, guarded, muffled, miserable. I had reading matter with me—the remains of a book, the cover gone, the pages held together by binder's thread and flakes of glue. I carried these fifty or sixty pages in the pocket of my short sheepskin. With the one hand I had free I couldn't manage this muti-

5. Chicago's downtown business district.
6. A reference to T. S. Eliot's poem *The Love Song of J. Alfred Prufrock* (1908) and Ezra Pound's *Hugh Selwyn Mauberley* (1919).

lated book. And on the Broadway–Clark car, reading was out of the question. I had to protect my lilies from the balancing straphangers and people pushing toward the front.

I got down at Ainslie Street holding high the package, which had the shape of a padded kite. The apartment house I was looking for had a courtyard with iron palings. The usual lobby: a floor sinking in the middle, kernels of tile, gaps stuffed with dirt, and a panel of brass mailboxes with earpiece-mouthpieces. No voice came down when I pushed the button; instead, the lock buzzed, jarred, rattled, and I went from the cold of the outer lobby to the overheated mustiness of the inner one. On the second floor one of the two doors on the landing was open, and overshoes and galoshes and rubbers were heaped along the wall. At once I found myself in a crowd of drinkers. All the lights in the house were on, although it was a good hour before dark. Coats were piled on chairs and sofas. All whiskey in those days was bootleg, of course. Holding the flowers high, I parted the mourners. I was quasi official. The message went out: "Let the kid through. Go right on, buddy."

The long passageway was full too, but the dining room was entirely empty. There, a dead girl lay in her coffin. Over her a cut-glass luster was hanging from a taped, deformed artery of wire pulled through the broken plaster. I hadn't expected to find myself looking down into a coffin.

You saw her as she was, without undertaker's makeup, a girl older than Stephanie, not so plump, thin, fair, her straight hair arranged on her dead shoulders. All buoyancy gone, a weight that counted totally on support, not so much lying as sunk in this gray rectangle. I saw what I took to be the pressure mark of fingers on her cheek. Whether she had been pretty or not was no consideration.

A stout woman (certainly the mother), wearing black, opened the swing door from the kitchen and saw me standing over the corpse. I thought she was displeased when she made a fist signal to come forward. As I passed her she drew both fists against her bosom. She said to put the flowers on the sink, and then she pulled the pins and crackled the paper. Big arms, thick calves, a bun of hair, her short nose thin and red. It was Behrens's practice to tie the lily stalks to slender green sticks. There was never any damage.

On the drainboard of the sink was a baked ham with sliced bread around the platter, a jar of French's mustard and wooden tongue depressors to spread it. I saw and I saw and I saw.

I was on my most discreet and polite behavior with the woman. I looked at the floor to spare her my commiserating face. But why should she care at all about my discreetness; how did I come into this except as a messenger and menial? If she wouldn't observe my behavior, whom was I behaving for? All she wanted was to settle the bill and send me on my way. She picked up her purse, holding it to her body as she had held her fists. "What do I owe Behrens?" she asked me.

"He said you could sign for this."

However, she wasn't going to deal in kindnesses. She said, "No." She said, "I don't want debts following me later on." She gave me a five-dollar bill, she added a tip of fifty cents, and it was I who signed the receipt, as well as I could on the enameled grooves of the sink. I folded the bill small and felt under the sheepskin coat for my watch pocket, ashamed to take money from her within sight of her dead daughter. I wasn't the object of the woman's severity, but her face somewhat frightened me. She leveled the same look at the walls, the door. I didn't figure here, however; this was no death of mine.

As if to take another reading of the girl's plain face, I looked again into the coffin on my way out. And then on the staircase I began to extract the pages from my sheepskin pocket, and in the lobby I hunted for the sentences I had read the night before. Yes, here they were:

Nature cannot suffer the human form within her system of laws. When given to her charge, the human being before us is reduced to dust. Ours is the most perfect form to be found on earth. The visible world sustains us until life leaves, and then it must utterly destroy us. Where, then, is the world from which the human form comes?

If you swallowed some food and then died, that morsel of food that would have nourished you in life would hasten your disintegration in death.

This meant that nature didn't make life; it only housed it.

In those days I read many such books. But the one I had read the previous night went deeper than the rest. You, my only child, are only too familiar with my lifelong absorption in or craze for further worlds. I used to bore you when I spoke of spirit, or pneuma, and of a continuum of spirit and nature. You were too well educated, respectably rational, to take stock in such terms. I might add, citing a famous scholar, that what is plausible can do without proof. I am not about to pursue this. Still, there would be a gap in what I have to tell if I were to leave out my significant book, and this after all is a narrative, not an argument.

Anyway, I returned my pages to the pocket of my sheepskin, and then I didn't know quite what to do. At four o'clock, with no more errands, I was somehow not ready to go home. So I walked through the snow to Argyle Street, where my brother-in-law practiced dentistry, thinking that we might travel home together. I prepared an explanation for turning up at his office. "I was on the North Side delivering flowers, saw a dead girl laid out, realized how close I was, and came here." Why did I need to account for my innocent behavior when it *was* innocent? Perhaps because I was always contemplating illicit things. Because I was always being accused. Because I ran a little truck farm of deceits—but self-examination, once so fascinating to me, has become tiresome.

My brother-in-law's office was a high, second-floor walkup: PHILIP HADDIS, D.D.S. Three bay windows at the rounded corner of the building gave you a full view of the street and of the lake, due east—the jagged flats of ice floating. The office door was open, and when I came through the tiny blind (windowless) waiting room and didn't see Philip at the big, back-tilted dentist's chair, I thought that he might have stepped into his lab. He was a good technician and did most of his own work, which was a big saving.

Philip wasn't tall, but he was very big, a burly man. The sleeves of his white coat fitted tightly on his bare, thick forearms. The strength of his arms counted when it came to pulling teeth. Lots of patients were referred to him for extractions.

When he had nothing in particular to do he would sit in the chair himself, studying the *Racing Form*[7] between the bent mantis leg of the drill, the gas flame, and the water spurting round and round in the green glass spit-sink.

7. A horse-racing periodical.

The cigar smell was always thick. Standing in the center of the dental cabinet was a clock under a glass bell. Four gilt weights rotated at its base. This was a gift from my mother. The view from the middle window was divided by a chain that couldn't have been much smaller than the one that stopped the British fleet on the Hudson.[8] This held the weight of the druggist's sign—a mortar and pestle outlined in electric bulbs. There wasn't much daylight left. At noon it was poured out; by four it had drained away. From one side the banked snow was growing blue, from the other the shops were shining warmth on it.

The dentist's lab was in a closet. Easygoing Philip peed in the sink sometimes. It was a long trek to the toilet at the far end of the building, and the hallway was nothing but two walls—a plaster tunnel and a carpet runner edged with brass tape. Philip hated going to the end of the hall.

There was nobody in the lab, either. Philip might have been taking a cup of coffee at the soda fountain in the drug-store below. It was possible also that he was passing the time with Marchek, the doctor with whom he shared the suite of offices. The connecting door was never locked, and I had occasionally sat in Marchek's swivel chair with a gynecology book, studying the colored illustrations and storing up the Latin names.

Marchek's starred glass pane was dark, and I assumed his office to be empty, but when I went in I saw a naked woman lying on the examining table. She wasn't asleep; she seemed to be resting. Becoming aware that I was there, she stirred, and then without haste, disturbing herself as little as possible, she reached for her clothing heaped on Dr. Marchek's desk. Picking out her slip, she put it on her belly—she didn't spread it. Was she dazed, drugged? No, she simply took her sweet time about everything, she behaved with exciting lassitude. Wires connected her nice wrists to a piece of medical apparatus on a wheeled stand.

The right thing would have been to withdraw, but it was already too late for that. Besides, the woman gave no sign that she cared one way or another. She didn't draw the slip over her breasts, she didn't even bring her thighs together. The covering hairs were parted. There were salt, acid, dark, sweet odors. These were immediately effective; I was strongly excited. There was a gloss on her forehead, an exhausted look about the eyes. I believed that I had guessed what she had been doing, but then the room was half dark, and I preferred to avoid any definite thought. Doubt seemed much better, or equivocation.

I remembered that Philip, in his offhand, lazy way, had mentioned a "research project" going on next door. Dr. Marchek was measuring the reactions of partners in the sexual act. "He takes people from the street, he hooks them up and pretends he's collecting graphs. This is for kicks; the science part is horseshit."

The naked woman, then, was an experimental subject.

I had prepared myself to tell Philip about the dead girl on Ainslie Street, but the coffin, the kitchen, the ham, the flowers were as distant from me now as the ice floes on the lake and the killing cold of the water.

"Where did you come from?" the woman said to me.

"From next door—the dentist's office."

8. Ship cables were used decisively in defeating the British at Plattsburg, New York, on Sept. 11, 1814.

"The doctor was about to unstrap me, and I need to get loose. Maybe you can figure out these wires."

If Marchek should be in the inner room, he wouldn't come in now that he heard voices. As the woman raised both her arms so that I could undo the buckles, her breasts swayed, and when I bent over her the odor of her upper body made me think of the frilled brown papers in a box after the chocolates had been eaten—a sweet aftersmell and acrid cardboard mixed. Although I tried hard to stop it, my mother's chest mutilated by cancer surgery passed through my mind. Its gnarled scar tissue. I also called in Stephanie's closed eyes and kissing face—anything to spoil the attraction of this naked young woman. It occurred to me as I undid the clasps that instead of disconnecting her I was hooking myself. We were alone in the darkening office, and I wanted her to reach under the sheepskin and undo my belt for me.

But when her hands were free she wiped the jelly from her wrists and began to dress. She started with her bra, several times lowering her breasts into the cups, and when her arms went backward to fasten the hooks she bent far forward, as if she were passing under a low bough. The cells of my body were like bees, drunker and drunker on sexual honey (I expect that this will change the figure of Grandfather Louie, the old man remembered as this or that but never as a hive of erotic bees).

But I couldn't be blind to the woman's behavior even now. It was very broad; she laid it on. I saw her face in profile, and although it was turned downward, there was no mistaking her smile. To use an expression from the thirties, she was giving me the works. She knew I was about to fall on my face. She buttoned every small button with deliberate slowness, and her blouse had at least twenty such buttons, yet she was still bare from the waist down. Though we were so minor, she and I, a schoolboy and a floozy, we had such major instruments to play. And if we were to go further, whatever happened would never get beyond this room. It would be between the two of us, and nobody would ever hear of it. Still, Marchek, that pseudoexperimenter, was probably biding his time in the next room. An old family doctor, he must have been embarrassed and angry. And at any moment, moreover, my brother-in-law Philip might come back.

When the woman slipped down from the leather table she gripped her leg and said she had pulled a muscle. She lifted one heel onto a chair and rubbed her calf, swearing under her breath and looking everywhere with swimming eyes. And then, after she had put on her skirt and fastened her stockings to the garter belt, she pushed her feet into her pumps and limped around the chair, holding it by the arm. She said, "Will you please reach me my coat? Just put it over my shoulders."

She, too, wore a raccoon. As I took it from the hook I wished it had been something else. But Stephanie's coat was newer than this one and twice as heavy. These pelts had dried out, and the fur was thin. The woman was already on her way out, and stooped as I laid the raccoon over her back. Marchek's office had its own exit to the corridor.

At the top of the staircase, the woman asked me to help her down. I said that I would, of course, but I wanted to look once more for my brother-in-law. As she tied the woolen scarf under her chin she smiled at me, with an Oriental wrinkling of her eyes.

Not to check in with Philip wouldn't have been right. My hope was that he would be returning, coming down the narrow corridor in his burly, sauntering, careless way. You won't remember your Uncle Philip. He had played college football, and he still had the look of a tackle, with his swelling, compact forearms. (At Soldier Field[9] today he'd be physically insignificant; in his time, however, he was something of a strongman.)

But there was the long strip of carpet down the middle of the wall-valley, and no one was coming to rescue me. I turned back to his office. If only a patient were sitting in the chair and I could see Philip looking into his mouth, I'd be on track again, excused from taking the woman's challenge. One alternative was to say that I couldn't go with her, that Philip expected me to ride back with him to the Northwest Side. In the empty office I considered this lie, bending my head so that I wouldn't confront the clock with its soundless measured weights revolving. Then I wrote on Philip's memo pad: "Louie, passing by." I left it on the seat of the chair.

The woman had put her arms through the sleeves of the collegiate, rahrah raccoon and was resting her fur-bundled rear on the banister. She was passing her compact mirror back and forth, and when I came out she gave the compact a snap and dropped it into her purse.

"Still the charley horse?"

"My lower back too."

We descended, very slow, both feet on each tread. I wondered what she would do if I were to kiss her. Laugh at me, probably. We were no longer between the four walls where anything might have happened. In the street, space was unlimited. I had no idea how far we were going, how far I would be able to go. Although she was the one claiming to be in pain, it was I who felt sick. She asked me to support her lower back with my hand, and there I discovered what an extraordinary action her hips could perform. At a party I had overheard an older woman saying to another lady, "I know how to make them burn." Hearing this was enough for me.

No special art was necessary with a boy of seventeen, not even so much as being invited to support her with my hand—to feel that intricate, erotic working of her back. I had already *seen* the woman on Marchek's examining table and had also felt the full weight of her when she leaned—when she laid her female substance on me. Moreover, she fully knew my mind. She was the thing I was thinking continually, and how often does thought find its object in circumstances like these—the object *knowing* that it has been found? The woman knew my expectations. She *was*, in the flesh, those expectations. I couldn't have sworn that she was a hooker, a tramp. She might have been an ordinary family girl with a taste for trampishness, acting loose, amusing herself with me, doing a comic sex turn as in those days people sometimes did.

"Where are we headed?"

"If you have to go, I can make it on my own," she said. "It's just Winona Street, the other side of Sheridan Road."

"No, no. I'll walk you there."

She asked whether I was still at school, pointing to the printed pages in my coat pocket.

9. A sports stadium in Chicago.

I observed when we were passing a fruit shop (a boy of my own age emptying bushels of oranges into the lighted window) that, despite the woman's thick-cream color, her eyes were Far Eastern, black.

"You should be about seventeen," she said.

"Just."

She was wearing pumps in the snow and placed each step with care.

"What are you going to be—have you picked your profession?"

I had no use for professions. Utterly none. There were accountants and engineers in the soup lines. In the world slump, professions were useless. You were free, therefore, to make something extraordinary of yourself. I might have said, if I hadn't been excited to the point of sickness, that I didn't ride around the city on the cars to make a buck or to be useful to the family, but to take a reading of this boring, depressed, ugly, endless, rotting city. I couldn't have thought it then, but I now understand that my purpose was to interpret this place. Its power was tremendous. But so was mine, potentially. I refused absolutely to believe for a moment that people here were doing what they thought they were doing. Beneath the apparent life of these streets was their real life, beneath each face the real face, beneath each voice and its words the true tone and the real message. Of course, I wasn't about to say such things. It was beyond me at that time to say them. I was, however, a high-toned kid, "La-di-dah," my critical, satirical brother Albert called me. A high purpose in adolescence will expose you to that.

At the moment, a glamorous, sexual girl had me in tow. I couldn't guess where I was being led, nor how far, nor what she would surprise me with, nor the consequences.

"So the dentist is your brother?"

"In-law—my sister's husband. They live with us. You're asking what he's like? He's a good guy. He likes to lock his office on Friday and go to the races. He takes me to the fights. Also, at the back of the drugstore there's a poker game. . . ."

"*He* doesn't go around with books in his pocket."

"Well, no, he doesn't. He says, 'What's the use? There's too much to keep up or catch up with. You could never in a thousand years do it, so why knock yourself out?' My sister wants him to open a Loop office, but that would be too much of a strain. I guess he's for inertia. He's not ready to do more than he's already doing."

"So what are you reading—what's it about?"

I didn't propose to discuss anything with her. I wasn't capable of it. What I had in mind just then was entirely different.

But suppose I had been able to explain. One does have a responsibility to answer genuine questions: "You see, miss, this is the visible world. We live in it, we breathe its air and eat its substance. When we die, however, matter goes to matter, and then we're annihilated. Now, which world do we really belong to, this world of matter or another world, from which matter takes its orders?"

Not many people were willing to talk about such notions. They made even Stephanie impatient. "When you die, that's it. Dead is dead," she would say. She loved a good time. And when I wouldn't take her downtown to the Oriental Theatre she didn't deny herself the company of other boys. She brought back off-color vaudeville jokes. I think the Oriental was part of a national entertainment circuit. Jimmy Savo, Lou Holtz, and Sophie Tucker played there. I was sometimes too solemn for Stephanie. When she gave imitations of Jimmy Savo singing "River, Stay Away from My Door," bringing her knees together and holding herself tight, she didn't break me up, and she was disappointed.

You would have thought that the book or book fragment in my pocket was a talisman from a fairy tale to open castle gates or carry me to mountaintops. Yet when the woman asked me what it was, I was too scattered to tell her. Remember, I still kept my hand as instructed on her lower back, tormented by that sexual grind of her movements. I was discovering what the lady at the party had meant by saying, "I know how to make them burn." So of course I was in no condition to talk about the Ego and the Will, or about the secrets of the blood. Yes, I believed that higher knowledge was shared out among all human beings. What else was there to hold us together but this force hidden behind daily consciousness? But to be coherent about it now was absolutely out of the question.

"Can't you tell me?" she said.

"I bought this for a nickel from a bargain table."

"That's how you spend your money?"

I assumed her to mean that I didn't spend it on girls.

"And the dentist is a good-natured, lazy guy," she went on. "What has he got to tell you?"

I tried to review the mental record. What did Phil Haddis say? He said that a stiff prick has no conscience. At the moment it was all I could think of. It amused Philip to talk to me. He was a chum. Where Philip was indulgent, my brother Albert, your late uncle, was harsh. Albert might have taught me something if he had trusted me. He was then a night-school law student clerking for Rowland, the racketeer congressman. He was Rowland's bagman, and Rowland hired him not to read law but to make collections. Philip suspected that Albert was skimming, for he dressed sharply. He wore a derby (called, in those days, a Baltimore heater) and a camel's hair topcoat and pointed, mafioso shoes. Toward me, Albert was scornful. He said, "You don't understand fuck-all. You never will."

We were approaching Winona Street, and when we got to her building she'd have no further use for me and send me away. I'd see no more than the flash of the glass and then stare as she let herself in. She was already feeling in her purse for the keys. I was no longer supporting her back, preparing instead to mutter "bye-bye," when she surprised me with a sideward nod, inviting me to enter. I think I had hoped (with sex-polluted hope) that she would leave me in the street. I followed her through another tile lobby and through the inner door. The staircase was fiercely heated by coal-fueled radiators, the skylight three stories up was wavering, the wallpaper had come unstuck and was curling and bulging. I swallowed my breath. I couldn't draw this heat into my lungs.

This had been a deluxe apartment house once, built for bankers, brokers, and well-to-do professionals. Now it was occupied by transients. In the big front room with its French windows there was a crap game. In the next room people were drinking or drowsing on the old chesterfields.[1] The woman led

1. Overstuffed sofas usually with upright armrests.

me through what had once been a private bar—some of the fittings were still in place. Then I followed her through the kitchen—I would have gone anywhere, no questions asked. In the kitchen there were no signs of cooking, neither pots nor dishes. The linoleum was shredding, brown fibers standing like hairs. She led me into a narrower corridor, parallel to the main one. "I have what used to be a maid's room," she said. "It's got a nice view of the alley, but there is a private bathroom."

And here we were—an almost empty space. So this was how whores operated—assuming that she was a whore: a bare floor, a narrow cot, a chair by the window, a lopsided clothespress against the wall. I stopped under the light fixture while she passed behind, as if to observe me. Then from the back she gave me a hug and a small kiss on the cheek, more promissory than actual. Her face powder, or perhaps it was her lipstick, had a sort of green-banana fragrance. My heart had never beaten as hard as this.

She said, "Why don't I go into the bathroom awhile and get ready while you undress and lie down in bed. You look like you were brought up neat, so lay your clothes on the chair. You don't want to drop them on the floor."

Shivering (this seemed the one cold room in the house), I began to pull off my things, beginning with the winter-wrinkled boots. The sheepskin I hung over the back of the chair. I pushed my socks into the boots and then my bare feet recoiled from the grit underfoot. I took off everything, as if to disassociate my shirt, my underthings, from whatever it was that was about to happen, so that only my body could be guilty. The one thing that couldn't be excepted. When I pulled back the cover and got in, I was thinking that the beds in Bridewell prison[2] would be like this. There was no pillowcase; my head lay on the ticking. What I saw of the outside was the utility wires hung between the poles like lines on music paper, only sagging, and the glass insulators like clumps of notes. The woman had said nothing about money. Because she liked me. I couldn't believe my luck—luck with a hint of disaster. I blinded myself to the Bridewell metal cot, not meant for two. I felt also that I couldn't hold out if she kept me waiting long. And what feminine thing was she doing in there—undressing, washing, perfuming, changing?

Abruptly, she came out. She had been waiting, nothing else. She still wore the raccoon coat, even the gloves. Without looking at me she walked very quickly, almost running, and opened the window. As soon as the window shot up, it let in a blast of cold air, and I stood up on the bed but it was too late to stop her. She took my clothes from the back of the chair and heaved them out. They fell into the alley. I shouted, "What are you doing!" She still refused to turn her head. As she ran away, tying the scarf under her chin, she left the door open. I could hear her pumps beating double time in the hallway.

I couldn't run after her, could I, and show myself naked to the people in the flat? She had banked on this. When we came in, she must have given the high sign to the man she worked with, and he had been waiting in the alley. When I ran to look out, my things had already been gathered up. All I saw was the back of somebody with a bundle under his arm hurrying in the walkway between two garages. I might have picked up my boots—those she

2. A reformatory in London.

had left me—and jumped from the first-floor window, but I couldn't chase the man very far, and in a few minutes I would have wound up on Sheridan Road naked and freezing.

I had seen a drunk in his union suit, bleeding from the head after he had been rolled and beaten, staggering and yelling in the street. I didn't even have a shirt and drawers. I was as naked as the woman herself had been in the doctor's office, stripped of everything, including the five dollars I had collected for the flowers. And the sheepskin my mother had bought for me last year. Plus the book, the fragment of an untitled book, author unknown. This may have been the most serious loss of all.

Now I could think on my own about the world I really belonged to, whether it was this one or another.

I pulled down the window, and then I went to shut the door. The room didn't seem lived in, but suppose it had a tenant, and what if he were to storm in now and rough me up? Luckily there was a bolt to the door. I pushed it into its loop and then I ran around the room to see what I could find to wear. In the lopsided clothespress, nothing but wire hangers, and in the bathroom, only a cotton hand towel. I tore the blanket off the bed; if I were to slit it I might pull it over my head like a serape, but it was too thin to do me much good in freezing weather. When I pulled the chair over to the clothespress and stood on it, I found a woman's dress behind the molding, and a quilted bed jacket. In a brown paper bag there was a knitted brown tam.[3] I had to put these things on. I had no choice.

It was now, I reckoned, about five o'clock. Philip had no fixed schedule. He didn't hang around the office on the off chance that somebody might turn up with a toothache. After his last appointment he locked up and left. He didn't necessarily set out for home; he was not too keen to return to the house. If I wanted to catch him I'd have to run. In boots, dress, tam, and jacket, I made my way out of the apartment. Nobody took the slightest interest in me. More people (Philip would have called them transients) had crowded in—it was even likely that the man who had snatched up my clothes in the alley had returned, was among them. The heat in the staircase now was stifling, and the wallpaper smelled scorched, as if it were on the point of catching fire. In the street I was struck by a north wind straight from the Pole, and the dress and sateen jacket counted for nothing. I was running, though, and had no time to feel it.

Philip would say, "Who was this floozy? Where did she pick you up?" Philip was unexcitable, always mild, amused by me. Anna would badger him with the example of her ambitious brothers—they hustled, they read books. You couldn't fault Philip for being pleased. I anticipated what he'd say—"Did you get in? Then at least you're not going to catch the clap." I depended on Philip now, for I had nothing, not even seven cents for carfare. I could be certain, however, that he wouldn't moralize at me, he'd set about dressing me, he'd scrounge a sweater among his neighborhood acquaintances or take me to the Salvation Army shop on Broadway if that was still open. He'd go about this in his slow-moving, thick-necked, deliberate way. Not even dancing

3. Short for tam-o'-shanter; a woolen cap of Scottish origin that is wide and flat on top and has a pompon in the center.

would speed him up; he spaced out the music to suit him when he did the fox-trot and pressed his cheek to Anna's. He wore a long, calm grin. My private term for this particular expression was Pussy-Veleerum. I saw Philip as fat but strong, strong but cozy, purring but inserting a joking comment. He gave a little suck at the corner of the mouth when he was about to take a swipe at you, and it was then that he was Pussy-Veleerum. A name it never occurred to me to speak aloud.

I sprinted past the windows of the fruit store, the delicatessen, the tailor's shop. I could count on help from Philip. My father, however, was an intolerant, hasty man. Slighter than his sons, handsome, with muscles of white marble (so they seemed to me), laying down the law. It would put him in a rage to see me like this. And it was true that I had failed to consider: my mother dying, the ground frozen, a funeral coming, the dug grave, the packet of sand from the Holy Land to be scattered on the shroud. If I were to turn up in this filthy dress, the old man, breaking under his burdens, would come down on me in a blind, Old Testament rage. I never thought of this as cruelty but as archaic right everlasting. Even Albert, who was already a Loop lawyer, had to put up with the old man's blows—outraged, his eyes swollen and maddened, but he took it. It never seemed to any of us that my father was cruel. We had gone over the limit, and we were punished.

There were no lights in Philip's D.D.S office. When I jumped up the stairs, the door with its blank starred glass was locked. Frosted panes were still rare. What we had was this star-marred product for toilets and other private windows. Marchek—whom nowadays we could call a voyeur—was also, angrily, gone. I had screwed up his experiment. I tried the doors, thinking that I could spend the night on the leather examining table where the beautiful nude had lain. From the office I could also make telephone calls. I did have a few friends, although there were none who might help me. I wouldn't have known how to explain my predicament to them. They'd think I was putting them on, that it was a practical joke—"This is Louie. A whore robbed me of my clothes and I'm stuck on the North Side without carfare. I'm wearing a dress. I lost my house keys. I can't get home."

I ran down to the drugstore to look for Philip there. He sometimes played five or six hands of poker in the druggist's back room, trying his luck before getting on the streetcar. I knew Kiyar, the druggist, by sight. He had no recollection of me—why should he have? He said, "What can I do for you, young lady?"

Did he really take me for a girl, or a tramp off the street, or a gypsy from one of the storefront fortune-teller camps? Those were now all over town. But not even a gypsy would wear this blue sateen quilted boudoir jacket instead of a coat.

"I wonder, is Phil Haddis the dentist in the back?"

"What do you want with Dr. Haddis—have you got a toothache, or what?"

"I need to see him."

The druggist was a compact little guy, and his full round bald head was painfully sensitive looking. In its sensitivity it could pick up any degree of disturbance, I thought. Yet there was a canny glitter coming through his specs, and Kiyar had the mark of a man whose mind never would change once he had made it up. Oddly enough, he had a small mouth, baby's lips.

He had been on the street—how long? Forty years? In forty years you've seen it all and nobody can tell you a single thing.

"Did Dr. Haddis have an appointment with you? Are you a patient?"

He knew this was a private connection. I was no patient.

"No. But if I was out here he'd want to know it. Can I talk to him one minute?"

"He isn't here."

Kiyar had walked behind the grille of the prescription counter. I mustn't lose him. If he went, what would I do next? I said, "This is important, Mr. Kiyar." He waited for me to declare myself. I wasn't about to embarrass Philip by setting off rumors. Kiyar said nothing. He may have been waiting for me to speak up. Declare myself. I assume he took pride in running a tight operation, giving nothing away. To cut through to the man I said, "I'm in a spot. I left Dr. Haddis a note before, but when I came back I missed him."

At once I recognized my mistake. Druggists were always being appealed to. All those pills, remedy bottles, bright lights, medicine ads, drew wandering screwballs and moochers. They all said they were in bad trouble.

"You can go to the Foster Avenue station."

"The police, you mean."

I had thought of that too. I could always tell them my hard-luck story and they'd keep me until they checked it out and someone would come to fetch me. That would probably be Albert. Albert would love that. He'd say to me, "Well, aren't you the horny little bastard." He'd play up to the cops too, and amuse them.

"I'd freeze before I got to Foster Avenue," was my answer to Kiyar.

"There's always the squad car."

"Well, if Phil Haddis isn't in the back maybe he's still in the neighborhood. He doesn't always go straight home."

"Sometimes he goes over to the fights at Johnny Coulon's. It's a little early for that. You could try the speakeasy[4] down the street, on Kenmore. It's an English basement, side entrance. You'll see a light by the fence. The guy at the slot is called Moose."

He didn't offer so much as a dime from his till. If I had said that I was in a scrape and that Phil was my sister's husband he'd probably have given me carfare. But I hadn't confessed, and there was a penalty for that.

Going out, I crossed my arms over the bed jacket and opened the door with my shoulder. I might as well have been wearing nothing at all. The wind cut at my legs, and I ran. Luckily I didn't have far to go. The iron pipe with the bulb at the end of it was halfway down the block. I saw it as soon as I crossed the street. These illegal drinking parlors were easy to find; they were meant to be. The steps were cement, four or five of them bringing me down to the door. The slot came open even before I knocked, and instead of the doorkeeper's eyes, I saw his teeth.

"You Moose?"

"Yah. Who?"

"Kiyar sent me."

4. During Prohibition, a place to buy alcoholic drinks illegally.

"Come on."

I felt as though I were falling into a big, warm, paved cellar. There was little to see, almost nothing. A sort of bar was set up, a few hanging fixtures, some tables from an ice cream parlor, wire-backed chairs. If you looked through the window of an English basement your eyes were at ground level. Here the glass was tarred over. There would have been nothing to see anyway: a yard, a wooden porch, a clothesline, wires, a back alley with ash heaps.

"Where did you come from, sister?" said Moose.

But Moose was a nobody here. The bartender, the one who counted, called me over and said, "What is it, sweetheart? You got a message for somebody?"

"Not exactly."

"Oh? You needed a drink so bad that you jumped out of bed and ran straight over—you couldn't stop to dress?"

"No, sir. I'm looking for somebody—Phil Haddis? The dentist?"

"There's only one customer. Is that him?"

It wasn't. My heart sank into river mud.

"It's not a drunk you're looking for?"

"No."

The drunk was on a high stool, thin legs hanging down, arms forward, and his head lying sidewise on the bar. Bottles, glasses, a beer barrel. Behind the barkeeper was a sideboard pried from the wall of an apartment. It had a long mirror—an oval laid on its side. Paper streamers curled down from the pipes.

"Do you know the dentist I'm talking about?"

"I might. Might not," said the barkeeper. He was a sloppy, long-faced giant—something of a kangaroo look about him. That was the long face in combination with the belly. He told me, "This is not a busy time. It's dinner, you know, and we're just a neighborhood speak."

It was no more than a cellar, just as the barman was no more than a Greek, huge and bored. Just as I myself, Louie, was no more than a naked male in a woman's dress. When you had named objects in this elementary way, hardly anything remained in them. The barman, on whom everything now depended, held his bare arms out at full reach and braced on his spread hands. The place smelled of yeast sprinkled with booze. He said, "You live around here?"

"No, about an hour on the streetcar."

"Say more."

"Humboldt Park is my neighborhood."

"Then you got to be a Uke, a Polack, a Scandihoof,[5] or a Jew."

"Jew."

"I know my Chicago. And you didn't set out dressed like that. You'da frozen to death inside of ten minutes. It's for the boudoir, not winter wear. You don't have the shape of a woman, neither. The hips aren't there. Are you covering a pair of knockers? I bet not. So what's the story, are you a morphodite?[6] Let me tell you, you got to give this Depression credit. Without it you'd never find out what kind of funny stuff is going on. But one thing I'll never believe is that you're a young girl and still got her cherry."

5. Slang for Ukrainian, Pole, and Scandinavian, respectively.

6. I.e., hermaphrodite.

"You're right as far as that goes, but the rest of it is that I haven't got a cent, and I need carfare."

"Who took you, a woman?"

"Up in her room when I undressed, she grabbed my things and threw them out the window."

"Left you naked so you couldn't chase her . . . I would have grabbed her and threw her on the bed. I bet you didn't even get in."

Not even, I repeated to myself. Why didn't I push her down while she was still in her coat, as soon as we entered the room—pull up her clothes, as he would have done? Because he was born to do that. While I was not. I wasn't intended for it.

"So that's what happened. You got taken by a team of pros. She set you up. You were the mark. Jewish fellows aren't supposed to keep company with those bad cunts. But when you get out of your house, into the world, you want action like anybody else. So. And where did you dig up this dress with the fancy big roses? I guess you were standing with your sticker sticking out and were lucky to find anything to put on. Was she a good looker?"

Her breasts, as she lay there, had kept their shape. They didn't slip sideward. The inward lines of her legs, thigh swelling toward thigh. The black crumpled hairs. Yes, a beauty, I would say.

Like the druggist, the barman saw the fun of the thing—an adolescent in a fix, a soiled dress, the rayon or sateen bed jacket. It was a lucky thing for me that business was at a standstill. If he had had customers, the barman wouldn't have given me the time of day. "In short, you got mixed up with a whore and she gave you the works."

For that matter, I had no sympathy for myself. I confessed that I had this coming, a high-minded Jewish schoolboy, too high-and-mighty to be Orthodox and with his eye on a special destiny. At home, inside the house, an archaic rule; outside, the facts of life. The facts of life were having their turn. Their first effect was ridicule. To throw my duds into the alley was the woman's joke on me. The druggist with his pain-sensitive head was all irony. And now the barman was going to get his fun out of my trouble before he, maybe, gave me the seven cents for carfare. Then I could have a full hour of shame on the streetcar. My mother, with whom I might never speak again, used to say that I had a line of pride straight down the bridge of my nose, a foolish stripe that she could see.

I had no way of anticipating what her death would signify.

The barman, having me in place, was giving me the business. And Moose ("Moosey," the Greek called him) had come away from the door so as not to miss the entertainment. The Greek's kangaroo mouth turned up at the corners. Presently his hand went up to his head and he rubbed his scalp under the black, spiky hair. Some said they drank olive oil by the glass, these Greeks, to keep their hair so rich. "Now give it to me again, about the dentist," said the barman.

"I came looking for him, but by now he's well on his way home."

He would by then be on the Broadway–Clark car, reading the Peach edition of the *Evening American*, a broad man with an innocent pout to his face, checking the race results. Anna had him dressed up as a professional man, but he let the fittings—shirt, tie, buttons—go their own way. His instep was fat and swelled inside the narrow shoe she had picked for him. He wore the fedora correctly. Toward the rest he admitted no obligation.

Anna cooked dinner after work, and when Philip came in, my father would begin to ask, "Where's Louie?" "Oh, he's out delivering flowers," they'd tell him. But the old man was nervous about his children after dark, and if they were late he waited up, walking—no, trotting—up and down the long apartment. When you tried to slip in, he caught you and twisted you tight by the neckband. He was small, neat, slender, a gentleman, but abrupt, not unworldly—he wasn't ignorant of vices; he had lived in Odessa and even longer in St. Petersburg—but he had no patience. The least thing might craze him. Seeing me in this dress, he'd lose his head at once. *I* lost *mine* when that woman showed me her snatch with all the pink layers, when she raised up her arm and asked me to disconnect the wires, when I felt her skin and her fragrance came upward.

"What's your family, what does your dad do?" asked the barman.

"His business is wood fuel for bakers' ovens. It comes by freight car from northern Michigan. Also from Birnamwood, Wisconsin. He has a yard off Lake Street, east of Halsted."

I made an effort to give the particulars. I couldn't afford to be suspected of invention now.

"I know where that is. Now, that's a neighborhood just full of hookers and cathouses. You think you can tell your old man what happened to you, that you got picked up by a cutie and she stole your clothes off you?"

The effect of this question was to make me tight in the face, dim in the ears. The whole cellar grew small and distant, toylike but not for play.

"How's your old man to deal with—tough?"

"Hard," I said.

"Slaps the kids around? This time you've got it coming. What's under the dress, a pair of bloomers?"[7]

I shook my head.

"Your behind is bare? Now you know how it feels to go around like a woman."

The Greek's great muscles were dough-colored. You wouldn't have wanted him to take a headlock on you. That's the kind of man the Organization hired. The Capone people were now in charge.[8] The customers would be like celluloid Kewpie dolls to the Greek. He looked like one of those boxing kangaroos in the movies, and he could do a standing jump over the bar. Yet he enjoyed playing zany. He could curve his long mouth up at the corners like the happy face in a cartoon.

"What were you doing on the North Side?"

"Delivering flowers."

"Hustling after school but with ramming on your brain. You got a lot to learn, buddy boy. Well, enough of that. Now, Moosey, take this flashlight and see if you can scrounge up a sweater or something in the back basement for this down-on-his-luck kid. I'd be surprised if the old janitor hasn't picked the stuff over pretty good. If mice have nested in it, shake out the turds. It'll help on the trip home."

7. A woman's undergarment.
8. In Chicago, Al Capone ran America's largest organized crime network.

I followed Moose into the hotter half of the cellar. His flashlight picked out the laundry tubs with the hand-operated wringers mounted on them, the padlocked wooden storage bins. "Turn over some of these cardboard boxes. Mostly rags, is my guess. Dump 'em out, that's the easiest."

I emptied a couple of big cartons. Moose passed the light back and forth over the heaps. "Nothing much, like I said."

"Here's a flannel shirt," I said. I wanted to get out. The smell of heated burlap was hard to take. This was the only wearable article. I could have used a pullover or a pair of pants. We returned to the bar. As I was putting on the shirt, which revolted me (I come of finicky people whose fetish is cleanliness), the barman said, "I tell you what, you take this drunk home—this is about time for him, isn't it, Moosey? He gets plastered here every night. See he gets home and it'll be worth half a buck to you."

"I'll do it," I said. "It all depends on how far away he lives. If it's far, I'll be frozen before I get there."

"It isn't far. Winona, west of Sheridan, isn't far. I'll give you the directions. This guy is a city-hall payroller. He has no special job, he works direct for the ward committeeman. He's a lush with two little girls to bring up. If he's sober enough he cooks their dinner. Probably they take more care of him than he does of them."

"First I'll take charge of his money," said the barman. "I don't want my buddy here to be rolled. I don't say you would do it, but I owe this to a customer."

Bristle-faced Moose began to empty the man's pockets—his wallet, some keys, crushed cigarettes, a red bandanna that looked foul, matchbooks, greenbacks, and change. All these were laid out on the bar.

When I look back at past moments, I carry with me an apperceptive mass that ripens and perhaps distorts, mixing what is memorable with what may not be worth mentioning. Thus I see the barman with one big hand gathering in the valuables as if they were his winnings, the pot in a poker game. And then I think that if the kangaroo giant had taken this drunk on his back he might have bounded home with him in less time than it would have taken me to support him as far as the corner. But what the barman actually said was, "I got a nice escort for you, Jim."

Moose led the man back and forth to make sure his feet were operating. His swollen eyes now opened and then closed again. "McKern," Moose said, briefing me. "Southwest corner of Winona and Sheridan, the second building on the south side of the street, and it's the second floor."

"You'll be paid when you get back," said the barman.

The freeze was now so hard that the snow underfoot sounded like metal foil. Though McKern may have sobered up in the frigid street, he couldn't move very fast. Since I had to hold on to him, I borrowed his gloves. He had a coat with pockets to put his hands in. I tried to keep behind him and get some shelter from the wind. That didn't work. He wasn't up to walking. I had to hold him. Instead of a desirable woman, I had a drunkard in my arms. This disgrace, you see, while my mother was surrendering to death. At about this hour, upstairs neighbors came down and relatives arrived and filled the kitchen and the dining room—a deathwatch. I should have been there, not on the far North Side. When I had earned the carfare, I'd still be an hour from home on a streetcar making four stops to the mile.

Toward the last, I was dragging McKern. I kept the street door open with my back while I pulled him into the dim lobby by the arms.

The little girls had been waiting and came down at once. They held the inner door for me while I brought their daddy upstairs with a fireman's-carry and laid him on his bed. The children had had plenty of practice at this. They undressed him down to the long johns and then stood silent on either side of the room. This, for them, was how things were. They took deep oddities calmly, as children generally will. I had spread his winter coat over him.

I had little sympathy for McKern, in the circumstances. I believe I can tell you why: He had surely passed out many times, and he would pass out again, dozens of times before he died. Drunkenness was common and familiar, and therefore accepted, and drunks could count on acceptance and support and relied on it. Whereas if your troubles were uncommon, unfamiliar, you could count on nothing. There was a convention about drunkenness, established in part by drunkards. The founding proposition was that consciousness is terrible. Its lower, impoverished forms are perhaps the worst. Flesh and blood are poor and weak, susceptible to human shock. Here my descendant will hear the voice of Grandfather Louie giving one of his sermons on higher consciousness and interrupting the story he promised to tell. You will hold him to his word, as you have every right to do.

The older girl now spoke to me. She said, "The fellow phoned and said a man was bringing Daddy home, and you'd help with supper if Daddy couldn't cook it."

"Yes. Well . . . ?"

"Only you're not a man—you've got a dress on."

"It looks like it, doesn't it. Don't you worry; I'll come to the kitchen with you."

"Are you a lady?"

"What do you mean—what does it look like? All right, I'm a lady."

"You can eat with us."

"Then show me where the kitchen is."

I followed them down a corridor narrowed by clutter—boxes of canned groceries, soda biscuits, sardines, pop bottles. When I passed the bathroom, I slipped in for quick relief. The door had neither a hook nor a bolt; the string of the ceiling fixture had snapped off. A tiny night-light was plugged into the baseboard. I thanked God it was so dim. I put up the board while raising my skirt, and when I had begun I heard one of the children behind me. Over my shoulder I saw that it was the younger one, and as I turned my back (*everything* was happening today) I said, "Don't come in here." But she squeezed past and sat on the edge of the tub. She grinned at me. She was expecting her second teeth. Today all females were making sexual fun of me, and even the infants were looking lewd. I stopped, letting the dress fall, and said to her, "What are you laughing about?"

"If you were a girl, you'd of sat down."

The kid wanted me to understand that she knew what she had seen. She pressed her fingers over her mouth, and I turned and went to the kitchen.

There the older girl was lifting the black cast-iron skillet with both hands. On dripping paper, the pork chops[9] were laid out—nearby, a Mason jar of

9. Jews are forbidden to eat pork.

grease. I was competent enough at the gas range, which shone with old filth. Loath to touch the pork with my fingers, I forked the meat into the spitting fat. The chops turned my stomach. My thought was, "I'm into it now, up to the ears." The drunk in his bed, the dim secret toilet, the glaring tungsten twist over the gas range, the sputtering droplets stinging the hands. The older girl said, "There's plenty for you. Daddy won't be eating dinner."

"No, not me. I'm not hungry," I said.

All that my upbringing held in horror geysered up, my throat filling with it, my guts griping.

The children sat at the table, an enamel rectangle. Thick plates and glasses, a waxed package of sliced white bread, a milk bottle, a stick of butter, the burning fat clouding the room. The girls sat beneath the smoke, slicing their meat. I brought them salt and pepper from the range. They ate without conversation. My chore (my duty) done, there was nothing to keep me. I said, "I have to go."

I looked in at McKern, who had thrown down the coat and taken off his drawers. The parboiled face, the short nose pointed sharply, the life signs in the throat, the broken look of his neck, the black hair of his belly, the short cylinder between his legs ending in a spiral of loose skin, the white shine of the shins, the tragic expression of his feet. There was a stack of pennies on his bedside table. I helped myself to carfare but had no pocket for the coins. I opened the hall closet feeling quickly for a coat I might borrow, a pair of slacks. Whatever I took, Philip could return to the Greek barman tomorrow. I pulled a trench coat from a hanger, and a pair of trousers. For the third time I put on stranger's clothing—this is no time to mention stripes or checks or make exquisite notations. Escaping, desperate, I struggled into the pants on the landing, tucking in the dress, and pulled on the coat as I jumped down the stairs, knotting tight the belt and sticking the pennies, a fistful of them, into my pocket.

But still I went back to the alley under the woman's window to see if her light was on, and also to look for pages. The thief or pimp perhaps had chucked them away, or maybe they had dropped out when he snatched the sheepskin. Her window was dark. I found nothing on the ground. You may think this obsessive crankiness, a crazy dependency on words, on printed matter. But remember, there were no redeemers in the streets, no guides, no confessors, comforters, enlighteners, communicants to turn to. You had to take teaching wherever you could find it. Under the library dome downtown, in mosaic letters, there was a message from Milton,[1] so moving but perhaps of no utility, perhaps aggravating difficulties: A GOOD BOOK, it said, IS THE PRECIOUS LIFE'S BLOOD OF A MASTER SPIRIT.

These are the plain facts, they have to be uttered. This, remember, is the New World, and here one of its mysterious cities. I should have hurried directly, to catch a car. Instead I was in a back alley hunting pages that would in any case have blown away.

I went back to Broadway—it *was* very broad—and waited on a safety island. Then the car came clanging, red, swaying on its trucks, a piece of Iron Age technology, double cane seats framed in brass. Rush hour was long past. I

1. John Milton (1608–1674), English poet and author of *Paradise Lost*; the quotation is from his *Areopagitica* (1644).

sat by a window, homebound, with flashes of thought like tracer bullets slanting into distant darkness. Like London in wartime. At home, what story would I tell? I wouldn't tell any. I never did. It was assumed anyway that I was lying. While I believed in honor, I did often lie. Is a life without lying conceivable? It was easier to lie than to explain myself. My father had one set of assumptions, I had another. Corresponding premises were not to be found.

I owed five dollars to Behrens. But I knew where my mother secretly hid her savings. Because I looked into all books, I had found the money in her *mahzor*, the prayer book for the High Holidays, the days of awe. As yet I hadn't taken anything. She had hoped until this final illness to buy passage to Europe to see her mother and her sister. When she died I would turn the money over to my father, except for ten dollars, five for the florist and the rest for Von Hügel's *Eternal Life*[2] and *The World as Will and Idea.*[3]

The after-dinner guests and cousins would be gone when I reached home. My father would be on the lookout for me. It was the rear porch door that was locked after dark. The kitchen door was generally off the latch. I could climb over the wooden partition between the stairs and the porch. I often did that. Once you got your foot on the doorknob you could pull yourself over the partition and drop to the porch without noise. Then I could see into the kitchen and slip in as soon as my patrolling father had left it. The bedroom shared by all three brothers was just off the kitchen. I could borrow my brother Len's cast-off winter coat tomorrow. I knew which closet it hung in. If my father should catch me I could expect hard blows on my shoulders, on the top of my head, on my face. But if my mother had, tonight, just died, he wouldn't hit me.

This was when the measured, reassuring, sleep-inducing turntable of days became a whirlpool, a vortex darkening toward the bottom. I had had only the anonymous pages in the pocket of my lost sheepskin to interpret it to me. They told me that the truth of the universe was inscribed into our very bones. That the human skeleton was itself a hieroglyph. That everything we had ever known on earth was shown to us in the first days after death. That our experience of the world was desired by the cosmos, and needed by it for its own renewal.

I do not think that these pages, if I hadn't lost them, would have persuaded me forever or made the life I led a different one.

I am writing this account, or statement, in response to an eccentric urge swelling toward me from the earth itself.

Failed my mother! That may mean, will mean, little or nothing to you, my only child, reading this document.

I myself know the power of nonpathos, in these low, devious days.

On the streetcar, heading home, I braced myself, but all my preparations caved in like sand diggings. I got down at the North Avenue stop, avoiding my reflection in the shop-windows. After a death, mirrors were immediately covered. I can't say what this pious superstition means. Will the soul of your dead be reflected in a looking glass, or is this custom a check to the vanity of the living?

2. A reference to Roman Catholic philosopher and theologian Baron Friedrich Von Hügel's (1852–1925) 1912 work.

3. A major work by German philosopher Arthur Schopenhauer (1788–1860).

I ran home, approached by the back alley, made no noise on the wooden backstairs, reached for the top of the partition, placed my foot on the white porcelain doorknob, went over the top without noise, and dropped down on our porch. I didn't follow the plan I had laid for avoiding my father. There were people sitting at the kitchen table. I went straight in. My father rose from his chair and hurried toward me. His fist was ready. I took off my tam or woolen beret and when he hit me on the head the blow filled me with gratitude. If my mother had already died, he would have embraced me instead.

Well, they're all gone now, and I have made my preparations. I haven't left a large estate, and this is why I have written this memoir, a sort of addition to your legacy.

Magazine, 1990
Book, 1991

ALFRED KAZIN
1915–1998

"Every time I go back to Brownsville it is as if I had never been away." The opening sentence of Alfred Kazin's *A Walker in the City* (1951) anchors the springing trajectory of his life and writing. Born in New York to Yiddish-speaking Russian immigrants on June 5, 1915—his father was a house painter and socialist, his mother a dressmaker who had worked in the Triangle Shirtwaist Factory—Kazin very early knew himself to be "the first American child, their offering to the strange new God; I was to be the monument of their liberation from the shame of being—what they were." He grew up in Brooklyn's Brownsville section, which the old folks called "Brunzvil" or "Bronzeville," where Henry Roth's family settles in *Call It Sleep*. Kazin's homey Sabbaths, his voracious reading, his agony at stammering in school when correct English ensured success, his long teenage walks through the city, his path between the synagogue and the subway under the East River to "New York": all these exemplify a first generation on the way to "making it" in America.

For the frontispiece to *A Walker in the City*, Kazin chose Alfred Stieglitz's photo of immigrants belowdecks, *The Steerage*; on the title page opposite, he put a verse from Walt Whitman's *Crossing Brooklyn Ferry*: "The glories strung like beads on my smallest sights and hearings—on the walk in the street, and the passage over the river." Between that bottom-rung aspiration and the golden land's self-laureled poet runs the arc of Alfred Kazin's career, and he remained true to both poles. Indeed, with his books of memoirs and journals, he seems a storybook character himself, typifying the generation that grew up in the depression and came of age just before the war.

In 1938, having attended City College and Columbia in New York, Kazin brashly began at the age of twenty-three a survey of major American literature from the later nineteenth century to the present. As Mary Antin, a generation before, had possessed the promised land in the Boston Public Library, Kazin would go every day to New York's Forty-second Street library and read from morning till evening, then take the subway back to Brooklyn. Emerson, Whitman, Dickinson, Rebecca Harding Davis, Edith Wharton, Sarah Orne Jewett, William and Henry James, William Dean Howells, Mark Twain, Henry Adams, Theodore Dreiser, John Dewey, plus Thomas Eakins, Albert Pinkham Ryder, John James Audubon: Kazin took "fresh instant delight in American landscape and culture." In 1942, he saw his first book come out. Its very title, *On Native Grounds*, had a personal as well as a literary point, as if to declare: "Here I now stand." Kazin's preface calls the book "an effort at moral history, which is greater than literary history."

On Native Grounds quotes in passing the political economist Thorstein Veblen about "the gifted Jew escap[ing] from the cultural environment created and fed by the particular genius of his own people. . . . It is by loss of allegiance, or at best by force of a divided allegiance to the people of his origin, that he finds himself in the vanguard of American inquiry. . . . He becomes a disturber of the intellectual peace," "an intellectual wayfaring man." Possibly Kazin was also thinking of himself by these terms of divided allegiance. In February 1944, when he already knew of the Nazi genocide, he could still say: "I learned long ago to accept the fact that I was Jewish without being a part of any meaningful Jewish life or culture." But by the war's end, a certain Jewish meaning was lodged in him to stay. In London one day, Kazin heard a broadcast of the first Sabbath service from liberated Bergen-Belsen. "I weep with them as they say the Shema and say it with them," he wrote in his journal then. Kazin a few years later opened *The Kitchen*, which memorializes a richly fraught American Jewish childhood, by recollecting that moment from 1945. And years later, after considering Rilke's famous line "You must change your life" to title a memoir, he ended up calling it simply *New York Jew* (1978).

Starting with *On Native Grounds*, Kazin flourished for five decades and more as a critic, editor, teacher, memoirist, and friend of such people as Isaac Rosenfeld, Saul Bellow, Lionel Trilling, Edmund Wilson, Hannah Arendt. His literary affinities show up in the editions he published: Blake, Fitzgerald, Dreiser, Melville, Emerson, Hawthorne, James, Whitman; and an insistent humanism marks his book titles: *The Inmost Leaf, An American Procession, Bright Book of Life, Writing Was Everything*. Alfred Kazin brought to American literature a mix of curiosity, freshness, sympathy, urgency, and, above all, gratitude that T. S. Eliot, for instance, with his family in this country since the 1600s, could not bring.

"Home is where one starts from": Kazin took from Eliot this epigraph and the title for his published journals, *A Lifetime Burning in Every Moment* (1996). It may well be that he is remembered even more for his vivid and often lyrical autobiographical writing than for his criticism. Although he would not have subscribed to Malamud's "Every man is a Jew," Kazin did feel that Jews, thanks to their precarious history, "naturally see existence as tension, issue, and drama, woven out of so many contradictions that only a work of art may appear to *hold* these contradictions, to compose them." So *A Walker in the City*, like Nabokov's *Speak, Memory*, engages us as strongly as any novel.

Alfred Kazin died on June 5, 1998. At a funeral gathering, his son read *The Kitchen*.

From A Walker in the City

The Kitchen

The last time I saw our kitchen this clearly was one afternoon in London at the end of the war, when I waited out the rain in the entrance to a music store. A radio was playing into the street, and standing there I heard a broadcast of the first Sabbath service from Belsen Concentration Camp.[1] When

1. I.e., Bergen-Belsen, a German concentration camp.

the liberated Jewish prisoners recited the *Hear O Israel, the Lord Our God, the Lord is One*,[2] I felt myself carried back to the Friday evenings at home, when with the Sabbath at sundown a healing quietness would come over Brownsville.

It was the darkness and emptiness of the streets I liked most about Friday evening, as if in preparation for that day of rest and worship which the Jews greet "as a bride"—that day when the very touch of money is prohibited, all work, all travel, all household duties, even to the turning on and off of a light—Jewry had found its way past its tormented heart to some ancient still center of itself. I waited for the streets to go dark on Friday evening as other children waited for the Christmas lights. Even Friday morning after the tests were over glowed in anticipation. When I returned home after three, the warm odor of a coffee cake baking in the oven and the sight of my mother on her hands and knees scrubbing the linoleum on the dining room floor filled me with such tenderness that I could feel my senses reaching out to embrace every single object in our household. One Friday, after a morning in school spent on the voyages of Henry Hudson,[3] I returned with the phrase *Among the discoverers of the New World* singing in my mind as the theme of my own new-found freedom on the Sabbath.

My great moment came at six, when my father returned from work, his overalls smelling faintly of turpentine and shellac, white drops of silver paint still gleaming on his chin. Hanging his overcoat in the long dark hall that led into our kitchen, he would leave in one pocket a loosely folded copy of the New York *World;* and then everything that beckoned to me from that other hemisphere of my brain beyond the East River[4] would start up from the smell of fresh newsprint and the sight of the globe on the front page. It was a paper that carried special associations for me with Brooklyn Bridge. They published the *World* under the green dome on Park Row overlooking the bridge; the fresh salt air of New York harbor lingered for me in the smell of paint and damp newsprint in the hall. I felt that my father brought the outside straight into our house with each day's copy of the *World*. The bridge somehow stood for freedom; the *World* for that rangy kindness and fraternalism and ease we found in Heywood Broun.[5] My father would read aloud from "It Seems To Me" with a delighted smile on his face. "A very clear and courageous man!" he would say. "Look how he stands up for our Sacco and Vanzetti![6] A real social conscience, that man! Practically a Socialist!" Then, taking off his overalls, he would wash up at the kitchen sink, peeling and gnawing the paint off his nails with Gold Dust Washing Powder as I poured it into his hands, smacking his lips and grunting with pleasure as he washed himself clean of the job at last, and making me feel that I was really helping him, that I, too, was contributing to the greatness of the evening and the coming day.

By sundown the streets were empty, the curtains had been drawn, the world put to rights. Even the kitchen walls had been scrubbed and now gleamed in the Sabbath candles. On the long white tablecloth were the

2. The Shema, credo of Judaism.
3. Hudson (1565–1611) was the English navigator and explorer who discovered the Hudson River.
4. The river that separates Brooklyn and Manhattan. "New York *World*": one of New York's daily newspapers (1860–1931).
5. New York journalist (1888–1939) noted for his liberal social and political opinions, and for his column *It Seems to Me*.
6. Italian American anarchists executed (1927) after a controversial seven-year murder trial in Massachussetts.

"company" dishes, filled for some with *gefillte* fish[7] on lettuce leaves, ringed by red horseradish, sour and half-sour pickles, tomato salad with a light vinegar dressing; for others, with chopped liver in a bed of lettuce leaves and white radishes; the long white *khalleh*, the Sabbath loaf; chicken soup with noodles *and* dumplings; chicken, meat loaf, prunes, and sweet potatoes that had been baked all day into an open pie; compote of prunes and quince, apricots and orange rind; applesauce; a great brown nutcake filled with almonds, the traditional *lekakh*;[8] all surrounded by glasses of port wine, seltzer bottles with their nozzles staring down at us waiting to be pressed; a samovar[9] of Russian tea, *svetouchnee*[1] from the little red box, always served in tall glasses, with lemon slices floating on top. My father and mother sipped it in Russian fashion, through lumps of sugar held between the teeth.

Afterwards we went into the "dining room" and, since we were not particularly orthodox, allowed ourselves little pleasures outside the Sabbath rule—an occasional game of Casino[2] at the dining-room table where we never dined; and listening to the victrola.[3] The evening was particularly good for me whenever the unmarried cousin who boarded with us had her two closest friends in after supper.

They were all dressmakers, like my mother; had worked with my mother in the same East Side sweatshops; were all passionately loyal members of the International Ladies Garment Workers Union; and were all unmarried. We were their only family. Despite my mother's frenzied matchmaking, she had never succeeded in pinning a husband down for any of them. As she said, they were all too *particular*—what a calamity for a Jewish woman to remain unmarried! But my cousin and her friends accepted their fate calmly, and prided themselves on their culture and their strong *progressive* interests. They felt they belonged not to the "kitchen world," like my mother, but to the enlightened tradition of the old Russian intelligentsia. Whenever my mother sighed over them, they would smile out of their greater knowledge of the world, and looking at me with a pointed appeal for recognition, would speak of novels they had read in Yiddish and Russian, of *Winesburg, Ohio*,[4] of some article in the *Nation*.[5]

Our cousin and her two friends were of my parents' generation, but I could never believe it—they seemed to enjoy life with such outspokenness. They were the first grown-up people I had ever met who used the word *love* without embarrassment. *"Libbe!*[6] *Libbe!"* my mother would explode whenever one of them protested that she could not, after all, marry a man she did not love. "What is this love you make such a stew about? You do not like the way he holds his cigarette? Marry him first and it will all come out right in the end!" It astonished me to realize there was a world in which even unmarried women no longer young were simply individual human beings with lives of their own. *Our* parents, whatever affection might offhandedly be expressed between them, always had the look of being com-

7. Balls or small loaves of seasoned ground fish that are usually poached in a fish stock (Yiddish).
8. Honey cake (Yiddish).
9. An urn with a spigot at its base used in Russia to boil water for tea.
1. It is sold in America under the brand name Swee-touch-nee.
2. A card game.
3. Phonograph (trademark).
4. A work (1919) by Sherwood Anderson (1876–1941).
5. A progressive weekly magazine.
6. Love (Yiddish).

mitted to something deeper than *mere* love. Their marriages were neither happy nor unhappy; they were arrangements. However they had met—whether in Russia or in the steerage[7] or, like my parents, in an East Side boarding house—whatever they still thought of each other, *love* was not a word they used easily. Marriage was an institution people entered into—for all I could ever tell—only from immigrant loneliness, a need to be with one's own kind that mechanically resulted in the *family*. The *family* was a whole greater than all the individuals who made it up, yet made sense only in their untiring solidarity. I was perfectly sure that in my parents' minds *libbe* was something exotic and not wholly legitimate, reserved for "educated" people like their children, who were the sole end of their existence. My father and mother worked in a rage to put us above their level; they had married to make *us* possible. We were the only conceivable end to all their striving; we were their America.

So far as I knew, love was not an element admissible in my parents' experience. Any open talk of it between themselves would have seemed ridiculous. It would have suggested a wicked self-indulgence, a preposterous attention to one's own feelings, possible only to those who were free enough to choose. They did not consider themselves free. They were awed by us, as they were awed by their own imagined unworthiness, and looked on themselves only as instruments toward the ideal "American" future that would be lived by their children. As poor immigrants who had remained in Brownsville, painfully conscious of the *alrightniks*[8] on Eastern Parkway—oh, those successes of whom I was always hearing so much, and whom we admired despite all our socialism!—everything in their lives combined to make them look down on love as something *they* had no time for. Of course there was a deep resentment in this, and when on those Friday evenings our cousin or her two friends openly mentioned the unheard-of collapse of someone's marriage—

"Sórelle and Berke? I don't believe it."

"But it's true."

"You must be joking!"

"No, it's true!"

"You're joking! You're joking!"

"No, it's true!"

—I noticed that my parents' talk had an unnaturally hard edge to it, as if those who gave themselves up to love must inevitably come to grief. Love, they could have said, was not *serious*. Life was a battle to "make sure"; it had no place, as we had no time, for whims.

Love, in fact, was something for the movies, which my parents enjoyed, but a little ashamedly. They were the land of the impossible. On those few occasions when my mother closed her sewing machine in the evening and allowed herself a visit to the Supreme, or the Palace, or the Premier,[9] she would return, her eyes gleaming with wonder and some distrust at the strangeness of it all, to report on erotic fanatics who were, thank God, like no one we knew. What heedlessness! What daring! What riches! To my mother riches alone were the gateway to romance, for only those who had

7. The cheapest section, belowdecks, of a passenger ship.

8. Immigrants who have done well for themselves.

9. Movie houses.

money enough could afford the freedom, and the crazy boldness, to give themselves up to love.

Yet there they were in our own dining room, our cousin and her two friends—women, grown-up women—talking openly of the look on Garbo's face when John Gilbert[1] took her in his arms, serenely disposing of each new *khayimyankel*,[2] poor wretch, my mother had picked for them, and arguing my father down on small points of Socialist doctrine. As they sat around the cut-glass bowl on the table—cracking walnuts, expertly peeling the skin off an apple in long even strips, cozily sipping at a glass of tea—they crossed their legs in comfort and gave off a deliciously musky fragrance of face powder that instantly framed them for me in all their dark coloring, brilliantly white teeth, and the rosy Russian blouses that swelled and rippled in terraces of embroidery over their opulent breasts.

They had a great flavor for me, those three women: they were the positive center of that togetherness that always meant so much to me in our dining room on Friday evenings. It was a quality that seemed to start in the prickly thickness of the cut-glass bowl laden with nuts and fruits; in the light from the long black-shaded lamp hanging over the table as it shimmered against the thick surfaces of the bowl and softened that room where the lace curtains were drawn against the dark and empty streets—and then found its unexpectedly tender voice in the Yiddish folksongs and Socialist hymns they taught me—*"Let's Now Forgive Each Other"*; *"Tsuzamen, Tsuzamen, All Together, Brothers!"* Those Friday evenings, I suddenly found myself enveloped in some old, primary Socialist idea that men could go beyond every barrier of race and nation and language, even of class! into some potential loving union of the whole human race. I was suddenly glad to be a Jew, as these women were Jews—simply and naturally glad of those Jewish dressmakers who spoke with enthusiastic familiarity of Sholem Aleichem and Peretz, Gorky and Tolstoy, who glowed at every reminiscence of Nijinsky, of Nazimova in *The Cherry Orchard*, of Pavlova in "The Swan."[3]

Often, those Friday evenings, they spoke of *der heym*, "Home," and then it was hard for me. *Heym* was a terrible word. I saw millions of Jews lying dead under the Polish eagle[4] with knives in their throats. I was afraid with my mother's fears, thought I should weep when she wept, lived again through every pogrom whose terrors she chanted. I associated with that old European life only pain, mud, and hopelessness, but I was of it still, through her. Whenever she would call through the roll of her many brothers and sisters and their children, remembering at each name that this one was dead, that one dead, another starving and sure soon to die—who knew *how* they were living these days in that miserable Poland?—I felt there was some

1. Gilbert (ca. 1899–1936), a popular Hollywood actor mostly remembered for his costarring roles opposite the equally popular Swedish-born Hollywood actress Greta Garbo (1905–1990).

2. From the Yiddish male names Chaim and Yankel—i.e., an ordinary fellow, a Joe Shmo.

3. Russian prima ballerina Anna Pavlova (1882–1931), famous for her depiction of the Dying Swan in Fokine's ballet *Le Cygne*. "Sholem Aleichem": pseudonym of Sh. Rabinovitch (1859–1916), Russian Jewish writer known as the "Jewish Mark Twain." "Peretz": I. L. Peretz (ca. 1851–1915), prolific Polish Jewish writer who brought Yiddish literature into modern times. "Gorky": Maxim Gorky (1868–1936), Russian bolshevik writer who helped develop the official aesthetic of socialist realism. "Tolstoy": Count Leo Tolstoy (1828–1910), Russian novelist and moral philosopher. "Nijinsky": Vaslav Nijinsky (1890–1950), Russian dancer and choreographer of Polish descent who rejected classical ballet for a more free-form approach to dance. "Nazimova": Alla Nazimova (1878–1945), Russian American actress who appeared in the 1928 stage version of Anton Chekhov's *The Cherry Orchard* (1904).

4. The national emblem of Poland.

supernatural Polish eagle across the sea whose face I should never see, but which sent out dark electrical rays to hold me fast.

In many ways *der heym* was entirely dim and abstract, nothing to do with me at all, alien as the skullcap and beard and frock coat of my mother's father, whom I never saw, but whose calm orthodox dignity stared up at me from an old cracked photograph at the bottom of the bureau drawer. Yet I lived each of my mother's fears from Dugschitz to Hamburg to London to Hester Street[5] to Brownsville through and through with such fidelity that there were times when I wished I had made that journey too, wished I could have seen Czarist Russia, since I had in any event to suffer it all over again. I often felt odd twinges of jealousy because my parents could talk about that more intense, somehow less *experimental* life than ours with so many private smiles between themselves. It was bewildering, it made me long constantly to get at some past nearer my own New York life, my having to live with all those running wounds of a world I had never seen.

Then, under cover of the talk those Friday evenings, I would take up *The Boy's Life of Theodore Roosevelt* again, and moodily call out to those strangers on the summer veranda in Oyster Bay[6] until my father spoke *his* tale of arriving in America. That was hard, too, painful in another way—yet it always made him curiously lighthearted and left me swimming in space. For he had gone off painting box cars on the Union Pacific, had been as far west as Omaha, had actually seen Sidney Hillman[7] toiling in Hart, Schaffner and Marx's Chicago factory, had heard his beloved Debs[8] making fools of Bryan[9] and Taft[1] in the 1908 campaign, had been offered a homestead in Colorado! *Omaha* was the most beautiful word I had ever heard, *homestead* almost as beautiful; but I could never forgive him for not having accepted that homestead.

"What would I have done there? I'm no farmer."

"You should have taken it! Why do we always live here!"

"It would have been too lonely. Nobody I knew."

"What a chance!"

"Don't be childish. Nobody I knew."

"Why? Why?"

"Alfred, what do you want of us poor Jews?"

So it was: we had always to be together: believers and non-believers, we were a people; I was of that people. Unthinkable to go one's own way, to doubt or to escape the fact that I was a Jew. I had heard of Jews who pretended they were not, but could not understand them. We had all of us lived together so long that we would not have known how to separate even if we had wanted to. The most terrible word was *aleyn*, alone. I always had the same picture of a man desolately walking down a dark street, newspapers

5. A street on New York's Lower East Side where Jewish immigrants concentrated. "Dugschitz": a town in Belorussia, west of Vitebsk; also Dokshitsky.

6. A town on Long Island, New York, the site of Theodore Roosevelt's family home.

7. An American labor leader and cofounder of the CIO (1887–1946).

8. Eugene V. Debs (1855–1926), labor organizer and Socialist party candidate for president five times from 1900 to 1920. "Hart, Schaffner and Marx": a New York City men's clothing store.

9. William Jennings Bryan (1860–1925), Democratic and Populist leader who ran unsuccessfully three times for the U.S. presidency (1896, 1900, 1908).

1. William Howard Taft (1857–1930), twenty-seventh president of the United States and tenth Chief Justice.

and cigarette butts contemptuously flying in his face as he tasted in the dusty grit the full measure of his strangeness. *Aleyn! Aleyn!* My father had been alone here in America as a boy. His father, whose name I bore, had died here at twenty-five of pneumonia caught on a garment workers' picket line, and his body flung in with thousands of other Jews who had perished those first years on the East Side. My father had never been able to find his father's grave. *Aleyn! Aleyn!* Did immigrant Jews, then, marry only out of loneliness? Was even Socialism just a happier way of keeping us together?

I trusted it to do that. Socialism would be one long Friday evening around the samovar and the cut-glass bowl laden with nuts and fruits, all of us singing *Tsuzamen, tsuzamen, ale tsuzamen!* Then the heroes of the Russian novel—*our* kind of people—would walk the world, and I—still wearing a circle-necked Russian blouse "*à la Tolstoy*"—would live forever with those I loved in that beautiful Russian country of the mind. Listening to our cousin and her two friends I, who had never seen it, who associated with it nothing but the names of great writers and my father's saying as we went through the Brooklyn Botanic Garden—"Nice! but you should have seen the Czar's summer palace at Tsarskoye-Selo!"[2]—suddenly saw Russia as the grand antithesis to all bourgeois ideals, the spiritual home of all truly free people. I was perfectly sure that there was no literature in the world like the Russian; that the only warm hearts in the world were Russian, like our cousin and her two friends; that other people were always dully materialist, but that the Russian soul, like Nijinsky's dream of pure flight, would always leap outward, past all barriers, to a lyric world in which my ideal socialism and the fiery moodiness of Tchaikovsky's *Pathétique*[3] would be entirely at home with each other. *Tsuzamen, alle tsuzamen!* How many millions would be with us! China was in our house those Friday evenings, Africa, the Indian masses. And it was those three unmarried dressmakers from the rank and file who fully wrapped me in that spell, with the worldly clang of their agate beads and the musky fragrance of their face powder and their embroidered Russian blouses, with the great names of Russian writers ringing against the cut-glass bowl under the black lamp. Never did the bowl look so laden, never did apples and tea smell so good, never did the samovar pour out with such steaming bounty, as on those Friday evenings when I tasted in the tea and the talk the evangelical heart of our cousin and her two friends, and realized that it was we—we!—who would someday put the world on its noblest course.

"*Kinder,*[4] kinder," my mother would say. "Enough *discusye*.[5] Maybe now a little music? Alfred, play *Scheherazade!*"[6]

You could melt their hearts with it; the effect of the violin on almost everyone I knew was uncanny. I could watch them softening, easing, already on the brink of tears—yet with their hands at rest in their laps, they stared straight ahead at the wall, breathing hard, an unforeseen smile of rapture on their mouths. Any slow movement, if only it were played lingeringly and sagely enough, seemed to come to them as a reminiscence of a reminiscence. It seemed to have something to do with our being Jews. The depths of Jewish memory the violin could throw open apparently had no limit—for every slow

2. A city in northwestern Russia just south of St. Petersburg, now called Pushkin.
3. Peter Ilich Tchaikovsky's (1840–1893) sixth symphony (1893).
4. Children (Yiddish).
5. Discussion (Yiddish).
6. A symphonic suite (1888) by Russian composer Nikolai Rimsky-Korsakov (1844–1908).

movement was based on something "Russian," every plaintive melody even in Beethoven or Mozart was "Jewish." I could skip from composer to composer, from theme to theme, without any fear, ever, of being detected, for all slow movements fell into a single chant of *der heym* and of the great *Kol Nidre*[7] sung in the first evening hours of the Day of Atonement,[8] in whose long rending cry—of contrition? of grief? of hopeless love for the Creator?—I relived all of the Jews' bitter intimacy with death.

Then I cranked up the old brown Victor,[9] took our favorite records out of the red velvet pleated compartments, and we listened to John McCormack singing *Ave Maria*, Amelita Galli-Curci singing *Caro Nome* ("How ugly she is!" my parents would say wonderingly. "Have you seen her picture? Incredible! But how she sings!"), and Alma Gluck singing *Comin' Thro' the Rye*. The high point was Caruso singing from *La Juive*. He inspired in my father and mother such helpless, intimidated adoration that I came to think of what was always humbly referred to as his *golden voice* as the invocation of a god. The pleasure he gave us was beyond all music. When Mischa Elman[1] played some well-known melody we sighed familiarly at each other—his tone was so *warm*; he bubbled slowly in my ears like the sound of chicken fat crackling in the pan. But Caruso, "that *Italyéner*,"[2] seemed to me the echo of some outrageously pagan voice at the roof of the world. While I pushed at the hand-crank and the wheezy sounds of the orchestra in the background came to me as the whispered turnings, sighs and alarms of the crowd around the circus pit, there on high, and rising higher and higher with each note, that voice, that *golden voice*, leaped its way from one trapeze to another. We sat hunched in our wonder, our adoration, our fear. Would he make it? Could any human being find that last impossible rung?

Rachel! Quand du Seigneur la grâce tutélaire . . .[3]

Then, suddenly bounding back to earth again, there he was before us again, secretly smiling, the tones welling out of him with such brazen strength, such irresistible energy, that he left us gasping. I could see him standing inside the victrola box—a centaur[4] just out of the woods, not quite human, with that enigmatic, almost contemptuous smile on his face. "What a voice!" my father would say over and over, deeply shaken. "What a voice! It's not human! Never was there a voice like it! Only the other day I was reading that when they opened him up after he died they found his vocal chords were absolutely unique!" Then, his face white with pleasure, with amazement, with wonder: "Oh that *Italyéner!* Oh that *Italyéner!* What a power he has, that *Italyéner!*"

In Brownsville tenements the kitchen is always the largest room and the center of the household. As a child I felt that we lived in a kitchen to which

7. The chant that opens the Yom Kippur service.
8. Yom Kippur, the most solemn Jewish holy day, when sins are confessed and expiated, and Jews are reconciled with God.
9. An early phonograph company.
1. American violinist (1891–1967) noted for his virtuosity and warmth. "John McCormack": Irish American concert and opera star (1884–1945). "*Ave Maria*": a reference to a very popular setting of the Hail Mary. "Amelita Galli-Curci singing *Caro Nome*": Galli-Curci was an American coloratura soprano famous for her Gilda in Verdi's opera *Rigoletto*, from which the aria *Caro Nome* (Dear Name) comes. "Alma Gluck": American opera and concert singer (1884–1938). "Caruso singing from *La Juive*": Enrico Caruso (1873–1921), great lyric tenor who performed in J. F. Halévy's (1799–1862) opera *La Juive* (The Jewess, 1835), among other vehicles.
2. Italian (Yiddish).
3. "Rachel! When the Lord's protective grace," an aria from *La Juive*.
4. In Greek mythology, a race of beings that are half human and half horse.

four other rooms were annexed. My mother, a "home" dressmaker, had her workshop in the kitchen. She told me once that she had begun dressmaking in Poland at thirteen; as far back as I can remember, she was always making dresses for the local women. She had an innate sense of design, a quick eye for all the subtleties in the latest fashions, even when she despised them, and great boldness. For three or four dollars she would study the fashion magazines with a customer, go with the customer to the remnants store on Belmont Avenue to pick out the material, argue the owner down—all remnants stores, for some reason, were supposed to be shady, as if the owners dealt in stolen goods—and then for days would patiently fit and baste and sew and fit again. Our apartment was always full of women in their housedresses sitting around the kitchen table waiting for a fitting. My little bedroom next to the kitchen was the fitting room. The sewing machine, an old nut-brown Singer with golden scrolls painted along the black arm and engraved along the two tiers of little drawers massed with needles and thread on each side of the treadle, stood next to the window and the great coal-black stove which up to my last year in college was our main source of heat. By December the two outer bedrooms were closed off, and used to chill bottles of milk and cream, cold borscht[5] and jellied calves' feet.

The kitchen held our lives together. My mother worked in it all day long, we ate in it almost all meals except the Passover *seder*,[6] I did my homework and first writing at the kitchen table, and in winter I often had a bed made up for me on three kitchen chairs near the stove. On the wall just over the table hung a long horizontal mirror that sloped to a ship's prow at each end and was lined in cherry wood. It took up the whole wall, and drew every object in the kitchen to itself. The walls were a fiercely stippled whitewash, so often rewhitened by my father in slack seasons that the paint looked as if it had been squeezed and cracked into the walls. A large electric bulb hung down the center of the kitchen at the end of a chain that had been hooked into the ceiling; the old gas ring and key still jutted out of the wall like antlers. In the corner next to the toilet was the sink at which we washed, and the square tub in which my mother did our clothes. Above it, tacked to the shelf on which were pleasantly ranged square, blue-bordered white sugar and spice jars, hung calendars from the Public National Bank on Pitkin Avenue and the Minsker Progressive Branch of the Workman's Circle;[7] receipts for the payment of insurance premiums, and household bills on a spindle; two little boxes engraved with Hebrew letters. One of these was for the poor, the other to buy back the Land of Israel. Each spring a bearded little man would suddenly appear in our kitchen, salute us with a hurried Hebrew blessing, empty the boxes (sometimes with a sidelong look of disdain if they were not full), hurriedly bless us again for remembering our less fortunate Jewish brothers and sisters, and so take his departure until the next spring, after vainly trying to persuade my mother to take still another box. We did occasionally remember to drop coins in the boxes, but this was usually only on the dreaded morning of "midterms" and final examinations, because my mother thought it would bring me luck. She was extremely superstitious, but embarrassed about it, and always laughed at herself whenever, on the morn-

5. A soup made primarily of beets and served hot or cold, often with sour cream.
6. The service and dinner on Passover eve.
7. A Jewish socialist organization. This branch was populated by Jews from Minsk.

ing of an examination, she counseled me to leave the house on my right foot. "I know it's silly," her smile seemed to say, "but what harm can it do? It may calm God down."

The kitchen gave a special character to our lives; my mother's character. All my memories of that kitchen are dominated by the nearness of my mother sitting all day long at her sewing machine, by the clacking of the treadle against the linoleum floor, by the patient twist of her right shoulder as she automatically pushed at the wheel with one hand or lifted the foot to free the needle where it had got stuck in a thick piece of material. The kitchen was her life. Year by year, as I began to take in her fantastic capacity for labor and her anxious zeal, I realized it was ourselves she kept stitched together. I can never remember a time when she was not working. She worked because the law of her life was work, work and anxiety; she worked because she would have found life meaningless without work. She read almost no English; she could read the Yiddish paper, but never felt she had time to. We were always talking of a time when I would teach her how to read, but somehow there was never time. When I awoke in the morning she was already at her machine, or in the great morning crowd of housewives at the grocery getting fresh rolls for breakfast. When I returned from school she was at her machine, or conferring over *McCall's*[8] with some neighborhood woman who had come in pointing hopefully to an illustration—"Mrs. Kazin! Mrs. Kazin! Make me a dress like it shows here in the picture!" When my father came home from work she had somehow mysteriously interrupted herself to make supper for us, and the dishes cleared and washed, was back at her machine. When I went to bed at night, often she was still there, pounding away at the treadle, hunched over the wheel, her hands steering a piece of gauze under the needle with a finesse that always contrasted sharply with her swollen hands and broken nails. Her left hand had been pierced through when as a girl she had worked in the infamous Triangle Shirtwaist Factory[9] on the East Side. A needle had gone straight through the palm, severing a large vein. They had sewn it up for her so clumsily that a tuft of flesh always lay folded over the palm.

The kitchen was the great machine that set our lives running; it whirred down a little only on Saturdays and holy days. From my mother's kitchen I gained my first picture of life as a white, overheated, starkly lit workshop redolent with Jewish cooking, crowded with women in housedresses, strewn with fashion magazines, patterns, dress material, spools of thread—and at whose center, so lashed to her machine that bolts of energy seemed to dance out of her hands and feet as she worked, my mother stamped the treadle hard against the floor, hard, hard, and silently, grimly at war, beat out the first rhythm of the world for me.

Every sound from the street roared and trembled at our windows—a mother feeding her child on the doorstep, the screech of the trolley cars on Rockaway Avenue, the eternal smash of a handball against the wall of our house, the clatter of *"der Italyéner"* 's cart packed with watermelons, the singsong of the old-clothes men walking Chester Street, the cries *"Árbes! Árbes!*

8. A popular "women's" magazine.
9. A New York sweatshop that was the site of a fire that killed many immigrant workers (mostly women) and brought demands for safer working conditions.

Kinder! Kinder! Heyse guteárbes!"[1] All day long people streamed into our apartment as a matter of course—"customers," upstairs neighbors, downstairs neighbors, women who would stop in for a half-hour's talk, salesmen, relatives, insurance agents. Usually they came in without ringing the bell—everyone knew my mother was always at home. I would hear the front door opening, the wind whistling through our front hall, and then some familiar face would appear in our kitchen with the same bland, matter-of-fact inquiring look: no need to stand on ceremony: my mother and her kitchen were available to everyone all day long.

At night the kitchen contracted around the blaze of light on the cloth, the patterns, the ironing board where the iron had burned a black border around the tear in the muslin cover; the finished dresses looked so frilly as they jostled on their wire hangers after all the work my mother had put into them. And then I would get that strangely ominous smell of tension from the dress fabrics and the burn in the cover of the ironing board—as if each piece of cloth and paper crushed with light under the naked bulb might suddenly go up in flames. Whenever I pass some small tailoring shop still lit up at night and see the owner hunched over his steam press; whenever in some poorer neighborhood of the city I see through a window some small crowded kitchen naked under the harsh light glittering in the ceiling, I still smell that fiery breath, that warning of imminent fire. I was always holding my breath. What I must have felt most about ourselves, I see now, was that we ourselves were like kindling—that all the hard-pressed pieces of ourselves and all the hard-used objects in that kitchen were like so many slivers of wood that might go up in flames if we came too near the white-blazing filaments in that naked bulb. Our tension itself was fire, we ourselves were forever burning—to live, to get down the foreboding in our souls, to make good.

Twice a year, on the anniversaries of her parents' deaths, my mother placed on top of the ice-box an ordinary kitchen glass packed with wax, the *yortsayt*,[2] and lit the candle in it. Sitting at the kitchen table over my homework, I would look across the threshold to that mourning-glass, and sense that for my mother the distance from our kitchen to *der heym*, from life to death, was only a flame's length away. Poor as we were, it was not poverty that drove my mother so hard; it was loneliness—some endless bitter brooding over all those left behind, dead or dying or soon to die; a loneliness locked up in her kitchen that dwelt every day on the hazardousness of life and the nearness of death, but still kept struggling in the lock, trying to get us through by endless labor.

With us, life started up again only on the last shore. There seemed to be no middle ground between despair and the fury of our ambition. Whenever my mother spoke of her hopes for us, it was with such unbelievingness that the likes of us would ever come to anything, such abashed hope and readiness for pain, that I finally came to see in the flame burning on top of the ice-box death itself burning away the bones of poor Jews, burning out in us everything but courage, the blind resolution to live. In the light of that mourning-candle, there were ranged around me how many dead and dying—

1. "Chickpeas! Chickpeas! Children! Children! Good hot [roasted] chickpeas" (Yiddish).

2. Anniversary of a parent's death, which is commemorated each year (Yiddish).

how many eras of pain, of exile, of dispersion, of cringing before the powers of this world!

It was always at dusk that my mother's loneliness came home most to me. Painfully alert to every shift in the light at her window, she would suddenly confess her fatigue by removing her pince-nez,[3] and then wearily pushing aside the great mound of fabrics on her machine, would stare at the street as if to warm herself in the last of the sun. "How sad it is!" I once heard her say. "It grips me! It grips me!" Twilight was the bottommost part of the day, the chillest and loneliest time for her. Always so near to her moods, I knew she was fighting some deep inner dread, struggling against the returning tide of darkness along the streets that invariably assailed her heart with the same foreboding—Where? Where now? Where is the day taking us now?

Yet one good look at the street would revive her. I see her now, perched against the windowsill, with her face against the glass, her eyes almost asleep in enjoyment, just as she starts up with the guilty cry—"What foolishness is this in me!"—and goes to the stove to prepare supper for us: a moment, only a moment, watching the evening crowd of women gathering at the grocery for fresh bread and milk. But between my mother's pent-up face at the window and the winter sun dying in the fabrics—"Alfred, see how beautiful!"—she has drawn for me one single line of sentience.

The unmarried cousin who boarded with us had English books in her room—the only English books in our house I did not bring into it myself. Half an hour before supper, I liked nothing better than to stray into her room, and sitting on the India print spread of her bed next to the yellow wicker bookstand, look through her books and smell the musky face powder that filled her room. There was no closet: her embroidered Russian blouses and red velvet suits hung behind a curtain, and the lint seemed to float off the velvet and swim in multicolored motes through the air. On the wall over her bed hung a picture of two half-nude lovers fleeing from a storm, and an oval-framed picture of Psyche perched on a rock. On the wicker bookstand, in a star-shaped frame of thick glass, was a photograph of our cousin's brother, missing since the Battle of Tannenberg,[4] in the uniform of a Czarist Army private.

In that wicker bookstand, below the blue set of Sholem Aleichem in Yiddish and the scattered volumes of Russian novels, were the books I would never have to drag from the Stone Avenue Library myself—THE WORLD'S GREATEST SELECTED SHORT STORIES; a biography of Alfred E. Smith[5] entitled *Up From the City Streets*; a Grosset and Dunlap edition of *The Sheik*;[6] and in English, a volume of stories by Alexander Kuprin.[7] Day after day at five-thirty, half an hour before supper, I would sit myself carefully on the India print, and fondle those books with such rapture that they were actually *there*, for me to look through whenever I liked, that on some days I could

3. Eyeglasses clipped to the nose by a spring.
4. An east Prussian village. Early during the First World War (August 1914), Germany defeated the Russian armies there. "Psyche": in classical mythology, the princess who aroused Venus's jealousy and Cupid's love.
5. Smith (1873–1944) was a U.S. politician, a four-time Democratic governor of New York, and the first Roman Catholic to run for the U.S. presidency (1928).
6. A popular romance (1921) by E. M. Hull and published by Grosset and Dunlap. Rudolph Valentino starred in the silent movie.
7. Russian novelist and short-story writer, Kuprin (1870–1938) was an exponent of critical realism.

not bear to open them at all, but sat as close to the sun in the windows as I could, breathing the lint in, and the sun still hot on the India spread.

On the roof just across the street, the older boys now home from work would spring their pigeons from the traps. You could see the feathers glistening faintly in the last light, beating thinly against their sides—they, too, sucking air as the birds leaped up from their wire cages. Then, widening and widening their flight each time they came over our roof again, they went round a sycamore and the spire of the church without stopping. The sun fell straight on the India spread—how the thin prickly material burned in my nostrils—and glowed along the bony gnarled bumps in the legs of the yellow wicker bookstand. Happiness was warmth. Beyond Chester Street, beyond even Rockaway, I could see to where the Italians lived on broken streets that rose up to a hill topped by a church. The church seemed to be thickly surrounded by trees. In his star-shaped glass on the bookstand, that Russian soldier missing since the Battle of Tannenberg looked steadily at me from under his round forage cap. His chest bulged against two rows of gold buttons up and down his black blouse. Where? Where now? Had they put him, too, into a great pit? Suddenly it did not matter. Happiness was the sun on the India spread, the hot languid sands lapping at the tent of the Sheik—*"Monseigneur! My desert prince!"*—the summer smell of the scum on the East River just off Oliver Street where Alfred E. Smith worked in the Fulton Fish Market. In the Kuprin stories an old man and a boy went wandering up a road in the Crimea.[8] There was dust on the road, dust on the leaves—*hoo! hoo! my son! how it is hot!* But they were happy. It was summer in the Crimea, and just to walk along with them made me happy. When they got hungry they stopped at a spring, took black bread, salt, and tomatoes out of their knapsacks, and ate. The ripe open tomatoes gushed red from their mouths, the black bread and salt were good, very good, and when they leaned over to drink at the spring, the water was so icy cold it made my teeth ache. I read that story over and over, sometimes skipping pages to get to the part about the bread, the salt, the tomatoes, the icy water. *I could taste that bread, that salt, those tomatoes, that icy spring.*

Now the light begins to die. Twilight is also the mind's grazing time. Twilight is the bottom of that arc down which we had fallen the whole long day, but where I now sit at our cousin's window in some strange silence of attention, watching the pigeons go round and round to the leafy smell of soupgreens from the stove. In the cool of that first evening hour, as I sit at the table waiting for supper and my father and the New York *World*, everything is so rich to overflowing, I hardly know where to begin.

1951

8. A peninsula on the Black Sea in southern Russia at the time of writing, now in the Ukraine. "Fulton Fish Market": a thriving fish market on Fulton Street, in Manhattan's Lower East Side.

IRVING HOWE
1920–1993

"What is the likely future of American Jewish writing? Has it already passed its peak of achievement and influence? Can we expect a new generation of writers to appear who will contribute to American literature a distinctive sensibility and style derived from the Jewish experience in this country?" Posing these questions in 1976, Irving Howe had just published his monumental *World of Our Fathers: The Journey of the Eastern European Jews to America and the Life They Found and Made*. He was open but skeptical: "My own view is that American Jewish fiction has probably moved past its high point. Insofar as this body of writing draws heavily from the immigrant experience, it must suffer a depletion of resources, a thinning-out of materials and memories. . . . There remains, to be sure, the problem of 'Jewishness,' and the rewards and difficulties of definition it may bring us. But this problem, though experienced as an urgent one by at least some people, does not yield a thick enough sediment of felt life to enable a new outburst of writing about American Jews."

Younger writers, Howe admits, claim that "there is a postimmigrant Jewish experience in America which can be located in its own milieu, usually suburbs or middle-class urban neighborhoods. . . . Is not their phase of Jewish life in America as authentic and interesting as that of the earlier immigrants? Do they not have a right, also, to make of their involvements and confusions with Jewishness the foundation of stories and novels?" Of course, in limiting his question to the genre of prose fiction, Howe assumes that only a pervasive social matrix can engender authentic writing. And anyway it was premature, in 1976, to announce the end of American Jewish fiction; probably, for the indefinite future, it will remain premature. Yet Howe's doubts about the postimmigrant Jewish experience remain compelling: "Does that experience go deep enough into the lives of the younger, 'Americanized' Jews? Does it form the very marrow of their being? Does it provide images of conflict, memories of exaltation and suffering, such as enable the creating of stories?"

Irving Howe was born on June 11, 1920, in the Bronx, New York, to poor immigrant parents, David and Nettie (Goldman) Horenstein (he changed his name early on while writing for the leftist paper *Labor Action*). After earning a B.Sc. at City College of New York, he went to Brooklyn College but quit when he found "the routine of graduate study appalling." Opposing American entry into World War II as a doctrinaire Marxist, he was drafted and stationed with the army for three years in Alaska. After the war, he edited a selection of Rabbi Leo Baeck's work (1948), published studies of Sherwood Anderson (1951) and William Faulkner (1952), and compiled *A Treasury of Yiddish Stories* (1954), the first of five collections of Yiddish writing coedited with Eliezer Greenberg. As Howe engaged with the richly conflicted literary imagination, his early political dogmatism mutated into democratic socialism, a radical meliorative movement. He cofounded and edited the magazine *Dissent* (1953–93), and wrote *Politics and the Novel* (1957) and *A World More Attractive* (1963), where his Sholom Aleichem essay appeared.

In his edition of *Jewish-American Stories* (1977), whose introduction doubted the future viability of that genre, Howe included Sholom Aleichem plus the Russian Isaac Babel. Although their work had nothing to do with America, it reveals a continuity from the Old World to the New, and it influenced writers such as Bellow, Malamud, Paley, Ozick. Howe's affection for Sholom Aleichem—for his "moral poise" of "sympathy and skepticism," his "power to see the world as it is, to love it and yet not succumb to it"—speaks for himself as well. It also shows why he could not esteem Philip Roth's "contempt" for (Jewish) humankind. But there is more to Roth than satiric animus, just as there is more than Howe recognized to Jewish American experience: a chastening responsiveness to the Holocaust, a questioning of Israeli vis-à-vis Diaspora centrality, a reintegration of traditional Judaism, an opening of women's voices.

What finally distinguishes Irving Howe from the postwar intellectuals addressing themselves to Jewish American identity is his own masterful prose. *World of Our Fathers*, however encyclopedic its narrative, stays alive and absorbing on every page. His various introductions, doing so much so succinctly, are the despair of any other introduction (or headnote) writer. Not only lucid and unerring, informative and insightful, a single Howe sentence can enfold, in its asides and alternatives, the rich complexity of Jewish American experience.

Howe died on May 5, 1993.

Sholom Aleichem:[1] Voice of Our Past

Fifty or sixty years ago the Jewish intelligentsia, its head buzzing with Zionist, Socialist and Yiddishist ideas, tended to look down upon Sholom Aleichem. His genius was acknowledged, but his importance skimped. To the intellectual Jewish youth in both Warsaw and New York he seemed old-fashioned, lacking in complexity and rebelliousness—it is even said that he showed no appreciation of existentialism. Sh. Niger,[2] the distinguished Yiddish critic, tried to explain this condescension by saying that laughter, the characteristic effect of Sholom Aleichem's stories, is for children and old people, not the young. Perhaps so; the young are notoriously solemn. But my own explanation would be that the Jewish intellectuals simply did not know what to make of Sholom Aleichem: they did not know how to respond to his moral poise and his invulnerability to ideological fashions.

With the passage of the years embarrassment has been replaced by indifference. Soon we shall be needing an historical expedition, armed with footnotes, to salvage his work. Even today we cannot be quite certain that our affection for him rests upon a strict regard for the words he put on the page, rather than a parochial nostalgia.

It has been customary to say that Sholom Aleichem speaks for a whole people, but saying this we might remember that his people have not spoken very well for him. The conventional estimate—that Sholom Aleichem was a folksy humorist, a sort of jolly gleeman of the *shtetl*[3]—is radically false. He needs to be rescued from his reputation, from the quavering sentimentality which keeps him at a safe distance.

When we say that Sholom Aleichem speaks for a whole culture, we can mean that in his work he represents all the significant levels of behavior and class in the *shtetl* world, thereby encompassing the style of life of the east European Jews in the nineteenth century. In that sense, however, it may be doubted that he does speak for the whole *shtetl* culture. For he does not command the range of a Balzac or even a Faulkner,[4] and he does not present

1. Literally, "Peace unto you" (Hebrew). Pseudonym of Sh. Rabinovitch (1859–1916), Russian Jewish author, primarily of stories. He settled in New York in 1914.
2. Shmuel Niger (1883–1955), literary critic.
3. A small Jewish town or village in Eastern Europe.
4. William Faulkner (1897–1962), American novelist and short-story writer well known for his Yaknapatawpha cycle, a fable of the American South. "Balzac": French novelist and short-story writer Honoré de Balzac (1799–1850), creator of the realistic novel.

himself as the kind of writer who is primarily concerned with social representation. The ambition, or disease, of literary "scope" leaves him untouched.

Nor can we mean, in saying that Sholom Aleichem speaks for a whole culture, that he advances the conscious program of that culture. Toward the dominant Jewish ideologies of his time Sholom Aleichem showed a characteristic mixture of sympathy and skepticism, and precisely this modesty enabled him to achieve a deeper relation to the *folksmassen* than any Jewish political leader. He never set himself up as cultural spokesman or institution, in the style of Thomas Mann[5] at his worst; he had no interest in boring people.

Sholom Aleichem speaks for the culture of the east European Jews because he embodies—not represents—its essential values in the very accents and rhythm of his speech, in the inflections of his voice and the gestures of his hands, in the pauses and suggestions between the words even more than the words themselves. To say that a writer represents a culture is to imply that a certain distance exists between the two. But that is not at all the relationship between Sholom Aleichem and the culture of the east European Jews: it is something much more intimate and elusive, something for which, having so little experience of it, we can barely find a name. In Sholom Aleichem everything that is deepest in the ethos of the east European Jews is brought to fulfillment and climax. He is, I think, the only modern writer who may truly be said to be a culture-hero, a writer whose work releases those assumptions of his people, those tacit gestures of bias, which undercut opinion and go deeper into communal life than values.

II

In his humorous yet often profoundly sad stories, Sholom Aleichem gave to the Jews what they instinctively felt was the right and true judgment of their experience: a judgment of love through the medium of irony. Sholom Aleichem is the great poet of Jewish humanism and Jewish transcendence over the pomp of the world. For the Jews of Eastern Europe he was protector and advocate; he celebrated their communal tradition; he defended their style of life and constantly underlined their passionate urge to dignity. But he was their judge as well: he ridiculed their pretensions, he mocked their vanity, and he constantly reiterated the central dilemma, that simultaneous tragedy and joke, of their existence—the irony of their claim to being a Chosen People, indeed, the irony of their existence at all.

Sholom Aleichem's Yiddish is one of the most extraordinary verbal achievements of modern literature, as important in its way as T. S. Eliot's revolution in the language of English verse or Berthold Brecht's[6] infusion of street language into the German lyric. Sholom Aleichem uses a sparse and highly controlled vocabulary; his medium is so drenched with irony that the material which comes through it is often twisted and elevated into direct tragic statement—irony multiplies upon itself to become a deep winding sadness. Many of his stories are monologues, still close to the oral folk tradition, full

5. German author and recipient, in 1929, of the Nobel Prize for literature (1875–1955). "*Folksmassen*": the masses, the people (Yiddish).

6. Bertolt Brecht (1898–1956), German playwright and poet of political and social criticism. "T. S. Eliot's revolution": Thomas Stearns Eliot (1888–1965), the American poet whose *The Waste Land* (1922) exemplified modernist sensibility and expression.

of verbal by-play, slow in pace, winding in direction, but always immediate and warm in tone. His imagery is based on an absolute mastery of the emotional rhythm of Jewish life; describing the sadness of a wheezing old clock, he writes that it was "a sadness like that in the song of an old, worn-out cantor toward the end of Yom Kippur"—and how sad that is only someone who has heard such a cantor and therefore knows the exquisite rightness of the image can really say.

The world of Sholom Aleichem is bounded by three major characters, each of whom has risen to the level of Jewish archetype: Tevye the Dairyman; Menachem Mendel the *luftmensch*;[7] and Mottel the cantor's son, who represents the loving, spontaneous possibilities of Jewish childhood. Tevye remains rooted in his little town, delights in displaying his uncertain Biblical learning, and stays close to the sources of Jewish survival. Solid, slightly sardonic, fundamentally innocent, Tevye is the folk voice quarreling with itself, criticizing God from an abundance of love, and realizing in its own low-keyed way all that we mean, or should mean, by humaneness.

Tevye represents the generation of Jews that could no longer find complete deliverance in the traditional God yet could not conceive of abandoning Him. No choice remained, therefore, but to celebrate the earthly condition: poverty and hope. For if you had become skeptical of deliverance from above and had never accepted the heresy of deliverance from below, what could you do with poverty but celebrate it? "In Kasrilevke,"[8] says Tevye, "there are experienced authorities on the subject of hunger, one might say specialists. On the darkest night, simply by hearing your voice, they can tell if you are hungry and would like a bite to eat, or if you are really starving." Tevye, like the people for whom he speaks, is constantly assaulted by outer forces. The world comes to him, most insidiously, in the form of undesired sons-in-law: one who is poverty-stricken but romantic; another who is a revolutionist and ends in Siberia; a third—could anything be worse?—who is a gentile; and a fourth—this *is* worse—who is a Jew but rich, coarse, and unlearned.

Menachem Mendel, Tevye's opposite, personifies the element of restlessness and soaring, of speculation and fancy-free idealization, in Jewish character. He has a great many occupations: broker, insurance agent, matchmaker, coal dealer, and finally—it is inevitable—writer; but his fundamental principle in life is to keep moving. The love and longing he directs toward his unfound millions are the love and longing that later Jews direct toward programs and ideologies. He is the utopian principle of Jewish life; he is driven by the modern demon. Through Tevye and Menachem Mendel, flanked by little Mottel, Sholom Aleichem creates his vision of the Yiddish world.

There is a strong element of fantasy, even surrealism, in Sholom Aleichem. Strange things happen: a tailor becomes enchanted, a clock strikes thirteen, money disappears in the synagogue during Yom Kippur, a woman's corpse is dragged across the snow, a timid little Jew looks at himself in the mirror and sees the face of a Czarist officer. Life is precarious, uncertain, fearful, yet always bound by a sense of community and affection.

7. Literally, "man of the air," someone who seems to subsist on nothing (Yiddish).

8. A shtetl invented by Sholom Aleichem.

III

Sholom Aleichem came at a major turning point in the history of the east European Jews: between the unquestioned dominance of religious belief and the appearance of modern ideologies, between the past of traditional Judaism and the future of Jewish politics, between a totally integrated culture and a culture that by a leap of history would soon plunge into the midst of modern division and chaos. Yet it was the mark of Sholom Aleichem's greatness that, coming as he did at this point of transition, he betrayed no moral imbalance or uncertainty of tone. He remained unmoved by the fanaticisms of his time, those that were Jewish and those that were not; he lost himself neither to the delusions of the past nor the delusions of the future. His work is the fulfillment—pure, relaxed, humane—of that moment in the history of the Jews in which a people lives securely with itself, untroubled by any dualism, hardly aware of a distinction, between the sacred and secular.

The world he presented was constantly precarious and fearful, yet the vision from which it was seen remained a vision of absolute assurance. It was a vision controlled by that sense of Jewish humaneness which held the best of—even as it transcended—both the concern with the other world that had marked the past and the eagerness to transform this world that would mark the future. His work abounds in troubles, but only rarely does it betray anxiety.

In reading Sholom Aleichem one seldom thinks to wonder about his opinions. He stands between the age of faith and the age of ideology, but I doubt that there has ever been a reader naive enough to ask whether Sholom Aleichem *really* believed in God. For him it was not a living question, no more than it was for the people who read him. To say that he believed in God may be true, but it is also irrelevant. To say that he did not believe in God is probably false, but equally irrelevant.

What Sholom Aleichem believed in was the Jews who lived with him and about him, most of them Jews still believing in God. Or perhaps he believed in those Jews who lived so completely in the orbit of their fathers—fathers who had surely believed in God—that there was no need for them to ask such questions.

In Sholom Aleichem's stories God is there, not because He is God, not because there is any recognition or denial of His heavenly status, but simply because He figures as an actor in the life of the Jews. God becomes absorbed into the vital existence of the people, or to put it more drastically: God is there because Tevye is there.

But Tevye, does *he* believe in God? Another hopeless question. Tevye believes in something more important than believing in God; he believes in talking to God. And Tevye talks to God as to an old friend whom one need not flatter or assuage: Tevye, as we say in American slang, gives Him an earful.

Tevye, we may assume, makes God extremely uncomfortable—though also a little proud at the thought that, amid the countless failures of His world, He should at least have created a Tevye who can make him so sublimely uncomfortable. And how does Tevye do this? By telling God the complete truth. It is not a pretty truth, and if God would care to dispute anything Tevye has told him, Tevye is entirely prepared to discuss it with Him further. But whatever other mistakes He may have made, God is too clever to get into an argument with Tevye. God knows that Tevye does not fear Him: a Jew is afraid of people, not of God. So perhaps you can see how absurd it is to ask whether Sholom Aleichem *really* believed in God: —Sholom Aleichem who created a character to serve as the conscience of God.

All this comes through in Sholom Aleichem's stories as a blend of rapture and the absurd, sublimity and household ordinariness. Nor is it confined to Sholom Aleichem alone. In the poems of Jacob Glatstein,[9] one of the great living Yiddish writers, there is a whole series of loving and estranged monologues to God. Glatstein writes: "I love my sorrowful God /My companion . . . I love to sit with Him upon a stone /And to pour out all my words . . . And there He sits with me, my friend, my companion, clasping me /And shares His last bite of food with me." Later, in the same poem, Glatstein adds: "The God of my unbelief is magnificent . . . My God sleeps and I watch over him/ My weary brother dreams the dream of my people."

Had Tevye lived through the events of the past thirty years, that is how he would have felt.

IV

Sholom Aleichem believed in Jews as they embodied the virtues of powerlessness and the healing resources of poverty, as they stood firm against the outrage of history, indeed, against the very idea of history itself. Whoever is unable to conceive of such an outlook as at least an extreme possibility, whoever cannot imagine the power of a messianism turned away from the apocalyptic future and inward toward a living people, cannot understand Sholom Aleichem or the moment in Jewish experience from which he stems.

It is here that the alien reader may go astray. He may fail to see that for someone like Tevye everything pertaining to Jewishness can be a curse and an affliction, a wretched joke, a source of mockery and despair, but that being a Jew is nevertheless something to be treasured. Treasured, because in the world of Tevye there was a true matrix of human sociability.

The stories Sholom Aleichem told his readers were often stories they already knew, but then, as the Hasidic[1] saying goes, they cared not for the words but the melody. What Sholom Aleichem did was to give back to them the very essence of their life and hope, in a language of exaltation: the exaltation of the ordinary.

When Tevye talked to his horse, it was the same as if he were talking to his wife. When he talked to his wife, it was the same as if he were talking to God. And when he talked to God, it was the same as if he were talking to his horse. That, for Tevye, was what it meant to be a Jew.

Kierkegaard[2] would never have understood it.

V

Between Sholom Aleichem and his readers there formed a community of outcasts: *edele kaptzunim*. Millions of words flowed back and forth, from writer to reader and reader to writer, for no people has ever talked so much

9. Polish-born Yiddish poet and critic (1896–1971).
1. Of Hasidism, a devout mystical Jewish sect.
2. Søren Kierkegaard (1813–1855), Danish philosopher and theologian, regarded as the founder of existentialist philosophy and noted for his views on angst and suffering.

in all recorded history; yet their companionship did not rest upon or even require words.

The last thing I wish to suggest here is an image of the sweetly pious or sentimental. Sholom Aleichem did not hesitate to thrust his barbs at his readers, and they were generous at reciprocating. Having love, they had no need for politeness. But the love of which I speak here is sharply different from that mindless ooze, that collapse of will, which the word suggests to Americans. It could be argumentative, fierce, bitter, violent; it could be ill-tempered and even vulgar; only one thing it could not be: lukewarm.

The Jews never fooled Sholom Aleichem. Peretz, I think, was sometimes deceived by the culture of the east European Jews, and Sholem Asch[3] tried to deceive it at the end of his career. But with Sholom Aleichem, even as he was the defender of the Jews and their culture, there was always a sly wrinkle near his eyes which as soon as Jews saw it, they said to themselves: *Im ken men nisht upnaren*, him you cannot deceive. That is why, when you go through his stories, you find so little idealization, so little of that cozy self-indulgence and special pleading which is the curse of Jewish life. Between Sholom Aleichem and his readers there is a bond of that wary respect which grows up among clever men who recognize each other's cleverness, enjoy it and are content.

Middleton Murry[4] once said of Thomas Hardy[5] that "the contagion of the world's slow stain has not touched him." This magnificent remark must have referred to something far more complex and valuable than innocence, for no one could take Hardy to be merely innocent; it must have referred to the artist's final power, the power to see the world as it is, to love it and yet not succumb to it; and that is the power one finds in Sholom Aleichem.

1963

3. Polish-born American novelist and playwright who wrote in Yiddish and English (1880–1957). "Peretz": I. L. Peretz (1852–1915), Polish author, the "father of modern Jewish literature."

4. John Middleton Murry (1889–1956), English literary critic and editor.

5. English novelist and poet whose works are noted for their pessimism (1840–1928).

HOWARD NEMEROV
1920–1991

"You've lost your religion, the Rabbi said. / It wasn't much to keep, said I." Howard Nemerov's *Debate with the Rabbi* (1962) opens with what may sound facile or callow unless we hear it echoing Yeats's *Crazy Jane Talks with the Bishop*, where earthy sense refutes sacrosanctity. Nemerov's *Debate* ends: "You go on in your obstinacy. / We Jews are that way, I replied." The poet's obstinacy, as a nonpracticing Jew, meant finding his own way as a writer. "Poetry is a way of getting something right in language," he said, trying to simplify away from creeds and commandments. Or, more reachingly: "The purpose of poetry is to persuade, fool, or compel God into speaking."

One thing Nemerov did not let go, as he outgrew sternly formal verse plus the influence of Yeats, Eliot, Stevens, and possibly Robert Lowell, was the Bible. *Lion and Honeycomb* (1962) stems from Samson's riddle about bees in a lion's carcass:

"out of the strong came something sweet" (Judges 14.14). It was "Hard work learning to rime," the poem insists, but "Harder learning not to"—learning to make something "Perfected and casual as to a child's eye / Soap bubbles are, and skipping stones." These sweet things are "remembrances from childhood," Nemerov once said, things whose "gaiety, marvelousness, energy, maintained itself against gravity, even against possibility, in a hard world."

Howard Nemerov was born on March 1, 1920, in New York City to David Nemerov, an art connoisseur and head of his wife's family's exclusive clothing store, and Gertrude Russek Nemerov. On graduating from Harvard in 1941, he enlisted in the Canadian Air Force, then flew fighter planes in the U.S. Army Air Force (1944–45). He married in 1944, had three sons, and taught in various places, including, from 1969 on, Washington University, St. Louis. Publishing fiction, essays, and mainly poetry, he won the Pulitzer prize, National Book Award, and Bollingen Prize, and was U.S. Poet Laureate from 1988 to 1990.

Like Nicodemus, a Jew of the Pharisees who devoutly questioned Jesus by night, Nemerov situated himself vis-à-vis Christianity, finding Sarah's blood "sweeter than honey" but Abraham's "wild seed . . . cold." His voice in the early poems has a prophetic severity. "Poetry is a kind of spiritual exercise," he said, "a (generally doomed but stoical) attempt to pray one's humanity back into the universe." Over the decades, he continued siding with Freud, who "makes it tough on us," but his poems find a freer energy, wit, equilibrium. Sardonic views trade off with common acceptance, severity with humor; "If you are seated among the angels it is still on your butt." His verse play *Cain* gives the last word to Adam, promising to sustain love "in pleasure and in bitterness all ways." Nemerov died on July 5, 1991.

Lot's Wife[1]

I have become a gate
To the ruined city, dry,
Indestructible by fire.
A pillar of salt, a white
Salt boundary stone
On the edge of destruction.

A hard lesson to learn,
A swift punishment; and many
Now seek to escape
But look back, or to escape
By looking back: and they
Too become monuments.

Remember me, Lot's wife,
Standing at the furthest
Commark[2] of lust's county,
Unwilling to enjoy,
Unable to escape, I make
Salt the rain of the world.

1947

1. In Genesis 19, before destroying the sinful cities Sodom and Gomorrah, angels of the Lord allow Lot and his family to escape provided they do not look back at the destruction or stop. Lot's wife looks back and is turned into a pillar of salt.
2. Border country.

A Song of Degrees[1]

Though the road lead nowhere
I have followed the road
In its blind turnings, its descents
And the long levels where the emptiness ahead
Is inescapably seen.

I have cried for justice, I have cried
For mercy, now I desire neither.
A man may grow strong in his wandering,
His foot strong as a wheel
Turning the endless road.

Foot and hand hardened to horn,
Nose but a hook of bone, and eyes
Not liquid now but stone—I
To myself violent, fiercely exult
In Zion[2] everywhere.

1950

Nicodemus[1]

I

I went under cover of night
By back streets and alleyways,
Not as one secret and ashamed
But with a natural discretion.

I passed by a boy and a girl
Embraced against the white wall
In parts of shadow, parts of light,
But though I turned my eyes away, my mind shook
Whether with dryness or their driving blood;
And a dog howled once in a stone corner.

II

Rabbi, I said,
How is a man born, being old?
From the torn sea into the world
A man may be forced only the one time
To suffer the indignation of the child,
His childish distempers and illnesses.
I would not, if I could, be born again

1. Psalms 120–134 are called *Shir HaMahalot*, Song of Degrees or Song of Ascent, as they may have been sung by Jewish pilgrims as they ascended to Jerusalem.

2. The Jewish people or homeland; also, an ideal society.

1. In John 3, Nicodemus visits and questions Jesus by night, and later defends him against other Pharisees.

To suffer the miseries of the child,
The perpetual nearness to tears,
The book studied through burning eyes,
The particular malady of being always ruled
To ends he does not see or understand.

A man may be forced only the one time
To the slow perception of what is meant
That is neither final nor sufficient,
To the slow establishment of a self
Adequate to the ceremony and respect
Of other men's eyes; and to the last
Knowledge that nothing has been done,
The bitter bewilderment of his age,
A master in Israel and still a child.

III

Rabbi, all things in the springtime
Flower again, but a man may not
Flower again. I regret
The sweet smell of lilacs and the new grass
And the shoots put forth of the cedar
When we are done with the long winter.

Rabbi, sorrow has mothered me
And humiliation been my father,
But neither the ways of the flesh
Nor the pride of the spirit took me,
And I am exalted in Israel
For all that I know I do not know.

Now the end of my desire is death
For my hour is almost come.
I shall not say with Sarah
That God hath made me to laugh,[2]
Nor the new word shall not be born
Out of the dryness of my mouth.

Rabbi, let me go up from Egypt
With Moses to the wilderness of Sinai
And to the country of the old Canaan
Where, sweeter than honey, Sarah's blood
Darkens the cold cave[3] in the field
And the wild seed of Abraham is cold.

1950

2. In Genesis 18.12, Sarah, wife of Abraham, laughs when God tells her she will bear a son in her old age.

3. In Genesis 23, Abraham buys a cave in the field of Machpelah as burial ground for Sarah and himself.

GRACE PALEY
b. 1922

"I lived my childhood in a world so dense with Jews that I thought we were the great imposing majority and kindness had to be extended to the others because, as my mother said, everyone wants to live like a person. In school I met my friend Adele, who, together with her mother and father, were not Jewish. Despite this they often seemed to be in a good mood." Grace Paley's matter-of-fact Jewishness and wry humor, plus that "stretch to the stranger" entailed by Exodus, mark her offhand statements as well as her tightly crafted stories. Though her parents were secular, they held a Seder at which her father (in Russian or Yiddish or English) would tell how they had been "brought out of bondage for some reason. . . . We had been strangers and slaves in Egypt and therefore knew what we were talking about when we cried out against pain and oppression. In fact, we were obligated by knowledge to do so."

In her stories, Paley's commitment to social justice and political activism shows up almost casually, as an inevitable part of the scene, while human elements hold the foreground: dogged mothers, gutsy spinsters, brash children, immigrant parents trying to navigate the "creeping pogrom" (*The Loudest Voice*) that is Christian America—and, always, talk, schmoozing. "My father talked an awful lot, when he had time, and my aunts told stories," says Paley. "You have to really understand how people speak, and you have to reconstruct it. . . . Most pleasure in writing, you know, is in inventing." Especially her strong-mettled women, with a Yiddish or life-worn or street-smart pulse to their speech, invigorate the stories of someone who all her life has been listening gratefully.

Grace Paley was born on December 11, 1922, in the Bronx, New York, to Ukrainian-born anticzarist revolutionaries who had been exiled to Siberia around 1904 and were

> . . . present for the pogrom of
> 1905   in which
> our Rusya   our brother our uncle
>   waving the workers' flag
> was murdered.

Paley's parents came to America in 1905, and her father became a doctor. Grace briefly attended Hunter College and New York University, married at nineteen, had two children, and was separated soon afterward. Alongside the urban neighborhood social-political life that was to furnish her stories, she studied with W. H. Auden at the New School and wrote only poetry into her thirties (collected in *Leaning Forward* [1985] and *New and Selected Poems* [1992]). Her first book, *The Little Disturbances of Man: Stories of Women and Men at Love* (1959), was greeted by Philip Roth: "An understanding of loneliness, lust, selfishness, and fatigue that is splendidly comic and unladylike. Grace Paley has deep feelings, a wild imagination, and a style [of] toughness and bumpiness." Her later collections were *Enormous Changes at the Last Minute* (1974) and *Later the Same Day* (1985).

An often-used photo shows a middle-aged Grace Paley outdoors at a wintertime protest, standing in a down jacket and wool cap, a quizzical expression on her face, hands thrust into pockets under a white smock with crude lettering: MONEY   ARMS   WAR   PROFITS   WALL STREET. Like Tillie Olsen and Muriel Rukeyser as well as her nearer contemporaries Denise Levertov and Adrienne Rich, Paley has acted on her politics. Sometimes she gets criticized for taking unbalanced views—chiefly of the conflict in Vietnam. Rooted stubbornly in the Jewish socialism of her childhood, Paley's political feelings are "almost always," she says, "on the side of the underdog."

Her best storytelling, though, seems simple without in the least being simplistic or tendentious. Strict plotting, claims the daughter in *A Conversation with My Father*, "takes all hope away. Everyone, real or invented, deserves the open destiny of life." Reading to an audience, Paley stands a little like Norman Mailer, firmly spread-legged, on a booster behind the podium, chewing gum, delivering dialogue and narrative in a Bronx accent also from her childhood.

Asked about influences, Paley will mention James Joyce and also Gertrude Stein, who declared in *The Making of Americans:* "The old people in a new world, the new people made out of the old, that is the story that I mean to tell, for that is what really is and what I really know." Paley also muses on the Jewish storyteller Isaac Babel: "When I read him now, I think that he had the same grandparents I had and that those grandparents influenced him in Russia and me here."

The Loudest Voice

There is a certain place where dumb-waiters[1] boom, doors slam, dishes crash; every window is a mother's mouth bidding the street shut up, go skate somewhere else, come home. My voice is the loudest.

There, my own mother is still as full of breathing as me and the grocer stands up to speak to her. "Mrs. Abramowitz," he says, "people should not be afraid of their children."

"Ah, Mr. Bialik," my mother replies, "if you say to her or her father 'Ssh,' they say, 'In the grave it will be quiet.' "

"From Coney Island[2] to the cemetery," says my papa. "It's the same subway; it's the same fare."

I am right next to the pickle barrel. My pinky is making tiny whirlpools in the brine. I stop a moment to announce: "Campbell's Tomato Soup. Campbell's Vegetable Beef Soup. Campbell's S-c-otch Broth . . ."

"Be quiet," the grocer says, "the labels are coming off."

"Please, Shirley, be a little quiet," my mother begs me.

In that place the whole street groans: Be quiet! Be quiet! but steals from the happy chorus of my inside self not a little or a jot.

There, too, but just around the corner, is a red brick building that has been old for many years. Every morning the children stand before it in double lines which must be straight. They are not insulted. They are waiting anyway.

I am usually among them. I am, in fact, the first, since I begin with "A."

One cold morning the monitor tapped me on the shoulder. "Go to Room 409, Shirley Abramowitz," he said. I did as I was told. I went in a hurry up a down staircase to Room 409, which contained sixth-graders. I had to wait at the desk without wiggling until Mr. Hilton, their teacher, had time to speak.

After five minutes he said, "Shirley?"

"What?" I whispered.

He said, "My! My! Shirley Abramowitz! They told me you had a particularly loud, clear voice and read with lots of expression. Could that be true?"

"Oh yes," I whispered.

1. In old apartment buildings, a small rope-and-pulley elevator used to lower trash to the basement.
2. A section of Brooklyn, New York, on the Atlantic Ocean famous for its amusement area and easily accessible by public transportation.

"In that case, don't be silly; I might very well be your teacher someday. Speak up, speak up."

"Yes," I shouted.

"More like it," he said. "Now, Shirley, can you put a ribbon in your hair or a bobby pin? It's too messy."

"Yes!" I bawled.

"Now, now, calm down." He turned to the class. "Children, not a sound. Open at page 39. Read till 52. When you finish, start again." He looked me over once more. "Now, Shirley, you know, I suppose, that Christmas is coming. We are preparing a beautiful play. Most of the parts have been given out. But I still need a child with a strong voice, lots of stamina. Do you know what stamina is? You do? Smart kid. You know, I heard you read 'The Lord is my shepherd'[3] in Assembly yesterday. I was very impressed. Wonderful delivery. Mrs. Jordan, your teacher, speaks highly of you. Now listen to me, Shirley Abramowitz, if you want to take the part and be in the play, repeat after me, 'I swear to work harder than I ever did before.' "

I looked to heaven and said at once, "Oh, I swear." I kissed my pinky and looked at God.

"That is an actor's life, my dear," he explained. "Like a soldier's, never tardy or disobedient to his general, the director. Everything," he said, "absolutely everything will depend on you."

That afternoon, all over the building, children scraped and scrubbed the turkeys and the sheaves of corn off the schoolroom windows. Goodbye Thanksgiving. The next morning a monitor brought red paper and green paper from the office. We made new shapes and hung them on the walls and glued them to the doors.

The teachers became happier and happier. Their heads were ringing like the bells of childhood. My best friend Evie was prone to evil, but she did not get a single demerit for whispering. We learned "Holy Night" without an error. "How wonderful!" said Miss Glacé, the student teacher. "To think that some of you don't even speak the language!" We learned "Deck the Halls" and "Hark! The Herald Angels". . . . They weren't ashamed and we weren't embarrassed.

Oh, but when my mother heard about it all, she said to my father: "Misha, you don't know what's going on there. Cramer is the head of the Tickets Committee."

"Who?" asked my father. "Cramer? Oh yes, an active woman."

"Active? Active has to have a reason. Listen," she said sadly, "I'm surprised to see my neighbors making tra-la-la for Christmas."

My father couldn't think of what to say to that. Then he decided: "You're in America! Clara, you wanted to come here. In Palestine the Arabs would be eating you alive. Europe you had pogroms.[4] Argentina is full of Indians. Here you got Christmas. . . . Some joke, ha?"

"Very funny, Misha. What is becoming of you? If we came to a new country a long time ago to run away from tyrants, and instead we fall into a creeping pogrom, that our children learn a lot of lies, so what's the joke? Ach, Misha, your idealism is going away."

"So is your sense of humor."

3. Psalm 23.

4. Violent attacks on Jewish communities.

"That I never had, but idealism you had a lot of."

"I'm the same Misha Abramovitch, I didn't change an iota. Ask anyone."

"Only ask me," says my mama, may she rest in peace. "I got the answer."

Meanwhile the neighbors had to think of what to say too.

Marty's father said: "You know, he has a very important part, my boy."

"Mine also," said Mr. Sauerfeld.

"Not my boy!" said Mrs. Klieg. "I said to him no. The answer is no. When I say no! I mean no!"

The rabbi's wife said, "It's disgusting!" But no one listened to her. Under the narrow sky of God's great wisdom she wore a strawberry-blond wig.[5]

Every day was noisy and full of experience. I was Right-hand Man. Mr. Hilton said: "How could I get along without you, Shirley?"

He said: "Your mother and father ought to get down on their knees every night and thank God for giving them a child like you."

He also said: "You're absolutely a pleasure to work with, my dear, dear child."

Sometimes he said: "For God's sakes, what did I do with the script? Shirley! Shirley! Find it."

Then I answered quietly: "Here it is, Mr. Hilton."

Once in a while, when he was very tired, he would cry out: "Shirley, I'm just tired of screaming at those kids. Will you tell Ira Pushkov not to come in till Lester points to that star the second time?"

Then I roared: "Ira Pushkov, what's the matter with you? Dope! Mr. Hilton told you five times already, don't come in till Lester points to that star the second time."

"Ach, Clara," my father asked, "what does she do there till six o'clock she can't even put the plates on the table?"

"Christmas," said my mother coldly.

"Ho! Ho!" my father said. "Christmas. What's the harm? After all, history teaches everyone. We learn from reading this is a holiday from pagan times also, candles, lights, even Chanukah. So we learn it's not altogether Christian. So if they think it's a private holiday, they're only ignorant, not patriotic. What belongs to history, belongs to all men. You want to go back to the Middle Ages? Is it better to shave your head with a secondhand razor? Does it hurt Shirley to learn to speak up? It does not. So maybe someday she won't live between the kitchen and the shop. She's not a fool."

I thank you, Papa, for your kindness. It is true about me to this day. I am foolish but I am not a fool.

That night my father kissed me and said with great interest in my career, "Shirley, tomorrow's your big day. Congrats."

"Save it," my mother said. Then she shut all the windows in order to prevent tonsillitis.

In the morning it snowed. On the street corner a tree had been decorated for us by a kind city administration. In order to miss its chilly shadow our neighbors walked three blocks east to buy a loaf of bread. The butcher pulled down black window shades to keep the colored lights from shining on his chickens. Oh, not me. On the way to school, with both my hands I tossed it a kiss of tolerance. Poor thing, it was a stranger in Egypt.

5. Married Jewish women who are strictly orthodox wear a wig.

I walked straight into the auditorium past the staring children. "Go ahead, Shirley!" said the monitors. Four boys, big for their age, had already started work as propmen and stagehands.

Mr. Hilton was very nervous. He was not even happy. Whatever he started to say ended in a sideward look of sadness. He sat slumped in the middle of the first row and asked me to help Miss Glacé. I did this, although she thought my voice too resonant and said, "Show-off!"

Parents began to arrive long before we were ready. They wanted to make a good impression. From among the yards of drapes I peeked out at the audience. I saw my embarrassed mother.

Ira, Lester, and Meyer were pasted to their beards by Miss Glacé. She almost forgot to thread the star on its wire, but I reminded her. I coughed a few times to clear my throat. Miss Glacé looked around and saw that everyone was in costume and on line waiting to play his part. She whispered, "All right . . ." Then:

Jackie Sauerfeld, the prettiest boy in first grade, parted the curtains with his skinny elbow and in a high voice sang out:

"Parents dear
We are here
To make a Christmas play in time.
It we give
In narrative
And illustrate with pantomime."

He disappeared.

My voice burst immediately from the wings to the great shock of Ira, Lester, and Meyer, who were waiting for it but were surprised all the same.

"I remember, I remember, the house where I was born . . ."

Miss Glacé yanked the curtain open and there it was, the house—an old hayloft, where Celia Kornbluh lay in the straw with Cindy Lou, her favorite doll. Ira, Lester, and Meyer moved slowly from the wings toward her, sometimes pointing to a moving star and sometimes ahead to Cindy Lou.

It was a long story and it was a sad story. I carefully pronounced all the words about my lonesome childhood, while little Eddie Braunstein wandered upstage and down with his shepherd's stick, looking for sheep. I brought up lonesomeness again, and not being understood at all except by some women everybody hated. Eddie was too small for that and Marty Groff took his place, wearing his father's prayer shawl. I announced twelve friends, and half the boys in the fourth grade gathered round Marty, who stood on an orange crate while my voice harangued. Sorrowful and loud, I declaimed about love and God and Man, but because of the terrible deceit of Abie Stock we came suddenly to a famous moment. Marty, whose remembering tongue I was, waited at the foot of the cross. He stared desperately at the audience. I groaned, "My God, my God, why hast thou forsaken me?"[6] The soldiers who were sheiks grabbed poor Marty to pin him up to die, but he wrenched free, turned again to the audience, and spread his arms aloft to show despair and the end. I murmured at the top of my voice, "The rest is silence, but as

6. Christ's last words (Matthew 27.46; cf. Psalms 22.1).

everyone in this room, in this city—in this world—now knows, I shall have life eternal."

That night Mrs. Kornbluh visited our kitchen for a glass of tea.

"How's the virgin?" asked my father with a look of concern.

"For a man with a daughter, you got a fresh mouth, Abramovitch."

"Here," said my father kindly, "have some lemon, it'll sweeten your disposition."

They debated a little in Yiddish, then fell in a puddle of Russian and Polish. What I understood next was my father, who said, "Still and all, it was certainly a beautiful affair, you have to admit, introducing us to the beliefs of a different culture."

"Well, yes," said Mrs. Kornbluh. "The only thing . . . you know Charlie Turner—that cute boy in Celia's class—a couple others? They got very small parts or no part at all. In very bad taste, it seemed to me. After all, it's their religion."

"Ach," explained my mother, "what could Mr. Hilton do? They got very small voices; after all, why should they holler? The English language they know from the beginning by heart. They're blond like angels. You think it's so important they should get in the play? Christmas . . . the whole piece of goods . . . they own it."

I listened and listened until I couldn't listen any more. Too sleepy, I climbed out of bed and kneeled. I made a little church of my hands and said, "Hear, O Israel . . ." Then I called out in Yiddish, "Please, good night, good night. Ssh." My father said, "Ssh yourself," and slammed the kitchen door.

I was happy. I fell asleep at once. I had prayed for everybody: my talking family, cousins far away, passersby, and all the lonesome Christians. I expected to be heard. My voice was certainly the loudest.

1959

A Conversation with My Father

My father is eighty-six years old and in bed. His heart, that bloody motor, is equally old and will not do certain jobs any more. It still floods his head with brainy light. But it won't let his legs carry the weight of his body around the house. Despite my metaphors, this muscle failure is not due to his old heart, he says, but to a potassium shortage. Sitting on one pillow, leaning on three, he offers last-minute advice and makes a request.

"I would like you to write a simple story just once more," he says, "the kind de Maupassant[1] wrote, or Chekhov,[2] the kind you used to write. Just recognizable people and then write down what happened to them next."

I say, "Yes, why not? That's possible." I want to please him, though I don't remember writing that way. I *would* like to try to tell such a story, if he means the kind that begins: "There was a woman . . ." followed by plot, the absolute line between two points which I've always despised. Not for literary reasons,

1. Guy de Maupassant (1850–1893), French naturalist writer of short stories and novels; a protégé of Flaubert.

2. Anton Chekhov (1860–1904), Russian playwright and master of the modern short story.

but because it takes all hope away. Everyone, real or invented, deserves the open destiny of life.

Finally I thought of a story that had been happening for a couple of years right across the street. I wrote it down, then read it aloud. "Pa," I said, "how about this? Do you mean something like this?"

> Once in my time there was a woman and she had a son. They lived nicely, in a small apartment in Manhattan. This boy at about fifteen became a junkie, which is not unusual in our neighborhood. In order to maintain her close friendship with him, she became a junkie too. She said it was part of the youth culture, with which she felt very much at home. After a while, for a number or reasons, the boy gave it all up and left the city and his mother in disgust. Hopeless and alone, she grieved. We all visit her.

"O.K., Pa, that's it," I said, "an unadorned and miserable tale."

"But that's not what I mean," my father said. "You misunderstood me on purpose. You know there's a lot more to it. You know that. You left everything out. Turgenev[3] wouldn't do that. Chekhov wouldn't do that. There are in fact Russian writers you never heard of, you don't have an inkling of, as good as anyone, who can write a plain ordinary story, who would not leave out what you have left out. I object not to facts but to people sitting in trees talking senselessly, voices from who knows where . . ."

"Forget that one, Pa, what have I left out now? In this one?"

"Her looks, for instance."

"Oh. Quite handsome, I think. Yes."

"Her hair?"

"Dark, with heavy braids, as though she were a girl or a foreigner."

"What were her parents like, her stock? That she became such a person. It's interesting, you know."

"From out of town. Professional people. The first to be divorced in their county. How's that? Enough?" I asked.

"With you, it's all a joke," he said. "What about the boy's father? Why didn't you mention him? Who was he? Or was the boy born out of wedlock?"

"Yes," I said. "He was born out of wedlock."

"For Godsakes, doesn't anyone in your stories get married? Doesn't anyone have the time to run down to City Hall before they jump into bed?"

"No," I said. "In real life, yes. But in my stories, no."

"Why do you answer me like that?"

"Oh, Pa, this is a simple story about a smart woman who came to N.Y.C. full of interest love trust excitement very up to date, and about her son, what a hard time she had in this world. Married or not, it's of small consequence."

"It is of great consequence," he said.

"O.K.," I said.

"O.K. O.K. yourself," he said, "but listen. I believe you that she's good-looking, but I don't think she was so smart."

"That's true," I said. "Actually that's the trouble with stories. People start out fantastic. You think they're extraordinary, but it turns out as the work goes along, they're just average with a good education. Sometimes the other

3. Ivan Turgenev (1818–1883), Russian novelist, poet, and playwright.

way around, the person's a kind of dumb innocent, but he outwits you and you can't even think of an ending good enough."

"What do you do then?" he asked. He had been a doctor for a couple of decades and then an artist for a couple of decades and he's still interested in details, craft, technique.

"Well, you just have to let the story lie around till some agreement can be reached between you and the stubborn hero."

"Aren't you talking silly, now?" he asked. "Start again," he said. "It so happens I'm not going out this evening. Tell the story again. See what you can do this time."

"O.K.," I said. "But it's not a five-minute job." Second attempt:

> Once, across the street from us, there was a fine handsome woman, our neighbor. She had a son whom she loved because she'd known him since birth (in helpless chubby infancy, and in the wrestling, hugging ages, seven to ten, as well as earlier and later). This boy, when he fell into the fist of adolescence, became a junkie. He was not a hopeless one. He was in fact hopeful, an ideologue and successful converter. With his busy brilliance, he wrote persuasive articles for his high-school newspaper. Seeking a wider audience, using important connections, he drummed into Lower Manhattan newsstand distribution a periodical called *Oh! Golden Horse!*
>
> In order to keep him from feeling guilty (because guilt is the stony heart of nine tenths of all clinically diagnosed cancers in America today, she said), and because she had always believed in giving bad habits room at home where one could keep an eye on them, she too became a junkie. Her kitchen was famous for a while—a center for intellectual addicts who knew what they were doing. A few felt artistic like Coleridge[4] and others were scientific and revolutionary like Leary.[5] Although she was often high herself, certain good mothering reflexes remained, and she saw to it that there was lots of orange juice around and honey and milk and vitamin pills. However, she never cooked anything but chili, and that no more than once a week. She explained, when we talked to her, seriously, with neighborly concern, that it was her part in the youth culture and she would rather be with the young, it was an honor, than with her own generation.
>
> One week, while nodding through an Antonioni[6] film, this boy was severely jabbed by the elbow of a stern and proselytizing girl, sitting beside him. She offered immediate apricots and nuts for his sugar level, spoke to him sharply, and took him home.
>
> She had heard of him and his work and she herself published, edited, and wrote a competitive journal called *Man Does Live By Bread Alone*. In the organic heat of her continuous presence he could not help but become interested once more in his muscles, his arteries, and nerve connections. In fact he began to love them, treasure them, praise them with funny little songs in *Man Does Live* . . .

4. Samuel Taylor Coleridge (1772–1834), English Romantic poet, critic, and philosopher who was addicted to opium, which he took against a painful disease.
5. Timothy Leary (1920–1996) was an American teacher, psychologist, and author, and a leading proponent of mind-altering drugs.
6. Michelangelo Antonioni (b. 1912), Italian film director, noted for his avoidance of realistic narrative.

the fingers of my flesh transcend
my transcendental soul
the tightness in my shoulders end
my teeth have made me whole

To the mouth of his head (that glory of will and determination) he brought hard apples, nuts, wheat germ, and soybean oil. He said to his old friends, From now on, I guess I'll keep my wits about me. I'm going on the natch. He said he was about to begin a spiritual deep-breathing journey. How about you too, Mom? he asked kindly.

His conversion was so radiant, splendid, that neighborhood kids his age began to say that he had never been a real addict at all, only a journalist along for the smell of the story. The mother tried several times to give up what had become without her son and his friends a lonely habit. This effort only brought it to supportable levels. The boy and his girl took their electronic mimeograph and moved to the bushy edge of another borough. They were very strict. They said they would not see her again until she had been off drugs for sixty days.

At home alone in the evening, weeping, the mother read and reread the seven issues of *Oh! Golden Horse!* They seemed to her as truthful as ever. We often crossed the street to visit and console. But if we mentioned any of our children who were at college or in the hospital or dropouts at home, she would cry out, My baby! My baby! and burst into terrible, face-scarring, time-consuming tears. The End.

First my father was silent, then he said, "Number One: You have a nice sense of humor. Number Two: I see you can't tell a plain story. So don't waste time." Then he said sadly, "Number Three: I suppose that means she was alone, she was left like that, his mother. Alone. Probably sick?"

I said, "Yes."

"Poor woman. Poor girl, to be born in a time of fools, to live among fools. The end. The end. You were right to put that down. The end."

I didn't want to argue, but I had to say, "Well, it is not necessarily the end, Pa."

"Yes," he said, "what a tragedy. The end of a person."

"No, Pa," I begged him. "It doesn't have to be. She's only about forty. She could be a hundred different things in this world as time goes on. A teacher or a social worker. An ex-junkie! Sometimes it's better than having a master's in education."

"Jokes," he said. "As a writer that's your main trouble. You don't want to recognize it. Tragedy! Plain tragedy! Historical tragedy! No hope. The end."

"Oh, Pa," I said. "She could change."

"In your own life, too, you have to look it in the face." He took a couple of nitroglycerin.[7] "Turn to five," he said, pointing to the dial on the oxygen tank. He inserted the tubes into his nostrils and breathed deep. He closed his eyes and said, "No."

I had promised the family to always let him have the last word when arguing, but in this case I had a different responsibility. That woman lives across the street. She's my knowledge and my invention. I'm sorry for her. I'm not

7. In pill form, a heart medicine.

going to leave her there in that house crying. (Actually neither would Life, which unlike me has no pity.)

Therefore: She did change. Of course her son never came home again. But right now, she's the receptionist in a storefront community clinic in the East Village. Most of the customers are young people, some old friends. The head doctor has said to her, "If we only had three people in this clinic with your experiences . . ."

"The doctor said that?" My father took the oxygen tubes out of his nostrils and said, "Jokes. Jokes again."

"No, Pa, it could really happen that way, it's a funny world nowadays."

"No," he said. "Truth first. She will slide back. A person must have character. She does not."

"No, Pa," I said. "That's it. She's got a job. Forget it. She's in that storefront working."

"How long will it be?" he asked. "Tragedy! You too. When will you look it in the face?"

Magazine, 1972
Book, 1974

In This Country, but in Another Language, My Aunt Refuses to Marry the Men Everyone Wants Her To

My grandmother sat in her chair. She said, When I lie down at night I can't rest, my bones push each other. When I wake up in the morning I say to myself, What? Did I sleep? My God, I'm still here. I'll be in this world forever.

My aunt was making the bed. Look, your grandmother, she doesn't sweat. Nothing has to be washed—her stockings, her underwear, the sheets. From this you wouldn't believe what a life she had. It wasn't life. It was torture.

Doesn't she love us? I asked.

Love you? my aunt said. What else is worth it? You children. Your cousin in Connecticut.

So. Doesn't that make her happy?

My aunt said, Ach, what she saw!

What? I asked. What did she see?

Someday I'll tell you. One thing I'll tell you right now. Don't carry the main flag. When you're bigger, you'll be in a demonstration or a strike or something. It doesn't have to be you, let someone else.

Because Russya carried the flag, that's why? I asked.

Because he was a wonderful boy, only seventeen. All by herself, your grandmother picked him up from the street—he was dead—she took him home in the wagon.

What else? I asked.

My father walked into the room. He said, At least *she* lived.

Didn't you live too? I asked my aunt.

Then my grandmother took her hand. Sonia. One reason I don't close my eyes at night is I think about you. You know it. What will be? You have no life.

Grandmother, I asked, what about us?

My aunt sighed. Little girl. Darling, let's take a nice walk.

At the supper table nobody spoke. So I asked her once more: Sonia, tell me no or yes. Do you have a life?

Ha! she said. If you really want to know, read Dostoevsky.[1] Then they all laughed and laughed.

My mother brought tea and preserves.

My grandmother said to all our faces, Why do you laugh?

But my aunt said, Laugh!

Magazine, 1983
Book, 1985

1. Fyodor Dostoevsky (1821–1881), Russian novelist whose work had immense influence on 20th-century fiction.

ANTHONY HECHT
b. 1923

"How often you have thought about that camp, / As though in some strange way you were driven to." Musing to himself in his poem *The Book of Yolek* (1990), Anthony Hecht calls up the August 1942 "evacuation" of Dr. Janusz Korczak's Krochmalna Street orphanage in the Warsaw ghetto. Wherever he may be, sauntering down a fern trail "among midsummer hills" or dining "safe at home," the poet will be visited by Yolek, a five year old murdered amidst "the smell of smoke, and the loudspeakers" of Treblinka. For this dismal meditation, Hecht chose a seemingly discrepant kind of verse: the sestina, an elaborate, virtuosic form invented by medieval Provençal troubadours. Still, similar acts of memory and imagination can be found in many American poets who write about the Holocaust although—and because—they were not actually vulnerable *there* and *then*.

Anthony Hecht was born on January 16, 1923, in New York City, graduated from Bard College in 1944, and served three years in the army. As an infantry rifleman, he saw half his company lost, a man's head blown off, and was among the first troops to liberate the Nazi camp of Flossenbürg, north of Munich. Hecht's first two collections, not notably Jewish in orientation, were praised for their "Baroque exuberance," their erudition, wit, and mastery of classical and "courtly tradition." His next book, *The Hard Hours* (1967), which won the Pulitzer prize, marked a change; well-wrought poetic form had to accommodate the intractable facts of personal and historical experience. This volume, poet Richard Howard said, contains some of "the most agonizing poems to have appeared in America," and in the same sentence Howard praises "Hecht's truly burnished gifts." " 'More Light! More Light!' " sets Goethe's heroic last words above rhymed quatrains that depict Jews digging their own graves at Buchenwald, near Goethe's revered shrine at Weimar. And Hecht uses Hamlet's caution against tragical bombast, *It Out-Herods Herod. Pray You, Avoid It,* to title a kind of nursery rhyme about his children and about himself, "Who could not, at one time, / Have saved them from the gas."

The Room, also from *The Hard Hours*, pulls out all the stops of modernist poetics to compose stanzas befitting the European Jewish catastrophe: divine invocation, Hebraic and Christian biblical allusion and archaic eloquence, double entendres and punning overtones, ironic quotations, loaded similes (pollen, aquarium), bitterly sarcastic rhymes—"Made into soap" with the whispering "Pope," "cement floor" with the bureaucratic "deplore," "kill" with the Psalmic *"hill,"* and lastly a deft adjustment of Psalm 3.4 into iambic pentameter. To insist on imagination's prerogative—"I am there, I am there. I am pushed through / With the others"—and to use the pronoun "We" strain credibility somewhat like Irving Feldman's self-confessed fantasy of the Pripet Marshes.

What *The Room* enacts is Elie Wiesel's difficult axiom: just as Jews throughout history all stood at Sinai, now they have stood at Auschwitz. True, Hecht's "We are crowded in here naked" differs authorially from Paul Celan's "we" drinking "black milk of daybreak" in *Todesfuge* (Deathfugue, 1944–45). Yet unlike younger (and some older) American poets, Hecht was really there in wartime Europe, as the middle of *The Room* attests. Finally, this poem's deep craft authenticates its urgency.

The Room

Father, adonoi,[1] author of all things,
    of the three states,
the soft light on the barn at dawn,
    a wind that sings
in the bracken, fire in iron grates,
    the ram's horn,[2]
Furnisher, hinger of heaven, who bound
    the lovely Pleaides,[3]
entered the perfect treasuries of the snow,[4]
    established the round
course of the world, birth, death and disease
    and caused to grow
veins, brain, bones in me, to breathe and sing
    fashioned me air,
Lord, who, governing cloud and waterspout,
    o my King,
held me alive till this my forty-third year—
    in whom we doubt[5]—
Who was that child of whom they tell
    in lauds and threnes?[6]
whose holy name all shall pronounce
    Emmanuel,[7]
which being interpreted means,
    "Gott mit uns"?

I saw it on their belts.[8] A young one, dead,
Left there on purpose to get us used to the sight

1. "My Lord," God (Hebrew).
2. Shofar. In the time of Solomon's Temple, it was blown on solemn and other occasions; it is now blown on the Jewish New Year (Rosh Hashanah) and the Day of Atonement (Yom Kippur).
3. A constellation of six stars.
4. Cf. Job 38.22: "Hast thou entered into the treasures of the snow?" (King James version).
5. Cf. U.S. motto: "In God we trust."
6. Praises (Latin) and laments (Greek).
7. "God with us" (Hebrew). Cf. Isaiah 7.14; see also Matthew 1.23: "They shall call his name Emmanuel, which being interpreted is, God with us."
8. German army belt buckles bore an iron cross and the words *"Gott mit uns"* (God with us).

When we first moved in. Helmet spilled off, head
Blond and boyish and bloody. I was scared that night.
And the sign was there,
The sign of the child, the grave, worship and loss,
Gunpowder heavy as pollen in winter air,
An Iron Cross.

It is twenty years now, Father. I have come home.
But in the camps, one can look through a huge square
Window, like an aquarium, upon a room
The size of my livingroom filled with human hair.[9]
Others have shoes, or valises
Made mostly of cardboard, which once contained
Pills, fresh diapers. This is one of the places
Never explained.

Out of one trainload, about five hundred in all,
Twenty the next morning were hopelessly insane.
And some there be[1] *that have no memorial,*
That are perished as though they had never been.
Made into soap.[2]
Who now remembers "The Singing Horses of Buchenwald"?[3]
"Above all, the saving of lives," whispered the Pope.[4]
Die Vögelein schweigen im Walde,[5]

But for years the screaming continued, night and day,
And the little children were suffered[6] to come along, too.
At night, Father, in the dark, when I pray,
I am there, I am there. I am pushed through
With the others to the strange room
Without windows; whitewashed walls, cement floor.
Millions, Father, millions have come to this pass,
Which a great church has voted to "deplore."

Are the vents in the ceiling, Father, to let the spirit depart?
We are crowded in here naked, female and male.
An old man is saying a prayer. And now we start
To panic, to claw at each other, to wail
As the rubber-edged door closes on chance and choice.
He is saying a prayer for all whom this room shall kill.
"I cried unto the Lord God with my voice,
And He has heard me out His holy hill."[7]

1967

9. At Auschwitz, there was a storage room for hair that the Nazis took off of victims to make cloth.
1. From Ecclesiasticus 4.1 (Apocrypha).
2. The Nazis allegedly used the corpses of their death-camp victims to manufacture soap.
3. These prisoners were forced to sing as they dragged wagons.
4. Alludes to the belief that Pope Pius XII—Eugenio Pacelli (1876–1958)—did not speak out enough against Nazi anti-Semitism.
5. "The little birds are silent" (German), from Goethe's *Wanderer's Night Song*, set to music by Schubert and others.
6. Cf. Mark 10.14: "Suffer [allow] the little children to come unto me."
7. Cf. Psalm 3.4.

The Book of Yolek[1]

Wir haben ein Gesetz,
Und nach dem Gesetz soll er sterben.[2]

The dowsed coals fume and hiss after your meal
Of grilled brook trout, and you saunter off for a walk
Down the fern trail, it doesn't matter where to,
Just so you're weeks and worlds away from home,
And among midsummer hills have set up camp
In the deep bronze glories of declining day.

You remember, peacefully, an earlier day
In childhood, remember a quite specific meal:
A corn roast and bonfire in summer camp.
That summer you got lost on a Nature Walk;
More than you dared admit, you thought of home;
No one else knows where the mind wanders to.

The fifth of August, 1942.
It was morning and very hot. It was the day
They came at dawn with rifles to The Home
For Jewish Children, cutting short the meal
Of bread and soup, lining them up to walk
In close formation off to a special camp.

How often you have thought about that camp,
As though in some strange way you were driven to.
And about the children, and how they were made to walk.
Yolek who had bad lungs, who wasn't a day
Over five years old, commanded to leave his meal
And shamble between armed guards to his long home.

We're approaching August again. It will drive home
The regulation torments of that camp
Yolek was sent to, his small, unfinished meal,
The electric fences, the numeral tattoo,
The quite extraordinary heat of the day
They all were forced to take that terrible walk.

Whether on a silent, solitary walk
Or among crowds, far off or safe at home,
You will remember, helplessly, that day,
And the smell of smoke, and the loudspeakers of the camp.
Wherever you are, Yolek will be there, too.
His unuttered name will interrupt your meal.

1. This title echoes *The Book of Yukel*, a post-Holocaust story by Egyptian-born, French-speaking Jewish writer Edmond Jabès (1912–1991).

2. From the Gospel of John 19.7, in Martin Luther's translation, attributed to the Jews before Jesus' crucifixion: "We have a law, and by our law he ought to die."

Prepare to receive him in your home some day.
Though they killed him in the camp they sent him to,
He will walk in as you're sitting down to a meal.

Magazine, 1982
Book, 1990

SHIRLEY KAUFMAN
b. 1923

"American hyphen Israeli," Shirley Kaufman describes herself. Born in Seattle, Washington, on June 5, 1923, to parents who had emigrated from Eastern Europe, she lived in San Francisco for many years before making her home in Jerusalem in 1973. She uses poetry to come to terms with herself—a self that has been uprooted. Kaufman's work, with its allusions to her religion, her life in Israel, and her life in America, takes on the characteristic of a photo album as she continually creates and re-creates snapshots of her life. As she moves between cultures and identities, Kaufman seeks to hone her language with a more careful observance of "the particulars of [her] experience."

While she has left behind the physical locations in which she initially wrote poetry, Kaufman writes that "I have . . . not moved far from the sources that nurtured me: The Bible, Whitman, Rilke, Lorca, Chinese poets and Zen, the feminist, political breakthrough of Muriel Rukeyser and Adrienne Rich, the Objectivism of Williams and especially of George Oppen, his 'clarity'. I still want poems that are honest, exact, and authentic as witness to our difficult and often unfathomable world."

As the selected poems illustrate, Kaufman's voice serves as a witness to all who balance between tradition and contemporary life. In *His Wife,* for example, Kaufman both succinctly re-creates and effortlessly mitigates the story of Lot's wife, and she has written numerous other poems re-imagining biblical women. Such poems not only demonstrate her identification with other Jewish American writers (many of whom draw on biblical themes and stories), but also with a larger population of postwar authors.

The author of eight volumes of her own poetry, Kaufman is also an accomplished translator and has published several books of translations from Hebrew poetry. In addition, she collaborated with Judith Herzberg on the translation of Herzberg's Dutch poems *But What: Selected Poems*, which won a Columbia University Translation Prize.

His Wife[1]

But it was right that she
looked back. Not to be
curious, some lumpy

1. Lot (Genesis 19) is saved from the destruction of Sodom and Gomorrah by Abraham. His wife, however, disobeys God's orders and looks back at the destruction of the two cities. In punishment, she becomes a pillar of salt.

reaching of the mind
that turns all shapes to pillars.
But to be only who she was
apart from them, the place
exploding, and herself
defined. Seeing them melt
to slag heaps and the flames
slide into their mouths.
Testing her own lips then,
the coolness, till
she could taste the salt.

1970

Bunk Beds

I

My face in the mirror and his eyes
back of my eyes and back
of us both the money carefully
counted in a purse like licorice
buttons, bottle caps,

or *groszy*[2] in Ulanov,[3] mud
in the streets where you can't
see it, up to your ankles
as you find your way to the river,
lose and find it again.

Poland, whatever they call it
when the borders change,
a river of mud where
nobody fishes, Poland
around you like a swamp.

His brother reads Schiller[4]
by the small lamp
at the toll bridge, all
the unholy books you never
should open. His secret

longing to be keeper
of the bridge like Jack,
to read the books in German
stopping the wagons
to collect the tolls.

2. A small coin or penny (Yiddish).
3. A town in the Ukraine.
4. Friedrich von Schiller (1759–1805), German playwright, poet, critic, and philosopher.

II

Books and money. Money and never mind
the books. You might say water
under the bridge or mud,
or how do you feed a wife
and child. Telling us money

got him to the next town,
money bought him a coat
that wasn't his brother's, money
peddling eggs from door to door
so he could buy the ticket

to America where there was more
of it in bunk beds
than anyone dreamed. Everything
smelled of varnish even
in spring. He cut the cost

and piled them one on top
of the other like blocks or bricks
or candy bars, like pieces
of dough you play with
till the stuff gets spongy,

doubles in size. You
punch it down and watch it
rise, cinnamon buns,
the Dow Jones,[5] what do you
think? It grows on trees?

III

There in the photograph his smile
suggests what passes for happiness,
the slight blur of his arm
feeling the weight of the biggest
salmon he ever caught.

When he had trouble sleeping
he told me he thought of salmon
on his line, reeling
the big ones in, their scales
in the sun like silver coins.

I hold his hand until
the soft skin tightens with a
jerk and I let go. His head
strains upward and his lips
as if the air is somewhere

5. The name of an index on the New York Stock Exchange. The rise and fall of the Dow Jones indicates the health of the stock market on any given day.

beyond his reach, as if
he sucks a pineapple soda
while the small bits of fruit
get stuck in the straw. It is his
death he sucks on and it comes

in quick gasps thicker than
syrup at the bottom of the glass.
His mouth gives up then, open
and round like a young trout, size
of a dollar with the dollar gone.

1979

Stones

When you live in Jerusalem you begin
to feel the weight of stones.
You begin to know the word
was made stone, not flesh.[1]

They dwell among us. They crawl
up the hillsides and lie down
on each other to build a wall.
They don't care about prayers,
the small slips of paper
we feed them between the cracks.[2]

They stamp at the earth
until the air runs out
and nothing can grow.

They stare at the sun without blinking
and when they've had enough,
make holes in the sky
so the rain will run down their faces.

They sprawl all over the town
with their pitted bodies. They want
to be water, but nobody
strikes them anymore.[3]

Sometimes at night I hear them
licking the wind to drive it crazy.
There's a huge rock lying on my chest
and I can't get up.

1984

1. I.e., the word of God, divine revelation. In Christianity, the Logos, second person of the Trinity—Jesus Christ; see John 1.14: "And the Word was made flesh."

2. A reference to the Western, or Wailing, Wall, the only remnant of Solomon's Temple in Jerusalem, where visitors stick slips of paper, with prayers or petitions on them, between the stones.

3. In Numbers 20.11, Moses strikes a rock with his rod, and water comes out.

DENISE LEVERTOV
1923–1997

"Insofar as poetry has a social function it is to awaken sleepers by other means than shock." Denise Levertov was speaking not about content, but form, or rather formlessness—"the sloppy garbage that seemed in 1959 to be suddenly appearing everywhere in [Allen Ginsberg's] wake." Poems such as *Howl* she did admire for being "intricately structured": "the force is there, and the horror, but they are there precisely *because* these are works of art." For Levertov, the artistic principle consists in "organic form," stemming from Coleridge and Emerson by way of Gerard Manley Hopkins and Charles Olson: "There is a form in all things (and in our experience) which the poet can discover and reveal." Poems do not start with ideas or subjects; they follow the "exploratory" process of articulating an experience whereby "form is never more than a *revelation* of content."

Candles in Babylon, the title poem of a 1982 collection, enacts that revelation through its syntax, linking prepositions and present participles, breaking a simple "return . . . home" with the line "from this place of terror" and ending with "just begun." This poem's single sentence also embodies the rich provenance of a Levertov lyric. "Babylon" evokes the destruction and exile of Jerusalem, along with Isaiah's "Awake, awake; put on thy strength, O Zion" (52.1). At the same time, it echoes a Bach cantata and especially a deeply remembered nursery rhyme to impel the private and public poet's hope that we may get "back again" home from apathy and terror. Levertov sometimes regretted that younger readers no longer had an upbringing that made such things as the Bible and nursery rhymes intimate, instinctual.

Denise Levertov was born on October 24, 1923, in Ilford, Essex, near London. "My mother was descended from the Welsh tailor and mystic Angel Jones of Mold, my father from the noted Hasid, Schneour Zalman (d. 1813), 'the Rav of Northern White Russia.' My father had experienced conversion to Christianity as a student at Königsberg in the 1890s. His lifelong hope was towards the unification of Judaism and Christianity." Denise never attended any school except ballet; she did lessons at home, was greatly read to, and "had a house full of books. . . . Jewish booksellers, German theologians, Russian priests from Paris, and Viennese opera singers, visited the house; and perhaps my earliest memory is of being dandled by the ill-fated son of Theodor Herzl, the great Zionist."

After the war years and air raids in London as a civilian nurse, Levertov married the American writer Mitch Goodman, came to the United States in 1948, and in 1949 had a son, sharing her early experience of motherhood with Adrienne Rich in New York City. Without the influence of William Carlos Williams and Wallace Stevens, along with Olson, Robert Creeley, Robert Duncan, plus Muriel Rukeyser's blending of "the engaged and the lyrical," she says, "I could not have developed from a British Romantic with almost Victorian background to an American poet of any vitality."

To identify Denise Levertov as a Jewish American poet, however, may seem dubious. In over twenty collections, very few poems manifest that affinity, much less allegiance, and even her biblical allusions summon the New Testament as much as the "Old." The title poem from *O Taste and See* (1964) finds Psalm 34.8 on a subway Bible poster: "O taste and see that the Lord is good." Grief, mercy, language, tangerine, plum, quince, she says, are for us to "transform / into our flesh our / deaths," for us "being / hungry, and plucking / the fruit." Or Levertov can call a later poem *Daily Bread* (1992) and embed a verse from Psalm 118: "This is the day that the Lord hath made, / let us rejoice and be glad in it." Possibly, implicitly, her poetry, like her father, wants "the unification of Judaism and Christianity."

Levertov's Jewishness derives from her father, Paul (born Saul or Shaul) Philip

Levertoff (1878–1954). She begins *Tesserae* (1995), a gathering of memories, by recalling "my father's great-grandfather, the Rav of Northern White Russia"—Schneour (Shneur) Zalman, the founder of Habad Hasidism, an ancestor in the maternal line of Denise's father. From Paul Levertoff, ordained an Anglican priest, his daughter imbibed a Hasidic fervency; he used to tell her about a peddler from his childhood near Vitebsk, a peddler with a "sack full of wings" whom Marc Chagall later depicted.

Her father broke with his parents and with Judaism "to be, as he believed, the more fully a Jew," Levertov writes—"a *Jewish Christian.*" When Denise was five, Levertoff published *St. Paul in Jewish Thought* (1928), which at one point speaks of certain Jewish qualities vital to Christianity: "This union of a deep faith in God with the highest concentration of human energy." Then he goes on, uncannily, to identify what would become the very ground of Denise Levertov's poetic creed: "Jewish materialism is *religious* materialism, or, rather, realism. For every idea and every ideal the Jew demands a visible and touchable materialisation. . . . He is capable and prepared to acknowledge the highest spiritual truth, but only on condition that he should at the same time see and feel its real working. He believes in the invisible . . . but he desires that this invisible should become visible and reveal its power; that it should permeate everything material."

This desire permeates poem after poem, such as one from Denise Levertov's last and longest teaching job, at Stanford. *In California* (1988) starts with morning light

> emblazoning
> summits of palm and pine,
>
> the dew
> lingering,
> scripture of scintillas.

And the spiritual materialism Paul Levertoff prized drives *The Jacob's Ladder,* with its emphatic "not" in line 1 and its "rosy stone." Levertov called her poetic vocation, in its gradual arc toward Catholicism, "work that enfaiths."

Even Jacob's ladder, a primal Judaic image, takes a Christian tinge in Levertov's hands, for she had in mind the steep stone steps of a colonial church in Oaxaca, Mexico. Vis-à-vis commonplace material things and common people alike, she kept a "Franciscan sense of wonder" (her phrase for William Carlos Williams). Her sensuous lyric utterance, in the voice and on the page, derives from the imagery and cadences of both the King James Bible and the Anglican Book of Common Prayer. Her quick and single-minded political emotions—against the Vietnam War, nuclear arms, U.S. interference in Central America, wastage of the environment—witness a sense of sacredness, an increasingly Christian sacramental spirit that nonetheless gains from being rooted in biblical and Hasidic Judaism.

Denise Levertov died in Seattle on December 20, 1997.

Illustrious Ancestors

The Rav[1]
of Northern White Russia declined,
in his youth, to learn the
language of birds, because

1. Shneur Zalman (1745–1813), an ancestor of Levertov's father, founded the Habad branch of Hasidism, a Jewish mystical sect.

the extraneous did not interest him; nevertheless
when he grew old it was found
he understood them anyway, having
listened well, and as it is said, 'prayed
with the bench and the floor.' He used
what was at hand—as did
Angel Jones of Mold,[2] whose meditations
were sewn into coats and britches.
Well, I would like to make,
thinking some line still taut between me and them,
poems direct as what the birds said,
hard as a floor, sound as a bench,
mysterious as the silence when the tailor
would pause with his needle in the air.

1958

The Jacob's Ladder[1]

The stairway is not
a thing of gleaming strands
a radiant evanescence
for angels' feet that only glance in their tread, and need not
touch the stone.

It is of stone.
A rosy stone[2] that takes
a glowing tone of softness
only because behind it the sky is a doubtful, a doubting
night gray.

A stairway of sharp
angles, solidly built.
One sees that the angels must spring
down from one step to the next, giving a little
lift of the wings:

and a man climbing
must scrape his knees, and bring
the grip of his hands into play. The cut stone
consoles his groping feet. Wings brush past him.
The poem ascends.

1961

2. A Welsh tailor-mystic, ancestor of Levertov's mother.
1. In Genesis 28.12, Jacob dreams of a ladder reaching to heaven with "angels of God ascending and descending on it."
2. The steps Levertov has in mind are actually those of a colonial Mexican church.

Candles in Babylon[1]

Through the midnight streets of Babylon
between the steel towers of their arsenals,
between the torture castles with no windows,
we race by barefoot, holding tight
our candles,[2] trying to shield
the shivering flames, crying
'Sleepers Awake!'
hoping
the rhyme's promise was true,
that we may return
from this place of terror
home to a calm dawn and
the work we had just begun.

1982

1. The place of exile and captivity, when Solomon's Temple and Jerusalem were destroyed 586 B.C.E.

2. Cf. the English nursery rhyme: "How many miles to Babylon? / Threescore miles and ten. / Can I get there by candlelight? / Yes, and back again."

NORMAN MAILER
b. 1923

Norman Mailer was born in Long Branch, New Jersey, the son of Isaac Barnet ("Barney") Mailer, a Russian Jewish immigrant who served in the British army during World War I, and Fanny Schneider Mailer, whose family was in the resort-hotel business in Long Branch. In 1927, the family moved to the Eastern Parkway section (in Crown Heights) of Brooklyn. Although this was, in his own words, "the most secure Jewish environment in America," and he had a conventional Orthodox/Conservative upbringing—Hebrew school and Bar Mitzvah—he asserts in the selection that follows, "I left what part of me belonged to Brooklyn and the Jews on the streets of Crown Heights." Mailer's work occasionally includes Jewish and part-Jewish characters, good and bad, but the almost deliberate avoidance of what seem to be centrally and recognizably Jewish issues in the greatest part of his prolific output over six decades has been noted and decried by almost all critics concerned with Jewish American literature. That is not the least of the issues that have made Norman Mailer a controversial figure for most of his literary life.

That life began at Harvard University, which he entered in 1939. There he published his first story, in the *Harvard Advocate*, during his sophomore year and decided to become a writer rather than an aeronautical engineer. After graduation in 1943, he married his first wife (they had a child together, but he divorced her and went on to have five other wives and five children) and entered the army as an infantryman in 1944. He served until 1946 in the Pacific theater, the setting of his first novel, *The Naked and the Dead* (1948). A highly successful war novel, it made him a literary star, a major figure at the age of twenty-five—a dizzying experience. The book was influenced by the writers he had read and admired in college—chiefly, James T. Farrell, John Dos Passos, and Ernest Hemingway—a realistic and socially conscious tradition that Mailer seems thereafter to have found unproductive, and much of his later work is a restless search for an original form appropriate to a changing time.

Among his many novels are *Barbary Shore* (1951), an almost surreal novel of ideas that works through his early leftist ideologies; *The Deer Park* (1955), a sexually daring Hollywood novel; *An American Dream* (1965), which recalls the Kennedy era and the connections among sex, violence, and power (a subject that occupies much of his work); *Why Are We in Vietnam?* (1967), an extraordinary tour de force of language (often obscene) that probes those connections most originally; *The Executioner's Song* (1979), an elaborate, very long (over 1,000 pages) retelling of the story of the Utah murderer Gary Gilmore; *Ancient Evenings* (1983), a long, pre–Judeo-Christian imagining of Egyptian life, sex (including sodomy and incest), mystery, and death told by a narrator who is a ghost with telepathic powers; *Harlot's Ghost* (1991), weighing in at 1,310 pages, about the intricacies and madness of CIA intelligence operations; and, most recently, *The Gospel According to the Son* (1997), a religious fiction about Jesus Christ. No wonder Mailer is difficult to categorize and often controversial.

In addition, his best—and worst—work is in other forms. Among these are certain short stories—*The Time of Her Time* (1959), which appears to advocate rape and violence perpetrated on a Jewish woman; *The White Negro* (1957), which extols violence and drugs as a way to free the instincts and the self from a repressive society; the long antifeminist polemic *The Prisoner of Sex* (1971). He has also written on political conventions, bullfighting, prizefighting, the moon shot, and Marilyn Monroe. The one work that many regard as outstanding is *The Armies of the Night* (1968), the story of the march on the Pentagon protesting the Vietnam War in which Mailer participated and was briefly arrested. It helped invent the New Journalism, in which the reporter is participant or reacter as well as observer, and it was awarded the Pulitzer prize and the National Book Award. Alfred Kazin considered it "just as brilliant a personal testimony as Whitman's diary of the civil war."

Against such high praise, one can also cite criticism that regards much of Mailer's work as pretentious, long-winded, occasionally absurd, often reckless and dangerous. Jewish critics have found much to object to in this "nice Jewish boy from Brooklyn" who consciously has attempted to expunge that "nice boy" side of himself. One critic, Helen Weinberg, however, has argued that he can be seen as being in the Jewish mystical tradition—prophetic, Hasidic, messianic. When his then-friend Norman Podhoretz, editor of *Commentary*, invited him in the early 1960s to contribute to his magazine, Mailer responded with five pieces, one to run every two months, of commentaries on the recently reissued *Tales of the Hasidim*, gathered and edited by Martin Buber. The *Commentary* editors claimed that Buber's collection had a greater impact on non-Jewish writers than any other book in recent times. More to the point, and probably an enticement to Mailer, was their claim that these tales had an even greater impact upon Jewish writers and intellectuals—especially upon those not identified with the organized Jewish community. Mailer was hooked. The selections that follow are the first and last of these pieces, which appeared in December 1962 and August 1963. At the least, they show that this "non-Jewish Jew" deserves a place in this anthology as well as in the ranks of important American writers.

Responses & Reactions

The tradition of the Hasidim[1] is naturally and passionately existential. It is a tradition which lives apart from the regular, grave, solemn, aspects of Judaism, which are the ground and tablet of the essentialist. Disraeli once made a speech in Commons[2] to the effect that the most damaging mistake a conservative party could make was to persecute the Jews, since they were naturally conservative and turned to radical ideas only when they were deprived of an organic place in society. The statement is certainly not without interest, but may grasp no more than a part of the truth. It is more likely the instinct of the Jews to be attracted to large whole detailed views of society, to seek intellectual specifications of the social machine, and to enter precisely those occupations which subtly can offer institutional, personal, and legislative possibilities to a man of quick wit and sensible cohesive culture. The precise need of the essentialist, the authoritarian, or the progressive is to have a social machine upon which one can apply oneself. Later, having earned sufficient and satisfactory power, one may tinker with the machine. It is small wonder that the four corners of modern Protestantism are pegged on Judaistic notions, upon a set of social ideas given bulk and mass only by a most determinedly circumscribed conception of heaven, hell, divine compassion, and eternal punishment. For modern man, Judaeo-Christian man, the social world before him tends to become all of existence.

Yet if the Jews have a greatness, an irreducible greatness, I wonder if it is not to be found in the devil of their dialectic, which places madness next to practicality, illumination side by side with duty, and arrogance in bed with humility. The Jews first saw God in the desert—that dramatic terrain of the present tense stripped of the past, blind to the future. The desert is a land where man may feel insignificant or feel enormous. On the desert can perish the last of one's sensitivities; one's end can wither in the dwarf's law of a bleak nature. Or to the contrary, left alone and in fever, a solitary witness, no animal or vegetable close to him, man may come to feel immensely alive, more portentous in his own psychic presence than any manifest of nature. In the desert, man may flee before God, in terror of the apocalyptic voice of *His* lightning, *His* thunder; or, as dramatically, in a style that no Christian would ever attempt, man dares to speak directly to God, bargains with Him, upbraids Him, rises to scold Him, stares into God's eye like a proud furious stony-eyed child. It may be the anguish of the Jew that he lives closer to God and farther away than men of other religions; certainly it must be true that the Jewish ritual leads one closer to the family, the community, to one's duty, but does not encourage a transcendent vault into the presence of any Power or Divine. It is even possible the Orthodox ritual may have evolved out of some sense in the Community that the Jews had better not dare a rhapsodic and *personal* communion with God, not by themselves, not divorced from ritual, not alone, precisely not alone because they had such voracious

1. "Hasidim": members of a religious revival movement of Jewish mystics that originated in Poland and the Ukraine in the 18th century (Hebrew).
2. I.e., the House of Commons, the democratically elected and more important of the two Houses of the English Parliament. (The House of Lords, which recently voted itself out of existence, was, for the most part, ceremonial.) "Disraeli": Benjamin Disraeli (1804–1881), an English novelist of Jewish descent and a prominent statesman who was prime minister in 1868 and from 1874 to 1880. He pursued an aggressive and imperial foreign policy, becoming a great favorite of Queen Victoria.

instincts and such passionate desires for ecstatic union that they might burn with madness and destroy the race. Given their sober gloomy estimate of reality, they would find malaise and nausea in any communion with God which was too private. It would seem a condition somewhat obscene. This tension may even have helped to create their humor. "What of the *kinder* if I dance naked in the streets?"

These remarks are to offer background for a venture. Every other month in this magazine, a short story, or two, or possibly three, all very short, from Martin Buber's[3] *Tales of the Hasidim* will be printed, followed by a terse commentary by me. Since the gravamen of my own most special ignorance may well be, "Do you dare?" I rush to provide an explanation, a capsule of biography. Seven years ago, riding the electric rail of long nights on marijuana, I used to dip into *The Early Masters* and *The Later Masters*[4] and find some peculiar consolation—these pieces were the first bits of Jewish devotional prose I read which were not deadening to me. Out of the cave of history came a thin filament of the past, the first to which I paid attention.

But I break the capsule to offer the salt of quick detail. I had, of course, grown up in Brooklyn, my parents were modestly Orthodox, then Conservative. I went to a Hebrew School. The *melamed*[5] had a yellow skin, yellow as atabrine. I passed through the existential rite of a Bar Mitzvah.[6] I was a Jew out of loyalty to the underdog. I would never say I was not a Jew, but I looked to take no strength from the fact. What Hebrew I learned was set out to atrophy. I left what part of me belonged to Brooklyn and the Jews on the streets of Crown Heights. In college, it came over me like a poor man's rich fever that I had less connection to the past than anyone I knew.

Today, one does not feel necessarily more a Jew. One is rather a member of a new Diaspora—those veterans without honor of the Beat Generation.[7] But I have a debt to Buber. I have a fondness for the Hasidim. There was a recognition those seven or eight years ago that if I had nothing else in my mind or desire which belonged to Jewish culture, that if I were some sort of dispossessed American, dispossessed even of category, still I had, I had at least, a rudimentary sense of clan across the centuries. *The Tales of the Hasidim* did not make me feel like a Jew, so much as they made me realize what kind of Jew I would or might have been two hundred years ago. I would never, no never, have been a member of the Jewish Establishment. But some bright troublemaking young Reb[8] with a wild beard, an odium for ceremony, a nose for the psychic épée, and a determined taste for the dramatic in words,

3. Jewish philosopher (1878–1965) born in Vienna, prominent in the intellectual life of Germany until he settled permanently in Israel in 1938. He was an early interpreter of Hasidism; his thought developed from mysticism to existentialism. Among his most influential works are *Life of Dialogue* and *I and Thou* (1923).

4. *The Early Masters* and *The Later Masters* (both 1961) appeared originally as *Tales of the Hasidim*, trans. Olga Marx, 2 vols. (New York: Shocken, 1947–48).

5. A teacher (Hebrew and Yiddish), usually of smaller children.

6. In Judaism, the ceremony by which a male of thirteen is accepted in the congregation of men. The youth usually is required to read part of the weekly Torah portion and often then makes a short speech (Hebrew).

7. A term applied to certain American writers of the 1950s. They rejected conventional social and artistic forms, employing direct expression, the rhythms of speech, jazz, and bebop spontaneity in their work. They valued experiences (including the use of drugs, alcohol, sexuality) that they believed produced beatific visions—to many of them a version of Zen philosophy. Jack Kerouac, Allen Ginsberg, Gregory Corso, William Burroughs were among the best known of the so-called "Beats" of that generation.

8. A respectful form of address, like "Mister." It could be a shortened form, too, of *rebbe* (Yiddish), which is a term used for Hasidic leaders and spiritual guides.

in writings, in acts, in the life of dialogue—that was not altogether impossible. For the first time in years I could quit seeing myself as a prime creation, some prize mystery dropped on earth void of antecedents. Granted the intoxication of a historic past (it is like an orphan discovering that in fact he has a beautiful mother) I spent a few days scribbling aphorisms on the end-pages of the hard-bound Schocken[9] edition I owned. Most of these remarks have that sentimental gnomic intensity which a literary mind vaulted too soon into religion will emit:

> Anxiety is the noise man makes as he flees his soul.
>
> False Humility: What man is so arrogant as to declare that his past works led people in bad directions rather than in good ones?
>
> Arrogance is better than indifference, for indifference is the drugged sleep of the soul, while arrogance is the record of a man's struggle against his soul, and by so describing it there may come the day when he will find it.

They are half-tolerable at best, these pietisms; they are really funny: I was writing "soul" with the same fretful grinding of the jaws once used for proving the soul could not exist—something emetic about a good atheist turning into a high-strung saint on a flight of drugs. But one didn't know that then. No photographers were at hand. One merely felt beatific and too worshipful of sedation—the nerves were raddled. Once in a while, religious shafts and dark psychic clouds parted long enough to give an aphorism which was fair:

> We laugh when we recognize a great truth and in the same instant conceal it.

In fact, Buber was indigestible—I was finishing *The Deer Park*. So one had to quit. One left the *Tales of the Hasidim* alone. Over other years, they were used for blackjacking cultural bullies—"Oh, you haven't read *The Early Masters?* Oh."

Once in a while, one would return for a look. The *Tales* had a continuing charm. One could read them as one would turn to a poet who was mild but a favorite.

Along the way, I was seeking to shape some existential leaps into a bit of coherent philosophy. It was never easy. I seemed to have no intellectual tools but the adz and the broad axe. The point of departure, opposed to Sartre,[1] was without a shiver, religious. There was the steadiest belief in Heaven, Hell, and Something Other, something much worse. Since the formal equipment for this structural voyage was as complete as a Beat poet's mountain pack, one found that the *Tales* began to take on a special character. They became the antiquated but conceivable vehicle for a small intellectual raid into the corporated aisles of modern theology. The Talmudist,[2] that poor gun, was now unwinding his filament out from the cave.

With what a difference. The *reactions* to the *Tales of the Hasidim* will be

9. A publishing company, Schocken Books, founded by Salman Schocken in Germany in 1933, began publishing in the United States in 1945. In addition to its historic commitment to the publishing of Judaica, Schocken Books (since 1987 part of Random House, Inc.) specializes in the areas of religious, cultural, and women's studies.

1. Jean-Paul Sartre (1905–1980), French existentialist philosopher, playwright, and novelist.

2. One versed in the Talmud (Hebrew for "instruction" and "to learn"), the collected writings, compiled over centuries, constituting Jewish civil and religious law.

the natural work of a non-Jewish Jew, an alienated American, an existentialist without portfolio. As such, obligatorily, they will have a modern, an irreplaceable value—they are document. As such they are entitled to appeal across the spectrum from A. Hays Sulzberger[3] to Allen Ginsberg.[4]

For sample, two short tales are put here with a garnish of comment. Normally the display will be reversed; greens will endeavor to grow from Hasidic seeds.

The Soul and the Evil Urge[5]

The soul says (to the Evil Urge): "When you try to lead me left, I will not heed you and go to the right. But should you by any chance advise me to go right in your company, I'd prefer to go left."

Which is a way of saying that if you, Evil Urge, tell me to marry, my soul knows it is wise to remain in sin. But, of course, says the Soul, how may I distinguish myself from the Beatific raptures of the Evil Urge?

The Test[6]

Rabbi Yitzhak of Vorki once took his sons to see his teacher Rabbi Bunam, who gave each of them a glass of bock beer and asked them what it was. The elder boy said: "I don't know." Menahem Mendel, the younger, who was three years old at the time, said: "Bitter and good."

"This one will become the leader of a great congregation," said Rabbi Bunam.

Or as St. Thomas of Aquinas[7] said, "Trust the authority of your senses."

1962

Responses & Reactions V

The Fear of God

Once Zusya prayed to God: "Lord, I love you so much, but I do not fear you enough! Lord, I love you so much, but I do not fear you enough! Let me stand in awe of you like your angels, who are penetrated by your awe-inspiring name." And God heard his prayer, and his name penetrated the hidden heart of Zusya as it does those of the angels. But Zusya crawled under the bed like a little dog, and animal fear shook him until he howled: "Lord, let me love you like Zusya again!" And God heard him this time also.

There is an existential logic in this story which leads to a root in the meaning of miracles. Zusya is ambitious, he is intellectually ambitious, he wishes

3. Arthur Hays Sulzberger (1891–1968). Newspaper publisher, born in New York City. Upon the death of his father-in-law, Adolph S. Ochs, he became publisher of the *New York Times* in 1935. His son, Arthur Ochs Sulzberger (b. 1926) took over as publisher in 1963.

4. Ginsberg (1926–1997), born in Newark, New Jersey, has long been identified as a chief figure in the Beat Generation. He is best known for his long poem *Howl* (1956), which attacked American values of the 1950s.

5. Martin Buber, *The Later Masters*, p. 163 (paraphrased) [adapted from Mailer's note].

6. *Ibid.*, p. 298 [Mailer's note].

7. A Catholic theologian of the 13th century who attempted to reconcile the philosophy of Aristotle with the Christian faith. He held that faith and reason were the sources of knowledge. His theories formed the basis of 13th-century Scholasticism (the upholding of traditional doctrines and methods).

to feel a fear of God because he is secretly confident he will be able to withstand that fear and so acquire more knowledge of the universe, more revelation of the secrets of God and Nature. The request is Faustian.[1] Yet God in revealing Himself further to Zusya terrifies him profoundly. Why? Does He terrify Zusya because He is Jehovah, a God of wrath and rectitude, an essentialist's God? Or is the fear which comes over Zusya a part of the profound fear God feels Himself, a fear that His conception of Being (that noble conception of man as a creature of courage and compassion, art, tenderness, skill, stamina, and imagination, exactly the imagination to carry this conception of Being out into the dark emptiness of the universe, there to war against other more malignant conceptions of Being), yes, a fear that precisely this noble conception will not prevail, and instead a wasteful, slovenly, slothful, treacherous, cowardly, and monotonous conception of Being will become the future of man—such a fear must for a God be insupportable. It is the heart of existential logic that God's ultimate victory over the Devil is no more uncertain than the Devil's victory over God—either may conquer man and so give Being a characteristic Good or Evil, or indeed each may exhaust the other, until Being ceases to exist or sinks through seas of entropy into a Being less various, less articulated, less organic, more like plastic than the Nature we know. What a fear is this fear in God that He may lose eventually to the Devil. What abysses of anxiety and pits of woe in such a contemplation. Zusya asking to fear God more, is given instead a vision of God's fear. Like any other man, Zusya draws back in terror.

But is not one of the secrets of the miracle just here? The miracle is revealed to those who can bear to undergo the terror which accompanies it. If intimacy with God is not merely a communion of love but a sharing of the Divine terror, then the beauty of any miracle delivered by God is always accompanied by a fear proportionate to the beauty. Because a miracle is not merely a breach in the laws of nature, but a revelation of the nature of the God behind Nature. If one cannot undergo the fear, one does not deserve the revelation. So our taste for miracles has left us. Man in the Middle Ages lived with dread as a natural accompaniment to his day. His senses uninsulated by the daily use of daily drugs (nicotine, caffeine, aspirin, alcohol, so forth), his mind not guarded by a society which was anti-supernatural, medieval man lived with gods, devils, angels, and demons, with witches, warlocks, and spirits. Miracles, while terrifying, were nonetheless a mark of merit. One was honored to receive them. Whereas we reach quickly and in terror for a chemical which will flatten an affect, deaden our senses, damp our madness, or forestall a miracle. Conversely, we also look to a drug to induce a hallucination—because any visitation produced by a drug is exempt from the terror of engaging the supernatural. For we know, even as the experience is upon us, that we are not privy to a vision beyond the lip of death, but merely are offered a derangement of the senses produced by chemicals. Our modern pleasure is that one is witnessing not a miracle but miracle-in-a-theater.

1. Dr. Johann Faust was the hero of medieval legends, adapted in plays, stories, and novels in later and modern times, as an example of one who sells his soul to the devil in exchange for knowledge and power.

"And the Fire Abated
The tale is told:
The rabbi of Kalev once spent the Sabbath in a nearby village as the guest of one of the hasidim. When the hour to receive the Sabbath had come, someone suddenly screamed, and a servant rushed in and cried that the barn in which the grain was stored was on fire. The owner wanted to run out, but the rabbi took him by the hand. "Stay!" he said. "I am going to tell you a story." The hasid stayed.
"When our master Rabbi Zusya was young," said the zaddik,[2] *"he stoked the stoves in the house of the Great Maggid,*[3] *for this duty was always assigned to the youngest disciples. Once when he was saying the psalms with great fervor just before the coming of the Sabbath, he was startled by screams from within the house. Sparks had fallen from the stove which he had filled with wood, and since no one was in the living room, a fire had started.*
" 'Zusya!" he was reproached. 'There's a fire!'
" 'No matter,' he replied. 'Is it not written: And the fire abated!' At that very same moment the fire abated."
The rabbi of Kalev fell silent. The hasid, whom he still held by the hand, did not dare move. A moment passed and someone called in at the window that the fire in the barn had gone out.

Mood is the earth of the miracle, its garden, its terrain. The mood created by a fire is always in some part Satanic. One senses an avid implacable relentless impatience, a greed to consume, a determination to destroy the material before it, indeed a lunatic intensity within the fire to appropriate the Time which is embodied in the object which is burning. That is why a fire in a fireplace offers comfort. The fire in this case is smaller than ourselves; the material it consumes, the Time it accelerates, are subservient to the mood of calm and benevolence with which we study the fire. We have the ability at any moment to put it out. We are not confronting the force of the devil but rather devil-in-a-theater. In effect, we are dealing with a commonplace miracle. We invoke the supernatural power of fire, but we control it. To primitive man fire was of course always a miracle, a dangerous miracle. He did not know, he could not know—for he had not yet codified the resources of fire—that he would necessarily be able to control it in every contingency. So he approached fire with profound respect, and prayed to various spirits as he put out a fire in order that the demons in the flame be not offended. How natural for him to assume that the intensity of the fire came from the rabidity of the evil contained within the material. By this understanding, it is not insignificant that the grain of the Hasid catches on fire. The grain is his hoarded wealth, his greed, his covetousness. If his heart has been impure and his plans for what he will do with the money he obtains from the sale of the grain are unholy, then the grain—by this unspoken logic—becomes filled with everything which is evil in the Hasid's soul, and

2. "Righteous" (Hebrew). One who lives by his faith scrupulously. His religious value is based on his saintly personality rather than on his scholarly knowledge. In Hasidism, he is the intermediary between man and God, held in reverence by his followers.
3. *Maggid* (Hebrew) is the term for preacher. Preachers were a characteristic feature of Russian and Polish communities, and in the 18th century wandering preachers were the principal means of spreading Hasidism. The Great Maggid was Rabbi Dov Baer, the Maggid of Mezritch, the greatest of the disciples of the Baal Shem Tov, founder of Hasidism.

so begins to smolder, then bursts into flame. The Hasid is ready to run to the barn, the rabbi restrains him. When the Hasid pauses to listen to the speech of the rabbi, he is in effect ready to relinquish his wealth. So what has been evil in him expires, and what has been heat for the flame in the grain is now cooled. Thus might go the religious logic. The question is whether this logic is utterly without foundation in the real. For philosophically is it not as plausible to assume we have a spirit which is communicable to other people and to the very properties of our environment as it is to assume that spirit does not exist or is not communicable? And is it not equally or almost equally comfortable to assume that a fire may be extinguished by a dramatic shift in mood? Let the burden fall on the philosopher who would prove that the existence of a fire can never be affected by a mood.

1963

LOUIS SIMPSON
b. 1923

"I had no formal Jewish education, unless reading the Old Testament in English can be thought of as an education . . . the psalms of David, translated into English, became a part of my thinking. To this day the imagery of desert and rocky places presents itself to my mind's eye as though it were my native ground. I do not need to be told how the Jews lived three thousand years ago—I understand the despair of the people in the wilderness better than I understand their lives in the suburbs." Louis Simpson, receiving the Jewish Book Council Award in 1981, also identified a Jew's chief traits: "to be curious about the purpose of life, to find a justifying design in experience. . . . He believes that life is lived to some purpose, and that it is good. The Jew believes that ultimately there is a community of man and God." To show these things, "I have had to tell stories, and this places me in the tradition of the Jewish people. . . . I find it hard not to think of Anton Chekhov as a Jew. He has the pathos, the sense of dispersal, the desire to bring things back together, and the humor, that are found in the best Jewish writers." And finally, in this self-revealing tally of traits, Simpson notes that Jews, being often "strangers to the place where they lived," developed the humor "that turns a sad situation around so that we can see the comical side." But he adds that other races and nations share these qualities. It's only that Jews have cultivated and preserved them, "as they themselves have been preserved."

Louis Simpson was born on March 27, 1923, in Kingston, Jamaica, to Aston and Rosalind Marantz Simpson. His father, a native British West Indian, was a respected lawyer. His mother, from the southern Russian town of Lutsk, came to America with her family around 1908, worked in the garment district and as an actress in silent films, then settled in Jamaica. Louis, with no sense of himself as a Jew, was sent to a boarding school and left Jamaica for New York at seventeen, enrolling in Columbia College. Drafted in 1943, "I began with the tanks and finished with the 101st Airborne Division. We fought in Normandy, Holland, Belgium, and Germany. I came back from the war much changed. To this day when I see an open field I think, How are we going to get across that?" Simpson was decorated several times, with two Purple Hearts, and suffered a brief breakdown after the war.

Back at Columbia, he "wrote furiously," including memorable war poems such as *Carentan O Carentan*, in rhymed quatrains. One day he gave a poetry reading—

introduced by the British poet Stephen Spender—with fellow students Allen Ginsberg and John Hollander, and was astonished when Spender said the "main difference between English and American poetry was that Englishmen had experienced the war and Americans hadn't." Simpson has had three children, taught at Berkeley (1959–67) and SUNY, Stony Brook, written much literary criticism and autobiography, and received a Pulitzer prize for *At the End of the Open Road* (1963).

"The Open Road goes to the used-car lot," Simpson writes in that book, separating Walt Whitman's impossible claim for a nation of poets from "the Whitman who uses his own eyes and ears, who describes things, who expresses his own sly humor or pathos." Humor joins pathos in *A Story about Chicken Soup*, another poem from the early 1960s, when Simpson was in Berkeley. And several memories undergird this poem: "At bedtime Mother would read us stories. . . . Or else she would tell stories about Russia when she was a child. Russia was covered with snow and the wind was freezing cold. Wolves howled in the distance. People rode in sleighs with jingling bells. In Russia there were cossacks. . . . 'What are cossacks?' " her son asked. And from about 1941: "On Fridays I used to go to Brooklyn" (to visit his grandmother). "She was Jewish—and I was a Jew. I had not known this before I met her. . . . She lit the candles and prayed, and carried the prayer with a sweeping motion into her heart. Then she served the meal—chicken soup, [etc.]. . . . She wept for her people in Russia."

In *A Story about Chicken Soup*, Simpson first opened himself loyally, as it were, to his Russian Jewish origins; the process culminated in *Adventures of the Letter I* (1971) and *Caviare at the Funeral* (1980). This peom's quasi-facetious irreverence may mislead us: "I know it's in bad taste to say it, / But it's true. The Germans killed them all." Yet that tone sounds clearly when Simpson recites his "story." "Imagine," he tells us both colloquially and urgently. Maybe only humor can hold the pathos of being distant from the perished "old country." Only a charnel pun, "They are all eyes," and an understated "mudhole" for pre-Holocaust Eastern European Jewry can bear the irony of 1960s California: "Not to walk in the painted sunshine . . . But to live in the tragic world forever."

A Story about Chicken Soup

In my grandmother's house there was always chicken soup
And talk of the old country—mud and boards,
Poverty,
The snow falling down the necks of lovers.

Now and then, out of her savings
She sent them a dowry. Imagine
The rice-powdered[1] faces!
And the smell of the bride, like chicken soup.

But the Germans killed them.
I know it's in bad taste to say it,
But its' true. The Germans killed them all.

In the ruins of Berchtesgaden[2]
A child with yellow hair
Ran out of a doorway.

1. Rice is often tossed at the bride after a wedding as a symbol of fertility.
2. A town in southern Germany where the chalets of Hitler, Göring, Bormann, and other Nazi leaders were located, along with other installations.

A German girl-child—
Cuckoo, all skin and bones—
Not even enough to make chicken soup.
She sat by the stream and smiled.

Then as we splashed in the sun
She laughed at us.
We had killed her mechanical brothers,
So we forgave her.

The sun is shining.
The shadows of the lovers have disappeared.
They are all eyes; they have some demand on me—
They want me to be more serious than I want to be.

They want me to stick in their mudhole
Where no one is elegant.
They want me to wear old clothes,
They want me to be poor, to sleep in a room with many others—

Not to walk in the painted sunshine
To a summer house,[3]
But to live in the tragic world forever.

1963

Dvonya

In the town of Odessa
there is a garden
and Dvonya is there,
Dvonya whom I love
though I have never been in Odessa.

I love her black hair, and eyes
as green as a salad
that you gather in August
between the roots of alder,
her skin with an odor of wildflowers.

We understand each other perfectly.
We are cousins twice removed.
In the garden we drink our tea,
discussing the plays of Chekhov[1]
as evening falls and the lights begin to twinkle.

But this is only a dream.
I am not there
with my citified speech,
and the old woman is not there
peering between the curtains.

3. A small structure in a garden for shade and rest.
1. Anton Chekhov (1860–1904), Russian playwright and short-story writer.

We are only phantoms, bits of ash,
like yesterday's newspaper
or the smoke of chimneys.
All that passed long ago
on a summer night in Odessa.

1971

GERALD STERN
b. 1925

"I'm a rabbi!" Gerald Stern exclaims jokingly in a 1984 interview. "I was raised Orthodox and quit when I was thirteen years and one day. I never had a negative feeling towards my religion, though I was sometimes bored." This stance might seem to say it all, but in practice, Judaism and Jewishness press closely on Stern's poetic consciousness. He recalls, "My grandfather was a holy man and killed chickens [as a ritual slaughterer] and taught boys, and wrote essays on Tolstoy and Goethe"; his father "came to America in 1905, huge wolves / snapped at the horse's legs"; a lucky American, he acknowledges his Russian Jewish "counterpart . . . / I don't like to see him born / in a little village fifty miles from Kiev"; his touch for rhythm and repetition "comes partly from Whitman, partly from the Bible."

Born in Pittsburgh, Pennsylvania, in 1925 to Eastern European immigrants, Stern taught at Columbia, New York University, the University of Pittsburgh, Sarah Lawrence, and, until his retirement in 1995, at the Writers' Workshop in Iowa City for fourteen years. He published nine books of poetry but came into national prominence only in his fifties with *Lucky Life* (1977), which won the National Book Critics Circle Award and the Lamont Prize. His 1998 collection *This Time* won the National Book Award. He presently lives in rural Pennsylvania and New York City.

In his poem *Behaving Like a Jew*, from *Lucky Life*, Stern says, "I am going to be unappeased at the opossum's death. / I am going to behave like a Jew." Which means, "I am not going to . . . praise the beauty and the balance / and lose myself in the immortal lifestream." For Stern, then, behaving like a Jew means not passively accepting what cannot be altered. His writing passes credibly from beauty and awe to catastrophe, from pedestrian concerns to the spiritual questions that lie just beneath the surface of our daily toils.

Gerald Stern has been writing poetry for fifty years on widely varied subjects. But his verse has persisted in a celebratory vein whose blended humor and sadness, candor and irony keep it authentic.

Lucky Life

Lucky life isn't one long string of horrors
and there are moments of peace, and pleasure, as I lie in between the
blows.
Lucky I don't have to wake up in Phillipsburg, New Jersey,

on the hill overlooking Union Square or the hill overlooking
Kuebler Brewery or the hill overlooking SS. Philip and James
but have my own hills and my own vistas to come back to.

Each year I go down to the island I add
one more year to the darkness;
and though I sit up with my dear friends
trying to separate the one year from the other,
this one from the last, that one from the former,
another from another,
after a while they all get lumped together,
the year we walked to Holgate,
the year our shoes got washed away,
the year it rained,
the year my tooth brought misery to us all.

This year was a crisis. I knew it when we pulled
the car onto the sand and looked for the key.
I knew it when we walked up the outside steps
and opened the hot icebox and began the struggle
with swollen drawers and I knew it when we laid out
the sheets and separated the clothes into piles
and I knew it when we made our first rush onto
the beach and I knew it when we finally sat
on the porch with coffee cups shaking in our hands.

My dream is I'm walking through Phillipsburg, New Jersey,
and I'm lost on South Main Street. I am trying to tell,
by memory, which statue of Christopher Columbus
I have to look for, the one with him slumped over
and lost in weariness or the one with him
vaguely guiding the way with a cross and globe in
one hand and a compass in the other.
My dream is I'm in the Eagle Hotel on Chamber Street
sitting at the oak bar, listening to two
obese veterans discussing Hawaii in 1942,
and reading the funny signs over the bottles.
My dream is I sleep upstairs over the honey locust
and sit on the side porch overlooking the stone culvert
with a whole new set of friends, mostly old and humorless.

Dear waves, what will you do for me this year?
Will you drown out my scream?
Will you let me rise through the fog?
Will you fill me with that old salt feeling?
Will you let me take my long steps in the cold sand?
Will you let me lie on the white bedspread and study
the black clouds with the blue holes in them?
Will you let me see the rusty trees and the old monoplanes one more year?
Will you still let me draw my sacred figures
and move the kites and the birds around with my dark mind?

Lucky life is like this. Lucky there is an ocean to come to.
Lucky you can judge yourself in this water.
Lucky you can be purified over and over again.
Lucky there is the same cleanliness for everyone.
Lucky life is like that. Lucky life. Oh lucky life.
Oh lucky lucky life. Lucky life.

1977

Sixteen Minutes

There in the sky above Lewisburg[1]
were two land masses that looked so much like clouds
that when two birds flew through them
they flew through livid chimneys and smoking hillsides.

One was Ireland and one was Long Island,[2]
side by side at last,
completely forgetful of the other two masses,
one to the east of those islands, one to the west.

I parked my car, as I do, at a deadly corner
to watch them change or come together as one more
land mass or even to join the other continents
they left behind in Wal-Mart's[3] cloudy parking.

I noted everything
including the great salt ponds in eastern Long Island,
including the dark blood all over Ireland,
caused, as it were, by the sun.

Wild ducks flew over one place
and wild geese over the other;
crows, with strips of something hanging from their mouths,
flew between them.

I tried, without going to the library,
to unravel the history. Especially
I thought of illegal landings and I thought
of the little white potato passing between them.

Strange to think that they had different poets,
so close they were together, and strange to think
how it would be if ours were closer or theirs
were closer to us or if they drifted together

1. A city in central-western Pennsylvania.
2. A popular and populous island east of Manhattan.
3. A reference to one of the numerous discount department stores of that name.

east of New York and west of England or in
the lower sky above this Lewisburg east
of Clarion, Pennsylvania, west of Bloomsburg,
three hours from Philadelphia, five from Pittsburgh.

Odd to think of the Jews and Irish too,
how we married each other,
how my own children have pink faces,
how we hated each other, Jews and Irish,

and fought each other, how the Jews were horrified
by one thing, how the Irish were enraged
by another, how the Irgun[4] on our side
and the I.R.A.[5] on theirs both battled English

smugness and deceit, how they both saw through it,
and how the English were appalled by them both,
not to mention the Irish down from Canada
who settled in Queens,[6] not to mention the mayor

of Dublin himself a Jew[7] whom I saw plant
a tree in the old Sephardic graveyard on Arch Street
in Philadelphia I am sure who traveled
from Jewish place to Jewish place and planted

and talked and drank and told a joke albeit
wearing a top hat not a derby and not a
cap—the thing we had in common—certainly
not a beret and not a yarmulke, the wind

our enemy, destroying a couple of counties
in both good places, me not wanting to see
the world in shreds. Language too we had
together, I would call it subversive, and spoke we

still another tongue and spoke we this tongue
as gorgeous strangers; and theater, I would name
theater, and comedians and actors and lightweight boxers
and singers, by the dozen, and music of tears

you might call soft from time to time and blarney,
a Jewish characteristic, mostly though
self-reproach—we couldn't help it—one cloud
turned black, and then the other, they were raking

4. The Jewish right-wing underground movement that seceded from the World Zionist Organization to protest more actively the British presence in post–World War II Palestine. Their methods were often extremely violent, and many considered them terrorists, while others would argue that they did much to help found the State of Israel.
5. An acronym for the Irish Republican Army, founded in 1919, which is an unofficial semimilitary group that has violently protested the British presence in Northern Ireland. Depending upon one's political leaning, the members of the IRA are considered either freedom fighters or terrorists.
6. One of the five boroughs of New York City, located in western Long Island.
7. A reference to Robert Briscoe, lord mayor of Dublin from 1956 to 1957 and from 1961 to 1962.

their own furnaces; there was a little
crime too, and there was the mother, we both
sang "Mammy," how could we help it?—Mammy, Mammy,[8]
I'd walk a million miles for one of your towels

Oh Mammy; but God we were different. Did I say
how one cloud was different from the other and how
I sat there for sixteen minutes till one island
then the other fell apart? Truth was

they fell apart slowly, truth was a larger
island came in view, I guess it was Greenland
or part of Alaska had mingled with Siberia
and carried it my way; I almost made a new

religion in those sixteen minutes and a new
language, Judish, and a foggy city
called Irishaloyem—that would mean
Peace to the Irish. I say peace to the Irish

and I say peace to the Jews, and I say—grudgingly—
peace to Greenland and peace to the monster Siberia
with Alaska in its mouth and peace to
the hills of Pennsylvania and mostly peace

to the inmates of Lewisburg Penitentiary
and to the Irishman there we held illegally
and Thornburgh[9] extradited as a last vicious act
to make Bush[1] smile and Queen Elizabeth[2] chuckle,

and Jimmy Hoffa[3] and the Berrigan brothers[4]
and Greenglass[5] the rat who checked his atom bomb in
before they gave him a number and Morton Sobel[6]
who spent twenty years here because he kept his bomb

in a cardboard suitcase underneath a girder
on the Williamsburg Bridge; and good Alger Hiss,[7] he came here

8. A reference to a song made popular by Jewish performer Al Jolson (1886–1950), who frequently performed in blackface. The song actually says "smiles," not "towels" (line 68).
9. Richard L. Thornburgh (b. 1932) was the governor of Pennsylvania from 1979 to 1987. He was also U.S. attorney general during the Bush administration.
1. A reference to George Bush (b. 1924), the forty-first president of the United States, a political conservative.
2. Queen Elizabeth II (b. 1926) has been the sovereign head of the United Kingdom and Northern Ireland since 1952.
3. Hoffa (1913–1975), a notorious and controversial American labor leader, served as head of the Teamsters Union from 1957 to 1971. Alleged to have been involved with organized crime, he disappeared under mysterious circumstances, and his fate remains unknown.
4. I.e., Philip and Daniel, political activists in the American 1960s. Daniel Berrigan, a Catholic priest, went to jail for the first time in 1967 after being arrested in a protest against the Vietnam War.
5. Greenglass was the maiden name of Ethel Rosenberg (1915–1953). She and her husband, Julius (1918–1953), were the first Americans to be executed for treason. Ethel's brother, David Greenglass, gave the Rosenbergs the data that they later allegedly supplied to the Soviet Union. The Rosenbergs' case was highly controversial, many believing that they were unjustly convicted and unfairly executed.
6. Another alleged conspirator in the Rosenberg episode.
7. Hiss (1904–1996), a member of the State Department, was named as a communist and a traitor in 1950 during the Red Scare. His guilt or innocence is still debated today.

for the air and for the food, he had
a cardboard suitcase too with a bomb inside it;

and peace to that Irish Jew, Wilhelm Reich,[8]
who died inside his cage in 1957
and to the love he brought us and to his exploding
cells and to the cloud that carried him up;

and to the shawls we wore and to our moaning
and to the stone walls we moaned against and the moon
we always kept track of, the moon that ruled our lives
through all the killing and hounding, we all but worshipped.

1995

8. Reich (1897–1957) was an Austrian psychoanalyst who lived in Lewisburg, Pennsylvania, the same town in which Stern lived for many years. He was most famous for his work on sexual health and neurosis. Reich's controversial experiments brought him into conflict with the authorities in the early 1950s. Reich was convicted of contempt of court and died in prison.

ALLEN GINSBERG
1926–1997

"Allee samee," Allen Ginsberg was wont to reply when asked about his religious or ethnic affiliation. And he was right, for himself at least, given the deep expanse he claimed for that affiliation. William Blake, the biblical prophets, Buddhist meditation, all fed the same visionary inspiration in his most characteristic poetry. Take the closing cadence of *Sunflower Sutra,* conceived soon after Ginsberg's spectacular 1955 presentation of *Howl* in San Francisco:

> —We're not our skin of grime, we're not our dread bleak dusty imageless locomotive, we're all golden sunflowers inside, blessed by our own seed & hairy naked accomplishment-bodies growing into mad black formal sunflowers in the sunset, spied on by our eyes under the shadow of the mad locomotive riverbank sunset Frisco hilly tincan evening sitdown vision.

The golden sunflower stems from Blake, the sutra (thread) from Buddhist scripture, and the drawn-out breath-line from Hebraic verse.

Or listen to Ginsberg relate his prime revelatory moment. Desolate in an east Harlem sublet in 1948, he is lying in bed with Blake's *The Sunflower*—"Seeking that sweet golden clime"—open on his lap: "Suddenly I realized that the poem was talking about *me* . . . and suddenly, simultaneously with understanding it, heard a very deep earthen grave voice in the room. . . . Like the voice of the Ancient of Days. But the peculiar quality of the voice was something unforgettable because it was like God had a human voice, with all the infinite tenderness and anciency and mortal gravity of a living Creator speaking to his son." In the sky outside his window and the carved cornices on the old tenement, he sensed a living spirit: "I suddenly realized that *this* existence was *it*! . . . Never deny the voice—no, never *forget* it."

Where did this nice Jewish boy come from, to be visited by the Ancient of Days in east Harlem? Irwin Allen Ginsberg was born in Newark, New Jersey, on June 3, 1926, the son of Naomi Levy Ginsberg, Russian émigrée and avid Marxist, and Louis Ginsberg, high-school teacher and lyric poet. From a 1985 interview: "They were old-fashioned delicatessen philosophers. My father would go around the house either reciting Emily Dickinson and Longfellow under his breath or attacking T. S. Eliot for ruining poetry with his 'obscurantism.' My mother made up bedtime stories that all went something like: 'The good king rose forth from his castle, saw the suffering workers and healed them.' " And from his own 1960 biographical note: "High school in Paterson till 17, Columbia College, merchant marine, Texas and Denver, copyboy, Times Square, amigos in jail, dishwashing, book reviews, Mexico City, market research, satori in Harlem, Yucatan and Chiapas 1954, West Coast Howl 1955, Arctic Sea Trip & then Tangier, Venice, Amsterdam, Paris, London, readings Oxford Harvard Columbia Chicago, New York Kaddish 1959."

At Columbia, Ginsberg studied literature with Mark Van Doren and especially Lionel Trilling, whom he felt close to "because we were both Jewish and he sort of empathized with me." Later, studying with the art historian Meyer Schapiro, he "got all hung up on Cézanne." He also fell in with William Burroughs, Jack Kerouac, Gregory Corso, Neal Cassady, and other "angelheaded hipsters," experimenting with drugs, homosexuality, poetry. In a psychiatric institution, where he'd gone in lieu of jail when a friend storing stolen goods with him was convicted, Ginsberg met the "intuitive Bronx dadaist" Carl Solomon, an inspiration for *Howl*. Yet the same budding poet could go home to Paterson, New Jersey, in 1950 and write to the town's eminent older poet William Carlos Williams, speaking of the "misery I see (like a tide out of my own fantasy) but mainly the splendor which I carry within me," and sending his poems, including "a mad song (to be sung by Groucho Marx to a Bop background)." Williams's touch for common, earthy things and people, his colloquial bent, plus the extended verse line he was trying at the time, helped Ginsberg toward his own voice.

Nothing, though, could have presaged the explosion of *Howl*. Having gone to San Francisco in 1954 and taken a room around the corner from Lawrence Ferlinghetti's City Lights bookshop, Ginsberg joined with Kenneth Rexroth, Gary Snyder, Robert Duncan, Philip Whalen, and met Peter Orlovsky, who became his longtime companion. At a gathering in a converted auto repair shop on Fillmore Street on October 13, 1955—exactly one century, as it happens, after Whitman published *Leaves of Grass*—Ginsberg recited the first part of *Howl*:

I saw the best minds of my generation destroyed by madness, starving hysterical
  naked,
dragging themselves through the negro streets at dawn looking for an angry fix,
angelheaded hipsters burning for the ancient heavenly connection to the starry
  dynamo in the machinery of night. . . .

With this "Hebraic-Melvillean bardic breath" (as he said), which also owed to Kerouac's "inspired prose line" and to cantorial chant, Ginsberg opened up for poetry a culture of down-and-out Beatness, drugs, rebellion, sex, and ecstasy in the midst of the Eisenhower and McCarthy years.

Propelling his "spontaneous bop prosody," Ginsberg's sense "that each line has to be contained within the elastic of one breath" gives *Howl* visionary reach. The rhythm surges with prophetic force: "Moloch whose eyes are a thousand blind windows!" The words agglomerate into daubings of urban actuality. But while Ginsberg says he wrote *Howl* on peyote and espouses "first thought, best thought," the poem's typescript shows deliberate revision.

Howl and Other Poems (City Lights, 1956) carried an introduction by Williams, noting the "horrifying . . . depths" the poet had traversed. "It is the belief in the art of poetry that has gone hand in hand with this man into his Golgotha, from that charnel house, similar in every way, to that of the Jews in the past war." Apart from this rather excessive estimate, Williams welcomed "a well-made poem." But the poem's rude language provoked San Francisco authorities into charging City Lights with obscenity. After a two-month trial, the judge ruled that *Howl* was not without "redeeming social importance" (over the next decade it went through fifteen printings).

Later, Ginsberg added the *Footnote to Howl.* Its exclamatory liturgic impetus—"Holy! Holy! Holy!"—not only recalls Blake and Whitman, but resonates against Isaiah's calling (6.3) : *Kadosh, Kadosh, Kadosh* . . . (Holy, holy, holy, is the Lord of hosts: the whole earth is full of his glory). Ginsberg's lines also recapitulate his besetting concerns, people, and places. "Footnote to Howl is too lovely and serious a joke to explain," he told John Hollander in 1958. "It's dedicated to my mother who died in the madhouse and it says I loved her anyway & that even in worst conditions life is holy."

Ginsberg had mailed his mother a dittoed copy of *Howl.* The night before her death on Long Island in June 1956, she wrote him in San Francisco: "I wish you get married. Do you like farming? It's as good a job as any. . . . I wish I were out of here and home at the time you were young; then I would be young. . . . I hope you are not taking drugs as suggested by your poetry. That would hurt me. Don't go in for ridiculous things." At her funeral, there were not ten men for a *minyan* to say the mourners' Kaddish, so that was left to her son. Months later in a Paris café, Ginsberg began his *Kaddish,* then finished it on New York's Lower East Side in 1959: two days on "amphetamine plus a little bit of morphine, plus some dexedrine later on to keep me going."

The elegy's strongly cadenced opening calls up Ray Charles, "the rhythm the rhythm," but an older measure can be heard, the habitual dactyls of Walt Whitman's first lines: "Starting from Paumanok" or "Out of the cradle endlessly rocking."

Strange now to think of you, gone without corsets & eyes, while I walk on the
    sunny pavement of Greenwich Village.
downtown Manhattan, clear winter noon, and I've been up all night, talking,
    talking, reading the Kaddish aloud, listening to Ray Charles blues shout blind
    on the phonograph
the rhythm the rhythm—and your memory in my head three years after—And
    read Adonais' last triumphant stanzas aloud—wept, realizing how we suffer—
And how Death is that remedy all singers dream of, sing, remember, prophesy
    as in the Hebrew Anthem, or the Buddhist Book of Answers . . .

And a yet older repetitive cadence is present in Ginsberg's opening: *tushbehata v'nehemata* . . . , the incantatory Aramaic of the Kaddish itself.

Kaddish (meaning "holy"), the traditional mourners' prayer, contains no lament of death, but only sanctification, praise of God, and peace. It may seem hard to find praise in a harrowing, humiliating account of Naomi Ginsberg's paranoia and degeneration: "scars of operations, pancreas, belly wounds, abortions, appendix, stitching of incisions pulling down in the fat like hideous thick zippers—ragged long lips between her legs." But her son meant "Only to have not forgotten," he says in Part III. The unsparing honesty of Ginsberg's language, exposing his own pain opposite hers, may possibly earn a sort of peace, as in his summons:

Communist beauty, sit here married in the summer among daisies . . .
blessed daughter come to America, I long to hear your voice again . . .

and in her own vision:

'Yesterday I saw God. What did he look like? Well, in the afternoon I climbed up a ladder—he has a cheap cabin in the country, like Monroe, N.Y. the chicken farms in the wood. He was a lonely old man with a white beard.

'I cooked supper for him. I made him a nice supper—lentil soup, vegetables, bread & butter—miltz—he sat down at the table and ate, he was sad.

'I told him, Look at all those fightings and killings down there, What's the matter? Why don't you put a stop to it?

'I try, he said—That's all he could do, he looked tired. He's a bachelor so long, and he likes lentil soup.'

This "once long-tressed Naomi of Bible— / or Ruth who wept in America" wrote one last letter: "Get married Allen don't take drugs—the key is in the bars, in the sunlight in the window. Love, your mother."

After *Kaddish and Other Poems* (1961), Ginsberg intensified the traveling—Europe, Asia, America—and public demonstration that shaped his notoriety. In Jerusalem in 1961, he visited Martin Buber, who urged him toward human-to-human relationships rather than human-nonhuman. Prague students crowned him King of the May in 1963, and he declared himself a "Buddhist Jew." Indian gurus told him to live in his body, in his heart. In Japan, he felt a need to renounce drugs and even his Blakean vision. In Venice, Ezra Pound admitted to him: "The worst mistake I made was the stupid suburban prejudice of anti-Semitism." Ginsberg's turn toward the human meant political protest for sexual and drug liberation, for underdogs and misfits and outcasts, against the Vietnam War, nuclear arms, ecological desecration. "America, I'm putting my queer shoulder to the wheel," he announced in 1956, and that he did—with finger cymbals and harmonium, at peace rallies and Be-ins, universities and courtrooms, in Wichita and throughout "these states."

Allen Ginsberg died on April 5, 1997. Was he a charlatan or a salutary spirit? For Harold Bloom, *Kaddish* is "not an *imaginative* suffering for the reader," but like being "compelled to watch the hysteria of strangers." Yet for Saul Bellow, "Under all this self-revealing candor is purity of heart." With comic brio (and a lot of help from his friends), Ginsberg did change the face of American poetry. The word for him is *chutzpah*.

Footnote to Howl

Holy! Holy! Holy! Holy! Holy! Holy! Holy! Holy! Holy! Holy! Holy! Holy! Holy! Holy! Holy!
The world is holy! The soul is holy! The skin is holy! The nose is holy! The tongue and cock and hand and asshole holy!
Everything is holy! everybody's holy! everywhere is holy! everyday is in eternity! Everyman's an angel!
The bum's as holy as the seraphim! the madman is holy as you my soul are holy!
The typewriter is holy the poem is holy the voice is holy the hearers are holy the ecstasy is holy!
Holy Peter holy Allen holy Solomon holy Lucien holy Kerouac holy Huncke holy Burroughs holy Cassady[1] holy the unknown buggered and suffering beggars holy the hideous human angels!
Holy my mother in the insane asylum! Holy the cocks of the grandfathers of Kansas!
Holy the groaning saxophone! Holy the bop apocalypse! Holy the jazzbands marijuana hipsters peace peyote pipes & drums!
Holy the solitudes of skyscrapers and pavements! Holy the cafeterias filled with the millions! Holy the mysterious rivers of tears under the streets!
Holy the lone juggernaut! Holy the vast lamb of the middleclass! Holy the crazy shepherds of rebellion! Who digs Los Angeles IS Los Angeles!

1. The poet himself and his circle of friends: Peter Orlovsky, Carl Solomon, Lucien Carr, Jack Kerouac, Herbert Huncke, William Burroughs, Neal Cassady.

Holy New York Holy San Francisco Holy Peoria & Seattle Holy Paris Holy Tangiers Holy Moscow Holy Istanbul!
Holy time in eternity holy eternity in time holy the clocks in space holy the fourth dimension holy the fifth International[2] holy the Angel in Moloch![3]
Holy the sea holy the desert holy the railroad holy the locomotive holy the visions holy the hallucinations holy the miracles holy the eyeball holy the abyss!
Holy forgiveness! mercy! charity! faith! Holy! Ours! bodies! suffering! magnanimity!
Holy the supernatural extra brilliant intelligent kindness of the soul!

Berkeley, 1955 1956

From Kaddish

II

Over and over—refrain—of the Hospitals—still haven't written your history—leave it abstract—a few images
run thru the mind—like the saxophone chorus of houses and years—remembrance of electrical shocks.
By long nites as a child in Paterson[1] apartment, watching over your nervousness—you were fat—your next move—
By that afternoon I stayed home from school to take care of you—once and for all—when I vowed forever that once man disagreed with my opinion of the cosmos, I was lost—
By my later burden—vow to illuminate mankind—this is release of particulars—(mad as you)—(sanity a trick of agreement)—
But you stared out the window on the Broadway Church corner, and spied a mystical assassin from Newark,[2]
So phoned the Doctor—'OK go way for a rest'—so I put on my coat and walked you downstreet—On the way a grammarschool boy screamed, unaccountably—'Where you goin Lady to Death'? I shuddered—
and you covered your nose with motheaten fur collar, gas mask against poison sneaked into downtown atmosphere, sprayed by Grandma—
And was the driver of the cheesebox Public Service bus a member of the gang? You shuddered at his face, I could hardly get you on—to New York, very Times Square, to grab another Greyhound—
where we hung around 2 hours fighting invisible bugs and jewish sickness—breeze poisoned by Roosevelt[3]—
out to get you—and me tagging along, hoping it would end in a quiet room in a Victorian house by a lake.
Ride 3 hours thru tunnels past all American industry, Bayonne[4] preparing for World War II, tanks, gas fields, soda factories, diners, locomotive

2. A meeting of the international communist organization (1924).
3. A cult god in ancient Israel to whom children were sacrificed (see 2 Kings 23.10; Jeremiah 32.35).
1. The city in New Jersey where Ginsberg grew up. American poet William Carlos Williams (1883–1963) also lived there.
2. A city in and port of entry to New Jersey; the place where Ginsberg was born.
3. I.e., Franklin Delano Roosevelt (1882–1945), thirty-second president of the United States (1932–45).
4. A New Jersey port city with a navy supply depot and heavy industry.

roundhouse fortress—into piney woods New Jersey Indians—calm towns—long road thru sandy tree fields—

Bridges by deerless creeks, old wampum[5] loading the streambed—down there a tomahawk or Pocahontas[6] bone—and a million old ladies voting for Roosevelt in brown small houses, roads off the Madness highway—

perhaps a hawk in a tree, or a hermit looking for an owl-filled branch—

All the time arguing—afraid of strangers in the forward double seat, snoring regardless—what busride they snore on now?

'Allen, you don't understand—it's—ever since those 3 big sticks up my back—they did something to me in Hospital, they poisoned me, they want to see me dead—3 big sticks, 3 big sticks—

'The Bitch! Old Grandma! Last week I saw her, dressed in pants like an old man, with a sack on her back, climbing up the brick side of the apartment

'On the fire escape, with poison germs, to throw on me—at night—maybe Louis is helping her—he's under her power—

'I'm your mother, take me to Lakewood' (near where Graf Zeppelin[7] had crashed before, all Hitler in Explosion) 'where I can hide.'

We got there—Dr. Whatzis rest home—she hid behind a closet—demanded a blood transfusion.

We were kicked out—tramping with Valise to unknown shady lawn houses—dusk, pine trees after dark—long dead street filled with crickets and poison ivy—

I shut her up by now—big house REST HOME ROOMS—gave the landlady her money for the week—carried up the iron valise—sat on bed waiting to escape—

Neat room in attic with friendly bedcover—lace curtains—spinning wheel rug—Stained wallpaper old as Naomi. We were home.

I left on the next bus to New York—laid my head back in the last seat, depressed—the worst yet to come?—abandoning her, rode in torpor—I was only 12.

Would she hide in her room and come out cheerful for breakfast? Or lock her door and stare thru the window for sidestreet spies? Listen at keyholes for Hitlerian invisible gas? Dream in a chair—or mock me, by—in front of a mirror, alone?

12 riding the bus at nite thru New Jersey, have left Naomi to Parcae[8] in Lakewood's haunted house—left to my own fate bus—sunk in a seat—all violins broken—my heart sore in my ribs—mind was empty—Would she were safe in her coffin—

Or back at Normal School[9] in Newark, studying up on America in a black skirt—winter on the street without lunch—a penny a pickle—home at night to take care of Elanor[1] in the bedroom—

First nervous breakdown was 1919—she stayed home from school and lay in a dark room for three weeks—something bad—never said what—every noise hurt—dreams of the creaks of Wall Street—

Before the gray Depression—went upstate New York—recovered—Lou took photo of her sitting crossleg on the grass—her long hair wound with

5. Beads of polished shells strung together and used by North American Indians as money (Narraganset).

6. A Powhatan Indian princess (ca. 1595–1617) who helped maintain peace between the Indians and the settlers in colonial Virginia. She married a settler, went to England, and died there.

7. The *Graf Zeppelin* was a dirigible that started and finished a twenty-one-day trip around the world in Lakehurst (not Lakewood, as Ginsberg states), New Jersey.

8. Fate.

9. A school for teacher training.

1. Naomi's sister.

flowers—smiling—playing lullabies on mandolin—poison ivy smoke in left-wing summer camps and me in infancy saw trees—

or back teaching school, laughing with idiots, the backward classes—her Russian specialty—morons with dreamy lips, great eyes, thin feet & sicky fingers, swaybacked, rachitic—

great heads pendulous over Alice in Wonderland, a blackboard full of C A T.

Naomi reading patiently, story out of a Communist fairy book—Tale of the Sudden Sweetness of the Dictator—Forgiveness of Warlocks[2]—Armies Kissing—

Deathsheads Around the Green Table—The King & the Workers—Paterson Press printed them up in the '30s till she went mad, or they folded, both.

O Paterson! I got home late that nite. Louis was worried. How could I be so—didn't I think? I shouldn't have left her. Mad in Lakewood. Call the Doctor. Phone the home in the pines. Too late.

Went to bed exhausted, wanting to leave the world (probably that year newly in love with R——my high school mind hero, jewish boy who came a doctor later—then silent neat kid—

I later laying down life for him, moved to Manhattan—followed him to college—Prayed on ferry to help mankind if admitted—vowed, the day I journeyed to Entrance Exam—

by being honest revolutionary labor lawyer—would train for that—inspired by Sacco Vanzetti, Norman Thomas, Debs, Altgeld, Sandburg, Poe—Little Blue Books.[3] I wanted to be President, or Senator.

ignorant woe—later dreams of kneeling by R's shocked knees declaring my love of 1941—What sweetness he'd have shown me, tho, that I'd wished him & despaired—first love—a crush—

Later a mortal avalanche, whole mountains of homosexuality, Matterhorns of cock, Grand Canyons of asshole—weight on my melancholy head—

meanwhile I walked on Broadway imagining Infinity like a rubber ball without space beyond—what's outside?—coming home to Graham Avenue still melancholy passing the lone green hedges across the street, dreaming after the movies—)

The telephone rang at 2 A.M.—Emergency—she'd gone mad—Naomi hiding under the bed screaming bugs of Mussolini—Help! Louis! Buba![4] Fascists! Death!—the landlady frightened—old fag attendant screaming back at her—

Terror, that woke the neighbors—old ladies on the second floor recovering from menopause—all those rags between thighs, clean sheets, sorry over lost babies—husbands ashen—children sneering at Yale, or putting oil in hair at CCNY—or trembling in Montclair State Teachers College like Eugene[5]—

Her big leg crouched to her breast, hand outstretched Keep Away, wool

2. Male witches.

3. Series of breast-pocket-sized popular literature. "Sacco Vanzetti": Nicola Sacco and Bartolomeo Vanzetti were Italian American anarchists executed (1927) after a controversial seven-year murder trial in Massachusetts. "Norman Thomas": American socialist (1884–1968). "Debs": Eugene V. Debs (1855–1926), labor organizer and Socialist-party candidate for president five times. "Altgeld": John Peter Altgeld (1847–1902), governor of Illinois who supported the 1894 Pullman railway workers' strike and pardoned three people convicted in the Haymarket Riot of 1886. "Sandburg": Carl Sandburg (1878–1967), American writer. "Poe": Edgar Allan Poe (1809–1849), American poet and short-story writer.

4. Grandmother, old woman (Yiddish).

5. Ginsberg's older brother. "CCNY": City College of New York.

dress on her thighs, fur coat dragged under the bed—she barricaded herself under bedspring with suitcases.

Louis in pajamas listening to phone, frightened—do now?—Who could know?—my fault, delivering her to solitude?—sitting in the dark room on the sofa, trembling, to figure out—

He took the morning train to Lakewood, Naomi still under bed—thought he brought poison Cops—Naomi screaming—Louis what happened to your heart then? Have you been killed by Naomi's ecstasy?

Dragged her out, around the corner, a cab, forced her in with valise, but the driver left them off at drugstore. Bus stop, two hours' wait.

I lay in bed nervous in the 4-room apartment, the big bed in living room, next to Louis' desk—shaking—he came home that nite, late, told me what happened.

Naomi at the prescription counter defending herself from the enemy—racks of children's books, douche bags, aspirins, pots, blood—'Don't come near me—murderers! Keep away! Promise not to kill me!'

Louis in horror at the soda fountain—with Lakewood girlscouts—Coke addicts—nurses—busmen hung on schedule—Police from country precinct, dumbed—and a priest dreaming of pigs on an ancient cliff?

Smelling the air—Louis pointing to emptiness?—Customers vomiting their Cokes—or staring—Louis humiliated—Naomi triumphant—The Announcement of the Plot. Bus arrives, the drivers won't have them on trip to New York.

Phonecalls to Dr. Whatzis, 'She needs a rest,' The mental hospital—State Greystone Doctors—'Bring her here, Mr. Ginsberg.'

Naomi, Naomi—sweating, bulge-eyed, fat, the dress unbuttoned at one side—hair over brow, her stocking hanging evilly on her legs—screaming for a blood transfusion—one righteous hand upraised—a shoe in it—barefoot in the Pharmacy—

The enemies approach—what poisons? Tape recorders? FBI? Zhdanov[6] hiding behind the counter? Trotsky[7] mixing rat bacteria in the back of the store? Uncle Sam in Newark, plotting deathly perfumes in the Negro district? Uncle Ephraim, drunk with murder in the politician's bar, scheming of Hague?[8] Aunt Rose passing water thru the needles of the Spanish Civil War?

till the hired $35 ambulance came from Red Bank——Grabbed her arms—strapped her on the stretcher—moaning, poisoned by imaginaries, vomiting chemicals thru Jersey, begging mercy from Essex County to Morristown[9]—

And back to Greystone where she lay three years—that was the last breakthrough, delivered her to Madhouse again—

On what wards—I walked there later, oft—old catatonic ladies, gray as cloud or ash or walls—sit crooning over floorspace—Chairs—and the wrinkled hags acreep, accusing—begging my 13-year-old mercy—

'Take me home'—I went alone sometimes looking for the lost Naomi, taking Shock—and I'd say, 'No, you're crazy Mama,—Trust the Drs.'—

6. Andrei Zhdanov (1896–1948), a member of Stalin's Politburo who assisted in the purges.
7. Leon Trotsky (Lev Davidovich Bronstein, 1879–1940), Russian revolutionary and communist leader.
8. Capital of the Netherlands; site of the international courts of arbitration and justice.
9. Red Bank, Essex County, and Morristown are all places in New Jersey.

And Eugene, my brother, her elder son, away studying Law in a furnished room in Newark—
came Paterson-ward next day—and he sat on the broken-down couch in the living room—'We had to send her back to Greystone'—
—his face perplexed, so young, then eyes with tears—then crept weeping all over his face—'What for?' wail vibrating in his cheekbones, eyes closed up, high voice—Eugene's face of pain.
Him faraway, escaped to an Elevator in the Newark Library, his bottle daily milk on windowsill of $5 week furn room downtown at trolley tracks—
He worked 8 hrs. a day for $20/wk—thru Law School years—stayed by himself innocent near negro whorehouses.
Unlaid, poor virgin—writing poems about Ideals and politics letters to the editor Pat Eve News—(we both wrote, denouncing Senator Borah[1] and Isolationists—and felt mysterious toward Paterson City Hall—
I sneaked inside it once—local Moloch tower with phallus spire & cap o' ornament, strange gothic Poetry that stood on Market Street—replica Lyons' Hotel de Ville[2]—
wings, balcony & scrollwork portals, gateway to the giant city clock, secret map room full of Hawthorne—dark Debs in the Board of Tax—Rembrandt[3] smoking in the gloom—
Silent polished desks in the great committee room—Aldermen? Bd of Finance? Mosca the hairdresser aplot—Crapp the gangster issuing orders from the john—The madmen struggling over Zone, Fire, Cops & Backroom Metaphysics—we're all dead—outside by the bus stop Eugene stared thru childhood—
where the Evangelist preached madly for 3 decades, hard-haired, cracked & true to his mean Bible—chalked Prepare to Meet Thy God on civic pave—
or God is Love on the railroad overpass concrete—he raved like I would rave, the lone Evangelist—Death on City Hall—)
But Gene, young,—been Montclair Teachers College 4 years—taught half year & quit to go ahead in life—afraid of Discipline Problems—dark sex Italian students, raw girls getting laid, no English, sonnets disregarded—and he did not know much—just that he lost—
so broke his life in two and paid for Law—read huge blue books and rode the ancient elevator 13 miles away in Newark & studied up hard for the future
just found the Scream of Naomi on his failure doorstep, for the final time, Naomi gone, us lonely—home—him sitting there—
Then have some chicken soup, Eugene. The Man of Evangel wails in front of City Hall. And this year Lou has poetic loves of suburb middle age—in secret—music from his 1937 book—Sincere—he longs for beauty—
No love since Naomi screamed—since 1923?—now lost in Greystone ward—new shock for her—Electricity, following the 40 Insulin.
And Metrazol[4] had made her fat.

So that a few years later she came home again—we'd much advanced and planned—I waited for that day—my Mother again to cook &—play the

1. Senator William Edgar Borah (1865–1940), chairman of the Senate foreign relations committee, was a vigorous isolationist.
2. City hall. "Lyons": a city in east-central France.
3. A reference to Rembrandt van Rijn (1606–1669), Dutch artist famous for his effects of light and shadow. "Hawthorne": i.e., Nathaniel Hawthorne (1804–1864), American writer famous for his short stories and such novels as *The Scarlet Letter* (1850).
4. A brand of stimulant.

piano—sing at mandolin—Lung Stew, & Stenka Razin, & the communist line on the war with Finland—and Louis in debt—suspected to be poisoned money—mysterious capitalisms

—& walked down the long front hall & looked at the furniture. She never remembered it all. Some amnesia. Examined the doilies—and the dining room set was sold—

the Mahogany table—20 years love—gone to the junk man—we still had the piano—and the book of Poe—and the Mandolin, tho needed some string, dusty—

She went to the backroom to lie down in bed and ruminate, or nap, hide—I went in with her, not leave her by herself—lay in bed next to her—shades pulled, dusky, late afternoon—Louis in front room at desk, waiting—perhaps boiling chicken for supper—

'Don't be afraid of me because I'm just coming back home from the mental hospital—I'm your mother—'

Poor love, lost—a fear—I lay there—Said, 'I love you Naomi,'—stiff, next to her arm. I would have cried, was this the comfortless lone union?—Nervous, and she got up soon.

Was she ever satisfied? And—by herself sat on the new couch by the front windows, uneasy—cheek leaning on her hand—narrowing eye—at what fate that day—

Picking her tooth with her nail, lips formed an O, suspicion—thought's old worn vagina—absent sideglance of eye—some evil debt written in the wall, unpaid—& the aged breasts of Newark come near—

May have heard radio gossip thru the wires in her head, controlled by 3 big sticks left in her back by gangsters in amnesia, thru the hospital—caused pain between her shoulders—

Into her head—Roosevelt should know her case, she told me—Afraid to kill her, now, that the government knew their names—traced back to Hitler—wanted to leave Louis' house forever.

One night, sudden attack—her noise in the bathroom—like croaking up her soul—convulsions and red vomit coming out of her mouth—diarrhea water exploding from her behind—on all fours in front of the toilet—urine running between her legs—left retching on the tile floor smeared with her black feces—unfainted—

At forty, varicosed, nude, fat, doomed, hiding outside the apartment door near the elevator calling Police, yelling for her girlfriend Rose to help—

Once locked herself in with razor or iodine—could hear her cough in tears at sink—Lou broke through glass green-painted door, we pulled her out to the bedroom.

Then quiet for months that winter—walks, alone, nearby on Broadway, read Daily Worker[5]—Broke her arm, fell on icy street—

Began to scheme escape from cosmic financial murder plots—later she ran away to the Bronx to her sister Elanor. And there's another saga of late Naomi in New York.

Or thru Elanor or the Workmen's Circle,[6] where she worked, addressing envelopes, she made out—went shopping for Campbell's tomato soup—saved money Louis mailed her—

5. A New York Communist newspaper.
6. A Jewish social and cultural organization with strong pro-labor and socialist leanings.

Later she found a boyfriend, and he was a doctor—Dr. Isaac worked for National Maritime Union—now Italian bald and pudgy old doll—who was himself an orphan—but they kicked him out—Old cruelties—

Sloppier, sat around on bed or chair, in corset dreaming to herself—'I'm hot—I'm getting fat—I used to have such a beautiful figure before I went to the hospital—You should have seen me in Woodbine[7]—This in a furnished room around the NMU hall, 1943.

Looking at naked baby pictures in the magazine—baby powder advertisements, strained lamb carrots—'I will think nothing but beautiful thoughts.'

Revolving her head round and round on her neck at window light in summertime, in hypnotize, in doven-dream recall—

'I touch his cheek, I touch his cheek, he touches my lips with his hand, I think beautiful thoughts, the baby has a beautiful hand.'—

Or a No-shake of her body, disgust—some thought of Buchenwald[8]—some insulin passes thru her head—a grimace nerve shudder at Involuntary (as shudder when I piss)—bad chemical in her cortex—'No don't think of that. He's a rat.'

Naomi: 'And when we die we become an onion, a cabbage, a carrot, or a squash, a vegetable.' I come downtown from Columbia and agree. She reads the Bible, thinks beautiful thoughts all day.

'Yesterday I saw God. What did he look like? Well, in the afternoon I climbed up a ladder—he has a cheap cabin in the country, like Monroe, N.Y. the chicken farms in the wood. He was a lonely old man with a white beard.

'I cooked supper for him. I made him a nice supper—lentil soup, vegetables, bread & butter—miltz[9]—he sat down at the table and ate, he was sad.

'I told him, Look at all those fightings and killings down there, What's the matter? Why don't you put a stop to it?

'I try, he said—That's all he could do, he looked tired. He's a bachelor so long, and he likes lentil soup.'

Serving me meanwhile, a plate of cold fish—chopped raw cabbage dript with tapwater—smelly tomatoes—week-old health food—grated beets & carrots with leaky juice, warm—more and more disconsolate food—I can't eat it for nausea sometimes—the Charity of her hands stinking with Manhattan, madness, desire to please me, cold undercooked fish—pale red near the bones. Her smells—and oft naked in the room, so that I stare ahead, or turn a book ignoring her.

One time I thought she was trying to make me come lay her—flirting to herself at sink—lay back on huge bed that filled most of the room, dress up round her hips, big slash of hair, scars of operations, pancreas, belly wounds, abortions, appendix, stitching of incisions pulling down in the fat like hideous thick zippers—ragged long lips between her legs—What, even, smell of asshole? I was cold—later revolted a little, not much—seemed perhaps a good idea to try—know the Monster of the Beginning Womb—Perhaps—that way. Would she care? She needs a lover.

Yisborach, v'yistabach, v'yispoar, v'yisroman, v'yisnaseh, v'yishador, v'yishalleh, v'yishallol, sh'meh d'kudsho, b'rich hu.[1]

And Louis reestablishing himself in Paterson grimy apartment in negro

7. A borough of Cape May County in southern New Jersey.
8. A village in central Germany, site of one of the worst of World War II's Nazi concentration camps. "Doven": daven (origin unknown), pray (Yiddish).
9. Spleen.
1. A passage from the Kaddish (Aramaic).

district—living in dark rooms—but found himself a girl he later married, falling in love again—tho sere & shy—hurt with 20 years Naomi's mad idealism.

Once I came home, after longtime in N.Y., he's lonely—sitting in the bedroom, he at desk chair turned round to face me—weeps, tears in red eyes under his glasses—

That we'd left him—Gene gone strangely into army—she out on her own in N.Y., almost childish in her furnished room. So Louis walked downtown to postoffice to get mail, taught in highschool—stayed at poetry desk, forlorn—ate grief at Bickford's[2] all these years—are gone.

Eugene got out of the Army, came home changed and lone—cut off his nose in jewish operation—for years stopped girls on Broadway for cups of coffee to get laid—Went to NYU, serious there, to finish Law.—

And Gene lived with her, ate naked fishcakes, cheap, while she got crazier—He got thin, or felt helpless, Naomi striking 1920 poses at the moon, half-naked in the next bed.

bit his nails and studied—was the weird nurse-son—Next year he moved to a room near Columbia—though she wanted to live with her children—

'Listen to your mother's plea, I beg you'—Louis still sending her checks—I was in bughouse that year 8 months—my own visions unmentioned in this here Lament—

But then went half mad—Hitler in her room, she saw his mustache in the sink—afraid of Dr. Isaac now, suspecting that he was in on the Newark plot—went up to Bronx to live near Elanor's Rheumatic Heart—

And Uncle Max never got up before noon, tho Naomi at 6 A.M. was listening to the radio for spies—or searching the windowsill,

for in the empty lot downstairs, an old man creeps with his bag stuffing packages of garbage in his hanging black overcoat.

Max's sister Edie works—17 years bookkeeper at Gimbels[3]—lived downstairs in apartment house, divorced—so Edie took in Naomi on Rochambeau Ave—

Woodlawn Cemetery across the street, vast dale of graves where Poe once—Last stop on Bronx subway—lots of communists in that area.

Who enrolled for painting classes at night in Bronx Adult High School—walked alone under Van Cortlandt Elevated[4] line to class—paints Naomiisms—

Humans sitting on the grass in some Camp No-Worry summers yore—saints with droopy faces and long-ill-fitting pants, from hospital—

Brides in front of Lower East Side with short grooms—lost El trains running over the Babylonian apartment rooftops in the Bronx—

Sad paintings—but she expressed herself. Her mandolin gone, all strings broke in her head, she tried. Toward Beauty? or some old life Message?

But started kicking Elanor, and Elanor had heart trouble—came upstairs and asked her about Spydom for hours,—Elanor frazzled. Max away at office, accounting for cigar stores till at night.

'I am a great woman—am truly a beautiful soul—and because of that they (Hitler, Grandma, Hearst, the Capitalists, Franco,[5] Daily News, the '20s,

2. An inexpensive cafeteria chain.
3. A popular department store.
4. A railway line, elevated above the street, that ends/begins its run in the northwest Bronx.
5. Francisco Franco (1892–1975), a Spanish general who became dictator of Spain after its civil war (1936). "Hearst": William Randolph Hearst (1863–1951), U.S. newspaper and magazine publisher.

Mussolini, the living dead) want to shut me up—Buba's the head of a spider network—'

Kicking the girls, Edie & Elanor—Woke Edie at midnite to tell her she was a spy and Elanor a rat. Edie worked all day and couldn't take it—She was organizing the union.—And Elanor began dying, upstairs in bed.

The relatives call me up, she's getting worse—I was the only one left—Went on the subway with Eugene to see her, ate stale fish—

'My sister whispers in the radio—Louis must be in the apartment—his mother tells him what to say—LIARS!—I cooked for my two children—I played the mandolin—'

Last night the nightingale woke me / Last night when all was still / it sang in the golden moonlight / from on the wintry hill. She did.

I pushed her against the door and shouted 'DON'T KICK ELANOR!'—she stared at me—Contempt—die—disbelief her sons are so naive, so dumb—'Elanor is the worst spy! She's taking orders!'

'—No wires in the room!'—I'm yelling at her—last ditch, Eugene listening on the bed—what can he do to escape that fatal Mama—'You've been away from Louis years already—Grandma's too old to walk—'

We're all alive at once then—even me & Gene & Naomi in one mythological Cousinesque room—screaming at each other in the Forever—I in Columbia jacket, she half undressed.

I banging against her head which saw Radios, Sticks, Hitlers—the gamut of Hallucinations—for real—her own universe—no road that goes elsewhere—to my own—No America, not even a world—

That you go as all men, as Van Gogh,[6] as mad Hannah, all the same—to the last doom—Thunder, Spirits, Lightning!

I've seen your grave! O strange Naomi! My own—cracked grave! Shema Y'Israel—I am Svul Avrum[7]—you—in death?

Your last night in the darkness of the Bronx—I phonecalled—thru hospital to secret police

that came, when you and I were alone, shrieking at Elanor in my ear—who breathed hard in her own bed, got thin—

Nor will forget, the doorknock, at your fright of spies,—Law advancing, on my honor—Eternity entering the room—you running to the bathroom undressed, hiding in protest from the last heroic fate—

staring at my eyes, betrayed—the final cops of madness rescuing me—from your foot against the broken heart of Elanor,

your voice at Edie weary of Gimbels coming home to broken radio—and Louis needing a poor divorce, he wants to get married soon—Eugene dreaming, hiding at 125 St., suing negroes for money on crud furniture, defending black girls—

Protests from the bathroom—Said you were sane—dressing in a cotton robe, your shoes, then new, your purse and newspaper clippings—no—your honesty—

as you vainly made your lips more real with lipstick, looking in the mirror to see if the Insanity was Me or a carful of police.

or Grandma spying at 78—Your vision—Her climbing over the walls of

6. Vincent van Gogh (1853–1890), Dutch painter who became mentally ill in his last years and committed suicide.

7. Probably "Srul Avrum" (Yiddish), for Israel Abraham, possibly Ginsberg's Hebrew given name. "Shema Y'Israel": "Hear, O Israel" (Hebrew), the opening of the watchword of Judaism.

the cemetery with political kidnapper's bag—or what you saw on the walls of the Bronx, in pink nightgown at midnight, staring out the window on the empty lot—
Ah Rochambeau Ave.—Playground of Phantoms—last apartment in the Bronx for spies—last home for Elanor or Naomi, here these communist sisters lost their revolution—
'All right—put on your coat Mrs.—let's go—We have the wagon downstairs—you want to come with her to the station?'
The ride then—held Naomi's hand, and held her head to my breast, I'm taller—kissed her and said I did it for the best—Elanor sick—and Max with heart condition—Needs—
To me—'Why did you do this?'—'Yes Mrs., your son will have to leave you in an hour'—The Ambulance
came in a few hours—drove off at 4 A.M. to some Bellevue in the night downtown—gone to the hospital forever. I saw her led away—she waved, tears in her eyes.

Two years, after a trip to Mexico—bleak in the flat plain near Brentwood, scrub brush and grass around the unused RR train track to the crazyhouse—
new brick 20 story central building—lost on the vast lawns of madtown on Long Island—huge cities of the moon.
Asylum spreads out giant wings above the path to a minute black hole—the door—entrance thru crotch—
I went in—smelt funny—the halls again—up elevator—to a glass door on a Women's Ward—to Naomi—Two nurses buxom white—They led her out, Naomi stared—and I gaspt—She'd had a stroke—
Too thin, shrunk on her bones—age come to Naomi—now broken into white hair—loose dress on her skeleton—face sunk, old! withered—cheek of crone—
One hand stiff—heaviness of forties & menopause reduced by one heart stroke, lame now—wrinkles—a scar on her head, the lobotomy—ruin, the hand dipping downwards to death—

O Russian faced, woman on the grass, your long black hair is crowned with flowers, the mandolin is on your knees—
Communist beauty, sit here married in the summer among daisies, promised happiness at hand—
holy mother, now you smile on your love, your world is born anew, children run naked in the field spotted with dandelions,
they eat in the plum tree grove at the end of the meadow and find a cabin where a white-haired negro teaches the mystery of his rainbarrel—
blessed daughter come to America, I long to hear your voice again, remembering your mother's music, in the Song of the Natural Front[8]—
O glorious muse that bore me from the womb, gave suck first mystic life & taught me talk and music, from whose pained head I first took Vision—
Tortured and beaten in the skull—What mad hallucinations of the damned that drive me out of my own skull to seek Eternity till I find Peace for Thee, O Poetry—and for all humankind call on the Origin
Death which is the mother of the universe!—Now wear your nakedness

8. Cf. National Front—a broad political movement.

forever, white flowers in your hair, your marriage sealed behind the sky—no revolution might destroy that maidenhood—
O beautiful Garbo of my Karma—all photographs from 1920 in Camp Nicht-Gedeiget[9] here unchanged—with all the teachers from Newark—Nor Elanor be gone, nor Max await his specter—nor Louis retire from this High School—

Back! You! Naomi! Skull on you! Gaunt immortality and revolution come—small broken woman—the ashen indoor eyes of hospitals, ward grayness on skin—
'Are you a spy?' I sat at the sour table, eyes filling with tears—'Who are you? Did Louis send you?—The wires—'
in her hair, as she beat on her head—'I'm not a bad girl—don't murder me!—I hear the ceiling—I raised two children—'
Two years since I'd been there—I started to cry—She stared—nurse broke up the meeting a moment—I went into the bathroom to hide, against the toilet white walls
'The Horror' I weeping—to see her again—'The Horror'—as if she were dead thru funeral rot in—'The Horror!'
I came back she yelled more—they led her away—'You're not Allen—' I watched her face—but she passed by me, not looking—
Opened the door to the ward,—she went thru without a glance back, quiet suddenly—I stared out—she looked old—the verge of the grave—'All the Horror!'

Another year, I left N.Y.—on West Coast in Berkeley cottage dreamed of her soul—that, thru life, in what form it stood in that body, ashen or manic, gone beyond joy—
near its death—with eyes—was my own love in its form, the Naomi, my mother on earth still—sent her long letter—& wrote hymns to the mad—Work of the merciful Lord of Poetry.
that causes the broken grass to be green, or the rock to break in grass—or the Sun to be constant to earth—Sun of all sunflowers and days on bright iron bridges—what shines on old hospitals—as on my yard—
Returning from San Francisco one night, Orlovsky in my room—Whalen[1] in his peaceful chair—a telegram from Gene, Naomi dead—
Outside I bent my head to the ground under the bushes near the garage—knew she was better—
at last—not left to look on Earth alone—2 years of solitude—no one, at age nearing 60—old woman of skulls—once long-tressed Naomi of Bible—
or Ruth who wept in America—Rebecca aged in Newark—David[2] remembering his Harp, now lawyer at Yale
or Srul Avrum—Israel Abraham—myself—to sing in the wilderness toward God—O Elohim![3]—so to the end—2 days after her death I got her letter—

9. "Don't Worry" (Yiddish). "Garbo": Greta Garbo (1905–1990), popular Swedish-born Hollywood actress. "Karma": destiny (Sanskrit).
1. Philip Whalen (b. 1923), American Buddhist poet.
2. A Hebrew shepherd who pleased King Saul with his harp playing (1 Samuel 16) and who later became king of Israel. "Naomi": the Israelite mother-in-law of Ruth. "Ruth": a Moabite princess who married an Israelite. Upon his death, Ruth accompanied her mother-in-law, Naomi, to Jerusalem, where she became a righteous convert. She is an ancestor of King David. "Rebecca": the wife of Isaac, the mother of Jacob and Esau, and one of the Matriarchs.
3. Biblical name for God (Hebrew).

Strange Prophecies anew! She wrote—'The key is in the window, the key is in the sunlight at the window—I have the key—Get married Allen don't take drugs—the key is in the bars, in the sunlight in the window.

Love,
your mother'

which is Naomi—

1959 1961

From HYMMNN

IV

O mother
what have I left out
O mother
what have I forgotten
O mother
farewell
with a long black shoe
farewell
with Communist Party and a broken stocking
farewell
with six dark hairs on the wen of your breast
farewell
with your old dress and long black beard around the vagina
farewell
with your sagging belly
with your fear of Hitler
with your mouth of bad short stories
with your fingers of rotten mandolins
with your arms of fat Paterson porches
with your belly of strikes and smokestacks
with your chin of Trotsky and the Spanish War
with your voice singing for the decaying overbroken workers
with your nose of bad lay with your nose of the smell of pickles of Newark
with your eyes
with your eyes of Russia
with your eyes of no money
with your eyes of false China
with your eyes of Aunt Elanor in an oxygen tent
with your eyes of starving India
with your eyes pissing in the park
with your eyes of America taking a fall
with your eyes of your failure at the piano
with your eyes of your relatives in California
with your eyes of Ma Rainey[1] dying in an ambulance
with your eyes of Czechoslovakia attacked by robots
with your eyes going to painting class at night in the Bronx

1. Gertrude Pridgett ("Ma") Rainey (1886–1939), the first of the great African American blues singers.

with your eyes of the killer Grandma you see on the horizon from the Fire-Escape
with your eyes running naked out of the apartment screaming into the hall
with your eyes being led away by policemen to an ambulance
with your eyes strapped down on the operating table
with your eyes with the pancreas removed
with your eyes of appendix operation
with your eyes of abortion
with your eyes of ovaries removed
with your eyes of shock
with your eyes of lobotomy
with your eyes of divorce
with your eyes of stroke
with your eyes alone
with your eyes
with your eyes
with your Death full of Flowers

V

Caw caw caw crows shriek in the white sun over grave stones in Long Island[2]
Lord Lord Lord Naomi underneath this grass my halflife and my own as hers
caw caw my eye be buried in the same Ground where I stand in Angel
Lord Lord great Eye that stares on All and moves in a black cloud
caw caw strange cry of Beings flung up into sky over the waving trees
Lord Lord O Grinder of giant Beyonds my voice in a boundless field in Sheol[3]
Caw caw the call of Time rent out of foot and wing an instant in the universe
Lord Lord an echo in the sky the wind through ragged leaves the roar of memory
caw caw all years my birth a dream caw caw New York the bus the broken shoe the vast highschool caw caw all Visions of the Lord
Lord Lord Lord caw caw caw Lord Lord Lord caw caw caw Lord

Paris, December 1957–New York, 1959 1961

2. An island east of Manhattan that extends east-northeast into the Atlantic and contains the New York City boroughs of Brooklyn and Queens as well as Nassau and Suffolk counties.
3. Abode of the dead (Hebrew).

IRVING FELDMAN
b. 1928

" 'Irving Feldman?' 'Irving *Feldman*?' '*Oiving* Feldman?' " Quoting this remark from Beat celebrity Gregory Corso, who around 1962 had crashed a party at his house, the author himself wonders ironically how, under such a name as his, Irving Feldman, one can possibly aspire to the estate of poet. Corso's banter sounds misguided, especially coming from the comrade of one Allen Ginsberg. But Irving Feldman throughout his career has anyway been asking what it means for him to be a poet—asking this in poems entitled *Prometheus* as well as *Moses on Pisgah, Manhattan* as well as *The Pripet Marshes, Song* as well as *Psalm*. And here he is, praised by the urbane southern critic John Crowe Ransom ("a very sound poet"), aligned by John Hollander with Hart Crane as well as Kafka, associating himself as much with Goya as with the biblical prophets.

In November 1965, at New York's 92nd Street Y, Cynthia Ozick introduced him: "Irving Feldman is a Jewish poet. This is *not* a delimiting category. [The prophet] Micah is also a Jewish poet. . . . The word of God is not what impresses us in Feldman's Jewish poetry. Rather, it is Feldman's word *to* God. *Be*, he seems to implore or command or dare God whose being he cannot accept." In beginning his poem *To the Six Million* (1965), Feldman asks: "But who is the god rising from death?" In closing *Psalm*: "Do not deny your blessing, speak to us."

Irving Feldman was born on September 22, 1928, in Coney Island, Brooklyn, New York. He went to City College of New York and Columbia University, and has taught in Puerto Rico, France, and the United States. His wrestling with Judaic presences pervades his earlier more than his later books. Yet a couplet from *To the Six Million*—"There is someone missing. / Is it I who am missing?"—speaks a Diaspora Jew's Isaaclike sense of uneasy survivorhood that informs his work. (Richard Howard has called this plight that of a "stand-up Jewish tragic.") Feldman's later poems, whether in colloquial or charged or comic language, mix gratitude with skepticism at the variegations of "theme park America."

The poet of *The Pripet Marshes* risks sounding presumptuous, callow, sentimental in imagining himself before and during the Holocaust. The Nazistic verbs "seize" and "transport" give way to "I can be a God," and presumption dissolves in honesty: "the Pripet Marshes, which I have never seen," "I can't hold out any longer." This poem "attempts to dizzy God, to spite God, even to rival God by toying with history," Ozick said in 1965. "It is the only piece of American literature yet written which makes real for us, for *us* in our own bodies and sensibilities, what happened to *them*." At the same time, "the leap of Imagination can't carry beyond history," Feldman has said. "I find in myself no pathos, no nostalgia for a pre-Holocaust era—only bleakness and silence."

The Pripet Marshes[1]

Often I think of my Jewish friends and seize them as they are and transport them in my mind to the *shtetlach*[2] and ghettos,

And set them walking the streets, visiting, praying in *shul*,[3] feasting and dancing. The men I set to arguing, because I love dialectic and song—my ears tingle when I hear their voices—and the girls and women I set to promenading or to cooking in the kitchens, for the sake of their tiny feet and clever hands.

And put kerchiefs and long dresses on them, and some of the men I dress in black and reward with beards. And all of them I set among the mists of the Pripet Marshes, which I have never seen, among wooden build-

1. A vast marshland in Eastern Europe, covering parts of Belorussia and the Ukraine and including the cities of Minsk and Pinsk.

2. Small Jewish towns or villages of Eastern Europe (Yiddish).

3. Synagogue (Yiddish).

ings that loom up suddenly one at a time, because I have only heard of them in stories, and that long ago.

It is the moment before the Germans will arrive.

Maury is there, uncomfortable, and pigeon-toed, his voice is rapid and slurred, and he is brilliant;
And Frank who is goodhearted and has the hair and yellow skin of a Tartar[4] and is like a flame turned low;
And blonde Lottie who is coarse and miserable, her full mouth is turning down with a self-contempt she can never hide, while the steamroller of her voice flattens every delicacy;
And Marian, her long body, her face pale under her bewildered black hair and of the purest oval of those Greek signets she loves; her head tilts now like the heads of the birds she draws;
And Adele who is sullen and an orphan and so like a beaten creature she trusts no one, and who doesn't know what to do with herself, lurching with her magnificent body like a despoiled tigress;
And Munji, moping melancholy clown, arms too short for his barrel chest, his penny-whistle nose, and mocking nearsighted eyes that want to be straightforward and good;
And Abbie who, when I listen closely, is speaking to me, beautiful with her large nose and witty mouth, her coloring that always wants lavender, her vitality that body and mind can't quite master;
And my mother whose gray eyes are touched with yellow, and who is as merry as a young girl;
And my brown-eyed son who is glowing like a messenger impatient to be gone and who may stand for me.
I cannot breathe when I think of him there.
And my red-haired sisters, and all my family, our embarrassed love bantering our tenderness away.

Others, others, in crowds filling the town on a day I have made sunny for them; the streets are warm and they are at their ease.

How clearly I see them all now, how miraculously we are linked! And sometimes I make them speak Yiddish in timbres whose unfamiliarity thrills me.

But in a moment the Germans will come.

What, will Maury die? Will Marian die?

Not a one of them who is not transfigured then!

The brilliant in mind have bodies that glimmer with a total dialectic;
The stupid suffer an inward illumination; their stupidity is a subtle tenderness that glows in and around them;
The sullen are surrounded with great tortured shadows raging with pain, against whom they struggle like titans;

4. A person from Tatarstan (formerly Tatar Autonomous Soviet Socialist Republic) in east-central Russia.

In Frank's low flame I discover an enormous perspectiveless depth;
The gray of my mother's eyes dazzles me with our love;
No one is more beautiful than my red-haired sisters.
And always I imagine the least among them last, one I did not love, who was almost a stranger to me.
I can barely see her blond hair under the kerchief; her cheeks are large and faintly pitted, her raucous laugh is tinged with shame as it subsides; her bravado forces her into still another lie;
But her vulgarity is touched with a humanity I cannot exhaust, her wretched self-hatred is as radiant as the faith of Abraham, or indistinguishable from that faith.
I can never believe my eyes when this happens, and I want to kiss her hand, to exchange a blessing

In the moment when the Germans are beginning to enter the town.

But there isn't a second to lose, I snatch them all back,
For, when I want to, I can be a God.
No, the Germans won't have one of them!
This is my people, they are mine!

And I flee with them, crowd out with them; I hide myself in a pillowcase stuffed with clothing, in a woman's knotted handkerchief, in a shoebox.
And one by one I cover them in mist, I take them out.
The German motorcycles zoom through the town,
They break their fists on the hollow doors.
But I can't hold out any longer. My mind clouds over.
I sink down as through drugged[5] or beaten.

1965

Psalm

There is no singing without God.
Words sound in air, mine
are flying, their wombs empty.
Whining for the living weight, they bear
themselves, a din of echoes,
and vanish: a subsiding
noise, a flatulence, a nothing
that stinks.
The glory of man shall fly away like a bird
—no birth, no pregnancy, no conception.

A people dies intestate, its benediction
lost. And the future succeeds, unfathered,
a mute, responding to no sign,
foraging its own fields at night,

5. Originally, Feldman used the word "drunk" here. He changed it to indicate an involuntary state.

hiding by day.
Withheld in the unuttered
blessing, God labors, and is not born.

But if I enter, vanished bones
of the broken temple, lost people,
and go in the sanctum of the scattered
house, saying words like these,
forgive—my profaneness is
insufferable to me—and bless, make fertile
my words, give them a radiant burden!
Do not deny your blessing, speak to us.

1970

PHILIP LEVINE
b. 1928

Philip Levine's poetic stand is stubbornly humane, his poetic subjects, ordinary, working people like the ones he grew up with in Detroit, where he was born and raised. During World War II and through the 1950s, Levine worked in Detroit's factories—auto plants, a bottling company, a chemical factory—"in a succession of stupid jobs," which led to his resolve "to find a voice for the voiceless." That voice emerges from two resonant elements in his poetry—a gritty physical reality that is coupled with a deep spiritual reach; in the pedestrian experiences of American workers, Levine finds a complex cord of meaning. Though his poems may seem unassuming, straightforward narratives of trivial events, the steady rhythm of the verse carries the reader toward something larger. His poems gently build momentum, the run-on lines propelling the piece forward until the end, where we recognize a quiet revelation.

Unlike some other poets of his generation, Levine did not reclaim his Jewishness later in his career, nor does his Jewishness constitute a new identity for him. Rather, he has always presented it as one of many ingredients in his personal history, and it serves as a point of empathic connection to others. Writing of two years he spent in Spain, Levine notes: "I began to become a Catalan. I think half of them are Jews anyway, and they look very Jewish. They look a lot like me." In *The Sweetness of Bobby Hefka*, reprinted here, Levine tells a grade-school anecdote whose narrative, set against the backdrop of World War II, gradually probes the connections of Jews to African Americans and to other immigrant groups. In Levine's recollections of his childhood, World War II often sets into relief what it meant for him to grow up Jewish.

Neither avant-garde nor given to postmodern skepticism and irony, Levine's writing is disarmingly honest. Some critics dismiss him as sentimental, yet other writers as well as readers prize him passionately. Poet Ira Sadoff claims that "at a time when American poetry has become self-conscious, exploring the psyche almost to the point of narcissism, Philip Levine, one of our finest poets, continues to write poetry that explores the relationship between the self and the other, between personal and social worlds."

Levine received an M.F.A. from the University of Iowa in 1957 and in 1958 moved to Fresno, California, where he taught at the University of California. He has also taught at Tufts and New York University. Since his first book, *On the Edge* (1963), Levine has published sixteen volumes of poetry, among them *Ashes: Poems Old and New* (1979), which received the National Book Critics Circle Award and the first American Book Award for Poetry; *What Work Is* (1991), which won the National Book Award; and *The Simple Truth* (1994), which won the Pulitzer prize.

Zaydee[1]

Why does the sea burn? Why do the hills cry?
My grandfather opens a fresh box
of English Ovals, lights up, and lets the smoke
drift like clouds from his lips.

Where did my father go in my fifth autumn?
In the blind night of Detroit
on the front porch, Grandfather points up
at a constellation shaped like a cock and balls.

A tiny man, at 13 I outgrew his shirts.
I then beheld a closet of stolen suits,
a hive of elevator shoes, crisp hankies,
new bills in the cupboard, old in the wash.

I held the spotted hands that passed over
the breasts of airlines stewardesses,
that moved in the fields like a wind
stirring the long hairs of grain.

Where is the ocean? the flying fish?
the God who speaks from a cloud?
He carries a card table out under the moon
and plays gin rummy and cheats.

He took me up in his arms
when I couldn't walk and carried me
into the grove where the bees sang
and the stream paused forever.

He laughs in the movies, cries in the streets,
the judges in their gowns are monkeys,
the lawyers mice, a cop is a fat hand.
He holds up a strawberry and bites it.

He sings a song of freestone peaches
all in a box,
in the street he sings out Idaho potatoes
California, California oranges.

1. Grandfather (Yiddish).

He sings the months in prison,
sings salt pouring down the sunlight,
shovelling all night in the stove factory
he sings the oven breathing fire.

Where did he go when his autumn came?
He sat before the steering wheel
of the black Packard, he turned the key,
pressed the starter, and he went.

The maples blazed golden and red
a moment and then were still,
the long streets were still and the snow
swirled where I lay down to rest.

1974

On a Drawing by Flavio[1]

Above my desk
the Rabbi of Auschwitz[2]
bows his head and prays
for us all, and the earth
which long ago inhaled
his last flames turns
its face toward the light.
Outside the low trees
take the first gray shapes.
At the cost of such
death must I enter
this body again,
this body which is
itself closing on
death? Now the sun
rises above a stunning
valley, and the orchards
thrust their burning
branches into the day.
Do as you please, says
the sun without uttering
a word. But I can't.
I am this hand that
would raise itself
against the earth
and I am the earth too.
I look again and closer
at the Rabbi and at last

1. The poem is based on a drawing by Levine's friend, Italian anarchist artist Flavio Constantini, who took a photo of the Warsaw ghetto and superimposed his own drawing on top of it.

2. A notorious concentration camp in Poland during World War II.

see he has my face
that opened its eyes
so many years ago
to death. He has these
long tapering fingers
that long ago reached
for our father's hand
long gone to dirt, these
fingers that hold
hand to forearm,
forearm to hand because
that is all that God
gave us to hold.

1979

Sources

Fish scales, wet newspapers, unopened cans
of syrupy peaches, smoking tires,
houses that couldn't contain
even a single family without someone
going nuts, raping his own child
or shotgunning his wife. The oily floors
of filling stations where our cars
surrendered their lives and we called
it quits and went on foot to phone
an indifferent brother for help.
No, these are not the elements
of our lives, these are what we left
for our children to puzzle our selves
together so they might come to know
who they are.
But they won't wait.
This one has borrowed a pickup and a bag
of nails and will spend the light of day
under the California sun singing the songs
the radio lets loose and pounding together
a prefabricated barn. This one lies
back at night before a television set,
a beer in one hand, and waits for
the phone to ring him awake, for
a voice out of the night to tell him
the meaning of the names that fell
together and by which he knows himself.
Out there in the harbor of New York
is Ellis Island,[1] almost empty now

1. In upper New York Bay, this island served as the debarkation point and immigration station for millions between 1892 and 1943. It also served as a detention center for aliens and deportations until 1954.

except for the wind that will never leave.
He thinks of the little girl, her name
pinned to her dress, all she is
held in a little bag.
My distant sons,
my unborn daughters, myself, we
can go on smiling in the face
of the freezing winds that tear down
the Hudson Valley[2] and out to sea, winds
that turn our eyes to white tears, or under
the bland blue sky of this our Western
valley where you sweat until you
cannot hold your own hands. What do we have
today? A morning paper full of lies.
A voice out of nowhere that says, Keep
punching. Darkness that falls each night.
Sea winds that smell of fish scales.
Borrowed cars that won't start and if they did
would go nowhere. Names that mean Lover
of Horses, Hammer, First and Only, Last
but Not Least, Beloved of God. Each other.

1981

The Sweetness of Bobby Hefka

What do you make of little Bobby Hefka
in the 11th grade admitting to Mr. Jaslow
that he was a racist and if Mr. Jaslow
was so tolerant how come he couldn't
tolerate Bobby? The class was stunned.
"How do you feel about the Jews?"
asked my brother Eddie, menacingly.
"Oh, come on, Eddie," Bobby said,
"I thought we were friends." Mr. Jaslow
banged the desk to regain control.
"What is it about Negroes you do not like?"
he asked in his most rational voice,
which always failed to hide the fact
he was crazy as a bed bug, claiming
Capek's *RUR*[1] was far greater than *Macbeth*.
Bobby was silent for a long minute, thinking.
"Negroes frighten me," he finally said,
"they frighten my mother and father who never
saw them in Finland, they scare my brother
who's much bigger than me." Then he added

2. The area that Levine refers to is west of New York City and extends north into New York State.
1. Karel Čapek (1890–1938), Czech writer whose works often depict the dangers of technological progress. In *R.U.R.* (1920), a man constructs a robot (Čapek invented the word) which dominates and destroys him.

the one name, Joe Louis,[2] who had been
busy cutting down black and white men
no matter what their size. Mr. Jaslow
sighed with compassion. We knew that
before the class ended he'd be telling us
a great era for men and women was imminent
if only we could cross the threshold
into humanitarianism, into the ideals
of G. B. Shaw,[3] Karel Capek, and Mr. Jaslow.
I looked across the room to where Bobby
sat in the back row next to the windows.
He was still awake, his blue eyes wide.
Beyond him the dark clouds of 1945
were clustering over Linwood, the smokestack
of the power plant gave its worst
to a low sky. Lacking the patience to wait
for combat, Johnny Mooradian had quit school
a year before, and Johnny was dead on an atoll
without a name. Bobby Hefka had told the truth
—to his own shame and pride—and the rains
came on. Nothing had changed for a roomful
of 17 year olds more scared of life than death.
The last time I saw Bobby Hefka he was driving
a milk truck for Dairy Cream, he was married,
he had a little girl, he still dreamed
of going to medical school. He listened
in sorrow to what had become of me. He handed
me an icy quart bottle of milk, a gift
we both held on to for a silent moment
while the great city roared around us, the trucks
honking and racing their engines to make him move.
His eyes were wide open. Bobby Hefka loved me.

1991

2. Louis (1914–1981), the "Brown Bomber," was a world-famous African American heavyweight boxer from 1937 to 1949.

3. George Bernard Shaw (1856–1950), Irish-born comic dramatist, literary critic, and socialist propagandist.

CYNTHIA OZICK
b. 1928

"If we blow into the narrow end of the *shofar*, we will be heard far. But if we choose to be Mankind rather than Jewish and blow into the wider part, we will not be heard at all; for us America will have been in vain." In Israel in 1970, Cynthia Ozick issued this call to "build in Diaspora a permanent body of Jewish literature." To reconsecrate the English language of Jewish American writers she imagined something akin to Yiddish, which "became the instrument of our peoplehood on the European continent, and . . . a spectacular body of literature at last sprang out of it." Although Ozick did not go on holding to so strict a prescription, her writings and public statements have mainly evinced Jewish history and concerns or Judaic religion and culture. What's more, the narrow end of the shofar, the ram's horn that recalls Isaac's near-sacrifice, has served her in stories touching on the Holocaust, such as *The Shawl* and (indirectly) *Envy; or, Yiddish in America.*

Cynthia Ozick was born on April 17, 1928, and grew up in Pelham Bay, then a semirural area of the Bronx. There, her parents, Russian immigrants, tended a struggling pharmacy through the depression. Ozick "experienced a great deal of anti-Semitism in my neighborhood and school—being called a Christ-killer and all of that." She was also turned away, as a girl, from Hebrew school, but her grandmother insisted that she be let in. After graduating from New York University, she wrote a master's thesis at Ohio State on Henry James's late novels. "Besotted with the religion of literature," Ozick spent seven years trying to write a Jamesian "Work of Art," then seven more years on her first novel. *Trust* (1966) was greeted as "almost Tolstoyan . . . and her prose at intervals attains a Jamesian sonority."

It was Ozick's stories that first made her mark. *The Pagan Rabbi,* published originally in 1966, starts from a saying in *Ethics of the Fathers* that sets the love of nature below sacred study. In this tale, a brilliant young New York rabbi struggles between Moses and Pan, couples ecstatically with a wood nymph, loses his soul, and ends by hanging himself in a tree. Recalling Isaac Bashevis Singer, this fantasy appeared in Ozick's collection *The Pagan Rabbi* (1971) next to a realistic story that actually involves Singer. *Envy; or, Yiddish in America* (1969) presents an immigrant Yiddish poet named Edelshtein (based on poets such as Jacob Glatstein) who desperately seeks a translator to "lift me out of the ghetto" so that "the prayer-load that spilled upward from the mass graves should somehow survive." Meanwhile, Ostrover, a satiric version of Singer, is amply translated and published. "Ostrover's the world. A pantheist, a pagan, a goy," cries Edelshtein. "For humanity he speaks? . . . And to speak for Jews isn't to speak for humanity?"

Clearly, the endlessly vexed question of what it means to be Jewish preoccupies Ozick, especially in America and after the Holocaust. For her as a writer of fiction, this question has taken particular form in the opposition between Hellenism and Hebraism or aesthetics and morality. She cites the second commandment, "Thou shalt have no other gods before me," which prohibits making any likeness of things in heaven or earth. Even though her own work consistently pushes us and her characters toward moral distinctions, fiction writing has seemed to Ozick an idolatry, yet a necessary idolatry.

One can sense the force of this dilemma in her virtuosic metaphor making. "A darkness inside a cloud," Edelshtein calls the Yiddish language. Sometimes Ozick's metaphors become rather rich; but often they achieve a magical efficacy, as in *The Shawl*'s imagery of sound, light, and animality. And her title essay in *Metaphor and Memory* (1989) finds the revelatory Judaic—as well as literary—idea in a verse from Leviticus (19.34): "The stranger that sojourneth with you shall be unto you as the home-born among you, and you shall love him as yourself; because you were strangers in the land of Egypt." Here is "history as metaphor, memory raised to parable," Ozick says. "Without the metaphor of memory and history, we cannot imagine the life of the Other."

Ozick published several collections of essays and reviews that range tellingly over Western literature and questions of writing. Reviewing a book by Bruno Schulz, a Polish Jew gunned down by the SS in 1942, she aligns him with Kafka, Babel, Singer, and Jerzy Kosinski, and mentions Schulz's final manuscript, a novel called *The Messiah* that was lost after his death. Then years later, Ozick wrote *The Messiah of Stockholm* (1987), imagining that Schulz's manuscript has resurfaced: an obsessive Swedish critic believing himself Schulz's son announces, "*The Messiah*'s turned up! Here!" This slender redemptive thread in Ozick's phantasmagoric tale goes some way toward relieving her sense of literature as idolatry.

Along with the charged imagination and prose style that move her theological impulse, Ozick has a comic side. It emerges in *The Puttermesser Papers* (1997), wherein a female Jewish mayor of New York creates a girl golem to cleanse—not Prague, like Rabbi Loew's sixteenth-century golem, but "New York!" And Ozick has a feminist persuasion, too: "Feminism is simply another way of saying humanism."

Envy; or, Yiddish in America

Edelshtein, an American for forty years, was a ravenous reader of novels by writers "of"—he said this with a snarl—"Jewish extraction." He found them puerile, vicious, pitiable, ignorant, contemptible, above all stupid. In judging them he dug for his deepest vituperation—they were, he said, *"Amerikaner-geboren."* Spawned in America, pogroms a rumor, *mamoloshen*[1] a stranger, history a vacuum. Also many of them were still young, and had black eyes, black hair, and red beards. A few were blue-eyed, like the *cheder-yinglach* of his youth. Schoolboys. He was certain he did not envy them, but he read them like a sickness. They were reviewed and praised, and meanwhile they were considered Jews, and knew nothing. There was even a body of Gentile writers in reaction, beginning to show familiarly whetted teeth: the Jewish Intellectual Establishment was misrepresenting American letters, coloring it with an alien dye, taking it over, and so forth. Like Berlin and Vienna in the twenties. *Judenrein ist Kulturrein*[2] was Edelshtein's opinion. Take away the Jews and where, O so-called Western Civilization, is your literary culture?

For Edelshtein Western Civilization was a sore point. He had never been to Berlin, Vienna, Paris, or even London. He had been to Kiev, though, but only once, as a young boy. His father, a *melamed*,[3] had traveled there on a tutoring job and had taken him along. In Kiev they lived in the cellar of a big house owned by rich Jews, the Kirilovs. They had been born Katz, but bribed an official in order to Russify their name. Every morning he and his father would go up a green staircase to the kitchen for a breakfast of coffee and stale bread and then into the schoolroom to teach *chumash*[4] to Alexei Kirilov, a red-cheeked little boy. The younger Edelshtein would drill him while his father dozed. What had become of Alexei Kirilov? Edelshtein, a widower in New York, sixty-seven years old, a Yiddishist (so-called), a poet, could stare at anything at all—a subway car-card, a garbage can lid, a street-light—and cause the return of Alexei Kirilov's face, his bright cheeks, his Ukraine-accented Yiddish, his shelves of mechanical toys from Germany—trucks, cranes, wheelbarrows, little colored autos with awnings overhead. Only Edelshtein's father was expected to call him Alexei—everyone else, including the young Edelshtein, said Avremeleh. Avremeleh had a knack of getting things by heart. He had a golden head. Today he was a citizen of the Soviet Union. Or was he finished, dead, in the ravine at Babi Yar? Edelshtein remembered every coveted screw of the German toys. With his father he left Kiev in the spring and returned to Minsk.[5] The mud, frozen into peaks, was

1. Mother tongue (Yiddish).
2. "Jew-free is culture-free" (German).
3. Teacher (Hebrew).
4. Torah, Five Books of Moses (Hebrew).
5. A city in western Russia (now Belorussia) with a large Jewish population. "Babi Yar": a place near Kiev where over 33,000 Jews were murdered and buried in September 1941.

melting. The train carriage reeked of urine and the dirt seeped through their shoelaces into their socks.

And the language was lost, murdered. The language—a museum. Of what other language can it be said that it died a sudden and definite death, in a given decade, on a given piece of soil? Where are the speakers of ancient Etruscan? Who was the last man to write a poem in Linear B? Attrition, assimilation. Death by mystery not gas. The last Etruscan walks around inside some Sicilian. Western Civilization, that pod of muck, lingers on and on. The Sick Man of Europe[6] with his big globe-head, rotting, but at home in bed. Yiddish, a littleness, a tiny light—oh little holy light!—dead, vanished. Perished. Sent into darkness.

This was Edelshtein's subject. On this subject he lectured for a living. He swallowed scraps. Synagogues, community centers, labor unions underpaid him to suck on the bones of the dead. Smoke. He traveled from borough to borough, suburb to suburb, mourning in English the death of Yiddish. Sometimes he tried to read one or two of his poems. At the first Yiddish word the painted old ladies of the Reform Temples would begin to titter from shame, as at a stand-up television comedian. Orthodox and Conservative men fell instantly asleep. So he reconsidered, and told jokes:

> Before the war there was held a great International Esperanto Convention. It met in Geneva. Esperanto scholars, doctors of letters, learned men, came from all over the world to deliver papers on the genesis, syntax, and functionalism of Esperanto. Some spoke of the social value of an international language, others of its beauty. Every nation on earth was represented among the lecturers. All the papers were given in Esperanto. Finally the meeting was concluded, and the tired great men wandered companionably along the corridors, where at last they began to converse casually among themselves in their international language: *"Nu, vos macht a yid?"*[7]

> After the war a funeral cortège was moving slowly down a narrow street on the Lower East Side. The cars had left the parking lot behind the chapel in the Bronx and were on their way to the cemetery in Staten Island.[8] Their route took them past the newspaper offices of the last Yiddish daily left in the city. There were two editors, one to run the papers off the press and the other to look out the window. The one looking out the window saw the funeral procession passing by and called to his colleague: "Hey Mottel, print one less!"

But both Edelshtein and his audiences found the jokes worthless. Old jokes. They were not the right kind. They wanted jokes about weddings—spiral staircases, doves flying out of cages, bashful medical students—and he gave them funerals. To speak of Yiddish was to preside over a funeral. He was a rabbi who had survived his whole congregation. Those for whom his tongue was no riddle were specters.

The new Temples scared Edelshtein. He was afraid to use the word *shul*

6. The Ottoman or Turkish Empire before World War I.
7. "So what's a Jew up to?" or "So, how are you?" (Yiddish).
8. One of the boroughs of New York City, located in New York Harbor. "Lower East Side": an area of Manhattan where Jews and other immigrants settled between 1880 and 1920 and afterward. "Bronx": one of the boroughs of New York City, located north and east of Manhattan.

in these palaces—inside, vast mock-bronze Tablets, mobiles of outstretched hands rotating on a motor, gigantic dangling Tetragrammatons[9] in transparent plastic like chandeliers, platforms, altars, daises, pulpits, aisles, pews, polished-oak bins for prayerbooks printed in English with made-up new prayers in them. Everything smelled of wet plaster. Everything was new. The refreshment tables were long and luminous—he saw glazed cakes, snow-heaps of egg salad, herring, salmon, tuna, whitefish, gefilte fish, pools of sour cream, silver electric coffee urns, bowls of lemon-slices, pyramids of bread, waferlike teacups from the Black Forest,[1] Indian-brass trays of hard cheeses, golden bottles set up in rows like ninepins, great sculptured butter-birds, Hansel-and-Gretel houses of cream cheese and fruitcake, bars, butlers, fat napery, carpeting deep as honey. He learned their term for their architecture: "soaring." In one place—a flat wall of beige brick in Westchester—he read Scripture riveted on in letters fashioned from 14-karat gold molds: "And thou shalt see My back; but My face shall not be seen." Later that night he spoke in Mount Vernon,[2] and in the marble lobby afterward he heard an adolescent girl mimic his inflections. It amazed him: often he forgot he had an accent. In the train going back to Manhattan he slid into a miniature jogging doze—it was a little nest of sweetness there inside the flaps of his overcoat, and he dreamed he was in Kiev, with his father. He looked through the open schoolroom door at the smoking cheeks of Alexei Kirilov, eight years old. "Avremeleh," he called, "Avremeleh, *kum tsu mir, lebst ts' geshtorben?*"[3] He heard himself yelling in English: Thou shalt see my asshole! A belch woke him to hot fear. He was afraid he might be, unknown to himself all his life long, a secret pederast.

He had no children and only a few remote relations (a druggist cousin in White Plains, a cleaning store in-law hanging on somewhere among the blacks in Brownsville),[4] so he loitered often in Baumzweig's apartment—dirty mirrors and rusting crystal, a hazard and invitation to cracks, an abandoned exhausted corridor. Lives had passed through it and were gone. Watching Baumzweig and his wife—gray-eyed, sluggish, with a plump Polish nose—it came to him that at this age, his own and theirs, it was the same having children or not having them. Baumzweig had two sons, one married and a professor at San Diego, the other at Stanford, not yet thirty, in love with his car. The San Diego son had a son. Sometimes it seemed that it must be in deference to his childlessness that Baumzweig and his wife pretended a detachment from their offspring. The grandson's photo—a fat-lipped blond child of three or so—was wedged between two wine glasses on top of the china closet. But then it became plain that they could not imagine the lives of their children. Nor could the children imagine their lives. The parents were too helpless to explain, the sons were too impatient to explain. So they had given each other up to a common muteness. In that apartment Josh and Mickey had grown up answering in English the Yiddish of their parents.

9. The four-letter Hebrew name of God. "*Shul*": synagogue (Yiddish). "Tablets": replicas of the stone tablet engraved with the Ten Commandments that was received by Moses at Mount Sinai.
1. Known as the Schwarzwald, this tourist resort is in southwest Germany. "Gefilte fish": ground, seasoned fish made into balls or small loaves, then usually poached in stock and served cold (Yiddish).
2. A city in Westchester County, New York, north of the Bronx. "And thou shalt see . . .": cf. Exodus 33.23.
3. "Come to me, are you alive or dead?" (Yiddish).
4. A section of Brooklyn, formerly home to many immigrant Jews. "White Plains": a city in Westchester County, New York; a suburb of New York City.

Mutes. Mutations. What right had these boys to spit out the Yiddish that had bred them, and only for the sake of Western Civilization? Edelshtein knew the titles of their Ph.D. theses: literary boys, one was on Sir Gawain and the Green Knight, the other was on the novels of Carson McCullers.[5]

Baumzweig's lethargic wife was intelligent. She told Edelshtein he too had a child, also a son. "Yourself, yourself," she said. "You remember yourself when you were a little boy, and *that* little boy is the one you love, *him* you trust, *him* you bless, *him* you bring up in hope to a good manhood." She spoke a rich Yiddish, but high-pitched.

Baumzweig had a good job, a sinecure, a pension in disguise, with an office, a part-time secretary, a typewriter with Hebrew characters, ten-to-three hours. In 1910 a laxative manufacturer—a philanthropist—had founded an organization called the Yiddish-American Alliance for Letters and Social Progress. The original illustrious members were all dead—even the famous poet Yehoash[6] was said to have paid dues for a month or so—but there was a trust providing for the group's continuation, and enough money to pay for a biannual periodical in Yiddish. Baumzweig was the editor of this, but of the Alliance nothing was left, only some crumbling brown snapshots of Jews in derbies. His salary check came from the laxative manufacturer's grandson—a Republican politician, an Episcopalian. The name of the celebrated product was LUKEWARM: it was advertised as delightful to children when dissolved in lukewarm cocoa. The name of the obscure periodical was *Bitterer Yam*, Bitter Sea, but it had so few subscribers that Baumzweig's wife called it Invisible Ink. In it Baumzweig published much of his own poetry and a little of Edelshtein's. Baumzweig wrote mostly of Death, Edelshtein mostly of Love. They were both sentimentalists, but not about each other. They did not like each other, though they were close friends.

Sometimes they read aloud among the dust of empty bowls their newest poems, with an agreement beforehand not to criticize: Paula should be the critic. Carrying coffee back and forth in cloudy glasses, Baumzweig's wife said: "Oh, very nice, very nice. But so sad. Gentlemen, life is not that sad." After this she would always kiss Edelshtein on the forehead, a lazy kiss, often leaving stuck on his eyebrow a crumb of Danish: very slightly she was a slattern.

Edelshtein's friendship with Baumzweig had a ferocious secret: it was moored entirely to their agreed hatred for the man they called *der chazer*. He was named Pig because of his extraordinarily white skin, like a tissue of pale ham, and also because in the last decade he had become unbelievably famous. When they did not call him Pig they called him *shed*—Devil. They also called him Yankee Doodle. His name was Yankel Ostrover, and he was a writer of stories.

They hated him for the amazing thing that had happened to him—his fame—but this they never referred to. Instead they discussed his style: his Yiddish was impure, his sentences lacked grace and sweep, his paragraph transitions were amateur, vile. Or else they raged against his subject matter, which was insanely sexual, pornographic, paranoid, freakish—men who embraced men, women who caressed women, sodomists of every variety,

5. A popular American author whose works depict the lives of lonely people (1917–1967): "Sir Gawain and the Green Knight": a Middle English romance.

6. Pseudonym of Yehoash-Solomon Bloomgarden (1872–1927), Yiddish poet and Bible translator.

boys copulating with hens, butchers who drank blood for strength behind the knife. All the stories were set in an imaginary Polish village, Zwrdl, and by now there was almost no American literary intellectual alive who had not learned to say Zwrdl when he meant lewd. Ostrover's wife was reputed to be a high-born Polish Gentile woman from the "real" Zwrdl, the daughter in fact of a minor princeling, who did not know a word of Yiddish and read her husband's fiction falteringly, in English translation—but both Edelshtein and Baumzweig had encountered her often enough over the years, at this meeting and that, and regarded her as no more impressive than a pot of stale fish. Her Yiddish had an unpleasant gargling Galician[7] accent, her vocabulary was a thin soup—they joked that it was correct to say she spoke no Yiddish—and she mewed it like a peasant, comparing prices. She was a short square woman, a cube with low-slung udders and a flat backside. It was partly Ostrover's mockery, partly his self-advertising, that had converted her into a little princess. He would make her go into their bedroom to get a whip he claimed she had used on her bay, Romeo, trotting over her father's lands in her girlhood. Baumzweig often said this same whip was applied to the ear-lobes of Ostrover's translators, unhappy pairs of collaborators he changed from month to month, never satisfied.

Ostrover's glory was exactly in this: that he required translators. Though he wrote only in Yiddish, his fame was American, national, international. They considered him a "modern." Ostrover was free of the prison of Yiddish! Out, out—he had burst out, he was in the world of reality.

And how had he begun? The same as anybody, a columnist for one of the Yiddish dailies, a humorist, a cheap fast article-writer, a squeezer-out of real-life tales. Like anybody else, he saved up a few dollars, put a paper clip over his stories, and hired a Yiddish press to print up a hundred copies. A book. Twenty-five copies he gave to people he counted as relatives, another twenty-five he sent to enemies and rivals, the rest he kept under his bed in the original cartons. Like anybody else his literary gods were Chekhov and Tolstoy, Peretz and Sholem Aleichem.[8] From this, how did he come to *The New Yorker*, to *Playboy*, to big lecture fees, invitations to Yale and M.I.T. and Vassar, to the Midwest, to Buenos Aires, to a literary agent, to a publisher on Madison Avenue?

"He sleeps with the right translators," Paula said. Edelshtein gave out a whinny. He knew some of Ostrover's translators—a spinster hack in dresses below the knee, occasionally a certain half-mad and drunken lexicographer, college boys with a dictionary.

Thirty years ago, straight out of Poland via Tel Aviv, Ostrover crept into a toying affair with Mireleh, Edelshtein's wife. He had left Palestine during the 1939 Arab riots, not, he said, out of fear, out of integrity rather—it was a country which had turned its face against Yiddish. Yiddish was not honored in Tel Aviv or Jerusalem. In the Negev[9] it was worthless. In the God-given State of Israel they had no use for the language of the bad little interval between Canaan and now. Yiddish was inhabited by the past, the new Jews

7. From an area that has belonged to Poland, Germany, and the Ukraine. Before World War I, it had a large Jewish population.
8. Pseudonym of Sh. Rabinovitch (1859–1916), Russian Jewish author. "Chekhov": Anton Chekhov (1860–1904), Russian playwright and short-story writer. "Tolstoy": Count Leo Tolstoy (1828–1910), Russian novelist and moral reformer. "Peretz": I. L. Peretz (1852–1915), Polish Jewish writer, called the "father of modern Yiddish literature."
9. A desert region in the south of Israel.

did not want it. Mireleh liked to hear these anecdotes of how rotten it was in Israel for Yiddish and Yiddishists. In Israel the case was even lamer than in New York, thank God! There was after all a reason to live the life they lived: it was worse somewhere else. Mireleh was a tragedian. She carried herself according to her impression of how a barren woman should sit, squat, stand, eat and sleep, talked constantly of her six miscarriages, and was vindictive about Edelshtein's sperm-count. Ostrover would arrive in the rain, crunch down on the sofa, complain about the transportation from the Bronx to the West Side, and begin to woo Mireleh. He took her out to supper, to his special café, to Second Avenue vaudeville, even home to his apartment near Crotona Park to meet his little princess Pesha. Edelshtein noticed with self-curiosity that he felt no jealousy whatever, but he thought himself obliged to throw a kitchen chair at Ostrover. Ostrover had very fine teeth, his own; the chair knocked off half a lateral incisor, and Edelshtein wept at the flaw. Immediately he led Ostrover to the dentist around the corner.

The two wives, Mireleh and Pesha, seemed to be falling in love: they had dates, they went to museums and movies together, they poked one another and laughed day and night, they shared little privacies, they carried pencil-box rulers in their purses and showed each other certain hilarious measurements, they even became pregnant in the same month. Pesha had her third daughter, Mireleh her seventh miscarriage. Edelshtein was griefstricken but elated. "*My* sperm-count?" he screamed. "*Your* belly! Go fix the machine before you blame the oil!" When the dentist's bill came for Ostrover's jacket crown, Edelshtein sent it to Ostrover. At this injustice Ostrover dismissed Mireleh and forbade Pesha to go anywhere with her ever again.

About Mireleh's affair with Ostrover Edelshtein wrote the following malediction:

> *You, why do you snuff out my sons, my daughters?*
> *Worse than Mother Eve, cursed to break waters*
> *for little ones to float out upon in their tiny barks of skin,*
> *you, merciless one, cannot even bear the fruit of sin.*

It was published to much gossip in *Bitterer Yam* in the spring of that year—one point at issue being whether "snuff out" was the right term in such a watery context. (Baumzweig, a less oblique stylist, had suggested "drown.") The late Zimmerman, Edelshtein's cruelest rival, wrote in a letter to Baumzweig (which Baumzweig read on the telephone to Edelshtein):

> Who is the merciless one, after all, the barren woman who makes the house peaceful with no infantile caterwauling, or the excessively fertile poet who bears the fruit of his sin—namely his untalented verses? He bears it, but who can bear it? In one breath he runs from seas to trees. Like his ancestors the amphibians, puffed up with arrogance. Hersheleh Frog! Why did God give Hersheleh Edelshtein an unfaithful wife? To punish him for writing trash.

Around the same time Ostrover wrote a story: two women loved each other so much they mourned because they could not give birth to one another's children. Both had husbands, one virile and hearty, the other impotent, with a withered organ, a *shlimazal*.[1] They seized the idea of making a tool out of

1. An unlucky person (Yiddish).

one of the husbands: they agreed to transfer their love for each other into the man, and bear the child of their love through him. So both women turned to the virile husband, and both women conceived. But the woman who had the withered husband could not bear her child: it withered in her womb. "As it is written," Ostrover concluded, "Paradise is only for those who have already been there."

A stupid fable! Three decades later—Mireleh dead of a cancerous uterus, Pesha encrusted with royal lies in *Time* magazine (which photographed the whip)—this piece of insignificant mystification, this *pollution*, included also in Ostrover's *Complete Tales* (Kimmel & Segal, 1968), was the subject of graduate dissertations in comparative literature, as if Ostrover were Thomas Mann,[2] or even Albert Camus.[3] When all that happened was that Pesha and Mireleh had gone to the movies together now and then—and such a long time ago! All the same, Ostrover was released from the dungeon of the dailies, from *Bitterer Yam* and even seedier nullities, he was free, the outside world knew his name. And why Ostrover? Why not somebody else? Was Ostrover more gifted than Komorsky? Did he think up better stories than Horowitz? Why does the world outside pick on an Ostrover instead of an Edelshtein or even a Baumzweig? What occult knack, what craft, what crooked convergence of planets drove translators to grovel before Ostrover's naked swollen sentences with their thin little threadbare pants always pulled down? Who had discovered that Ostrover was a "modern"? His Yiddish, however fevered on itself, bloated, was still Yiddish, it was still *mamaloshen*, it still squeaked up to God with a littleness, a familiarity, an elbow-poke, it was still pieced together out of *shtetl*[4] rags, out of a baby *aleph*, a toddler *beys*[5]—so why Ostrover? Why only Ostrover? Ostrover should be the only one? Everyone else sentenced to darkness, Ostrover alone saved? Ostrover the survivor? As if hidden in the Dutch attic like that child. *His* diary, so to speak, the only documentation of what was. Like Ringelblum[6] of Warsaw. Ostrover was to be the only evidence that there was once a Yiddish tongue, a Yiddish literature? And all the others lost? Lost! Drowned. Snuffed out. Under the earth. As if never.

Edelshtein composed a letter to Ostrover's publishers:

Kimmel & Segal
244 Madison Avenue, New York City

My dear Mr. Kimmel, and very honored Mr. Segal:

I am writing to you in reference to one Y. Ostrover, whose works you are the company that places them before the public's eyes. Be kindly enough to forgive all flaws of English Expression. Undoubtedly, in the course of his business with you, you have received from Y. Ostrover, letters in English, even worse than this. (I HAVE NO TRANSLATOR!) We

2. German author who became a U.S. citizen and who, in 1929, won the Nobel prize for literature (1875–1955).
3. French author famous for his treatment of alienation, absurdity and nihilism (1913–1960). He received the 1957 Nobel prize for literature.
4. Small East European Jewish town or village (Yiddish).
5. *Aleph* and *beys* are the first two letters of the Hebrew alphabet.
6. Emmanuel Ringelblum (1900–1944), Jewish resister, social historian, and author of *Notes from the Warsaw Ghetto*.

immigrants, no matter how long already Yankified, stay inside always green and never attain to actual native writing Smoothness. For one million green writers, one Nabokov,[7] one Kosinski.[8] I mention these to show my extreme familiarness with American Literature in all Contemporaneous avatars. In your language I read, let us say, wolfishly. I regard myself as a very Keen critic, esp. concerning so-called Amer.-Jewish writers. If you would give time I could willingly explain to you many clear opinions I have concerning these Jewish-Amer. boys and girls such as (not alphabetical) Roth Philip/ Rosen Norma/ Melammed Bernie/ Friedman B. J./ Paley Grace/ Bellow Saul/ Mailer Norman. Of the latter having just read several recent works including political I would like to remind him what F. Kafka,[9] rest in peace, said to the German-speaking, already very comfortable, Jews of Prague, Czechoslovakia: "Jews of Prague! You know more Yiddish than you think!"

Perhaps, since doubtless you do not read the Jewish Press, you are not informed. Only this month all were taken by surprise! In that filthy propaganda *Sovietish Heymland*[1] which in Russia they run to show that their prisoners the Jews are not prisoners—a poem! By a 20-year-old young Russian Jewish girl! Yiddish will yet live through our young. Though I doubt it as do other pessimists. However, this is not the point! I ask you—what does the following personages mean to you, you who are Sensitive men, Intelligent, and with closely-warmed Feelings! Lyessin, Reisen, Yehoash! H. Leivik himself! Itzik Manger, Chaim Grade, Aaron Zeitlen, Jacob Glatshtein, Eliezer Greenberg! Molodowsky and Korn, ladies, gifted! Dovid Ignatov, Morris Rosenfeld, Moishe Nadir, Moishe Leib Halpern, Reuven Eisland, Mani Leib, Zisha Landau! I ask you! Frug, Peretz, Vintchevski, Bovshover, Edelshtat! Velvl Zhbarzher, Avrom Goldfaden! A. Rosenblatt! Y. Y. Schwartz, Yoisef Rollnick! These are all our glorious Yiddish poets. And if I would add to them our beautiful recent Russian brother-poets that were killed by Stalin with his pockmarks, for instance Peretz Markish, would you know any name of theirs? No! THEY HAVE NO TRANSLATORS!

Esteemed Gentlemen, you publish only one Yiddish writer, not even a Poet, only a Story-writer. I humbly submit you give serious wrong Impressions. That we have produced nothing else. I again refer to your associate Y. Ostrover. I do not intend to take away from him any possible talent by this letter, but wish to WITH VIGOROUSNESS assure you that others also exist without notice being bothered over them! I myself am the author and also publisher of four tomes of poetry: *N'shomeh un Guf, Zingen un Freyen, A Velt ohn Vint, A Shtundeh mit Shney*. To wit, "Soul and Body," "Singing and Being Happy," "A World with No Wind," "An Hour of Snow," these are my Deep-Feeling titles.

Please inform me if you will be willing to provide me with a translator for these very worthwhile pieces of hidden writings, or, to use a Hebrew Expression, "Buried Light."

Yours very deeply respectful.

7. Vladimir Nabokov (1899–1977), popular Russian-born American author (*Lolita*).
8. Jerzy Kosinski (1933–1991), popular Polish-born American author (*The Painted Bird*).
9. Franz Kafka (1883–1924), German-speaking Jewish author born in Prague.
1. Literally, "Soviet Homeland" (Yiddish), the name of a Soviet-controlled Yiddish journal.

He received an answer in the same week.

Dear Mr. Edelstein:

Thank you for your interesting and informative letter. We regret that, unfortunately, we cannot furnish you with a translator. Though your poetry may well be of the quality you claim for it, practically speaking, reputation must precede translation.

Yours sincerely.

A lie! Liars!

Dear Kimmel, dear Segal,

Did YOU, Jews without tongues, ever hear of Ostrover before you found him translated everywhere? In Yiddish he didn't exist for you! For you Yiddish has no existence! A darkness inside a cloud! Who can see it, who can hear it? The world has no ears for the prisoner! You sign yourself "Yours." You're not mine and I'm not Yours!

Sincerely.

He then began to search in earnest for a translator. Expecting little, he wrote to the spinster hack.

Esteemed Edelshtein [she replied]:

To put it as plainly as I can—a plain woman should be as plain in her words—you do not know the world of practicality, of reality. Why should you? You're a poet, an idealist. When a big magazine pays Ostrover $500, how much do I get? Maybe $75. If he takes a rest for a month and doesn't write, what then? Since he's the only one they want to print he's the only one worth translating. Suppose I translated one of your nice little love songs? Would anyone buy it? Foolishness even to ask. And if they bought it, should I slave for the $5? You don't know what I go through with Ostrover anyhow. He sits me down in his dining room, his wife brings in a samovar of tea—did you ever hear anything as pretentious as this—and sits also, watching me. She has jealous eyes. She watches my ankles, which aren't bad. Then we begin. Ostrover reads aloud the first sentence the way he wrote it, in Yiddish. I write it down, in English. Right away it starts. Pesha reads what I put down and says, "That's no good, you don't catch his idiom." Idiom! She knows! Ostrover says, "The last word sticks in my throat. Can't you do better than that? A little more robustness." We look in the dictionary, the thesaurus, we scream out different words, trying, trying. Ostrover doesn't like any of them. Suppose the word is "big." We go through huge, vast, gigantic, enormous, gargantuan, monstrous, etc., etc., etc., and finally Ostrover says—by now it's five hours later, my tonsils hurt, I can hardly stand—"all right, so let it be 'big.' Simplicity above all." Day after day like this! And for $75 is it worth it? Then after this he fires me and gets himself a college boy! Or that imbecile who cracked up over the mathematics dictionary! Until he needs me. However I get a little glory out of it. Everyone says, "There goes Ostrover's translator." In actuality I'm his pig, his stool (I mean that in both senses, I assure you). You write that he has no talent. That's your opinion, maybe you're not wrong, but let me tell you he has a talent for pressure. The way among *them* they write careless novels, hoping they'll be transformed into beautiful movies and sometimes it happens—that's how it is with him. Never mind the quality of his Yiddish, what will it turn into when it becomes English? Transformation is all he cares for—and in English he's a cripple—like, please excuse me, yourself and everyone of your generation. But Ostrover has the sense to be a suitor. He keeps all his translators in a perpetual frenzy of envy for each other, but they're just rubble and offal to him, they aren't the object of his suit. What he woos is *them*. Them! You understand me, Edelshtein? He stands on the backs of hacks to reach. I know you call me hack, and it's all right, by myself I'm what you think me, no imagination, so-so ability (I too once wanted to be a poet, but that's another life)—with Ostrover on my back I'm something else: I'm "Ostrover's translator." You think that's nothing? It's an entrance into *them*. I'm invited everywhere, I go to the same parties Ostrover goes to. Everyone looks at me and thinks I'm a bit freakish, but they say: "It's Ostrover's translator." A marriage. Pesha, that junk-heap, is less married to Ostrover than I am. Like a wife, I have the supposedly passive role. Supposedly: who knows what goes on in the bedroom? An unmarried person like myself becomes good at guessing at these matters. The same with translation. Who makes the language Ostrover is famous for? You ask: what has persuaded *them* that he's a "so-called modern"?—a sneer. Aha. *Who* has read James Joyce, Ostrover or I? I'm fifty-three years old. I wasn't born back of Hlusk[2] for nothing, I didn't go to Vassar for nothing—do you understand me? I got caught in between, so I got squeezed. Between two organisms. A cultural hermaphrodite, neither one nor the other. I have a forked tongue. When I fight for five hours to make Ostrover say "big" instead of "gargantuan," when I take out all the nice homey commas he sprinkles like a fool, when I drink his wife's stupid tea and then go home with a watery belly—*then* he's being turned into a "modern," you see? I'm the one! No one recognizes this, of course, they think it's something inside the stories themselves, when actually it's the way I dress them up and paint over them. It's all cosmetics, I'm a cosmetician, a painter, the one they pay to do the same job on the corpse in the mortuary, among *them* . . . don't, though, bore me with your criticisms. I tell you his Yiddish doesn't matter. Nobody's Yiddish matters. Whatever's in Yiddish doesn't matter.

The rest of the letter—all women are long-winded, strong-minded—he did not read. He had already seen what she was after: a little bit of money, a little bit of esteem. A miniature megalomaniac: she fancied herself the *real* Ostrover. She believed she had fashioned herself a genius out of a rag. A rag turned into a sack, was that genius? She lived out there in the light, with *them:* naturally she wouldn't waste her time on an Edelshtein. In the bleak-

2. Now Glusk, a town in Belorussia, south of Pinsk.

ness. Dark where he was. An idealist! How had this good word worked itself up in society to become an insult? A darling word nevertheless. Idealist. The difference between him and Ostrover was this: Ostrover wanted to save only himself, Edelshtein wanted to save Yiddish.

Immediately he felt he lied.

With Baumzweig and Paula he went to the 92nd Street Y[3] to hear Ostrover read. "Self-mortification," Paula said of this excursion. It was a snowy night. They had to shove their teeth into the wind, tears of suffering iced down their cheeks, the streets from the subway were Siberia. "Two Christian saints, self-flagellation," she muttered, "with chains of icicles they hit themselves." They paid for the tickets with numb fingers and sat down toward the front. Edelshtein felt paralyzed. His toes stung, prickled, then seemed diseased, grangrenous, furnace-like. The cocoon of his bed at home, the pen he kept on his night table, the first luminous line of his new poem lying there waiting to be born—*Oh that I might like a youth be struck with the blow of belief*—all at once he knew how to go on with it, what it was about and what he meant by it, the hall around him seemed preposterous, unnecessary, why was he here? Crowds, huddling, the whine of folding chairs lifted and dropped, the babble, Paula yawning next to him with squeezed and wrinkled eyelids, Baumzweig blowing his flat nose into a blue plaid handkerchief and exploding a great green flower of snot, why was he in such a place at this? What did such a place have in common with what he knew, what he felt?

Paula craned around her short neck inside a used-up skunk collar to read the frieze, mighty names, golden letters, Moses, Einstein, Maimonides, Heine.[4] Heine. Maybe Heine knew what Edelshtein knew, a convert. But these, ushers in fine jackets, skinny boys carrying books (Ostrover's), wearing them nearly, costumed for blatant bookishness, blatant sexuality, in pants crotch-snug, penciling buttocks on air, mustachioed, some hairy to the collarbone, shins and calves menacing as hammers, and girls, tunics, knees, pants, boots, little hidden sweet tongues, black-eyed. Woolly smell of piles and piles of coats. For Ostrover! The hall was full, the ushers with raised tweed wrists directed all the rest into an unseen gallery nearby: a television screen there, on which the little gray ghost of Ostrover, palpable and otherwise white as a washed pig, would soon flutter. The Y. Why? Edelshtein also lectured at Y's—Elmhurst, Eastchester, Rye, tiny platforms, lecterns too tall for him, catalogues of vexations, his sad recitations to old people. Ladies and Gentlemen, they have cut out my vocal cords, the only language I can freely and fluently address you in, my darling *mamaloshen*, surgery, dead, the operation was a success. Edelshtein's Y's were all old people's homes, convalescent factories, asylums. To himself he sang,

Why	*Farvos di Vy?*
the Y?	*Ich reyd*
Lectures	*ohn freyd*
to specters,	*un shey dim tantsen derbei,*

3. I.e., the YMHA, Young Men's Hebrew Association, on the Upper East Side of Manhattan. It is the scene of many important cultural events.
4. Heinrich Heine (1797–1856), German Jewish poet and critic. "Maimonides": i.e., Moses ben Maimon (1135–1204), Spanish Jewish philosopher, physician, and codifier of the Talmud.

aha! specters, if my tongue has no riddle for you, Ladies and Gentlemen, you are specter, wraith, phantom, I have invented you, you are my imagining, there is no one here at all, an empty chamber, a vacant valve, abandoned, desolate. Everyone gone. *Pust vi dem kalten shul mein harts*[5] (another first line left without companion-lines, fellows, followers), the cold study-house, spooks dance there. Ladies and Gentlemen, if you find my tongue a riddle, here is another riddle: How is a Jew like a giraffe? A Jew too has no vocal cords. God blighted Jew and giraffe, one in full, one by half. And no salve. Baumzweig hawked up again. Mucus the sheen of the sea. In God's Creation no thing without beauty however perverse. *Khrakeh khrakeh.*[6] Baumzweig's roar the only noise in the hall. "Shah," Paula said, *"ot kumt der shed."*[7]

Gleaming, gleaming, Ostrover stood—high, far, the stage broad, brilliant, the lectern punctilious with microphone and water pitcher. A rod of powerful light bored into his eye sockets. He had a moth-mouth as thin and dim as a chalk line, a fence of white hair erect over his ears, a cool voice.

"A new story," he announced, and spittle flashed on his lip. "It isn't obscene, so I consider it a failure."

"Devil," Paula whispered, "washed white pig, Yankee Doodle."

"Shah," Baumzweig said, *"lomir heren."*[8]

Baumzweig wanted to hear the devil, the pig! Why should anyone want to hear him? Edelshtein, a little bit deaf, hung forward. Before him, his nose nearly in it, the hair of a young girl glistened—some of the stage light had become enmeshed in it. Young, young! Everyone young! Everyone for Ostrover young! A modern.

Cautiously, slyly, Edelshtein let out, as on a rope, little bony shiverings of attentiveness. Two rows in front of him he glimpsed the spinster hack, Chaim Vorovsky the drunken lexicographer whom too much mathematics had crazed, six unknown college boys.

Ostrover's story:

> Satan appears to a bad poet. "I desire fame," says the poet, "but I cannot attain it, because I come from Zwrdl, and the only language I can write is Zwrdlish. Unfortunately no one is left in the world who can read Zwrdlish. That is my burden. Give me fame, and I will trade you my soul for it."
>
> "Are you quite sure," says Satan, "that you have estimated the dimensions of your trouble entirely correctly?" "What do you mean?" says the poet. "Perhaps," says Satan, "the trouble lies in your talent. Zwrdl or no Zwrdl, it's very weak." "Not so!" says the poet, "and I'll prove it to you. Teach me French, and in no time I'll be famous." "All right," says Satan, "as soon as I say Glup you'll know French perfectly, better than de Gaulle.[9] But I'll be generous with you. French is such an easy language, I'll take only a quarter of your soul for it."
>
> And he said Glup. And in an instant there was the poet, scribbling away in fluent French. But still no publisher in France wanted him and he

5. "My heart is empty as a cold synagogue" (Yiddish).
6. Hawking sounds made when clearing the throat.
7. "Quiet, here comes that devil" (Yiddish).
8. "Let us listen" (Yiddish).
9. Charles de Gaulle (1890–1970), French general during World War II and president of France.

remained obscure. Back came Satan: "So the French was no good, *mon vieux? Tant pis!*"[1] "Feh," says the poet, "what do you expect from a people that kept colonies, they should know what's good in the poetry line? Teach me Italian, after all even the Pope dreams in Italian." "Another quarter of your soul," says Satan, ringing it up in his portable cash register. And Glup! There he was again, the poet, writing *terza rima*[2] with such fluency and melancholy that the Pope would have been moved to holy tears of praise if only he had been able to see it in print—unfortunately every publisher in Italy sent the manuscript back with a plain rejection slip, no letter.

"What? Italian no good either?" exclaims Satan. "*Mamma mia,* why don't you believe me, little brother, it's not the language, it's you." It was the same with Swahili and Armenian, Glup!—failure, Glup!—failure, and by now, having rung up a quarter of it at a time, Satan owned the poet's entire soul, and took him back with him to the Place of Fire. "I suppose you'll burn me up," says the poet bitterly. "No, no," says Satan, "we don't go in for that sort of treatment for so silken a creature as a poet. Well? Did you bring everything? I told you to pack carefully! Not to leave behind a scrap!" "I brought my whole file," says the poet, and sure enough, there it was, strapped to his back, a big black metal cabinet. "Now empty it into the Fire," Satan orders. "My poems! Not all my poems? My whole life's output?" cries the poet in anguish. "That's right, do as I say," and the poet obeys, because, after all, he's in hell and Satan owns him. "Good," says Satan, "now come with me, I'll show you to your room."

A perfect room, perfectly appointed, not too cold, not too hot, just the right distance from the great Fire to be comfortable. A jewel of a desk, with a red leather top, a lovely swivel chair cushioned in scarlet, a scarlet Persian rug on the floor, nearby a red refrigerator stocked with cheese and pudding and pickles, a glass of reddish tea already steaming on a little red table. One window without a curtain. "That's your Inspiring View," says Satan, "look out and see." Nothing outside but the Fire cavorting splendidly, flecked with unearthly colors, turning itself and rolling up into unimaginable new forms. "It's beautiful," marvels the poet. "Exactly," says Satan. "It should inspire you to the composition of many new verses." "Yes, yes! May I begin, your Lordship?" "That's why I brought you here," says Satan. "Now sit down and write, since you can't help it anyhow. There is only one stipulation. The moment you finish a stanza you must throw it out of the window, like this." And to illustrate, he tossed out a fresh page.

Instantly a flaming wind picked it up and set it afire, drawing it into the great central conflagration. "Remember that you are in hell," Satan says sternly, "here you write only for oblivion." The poet begins to weep. "No difference, no difference! It was the same up there! O Zwrdl, I curse you

1. "My friend? Too bad!" (French).
2. An intricate rhyme scheme perfected by Dante (Italian).

> that you nurtured me!" "And still he doesn't see the point!" says Satan, exasperated. "Glup glup glup glup glup glup glup! Now write." The poor poet began to scribble, one poem after another, and lo! suddenly he forgot every word of Zwrdlish he ever knew, faster and faster he wrote, he held on to the pen as if it alone kept his legs from flying off on their own, he wrote in Dutch and in English, in German and in Turkish, in Santali and in Sassak, in Lapp and in Kurdish, in Welsh and in Rhaeto-Romanic, in Niasese and in Nicobarese, in Galcha and in Ibanag, in Ho and in Khmer, in Ro and in Volapük, in Jagatai and in Swedish, in Tulu and in Russian, in Irish and in Kalmuck! He wrote in every language but Zwrdlish, and every poem he wrote he had to throw out the window because it was trash anyhow, though he did not realize it. . . .

Edelshtein, spinning off into a furious and alien meditation, was not sure how the story ended. But it was brutal, and Satan was again in the ascendancy: he whipped down aspiration with one of Ostrover's sample aphorisms, dense and swollen as a phallus, but sterile all the same. The terrifying laughter, a sea-wave all around: it broke toward Edelshtein, meaning to lash him to bits. Laughter for Ostrover. Little jokes, little jokes, all they wanted was jokes! "Baumzweig," he said, pressing himself down across Paula's collar (under it her plump breasts), "he does it for spite, you see that?"

But Baumzweig was caught in the laughter. The edges of his mouth were beaten by it. He whirled in it like a bug. "Bastard!" he said.

"Bastard," Edelshtein said reflectively.

"He means *you,*" Baumzweig said.

"Me?"

"An allegory. You see how everything fits. . . ."

"If you write letters, you shouldn't mail them," Paula said reasonably. "It got back to him you're looking for a translator."

"He doesn't need a muse, he needs a butt. Naturally it got back to him," Baumzweig said. "That witch herself told him."

"Why me?" Edelshtein said. "It could be you."

"I'm not a jealous type," Baumzweig protested. "What he has you want." He waved over the audience: just then he looked as insignificant as a little bird.

Paula said, "You both want it."

What they both wanted now began. Homage.

Q. Mr. Ostrover, what would you say is the symbolic weight of this story?
A. The symbolic weight is, what you need you deserve. If you don't need to be knocked on the head you'll never deserve it.
Q. Sir, I'm writing a paper on you for my English class. Can you tell me please if you believe in hell?
A. Not since I got rich.
Q. How about God? Do you believe in God?
A. Exactly the way I believe in pneumonia. If you have pneumonia, you have it. If you don't, you don't.
Q. Is it true your wife is a Countess? Some people say she's really only Jewish.
A. In religion she's a transvestite, and in actuality she's a Count.
Q. Is there really such a language as Zwrdlish?

A. You're speaking it right now, it's the language of fools.
Q. What would happen if you weren't translated into English?
A. The pygmies and the Eskimos would read me instead. Nowadays to be Ostrover is to be a worldwide industry.
Q. Then why don't you write about worldwide things like wars?
A. Because I'm afraid of loud noises.
Q. What do you think of the future of Yiddish?
A. What do you think of the future of the Doberman pinscher?
Q. People say other Yiddishists envy you.
A. No, it's I who envy them. I like a quiet life.
Q. Do you keep the Sabbath?
A. Of course, didn't you notice it's gone?—I keep it hidden.
Q. And the dietary laws? Do you observe them?
A. Because of the moral situation of the world I have to. I was heartbroken to learn that the minute an oyster enters my stomach, he becomes an anti-Semite. A bowl of shrimp once started a pogrom against my intestines.

Jokes, jokes! It looked to go on for another hour. The condition of fame, a Question Period: a man can stand up forever and dribble shallow quips and everyone admires him for it. Edelshtein threw up his seat with a squeal and sneaked up the aisle to the double doors and into the lobby. On a bench, half-asleep, he saw the lexicographer. Usually he avoided him—he was a man with a past, all pasts are boring—but when he saw Vorovsky raise his leathery eyelids he went toward him.

"What's new, Chaim?"

"Nothing. Liver pains. And you?"

"Life pains. I saw you inside."

"I walked out, I hate the young."

"You weren't young, no."

"Not like these. I never laughed. Do you realize, at the age of twelve I had already mastered calculus? I practically reinvented it on my own. You haven't read Wittgenstein,[3] Hersheleh, you haven't read Heisenberg,[4] what do you know about the empire of the universe?"

Edelshtein thought to deflect him: "Was it your translation he read in there?"

"Did it sound like mine?"

"I couldn't tell."

"It was and it wasn't. Mine, improved. If you ask that ugly one, she'll say it's hers, improved. Who's really Ostrover's translator? Tell me, Hersheleh, maybe it's you. Nobody knows. It's as they say—by several hands, and all the hands are in Ostrover's pot, burning up. I would like to make a good strong b.m. on your friend Ostrover."

"*My* friend? He's not my friend."

"So why did you pay genuine money to see him? You can see him for free somewhere else, no?"

"The same applies to yourself."

3. Ludwig Wittgenstein (1889–1951), Austrian-born British philosopher of Jewish descent.
4. Werner Heisenberg (1901–1976), German theoretical physicist of quantum mechanics. He won the Nobel prize for physics in 1932.

"Youth, I brought youth."

A conversation with a madman: Vorovsky's *meshugas*[5] was to cause other people to suspect him of normality. Edelshtein let himself slide to the bench—he felt his bones accordion downward. He was in the grip of a mournful fatigue. Sitting eye to eye with Vorovsky he confronted the other's hat—a great Russian-style fur monster. A nimbus of droshky[6]-bells surrounded it, shrouds of snow. Vorovsky had a big head, with big kneaded features, except for the nose, which looked like a doll's, pink and formlessly delicate. The only sign of drunkenness was at the bulbs of the nostrils, where the cartilage was swollen, and at the tip, also swollen. Of actual madness there was, in ordinary discourse, no sign, except a tendency toward elusiveness. But it was known that Vorovsky, after compiling his dictionary, a job of seventeen years, one afternoon suddenly began to laugh, and continued laughing for six months, even in his sleep: in order to rest from laughing he had to be given sedatives, though even these could not entirely suppress his laughter. His wife died, and then his father, and he went on laughing. He lost control of his bladder, and then discovered the curative potency, for laughter, of drink. Drink cured him, but he still peed publicly, without realizing it; and even his cure was tentative and unreliable, because if he happened to hear a joke that he liked he might laugh at it for a minute or two, or, on occasion, three hours. Apparently none of Ostrover's jokes had struck home with him—he was sober and desolate-looking. Nevertheless Edelshtein noticed a large dark patch near his fly. He had wet himself, it was impossible to tell how long ago. There was no odor. Edelshtein moved his buttocks back an inch. "Youth?" he inquired.

"My niece. Twenty-three years old, my sister Ida's girl. She reads Yiddish fluently," he said proudly. "She writes."

"In Yiddish?"

"Yiddish," he spat out. "Don't be crazy, Hersheleh, who writes in Yiddish? Twenty-three years old, she should write in Yiddish? What is she, a refugee, an American girl like that? She's crazy for literature, that's all, she's like the rest in there, to her Ostrover's literature. I brought her, she wanted to be introduced."

"Introduce me," Edelshtein said craftily.

"She wants to be introduced to someone famous, where do you come in?"

"Translated I'd be famous. Listen, Chaim, a talented man like you, so many languages under your belt, why don't you give me a try? A try and a push."

"I'm no good at poetry. You should write stories if you want fame."

"I don't want fame."

"Then what are you talking about?"

"I want—" Edelshtein stopped. What did he want? "To reach," he said.

Vorovsky did not laugh. "I was educated at the University of Berlin. From Vilna to Berlin, that was 1924. Did I reach Berlin? I gave my whole life to collecting a history of the human mind, I mean expressed in mathematics. In mathematics the final and only poetry possible. Did I reach the empire of the universe? Hersheleh, if I could tell you about reaching, I would tell you this: reaching is impossible. Why? Because when you get where you wanted to reach to, that's when you realize that's not what you want to reach to.—Do

5. Craziness (Yiddish).

6. A Russian carriage.

you know what a bilingual German-English mathematical dictionary is good for?"

Edelshtein covered his knees with his hands. His knuckles glimmered up at him. Row of white skulls.

"Toilet paper," Vorovsky said. "Do you know what poems are good for? The same. And don't call me cynic, what I say isn't cynicism."

"Despair maybe," Edelshtein offered.

"Despair up your ass. I'm a happy man. I know something about laughter." He jumped up—next to the seated Edelshtein he was a giant. Fists gray, thumbnails like bone. The mob was pouring out of the doors of the auditorium. "Something else I'll tell you. Translation is no equation. If you're looking for an equation, better die first. There are no equations, equations don't happen. It's an idea like a two-headed animal, you follow me? The last time I saw an equation it was in a snapshot of myself. I looked in my own eyes, and what did I see there? I saw God in the shape of a murderer. What you should do with your poems is swallow your tongue. There's my niece, behind Ostrover like a tail. Hey Yankel!" he boomed.

The great man did not hear. Hands, arms, heads enclosed him like a fisherman's net. Baumzweig and Paula paddled through eddies, the lobby swirled. Edelshtein saw two little people, elderly, overweight, heavily dressed. He hid himself, he wanted to be lost. Let them go, let them go—

But Paula spotted him. "What happened? We thought you took sick."

"It was too hot in there."

"Come home with us, there's a bed. Instead of your own place alone."

"Thank you no. He signs autographs, look at that."

"Your jealousy will eat you up, Hersheleh."

"I'm not jealous!" Edelshtein shrieked; people turned to see. "Where's Baumzweig?"

"Shaking hands with the pig. An editor has to keep up contacts."

"A poet has to keep down vomit."

Paula considered him. Her chin dipped into her skunk ruff. "How can you vomit, Hersheleh? Pure souls have no stomachs, only ectoplasm. Maybe Ostrover's right, you have too much ambition for your size. What if your dear friend Baumzweig didn't publish you? You wouldn't know your own name. My husband doesn't mention this to you, he's a kind man, but I'm not afraid of the truth. Without him you wouldn't exist."

"With him I don't exist," Edelshtein said. "What is existence?"

"I'm not a Question Period," Paula said.

"That's all right," Edelshtein said, "because I'm an Answer Period. The answer is period. Your husband is finished, period. Also I'm finished, period. We're already dead. Whoever uses Yiddish to keep himself alive is already dead. Either you realize this or you don't realize it. I'm one who realizes."

"I tell him all the time he shouldn't bother with you. You come and you hang around."

"Your house is a gallows, mine is a gas chamber, what's the difference?"

"Don't come any more, nobody needs you."

"My philosophy exactly. We are superfluous on the face of the earth."

"You're a scoundrel."

"Your husband's a weasel, and you're the wife of a weasel."

"Pig and devil yourself."

"Mother of puppydogs." (Paula, such a good woman, the end, he would never see her again!)

He blundered away licking his tears, hitting shoulders with his shoulder, blind with the accident of his grief. A yearning all at once shouted itself in his brain:

EDELSHTEIN: Chaim, teach me to be a drunk!
VOROVSKY: First you need to be crazy.
EDELSHTEIN: Teach me to go crazy!
VOROVSKY: First you need to fail.
EDELSHTEIN: I've failed, I'm schooled in failure, I'm a master of failure!
VOROVSKY: Go back and study some more.

One wall was a mirror. In it he saw an old man crying, dragging a striped scarf like a prayer shawl. He stood and looked at himself. He wished he had been born a Gentile. Pieces of old poems littered his nostrils, he smelled the hour of their creation, his wife in bed beside him, asleep after he had rubbed her to compensate her for bitterness. *The sky is cluttered with stars of David. . . . If everything is something else, then I am something else. . . . Am I a thing and not a bird? Does my way fork though I am one? Will God take back history? Who will let me begin again. . . .*

OSTROVER: Hersheleh, I admit I insulted you, but who will know? It's only a make-believe story, a game.

EDELSHTEIN: Literature isn't a game! Literature isn't little stories!

OSTROVER: So what is it, Torah? You scream out loud like a Jew, Edelshtein. Be quiet, they'll hear you.

EDELSHTEIN: And you, Mr. Elegance, you aren't a Jew?

OSTROVER: Not at all, I'm one of *them*. You too are lured, aren't you, Hersheleh? Shakespeare is better than a shadow, Pushkin[7] is better than a pipsqueak, hah?

EDELSHTEIN: If you become a Gentile you don't automatically become a Shakespeare.

OSTROVER: Oho! A lot you know. I'll let you in on the facts, Hersheleh, because I feel we're really brothers, I feel you straining toward the core of the world. Now listen—did you ever hear of Velvl Shikkerparev? Never. A Yiddish scribbler writing romances for the Yiddish stage in the East End, I'm speaking of London, England. He finds a translator and overnight he becomes Willie Shakespeare. . . .

EDELSHTEIN: Jokes aside, is this what you advise?

OSTROVER: I would advise my own father no less. Give it up, Hersheleh, stop believing in Yiddish.

EDELSHTEIN: But I don't believe in it!

OSTROVER: You do. I see you do. It's no use talking to you, you won't let go. Tell me, Edelshtein, what language does Moses speak in the world-to-come?

EDELSHTEIN: From babyhood I know this. Hebrew on the Sabbath, on weekdays Yiddish.

7. Alexander Pushkin (1799–1837), Russian Romantic poet.

OSTROVER: Lost soul, don't make Yiddish into the Sabbath-tongue! If you believe in holiness, you're finished. Holiness is for make-believe.
EDELSHTEIN: I want to be a Gentile like you!
OSTROVER: I'm only a make-believe Gentile. This means that I play at being a Jew to satisfy them. In my village when I was a boy they used to bring in a dancing bear for the carnival, and everyone said, "It's human!"—They said this because they knew it was a bear, though it stood on two legs and waltzed. But it was a bear.

Baumzweig came to him then. "Paula and her temper. Never mind, Hersheleh, come and say hello to the big celebrity, what can you lose?" He went docilely, shook hands with Ostrover, even complimented him on his story. Ostrover was courtly, wiped his lip, let ooze a drop of ink from a slow pen, and continued autographing books. Vorovsky lingered humbly at the rim of Ostrover's circle: his head was fierce, his eyes timid; he was steering a girl by the elbow, but the girl was mooning oven an open flyleaf, where Ostrover had written his name. Edelshtein, catching a flash of letters, was startled: it was the Yiddish version she held.

"Excuse me," he said.

"My niece," Vorovsky said.

"I see you read Yiddish," Edelshtein addressed her. "In your generation a miracle."

"Hannah, before you stands H. Edelshtein the poet."

"Edelshtein?"

"Yes."

She recited, *"Little fathers, little uncles, you with your beards and glasses and curly hair. . . ."*

Edelshtein shut his lids and again wept.

"If it's the same Edelshtein?"

"The same," he croaked.

"My grandfather used to do that one all the time. It was in a book he had, *A Velt ohn Vint*.[8] But it's not possible."

"Not possible?"

"That you're still alive."

"You're right, you're right," Edelshtein said, struck. "We're all ghosts here."

"My grandfather's dead."

"Forgive him."

"*He* used to read you! And he was an old man, he died years ago, and you're still alive—"

"I'm sorry," Edelshtein said. "Maybe I was young then, I began young."

"Why do you say ghosts? Ostrover's no ghost."

"No, no," he agreed. He was afraid to offend. "Listen, I'll say the rest for you. I'll take a minute only, I promise. Listen, see if you can remember from your grandfather—"

Around him, behind him, in front of him Ostrover, Vorovsky, Baumzweig, perfumed ladies, students, the young, the young, he clawed at his wet face and declaimed, he stood like a wanton stalk in the heart of an empty field:

8. "A World with No Wind" (Yiddish).

How you spring out of the ground covered with poverty!
In your long coats, fingers rolling wax, tallow eyes.
How can I speak to you, little fathers?
You who nestled me with lyu, lyu, lyu,
lip-lullaby. Jabber of blue-eyed sailors,
how am I fallen into a stranger's womb?

Take me back with you, history has left me out.
You belong to the Angel of Death,
I to you.
Braided wraiths, smoke,
let me fall into your graves,
I have no business being your future.

He gargled, breathed, coughed, choked, tears invaded some false channel in his throat—meanwhile he swallowed up with the seizure of each bawled word this niece, this Hannah, like the rest, boots, rough full of hair, a forehead made on a Jewish last, chink eyes—

At the edge of the village a little river.
Herons tip into it pecking at their images
when the waders pass whistling like Gentiles.
The herons hang, hammocks above the sweet summer-water.
Their skulls are full of secrets, their feathers scented.
The village is so little it fits into my nostril.
The roofs shimmer tar,
the sun licks thick as cow.
No one knows what will come.
How crowded with mushrooms the forest's dark floor.

Into his ear Paula said, "Hersheleh, I apologize, come home with us, please, please, I apologize." Edelshtein gave her a push, he intended to finish. *"Littleness,"* he screamed,

I speak to you.
We are such a little huddle.
Our little hovels, out grandfather's hard hands, how little,
our little, little words,
this lullaby
sung at the tip of your grave,

he screamed.

Baumzweig said, "That's one of your old good ones, the best."

"The one on my table, in progress, is the best," Edelshtein screamed, clamor still high over his head; but he felt soft, rested, calm; he knew how patient.

Ostrover said, "That one you shouldn't throw out the window."

Vorovsky began to laugh.

"This is the dead man's poem, now you know it," Edelshtein said, looking all around, pulling at his shawl, pulling and pulling at it: this too made Vorovsky laugh.

"Hannah, better take home your uncle Chaim," Ostrover said: handsome, all white, a public genius, a feather.

Edelshtein discovered he was cheated, he had not examined the girl sufficiently.

He slept in the sons' room—bunk beds piled on each other. The top one was crowded with Paula's storage boxes. He rolled back and forth on the bottom, dreaming, jerking awake, again dreaming. Now and then, with a vomitous taste, he belched up the hot cocoa Paula had given him for reconciliation. Between the Baumzweigs and himself a private violence: lacking him, whom would they patronize? They were moralists, they needed someone to feel guilty over. Another belch. He abandoned his fine but uninnocent dream—young, he was kissing Alexei's cheeks like ripe peaches, he drew away . . . it was not Alexei, it was a girl, Vorovsky's niece. After the kiss she slowly tore the pages of a book until it snowed paper, black bits of alphabet, white bits of empty margin. Paula's snore traveled down the hall to him. He writhed out of bed and groped for a lamp. With it he lit up a decrepit table covered with ancient fragile model airplanes. Some had rubber-band propellers, some were papered over a skeleton of balsa-wood ribs. A game of Monopoly lay under a samite[9] tissue of dust. His hand fell on two old envelopes, one already browning, and without hesitation he pulled the letters out and read them:

> Today was two special holidays in one, Camp Day and Sacco and Vanzetti[1] Day. We had to put on white shirts and white shorts and go to the casino to hear Chaver[2] Rosenbloom talk about Sacco and Vanzetti. They were a couple of Italians who were killed for loving the poor. Chaver Rosenbloom cried, and so did Mickey but I didn't. Mickey keeps forgetting to wipe himself in the toilet but I make him.

> Paula and Ben: thanks so much for the little knitted suit and the clown rattle. The box was a bit smashed in but the rattle came safe anyhow. Stevie will look adorable in his new blue suit when he gets big enough for it. He already seems to like the duck on the collar. It will keep him good and warm too. Josh has been working very hard these days preparing for a course in the American Novel and asks me to tell you he'll write as soon as he can. We all send love, and Stevie sends a kiss for Grandma and Pa. *P. S.* Mickey drove down in a pink Mercedes last week. We all had quite a chat and told him he should settle down!

Heroes, martyrdom, a baby. Hatred for these letters made his eyelids quiver. Ordinariness. Everything a routine. Whatever man touches becomes banal like man. Animals don't contaminate nature. Only man the corrupter, the anti-divinity. All other species live within the pulse of nature. He despised these ceremonies and rattles and turds and kisses. The pointlessness of their babies. Wipe one generation's ass for the sake of wiping another generation's ass: this was his whole definition of civilization. He pushed back the airplanes, cleared a front patch of table with his elbow, found his pen, wrote:

9. Heavy silk fabric.
1. Nicola Sacco and Bartolomeo Vanzetti were Italian-born American anarchists executed in 1927 after their controversial murder trial that lasted for seven years in Massachusetts.
2. Comrade (Yiddish).

Dear Niece of Vorovsky:

It is very strange to me to feel I become a Smasher, I who was born to being humane and filled with love for our darling Human Race.

But nausea for his shadowy English, which he pursued in dread, passion, bewilderment, feebleness, overcame him. He started again in his own tongue—

Unknown Hannah:

I am a man writing you in a room of the house of another man. He and I are secret enemies, so under his roof it is difficult to write the truth. Yet I swear to you I will speak these words with my heart's whole honesty. I do not remember either your face or your body. Vaguely your angry voice. To me you are an abstraction. I ask whether the ancients had any physical representation of the Future, a goddess Futura, so to speak. Presumably she would have blank eyes, like Justice. It is an incarnation of the Future to whom this letter is addressed. Writing to the Future one does not expect an answer. The Future is an oracle for whose voice one cannot wait in inaction. One must do to be. Although a Nihilist,[3] not by choice but by conviction, I discover in myself an unwillingness to despise survival. Often I have spat on myself for having survived the death-camps—survived them drinking tea in New York!—but today when I heard carried on your tongue some old syllables of mine I was again wheedled into tolerance of survival. The sound of a dead language on a live girl's tongue! That baby should follow baby is God's trick on us, but surely we too can have a trick on God? If we fabricate with our syllables an immortality passed from the spines of the old to the shoulders of the young, even God cannot spite it. If the prayer-load that spilled upward from the mass graves should somehow survive! If not the thicket of lamentation itself, then the language on which it rode. Hannah, youth itself is nothing unless it keeps its promise to grow old. Grow old in Yiddish, Hannah, and carry fathers and uncles into the future with you. Do this. You, one in ten thousand maybe, who were born with the gift of Yiddish in your mouth, the alphabet of Yiddish in your palm, don't make ash of these! A little while ago there were twelve million people—not including babies—who lived inside this tongue, and now what is left? A language that never had a territory except Jewish mouths, and half the Jewish mouths on earth already stopped up with German worms. The rest jabber Russian, English, Spanish, God knows what. Fifty years ago my mother lived in Russia and spoke only broken Russian, but her Yiddish was like silk. In Israel they give the language of Solomon to machinists. Rejoice—in Solomon's time what else did the mechanics speak? Yet whoever forgets Yiddish courts amnesia of history. Mourn—the forgetting has already happened. A thousand years of our travail forgotten. Here and there a word left for vaudeville jokes. Yiddish, I call on you to choose! Yiddish! Choose death or death. Which is to say death through forgetting or death through translation. Who will redeem you? What act of salvation

3. One who rejects all religious and moral principles or believes that nothing has real existence.

> will restore you? All you can hope for, you tattered, you withered, is translation in America! Hannah, you have a strong mouth, made to carry the future—

But he knew he lied, lied, lied. A truthful intention is not enough. Oratory and declamation. A speech. A lecture. He felt himself an obscenity. What did the death of Jews have to do with his own troubles? His cry was ego and more ego. His own stew, foul. Whoever mourns the dead mourns himself. He wanted someone to read his poems, no one could read his poems. Filth and exploitation to throw in history. As if a dumb man should blame the ears that cannot hear him.

He turned the paper over and wrote in big letters:

EDELSHTEIN GONE,

and went down the corridor with it in pursuit of Paula's snore. Taken without ridicule a pleasant riverside noise. Bird. More cow to the sight: the connubial bed, under his gaze, gnarled and lumped—in it this old male and this old female. He was surprised on such a cold night they slept with only one blanket, gauzy cotton. They lay like a pair of kingdoms in summer. Long ago they had been at war, now they were exhausted into downy truce. Hair all over Baumzweig. Even his leg-hairs gone white. Nightstands, a pair of them, on either side of the bed, heaped with papers, books, magazines, lampshades sticking up out of all that like figurines on a prow—the bedroom was Baumzweig's second office. Towers of back issues on the floor. On the dresser a typewriter besieged by Paula's toilet water bottles and face powder. Fragrance mixed with urinous hints. Edelshtein went on looking at the sleepers. How reduced they seemed, each breath a little demand for more, more, more, a shudder of jowls; how they heaved a knee, a thumb; the tiny blue veins all over Paula's neck. Her nightgown was stretched away and he saw that her breasts had dropped sidewise and, though still very fat, hung in pitiful creased bags of mole-dappled skin. Baumzweig wore only his underwear: his thighs were full of picked sores.

He put EDELSHTEIN GONE between their heads. Then he took it away—on the other side was his real message: secret enemies. He folded the sheet inside his coat pocket and squeezed into his shoes. Cowardly. Pity for breathing carrion. All pity is self-pity. Goethe on his deathbed: more light!

In the street he felt liberated. A voyager. Snow was still falling, though more lightly than before, a night-colored blue. A veil of snow revolved in front of him, turning him around. He stumbled into a drift, a magnificent bluish pile slanted upward. Wetness pierced his feet like a surge of cold blood. Beneath the immaculate lifted slope he struck stone—the stair of a stoop. He remembered his old home, the hill of snow behind the study-house, the smoky fire, his father swaying nearly into the black fire and chanting, one big duck, the stupid one, sliding on the ice. His mother's neck too was finely veined and secretly, sweetly, luxuriantly odorous. Deeply and gravely he wished he had worn galoshes—no one reminds a widower. His shoes were infernos of cold, his toes dead blocks. Himself the only life in the street, not even a cat. The veil moved against him, turning, and beat on his pupils. Along the curb cars squatted under humps of snow, blue-backed tortoises. Nothing moved in the road. His own house was far, Vorovsky's nearer, but he could not read the street sign. A building with a canopy. Vorovsky's hat. He made himself very small, small as a mouse, and curled himself up in the fur of it. To be very, very little and to live in a hat. A little wild creature in a burrow. Inside warm, a mound of seeds nearby, licking himself for cleanliness, all sorts of weather leaping down. His glasses fell from his face and with an odd tiny crack hit the lid of a garbage can. He took off one glove and felt for them in the snow. When he found them he marveled at how the frames burned. Suppose a funeral on a night like this, how would they open the earth? His glasses were slippery as icicles when he put them on again. A crystal spectrum delighted him, but he could not see the passageway, or if there was a canopy. What he wanted from Vorovsky was Hannah.

There was no elevator. Vorovsky lived on the top floor, very high up. From his windows you could look out and see people so tiny they became patterns. It was a different building, not this one. He went down three fake-marble steps and saw a door. It was open: inside was a big black room knobby with baby carriages and tricycles. He smelled wet metal like a toothpain: life! Peretz tells how on a bitter night a Jew outside the window envied peasants swigging vodka in a hovel—friends in their prime and warm before the fire. Carriages and tricycles, instruments of Diaspora. Baumzweig with his picked sores was once also a baby. In the Diaspora the birth of a Jew increases nobody's population, the death of a Jew has no meaning. Anonymous. To have died among the martyrs—solidarity at least, a passage into history, one of the marked ones, *kiddush ha-shem*.[4]—A telephone on the wall. He pulled off his glasses, all clouded over, and took out a pad with numbers in it and dialed.

"Ostrover?"

"Who is this?"

"*Yankel* Ostrover, the writer, or Pisher Ostrover the plumber?"

"What do you want?"

"To leave evidence," Edelshtein howled.

"Never mind! Make an end! Who's there?"

"The Messiah."

"Who is this?—Mendel, it's you?"

"Never."

"Gorochov?"

"That toenail? Please. Trust me."

"Fall into a hole!"

"This is how a man addresses his Redeemer?"

"It's five o'clock in the morning! What do you want? Bum! Lunatic! Cholera! Black year! Plague! Poisoner! Strangler!"

"You think you'll last longer than your shroud, Ostrover? Your sentences are an abomination, your style is like a pump, a pimp has a sweeter tongue—"

"Angel of Death!"

He dialed Vorovsky but there was no answer.

The snow had turned white as the white of an eye. He wandered toward

4. The sanctification of God; martyrdom (Hebrew).

Hannah's house, though he did not know where she lived, or what her name was, or whether he had ever seen her. On the way he rehearsed what he would say to her. But this was not satisfactory, he could lecture but not speak into a face. He bled to retrieve her face. He was in pursuit of her, she was his destination. Why? What does a man look for, what does he need? What can a man retrieve? Can the future retrieve the past? And if retrieve, how redeem? His shoes streamed. Each step was a pond. The herons in spring, red-legged. Secret eyes they have: the eyes of birds—frightening. Too open. The riddle of openness. His feet poured rivers. Cold, cold.

Little old man in the cold,
come hop up on the stove,
your wife will give you a crust with jam.
Thank you, muse, for this little psalm.

He belched. His stomach was unwell. Indigestion? A heart attack? He wiggled the fingers of his left hand: though frozen they tingled. Heart. Maybe only ulcer. Cancer, like Mireleh? In a narrow bed he missed his wife. How much longer could he expect to live? An unmarked grave. Who would know he had ever been alive? He had no descendants, his grandchildren were imaginary. *O my unborn grandson* . . . Hackneyed. *Ungrandfathered ghost* . . . Too baroque. Simplicity, purity, truthfulness.

He wrote:

Dear Hannah:

You made no impression on me. When I wrote you before at Baumzweig's I lied. I saw you for a second in a public place, so what? Holding a Yiddish book. A young face on top of a Yiddish book. Nothing else. For me this is worth no somersault. Ostrover's vomit!—that popularizer, vulgarian, panderer to people who have lost the memory of peoplehood. A thousand times a pimp. Your uncle Chaim said about you: "She writes." A pity on his judgment. Writes! Writes! Potatoes in a sack! Another one! What do you write? When will you write? How will you write? Either you'll become an editor of *Good Housekeeping*, or, if serious, join the gang of so-called Jewish novelists. I've sniffed them all, I'm intimate with their smell. Satirists they call themselves. Picking at their crotches. What do they *know*, I mean of *knowledge*? To satirize you have to know something. In a so-called novel by a so-called Jewish novelist ("*activist-existential*"—listen, I understand, I read everything!)—Elkin, Stanley, to keep to only one example—the hero visits Williamsburg[5] to contact a so-called "miracle rabbi." Even the word *rabbi*! No, listen—to me, a descendant of the Vilna Gaon[6] myself, the *guter yid* is a charlatan and his *chasidim*[7] are victims, never mind if willing or not. But that's not the point. You have to KNOW SOMETHING! At least the difference between a *rav* and a *rebbeh*![8] At least a *pinteleh*[9] here and

5. A section of Brooklyn where Orthodox Jews congregate. "Elkin, Stanley": Jewish American comic novelist (1930–1995).
6. Elijah ben Solomon (1720–1797), revered Lithuanian Jewish scholar and a vigorous opponent of Hasidism.
7. I.e., Hasidim, followers of Jewish mystical movement. *"Guter yid"*: good Jew (Yiddish).
8. A Hasidic rabbi, a learned man. *"Rav"*: an Orthodox (non-Hasidic) rabbi.
9. A little point, a dot; the least little bit of Jewish learning a Jew should have (Yiddish).

> there! Otherwise where's the joke, where's the satire, where's the mockery? American-born! An ignoramus mocks only himself. *Jewish* novelists! Savages! The allrightnik's[1] children, all they know is to curse the allrightnik! Their Yiddish! One word here, one word there. *Shikseh*[2] on one page, *putz*[3] on the other, and that's the whole vocabulary! And when they give a try at phonetic rendition! Darling God! If they had mothers and fathers, they crawled out of the swamps. Their grandparents were tree-squirrels if that's how they held their mouths. They know ten words for, excuse me, penis, and when it comes to a word for learning they're impotent!

Joy, joy! He felt himself on the right course at last. Daylight was coming, a yellow elephant rocked silently by in the road. A little light burned eternally on its tusk. He let it slide past, he stood up to the knees in the river at home, whirling with joy. He wrote:

TRUTH!

But this great thick word, Truth!, was too harsh, oaken; with his finger in the snow he crossed it out.

> I was saying: indifference. I'm indifferent to you and your kind. Why should I think you're another species, something better? Because you knew a shred of a thread of a poem of mine? Ha! I was seduced by my own vanity. I have a foolish tendency to make symbols out of glimpses. My poor wife, peace on her, used to ridicule me for this. Riding in the subway once I saw a beautiful child, a boy about twelve. A Puerto Rican, dusky, yet he had cheeks like pomegranates. I once knew, in Kiev, a child who looked like that. I admit to it. A portrait under the skin of my eyes. The love of a man for a boy. Why not confess it? Is it against the nature of man to rejoice in beauty? "This is to be expected with a childless man"—my wife's verdict. That what I wanted was a son. Take this as a complete explanation: if an ordinary person cannot

The end of the sentence flew like a leaf out of his mind . . . it was turning into a quarrel with Mireleh. Who quarrels with the dead? He wrote:

> Esteemed Alexei Yosifovitch:
>
> You remain. You remain. An illumination. More than my own home, nearer than my mother's mouth. Nimbus. Your father slapped my father. You were never told. Because I kissed you on the green stairs. The shadow-place on the landing where I once saw the butler scratch his pants. They sent us away shamed. My father and I, into the mud.

Again a lie. Never near the child. Lying is like a vitamin, it has to fortify everything. Only through the doorway, looking, looking. The gleaming face: the face of flame. Or would test him on verb-forms: *kal, nifal, piel, pual, hifil, hofal, hispael.*[4] On the afternoons the Latin tutor came, crouched outside the threshold, Edelshtein heard *ego, mei, mihi, me, me.*

1. A Jewish immigrant who has done all right in America.
2. A Gentile woman.
3. Penis (Yiddish slang).
4. Hebrew verb forms.

May may. Beautiful foreign nasal chant of riches. Latin! Dirty from the lips of idolators. An apostate family. Edelshtein and his father took their coffee and bread, but otherwise lived on boiled eggs: the elder Kirilov one day brought home with him the *mashgiach*[5] from the Jewish poorhouse to testify to the purity of the servants' kitchen, but to Edelshtein's father the whole house was *treyf*,[6] the *mashgiach* himself a hired impostor. Who would oversee the overseer? Among the Kirilovs with their lying name money was the best overseer. Money saw to everything. Though they had their particular talent. Mechanical. Alexei Y. Kirilov, engineer. Bridges, towers. Consultant to Cairo. Builder of the Aswan Dam,[7] assistant to Pharaoh for the latest Pyramid. To set down such a fantasy about such an important Soviet brain . . . poor little Alexei, Avremeleh, I'll jeopardize your position in life, little corpse of Babi Yar.

Only focus. Hersh! Scion of the Vilna Gaon! Prince of rationality! Pay attention!

He wrote:

> The gait—the prance, the hobble—of Yiddish is not the same as the gait of English. A big headache for a translator probably. In Yiddish you use more words than in English. Nobody believes it but it's true. Another big problem is form. The moderns take the old forms and fill them up with mockery, love, drama, satire, etc. Plenty of play. But STILL THE SAME OLD FORMS, conventions left over from the last century even. It doesn't matter who denies this, out of pride: it's true. Pour in symbolism, impressionism, be complex, be subtle, be daring, take risks, break your teeth—whatever you do, it still comes out Yiddish. *Mamaloshen* doesn't produce *Wastelands*.[8] No alienation, no nihilism, no dadaism. With all the suffering no smashing! No INCOHERENCE! Keep the latter in mind, Hannah, if you expect to make progress. Also: please remember that when a goy from Columbus, Ohio, says "Elijah the Prophet" he's not talking about *Eliohu hanovi*. Eliohu is one of us, a *folksmensh*,[9] running around in second-hand clothes. Theirs is God knows what. The same biblical figure, with exactly the same history, once he puts on a name from King James, COMES OUT A DIFFERENT PERSON. Life, history, hope, tragedy, they don't come out even. They talk Bible Lands, with us it's *eretz yisroel*.[1] A misfortune.

Astonished, he struck up against a kiosk. A telephone! On a street corner! He had to drag the door open, pulling a load of snow. Then he squeezed inside. His fingers were sticks. Never mind the pad, he forgot even where the pocket was. In his coat? Jacket? Pants? With one stick he dialed Vorovsky's number: from memory.

"Hello, Chaim?"

"This is Ostrover."

"Ostrover! Why Ostrover? What are you doing there? I want Vorovsky."

"Who's this?"

5. Supervisor (Hebrew).
6. Not kosher.
7. The dam spanning the Nile River in Egypt; built between 1898 and 1902.
8. I.e., great poems such as T. S. Eliot's *The Waste Land* (1922).
9. Man of the people (Yiddish). "Dadaism": an early 20th-century movement in the arts that was based on the deliberately irrational and on the negation of traditional values. "Goy": a non-Jew (Hebrew).
1. The land of Israel (Yiddish).

"Edelshtein."

"I thought so. A persecution, what is this? I could send you to jail for tricks like before—"

"Quick, give me Vorovsky."

"I'll *give* you."

"Vorovsky's not home?"

"How do I know if Vorovsky's home? It's dawn, go ask Vorovsky!"

Edelshtein grew weak: "I called the wrong number."

"Hersheleh, if you want some friendly advice you'll listen to me. I can get you jobs at fancy out-of-town country clubs, Miami Florida included, plenty of speeches your own style, only what they need is rational lecturers not lunatics. If you carry on like tonight you'll lose what you have."

"I don't have anything."

"Accept life, Edelshtein."

"Dead man, I appreciate your guidance."

"Yesterday I heard from Hollywood, they're making a movie from one of my stories. So now tell me again who's dead."

"The puppet the ventriloquist holds in his lap. A piece of log. It's somebody else's language and the dead doll sits there."

"Wit, you want them to make movies in Yiddish now?"

"In Talmud[2] if you save a single life it's as if you saved the world. And if you save a language? Worlds maybe. Galaxies. The whole universe."

"Hersheleh, the God of the Jews made a mistake when he didn't have a son, it would be a good occupation for you."

"Instead I'll be an extra in your movie. If they shoot the *shtetl* on location in Kansas send me expense money. I'll come and be local color for you. I'll put on my *shtreiml*[3] and walk around, the people should see a real Jew. For ten dollars more I'll even speak *mamaloshen*."

Ostrover said, "It doesn't matter what you speak, envy sounds the same in all languages."

Edelshtein said, "Once there was a ghost who thought he was still alive. You know what happened to him? He got up one morning and began to shave and he cut himself. And there was no blood. No blood at all. And he still didn't believe it, so he looked in the mirror to see. And there was no reflection, no sign of himself. He wasn't there. But he still didn't believe it, so he began to scream, but there was no sound, no sound at all—"

There was no sound from the telephone. He let it dangle and rock.

He looked for the pad. Diligently he consulted himself: pants cuffs have a way of catching necessary objects. The number had fallen out of his body. Off his skin. He needed Vorovsky because he needed Hannah. Worthwhile maybe to telephone Baumzweig for Vorovsky's number, Paula could look it up—Baumzweig's number he knew by heart, no mistake. He had singled out his need. Svengali, Pygmalion, Rasputin, Dr. (jokes aside) Frankenstein.[4]

2. Rabbinic commentary on the Torah.
3. A hat worn by Orthodox Jewish men.
4. In Mary Shelley's novel *Frankenstein*, the doctor is the creator of a monster who eventually destroys him. The name has popularly become attached to the monster himself. "Svengali": the evil hypnotist in the novel *Trilby* (1894) by George du Maurier; he forces others to do his bidding. "Pygmalion": in Ovid's *Metamorphoses* (8 C.E.), the sculptor who creates a statue of the ideal woman and then falls in love with it. "Rasputin": Grigory Yefimovich Rasputin (ca. 1872–1916) was a Siberian peasant and mystic who was very influential at the Russian court from 1905 on, despite his womanizing.

What does it require to make a translator? A secondary occupation. Parasitic. But your own creature. Take this girl Hannah and train her. His alone. American-born but she had the advantage over him, English being no worm on her palate; also she could read his words in the original. Niece of a vanquished mind—still, genes are in reality God, and if Vorovsky had a little talent for translation why not the niece?—Or the other. Russia. The one in the Soviet Union who wrote two stanzas in Yiddish. In Yiddish! And only twenty! Born 1948, same year they made up to be the Doctors' Plot,[5] Stalin already very busy killing Jews, Markish, Kvitko, Kushnirov, Hofshtein, Mikhoels, Susskin, Bergelson, Feffer, Gradzenski with the wooden leg. All slaughtered. How did Yiddish survive in the mouth of that girl? Nurtured in secret. Taught by an obsessed grandfather, a crazy uncle: Marranos.[6] The poem reprinted, as they say, in the West. (The West! If a Jew says "the West," he sounds like an imbecile. In a puddle what's West, what's East?) Flowers, blue sky, she yearns for the end of winter: very nice. A zero, and received like a prodigy! An aberration! A miracle! Because composed in the lost tongue. As if some Neapolitan child suddenly begins to prattle in Latin. Not the same. Little verses merely. Death confers awe. Russian: its richness, directness. For "iron" and "weapon" the same word. A *thick* language, a world-language. He visualized himself translated into Russian, covertly, by the Marranos' daughter. To be circulated, in typescript, underground: to be read, read!

> Understand me, Hannah—that our treasure-tongue is derived from strangers means nothing. 90 per cent German roots, 10 per cent Slavic: irrelevant. The Hebrew take for granted without percentages. We are a people who have known how to forge the language of need out of the language of necessity. Our reputation among ourselves as a nation of scholars is mostly empty. In actuality we are a mob of working people, laborers, hewers of wood, believe me. Leivik, our chief poet, was a house painter. Today all pharmacists, lawyers, accountants, haberdashers, but tickle the lawyer and you'll see his grandfather sawed wood for a living. That's how it is with us. Nowadays the Jew is forgetful, everybody with a profession, every Jewish boy a professor—justice seems less urgent. Most don't realize this quiet time is only another Interim. Always, like in a terrible Wagnerian storm,[7] we have our interludes of rest. So now. Once we were slaves, now we are free men, remember the bread of affliction. But listen. Whoever cries Justice! is a liberated slave. Whoever honors Work is a liberated slave. They accuse Yiddish literature of sentimentality in this connection. Very good, true. True, so be it! A dwarf at a sewing machine can afford a little loosening of the heart. I return to Leivik. He could hang wallpaper. I once lived in a room he papered—yellow vines. Rutgers Street that was. A good job, no bubbles, no peeling. This from a poet of very morbid tendencies. Mani Leib fixed shoes. Moishe Leib Halpern[8] was a waiter, once in a while a handyman. I could

5. An anti-Jewish propaganda episode under Stalin in 1953 in which nine prominent doctors, most of them Jewish, were accused of murdering by medical means two members of the Politburo, A. A. Zhdanov and A. S. Scherbakov.

6. Jews ostensibly converted to Christianity, especially after the Spanish Inquisition.

7. Richard Wagner (1813–1883) was a German opera composer who was noted for (among other things) his larger-than-life musical effects.

8. H. Leivik (1888–1962), Mani Leib (1883–1953), and Moishe Leib Halpern (1886–1932) were popular American Yiddish poets.

tell you the names of twenty poets of very pure expression who were operators, pressers, cutters. In addition to fixing shoes Mani Leib was also a laundryman. I beg you not to think I'm preaching Socialism. To my mind politics is dung. What I mean is something else: Work is Work, and Thought is Thought. Politics tries to mix these up, Socialism especially. The language of a hard-pressed people works under the laws of purity, dividing the Commanded from the Profane. I remember one of my old teachers. He used to take attendance every day and he gave his occupation to the taxing council as "attendance-taker"—so that he wouldn't be getting paid for teaching Torah. This with five pupils, all living in his house and fed by his wife! Call it splitting a hair if you want, but it's the hair of a head that distinguished between the necessary and the merely needed. People who believe that Yiddish is, as they like to say, "richly intermixed," and that in Yiddishkeit the presence of the Covenant,[9] of Godliness, inhabits humble things and humble words, are under a delusion or a deception. The slave knows exactly when he belongs to God and when to the oppressor. The liberated slave who is not forgetful and can remember when he himself was an artifact, knows exactly the difference between God and an artifact. A language also knows whom it is serving at each moment. I am feeling very cold right now. Of course you see that when I say liberated I mean self-liberated. Moses not Lincoln, not Franz Josef.[1] Yiddish is the language of auto-emancipation. Theodor Herzl[2] wrote in German but the message spread in *mamaloshen*—my God cold. Naturally the important thing is to stick to what you learned as a slave including language, and not to speak their language, otherwise you will become like them, acquiring their confusion between God and artifact and consequently their taste for making slaves, both of themselves and others.

Slave of rhetoric! This is the trouble when you use God for a Muse. Philosophers, thinkers—all cursed. Poets have it better: most are Greeks and pagans, unbelievers except in natural religion, stones, stars, body. This cube and cell. Ostrover had already sentenced him to jail, little booth in the vale of snow; black instrument beeped from a gallows. The white pad—something white—on the floor. Edelshtein bent for it and struck his jaw. Through the filth of the glass doors morning rose out of the dark. He saw what he held:

"ALL OF US ARE HUMANS TOGETHER
BUT SOME HUMANS SHOULD DROP DEAD."

DO YOU FEEL THIS?

IF SO CALL TR 5-2530 IF YOU WANT TO
KNOW WHETHER YOU WILL SURVIVE IN
CHRIST'S FIVE-DAY INEXPENSIVE
ELECT-PLAN

*

9. The agreement between God and his people, Israel, promising his protection and blessing for their faithfulness. "Yiddishkeit": Jewishness, especially the Eastern European kind.

1. The emperor of Austria from 1848 to 1916.
2. Hungarian-born Austrian writer and the founder of Zionism (1860–1904).

"AUDITORY PHRENOLOGY"[3]
PRACTICED FREE FREE

*

(PLEASE NO ATHEISTS OR CRANK CALLS
WE ARE SINCERE SCIENTIFIC SOUL-SOCIOLOGISTS)

*

ASK FOR ROSE OR LOU
WE LOVE YOU

He was touched and curious, but withdrawn. The cold lit him unfamiliarly: his body a brilliant hollowness, emptied of organs, cleansed of debris, the inner flanks of him perfect lit glass. A clear chalice. Of small change he had only a nickel and a dime. For the dime he could CALL TR 5-2530 and take advice appropriate to his immaculateness, his transparency. Rose or Lou. He had no satire for their love. How manifold and various the human imagination. The simplicity of an ascent lured him, he was alert to the probability of levitation but disregarded it. The disciples of Reb Moshe of Kobryn[4] also disregarded feats in opposition to nature—they had no awe for their master when he hung in air, but when he slept—the miracle of his lung, his breath, his heartbeat! He lurched from the booth into rushing daylight. The depth of snow sucked off one of his shoes. The serpent too prospers without feet, so he cast off his and weaved on. His arms, particularly his hands, particularly those partners of mind his fingers, he was sorry to lose. He knew his eyes, his tongue, his stinging loins. He was again tempted to ascend. The hillock was profound. He outwitted it by creeping through it, he drilled patiently into the snow. He wanted to stand then, but without legs could not. Indolently he permitted himself to rise. He went only high enough to see the snowy sidewalks, the mounds in gutters and against stoops, the beginning of business time. Lifted light. A doorman fled out of a building wearing earmuffs, pulling a shovel behind him like a little tin cart. Edelshtein drifted no higher than the man's shoulders. He watched the shovel pierce the snow, tunneling down, but there was no bottom, the earth was without foundation.

He came under a black wing. He thought it was the first blindness of Death but it was only a canopy.

The doorman went on digging under the canopy; under the canopy Edelshtein tasted wine and felt himself at a wedding, his own, the canopy covering his steamy gold eyeglasses made blind by Mireleh's veil. Four beings held up the poles:[5] one his wife's cousin the postman, one his own cousin the druggist; two poets. The first poet was a beggar who lived on institutional charity—Baumzweig; the second, Silverman, sold ladies' elastic stockings, the kind for varicose veins. The postman and the druggist were still alive, only one of them retired. The poets were ghosts, Baumzweig picking at himself in bed also a ghost, Silverman long dead, more than twenty years—*lideleh-shreiber*[6] they called him, he wrote for the popular theater. "Song to Steerage":[7] *Steerage, steerage, I remember the crowds, the rags we took with*

3. The practice of determining character from the conformation of the skull.
4. A 19th-century Hasidic rabbi. Kobryn is a town in western Russia (now Belorussia), east of Warsaw.
5. At Jewish weddings, a bridal canopy (*chupah*) is held up by four attendants.
6. Writer of little songs (Yiddish).
7. The cheapest quarters on a passenger ship.

us we treated like shrouds, we tossed them away when we spied out the shore, going re-born through the Golden Door. . . . Even on Second Avenue 1905 was already stale, but it stopped the show, made fevers, encores, tears, yells. Golden sidewalks. America the bride, under her fancy gown nothing. Poor Silverman, in love with the Statue of Liberty's lifted arm, what did he do in his life besides raise up a post at an empty wedding, no progeny?

The doorman dug out a piece of statuary, an urn with a stone wreath. Under the canopy Edelshtein recognized it. Sand, butts, a half-naked angel astride the wreath. Once Edelshtein saw a condom in it. Found! Vorovsky's building. There is no God, yet who brought him here if not the King of the Universe? Not so bad off after all, even in a snowstorm he could find his way, an expert, he knew one block from another in this desolation of a world.

He carried his shoe into the elevator like a baby, an orphan, a redemption. He could kiss even a shoe.

In the corridor laughter, toilets flushing; coffee stabbed him.

He rang the bell.

From behind Vorovsky's door, laughter, laughter!

No one came.

He rang again. No one came. He banged. "Chaim, crazy man, open up!" No one came. "A dead man from the cold knocks, you don't come? Hurry up, open, I'm a stick of ice, you want a dead man at your door? Mercy! Pity! Open up!"

No one came.

He listened to the laughter. It had a form; a method, rather; some principle, closer to physics than music, of arching up and sinking back. Inside the shape barks, howls, dogs, wolves, wilderness. After each fright a crevice to fall into. He made an anvil of his shoe and took the doorknob for an iron hammer and thrust. He thrust, thrust. The force of an iceberg.

Close to the knob a panel bulged and cracked. Not his fault. On the other side someone was unused to the lock.

He heard Vorovsky but saw Hannah.

She said: "What?"

"You don't remember me? I'm the one what recited to you tonight my work from several years past, I was passing by in your uncle's neighborhood—"

"He's sick."

"What, a fit?"

"All night. I've been here the whole night. The whole night—"

"Let me in."

"Please go away. I just told you."

"In. What's the matter with you? I'm sick myself, I'm dead from cold! Hey, Chaim! Lunatic, stop it!"

Vorovsky was on his belly on the floor, stifling his mouth with a pillow as if it were a stone, knocking his head down on it, but it was no use, the laughter shook the pillow and came yelping out, not muffled but increased, darkened. He laughed and said "Hannah" and laughed.

Edelshtein took a chair and dragged it near Vorovsky and sat. The room stank, a subway latrine.

"Stop," he said.

Vorovsky laughed.

"All right, merriment, very good, be happy. You're warm, I'm cold. Have mercy, little girl—tea. Hannah. Boil it up hot. Pieces of flesh drop from me." He heard that he was speaking Yiddish, so he began again for her. "I'm sorry. Forgive me. A terrible thing to do. I was lost outside, I was looking, so now I found you, I'm sorry."

"It isn't a good time for a visit, that's all."

"Bring some tea also for your uncle."

"He can't."

"He can maybe, let him try. Someone who laughs like this is ready for a feast—*flanken, tsimmis, rosselfleysh*[8]—" In Yiddish he said, "In the world-to-come people dance at a parties like this, all laughter, joy. The day after the Messiah people laugh like this."

Vorovsky laughed and said "Messiah" and sucked the pillow, spitting. His face was a flood: tears ran upside down into his eyes, over his forehead, saliva sprang in puddles around his ears. He was spitting, crying, burbling, he gasped, wept, spat. His eyes were bloodshot, the whites showed like slashes, wounds; he still wore his hat. He laughed, he was still laughing. His pants were wet, the fly open, now and then seeping. He dropped the pillow for tea and ventured a sip, with his tongue, like an animal full of hope—vomit rolled up with the third swallow and he laughed between spasms, he was still laughing, stinking, a sewer.

Edelshtein took pleasure in the tea, it touched him to the root, more gripping on his bowel than the coffee that stung the hall. He praised himself with no meanness, no bitterness: prince of rationality! Thawing, he said, "Give him *schnapps*,[9] he can hold *schnapps*, no question."

"He drank and he vomited."

"Chaim, little soul," Edelshtein said, "what started you off? Myself. I was there. I said it, I said graves, I said smoke. I'm the responsible one. Death. Death, I'm the one who said it. Death you laugh at, you're no coward."

"If you want to talk business with my uncle come another time."

"Death is business?"

Now he examined her. Born 1945, in the hour of the death-camps. Not selected. Immune. The whole way she held herself looked immune—by this he meant American. Still, an exhausted child, straggled head, remarkable child to stay through the night with the madman. "Where's your mother?" he said. "Why doesn't she come and watch her brother? Why does it fall on you? You should be free, you have your own life."

"You don't know anything about families."

She was acute: no mother, father, wife, child, what did he know about families? He was cut off, a survivor. "I know your uncle," he said, but without belief: in the first place Vorovsky had an education. "In his right mind your uncle doesn't want you to suffer."

Vorovsky, laughing, said "Suffer."

"He likes to suffer. He wants to suffer. He admires suffering. All you people want to suffer."

Pins and needles: Edelshtein's fingertips were fevering. He stroked the heat of the cup. He could feel. He said, " 'You people'?"

"You Jews."

8. Pot roast. "*Flanken*": short ribs of beef. "*Tsimmis*": a long-cooking stew, usually vegetarian or meat.

9. Strong liquor (German).

"Aha. Chaim, you hear? Your niece Hannah—on the other side already, never mind she's acquainted with *mamaloshen*. In one generation, 'you Jews.' You don't like suffering? Maybe you respect it?"

"It's unnecessary."

"It comes from history, history is also unnecessary?"

"History's a waste."

America the empty bride. Edelshtein said, "You're right about business. I came on business. My whole business is waste."

Vorovsky laughed and said "Hersheleh Frog Frog Frog."

"I think you're making him worse," Hannah said. "Tell me what you want and I'll give him the message."

"He's not deaf."

"He doesn't remember afterward—"

"I have no message."

"Then what do you want from him?"

"Nothing. I want from you."

"Frog Frog Frog Frog Frog."

Edelshtein finished his tea and put the cup on the floor and for the first time absorbed Vorovsky's apartment: until now Vorovsky had kept him out. It was one room, sink and stove behind a plastic curtain, bookshelves leaning over not with books but journals piled flat, a sticky table, a sofa-bed, a desk, six kitchen chairs, and along the walls seventy-five cardboard boxes which Edelshtein knew harbored two thousand copies of Vorovsky's dictionary. A pity on Vorovsky, he had a dispute with the publisher, who turned back half the printing to him. Vorovsky had to pay for two thousand German-English mathematical dictionaries, and now he had to sell them himself, but he did not know what to do, how to go about it. It was his fate to swallow what he first excreted. Because of a mishap in business he owned his life, he possessed what he was, a slave, but invisible. A hungry snake has to eat its tail all the way down to the head until it disappears.

Hannah said: "What could I do for you"—flat, not a question.

"Again 'you.' A distinction, a separation. What I'll ask is this: annihilate 'you,' annihilate 'me.' We'll come to an understanding, we'll get together."

She bent for his cup and he saw her boot. He was afraid of a boot. He said mildly, nicely, "Look, your uncle tells me you're one of us. By 'us' he means writer, no?"

"By 'us' you mean Jew."

"And you're not a Jew, *meydeleh*?"[1]

"Not your kind."

"Nowadays there have to be kinds? Good, bad, old, new—"

"Old and new."

"All right! So let it be old and new, fine, a reasonable beginning. Let old work with new. Listen, I need a collaborator. Not exactly a collaborator, it's not even complicated like that. What I need is a translator."

"My uncle the translator is indisposed."

At that moment Edelshtein discovered he hated irony. He yelled, "Not your uncle. You! You!"

1. Girl (Yiddish).

Howling, Vorovsky crawled to a tower of cartons and beat on them with his bare heels. There was an alteration in his laughter, something not theatrical but of the theater—he was amused, entertained, clowns paraded between his legs.

"You'll save Yiddish," Edelshtein said, "you'll be like a Messiah to a whole generation, a whole literature, naturally you'll have to work at it, practice, it takes knowledge, it takes a gift, a genius, a born poet—"

Hannah walked in her boots with his dirty teacup. From behind the plastic he heard the faucet. She opened the curtain and came out and said: "You old men."

"Ostrover's pages you kiss!"

"You jealous old men from the ghetto," she said.

"And Ostrover's young, a young prince? Listen! You don't see, you don't follow—translate me, lift me out of the ghetto, it's my life that's hanging on you!"

Her voice was a whip. "Bloodsuckers," she said. "It isn't a translator you're after, it's someone's soul. Too much history's drained your blood, you want someone to take you over, a dybbuk[2]—"

"Dybbuk! Ostrover's language. All right, I need a dybbuk, I'll become a golem,[3] I don't care, it doesn't matter! Breathe in me! Animate me! Without you I'm a clay pot!" Bereaved, he yelled, "Translate me !"

The clowns ran over Vorovsky's charmed belly.

Hannah said: "You think I have to read Ostrover in translation? You think translation has anything to do with what Ostrover is?"

Edelshtein accused her, "Who taught you to read Yiddish?—A girl like that, to know the letters worthy of life and to be ignorant! 'You Jews,' 'you people,' you you you!"

"I learned, my grandfather taught me, I'm not responsible for it, I didn't go looking for it, I was smart, a golden head, same as now. But I have my own life, you said it yourself, I don't have to throw it out. So pay attention, Mr. Vampire: even in Yiddish Ostrover's not in the ghetto. Even in Yiddish he's not like you people."

"He's not in the ghetto? Which ghetto, what ghetto? So where is he? In the sky? In the clouds? With the angels? Where?"

She meditated, she was all intelligence. "In the world," she answered him.

"In the marketplace. A fishwife, a *kochleffel*,[4] everything's his business, you he'll autograph, me he'll get jobs, he listens to everybody."

"Whereas you people listen only to yourselves."

In the room something was absent.

Edelshtein, pushing into his snow-damp shoe, said into the absence, "So? You're not interested?"

"Only in the mainstream. Not in your little puddles."

"Again the ghetto. Your uncle stinks from the ghetto? Graduated, 1924, the University of Berlin, Vorovsky stinks from the ghetto? Myself, four God-given books not one living human being knows, I stink from the ghetto? God, four thousand years since Abraham hanging out with Jews, God also stinks from the ghetto?"

2. An evil spirit, a demon, who takes possession of someone (Hebrew).
3. An artificial creature that has had life breathed into it (Yiddish, from the Hebrew). Cf. Psalm 139.16.
4. Busybody (Yiddish).

"Rhetoric," Hannah said. "Yiddish literary rhetoric. That's the style."

"Only Ostrover doesn't stink from the ghetto."

"A question of vision."

"Better say visions. He doesn't know real things."

"He knows a reality beyond realism."

"American literary babies! And in your language you don't have a rhetoric?" Edelshtein burst out. "Very good, he's achieved it, Ostrover's the world. A pantheist, a pagan, a goy."

"That's it. You've nailed it. A Freudian, a Jungian,[5] a sensibility. No little love stories. A contemporary. He speaks for everybody."

"Aha. Sounds familiar already. For humanity he speaks? Humanity?"

"Humanity," she said.

"And to speak for Jews isn't to speak for humanity? We're not human? We're not present on the face of the earth? We don't suffer? In Russia they let us live? In Egypt they don't want to murder us?"

"Suffer suffer," she said. "I like devils best. They don't think only about themselves and they don't suffer."

Immediately, looking at Hannah—my God, an old man, he was looking at her little waist, underneath it where the little apple of her womb was hidden away—immediately, all at once, instantaneously, he fell into a chaos, a trance, of truth, of actuality: was it possible? He saw everything in miraculous reversal, blessed—everything plain, distinct, understandable, true. What he understood was this: that the ghetto was the real world, and the outside world only a ghetto. Because in actuality who was shut off? Who then was really buried, removed, inhabited by darkness? To whom, in what little space, did God offer Sinai? Who kept Terach[6] and who followed Abraham? Talmud explains that when the Jews went into Exile, God went into Exile also. Babi Yar is maybe the real world, and Kiev with its German toys, New York with all its terrible intelligence, all fictions, fantasies. Unreality.

An infatuation! He was the same, all his life the same as this poisonous wild girl, he coveted mythologies, specters, animals, voices. Western Civilization his secret guilt, he was ashamed of the small tremor of his self-love, degraded by being ingrown. Alexei with his skin a furnace of desire, his trucks and trains! He longed to be Alexei. Alexei with his German toys and his Latin! Alexei whose destiny was to grow up into the world-at-large, to slip from the ghetto, to break out into engineering for Western Civilization! Alexei, I abandon you! I'm at home only in a prison, history is my prison, the ravine my house, only listen—suppose it turns out that the destiny of the Jews is vast, open, eternal, and that Western Civilization is meant to dwindle, shrivel, shrink into the ghetto of the world—what of history then? Kings, Parliaments, like insects, Presidents like vermin, their religion a row of little dolls, their art a cave smudge, their poetry a lust—Avremeleh, when you fell from the ledge over the ravine into your grave, for the first time you fell into reality.

To Hannah he said: "I didn't ask to be born into Yiddish. It came on me."

He meant he was blessed.

"So keep it," she said, "and don't complain."

With the whole ferocity of his delight in it he hit her mouth. The madman

5. A follower of Carl Jung (1875–1961), Swiss psychologist and psychiatrist. "Freudian": a follower of Sigmund Freud (1856–1939), Austrian neurologist and founder of psychoanalysis.

6. Abraham's father.

again struck up his laugh. Only now was it possible to notice that something had stopped it before. A missing harp. The absence filled with bloody laughter, bits of what looked like red pimento hung in the vomit on Vorovsky's chin, the clowns fled, Vorovsky's hat with its pinnacle of fur dangled on his chest—he was spent, he was beginning to fall into the quake of sleep, he slept, he dozed, roars burst from him, he hiccuped, woke, laughed, an enormous grief settled in him, he went on napping and laughing, grief had him in its teeth.

Edelshtein's hand, the cushiony underside of it, blazed from giving the blow. "You," he said, "you have no ideas, what are you?" A shred of learning flaked from him, what the sages said of Job ripped from his tongue like a peeling of the tongue itself, *he never was, he never existed*. "You were never born, you were never created!" he yelled. "Let me tell you, a dead man tells you this, at least I had a life, at least I understood something!"

"Die," she told him. "Die now, all you old men, what are you waiting for? Hanging on my neck, him and now you, the whole bunch of you, parasites, hurry up and die."

His palm burned, it was the first time he had ever slapped a child. He felt like a father. Her mouth lay back naked on her face. Out of spite, against instinct, she kept her hands from the bruise—he could see the shape of her teeth, turned a little one on the other, imperfect, again vulnerable. From fury her nose streamed. He had put a bulge in her lip.

"Forget Yiddish!" he screamed at her. "Wipe it out of your brain! Extirpate it! Go get a memory operation! You have no right to it, you have no right to an uncle, a grandfather! No one ever came before you, you were never born! A vacuum!"

"You old atheists," she called after him. "You dead old socialists. Boring! You bore me to death. You hate magic, you hate imagination, you talk God and you hate God, you despise, you bore, you envy, you eat people up with your disgusting old age—cannibals, all you care about is your own youth, you're finished, give somebody else a turn!"

This held him. He leaned on the door frame. "A turn at what? I didn't offer you a turn? An opportunity of a lifetime? To be published now, in youth, in babyhood, early in life? Translated I'd be famous, this you don't understand. Hannah, listen," he said, kindly, ingratiatingly, reasoning with her like a father, "you don't have to like my poems, do I ask you to *like* them? I don't ask you to like them, I don't ask you to respect them, I don't ask you to love them. A man my age, do I want a lover or a translator? Am I asking a favor? No. Look," he said, "one thing I forgot to tell you. A business deal. That's all. Business, plain and simple. I'll pay you. You didn't think I wouldn't pay, God forbid?"

Now she covered her mouth. He wondered at his need to weep; he was ashamed.

"Hannah, please, how much? I'll pay, you'll see. Whatever you like. You'll buy anything you want. Dresses, shoes—" *Gottenyu,*[7] what could such a wild beast want? "You'll buy more boots, all kinds of boots, whatever you want, books, everything—" He said relentlessly, "You'll have from me money."

"No," she said, "no."

7. "Dear God!" (Yiddish).

"Please. What will happen to me? What's wrong? My ideas aren't good enough? Who asks you to believe in my beliefs? I'm an old man, used up, I have nothing to say any more, anything I ever said was all imitation. Walt Whitman I used to like. Also John Donne. Poets, masters. We, what have we got? A Yiddish Keats?[8] Never—" He was ashamed, so he wiped his cheeks with both sleeves. "Business. I'll pay you," he said.

"No."

"Because I laid a hand on you? Forgive me, I apologize. I'm crazier than he is, I should be locked up for it—"

"Not because of that."

"Then why not? *Meydeleh*, why not? What harm would it do you? Help out an old man."

She said desolately, "You don't interest me. I would have to be interested."

"I see. Naturally." He looked at Vorovsky. "Goodbye, Chaim, regards from Aristotle. What distinguishes men from the beasts is the power of ha-ha-ha. So good morning, ladies and gentlemen. Be well. Chaim, live until a hundred and twenty. The main thing is health."

In the street it was full day, and he was warm from the tea. The road glistened, the sidewalks. Paths crisscrossed in unexpected places, sleds clanged, people ran. A drugstore was open and he went in to telephone Baumzweig: he dialed, but on the way he skipped a number, heard an iron noise like a weapon, and had to dial again. "Paula," he practiced, "I'll come back for a while, all right? For breakfast maybe," but instead he changed his mind and decided to CALL TR 5-2530. At the other end of the wire it was either Rose or Lou. Edelshtein told the eunuch's voice, "I believe with you about some should drop dead. Pharaoh, Queen Isabella, Haman, that pogromchik King Louis they call in history Saint, Hitler, Stalin, Nasser[9]—" The voice said, "You're a Jew?" It sounded Southern but somehow not Negro—maybe because schooled, polished: "Accept Jesus as your Saviour and you shall have Jerusalem restored." "We already got it," Edelshtein said. *Meshiachtseiten!*[1] "The terrestrial Jerusalem has no significance. Earth is dust. The Kingdom of God is within. Christ released man from Judaic exclusivism." "Who's excluding who?" Edelshtein said. "Christianity is Judaism universalized. Jesus is Moses publicized for ready availability. Our God is the God of Love, your God is the God of Wrath. Look how He abandoned you in Auschwitz."[2] "It wasn't only God who didn't notice." "You people are cowards, you never even tried to defend yourselves. You got a wide streak of yellow, you don't know how to hold a gun." "Tell it to the Egyptians,"[3] Edelshtein said. "Everyone you come into contact with turns into your enemy. When you were in Europe every nation despised you. When you moved to

8. John Keats (1795–1821), an English Romantic lyric poet. "Walt Whitman": considered the great poet of America democracy (1819–1892). "John Donne": one of the finest of the Metaphysical poets (1572–1631).

9. Gamal Abdel Nasser (1918–1970), Egypt's prime minister and president, fought losing wars against Israel in 1956 and 1967. "Queen Isabella": the Spanish monarch during whose reign the Inquisition against non-Christians resulted in the death or expulsion of many Jews (1451–1504). "Haman": in the biblical Book of Esther, King Ahasuerus's vizier who persecuted and plotted against the Jews. He was finally executed. "Pogromchik": one who foments a pogrom or anti-Jewish riot. "King Louis they call in history Saint": i.e., Louis IX (1214–1270), who led the seventh Crusade to the Holy Land, which brought about many Jewish deaths.

1. Time of the Messiah (Yiddish).

2. A Nazi concentration and death camp in Poland during World War II.

3. An allusion to the Six Day War of June 1967 in which Israel defeated Egypt and other invading Arab countries.

take over the Middle East the Arab Nation, spic faces like your own, your very own blood-kin, began to hate you. You are a bone in the throat of all mankind." "Who gnaws at bones? Dogs and rats only." "Even your food habits are abnormal, against the grain of quotidian delight. You refuse to seethe a lamb in the milk of its mother. You will not eat a fertilized egg because it has a spot of blood on it. When you wash your hands you chant. You pray in a debased jargon, not in the beautiful sacramental English of our Holy Bible." Edelshtein said, "That's right, Jesus spoke the King's English." "Even now, after the good Lord knows how many years in America, you talk with a kike[4] accent. You kike, you Yid."

Edelshtein shouted into the telephone, "Amalekite![5] Titus![6] Nazi! The whole world is infected by you anti-Semites! On account of you children become corrupted! On account of you I lost everything, my whole life! On account of you I have no translator!"

Magazine, 1969
Book, 1971

The Shawl[1]

Stella, cold, cold, the coldness of hell. How they walked on the roads together, Rosa with Magda curled up between sore breasts, Magda wound up in the shawl. Sometimes Stella carried Magda. But she was jealous of Magda. A thin girl of fourteen, too small, with thin breasts of her own, Stella wanted to be wrapped in a shawl, hidden away, asleep, rocked by the march, a baby, a round infant in arms. Magda took Rosa's nipple, and Rosa never stopped walking, a walking cradle. There was not enough milk; sometimes Magda sucked air; then she screamed. Stella was ravenous. Her knees were tumors on sticks, her elbows chicken bones.

Rosa did not feel hunger; she felt light, not like someone walking but like someone in a faint, in trance, arrested in a fit, someone who is already a floating angel, alert and seeing everything, but in the air, not there, not touching the road. As if teetering on the tips of her fingernails. She looked into Magda's face through a gap in the shawl: a squirrel in a nest, safe, no one could reach her inside the little house of the shawl's windings. The face, very round, a pocket mirror of a face: but it was not Rosa's bleak complexion, dark like cholera, it was another kind of face altogether, eyes blue as air, smooth feathers of hair nearly as yellow as the Star[2] sewn into Rosa's coat. You could think she was one of *their* babies.

Rosa, floating, dreamed of giving Magda away in one of the villages. She could leave the line for a minute and push Magda into the hands of any woman on the side of the road. But if she moved out of line they might shoot. And even if she fled the line for half a second and pushed the shawl-bundle

4. An offensive term meaning "Jewish."
5. A tribal enemy of Israel in the Bible.
6. The Roman emperor (79–81 C.E.) who destroyed the Temple in Jerusalem.
1. The epigraph to Ozick's book *The Shawl* is the closing lines (in German) of Paul Celan's *Death-fugue*: "Your golden hair Margareta / your ashen hair Shulamith."
2. I.e., the Star of David, a Jewish symbol, which Jews were forced to wear under the Nazi occupation of Europe.

at a stranger, would the woman take it? She might be surprised, or afraid; she might drop the shawl, and Magda would fall out and strike her head and die. The little round head. Such a good child, she gave up screaming, and sucked now only for the taste of the drying nipple itself. The neat grip of the tiny gums. One mite of a tooth tip sticking up in the bottom gum, how shining, an elfin tombstone of white marble gleaming there. Without complaining, Magda relinquished Rosa's teats, first the left, then the right; both were cracked, not a sniff of milk. The duct-crevice extinct, a dead volcano, blind eye, chill hole, so Magda took the corner of the shawl and milked it instead. She sucked and sucked, flooding the threads with wetness. The shawl's good flavor, milk of linen.

It was a magic shawl, it could nourish an infant for three days and three nights. Magda did not die, she stayed alive, although very quiet. A peculiar smell, of cinnamon and almonds, lifted out of her mouth. She held her eyes open every moment, forgetting how to blink or nap, and Rosa and sometimes Stella studied their blueness. On the road they raised one burden of a leg after another and studied Magda's face. "Aryan," Stella said, in a voice grown as thin as a string; and Rosa thought how Stella gazed at Magda like a young cannibal. And the time that Stella said "Aryan," it sounded to Rosa as if Stella had really said "Let us devour her."

But Magda lived to walk. She lived that long, but she did not walk very well, partly because she was only fifteen months old, and partly because the spindles of her legs could not hold up her fat belly. It was fat with air, full and round. Rosa gave almost all her food to Magda, Stella gave nothing; Stella was ravenous, a growing child herself, but not growing much. Stella did not menstruate. Rosa did not menstruate. Rosa was ravenous, but also not; she learned from Magda how to drink the taste of a finger in one's mouth. They were in a place without pity, all pity was annihilated in Rosa, she looked at Stella's bones without pity. She was sure that Stella was waiting for Magda to die so she could put her teeth into the little thighs.

Rosa knew Magda was going to die very soon; she should have been dead already, but she had been buried away deep inside the magic shawl, mistaken there for the shivering mound of Rosa's breasts; Rosa clung to the shawl as if it covered only herself. No one took it away from her. Magda was mute. She never cried. Rosa hid her in the barracks, under the shawl, but she knew that one day someone would inform; or one day someone, not even Stella, would steal Magda to eat her. When Magda began to walk Rosa knew that Magda was going to die very soon, something would happen. She was afraid to fall asleep; she slept with the weight of her thigh on Magda's body; she was afraid she would smother Magda under her thigh. The weight of Rosa was becoming less and less; Rosa and Stella were slowly turning into air.

Magda was quiet, but her eyes were horribly alive, like blue tigers. She watched. Sometimes she laughed—it seemed a laugh, but how could it be? Magda had never seen anyone laugh. Still, Magda laughed at her shawl when the wind blew its corners, the bad wind with pieces of black in it, that made Stella's and Rosa's eyes tear. Magda's eyes were always clear and tearless. She watched like a tiger. She guarded her shawl. No one could touch it; only Rosa could touch it. Stella was not allowed. The shawl was Magda's own baby, her pet, her little sister. She tangled herself up in it and sucked on one of the corners when she wanted to be very still.

Then Stella took the shawl away and made Magda die.

Afterward Stella said: "I was cold."

And afterward she was always cold, always. The cold went into her heart: Rosa saw that Stella's heart was cold. Magda flopped onward with her little pencil legs scribbling this way and that, in search of the shawl; the pencils faltered at the barracks opening, where the light began. Rosa saw and pursued. But already Magda was in the square outside the barracks, in the jolly light. It was the roll-call arena. Every morning Rosa had to conceal Magda under the shawl against a wall of the barracks and go out and stand in the arena with Stella and hundreds of others, sometimes for hours, and Magda, deserted, was quiet under the shawl, sucking on her corner. Every day Magda was silent, and so she did not die. Rosa saw that today Magda was going to die, and at the same time a fearful joy ran in Rosa's two palms, her fingers were on fire, she was astonished, febrile: Magda, in the sunlight, swaying on her pencil legs, was howling. Ever since the drying up of Rosa's nipples, ever since Magda's last scream on the road, Magda had been devoid of any syllable; Magda was a mute. Rosa believed that something had gone wrong with her vocal cords, with her windpipe, with the cave of her larynx; Magda was defective, without a voice; perhaps she was deaf; there might be something amiss with her intelligence; Magda was dumb. Even the laugh that came when the ash-stippled wind made a clown out of Magda's shawl was only the air-blown showing of her teeth. Even when the lice, head lice and body lice, crazed her so that she became as wild as one of the big rats that plundered the barracks at daybreak looking for carrion, she rubbed and scratched and kicked and bit and rolled without a whimper. But now Magda's mouth was spilling a long viscous rope of clamor.

"Maaaa—"

It was the first noise Magda had ever sent out from her throat since the drying up of Rosa's nipples.

"Maaaa . . . aaa!"

Again! Magda was wavering in the perilous sunlight of the arena, scribbling on such pitiful little bent shins. Rosa saw. She saw that Magda was grieving for the loss of her shawl, she saw that Magda was going to die. A tide of commands hammered in Rosa's nipples: Fetch, get, bring! But she did not know which to go after first, Magda or the shawl. If she jumped out into the arena to snatch Magda up, the howling would not stop, because Magda would still not have the shawl; but if she ran back into the barracks to find the shawl, and if she found it, and if she came after Magda holding it and shaking it, then she would get Magda back, Magda would put the shawl in her mouth and turn dumb again.

Rosa entered the dark. It was easy to discover the shawl. Stella was heaped under it, asleep in her thin bones. Rosa tore the shawl free and flew—she could fly, she was only air—into the arena. The sunheat murmured of another life, of butterflies in summer. The light was placid, mellow. On the other side of the steel fence, far away, there were green meadows speckled with dandelions and deep-colored violets; beyond them, even farther, innocent tiger lilies, tall, lifting their orange bonnets. In the barracks they spoke of "flowers," of "rain": excrement, thick turd-braids, and the slow stinking maroon waterfall that slunk down from the upper bunks, the stink mixed with a bitter fatty floating smoke that greased Rosa's skin. She stood for an instant at the margin of the arena. Sometimes the electricity inside the fence would seem to hum; even Stella said it was only an imagining, but Rosa heard real sounds in the wire: grainy sad voices. The farther she was from the fence, the more clearly the voices crowded at her. The lamenting voices strummed so convincingly, so passionately, it was impossible to suspect them of being phantoms. The voices told her to hold up the shawl, high; the voices told her to shake it, to whip with it, to unfurl it like a flag. Rosa lifted, shook, whipped, unfurled. Far off, very far, Magda leaned across her air-fed belly, reaching out with the rods of her arms. She was high up, elevated, riding someone's shoulder. But the shoulder that carried Magda was not coming toward Rosa and the shawl, it was drifting away, the speck of Magda was moving more and more into the smoky distance. Above the shoulder a helmet glinted. The light tapped the helmet and sparkled it into a goblet. Below the helmet a black body like a domino and a pair of black boots hurled themselves in the direction of the electrified fence. The electric voices began to chatter wildly. "Maamaa, maaamaaa," they all hummed together. How far Magda was from Rosa now, across the whole square, past a dozen barracks, all the way on the other side! She was no bigger than a moth.

All at once Magda was swimming through the air. The whole of Magda traveled through loftiness. She looked like a butterfly touching a silver vine. And the moment Magda's feathered round head and her pencil legs and balloonish belly and zigzag arms splashed against the fence, the steel voices went mad in their growling, urging Rosa to run and run to the spot where Magda had fallen from her flight against the electrified fence; but of course Rosa did not obey them. She only stood, because if she ran they would shoot, and if she tried to pick up the sticks of Magda's body they would shoot, and if she let the wolf's screech ascending now through the ladder of her skeleton break out, they would shoot; so she took Magda's shawl and filled her own mouth with it, stuffed it in and stuffed it in, until she was swallowing up the wolf's screech and tasting the cinnamon and almond depth of Magda's saliva; and Rosa drank Magda's shawl until it dried.

Magazine, 1980
Book, 1989

ELIE WIESEL
b. 1928

"So, learn to be silent." The burden of Elie Wiesel's speaking, teaching, and writing has been to guide the world at large, not just Jews, toward silence in face of an unspeakable event: the Nazi genocide, the European Jewish catastrophe. "But how to do this?" he asks in *Why I Write* (1978). "All words seemed inadequate. . . . Where was I to discover a fresh vocabulary, a primeval language? The language of night was not human." Not actually silence, then, but the process of learning what to be silent about and why has taken Wiesel through over twenty-five novels, plays, biblical and Hasidic portraits and legends, essay collections, memoirs—plus his regular teaching and ceaseless speaking engagements, from New York public schools to the Nobel prize ceremony. A paradox may reside here, not necessarily due to Wiesel, but to history and society: "Learn to be silent."

Elie Wiesel was born on September 30, 1928, a few days before Simchas Torah (Joy of the Torah), when the year's cycle of Bible readings commences anew. His birthplace, Sighet in the Carpathian Mountains, was a largely Jewish town that passed from Romania to Hungary in 1940; thus his ambient languages were Yiddish, Hebrew, Romanian, Hungarian, and also German. Wiesel's father, Shlomo, was a shopkeeper, his adored mother, Sarah, the daughter of Dodye Feig. From Reb Dodye—"cultured and erudite . . . a festival for the heart and mind . . . a marvelous singer"—Elie imbibed a fervent Hasidism, and he steeped himself in Talmud.

It was not until Passover 1944, when he was fifteen, that Hungarians and German Nazis set up a ghetto in Sighet and deported the town's Jews. Elie's mother and the youngest of his three sisters perished in Auschwitz; he himself stayed with his father, who died after the death march to Buchenwald in January 1945. Upon liberation, Wiesel went to France. In 1949, he became a foreign correspondent for the Tel Aviv daily *Yediot Aharonot*; in 1958, he settled in New York, covered the United Nations, and worked for the Yiddish daily *Forward*.

Years after the nightmare of 1944–45, Wiesel wrote a Yiddish memoir of his experience. Cutting it from 862 to 245 pages, he published *Un di velt hot geshvign* (And the World Stayed Silent, 1956). Cut even further, the French version was entitled *La Nuit* (Night, 1958), symbolizing the horror rather than shaking a prophetic fist. Now Wiesel's style, recalling Albert Camus's *The Stranger* and *The Plague* as well as Samuel Beckett's stripped tableaux, was spare, mostly understated, and refrained from moral or psychological comment. For instance, at the book's end, after his image of a corpse gazing in the mirror, Wiesel's Yiddish version had turned angry and skeptical: "Ilse Koch, the sadist of Buchenwald, is a happy wife and mother. War criminals stroll in the streets of Hamburg and Munich. The past has been erased, buried."

As for an American edition, dozens of publishers "sent their regrets," says Wiesel. "Some thought the book too slender (American readers seemed to prefer fatter volumes), others too depressing (American readers seemed to prefer optimistic books). Some felt its subject was too little known, others that it was too well known." Scribner's had "certain misgivings" because it was merely "a document." Finally, Hill and Wang bought the book, giving Wiesel an advance of $100. *Night* came out in 1960, around the time of Adolf Eichmann's arrest in Argentina. For several years it sold little, but it has become, after Anne Frank's diary, the most frequently read story to emerge from the Holocaust.

What kind of book is *Night*, what genre—memoir or novel? And what makes it part of Jewish American literature? The two questions bear on each other because most Americans, at our distant remove of time and space, cannot organically absorb what happened in Nazi-ridden Europe from 1939 to 1945. Elie Wiesel, trying (as he says) to "unite the language of man with the silence of the dead," gave shape to his account. The rhythm of Jewish holidays, the allusions to liturgy, the image of night, the figure of sons and fathers: such things make *Night* seem a Bildungsroman, a novel depicting one young person's growth and "education," however grim. Yet Wiesel meant this book to be stark, like the ghetto chronicles.

Of course, memory and the act of writing inevitably recompose the past, reenvision the fact of things, so that *Night* is a strange amalgam. American readers did not immediately respond, but before long this book became almost an article of faith, a spiritual and moral touchstone. No American writer—not Malamud or Roth, not even Bellow or Singer—could possess the gravitas to say: *Le silence de Dieu est Dieu*, "The silence of God *is* God." Nor could they, for that matter, have spoken as simply to Ronald Reagan when, in 1985, the president accompanied Germany's chancellor to lay a wreath at the Bitburg cemetery, where SS men are buried: "That place, Mr. President, is not your place. Your place is with the victims of the SS."

Wiesel has divided his professional life between public activities and writing. In 1965, during the cold war, he went to Russia to witness the plight of Soviet Jewry, long before the emigration movement; from this came *The Jews of Silence* (1966). In 1979, while leading the effort to establish a Holocaust museum in Washington, he went as a witness to Cambodia. He received the 1986 Nobel Peace Prize. Meanwhile, in 1969, he married Marion Wiesel, who translates his work from French, and they had a son in 1972.

Between 1961 and 1970, Wiesel published the novels *Dawn, The Accident, The Gates of the Forest, The Town beyond the Wall,* and *A Beggar in Jerusalem*. His lectures at the 92nd Street Y in New York City produced *Souls on Fire* (1972), portraits and legends of Hasidism, the popular movement of devotion and ecstatic prayer and song founded in the eighteenth century by Israel ben Eliezer Ba'al Shem Tov. Then came *Messengers of God* (1976), personal meditations on Adam and Eve, Cain and Abel, Abraham and Isaac, Jacob, Joseph, Moses, Job—figures who gripped Wiesel as a child. "Of all the Biblical tales, the one about Isaac is perhaps the most timeless and most relevant to our generation," he writes, since the word *holocaust* originally designates a sacrifice, burnt offering.

Besides Hasidism and Bible, Elie Wiesel's antecedents are Camus, Beckett, Malraux, Dostoyevsky, Racine—not Henry James, whom Cynthia Ozick adored, or Allen Ginsberg's Walt Whitman. Yet the Romanian Jew, French novelist, and American citizen first spoke for survivors to an American public unaware of them in its midst and insisted on keeping memory alive.

From Night

Chapter 3. [*Arrival at Auschwitz-Birkenau*]

The cherished objects we had brought with us thus far were left behind in the train, and with them, at last, our illusions.

Every two yards or so an SS[1] man held his tommy gun trained on us. Hand in hand we followed the crowd.

An SS noncommissioned officer came to meet us, a truncheon in his hand. He gave the order:

"Men to the left! Women to the right!"

Eight words spoken quietly, indifferently, without emotion. Eight short, simple words. Yet that was the moment when I parted from my mother. I had not had time to think, but already I felt the pressure of my father's hand: we were alone. For a part of a second I glimpsed my mother and my sisters moving away to the right. Tzipora held Mother's hand. I saw them disappear into the distance; my mother was stroking my sister's fair hair, as though to protect her, while I walked on with my father and the other men. And I did not know that in that place, at that moment, I was parting from my mother and Tzipora forever. I went on walking. My father held onto my hand.

Behind me, an old man fell to the ground. Near him was an SS man, putting his revolver back in its holster.

My hand shifted on my father's arm. I had one thought—not to lose him. Not to be left alone.

The SS officers gave the order:

1. Abbreviation for *Schutzstaffel*, literally "protection echelon" (German). This unit of Nazis was in charge of intelligence, central security, policing action, and mass murder of "inferiors" and "undesirables."

"Form fives!"

Commotion. At all costs we must keep together.

"Here, kid, how old are you?"

It was one of the prisoners who asked me this. I could not see his face, but his voice was tense and weary.

"I'm not quite fifteen yet."

"No. Eighteen."

"But I'm not," I said. "Fifteen."

"Fool. Listen to what *I* say."

Then he questioned my father, who replied:

"Fifty."

The other grew more furious than ever.

"No, not fifty. Forty. Do you understand? Eighteen and forty."

He disappeared into the night shadows. A second man came up, spitting oaths at us.

"What have you come here for, you sons of bitches? What are you doing here, eh?"

Someone dared to answer him.

"What do you think? Do you suppose we've come here for our own pleasure? Do you think we asked to come?"

A little more, and the man would have killed him.

"You shut your trap, you filthy swine, or I'll squash you right now! You'd have done better to have hanged yourselves where you were than to come here. Didn't you know what was in store for you at Auschwitz? Haven't you heard about it? In 1944?"

No, we had not heard. No one had told us. He could not believe his ears. His tone of voice became increasingly brutal.

"Do you see that chimney over there? See it? Do you see those flames? (Yes, we did see the flames.) Over there—that's where you're going to be taken. That's your grave, over there. Haven't you realized it yet? You dumb bastards, don't you understand anything? You're going to be burned. Frizzled away. Turned into ashes."

He was growing hysterical in his fury. We stayed motionless, petrified. Surely it was all a nightmare? An unimaginable nightmare?

I heard murmurs around me.

"We've got to do something. We can't let ourselves be killed. We can't go like beasts to the slaughter. We've got to revolt."

There were a few sturdy young fellows among us. They had knives on them, and they tried to incite the others to throw themselves on the armed guards.

One of the young men cried:

"Let the world learn of the existence of Auschwitz. Let everybody hear about it, while they can still escape. . . ."

But the older ones begged their children not to do anything foolish:

"You must never lose faith, even when the sword hangs over your head. That's the teaching of our sages. . . ."

The wind of revolt died down. We continued our march toward the square. In the middle stood the notorious Dr. Mengele[2] (a typical SS officer: a cruel

2. Known as the "angel of death," Josef Mengele (1911–ca. 1979), camp doctor at Auschwitz, conducted medical experiments on twins, dwarfs, giants, and others, and was responsible, directly and indirectly, for the deaths of many of Auschwitz's prisoners.

face, but not devoid of intelligence, and wearing a monocle); a conductor's baton in his hand, he was standing among the other officers. The baton moved unremittingly, sometimes to the right, sometimes to the left.

I was already in front of him:

"How old are you?" he asked, in an attempt at a paternal tone of voice.

"Eighteen." My voice was shaking.

"Are you in good health?"

"Yes."

"What's your occupation?"

Should I say that I was a student?

"Farmer," I heard myself say.

This conversation cannot have lasted more than a few seconds. It had seemed like an eternity to me.

The baton moved to the left. I took half a step forward. I wanted to see first where they were sending my father. If he went to the right, I would go after him.

The baton once again pointed to the left for him too. A weight was lifted from my heart.

We did not yet know which was the better side, right or left; which road led to prison and which to the crematory. But for the moment I was happy; I was near my father. Our procession continued to move slowly forward.

Another prisoner came up to us:

"Satisfied?"

"Yes," someone replied.

"Poor devils, you're going to the crematory."

He seemed to be telling the truth. Not far from us, flames were leaping up from a ditch, gigantic flames. They were burning something. A lorry drew up at the pit and delivered its load—little children. Babies! Yes, I saw it—saw it with my own eyes . . . those children in the flames. (Is it surprising that I could not sleep after that? Sleep had fled from my eyes.)

So this was where we were going. A little farther on was another and larger ditch for adults.

I pinched my face. Was I still alive? Was I awake? I could not believe it. How could it be possible for them to burn people, children, and for the world to keep silent? No, none of this could be true. It was a nightmare. . . . Soon I should wake with a start, my heart pounding, and find myself back in the bedroom of my childhood, among my books. . . .

My father's voice drew me from my thoughts:

"It's a shame . . . a shame that you couldn't have gone with your mother. . . . I saw several boys of your age going with their mothers. . . ."

His voice was terribly sad. I realized that he did not want to see what they were going to do to me. He did not want to see the burning of his only son.

My forehead was bathed in cold sweat. But I told him that I did not believe that they could burn people in our age, that humanity would never tolerate it. . . .

"Humanity? Humanity is not concerned with us. Today anything is allowed. Anything is possible, even these crematories. . . ."

His voice was choking.

"Father," I said, "if that is so, I don't want to wait here. I'm going to run to the electric wire. That would be better than slow agony in the flames."

He did not answer. He was weeping. His body was shaken convulsively. Around us, everyone was weeping. Someone began to recite the Kaddish, the prayer for the dead. I do not know if it has ever happened before, in the long history of the Jews, that people have ever recited the prayer for the dead for themselves.

"*Yitgadal veyitkadach shmé raba*. . . . May His Name be blessed and magnified. . . ."[3] whispered my father.

For the first time, I felt revolt rise up in me. Why should I bless His name? The Eternal, Lord of the Universe, the All-Powerful and Terrible, was silent. What had I to thank Him for?

We continued our march. We were gradually drawing closer to the ditch, from which an infernal heat was rising. Still twenty steps to go. If I wanted to bring about my own death, this was the moment. Our line had now only fifteen paces to cover. I bit my lips so that my father would not hear my teeth chattering. Ten steps still. Eight. Seven. We marched slowly on, as though following a hearse at our own funeral. Four steps more. Three steps. There it was now, right in front of us, the pit and its flames. I gathered all that was left of my strength, so that I could break from the ranks and throw myself upon the barbed wire. In the depths of my heart, I bade farewell to my father, to the whole universe; and, in spite of myself, the words formed themselves and issued in a whisper from my lips: *Yitgadal veyitkadach shmé raba*. . . . May His name be blessed and magnified. . . . My heart was bursting. The moment had come. I was face to face with the Angel of Death. . . .

No. Two steps from the pit we were ordered to turn to the left and made to go into a barracks.

I pressed my father's hand. He said:

"Do you remember Madame Shcächter,[4] in the train?"

Never shall I forget that night, the first night in camp, which has turned my life into one long night, seven times cursed and seven times sealed. Never shall I forget that smoke. Never shall I forget the little faces of the children, whose bodies I saw turned into wreaths of smoke beneath a silent blue sky.

Never shall I forget those flames which consumed my faith forever.

Never shall I forget that nocturnal silence which deprived me, for all eternity, of the desire to live. Never shall I forget those moments which murdered my God and my soul and turned my dreams to dust. Never shall I forget these things, even if I am condemned to live as long as God Himself. Never.

The barracks we had been made to go into was very long. In the roof were some blue-tinged skylights. The antechamber of Hell must look like this. So many crazed men, so many cries, so much bestial brutality!

There were dozens of prisoners to receive us, truncheons in their hands, striking out anywhere, at anyone, without reason. Orders:

"Strip! Fast! *Los*! Keep only your belts and shoes in your hands. . . ."

We had to throw our clothes at one end of the barracks. There was already

3. The first words of the Kaddish.
4. In Chapter 2 of *Night*, a woman in Wiesel's railway car who went mad during the journey to Auschwitz and saw "a terrible fire"—which, on arrival, became true.

a great heap there. New suits and old, torn coats, rags. For us, this was the true equality: nakedness. Shivering with the cold.

Some SS officers moved about in the room, looking for strong men. If they were so keen on strength, perhaps one should try and pass oneself off as sturdy? My father thought the reverse. It was better not to draw attention to oneself. Our fate would then be the same as the others. (Later, we were to learn that he was right. Those who were selected that day were enlisted in the *Sonder-Kommando*,[5] the unit which worked in the crematories. Bela Katz—son of a big tradesman from our town—had arrived at Birkenau[6] with the first transport, a week before us. When he heard of our arrival, he managed to get word to us that, having been chosen for his strength, he had himself put his father's body into the crematory oven.)

Blows continued to rain down.

"To the barber!"

Belt and shoes in hand, I let myself be dragged off to the barbers. They took our hair off with clippers, and shaved off all the hair on our bodies. The same thought buzzed all the time in my head—not to be separated from my father.

Chapter 9. [*Liberation*]

I had to stay at Buchenwald until April eleventh. I have nothing to say of my life during this period. It no longer mattered. After my father's death, nothing could touch me any more.

I was transferred to the children's block, where there were six hundred of us.

The front was drawing nearer.

I spent my days in a state of total idleness. And I had but one desire—to eat. I no longer thought of my father or of my mother.

From time to time I would dream of a drop of soup, of an extra ration of soup. . . .

On April fifth, the wheel of history turned.

It was late in the afternoon. We were standing in the block, waiting for an SS man to come and count us. He was late in coming. Such a delay was unknown till then in the history of Buchenwald. Something must have happened.

Two hours later the loudspeakers sent out an order from the head of the camp: all the Jews must come to the assembly place.

This was the end! Hitler was going to keep his promise.

The children in our block went toward the place. There was nothing else we could do. Gustav, the head of the block, made this clear to us with his truncheon. But on the way we met some prisoners who whispered to us:

"Go back to your block. The Germans are going to shoot you. Go back to your block, and don't move."

We went back to our block. We learned on the way that the camp resis-

5. Literally, "Special Squad" (German).
6. Site in Poland of a second concentration camp near Auschwitz.

tance organization had decided not to abandon the Jews and was going to prevent their being liquidated.

As it was late and there was great upheaval—innumerable Jews had passed themselves off as non-Jews—the head of the camp decided that a general roll call would take place the following day. Everybody would have to be present.

The roll call took place. The head of the camp announced that Buchenwald was to be liquidated. Ten blocks of deportees would be evacuated each day. From this moment, there would be no further distribution of bread and soup. And the evacuation began. Every day, several thousand prisoners went through the camp gate and never came back.

On April tenth, there were still about twenty thousand of us in the camp, including several hundred children. They decided to evacuate us all at once, right on until the evening. Afterward, they were going to blow up the camp.

So we were massed in the huge assembly square, in rows of five, waiting to see the gate open. Suddenly, the sirens began to wail. An alert! We went back to the blocks. It was too late to evacuate us that evening. The evacuation was postponed again to the following day.

We were tormented with hunger. We had eaten nothing for six days, except a bit of grass or some potato peelings found near the kitchens.

At ten o'clock in the morning the SS scattered through the camp, moving the last victims toward the assembly place.

Then the resistance movement decided to act. Armed men suddenly rose up everywhere. Bursts of firing. Grenades exploding. We children stayed flat on the ground in the block.

The battle did not last long. Toward noon everything was quiet again. The SS had fled and the resistance had taken charge of the running of the camp.

At about six o'clock in the evening, the first American tank stood at the gates of Buchenwald.

Our first act as free men was to throw ourselves onto the provisions. We thought only of that. Not of revenge, not of our families. Nothing but bread.

And even when we were no longer hungry, there was still no one who thought of revenge. On the following day, some of the young men went to Weimar to get some potatoes and clothes—and to sleep with girls. But of revenge, not a sign.

Three days after the liberation of Buchenwald[7] I became very ill with food poisoning. I was transferred to the hospital and spent two weeks between life and death.

One day I was able to get up, after gathering all my strength. I wanted to see myself in the mirror hanging on the opposite wall. I had not seen myself since the ghetto.

From the depths of the mirror, a corpse gazed back at me.

The look in his eyes, as they stared into mine, has never left me.

1958 (in French)
1960 (in English)

7. The German concentration camp to which Wiesel was transferred after Auschwitz.

Why I Write[1]

Why do I write? Perhaps in order not to go mad. Or, on the contrary, to touch the bottom of madness.

Like Samuel Beckett,[2] the survivor expresses himself "en désespoir de cause,"[3] because there is no other way.

Speaking of the solitude of the survivor, the great Yiddish and Hebrew poet and thinker Aaron Zeitlin[4] addresses those who have left him: his father, dead; his brother, dead; his friends, dead: "You have abandoned me," he says to them. "You are together, without me. I am here. Alone. And I make words."

So do I, just like him. I also say words, write words, reluctantly.

There are easier occupations, far more pleasant ones. But for the survivor, writing is not a profession, but an occupation, a duty. Camus[5] calls it "an honor." As he puts it: "I entered literature through worship." Other writers said: "Through anger, through love." Speaking for myself, I would say: "Through silence."

It was by seeking, by probing, silence that I began to discover the perils and power of the word.

I never intended to be a philosopher, or a theologian. The only role I sought was that of witness. I believed that, having survived by chance, I was duty-bound to give meaning to my survival, to justify each moment of my life. I knew the story had to be told. Not to transmit an experience is to betray it; this is what Jewish tradition teaches us. But how to do this? "When Israel is in exile, so is the word," says the Zohar.[6] The word has deserted the meaning it was intended to convey—impossible to make them coincide. The displacement, the shift, is irrevocable. This was never more true than right after the upheaval. We all knew that we could never, never say what had to be said, that we could never express in words, coherent, intelligible words, our experience of madness on an absolute scale. The walk through flaming night, the silence before and after the selection, the monotonous praying of the condemned, the Kaddish[7] of the dying, the fear and hunger of the sick, the shame and suffering, the haunted eyes, the demented stares. I thought that I would never be able to speak of them. All words seemed inadequate, worn, foolish, lifeless, whereas I wanted them to be searing. Where was I to discover a fresh vocabulary, a primeval language? The language of night was not human; it was primitive, almost animal—hoarse shouting, screams, muffled moaning, savage howling, the sound of beating. . . . A brute striking wildly, a body falling; an officer raises his arm and a whole community walks toward a common grave; a soldier shrugs his shoulders, and a thousand families are torn apart, to be reunited only by death. This is the concentration camp language. It negated all other language and took its place. Rather than link, it became wall. Could it be surmounted? Could the reader be brought to the other side? I knew the answer to be negative, and yet I also knew that

1. Translated by Rosette C. Lamont.
2. Playwright, novelist, poet who was born in Ireland and wrote in France (1906–1989); author of *Waiting for Godot*, an absurdist play.
3. "As a last resource" (French).
4. 1898–1973.
5. Albert Camus (1913–1960), French novelist, essayist, and playwright who often wrote of the absurdity of life.
6. Book of Splendor, a 13th-century text of esoteric Jewish mysticism, or Kabbalah, in Aramaic and Hebrew.
7. Aramaic hymn of praise to God, recited at the end of principal sections of all synagogue services, especially by mourners at services after the death of a close relative.

"no" had to become "yes." It was the wish, the last will of the dead. One had to break the shell enclosing the dark truth, and give it a name. One had to force man to look.

The fear of forgetting: the main obsession of all those who have passed through the universe of the damned. The enemy counted on people's disbelief and forgetfulness. How could one foil this plot? And if memory grew hollow, empty of substance, what would happen to all we had accumulated along the way?

Remember, said the father to his son, and the son to his friend. Gather the names, the faces, the tears. If, by a miracle, you come out of it alive, try to reveal everything, omitting nothing, forgetting nothing. Such was the oath we had all taken: "If, by some miracle, I emerge alive, I will devote my life to testifying on behalf of those whose shadow will fall on mine forever and ever."

This is why I write certain things rather than others: to remain faithful.

Of course, there are times of doubt for the survivor, times when one would give in to weakness, or long for comfort. I hear a voice within me telling me to stop mourning the past. I too want to sing of love and of its magic. I too want to celebrate the sun, and the dawn that heralds the sun. I would like to shout, and shout loudly: "Listen, listen well! I too am capable of victory, do you hear? I too am open to laughter and joy! I want to stride, head high, my face unguarded, without having to point to the ashes over there on the horizon, without having to tamper with facts to hide their tragic ugliness. For a man born blind, God himself is blind, but look, I see, I am not blind." One feels like shouting this, but the shout changes to a murmur. One must make a choice; one must remain faithful. A big word, I know. Nevertheless I use it, it suits me. Having written the things I have written, I feel I can afford no longer to play with words. If I say that the writer in me wants to remain loyal, it is because it is true. This sentiment moves all survivors; they owe nothing to anyone, but everything to the dead.

I owe them my roots and memory. I am duty-bound to serve as their emissary, transmitting the history of their disappearance, even if it disturbs, even if it brings pain. Not to do so would be to betray them, and thus myself. And since I feel incapable of communicating their cry by shouting, I simply look at them. I see them and I write.

While writing, I question them as I question myself. I believe I said it before, elsewhere: I write to understand as much as to be understood. Will I succeed one day? Wherever one starts from one reaches darkness. God? He remains the God of darkness. Man? Source of darkness. The killers' sneers, their victims' tears, the onlookers' indifference, their complicity and complacency, the divine role in all that: I do not understand. A million children massacred: I shall never understand.

Jewish children: they haunt my writings. I see them again and again. I shall always see them. Hounded, humiliated, bent like the old men who surround them as though to protect them, unable to do so. They are thirsty, the children, and there is no one to give them water. They are hungry, the children, but there is no one to give them a crust of bread. They are afraid, and there is no one to reassure them.

They walk in the middle of the road, like vagabonds. They are on the way to the station, and they will never return. In sealed cars, without air or food, they travel toward another world; they guess where they are going, they know it, and they keep silent. Tense, thoughtful, they listen to the wind, the call of death in the distance.

All these children, these old people, I see them. I never stop seeing them. I belong to them.

But they, to whom do they belong?

People tend to think that a murderer weakens when facing a child. The child reawakens the killer's lost humanity. The killer can no longer kill the child before him, the child inside him.

Not this time. With us, it happened differently. Our Jewish children had no effect upon the killers. Nor upon the world. Nor upon God.

I think of them, I think of their childhood. Their childhood is a small Jewish town, and this town is no more. They frighten me; they reflect an image of myself, one that I pursue and run from at the same time—the image of a Jewish adolescent who knew no fear, except the fear of God, whose faith was whole, comforting, and not marked by anxiety.

No, I do not understand. And if I write, it is to warn the reader that he will not understand either. "You will not understand, you will never understand," were the words heard everywhere during the reign of night. I can only echo them. You, who never lived under a sky of blood, will never know what it was like. Even if you read all the books ever written, even if you listen to all the testimonies ever given, you will remain on this side of the wall, you will view the agony and death of a people from afar, through the screen of a memory that is not your own.

An admission of impotence and guilt? I do not know. All I know is that Treblinka and Auschwitz[8] cannot be told. And yet I have tried. God knows I have tried.

Did I attempt too much or not enough? Out of some fifteen volumes, only three or four penetrate the phantasmagoric realm of the dead. In my other books, through my other books, I try to follow other roads. For it is dangerous to linger among the dead; they hold on to you, and you run the risk of speaking only to them. And so, I forced myself to turn away from them and study other periods, explore other destinies and teach other tales: the Bible and the Talmud,[9] Hasidism[1] and its fervor, the *Shtetl*[2] and its songs, Jerusalem and its echoes; the Russian Jews and their anguish, their awakening, their courage. At times, it seems to me that I am speaking of other things with the sole purpose of keeping the essential—the personal experience—unspoken. At times I wonder: And what if I were wrong? Perhaps I should not have heeded my own advice and stayed in my own world with the dead.

But then, I have not forgotten the dead. They have their rightful place even in the works about Rizhin and Koretz,[3] Jerusalem and Kolvillàg. Even in my biblical and Midrashic[4] tales, I pursue their presence, mute and motionless. The presence of the dead then beckons in such tangible ways that it affects even the most removed characters. Thus, they appear on

8. Nazi death and concentration camps.
9. Jewish religious teachings and commentary.
1. A Jewish mystical religious movement originating in 18th-century Eastern Europe.
2. A small Jewish town or village in Eastern Europe.
3. Eastern European towns where Hasidism flourished.
4. Pertaining to the exposition or interpretation of Hebrew Scripture. "Kolvillàg": a shtetl in Transylvania (Romania) invented by Wiesel for his novel *The Oath* (1973). A massacre of Jewish martyrs occurred in medieval Kolvillàg, and in the 16th century a Jewish sage flourished there.

Mount Moriah, where Abraham is about to sacrifice his son, a holocaust offering to their common God. They appear on Mount Nebo, where Moses enters solitude and death. And again in the Pardés[5] where a certain Elisha ben Abuya,[6] seething with anger and pain, decided to repudiate his faith. They appear in Hasidic and Talmudic legends in which victims forever need defending against forces that would crush them. Technically, so to speak, they are of course elsewhere, in time and space, but on a deeper, truer plane, the dead are part of every story, of every scene. They die with Isaac, lament with Jeremiah, they sing with the *Besht*,[7] and, like him, they wait for miracles—but alas, they will not come to pass.

"But what is the connection?" you will ask. Believe there is one. After Auschwitz everything brings us back to Auschwitz. When I speak of Abraham, Isaac, and Jacob, when I evoke Rabbi Yohanan ben Zakkai[8] and Rabbi Akiba,[9] it is the better to understand them in the light of Auschwitz. As for the Maggid of Mezeritch[1] and his disciples, it is to encounter the followers of their followers, that I attempt to reconstruct their spellbound, spellbinding universe. I like to imagine them alive, exuberant, celebrating life and hope. Their happiness is as necessary to me as it was once to themselves. And yet.

How did they manage to keep their faith intact? How did they manage to sing as they went to meet the Angel of Death? I know Hasidim who never vacillated; I respect their strength. I know others who chose rebellion, protest, rage; I respect their courage. For there comes a time when only those who do not believe in God will not cry out to him in wrath and anguish.

Do not judge either. Even the heroes perished as martyrs, even the martyrs died as heroes. Who would dare oppose knives to prayers? The faith of some matters as much as the strength of others. It is not ours to judge; it is only ours to tell the tale.

But where is one to begin? Whom is one to include? One meets a Hasid in all my novels. And a child. And an old man. And a beggar. And a madman. They are all part of my inner landscape. The reason why? Pursued and persecuted by the killers, I offer them shelter. The enemy wanted to create a society purged of their presence, and I have brought some of them back. The world denied them, repudiated them, so let them live at least within the feverish dreams of my characters.

It is for them that I write.

And yet, the survivor may experience remorse. He has tried to bear witness; it was all in vain.

After the liberation, illusions shaped one's hopes. We were convinced that a new world would be built upon the ruins of Europe. A new civilization was to see the light. No more wars, no more hate, no more intolerance, no fanaticism anywhere. And all this because the witnesses would speak. And speak they did, to no avail.

They will continue, for they cannot do otherwise. When man, in his grief,

5. A book (1549) by Galilean Kabbalist Moses ben Jacob Cordovero (1522–1570).
6. A 2d-century Jewish sage.
7. Acronym for the Ba'al Shem Tov, Israel ben Eliezer (ca. 1700–1760), the charismatic Polish founder (ca. 1750) of Hasidism.
8. First-century Jewish sage who, after the destruction of the Temple, founded an academy at Javneh.
9. Jewish sage, patriot, and martyr (ca. 50–135); the principal founder of rabbinic Judaism.
1. Rabbi Dov Baer of Mezhirech (d. 1772) succeeded the Ba'al Shem Tov as Hasidic leader.

falls silent, Goethe[2] says, then God gives him the strength to sing of his sorrows. From that moment on, he may no longer choose not to sing, whether his song is heard or not. What matters is to struggle against silence with words, or through another form of silence. What matters is to gather a smile here and there, a tear here and there, a word here and there, and thus justify the faith placed in you, a long time ago, by so many victims.

Why I write? To wrench those victims from oblivion. To help the dead vanquish death.

1978

2. Johann Wolfgang von Goethe (1749–1832), German Romantic poet, novelist, playwright, and natural philosopher; author of *Faust*.

JOHN HOLLANDER
b. 1929

"I suppose that the American Jewish poet can be either blessed or cursed by whatever knowledge he or she has of Jewish history and tradition," John Hollander says. "I obviously believe in the power of the blessing." Clearly, albeit subtly, this blessing has touched the poems anthologized here. Each forms a kind of midrash or commentary on sacred or canonical text—in the sense that "all poetry," as Hollander suggests, is "unofficial midrash." He has also set his hand and mind to things not-quite-canonical, such as Kabbalah mysticism and Yiddish poetry. And with all this, he remains steeped in Western mythological, classical, and Anglo-European Christian sources. He is as much at home with Virgil as with Jeremiah, with George Herbert and Andrew Marvell as with Mani Leyb and Moyshe-Leyb Halpern.

Born in New York City in 1929, Hollander took degrees from Columbia and Indiana universities. His first poetry collection, *A Crackling of Thorns* (1958), gratefully took its title from Ecclesiastes 7.6—"For as the crackling of thorns under a pot, so is the laughter of the fool" (King James version)—which carries far, Hollander adds. His poetry has been called dense, difficult, dexterous, erudite, academic, elegant, urbane, witty. At its best, it marshals all such qualities within verbally inventive, intricate verse, wedding thought to passion.

In *Adam's Task,* Hollander combines the real and the imagined. With an epigraph from Genesis, he humorously reworks the biblical account of Adam's naming of the beasts. Combining the grandiosity of the task with Adam's seemingly offhand gibberish, Hollander illustrates just how easily the imagination, where the phonetics of language breathe, becomes reality through the naming of the animals. *The Ninth of Ab* builds on Israel's mourning over the destruction of the Temple but enlarges it, linking our modern situation to the destruction of the city as seen in Jeremiah and 2 Kings.

Hollander's foray into biblical topics has impressed literary critics, especially Harold Bloom, who has written that Hollander "has developed into an American-Jewish high Romantic, esoteric and elegiac and daring to write long poems in the Sublime mode."

For four decades, John Hollander has been a Renaissance man in contemporary American letters. He has written over twenty books of poetry, half a dozen books of criticism, and several books on poetic form including the influential and delightful *Rhyme's Reason* (1981). He has also edited books of critical essays as well as anthologies of literature, and has translated several Yiddish poets. He received the Yale Younger Poets Award in 1958 and the Bollingen Prize in Poetry in 1983. Hollander is currently a member of the English faculty at Yale University.

The Ninth of Ab[1]

August is flat and still, with ever-thickening green
  Leaves, clipped in their richness; hoarse sighs in the grass,
    Moments of mowing, mark out the lengthening summer. The ground
We children play on, and toward which maples tumble their seed.
  Reaches beneath us all, back to the sweltering City:
    Only here can it never seem yet a time to be sad in.
Only the baking concrete, the softening asphalt, the wail
  Of wall and rampart made to languish together in wild
    Heat can know of the suffering of summer. But here, or in woods
Fringing a pond in Pennsylvania, where dull-red newts
  The color of coals glow on the mossy rocks, the nights
    Are starry, full of promise of something beyond them, north
Of the north star, south of the warm dry wind, or east of the sea.
  There are no cities for now. Even in the time of songs
    Of lamenting for fallen cities, this spectacular sunset
Over the ninth hole of the golf-course of the hotel
  Should lead to no unusual evening, and the tall
    Poplars a mile away, eventually fading to total
Purple of fairway and sky and sea, should reman unlit
  By flaring of urban gloom. But here in this room, when the last
    Touches of red in the sky have sunk, these few men, lumped
Toward the end away from the windows, some with bleachy white
  Handkerchiefs comically knotted at each corner, worn
    In place of black skullcaps, read what was wailed at a wall
In the most ruined of cities. Only the City is missing.
  Behold their sitting down and their rising up. I am their music,
    (Music of half-comprehended Hebrew, and the muddied
Chaos of *Lamentations*)[2]

                    The City, a girl with the curse,
  Unclean, hangs on in her wisdom, her filthiness in her skirts,
    Gray soot caked on the fringes of buildings, already scarred
With wearing. North, north of here, I know, though, that she waits
  For my return at the end of August across the wide
    River, on a slow ferry, crawling toward the walls
Of high Manhattan's westward face, her concrete cliffs
  Micaed with sunset's prophecies of stars, her hardened clay
    Preserved, her gold undimmed, her prewar streets uncluttered.

1. Ab, or Av, is the Hebrew month that occurs in July and/or the beginning of August. On the ninth of this month, Jews fast to commemorate the destruction of the First and Second Temples in Jerusalem.
2. The Book of Lamentations, one of five scrolls in the hagiographa or "Writings" portion of the Bible, consists of poetic chapters lamenting the destruction of Jerusalem in the person of a despoiled princess: "Behold their sitting down, and their rising up; I am their musick" (Lamentations 3.63; King James vesion).

But here in this hot, hushed room I sit perspiring
Among the intonations of old tropes of despair;
Already, dark in my heart's dank corners, grow alien spores;
These drops of sweat, tears for Tammuz;[3] these restless fidgetings,
Ritual turnings northward, away from here where fractured
And gutted walls seem still afire in history's forests,
Toward her, the City who claims me after each summer is over.
Returning is sweet and somehow embarrassing and awful,
But I shall be grateful to burn again in her twilight oven.

Meanwhile the cooling ground down toward the roots of the grass
Heightens the katydids' scherzo. The men disperse in a grove
Of spruces, while from the distant water-hazard, grunts
Of frogs resume their hold on the late-arriving night,
And the just-defunct chants, never perfunctory, but not
Immediate, have vanished into the familiar unknown.
When the days are prolonged, and every vision fails to blaze
Up into final truth, when memories merely blur
A sweated lens for a moment, night is enough of a blessing
And enough of a fulfillment. See! the three canonical stars[4]
Affirm what is always beyond danger of being disturbed
By force of will or neglect, returning and unstoppable.

1965

Adam's Task

And Adam gave names to all cattle, and to the fowl of the air, and to every beast of the field. . .

GEN. 2:20

Thou, paw-paw-paw; thou, glurd; thou, spotted
Glurd; thou, whitestap, lurching through
The high-grown brush; thou, pliant-footed,
Implex; thou, awagabu.

Every burrower, each flier
Came for the name he had to give:
Gay, first work, ever to be prior,
Not yet sunk to primitive.

Thou, verdle; thou, McFleery's pomma;
Thou; thou; thou—three types of grawl;
Thou, flisket; thou, kabasch; thou, comma-
Eared mashawk; thou, all; thou, all.

Were, in a fire of becoming,
Laboring to be burned away,

3. The postexilic name of the fourth month of the Jewish year; usually occurring in the modern months of June or July. The seventeenth of this month is a fast day commemorating, like the ninth of Ab, the destruction of the Temples.

4. For Jews, the Sabbath customarily begins Friday evening when three stars have appeared in the sky.

Then work, half-measuring, half-humming,
  Would be as serious as play.

Thou, pambler; thou, rivarn; thou, greater
  Wherret, and thou, lesser one;
Thou, sproal; thou, zant; thou, lily-eater.
  Naming's over. Day is done.

1971

The Ziz[1]

What is the Ziz?
                    It is not quite
Written how at the Beginning,
Along with the Behemoth[2] of
Earth and the deep Leviathan,[3]
A third was set forth (as if air
Could share a viceroy with fire,
A third only): This is the Ziz.

The Rabbi Aquila[4] then asked:

Can we thrall him and his entailed
Space in our glance? And can we cast
A look wide enough to draw up
A glimpse of fluttering over
The chimney-stacks, of flashing in
Huge fir-boughs, or among high crags
Sinking at dusk? How could we have
Lime or twigs or patience enough
To snare the Ziz? The Phoenix[5] lives
Blessedly in belts of hidden
Fire, guarding us from the hurt of
Light beyond sunlight: but where is
The Ziz? A gleaming, transparent
Class, kingdom of all the winged?
Pre-existing its instances,
It covers them, it covers us
With no shadow that we can see:
But the dark of its wings tinges
What flutters in the shadows' heart.

1. Mentioned in Psalm 50.11, the ziz is a bird of monstrous size, ruling all the other birds. Its wings are so large that when they are unfurled, day supposedly turns into night.
2. A creature described in Job 40.15–24 as an oxlike animal. At one time a real animal, the behemoth has taken on legendary details and mythic status.
3. In biblical and Talmudic texts, Leviathan refers to a marine animal, sometimes real and sometimes legendary. Cf. Job 41.1: "Canst thou draw out leviathan with an hook?" (King James version).
4. The rabbis in these three marginal glosses are all "joke-fictional," according to Hollander: *Aquila* (Latin) means "eagle"; *Jonah* (Hebrew *Yonah*) means "dove"; *Ben-Tarnegol* (Hebrew) means "son of rooster." Nonetheless, there was a 2d-century-C.E. translator of the Bible into Greek named Aquila, who converted to Judaism and studied under Rabbi Akiva, and a 4th-century Palestinian scholar named Jonah is frequently quoted in the Jerusalem Talmud.
5. A mythological bird that, after death, reconstitutes itself from its own ashes.

Even more, Rabbi Jonah said:

In their last whispered syllables
The muffled whatziz, the shrouded
Whooziz (trailing a sorrowful
Feather from beneath its cloak) tell
False tales of the Ziz: his is not
Theirs, nor he their wintry answer.
—Nor should we desire August light,
Showing a prematurely full
Sight of the Ziz entire, lest we
See and see and see our eyes out:
No: Praised be the cool, textual
Hearsay by which we beware the
Unvarying stare of the Ziz
In whose gaze curiosity
Rusts, and all quests are suspended.

At which Ben-Tarnegol recalled:

One day at the end of days, the
General Grand Collation will
Feature the deliciously
Prepared Ziz, fragrant far beyond
Spiciness, dazzling far beyond
The poor, bland sweetness of our meals;
Faster than feasting, eternal
Past the range of our enoughness:
So, promised in time, the future
Repast; but now, only vastness
We are blind to, a birdhood
To cover the head of the sky.

1975

PHILIP ROTH
b. 1933

"How are you connected to me as another man is not?" In a 1961 symposium, Philip Roth doubted that Judaism or Jewishness determined his identity. One thinks of Bernard Malamud's *The Last Mohican*, where Susskind demands succor from the story's protagonist "because you are a man. Because you are a Jew, aren't you?" Whatever Jewish consanguinity or Jewish faith or even the notion of Jewish writing may mean for Roth, there's no doubt that his imagination and his prose itself are grounded in Jewish experience. "I have always been far more pleased by my good fortune in being born a Jew than my critics may begin to imagine. It's a complicated, interesting, morally demanding, and very singular experience, and I like that. I find myself in the historic predicament of being Jewish, with all its implications. Who could ask for more?"

Here Roth has in mind those Jews who complained that the empathically satiric stories in his first book, *Goodbye, Columbus* (1959), were instead "self-hating," that they provided "fuel" for anti-Semitism. One story, *Defender of the Faith*, involved a wartime recruit, Sheldon Grossbart, exploiting the Jewish sympathies of his sergeant. Their problems were "problems for most people," Roth explained to Jewish groups in 1962 and 1963. And yet, he added, "I never for a moment considered that the characters in the story should be anything other than Jews . . . for me there was no choice." An honest, truthful portrayal of his characters, who, after all, spring from the same milieu Roth did, must finally make them all the more human—and credible. Thus, "to have made any serious alteration in the Jewish factuality of 'Defender of the Faith,' as it began to fill itself out in my imagination, would have so unsprung the tensions I felt in the story that I would no longer have had left a story that I wanted to tell, or one I believed myself able to."

Philip Roth was born in Newark, New Jersey, on March 19, 1933, to Bess Finkel Roth, the nurturing "historian of our childhood," and Herman Roth, the son of an Orthodox, Yiddish-speaking immigrant from Galicia. During the novelist's adolescence, his father doggedly survived "grave financial setback," making him "a figure of considerable pathos and heroism in my eyes, a cross . . . between Captain Ahab and Willy Loman." In 1954, Roth graduated with a B.A. in English from Bucknell University, then took an M.A. at the University of Chicago. He married in 1959, but after three years the "lurid and tragic" marriage ended. Meanwhile, *Goodbye, Columbus* earned him the National Book Award and other prizes plus teaching positions at Iowa and Princeton.

Eli, the Fanatic (1959), the major story in *Goodbye, Columbus,* exposed early on postwar American Jews who found themselves acculturating nicely when over a third of their people had just perished in Europe. (Malamud's stories came out in 1958, Elie Wiesel's *Night* in 1960.) How are they to countenance the wretched remnant of the Old World that they or their parents had striven to leave behind? From the moment he encounters Leo Tzuref, a survivor whose very name evokes Yiddish *tsuris* (trouble), Eli Peck feels off balance, caught between the neon lights of Woodenton and the dark yeshiva. He is so callow as to tell Tzuref it would have been better in prewar Europe "for Jews and Gentiles to live beside each other in amity"—amity! Roth's storytelling genius fashions a kind of medieval morality play in which Eli shuttles between two opposing forces—man's expedient law and God's absolute Law. What's more, on every page a precise comic touch lightens and enlivens without trivializing the story's charged matter. At times, Tzuref's Talmudic quibbling with Eli sounds dizzyingly like Chico and Groucho Marx ("Sanity Clause? Go on! There ain't no Sanity Claus!").

When the assimilated American lawyer becomes Eli, the Fanatic, taking on the greenhorn's black suit, we recall *Eliyahu hanavi*: Elijah, the prophet (1 Kings 21), taking on his mantle, zealous for the Lord and not Baal. Even here, risking comedy and satire—the "special underwear," the "new Byzantine mosaic entrance" to Ted's shoeshop, the ironic "Excuse me, rabbi, but you're wanted . . . in the temple"—Roth still deepens the crisis. Perhaps Eli has merely "flipped," as the slang has it. Or is a flip a conversion? Something does come to birth during this story, set in May 1948, just when the State of Israel was declared.

After two novels that were less well received than *Goodbye, Columbus*, Roth published *Portnoy's Complaint* (1969), which electrified his career overnight. This first-person explosion of male sexual selfhood appeared, as Murray Baumgarten points out, amidst urban unrest and conflagration, anti-Vietnam protest, 1960s sexual liberation, and the burgeoning women's movement. Its hero, Alexander Portnoy, flounders between repressed "Nice Jewish Boy" and aggressive "Jewboy," with neither stereotype suiting or satisfying him: "This is my life, my only life," he cries to his analyst, "and I'm living it in the middle of a Jewish joke!" In striving for salvation, Portnoy violates enough taboos to offend not only Jews: dirty words, dirty scenes involving obsessive masturbation, oral and anal sex, exhibitionism, voyeurism, fetishism, acted-out fantasies about shiksas, and a caustic caricature of an overprotective Jewish mother.

Flagrancy, however, was not his aim, Roth said in interviews, but, rather, "prose that has the turns, vibrations, intonations, and cadences, the spontaneity and ease, of spoken language, at the same time that it is solidly grounded on the page, weighted with the irony, precision, and ambiguity associated with a more traditional literary rhetoric." And besides, "the Jewish quality of books like mine doesn't really reside in their subject matter. Talking about Jewishness hardly interests me at all. It's a kind of sensibility if anything: the nervousness, the excitability, the arguing, the dramatizing, the indignation, the obsessiveness, the touchiness, the play-acting, above all, the talking. It isn't what it's talking about that makes a book Jewish—it's that the book won't shut up." So it seems fitting that the novel's last word belongs to Portnoy's German-Jewish analyst: "Now vee may perhaps to begin."

Was the propulsive narrative in *Portnoy's Complaint* influenced by Jewish stand-up comics such as Lenny Bruce, Shelley Berman, Mort Sahl? No, Roth says, but by "a sit-down comic named Franz Kafka." Teaching at the University of Pennsylvania during the gestation of *Portnoy's Complaint*, Roth assigned "a lot of Kafka": "the course might have been called 'Studies in Guilt and Persecution.'" He half-facetiously proposed a movie of Kafka's *The Castle* featuring the Marx brothers. And he dedicated to his students a unique piece of writing: *'I Always Wanted You to Admire My Fasting'; or, Looking at Kafka* (1973). Part One rehearses, in an intimate present tense, Kafka's escape from family and guilt up to 1924, when on his deathbed he is correcting proof for his story *A Hunger Artist*. Then, Part Two launches a tale, as delectable as it is impossible, of Kafka somehow surviving to become young Philip's Newark Hebrew teacher in 1942. When this Kafka dies, the obituary says, "He leaves no survivors." Yet he does.

To Kafka and, less stringently, to other Central and Eastern European authors, Philip Roth feels himself related, in spite—or maybe because—of his American immunity from their historical fate. He edited a valuable series called *The Other Europe*, presenting Milan Kundera, Tadeusz Borowski, Bruno Schulz, among others. He also went to Jerusalem to interview the survivor-novelist Aharon Appelfeld and to Turin, where he and Primo Levi, the Auschwitz memoirist, became "mysteriously close friends."

And another figure has incited Roth's imagination. In June 1979, when Anne Frank should have turned fifty, he published *The Ghost Writer*, a finely conceived and constructed parable of artistic identity. Herein one Nathan Zuckerman, Roth's "impersonation" of himself, visits an older writer (modeled on Malamud) in 1956 to find a literary father and shake off his doting parents, who are troubled by their son's Jewish satires: "If you had been living in Nazi Germany in the thirties, would you have written such a story?" Nathan meets a dark-haired young woman with a faint foreign accent, who he feverishly decides is Anne Frank—alive but incognito because the play about her has just opened on Broadway and her survival would vitiate its force. If only he could present her as his bride to his parents—*then* they'd see that he was no self-hating Jew. *The* Anne Frank! "Dear Folks: Anne is pregnant, and happier, she says, than she ever thought possible again."

More telling than this somewhat exploitative conceit is Roth-Zuckerman's rapture on the diary: "Oh, yes. She was a marvellous young writer. She was something for thirteen. It's like watching an accelerated film of a fetus sprouting a face, watching her mastering things. . . . Suddenly she's discovering reflection, suddenly there's portraiture, character sketches, suddenly there's a long intricate eventful happening so beautifully recounted it seems to have gone through a dozen drafts. And no poisonous notion of being *interesting* or *serious*. She just *is*." And then: "She's like some impassioned little sister of Kafka's, his lost little daughter—a kinship is even there in the face, I think."

Nathan Zuckerman persists in Roth's work on into his highly inventive, formally experimental novel *The Counterlife* (1987). There, besides the perennial interwoven themes of family constraint and sexual salvation, American Zionism figures centrally. As ever, Roth's brilliant impersonations make it hard to pinpoint authorial opinion. Just as he will never get the Holocaust off his mind or apologize for not having undergone it, Roth compellingly states the Israeli "counterlife" to Diaspora Jewishness: "a life free of Jewish cringing, deference, diplomacy, apprehension, alienation, self-pity, self-satire, self-mistrust, depression, clowning, bitterness, nervousness, inwardness, hypercriticalness, hypertouchiness, social anxiety, social assimilation—a way of life absolved, in short, of all the Jewish 'abnormalities,' those peculiarities of self-division whose traces remained imprinted in just about every engaging Jew I knew."

Roth went on tapping the vein of self-division in its various forms—past and present, family and self, conscience and concupiscence, Israel and America, fact and fiction—in succeeding novels: *Sabbath's Theater* (1995) won the National Book Award; *American Pastoral* (1997) won the Pulitzer prize. He also wrote one book of unalloyed candor, an absorbing memoir of his father's death: *Patrimony* (1991) is subtitled *A True Story*. Ultimately, the truth of Philip Roth's story may lie in two epigraphs he chose: a Yiddish proverb for *Goodbye, Columbus*—"The heart is half a prophet"—and a biblical figure for *Operation Shylock* (1993)—Jacob wrestling the angel until daybreak. Jacob's last word in that story is, "I will not let thee go until thou bless me."

Eli, the Fanatic[1]

Leo Tzuref stepped out from back of a white column to welcome Eli Peck. Eli jumped back, surprised; then they shook hands and Tzuref[2] gestured him into the sagging old mansion. At the door Eli turned, and down the slope of lawn, past the jungle of hedges, beyond the dark, untrampled horse path, he saw the street lights blink on in Woodenton. The stores along Coach House Road tossed up a burst of yellow—it came to Eli as a secret signal from his townsmen: "Tell this Tzuref where we stand, Eli. This is a modern community, Eli, we have our families, we pay taxes . . ." Eli, burdened by the message, gave Tzuref a dumb, weary stare.

"You must work a full day," Tzuref said, steering the attorney and his briefcase into the chilly hall.

Eli's heels made a racket on the cracked marble floor, and he spoke above it. "It's the commuting that's killing," he said, and entered the dim room Tzuref waved open for him. "Three hours a day . . . I came right from the train." He dwindled down into a harp-backed chair. He expected it would be deeper than it was and consequently jarred himself on the sharp bones of his seat. It woke him, this shiver of the behind, to his business. Tzuref, a bald shaggy-browed man who looked as if he'd once been very fat, sat back of an empty desk, halfway hidden, as though he were settled on the floor. Everything around him was empty. There were no books in the bookshelves, no rugs on the floor, no draperies in the big casement windows. As Eli began to speak Tzuref got up and swung a window back on one noisy hinge. "May and it's like August," he said, and with his back to Eli, he revealed the black

1. Elijah the Prophet, as he is known, was zealous for the Lord against Baal in the time of Ahab, king of Israel (1 Kings 17 ff.).
2. The Yiddish for *trouble* is *tsuris*.

circle on the back of his head. The crown of his head was missing! He returned through the dimness—the lamps had no bulbs—and Eli realized all he'd seen was a skullcap.[3] Tzuref struck a match and lit a candle, just as the half-dying shouts of children at play rolled in through the open window. It was as though Tzuref had opened it so Eli could hear them.

"Aah, now," he said. "I received your letter."

Eli poised, waiting for Tzuref to swish open a drawer and remove the letter from his file. Instead the old man leaned forward onto his stomach, worked his hand into his pants pocket, and withdrew what appeared to be a week-old handkerchief. He uncrumpled it; he unfolded it; he ironed it on the desk with the side of his hand. "So," he said.

Eli pointed to the grimy sheet which he'd gone over word-by-word with his partners, Lewis and McDonnell. "I expected an answer," Eli said. "It's a week."

"It was so important, Mr. Peck, I knew you would come."

Some children ran under the open window and their mysterious babble—not mysterious to Tzuref, who smiled—entered the room like a third person. Their noise caught up against Eli's flesh and he was unable to restrain a shudder. He wished he had gone home, showered and eaten dinner, before calling on Tzuref. He was not feeling as professional as usual—the place was too dim, it was too late. But down in Woodenton they would be waiting, his clients and neighbors. He spoke for the Jews of Woodenton, not just himself and his wife.

"You understood?" Eli said.

"It's not hard."

"It's a matter of zoning . . ." and when Tzuref did not answer, but only drummed his fingers on his lips, Eli said, "We didn't make the laws . . ."

"You respect them."

"They protect us . . . the community."

"The law is the law," Tzuref said.

"Exactly!" Eli had the urge to rise and walk about the room.

"And then of course"—Tzuref made a pair of scales in the air with his hands—"The law is not the law. When is the law that is the law not the law?" He jiggled the scales. "And vice versa."

"Simply," Eli said sharply. "You can't have a boarding school in a residential area." He would not allow Tzuref to cloud the issue with issues. "We thought it better to tell you before any action is undertaken."

"But a house in a residential area?"

"Yes. That's what residential means." The DP's[4] English was perhaps not as good as it seemed at first. Tzuref spoke slowly, but till then Eli had mistaken it for craft—or even wisdom. "Residence means home," he added.

"So this is my residence."

"But the children?"

"It is their residence."

"*Seventeen* children?"

"Eighteen," Tzuref said.

"But you *teach* them here."

"The Talmud. That's illegal?"

3. Yarmulke or yamalkah, a cap worn traditionally by Jewish men and boys for prayer.
4. Displaced person, forced from home by war.

"The law": the "Law" in Judaism denotes Mosaic Law, as in the Pentateuch.

"That makes it school."

Tzuref hung the scales again, tipping slowly the balance.

"Look, Mr. Tzuref, in America we call such a place a boarding school."

"Where they teach the Talmud?"

"Where they teach period. You are the headmaster, they are the students."

Tzuref placed his scales on the desk. "Mr. Peck," he said, "I don't believe it . . ." but he did not seem to be referring to anything Eli had said.

"Mr. Tzuref, that is the law. I came to ask what you intend to do."

"What I *must* do?"

"I hope they are the same."

"They are." Tzuref brought his stomach into the desk. "We stay." He smiled. "We are tired. The headmaster is tired. The students are tired."

Eli rose and lifted his briefcase. It felt so heavy packed with the grievances, vengeances, and schemes of his clients. There were days when he carried it like a feather—in Tzuref's office it weighed a ton.

"Goodbye, Mr. Tzuref."

"Sholom,"[5] Tzuref said.

Eli opened the door to the office and walked carefully down the dark tomb of a corridor to the door. He stepped out on the porch and, leaning against a pillar, looked down across the lawn to the children at play. Their voices whooped and rose and dropped as they chased each other round the old house. The dusk made the children's game look like a tribal dance. Eli straightened up, started off the porch, and suddenly the dance was ended. A long piercing scream trailed after. It was the first time in his life anyone had run at the sight of him. Keeping his eyes on the lights of Woodenton, he headed down the path.

And then, seated on a bench beneath a tree, Eli saw him. At first it seemed only a deep hollow of blackness—then the figure emerged. Eli recognized him from the description. There he was, wearing the hat, that hat which was the very cause of Eli's mission, the source of Woodenton's upset. The town's lights flashed their message once again: "Get the one with the hat. What a nerve, what a nerve . . ."

Eli started towards the man. Perhaps he was less stubborn than Tzuref, more reasonable. After all, it was the law. But when he was close enough to call out, he didn't. He was stopped by the sight of the black coat that fell down below the man's knees, and the hands which held each other in his lap. By the round-topped, wide-brimmed Talmudic hat, pushed onto the back of his head. And by the beard, which hid his neck and was so soft and thin it fluttered away and back again with each heavy breath he took. He was asleep, his sidelocks[6] curled loose on his cheeks. His face was no older than Eli's.

Eli hurried towards the lights.

The note on the kitchen table unsettled him. Scribblings on bits of paper had made history this past week. This one, however, was unsigned. "Sweetie," it said, "I went to sleep. I had a sort of Oedipal experience[7] with the baby today. Call Ted Heller."

5. "Peace" (Yiddish), or *shalom* (Hebrew), a word of greeting or farewell.

6. Hair worn uncut in front of or behind the ears by Orthodox Jewish males.

7. Sexual feelings of a child toward a parent of the opposite sex. Oedipus, according to Greek legend, killed his father and married his mother.

She had left him a cold soggy dinner in the refrigerator. He hated cold soggy dinners, but would take one gladly in place of Miriam's presence. He was ruffled, and she never helped that, not with her infernal analytic powers. He loved her when life was proceeding smoothly—and that was when she loved him. But sometimes Eli found being a lawyer surrounded him like quicksand—he couldn't get his breath. Too often he wished he were pleading for the other side; though if he were on the other side, then he'd wish he were on the side he was. The trouble was that sometimes the law didn't seem to be the answer, *law* didn't seem to have anything to do with what was aggravating everybody. And that, of course, made him feel foolish and unnecessary . . . Though that was not the situation here—the townsmen had a case. But not *exactly*, and if Miriam were awake to see Eli's upset, she would set about explaining his distress to him, understanding him, forgiving him, so as to get things back to Normal, for Normal was where they loved one another. The difficulty with Miriam's efforts was they only upset him more; not only did they explain little to him about himself or his predicament, but they convinced him of *her* weakness. Neither Eli nor Miriam, it turned out, was terribly strong. Twice before he'd faced this fact, and on both occasions had found solace in what his neighbors forgivingly referred to as "a nervous breakdown."

Eli ate his dinner with his briefcase beside him. Halfway through, he gave in to himself, removed Tzuref's notes, and put them on the table, beside Miriam's. From time to time he flipped through the notes, which had been carried into town by the one in the black hat. The first note, the incendiary:

> To whom it may concern:
>
> Please give this gentleman the following: Boys shoes with rubber heels and soles.
>
> 5 prs size 6c
> 3 prs size 5c
> 3 prs size 5b
> 2 prs size 4a
> 3 prs size 4c
> 1 pr size 7b
> 1 pr size 7c
>
> Total 18 prs. boys shoes. This gentleman has a check already signed. Please fill in correct amount.
>
> L. TZUREF
> Director, Yeshivah[8] of
> Woodenton, N.Y.
> (5/8/48)

"Eli, a regular greenhorn,"[9] Ted Heller had said. "He didn't say a word. Just handed me the note and stood there, like in the Bronx[1] the old guys who used to come around selling Hebrew trinkets."

8. Jewish academy of Talmudic learning.
9. An inexperienced or unsophisticated person, especially a newly arrived Jewish immigrant.
1. A borough of New York City, north and east of Manhattan. Many Jews moved to the suburbs from there.

"A Yeshivah!" Artie Berg had said. "Eli, in Woodenton, a Yeshivah! If I want to live in Brownsville,[2] Eli, I'll live in Brownsville."

"Eli," Harry Shaw speaking now, "the old Puddington place. Old man Puddington'll roll over in his grave. Eli, when I left the city, Eli, I didn't plan the city should come to me."

Note number two:

Dear Grocer:

Please give this gentleman ten pounds of sugar. Charge it to our account, Yeshivah of Woodenton, NY—which we will now open with you and expect a bill each month. The gentleman will be in to see you once or twice a week.

L. TZUREF, Director
(5/10/48)

P.S. Do you carry kosher meat?

"He walked right by my window, the greenie," Ted had said, "and he nodded, Eli. He's my *friend* now."

"Eli," Artie Berg had said, "he handed the damn thing to a *clerk* at Stop N' Shop—and in that hat yet!"

"Eli," Harry Shaw again, "it's not funny. Someday, Eli, it's going to be a hundred little kids with little *yamalkahs* chanting their Hebrew lessons on Coach House Road, and then it's not going to strike you funny."

"Eli, what goes on up there—my kids hear strange sounds."

"Eli, this is a modern community."

"Eli, we pay taxes."

"Eli."

"Eli!"

"Eli!"

At first it was only another townsman crying in his ear; but when he turned he saw Miriam, standing in the doorway, behind her belly.

"Eli, sweetheart, how was it?"

"He said no."

"Did you see the other one?" she asked.

"Sleeping, under a tree."

"Did you let him know how people feel?"

"He was sleeping."

"Why didn't you wake him up? Eli, this isn't an everyday thing."

"He was tired!"

"Don't shout, please," Miriam said.

" 'Don't shout. I'm pregnant. The baby is heavy.' " Eli found he was getting angry at nothing she'd said yet; it was what she was going to say.

"He's a very heavy baby the doctor says," Miriam told him.

"Then sit *down* and make my dinner." Now he found himself angry about her not being present at the dinner which he'd just been relieved that she wasn't present at. It was as though he had a raw nerve for a tail, that he kept stepping on. At last Miriam herself stepped on it.

2. A section of Brooklyn, a borough of New York City, once largely inhabited by immigrant Jews.

"Eli, you're upset. I understand."

"You *don't* understand."

She left the room. From the stairs she called, "I do, sweetheart."

It was a trap! He would grow angry knowing she would be "understanding." She would in turn grow more understanding seeing his anger. He would in turn grow angrier . . . The phone rang.

"Hello," Eli said.

"Eli, Ted. So?"

"So nothing."

"Who is Tzuref? He's an American guy?"

"No. A DP. German."

"And the kids?"

"DP's too. He teaches them."

"What? What subjects?" Ted asked.

"I don't know."

"And the guy with the hat, you saw the guy with the hat?"

"Yes. He was sleeping."

"Eli, he sleeps with the *hat*?"

"He sleeps with the hat."

"Goddam fanatics," Ted said. "This is the twentieth century, Eli. Now it's the guy with the hat. Pretty soon all the little Yeshivah boys'll be spilling down into town."

"Next thing they'll be after our daughters."

"Michele and Debbie wouldn't look at them."

"Then," Eli mumbled, "you've got nothing to worry about, Teddie," and he hung up.

In a moment the phone rang. "Eli? We got cut off. We've got nothing to worry about? You worked it out?"

"I have to see him again tomorrow. We can work something out."

"That's fine, Eli. I'll call Artie and Harry."

Eli hung up.

"I thought you said *nothing* worked out." It was Miriam.

"I did."

"Then why did you tell Ted *something* worked out?"

"It did."

"Eli, maybe you should get a little more therapy."

"That's enough of that, Miriam."

"You can't function as a lawyer by being neurotic. That's no answer."

"You're ingenious, Miriam."

She turned, frowning, and took her heavy baby to bed.

The phone rang.

"Eli, Artie. Ted called. You worked it out? No trouble?"

"Yes."

"When are they going?"

"Leave it to me, will you, Artie? I'm tired. I'm going to sleep."

In bed Eli kissed his wife's belly and laid his head upon it to think. He laid it lightly, for she was that day entering the second week of her ninth month. Still, when she slept, it was a good place to rest, to rise and fall with her breathing and figure things out. "If that guy would take off that crazy hat. I know it, what eats them. If he'd take off that crazy hat everything would be all right."

"What?" Miriam said.

"I'm talking to the baby."

Miriam pushed herself up in bed. "Eli, please, baby, shouldn't you maybe stop in to see Dr. Eckman, just for a little conversation?"

"I'm fine."

"Oh, sweetie!" she said, and put her head back on the pillow.

"You know what your mother brought to this marriage—a sling chair and a goddam New School enthusiasm for Sigmund Freud."[3]

Miriam feigned sleep, he could tell by the breathing.

"I'm telling the kid the truth, aren't I, Miriam? A sling chair, three months to go on a *New Yorker* subscription, and *An Introduction to Psychoanalysis*.[4] Isn't that right?"

"Eli, must you be aggressive?"

"That's all you worry about, is your insides. You stand in front of the mirror all day and look at yourself being pregnant."

"Pregnant mothers have a relationship with the fetus that fathers can't understand."

"Relationship my ass. What is my liver doing now? What is my small intestine doing now? Is my island of Langerhans[5] on the blink?"

"Don't be jealous of a little fetus, Eli."

"I'm jealous of your island of Lagerhans!"

"Eli, I can't argue with you when I know it's not me you're really angry with. Don't you see, sweetie, you're angry with yourself."

"You and Eckman."

"Maybe he could help, Eli."

"Maybe he could help you. You're practically lovers as it is."

"You're being hostile again," Miriam said.

"What do you care—it's only *me* I'm being hostile towards."

"Eli, we're going to have a beautiful baby, and I'm going to have a perfectly simple delivery, and you're going to make a fine father, and there's absolutely no reason to be obsessed with whatever is on your mind. All we have to worry about—" she smiled at him "—is a name."

Eli got out of bed and slid into his slippers. "We'll name the kid Eckman if it's a boy and Eckman if it's a girl."

"Eckman Peck sounds terrible."

"He'll have to live with it," Eli said, and he went down to his study where the latch on his briefcase glinted in the moonlight that came through the window.

He removed the Tzuref notes and read through them all again. It unnerved him to think of all the flashy reasons his wife could come up with for his reading and rereading the notes. "Eli, why are you so *preoccupied* with Tzuref?" "Eli, stop getting *involved*. Why do you think you're getting *involved*, Eli?" Sooner or later, everybody's wife finds their weak spot. His goddam luck he had to be neurotic! Why couldn't he have been born with a short leg.

3. Eminent Austrian psychologist and founder of psychoanalysis (1856–1939). "New School": i.e., the New School for Social Research, in New York City, founded in 1919 for progressive adult education.

4. A 1920 work by Sigmund Freud.

5. The islet of Langerhans is a group of endocrine cells in the pancreas that produces insulin.

He removed the cover from his typewriter, hating Miriam for the edge she had. All the time he wrote the letter, he could hear what she would be saying about his not being *able* to let the matter drop. Well, her trouble was that she wasn't *able* to face the matter. But he could hear her answer already: clearly, he was guilty of "a reaction formation." Still, all the fancy phrases didn't fool Eli: all she wanted really was for Eli to send Tzuref and family on their way, so that the community's temper would quiet, and the calm circumstances of their domestic happiness return. All she wanted were order and love in her private world. Was she so wrong? Let the world bat its brains out—in Woodenton there should be peace. He wrote the letter anyway:

Dear Mr. Tzuref:

Our meeting this evening seems to me inconclusive. I don't think there's any reason for us not to be able to come up with some sort of compromise that will satisfy the Jewish community of Woodenton and the Yeshivah and yourself. It seems to me that what most disturbs my neighbors are the visits to town by the gentleman in the black hat, suit, etc. Woodenton is a progressive suburban community whose members, both Jewish and Gentile, are anxious that their families live in comfort and beauty and serenity. This is, after all, the twentieth century, and we do not think it too much to ask that the members of our community dress in a manner appropriate to the time and place.

Woodenton, as you may not know, has long been the home of well-to-do Protestants. It is only since the war that Jews have been able to buy property here, and for Jews and Gentiles to live beside each other in amity. For this adjustment to be made, both Jews and Gentiles alike have had to give up some of their more extreme practices in order not to threaten or offend the other. Certainly such amity is to be desired. Perhaps if such conditions had existed in prewar Europe, the persecution of the Jewish people, of which you and those 18 children have been victims, could not have been carried out with such success—in fact, might not have been carried out at all.

Therefore, Mr. Tzuref, will you accept the following conditions? If you can, we will see fit not to carry out legal action against the Yeshivah for failure to comply with township Zoning ordinances No. 18 and No. 23. The conditions are simply:

1. The religious, educational, and social activities of the Yeshivah of Woodenton will be confined to the Yeshivah grounds.

2. Yeshivah personnel are welcomed in the streets and stores of Woodenton provided they are attired in clothing usually associated with American life in the 20th century.

If these conditions are met, we see no reason why the Yeshivah of Woodenton cannot live peacefully and satisfactorily with the Jews of Woodenton—as the Jews of Woodenton have come to live with the Gentiles of Woodenton. I would appreciate an immediate reply.

Sincerely,
ELI PECK, Attorney

Two days later Eli received his immediate reply:

Mr. Peck:

The suit the gentleman wears is all he's got.

Sincerely,
LEO TZUREF, Headmaster

Once again, as Eli swung around the dark trees and onto the lawn, the children fled. He reached out with his briefcase as if to stop them, but they were gone so fast all he saw moving was a flock of skullcaps.

"Come, come . . ." a voice called from the porch. Tzuref appeared from behind a pillar. Did he *live* behind those pillars? Was he just watching the children at play? Either way, when Eli appeared, Tzuref was ready, with no forewarning.

"Hello," Eli said.

"Sholom."

"I didn't mean to frighten them."

"They're scared, so they run."

"I didn't do anything."

Tzuref shrugged. The little movement seemed to Eli strong as an accusation. What he didn't get at home, he got here.

Inside the house they took their seats. Though it was lighter than a few evenings before, a bulb or two would have helped. Eli had to hold his briefcase towards the window for the last gleamings. He removed Tzuref's letter from a manila folder. Tzuref removed Eli's letter from his pants pocket. Eli removed the carbon of his own letter from another manila folder. Tzuref removed Eli's first letter from his back pocket. Eli removed the carbon from his briefcase. Tzuref raised his palms. ". . . It's all I've got . . ."

Those upraised palms, the mocking tone—another accusation. It was a crime to keep carbons! Everybody had an edge on him—Eli could do no right.

"I offered a compromise, Mr. Tzuref. You refused."

"Refused, Mr. Peck? What is, is."

"The man could get a new suit."

"That's all he's got."

"So you told me," Eli said.

"So I told you, so you know."

"It's not an insurmountable obstacle, Mr. Tzuref. We have stores."

"For that too?"

"On Route 12, a Robert Hall—"

"To take away the one thing a man's got?"

"Not take away, *replace*."

"But I tell you he has nothing. *Nothing*. You have that word in English? *Nicht? Gornisht?*"

"Yes, Mr. Tzuref, we have the word."

"A mother and a father?" Tzuref said. "No. A wife? No. A baby? A little ten-month-old baby? No! A village full of friends? A synagogue where you knew the feel of every seat under your pants? Where with your eyes closed you could smell the cloth of the Torah?" Tzuref pushed out of his chair, stirring a breeze that swept Eli's letter to the floor. At the window he leaned out, and looked, beyond Woodenton. When he turned he was shaking a finger at Eli. "And a medical experiment they performed on him yet! That leaves nothing, Mr. Peck. Absolutely nothing!"

"I misunderstood."

"No news reached Woodenton?"

"About the suit, Mr. Tzuref. I thought he couldn't afford another."

"He can't."

They were right where they'd begun. "Mr. Tzuref!" Eli demanded. "*Here?*" He smacked his hand to his billfold.

"Exactly!" Tzuref said, smacking his own breast.

"Then we'll buy him one!" Eli crossed to the window and taking Tzuref by the shoulders, pronounced each word slowly. "We-will-pay-for-it. All right?"

"Pay? What, diamonds!"

Eli raised a hand to his inside pocket, then let it drop. Oh stupid! Tzuref, father to eighteen, had smacked not what lay under his coat, but deeper, under the ribs.

"Oh . . ." Eli said. He moved away along the wall. "The suit is all he's got then."

"You got my letter," Tzuref said.

Eli stayed back in the shadow, and Tzuref turned to his chair. He swished Eli's letter from the floor, and held it up. "You say too much . . . all this reasoning . . . all these conditions . . ."

"What can I do?"

"You have the word 'suffer' in English?"

"We have the word suffer. We have the word law too."

"Stop with the law! You have the word suffer. Then try it. It's a little thing."

"They won't," Eli said.

"But you, Mr. Peck, how about you?"

"I am them, they are me, Mr. Tzuref."

"Aach! You are us, we are you!"

Eli shook and shook his head. In the dark he suddenly felt that Tzuref might put him under a spell. "Mr. Tzuref, a little light?"

Tzuref lit what tallow was left in the holders. Eli was afraid to ask if they couldn't afford electricity. Maybe candles were all they had left.

"Mr. Peck, who made the law, may I ask you that?"

"The people."

"No."

"Yes."

"Before the people."

"No one. Before the people there was no law." Eli didn't care for the conversation, but with only candlelight, he was being lulled into it.

"Wrong," Tzuref said.

"We make the law, Mr. Tzuref. It is our community. These are my neighbors. I am their attorney. They pay me. Without law there is chaos."

"What you call law, I call shame. The heart, Mr. Peck, the heart is law! God!" he announced.

"Look, Mr. Tzuref, I didn't come here to talk metaphysics. People use the law, it's a flexible thing. They protect what they value, their property, their well-being, their happiness—"

"Happiness? They hide their shame. And you, Mr. Peck, you are shameless?"

"We do it," Eli said, wearily, "for our children. This is the twentieth century . . ."

"For the goyim[6] maybe. For me the Fifty-eighth."[7] He pointed at Eli. "That is too old for shame."

Eli felt squashed. Everybody in the world had evil reasons for his actions. Everybody! With reasons so cheap, who buys bulbs. "Enough wisdom, Mr. Tzuref. Please. I'm exhausted."

"Who isn't?" Tzuref said.

He picked Eli's papers from his desk and reached up with them. "What do you intend for us to do?"

"What you must," Eli said. "I made the offer."

"So he must give up his suit?"

"Tzuref, Tzuref, leave me be with that suit! I'm not the only lawyer in the world. I'll drop the case, and you'll get somebody who won't talk compromise. Then you'll have no home, no children, nothing. Only a lousy black suit! Sacrifice what you want. I know what I would do."

To that Tzuref made no answer, but only handed Eli his letters.

"It's not me, Mr. Tzuref, it's them."

"They are you."

"No," Eli intoned, "I am me. They are them. You are you."

"You talk about leaves and branches. I'm dealing with under the dirt."

"Mr. Tzuref, you're driving me crazy with Talmudic wisdom.[8] This is that, that is the other thing. Give me a straight answer."

"Only for straight questions."

"Oh, God!"

Eli returned to his chair and plunged his belongings into his case. "Then, that's all," he said angrily.

Tzuref gave him the shrug.

"Remember, Tzuref, you called this down on yourself."

"*I* did?"

Eli refused to be his victim again. Double-talk proved nothing.

"Goodbye," he said.

But as he opened the door leading to the hall, he heard Tzuref.

"And your wife, how is she?"

"Fine, just fine." Eli kept going.

"And the baby is due when, any day?"

Eli turned. "That's right."

"Well," Tzuref said, rising. "Good luck."

"You know?"

Tzuref pointed out the window—then, with his hands, he drew upon himself a beard, a hat, a long, long coat. When his fingers formed the hem they touched the floor. "He shops two, three times a week, he gets to know them."

"He *talks* to them?"

"He sees them."

"And he can tell which is my wife?"

6. Gentiles, non-Jews (Yiddish, from the Hebrew).
7. The Jewish calendar reckons years as from the biblical Creation.
8. Analytic, argumentative skills developed from studying Talmud, the sacred interpretation of Judaic law.

"They shop at the same stores. He says she is beautiful. She has a kind face. A woman capable of love . . . though who can be sure."

"*He* talks about *us*, to *you*?" demanded Eli.

"You talk about us, to her?"

"Goodbye, Mr. Tzuref."

Tzuref said, "Sholom. And good luck—I know what it is to have children. Sholom," Tzuref whispered, and with the whisper the candles went out. But the instant before, the flames leaped into Tzuref's eyes, and Eli saw it was not luck Tzuref wished him at all.

Outside the door, Eli waited. Down the lawn the children were holding hands and whirling around in a circle. At first he did not move. But he could not hide in the shadows all night. Slowly he began to slip along the front of the house. Under his hands he felt where bricks were out. He moved in the shadows until he reached the side. And then, clutching his briefcase to his chest, he broke across the darkest spots of the lawn. He aimed for a distant glade of woods, and when he reached it he did not stop, but ran through until he was so dizzied that the trees seemed to be running beside him, fleeing not towards Woodenton but away. His lungs were nearly ripping their seams as he burst into the yellow glow of the Gulf station at the edge of town.

"Eli, I had pains today. Where were you?"

"I went to Tzuref."

"Why didn't you call? I was worried."

He tossed his hat past the sofa and onto the floor. "Where are my winter suits?"

"In the hall closet. Eli, it's May."

"I need a strong suit." He left the room, Miriam behind him.

"Eli, talk to me. Sit down. Have dinner. Eli, what are you doing? You're going to get moth balls all over the carpet."

He peered out from the hall closet. Then he peered in again—there was a zipping noise, and suddenly he swept a greenish tweed suit before his wife's eyes.

"Eli, I love you in that suit. But not now. Have something to eat. I made dinner tonight—I'll warm it."

"You've got a box big enough for this suit?"

"I got a Bonwit's[9] box, the other day. Eli, *why?*"

"Miriam, you see me doing something, let me do it."

"You haven't eaten."

"I'm *doing* something." He started up the stairs to the bedroom.

"Eli, would you please tell me what it is you want, and why?"

He turned and looked down at her. "Suppose this time you give me the reasons *before* I tell you what I'm doing. It'll probably work out the same anyway."

"Eli, I want to help."

"It doesn't concern you."

"But I want to help *you*," Miriam said.

"Just be quiet, then."

9. Bonwit Teller, an upscale department store on Manhattan's Fifth Avenue.

"But you're upset," she said, and she followed him up the stairs, heavily, breathing for two.

"Eli, what now?"

"A shirt." He yanked open all the drawers of their new teak dresser. He extracted a shirt.

"Eli, batiste? With a tweed suit?" she inquired.

He was at the closet now, on his knees. "Where are my cordovans?[1]

"Eli, why are you doing this so compulsively? You look like you *have* to do something."

"Oh, Miriam, you're supersubtle."

"Eli, stop this and talk to me. Stop it or I'll call Dr. Eckman."

Eli was kicking off the shoes he was wearing. "Where's the Bonwit box?"

"Eli, do you want me to have the baby right *here!*"

Eli walked over and sat down on the bed. He was draped not only with his own clothing, but also with the greenish tweed suit, the batiste shirt, and under each arm a shoe. He raised his arms and let the shoes drop onto the bed. Then he undid his necktie with one hand and his teeth and added that to the booty.

"Underwear," he said. "He'll need underwear."

"Who!"

He was slipping out of his socks.

Miriam kneeled down and helped him ease his left foot out of the sock. She sat with it on the floor. "Eli, just lie back. Please."

"Plaza 9-3103."

"What?"

"Eckman's number," he said. "It'll save you the trouble."

"Eli—"

"You've got that goddam tender 'You need help' look in your eyes, Miriam, don't tell me you don't."

"I don't."

"I'm not flipping," Eli said.

"I know, Eli."

"Last time I sat in the bottom of the closet and chewed on my bedroom slippers. That's what I did."

"I know."

"And I'm not doing that. This is not a nervous breakdown, Miriam, let's get that straight."

"Okay," Miriam said. She kissed the foot she held. Then, softly, she asked, "What *are* you doing?"

"Getting clothes for the guy in the hat. Don't tell me why, Miriam. Just let me do it."

"That's all?" she asked.

"That's all."

"You're not leaving?"

"No."

"Sometimes I think it gets too much for you, and you'll just leave."

"What gets too much?"

"I don't *know*, Eli. Something gets too much. Whenever everything's

1. Shoes made from a dark grayish-red leather, usually horsehide. "Batiste": a fine cloth.

peaceful for a long time, and things are nice and pleasant, and we're expecting to be even happier. Like now. It's as if you don't think we *deserve* to be happy."

"Damn it, Miriam! I'm giving this guy a new suit, is that all right? From now on he comes into Woodenton like everybody else, is that all right with you?"

"And Tzuref moves?"

"I don't even know if he'll take the suit, Miriam! What do you have to bring up moving!"

"Eli, I didn't bring up moving. Everybody did. That's what everybody wants. Why make everybody un*happy*. It's even a law, Eli."

"Don't tell me what's the law."

"All right, sweetie. I'll get the box."

"*I'll* get the box. Where is it?"

"In the basement."

When he came up from the basement, he found all the clothes neatly folded and squared away on the sofa: shirt, tie, shoes, socks, underwear, belt, and an old gray flannel suit. His wife sat on the end of the sofa, looking like an anchored balloon.

"Where's the green suit?" he said.

"Eli, it's your loveliest suit. It's my favorite suit. Whenever I think of you, Eli, it's in that suit."

"Get it out."

"Eli, it's a Brooks Brothers suit. You say yourself how much you love it."

"Get it out."

"But the gray flannel's more practical. For shopping."

"Get it out."

"You go overboard, Eli. That's your trouble. You won't do anything in moderation. That's how people destroy themselves."

"I do *everything* in moderation. That's my trouble. The suit's in the closet again?"

She nodded, and began to fill up with tears. "Why does it have to be *your* suit? Who are you even to decide to give a suit? What about the others?" She was crying openly, and holding her belly. "Eli, I'm going to have a baby. Do we need all *this*?" and she swept the clothes off the sofa to the floor.

At the closet Eli removed the green suit. "It's a J. Press,"[2] he said, looking at the lining.

"I hope to hell he's happy with it!" Miriam said, sobbing.

A half hour later the box was packed. The cord he'd found in the kitchen cabinet couldn't keep the outfit from popping through. The trouble was there was too much: the gray suit *and* the green suit, an oxford shirt as well as the batiste. But let him have two suits! Let him have three, four, if only this damn silliness would stop! And a hat—of course! God, he'd almost forgotten the hat. He took the stairs two at a time and in Miriam's closet yanked a hatbox from the top shelf. Scattering hat and tissue paper to the floor, he returned downstairs, where he packed away the hat he'd worn that day. Then he looked at his wife, who lay outstretched on the floor before the fireplace.

2. J. Press and Brooks Brothers are high-quality, conservative clothing stores in Manhattan.

For the third time in as many minutes she was saying, "Eli, this is the real thing."

"Where?"

"Right under the baby's head, like somebody's squeezing oranges."

Now that he'd stopped to listen he was stupefied. He said, "But you have two more weeks . . ." Somehow he'd really been expecting it was to go on not just another two weeks, but another nine months. This led him to suspect, suddenly, that his wife was feigning pain so as to get his mind off delivering the suit. And just as suddenly he resented himself for having such a thought. God, what had he become! He'd been an unending bastard towards her since this Tzuref business had come up—just when her pregnancy must have been most burdensome. He'd allowed her no access to him, but still, he was sure, for good reasons: she might tempt him out of his confusion with her easy answers. He could be tempted all right, it was why he fought so hard. But now a sweep of love came over him at the thought of her contracting womb, and his child. And yet he would not indicate it to her. Under such splendid marital conditions, who knows but she might extract some promise from him about his concern with the school on the hill.

Having packed his second bag of the evening, Eli sped his wife to Woodenton Memorial. There she proceeded not to have her baby, but to lie hour after hour through the night having at first oranges, then bowling balls, then basketballs, squeezed back of her pelvis. Eli sat in the waiting room, under the shattering African glare of a dozen rows of fluorescent bulbs, composing a letter to Tzuref.

> Dear Mr. Tzuref:
>
> The clothes in this box are for the gentleman in the hat. In a life of sacrifice what is one more? But in a life of no sacrifices even one is impossible. Do you see what I'm saying, Mr. Tzuref? I am not a Nazi[3] who would drive eighteen children, who are probably frightened at the sight of a firefly, into homelessness. But if you want a home here, you must accept what we have to offer. The world is the world, Mr. Tzuref. As you would say, what is, is. All we say to this man is change your clothes. Enclosed are two suits and two shirts, and everything else he'll need, including a new hat. When he needs new clothes let me know.
>
> We await his appearance in Woodenton, as we await friendly relations with the Yeshivah of Woodenton.

He signed his name and slid the note under a bursting flap and into the box. Then he went to the phone at the end of the room and dialed Ted Heller's number.

"Hello."

"Shirley, it's Eli."

"Eli, we've been calling all night. The lights are on in your place, but nobody answers. We thought it was burglars."

"Miriam's having the baby."

3. A member of the German National Socialist party, which came to power with Hitler in 1933.

"At home?" Shirley said. "Oh, Eli, what a fun-idea!"

"Shirley, let me speak to Ted."

After the ear-shaking clatter of the phone whacking the floor, Eli heard footsteps, breathing, throat-clearing, then Ted. "A boy or a girl?"

"Nothing yet."

"You've given Shirley the bug, Eli. Now she's going to have *our* next one at home."

"Good."

"That's a terrific way to bring the family together, Eli."

"Look, Ted, I've settled with Tzuref."

"When are they going?"

"They're not exactly going, Teddie. I settled it—you won't even know they're there."

"A guy dressed like 1000 B.C. and I won't know it? What are you thinking about, pal?"

"He's changing his clothes."

"Yeah, to what? Another funeral suit?"

"Tzuref promised me, Ted. Next time he comes to town, he comes dressed like you and me."

"What! Somebody's kidding somebody, Eli."

Eli's voice shot up. "If he says he'll do it, he'll do it!"

"And, Eli," Ted asked, "he said it?"

"He said it." It cost him a sudden headache, this invention.

"And suppose he doesn't change, Eli. Just suppose. I mean that *might* happen, Eli. This might just be some kind of stall or something."

"No," Eli assured him.

The other end was quiet a moment. "Look, Eli," Ted said, finally, "he changes. Okay? All right? But they're still up there, aren't they? *That* doesn't change."

"The point is you won't know it."

Patiently Ted said, "Is this what we asked of you, Eli? When we put our faith and trust in you, is that what we were asking? We weren't concerned that this guy should become a Beau Brummel,[4] Eli, believe me. We just don't think this is the community for them. And, Eli, we isn't me. The Jewish members of the community appointed me, Artie, and Harry to see what could be done. And we appointed you. And what's happened?"

Eli heard himself say, "What happened, happened."

"Eli, you're talking in crossword puzzles."

"My wife's having a baby," Eli explained, defensively.

"I realize that, Eli. But this is a matter of zoning, isn't it? Isn't that what we discovered? You don't abide by the ordinance, you go. I mean I can't raise mountain goats, say, in my backyard—"

"This isn't so simple, Ted. People are involved—"

"People? Eli, we've been through this and through this. We're not just dealing with people—these are religious fanatics is what they are. Dressing like that. What I'd really like to find out is what goes on up there. I'm getting more and more skeptical, Eli, and I'm not afraid to admit it. It smells like a lot of hocus-pocus abracadabra stuff to me. Guys like Harry, you know, they

4. A dandy, a foppish dresser.

think and they think and they're afraid to admit what they're thinking. I'll tell you. Look, I don't even know about this Sunday school business. Sundays I drive my oldest kid all the way to Scarsdale[5] to learn Bible stories . . . and you know what she comes up with? This Abraham in the Bible was going to kill his own *kid* for a sacrifice. She gets nightmares from it, for God's sake! You call that religion? Today a guy like that they'd lock him up. This is an age of science, Eli. I size people's feet with an X-ray machine, for God's sake. They've disproved all that stuff, Eli, and I refuse to sit by and watch it happening on my own front lawn."

"Nothing's happening on your front lawn, Teddie. You're exaggerating, nobody's sacrificing their kid."

"You're damn right, Eli—I'm not sacrificing mine. You'll see when you have your own what it's like. All the place is, is a hideaway for people who can't face life. It's a matter of *needs*. They have all these superstitions, and why do you think? Because they can't face the world, because they can't take their place in society. That's no environment to bring kids up in, Eli."

"Look, Ted, see it from another angle. We can convert them," Eli said, with half a heart.

"What, make a bunch of Catholics out of them? Look, Eli—pal, there's a good healthy relationship in this town because it's modern Jews and Protestants. That's the point, isn't it, Eli? Let's not kid each other, I'm not Harry. The way things are now are fine—like human beings. There's going to be no pogroms[6] in Woodenton. Right? 'Cause there's no fanatics, no crazy people —" Eli winced, and closed his eyes a second—"just people who respect each other, and leave each other be. Common sense is the ruling thing, Eli. I'm for common sense. Moderation."

"Exactly, exactly, Ted. I agree, but common sense, maybe, says make this guy change his clothes. Then maybe—"

"Common sense says that? Common sense says to me they go and find a nice place somewhere else, Eli. New York is the biggest city in the world, it's only 30 miles away—why don't they go there?"

"Ted, give them a chance. Introduce them to common sense."

"Eli, you're dealing with *fanatics*. Do they display common sense? Talking a dead language, that makes sense? Making a big thing out of suffering, so you're going oy-oy-oy all your life, that's common sense? Look, Eli, we've been through all this. I don't know if you know—but there's talk that *Life* magazine is sending a guy out to the Yeshivah for a story. With pictures."

"Look, Teddie, you're letting your imagination get inflamed. I don't think *Life's* interested."

"But I'm interested, Eli. And we thought you were supposed to be."

"I am," Eli said, "I am. Let him just change the clothes, Ted. Let's see what happens."

"They live in the medieval ages, Eli—it's some superstition, some *rule*."

"Let's just *see*," Eli pleaded.

"Eli, every day—"

"One more day," Eli said. "If he doesn't change in one more day. . . ."

"What?"

5. A residential suburb in Westchester County, north of New York City.

6. Organized anti-Jewish riots, as in Eastern Europe before World War II.

"Then I get an injunction first thing Monday. That's that."

"Look, Eli—it's not up to me. Let me call Harry—"

"You're the spokesman, Teddie. I'm all wrapped up here with Miriam having a baby. Just give me the day—them the day."

"All right, Eli. I want to be fair. But tomorrow, that's all. Tomorrow's the judgment day, Eli, I'm telling you."

"I hear trumpets," Eli said, and hung up. He was shaking inside—Teddie's voice seemed to have separated his bones at the joints. He was still in the phone booth when the nurse came to tell him that Mrs. Peck would positively not be delivered of a child until the morning. He was to go home and get some rest, he looked like *he* was having the baby. The nurse winked and left.

But Eli did not go home. He carried the Bonwit box out into the street with him and put it in the car. The night was soft and starry, and he began to drive the streets of Woodenton. Square cool windows, apricot-colored, were all one could see beyond the long lawns that fronted the homes of the townsmen. The stars polished the permanent baggage carriers atop the station wagons in the driveways. He drove slowly, up, down, around. Only his tires could be heard taking the gentle curves in the road.

What peace. What incredible peace. Have children ever been so safe in their beds? Parents—Eli wondered—so full in their stomachs? Water so warm in its boilers? Never. Never in Rome, never in Greece. Never even did walled cities have it so good! No wonder then they would keep things just as they were. Here, after all, were peace and safety—what civilization had been working toward for centuries. For all his jerkiness, that was all Ted Heller was asking for, peace and safety. It was what his parents had asked for in the Bronx, and his grandparents in Poland, and theirs in Russia or Austria, or wherever else they'd fled to or from. It was what Miriam was asking for. And now they had it—the world was at last a place for families, even Jewish families. After all these centuries, maybe there just had to be this communal toughness—or numbness—to protect such a blessing. Maybe that was the trouble with the Jews all along—too soft. Sure, to live takes guts . . . Eli was thinking as he drove on beyond the train station, and parked his car at the darkened Gulf station. He stepped out, carrying the box.

At the top of the hill one window trembled with light. What *was* Tzuref doing up there in that office? Killing babies—probably not. But studying a language no one understood? Practicing customs with origins long forgotten? Suffering sufferings already suffered once too often? Teddie was right—why keep it up! However, if a man chose to be stubborn, then he couldn't expect to survive. The world is give-and-take. What sense to sit and brood over a suit. Eli would give him one last chance.

He stopped at the top. No one was around. He walked slowly up the lawn, setting each foot into the grass, listening to the shh shhh shhhh his shoes made as they bent the wetness into the sod. He looked around. Here there was nothing. Nothing! An old decaying house—and a suit.

On the porch he slid behind a pillar. He felt someone was watching him. But only the stars gleamed down. And at his feet, off and away, Woodenton glowed up. He set his package on the step of the great front door. Inside the cover of the box he felt to see if his letter was still there. When he touched it, he pushed it deeper into the green suit, which his fingers still remembered from winter. He should have included some light bulbs. Then he slid back by the pillar again, and this time there was something on the lawn. It was the second sight he had of him. He was facing Woodenton and barely moving across the open space towards the trees. His right fist was beating his chest. And then Eli heard a sound rising with each knock on the chest. What a moan! It could raise hair, stop hearts, water eyes. And it did all three to Eli, plus more. Some feeling crept into him for whose deepness he could find no word. It was strange. He listened—it did not hurt to hear this moan. But he wondered if it hurt to make it. And so, with only stars to hear, he tried. And it did hurt. Not the bumblebee of noise that turned at the back of his throat and winged out his nostrils. What hurt buzzed down. It stung and stung inside him, and in turn the moan sharpened. It became a scream, louder, a song, a crazy song that whined through the pillars and blew out to the grass, until the strange hatted creature on the lawn turned and threw his arms wide, and looked in the night like a scarecrow.

Eli ran, and when he reached the car the pain was only a bloody scratch across his neck where a branch had whipped back as he fled the greenie's arms.

The following day his son was born. But not till one in the afternoon, and by then a great deal had happened.

First, at nine-thirty the phone rang. Eli leaped from the sofa—where he'd dropped the night before—and picked it screaming from the cradle. He could practically smell the hospital as he shouted into the phone, "Hello, yes!"

"Eli, it's Ted. Eli, he *did* it. He just walked by the store. I was opening the door, Eli, and I turned around and I swear I thought it was you. But it was him. He still walks like he did, but the clothes, Eli, the clothes."

"Who?"

"The greenie. He has on man's regular clothes. And the suit, it's a beauty."

The suit barreled back into Eli's consciousness, pushing all else aside. "What color suit?"

"Green. He's just strolling in the green suit like it's a holiday. Eli . . . is it a Jewish holiday?"

"Where is he now?"

"He's walking straight up Coach House Road, in this damn tweed job. Eli, it worked. You were right."

"We'll see."

"What next?"

"We'll see."

He took off the underwear in which he'd slept and went into the kitchen where he turned the light under the coffee. When it began to perk he held his head over the pot so it would steam loose the knot back of his eyes. It still hadn't when the phone rang.

"Eli, Ted again. Eli, the guy's walking up and down every street in town. Really, he's on a tour or something. Artie called me, Herb called me. Now Shirley calls that he just walked by our house. Eli, go out on the porch you'll see."

Eli went to the window and peered out. He couldn't see past the bend in the road, and there was no one in sight.

"Eli?" He heard Ted from where he dangled over the telephone table. He dropped the phone into the hook, as a few last words floated up to him—"Eliyousawhim . . . ?" He threw on the pants and shirt he'd worn the night before and walked barefoot on to his front lawn. And sure enough, his apparition appeared around the bend: in a brown hat a little too far down on his head, a green suit too far back on the shoulders, an unbuttoned-down button-down shirt, a tie knotted so as to leave a two-inch tail, trousers that cascaded onto his shoes—he was shorter than that black hat had made him seem. And moving the clothes was that walk that was not a walk, the tiny-stepped shlumpy[7] gait. He came round the bend, and for all his strangeness—it clung to his whiskers, signaled itself in his locomotion—he looked as if he belonged. Eccentric, maybe, but he belonged. He made no moan, nor did he invite Eli with wide-flung arms. But he did stop when he saw him. He stopped and put a hand to his hat. When he felt for its top, his hand went up too high. Then it found the level and fiddled with the brim. The fingers fiddled, fumbled, and when they'd finally made their greeting, they traveled down the fellow's face and in an instant seemed to have touched each one of his features. They dabbed the eyes, ran the length of the nose, swept over the hairy lip, until they found their home in the hair that hid a little of his collar. To Eli the fingers said, *I have a face, I have a face at least*. Then his hand came through the beard and when it stopped at his chest it was like a pointer—and the eyes asked a question as tides of water shifted over them. *The face is all right, I can keep it?* Such a look was in those eyes that Eli was still seeing them when he turned his head away. They were the hearts of his jonquils, that only last week had appeared—they were the leaves on his birch, the bulbs in his coach lamp, the droppings on his lawn: those eyes were the eyes in his head. They were his, he had made them. He turned and went into his house and when he peeked out the side of the window, between shade and molding, the green suit was gone.

The phone.

"Eli, Shirley."

"I saw him, Shirley," and he hung up.

He sat frozen for a long time. The sun moved around the windows. The coffee steam smelled up the house. The phone began to ring, stopped, began again. The mailman came, the cleaner, the bakery man, the gardener, the ice cream man, the League of Women Voters lady. A Negro woman spreading some strange gospel calling for the revision of the Food and Drug Act knocked at the front, rapped the windows, and finally scraped a half-dozen pamphlets under the back door. But Eli only sat, without underwear, in last night's suit. He answered no one.

Given his condition, it was strange that the trip and crash at the back door reached his inner ear. But in an instant he seemed to melt down into the crevices of the chair, then to splash up and out to where the clatter had been. At the door he waited. It was silent, but for a fluttering of damp little leaves on the trees. When he finally opened the door, there was no one there. He'd expected to see green, green, green, big as the doorway, topped by his hat, waiting for him with those eyes. But there was no one out there, except for the Bonwit's box which lay bulging at his feet. No string tied it and the top rode high on the bottom.

7. Drooping, careless (Yiddish).

The coward! He couldn't do it! He couldn't!

The very glee of that idea pumped fuel to his legs. He tore out across his back lawn, past his new spray of forsythia, to catch a glimpse of the bearded one fleeing naked through yards, over hedges and fences, to the safety of his hermitage. In the distance a pile of pink and white stones—which Harriet Knudson had painted the previous day—tricked him. "Run," he shouted to the rocks, "Run, you . . ." but he caught his error before anyone else did, and though he peered and craned there was no hint anywhere of a man about his own size, with white, white, terribly white skin (how white must be the skin of his body!) in cowardly retreat. He came slowly, curiously, back to the door. And while the trees shimmered in the light wind, he removed the top from the box. The shock at first was the shock of having daylight turned off all at once. Inside the box was an eclipse. But black soon sorted from black, and shortly there was the glassy black of lining, the coarse black of trousers, the dead black of fraying threads, and in the center the mountain of black: the hat. He picked the box from the doorstep and carried it inside. For the first time in his life he *smelled* the color of blackness: a little stale, a little sour, a little old, but nothing that could overwhelm you. Still, he held the package at arm's length and deposited it on the dining room table.

Twenty rooms on a hill and they store their old clothes with me! What am I supposed to do with them? Give them to charity? That's where they came from. He picked up the hat by the edges and looked inside. The crown was smooth as an egg, the brim practically threadbare. There is nothing else to do with a hat in one's hands but put it on, so Eli dropped the thing on his head. He opened the door to the hall closet and looked at himself in the full-length mirror. The hat gave him bags under the eyes. Or perhaps he had not slept well. He pushed the brim lower till a shadow touched his lips. Now the bags under his eyes had inflated to become his face. Before the mirror he unbuttoned his shirt, unzipped his trousers, and then, shedding his clothes, he studied what he was. What a silly disappointment to see yourself naked in a hat. Especially in that hat. He sighed, but could not rid himself of the great weakness that suddenly set on his muscles and joints, beneath the terrible weight of the stranger's strange hat.

He returned to the dining room table and emptied the box of its contents: jacket, trousers, and vest (*it* smelled deeper than blackness). And under it all, sticking between the shoes that looked chopped and bitten, came the first gleam of white. A little fringed serape, a gray piece of semiunderwear, was crumpled at the bottom, its thready border twisted into itself. Eli removed it and let it hang free. What is it? For warmth? To wear beneath underwear in the event of a chest cold? He held it to his nose but it did not smell from Vick's or mustard plaster. It was something special, some Jewish thing. Special food, special language, special prayers, why not special BVD's?[8] So fearful was he that he would be tempted back into wearing his traditional clothes—reasoned Eli—that he had carried and buried in Woodenton everything, including the special underwear. For that was how Eli now understood the box of clothes. The greenie was saying, Here, I give up. I refuse even to be tempted. We surrender. And that was how Eli continued

8. A brand of men's underwear. "Fringed serape": literally, a Mexican shawl; in this case, the small tallis, or fringed undergarment, worn by strictly observant Jewish men.

to understand it until he found he'd slipped the white fringy surrender flag over his hat and felt it clinging to his chest. And now, looking at himself in the mirror, he was momentarily uncertain as to who was tempting who into what. Why *did* the greenie leave his clothes? Was it even the greenie? Then who was it? And why? But, Eli, for Christ's sake, in an age of science things don't happen like that. Even the goddam pigs take drugs . . .

Regardless of who was the source of the temptation, what was its end, not to mention its beginning, Eli, some moments later, stood draped in black, with a little white underneath, before the full-length mirror. He had to pull down on the trousers so they would not show the hollow of his ankle. The greenie, didn't he wear socks? Or had he forgotten them? The mystery was solved when Eli mustered enough courage to investigate the trouser pockets. He had expected some damp awful thing to happen to his fingers should he slip them down and out of sight—but when at last he jammed bravely down he came up with a khaki army sock in each hand. As he slipped them over his toes, he invented a genesis: a G.I.'s present in 1945. Plus everything else lost between 1938 and 1945, he had also lost his socks. Not that he had lost the socks, but that he'd had to stoop to accepting these, made Eli almost cry. To calm himself he walked out the back door and stood looking at his lawn.

On the Knudson back lawn, Harriet Knudson was giving her stones a second coat of pink. She looked up just as Eli stepped out. Eli shot back in again and pressed himself against the back door. When he peeked between the curtain all he saw were paint bucket, brush, and rocks scattered on the Knudsons' pink-spattered grass. The phone rang. Who was it—Harriet Knudson? Eli, there's a Jew at your door. *That's me*. Nonsense, Eli, I saw him with my own eyes. *That's me, I saw you too, painting your rocks pink*. Eli, you're having a nervous breakdown again. Jimmy, Eli's having a nervous breakdown again. Eli, this is Jimmy, hear you're having a little breakdown, anything I can do, boy? Eli, this is Ted, Shirley says you need help. Eli, this is Artie, you need help. Eli, Harry, you need help . . . The phone rattled its last and died.

"God helps them who help themselves," intoned Eli, and once again he stepped out the door. This time he walked to the center of his lawn and in full sight of the trees, the grass, the birds, and the sun, revealed that it was he, Eli, in the costume. But nature had nothing to say to him, and so stealthily he made his way to the hedge separating his property from the field beyond and he cut his way through, losing his hat twice in the underbrush. Then, clamping the hat to his head, he began to run, the threaded tassels jumping across his heart. He ran through the weeds and wild flowers, until on the old road that skirted the town he slowed up. He was walking when he approached the Gulf station from the back. He supported himself on a huge tireless truck rim, and among tubes, rusted engines, dozens of topless oil cans, he rested. With a kind of brainless cunning, he readied himself for the last mile of his journey.

"How are you, Pop?" It was the garage attendant, rubbing his greasy hands on his overalls, and hunting among the cans.

Eli's stomach lurched and he pulled the big black coat round his neck.

"Nice day," the attendant said and started around to the front.

"Sholom," Eli whispered and zoomed off towards the hill.

The sun was directly overhead when Eli reached the top. He had come by way of the woods, where it was cooler, but still he was perspiring beneath his new suit. The hat had no sweatband and the cloth clutched his head. The children were playing. The children were always playing, as if it was that alone that Tzuref had to teach them. In their shorts, they revealed such thin legs that beneath one could see the joints swiveling as they ran. Eli waited for them to disappear around a corner before he came into the open. But something would not let him wait—his green suit. It was on the porch, wrapped around the bearded fellow, who was painting the base of a pillar. His arm went up and down, up and down, and the pillar glowed like white fire. The very sight of him popped Eli out of the woods onto the lawn. He did not turn back, though his insides did. He walked up the lawn, but the children played on; tipping the black hat, he mumbled, "Shhh . . . shhhh," and they hardly seemed to notice.

At last he smelled paint.

He waited for the man to turn to him. He only painted. Eli felt suddenly that if he could pull the black hat down over his eyes, over his chest and belly and legs, if he could shut out all light, then a moment later he would be home in bed. But the hat wouldn't go past his forehead. He couldn't kid himself—he was there. No one he could think of had forced him to do this.

The greenie's arm flailed up and down on the pillar. Eli breathed loudly, cleared his throat, but the greenie wouldn't make life easier for him. At last, Eli had to say "Hello."

The arm swished up and down; it stopped—two fingers went out after a brush hair stuck to the pillar.

"Good day," Eli said.

The hair came away; the swishing resumed.

"Sholom," Eli whispered and the fellow turned.

The recognition took some time. He looked at what Eli wore. Up close, Eli looked at what he wore. And then Eli had the strange notion that he was two people. Or that he was one person wearing two suits. The greenie looked to be suffering from a similar confusion. They stared long at one another. Eli's heart shivered, and his brain was momentarily in such a mixed-up condition that his hands went out to button down the collar of his shirt that somebody else was wearing. What a mess! The greenie flung his arms over his face.

"What's the matter . . ." Eli said. The fellow had picked up his bucket and brush and was running away. Eli ran after him.

"I wasn't going to hit . . ." Eli called. "Stop . . ." Eli caught up and grabbed his sleeve. Once again, the greenie's hands flew up to his face. This time, in the violence, white paint spattered both of them.

"I only want to . . ." But in that outfit Eli didn't really know what he wanted. "To talk . . ." he said finally. "For you to look at me. Please, just *look* at me . . ."

The hands stayed put, as paint rolled off the brush onto the cuff of Eli's green suit.

"Please . . . please," Eli said, but he did not know what to do. "Say something, speak *English*," he pleaded.

The fellow pulled back against the wall, back, back, as though some arm would finally reach out and yank him to safety. He refused to uncover his face.

"Look," Eli said, pointing to himself. "It's your suit. I'll take care of it."

No answer—only a little shaking under the hands, which led Eli to speak as gently as he knew how.

"We'll . . . we'll moth-proof it. There's a button missing"—Eli pointed—"I'll have it fixed. I'll have a zipper put in . . . Please, please—just look at me . . ." He was talking to himself, and yet how could he stop? Nothing he said made any sense—that alone made his heart swell. Yet somehow babbling on, he might babble something that would make things easier between them. "Look . . ." He reached inside his shirt to pull the frills of underwear into the light. "I'm wearing the special underwear, even . . . Please." he said, "*please, please, please*" he sang, as if it were some sacred word. "Oh, *please* . . ."

Nothing twitched under the tweed suit—and if the eyes watered, or twinkled, or hated, he couldn't tell. It was driving him crazy. He had dressed like a fool, and for what? For this? He reached up and yanked the hands away.

"There!" he said—and in that first instant all he saw of the greenie's face were two white droplets stuck to each cheek.

"Tell me—" Eli clutched his hands down to his sides—"Tell me, what can I do for you, I'll do it . . ."

Stiffly, the greenie stood there, sporting his two white tears.

"Whatever I can do . . . Look, look, what I've done *already*." He grabbed his black hat and shook it in the man's face.

And in exchange, the greenie gave him an answer. He raised one hand to his chest, and then jammed it, finger first, towards the horizon. And with what a pained look! As though the air were full of razors! Eli followed the finger and saw beyond the knuckle, out past the nail, Woodenton.

"What do you want?" Eli said. "I'll bring it!"

Suddenly the greenie made a run for it. But then he stopped, wheeled, and jabbed that finger at the air again. It pointed the same way. Then he was gone.

And then, all alone, Eli had the revelation. He did not question his understanding, the substance or the source. But with a strange, dreamy elation, he started away.

On Coach House Road, they were double-parked. The Mayor's wife pushed a grocery cart full of dog food from Stop N' Shop to her station wagon. The President of the Lions Club,[9] a napkin around his neck, was jamming pennies into the meter in front of the Bit-in-Teeth Restaurant. Ted Heller caught the sun as it glazed off the new Byzantine mosaic entrance to his shoe shop. In pinkened jeans, Mrs. Jimmy Knudson was leaving Halloway's Hardware, a paint bucket in each hand. Roger's Beauty Shoppe had its doors open—women's heads in silver bullets far as the eye could see. Over by the barbershop the pole spun, and Artie Berg's youngest sat on a red horse, having his hair cut; his mother flipped through *Look*,[1] smiling: the greenie had changed his clothes.

And into this street, which seemed paved with chromium, came Eli Peck. It was not enough, he knew, to walk up one side of the street. That was not

9. An American fraternal social organization.

1. A popular picture magazine.

enough. Instead he walked ten paces up one side, then on an angle, crossed to the other side, where he walked ten more paces, and crossed back. Horns blew, traffic jerked, as Eli made his way up Coach House Road. He spun a moan high up in his nose as he walked. Outside no one could hear him, but he felt it vibrate the cartilage at the bridge of his nose.

Things slowed around him. The sun stopped rippling on spokes and hubcaps. It glowed steadily as everyone put on brakes to look at the man in black. They always paused and gaped, whenever he entered the town. Then in a minute, or two, or three, a light would change, a baby squawk, and the flow continue. Now, though lights changed, no one moved.

"He shaved his beard," Eric the barber said.

"Who?" asked Linda Berg.

"The . . . the guy in the suit. From the place there."

Linda looked out the window.

"It's Uncle Eli," little Kevin Berg said, spitting hair.

"Oh, God," Linda said, "Eli's having a nervous breakdown."

"A nervous breakdown!" Ted Heller said, but not immediately. Immediately he had said "Hoooly . . ."

Shortly, everybody in Coach House Road was aware that Eli Peck, the nervous young attorney with the pretty wife, was having a breakdown. Everybody except Eli Peck. He knew what he did was not insane, though he felt every inch of its strangeness. He felt those black clothes as if they were the skin of his skin—the give and pull as they got used to where he bulged and buckled. And he felt eyes, every eye on Coach House Road. He saw headlights screech to within an inch of him, and stop. He saw mouths: first the bottom jaw slides forward, then the tongue hits the teeth, the lips explode, a little thunder in the throat, and they've said it: Eli Peck Eli Peck Eli Peck Eli Peck. He began to walk slowly, shifting his weight down and forward with each syllable: E–li–Peck–E–li–Peck–E–li–Peck. Heavily he trod, and as his neighbors uttered each syllable of his name, he felt each syllable shaking all his bones. He knew who he was down to his marrow—they were telling him. Eli Peck. He wanted them to say it a thousand times, a million times, he would walk forever in that black suit, as adults whispered of his strangeness and children made "Shame . . . shame" with their fingers.

"It's going to be all right, pal . . ." Ted Heller was motioning to Eli from his doorway. "C'mon, pal, it's going to be all right . . ."

Eli saw him, past the brim of his hat. Ted did not move from his doorway, but leaned forward and spoke with his hand over his mouth. Behind him, three customers peered through the doorway. "Eli, it's Ted, remember Ted . . ."

Eli crossed the street and found he was heading directly towards Harriet Knudson. He lifted his neck so she could see his whole face.

He saw her forehead melt down to her lashes. "Good morning, Mr. Peck."

"Sholom," Eli said, and crossed the street where he saw the President of the Lions.

"Twice before . . ." he heard someone say, and then he crossed again, mounted the curb, and was before the bakery, where a delivery man charged past with a tray of powdered cakes twirling above him. "Pardon me, Father," he said, and scooted into his truck. But he could not move it. Eli Peck had stopped traffic.

He passed the Rivoli Theater, Beekman Cleaners, Harris' Westinghouse, the Unitarian Church, and soon he was passing only trees. At Ireland Road he turned right and started through Woodenton's winding streets. Baby carriages stopped whizzing and creaked—"Isn't that . . ." Gardeners held their clipping. Children stepped from the sidewalk and tried the curb. And Eli greeted no one, but raised his face to all. He wished passionately that he had white tears to show them . . . And not till he reached his own front lawn, saw his house, his shutters, his new jonquils, did he remember his wife. And the child that must have been born to him. And it was then and there he had the awful moment. He could go inside and put on his clothes and go to his wife in the hospital. It was not irrevocable, even the walk wasn't. In Woodenton memories are long but fury short. Apathy works like forgiveness. Besides, when you've flipped, you've flipped—it's Mother Nature.

What gave Eli the awful moment was that he turned away. He knew exactly what he could do but he chose not to. To go inside would be to go halfway. There was more . . . So he turned and walked towards the hospital and all the time he quaked an eighth of an inch beneath his skin to think that perhaps he'd chosen the crazy way. To think that he'd *chosen* to be crazy! But if you chose to be crazy, then you weren't crazy. It's when you didn't choose. No, he wasn't flipping. He had a child to see.

"Name?"

"Peck."

"Fourth floor." He was given a little blue card.

In the elevator everybody stared. Eli watched his black shoes rise four floors.

"Four."

He tipped his hat, but knew he couldn't take it off.

"Peck," he said. He showed the card.

"Congratulations," the nurse said. ". . . the grandfather?"

"The father. Which room?"

She led him to 412. "A joke on the Mrs?" she said, but he slipped in the door without her.

"Miriam?"

"Yes?"

"Eli."

She rolled her white face towards her husband. "Oh, Eli . . . Oh, Eli."

He raised his arms. "What could I do?"

"You have a son. They called all morning."

"I came to see him."

"Like *that*!" she whispered harshly. "Eli, you can't go around like that."

"I have a son. I want to see him."

"Eli, why are you doing this to me!" Red seeped back into her lips. "*He's* not your fault," she explained. "Oh, Eli, sweetheart, why do you feel guilt about everything. Eli, change your clothes. I forgive you."

"Stop forgiving me. Stop understanding me."

"But I love you."

"That's something else."

"But, sweetie, you *don't* have to dress like that. You didn't do anything. You don't have to feel guilty because . . . because everything's all right. Eli, can't you see that?"

"Miriam, enough reasons. Where's my son?"

"Oh, please, Eli, don't flip now. I need you now. Is that why you're flipping—because I need you?"

"In your selfish way, Miriam, you're very generous. I want my son."

"Don't flip now. I'm afraid, now that he's out." She was beginning to whimper. "I don't know if I love him, now that he's out. When I look in the mirror, Eli, he won't be there . . . Eli, Eli, you look like you're going to your own funeral. Please, can't you leave well enough *alone*? Can't we just have a family?"

"No."

In the corridor he asked the nurse to lead him to his son. The nurse walked on one side of him, Ted Heller on the other.

"Eli, do you want some help? I thought you might want some help."

"No."

Ted whispered something to the nurse; then to Eli he whispered, "Should you be walking around like this?"

"Yes."

In his ear Ted said, "You'll . . . you'll frighten the kid . . ."

"There," the nurse said. She pointed to a bassinet in the second row and looked, puzzled, to Ted. "Do I go in?" Eli said.

"No," the nurse said. "She'll roll him over." She rapped on the enclosure full of babies. "Peck," she mouthed to the nurse on the inside.

Ted tapped Eli's arm. "You're not thinking of doing something you'll be sorry for . . . are you, Eli? Eli—I mean you know you're still Eli, don't you?"

In the enclosure, Eli saw a bassinet had been wheeled before the square window.

"Oh, Christ. . . ." Ted said. "You don't have this Bible stuff on the brain—" And suddenly he said, "You wait, pal." He started down the corridor, his heels tapping rapidly.

Eli felt relieved—he leaned forward. In the basket was what he'd come to see. Well, now that he was here, what did he think he was going to say to it? I'm your father, Eli, the Flipper? I am wearing a black hat, suit, and fancy underwear, all borrowed from a friend? How could he admit to this reddened ball—*his* reddened ball—the worst of all: that Eckman would shortly convince him he wanted to take off the whole business. He couldn't admit it! He wouldn't do it!

Past his hat brim, from the corner of his eye, he saw Ted had stopped in a doorway at the end of the corridor. Two interns stood there smoking, listening to Ted. Eli ignored it.

No, even Eckman wouldn't make him take it off! No! He'd wear it, if he chose to. He'd make the kid wear it! Sure! Cut it down when the time came. A smelly hand-me-down, whether the kid liked it or not!

Only Teddie's heels clacked; the interns wore rubber soles—for they were there, beside him, unexpectedly. Their white suits smelled, but not like Eli's.

"Eli," Ted said, softly, "visiting time's up, pal."

"How are you feeling, Mr. Peck? First child upsets everyone. . . ."

He'd just pay no attention; nevertheless, he began to perspire, thickly, and his hat crown clutched his hair.

"Excuse me—Mr. Peck. . . ." It was a new rich bass voice. "Excuse me, rabbi, but you're wanted . . . in the temple." A hand took his elbow, firmly;

then another hand, the other elbow. Where they grabbed, his tendons went taut.

"Okay, rabbi. Okay okay okay okay okay okay. . . ." He listened; it was a very soothing word, that okay. "Okay okay everything's going to be okay." His feet seemed to have left the ground some, as he glided away from the window, the bassinet, the babies. "Okay easy does it everything's all right all right—"

But he rose, suddenly, as though up out of a dream, and flailing his arms, screamed: *"I'm the father!"*

But the window disappeared. In a moment they tore off his jacket—it gave so easily, in one yank. Then a needle slid under his skin. The drug calmed his soul, but did not touch it down where the blackness had reached.

1959

From The Ghost Writer

Femme Fatale[1]

It was only a year earlier that Amy had told Lonoff her whole story. Weeping hysterically, she had phoned him one night from the Biltmore Hotel in New York; as best he could understand, that morning she had come down alone on a train from Boston to see the matinee performance of a play intending to return home again by train in the evening. Instead, after coming out of the theater she had taken a hotel room, where ever since she had been "in hiding."

At midnight, having only just finished his evening's reading and gone up to bed, Lonoff got into his car and drove south. By four he had reached the city, by six she had told him that it was the dramatization of Anne Frank's diary[2] she had come to New York to see, but it was midmorning before she could explain even somewhat coherently her connection with this new Broadway play.

"It wasn't the play—I could have watched that easily enough if I had been alone. It was the people watching with me. Carloads of women kept pulling up to the theater, women wearing fur coats, with expensive shoes and handbags. I thought, This isn't for me. The billboards, the photographs, the marquee, I could take all that. But it was the women who frightened me—and their families and their children and their homes. Go to a movie, I told

1. Literally, "disastrous woman" (French). A seductive woman who lures men into dangerous situations or attracts them by her mysterious charm.
2. Anne Frank (1929–1945) was born in Frankfurt, Germany, and immigrated with her family to Amsterdam after Hitler came to power (1933). Faced with deportation after German forces occupied the Netherlands, the Franks went into hiding on July 9, 1942, with four other Jews in the back rooms of her father, Otto's, business office. There, for two years, Anne kept a private diary in Dutch, recording her personal experiences and emotions, events in the secret annex, and reactions to events outside. On August 4, 1944, betrayed by Dutch informers, the Franks were discovered and sent via Westerbork, a transit camp north of Amsterdam, to Auschwitz. Anne's mother died there, while Anne and her sister, Margot, were transferred to the German concentration camp of Bergen-Belsen and died there of typhus in March 1945, one month before liberation. Otto Frank survived and, on returning to Amsterdam, found his daughter's diary. He published it in 1947 as *Het Achterhuis* (The House Behind). The diary appeared in the United States in 1952, and a Broadway version was staged in 1955. It has been translated into more than thirty languages, and the Frank family's hiding place on the Prinsengracht Canal in Amsterdam has become a museum and virtually a pilgrimage site.

myself, go instead to a museum. But I showed my ticket, I went in with them, and of course it happened. It had to happen. It's what happens there. The women cried. Everyone around me was in tears. Then at the end, in the row behind me, a woman screamed, 'Oh, no.' That's why I came running here. I wanted a room with a telephone in it where I could stay until I'd found my father. But all I did once I was here was sit in the bathroom thinking that if he knew, if I told him, then they would have to come out on the stage after each performance and announce, 'But she is really alive. You needn't worry, she survived, she is twenty-six now, and doing very well.' I would say to him. 'You must keep this our secret—no one but you must ever know.' But suppose he was found out? What if we both were? Manny, I couldn't call him. And I knew I couldn't when I heard that woman scream 'Oh, no.' I knew then what's been true all along: I'll never see him again. I have to be dead to everyone."

Amy lay on the rumpled bed, wrapped tightly in a blanket, while Lonoff listened in silence from a chair by the window. Upon entering the unlocked room, he had found her sitting in the empty bathtub, still wearing her best dress and her best coat: the coat because she could not stop trembling, in the tub because it was the farthest she could get from the window, which was twenty floors above the street.

"How pathetic, you must think. What a joke," she said.

"A joke? On whom? I don't see the joke."

"My telling this to you."

"I still don't get it."

"Because it's like one of your stories. An E. I. Lonoff story . . . called . . . oh, you'd know what to call it. You'd know how to tell it in three pages. A homeless girl comes from Europe, sits in the professor's class being clever, listens to his records, plays his daughter's piano, virtually grows up in his house, and then one day, when the waif is a woman and out on her own, one fine day in the Biltmore Hotel, she casually announces . . ."

He left his chair and came to sit beside her on the bed while she went to pieces again. "Yes," he said, "quite casually."

"Manny, I'm not a lunatic, I'm not a crackpot, I'm not some girl—you must believe me—trying to be interesting and imitate your art!"

"My dear friend," he replied, his arms around her now and rocking her like a child, "if this is all so—"

"Oh, Dad-da, I'm afraid it really is."

"Well, then, you have left my poor art far behind."

This is the tale that Amy told the morning after she had gone alone to the Cort Theatre to sit amid the weeping and inconsolable audience at the famous New York production of *The Diary of Anne Frank*. This is the story that the twenty-six-year-old young woman with the striking face and the fetching accent and the felicitous prose style and the patience, according to Lonoff, of a Lonoff, expected him to believe was true.

After the war she had become Amy Bellette. She had not taken the new name to disguise her identity—as yet there was no need—but, as she imagined at the time, to forget her life. She had been in a coma for weeks, first in the filthy barracks with the other ailing and starving inmates, and then in the squalid makeshift "infirmary." A dozen dying children had been rounded up by the SS[3] and placed beneath blankets in a room with twelve beds in order to impress the Allied armies advancing upon Belsen[4] with the amenities of concentration-camp living. Those of the twelve still alive when the British got there had been moved to an army field hospital. It was here that she finally came around. She understood sometimes less and sometimes more than the nurses explained to her, but she would not speak. Instead, without howling or hallucinating, she tried to find a way to believe that she was somewhere in Germany, that she was not yet sixteen, and that her family was dead. Those were the facts: now to grasp them.

"Little Beauty" the nurses called her—a silent, dark, emaciated girl—and so, one morning, ready to talk, she told them that the surname was Bellette. Amy she got from an American book she had sobbed over as a child. *Little Women.*[5] She had decided, during her long silence, to finish growing up in America now that there was nobody left to live with in Amsterdam. After Belsen she figured it might be best to put an ocean the size of the Atlantic between herself and what she needed to forget.

She learned of her father's survival while waiting to get her teeth examined by the Lonoffs' family dentist in Stockbridge.[6] She had been three years with foster families in England, and almost a year as a freshman at Athene College,[7] when she picked an old copy of *Time*[8] out of the pile in the waiting room, and just turning pages, saw a photograph of a Jewish businessman named Otto Frank.[9] In July of 1942, some two years after the beginning of the Nazi occupation, he had taken his wife and his two young daughters into hiding. Along with another Jewish family, the Franks lived safely for twenty-five months in a rear upper story of the Amsterdam building where he used to have his business offices. Then, in August 1944, their whereabouts were apparently betrayed by one of the workers in the warehouse below, and the hideout was uncovered by the police. Of the eight who'd been together in the sealed-off attic rooms, only Otto Frank survived the concentration camps. When he came back to Amsterdam after the war, the Dutch family who had been their protectors gave him the notebooks that had been kept in hiding by his younger daughter, a girl of fifteen when she died in Belsen: a diary, some ledgers she wrote in, and a sheaf of papers emptied out of her briefcase when the Nazis were ransacking the place for valuables. Frank printed and circulated the diary only privately at first, as a memorial to his family, but in 1947 it was published in a regular edition under the title *Het Achterhuis*—"The House Behind." Dutch readers, *Time* said, were greatly affected by the young teenager's record of how the hunted Jews tried to carry on a civilized life despite their deprivations and the terror of discovery.

Alongside the article—"A Survivor's Sorrows"—was the photograph of the diarist's father, "now sixty." He stood alone in his coat and hat in front of the building on the Prinsengracht Canal where his late family had improvised a last home.

3. Abbreviation of *Schutzstaffel,* literally "protection echelon" (German), the Nazi's elite police corp, in charge of intelligence, central security, policing action, and mass murder of "inferiors" and "undesirables."
4. A village near Hanover, Germany; the site of a Nazi concentration camp, liberated on April 15, 1945.
5. An autobiographical novel (1868–69) by American author Louisa May Alcott (1832–1888).
6. A resort town in the Berkshires of western Massachusetts.
7. A fictitious college in western Massachusetts.
8. A popular weekly picture newsmagazine, founded in 1923.
9. Anne Frank's father (1889–1980).

Next came the part of her story that Lonoff was bound to think improbable. She herself, however, could not consider it all that strange that she should be thought dead when in fact she was alive; nobody who knew the chaos of those final months—the Allies bombing everywhere, the SS in flight—would call that improbable. Whoever claimed to have seen her dead of typhus in Belsen had either confused her with her older sister, Margot, or had figured that she was dead after seeing her so long in a coma, or had watched her being carted away, as good as dead, by the Kapos.[1]

"Belsen was the third camp," Amy told him. "We were sent first to Westerbork, north of Amsterdam. There were other children around to talk to, we were back in the open air—aside from being frightened it really wasn't that awful. Daddy lived in the men's barracks, but when I got sick he managed somehow to get into the women's camp at night and to come to my bed and hold my hand. We were there a month, then we were shipped to Auschwitz. Three days and three nights in the freight cars. Then they opened the doors and that was the last I saw of him. The men were pushed in one direction, we were pushed in the other. That was early September. I saw my mother last at the end of October. She could hardly speak by then. When Margot and I were shipped from Auschwitz, I don't even know if she understood."

She told him about Belsen. Those who had survived the cattle cars lived at first in tents on the heath. They slept on the bare ground in rags. Days went by without food or fresh water, and after the autumn storms tore the tents from their moorings, they slept exposed to the wind and rain. When at last they were being moved into barracks, they saw ditches beyond the camp enclosure piled high with bodies—the people who had died on the heath from typhus and starvation. By the time winter came, it seemed as if everyone still alive was either sick or half mad. And then, while watching her sister slowly dying, she grew sick herself. After Margot's death, she could hardly remember the women in the barracks who had helped her, and knew nothing of what happened to them.

It was not so improbable either that after her long hospital convalescence she had not made her way to the address in Switzerland where the family had agreed to meet if they should ever lose touch with one another. Would a weak sixteen-year-old girl undertake a journey requiring money, visas—requiring hope—only to learn at the other end that she was as lost and alone as she feared?

No, no, the improbable part was this: that instead of telephoning *Time* and saying, "I'm the one who wrote the diary—find Otta Frank!" she jotted down in her notebook the date on the magazine's cover and, after a tooth had been filled, went off with her school books to the library. What was improbable—inexplicable, indefensible, a torment still to her conscience—was that, calm and studious as ever, she checked *The New York Times Index* and the *Readers' Guide to Periodical Literature* for "Frank, Anne" and "Frank, Otto" and *"Het Achterhuis,"* and, when she found nothing, went down to the library's lowest stacks, where the periodicals were shelved. There she spent the remaining hour before dinner rereading the article in *Time*. She read it

1. From the French *caporals* (corporals). In the Nazi camps, these were prisoners who were given oversight over other prisoners.

until she knew it by heart. She studied her father's photograph. Now sixty. And those were the words that did it—made of her once again the daughter who cut his hair for him in the attic, the daughter who did her lessons there with him as her tutor, the daughter who would run to his bed and cling to him under the covers when she heard the Allied bombers flying over Amsterdam: suddenly she was the daughter from whom he had taken the place of everything she could no longer have. She cried for a very long time. But when she went to dinner in the dormitory, she pretended that nothing catastrophic had once again happened to Otto Frank's Anne.

But then right from the beginning she had resolved not to speak about what she had been through. Resolutions were her strong point as a young girl on her own. How else could she have lasted on her own? One of the thousand reasons she could not bear Uncle Daniel, the first of her foster fathers in England, was that sooner or later he wound up telling whoever walked into the house about all that had happened to Amy during the war. And then there was Miss Giddings, the young teacher in the school north of London who was always giving the orphaned little Jewess tender glances during history class. One day after school Miss Giddings took her for a lemon-curd tart at the local tearoom and asked her questions about the concentration camps. Her eyes filled with tears as Amy, who felt obliged to answer, confirmed the stories she had heard but could never quite believe. "Terrible," Miss Giddings said, "so terrible." Amy silently drank her tea and ate her lovely tart, while Miss Giddings, like one of her own history students, tried in vain to understand the past. "Why is it," the unhappy teacher finally asked, "that for centuries people have hated you Jews?" Amy rose to her feet. She was stunned. "Don't ask me that!" the girl said—"ask the madmen who hate us!" And she had nothing further to do with Miss Giddings as a friend—or with anyone else who asked her anything about what they couldn't possibly understand.

One Saturday only a few months after her arrival in England, vowing that if she heard another plaintive "Belsen" out of Uncle Daniel's mouth she would run off to Southampton and stow away on an American ship—and having had about enough of the snooty brand of sympathy the pure-bred English teachers offered at school—she burned her arm while ironing a blouse. The neighbors came running at the sound of her screams and rushed her to the hospital emergency room. When the bandage was removed, there was a patch of purple scar tissue about half the size of an egg instead of her camp number.

After the accident, as her foster parents called it, Uncle Daniel informed the Jewish Welfare Board that his wife's ill health made it impossible for them to continue to have Amy in their home. The foster child moved on to another family—and then another. She told whoever asked that she had been evacuated from Holland with a group of Jewish schoolchildren the week before the Nazis invaded. Sometimes she did not even say that the schoolchildren were Jewish, an omission for which she was mildly rebuked by the Jewish families who had accepted responsibility for her and were troubled by her lying. But she could not bear them all laying their helpful hands upon her shoulders because of Auschwitz and Belsen. If she was going to be thought exceptional, it would not be because of Auschwitz and Belsen but because of what she had made of herself since.

They were kind and thoughtful people, and they tried to get her to understand that she was not in danger in England. "You needn't feel frightened or threatened in any way," they assured her. "Or ashamed of anything." "I'm not ashamed. That's the point." "Well, that isn't always the point when young people try to hide their Jewish origins." "Maybe it isn't with others," she told them, "but it is with me."

On the Saturday after discovering her father's photograph in *Time*, she took the morning bus to Boston, and in every foreign bookstore looked in vain for a copy of *Het Achterhuis*. Two weeks later she traveled the three hours to Boston again, this time to the main post office to rent a box. She paid for it in cash, then mailed the letter she was carrying in her handbag, along with a money order for fifteen dollars, to Contact Publishers in Amsterdam, requesting them to send, postage paid, to Pilgrim International Bookshop, P.O. Box 152, Boston, Mass., U.S.A., as many copies as fifteen dollars would buy of *Het Achterhuis* by Anne Frank.

She had been dead for him some four years; believing her dead for another month or two would not really hurt much more. Curiously she did not hurt more either, except in bed at night when she cried and begged forgiveness for the cruelty she was practicing on her perfect father, now sixty.

Nearly three months after she had sent the order off to her Amsterdam publisher, on a warm, sunny day at the beginning of August, there was a package too large for the Pilgrim Bookshop post-office box waiting to be picked up in Boston. She was wearing a beige linen skirt and a fresh white cotton blouse, both ironed the night before. Her hair, cut in pageboy style that spring, had been washed and set the previous night, and her skin was evenly tanned. She was swimming a mile every morning and playing tennis every afternoon and, all in all, was as fit and energetic as a twenty-year-old could be. Maybe that was why, when the postal clerk handed her the parcel, she did not tear at the string with her teeth or faint straightaway onto the marble floor. Instead, she walked over to the Common—the package mailed from Holland swinging idly from one hand—and wandered along until she found an unoccupied bench. She sat first on a bench in the shade, but then got up and walked on until she found a perfect spot in the sunshine.

After thoroughly studying the Dutch stamps—postwar issues new to her—and contemplating the postmark, she set about to see how carefully she could undo the package. It was a preposterous display of unruffled patience and she meant it to be. She was feeling at once triumphant and giddy. Forbearance, she thought. Patience. Without patience there is no life. When she had finally untied the string and unfolded, without tearing, the layers of thick brown paper, it seemed to her that what she had so meticulously removed from the wrappings and placed onto the lap of her clean and pretty American girl's beige linen skirt was her survival itself.

Van Anne Frank. Her book. Hers.

She had begun keeping a diary less than three weeks before Pim[2] told her that they were going into hiding. Until she ran out of pages and had to carry over onto office ledgers, she made the entries in a cardboard-covered notebook that he'd given her for her thirteenth birthday. She still remembered

2. Anne Frank's pet name for her father.

most of what happened to her in the achterhuis, some of it down to the most minute detail, but of the fifty thousand words recording it all, she couldn't remember writing one. Nor could she remember anything much of what she'd confided there about her personal problems to the phantom confidante she'd named Kitty—whole pages of her tribulations as new and strange to her as her native tongue.

Perhaps because *Het Achterhuis* was the first Dutch book she'd read since she'd written it, her first thought when she finished was of her childhood friends in Amsterdam, the boys and girls from the Montessori school where she'd learned to read and write. She tried to remember the names of the Christian children, who would have survived the war. She tried to recall the names of her teachers, going all the way back to kindergarten. She pictured the faces of the shopkeepers, the postman, the milk deliveryman who had known her as a child. She imagined their neighbors in the houses on Merwedeplein. And when she had, she saw each of them closing her book and thinking. Who realized she was so gifted? Who realized we had such a writer in our midst?

The first passage she reread was dated over a year before the birth of Amy Bellette. The first time round she'd bent back the corner of the page; the second time, with a pen from her purse, she drew a dark meaningful line in the margin and beside it wrote—in English, of course—"uncanny." (Everything she marked she was marking for him, or made the mark actually pretending to be him.) *I have an odd way of sometimes, as it were, being able to see myself through someone else's eyes. Then I view the affairs of a certain "Anne" at my ease, and browse through the pages of her life as if she were a stranger. Before we came here, when I didn't think about things as much as I do now, I used at times to have the feeling that I didn't belong to Mansa,*[3] *Pim, and Margot, and that I would always be a bit of an outsider. Sometimes I used to pretend I was an orphan . . .*

Then she read the whole thing from the start again, making a small marginal notation—and a small grimace—whenever she came upon anything she was sure he would consider "decorative" or "imprecise" or "unclear." But mostly she marked passages she couldn't believe that she had written as little more than a child. Why, what eloquence, Anne—it gave her gooseflesh, whispering her own name in Boston—what deftness, what wit! How nice, she thought, if I could write like this for Mr. Lonoff's English 12. "It's good," she heard him saying, "it's the best thing you've ever done, Miss Bellette."

But of course it was—she'd had a "great subject," as the girls said in English class. Her family's affinity with what families were suffering everywhere had been clear to her right from the beginning. *There is nothing we can do but wait as calmly as we can till the misery comes to an end. Jews and Christians wait, the whole earth waits; and there are many who wait for death.* But while writing these lines ("Quiet, emphatic feeling—that's the idea, E. I. L.") she had had no grandiose delusions about her little achterhuis diary's ever standing as part of the record of the misery. It wasn't to educate anybody other than herself—out of her great expectations—that she kept track of how trying it all was. Recording it was enduring it; the diary kept her company and it kept her sane, and whenever being her parents' child

3. Anne Frank's pet name for her mother.

seemed to her as harrowing as the war itself, it was where she went to confess. Only to Kitty was she able to speak freely about the hopelessness of trying to satisfy her mother the way Margot did; only to Kitty could she openly bewail her inability even to pronounce the word "Mumsie" to her aloud—and to concede the depth of her feeling for Pim, a father she wanted to want her to the exclusion of all others, *not only as his child, but for me—Anne, myself.*

Of course it had eventually to occur to any child so *mad on books and reading* that for all she knew she was writing a book of her own. But most of the time it was her morale that she was sustaining not, at fourteen, literary ambition. As for developing into a writer—she owed that not to any decision to sit down each day and try to be one but to their stifling life. That, of all things, seemed to have nurtured her talent! Truly, without the terror and the claustrophobia of the achterhuis, as a *chatterbox* surrounded by friends and *rollicking with laughter,* free to come and go, free to clown around, free to pursue her every last expectation, would she ever have written sentences so deft and so eloquent and so witty? She thought, Now maybe that's the problem in English 12—not the absence of the great subject but the presence of the lake and the tennis courts and Tanglewood.[4] The perfect tan, the linen skirts, my emerging reputation as the Pallas Athene[5] of Athene College—maybe that's what's doing me in. Maybe if I were locked up again in a room somewhere and fed on rotten potatoes and clothed in rags and terrified out of my wits, maybe then I could write a decent story for Mr. Lonoff!

It was only with the euphoria of *invasion fever,* with the prospect of the Allied landings and the German collapse and the coming of that golden age known around the achterhuis as *after the war,* that she was able to announce to Kitty that the diary had perhaps done more than just assuage her adolescent loneliness. After two years of honing her prose, she felt herself ready for the great undertaking: *my greatest wish is to become a journalist someday and later on a famous writer.* But that was in May of 1944, when to be famous someday seemed to her no more or less extraordinary than to be going back to school in September. Oh, that May of marvelous expectations! Never again another winter in the achterhuis. Another winter and she would have gone crazy.

The first year there it hadn't been that bad; they'd all been so busy settling in that she didn't have time to feel desperate. In fact, so diligently had they all worked to transform the attic into a *superpractical* home that her father had gotten everybody to agree to subdivide the space still further and take in another Jew. But once the Allied bombing started, the superpractical home became her torture chamber. During the day the two families squabbled over everything, and then at night she couldn't sleep, sure that the Gestapo[6] was going to come in the dark to take them away. In bed she began to have horrifying visions of Lies, her schoolfriend, reproaching her for being safe in bed in Amsterdam and not in a concentration camp, like all her Jewish friends: *"Oh, Anne, why have you deserted me? Help, oh, help me, rescue me from this hell!"* She would see herself *in a dungeon, without Mummy and*

4. Located in Lenox, western Massachusetts, the summer home of the Boston Symphony Orchestra and the site of the annual Berkshire Musical Festival.

5. The Greek goddess of wisdom.

6. Abbreviation of *Geheime Staatspolizei*, secret state police (German); Nazi Germany's secret police.

Daddy—and worse. Right down to the final hours of 1943 she was dreaming and thinking *the most terrible things*. But then all at once it was over. Miraculously. "And what did it. Professor Lonoff? See *Anna Karenina*.[7] See *Madame Bovary*.[8] See half the literature of the Western world." The miracle: desire. She would be back to school in September, but she would not be returning to class the same girl. She was no longer a girl. Tears would roll down her cheeks at the thought of a naked woman. Her unpleasant menstrual periods became a source of the strangest pleasure. At night in bed she was excited by her breasts. Just these sensations—but all at once forebodings of her miserable death were replaced with a craze for life. One day she was completely recovered, and the next she was, of course, in love. Their troubles had made her her own woman, at fourteen. She began going off on private visits to the secluded corner of the topmost floor, which was occupied exclusively by Peter, the Van Daans' seventeen-year-old son. That she might be stealing him away from Margot didn't stop her, and neither did her scandalized parents: first just teatime visits, then evening assignations—then the defiant letter to the disappointed father. On May 3rd of that marvelous May: *I am young and I possess many buried qualities: I am young and strong and am living a great adventure*. And two days later, to the father who had saved her from the hell that had swallowed up Lies, to the Pim whose favorite living creature she had always longed to be, a declaration of her independence, *in mind and body,* as she bluntly put it: *I have now reached the stage that I can live entirely on my own, without Mummy's support or anyone else's for that matter . . . I don't feel in the least bit responsible to any of you . . . I don't have to give an account of my deeds to anyone but myself . . .*

Well, the strength of a woman on her own wasn't all she'd imagined it to be. Neither was the strength of a loving father. He told her it was the most unpleasant letter he'd ever received, and when she began to cry with shame for having been *too low for words,* he wept along with her. He burned the letter in the fire, the weeks passed, and she found herself growing disenchanted with Peter. In fact, by July she was wondering how it would be possible, in their circumstances, to *shake him off,* a problem resolved for her on a sunny August Friday, when in the middle of the morning, as Pim was helping Peter with his English lessons and she was off studying by herself, the Dutch Green Police[9] arrived and dissolved forever the secret household still heedful of propriety, obedience, discretion, self-improvement, and mutual respect. The Franks, as a family, came to an end, and, fittingly enough, thought the diarist, so did her chronicle of their effort to go sensibly on as themselves, in spite of everything.

The third time she read the book through was on the way back to Stockbridge that evening. Would she ever read another book again? How, if she couldn't put this one down? On the bus she began to speculate in the most immodest way about what she had written—had "wrought." Perhaps what got her going was the rumbling, boundless, electrified, indigo sky that had been stalking the bus down the highway since Boston: outside the window the most out-

7. A Russian novel (1875–77) by Leo Tolstoy (1828–1910), which centers on the affair between married Anna and bachelor Count Vronsky.

8. A French novel (1857) by Gustave Flaubert (1821–1880), about a passionate, unsatisfied woman drawn into adultery.

9. Police who worked with German forces occupying the Netherlands.

landish El Greco[1] stage effects, outside a Biblical thunderstorm complete with baroque[2] trimmings, and inside Amy curled up with her book—and with the lingering sense of tragic grandeur she'd soaked up from the real El Grecos that afternoon in the Boston Museum of Fine Arts. And she was exhausted, which probably doesn't hurt fantastical thinking, either. Still spellbound by her first two readings of *Het Achterhuis,* she had rushed on to the Gardner[3] and the Fogg,[4] where, to top off the day, the self-intoxicated girl with the deep tan and the animated walk had been followed by easily a dozen Harvard Summer School students eager to learn her name. Three museums because back at Athene she preferred to tell everyone the truth, more or less, about the big day in Boston. To Mr. Lonoff she planned to speak at length about all the new exhibitions she'd gone to see at his wife's suggestion.

The storm, the paintings, her exhaustion—none of it was really necessary, however, to inspire the sort of expectations that resulted from reading her published diary three times through in the same day. Towering egotism would probably have been sufficient. Perhaps she was only a very young writer on a bus dreaming a very young writer's dreams.

All her reasoning, all her fantastical thinking about the ordained mission of her book followed from this: neither she nor her parents came through in the diary as anything like representative of religious or observant Jews. Her mother lit candles on Friday night and that was about the extent of it. As for celebrations, she had found St. Nicholas's Day,[5] once she'd been introduced to it in hiding, much more fun than Chanukah,[6] and along with Pim made all kinds of clever gifts and even written a Santa Claus poem to enliven the festivities. When Pim settled upon a children's Bible as her present for the holiday—so she might learn something about the New Testament—Margot hadn't approved. Margot's ambition was to be a midwife in Palestine. She was the only one of them who seemed to have given serious thought to religion. The diary that Margot kept, had it ever been found, would not have been quite so sparing as hers in curiosity about Judaism, or plans for leading a Jewish life. Certainly it was impossible for her to imagine Margot thinking, let alone writing with longing in her diary, *the time will come when we are people again, and not just Jews.*

She had written these words, to be sure, still suffering the aftereffects of a nighttime burglary in the downstairs warehouse. The burglary had seemed certain to precipitate their discovery by the police, and for days afterward everyone was weak with terror. And for her, along with the residue of fear and the dubious sense of relief, there was, of course, the guilt-tinged bafflement when she realized that, unlike Lies, she had again been spared. In the aftermath of that gruesome night, she went around and around trying to understand the meaning of their persecution, one moment writing about the misery of being Jews and only Jews to their enemies, and then in the next

1. I.e., Doménikos Theotokópoulos (1541–1614), Spanish painter, noted for his dramatic Mannerist style, including the use of vivid colors and shadowy settings.
2. A style prevalent in the 17th century, characterized by extravagance, complexity, bold ornamentation, and the grotesque.
3. Boston's Isabella Stewart Gardner Museum was the creation of art collector and patron Mrs. Gardner (1840–1924).
4. An art museum of Harvard University in Cambridge, Massachusetts.
5. The Dutch equivalent of Christmas.
6. A Jewish holiday, occurring in December, that commemorates the rededication of Jerusalem's Second Temple (165 B.C.E.) and the victory of Judas Maccabeus against the Syrians.

airily wondering if *it might even be our religion from which of the world and all peoples learn good. . . . We can never become just Netherlanders,* she reminded Kitty, *we will always remain Jews, but we want to, too*—only to close out the argument with an announcement one most assuredly would not have come upon in "The Diary of Margot Frank": *I've been saved again, now my first wish after the war is that I may become Dutch! I love the Dutch, I love this country, I love the language and want to work here. And even if I have to write to the Queen myself, I will not give up until I have reached my goal.*

No, that wasn't mother's Margot talking, that was father's Anne. To London to learn English, to Paris to look at clothes and study art, to Hollywood, California, to interview the stars as someone named "Anne Franklin"—while self-sacrificing Margot delivered babies in the desert. To be truthful, while Margot was thinking about God and the homeland, the only deities she ever seemed to contemplate at any length were to be found in the mythology of Greece and Rome, which she studied all the time in hiding, and adored. To be truthful, the young girl of her diary was, compared to Margot, only dimly Jewish, though in that entirely the daughter of the father who calmed her fears by reading aloud to her at night not the Bible but Goethe[7] in German and Dickens[8] in English.

But that was the point—that was what gave her diary the power to make the nightmare real. To expect the great callous and indifferent world to care about the child of a pious, bearded father living under the sway of the rabbis and the rituals—that was pure folly. To the ordinary person with no great gift for tolerating even the smallest of differences the plight of that family wouldn't mean a thing. To ordinary people it probably would seem that they had invited disaster by stubbornly repudiating everything modern and European—not to say Christian. But the family of Otto Frank, that would be another matter! How could even the most obtuse of the ordinary ignore what had been done to the Jews *just for being Jews,* how could even the most benighted of the Gentiles fail to get the idea when they read in *Het Achterhuis* that once a year the Franks sang a harmless Chanukah song, said some Hebrew words, lighted some candles, exchanged some presents—a ceremony lasting about ten minutes—and that was all it took to make them the enemy. It did not even take that much. It took nothing—that was the horror. And that was the truth. And that was the power of her book. The Franks could gather together by the radio to listen to concerts of Mozart, Brahms, and Beethoven;[9] they could entertain themselves with Goethe and Dickens and Schiller;[1] she could look night after night through the genealogical tables of all of Europe's royal families for suitable mates for Princess Elizabeth and Princess Margaret Rose;[2] she could write passionately in her diary of her love

7. Johann Wolfgang von Goethe (1749–1832), German poet, novelist, playwright, and philosopher; leading figure of the German Romantic period.
8. Charles Dickens (1812–1870), leading English novelist of the Victorian era.
9. Ludwig van Beethoven (1770–1827), German composer of the early Romantic movement. Wolfgang Amadeus Mozart (1756–1791), Austrian composer of the Enlightenment. Johannes Brahms (1833–1897), German Romantic composer and pianist.
1. Friedrich von Schiller (1759–1805), German dramatist, poet, and literary theorist.
2. Margaret Rose (b. 1930), the younger daughter of King George VI of England, married the earl of Snowdon. Elizabeth (b. 1926), daughter of King George VI of England, married Philip, duke of Edinburgh, in 1947 and became Queen Elizabeth II on February 6, 1952.

for Queen Wilhelmina[3] and her desire for Holland to be her fatherland—and none of it made any difference. Europe was not theirs nor were they Europe's, not even her Europeanized family. Instead, three flights up from a pretty Amsterdam canal, they lived crammed into a hundred square feet with the Van Daans, as isolated and despised as any ghetto Jews. First expulsion, next confinement, and then, in cattle cars and camps and ovens, obliteration. And why? Because the Jewish problem to be solved, the degenerates whose contamination civilized people could no longer abide, were they themselves, Otto and Edith Frank, and their daughters, Margot and Anne.

This was the lesson that on the journey home she came to believe she had the power to teach. But only if she were believed to be dead. Were *Het Achterhuis* known to be the work of a living writer, it would never be more than it was: a young teenager's diary of her trying years in hiding during the German occupation of Holland, something boys and girls could read in bed at night along with the adventures of the Swiss Family Robinson.[4] But dead she had something more to offer than amusement for ages 10–15; dead she had written, without meaning to or trying to, a book with the force of a masterpiece to make people finally see.

And when people had finally seen? When they had learned what she had the power to teach them, what then? Would suffering come to mean something new to them? Could she actually make them humane creatures for any longer than the few hours it would take to read her diary through? In her room at Athene—after hiding in her dresser the three copies of *Het Achterhuis*—she thought more calmly about her readers-to-be than she had while pretending to be one of them on the stirring bus ride through the lightning storm. She was not, after all, the fifteen-year-old who could, while hiding from a holocaust, tell Kitty, *I still believe that people are really good at heart*. Her youthful ideals had suffered no less than she had in the windowless freight car from Westerbork[5] and in the barracks at Auschwitz and on the Belsen heath. She had not come to hate the human race for what it was—what could it be but what it was?—but she did not feel seemly any more singing its praises.

What would happen when people had finally seen? The only realistic answer was Nothing. To believe anything else was only to yield to longings which even she, the great longer, had a right to question by now. To keep her existence a secret from her father so as to help improve mankind . . . no, not at this late date. The improvement of the living was their business, not hers; they could improve themselves, if they should ever be so disposed; and if not, not. Her responsibility was to the dead, if to anyone—to her sister, to her mother, to all the slaughtered schoolchildren who had been her friends. There was her diary's purpose, there was her ordained mission: to restore in print their status as flesh and blood . . . for all the good that would do them. An ax was what she really wanted, not print. On the stairwell at the end of her corridor in the dormitory there was a large ax with an enormous red

3. Wilhelmina (1880–1962), queen of the Netherlands (1890–1948), made hortatory radio broadcasts from London during the German occupation of her country.

4. Characters in a widely popular novel of the same name (English translation, 1814) by Swiss writer Johann Rudolf Wyss (1782–1830) about the romantic adventures of a family who survives in the wilderness.

5. A small Jewish transit camp in northeastern Netherlands run by the Germans after 1940. Anne Frank and her family were imprisoned there in August 1944.

handle, to be used in case of fire. But what about in case of hatred—what about murderous rage? She stared at it often enough, but never found the nerve to take it down from the wall. Besides, once she had it in her hands, whose head would she split open? Whom could she kill in Stockbridge to avenge the ashes and the skulls? If she even could wield it. No, what she had been given to wield was *Het Achterhuis, van Anne Frank*. And to draw blood with it she would have to vanish again into another achterhuis, this time fatherless and all on her own.

So she renewed her belief in the power of her less than three hundred pages, and with it the resolve to keep from her father, sixty, the secret of her survival. "For them," she cried, "for them," meaning all who had met the fate that she had been spared and was now pretending to. "For Margot, for my mother, for Lies."

Now every day she went to the library to read *The New York Times*. Each week she read carefully through the newsmagazines. On Sundays she read about all the new books being published in America: novels said to be "notable" and "significant," none of which could possibly be more notable and more significant than her posthumously published diary; insipid best-sellers from which real people learned about fake people who could not exist and would not matter if they did. She read praise for historians and biographers whose books, whatever their merit, couldn't possibly be as worthy of recognition as hers. And in every column in every periodical she found in the library—American, French, German, English—she looked for her own real name. It could not end with just a few thousand Dutch readers shaking their heads and going about their business—it was too important for that! "For them, for them"—over and over, week after week, "for them"—until at last she began to wonder if having survived in the achterhuis, if having outlived the death camps, if masquerading here in New England as somebody other than herself did not make something very suspect—and a little mad—of this seething passion to "come back" as the avenging ghost. She began to fear that she was succumbing to having not succumbed.

And why should she! Who was she pretending to be but who she would have been anyway if no achterhuis and no death camps had intervened? Amy was not somebody else. The Amy who had rescued her from her memories and restored her to life—beguiling, commonsensical, brave, and realistic Amy—was herself. Who she had every right to be! Responsibility to the dead? Rhetoric for the pious! There was nothing to give the dead—they were dead. "Exactly. The importance, so-called, of this book is a morbid illusion. And playing dead is melodramatic and disgusting. And hiding from Daddy is worse. No atonement is required," said Amy to Anne. "Just get on the phone and tell Pim you're alive. He is sixty."

Her longing for him now exceeded even what it had been in childhood, when she wanted more than anything to be his only love. But she was young and strong and she was living a great adventure, and she did nothing to inform him or anyone that she was still alive; and then one day it was just too late. No one would have believed her; no one other than her father would have wanted to. Now people came every day to visit their secret hideaway and to look at the photographs of the movie stars that she'd pinned to the wall beside her bed. They came to see the tub she had bathed in and the table where she'd studied. They looked out of the loft window where Peter and she had cuddled together watching the stars. They stared at the cupboard camouflaging the door the police had come through to take them away. They looked at the open pages of her secret diary. That was her handwriting, they whispered, those are her words. They stayed to look at everything in the achterhuis that she had ever touched. The plain passageways and serviceable little rooms that she had, like a good composition student, dutifully laid out for Kitty in orderly, accurate, workaday Dutch—the superpractical achterhuis was now a holy shrine, a Wailing Wall.[6] They went away from it in silence, as bereft as though she had been their own.

But it was they who were hers. "They wept for me," said Amy; "they pitied me; they prayed for me; they begged my forgiveness. I was the incarnation of the millions of unlived years robbed from the murdered Jews. It was too late to be alive now. I was a saint."

That was her story. And what did Lonoff think of it when she was finished? That she meant every word and that not a word was true.

After Amy had showered and dressed, she checked out of the hotel and he took her to eat some lunch. He phoned Hope from the restaurant and explained that he was bringing Amy home. She could walk in the woods, look at the foliage, sleep safely in Becky's bed; over a few days' time she would be able to collect herself, and then she could return to Cambridge.[7] All he explained about her collapse was that she appeared to him to be suffering from exhaustion. He had promised Amy that he would say no more.

On the ride back to the Berkshires,[8] while Amy told him what it had been like for her during the years when she was being read in twenty different languages by twenty million people, he made plans to consult Dr. Boyce. Boyce was at Riggs, the Stockbridge psychiatric hospital. Whenever a new book appeared, Dr. Boyce would send a charming note asking the author if he would kindly sign the doctor's copy, and once a year the Lonoffs were invited to the Boyces' big barbecue. At Dr. Boyce's request, Lonoff once reluctantly consented to meet with a staff study group from the hospital to discuss "the creative personality." He didn't want to offend the psychiatrist, and it might for a while pacify his wife, who liked to believe that if he got out and mixed more with people things would be better at home.

The study group turned out to have ideas about writing that were too imaginative for his taste, but he made no effort to tell them they were wrong. Nor did he think that he was necessarily right. They saw it their way, he saw it like Lonoff. Period. He had no desire to change anyone's mind. Fiction made people say all kinds of strange things—so be it.

The meeting with the psychiatrists had been underway for only an hour when Lonoff said it had been an enjoyable evening but he had to be getting home. "I have the evening's reading still ahead of me. Without my reading I'm not myself. However, you must feel free to talk about my personality when I'm gone." Boyce, smiling warmly, replied, "I hope we've amused you at least a little with our naïve speculations." "I would have liked to amuse *you*. I apologize for being boring." "No, no," said Boyce, "passivity in a man

6. The only remnant of Jerusalem's Second Temple, also known as Herod's Temple, destroyed in 70 C.E. during the Jewish rebellion against Rome. It is also known as the Western Wall.

7. A city in Massachusetts, 3 miles west of Boston; the site of Harvard, Radcliffe, and MIT.

8. A scenic range of hills and low mountains in western Massachusetts.

of stature has a charm and mystery all its own." "Yes?" said Lonoff. "I must tell my wife."

But an hour wasted some five years ago was hardly to the point. He trusted Boyce and knew that the psychiatrist would not betray his confidence when he went the next day to talk with him about his former student and quasi daughter, a young woman of twenty-six, who had disclosed to him that of all the Jewish writers, from Franz Kafka to E. I. Lonoff, she was the most famous. As for his own betrayal of the quasi daughter's confidence, it did not count for much as Amy elaborated further upon her consuming delusion.

"Do you know why I took this sweet name? It wasn't to protect me from my memories. I wasn't hiding the past from myself or myself from the past. I was hiding from hatred, from hating people the way people hate spiders and rats. Manny, I felt flayed. I felt as though the skin had been peeled away from half my body. Half my face had been peeled away, and everybody would stare in horror for the rest of my life. Or they would stare at the other half, at the half still intact; I could see them smiling, pretending that the flayed half wasn't there, and talking to the half that was. And I could hear myself screaming at them, I could see myself thrusting my hideous side right up into their unmarred faces to make them properly horrified. 'I was pretty! I was whole! I was a sunny, lively little girl! Look, look at what they did to me!' But whatever side they looked at, I would always be screaming. 'Look at the other! Why don't you look at the other!' That's what I thought about in the hospital at night. However they look at me, however they talk to me, however they try to comfort me, I will always be this half-flayed thing. I will never be young, I will never be kind or at peace or in love, and I will hate them all my life.

"So I took the sweet name—to impersonate everything that I wasn't. And a very good pretender I was, too. After a while I could imagine that I wasn't pretending at all, that I had become what I would have been anyway. Until the book. The package came from Amsterdam, I opened it, and there it was: my past, myself, my name, *my face intact*—and all I wanted was revenge. It wasn't for the dead—it had nothing to do with bringing back the dead or scourging the living. It wasn't corpses I was avenging—it was the motherless, fatherless, sisterless, venge-filled, hate-filled, shame-filled, half-flayed, seething thing. It was myself. I wanted tears, I wanted their Christian tears to run like Jewish blood, for me. I wanted their pity—and in the most pitiless way. And I wanted love, to be loved mercilessly and endlessly, just the way I'd been debased. I wanted my fresh life and my fresh body, cleansed and unpolluted. And it needed twenty million people for that. Twenty million ten times over.

"Oh, Manny, I want to live with you! That's what I need! The millions won't do it—it's you! I want to go home to Europe with you. Listen to me, don't say no, not yet. This summer I saw a small house for rent, a stone villa up on a hillside. It was outside Florence. It had a pink tile roof and a garden. I got the phone number and I wrote it down. I still have it. Oh, everything beautiful that I saw in Italy made me think of how happy you could be there—how happy I would be there, looking after you. I thought of the trips we'd take. I thought of the afternoons in the museums and having coffee later by the river. I thought of listening to music together at night. I thought of making your meals. I thought of wearing lovely night-gowns to bed. Oh, Manny, their Anne Frank is theirs; I want to be *your* Anne Frank. I'd like at last to be my own. Child Martyr and Holy Saint isn't a position I'm really qualified for any more. They wouldn't even have me, not as I am, longing for somebody else's husband, begging him to leave his loyal wife to run off with a girl half his age. Manny, does it matter that I'm your daughter's age and you're my father's? Of course I love the Dad-da in you, how could I not? And if you love the child in me, why shouldn't you? There's nothing strange in that—so does half the world. Love has to start somewhere, and that's where it starts in us. And as for who I am—well," said Amy, in a voice as sweet and winning as any he'd ever heard, "you've got to be somebody, don't you? There's no way around that."

At home they put her to bed. In the kitchen Lonoff sat with his wife drinking the coffee she'd made him. Every time he pictured Amy at the dentist's office reading about Otto Frank in *Time* magazine, or in the library stacks searching for her "real" name, every time he imagined her on Boston Common addressing to her writing teacher an intimate disquisition on "her" book, he wanted to let go and cry. He had never suffered so over the suffering of another human being.

Of course he told Hope nothing about who Amy thought she was. But he didn't have to, he could guess what she would say if he did: it was for him, the great writer, that Amy had chosen to become Anne Frank; that explained it all, no psychiatrist required. For him, as a consequence of her infatuation: to enchant him, to bewitch him, to break through the scrupulosity and the wisdom and the virtue into his imagination, and there, as Anne Frank, to become E. I. Lonoff's *femme fatale*.

1979

The Golden Age of the Broadway Song

Some of the nation's most memorable poetry has come from its songwriters—its Jewish songwriters. Consider for a moment these words:

> My funny valentine, sweet comic valentine,
> You make me smile with my heart.
> Your looks are laughable, unphotographable,
> Yet, you're my favorite work of art.
> Is your figure less than greek?
> Is your mouth a little weak?
> When you open it to speak, are you smart?
> But don't change a hair for me, Not if you care for me.
> Stay, little valentine, stay!
> Each day is Valentine's day.

Written by Lorenz Hart and set to music by Richard Rodgers, these lyrics were first heard by the audience of *Babes in Arms,* a Broadway musical of 1937. An American standard for over half a century, "My Funny Valentine" is just a single song from the golden age of Broadway—an era when the New York stage produced one smash-hit musical after another, an era when people left theaters whistling or humming songs they would remember for a lifetime. In that very same show, audiences also heard for the first time "I Wish I Were in Love Again" and "The Lady Is a Tramp."

Between 1920 and 1965, American songwriters lifted the musical to a new level of excellence, as this partial list attests: *Oklahoma!, Annie Get Your Gun, Brigadoon, South Pacific, Gentleman Prefer Blondes, Guys and Dolls, The King and I, Wonderful Town, Pajama Game, My Fair Lady, The Most Happy Fella, Peter Pan, Camelot, Funny Girl, West Side Story, Carousel, Gypsy, Pal Joey, Paint Your Wagon, How to Succeed in Business without Really Trying, A Funny Thing Happened on the Way to the Forum, Hello, Dolly!*, and *Fiddler on the Roof.* In high schools, in community theaters, and in revivals on Broadway, these musicals have been mounted again and again. The songs they introduced comprise a significant chunk of our national songbook: "I Got Rhythm," "I've Got a Crush on You," "Easter Parade," "Smoke Gets in Your Eyes," "Someone to Watch over Me," "This Can't Be Love," "I Could Write a Book," "Bewitched," "Oh, What a Beautiful Morning," "New York, New York," "There's No Business Like Show Business," "Almost Like Being in Love," "Some Enchanted Evening," "Diamonds Are a Girl's Best Friend," "Luck Be a Lady," "Hello, Young Lovers," "I Could Have Danced All Night," "Party's Over," "Maria," "Everything's Coming Up Roses," "Do-Re-Mi," "If Ever I Would Leave You," "Hello, Dolly!" and "Sunrise, Sunset."

Remarkably, Jewish American composers and lyricists wrote every one of these songs as well as the shows in which they were featured. With the very important exception of Cole Porter, Jewish Americans are responsible for this golden age of Broadway. Jerome Kern, Irving Berlin, George and Ira Gershwin, Richard Rodgers, Lorenz Hart, Oscar Hammerstein II, Jules Styne, Arthur Schwartz, Adolph Green, Betty Comden, Sheldon Harnick, Alan Jay Lerner, Frederick Loewe, Frank Loesser, Jerry Bock, Harold Arlen, Sammy Fain—these are some of the composers and lyricists who make up the pantheon of American songwriters. The melodies they composed and the lyrics they wrote return to us like old and familiar friends.

Yet to revisit the music and lyrics is to realize that few of these musicals have any explicit connection to Jewishness. They do not tell "Jewish" stories, nor do their melodies and lyrics "sound" Jewish. In most cases, even though the composers and lyricists were only tenuously connected to any religious heritage (George Gershwin was never bar mitzvahed), they identified themselves as ethnic Jews, and their careers tell a story of assimilation, accommodation, and achievement that was available to Jewish Americans in mid-century America. The story is also about the perfecting of an American art form: the popular musical. Finally, the story helps us distinguish the fragile threads by which Jewish identity was sewn, torn, and mended in the years between 1920 and 1965.

Why the musical? Why Broadway? What accounts for the extraordinary success of Jewish Americans in this business? The answer to these questions imparts crucial sociological information about Jewish American lifestyle. First, demographics played a role, for although Jews have never comprised more than a tiny percentage of the American population, Jews in New York City have made up almost one-third of the general population. Thus, proximity and availability help account for the hefty Jewish presence on Broadway.

World of Our Fathers, Irving Howe's influential text about Eastern European immigrants, notes other important factors. By the early 1900s, Howe reports, Jewish businessmen owned a large portion of New York's entertainment industry. The notoriously ruthless Shubert brothers, for instance, fought off organized crime and owned their own dynasty on Broadway for half a century. Florenz Ziegfeld's theater and his *Follies* productions not only established the model for the musical revue, but he, as well as other producers and directors, employed scores of aspiring Jewish American comics and songwriters "on their way up" as well as other Jewish Americans to stage his musical extravaganzas, write his lyrics, do his choreography. Jewish talent trying to break in to the business would never have to worry about anti-Semitism because Jews were in charge. And Jews were in charge because, to a certain degree, musicals were historically associated with lower-class tastes, with vaudeville and burlesque, and with a kind of lifestyle that established, "respectable" Americans shunned in favor of more genteel entertainment.

Because the upper echelons had no use for it, the theater industry had no quotas—no gates or gatekeepers, save the audience. To have a hit, you only had to find the right words, a catchy tune, a good story. And one hit meant you had the capital to finance the next one. Of the Jewish dominance in Hollywood, critic Neal Gabler writes, "The Jews saw an America of gentility, respectability and status, but they were prohibited from entering those precincts. But in the movies, there were none of the impediments imposed by loftier professions." This could also be said of popular theater, which, in fact, offered even more opportunities than the film industry, especially for immigrant communities, a large portion of which lived in New York City.

In vaudeville, the most popular theater of the early twentieth century, immigrant Americans flourished. They amused their fellow greenhorns, Irish, German, Dutch, all of whom would gather for the show in small auditoriums and local playhouses.

Immigrants also participated in minstrel shows, a popular entertainment originating in the nineteenth century. Presenting elements of black life in song, dance, and speech, minstrelsy was performed by whites imitating blacks. Whites blackened their faces with cork and wore costumes that typified for white audiences the unschooled, naïve, carefree black. In tattered clothing, the blackface performer sang and told jokes in dialect, danced, and played banjo and fiddle. Al Jolson, the son of a cantor, spent most of his career singing in blackface. He is best remembered by contemporary audiences for his rendition of "Mammy," a song immortalized in the first "talking" motion picture, *The Jazz Singer* (1928).

Vaudeville and minstrel-show acts would undoubtedly offend today's audiences, for they poked fun at ethnic stereotypes—usually (but not always) their own—a trend that Jewish vaudevillians joined with gusto. The popular and meshugener Frank Bush, for one, performed in a scrappy black coat, shabby pants, and long beard, delivering his lines in an exaggerated Eastern European accent. Vaudeville had no highbrow aspirations; it sought to appeal to a diverse, often uneducated audience. In fact, many immigrant performers got their start on the streets, which became a proving ground for the inexperienced. No subject was taboo. Yet those who succeeded found themselves in larger and larger theaters, playing to more demanding audiences and looking for more sophisticated ways to entertain an increasingly Americanized crowd.

Tin Pan Alley, the nickname for the district where composers and publishers of popular music in the early twentieth century worked, was another precursor to the golden age of the Broadway musical. Also a safe haven for Jews, Tin Pan Alley hired composers and lyricists on a permanent basis to write popular songs, offering a chance to anyone who could write a song and "plug" (promote) it. That plugging happened anywhere: bars, beer gardens, brothels, vaudeville theaters. When people heard and liked the songs, they bought the sheet music so that they could play the songs on their parlor pianos. Several of the most important music publishers were Jewish American businessmen, including Max Dreyfus and William Morris, the man that founded the powerful William Morris theatrical agency.

The life and career of Irving Berlin, who is commonly considered the greatest popular American songwriter of all time, exemplifies in many ways the paths that were taken by other Jewish American songwriters at the time. Berlin, born Israel Baline, immigrated to the United States in 1893, at the age of five, after the Cossacks had burned his family home to the ground. He and his family lived on the Lower East Side of New York, a large, bustling, notoriously poor community. His father, who had been a cantor in Russia, barely made a living as an itinerant cantor in the city. When Berlin's father died, Irving had to support the family. So he did the only thing he had ever seen his father do—he sang. At seventeen, he earned pocket money by singing from the balcony of a local nightclub. At eighteen, he became a singing waiter. His talents captured the attention of the businessmen of Tin Pan Alley. Joseph Stern, a Jewish American publisher, signed Berlin's first song, "Marie from Sunny Italy," in 1907. On that occasion, Israel Baline's first name became Irving and his last, Berlin, a transition that indicates Berlin's ambitions to be more than a Lower East Side vaudevillian. For the Jewish American composer, a new era of success and Americanization had begun.

The great popularity of "Alexander's Ragtime Band" (1911) made Berlin the uncontested leader of Tin Pan Alley. The sheet music for his songs, the equivalent of record sales, sold in the millions. Yet the true measure of success for a songwriter was a Broadway hit. In 1914, Berlin wrote his first musical and opened his own music publishing company. He went on to have a long and brilliant career—on Broadway and off. President Eisenhower gave him an award for writing "God Bless America," the moment that Berlin remembered as being his proudest. His most successful play, *Annie Get Your Gun* (1946), lavished Americans with a wealth of songs, including "There's No Business Like Show Business," "I Got the Sun in the Morning," "Doin' What Comes Natur'lly," and the famous duet "Anything You Can Do."

Annie Get Your Gun would not have been possible without the innovations to the musical that Jerome Kern and George Gershwin had initiated in the late 1920s and early 1930s. Before the 1920s, the musical resembled comic operetta: lighthearted but often frivolous, and sometimes crude, episodic, and chaotic rather than narrative. With *Show Boat* (1927), for which Kern wrote the music and Oscar Hammerstein II the lyrics, and based on a novel by Edna Ferber, the Broadway musical leapt forward. For the first time in a popular musical, the songs crucially contributed to the telling of a story that daringly dealt with weighty subjects—miscegenation and unhappy marriage. Most remarkable, perhaps, *Show Boat* featured noncomic, three-dimensional African American characters.

Kern's focus on African American culture was not unusual for the time; in fact, it parallels, though probably does not equal, George Gershwin's. Like Berlin and Kern, Gershwin got his start writing songs for Tin Pan Alley, earning fifteen dollars a week to play the piano and plug songs. Like Berlin, too, he was the son of Eastern European immigrants. Gershwin perceived no distinction between what critics saw as his popular work and his more "classically bent" compositions (*Rhapsody in Blue* or *An American in Paris*, for instance), and combined his popular and classical musical vocabularies in innovative ways that redefined the form and content of the Broadway musical.

His *Of Thee I Sing* (1931), using chants, marches, and mock serenades to satirize American politics, became the first musical to win a Pulitzer prize. This show, the awards committee noted, had made theater history: "Musical plays are always popular, and by injecting satire and point into them, a very large public is reached." But it was *Porgy and Bess* (1935), a dramatic opera about African American life in rural South Carolina, that many consider Gershwin's masterpiece. It features among its songs "Summertime," "It Ain't

Necessarily So," and "I Got Plenty o' Nuttin'." As is the case with much art or music that is ahead of its time, audiences did not greet *Porgy and Bess* with immediate acclaim—though the critics raved.

For over fifty years, critics have called *Porgy and Bess* the most important American opera ever written. Recently, however, scholarship has centered less on the work itself than on its reception and the controversial relationship between blacks and Jews in the music professions during the first half of the twentieth century. Research makes clear that Jewish Americans did enjoy a productive, though not a fully reciprocal, relationship with African Americans. Before he wrote *Porgy and Bess,* Gershwin spent eleven months living in a shack in the Sea Islands off South Carolina in order to absorb the experience of southern African Americans. In New York City, he searched out all types of African American music and often visited the nightclubs of Harlem. Berlin, too, had begun his career composing rags, taking inspiration from African American composer Scott Joplin, the "King of Ragtime," who pioneered that form. Harold Arlen, a cantor's son, wrote songs to be sung at Harlem's Cotton Club, the legendary African American night club that launched the careers of many jazz greats, including blues singer Ethel Waters. Waters had also appeared in an Irving Berlin revue, *As Thousands Cheer* (1915), singing a song called "Supper Time," about a lynching. In the most controversial crossover of all, Al Jolson, a Jewish American vaudevillian, spent a large part of his career singing in blackface.

From the vantage point of scholars today, the musical relationship between Jews and blacks in the first half of the twentieth century was complex and conflicted. Was singing in blackface a coarse form of ridicule, or did it express an affinity between the suffering of blacks and Jews? Was it a mask by which Jews could express their own woes, or was it merely a way for Jews to assimilate into the larger world of white racism? Some music historians have suggested that opportunistic Jewish Americans mined the world of African American music, benefiting from their resources to sell it in a way that African Americans could not. At the very least, the willingness of Jewish American songwriters to work closely with African American artists, some have argued, contributed to the songwriters' phenomenal success.

The complexity of the conundrum includes the apparent fact that the "discovery" of African American culture by Jewish songwriters occurs at the same time that Jews appear to misplace their own culture. After the first wave of ethnic and racial comedy in vaudeville, signs of visible Jewishness seem to have disappeared from Broadway until the 1960s. Assimilation, actual or aspired-to, is the most compelling reason. Though Richard Rodgers writes in his autobiography that he was identified with Jews for "for socioethnic reasons," he also states "that his family's Reform Judaism faded after his bar mitzvah." Gershwin and Berlin, as children of immigrants, may have been even more eager to shed—or camouflage—their socioethnic tags. Berlin not only changed his name, he wrote America's most famous Christmas song of all time, "White Christmas," as well as the popular standard "Easter Parade." Philip Roth has meditated upon the noteworthy fact that an Eastern European Jew wrote "White Christmas," hypothesizing that Berlin's blockbusters actually represent a profound moment of cultural subversion. Through his slightly lunatic alter ego in *Operation Shylock*, Roth proposes that

> God gave Moses the Ten Commandments and then He gave to Irving Berlin "White Christmas" and "Easter Parade." The two holidays that celebrate the divinity of Christ—the divinity that's the very heart of the Jewish rejection of Christianity—and what does Irving Berlin brilliantly do? He de-Christs them both! Easter he turns into a fashion show and Christmas into a holiday about snow. Gone is the gore and the murder of Christ! But nicely! Nicely! So nicely the goyim don't even know what hit 'em!

The incisiveness of Roth's humor should not be missed. Berlin had a Christian wife; publicity photos show the two of them merrily trimming a Christmas tree. "White Christmas," then, may be seen as Berlin's attempt to make Christmas something he could partake in, for his love of America and his famed devotion to his wife would make the holiday impossible to ignore.

Berlin's "White Christmas" sheds light on the success of Jewish American songwriters and the history of Jewish American assimilation in general. The ability to contribute to mainstream American culture provided a way of claiming that culture as one's own and of making oneself at home. Thus, Berlin went to great lengths to capture the American fancy. In his early days, he not only skillfully borrowed from African American ragtime, but wrote songs in Yiddish, Irish, and German idioms, adapting ethnic styles to popular tastes. Gershwin shared that talent for adapting various styles to the American palette. In response to the question of whether his subject's work seemed to spring from "Jewish roots," Gershwin's biographer wrote: "His work as a whole was geared primarily for American audiences and was expected to be performed according to American—not Jewish—performance practice standards. He emphasized the American aspects of his work by using only English texts and by pushing for performances of his work by singers and instrumentalists familiar with the language of Tin Pan Alley, Broadway, jazz."

Jewish American popular songwriters followed this tack closely. In order to do so, however, their works stayed far afield from Jewishness. In the landmark musical *Oklahoma!* (1943), Richard Rodgers and Oscar Hammerstein II depicted the American Southwest at the turn of the century, complete with cornfields, square dances, and cowboys, offering audiences a vision of pastoral America, a landscape altogether different from the New York neighborhoods that the two creators of the work had grown up in. The plots, too, could be unquestionably exotic or fantastical: a schoolteacher goes to Siam, finding romance, in *The King and I* (1951); a magical Scottish town awakens only one day every one hundred years in *Brigadoon* (1947); a romantic triangle involves King Arthur, Queen Guenevere, and Sir Lancelot in *Camelot* (1960).

Despite the plays' romantic bases, the writers never totally abandoned intellectual and social issues. Rodgers and Hammerstein's *South Pacific* (1949) and *The King and I* tackle the problem of interracial romance; Richard Adler and Jerry Ross's *The Pajama Game* (1954) tells the story of a union activist's uneasy romance with a member of management; Alan Jay Lerner and Frederick Loewe's *My Fair Lady* (1956) demonstrates that class barriers are not as impervious as they seem; Frank Loesser's *How to Succeed in Business without Really Trying* (1961) skewers big business and the

Horatio Alger myth. For many Jewish Americans, these themes hit close to home.

In its depiction of social issues, Leonard Bernstein and Stephen Sondheim's *West Side Story*, which opened in 1957, broke new ground in the American musical theater. *West Side Story* translates *Romeo and Juliet* into the contemporary world of ethnic street gangs—the Anglos versus the Puerto Ricans. Originally, the creators had sought to present the conflict as a Jewish boy's infatuation with an Italian Catholic girl, though they eventually decided that that type of conflict seemed dated. Given this discussion, it seems reasonable to assume that Bernstein and Sondheim also hesitated to call attention to their Jewish heritage. In any case, Bernstein, inspired by Latin American rhythms, fused those with jazz to elevate theater music. In addition, the ethnic content as well as the tone of the play had a great impact on the Broadway theater. Never before had there been a musical, according to Brooks Atkinson, theater critic for the *New York Times*, whose "tribal code of honor . . . is the code of hoodlums and gangsters . . . rooted in ignorance and evil. . . . It is part of the hideousness that lies under the scabby surface of the city."

Bernstein's identification with ethnic subjects kept him pursuing other Jewish themes in his music, including the ballet *Dybbuk* (1974). Stephen Sondheim, on the other hand, while continuing to be an innovative and brilliant force in American musical theater—his plays include *Gypsy* (1950), *Do I Hear a Waltz?* (1965), *Company* (1970), *A Little Night Music* (1973), and *Sweeney Todd* (1979)—has avoided ethnic character or religious identification. In *West Side Story*, however, both men had uttered the unspeakable; they had actually taken aim at ethnic division and racial hatred, and had made theater history by portraying a diverse—and divided—New York.

In the 1960s, Jewish American composers turned tentatively toward their own heritage for inspiration. A short-lived musical, *Milk and Honey* (1961), became the first ever to have an Israeli setting. In *Hello, Dolly!* (1964), the famous eponymous matchmaker, Dolly Levi, had a Jewish flavor, though, when played by Carol Channing, perhaps a lighter one than when Barbra Streisand played Dolly in the movie. Just two months after the debut of *Hello Dolly!*, *Funny Girl* opened. *Funny Girl* covers the major events in the life of famous (and Jewish) comedienne Fanny Brice. Because Streisand played the role of Brice with all of Brice's regional and ethnic idioms intact, few in the audience could ignore the Jewish tone, especially when the star sang "Sadie, Sadie."

It would take just a few more months, however, before Jewishness came completely out of the closet. For also in 1964, at the end of September, *Fiddler on the Roof* opened on Broadway. Adapted from the stories of Sholem Aleichem and from Arnold Perl's play *Tevya and His Daughters* (1957), *Fiddler* depicts Jewish life in czarist Russia at the turn of the century. The facts of Jewish life at that time would hardly seem to support a popular musical since the Jews in Russia lived with the constant threat of pogrom, not nearly enough to eat, and a fervent wish to come to America. Still, in Sheldon Harnick's lyrics, Jerry Bock's music, and Joseph Stein's book, life in the Russian shtetl becomes romantic, colorful, and sentimental. Featuring songs like "Tradition," "Matchmaker," and "Sunrise, Sunset," the play idealizes a world in which people's lives overflowed with community, tradition, and the neighbors' troubles. When the play ends, the characters mournfully separate and head to America. Ironically, *Fiddler on the Roof* appealed to American Jews nostalgic for a past that they had never experienced and that their ancestors had fought desperately to escape.

Fiddler on the Roof was seen by more than American Jews. With a first run of close to eight years, it became, at that time, the longest running musical in history. The remarkable mainstream success of *Fiddler* cleared away doubt that Broadway theatergoers would embrace the diverse cultures present in American life; it also paved the way for the opening of two new musicals in 1970 that dealt with Jewish themes: Jerry Bock and Sheldon Harnick's *The Rothschilds*, starring Hal Linden, and Richard Rodgers and Martin Charnin's *Two by Two*, which boasted Danny Kaye (Noah) and Madeline Kahn. Paradoxically, with the closing of *Fiddler* in 1972, the golden age of Broadway musicals and of Jewish American songwriters ended in some respects. Perhaps the same changes in American culture that had made it possible to stage a smash hit about shletl life also made it possible for Jewish Americans to choose more conventionally rewarding professions. For as Jewish Americans songwriters succeeded in creating four decades of remarkable American musicals, they had, at the same time, made American culture more tolerant toward the ethnic differences of its citizens. Their songs and stories move Jewish Americans from the wings to center stage.

OSCAR HAMMERSTEIN II
1895–1960

Oscar Hammerstein, librettist and producer, was born into an influential Jewish theater family of German origin (though Hammerstein's mother had him baptized as an Episcopalian). He was named after his grandfather, an impresario of Broadway musicals. His father, William, managed the Victoria Theatre; his uncle Arthur and cousins William and James all made their living staging, writing, and producing plays on Broadway. Hammerstein attended Columbia University, where he wrote lyrics for college shows. His first professional production was *The Light*, which opened in 1919; his first hit was *Rose Marie*, which he co-wrote with Oscar Harbach in 1924. Hammerstein's most successful collaborations were with the composer Richard Rodgers; together they wrote *Oklahoma!* (1943), *Carousel* (1945), *The King and I* (1951), and *The Sound of Music* (1959), among others.

Show Boat, based on Edna Ferber's successful novel about life on a Mississippi riverboat, took the American musical theater into new dramatic territory. Departing from the lightweight song-and-dance musical, Hammerstein's libretto and lyrics introduced audiences to three-dimensional characters who faced the hardships of failed marriage, miscegenation, and labor without respite. Hammerstein's lyrics and Jerome Kern's (1885–1945) score, while faithful to the tone and outline of the novel, brought to it songs that took on their own importance, such as "Make Believe" and "Can't Help Lovin' Dat Man," and the motif that brings power and unity to the work: "Ol' Man River."

From Show Boat

Ol' Man River

Dere's an ol' man called de Mississippi,
Dat's de ol' man dat I'd like to be.
What does he care if de world's got troubles?
What does he care if de land ain't free?

Ol' man river, Dat ol' man river,
He mus' know sumpin' But don't say nuthin',
He jes' keeps rollin', He keeps on rollin' along.

He don't plant taters, He don't plant cotton
An' dem dat plants em' Is soon forgotten,
But ol' man river, He jes' keeps rollin' along.

You an' me, we sweat an' strain,
Body all achin' an' racked wid' pain.
Tote dat barge! Lift dat bale!
Git a little drunk An' you land in jail.

I git weary An' sick of tryin',
I'm tired of livin' An' skeered of dyin';
But ol' man river, He jes' keeps rollin' along!

Colored folks work on de Mississippi,
Colored folks work while de white folks play.
Pullin' dem boats from de dawn to sunset,
Gittin' no rest till de Judgment Day.

Don't look up an' don't look down,
You don't dast make de white boss frown;
Bend yo' knees an' bow yo' head,
An' pull dat rope until yo're dead.

Let me go 'way from de Mississippi,
Let me go 'way from de white man boss.
Show me dat stream called de river Jordan,
Dat's de ol' stream dat I longs to cross!

Ol' man river, Dat ol' man river,
He mus' know sumpin' But don't say nuthin',
He jes' keeps rollin', He keeps on rollin' along.

1927

IRVING BERLIN
1888–1989

Born Israel Baline in Russia, Irving Berlin (1888–1989) gained worldwide fame with the song "Alexander's Ragtime Band" in 1911 and went on to write over 1,000 songs in what has become known as "the American style." Berlin contributed songs for Broadway musicals and revues, notably the *Ziegfeld Follies,* and wrote his first book musical for the Marx Brothers, whose film *Cocoanuts* (1925) included fourteen musical numbers. While Berlin wrote other successful book musicals—*Annie Get Your Gun* (1946) and *Call Me Madam* (1950)—he is best known for individual songs such as the holiday classics "White Christmas" and "Easter Parade," "Blue Skies" and "God Bless America," which was introduced to radio audiences by the singer Kate Smith in her Armistice Day broadcast in November 1938.

God Bless America

While the storm clouds gather far across the sea,
let us swear allegiance to a land that's free,
let us all be grateful for a land so fair,
as we raise our voices in a solemn prayer.
God bless America, land that I love.
Stand beside her and guide her,
thru the night with a light from above.
From the mountains to the prairies,
to the oceans white with foam,
God bless America, my home sweet home.

1938

LORENZ HART
1895–1943

"If it is possible to make an entertaining musical comedy out of an odious story," wrote critic Brooks Atkinson in the *New York Times,* " 'Pal Joey' is it." Lorenz Hart's (1895–1943) lyrics and Richard Rodgers's (1902–1979) music drew on John O'Hara's *New Yorker* stories about the affairs and betrayals of Joey Evans, a self-absorbed, second-rate nightclub performer in Chicago. In spite of Hart's drinking and emotional instability, his partnership with Rodgers, begun in Hart's college days, produced successful revues (*The Garrick Gaieties* [1925]) and musicals (*A Connecticut Yankee* [1927], *On Your Toes* [1936], *The Boys from Syracuse* [1938]), wherein the best of Hart's lyrics—"Where or When," "My Funny Valentine," "Bewitched"—tell of love but with a touch of irony and display a free, easy-rhyming use of the vernacular. These qualities, and the lilt of Rodgers's melodies, have given the songs a life beyond the shows that they were a part of.

From Pal Joey

Bewitched

He's a fool and don't I know it. But a fool can have his charms.
I'm in love and don't I show it, Like a babe in arms.
Love's the same old sad sensation. Lately I've not slept a wink
Since this half-pint imitation Put me on the blink.

Refrain
I'm wild again! Beguiled again! A simpering, whimpering child again.
Bewitched, bothered and bewildered am I.
Couldn't sleep And wouldn't sleep Until I could sleep where I
shouldn't sleep.
Bewitched, bothered and bewildered am I.
Lost my heart, but what of it? My mistake, I agree.
He's a laugh, but I love it Because the laugh's on me.
A pill he is, But still he is All wine and I'll keep him until he is
Bewitched, bothered and bewildered like me.

Seen a lot; I mean a lot! But now I'm like sweet seventeen a lot.
Bewitched, bothered, and bewildered am I.
I'll sing to him Each spring to him And worship the trousers that cling
to him.
Bewitched, bothered and bewildered am I.
When he talks He is seeking Words to get off his chest.
Horizontally speaking, He's at his very best.
Vexed again, Perplexed again, Thank God I can be oversexed again.
Bewitched, bothered and bewildered am I.

Sweet again, Petite again, And on my proverbial seat again.
Bewitched, bothered and bewildered am I.
What am I? Half shot am I. To think that he loves me, So hot am I.
Bewitched, bothered and bewildered am I.
Though at first we said "No, sir." Now we're two little dears.
You might say we are closer Than Roebuck is to Sears.
I'm dumb again And numb again, A rich, ready, ripe little plum again.
Bewitched, bothered and bewildered am I.

Encore
It is really quite funny Just how quickly he learns How to spend
all the money That Mister Simpson earns.
He's kept enough, He's slept enough, And yet, where it counts, he's
adept enough.
Bewitched, bothered and bewildered am I.

1941

FRANK LOESSER
1910–1969

Frank Loesser wrote several successful musicals—*Where's Charley?* (1948), *The Most Happy Fella* (1956), and *How to Succeed in Business without Really Trying* (1960)—but *Guys and Dolls* (1950) is his indisputable masterpiece. For technical brilliance and for vivid expression of character and atmosphere—in this case the quirky gamblers and chorus girls in Damon Runyon's colorful Times Square—Loesser's music and lyrics are a high-water mark for the American musical. Based on Damon Runyon's short story *The Idyll of Miss Sarah Brown*, Abe Burrows's libretto has the rare distinction of still being hilarious more than fifty years after the musical opened. The comic exuberance of *Guys and Dolls* comes through in almost every number: "Fugue for Tinhorns," "Sit Down, You're Rockin' the Boat," "Marry the Man Today," and "Adelaide's Lament," in which the nightclub chanteuse, Miss Adelaide, congestedly bemoans her fiancé of fourteen years' inability to give up gambling in exchange for married bliss.

From Guys and Dolls

Adelaide's Lament

The average unmarried female basicly insecure
Due to some long frustration may react
With psychosomatic symptoms difficult to endure
Affecting the upper respiratory tract.
In other words, just from waiting around for that plain little band of gold
A person can develop a cold.
You can spray her wherever you figure the streptococci lurk,
You can give her a shot for whatever she's got but it just won't work.
If she's tired of getting the fish-eye from the hotel clerk,
A person can develop a cold.

It says here
The female remaining single just in the legal sense
Shows a neurotic tendency. See note
Note:
Chronic, organic syndromes toxic or hypertense
Involving the eye, the ear, and the nose, and throat.
In other words, just from worrying whether the wedding is on or off
A person can develop a cough.
You can feed her all day with the Vitamin A and the Bromo Fizz
But the medicine never gets anywhere where the trouble is.
If she's getting a kind of a name for herself and the name ain't "his"
A person can develop a cough.
And furthermore just from stalling and stalling And stalling the wedding trip,
A person can develop La grippe.
When they get on the train for Niag'ra and she can hear church bells chime

The compartment is air-conditioned and the mood sublime
Then they get off at Saratoga for the fourteenth time,
A person can develop La Grippe, La grippe, La Post nasal drip
With the wheezes and the sneezes and a sinus that's really a pip!
From a lack of community property and a feeling she's getting too old,
A person can develop a bad bad cold.

1950

STEPHEN SONDHEIM
b. 1930

In a recent interview, Stephen Sondheim described *West Side Story* (1957), his Broadway debut, as a "completely maverick show," a musical that defied the popular taste for lighthearted escapist fare. Based loosely on *Romeo and Juliet*, Arthur Laurents's book sets the tragic story in one of New York's poor immigrant neighborhoods. Leonard Bernstein's score is singularly rich in dance music, orchestral and vocal, that heightens the edgy, youthful, often violent energy of the warring Jets and Sharks. Sondheim's lyrics, at turns joyous ("Maria," "Tonight") and biting ("America," "Gee, Officer Krupke"), introduces to theatergoers the maverick talent whose distinctive adult musicals—among them *Gypsy* (1959), *Company* (1970), *Follies* (1971), *Sweeney Todd* (1979), and *Sunday in the Park with George* (1984)—have made him one of the greatest artists in the American musical theater.

From West Side Story

America

Rosalia. Just for a successful visit. (nostalgically):
Puerto Rico, You lovely island,
Island of tropical breezes,
Always the pineapples growing,
Always the coffee blossoms blowing.

Anita (mockingly):
Puerto Rico, You ugly island,
Island of tropic diseases.
Always the hurricanes blowing,
Always the population growing,
And the money owing,
And the babies crying,
And the bullets flying.
I like the island Manhattan.
Smoke on your pipe and put that in!

Anita and Girls (except Rosalia):
I like to be in America!

O.K. by me in America!
Ev'rything free in America
For a small fee in America!

Rosalia:
I like the city of San Juan.

Anita:
I know a boat you can get on.

Rosalia:
Hundreds of flowers in full bloom.

Anita:
Hundreds of people in each room!

Anita and Girls (except Rosalia):
Automobile in America,
Chromium steel in America,
Wire-spoke wheel in America
Very big deal in America!

Rosalia:
I'll drive a Buick through San Juan.

Anita:
If there's a road you can drive on.

Rosalia:
I'll give my cousins a free ride.

Anita:
How you get all of them inside?

Anita and Girls (except Rosalia):
Immigrant goes to America,
Many hellos in America,
Nobody knows in America
Puerto Rico's in America!

Rosalia:
I'll bring a T.V. to San Juan.

Anita:
If there's a current to turn on!

Rosalia:
I'll give them new washing machine.

Anita:
What have they got there to keep clean?

Anita and Girls (except Rosalia):
I like the shores of America!
Comfort is yours in America!
Knobs on the doors in America,
Wall-to-wall floors in America!

Rosalia:
When I will go back to San Juan

Anita:
When you will shut up and get gone!

Rosalia:
Ev'ryone there will give big cheer!

Anita:
Ev'ryone there will have moved here!

1957

SHELDON HARNICK
b. 1924

Born and raised in Chicago, Sheldon Harnick attended Northwestern University, where he wrote the words and music for undergraduate revues. After graduating, he moved to New York City, where he wrote lyrics for popular songs. In 1955, his first Broadway musical, *The Amazing Adele,* was produced, but it was his collaboration with the composer Jerry Bock that led to success, first with *Fiorello!*, a story about New York City's popular and unconventional mayor Fiorello La Guardia, which won the Pulitzer prize in 1959, and five years later with *Fiddler on the Roof*.

A record-breaking hit on Broadway, *Fiddler on the Roof* is based on the stories of Sholem Aleichem—that is, the book, by Joseph Stein, reuses Sholem Aleichem's stories from the play *Tevya and His Daughters* (1957) by Arnold Perl. Teyve the Milkman's poignant puzzlement at the breakdown of traditional life in the Russian Jewish village of Anatevka is the source of Sheldon Harnick (lyrics) and Jerry Bock's (music) colorful, witty songs—"Tradition," "Sunrise, Sunset," "Matchmaker," and "If I Were a Rich Man" are among the best known—that skillfully blend Jewish ethnicity with nostalgic warmth, appealing to mainstream audiences worldwide.

From Fiddler on the Roof

If I Were a Rich Man

If I were a rich man,
Daidle, deedle, daidle, Digguh, digguh, deedle, daidle dum.
All day long I'd biddy, biddy bum—
If I were a wealthy man.

Wouldn't have to work hard,
Daidle, deedle, daidle, Digguh, digguh, deedle, daidle dum.
If I were a biddy, biddy rich,
Digguh, dighuh, deedle, daidle man.
I'd build a big tall house with rooms by the dozen, Right in the middle of the town.
A fine tin roof with real wooden floors below.
There would be one long staircase just going up And one even longer coming down.
And one more leading nowhere, just for show.
I'd fill my yard with chicks and turkeys and geese And ducks for the town to see and hear;
Squawking just as noisily as they can.
And each loud quack and cluck and gobble and honk Will land like a trumpet on the ear.
As if to say: here lives a wealthy man. (Sigh)
If I were a rich man,
Daidle, deedle, daidle, Digguh, digguh, digguh, deedle, daidle dum,
All day long I'd biddy, biddy bum—
If I were a wealthy man.
Wouldn't have to work hard,
Daidle, deedle, daidle, Digguh, digguh, deedle, daidle dum.
If I were a biddy, biddy rich,
Digguh, digguh, deedle, daidle man.
I see my wife, my Golde, looking like a rich man's wife With a proper double chin;
Supervising meals to her heart's delight.
I see her putting on airs and strutting like a peacock.
Oi! What a happy mood she's in, Screaming at the servants day and night.
The most important men in town will come to fawn on me.
They will ask me to advise them, like a Solomon, the wise.
"If you please, Reb Tevye, pardon me, Reb Tevye—"
Posing problems that would cross a Rabbi's eyes.
Boi-boi-boi-boi-boi-boi-boi-boi.
And it won't make one bit of diff'rence If I answer right or wrong.
When you're rich they think you really know.
If I were rich I'd have the time that I lack To sit in the synagogue and pray
And maybe have a seat by the eastern wall.
And I'd discuss the holy books with the learned men Seven hours ev'ry day.
Daidle, deedle, daidle, Digguh, digguh, deedle, daidle dum.
Lord who made the lion and the lamb, you decreed I should be what I am.
Would it spoil some vast, eternal plan—If I were a wealthy man?
This would be the sweetest thing of all. (Sigh)
If I were a rich man,
Daidle, deedle, daidle, Digguh, digguh, deedle, daidle dum.
All day long I'd biddy, biddy bum—
If I were a wealthy man.
Wouldn't have to work hard,

Daidle, deedle, daidle, Digguh, digguh, deedle, daidle dum.
Lord who made the lion and the lamb, You decreed I should be what I
am.
Would it spoil some vast, eternal plan—If I were a wealthy man?

1964

Wandering and Return: Literature since 1973

Always successful at acculturating, Jewish Americans in this period have found themselves woven into the cloth of national identity. As the last vestiges of institutionalized anti-Semitism disappear and isolated incidents of anti-Semitism decline, American Jews continue to rise to high levels in politics and culture. As secretaries of state, senators, presidential advisers, producers and directors, Nobel prizewinners and owners of championship sports teams, American Jews have participated in all aspects of mainstream American culture. Only 2.5 percent of the American population, Jews make up 20.0 percent of the professors and students at Ivy League universities and 10.0 percent of the Senate; they are also one-quarter of the writers, editors, and producers of the elite media, which include network news divisions, the top newsweeklies, and the four leading newspapers—the *New York Times,* the *Los Angeles Times,* the *Washington Post,* and the *Wall Street Journal.*

Reading statistics like these, it is easy to conclude that Jews are no longer outsiders—that, in fact, they are deeply embedded in the social structures of this nation. And perhaps they are. Yet sociological acceptance should not be confused with religious and cultural homogeneity. Even as these statistics suggest a narrative of progress, they also suggest several new challenges; such thorough integration has not been without cost. In this period more than any other, the success of acculturation has led to rapid assimilation and has posed a serious threat to the welfare of the Jewish American community. Only with great difficulty can American Jews continue to maintain an alternative religious practice and cultural distinction when they so wholly participate in a national culture that is largely based in Christian ritual and tradition. This challenge, as well as the fracture of other familiar touchstones that we will examine, called many to question what it actually meant to be Jewish in late twentieth-century America.

The literature in this section reflects these concerns. In these selections, the reader will find evidence of widespread assimilation and its critique. To the overarching question What does it mean to be Jewish in the final quarter of the American twentieth century? the writers here essay answers—and pose more questions: What does it mean to be Jewish when ties to ethnic heritage have loosened? When anti-Semitism is no longer as overt as it once was? When an American Jew can no longer wholly sympathize with Israeli politics? How does the Holocaust continue to shape Jewish American identity? What relationship do Jews have with a common past? What makes a Jew Jewish if he or she does not practice the rituals of Judaism? Will all Jewish Americans eventually assimilate? What is the future of Jewish Americans as a community in the United States?

Many of these questions have been asked in some form since the first Jew set foot on American soil. Yet this section takes 1973 as a dividing line because that year marks substantial changes in the lives of all Americans—especially Jewish Americans. In 1973, the United States ended its involvement in the Vietnam War, the Yom Kippur War broke out in Israel, the American government foundered with the Watergate cover-ups, the "sixties" as an American movement came to an end, and the multicultural 1970s began. These events left Jewish Americans thinking about their responsibilities, both private and political, and their inheritance, both national and ethnic. As interest in multiculturalism and feminism deepened, as Israel's role in world politics became more complex, and as the Holocaust drew renewed study, America's Jews, affected by all these things, wrestled with questions of heritage, loyalty, identity, and nationalism. And while the literature collected here sometimes displays the spiritual foundering of Jewish Americans, it also shows a renewed interest in preserving a unique and rich identity, and in renewing the bases on which one turns—or returns—to Jewish American identity and culture. For this reason, we have named this section *Wandering and Return.*

THE FORCES OF ASSIMILATION

The threat of anti-Semitism, as a cohesive force for Jewish Americans, is perhaps not the noblest or smartest flag around which to rally. Yet in previous generations, those who had drifted away from organized Judaism found in anti-Semitism a compelling reason to assert their difference: society treated them differently. Anti-Semitism in the United States has always been comparatively minor and perhaps not sufficient to galvanize American Jews of diverse regions and backgrounds around a common cause. Still, before the 1970s, genteel discrimination had kept Jews out of certain spheres of influence. That, combined with revelations about the Holocaust and their grandparents' memories of pogroms, could prompt even the most assimilated Jew to become defiant and insistent about his or her heritage. Yet, as the impress of European history continued to lighten and American society grew more tolerant, anti-Semitism would not remind Jews that they were Jews. In earlier periods of history, equality and brotherhood on the battlefields of World War II had substantially lessened anti-Semitism; in the 1970s, a much more thorough social integration was effected. At Princeton and Yale, at the corporate offices of IBM and Citicorps, as mail carriers and civil engineers, Jews studied and labored side by side with non-Jews. And, perhaps to no one's particular surprise though to many cries of dismay, Jews fell in love with non-Jews. And married them.

In 1990, the National Jewish Population Survey reported its findings to a shocked public. According to the survey, Jewish Americans had a lower rate of population growth than any other of the three major religions. America's Jews were graying more rapidly, joining synagogues less often, and giving less to Jewish charities than they ever had before. The most disturbing statistic—that between 1985 and 1990, 52 percent of Jews had intermarried—left the organized Jewish community in a state of crisis, for the survey also reported that only a quarter of these couples would raise their children as Jews. For some, the extinction of American Jewry seemed inevitable.

This threat joined another, one that seemed almost insuperable: a steady decline in the number of Jews whose primary identification was ethnic. For at least one hundred years previously, the large numbers of immigrants, especially from Eastern Europe, had enjoyed an ethnic culture rerooted in American soil. Like other immigrants, the traditions of the Old World were strongest among those who had made the crossing and grew weaker with each ensuing generation. While previous generations of American Jews could, in the absence of strong spiritual beliefs, link their Jewishness to certain traditional ways of living as well as to a common heritage, the generation that came of age in the 1970s would have to reestablish their ties to ethnic identity—if, in fact, they chose to do so. As Jews fanned out across the country and bagel stores became national franchises, the quaint Yiddishisms of their grandparents moved further back in their minds. For many, what remained of Jewishness was only a memory, however fond or treasured. In this sense, Jewish Americans can be compared to third-generation Italian Americans who have lost the ethnic speech, mannerisms, values of their ancestors but still closely follow their grandmothers' recipes for ragù.

Yet the analogy quickly loses currency, for the difference between Italian Americans and Jewish Americans is clear: Jewishness is more than an ethnicity—it is a religion. But religious commitment had declined. Added to this, of course, was the realization that Jewishness was not a race either. The kind of anti-Semitic ravings of the Third Reich—that Jews were racially different from other Caucasians—were largely silenced. With the decline of racial thinking and the waning of ethnic and religious traditions, American Jews, those who were affiliated with synagogues and those who were not, had to look hard at what was left to define them as Jews. As Max Apple reminds us in *The Eighth Day,* Jewishness would now be a matter of choice, something the individual might struggle to retain in the face of increasing claims on his or her attention.

MULTICULTURALISM, IDENTITY POLITICS, AND THE HOLOCAUST

At the same time that Jewish Americans were facing this identity crisis, the national celebration of diversity and multiculturalism reached its zenith. Jewish Americans, like other ethnic and racial Americans, began journeys to find their "roots"—after a popular 1977 miniseries based on a best-selling novel by Alex Haley in which an African American family traces its lineage in order to appreciate its own history and uniqueness. If, in the 1950s, Jews had labored to become more American and to adopt the ways of "real" Americans more fully, the 1970s began an opposite trend, a trend of identity seeking. Following the lead of other ethnic and racial cultures, Jewish Americans, now significantly distant from their immigrant past, explored their roots as well. And a vast majority could go only so far—for it did not take long for an American Jew of European descent to find the ancestor who had perished in the Holocaust. In the 1970s, Holocaust awareness intensified and in many ways would energize—though, some believed, detrimentally—the Jewish American community.

This increased consciousness of lineage merged with several other cultural turning points to produce a new public awareness of the Holocaust. Shortly, we will discuss Jewish Americans in relation to Israeli politics; here it is worth noting that the Yom Kippur War (1973), in which Egypt attacked Israel on the holiest day of the year, caused severe Israeli casualties and alerted many Jewish Americans to Israel's vulnerability. The fear that the Jewish nation could be wiped out reminded many of the genocide in Europe. Also during the 1970s and undoubtedly as a result of the factors described above, NBC aired the television miniseries *Holocaust* (1978). Even as Elie Wiesel called the series "misleading, complacent, and dangerous," millions watched it; and although not as realistic as some might have liked, the show, nevertheless, introduced to a new generation the horrors of the Holocaust. That very same year, President Carter authorized the first committee to plan the U.S. Holocaust Memorial Museum, which would be prominently situated adjacent to the Mall in Washington, D.C.

In the ensuing years, representations of the Holocaust in American culture have skyrocketed; aspects of the Holocaust regularly appear in all media: on television, in film, in college classrooms, in monuments in local parks. In 1993, Holocaust consciousness reached a peak of interest for Jews and non-Jews alike. The movie *Schindler's List*, produced and directed by the Jewish American Steven Spielberg, won the Academy Award for best picture, while in the same year the U.S. Holocaust Memorial Museum finally opened and boasted the largest attendance figures of any national museum. Yet nothing has been accomplished without controversy, nor has the Holocaust's heightened place in Jewish memory been without criticism.

Each milestone of memorializing the Holocaust has encountered its share of debate. Construction of the museum, for instance, stalled for years while the committee argued over the treatment of the Holocaust: Should it be cast as an event that is comparable to other atrocities and thus widen its implications for an American audience, or should it be portrayed as a unique event, incomparable to any other, and most meaningful to Jews? Further, the status of Jewish Americans, and how it has been measured in relation to other ethnic Americans, also came into question: Why should a "Jewish" museum, some argued, be part of the Smithsonian when there is no comparable museum commemorating the evils of slavery or the persecution of the American Indian?

Such arguments illustrate one of the unfortunate side effects of multiculturalism in the United States: the tendency to self-identify as a victim and to understand one's communal legacy as one largely of persecution. Those concerned with the future of Judaism soon realized that a religion could not—and should not—be maintained by pointing to catastrophe, devastation, and genocide. Over four thousand years of Jewish history and culture had been supplanted by the Holocaust. Michael Goldberg's influential book *Why Should Jews Survive?* called those Americans who overidentified with the Holocaust a cult and argued that the Holocaust had taken the place of God in Jewish American life and that the Jewish religion could and should provide a wellspring of spirit, tradition, religion, and scholarship.

For the imagination of Jewish American writers, however, the Holocaust has continued to exert an authoritative pull. In generations past, questions of whether those who had not actually experienced the event could respond to it had silenced American writers and artists. In this period, the silence ruptures. Various and emphatic voices echo throughout the arts and media—not only the voices of the children of survivors (for example, Art Spiegelman and Melvin Jules Bukiet), but those of Jews who had somehow established their own identity by forging this link with European history (Steven Spielberg). Though controversy has continued about the appropriateness of using the Holocaust as an artistic subject as well as a vehicle for forging a Jewish identity, even such writers who initially insisted that anyone who had not been there could not write about it found its pull irresistible. Cynthia Ozick eventually allowed, "I don't want to tamper or invent or imagine. And yet I have done it. I can't not do it. It comes, it invades."

Increased consciousness of the Holocaust has not been the only by-product of increasing attention to multiculturalism; the emphasis on cultural diversity has revitalized ethnic cultures in the United States. The reflowering of Jewish art forms has been extraordinary. Indeed, one might note that even as the number of American Jews declines, the quantity and diversity of Jewish forms of cultural expression has exploded. This anthology had room only for a sampling of these voices, and the writers we could not include (C. K. Williams and Marcia Falk, to name two) illustrate the richness of the contemporary world of Jewish American writing.

Popular culture, too, has exploded with images of Jewish life. In 1975, Hollywood would not produce *Hester Street;* independent filmmaker Joan Micklin Silver had to finance it herself. In the 1980s and 1990s, however, Jewish themes emerged prominently in *The Chosen* (1981), *An American Tail* (1986), *Crossing Delancey* (1988), *Enemies: A Love Story* (1989), *Driving Miss Daisy* (1989), *Avalon* (1990), *Mr. Saturday Night* (1992), and a multitude of movies about the Holocaust. On television, Dr. Joel Fleischman wrestled with what Jewish identity meant in Alaska on *Northern Exposure;* and we have seen a rebirth of Jewish humor and heroes in the popular sitcoms *Rhoda, Seinfeld*, and *The Nanny* as well as in the cartoons *The Simpsons* (Krusty the Clown) and *South Park* (Kyle Broslofski and family). The resurgence of klezmer—a festive Yiddish folk music—also demonstrates how thoroughly Jewish culture, history, and artistic forms are being rediscovered and celebrated.

For playwrights especially, the exploration of Jewish culture and identity has taken on a new prominence. Although it is Arthur Miller's (b. 1915) ethics rather than his ethnicity that has informed his plays, some have embraced such Jewish American concerns as otherness, scapegoatism, guilt, and punishment. Alfred Uhry, on the other hand, is open about his Jewish roots, as is attested to by *Driving Miss Daisy* (1988), which considers the relationship between an elderly Jewish woman and her black chauffeur in the South, *The Last Night of Ballyhoo* (1997), about Atlanta's assimilated Jews in 1939, and *Parade* (1999), a musical based on the 1915 lynching of Leo Frank, a Jewish pencil manufacturer from Atlanta who, in 1913, was falsely accused of the murder of a thirteen-year-old Gentile female employee.

The nostalgic view of shtetl life in *Fiddler on the Roof* (1964) opened the way for a variety of plays centered on the lives of Jewish Americans. Certainly, the best-known and most prolific participant has been playwright Neil

Simon, author of more than forty-nine plays and film scripts. Born in the Bronx in 1927, Simon began his career by writing for radio and television. His first play, *Come Blow Your Horn* (1961), a modest success, contained only the thinnest references to his Jewish roots in dialogue that occasionally took on a Yiddish cadence. By 1982, with the opening of *Brighton Beach Memoirs,* Simon's plays were firmly rooted in his Jewish identity and his family history. Part 1 of a trilogy that also includes *Biloxi Blues* and *Broadway Bound, Brighton Beach Memoirs* is a heavily autobiographical account of the Jeromes, a family that lives in an ethnic enclave of Brooklyn during World War II. The Jeromes' religion is clear; in fact, the play makes full use of the unadulterated cultural richness, as well as trials, of Simon's heritage. Thus, the fourteen-year-old Eugene (Simon's alter ago), putting his head in his hands one evening, can lament, "The ultimate tragedy . . . liver and cabbage for dinner! A Jewish medieval torture!" After dinner, the family listens to the radio, anxiously awaiting news of Hitler's advance in Europe. A professional landmark for Simon, *Brighton Beach Memoirs* energized a new generation of Jewish American playwrights.

Playwright Wendy Wasserstein (b. 1950) takes her inspiration from Simon's ethnically inflected comedies as well as her own coming-of-age during the 1970s. Wasserstein's comedies focus on women. *The Heidi Chronicles* (1988) traces the changing status and roles of women from the 1960s through the 1980s; *The Sisters Rosenzweig* (1993) explores the relationships of three women to each other and to the changing landscape of American Judaism. Both plays provide a sense of the particular cultural circumstances that produced its characters, each of whom firmly asserts her differences from mainstream culture, whether political, sexual, or cultural.

Tony Kushner, lauded among contemporary Jewish American playwrights, dismantles the myth of a monolithic American identity, denouncing capitalism and celebrating homosexuality, in his groundbreaking seven-hour, two-part fantasia-like *Angels in America: Millennium Approaches* (1993) and *Angels in America: Perestroika* (1994). Kushner's work shows us how far the representation of Jewishness on stage and in contemporary literature has traveled. In *Millennium Approaches*, a rabbi, the first character to appear on stage, delivers the eulogy for the main character's grandmother. On her coffin (a plain wooden box, as Judaic law requires), the Star of David appears prominently. With a heavy, but not comical, Eastern European accent, the rabbi intones,

> Your clay is the clay of some Litvak shtetl, your air the air of the steppes—because she carried the old world on her back across the ocean, in a boat, and she put it down on Grand Concourse Avenue, or in Flatbush, and she worked that earth into your bones, and you pass it to your children, this ancient, ancient culture and home. You can never make that crossing she made, for such Great Voyages in this world do not anymore exist. But every day of your lives the miles that voyage between that place and this one you cross. Every day. You understand me? In you that journey is. So . . . She was the last of the Mohicans, this one was. Pretty soon . . . all the old will be dead.

Kushner's words well summarize the project for many Jewish Americans and Jewish American writers during this period: How can we attach to the traditions of our ancestors?

AMERICAN JEWS AND ISRAEL

If, in 1967, Israel's decisive victory over Egypt, Jordan, and Syria in the Six Day War had left Israelis and American Jews euphoric, Israel's defeat in the Yom Kippur War in 1973 brought with it feelings of disillusionment and despair. While Israelis began to feel the legacy of a war that had produced tremendous bloodshed and casualties, Jewish Americans felt more keenly the possibility that Israel would not withstand its enemies. In the 1980s, American Jews responded to this threat by supplying the State of Israel with huge donations and support. In fact, in 1990, the United Jewish Appeal, the charity that supports Israel with $300 million a year, was reported to have received more than any other American charity in history—close to $1 billion.

Changes in Israeli politics brought changes for Jewish Americans. The memories of the 1973 war and its harrowing violence provoked new Israeli protest, protest that joined already thunderous Palestinian protest. The Israeli political Left grew stronger, arguing that extreme nationalism had exercised a corrosive force on national character and that compromise and moderation might lead to peace—the ultimate prize. Religious and national rightists, on the other hand, argued that peace would never be achieved without military force and that the Arabs and Palestinians could not be trusted to negotiate honestly.

The factionalization of Israeli politics has had a detrimental effect on the relationship of American Jews and Israel. To some extent, this seems peculiar since polarization of political parties is a normal, if unhappy, certitude of most governments. But Jewish Americans as well as many non-Jewish Americans had viewed Israel through an idealistic cloud—in battle, powerful and triumphant; the kibbutz, a utopian fantasy; the deserts, transformed into a land of milk and honey. Yet the bitter factionalism of the 1980s and 1990s within Israel and the assassination, by a rightist, of moderate prime minister Yitzhak Rabin made many Jewish Americans question their idealization of Israel. Similarly, the rise of Jewish religious right-wing fundamentalists also disenchanted Jewish American philanthropists, who by and large were secular Jews and who demanded a closer accounting of where their donations would be received and to what uses they might be applied. The 1990s saw American philanthrophy to Israel drop to an all-time low.

RETURN

The rise of assimilation and intermarriage, the difficulties of ethnic identity in the New World, the problematization of representations of the Holocaust, and the complications of Israeli politics—all played a part in the spiritual and actual wandering of American Jews in the last three decades. The stories of Max Apple and Bruce Jay Friedman in this section humorously describe that wandering but forcefully invite the reader to question what remains of his or her Jewishness. For many of these writers, that answer will be found in a common history: certainly, poet Allen Grossman sees his Jewishness as determined by an ancestral burden that defines and provides meaning in an otherwise chaotic cosmos. But for Grossman as well as virtually all the writers in this section, the decision to find meaning in his Jewish lineage is a choice consciously willed and cultivated. Similarly, Adrienne Rich's decision to define herself as a Jewish poet is not inevitable; for the decades prior to the 1970s, she had not done so. But if we are to understand that Jewishness has become a choice, a conscious and willed decision on the part of those participants, then we should also understand that it is an alliance that has a recommitted membership.

This determination to reclaim Jewishness as a way of organizing one's experience defines this period in literature and has had reverberations in the larger culture as well. Along with the writers who have described Jewish life, the organized Jewish American community has responded to external pressures by increasing its commitment to Jewish education and rededicating itself to nourishing traditions. A return to observance and the life of the synagogue has given many Jewish Americans a new meaning of Jewishness. In Allegra Goodman's story *The Four Questions,* for instance, Miriam, frustrated by her parents' formless and secular Seder, preaches a return to Jewish ritual. Similarly, Jacqueline Osherow's poetry finds much beauty and inspiration in the Bible and in Yiddish, which she fights to keep alive.

Although intermarriage continues to exert pressure on the community, many Jewish organizations have worked toward educating the children of intermarried parents in the hope that they will choose to be Jewish. Rather than looking to the past to find the thread of victimization, Jewish educators encourage students to look at history for inspirational narratives of self-definition. In his work and the story included here, *Lazar Malkin Enters Heaven,* Steve Stern looks at an unusual community of Jews in the South to describe a vivid and enriching way to approach one's spirituality. By considering the matriarchal lineage of Judaism, feminists like E. M. Broner and Marge Piercy have reinvented traditions for a new generation of Jewish women. And postmodern writers like Jerome Rothenberg and Charles Bernstein recycle the idioms of their immigrant ancestors to forge a new language that has influenced the poetic avant-garde. Together, the writers in this section offer both traditional and innovative approaches to understanding what it means to be Jewish in the United States in the last quarter of the twentieth century.

CHAIM POTOK
b. 1929

The popular writer Chaim Potok does not write about Jewish faith and culture from a liminal perspective, as is the case with many other Jewish American authors; he contemplates the religion from within. A writer who puts his Orthodox Jewish faith at the center of his novels, Potok depicts the American Jew as a person concerned with reconciling religious belief and secular life. In Potok's novels, the Jewish American experience inevitably involves the practicing of religious ritual; it is not a quest to escape, redefine, or supplant religious belief.

In his hugely successful first novel, *The Chosen* (1967), Potok begins his search to find the place for Judaism in the modern world. As the protagonists struggle to come to terms with their religion (and disputing factions within that religion), they are forced to come to terms with their own identities. Judaism functions as the central catalyst rather than as a marginal consideration. Similar themes are explored in *The Promise* (1969), the sequel to *The Chosen*, and the idea continues in *My Name Is Asher Lev* (1972), the novel excerpted here.

The story of a Hasidic Jew in Brooklyn, *My Name Is Asher Lev* explores the conflicts inherent in Asher's desire to follow the religious practices of his community, while also needing to express himself as an artist. Wanting to please his parents and be true to his profession, Asher finds himself trying to reconcile his religious beliefs with his secular life. His artistic vision and integrity, which drives him to imagine, and then paint, his father on the Cross portrays the often antagonistic relationship between the "people of the book" and the assimilated Jew. Potok himself felt the disapproval of his parents and his Talmud teacher, who viewed art as a waste of time and a distraction from serious study.

Since the publication of *My Name Is Asher Lev,* Potok continues to tread the fine line between an author of Jewish moral doctrine and an author of contemporary fiction with *The Book of Lights* (1981), *Davita's Harp* (1985), and *The Gift of Asher Lev* (1990).

Potok was educated in Orthodox Jewish schools. In 1950, he graduated from Yeshiva University in New York with a B.A. in English; he received his M.H.L. and rabbinic ordination in 1954 at the Jewish Theological Seminary, New York, and went on to earn his Ph.D. in philosophy in 1965 at the University of Pennsylvania. Potok received the Edward Lewis Wallant Award and was nominated for the National Book Award for *The Chosen.*

From My Name Is Asher Lev

By the first of September of that year, I had begun a new painting—the old man with the pigeons in the Piazza del Duomo.[1] I wrote Anna Schaeffer [2] to let her know I was alive and well and working in Paris. She wrote me back immediately. Now I was a real painter, she said. Asher Lev in Paris. It had a ring to it. Asher Lev in Paris. I should stay away from cafés and night life and paint pictures that would make us rich. I should stay away from the artists of the New School of Paris;[3] they were timid bores. I should paint and paint and make her happy and rich. She did not mention Jacob Kahn.[4]

Four weeks later, on a day when I could feel the cold of the fall begin to settle into the city, I received a package from her in the mail. I opened it and saw a new dark-blue beret. There was a card: "From an impossible old lady to an impossible young man. Affectionately, Anna."

I put the beret into a drawer and continued to wear my fisherman's cap.

I remember the winter rain and the way it washed across the roofs of the houses and stained the beige facades of the walls. The house stood near the

1. A square in Naples, Italy, where the Duomo, a historic church, sits.
2. In the text, Anna is a motherly character who has taken Asher under her wing.
3. A group of foreign artists in Montparnasse who sought artistic freedom and fellowship. Many of these artists were Jewish, including Marc Chagall and Amedeo Modigliani.
4. In the novel, Jacob Kahn is a famous older Jewish painter who has mentored Asher Lev.

head of a steep narrow cobblestone street, and from the windows of the apartment I could see the rain flow in swift rivulets along the stone curbs, then follow the turn of the curbs into the wide boulevard below. It was cold in the rain but I did not have to walk in it often. I lived and painted in the apartment; I ate in the yeshiva's[5] dining room, prayed in its synagogue, and attended an occasional lecture on Hasidus.[6] Sometimes, gazing out the window at one of the blue windless days of winter, I would feel the need to leave the apartment. Then I would walk beneath the chestnut trees of the city's boulevards or take the Metro to the Louvre or to the Jeu de Paume[7] near the Place de la Concorde. I did not stay away from the artists of the New School of Paris, as some call it; and I did not find them to be bores.

I had stretched my own canvases. They stood stacked against a wall of the room I had turned into a studio. In the early morning, I would pray and eat breakfast in the yeshiva, then go back along the boulevard and up the steep street to the house. There would be schoolchildren on the street then and men pulling away from the curb in little cars and shopkeepers opening their stores. I would climb the narrow stairs to my apartment and come into the studio and stare at the white canvases against the wall.

Weeks passed and became months. It rained. The skies were dark often now. Few people walked the narrow street. The canvases remained bare.

Away from my world, alone in an apartment that offered me neither memories nor roots, I began to find old and distant memories of my own, long buried by pain and time and slowly brought to the surface now by the sight of waiting white canvases and by the winter emptiness of the small Parisian street. It was time now for that. I had painted my visible street until there was nothing left of it for me to put onto canvas. Now I would have to paint the street that could not be seen.

I remembered my mythic ancestor. He had never been too difficult to bring to memory. But now I could recall tales told to a wondering child about a Jew who had made a Russian nobleman rich by tending his estates. The nobleman was a despotic goy,[8] a degenerate whose debaucheries grew wilder as he grew wealthier. The Jew, my mythic ancestor, made him wealthier. Serfs were on occasion slain by that nobleman during his long hours of drunken insanity, and once houses were set on fire by a wildly thrown torch and a village was burned. You see how a goy behaves, went the whispered word to the child. A Jew does not behave this way. But the Jew had made him wealthy, wondered the child. Is not the Jew also somehow to blame? The child had never given voice to that question. Now the man who had once been the child asked it again and wondered if the giving and the goodness and the journeys of that mythic ancestor might have been acts born in the memories of screams and burning flesh. A balance had to be given the world; the demonic had to be reshaped into meaning. Had a dream-haunted Jew spent the rest of his life sculpting form out of the horror of his private night?

I did not know. But I sensed it as truth.

5. An institution where Jewish law, the Talmud, is studied.
6. Of or relating Hasidism, the most devout and spiritual sect of the Jewish religion, often associated with mysticism and high emotionalism.
7. The Jeu de Paume, once a famous tennis court, was, at the time this text was written, a garden behind the Louvre. "Metro": the Paris subway. "Louvre": a museum in Paris.
8. Non-Jew (Yiddish).

I began to paint my mythic ancestor. Over and over again, I painted him now, in his wealth and his journeys, in the midst of fire and death and dreams, a weary Jew traveling to balance the world.

I remembered my grandfather, the scholar, the recluse, the dweller in the study halls of synagogues and academies of learning. What had transformed him from recluse and scholar to emissary for the Rebbe's father? Had the encounter with the journeying Ladover Hasid[9] brought back to memory the journeys of his ancestor? I wondered how a journeying ancestor could suddenly transform a recluse into a journeying Hasid. Had something inarticulate been handed down from generation to generation that came to life in each individual at a time most appropriate to him?

I did not know. But I sensed it as truth.

I painted my grandfather. Over and over again, I painted him now, seated in dusty rooms with sacred books, traveling across endless Russian steppes, dead on a dark street with an axe in his skull, his journey incomplete.

Outside my window, there was snow. A cold wind blew through the boulevards and stripped the last dead leaves from the trees.

I remembered my father during my mother's illness. He had been as torn by her illness as by his inability to journey for the Rebbe. I had never been able to understand that torment. Now I wondered if journeying meant to him more than a way of bringing God into the world. Was journeying an unknowing act of atonement? In the dim past, a village had burned to the ground and people had died. The Gemorra[1] teaches us that a man who slays another man slays not only one individual but all the children and children's children that individual might have brought into life. Traditions are born by the power of an initial thrust that hurls acts and ideas across the centuries. Had the death by fire of those individuals been such a thrust? Was my ancestor's act of atonement to extend through all the generations of our family line? Had he unwittingly transmitted the need for such an act to his children; had they transmitted it to their children?

I did not know. But I sensed it as truth.

I remembered my mother and the long quiet conversations between her and my father when I had been a child. Surely she had sensed the depth of his feelings about his journeys. She, too, had told me stories about my mythic ancestor. Had she somehow dimly perceived the true nature of my ancestor's journey? Then, perceiving it, had she joined her brother's incompleted task to my father's beginning journeys and thereby, without being fully aware of what she was doing, made possible the continuation of the line of atonement? Had I, with my need to give meaning to paper and canvas rather than to people and events, interrupted an act of eternal atonement?

I did not know.

Now I thought of my mother and began to sense something of her years of anguish. Standing between two different ways of giving meaning to the world, and at the same time possessed by her own fears and memories, she had moved now toward me, now toward my father, keeping both worlds of meaning alive, nourishing with her tiny being, and despite her torments, both me and my father. Paint pretty pictures, Asher, she had said. Make the world

9. A Hasid from a particular sect.

1. The Talmud is divided into the Mishnah and the Gemorra. The Mishnah gives a simple statement of a law or precept; the Gemorra presents the commentaries on it.

pretty. Show me your good drawings, Asher. Why have you stopped drawing? She had kept the gift alive during the dead years; and she had kept herself alive by picking up her dead brother's work and had kept my father alive by enabling him to resume his journeys. Trapped between two realms of meaning, she had straddled both realms, quietly feeding and nourishing them both, and herself as well. I could only dimly perceive such an awesome act of will. But I could begin to feel her torment now as she waited by our living-room window for both her husband and her son. What did she think of as she stood by the window? Of the phone call that had informed my father of her brother's death? Would she wait now in dread all the rest of her life, now for me, now for my father, now for us both—as she had once waited for me to return in a museum, as she had once waited for my father to return in a snowstorm? And I could understand her torment now; I could see her waiting endlessly with the fear that someone she loved would be brought to her dead. I could feel her anguish.

Then I found I could no longer paint and I walked the winter streets of the city and felt its coldness. There was snow and rain and the city lay bleak and spent beneath the dark skies. I wandered through museums and galleries. I walked the winding streets of Montmartre[2] and peered through the misty windows of its shops and restaurants. I walked up the mountain of steps to the Sacré-Coeur[3] and wandered through its awesome dimness. I remember that during all this walking and wandering letters went back and forth between me and my parents and between me and Anna Schaeffer. My father had fallen and hurt his leg, but was well now. Jacob Kahn's show had been very well received. My uncle was fine. Yudel Krinsky[4] was fine. It was all vague. Even the walking and wandering was vague. I could not paint.

The rains ended. There were days of blue and warming air. One day, I sat in a café over a warm Coke around the corner from the Sacré-Coeur and found myself drawing the contour of the Duomo *Pietà*[5] on red tablecloth. I looked at it and paid for the Coke and returned to the apartment.

I sat at my table in the apartment and drew the *Pietà* again, leaving the faces blank. I drew it a third time and made the two Marys into bearded males and made the central figure into one of the Marys. Then I drew the central figure of Jesus, alone, head bent and arm twisted, alone, unsupported. Then I left the apartment and went down the narrow stairs and came out onto the street. I walked beneath the trees of the boulevard and was astonished to discover tiny green buds on the branches. Was the winter gone? Was it spring?

I returned to the apartment and sat at the table and thought of the *David*[6] and its spatial and temporal shift. I looked at the painting of the old man with the pigeons that stood against a wall. And it was then that it came, though I think it had been coming for a long time and I had been choking it and hoping it would die. But it does not die. It kills you first. I knew there would be no other way to do it. No one says you have to paint ultimate anguish and torment. But if you are driven to paint it, you have no other way.

2. A neighborhood in Paris populated by artists, galleries, and cafés.
3. Literally, "Sacred Heart," Sacré-Coeur is a large, beautiful church in Montmartre.
4. Yudel Krinsky was an actual Hasidic rabbi, whom, in the novel, Asher fears displeasing.
5. As a theme in Christian art, a Pietà depicts the seated Virgin supporting the body of the dead Christ on her lap.
6. Famous sculpture by Michelangelo (1475–1564) in Florence, Italy.

The preliminary drawings came easily then. After a while, I put them away. It was Passover, and I rested.

On a warm spring day, with the sun streaming through the tall window and leaves now on the chestnut trees of the boulevard, I started the painting. I sketched it in charcoal on the huge canvas, drawing the long vertical of the center strip of wood in the living-room window of our Brooklyn apartment and the slanted horizontal of the bottom of our Venetian blind as it used to lie stuck a little below the top frame. I drew my mother behind those two lines, her right hand resting upon the upper right side of the window, her left hand against the frame over her head, her eyes directly behind the vertical line but burning through it. I drew the houses of our street and the slanting lines of the blind and the verticals and horizontals of near and distant telephone poles. Then I went away from it and came back the next day and reworked some of the geometry of its forms. Then I painted it—in ochres and grays, in dark smoky alizarins, in tones of Prussian and cobalt blue. I worked a long time on my mother's eyes and face. I had used a siccative. The paint dried quickly. I took the canvas down and put it against a wall. I felt vaguely unclean, as if I had betrayed a friend.

The following day, I put a fresh canvas on the easel. It was a small canvas and I thought I would fill it quickly. But I found I could not paint. I stood and stared at the canvas. I put the charcoal stick away and tried to do a drawing on paper. I could not draw. I came out of the house and walked down the cobblestone street to the boulevard. Girls in summer dresses walked beneath the trees. I returned to the apartment and looked at the blank canvas. I found I was sweating. I felt the sweat on my forehead and back. I removed the clean canvas from the easel and put the large canvas of my mother in its place. Then I looked a very long time at the painting and knew it was incomplete. It was a good painting but it was incomplete. The telephone poles were only distant reminders of the brutal reality of a crucifix. The painting did not say fully what I had wanted to say; it did not reflect fully the anguish and torment I had wanted to put into it. Within myself, a warning voice spoke soundlessly of fraud.

I had brought something incomplete into the world. Now I felt its incompleteness. "Can you understand what it means for something to be incomplete?" my mother had once asked me. I understood, I understood.

I turned away from the painting and walked to the yeshiva. I had supper and prayed the evening service. I returned to the apartment. Children played on the cobblestone street below my window. I stared at the painting and felt cold with dread. Then I went to bed and lay awake in the darkness, listening to the sounds of the street through my open window: a quarrel, a distant cough, a passing car, the cry of a child—all of it filtered through my feeling of cold dread. I slept very little. In the morning, I woke and prayed and knew what had to be done.

Yes, I could have decided not to do it. Who would have known? Would it have made a difference to anyone in the world that I had felt a sense of incompleteness about a painting? Who would have cared about my silent cry of fraud? Only Jacob Kahn, and perhaps one or two others, might have sensed its incompleteness. And even they could never have known how incomplete it truly was, for by itself it was a good painting. Only I would have known.

But it would have made me a whore to leave it incomplete. It would have made it easier to leave future work incomplete. It would have made it more and more difficult to draw upon that additional aching surge of effort that is always the difference between integrity and deceit in a created work. I would not be the whore to my own existence. Can you understand that? I would not be the whore to my own existence.

I stretched a canvas identical in size to the painting now on the easel. I put the painting against a wall and put the fresh canvas in its place. With charcoal, I drew the frame of the living-room window of our Brooklyn apartment. I drew the strip of wood that divided the window and the slanting bottom of the Venetian blind a few inches form the top of the window. On top—not behind this time, but on top—of the window I drew my mother in her housecoat, with her arms extended along the horizontal of the blind, her wrists tied to it with the cords of the blind, her legs tied at the ankles to the vertical of the inner frame with another section of the cord of the blind. I arched her body and twisted her head. I drew my father standing to her right, dressed in a hat and coat and carrying an attaché case. I drew myself standing to her left, dressed in paint-spattered clothes and a fisherman's cap and holding a palette and a long spearlike brush. I exaggerated the size of the palette and balanced it by exaggerating the size of my father's attaché case. We were looking at my mother and at each other. I split my mother's head into balanced segments, one looking at me, one looking at my father, one looking upward. The torment, the tearing anguish I felt in her, I put into her mouth, into the twisting curve of her head, the arching of her slight body, the clenching of her small fists, the taut downward pointing of her thin legs. I sprayed fixative on the charcoal and began to put on the colors, working with the same range of hues I had utilized in the previous painting—ochres, grays, alizarin, Prussian and cobalt blue—and adding tones of burnt sienna and cadmium red medium for my hair and beard. I painted swiftly in a strange nerveless frenzy of energy. For all the pain you suffered, my mama. For all the torment of your past and future years, my mama. For all the anguish this picture of pain will cause you. For the unspeakable mystery that brings good fathers and sons into the world and lets a mother watch them tear at each other's throats. For the Master of the Universe, whose suffering world I do not comprehend. For dreams of horror, for nights of waiting, for memories of death, for the love I have for you, for all the things I remember, and for all the things I should remember but have forgotten, for all these I created this painting—an observant Jew working on a crucifixion because there was no aesthetic mold in his own religious tradition into which he could pour a painting of ultimate anguish and torment.

I do not remember how long it took me to do that painting. But on a day of summer rain that cooled the streets and ran in streams across my window, the painting was finally completed. I looked at it and saw it was a good painting. I left it on the easel and went to the yeshiva in the rain and had supper and prayed. Then I walked through the streets of the city and felt the rain on my face and remembered how I had once watched the rain of another street through windows that seemed so distant now and that I suddenly wanted to see once again.

A few days later, I thought I would destroy the paintings. I had done them; that was enough. They did not have to remain alive. But I could not destroy them. I began to paint in a delirium of unceasing energy. All through that summer, I painted my hidden memories of our street. Sometime during that summer, Avraham Cutler[7] introduced me to a family and I returned the greetings of a girl with short dark-brown hair and brown eyes. Later, there were more greetings. Someone once said that there are things about which one ought to write a great deal or nothing at all. About those greetings, I choose to write nothing at all.

Looking old and elegant and rich, Anna Schaeffer showed up at the apartment one fall day on one of her European talent hunts.

She gazed a long time at the two large paintings.

"They are crucifixions," she said very quietly.

I said nothing.

"Asher Lev," she murmured. "Asher Lev." That was all she seemed able to say. She stared at the paintings. A long time later, she looked at me and said, "They are both great paintings." Then she added, "This one is truer than the other," and pointed to the second of the two canvases.

I was quiet.

She looked again at the paintings. Then she said, "What will you do now?"

"I don't know."

"Will you come back to America for the show?"

"Yes."

We were quiet then, gazing together at the paintings.

"How is Jacob Kahn?" I said.

"He is working to reach ninety." After a moment, she said, "Where is the beret I sent you?"

"In a drawer."

"You should wear it."

"No."

"All right," she said gently. "Now, please, you will go outside and take a very long walk."

We shook hands. I walked for hours through narrow streets and along wide boulevards. When I returned, the paintings were gone. I looked out the window of the room that was my studio, and I wept.

She wrote me a few weeks later and told me that all the paintings had arrived safely. She had scheduled the show for February. Would I object if she called the two large paintings *Brooklyn Crucifixion I* and *Brooklyn Crucifixion II*? She needed titles for the catalogue. I wrote back saying the titles were appropriate.

The weeks passed. The leaves fell from the trees. The city turned cold and dark. I walked the streets. I returned to the Bateau Lavoir.[8] I visited galleries and museums. I spent hours with the girl and her family. I wandered about with a sense of dread and oncoming horror.

In the last week of January, I flew to New York and arrived at night in a snowstorm five days before the opening of my show.

1972

7. A character introduced earlier in the novel. A Hasidic Jew, Cutler reestablishes Asher's link to the strict religious community of his home.

8. An artist's residence in Montmartre, famous for having housed Pablo Picasso and Juan Gris.

ADRIENNE RICH
b. 1929

"Being Jewish has meant:—being a question, not only as in 'the Jewish Question,' but as a woman, a lesbian, a patrilineal Jew, a non-Zionist, within the whole argument and contestation about 'being Jewish.' " Adrienne Rich's answer to an interviewer's question in 1999 speaks to her ongoing exploration of her identity as an American Jew, an exploration begun as a high-school girl growing up in Baltimore in the 1940s. In her 1982 essay *Split at the Root: An Essay on Jewish Identity,* Rich recalls a long poem she wrote in 1960, where she describes herself as "neither Gentile nor Jew, / Yankee nor rebel." With these lines, Rich acknowledges her complicated lineage. Rich's father was a Jew who grew up in Birmingham, Alabama, and her mother, a southern Protestant; therefore, as Rich notes, she could not, at least by Jewish law, "count herself as a Jew." Neither could she count herself as southern since her paternal grandparents had immigrated to the United States from Austria and Hungary, and their European past was a strong presence in the house in which Rich grew up. Through the course of her education at Radcliffe, her seventeen-year marriage to a Jewish husband from an observant family, and her experience as a mother raising three Jewish sons, Rich shaped her own Jewish identity—one based on commitment to the ethics of the Jewish tradition as much as on genealogy.

To speak solely of Rich's identity as a Jewish American poet is to limit her, for she is a leading American poet of the postwar period. Her first book of poetry, *A Change of World* (1951), published when she was only twenty-two, won the Yale Younger Poets Award. It appeared that Rich would enjoy success as a poet in the modernist tradition of Eliot and Auden, the latter of whom had chosen her book for the Yale prize, praising her poems "for speaking quietly and respecting their elders." But as Rich struggled to write while raising three small sons, her poetry took a different, more personal, direction, responding to the changes in American poetry that the San Francisco Renaissance inaugurated and to the political movements of the 1960s. With *Snapshots of a Daughter-in-Law* (1963), Rich's poems spoke in a new voice to a generation of women struggling to find their voices. In her groundbreaking essay *When We Dead Awaken: Writing as Re-Vision* (1971) and the title poem of *Diving into the Wreck* (1973), Rich's radical redefinition of history provided core texts for the feminist movement.

In the 1980s, Rich's Jewish heritage became central to her activism—she worked with New Jewish Agenda, a national organization of progressive Jews, and cofounded the Jewish feminist magazine *Bridges*—and to her poetry. In *Your Native Land, Your Life* (1986), Rich searches her Jewish past in an effort to understand the effect of the Holocaust on her writing (*Sources,* excerpted here) and how her identity as a Jew elides with her identity as a woman, a lesbian, and a poet (*Yom Kippur 1984*). It is from these multiple marginal identities that Rich fuses her poetic vision. Her poetry and prose of the 1990s extended her imaginative and formal reach to find the connections between the marginalized and oppressed in history and in contemporary life worldwide and to locate a place of connection and social change in poetry.

Trying to Talk with a Man

Out in the desert we are testing bombs,

that's why we came here.

Sometimes I feel an underground river
forcing its way between deformed cliffs
an acute angle of understanding
moving itself like a locus[1] of the sun
into this condemned scenery.

What we've had to give up to get here—
whole LP collections, films we starred in
playing in the neighborhoods, bakery windows
full of dry, chocolate-filled Jewish cookies,
the language of love-letters, of suicide notes,
afternoons on the riverbank
pretending to be children

Coming out to this desert
we meant to change the face of
driving among dull green succulents
walking at noon in the ghost town
surrounded by a silence

that sounds like the silence of the place
except that it came with us
and is familiar
and everything we were saying until now
was an effort to blot it out—
coming out here we are up against it

Out here I feel more helpless
with you than without you
You mention the danger
and list the equipment
we talk of people caring for each other
in emergencies—laceration, thirst—
but you look at me like an emergency

Your dry heat feels like power
your eyes are stars of a different magnitude
they reflect lights that spell out: EXIT
when you get up and pace the floor

talking of the danger
as if it were not ourselves
as if we were testing anything else.

1971 1973

1. Site; in mathematics, the set of all elements that satisfy a given requirement.

Yom Kippur[1] 1984

I drew solitude over me, on the long shore.
—Robinson Jeffers, "Prelude"[2]

For whoever does not afflict his soul throughout this day, shall be cut off from his people.
—Leviticus 23:29

What is a Jew in solitude?
What would it mean not to feel lonely or afraid
far from your own or those you have called your own?
What is a woman in solitude: a queer woman or man?
In the empty street, on the empty beach, in the desert
what in this world as it is can solitude mean?

The glassy, concrete octagon suspended from the cliffs
with its electric gate, its perfected privacy
is not what I mean
the pick-up with a gun parked at a turn-out in Utah or the Golan Heights[3]
is not what I mean
the poet's tower facing the western ocean, acres of forest planted to the
east, the woman reading in the cabin, her attack dog suddenly risen
is not what I mean

Three thousand miles from what I once called home
I open a book searching for some lines I remember
about flowers, something to bind me to this coast as lilacs in the dooryard[4]
once
bound me back there—yes, lupines on a burnt mountainside,
something that bloomed and faded and was written down
in the poet's book, forever:
Opening the poet's book
I find the hatred in the poet's heart: . . . *the hateful-eyed*
and human-bodied are all about me: you that love multitude may have them

Robinson Jeffers, multitude
is the blur flung by distinct forms against these landward valleys
and the farms that run down to the sea; the lupines
are multitude, and the torched poppies, the grey Pacific unrolling its
scrolls of surf,
and the separate persons, stooped
over sewing machines in denim dust, bent under the shattering skies of
harvest
who sleep by shifts in never-empty beds have their various dreams
Hands that pick, pack, steam, stitch, strip, stuff, shell, scrape, scour,
belong to a brain like no other

1. I.e., the Day of Atonement, the holiest day of the Jewish year.
2. American poet Robinson Jeffers (1887–1962) is best known for his long-lined free verse and his discussion of large philosophical themes. The epigraph and quotations from Jeffers (in italics within Rich's poem) can be found in the *The Women at Point Sur and Other Poems* (1977).
3. The piece of land that Israel annexed from Syria in 1967; its ownership is still a highly controversial issue in Middle Eastern politics.
4. A reference to Walt Whitman's *When Lilacs Last in the Dooryard Bloom'd*, a tribute to assassinated president Abraham Lincoln.

Must I argue the love of multitude in the blur or defend
a solitude of barbed-wire and searchlights, the survivalist's final solution,
have I a choice?

To wander far from your own or those you have called your own
to hear strangeness calling you from far away
and walk in that direction, long and far, not calculating risk
to go to meet the Stranger without fear or weapon, protection nowhere on
your mind
(the Jew on the icy, rutted road on Christmas Eve prays for another Jew
the woman in the ungainly twisting shadows of the street: *Make those be*
a woman's footsteps; as if she could believe in a woman's god)

Find someone like yourself. Find others.
Agree you will never desert each other.
Understand that any rift among you
means power to those who want to do you in.
Close to the center, safety; toward the edges, danger.
But I have a nightmare to tell: I am trying to say
that to be with my people is my dearest wish
but that I also love strangers
that I crave separateness
I hear myself stuttering these words
to my worst friends and my best enemies
who watch for my mistakes in grammar
my mistakes in love.
This is the day of atonement; but do my people forgive me?
If a cloud knew loneliness and fear, I would be that cloud.

To love the Stranger, to love solitude—am I writing merely about privilege
about drifting from the center, drawn to edges,
a privilege we can't afford in the world that is,
who are hated as being of our kind: faggot kicked into the icy river, woman
dragged from her stalled car
into the mist-struck mountains, used and hacked to death
young scholar shot at the university gates on a summer evening walk, his
prizes and studies nothing, nothing availing his Blackness
Jew deluded that she's escaped the tribe, the laws of her exclusion, the
men too holy to touch her hand; Jew who has turned her back
on *midrash* and *mitzvah* (yet wears the *chai*[5] on a thong between her
breasts) hiking alone
found with a swastika carved in her back at the foot of the cliffs (did she
die as queer or as Jew?)

Solitude, O taboo, endangered species
on the mist-struck spur of the mountain, I want a gun to defend you
In the desert, on the deserted street, I want what I can't have:
your elder sister, Justice, her great peasant's hand outspread
her eye, half-hooded, sharp and true

5. Life (Hebrew). *Chai*, fashioned into a charm, is often worn on a necklace. "*Midrash*": the scholarly interpretation of biblical stories. "*Mitzvah*": a good deed; often attributed to religious duty.

And I ask myself, have I thrown courage away?
have I traded off something I don't name?
To what extreme will I go to meet the extremist?
What will I do to defend my want or anyone's want to search for her spirit-vision
far from the protection of those she has called her own?
Will I find O solitude
your plumes, your breasts, your hair
against my face, as in childhood, your voice like the mockingbird's
singing *Yes, you are loved, why else this song?*
in the old places, anywhere?

What is a Jew in solitude?
What is a woman in solitude, a queer woman or man?
When the winter flood-tides wrench the tower from the rock, crumble the prophet's headland, and the farms slide into the sea
when leviathan is endangered and Jonah becomes revenger[6]
when center and edges are crushed together, the extremities crushed together on which the world was founded
when our souls crash together, Arab and Jew, howling our loneliness within the tribes
when the refugee child and the exile's child re-open the blasted and forbidden city
when we who refuse to be women and men as women and men are chartered, tell our stories of solitude spent in multitude
in that world as it may be, newborn and haunted, what will solitude mean?

1984–1985 1986

From Sources

VII

For years I struggled with you: your categories, your theories, your will, the cruelty which came inextricable from your love. For years all arguments I carried on in my head were with you. I saw myself, the eldest daughter raised as a son, taught to study but not to pray, taught to hold reading and writing sacred: the eldest daughter in a house with no son, she who must overthrow the father, take what he taught her and use it against him. All this in a castle of air, the floating world of the assimilated who know and deny they will always be aliens.

After your death I met you again as the face of patriarchy, could name at last precisely the principle you embodied, there was an ideology at last which let me dispose of you, identify the suffering you caused, hate you righteously as part of a system, the kingdom of the fathers. I saw the power and arrogance of the male as your true watermark; I did not see beneath it the suffering of the Jew, the alien stamp you bore, because you had deliberately

6. From the story of Jonah and the whale in the Book of Jonah 2.1: "And the Lord provided a huge fish to swallow Jonah; and Jonah remained in the fish's belly three days and three nights."

arranged that it should be invisible to me. It is only now, under a powerful, womanly lens, that I can decipher your suffering and deny no part of my own.

August 1981–August 1982 1986

From Eastern War Time[1]

10

Memory says: Want to do right? Don't count on me.
I'm a canal in Europe where bodies are floating
I'm a mass grave I'm the life that returns
I'm a table set with room for the Stranger[2]
I'm a field with corners left for the landless
I'm accused of child-death of drinking blood
I'm a man-child praising God he's a man
I'm a woman bargaining for a chicken
I'm a woman who sells for a boat ticket
I'm a family dispersed between night and fog
I'm an immigrant tailor who says *A coat*
is not a piece of cloth only[3] I sway
in the learnings of the master-mystics
I have dreamed of Zion I've dreamed of world revolution
I have dreamed my children could live at last like others
I have walked the children of others through ranks of hatred
I'm a corpse dredged from a canal in Berlin
a river in Mississippi I'm a woman standing
with other women dressed in black
on the streets of Haifa, Tel Aviv, Jerusalem[4]
there is spit on my sleeve there are phonecalls in the night
I am a woman standing in line for gasmasks
I stand on a road in Ramallah[5] with naked face listening
I am standing here in your poem unsatisfied
lifting my smoky mirror

1989–1990 1991

1. Based on Rich's memories of World War II.
2. Jews usually leave an empty seat at the Seder table.
3. See Barbara Myerhoff, *Number Our Days* (New York: Simon & Schuster, 1978), p. 44. Myerhoff quotes Shmuel Goldman, immigrant Socialist garment-worker: "It is not the way of a Jew to make his work like there was no human being to suffer when it's done badly. A coat is not a piece of cloth only. The tailor is connected to the one who wears it and he should not forget it" [Rich's note].
4. Israeli cities.
5. Town north of Jerusalem once occupied by Israel.

E. M. BRONER
b. 1930

"Every time I am impatient with, outraged and humiliated by the way traditional religion (mine in particular) treats women, I'm reminded again by the world that I can't separate my Judaism from myself, because the world defines me always as a Jew. In my writing I try, in various ways, to both accept and expand my own mythos."

In what could be described as the necessary coupling of the female Jewish voice and the feminist voice, E. M. Broner critiques the traditional Judeo-Christian patriarchy that infiltrates and often marginalizes the lives of women. Born in Detroit to Paul Masserman, a journalist and Jewish historian, and Beatrice Weckstein Masserman, who acted in the Yiddish theater in Poland, Broner's childhood was steeped in Jewish tradition and culture, which she rebels against in her writing.

Broner has written articles, plays, and short stories but is most widely known for her novels. Her ability to manipulate the physical form of a work, to create a structure that complements her major themes, is evident in her novella *Journal/Nocturnal and Seven Stories* (1986), for example, where she breaks the traditional page by offering a story told in columns: each page is divided into two columns, and each column tells one-half of the narrator's double life. In *Her Mothers* (1975), Broner uses a refrain to draw the book together, simultaneously creating and re-creating a chorus of female voices. *A Weave of Women* (1978), from which the following selection is taken, also diverges from traditional structure: narration and character development are not confined to a single voice, but are shared by twelve different women creating, paradoxically, a physical, emotional, and spiritual community within a collective expression of female autonomy.

Broner has garnered criticism for her style, sometimes called disruptive. The majority of her literary critics, however, have found her craft and her crusade against the patriarchal traditions of conventional Judaism innovative and compelling. By adding to and transforming the rituals and traditions of her heritage, Broner carves a distinctive place among her postmodern peers.

In addition to her writing, Broner has been a reviewer for *Ms.* and a frequent speaker at women's conferences. She splits her time between Wayne State University in Detroit, Michigan, and Sarah Lawrence College in Bronxville, New York.

From A Weave of Women

Chapter 1

THE BIRTH

They embrace and face Jordan. They are turned golden in the evening light, like the stone. There are several of them. The weeping one will not turn to salt.[1] In fact, she drinks her tears. She is a full-bellied sabra[2] and her fruit is sucking away inside.

The women breathe with Simha. Heavy labor has not started yet. They sit in the doorway of their stone house in the Old City.[3] They move inside and breathe with Simha into the stones.

1. Refers to the biblical story of Lot's wife (Genesis 19). When Sodom and Gomorrah were to be destroyed, Lot and his wife were permitted to leave uninjured if they did not look back. When Lot's wife looked, God turned her into a pillar of salt.

2. Any person born in Israel.

3. The area of Jerusalem surrounding the Western Wall, which, until the early 19th century, constituted the entire city.

Simha groans. They echo. Simha loses her water. The Dead Sea. The River Jordan. The Nile. They wait for the baby to float on a basket[4] from Simha's reeds.

They have notified two midwives. It is a mistake. The doctors have refused home delivery. A nurse warned them against it.

Deedee leans against the stones and tells of a friend who bore a son on Christmas Eve under the Christmas tree.

"Was it planned?"

"No. It was an accident."

"Which?"

"Both the pregnancy and the birth."

"What happened to the baby?"

"He was put into the Dirty Baby Ward at the hospital because he was covered with pine needles."

The midwives arrive. One is a Jews for Jesus girl, dressed modestly in kerchief, long skirt, covered arms. She knows her Old and New Testaments but not her Biology. The other is a Swede who is into health. She worked as a volunteer at a border kibbutz[5] and volunteered herself to a kibbutz member. She arrives nursing her new baby. The Swede is intent on smearing ointment onto her sore nipples. The other midwife is reading Leviticus[6] in variant texts.

Simha exclaims. She is in pain. The women are joyous. Pain quickens the moment to birth. Pain quickens the excitation.

They see the cervix. It is purple, a reddish purple.

The midwives look disturbed.

"Hot water?" asks the social worker.

They don't think so.

Simha is sitting on a stool. The women put a soft blanket between Simha's knees.

One midwife tries to hear the baby's heartbeat. She cannot. The Swede listens and hears the regular beat. The midwives do not know how many fingers Simha is dilated. Simha shouts at them from her stool. They leave.

The social worker goes to a house with a phone and, from there, she telephones accomplished women. She phones Martin Buber's[7] granddaughter, Golda Meir's[8] cousin, Ben Gurion's[9] niece. She phones women in the parliament, the law courts, at the university.

Gradually the experts gather. They surround Simha, crouched on her stool. They have books of instructions in several languages.

Antoinette is in the room, a Shakespearean from London. Joan is there, a playwright, a Britisher, but from Manchester. A scientist arrives, originally from Germany. Dahlia is there, a singer from Beer Sheva.[1] Tova has been

4. A reference to the story of Moses (Exodus 2.1–9) in which he is rescued from a riverbank after being sent downstream by his birth mother to save his life.

5. Israeli collective settlement, often agricultural, in which all profit is held in common and is reinvested in the community.

6. The third of the five Books of Moses, Leviticus expands upon the laws presented in Exodus.

7. Highly influential German-Jewish religious philosopher (1878–1965) whose philosophy proposed a more personal and individual relationship with God.

8. A founder and the fourth prime minister of Israel (1898–1978).

9. Zionist statesman, political leader, and defense minister (1886–1973) who became the first prime minister of Israel.

1. An Israeli city in the Negev region that in biblical times was the country's economic, social, and political center.

there all along, the curly-haired actress from New York. Hepzibah jitneys down from Haifa wearing her padded scarf against the wrath of the Father-Lord. Mickey arrives in the midst of her divorce. Gloria, the redhead, has been there for the fun. She came over from California for the fun. Another social worker arrives from Tel Aviv, serious Polish Vered.

Simha has left her stool for the mattress on the floor. Her labor has stopped and she dozes. Why is the baby so bad? It will do nothing on time or within reason. It will cry and the mother will never know why. Simha, matted hair, parched lips, is having nightmares.

The scientist says this is not her field of expertise but nothing seems wrong, the head down, labor proceeding.

Hepzibah barely refrains from covering Simha's full, long hair with a kerchief.[2] Simha is not married and, therefore, does not need a head covering, but perhaps the rules are different when it comes to unwed mothers.

Deedee is both intense and amused. The Jews are something else! She is Irish and prefers her own, and then the Greeks and then the Jews. But Israel is warm and she has women friends here who will neither let her starve nor weep.

They are up all night on this night of vigil. The women brew tea. The redhead, Gloria, knows a special way to make Turkish coffee that she learned from an Arab cab driver. He added cardamom seed. She talks on about the cab ride. All of her tales wander, often with cab drivers, jitney drivers, young students from the university who cannot resist her and follow her across the wadi near campus.

The women drink the thick coffee. They are not sleepy. It becomes chilly and they put naphtha[3] into the heater. They open the door a moment. The bad odor escapes, the blue flames light and the early morning air is warmed.

The Shakespearean has a crisp accent and a bustling manner.

"Did someone call the father?" she asks.

Gloria from California did.

At dawn the father runs into the little stone house. He has hitchhiked from his kibbutz. Gloria's message was delivered to the dining room and shouted from table to table. Ah! He is on his shift in the cow shed. His brother takes over and his mother gives him a basket of freshly baked bread from the kibbutz oven, also her own jam and a plant from her garden.

The kibbutz, accepting paternity, sends wishes of easy birth and warm blankets to receive the son.

A daughter is born.

By the time of the birth the father does not care what comes from Simha's cave, what small, furtive animal that is gnawing at her and making her scream. When the animal slides out, it has soft hair on its head and soft fur on its body. It is a daughter-puppy.

The women prepare the mother.

Mickey, in the midst of her divorce and of her hatred, combs Simha's hair. She braids it. She brushes it out again and puts it up. She lets it hang down Simha's back.

Antoinette gathers flowers from the valley of the Old City.

2. Jewish religious tradition in which all married women must cover their heads, obeyed today only in the Orthodox and Hasidic traditions.

3. Petroleum.

"There's rosemary, that's for remembrance . . . And there is pansies, that's for thought. There's fennel for you, and columbines . . . daisy . . . violets. . . ."

"That's morbid," says Joan. "Ophelia of all things!"[4]

Antoinette does not deign to reply. What does a Manchester person know of repartee, of the deft thrust? She wraps herself in London imperial dignity.

Gloria stares at the father of the child. He fell asleep wearily. He interests her, the natural man who eats hungrily without good or bad manners, sleeps easily, loves shyly. Gloria looks at his kibbutz stomach stretching the buttons of his cotton shirt. His hand is curled. She touches it and it jerks.

Hepzibah takes out her Daily Prayer Book. Terry, the social worker, readies a manifesto. Gerda, the scientist born in Germany, looks at this new marvel of science.

Dahlia from Beer Sheva goes out to exercise her face and chest. The total person sings, not just the vocal cords. She returns red-cheeked and lively-eyed. She sings to Simha of happiness, of bodies, of seas of the moon, of inner caverns that hold tropical fish, of waters that flood and the fish swims clear. The fish has no gills and now must sing instead of gulping.

Tova, the actress, strokes and smoothes the baby daughter. No one will spank her, croons Tova. Life is not a slap on the behind.

The women stroke the animal, pet it behind its ears, pet its scaly legs, its stretching turtle neck, its lumpy head.

Tova brings the stage property—an Indian bedspread with monkeys and fruit-bearing trees. Simha is sat up on the chattering monkey and the lush tree. A garland is twined for her hair.

Gloria tries again to awaken the kibbutznik. He opens his eyes, looks into Gloria's goyishe[5] pale blue and smiles. He has forgotten Simha, who was his happiness. He has forgotten the new daughter. He looks at Gloria's incandescent hair, her straight nose, her American long legs.

The women watch him silently. The kibbutznik feels a crick in his neck. He is a father. He must speak up at kibbutz meetings, in public, and ask for her maintenance. He is the lover of Simha, and she is a head taller than he. She has wide hips, pendulous breasts, large brown eyes, thick hair. He sighs. Never will he feel that canopy of red above him, those blue eyes sunlit upon his arrival. He belongs to furry animals and hairy, big women.

They surround the mattress and chant:

"Welcome to the new mother. Welcome to the new daughter."

Simha is happy but sloppy. She grabs at her breasts, which are beginning to fill and hurt. She cannot close her legs. The womb is sore. But she looks young again. That old woman who went into childbirth is rejuvenated.

Their home is a busy one and across the narrow street is a busier one. That is the Home for Wayward Girls, actually the Home for Jewish Wayward Girls. They are wayward because they ran away. Or because they stand along the roadside near the universities, secular or religious, crying out in the holy tongue, "Come and fuck me!"

4. A reference to William Shakespeare's *Hamlet* 4.5.

5. Non-Jewish (Yiddish).

Committees have met on these girls. Terry has sat on such a committee as Director of the Home. It is the committee decision that the girls are prostitutes because they are psychologically disturbed.

"No," says Terry, "economically disturbed."

She brings out charts on inflation, lack of education, illiteracy.

"What is left for these girls to do?" asks Terry.

"No one tells them to," says the committee.

But they, the girls, know it's what they have to do. And, afterward, their mothers scratch at their eyes. Their fathers whip them. The daughters have failed the religion and the socialist state.

The girls leave both religion and socialism. They wear pointy bras, beehive hairdos or they straighten and blow-dry Arabic-Jewish-African hair. They wear high-heeled chunky shoes and miniskirts when no one is mini anymore, not the Israeli policewomen or the women in the army, who have lengthened skirts to mid-knee.

Rina arrives for the ceremony, Rina from development town, court and prison. Rina wears a long skirt. She wears eyeliner along her almond eyes. She covers her pointy breasts with a shawl. Her parents threw her out because she was lazy in the house. Her lovers threw her out because she was fearful in bed.

Shula is invited, Shula the Westerner, the Pole. She is blonde and buxom. She spits on her parents. She does not honor their days in the land. She spits on her teachers. She does not follow the command to honor the teacher above all. She spits on the police. She spits on all uniforms: traffic, civil guard, nurses, beauty parlor.

"Who taught you to spit, Shula?"

"My grandmother. She spat on me when she saw me and said, 'An ugliness. May the Evil Eye leave her on this earth. May she only be seen as ugly and undesirable so that we never lose her.' And so I am—ugly and undesirable."

The ceremony begins.

Simha wears a wraparound skirt to cover either taut or flabby belly. The kibbutznik is present, bearing another basket from his kibbutz, sensible girls' clothing of strong kibbutz material.

He stares at both of the women, his daughter and his love. And he feels jealous. His daughter fits on the mother's hip, on her breast. There is no need for a father as there was no need for a husband, and he has traveled by bus a winding route for four hours to arrive in Jerusalem.

"Find a girl in the kibbutz," advises the kibbutz psychologist. "Forget her. She takes advantage of you."

Ah, she did! She did! His first love. She took advantage of him and deflowered him.

Gloria is there wearing a low-cut dress. She has found sun during this chilly weather, and her freckles reach into her cleavage.

The kibbutznik stares into the basket he is carrying.

Tova from New York is there. She has an Arab lover. He is too shy to attend, but he sends a song.

> Mother, I would leap from the mountain for you.
> Mother, I will never forget you.

Shh. It is Simha's prayer.

"I come into your house, O Mother God. You inclined your ear toward me, and I will whisper into it all the days of my life.

"The cords of life and death encompassed me. From the hollow of the grave, from the cave of the mouth of birth I called. I knew happiness and anguish. You delivered my soul from death into birth, my eyes from tears, my feet from falling. I shall walk before You in the land of the living."

The baby is poking at her own eyes. She grimaces. A thin cry.

Hepzibah says, "Let her become a comfort to Simha in her old age."

Hepzibah puts down her prayer book and kisses Simha.

"She may need it," murmurs Hepzibah.

Terry says, "Let there be peace. Grant this daughter of her people peace."

Ah, they do not know what will befall or that there will be no room for the daughter or for her people.

The kibbutznik says: "May she serve however she wishes, in the chicken house, the barn, the rose garden, the cotton field, the kitchen, the guesthouse. May she be a member of the community of people."

Simha knows why she chose him to be the father.

This is a story of the birth of Simha's daughter, of the births of other daughters, of the piercing of the women of these two houses. It is a story of women who are born in or arrive in the land, of some who stay and of many who leave.

It is a story of women who are ceremonious and correct with each other, who celebrate sermons and hermans, birth rites, death rites, sacrificial rites, exodus rites and exorcism rites.

It is the story of sanity and madness in the house of women.

1978

BRUCE JAY FRIEDMAN
b. 1930

The author of novels, plays, screenplays, and short stories, Bruce Jay Friedman has mastered all these genres as he maneuvers his way through the life and times of fiction's "lonely guy," Harry Towns. Paying close attention to America's most assimilated Jews, Friedman combines elements of comedy and tragedy, realism and fantasy in these portrayals.

Friedman found critical success quickly with his first novel, *Stern*, published in 1962. The story of a man determined to assimilate, the thirty-four-year-old title character seeks to reproduce suburban bliss but instead finds a world that has been perverted, fractured, and demoralized. Still comic, however, *Stern* offers an early look at a device that combines the shock of the absurd with the bite of satire; the novel provides a precursor to the dark humor of Kurt Vonnegut and Woody Allen.

Friedman's subsequent writings have all considered questions of contemporary ethnic identity. The story collected here, *When You're Excused, You're Excused*, originally published in *Far from the City of Class* (1963), captures the essence of Friedman's work. Depicting a man caught between his Jewish roots and a mass culture that glorifies superficial idolatry and the finer aspects of nihilism, *When You're Excused, You're Excused* illustrates the tawdry manipulation of traditional religion. The story asks readers to reevaluate the place that religion occupies in the contemporary world. As the protagonist fumbles his way through an evening of pumping iron and courting women, Jewish tradition is trampled with such precision that the target of Friedman's black humor—religious hypocrites—is clear.

In response to those critical of his black humor, Friedman has said that "it may be that if you are doing anything as high-minded as examining society, the very best way to go about it is by examining first its throwaways, the ones who can't or won't keep in step (in step with what?). And who knows? Perhaps 'bad' behavior of a certain kind is better than 'good' behavior."

Bruce Jay Friedman was born in 1930 in New York City. He has written six novels, including *Stern* (1962), *A Mother's Kisses* (1963), and *About Harry Towns* (1974); a number of collections of short stories and essays; and six plays, including *Scuba Duba: A Tense Comedy* (1967), *Steambath* (1971), and *Have You Spoken to Any Jews Lately?*. Friedman was nominated for Best Original Screenplay by the Academy of Motion Picture Arts and Sciences for the 1984 movie *Splash*.

When You're Excused, You're Excused

Having a gallstone removed at the age of thirty-seven almost frightened Mr. Kessler to death, and after he was healed up, he vowed he would get into the best shape of his life. He joined a local sports club called Vic Tanny's, and for six months took workouts every other night of the week, missing only three sessions for Asian flu. When one of his workouts came due on the eve of Yom Kippur, holiest day of the Jewish year, Mr. Kessler, who usually observed important religious holidays, said to his wife, "I've come to need these workouts and my body craves them like drugs. It's medicine and when I miss one I get edgy and feel awful. It doesn't make any difference that this is the most important holiday of all. I've got to go tonight. It's part of the religion that if you're sick you're excused from synagogue. It's in one of the psalms."

Mrs. Kessler was a woman of deep religious conviction but slender formal training. Her husband, as a result, was able to bully her around with references to obscure religious documents. Once he mentioned the psalms, rebuttal was out of the question, and she could only say, "All right, as long as it's in there."

Mr. Kessler did a great deal of aimless walking through the house for the rest of the day. His four-year-old son asked him, "Are any pirates good?" and Mr. Kessler said, "I don't feel like talking pirates." When the dark came and it was time for the gym, Mr. Kessler said to his wife, "All right, it isn't in the psalms, but it's in the religion somewhere, and it doesn't make any difference that it's such an important holiday. If you're excused, you're excused. That goes for Columbus Day and Washington's Birthday and if the Japs attack Pearl Harbor again, you're excused on that day, too. In fact, as a matter of principle, you're *especially* excused on Yom Kippur."

Mr. Kessler got his gym bundle together and his wife walked him to the driveway. "It seems dark and religious out here," she said.

"Nonsense," said Mr. Kessler.

He opened the door of his car and then said, "All right, I admit I'm not confident. I started to imagine there was a squadron of old rabbis prowling the streets taking down the names of Jews who were going off to gyms. When the railroad whistle sounded, I thought it was a ram's horn, and the wind tonight is like the wail of a thousand dying ghetto holdouts. But I've got to go there even if I just take a quick workout and skip my steambath. It's too bad it's Yom Kippur and I admit that's throwing me a little, but if you're excused, you're excused. On Yom Kippur or *double* Yom Kippur."

Mr. Kessler got behind the wheel and his young son hollered down from an open window, "Can a giant find you if you hide?"

"No giants when important things are going on," said Mr. Kessler, swinging out of the driveway and driving into the night.

Fifteen minutes later, he parked his car outside the gym and swept inside. He walked past the blonde receptionist who called out "Where's your wife?" and Mr. Kessler said, "She only came that once, and you know damned well her hips are past help. Why do you have to ask me that every time I come in here?"

He undressed in the locker room and gave his street clothing to Rico, the tiny attendant, who blew his nose and said, "I've got a cold, but I'm glad. It's good to have one. Guys come in here to lose colds and I'm glad to have one all year round. When you have a cold, you're always taking care of yourself and that's good."

Mr. Kessler said, "I never said anything to you before because I know you're supposed to be a charming old character, but you're an idiot. It's not good to have a cold. It's better not to have a cold. Any time. I just want to take a fast workout and go home and be in the house. I don't want to kid around."

Upstairs, in the workout room, a man with a thin body was lying on the floor in an awkward position, lifting a barbell in an unnatural movement. "Do you want to know this one?" the man asked. "Its the best exercise in the gym, getting a muscle no one else bothers with. It's right in the center of the arm and you can't see it. Its function is to push out all the other muscles. You don't have very much of a build while you're getting it started, but once she's going, all the other muscles shoot out and you look like an ape."

"I don't have time for any new exercises tonight," said Mr. Kessler. "I just want to get in and get out. Besides, I don't like the kind of body you have."

Mr. Kessler did a few warm-up exercises and then picked up a pair of light dumbbells to work his biceps. A handsome and heavily perspired young man with large shoulders came over and said, "Whew, it certainly is rough work. But when I was sixteen, I only weighed 110 and I said to myself, 'I'm going to look like something.' So each night, after working in Dad's filling station, I began to lift stuff in the family garage, getting to the point where I really had a nice build and then, in later years, joining up here. I vowed I would never again look like nothing."

"What makes you think that's such an exciting story?" said Mr. Kessler. "I've heard it a thousand times. I think *you* told it to me once and I don't want to hear it again as long as I live."

"What's eating you?" asked the handsome man.

"I just want to get in and get out and not hear any dull stories," said Mr. Kessler. He went over to a rowing machine, but a sparse-haired man who was doing vigorous waist-twisting Alpine calisthenics blocked his way. "Why don't you do those at home?" said Mr. Kessler. "You're in my way. I've seen you in here and you never use any of the equipment. You only do calisthenics and you're crazy to come here to do them. What are you, showing off?"

"I just like to do them here," said the man and let Mr. Kessler get at the rowing machine. Looking up at the clock, Mr. Kessler did half a dozen rows and then leaped up and caught the high bar, swinging back and forth a few times. A police sergeant who took clandestine workouts during duty hours came by and said, "Your lats are really coming out beautifully."

"Oh, really?" said Mr. Kessler. "Can you see the delts from back there?"

"Beauties," said the sergeant. "Both beauties."

"Thank you for saying that," said Mr. Kessler, swinging easily on the bar. "I can really feel them coming out now. I don't know why, but your saying they're coming out beautifully made me feel good for the first time tonight. I was rushing through my workout because we have this big holiday tonight and I felt guilty, but now I'm going to stay up here awhile. Six months ago I was sick with a bad gallstone and told everyone that if you're sick your only obligation is to yourself. Ahead of kids, your wife and the synagogue. Now I feel good up here and I'm not rushing. This is where I should be. I don't care if it's Yom Kippur or if the mayor's been killed by a bird turd."

"I don't say I follow all your arguments," said the sergeant, "but your lats are really coming up. I'll tell that to any man here in the gym, straight to his face."

"Thank you for feeling that way," said Mr. Kessler, dropping from the bar now and taking his place on a bench for some leg-raises. Sharing the bench with him was a tiny, dark-haired man with powerful forearms.

"It pays to work your forearms," said the little man. "You get them pumped up real good and even the big bastards will run."

"I'm one of the big bastards," said Mr. Kessler. "You can't tell because I'm sitting down."

"I couldn't see that," said the little man.

"It's all right," said Mr. Kessler. "It's just that maybe you ought to tell that story to a little bastard."

"I'm not telling it to anyone," said the little man.

Mr. Kessler did his legs and then went over to the board for some sit-ups. A man with a large head came over and said, "You look awfully familiar. From a long time ago."

"Public school," said Mr. Kessler, rising to shake hands with the man. "Your name is Block and your father was an attorney."

"Accountant," said the man. "But you're right about Block."

"You lived in the rooming house and there was something else about you. How come you're not in synagogue tonight?"

"I don't observe," said the man. "We never did. This is my first workout here."

"I do observe, but I was sick and I figure I'm excused. A long time ago I remember an old man in the temple didn't have to fast because his stomach was out of whack. That was orthodox and I figure if he was excused, I'm certainly excused. I was feeling bad for a while but not any more. If you're sick it doesn't matter if it's Yom Kippur or even if they make up a day holier than Yom Kippur. If you're excused, you're excused. What the hell *was* it about you?"

"I'd like to take off a little around the waist and pack some on the shoulders."

"I know," said Mr. Kessler. "*Blockhead*. They used to call you *Blockhead*. That's it, isn't it?"

"I don't like it now any more than I did then," said the man with the big head.

"Yes, but I just wanted to get it straight," said Mr. Kessler. "A thing like that can nag you."

Mr. Kessler did ten sets of sit-ups, and when he had worked up a good sweat, he went downstairs and showered. The massage room was empty and Mr. Kessler said to the attendant, "I want a massage. It doesn't matter that I've never had one before and that I associate it with luxury and extravagance. I want one. When I came in here I was going to get right out, but there's a principle involved. We have this big holiday, very big, but you're either excused from it or you're not. And I am. I was pretty sick."

"If I had the towel concession, I'd have it made," said the masseur, oiling up Mr. Kessler's body. "You can't make it on rubs alone. You've got to have rubs and rags."

"It's crazy that they're all sitting out there bent over in prayer and I'm in here, but when you're proving a point, sometimes things look ridiculous."

"If you have any influence at all," said the masseur, "try to get me towels. I can't make it on rubs alone."

Music poured into the gym now, and Mr. Kessler hummed along to several early Jerome Kern[1] tunes. His massage at an end, he got up from the table, showered, and then, as he dressed, told Rico, the locker room attendant, "I'm all tingling. I knew this was the right thing to do. Next year I'll be in the temple all bent over like they are, but I did the right thing tonight."

"All you need is a cold," said Rico.

"You know how I feel about that remark," said Mr. Kessler.

Upstairs, Mr. Kessler smiled at the blonde receptionist who grabbed him and began to lead him in a cha-cha across the front office. "I don't do this with girls," said Mr. Kessler, falling into step, "and I'm going right home. You have a ponytail and it's making me crazy."

"Where's your wife?" asked the girl, going off into a complicated cha-cha break that flustered Mr. Kessler.

"You ask me that all the time," said Mr. Kessler, picking up the beat again and doing primitive arm motions. "Look, it doesn't matter about her hips. Don't you understand a man can be in love with a woman with any size hips? Where's my wife, you ask? What do we need her for?"

"Do you want to go dancing?" asked the girl.

"I told you I don't do things with girls," said Mr. Kessler. "I shouldn't even be carrying on here in the lobby. What's your name?"

"Irish," said the girl.

"Irish?" said Mr. Kessler. "Do you have to be named the most gentile name

1. Popular composer (1885–1945) who was famous for his contributions to the American musical, including *Show Boat*.

there is? They're all out there wailing and beating their breasts for atonement and I'm with an Irish. But I've got to ask myself if it would be better if you were an Inge. I'm not doing anything wrong and even if I am it doesn't make any difference that I'm doing it tonight. I'm either excused or I'm not excused. I'm finished early and I'll go for about twenty minutes."

The girl put on a sweater and walked ahead of Mr. Kessler to his car. He started the motor and she said, "I don't want to dance just yet. I'd rather that you park somewhere and make love to me."

"I can't stand it when the girl says a thing like that," said Mr. Kessler. "That drives me out of my mind. Look, it was all right in there in the gym, but I'm feeling a little funny out here in the night air. As though I'm wandering around somewhere in the goddamned Sinai.[2] But that's just the kind of thing I've got to fight. I don't think there'll be anyone behind the Chinese restaurant now. All we're going to do is fool around a little, though."

The lights in the Chinese restaurant's parking field were dark when they got there and Mr. Kessler stopped the car and put his head into the receptionist's blonde hair and bit her ear. "You smell young. About that ear bite, though. I just feel that as long as I'm being so honest about Yom Kippur I can't do anything dishonest at all. The ear bite isn't mine. That is, it's just something I do. A long time ago, before my wife got big-hipped, we took a Caribbean cruise and she danced on deck with a Puerto Rican public relations man named Rodriguez. She acted funny after that and finally told me it was because he'd aroused her. I got it out of her that it was because he'd bitten her ear. I can't use an ear bite on her, of course, but I've been anxious to try one out and that's why I worked it in."

"Really make love to me," the receptionist whispered, putting herself against Mr. Kessler.

"There'll only be some light fooling around," said Mr. Kessler. "Do you know what the hell night this is? Uh oh. The voice you have just heard was that of the world's worst hypocrite. Am I proving anything if I just do some elaborate kissing about the neck and shoulders? A man is either excused or he's not excused. Oh, Jesus, you're wearing boyish-type underwear. You would be wearing something along those lines. That did it," he said, and fell upon her.

After a while, she said, "Now that you've had me, I want us to dance slowly knowing that you've had me."

"You're suggesting crazy things," said Mr. Kessler. "I'm calling my wife before I do any more of them."

They drove to a filling station and Mr. Kessler dialed his number and said, "I thought I'd get in and get out, but the car's broken. It's in the differential."

"You know I don't know what that is," said Mr. Kessler. "It's like telling me something is in the psalms."

"The garage has to run out and get some parts," he said.

"Do you feel funny about what you did?" asked Mrs. Kessler.

2. A mountainous region in Egypt. Mount Sinai is the site at which the Israelites received the Ten Commandments from God during their Exodus.

"I didn't do anything," he said. "Everybody forgets how sick I was. When you're sick, the religion understands."

Mr. Kessler hung up and the receptionist showed him the way to a dancing place. It was a cellar called Tiger Sam's, catering to Negroes and whites and specializing in barbecued ham hocks. They danced awhile and the receptionist said she was hungry. "I am, too," said Mr. Kessler. "It's going to be tough getting down that first bite because I know the fast isn't over until sundown tomorrow night, but it's about time I stopped thinking that way. I forget how sick I was."

The receptionist said she wanted the ham hocks, and Mr. Kessler said, "I confess I've had the urge to try them, but they're probably the most unkosher things in the world. I'm starting in again. Wouldn't I just be the most spineless man in America if I ordered eggs and told them to hold the hocks? I'll have the hocks."

When he had finished eating, Mr. Kessler began drinking double shots of bourbon until he slid off his stool and fell into the sawdust.

"I've gone past that point where I should have stopped. I only hope I don't get sentimental and run off into a synagogue. It's here where my heart starts breaking for every Jew who ever walked with a stoop and cried into a prayer book. That's just the kind of thing I've got to watch, though. It would be the best medicine in the world for me if an old Jewish refugee woman just happened to stumble in here by accident. Just so I could fail to hug and kiss her and apologize to her for all the world's crimes. And that would be that and I'd have proven that number one I was sick and number two when you're sick you're excused and number three when you're excused you're really excused."

A young Negro with a dancer's grace in his body came over, bowed to Mr. Kessler in the sawdust and said, "I'm Ben and should like to try the merengue with your lovely blonde companion. With your permission."

Mr. Kessler said it was all right and stayed in the sawdust while the two danced closely and primitively to a Haitian rhythm. Two Negro musicians sat on stools above Mr. Kessler. One handed another double bourbon down to him and said, "Like happy Yom Kippur, babe."

"I can't get to my feet," said Mr. Kessler. "You think that's funny and sort of like a jazz musician's joke, but it so happens I am Jewish. I ought to belt you one, but the point is even jokes shouldn't bother me if I'm excused from the holiday. If I got upset and belted you, it would show that I really haven't excused myself."

One of the musicians dangled a toilet bowl deodorizer in front of Mr. Kessler's nose while the other howled.

"I don't know where this fits into anything," said Mr. Kessler, "but I'm not going to get upset or start feeling sentimental."

The Negro named Ben came back now with his arm around the receptionist's waist and said, "I wonder if you two would join me at my apartment. I'm having a do there and am sure you'll love Benny's decor."

The two musicians carried Mr. Kessler out to a Sunbeam convertible and put him on the floor of the rear seat, slipping in above him. The receptionist got in alongside Ben, who drove to Harlem. The two musicians kept the deodorizer in Mr. Kessler's face. "I suppose you've got a reason for that," he said from the floor, as they howled in the night air and kept pushing it against his nose.

When the car stopped, Mr. Kessler said, "I can walk now," and stumbled along behind the four as they mounted the steps of a brownstone. Ben knocked on the door, two lights raps and a hard one, and a powerful pale-skinned man in leotards opened the door quickly to a huge single room, divided by a purple curtain. It was done in the style of a cave and there were bits of African sculpture on shelves, along with campaign pictures of New York's Governor Harriman.[3] A film flashed on one wall, demonstrating Martha Graham[4] ballet techniques, and some forty or fifty Negro-white couples in leotards stood watching it in the haze of the room, some assuming ballet poses along with the dancers. Ben got leotards for the new arrivals and led them behind the purple curtain so they could change. There, a man in a silk dressing gown sat reading *Popular Mechanics* on a divan shaped like a giant English muffin. Ben introduced him to Mr. Kessler and the receptionist as "Tor," his roommate, a noted anthropologist. "Why do I have to get into leotards?" asked Mr. Kessler as the receptionist and the two Negro musicians began to slip into theirs and the anthropologist looked on. "I'll bet my new Vic Tanny's body won't look bad in them, though." After he had changed, there was a scuffle outside the curtain. The film had stopped suddenly, fixing Martha Graham on the screen with one leg on the practice bar. Several couples were screaming. A police officer was on the floor, and Ben said to Mr. Kessler, "Get his legs. He came up here and got stuck and we've got to get him out."

"I've never committed a crime," said Mr. Kessler, smoothing his leotards and taking the policeman's legs. Something wine-colored and wet was on the officer's breast pocket. "What do you mean he got stuck? I don't want to be carrying him if he got stuck."

They stumbled down the stairs with him and then walked several blocks in the blackness, finally propping the officer's body against an ash can.

"I don't know about leaving him against an ash can," said Mr. Kessler. "This is one thing I'm sorry I had to do tonight. Not because it's tonight especially, but because I wouldn't want to do it any night. But if I had to do it at all, I suppose I'm glad it was tonight. Why should I worry about doing this on Yom Kippur? I can see worrying about it in general, but not because it's tonight. Not if I'm supposed to be excused."

They went back to the party. The film was off now and couples were dancing wildly in the murk to a three-man combo, each of whom was beating a bongo. They were hollering out a song in which the only lyrics were, "We're a bongo combo," repeated many times. One of the Negro musicians put a slim cigarette in Mr. Kessler's mouth and lit it. "Hey, wait a minute," said Mr. Kessler. "I know what kind of cigarette this is. I may have always had a yen to just try a puff of one, but that's one thing I'm absolutely not doing tonight. Not because it's tonight. I'd resist even more if it were just an ordinary night. In fact, the reason I haven't spit it out already is I want to show I'm not afraid of Yom Kippur. It's working already." Mr. Kessler sat down peacefully in the middle of perfumed, dancing, frenzied feet. "My senses are sharpened. I read that's what's supposed to happen." He saw the curtain part momentarily. Holding the anthropologist's purple dressing gown toreador

3. W. Averell Harriman (1891–1986), a statesman and a leading U.S. diplomat, was also the governor of New York from 1955 to 1959.

4. Famous choreographer and central figure in the modern dance movement (1894–1991).

style, the blonde receptionist, nude now, stood atop the English muffin. The noted Swede charged forward, making bull-like passes at her, one finger against each ear. A Negro girl with full lips leaned down and caught Mr. Kessler's head to her pistol-like bosoms, holding him there, senses sharpened, for what seemed like a season, and then Ben came whirling by in a series of *West Side Story*[5] leaps, chucking him flirtatiously under the chin and then kissing him wetly in the ear. Mr. Kessler got to his knees and screamed, "J'ACCUSE.[6] That isn't what I mean. What I mean is I'M EXCUSED, I'M EXCUSED," but no one heard him and he fell unconscious.

When he awakened, Ben and the two Negro musicians were helping him behind the wheel of his own car. Ben tapped the blonde receptionist on the behind and she slid in beside Mr. Kessler.

"We enjoyed your company terribly much," said Ben, and the two musicians howled. "Hope you enjoyed the decor and the Ivy League entertainment."

"What time is it?" Mr. Kessler asked the girl when the Negroes had driven off.

"Almost morning," said the receptionist.

"Well, at least they're out," said Mr. Kessler.

"Who's out of where?" she asked.

"The Jews are out of synagogue," said Mr. Kessler.

"I want you to meet my brothers," she said. "Maybe we can have a few beers before the sun comes up."

"The holiday is still on, but the important part is over," said Mr. Kessler. "Then tonight it's all over."

The receptionist showed Mr. Kessler the way to her white frame house. "I was divorced two years ago," she said. "Now I live with my two brothers. They're a hell of a lot of fun and I was lucky to have them."

The night was breaking when they got to the house. The receptionist introduced Mr. Kessler to the two brothers, both of whom were tall and freckled. The older brother served cans of beer for all, and when they had finished the beers, began to open a crate of grapefruits. "Our sales manager sent these back from the South," he said. "Aren't they honeys?" He picked up one of the grapefruits and rolled it to his younger brother, who fielded it like a baseball and threw it back. "You grabbed that one like Tommy Henrich,"[7] said the older brother, rolling it back. The younger brother picked it up, made a little skipping motion and flung it back again. "Hey, just like Johnny Logan,"[8] said the older one. He rolled it once again and when he got it back, said, "That was Marty Marion."[9]

"Or 'Phumblin' Phil' Weintraub," said Mr. Kessler.

The brothers stopped a second and then the older brother rolled the grape-

5. A popular Broadway musical (1957) and movie (1961), with music by Leonard Bernstein, lyrics by Stephen Sondheim, and book by Jerome Robbins and Arthur Laurents.

6. Literally, "I accuse" (French). Friedman refers the famous letter of the same name written by the French author Émile Zola (1840–1902), which protested the incarceration of the Jewish Frenchman, Alfred Dreyfus, for treason. His imprisonment, as Zola understood, was a landmark event in French history since the charges were specious. It is now commonly held that Dreyfus committed no crime but was a victim of anti-Semitism.

7. Outfielder Tommy "Old Reliable" Henrich (b. 1913) played ball for the New York Yankees from 1937 to 1942 and from 1947 to 1950.

8. Scrappy Johnny "Yatcha" Logan (b. 1927) played baseball for the Atlanta Braves and the Pittsburgh Pirates.

9. Known as "Slats" and "the Octopus," Marty Marion (b. 1917) was the premier defensive National League shortstop of his day.

fruit again. "George Stirnweiss,"[1] he hollered when his brother pegged it to him. He rolled it. He got it back. "Just like Bobby Richardson,"[2] he said.

"Or 'Phumblin' Phil' Weintraub," said Mr. Kessler.

"Who's that?" asked the older brother.

"That's it," said Mr. Kessler. He got to his feet with fists clenched and walked toward the older brother.

"You never should have said that," said Mr. Kessler.

"I didn't say anything," said the boy.

"Oh yes you did," said Mr. Kessler, through clenched teeth. "Maybe I went to Vic Tanny's and shacked up with a girl named Irish and got drunk and ate barbecued ham hocks. Maybe I hid a dead cop and smoked marijuana and went to a crazy party and got kissed by a Negro homosexual ballet dancer. But I'm not letting you get away with something like that."

He flew at the older brother now, knocked him down and began to tear at his ear. "He was all-hit-no-field and he played four years for the Giants in the early forties and faded when the regular players got out of service AND NO SON OF A BITCH IS GOING TO SAY ANYTHING ABOUT POOR 'PHUMBLIN' PHIL' WEINTRAUB ON YOM KIPPUR!"

The younger brother and the girl tugged at him with fury and finally dislodged him, but not before a little piece of the ear had come off. Then Mr. Kessler smoothed his leotards and went sobbing out the door.

"I may have been excused," they heard him call back in the early morning, "but I wasn't that excused."

1963

1. George "Snuffy" Stirnweiss (1918–1958), outstanding American League second baseman.

2. Respected as a multitalented competitor and a clean-living, God-fearing man, Richardson (b. 1935) played for the Yankees from 1957 to 1966.

HAROLD BLOOM
b. 1931

According to the Documentary Hypothesis, a theory of composition about the Hebrew Bible, four sources were stitched together to create the Pentateuch. These four sources are identified by initials: J, the Yahwist that calls God *Yahweh* (taken from the German *Jahwe*, from which we get the J); E, the Elohist (who uses the name *Elohim* for God); D, the author of Deuteronomy; and P, the Priestly source, which comprises most of the ritual law of the Bible. The hypothesis holds that these sources were sewn together by an anonymous Redactor, or editor.

Harold Bloom sets out to do a number of ambitious things in *The Book of J*. First, he tries to liberate the J text from its surroundings and print the Yahwist document separately. Second, he provides commentary side by side with the J text in order to persuade the reader that the writer was female, a close relation to the biblical David, and, therefore, probably of royal blood and living in Solomon's court. Third, he argues that this female author was the most brilliant of all Jewish writers, a precursor to Kafka (another writer that Bloom greatly admires), and that as an author, she was magnificent—dense, ironic, witty. Finally, Bloom wishes to blur the dividing line between what we consider literary writing and what we consider sacred writing—a task he had attempted from the opposite direction: in his earlier writings, he had tried to convince the reader that secular poetry, such as British Romantic poetry, is actually the holy texts of our culture.

Published in 1990, *The Book of J* met with acclaim, scrutiny, publicity, and controversy. While most critics agreed that the idea of a female author of the Old Testament was provocative, they also agreed that it had little support behind it. Still, the book was not read as scholarly biblical commentary; rather it was read as an imaginative, even fantastic, and appealing meditation on the Hebrew Bible. Or one might read it as a "misprision," to use a term central to the literary theory Bloom sets forth in *The Anxiety of Influence* (1973) and *A Map of Misreading* (1975)—the creative misreading of a text that creates another great text. *The Book of J* might well fall into that category. Finally, it can be read as an attempt by Bloom to find the epic poet of the Jewish canon, which, as he argued in *Ruin the Sacred Truths: Poetry and Belief from the Bible to the Present* (1989), contains only Freud, Kafka, and Gershom Scholem, the scholar of Jewish mysticism.

Perhaps the last explanation is most plausible since Bloom has been a prominent literary critic and canon maker for almost thirty years. *The Anxiety of Influence* virtually transformed the academic study of poetry. Using Freudian theory to map out a landscape of poetic influence, Bloom argued that every emerging poet engages in a struggle with a strong poetic "father" who appears to overpower him with his greatness. The emerging poet's response to that "anxiety," according to Bloom, is what produces great poetry. Bloom uses this theory to identify and advance a line of poets: in the British tradition, Bloom's criticism did much to elevate the Romantics; in the American tradition, Bloom distinguished Emerson, Whitman, Stevens, and Ashbery.

Engaging, brilliant, imaginative, controversial, bombastic, a withering critic of both popular culture and academic elitism, Harold Bloom is one of the most influential literary critics of his day. He is editor of dozens of literary works for students. His most recent works, *The Western Canon* (1994) and *Shakespeare and the Invention of the Human* (1998), have found large audiences outside of the academy. For two decades, he has taught at Yale University and New York University, where he has a well-earned reputation for genius and eccentricity, two traits that might well describe the project of *The Book of J*.

From The Book of J

[*Introduction*]

In Jerusalem, nearly three thousand years ago, an unknown author composed a work that has formed the spiritual consciousness of much of the world ever since. We possess only a fragmentary text of that work, embedded within what we call Genesis, Exodus, and Numbers, three of the divisions of Torah, or the Five Books of Moses. Since we cannot know the circumstances under which the work was composed, or for what purposes, ultimately we must rely upon our experience as readers to justify our surmises as to what it is that we are reading. Scholarship, however deeply grounded, can reach no agreement upon the dating of what I am calling the Book of J, or upon its surviving dimensions, or even upon whether it ever had an independent existence at all.

For reasons that I will expound, I am assuming that J lived at or nearby the court of Solomon's[1] son and successor, King Rehoboam of Judah,[2] under whom his father's kingdom fell apart soon after the death of Solomon in 922 B.C.E. My further assumption is that J was not a professional scribe but rather an immensely sophisticated, highly placed member of the Solomonic elite, enlightened and ironic. But my primary surmise is that J was a woman, and that she wrote for her contemporaries as a woman, in friendly competition with her only strong rival among those contemporaries, the male author of the court history narrative in 2 Samuel. Since I am aware that my vision of J will be condemned as a fancy or a fiction, I will begin by pointing out that all our accounts of the Bible are scholarly fictions or religious fantasies, and generally serve rather tendentious purposes. In proposing that J was a woman, at least I will not be furthering the interests of any religious or ideological group. Rather, I will be attempting to account, through my years of reading experience, for my increasing sense of the astonishing differences between J and every other biblical writer.

Feminist literary critics curiously condemn as what they term "essentialism" any attempt to describe particular literary characteristics as female rather than male. Surely feminist criticism should also exclude as "essentialism" every description of J's writing as possessing male characteristics. We simply do not know whether J was a man or a woman, but our moral imagination can calculate the passage of possibilities into probabilities when we compare J to the other strands in Genesis, Exodus, Numbers, or when we compare J to all other extant literature of the ancient Middle East. What is new in J? Where do J's crucial originalities cluster? What is it about J's tone, stance, mode of narrative, that was a difference that made a difference? One large area of answer will concern the representation of women as compared with that of men; another will concern irony, which seems to me the element of style in the Bible that is still most often and most weakly misread, even by the latest-model literary critics of the Hebrew Bible.

Misunderstandings of J's irony have continued for two millennia and have produced the curious issue of "anthropomorphism," of J's representation of Yahweh[3] as human-all-too-human. They have produced also the deadly issue of J's supposed misogyny and championing of "patriarchal religion." William Blake,[4] in *The Marriage of Heaven and Hell*, taught us that a crucial aspect of religious history is the process of "choosing forms of worship from poetic tales." That historical irony remains so prevalent, in its consequences, that it continues to affect all our lives. Jimmy Carter, former president of the United States, recently chided Salman Rushdie[5] for meddling with the poetic tales of the Koran,[6] and also denounced Martin Scorsese[7] for his liberties with the poetic tales of the New Testament. I myself do not believe that the Torah is any more or less the revealed Word of God than are Dante's *Com-*

1. In the Bible, Solomon is the son of David, king of Israel.
2. The name means in Hebrew "the Divine Kinsman has been generous." Rehoboam was king of Judah for seventeen years. His name is connected to one of the most important events in the history of Israel—the division of David's united monarchy into two separate kingdoms: Israel in the north and Judah in the south.
3. One of the Hebrew words for God.
4. William Blake (1757–1827), British poet, mystic, and engraver.
5. Salman Rushdie (b. 1947), Indian novelist and critic who, in his criticism of the Islamic nation, has been condemned by the Islamic community.
6. The sacred writings of the Islamic religion.
7. Martin Scorsese (b. 1942), American motion-picture director, writer, and producer, is famous for, among other things, his controversial movie *The Last Temptation of Christ* (1988), based on the novel by Nikos Kazantzakis. In it, Jesus is depicted as a tortured man, unsure of his role as the Messiah.

media, Shakespeare's *King Lear*, or Tolstoy's novels, all works of comparable literary sublimity. Yet even I am shadowed by the residual aura of the Book of J, despite my conviction that the distinction between sacred and secular texts results from social and political decisions, and thus is not a literary distinction at all. Because the peculiar status of the Bible, from at least the Return of Israel from Babylonian Exile on to the present day, is the decisive factor in the misreading of J, I must begin by speculating upon whether it is at all possible to recover the Book of J, even on my own rather free premises of imaginative surmise.

How does one begin to read more severely a writer whose work one has been misreading, necessarily and rather weakly, all of one's life? The investment, societal and individual, in the institutionalized misreading of J is extraordinarily comprehensive, since it is divided among Jews, Christians, Muslims, and members of the secular culture. There are profound reasons for not regarding the Bible as a literary text comparable to *Hamlet* and *Lear*, the *Commedia*, the *Iliad*, the poems of Wordsworth, or the novels of Tolstoy. Believers and historians alike clearly are justified in finding the Bible rather more comparable to the Koran or the Book of Mormon.[8] But what if one is neither a believer nor a historian? Or what if one is a believer, of some degree or kind, and yet still a reader, unable or unwilling to keep reminding oneself that the pages one reads are sacred or holy, at least to millions of others? If one is an Orthodox Jew, then one believes the marvelous fiction that the historical Moses wrote Genesis, Exodus, and Numbers, so that J never existed. J, whether female or male, may be a fiction also, but a less irrational fiction than the author Moses.

Religion can be the greatest of blessings or the greatest of curses. Historically it seems to have been both. There are myriads more Christians and Muslims than there are Jews, which means that the Hebrew Bible as such is more important in its revised form as the Old Testament than it can now be as itself. And there are many more normative Jews, few as they are compared with Christians and Muslims, than there are secular readers, Gentile and Jewish, who are prepared to read the Bible in something like the same spirit in which they read Shakespeare. This means that the Five Books of Moses, that grand work of the Redactor,[9] are more important than the Book of J. And yet, whether we speak of the Hebrew Bible or of the Old Testament, we are speaking of a work that takes as its original the writing of J. And that returns me to the profound reason for regarding the Bible as a library of literary texts, which to me and many other readers it must be. Yahweh, in transmogrified forms, remains the God of the Children of Abraham, of believing Jews, Christians, and Muslims. But Yahweh, in the Book of J, *is a literary character*, just as Hamlet is. If the history of religion is the process of choosing forms of worship from poetic tales, in the West that history is even more extravagant: it is the worship, in greatly modified and revised forms, of an extraordinarily wayward and uncanny literary character, J's Yahweh. Churches are founded upon metaphors, such as rocks and crosses, but the Western worship of God is in one sense more astonishing than the foun-

8. The Book of Mormon is accepted as holy Scripture, in addition to the Bible, in Mormon churches.

9. The word is defined as a person who puts a text into suitable literary form. In this context, it refers to a single man or woman who may have put many biblical texts into the form in which they now appear.

dation of any church. The original Yahweh of the Bible, J's, is a very complex and troublesome extended metaphor or figure of speech and thought. So is Hamlet. But we do not pray to Hamlet, or invoke him when we run for political office, or justify our opposition to abortion by appealing to him.

I am neither a believer nor a historian, but the dilemma I cite seems to me as much theirs as mine. Why does Yahweh attempt to murder Moses?[1] How can God sit under the terebinth trees at Mamre and devour roast calf and curds?[2] What can we do with a Supreme Being who goes nearly berserk at Sinai[3] and warns us he may break forth against the crowds, who clearly fill him with great distaste? As I insist throughout this book, J is anything but a naive writer; she is rather the most sophisticated of authors, as knowing as Shakespeare or Jane Austen.[4] I am frightened by the ironies of belief and of history when I contemplate the enormous differences between J's Yahweh and the God of Judaism, Christianity, and Islam, and indeed the God of the scholars and literary critics, both sectarian and secular. We, whoever we are, have been formed in part by strong misreadings of J. This is as it must be, but is there not value in returning to J, insofar as it can be done? The return may produce only another misreading, strong or weak, but the spirit of that misreading can be brought closer to what may have been J's own strong misreading of an archaic Jewish religion, or if not a religion, then a body of traditions and stories.

The largest assumption of nearly all writers on the Bible is that it is a theological work, as well as historical and literary. J was no theologian, and rather deliberately not a historian. To call J the composer of a national epic also seems to me misleading. Genre is an inoperative category when the strongest of authors are involved. Is Shakespeare's *Troilus and Cressida*[5] a comedy or a tragedy, or is it an ancient history play, or a satirical romance of chivalry? All and none. The Book of J fits no genre, though it established whatever genre the authors of the E, P, and D texts sought to follow. J tells stories, portrays theomorphic men and women, links myth to history, and implicitly utters the greatest of moral prophecies to post-Solomonic Judah and Israel. Yet J is something other than a storyteller, a creator of personalities (human and divine), a national historian and prophet, or even an ancestor of the moral fictions of Wordsworth, George Eliot,[6] and Tolstoy. There is always the other side of J: uncanny, tricky, sublime, ironic, a visionary of incommensurates, and so the direct ancestor of Kafka,[7] and of any writer, Jewish or Gentile, condemned to work in Kafka's mode. This other side of J will receive the largest share of my exegesis, because it is this antithetical element that all normative traditions—Judaic, Christian, Islamic, secular—have been unable to assimilate, and so have ignored, or repressed, or evaded.

Many contemporary literary critics of the highest distinction have turned their labors of cognition and description upon the Bible, but almost without

1. Exodus 4.24.
2. Genesis 18.1–8.
3. Bloom refers to Mount Sinai, upon which Moses received the Ten Commandments.
4. This British novelist (1775–1817) wrote six novels, *Pride and Prejudice* (1813) and *Sense and Sensibility* (1811) among them.
5. Shakespeare's play *Troilus and Cressida* (c. 1601) is typically regarded as a tragedy.
6. George Eliot (1819–1880) was a British novelist.
7. Franz Kafka (1883–1924), a Prague-born Austrian writer of Jewish descent. His writings center on the problematic relationship between modernity and humanity.

exception they chose to deal not with J but with R, the triumphant Redactor, who seems to have been of the Academy of Ezra, insofar as it existed. To that diverse company of eminent readers—Northrop Frye, Frank Kermode, Robert Alter, and Geoffrey Hartman[8] among them—the Bible is the received Bible of the normative traditions. Perhaps there can be no other Bible, in which case my attempt at a literary analysis of the Book of J is bound to be a failed experiment. But Frye's Bible is the Protestant Bible, in which the Hebrew Scriptures dwindle down to that captive prize of the Gentiles, the Old Testament. Kermode, shrewdest of empiricists, reads what is available to an objective scrutiny. Alter reads a work of "composite artistry," in which the artist is the Redactor, masterfully blending his somewhat incompatible sources. Hartman, questing after some shred of the normative garment, holds on fiercely to what he can, as though revisionism at last must touch its limit. Somewhere is such a kingdom, but not in the Hebrew Bible, not here, not now. Nothing is more arbitrary than the endless misprisions of J, who has served nearly every purpose except those I believe to have been her own. The God of the Jews and the Christians, of the Muslims, of the secular scholars and critics, is not the Yahweh of J. What J portrays, with loving irony, is an archaic Judaism now largely lost to us, though to call it a Judaism at all is bound to be an error. I know of only two paths back to some acquaintance with that lost strangeness. One is the way of the Israeli scholar of Kabbalah, Moshe Idel,[9] who finds in Kabbalah not a Gnosticism[1] but the surviving elements of an archaic vision that the Gnostics parodied. The other, equally speculative, is to search the giant fragments of J's text for just those areas of fable and surmise that the normative tradition could accommodate only with unease, if at all. But by what authority can such a search be undertaken, and for what purpose? What use can it be to recover a hypothetical Book of J?

The allegorization of Homer by Alexandrian Neoplatonists[2] and their heirs led eventually to the *Commedia* of Dante, though Dante never read Homer, who was hardly available to him. To recover J is to recover a great ironist, a revealer who works through the juxtaposing of incommensurates. Though I attempt throughout *not* to allegorize J but to seek her plain sense, I am aware that such a sense is unavailable to me. Presumably it was available to her contemporaries, so that we can find some clues to it in 2 Samuel, but it was lost forever by the time of the Deuteronomists, the Priestly Author, and the Redactor. Those who came after the Redactor read the Redactor, and explained away whatever of J could not be passed over in rabbinical silence. If J can be recovered, it must be by a reading that is partly outside every normative tradition whatsoever, or if inevitably inside, however unwillingly, then inside with a considerable difference. What matters most about J is what is sublime or uncanny, which can be recovered only by a criticism alert to the vagaries of the Sublime. But that returns us to the center of reading

8. Prominent literary critics of the twentieth century who have also written extensively about the Bible. "Academy of Ezra": an ironic reference to the devotees of poet Ezra Pound (1885–1972).

9. A contemporary scholar of Hasidism. "Kabbalah": the texts of Jewish mysticism.

1. Gnosticism, which means "knowing," as opposed to "believing," taught that knowledge, rather than mere faith, is the key to salvation.

2. In the third century, and originating in Alexandria, Neoplatonists combined Plato's ideas with oriental mysticism in order to construct a philosophical and religious system that strongly advocated a return to God through reason.

J: what are we to do about J's Yahweh, the uncanniest of all Western metaphors?

Jews, Christians, Muslims, and secularists fortunately are now less touchy about God than Jews are about Moses, Christians about Jesus, Muslims about Muhammad, and secularists about the idol they call Objectivity. Yahweh is less a personal possession, even for fundamentalist American Protestants, than Jesus is, and no one, in any case, is going to be tempted to make a film called *The Last Temptation of Yahweh*,[3] or to write novels in which Yahweh appears as a travestied character. Safely transcendentalized, the Yahweh of normative tradition has become a kind of gaseous vapor, fit only for representation through the resources of science fiction. J's Yahweh is quite another story, an imp who behaves sometimes as though he is rebelling against his Jewish mother, J. Like J herself, we ought always to be prepared to be surprised by him, which is the only way we can avoid being surprised.

No one in the West can now hope to read the Bible without having been conditioned by it, or by the various misreadings it has engendered. Throughout my commentary on the Book of J, I have tried to keep in mind certain observations by Ralph Waldo Emerson,[4] founder of the American Religion, which is post-Christian yet somehow also Protestant, or shall we say Protestant-Gnostic. Emerson, properly wary of those who convert the Bible into an idol, warned against mistaking the figure for the figuration of Jesus Christ, in a great sentence of "The Divinity School Address": "The idioms of his language and the figures of his rhetoric have usurped the place of his truth; and churches are not built on his principles, but on his tropes." Much the same can be said of Moses, or of Freud, or of many another founder. In two journal entries Emerson beautifully caught the double edge of what is now even more problematic about the Bible. In 1839 he wrote, "People imagine that the place which the Bible holds in the world, it owes to miracles. It owes it simply to the fact that it came out of a profounder depth of thought than any other book." And yet in 1865 the American sage remarked that "the Bible wears black cloth. It comes with a certain official claim against which the mind revolts." The two statements retain their force, and help define my own project for me. J's cognitive power is unmatched among Western writers until Shakespeare, yet J, converted to the official uses of the rabbis, priests, ministers, and their scholarly servants, is made to wear black cloth, hardly appropriate garb for that ironic and sophisticated lady (or enigmatic gentleman, if you would have it so).

I am aware that it may be vain labor, up Sinai all the way, as it were, to seek a reversal of twenty-five hundred years of institutionalized misreading, a misreading central to Western culture and society. Yet the Book of J, though fragmentary, is hardly Mr. David Rosenberg's[5] creation or my own. All I have done is to remove the Book of J from its context in the Redactor's Torah and then to read what remains, which is the best and most profound writing in the Hebrew Bible. What emerges is an author not so much lost as

3. Another allusion to the movie *The Last Temptation of Christ*.

4. Emerson (1803–1882), an American lecturer, poet, essayist, was a leading proponent of transcendentalism and is often considered a leading spokesman for Unitarianism, which Bloom here refers to as the "American Religion."

5. Rosenberg, Bloom's coauthor, translated *The Book of J* into English.

barricaded from us by normative moralists and theologians, who had and have designs upon us that are altogether incompatible with J's vision.

1990

E. L. DOCTOROW
b. 1931

Critically acclaimed author E. L. Doctorow writes historical novels that blur the line between truth and fiction. A student of philosophy and a child of the 1930s, the radical Left, and socialist doctrine, Doctorow's subject matter reflects the place and time in which he grew up—a culturally dense New York City in the first part of the twentieth century. In this setting, many of Doctorow's novels find their home.

Using fictionalized accounts of the lives of well-known historical figures, Doctorow recasts American history, creating through the body of his work a literary world that illuminates what he calls "one of the most personal relationships" in the twentieth century: that of the person and the state. By melding history and fiction, Doctorow succeeds in exploring that relationship, most dramatically in *The Book of Daniel* (1971), a fictionalized retelling of the execution of Ethel and Julius Rosenberg, a Jewish couple electrocuted in 1953 for allegedly giving state secrets to the Russians. *The Book of Daniel* explores the biblical and national themes of alienation, taking as much from the Old Testament as it does from modern American history. As Daniel struggles to understand the political unrest of the 1960s, the decade in which he lives, he also tries to connect its version of leftist ideology to the radicalism of his parents. He discovers that even during his own turbulent decade, no activist appreciates his parents' sacrifice. As a result, the reader sees the 1950s and 1960s linked in Doctorow's striking perception that each of these decades contained its share of hypocrisy, blindness, and conformity.

Doctorow labels himself a novelist first and only secondarily a "political novelist." An aversion to large political schemes deters him from adopting such a moniker. As he points out, all schemes, political or not, seem to be vulnerable to "human venery, greed, and insanity." Therefore, although his fiction easily demonstrates a passion for justice, it does so without programmatic recommendations. Rather, his passion for justice and judicial clarity inform of his fiction.

Doctorow's most popular novel, *Ragtime* (1975), which was also made into a film and a successful Broadway musical, prominently features the Jewish immigrant Tateh, who eventually moves to California and produces movies reminiscent of *Our Gang* comedies. In this novel also appear Evelyn Nesbitt, Stanford White, Booker T. Washington, Harry Houdini, and Emma Goldman. Doctorow states, "I was also in touch with, what turned out to be, although I couldn't realize it at the time, the last vestiges of Jewish immigrant culture. Those vestiges were in my grandparents, and to a lesser extent in my parents, who were born here. But it was enough for me to pick up on that wonderful sort of beautiful trade-union spirit of the early twentieth century—the expectation that this was a country where you could work out some justice for yourself and everyone else in your situation if you worked at it. So I was lucky in that sense. I was nourished by that Jewish humanist, not terribly religious, spirituality."

In *Heist*, the story printed below, Doctorow examines the costs and benefits of spirituality on the human soul. A down-and-out minister and a young, robust rabbi attempt to unravel the significance of a stolen crucifix that has been left on the roof of the rabbi's new synagogue of "evolutionary Judaism." *Heist* takes place in the New York City of the 1990s. Full of crime, crack addicts, unhelpful policemen, and Caribbean nannies, the story asks in what form we can continue to practice religion—whether it is Judaism or Christianity.

Doctorow grew up in New York City and was educated at Kenyon College and Columbia University. He has written nine novels and has earned the PEN/Faulkner Award for fiction, the National Book Critics Circle Arts and Letters Award, and the National Book Award. Doctorow teaches creative writing at New York University.

Heist

Sunday afternoon. A peddler in a purple chorister's robe selling watches in Battery Park.[1] Fellow with dreadlocks, a sweet smile, sacral presence. Doing well.

Rock doves[2] everywhere aswoop, the grit of the city in their wings. And the glare of the oil-slicked bay, and a warm-throated autumn breeze like a woman blowing in my ears.

At my back, the financial skyline of lower Manhattan sunlit into an islanded cathedral, a religioplex.

And here's the ferry from Ellis Island.[3] Listing to starboard, her three decks jammed to the rails. Sideswipes bulkhead for contemptuous New York landing. Oof. Pilings groan, crack like gunfire. Man on the promenade breaks into a run. How can I be lonely in this city?

Tourists stampeding down the gangplank. Cameras, camcorders, and stupefied children slung from their shoulders. Sun hats and baseball caps insouciant this morning, now their serious, unfortunate fashion.

Lord, there is something so exhausted about the New York waterfront, as if the smell of the sea were oil, as if boats were buses, as if all Heaven were a garage hung with girlie calendars, the months to come already leafed and fingered in black grease.

But I went back to the peddler in the choir robe and said I liked the look. Told him I'd give him a dollar if he'd let me see the label. The smile dissolves.

You crazy, mon?

I was in my mufti grunge—jeans, leather jacket over plaid shirt over T-shirt. Not even cruciform I.D. to flash at him.

Lifts his tray of watches out of reach: Get away, you got no business wit me. Looking left and right as he says it.

And then later on my walk, at Astor Place, where they lay their goods on plastic shower curtains on the sidewalk: three of the sacristy's purple choir robes neatly folded and stacked between a "Best of the Highwaymen"[4] LP and the autobiography of George Sanders.[5] I picked one and turned back the

1. A park and major ferry slip on the southern tip of Manhattan. It is crowded with tourists departing for or coming back from the Statue of Liberty and Ellis Island as well as with commuters to and from Staten Island.
2. Pigeons.
3. The historic point of entry for immigrants to the United States, now a tourist site.
4. A country band of the mid-1980s and 1990s featuring Willie Nelson, Waylon Jennings, Kris Kristofferson, and Johnny Cash.
5. British-born (1906–1972) motion-picture actor, known for his suaveness and facade of ennui.

neck, and there was the label, Churchpew Crafts, and the laundry mark from Mr. Chung. The peddler, a solemn young mestizo[6] with that bowl of black hair they have, wanted ten dollars each. I thought that was reasonable.

They come over from Senegal, or up from the Caribbean, or from Lima, San Salvador, Oaxaca, and find a piece of sidewalk and go to work. The world's poor lapping our shores, like the rising of the global-warmed sea. I remember how, on the way to Machu Picchu,[7] I stopped in the town of Cuzco[8] and watched the dances and listened to the street bands. I was told when I found my camera missing that I could buy it back the next morning in the market street behind the cathedral. Sure enough, next morning there were the women of Cuzco, in their woven ponchos of red and ochre, braids depending from their black derbies, broad Olmec[9] heads smiling shyly. They were fencing the stuff. Merciful heavens, I was pissed. But, surrounded by Anglos ransacking the stalls as if searching for their lost dead, how, my Lord Jesus, could I not accept the justice of the situation?

As I did at Astor Place in the shadow of the great, mansarded, brownstone-voluminous Cooper Union[1] people's college with the birds flying up from the square.

A block east, on St. Mark's, a thrift shop had the altar candlesticks that were heisted along with the robes. Twenty-five dollars the pair. While I was at it, I bought half a dozen used paperback detective novels. To learn the trade.

I'm lying, Lord, I just read the damn things when I'm depressed. The paperback detective never fails me. His rod and his gaff,[2] they comfort me. Sure, a life is lost here and there, but the paperback's world is ordered, circumscribed, dependable in its punishments. More than I can say for Yours.

I know You are on this screen with me. If Thos. Pemberton, D.D.,[3] is losing his life, he's losing it here, to his watchful God. Not just over my shoulder do I presumptively locate You, or in the Anglican starch of my collar, or in the rectory walls, or in the coolness of the chapel stone that frames the door, but in the blinking cursor . . .

Tuesday eve. Up to Lenox Hill[4] to see my terminal: ambulances backing into the emergency bay with their beepings and blinding strobe lights. They used to have "Quiet" signs around hospitals. Doctors' cars double-parked, patients strapped on gurneys double-parked on the sidewalk, smart young Upper East Side workforce pouring out of the subway walking past not looking. Looking.

It gets dark earlier now. Lights coming on in the apartment buildings. If only I was rising to a smart one-bedroom. A lithe young woman home from her interesting job, listening for my ring. Uncorking the wine, humming, wearing no underwear.

In the lobby, a stoic crowd primed for visiting hours with bags and bundles

6. A person of mixed European and Native American ancestry.
7. A site in Peru of ancient Incan ruins.
8. A Peruvian city. Once known as the "City of the Sun," it was the capital of the Incan Empire.
9. A Mesoamerican civilization of ca. 1000–400 B.C.E. along the southern Gulf of Mexico.
1. An art, architecture, and engineering college near Union Square.
2. An ironic misquotation of Psalm 23.4 ("Your rod and Your staff—they comfort me").
3. Doctor of Divinity.
4. I.e., Lenox Hill Hospital.

and infants squirming in laps. And that profession of the plague of our time, the security guard, in various indolent versions.

My terminal's room door slapped with a "Restricted Area" warning. I push in, all smiles.

You got medicine, Father? You gonna make me well? Then get the fuck outta here. The fuck out, I don't need your bullshit.

Enormous eyes all that's left of him. An arm bone aims the remote like a gun, and there in the hanging set the smiling girl spins the big wheel.

My comforting pastoral visit concluded, I pass down the hall, where several neatly dressed black people wait outside a private room. They hold gifts in their arms. I smell non-hospital things. A whiff of fruit pie still hot from the oven. Soups. Simmering roasts. I stand on tip-toe. Who is that? Through the flowers, like a Gauguin,[5] a handsome, light-complected black woman sitting up in bed. Turbaned. Regal. I don't hear the words, but her melodious, deep voice of prayer knows whereof it speaks. The men with their hats in their hands and their heads bowed. The women with white kerchiefs. On the way out I inquire of the floor nurse.

S.R.O.[6] twice a day, she says. We get all of Zion[7] up here. The only good thing, since Sister checked in I don't have to shop for supper. Yesterday I brought home baked pork chops. You wouldn't believe how good they were.

Another one having trouble with my bullshit—the widow code-name Moira. In her new duplex that looks across the river to the Pepsi-Cola sign she's been reading Pagels[8] on early Christianity.

It was all politics, wasn't it? she asks me.

Yes, I sez to her.

And so whoever won, that's why we have what we have now?

Well, with a nod at the Reformation,[9] I suppose, yes.

She lies back on the pillows. So it's all made up, it's an invention?

Yes, I sez, taking her in my arms. And you know for the longest time it actually worked.

Used to try to make her laugh at the dances at Spence.[1] Couldn't then, can't now. A gifted melancholic, Moira. The lost husband an add-on.

But she was one of the few in the old crowd who didn't think I was throwing my life away.

Wavy thick brown hair parted in the middle. Glimmering dark eyes, set a bit too wide. Figure not current, lacking tone, Glory to God in the highest.

From the corner of her full-lipped mouth her tongue emerges and licks away a teardrop.

And then, Jesus, the surprising condolence of her wet salted kiss.

For the sermon:

Open with that scene in the hospital, those good and righteous folk praying at the bedside of their minister. The humility of those people, their faith

5. French artist Paul Gauguin (1848–1902), famous for his colorful paintings of Tahiti and its natives.

6. Standing room only.

7. I.e., the entire congregation.

8. One of the few theologians read by both academics and the general public, Pagels (b. 1943) is best known for her accessible readings of early Christian texts.

9. The 16th-century movement against the Catholic Church that led to the establishment of Protestantism.

1. An elite private preparatory school in Manhattan.

glowing like light around them, put me in such longing . . . to share their innocence.

But then I asked myself: Why must faith rely on innocence? Must it be blind? Why must it come of people's *need* to believe?

We are all of us so pitiful in our desire to be unburdened, we will embrace Christianity's rule or any other claim of God's authority for that matter. God's authority, is a powerful claim and reduces us all, wherever we are in the world, whatever our tradition, to beggarly gratitude.

So where is the truth to be found? Who are the elect blessedly walking the true path to Salvation . . . and who are the misguided others? Can we tell? Do we know? We think we know—of course we think we know. We have our belief. But how do we distinguish our truth from another's falsity, we of the true faith, except by the story we cherish? Our story of God. But, my friends, I ask you: Is God a story? Can we, each of us examining our faith—I mean its pure center, not its comforts, not its habits, not its ritual sacraments—can we believe anymore in the heart of our faith that God is our story of Him? What, for instance, has the industrialized carnage, the continentally engineered terrorist slaughter of the Holocaust done to our story? Do we dare ask? What mortification, what ritual, what practice would have been a commensurate Christian response to the Holocaust? Something to assure us of the truth of our story? Something as earthshaking in its way as Auschwitz and Dachau[2]—a mass exile, perhaps? A lifelong commitment of millions of Christians to wandering, derelict, over the world? A clearing out of the lands and cities a thousand miles in every direction from each and every death camp? I don't know what it would be—but I know I'd recognize it if I saw it. If we go on with our story, blindly, after something like that, is it not merely innocent but also foolish, and possibly a defamation, a profound impiety? To presume to contain God in this unknowing story of ours, to hold Him, circumscribe Him, the author of everything we can conceive and everything we cannot conceive . . . in *our* story of *Him? Of Her? Of whom?* What in the name of our faith—what in God's name!—do we think we are talking about!

Wednesday lunch.

Well, Father, I hear you delivered yourself of another doozy.

How do you get your information, Charley. My little deacon, maybe, or my Kapellmeister?[3]

Be serious.

No, really, unless you've got the altar bugged. Because, God knows, there's nobody but us chickens. Give me an uptown parish, why don't you, where the subway doesn't shake the rafters. Give me one of God's midtown showplaces of the pious rich and famous, and I'll show you what doozy means.

Now, listen, Pem, he says. This is unseemly. You are doing and saying things that are . . . ecclesiastically worrying.

He frowns at his grilled fish as if wondering what it's doing there. His well-chosen Pinot Grigio[4] shamelessly neglected as he sips ice water.

Tell me what I should be talking about, Charley. My five parishioners are

2. Concentration camps in World War II.
3. Musical director (German).
4. A light, dry Italian white wine made from Pinot Gris grapes.

serious people. I mean, is this only a problem for Jewish theology? Mormon? Swedenborgian?[5]

There's a place for doubt. And it's not the altar of St. Timothy's.

Funny you should say that. Doubt is my next week's sermon: the idea is that in our time it is no more likely that a religious person will live a moral life than that an irreligious person will. What do you think?

A tone has crept in, a pride of intellect, something is not right—

And it may be that we guardians of the sacred texts are in spirit less God-fearing than the average secular individual in a modern industrial democracy who has quietly accepted the ethical teachings and installed them in himself and or herself.

Lays the knife and fork down, composes his thoughts: You've always been your own man, Pem, and in the past I've had a sneaking admiration for the freedom you've found within church discipline. We all have. And in a sense you've paid for it, we both know that. In terms of talent and brains, the way you burned up Yale, you probably should have been my bishop. But in another sense it is harder to do what I do, be the authority that your kind is always testing.

My kind?

Please think about this. The file is getting awfully thick. You are headed for an examination, a Presentment.[6] Is that what you want?

His blue eyes look disarmingly into mine. Boyish shock of hair, now gray, falling over the forehead. Then his famous smile flashes over his face and instantly fades, having been the grimace of distraction of an administrative mind.

What I know of such things, Pem, I know well. Self-destruction is not one act, or even one kind of act. It is the whole man coming apart in every direction, all three hundred and sixty degrees.

Amen to that, Charley. You don't suppose there's time for a double espresso?

All right, that wise old dog Tillich[7]—Paulus Tillichus—how does he construe the sermon? Picks a text and worries the hell out of it. Sniffs at the words, paws them: what, when you get right down to it, is a *demon*? You say you want to be *saved*? But what does that mean? When you pray for *eternal life*, what do you think you're asking for? Paulus, God's philologist, this Merriam-Webster[8] of the D.D.s, this German . . . shepherd. I loved him. The suspense he held us in—teetering on the edge of secularism, arms waving wildly. Of course, he saved us every time, pulled back from the abyss, and we were O.K. after all, back with Jesus. Until the next sermon, the next lesson. Because if God is to live, the words of faith must be renewed. The words must be reborn.

Oh, did we flock to him. Enrollments soared.

But that was then and this is now.

5. Emanuel Swedenborg (1688–1772) was a Swedish scientist and Christian mystic who inspired a "new church" based on a psychical and spiritual interpretations of the Scriptures.

6. The act of presenting a clergyman to a church authority.

7. Paul Tillich (1886–1965), who was born in Prussia and raised in Germany, and who became a U.S. citizen, was a Protestant theologian and philosopher who reached a popular audience with his mixture of existential and Christian philosophies.

8. A reference to a well-known American dictionary.

We're back in Christendom, Paulus. People are born again, not words. You can see it on television.

Friday morning. Following his intuition, Divinity Detective wandered over to the restaurant-supply district on the Bowery, below Houston, where the trade is brisk in used steam tables, walk-in freezers, grills, sinks, pots, woks, and bins of cutlery. Back behind the Taipei Trading Company was the antique gas-operated fridge too recently acquired to have a sales tag, with the mark of my shoe sole still on the door where I kicked it when it wouldn't stay closed. And in one of the bins of the used-dish department the tea things from our pantry, white with a green trim, gift from the dear departed Ladies' Auxiliary.

Practically named my own price, Lord. With free delivery. A steal.

Evening. I walk over to Tompkins Square, find my friend on his bench.

This has got to stop, I say to him.

My, you riled up.

Wouldn't you be?

Not like the Pops I know.

I thought we had an understanding. I thought there was mutual respect.

They is. Have a seat.

Sparrows working the benches in the dusk.

Told you wastin' your time, but I ast aroun like I said I would. No one here hittin' on Tim's.

Not from here?

Thasit.

How can you be sure?

This regulated territory.

Regulated! That's funny.

Now who's not showin' respeck. This my parish we talkin' bout. Church of the Sweet Vision. They lean on me, see what I'm sayin'? I am known for my compassion. You dealin' with foreigners or some such, thas my word to you.

Ah, hell. I suppose you're right.

No problem. Unsnaps attaché case: Here, my very own personal blend. No charge. Relax yoursel.

Thanks.

Toke of my affection.

Monday night, a new tack. I waited in the balcony with my BearScare six-volt Superbeam. If something stirred, I'd just press the button and my Superbeam would hit the altar at a hundred and eighty-six thousand miles per second—same cruising speed as the finger of God.

The amber crime-preventing lights on the block make a perfect indoor crime site of my church. Intimations of a kind of tarnished air in the vaulted spaces. The stained-glass figures yellowed into lurid obsolescence. How many years has this church been home to me? But all I had to do was sit up in the back for a few hours to understand the truth of its stolid indifference. How an oak pew creaks. How a passing police siren in its two Doppler pitches is like a crisis being filed away in the stone walls.

And then, Lord, I confess, I dozed. Father Brown would never have done that. But there was this crash, as if a waiter had dropped a whole load of dishes. That brought me up smartly. Wait a minute, I thought, churches don't have waiters—they're hitting the pantry again! I had figured them for the altar. I raced my bulk down the stairs, my Superbeam held aloft like a club. "Cry God for Tommy, England, and St. Tim!" How long had I been asleep? I stood in the doorway, found the light switch, and, when you do that, for an instant the only working sense is the sense of smell: hashish in that empty pantry. Male body odor. But also the pungent sanguinary scent of female hormone. And something else, something else. Like lipstick, or lollipop.

The dish cabinets—some of the panes shattered, broken cups and saucers on the floor, a cup still rocking.

A whiff of cool air. They'd gone out the alley door. An ungainly something moving out there. A deep metallic *bong* sounds up through my heels. Someone curses. It is me, fumbling with the damn searchlight. I swing the beam out and see a shadow rising with distinction, something with right angles in the vanished instant of the turned corner.

I ran back into the church and let my little light shine. Behind the altar where the big brass cross should have been was a shadow of your crucifix, Lord, in the unfaded paint of my predecessor's poor taste.

What the real detective said: Take my word for it, padre. I been in this precinct ten years. They'll hit a synagogue for the whatchamacallit, the Torah. Because it's handwritten, not a mass-produced item. It'll bring, a minimum, five K. Whereas the book value for your cross has got to be zilch. Nada. No disrespect, we're practically related, I'm Catholic, go to Mass, but on the street there is no way it is anything but scrap metal. Jesus! Whata buncha sickos.

Mistake talking to the *Times*. Such a sympathetic young man. I didn't understand anything till they took the cross, I told him. I thought they were just crackheads looking for a few dollars. Maybe they didn't understand it themselves. Am I angry? No. I'm used to this, I am used to being robbed. When the diocese took away my food-for-the-homeless program and merged it with one across town, I lost most of my parishioners. That was a big-time heist. So even before this happened I was tapped out. These people, whoever they are, have lifted our cross. It bothered me at first. But on further reflection maybe Christ goes where He is needed.

Phone ringing off the hook. I'm getting my very own Presentment. But also pledges of support, checks rolling in. Including some of the old crowd, pals now of my dear wife, who had thought my vocabulary quaint, like a performance of Mozart[9] on period instruments. Tommy Pemberton will scrape a few pieties for us on his viola da gamba.[1] I count nine hundred and change here. Have I stumbled on a new scam? I tell you, Lord, these people just don't get it. What am I supposed to do, put up a fence? Electrify it?

9. Wolfgang Amadeus Mozart (1756–1791), composer and musician of the Enlightenment who is commonly thought of as one of the greatest musical figures of the Western world.

1. The bass member of the viol family, having the range of today's cello; popular in Europe from the 15th through the 17th century.

The TV newspeople swarming all over. Banging on my door. Mayday, Mayday! I will raise the sash behind this desk, drop nimbly to the rubbled lot, pass under the window of Ecstatic Reps, where the lady with the big hocks is doing the treadmill, and I'm gone. Thanks heaps, Metro section.[2]

Trish giving a dinner when I got here. The caterer's man who let me in thought I was a latecomer. Now that I think about it, I was looking straight ahead as I passed the dining room, a millisecond, right? Yet I saw everything: which silver, the floral centerpiece. She's doing the veal-paillard dinner. Château Latour in the Steuben decanters.[3] Oh, what a waste. Two of the hopefuls present, the French U.N. diplomat, the boy-genius mutual-fund manager. Odds on the Frenchman. The others all extras. Amazing the noise ten people can make around a table. And, in this same millisecond of candlelight, Trish's glance over the rim of the wineglass raised to her lips, those cheekbones, the blue amused eyes, the frosted coif. That fraction of an instant of my passage in the doorway was all she needed from the far end of the table to see what she had to see of me, to understand, to know why I'd slunk home. But isn't it terrible that after it's over between us the synapses continue firing coördinately? What do You have to say about that, Lord? All the problems we have with You, we haven't even gotten around to your small-time perversities. I mean when an instant is still the capacious, hoppingly alive carrier of all our intelligence. And it's the same damn dumb biology when, however moved I am by another woman, the tips of my fingers are recording that she isn't Trish.

But the dining room was the least of it. It's a long walk down the hall to the guest room when the girls are home for the weekend.

We are on battery pack, Lord, I forgot the A.C. gizmo. And I am exhausted—forgive me.

Off the scanner:

dear father if u want to now where yor cross luk in 7531 w 168 street apt 2A where the santeria oombalah father casts the sea shels an scarifises chickns.

Sure.

Dear Mr. Pemberton, We are two missionaries of the church of Jesus Christ of Latter-day Saints (Mormon) assigned to the Lower Eastside of New York . . .

Nuffuvthat.

Dear Father, We have read of your troubles with those aliens who presume to desecrate the Christian church and smirch the Living God. Lest you despair, I am one of a group in nearby New Jersey who have dedicated ourselves to defending the Republic and the Sacred name of Jesus from interlopers wherever they may arise, even if from the federal government. And I mean defend—with skill, and organizational knowhow and the only thing these people understand, The Gun that is our prerogative to hold as free white Americans . . .

Right on.

2. The local section of the *New York Times*.
3. Steuben creates the highest-quality American crystal. "Château Latour": a very fine, expensive French red bordeaux.

O.k., action to report.

Yesterday, Monday, I get a message on the machine from a Rabbi Joshua Gruen, of the Synagogue of Evolutionary Judaism, on West Ninety-eighth: it is in my interest that we meet as soon as possible. Hmm. Clearly not one of the kooks. I call back. Cordial, but will answer no questions over the phone. So O.K., this is what detectives do, Lord, they investigate. Sounded a serious young man, one religioso to another—mufti or collar? I go for the collar.

The synagogue a brownstone between West End and Riverside Drive. A steep flight of granite steps to the front door. I deduce that Evolutionary Judaism includes aerobics. Confirmed when I am admitted. Joshua (my new friend) a trim five-nine in sweatshirt, jeans, running shoes. Gives me a firm handshake. Maybe thirty-two, thirty-four, good chin, well-curved forehead. A knitted yarmulke riding the top of his wavy black hair.

Shows me his synagogue: a converted parlor cum living room with an ark at one end, a platform table to read the Torah on, shelves with prayer books, and a few rows of bridge chairs, and that's it.

Second floor, introduces me to his wife, who puts her caller on hold, stands up from her desk to shake hands, she, too, a rabbi, Sarah Blumenthal, in blouse and slacks, pretty smile, high cheekbones, no cosmetics, needs none, light hair short, au courant cut, granny specs, Lord my heart. She is one of the assistant rabbis at Temple Emanu-El. What if Trish went for her D.D., wore the collar, celebrated the Eucharist with me? O.K., laugh, but it's not funny when I think about it, not funny at all.

Third floor, I meet the children, boys two and four, in their native habitat of primary-color wall boxes filled with stuffed animals. They cling to the flanks of their dark Guatemalan nanny, who is also introduced like a member of the family . . .

On the back wall of the third-floor landing is an iron ladder. Joshua Gruen ascends, opens a trapdoor, climbs out. A moment later his head appears against the blue sky. He beckons me upward, poor winded Pem so stress-tested and entranced . . . so determined to make it look effortless I can think of nothing else.

I stand finally on the flat roof, the old apartment houses of West End Avenue and Riverside Drive looming at either end of this block of chimneyed brownstone roofs, and try to catch my breath while smiling at the same time. The autumn sun behind the apartment houses, the late-afternoon river breeze on my face. I'm feeling the exhilaration and slight vertigo of roof-standing . . . and don't begin to think—until snapped to attention by the Rabbi's puzzled, frankly inquiring gaze that asks why do I think he's brought me here—why he's brought me here. His hands in his pockets, he points with his chin to the Ninety-eighth Street frontage, where, lying flat on the black tarred roof, its transverse exactly parallel to the front of the building, its upright pressed against the granite pediment, the eight-foot hollow brass cross of St. Timothy's, Episcopal, lies tarnished and shining in the autumn sun.

I suppose I knew I'd found it from the moment I heard the Rabbi's voice on the answering machine. I bend down for a closer look. There are the old nicks and dents. Some new ones, too. It's not all of a piece, which I hadn't known: the arms are bolted to the upright in a kind of mortise-and-tenon[4] idea. I lift it at the foot. It is not that heavy but clearly too much cross to bear on the stations of the I.R.T.

I'd been just about convinced it was, in fact, a new sect of some kind. You do let this happen, Lord, ideas of You bud with the profligacy of viruses. I thought, Well, I'll keep a vigil from across the street, watch them take my church apart brick by brick. Maybe I'll help them. They'll reassemble it somewhere as a folk church of some kind. A bizarre expression of their simple faith. Maybe I'll drop in, listen to the sermon now and then. Learn something . . .

Then my other idea, admittedly paranoid: it would end up as an installation in SoHo.[5] Some crazy artist—let me wait a few months, a year, and I'd look in a gallery window and see it there, duly embellished, a statement. People standing there drinking white wine. So that was the secular version. I thought I had all bases covered. I am shaken.

How did Rabbi Joshua Gruen know it was there?

An anonymous phone call. A man's voice. Hello, Rabbi Gruen? Your roof is burning.

The roof was burning?

If the children had been in the house I would have gotten them out and called the fire department. As it was, I grabbed our kitchen extinguisher and up I came. Not the smartest thing. Of course, the roof was not burning. But, modest as it is, this is a synagogue. A place for prayer and study. And, as you see, a Jewish family occupies the upper floors. So was he wrong, the caller?

He bites his lip, dark-brown eyes looking me in the eye. It is an execrable symbol to him. Burning its brand on his synagogue. Burning down, floor through floor, like the template of a Christian church. I want to tell him I'm on the Committee for Ecumenical Theology of the Trans-Religious Fellowship. A member of the National Conference of Christians and Jews.

This is deplorable. I am really sorry about this.

It's hardly your fault.

I know, I say. But this city is getting weirder by the minute.

The rabbis offer me a cup of coffee.

We sit in the kitchen. I feel quite close to them, both our houses of worship desecrated, the entire Judeo-Christian heritage trashed.

This gang's been preying on me for months. And for what they've gotten for their effort, I mean one hit on a dry cleaner would have done as much. Listen, Rabbi—

Joshua.

Joshua. Do you read detective stories?

He clears his throat, blushes.

Only all the time, Sarah Blumenthal says, smiling at him.

Well, let's put our minds together. We've got two mysteries going here.

Why two?

This gang. I can't believe their intent was, ultimately, to commit an anti-Semitic act. They have no intent. They lack sense. They're like overgrown

4. Two pieces of building material that are repeatedly cut in a dovetail pattern so as to lock into one another, creating a joint.

5. An abbreviation for "south of Houston" Street, an area in lower Manhattan.

children. They're not of this world. And all the way from the Lower East Side to the Upper West Side? No, that's asking too much of them.

So this is someone else?

It must be. A good two weeks went by. Somebody took the cross off their hands—if they didn't happen to find it in a Dumpster. I mean, the police told me it had no value, but if someone wants it it has value, right? And then this second one or more persons had the intent. But how did they get it onto the roof? And nobody saw them, nobody heard them?

I was on the case now, asking questions, my nostrils flaring. I was enjoying myself. Good Lord, Lord, should I have been a detective? Was that my true calling?

Angelina, whom I think you met with the children: she heard noises from the roof one morning. We were already gone. That was the day I went to see my father, Sarah says, looking to Joshua for confirmation.

And I'd gone running, Joshua says.

But the noise didn't last long and Angelina thought no more of it—thought that it was a repairman of some sort. I assume they came up through one of the houses on the block. The roofs abut.

Did you go down the block? Did you ring bells?

Joshua shook his head.

What about the cops?

They exchanged glances. Please, says Joshua. The congregation is new, just getting its legs. We're trying to make something viable for today—theologically, communally. A dozen or so families, just a beginning. A green shoot. The last thing we want is for this to get out. We don't need that kind of publicity. Besides, he says, that's what they want, whoever did this.

We don't accept the I.D. of victim, says Sarah Blumenthal, looking me in the eye.

And now I tell You, Lord, as I sit here back in my own study, in this bare ruined choir, I am exceptionally sorry for myself this evening, lacking as I do a companion like Sarah Blumenthal. This is not lust, and You know I would admit it if it were. No, but I think how quickly I took to her, how comfortable I was made, how naturally welcomed I felt under these difficult circumstances, there is a freshness and honesty about these people, both of them, I mean, they were so present in the moment, so self-possessed, a wonderful young couple with a quietly dedicated life, such a powerful family stronghold they make, and, oh Lord, he is one lucky rabbi, Joshua Gruen, to have such a beautiful devout by his side.

It was Sarah, apparently, who made the connection. He was sitting there trying to figure out how to handle it and she had come in from a conference somewhere and when he told her what was on the roof she wondered if that was the missing crucifix she had read about in the newspaper.

I hadn't read the piece and I was skeptical.

You thought it was just too strange, a news story right in your lap, Sarah says.

That's true. News is somewhere else. And to realize that you know more than the reporter knew? But we found the article.

He won't let me throw out anything, Sarah says.

Fortunately, in this case, says the husband to the wife.

It's like living in the Library of Congress.

So, thanks to Sarah, we now have the rightful owner.

She glances at me, colors a bit. Removes her glasses, the scholar, and pinches the bridge of her nose. I see her eyes in the instant before the specs go back on. Nearsighted, like a little girl I loved in grade school.

I am extremely grateful, I say to my new friends. This is, in addition to everything else, a mitzvah[6] you've performed. Can I use your phone? I'm going to get a van up here. We can take it apart, wrap it up, and carry it right out the front door and no one will be the wiser.

I'm prepared to share the cost.

Thank you, that won't be necessary. I don't need to tell you, but my life has been hell lately. This is good coffee, but you don't happen to have something to drink, do you?

Sarah going to a wall cabinet. Will Scotch do?

Joshua, sighing, leans back in his chair. I could use something myself.

The situation now: my cross dismantled and stacked like building materials behind the altar. It won't be put back together and hung in time for Sunday worship. That's fine, I can make a sermon out of that. The shadow is there, the shadow of the cross on the apse. We will offer our prayers to God in the name of His Indelible Son, Jesus Christ. Not bad, Pem, you can still pull these things out of a hat when you want to.

What am I to make of this strange night culture of stealth sickos, these mindless thieves of the valueless giggling through the streets, carrying what? whatever it was! through the watery precincts of urban nihilism . . . their wit, their glimmering dying recognition of something that once had a significance they laughingly cannot remember. Jesus, there's not even sacrilege there. A dog stealing a bone knows more what he's up to.

A phone call just now from Joshua. If we're going to be detectives about this, we start with what we know, isn't that what you did? What I know, what I start with, is that no Jewish person would have stolen your crucifix. It would not occur to him. Even in the depths of some drug-induced confusion.

I shouldn't think so, I say, thinking, Why does Joshua feel he has to rule this out?

But as you also said something like this has no street value unless someone wants it. Then it has value.

To an already in place, raging anti-Semite, for example.

Yes, that's the likelihood. This is a mixed neighborhood. There may be people who don't like a synagogue on their block. I've not been made aware of this, but it's always possible.

Right.

But it's also possible . . . placing that cross on my roof, well, that is something that could have been arranged by an ultra-orthodox fanatic. That's possible, too.

Good God!

We have our extremists, our fundamentalists, just as you have. There are some for whom what Sarah and I are doing, struggling to redesign, revalidate

6. In the colloquial sense, a good deed.

our faith—well, in their eyes it is tantamount to apostasy. What do you think of that for a theory?

Very generous of you, Joshua. But I don't buy it, I say. I mean, I can't think that it's likely. Why would it be?

The voice that told me my roof was burning? That was a Jewish thing to say. Of course, I don't know for sure, I may be all wrong. But it's something to think about. Tell me, Father—

Tom—

Tom. You're a bit older, you've seen more, given more thought to these things. Wherever you look in the world now, God belongs to the atavists. And they're so fierce, these people, so sure of themselves—as if all human knowledge since Scripture were not also God's revelation! I mean, is time a loop? Do you have the same feeling I have—that everything seems to be running backward? That civilization is in reverse?

Oh, my dear Rabbi . . . where does that leave us? Because maybe that's what faith is. That's what faith does. Whereas I am beginning to think that to hold in abeyance and irresolution any firm conviction of God, or of an afterlife with Him, warrants walking in His Spirit, somehow.

Monday. The front doors are padlocked. In the rectory kitchen, leaning back on the two hind legs of his chair and reading *People*, is St. Timothy's newly hired, classically indolent private security guard.

I am comforted, too, by the woman at Ecstatic Reps. She is there, as usual, walking in place, earphones clamped on her head, her large hocks in their black tights shifting up and dropping back down like Sisyphean boulders.[7] As the afternoon darkens, she'll be broken up and splashed in the greens and pale lavenders of the light refractions on the window.

So everything is as it should be, the world's in its place. The wall clock ticks. I have nothing to worry about except what I'm going to say to the Bishop's examiners who will determine the course of the rest of my life.

This is what I will say for starters: "My dear colleagues, what you are here to examine today is not in the nature of a spiritual crisis. Let's get that clear. I have not broken down, cracked up, burned out, or caved in. True, my personal life is a shambles, my church is like a war ruin, and, since I am not one to seek counsel or join support groups, and God, as usual, has ignored my communications (let's be honest, Lord, not a letter, not a card), I do feel somewhat isolated. I will even admit that for the past few years, no, the past several years, I have not known what to do when in despair except walk the streets. Nevertheless, my ideas have substance, and, while you may find some of them alarming, I would entreat—would suggest, would recommend, would advise—I would advise you to confront them on their merits, and not as evidence of the psychological decline of a mind you once had some respect for. I mean, for which you once had some respect."

That's O.K. so far, isn't it, Lord? Sort of taking it to them? Maybe a bit touchy. After all, what could they have in mind? In order of probability: one,

7. In Greek mythology, King Sisyphus of Corinth was condemned to eternally roll a huge stone up a hill in Hades only to have it roll down again as it neared the top.

a warning; two, a formal reprimand; three, censure; four, a month or so in therapeutic retreat followed by a brilliantly remote reassignment wherein I'm never to be heard from again; five, early retirement with or without full benefits; six, defrocking; seven, the Big Ex. Whatthahell! By the way, Lord, what are these "ideas of substance" I've promised them in the above? The phrase came trippingly off the tongue. I trust You will enlighten me. What with today's shortened attention span I don't need ninety-five, I can get by with just one or two. The point is, whatever I say will alarm them. Nothing of a church is shakier than its doctrine. That's why they guard it with their lives. I mean, just to lay the "H" word on the table, it heresy, is a legal concept, that's all. The shock is supposed to be Yours but the affront is to sectarian legality. A heretic can be of no more concern to You than someone kicked out of a building coöperative for playing the piano after ten. . . . So I pray, Lord, don't let me come up with something worth only a reprimand. Let me have the good stuff. Speak to me. Send me an E-mail. You were once heard to speak:

You Yourself are a word, though deemed by some to be unutterable,

You are said to be The Word, and I don't doubt You are the Last Word.

You're the Lord our Narrator, who made a text from nothing, at least that is our story of You.

So here is your servant, the Reverend Dr. Thomas Pemberton, the almost no longer rector of St. Timothy's, Episcopal, addressing You in one of your own inventions, one of your intonational systems of clicks and grunts, glottal stops and trills.

Will You show him no mercy, this poor soul tormented in his nostalgia for Your Only Begotten Son? He has failed his training as a detective, having solved nothing.

May he nevertheless pursue You? God? The Mystery?

1997

JEROME ROTHENBERG
b. 1931

"A swinging orgy of Martin Buber, Marcel Duchamp, Gertrude Stein, and Sitting Bull" and "no one writing poetry today has dug deeper into the roots of poetry"—this is how poet Kenneth Rexroth describes the teacher, scholar, editor, anthologist, and widely influential member of the poetic avant-garde Jerome Rothenberg. Born in New York City and educated at the City College of New York, he published his first book of poems in 1960 and has been publishing experimental and innovative poetry since then. Between the years 1970 and 1985, Rothenberg greatly influenced the development of American poetic expression by developing "ethnopoetics," a field that explored and celebrated the literatures of diverse cultures through the lenses of translation, ethnography, anthropology, linguistics, and poetics.

Early in his career, Rothenberg began exploring alternative poetic structures, using found poetry and collage, and working on the development of experimental dialogues and narrative. He then combined these postmodern explorations with his interest in oral culture and the primitive languages of man. In his anthology *Technicians of the Sacred* (1968), he rediscovered long-abandoned sites of poetry: picture poems, dreams and visions, and the scenarios of ritual events. From there, he rapidly moved on to studying American Indian poetry, collaborating with the Seneca to translate a series of Navajo horse-blessing songs and editing *Shaking the Pumpkin: Traditional Poetry of the Indian North Americas* (1972).

In the 1970s, Rothenberg's interest in primitive and tribal poetries returned him to his own ancestral past. In three collections—*Poland/1931* (1970), *A Book of Testimony* (1971), and *Esther K. Comes to America* (1973)—Rothenberg adapts the tribal form to a Jewish sensibility and revives the Eastern European past of American Jews. This trilogy, which includes Rothenberg's most important work, examines the impact of ethnicity, religion, and time on identity formation. By furnishing verbal collages that incorporate the sacred and secular—the Bible, the Kabbalah, Yiddish folk culture—Rothenberg renders a picture of the Jewish American unconscious replete with images of Adonai and Esau, the Baal Shem and crazed Buffalo Bills.

In 1989, Rothenberg published *Khurbn and Other Poems*, a book largely dedicated to representing the Holocaust.

Rothenberg's inventive and original literary techniques have strongly influenced the development of postmodern American poetry. His reputation and stature have grown as his interests have tapped into and influenced movements in the cultural avant-garde. His ethnopoetics, in the act of digging deeply into one's own roots, perfectly captured the essence of the 1970s; his experimentation with narrative and form have also inspired the poetic avant-garde of the 1980s and 1990s.

Rothenberg has taught at a number of colleges and universities, including the City College of New York and the University of California, San Diego.

Dibbukim (Dibbiks)[1]

spirits of the dead   lights
flickering (he said) their ruakh[2]
will never leave the earth
instead they crowd the forests the fields
around the privies the hapless spirits
wait millions of souls
turned into ghosts at once
the air is full of them
they are standing each one beside a tree
under its shadows or the moon's
but they cast no shadows on their own
this moment & the next they are pretending
to be rocks   but who is fooled
who is fooled here   by the dead   the jews
the gypsies   the leadeyed polish patriot
living beings reduced to symbols
of what it had been to be alive
"o do not touch them" the mother cries

1. Spirits that enter a living person's body, controlling it until they are exorcised by a religious rite (Hebrew).
2. Soul (Hebrew).

fitful, as almost in a dream
she draws the child's hand to her heart
in terror   but the innocent dead
grow furious they break down doors
drop slime onto your tables
they tear their tongues out by the roots
& smear your lamps your children's lips
with blood a hole drilled in the wall
will not deter them
from stolen homes stone architectures
they hate they are the convoys of the dead
the ghostly drivers still searching
the roads to malkin[3]   ghost carts overturned
ghost autos in blue ditches
if only our eyes were wild enough
to see them our hearts to know their terror
the terror of the man who walks alone
their victim whose house whose skin
they crawl in   incubus & succubus
a dibbik leaping from a cow to lodge inside
his throat   clusters of jews
who swarm here mothers without hair
blackbearded fathers
they lap up fire   water   slime
entangle the hairs of brides
or mourn their clothing hovering
over a field of rags   half-rotted shoes
& tablecloths   old thermos bottles   rings
lost tribes in empty synagogues
at night their voices
carrying across the fields
to rot your kasha[4] your barley
stricken beneath their acid rains
no holocaust because no sacrifice
no sacrifice to give the lie
of meaning   & no meaning   after auschwitz
there is only poetry   no hope
no other language left to heal
no language   & no faces
because no faces left   no names
no sudden recognitions on the street
only the dead still swarming   only khurbn[5]
a dead man in a rabbi's clothes
who squats   outside the mortuary house
who guards their privies who is called
master of shit   an old alarm clock
hung around his neck   who holds
a wreath of leaves under his nose

3. Although the dictionary defines *malkin* as a servant woman, in this context Rothenberg may be referring to a city in the Ukraine.

4. Buckwheat groats.

5. Destruction; sometimes used as a synonym for the Holocaust (Hebrew and Yiddish).

from eden   "to drive out
"the stinking odor of this world"

1960

Cokboy

Part One

saddlesore I came
a jew among
the indians
vot em I doink in dis strange place[1]
mit deez pipple mit strange eyes
could be it's trouble
could be   could be
(he says) a shadow
ariseth from his buckwheat
has tomahawk in hand
shadow of an axe inside his right eye
of a fountain pen inside his left
vot em I doink here
how vass I lost tzu get here
am a hundred men
a hundred fifty different shadows
jews & gentiles
who bring the Law to Wilderness[2]
(he says) this man
is me   my grandfather
& other men-of-letters
men with letters carrying the mail
lithuanian pony-express riders
the financially crazed Buffalo Bill[3]
still riding in the lead
hours before avenging the death of Custer[4]
making the first 3-D movie of those wars
or years before it
the numbers vanishing in kabbalistic[5] time
that brings all men together
& the lonely rider
saddlesore
is me   my grandfather
& other men of letters
jews & gentiles entering

1. Throughout the poem, Rothenberg transcribes English as if spoken with a heavy Eastern European accent. "Cokboy" is the Yiddishized version of "cowboy"; "vot em I doink" is "what am I doing"; and so on.
2. As Moses received the law at Mount Sinai, so this Jew brings the Jewish law to America.
3. William "Buffalo Bill" Cody (1846–1917), an Indian scout and Western hero remembered for his Wild West shows.
4. George Armstrong Custer (1839–1876), a general who distinguished himself in the Civil War but then suffered a complete rout by American Indians in the Battle of Little Bighorn (1876), in which he died.
5. Referring to the Kabbalah, the text of Jewish mysticism.

the domain of Indian
who bring the Law to Wilderness
in gold mines & shaky stores
the fur trade heavy agriculture
ballots bullets barbers
who threaten my beard your hair
but patronize me
& will make our kind the Senator from Arizona
the champion of their Law
who hates us both
but dresses as a jew one day an indian
the next a little christian shmuck[6]
vot em I doink here
dis place is maybe crazy
has all the letters going backwards
(he says) so who can read the signboards
to the desert
who can shake his way out of the woods
ford streams the grandmothers
were living near
with snakes inside their cunts
teeth maybe
maybe chainsaws
when the Baal Shem[7] visited America
he wore a shtreiml[8]
the locals all thought he was a cowboy
maybe from Mexico
"a cokboy?"
no a cowboy
I will be more than a credit to my community
& race
but will search for my brother Esau[9] among these redmen
their nocturnal fires I will share
piss strained from my holy cock
will bear seed of Adonoi[1]
& feed them visions
I will fill full a clamshell
will pass it around from mouth to mouth
we will watch the moonrise
through each other's eyes
the distances vanishing in kabbalistic time
(he says) the old man watches
from the cliffs a city
overcome with light
the man & the city disappear
he looks & sees another city
this one is made of glass

6. Literally, a penis; colloquially, a jerk (Yiddish).
7. Literally, master of God's name (Hebrew); a title given to one who has special knowledge of the holy and who can work miracles.
8. Fur-edged hat worn on the Sabbath and holidays by rabbis and very observant Jews (Yiddish).
9. The son of Isaac and elder twin brother of Jacob, Esau allegedly stole his brother's birthright. In the Talmud, Esau is synonymous with villainy.
1. Lord (Hebrew).

inside the buildings stand
immobile statues
brown-skinned faces
catch the light
an elevator
moving up & down
in the vision of the Cuna *nele*
the vision of my grandfather
vision of the Baal Shem in America
the slaves in steerage
what have they seen in common
by what light their eyes
have opened into stars
I wouldn't know
what I was doing here
this place has all the letters going
backwards a reverse in time
towards wilderness
the old jew strains at his gaberdine
it parts for him
his spirit rushes up the mountainside
& meets an eagle
no an iggle
captain commanders dollinks delicious madmen
murderers opening the continent up to exploitation
cease & desist (he says)
let's speak (he says)
feels like a little gas down here (he says)
(can't face the mirror without crying)
& the iggle lifts him
like an elevator
to a safe place above the sunrise
there gives a song to him
the Baal Shem's song
repeated without words for centuries
"hey heya heya" but translates it
as "yuh-buh-buh-buh-buh-buh-bum"
when the Baal Shem (yuh-buh) learns to do a bundle
what does the Baal Shem (buh-buh) put into the bundle?
silk of his prayershawl-bag beneath
cover of beaverskin above
savor of esrog[2] fruit within
horn of a mountaingoat between
feather of dove around the sides
clove of a Polish garlic at its heart
he wears when traveling
in journeys through kabbalistic forests
cavalry of the Tsars[3] on every side

2. Citron, which is used during the celebration of Sukkot as a symbol of gratitude to God for the harvest. In lines 125–27 of this poem, Rothenberg mentions other superstitious practices that supposedly bring luck.

3. A reference to the army of the tsars, rulers of Russia and enemies of the Jewish people.

men with fat moustaches yellow eyes & sabers
who stalk the gentle soul
at night through the Wyoming steppes
(he says) vot em I doink here
I could not find mine het
would search the countryside on hands & knees
until behind a rock in Cody[4]
old indian steps forth
the prophecies of both join at this point
like smoke a pipe is held
between them dribbles through their lips
the keen tobacco
"cowboy?"
cokboy (says the Baal Shem)
places a walnut in his handkerchief & cracks it
on a boulder each one eats
the indian draws forth a deck of cards
& shuffles
"game?"
they play at wolves & lambs
the fire crackles in the pripitchok[5]
in a large tent somewhere in America
the story of the coming-forth begins

1960

4. A city in northwest Wyoming on the Shoshone River.

5. Small stove or hearth (Yiddish).

ALLEN GROSSMAN
b. 1932

"The purpose of poetry," says Allen Grossman in *The Sight Singer* (1992), "is to construct that additional possession which the heart requires in order to make its love effective by means of the poem's mediation of a power not inherent or intrinsic or immanent in the world." As a teacher, scholar, and poet, Grossman has inspired scores of students to go on to teach and write. His influence in the classroom and beyond stems from his inspirational lessons about the power of the written word. In his own poetry, in interviews, and in lectures, Grossman preaches with great eloquence and passion about the redemptive power of poetry.

A contemporary reader first coming to Grossman's poetry might be surprised at the formal level of its diction. Elevated in style, tone, and subject, his poetry exhibits great rhetorical flourishes and an austere formalism. These qualities combine with the mythic, or prophetic, tone to make the poems operate on a grand scale, recalling the mystical tone of Yeats and such biblical writings as the Prophets. The cadences of Grossman's poetry as well as its subject matter—large spiritual questions on life and death, the afterlife, gods and goddesses—give his work a theological cast. Yet it is the ethical commitment to the holiness of individual suffering that often makes his poetry seem religious. Gerald Stern has called Grossman "the poet of lamentations" because "he demonstrates how the loss of holiness and well-being and purpose can be translated into dramatic renderings of individual loss." *Poland of Death,* the poem excerpted here, displays the elemental themes about which Grossman is always concerned: mother, father, life, death, and the spiritual connections one makes across generations and through death.

Allen Grossman grew up in Minneapolis, was educated at Harvard and Brandeis, where he earned his Ph.D., and then taught for over thirty years. In 1989, Grossman won a MacArthur Prize. He currently teaches in the Humanities Department at Johns Hopkins University.

Poland of Death (IV)

1.

It is the duty of every man,
And woman, to write the life of the mother.
But the life of the father is written by
The father alone. —Now he is of great size
In Poland of Death, and his garment is sewn
Of superior cloth. I came upon him down
An alley of that place, sitting on a wall,
At the intersection of two walls, looking wise:
Known there as Louis of Minneapolis,
The *maître à pensée*[1] of the necropolis.
And his song was, "When the deep purple falls. . . ."

2.

As I came up, he cast me a sharp glance
And stopped short at the middle of the verse
("Sleepy garden walls . . .")—meaning, "This is
Your last chance to say something." "*Say* something!"
"How do you like my suit?" And so I say
To him, "You looked better naked and small."
And he says, "What's given here can never be
Refused, or lost. That's the rule. Take this nail!"
Then he started an old song I didn't like
At all. Something of the "matter of the race"—
At very least the long and sonorous breath

3.

Of a dark language. —O Poland of Death!
I asked a beggar-woman of the cemetery
What he sang, the young one smelling of sea
And milk who sweeps the sill. "Louis," she replies,
"Is a proud Jew now, dwelling among the dead,
A big Rabbi of rats dressed in a suit
That fits. A prince!" And then—before my eyes—
On the vapors of the universe—the head

1. Master of thought, or master thinker (French).

Of Louis hung—like Brutus, the conspirator;[2]
And its song poured back centuries of rain
From the Etruscan[3] jar of an old man's voice

4.

Into the water-wells of the abyss:
"Now I know everything," it sang, "being in
The right place! —How did I get so wise?
When I proceeded Doctor of Philosophy
Torches smoked and flamed from every tower.
(Let the flame leap up, the heart ignite and burn!)
The celebrations of commencement were elaborate,
And I was clothed then, as you see me now,
In a suit that fits, sewn of superior cloth,
Invulnerable to the rust, the moth,
And the diurnal changes of the light

5.

In the air. My boy, the truth is great."
"Louis," I cried, "soon I am going to die.
The world is nearing its end. Say something
I can understand!" So he pulled out a beret
Of reddish brown, put it on his head, and smiled
Like a prince, as the woman said, or king—
(Of grave-diggers, as it seems, or wolves or Jews).
And I heard, then, the father calling to the son
And the son responding to the father from afar,
And the daughter to the mother, and the mother
To the children—voices like falling water,

6.

Or the shadow of swans, the sigh of the swan's
  feather:
"After a thousand years the Devil will be loosed
On a day, and in the morning of that day
This Louis will ride forth in his 1950
Chevrolet of prophecy—with feet, hands,
And four on the floor (Ezekiel I).
And the Rektor of the University
The Archbishop, the Lord Mayor and the General
Of Artillery, will applaud his face
And he will meet the host in the air,
Igniting the *auto-da-fé*[4] of the sun."

7.

But all I understood, in fact, was the next phrase
On of the song he was singing as he sat

2. I.e., Marcus Brutus, Julius Caesar's friend who conspired to kill him.
3. Of or pertaining to Etruria, an ancient country in central Italy known for its highly cultured civilization. It was at its height ca. 500 B.C.
4. Literally, "act of the faith"; broadly, the burning of a heretic (Portuguese).

At the intersection (you will remember it)
Of two walls, "When the deep purple falls."
This time he got as far as the "nightingales."
Then stopped, and shouted, "This is the story
Of my life. I am the Professor now
Bigger than the Lord God. *He* was seduced
And made the world against His will—by art.
My son, I never married. I have no children.
I was smart. My father was a butcher, an empiricist

8.

Who knew the Law. (And that explains, in case
You want to *know*, why I hate cats! . . .)
When the end comes, like a dark wife at last,
It will be among the nightingales and rats
Of the necropolis, as the 'purple' falls
On Poland of Death." He turned his face, then,
And stopped his voice, never to speak again.
The Etruscan jar rang. I said to him: "Louis
I will sing you a new song." And the abyss
Supplied its word, "Halleluya!" *Praise
The Lord*. Then the beggar-woman of the cemetery

9.

Saw her chance, and gave the old man on the wall
A proper kiss. For what? For being wise,
And (after all) unmarried, and for dressing well.
Happy, happy Louis! The new song was this:
"Father, not father, *O roi magicien!*[5]
Mother, not mother, O name of Beatrice!
Does the cloth forget the weaver, does the field
Of millet in its season no longer remember the sower,
Or the birds that feed on it honor in later summer
The labor that laid it down? O Yes! And the pot
The woman's hand who made it has forgot.

10.

How much less the mind, reading and running hard,
Touches the world. (O touch me, *roi thaumaturge!*)[6]
Therefore, Louis of Minneapolis at ease upon a wall,
Sucking on a nail—the Jew in charge—
Demands a word when the deep purple falls.
What do I hear? An audible air of voices
Calling out and answering: *'Au revoir,
Ma femme chère,' 'Mon frère,' 'Ma soeur,' 'Mon père.'*[7]
What do I see? Poland of Death! Louis driven out
(The Doctor in his garment of superior cloth)
Into the field behind the wall and shot!

5. Magician king (French).
6. Miracle worker–king (French).
7. "Good-bye, My dear wife, My brother, My sister, My father" (French).

'What is the past?' 'What passes?' 'What is to come
When I have died?' . . . *What is to come?* No figure
Has it yet, no form. —Night falls in a room.
Someone in the dark is scratching with a nail:
The chronicler. Upon the road to the necropolis
Approaches always the chrome of battlecars,
Convertibles in columns like descended stars.
What is the past? —Night falls in a room. A king
Gives laws in the abyss on a drowned throne.
What passes? —The *auto-da-fé* of the sun.
What is the WORD? Halleluya. The Lord is ONE."[8]

1992

8. A reference to the Shema, the central prayer of the Jewish faith, which asserts the belief in one God.

TOVA REICH
b. 1932

Tova Reich has written three novels, all controversial and all deeply satirical, about Jewish American life, particularly the Orthodox community and how women fare within it. In her first novel, *Mara* (1978), an eighteen-year-old girl rebels against her devout but ruthless mother and father, the latter of whom is a rabbi. Her second novel, *Master of the Return* (1988), also takes aim at the ultra-Orthodox, this time through the perspective of the Hasid Shmuel Himmelhoch, an absurdly self-righteous zealot. In her third and most accomplished novel, *The Jewish War* (1995), Reich broadens her target to include the Jewish American community, Israel, and the politics of the Middle East. Telling the farcical story of Jerry Goldberg, a Bronx boy who has himself anointed king of Judea, Reich manages to skewer the Catskills, the Holocaust, and Zionism. While the satire can be laugh-out-loud funny, reviewer Rosellen Brown observes that "the author appears determined to show us what such meshugas can lead to . . . as if to remind us that this isn't mischief, folks, it's serious tragedy."

Although raised in an Orthodox Jewish home and descended from a long line of rabbis, Reich, throughout her work, shows uneasiness about the political and spiritual fate of the women of the Orthodox Jewish community. Such is the case in *The Lost Girl,* originally printed in *Harper's* (1995) and reprinted here. Told partially through the perspective of Yehiel Berman, an Orthodox rabbi and principal of a Yeshiva for adolescent girls, the story illustrates the limited choices for women in this community as well as the cruel blanket of ignorance and isolation that keeps these girls in fear of their bodies and each other. Despite the harsh treatment that Reich seems to bestow on Orthodox Jewry in this story, critic Andrew Furman points out that "Reich does not reject ultra-orthodox Judaism . . . rather she envisions its feminization."

Reich wrote the *Hers* column for the *New York Times* from 1978 to 1981 and contributes frequently to the *Washington Post* and *Harper's*. She lives in Chevy Chase, Maryland.

The Lost Girl

It was not the first time that Rabbi Yehiel Berman had had dealings with the media, but on all those previous occasions it had been what he classified as the "Anglo-Jewish press," and to them he could comment in a kind of shorthand. By them he could count on being understood. Whatever was spoken was spoken within the walls of the family compound, as it were. He would be given the benefit of the doubt, and, ultimately, if necessary, he would be forgiven. But in the matter of the lost girl, Feigie Singer, and all the publicity attendant on that mess, it was no less than the mighty *New York Times* that had approached him, and Rabbi Berman had made the grievous error of taking seriously an unquestioned fact lodged many years earlier in his consciousness and accepted by him in innocent good faith—namely, the fact that the *Times* was a Jewish organ.

So when the *Times* reporter approached him for a comment on the Singer case, he had spoken openly, as one speaks to a brother, or at the very least a cousin. Because even a cousin several times removed would understand that there are two forms of speech—one meant for the inner precincts and the other for the outside sphere. And even that cousin, however many times cut off, would recognize that it is in their mutual interest to take the words spoken within the chambers and refine them for consumption by a hostile world where the one thing you could depend on was any excuse to pounce on the Jews—"All Jews irregardless," as Rabbi Berman liked to put it, no matter how distant the cousinship. The least Rabbi Berman could have expected from that reporter, a Jewish fellow named Sean Markowitz, as a matter of fact, was to apply some basic common sense in the interest of Jewish survival. As Rabbi Berman admonished this traitor afterward, when it was already too late, when his so-called offensive remark had been spread far and wide in the newspaper without commentary or spin, in a bitter phone call at that time the rabbi had counseled Markowitz that he would do well in the future to recite the *Shema*[1] with intense fervor, to pray "Hear, O Israel" each and every time he sat down at his desk to write even a single word about the Jewish people, in order to remind himself of his awesome responsibility, his heavy burden, lest he do, as he had certainly done with the rabbi's quote, severe harm to his own tribe and, by extension, whether he acknowledged this or not, to himself.

Above all, the rabbi had sought to drum a little empathy into the uselessly educated brain of this arrogant kid. Do not judge your friend until you reach his place, the sages teach. And who, who in this world, could ever imagine what it must be like to be in Rabbi Berman's position? To be the principal of an all-girls high school, to bear the weight of molding and shaping, day in and day out, the minds and souls of three hundred girls in the most difficult ages of fourteen through eighteen, to be charged with preparing these specimens for the critical task of Jewish wifehood and motherhood, in short, for the continuation of our people—this was the hard reality that Rabbi Berman had to face, a reality quite beyond the comprehension of the Markowitzes of

1. Literally, "Hear," the first word of the opening line of the prayer after which it is named (Hebrew). The Shema is an affirmation of monotheism, and is to be recited upon first waking up and before going to sleep, and in times of stress or crisis. Pious Jews hope to die with the words of the Shema on their lips.

this world. Did Markowitz realize, for instance, that by the age of twenty, God willing, most or all of these girls would already be married off to yeshiva[2] boys who sit and learn all day? Some were even engaged in their junior year of high school. A year at a women's seminary in Israel after graduation, night classes at Brooklyn College, some secretarial work or maybe in computers, marking time, as it were, and then, with God's help, they would be settled away. By twenty, many were already pushing a baby in a carriage down Thirteenth Avenue with another on the way, and if they were not fixed up by then it would truly be *och und vey*,[3] a serious problem, bad news for these girls and their families, a looming calamity in fact, because already a new crop of eighteen-year-olds would be coming up, and the chances these old goods had then of fulfilling the destiny that he, Rabbi Berman, and the institution he headed were preparing them for would be drastically reduced, reduced exponentially.

Now, was this a reality that Markowitz and his ilk could absorb? Did Markowitz have even an inkling of an idea of what it meant to be in the rabbi's shoes? Statistically speaking, in any given week at the school, the rabbi had once calculated, approximately one quarter of these girls, about seventy-five girls in all, had their periods. Could anyone imagine what it must be like to be living in the middle of all that? Sometimes he felt as if he were drowning in a thick soup. The constant smell of talcum, of old perspiration in woolen sweaters, the endless dieting and self-dissatisfaction, the pimples, the greasy hair, the preening, the sudden bursts of weeping, the shrieking, the jumping up and down, the hugging and kissing, the gossip, envy, rivalry, intrigue, the cliques, the moodiness, the obligation to chide this or that one for wearing makeup, shoes that made noise, colors that were too bright, sleeves that were too short, for snatching the excuse of warm weather not to wear any stockings at all—an obligation that naturally carried with it the necessity of looking closely at these growing girls when for the sake of the purity of his spirit he would, of course, have preferred not to—all of this was a headache beyond description.

And, to make matters worse, if you didn't count the public high school teachers who came into the building in the late afternoon for the secular subjects, since all of the religious classes were taught by married women in wigs and head scarves and hats, he, Rabbi Yehiel Berman, was the only man on the premises the entire day, not including Reb Avraham Washington, the janitor. But Reb Washington was a special case, a black man who had been their custodian for years, who had been so influenced and impressed by the Jewish lifestyle that he had actually converted, married the longtime secretary, the widow Mrs. Halpern, and now he could be seen in his full beard and side curls, shuffling around the facility with his mops and pails, wearing a black felt that over his black velvet yarmulke[4] and a great fringed ritual garment on top of his white shirt. Yet, in a very real sense, Reb Avraham Washington, no matter how sincere his convictions, could never really be considered a player, and, for all intents and purposes, he, Rabbi Yehiel Berman, was the only male on the scene.

2. School for the study of the sacred Hebrew texts (Hebrew).
3. Literally, aches and woes; more colloquially, as Reich indicates, serious trouble (Yiddish).
4. A skullcap worn especially by Orthodox and Conservative Jewish males.

So when the Singer girl had gotten lost that spring during the Lag B'Omer[5] outing, when she had not come out of the woods after wandering for over an hour with all the other girls, when she had not returned to the buses waiting in the parking lot, when, to the rabbi's utter astonishment, the disappearance of this skinny little girl had inspired the extraordinary spectacle of swarms of Hasidim[6] in black garb from Massachusetts to Maryland, as well as other—secular—men, descending on these woods in upstate New York in search of this female and the whole business had become big news, this guy Markowitz from the *Times* naturally sought out Rabbi Berman, as the principal of the school, for a comment. Markowitz's attitude had been openly hostile and confrontational from the outset. Wasn't the rabbi aware that this particular forest was notoriously confusing, complex, overgrown, filled with traps and illusions? How could he have allowed such young and vulnerable girls to wander in there alone? What form of supervision had been provided for these students, city girls that they were, innocent entirely of raw nature?

And even though Rabbi Berman knew that a wise man answers the first question first and the second second, everything in order, he hastened, in this instance, to take on at once the final query for which he had a ready response. There were fifteen chaperons in charge of the girls, he told Markowitz proudly, trained teachers from our school, one adult per every group of twenty adolescents. He did not add that the women had most likely remained in the parking lot, chatting in clumps—chatting, as usual, about this and that, about children, about where to get the best prices, comparing outfits—while the girls went off into the woods. He assumed that this had been the case, based on his past experience observing teachers in the yard overseeing students during free time, but why should he have volunteered such compromising information to Markowitz if he had not witnessed it with his own eyes? Because, naturally, he himself had not gone on the trip with the student body due to the delicate and essentially forbidden circumstance into which he would have been forced—of riding in close quarters for such a long period of time in the exclusive company of the opposite sex. True, the bus drivers were male, but they, of course, were gentiles.

Then, having successfully cleared away the issue of adequate supervision, Rabbi Berman diplomatically attempted to draw Markowitz closer, to establish some sort of bond of kinship between them, to bring him over to their side. "What kind of name is Sean for a Jewish boy?" he inquired with amused familiarity. Most likely, the rabbi went on to conjecture, he had been named for some ancestor called Samuel, Shmuel—Shmiel or Shmulik, in the Yiddish way. "So tell me, Shmulik," the rabbi said, "when was the last time you put on tefillin[7] since your bar mitzvah?"

But Markowitz wasn't buying. He persisted in questioning the rabbi, not only about the supervision for the trip—obviously he had found the answer unsatisfactory—but also about all the other arrangements and preparations, as well as about the steps they had taken upon discovering that a girl was

5. A minor Jewish holiday falling on the thirty-third day of the counting of the omer (barley sheaves).

6. The adherents of a sect of Judaism that is highly devout and mystical.

7. Two black leather boxes that contain portions of the Talmud and that are strapped to the left arm and forehead of Jewish men during morning prayer.

missing, until, in exasperation, and, really, in an attempt, misguided perhaps but well intentioned nonetheless, to bring some relief, some lightness, to a grim situation, Rabbi Berman had come out with the statement that had gotten him into so much trouble. "Look, Shmiel," he said, "we went into the woods with 300 girls and came out with 299. Now, you learned arithmetic. If you consider all girls equal, so that each one is worth the same amount of points, on a final exam that would give you a score of about 99.7 out of 100—a sure A, maybe even an A plus. Not a bad showing in anybody's book—am I right?" For this comment even members of his own community had chastised him, accusing him of insensitivity, of failing to place the proper value on one human life. Rabbi Yehiel Berman had been completely misunderstood.

And, after all, who was this girl Feigie Singer to inspire such a fuss? Of course, she was a human being—that goes without saying. Naturally, she was not a nothing, God forbid. But such a small, timid creature, the youngest in a family of thirteen—her father drove a fruit and vegetable truck, selling door to door, housewives bought from him out of pity—this was a girl who scarcely made any impression at all. You barely noticed her, she was hardly there even when she wasn't lost. It was a wonder, in a way, that they even realized she was missing. In this assessment, which, thank God, the rabbi had had the good sense to refrain from verbalizing, he was nevertheless backed up by two student leaders, Pessie Glick and Dvorah Birnbaum, who told Markowitz that Feigie was an exceptionally quiet girl, afraid of every little thing, you could practically see her heart pounding and fluttering like a naked newborn chick under her blouse, definitely not the type to go wandering off alone in the woods. Oh, they were very worried that something terrible had happened to her, Pessie and Dvorah said.

She had, in fact, been walking with them when she disappeared, cowering and trembling at every little movement and noise. Then, suddenly, they had turned around and Feigie was gone. The woods were extremely tangled and dark and moist. There was a man in there, they reported. They had seen him with their own eyes. Several times they saw him, though not while they were with Feigie. Later, only, after she had vanished. He was wearing a uniform of some sort—a forest ranger, they thought—rubber boots, a wide-brimmed hat with a leather band, a heavy wooden stick in his hand. They themselves circled aimlessly for another hour at least after Feigie disappeared, utterly lost and confused, clutching each other's hand, before they had finally, thank God, seen a clearing of light and found their way out into the parking lot.

And these two girls, Rabbi Berman noted, Pessie and Dvorah, were from the school's elite, from very good backgrounds, handsome, well-dressed girls. They would no doubt be married off within a year to excellent prospects from comfortable, well-connected families, families that would support them over the first few years while the boy sat and learned Torah all day and maybe studied at night for an accounting or an actuarial degree and the couple started a family of its own. Little Feigie Singer must have been honored, thrilled, to be allowed to walk in the woods in their company, alongside such important girls, Rabbi Berman was sure. Such, he knew, was the politics of a girls' high school. If it had been the Glick or the Birnbaum girl who had disappeared, it would have been a different story entirely. Whether Markowitz realized it or not, he was getting his inside information from the most prestigious teenage source possible, the cream of the cream. What Pessie and Dvorah said to him should have put the status of the Singer girl clearly into perspective.

So when the searchers brought Feigie Singer out of the woods nearly three days later, a little hungry, a little tired, a little soiled, but, to the uncritical eye, at least externally undamaged, it was a shock, almost like a blow, to Pessie and Dvorah, and to their entire school community for that matter, and it was a surprise even to the rabbi himself, he had to admit, that she was escorted out like a heroine, like a princess from an ancient tale. Yet even so, even though this meek girl had been welcomed like a celebrity when she was rescued, and masses gathered to dance and rejoice at her salvation, and even though Rabbi Yehiel Berman observed over the ensuing months that she had begun to grow considerably and to ripen, you should excuse me, in a recognizably womanly fashion, he had nevertheless regarded it as necessary at the time of her deliverance to urge her parents to collect notarized letters and affidavits from doctors and other examining authorities testifying to the fact that nothing compromising had happened to her during those days when she had been alone in the woods. This would be a wise precaution, Rabbi Berman had advised, in anticipation of the time, only a few years hence, when they would be seeking a suitable match for her, and the boys' families would recall the event and, naturally, they would pause and wonder.

When they found her in the early morning hours of the third day, she was inside the hollow shell of the dead tree trunk in which she had finally settled to await her fate. It was like a cradle, she imagined, high and protected on each side, soft and damp in the interior with decaying matter that peeled off and clung to her clothing, tangled in her hair, and when she curled up to sleep it seemed to her to be almost rocking. Her parents, of course, would have realized that she had not come home, but what resources could they muster to try to find her, downtrodden and careworn as they were? They were not the kind of people who liked to call attention to themselves, and a daughter who does not return home, that was in a way a shameful thing, not something they would want to get around. Pessie and Dvorah would probably have noticed that she was gone, most likely they would have reported her missing, though while she was walking beside them in the woods they seemed hardly to have noticed her. They didn't even bother to shake her off or to lower their voices to whisper their secrets but went on chatting intimately with each other as if they were entirely alone.

They really were magnificent girls, Pessie and Dvorah, tall and stately, Pessie with her red hair streaming down her back, held with a black velvet barrette, Dvorah's rich, dark curls framing the smooth paleness of her face. These were truly girls at the cusp of their bridal season, beautifully packaged, as it were, in designer clothing that their mothers single-mindedly hunted out for them from fashionable, bejeweled women in gorgeous blonde pageboy wigs who operated discount boutiques in the basements of their Borough Park homes. For her part, Feigie was wearing the long, drab, khaki-colored skirt and the well-washed blouse with the tiny yellow flowers and sleeves buttoned at the wrists handed down from her sisters, white socks, and sneakers. Her only ornaments were the small gold studs in her ears, which her mother had insisted she have pierced, and the gold ring with the tiny amethyst birthstone that she had been given three months earlier, on her fourteenth birthday. Pessie had milky pearls in her ears, and Dvorah elegant gold hoops, and they were each carrying fine leather pocketbooks slung stylishly over their shoulders while she, Feigie, had all of her possessions for this outing—her cream cheese and jelly sandwich wrapped in aluminum foil, her old Instamatic camera, her little prayer book, and a few dollars—in a lump at the bottom of a plastic Waldbaum's shopping bag that she clutched in her hand.

She could never imagine ever flowering as gloriously as they, even in three years time, even when she, too, would become a senior. She could never imagine ever being able to converse as amusingly or as easily or as confidently as they. How did they always know the right thing to say? She walked along silently beside them, trying to absorb every detail of their manner and speech, trying not to embarrass herself by starting at every sound and rustle in the woods, straining to keep up even though she was growing increasingly weary and alarmed as they penetrated deeper and deeper among the trees, her heart beating so that she was afraid they could hear it, a dragging ache radiating down her back, across her belly, into her thighs.

Would she ever possess the power to talk as fluidly, as brazenly about Rabbi Berman, for example, as they did? It seemed to Feigie to be a veritable gift, quite beyond her. They actually called him Berman. Last week Berman had asked her if she was wearing stockings, Dvorah told Pessie. Would you believe? He even put out his hand as if to slide it down her leg. Just checking, you know. Dvorah giggled. Hadn't he ever heard of sheer panty hose, for heaven's sake? Yeah, Pessie said, just two days ago Berman stopped her in the hallway and told her that her earrings were too long and dangly. He looked like he was about to rip them right out of her ears. There was definitely something wrong with the guy.

What could Feigie possibly contribute to the conversation? Rabbi Berman never looked at her, and ever since that one and only conversation she had had with him, when it had been her turn to be called into his office in the early autumn for the routine interview with each new freshman, she took pains to avoid him, ducking into classrooms when she saw him coming down the hall, staying out of his line of sight as much as was humanly possible. Without even looking up, he had indicated with his hand for her to sit down in the chair on the other side of his desk after she had knocked and come into his office that morning for the interview, and, with his eyes glued to the sheet of paper in front of him, he had said, "So, you're the daughter of Moishe Singer the fruit man. Didn't we have a couple of your sisters here? How're they doing? Are they married yet?" Feigie could tell that Rabbi Berman didn't even remember her sisters' names. Then he looked up, stared at her as if he were probing to her essence for an endless stretch of time, with his elbows planted on his desk and his bearded chin resting on a sling formed by his enlaced fingers and the bowl of his black velvet yarmulke tipped back exposing a half-moon of closely cropped gray hair, and finally, with his eyes still unyieldingly upon her, he had spoken. "So, tell me, Singer," he had said, "what do you plan to do about those pimples of yours?" For fifteen minutes after that interview, she had sat on a toilet in one of the cubicles in the third-floor bathroom, her shoulders heaving, sobbing into her two hands pressed against her mouth. She could never imagine Rabbi Berman saying such a thing to Pessie or to Dvorah.

With God's help she could avoid him, she figured, at least until the second semester of her last year, when every graduating senior was required to take his course on the Laws of Family Purity. But that was a long time from now. Meanwhile she would try not to worry about it. And even then, when the time came, she could sit silently in a corner of the classroom, staring down into her lap. She would practice making herself transparent. He would not find her, he would not look for her. She was not interesting to him. This subject, those laws, were what Pessie and Dvorah were discussing now. "The main point," Pessie was saying, "was that during those two weeks every month when you're not allowed to—you know—the main thing, like Berman said, is not to do anything to tempt your husband. Like, to excite him. Men are different that way—you know what I'm saying?" "Yeah," Dvorah responded, "but still you have to look good, even then. I mean, you still just can't get into bed with, like, cold cream or something smeared all over your face."

The two girls nodded. They were passing through a small clearing in the woods, and a shaft of light filtered down through the trees. Two squirrels ran out directly in their path, chasing each other, startling them. For the first time, Feigie remembered the animals that must inhabit these woods. Yet all of this talk, the moment to which she was privileged, however frightening, however much her back and her legs hurt, this moment was stunning, like a revelation she could only partially comprehend. She listened as the two girls went on to analyze the significant members of their class, one by one, their looks and their personalities, their position in the group and their prospects, their good points and their bad, and then as they proceeded to scrutinize each other, commenting on each other's clothing and hairstyles, offering constructive criticism, touching lightly here and there to make a helpful point about possible improvements.

The conversation, in its way, was becoming more and more wonderful and deep to Feigie. And then it passed into a realm utterly mysterious, even fabulous. They began to speak in what, to Feigie's ears, sounded almost like a cryptic tongue, like secret knowledge from a hidden world. Their words struck her, each one discretely, like little pellets. He called again last night, Dvorah reported to Pessie. Yes, it was the same guy. For sure. The same voice. I'd recognize it anywhere. Yes, he said the same thing. The same thing in the same words. Tell your friend Pessie Glick that I'm going to kill her. That's what he said. That he's going to kill you. It's really scary. And when I said to him, like you told me to, to call you up himself and tell you what he has against you, he just hung up. Like he always does. Just hung up.

Pessie turned coolly to face her friend. She said, "Well, as a matter of fact, he did call me last night finally, and we straightened the whole thing out, so he won't be bothering you anymore, D'vo."

"He called you? You're kidding! I don't believe it. That's really incredible." Dvorah's shock was alive in those woods, and dangerous, like a flash of lightning. Feigie could almost feel the current pass through those two superior girls, straight to her, to her, little Feigie Singer, to sear and to illuminate her, but she couldn't completely absorb it, it was too strong, she could not take it in, at least not then, she was feeling more and more sick, it was impossible to hide it from herself any longer. Her belly was tightening like a fist. The muscles in her thighs were pulled to a screech. The pain was breathtaking. She could see it as a separate entity in front of her. She needed to go off alone, to curl up like a wounded animal in a secluded place. She needed to be able to look at this thing. She could not continue. Most likely Pessie and Dvorah had never been struck so urgently, overwhelmed in such a mortifying, public way. She could not even picture them going to the bathroom. They seemed to be above all that. But she had to get some relief, and as the two girls immersed themselves ever deeper in their exotic language, Feigie slipped away and was lost.

She found a dark, mossy place within a heavy growth of trees. She set down her bag, slipped off her underpants, and crouched to the ground. She knew at once, with an ancient inborn knowledge, that something was different. With her fingers she felt the sticky warmth and wet. The smell was sweet and organic and intimate, hers. But no one else could love it, she was sure. So it had come to her at last. It was the end. She knew its name, of course, from her sisters, she just knew, yet she never truly expected it for herself. But it had befallen her nevertheless, as they claimed it befell all women, and now there was no longer any doubt that she would also, in the course of time, die. She had been sucked, whether she willed it or not, into the cycle. She took her little camera out of the plastic bag and pressed the flash. Her underwear was dark and soaked, she saw by the sharp snap of light, and her khaki skirt, when she flipped it back to front, was stained unmistakably. It was hopeless. Everyone would see. Pessie and Dvorah and Rabbi Berman—everyone. They would mock her. They would figure her out. She could not possibly go back now. She gathered some large flat leaves and placed them inside her underwear between her thighs. There was no escape. All choice had been taken from her. She could never leave the woods.

She waited for as long as she could bear to be safely lost, and then she rose and began to walk. She wanted to take out her prayer book and pray, but her hands were polluted from what she had just touched. First, she needed to find water. She had to wash, to purify herself. There were low signs stuck in the earth, she saw, painted with arrows. No, she would not follow them. She did not want to find her way out. But what if she came upon something, what if she came upon a man, say, prowling in this forest, what would she do then? What could she give to satisfy him? The money in her bag, her camera, her sandwich, the paltry jewels from her ears, her finger? She would grab the knife out of his hand. She would lay it across her hair and cut it all off. And she would give it to him. Her hair. She pulled out the rubber band off her braid and slipped it around her wrist. She shook her hair loose, letting it fall free over her shoulders, down her back. But if it was an animal that came upon her in these woods, lured by the smell of her blood, what then? What would she have to give?

The pain gathered intensity, it seemed almost loud, coming over her in great, constricting waves. It was tied to the blood. She passed a signpost emblazoned with arrows that seemed to be pointing skyward. She had never until now seen one like that. How could she possibly obey it, make the ascent, the sacrifice? Behind and alongside her as she advanced there was a rush of noise and movement. She began to climb in stiff long strides, not wanting to run, not wanting to show she was afraid, as she used to do when she was a child going down a long dark hallway, absolutely sure someone, something, a monster, was pursuing her, feeling it upon her back, draining her toward him. She was no longer a child. The strange sign appeared again, and then again, as if the creature that was trailing her in the shadows were picking it up as soon as she passed and running ahead to plant it at the next station, and then the next one, leading her to her destination, to the last of all possible signs, the sign that said, Enter.

She went inside. It was a cave. Here she would pass the night. She was hungry. She stretched out her hand, collected some leaves, squeezed and rubbed them in her palms, releasing the moisture. In this way she washed. She unwrapped her sandwich, taking a few bites, remembering to say the blessing before and after. Then she sealed it again in its foil and replaced it in her plastic bag, for later. She moved her lips in prayer, every chanted prayer by heart that could soothe her to sleep. A steady murmur and hum in the cave accompanied her prayers. Only when the full moon came up and cast a beam of light through the opening did she see who sang with her—a choir of snakes, tangled and snarled and intertwined in a kind of ecstasy. She ran out screaming. She was still lithe and spare—this might be the last time she could still run like a girl—she ran in the night and fell exhausted in the density of the forest, in a nest of pine needles and dead leaves.

When the dawn came up on the second day the woods seemed to be filling with men. She lay on her stomach under a thick blanket of forest droppings, alert, watching, her entire body concealed, only her eyes peering out, only the top of her hair visible, brown like the floor of these woods. A warm rain was falling. She emptied her plastic bag, stuffing the contents into her pockets, bit out three slits, for her eyes, her nose, and drew it over her head. They would never find her. What they would see, if they could see anything at all, would be litter, garbage, a discarded grocery sack. They would not see what was inside.

The pain, which had subsided in the night, began to mass once more. Between her legs there was a thickness, like paste. She bore down, struggled to push it out, strained to be delivered of this blood. Everywhere there were men, strange men, alien men from other worlds, worlds not her own, but also there were men she recognized, men in black hats, black coats, like brooding, great-winged birds. She watched them through the rain as they seemed to move entranced among the trees. What could such Jews be doing in these woods? Her Jews kept the sidewalks under their feet. Jews such as these—they gathered in forests only to be shot. Now and then, behind the rain, she imagined she heard them calling her name—Feigie, Feigie. But how could that be? Then she understood. These were the ones they called the Dead Hasidim, the enraptured ones who sought solitude in nature to commune with God. They were calling in Yiddish to the birds.

All day she watched them through the slits of her plastic bag, her body underground, the rain falling steadily. She felt herself beginning to be cleansed. Af-Bri was the name of the angel of rain. That was what Rabbi

Berman had told them at an assembly early in the school year, around the time you say the Prayer for Rain. *Af* for anger, rain that pours down in torrents and floods, *Bri* for health, sweet rain that refreshes and renews. For life and not for death—those were the words you chanted at the end of the prayer. "Remember that, girls," Rabbi Berman had said, "life, not death." Up there alone on that stage he looked for a moment almost like some mother's child. She could pity him.

When it was nearly dark, the woods emptied out. The rain had ended. Feigie took the plastic bag off her head and, like one who had passed through a grave sickness, shook off the earth that had covered her and rose. She began to walk among the trees, the wet ground giving under her feet. She gazed down at herself as she walked, and she thought, I am transformed, no one will recognize me.

She walked until the moon came out, until she found the cradle of the dead oak hollowed out for her. This is where she would remain. She climbed inside and curled up into herself against the cold, one arm underneath her body supporting her head, the other across her chest, the palm of her hand resting over her heart, stroking her breast. She did not know if this was allowed. In this way she fell asleep.

At dawn she awoke with her heart pounding, launched out of a dream of wolves and bears. She stood up in terror inside the shell of her dead tree. A black dog froze in place, its cold eyes upon her. Who is a Jew? The one with the inborn fear of dogs. Three men in the distance started and turned sharply. In the early morning light, she could see that each man was carrying a long weapon in his hands. Hunters. They were moving toward her. They had seen her. Nothing remained but surrender. As the groom draws closer to lift the veil over her face, the most pious of brides does not raise her eyes to look but keeps them cast down. She prays. Feigie sat down inside her cradle and took out her prayer book. She never lifted her eyes. Desperately, she prayed. Like a bride.

1995

MARGE PIERCY
b. 1936

Best known for her political novels, Marge Piercy is also an essayist, social activist, feminist, and poet. Much of Piercy's work of the 1960s and 1970s emerged from her involvement in the radical youth organization Students for a Democratic Society. She achieved prominence in the 1970s when her two novels *Small Changes* (1973) and *Woman on the Edge of Time* (1976) captured the attention of feminists as well as literary critics. The former novel was made into a miniseries for television; the latter, her most critically acclaimed novel, tells of Connie, a woman who has (mistakenly) been committed to a mental institution and whose travels into the future extend a coherent vision of the world as it should be juxtaposed against the world as it is.

Piercy has continued to write novels about outsiders: lesbians, urban African Americans, immigrants, and working-class Jews. In *Gone to Soldiers* (1987), Piercy, describing the lives of women during World War II, features several heroic women imprisoned in Auschwitz who struggle to define an affirmative Jewish identity, "a way of being Jewish," that is their own. Such exploration also could describe Piercy's own personal quest.

As a poet, Piercy also explores social issues; her work has challenged the assumption that poetry cannot take on thorny political terrain. Although some critics have dismissed Piercy's work as too polemical, others more sympathetic to her have understood her poetry as demonstrating the axiom that the political is personal and the personal political. In the 1980s, many of Piercy's most personal poems dealt with her experiences as a Jewish American woman and her attempts to fit into the longstanding religious traditions of her ancestors while devoting so much of her intellectual life to confronting the historically patriarchal rituals and structures of the faith.

Piercy is the author of twelve books of poetry and eleven novels; her work has been represented in over one hundred anthologies. Like Adrienne Rich, she enjoys the unusual distinction for a poet of having a wide and devoted constituency. She has taught at many universities, including the University of Michigan, where she was a distinguished visiting professor. She has been active in a number of Jewish organizations, including the Israeli Center for the Arts and Literature, ALEPH, and the Siddur Project. Currently, she lives in Cape Cod, Massachusetts, and is the poetry editor of the journal *Tikkun*.

Maggid[1]

The courage to let go of the door, the handle.
The courage to shed the familiar walls whose very
stains and leaks are comfortable as the little moles
of the upper arm; stains that recall a feast,
a child's naughtiness, a loud blattering storm
that slapped the roof hard, pouring through.

The courage to abandon the graves dug into the hill,
the small bones of children and the brittle bones
of the old whose marrow hunger had stolen;
the courage to desert the tree planted and only
begun to bear; the riverside where promises were
shaped; the street where their empty pots were broken.

The courage to leave the place whose language you learned
as early as your own, whose customs however dangerous or demeaning, bind you like a halter
you have learned to pull inside, to move your load;
the land fertile with the blood spilled on it;
the roads mapped and annotated for survival.

1. A popular preacher or an angel who conveys, in mysterious ways, teachings only to scholars worthy of such communications (Hebrew).

The courage to walk out of the pain that is known
into the pain that cannot be imagined,
mapless, walking into the wilderness, going
barefoot with a canteen into the desert;
stuffed in the stinking hold of a rotting ship
sailing off the map into dragons' mouths,

Cathay, India, Siberia, goldeneh medina[2]
leaving bodies by the way like abandoned treasure.
So they walked out of Egypt.[3] So they bribed their way
out of Russia under loads of straw; so they steamed
out of the bloody smoking charnelhouse of Europe
on overloaded freighters forbidden all ports—

out of pain into death or freedom or a different
painful dignity, into squalor and politics.
We Jews are all born of wanderers, with shoes
under our pillows and a memory of blood that is ours
raining down. We honor only those Jews who changed
tonight, those who chose the desert over bondage,

who walked into the strange and became strangers
and gave birth to children who could look down
on them standing on their shoulders for having
been slaves. We honor those who let go of everything but freedom, who ran, who revolted, who fought,
who became other by saving themselves.

1988

The Ram's Horn Sounding[1]

1.

Giant porcupine, I walk a rope braided
of my intestines and veins, beige and blue and red,
while clutched in my arms, you lie glaring
sore eyed, snuffling and sticking your spines at me.

Always I am finding quills worked into some unsuspected
muscle, an innocent pillow of fat pierced by you.
We sleep in the same bed nightly and you take it all.
I wake shuddering with cold, the quilt stripped from me.

No, not a porcupine: a leopard cub.
Beautiful you are as light and as darkness.
Avid, fierce, demanding with sharp teeth
to be fed and tended, you only want my life.

2. Golden land (Yiddish).
3. A reference to the biblical Exodus out of Egypt.
1. A reference to the shofar, the ram's horn that is sounded for the memorial blowing on Rosh Hashanah and other occasions.

Ancient, living, a deep and tortuous river
that rose in the stark mountains beyond the desert,
you have gouged through rocks with slow persistence
enduring, meandering in long shining coils to the sea.

2.

A friend who had been close before being recruited
by the CIA once sent me a postcard of the ghetto at Tetuàn[2]
yellowed like old pornography numbered 17,
a prime number as one might say a prime suspect.

The photographer stood well clear of the gate
to shoot old clothes tottering in the tight street,
beards matted and holy with grease,
children crooked under water jugs,
old men austere and busy as hornets.
Flies swarmed on the lens.
Dirt was the color.

Oh, I understood your challenge.
My Jewishness seemed to you sentimental,
perverse, planned obsolescence.
Paris was hot and dirty the night I first
met relatives who had survived the war.
My identity squatted whining on my arm
gorging itself on my thin blood.
A gaggle of fierce insistent speakers of ten
languages had different passports mother
from son, brother from sister, had four
passports all forged, kept passports
from gone countries (Transylvania, Bohemia,
old despotisms fading like Victorian wallpaper),
were used to sewing contraband into coat
linings. I smuggled for them across two borders.
Their wars were old ones.
Mine was just starting.

Old debater, it's easy in any manscape
to tell the haves from the have-nots.
Any ghetto is a kleinbottle.[3]
You think you are outside gazing idly in.
Winners write history; losers
die of it, like the plague.

3.

A woman and a Jew, sometimes more
of a contradiction than I can sweat out,
yet finally the intersection that is both
collision and fusion, stone and seed.

2. A city in north Morocco where a large population of Jews settled and prospered from 1511 until the late 1960s. "CIA": Central Intelligence Agency.

3. A single-sided bottle with no boundary; its inside is its outside; it contains itself (German).

Like any poet I wrestle the holy name
and know there is no wording finally
can map, constrain or summon that fierce
voice whose long wind lifts my hair

chills my skin and fills my lungs
to bursting. I serve the word
I cannot name, who names me daily,
who speaks me out by whispers and shouts.

Coming to the new year, I am picked
up like the ancient ram's horn to sound
over the congregation of people and beetles,
of pines, whales, marshhawks and asters.

Then I am dropped into the factory of words
to turn my little wheels and grind my own
edges, back on piece work again, knowing
there is no justice we don't make daily

like bread and love. Shekinah,[4]
stooping on hawk wings prying into my heart
with your silver beak; floating down
a milkweed silk dove of sunset;
riding the filmy sheets of rain like a ghost
ship with all sails still unfurled;
bless me and use me for telling and naming
the forever collapsing shades and shapes of life,

the rainbows cast across our eyes by the moment
of sun, the shadows we trail across the grass
running, the opal valleys of the night flesh,
the moments of knowledge ripping into the brain

and aligning everything into a new pattern
as a constellation learned organizes blur
into stars, the blood kinship with all green, hairy
and scaled folk born from the ancient warm sea.

1988

4. Divine Presence; most often a reference in rabbinic literature to the manifestation of the Divine Presence in human life (Hebrew).

MARK MIRSKY
b. 1939

To note that Mark Mirsky is the son of Orthodox Jewish parents and also a literary follower of postmodernist Donald Barthelme is to identify the two divergent, but ultimately complementary, aspects of Mirsky's work. His earliest novels—*Thou Worm Jacob* (1967), *Blue Hill Avenue* (1972), and *The Secret Table* (1975)—use postmodern literary invention to depict Blue Hill Avenue, a small Jewish community in Dorchester, Massachusetts, where he grew up. Through this technical and formal experimentation, Mirsky's portrayals of immigrant Jews take on new and rich dimensions. Rather than providing the more conventional narratives of Eastern European immigrant social history, Mirsky's novels and stories mix tradition, philosophy, and mysticism with the harsh realities of urban life in order to render a complex verbal collage of density, image, and texture. One reviewer of *The Secret Table*, a collection of stories, said that it is "the literary equivalent of a Marc Chagall window, full of metamorphosed denizens of Jewish fable."

In later works, Mirsky has sought to dig more deeply into his own experience to extract the meaning and roots of Judaism. Dissatisfied with the state of Jewish life in America, which, in *My Search for the Messiah* (1977), he calls "vulgar, shallow, and silly," Mirsky attempts to rediscover the mystical core of the Jewish experience. This search takes him to the foot of Mt. Sinai where he receives a personal revelation. In his next novel, *The Red Adam* (1989), the hero, Job Schwartz, living in a Protestant town in Connecticut in the eighteenth century, orders his life by means of a perverse reading of the Kabbalah and black magic; thus Mirsky provides a commentary on the nature of evil in the Judeo-Christian religious tradition.

In *Memory Candle,* the story reprinted here, the hero's desire to say Kaddish for his mother is interrupted by a near stream-of-consciousness record of his thoughts, feelings, and ambivalences. The narrative thread of the story fades as the details, texture, and poetry of the speaker's life become more prominent.

Mirsky has published seven books of novels and short stories and has edited, with David Stern, *Rabbinic Fantasies: Imaginative Narratives of Classical Hebrew Literature* (1990). He has also written a masterful history of the Russian city Pinsk, where his grandparents were born. He has taught at the City University of New York for over thirty years.

Memory Candle[1]

May 10, 1989.

It begins to oppress me the date, weeks before, to weigh on me, like an old debt that was only partly paid, which one doesn't wish to pay. It doesn't cost that much, but throws a way of moving through the day, out of whack. It is an obligation, strangely painful. Why?

I remember when my father imposed it. "Say it," he said. "It's an honor—to your mother."

It had to be said in front of others, of course, in some place, usually a downstairs room, or a half empty hall, musty but often sweet with the smell of damp old books.

When I was a child it meant nothing in my house whether you went, or

1. A memorial, or *yahrtzeit*, candle that is lit to commemorate the anniversary of a near relative's death.

you didn't, except in a social sense. It was nice if you went. Now and then my father might take the trouble to explain something there, but only to amuse himself, as part of his natural bent as a storyteller. That anything was serious about it—was never impressed upon me. If you made a fool of yourself, however, that was awful. You made *him* look like a fool. In fact, better not to get up, or make a show of what you might know, because you would *never* know as much as your father did, and therefore you looked silly from the point of view of the family, his, that is. He could do the whole thing. Not just on ordinary days, holidays too, what sounded like a tremendous rigmarole to a child, impressive, beyond reach, tunes, the right words, intersection of fine print and bold. (The book under your nose was only a reference. You had to know it by heart.)

My father would get up, easily, rise on the few stairs, to the *bimah*,[2] altar, bend over the book, begin. Everyone in the place took a deep breath—right from the first note. My father didn't use the voice in which he sang, which was deep and mellow. His own father, Grandfather, was known in Boston for an elegant cantorial delivery, and my great grandfather I was told by our family's oldest member, was a *baal tefillah* in Pinsk,[3] "master of the chant." Dad could go on and on in the car speeding along the Merritt Parkway down to Connecticut relatives singing Gilbert and Sullivan, trilling over and over, "a twisted cur, and elliptical bil-liard baaallls,"[4] our Dodge doing a dance back and forth across the white line down the center of the highway. Not a bit of that embellishment, its ringing, echoed when he got up to lead a service, though some of the fury of the patter, syllables puckering his lips in rapid fashion, the whole thing done—before it had hardly begun. It was a dry rush. The obligation was all, any show of enthusiasm an insult. It was typical of a certain kind of Litvak[5]—the dried herring delivery I was to be served up in a number of dusty basements after my father obliged me to my mother's memory.

Since I stumbled over the simplest elements of the language, fluency out of the question, the idea of having to go through it, even for the sake of Mother, was upsetting. Still I let my father wrap the straps around me, set me up.

Now it's too late to stop. Now the date has become part of a calendar which marks the year like the fall of leaves, the first green chives coming up out of the wet chill earth in the April backyard. I begin to feel it weeks before, although it has no mark on the calendars in the offices through which I trek. It can be in April, May, since it is a date tied to a moon's cycle, but the twinge starts in my kneecaps. Your mother's death—it's coming. Remember, remember, for to forget is to lose her, lose her one bit more.

Only it's forbidden to remember too much, too soon. It is the morning before that the dread settles in earnest over me. In the bed, the morning of the evening when I have to go, and do it, I see, waking up on sheets still

2. The raised area, with a reading desk, at the front of the sanctuary of the synagogue (Hebrew). Typically, the rabbi and the cantor stand on the *bimah* during services.

3. A town in Belorussia. It was formerly part of Poland, then the U.S.S.R. *"Baal tefillah"*: literally, a master of prayer (Hebrew). The term is often used to describe the cantor.

4. From act 2 of Gilbert and Sullivan's comic opera *The Mikado* (1885). (Note that the original lyric uses "cue," not "cur.") Sir William Gilbert (1836–1911) and Sir Arthur Sullivan (1842–1900) were the librettist and composer, respectively, of many such popular works.

5. A Jew from Lithuania.

clammy with dreams, the white candle suddenly flickering in the pantry, my father taking out his blue bag embroidered with symbols, flowers, in red and orange threads, filled with a silk *tallis*[6] threadbare but huge, bunching on the angry red boils in his neck, and spilling over his jacket shoulders and a smaller bag, a crushed green velvet faded away to brown and yellow strings. This is what he takes to these cavernous rooms and basements and in the smaller bag, bulging it, large leather boxes of his *tefillin*,[7] phylacteries, or *tefillin* inherited from my grandfather, enclosed in boxes of colored cardboard covered with the intaglio of kabbala.[8] He is going for his parents.

Did I go with him? The memory of wandering into cold halls with stale air early in the morning, scrambling over empty benches while he chanted in a corner with the meager count of ten, twelve men, taunts me. It is the candle I am sure of, flickering in an octagonal glass, holding the white wax which drips toward its own flame, self consumed, the sadness radiating from it, the sole source of light, painting shadows of the dead on the cream paint over plaster pantry walls late at night, looming on the linoleum, moving between stacks of dishes on the shelves, piled up in ziggurats to the ceiling.

Then the second morning, the day after, a tiny glow still there, the memorial light like a sick person guttered fitful, coughing last faint breaths, wanting to be, it seemed to me at five, six years old, with us. In the sad steps of my father moving about the kitchen, slumping against the counters, I did not doubt that the ghost of my grandfather, Israel, dogged the house. Dad's mother, Devorah, about whom he never talked, who died in his childhood, was an indistinct face in a photograph, prematurely old, blown from a small negative into a bitter presence against the living room walls. Her face was wary, angry, disapproving of me. The picture was taken in the weeks after Devorah's brother was murdered by the Poles in Pinsk. A kidney disease that would kill her in a few months was eating in her vitals. The will to see her husband, Israel, who had slipped away to America, nine years before, stiffened Devorah to shepherd their children over the Atlantic. Knowing only the photograph, not her story which no one cared to tell me, I could not see my grandmother, Devorah, in a flame.

Did my mother light candles? I don't think so. Her father was absent in the house, never part of her conversation. Her mother, Channah, lived in a dozen Yiddish remarks we had heard from the cradle, all sarcastic, putdowns. "*Mein groysse lappen*"—my big spoon, sung when I heaped for a portion larger than Mother thought due my plate, or I heaped hamburg patties, covetous. "*Iz nisht gefilte fish*"—not the real thing, okay, "something," but a *patchkee*, not what was asked or called for—not what she wanted. Some of this drum roll was rapped out half in English, "Don't mix *kashe* and *borscht*,"[9] i.e., opposites, dishes for different days of the week. My mother's favorite, "*Maishe Kepara*," a synonym for a hopelessly mixed up person, naturally, me, the Maishe in the house. Apart from these asides, the religion brought from Poland in my mother's family had washed away off the sea-

6. Prayer shawl (Hebrew).
7. Two black leather boxes that contain portions of the Talmud and that are strapped to the left arm and forehead of Jewish men during morning prayer (Hebrew).
8. The text of Jewish mysticism.
9. A soup made primarily of beets that is served hot or cold and garnished with sour cream. "*Kashe*": buckwheat groats, thought of as a cereal, actually an herb, and cooked like rice. This plant is a native of Russia.

board of America, leaving behind a mouthful of jokes, pebbles, smoothed by wealth.

The Grandparents' law on both sides of Mother's family, prayers, customs, were stowed away, creaky out of fashion furniture in the attics or cellars, a few displayed at weddings and funerals. Whatever came from Europe with the parents was dissipated among the comings and goings of the older siblings who practiced mostly disapproval. Twelve brothers and sisters; my mother, the next to youngest in the pictures that show her on the steps, in Harlem, Flatbush,[1] has that watchful, angry concentration I see in my daughter, an eye on her older brother about to bear off a gift she isn't getting. My mother lost her mother, Channah, before she could claim any attention and her father wandered off as a pariah while her older sisters brought her up.

My father had found his father, Israel again after a nine year lapse, separated by family quarrels, immigration, World War One. Israel walked on the boat in the hour that his wife, Devorah died and his three children, my father at twelve, the oldest, clung to the tall stranger's coattails as they came down the gangplank into a strange land. My father talked often about Israel's death, blaming himself, and the doctors who sent Grandfather home early from the hospital after a bout of pneumonia. Dad would tell me the story every year, on the day, or the day before, the *Yahrtzeit*.[2] I don't remember Dad said they gave my grandfather, Israel, penicillin against his infection but I see Grandpa getting up, proudly in his high silk hat, frock coat, in the round bowl of the Fowler Street schul.[3] The congregation is packed up into the balconies, over a thousand, not a seat empty, standing in the outer vestibules with the swinging doors open, and the noisemakers, big wooden clackers and little tin *gregors*,[4] cap pistols, wind up machine guns, bicycle horns, party tooters, ready to unleash pandemonium, and clutching the *Megillah*, Scroll of Esther, my grandfather starting the chant, at the cry "Haman!" falling over the bimah, off the platform. Rushed to the hospital, he died. Heart attack!

In a search for my family history I have heard other versions. There was a meeting at the Beth El synagogue the night before the holiday. The finances of Beth El cemetery came up. My grandfather was attacked by one of his enemies on the synagogue board—this collected from an aunt. The rabbi of the congregation, still alive, in Jerusalem, forty years after Israel's death, told me of a meeting just before the holiday service in which my grandfather with no warning, collapsed in the rabbi's arms.

Now I see it, his suit jacket half off, white sleeve folded above the elbow, the arm of my father naked, hairy, coming out of his shirt, wound seven times with the flat black phylactery strap, the boxes, a bit absurd, on his forehead, arm—but it is death naked in his white, hairy arm, rarely exposed, his mutter about Grandfather, falling on the bimah, in the middle of reading the Megillah, and the hospital, "the damn hospital" that had sent him home early, as my father in his pew wrapped the thongs up skillfully in front of me, through dim, morning light.

1. A Brooklyn neighborhood. "Harlem": a Manhattan neighborhood. Both were once heavily Jewish.
2. Literally, year's time, anniversary. The annual commemoration of death of a near relative; it includes the lighting of a memorial candle.
3. Synagogue (Yiddish).
4. Mirsky is describing the events at a Purim festival. A *gregor* is a noisemaker that is used when evil Haman's name is mentioned during the reading of the Megillah (Book of Esther, which relates the story of Purim).

In the wax of the candle, wasting away, those last moments in my mother's life, drip, painfully, into the light, catch fire, disappear. That hour, she waved me from the foot of a bed in the afternoon, and her hoarse voice, "Go away! Go away!" As if she was before some last nakedness—for I had taken her body up from the bed covers, washed it, moved it, handled it like a relic, a dozen times with the nurses turning her constantly during my visits in the final months to help her flesh resist the bed sores. There was no longer in that body the power that flashed between the cracks of half opened doors in childhood, a tower, or emerged in a bathing suit shimmering briefly, white, pink, black haired, as her slim frame, large bosomed, jumped from a rock, cleaved the cold Atlantic waters, salty and warm when I went crying to it. I cradled a set of bones, barely covered, from which my mother's voice still spoke, articulated. No, it was the bare stripped away last throes she barred me from, and I went home not knowing it, but frightened, wanting as she ordered, to flee her.

A former girlfriend was living in Cambridge, a few miles away from our family flat in Mattapan, a Boston suburb. Not the woman I was living with but I needed to be close to a female who was sympathetic that night. I called and invited her to our house for supper where my sister, her two little girls were staying. They had come from the far west to wait with my father and me for the death rattle.

I brought the friend back to her rooms in Cambridge, early, her sweetness making the gloom more awful. I took the oldest of my two nieces, five years old, along for company. I was afraid to be alone, even for fifteen minutes, in the car. It was only nine o'clock on the way home to Mattapan from Cambridge and we passed the hospital. I wanted to go in. I didn't. It was unusual not to stop. One of us, I, my father, my sister, had been by the bed for weeks now through most of the night. Was it my turn? I don't know. Going by the driveway for the hospital which loomed in brick towers beside the highway, I remembered my mother's hand, pushing the air, pushing me away. My niece beside me, I went on driving, went to what had been home to my mother and father for fifteen years, a rented floor in a brick Mattapan two decker.

The call woke us two hours later. It was Friday night. Later that would mean something. I only recall starting up in the sheets as my father cried, "She's dead!" at the telephone, ripping my white undershirt in two, as if making up a bandage right away against the terror, although it was because I had been told that you were supposed to tear your clothes. I wondered what else I should tear, my hair, my suit, the bedspread. I went into the hospital and the body was already wrapped. "It's moving," I told the nurse. "I see it moving."

"No, no," they said gently, pushing me out of the room, away from the body to which I had bent, trying to bite through the white adhesive tape which was wound around it from head to foot. "You are imagining it."

I wasn't. I wanted it unwound. Only it was too late. No one will do that for you. So I let myself be taken home. I went to bed. That's when it happened.

I felt her. She came for me. I was lying in the bed, in the darkness still, two or three in the morning, not asleep, not awake. When I felt her, saw something of her, a force, a wind with a shape, come down and begin to pull me up after her, taking me with her, toward something I knew was evil, dangerous, and I pushed her away.

Why did I do that? Was it you? What could I have wanted, more, Mother, than to have gone with you, yet I too pushed you, pushed you away. For you were angry, so angry I was afraid.

I was alone. Afraid to lie back, go to sleep, knowing that in sleep, she would come again, and for some reason, in fear.

In that moment I did not let myself take the hand that had only twelve hours ago pushed me away. I recognized my mother's face in the spirit furious over me, wanting to tear me away from the bed. But I recoiled from the force which had half drawn me up in the sheets after her.

Now collecting among the few surviving sisters, bits of my mother's childhood so carefully screened from me, I understand the anger under the calm hands that were only laid upon me in days of sickness; my fevers, the grippe, measles, fits of hysteria. I go over the photographs and I see her looking into the camera for love. The teeth marks she left in my lips at the corridor door of the ward of the dying, one afternoon in the last months sink into my flesh. "I was my mother's favorite," the next oldest of her sisters says. "My mother, Channah, used to take me into the bed and when I was too old, she put the last, the youngest, the one after your mother, there. Channah wanted to keep her husband who had given her twelve children out." So my mother was caught between the favorite, her next oldest sister who was sickly, and the youngest, the baby. According to the aunts, Channah sent her husband, my grandfather, away from the house, kept him out of the business which had originally been his, but which he made, I guess, a mess of. He was harrying his own children and her, unbalanced.

I remember what my father told me, that my mother had shrugged at the news of her father's death and had no plans to go down to the Connecticut town, to join her brothers and sisters at the funeral. It was impossible to get my mother to talk about her father and it was a surprise to me when I learned that he had lived some years after her mother. Yet his name had been given to me, in an abbreviation, as my middle one, Joseph, as Jay, though whether it was his or my father's mother's father, another Joseph, was left ambiguous.

As I stared at death in its long wasting, eating away my mother's face in the last few months, I saw the angular, stern bones of my oldest uncle, aunts, who bore the brunt of this missing grandfather, rise, the flesh sinking. I did not understand. I thought my mother was angry at me.

In my dreams she stalks with a bitter separation. She appears in a corridor of one of our rented houses, or the home we briefly owned with tenants on the top floors. She won't talk to my father and for me she has barely a word. She is alone, but she doesn't need us, not me, my sister, my father. She is living in Florida, by herself, a last minute miracle giving her life but without joy, hope. Not the woman who tugged at my arm in the final month and asked me, "Is it?" afraid still to give the malignancy a name.

"What do you think it is?" was all I could say.

She nodded. Mouthed the word silently. We didn't speak the word, which she and my father had refused to use. "All I want is six months," she whispered. "Six months is enough." We did not love her, not enough. We didn't arrange to take her home though she asked us to. The nurses were keeping her alive, we said. My father shouted at me when at last, I started in . . .

"You told me in my office, yourself, you couldn't take . . ."

"Stop," she whispers. Now, over the paper, as I write this, "Enough. Go away." She doesn't want to see my father, my sister, me, naked, around her bed. In showing us, I throw harsh illumination on her, as if she was always flayed out, helpless, a body being consumed by itself. No, she takes my hand as the young girl, who once bent to hoist me over a barbed wire fence to a forbidden garden, then bounded over herself, in shorts, ankle socks, loafers, laughing.

Her need to take me up the night the bandage was wound around her was part of a romance we had hidden, never given a name, and I tore myself apart from those arms that seized me, her last anchor, hope, and now I watch the flame, in its last flicker, each year, and wonder, jerking at the light.

1995

ROBERT PINSKY
b. 1940

Since 1997, when Robert Pinsky was appointed the thirty-ninth poet laureate of the United States, an appointment he held for an unprecedented three terms, he has become perhaps America's most recognized contemporary poet, speaking for poetry as a democratic and a vocal art at public readings across the country, on television, on the internet, and in print interviews. Pinsky's special undertaking as poet laureate, the Favorite Poem Project, put that democratic, vocal ideal of poetry into practice by encouraging community poetry readings across America that have led to the creation of video, audio, and print archives documenting thousands of individual Americans reading and talking about a poem of their choice.

The Favorite Poem Project, Pinsky's role as poetry editor of the internet weekly *Slate*, his collaboration on the computer game *Mindwheel*, his widely praised translation of Dante's *Inferno* (1994), a Book-of-the-Month Club Editor's Choice, all suggest the range of Pinsky's interests and influence but not their depth, for Pinsky has been a distinguished poet, critic, translator, and teacher for thirty years. Of his first book, *Sadness and Happiness* (1975), Louis Martz wrote that the poems "pointed the way towards the future of poetry." In the collections published since then, most recently *The Figured Wheel: New and Collected Poems, 1966–1996*, and in his works of criticism, Pinsky has claimed a distinct poetic territory: he holds that poetry should share the qualities of speech and prose, qualities he identifies in *The Situation of Poetry* (1976) as "Clarity, Flexibility, Efficiency, and Cohesiveness." It follows, then, that conversation, reminiscences, jokes, and the sounds of everyday American life infuse Pinsky's poetry but are given music by Pinsky's formal gifts. Pinsky's poetic subjects likewise come from everyday experience; he often locates his poems in the comfortable, familiar worlds of "small-town main street" life.

One of Pinsky's most moving poems, *History of My Heart*, from the volume of that same name (published 1984), deals with two favorite topics: his childhood and its relationship to history—large and small, personal and public. Pinsky's Jewish identity is a central strand of the poem. He grew up in Long Branch, New Jersey, a once famous ocean resort town whose ethnic makeup was primarily Italian and Jewish. His family was "nominally orthodox," and he lived in a "gorgeous, fading European reality" whose influence he has worked to decipher. As a secular Jew coming of age in the 1950s, he felt both inside and outside of mainstream American culture, a state of being he vividly captures in the poem *Night Game*, which recalls the heroism of Brooklyn Dodger Sandy Koufax—the rare Jewish professional athlete. When Koufax refused to pitch a World Series game because it fell on Yom Kippur, he became a legend to Jewish Americans everywhere.

Author of seven books of poems and four books of criticism, Pinsky attended Rutgers and then Stanford University. He taught at the University of California, Berkeley, and at Wellesley College before joining the graduate creative writing faculty at Boston University in 1988.

The Night Game

Some of us believe
We would have conceived romantic
Love out of our own passions
With no precedents,
Without songs and poetry—
Or have invented poetry and music
As a comb of cells for the honey.

Shaped by ignorance,
A succession of new worlds,
Congruities improvised by
Immigrants or children.

I once thought most people were Italian,
Jewish or Colored.
To be white and called
Something like *Ed Ford*[1]
Seemed aristocratic,
A rare distinction.

Possibly I believed only gentiles
And blonds could be left-handed.

Already famous
After one year in the majors,
Whitey Ford was drafted by the Army
To play ball in the flannels
Of the Signal Corps, stationed
In Long Branch, New Jersey.

A night game, the silver potion
Of the lights, his pink skin
Shining like a burn.

1. A reference to the Yankee's Edward "Whitey" Ford (b. 1928), the youngest pitcher ever to win a World Series. Because they were both teams in New York City, the Yankees and the Dodgers were each other's fiercest competitor.

Never a player
I liked or hated: a Yankee,
A mere success.

But white the chalked-off lines
In the grass, white and green
The immaculate uniform,
And white the unpigmented
Halo of his hair
When he[2] shifted his cap:

So ordinary and distinct,
So close up, that I felt
As if I could have made him up,
Imagined him as I imagined

The ball, a scintilla
High in the black backdrop
Of the sky. Tight red stitches.
Rawlings.[3] The bleached

Horsehide white: the color
Of nothing. Color of the past
And of the future, of the movie screen
At rest and of blank paper.

"I could have." The mind. The black
Backdrop, the white
Fly picked out by the towering
Lights. A few years later

On a blanket in the grass
By the same river
A girl and I came into
Being together
To the faint muttering
Of unthinkable
Troubadours and radios.

The emerald
Theater, the night.
Another time,
I devised a left-hander
Even more gifted
Than Whitey Ford: a Dodger.
People were amazed by him.

2. This is the first mention of the unnamed pitcher to whom the poet refers—Sandy Koufax (b. 1936), a left-handed pitching sensation for the Brooklyn Dodgers.
3. The name of a company that makes baseball equipment.

Once, when he was young,
He refused to pitch on Yom Kippur.[4]

1990

Visions of Daniel[1]

Magician, appointed officer
Of the crown. He thrived, he never
Seemed to get older.

Golden curly head.
Smooth skin, unreadable tawny eyes,
Former favorite, they said,
Of the chief eunuch of Nebuchadnezzar,
Who taught him the Chaldean language and courtly ways
And gave him his name of a courtier:
"Daniel who was called Belteshazzar"
In silk and Egyptian linen.
Proprietor, seer.

The Jews disliked him,
He smelled of pagan incense and char.
Pious gossips in the souk
Said he was unclean,
He had smeared his body with thick
Yellowish sperm of lion
Before he went into the den,
The odor and color
Were indelible, he would reek
Of beast forever.

Wheat-color. Faint smell as of smoke.
The Kings of Babylon feared him
For generations.

And Daniel who was called in Chaldean
Belteshazzar, meaning spared-by-the-lion
Said as for thee O King I took

4. Day of Atonement, the holiest day of the Jewish calendar, falling in late September or early October.

1. This poem retells the first half of the Book of Daniel, a biblical text. In this story, Daniel is taken to Babylon as a child and is raised in the court of King Nebuchadnezzar, who renames him Belteshazzar. The people of Babylon, as well as their language, are called Chaldean. Although he was only supposed to remain there for three years, the king favors Daniel and he stays until adulthood. His intelligence and prophetic powers make Daniel the king's most important adviser. The king's son, Belshazzar, sees the words "Mene Mene Tekel Upharsin" and asks Daniel to read them. The words have been translated as "You have been counted; You have been counted; and you have been found wanting." Daniel interprets them to mean that Nebuchadnezzar and his family have come to the end of their reign. Even after that event comes to pass, Daniel retains his powerful position as adviser to the new king, Darius the Mede, and afterward Cyrus the Persian. In the second half of the Book of Daniel—not recounted here—Daniel provides interpretations of dreams and visions of the kings.

Thy thoughts into my mind
As I lay upon my bed: You saw O King a great
Image with His head of gold His heart
And arms of silver His belly and thighs of brass
His legs of iron His feet
Part of iron and part of clay
And then alas
O Nebuchadnezzar the image fell

And clay and iron
And brass and gold and silver
Lay shattered like chaff on the
Threshingfloor in summer.

Terrified Nebuchadnezzar
Went on all fours, driven
To eat grass like the oxen.
His body wet by the dews of heaven,
Hair matted like feathers, fingers
Hooked like the claw of the raven.

Interpreter, survivor,
Still youthful years later
When Nebuchadnezzar's son Belshazzar
Saw a bodiless hand
Scrawl meaningless words on the plaster
Mene Tekel Upharsin,
Interpreted by Daniel, You are finished,
God has weighed you and found you
Wanting, your power will be given
To the Medes and the Persians.
And both King Darius the Mede
And King Cyrus the Persian
Feared him and honored him.

Yellow smoking head,
High royal administrator.
Unanointed. He declined
To bow to images.

Then one night God sent him a vision
Of the world's entire future
Couched in images: The lion
With the wings of an eagle
And feet of a man, the bear
With the mouth in its side
That said, Devour Much Flesh,
The four-headed leopard
Of dominion, and lastly
The beast with iron teeth
That devoured and broke

And stamped and spat
Fiery streams before him.

And he wrote, I the Jew Daniel
Saw the horn of the fourth beast
Grow eyes and a mouth and the horn
Made war with the saints and
Prevailed against them.

Also, he saw a man clothed in linen
Who stood upon the waters
And said, As to the abomination
And the trial and the making white
Go thy way O Daniel, for the words
Are closed up and sealed till the end.

For three weeks after this night vision
I Daniel, he wrote, ate no pleasant
Bread nor wine, my comeliness
Turned to corruption, I retained
No strength, my own countenance
Changed in me. But I kept the
Matter in my heart, I was mute
And set my face toward the earth.
And afterward I rose up
And did the king's business.

Appalled initiate. Intimate of power.
Scorner of golden images, governor.
In the drinking places they said
He had wished himself unborn,
That he had no navel.

So tawny Belteshazzar or Daniel
With his unclean smell of lion
And his night visions,
Who took the thoughts of the King
Into his mind O Jews, prospered
In the reign of Nebuchadnezzar
And of his son Belshazzar
And in the reign of Darius
And the reign of Cyrus the Persian.

1990

Avenue

They stack bright pyramids of goods and gather
Mop-helves in sidewalk barrels. They keen, they boogie.
Paints, fruits, clean bolts of cottons and synthetics,
Clarity and plumage of October skies.

Way of the costermonger's[1] wooden barrow
And also the secular marble cinquefoil and lancet
Of the great store. They persist. The jobber tells
The teller in the bank and she retells

Whatever it is to the shopper and the shopper
Mentions it to the retailer by the way.
They mutter and stumble, derelict. They write
These theys I write. Scant storefront pushbroom Jesus

Of Haitian hardware—they travel in shadows, they flog
Sephardic softgoods. They strain. Mid-hustle they faint
And shrivel. Or snoring on grates they rise to thrive.
Bonemen and pumpkins of All Saints. Kol Nidre,[2]

Blunt shovel of atonement, a blade of song
From the terra-cotta temple: Lord, forgive us
Our promises, we chant. Or we churn our wino
Syllables and stares on the Avenue. We, they—

Jack. Mrs. Whisenant from the bakery. Sam Lee.
This is the way, its pavement crackwork burnished
With plantain. In strollers they bawl and claw. They flourish.
Furniture, Florist, Pets. My mongrel tongue

Of *nudnik*[3] and *criminentlies*,[4] the tarnished flute
And brogue of quidnuncs[5] in the bars, in Casey's
Black amber air of spent Hiram Walker, attuned.
Sweet ash of White Owl.[6] Ten High. They touch. Eyes blurred

Stricken with passion as in a Persian lyric
They flower and stroke. They couple. From the Korean,
Staples and greens. From the Christian Lebanese,
Home electronics. Why is that Friday "Good"?

Why "Day of Atonement" for release from vows?
Because we tried us, to be at one, because
We say as one we traffic, we dice, we stare.
Some they remember that won't remember them—

Their headlights found me stoned, like a bundled sack
Lying in the Avenue, late. They didn't speak
My language. For them, a small adventure. They hefted
Me over the curb and bore me to an entry

1. Archaic term for apple seller; now a term used in London to mean one who sells fruits and vegetables in the street.
2. Kol Nidre is the evening service that begins Yom Kippur, the Day of Atonement. On this night, one may be forgiven for previous promises made to God that have not been fulfilled.
3. Pest (Yiddish).
4. This is not standard Yiddish but probably a combination of Yiddish and English, meant to suggest criminals or vandals.
5. Nosy people or busybodies (Latin).
6. These are brand names for alcoholic beverages.

Out of the way. Illuminated footwear
On both sides. How I stank. Dead drunk. They left me
Breathing in my bower between the Halloween
Brogans and pumps on crystal pedestals.

But I was dead to the world. The midnight city
In autumn. Day of attainment, tall saints
Who saved me. My taints, day of anointment. Oil
Of rose and almond in the haircutting parlor,

Motor oil swirling rainbows in gutter water.
Ritually unattainted, the congregation
File from the place of worship and resume
The rumbling drum and hautbois[7] of conversation,

Speech of the granary, of the cloven lanes
Of traffic, of salvaged silver. Not shriven and yet
Not rent, they stride the Avenue, banter, barter.
Capering, on fire, they cleave to the riven hub.

1996

7. Oboe.

MAX APPLE
b. 1941

Beginning with his first novel, *Zip* (1978), about nice Jewish Ira Goldstein, manager of the Puerto Rican boxer Jesus, Max Apple's affection for American and Jewish American culture is clear. In *Free Agents*, the 1984 collection of stories in which *The Eighth Day* originally appeared, Apple's subjects range from ice fishing and Aristotle to Japanese American lobbyists and circumcision. In a review for the *Los Angeles Times*, critic Ralph Sipper wrote that "the unifying principle in all these send-ups is an author who expresses himself in some of the niftiest satirical prose since Jonathan Swift."

For Apple (like Swift, perhaps), no subject is sacred—or, more accurately in Apple's case, nothing and everything is sacred. In *The Eighth Day*, a couple, one of whom is Jewish and one Gentile, struggle to know themselves by returning to the moment of their birth. The male, however, cannot fully complete this New Age ritual because he cannot remember his life before the eighth day—that is, the day of circumcision for the Jewish male. Because the protagonist cannot remember past that point, Apple tells us that there is no "past that point"—the protagonist's life began when he was circumcised, when his Jewish identity was given to him. For Apple, circumcision is more than religious ritual; it is a reaffirmation of culture, at once an opportunity for both humorous repartee and serious reflection. This story, like all of Apple's fiction, may now and then be crude, but it is never irreverent. What Apple gives us is satire without the sneer.

In the 1990s, Apple published two nonfiction accounts of life with his grandparents. *Roommates: My Grandfather's Story* (1994) tells of Apple sharing his living quarters with his grandfather for almost his entire life, including when the writer was in graduate school. This memoir received more praise than any of his previous work. In the *New Leader*, Tova Reich called the book "nothing less than a blessing," while the *New York Times* praised its straightforward prose and moving detail, its "full sentiment, but lack of treacle." In *I Love Gootie: My Grandmother's Story* (1998), Apple describes his Yiddish-speaking, Lithuanian grandmother, who also lived with his family in Grand Rapids, Michigan. Among other feats, this novel skillfully juxtaposes how he dealt with the onset of teenage acne in the context of his grandmother's crazy black and bitter memories of the shtetl. Ultimately, he decides that she was "born before love was invented." For Apple, however, no bitterness follows this revelation.

Apple has published eight books. He teaches at Rice University and lives in San Francisco, where, "out of respect for his history," he keeps a kosher home.

The Eighth Day[1]

I was always interested in myself, but I never thought I went back so far. Joan and I talked about birth almost as soon as we met. I told her I believed in the importance of early experience.

"What do you mean by early?" she asked. "Before puberty, before loss of innocence?"

"Before age five," I said.

She sized me up. I could tell it was the right answer.

She had light-blond hair that fell over one eye. I liked the way she moved her hair away to look at me with two eyes when she got serious.

"How soon before age five?" She took a deep breath before she asked me that. I decided to go the limit.

"The instant of birth," I said, though I didn't mean it and had no idea where it would lead me.

She gave me the kind of look then that men would dream about if being men didn't rush us so.

With that look Joan and I became lovers. We were in a crowded restaurant watching four large goldfish flick their tails at each other in a display across from the cash register. There was also another couple, who had introduced us.

Joan's hand snuck behind the napkin holder to rub my right index finger. With us chronology went backwards. Birth led us to love.

II

Joan was twenty-six and had devoted her adult life to knowing herself.

"Getting to know another person, especially one from the opposite gender, is fairly easy." She said this after our first night together. "Apart from reproduction it's the main function of sex. The biblical word 'to know' someone is exactly right. But nature didn't give us any such easy and direct ways to know ourselves. In fact, it's almost perverse how difficult it is to find out anything about the self."

1. According to Jewish law, male children must be circumcised on the eighth day after their birth to enter into the covenant with God.

She proposed herself up on an elbow to look at me, still doing all the talking.

"You probably know more about my essential nature from this simple biological act than I learned from two years of psychoanalysis."

Joan had been through Jung, Freud, LSD,[2] philosophy, and primitive religion. A few months before we met, she had re-experienced her own birth in primal therapy. She encouraged me to do the same. I tried and was amazed at how much early experience I seemed able to remember, with Joan and the therapist to help me. But there was a great stumbling block, one that Joan did not have. On the eighth day after my birth, according to the ancient Hebrew tradition, I had been circumcised. The circumcision and its pain seemed to have replaced in my consciousness the birth trauma. No matter how much I tried, I couldn't get back any earlier than the eighth day.

"Don't be afraid," Joan said. "Go back to birth. Think of all experience as an arch."

I thought of the golden arches of McDonald's. I focused. I howled. The therapist immersed me in warm water. Joan, already many weeks past her mother's postpartum depression, watched and coaxed. She meant well. She wanted me to share pain like an orgasm, like lovers in poems who slit their wrists together. She wanted us to be as content as trees in the rain forest. She wanted our mingling to begin in utero.[3]

"Try," she said.

The therapist rubbed Vaseline on my temples and gripped me gently with Teflon-coated kitchen tongs. Joan shut off all the lights and played in stereo the heartbeat of a laboring mother.

For thirty seconds I held my face under water. Two rooms away a tiny flashlight glowed. The therapist squeezed my ribs until I bruised. The kitchen tongs hung from my head like antennae. But I could go back no farther than the hairs beneath the chin of the man with the blade who pulled at and then slit my tiny penis, the man who prayed and drank wine over my foreskin. I howled and I gagged.

"The birth canal," Joan and the therapist said.

"The knife," I screamed, "the blood, the tube, the pain between my legs."

Finally we gave up.

"You Hebrews," Joan said. "Your ancient totems cut you off from the centers of your being. It must explain the high density of neurosis among Jewish males."

The therapist said that the subject ought to be studied, but she didn't think anyone would give her a grant.

I was a newcomer to things like primal therapy, but Joan had been born for the speculative. She was the Einstein of pseudoscience. She knew tarot, phrenology, and metaposcopy the way other people knew about baseball or cooking. All her time was spare time except when she didn't believe in time.

When Joan could not break down those eight days between my birth and my birthright, she became, for a while, seriously anti-Semitic. She used sur-

2. Lysergic acid diethylamide, a strong hallucinogen that induces psychotic symptoms similar to those of schizophrenia. In the 1960s and 1970s, it became popular because of its perceived "mind-expanding" capabilities. "Jung, Freud": a reference to Sigmund Freud (1856–1931), the founder of psychoanalysis, and his compatriot Carl Jung (1875–1961).

3. In the uterus, before birth (Latin).

gical tape to hunch my penis over into a facsimile of precircumcision. She told me that smegma was probably a healthy secretion. For a week she cooked nothing but pork. I didn't mind, but I worried a little about trichinosis because she liked everything rare.

Joan had an incredible grip. Her older brother gave her a set of Charles Atlas Squeezers when she was eight. While she read, she still did twenty minutes a day with each hand. If she wanted to show off, she could close the grip exerciser with just her thumb and middle finger. The power went right up into her shoulders. She could squeeze your hand until her nipples stood upright. She won spending money arm wrestling with men in bars. She had broken bones in the hands of two people, though she tried to be careful and gentle with everyone.

I met Joan just when people were starting to bore her, all people, and she had no patience for pets either. She put up with me, at least at the beginning, because of the primal therapy. Getting me back to my birth gave her a project. When the project failed and she also tired of lacing me with pork, she told me one night to go make love to dark Jewesses named Esther or Rebecca and leave her alone.

I hit her.

"Uncharacteristic for a neurotic Jewish male," she said.

It was my first fight since grade school. Her hands were much stronger than mine. In wrestling she could have killed me, but I stayed on the balls of my feet and kept my left in her face. My reach was longer so she couldn't get me in her grip.

"I'll pull your cock off!" she screamed and rushed at me. When my jab didn't slow her, I hit her a right cross to the nose. Blood spurted down her chin. She got one hand on my shirt and ripped it so hard she sprained my neck. I hit her in the midsection and then a hard but openhanded punch to the head.

"Christ killer, cocksucker," she called me, "wife beater." She was crying. The blood and tears mingled on her madras shirt. It matched the pattern of the fabric. I dropped my arms. She rushed me and got her hands around my neck.

"I must love you," I said, "to risk my life this way."

She loosened her grip but kept her thumbs on my jugular. Her face came down on mine, making us both a bloody mess. We kissed amid the carnage. She let go, but my neck kept her fingerprints for a week.

"I'd never kill anyone I didn't love," she said. We washed each other's faces. Later she said she was glad she hadn't pulled my cock off.

After the fight we decided, mutually, to respect one another more. We agreed that the circumcision was a genuine issue. Neither of us wanted it to come between us.

"Getting to the bottom of anything is one of the great pleasures of life," Joan said. She also believed a fresh start ought to be just that, not one eight days old.

So we started fresh and I began to research my circumcision. Since my father had been dead for ten years, my mother was my only source of information. She was very reluctant to talk about it. She refused to remember the time of day or even whether it happened in the house or the hospital or the synagogue.

"All I know," she said, "is that Reb Berkowitz did it. He was the only one in town. Leave me alone with this craziness. Go swallow dope with all your friends. It's her, isn't it? To marry her in a church you need to know about your circumcision? Do what you want; at least the circumcision is one thing she can't change."

Listening in on the other line, Joan said, "They can even change sex now. To change the circumcision would be minor surgery, but that's not the point."

"Go to hell," my mother said and hung up. My mother and I had not been on good terms since I quit college. She is closer to my two brothers, who are CPAs and have an office together in New Jersey. But, to be fair to my mother, she probably wouldn't want to talk about their circumcisions either.

From the United Synagogue Yearbook which I found in the library of Temple Beth-El only a few blocks from my apartment I located three Berkowitzes. Two were clearly too young to have done me, so mine was Hyman J., listed at Congregation Adath Israel, South Bend, Indiana.

"They all have such funny names," Joan said. "If he's the one, we'll have to go to him. It may be the breakthrough you need."

"Why?" my mother begged, when I told her we were going to South Bend to investigate. "For God's sake, why?"

"Love," I said. "I love her, and we both believe it's important to know this. Love happens to you through bodies."

"I wish," my mother said, "that after eight days they could cut the love off too and then maybe you'd act normal."

South Bend was a three-hundred-mile drive. I made an appointment with the synagogue secretary to meet Hyman Berkowitz late in the afternoon. Joan and I left before dawn. She packed peanut butter sandwiches and apples. She also took along the portable tape recorder so we could get everything down exactly as Berkowitz remembered it.

"I'm not all that into primal therapy anymore," she said as we started down the interstate. "You know that this is for your sake, that even if you don't get back to the birth canal this circumcision thing is no small matter. I mean, it's almost accidental that it popped up in primal; it probably would have affected you in psychoanalysis as well. I wonder if they started circumcising before or after astrology was a very well-developed Egyptian science. Imagine taking infants and mutilating them with crude instruments."

"The instruments weren't so crude," I reminded her. "The ancient Egyptians used to do brain surgery. They invented eye shadow and embalming. How hard was it to get a knife sharp, even in the Bronze Age?"

"Don't be such a defensive Jewish boy," she said. "After all, it's your pecker they sliced, and at eight days too, some definition of the age of reason."

For people who are not especially sexual, Joan and I talk about it a lot. She has friends who are orgiasts. She has watched though never participated in group sex.

"Still," she says, "nothing shocks me like the thought of cutting the foreskin of a newborn."

III

"It's no big deal," Berkowitz tells us late that afternoon. His office is a converted lavatory. The frosted glass windows block what little daylight there still is. His desk is slightly recessed in the cavity where once a four-legged tub stood. His synagogue is a converted Victorian house. Paint is peeling from all the walls. Just off the interstate we passed an ultramodern temple.

"Ritual isn't in style these days," he tells Joan when she asks about his surroundings. "The clothing store owners and scrap dealers have put their money into the Reformed. They want to be more like the goyim."[4]

"I'm a goy," Joan says. She raises her head proudly to display a short straight nose. Her blond hair is shoulder length.

"So what else is new?" Berkowitz laughs. "Somehow, by accident, I learned how to talk to goyim too." She asks to see his tools.

From his desk drawer he withdraws two flannel-wrapped packets. They look like place settings of sterling silver. It takes him a minute or two to undo the knots. Before us lies a long thin pearl-handled jackknife.

"It looks like a switchblade," Joan says. "Can I touch it?" He nods.

She holds the knife and examines the pearl handle for inscriptions.

"No writing?"

"Nothing," says Berkowitz. "We don't read knives."

He takes it from her and opens it. The blade is as long as a Bic pen. Even in his dark office the sharpness glows.

"All that power," she says, "just to snip at a tiny penis."

"Wrong," says Berkowitz. "For the shmekel[5] I got another knife. This one kills chickens."

Joan looks puzzled and nauseated.

"You think a person can make a living in South Bend, Indiana, on newborn Jewish boys? You saw the temple. I've got to compete with a half dozen Jewish pediatricians who for the extra fifty bucks will say a prayer too. When I kill a chicken, there's not two cousins who are surgeons watching every move. Chickens are my livelihood. Circumcising is a hobby."

"You're cute," Joan tells him.

H. Berkowitz blushes. "Shiksas[6] always like me. My wife worries that someday I'll run off with a convert. You came all this way to see my knife?" He is a little embarrassed by his question.

I try to explain my primal therapy, my failure to scream before the eighth day.

"In my bones, in my body, all I can remember is you, the knife, the blood."

"It's funny," Berkowitz says, "I don't remember you at all. Did your parents make a big party, or did they pay me a little extra or something? I don't keep records, and believe me, foreskins are nothing to remember."

"I know you did mine."

"I'm not denying. I'm just telling you it's not so special to me to remember it."

"Reverend," Joan says, "you may think this is all silly, but here is a man who wants to clear his mind by reliving his birth. Circumcision is standing in the way. Won't you help him?"

"I can't put it back."

4. Non-Jews (Yiddish).
5. Slang for penis (Yiddish).
6. Non-Jewish females (Yiddish).

"Don't joke with us, Reverend. We came a long way. Will you do it again?"

"Also impossible," he says. "I never leave a long enough piece of foreskin. Maybe some of the doctors do that, but I always do a nice clean job. Look."

He motions for me to pull out my penis. Joan also instructs me to do so. It seems oddly appropriate in this converted bathroom.

"There," he says, admiringly. "I recognize my work. Clean, tight, no flab."

"We don't really want you to cut it," Joan says. "He just wants to relive the experience so that he can travel back beyond it to the suffering of his birth. Right now your circumcision is a block in his memory."

Berkowitz shakes his head. I zip my fly.

"You're sure you want to go back so far?"

"Not so completely," I admit, but Joan gives me a look.

"Well," Berkowitz says, "in this business you get used to people making jokes, but if you want it, I'll try. It's not like you're asking me to commit a crime. There's not even a rabbinic law against pretending to circumcise someone a second time."

IV

The recircumcision takes place that night at Hyman Berkowitz's house. His wife and two children are already asleep. He asks me to try to be quiet. I am lying on his dining room table under a bright chandelier.

"I'd just as soon my wife not see this," Berkowitz says. "She's not as up to date as I am."

I am naked beneath a sheet on the hard table.

Berkowitz takes a small double-edged knife out of a torn and stained case. I can make out the remnants of his initials on the case. The instrument is nondescript stainless steel. If not for his initials, it might be mistaken for an industrial tool. I close my eyes.

"The babies," he says, "always keep their eyes open. You'd be surprised how alert they are. At eight days they already know when something's happening."

Joan puts a throw pillow from the sofa under my head.

"I'm proud of you," she whispers. "Most other men would never dare to do this. My instincts were right about you." She kisses my cheek.

Berkowitz lays down his razor.

"With babies," he says, "there's always a crowd around, at least the family. The little fellow wrapped in a blanket looks around or screams. You take off the diaper and one-two it's over." He hesitates. "With you it's like I'm a doctor. It's making me nervous, all this talking about it. I've been a mohel[7] thirty-four years and I started slaughtering chickens four years before that. I'm almost ready for Social Security. Just baby boys, chickens, turkeys, occasionally a duck. Once someone brought me a captured deer. He was so beautiful. I looked in his eyes. I couldn't do it. The man understood. He put the deer back in his truck, drove him to the woods, and let him go. He came back later to thank me."

"You're not really going to have to do much," Joan says, "just relive the thing. Draw a drop of blood, that will be enough: one symbolic drop."

7. One who performs circumcisions.

"Down there there's no drops," Berkowitz says. "It's close to arteries; the heart wants blood there. It's the way the Almighty wanted it to be."

As Berkowitz hesitates, I begin to be afraid. Not primal fear but very contemporary panic. Fear about what's happening right now, right before my eyes.

Berkowitz drinks a little of the Manischewitz wine he has poured for the blessing. He loosens his necktie. He sits down.

"I didn't have the voice to be a cantor," he says, "and for sure I wasn't smart enough to become a rabbi. Still, I wanted the religious life. I wanted some type of religious work. I'm not an immigrant, you know. I graduated from high school and junior college. I could have done lots of things. My brother is a dentist. He's almost assimilated in White Plains. He doesn't like to tell people what his older brother does.

"In English I sound like the Mafia, 'a ritual slaughterer.' " Berkowitz laughs nervously. "Every time on the forms when it says Job Description, I write 'ritual slaughterer.' I hate how it sounds."

"You've probably had second thoughts about your career right from the start," Joan says.

"Yes, I have. God's work, I tell myself, but why does God want me to slit the throats of chickens and slice the foreskins of babies? When Abraham did it, it mattered; now, why not let the pediatricians mumble the blessing, why not electrocute the chickens?"

"Do you think God wanted you to be a dentist," Joan asks, "or an insurance agent? Don't be ashamed of your work. What you do is holiness. A pediatrician is not a man of God. An electrocuted chicken is not an animal whose life has been taken seriously."

Hyman Berkowitz looks in amazement at my Joan, a twenty-six-year-old gentile woman who has already relived her own birth.

"Not everyone understands this," Berkowitz says. "Most people when they eat chicken think of the crust, the flavor, maybe of Colonel Sanders.[8] They don't consider the life of the bird that flows through my fingers."

"You are indeed a holy man," Joan says.

Berkowitz holds my penis in his left hand. The breeze from the air conditioner makes the chandelier above me sway.

"Do it," I say.

His knife, my first memory, I suddenly think, may be the last thing I'll ever see. I feel a lot like a chicken. I already imagine that he'll hang me upside down and run off with Joan.

She'll break your hands, I struggle to tell him. You'll be out of a job. Your wife was right about you.

The words clot in my throat. I keep my eyes shut tightly.

"I can't do it," Berkowitz says. "I can't do this, even symbolically, to a full-grown male. It may not be against the law; still, I consider it an abomination."

I am so relieved I want to kiss his fingertips.

Joan looks disappointed but she, too, understands.

"A man," Hyman Berkowitz says, "is not a chicken."

I pull on my trousers and give him gladly the fifty-dollar check that was to have been his professional fee. Joan kisses his pale cheek.

8. A reference to Kentucky Fried Chicken (KFC), a popular food franchise founded by Harland "Colonel" Sanders (1890–1980).

The holy man, clutching his cheek, waves to us from his front porch. My past remains as secret, as mysterious, as my father's baldness. My mother in the throes of labor is a stranger I never knew. It will always be so. She is as lost to me as my foreskin. My penis feels like a blindfolded man standing before the executioner who has been saved at the last second.

"Well," Joan says, "we tried."

On the long drive home Joan falls asleep before we're out of South Bend. I cruise the turnpike, not sure of whether I'm a failure at knowing myself. At a roadside rest stop to the east of Indiana beneath a full moon, I wake Joan. Fitfully, imperfectly, we know each other.

"A man," I whisper, "is not a chicken." On the eighth day I did learn something.

1984

IRENA KLEPFISZ
b. 1941

In *Dreams of an Insomniac: Jewish Feminist Essays, Speeches, and Diatribes* (1990), Irena Klepfisz recalls that "her first conscious feeling about being Jewish was that it was dangerous, something to be hidden." Her earliest memories were of a life in hiding. Klepfisz, who was born in Poland in 1941, was two years old during the Warsaw uprising. After her father was killed in an air attack, she and her mother escaped the Warsaw ghetto and were hidden by peasants until the end of the war. Klepfisz and her mother immigrated first to Sweden and then to the United States when she was fourteen years old.

A poet, essayist, and translator, Klepfisz's political commitments have informed all aspects of her work. In her activism and writing, she has addressed Jewish identity, Jewish secularism and culture, feminism, homophobia, class, childlessness, the Holocaust and anti-Semitism, and the Israeli-Palestinian conflict. Klepfisz has been a major force in preserving Yiddish women's poetry and short fiction through translation; her translations of Kadya Molodowsky and Fradl Shtok introduced those poets to English-language readers. Klepfisz's poetry, published in *A Few Words in the Mother Tongue* (1990), reflects her interest in formal experimentation and the interplay of English and Yiddish, as in *Bashert* (Yiddish for "inevitable" or "meant to be") and *Fradel Schtok,* reprinted here.

Klepfisz has taught at the University of California at Santa Cruz, Michigan State University, and Wake Forest University, and is currently teaching at Barnard College and Centre College in Kentucky.

Bashert

These words are dedicated to those who died

These words are dedicated to those who died
because they had no love and felt alone in the world

because they were afraid to be alone and tried to stick it out
because they could not ask
because they were shunned
because they were sick and their bodies could not resist the
disease
because they played it safe
because they had no connections
because they had no faith
because they felt they did not belong and wanted to die

These words are dedicated to those who died
because they were loners and liked it
because they acquired friends and drew others to them
because they took risks
because they were stubborn and refused to give up
because they asked for too much

These words are dedicated to those who died
because a card was lost and a number was skipped
because a bed was denied
because a place was filled and no other place was left

These words are dedicated to those who died
because someone did not follow through
because someone was overworked and forgot
because someone left everything to God

because someone was late
because someone did not arrive at all
because someone told them to wait and they just couldn't
any longer

These words are dedicated to those who died
because death is a punishment
because death is a reward
because death is the final rest
because death is eternal rage

These words are dedicated to those who died

Bashert

These words are dedicated to those who survived

These words are dedicated to those who survived
because their second grade teacher gave them books
because they did not draw attention to themselves and got
lost
in the shuffle
because they knew someone who knew someone else who
could
help them and bumped them into a corner on a Thursday

afternoon
because they played it safe
because they were lucky

These words are dedicated to those who survived
because they knew how to cut corners
because they drew attention to themselves and always got picked
because they took risks
because they had no principles and were hard

These words are dedicated to those who survived
because they refused to give up and defied statistics
because they had faith and trusted in God
because they expected the worst and were always prepared
because they were angry
because they could ask
because they mooched off others and saved their strength
because they endured humiliation
because they turned the other cheek
because they looked the other way

These words are dedicated to those who survived
because life is a wilderness and they were savage
because life is an awakening and they were alert
because life is a flowering and they blossomed
because life is a struggle and they struggled
because life is a gift and they were free to accept it

These words are dedicated to those who survived

Bashert

1982

Fradel Schtok

Yiddish writer. B. 1890 in Skale, Galicia. Emigrated to New York in 1907. Became known when she introduced the sonnet form into Yiddish poetry. Author of *Erzeylungen* (Stories) in 1919, a collection in Yiddish. Switched to English and published *For Musicians Only* in 1927. Institutionalized and died in a sanitarium around 1930.

Language is the only homeland.

—Czeslow Milosz[1]

They make it sound easy: some disjointed
sentences   a few allusions   to

1. Milosz (b. 1911) is a Polish American poet, author, translator, critic, and recipient of the Nobel prize for literature (1980).

mankind.   But for me   it was not
so simple   more like   trying
to cover the distance   from here
to the corner   or between two sounds.

Think of it: *heym*   and   *home*   the meaning
the same   of course   exactly
but the shift   in vowel   was the ocean
in which I drowned.[2]

I tried.   I did   try.
First held with Yiddish   but you
know   it's hard.   You write   *gas*
and   *street*   echoes back
No resonance.   And—let's face it—
memory falters.
You try to keep track of the difference
like *got* and *god*   or *hoyz* and *house*
but they blur   and you start using
alley   when you mean *gesele*   or *avenue*
when it's a *bulevar*.

And before you know it
you're on   some alien path
standing   before a brick   house
the doorframe   slightly familiar.
Still   you can't place it
exactly.   Passers-by   stop.
Concerned   they speak   but you've
heard   all this   before   the vowels
shifting   up and down   the subtle
change   in the guttural sounds
and now   it's nothing more
nothing   more   than   babble.
And so   you accept it.
You're lost.   This time   you really
don't know   where you are.

Land or sea   the house floats before you.
Perhaps you once sat   at that window
and it was home   and looked out
on that *street* or *gesele*.   Perhaps
it was a dead end   perhaps a short cut.
Perhaps not.
A movement by the door.   They stand there
beckoning   mouths open and close:
Come in! Come in!   I understood   it was
a welcome.   *A dank! A dank!*[3]

2. The Yiddish words in this poem are all rough translations for the English words that Klepfisz supplies in the poem. Her point is that the translation from Yiddish to English never feels exactly right to her—something is lost.

3. Thank you (Yiddish).

I said till I heard the lock
snap behind me.

1990

STEVE STERN
b. 1947

Steve Stern occupies a distinctive place in contemporary Jewish American fiction: his work describes the idiosyncrasies of Jewish culture in conjunction with the eccentricities of a close-knit southern community. His second short-story collection, *Lazar Malkin Enters Heaven* (1986) introduces "the Pinch," a Jewish ghetto in Memphis, Tennessee, the city in which Stern was born and raised. This collection, his third book (he had previously published a collection of short stories, *Isaac and the Undertaker's Daughter* [1983], and a novel, *The Moon and Ruben Schein* [1984]), met with wide critical acclaim and established him as a unique voice in American fiction. Morris Dickstein, for instance, said Stern was one of the few Jewish writers to "show any familiarity with the night side of the Jewish imagination, the magical and fantastical side that goes back through cabalism." The *Los Angeles Times* called the stories "luminous, remarkable and full of dreamy brilliance."

Although semiautobiographical, these stories include characters from Jewish folklore; angels, golems, and dybbuks regularly arise in the Pinch, rendering these stories timeless and visionary. Stern has said that once he started to read Yiddish fiction, he found the origins of his own themes. One could easily compare the folk traditions and superstitions of the Pinch to Isaac Bashevis Singer's depiction of supernatural Old World communities. In the title story, reprinted below, the decrepit and stubborn Lazar Malkin argues with the angel of death about the possibility of paradise. Stern's latest book, *A Plague of Dreamers* (1994), consists of three novellas that continue to paint a vivid picture of life in the Pinch.

Stern has written short stories, novels, and books for children. He has taught at the Memphis College of Art, the University of Wisconsin, and, since 1988, Skidmore College in Saratoga Springs. *Lazar Malkin Enters Heaven* won the Edward Lewis Wallant Award in 1987, and in 2000, Stern won the National Jewish Book Award for fiction.

Lazar Malkin Enters Heaven

My father-in-law, Lazar Malkin, may he rest in peace, refused to die. This was in keeping with his lifelong stubbornness. Of course there were those who said that he'd passed away already and come back again, as if death were another of his so-called peddling trips, from which he always returned with a sackful of crazy gifts.

There were those in our neighborhood who joked that he'd been dead for years before his end. And there was more than a little truth in this. Hadn't he been declared clinically kaput not once but twice on the operating table? Over the years they'd extracted more of his internal organs than it seemed possible to do without. And what with his wooden leg, his empty left eye socket concealed by a gabardine patch, his missing teeth and sparse white hair, there was hardly enough of old Lazar left in this world to constitute a human being.

"Papa," my wife, Sophie, once asked him, just after the first of his miraculous recoveries, "what was it like to be dead?" She was sometimes untactful, my Sophie, and in this she took after her father—whose child she was by one of his unholy alliances. (Typically obstinate, he had always refused to marry.)

Lazar had looked at her with his good eye, which, despite being set in a face like last week's roast, was usually wet and amused.

"Why ask me?" he wondered, refusing to take the question seriously. "Ask Alabaster the cobbler, who ain't left his shop in fifty years. He makes shoes, you'd think he's building coffins. Ask Petrofsky whose lunch counter serves nobody but ghosts. Ask Gruber the shammes[1] or Milstein the tinsmith. Ask your husband, who is as good as wearing his sewing machine around his neck . . ."

I protested that he was being unfair, though we both knew that he wasn't. The neighborhood, which was called the Pinch, had been dead since the War.[2] Life and business had moved east, leaving us with our shops falling down around our ears. Myself and the others, we kidded ourselves that North Main Street would come back. Our children would come back again. The ready-made industry,[3] we kept insisting, was just a passing fancy; people would return to quality. So who needed luftmenschen[4] like Lazar to remind us that we were deceived?

"The Pinch ain't the world," he would inform us, before setting off on one of his mysterious peddling expeditions. He would haul himself into the cab of his corroded relic of a truck piled with shmattes[5] and tools got on credit from a local wholesale outfit. Then he would sputter off in some random direction for points unknown.

Weeks later he would return, his pockets as empty as the bed of his truck. But he always brought back souvenirs in his burlap sack, which he prized like the kid in the story who swapped a cow for a handful of beans.

"I want you to have this," he would say to Mr. Alabaster or Gruber or Schloss or myself. Then he would give us a harp made out of a crocodile's tail; he would give us a Negro's toe, a root that looked like a little man, a contraption called a go-devil, a singletree, the uses of which he had no idea. "This will make you wise," he told us. "This will make you amorous. This came from Itta Bena and this from Nankipoo"[6]—as if they were places as far away as China, which for all we knew they were.

"Don't thank me," he would say, like he thought we might be speechless with gratitude. Then he would borrow a few bucks and limp away to whatever hole in the wall he was staying in.

Most of my neighbors got rid of Lazar's fetishes and elixirs, complaining that it made them nervous to have them around. I was likewise inclined, but

1. The rabbi's personal assistant (Yiddish).
2. I.e., World War II.
3. Early in the 20th century, the clothing industry was revolutionized by the advent of "ready-made," or factory-produced, ready-to-wear garments.
4. Literally, high people (Yiddish) or people with their heads in the clouds; impractical people without visible means of support.
5. Rags (Yiddish).
6. A city in Mississippi. "Itta Bena": a town in Mississippi.

in deference to my wife I kept them. Rather than leave them lying around the apartment, however, I tossed them into the storage shed behind my shop.

No one knew how old Lazar really was, though it was generally agreed that he was far past the age when it was still dignified to be alive. None of us, after all, was a spring chicken anymore. We were worn out from the years of trying to supplement our pensions with the occasional alteration or the sale of a pair of shoelaces. If our time should be near, nobody was complaining. Funerals were anyhow the most festive occasions we had in the Pinch. We would make a day of it, traveling in a long entourage out to the cemetery, then back to North Main for a feast at the home of the bereaved. You might say that death was very popular in our neighborhood. So it aggravated us that Lazar, who preceded us by a whole generation, should persist in hanging around.

He made certain that most of what we knew about him was hearsay. It was his nature to be mysterious. Even Sophie, his daughter by one of his several scandals, knew only the rumors. As to the many versions of his past, she would tell me to take my pick. "I would rather not, if you don't mind," I said. The idea of Lazar Malkin as a figure of romance was a little more than I could handle. But that never stopped Sophie from regaling me by telling stories of her father the way another woman might sing to herself.

He lost his eye as a young man, when he refused to get out of the way of a rampaging Cossack[7] in his village of Podolsk.[8] Walking away from Kamchatka,[9] where he'd been sent for refusing to be drafted into the army of the Czar, the frostbite turned to gangrene and he lost his leg. Or was it the other way around? He was dismembered by a Cossack, snowblinded in one eye for good? . . . What did it matter? The only moral I got out of the tales of Lazar's mishegoss[1] was that every time he refused to do what was sensible, there was a little less of him left to refuse with.

It puzzled me that Sophie could continue to have such affection for the old kocker.[2] Hadn't he ruined her mother, among others, at a time when women did not go so willingly to their ruin? Of course, the living proofs of his wickedness were gone now. His old mistresses had long since passed on, and it was assumed there were no offspring other than Sophie. Though sometimes I was haunted by the thought of the surrounding countryside populated by the children of Lazar Malkin.

So what was the attraction? Did the ladies think he was some pirate with his eye patch and clunking artificial leg? That one I still find hard to swallow. Or maybe they thought that with him it didn't count. Because he refused to settle down to any particular life, it was as if he had no legitimate life at all. None worth considering in any case. And I cursed myself for the time I took to think about him, an old fool responsible for making my wife a bastard—though who could think of Sophie in such a light?

. . .

"You're a sick man, Lazar," I told him, meaning in more ways than one. "See a doctor."

7. Any member of a group of soldiers in southern Europe organized in the calvary in the czarist army. Cossacks were infamous for ravaging and pillaging the Jewish towns of Russia.

8. A Russian city south of Moscow.

9. A peninsula in northeast Russia.

1. Craziness (Yiddish).

2. Old turd (Yiddish).

"I never felt better, I'll dance on your grave," he insisted, asking me incidentally did I have a little change to spare.

I admit that this did not sit well with me, the idea of his hobbling a jig on my headstone. Lie down already and die, I thought, God forgive me. But from the way he'd been lingering in the neighborhood lately, postponing his journeys, it was apparent to whoever noticed that something was wrong. His unshaven face was the gray of dirty sheets, and his wizened stick of a frame was shrinking visibly. His odor, no longer merely the ripe stench of the unwashed, had about it a musty smell of decay. Despite my imploring, he refused to see a physician, though it wasn't like he hadn't been in the hospital before. (Didn't I have a bundle of his unpaid bills to prove it?) So maybe this time he knew that for what he had there wasn't a cure.

When I didn't see him for a while, I supposed that, regardless of the pain he was in, he had gone off on another of his peddling trips.

"Your father needs a doctor," I informed Sophie over dinner one night.

"He won't go," she said, wagging her chins like what can you do with such a man. "So I invited him to come stay with us."

She offered me more kreplach,[3] as if wide-open mouth meant that I must still be hungry. I was thinking of the times he'd sat at our table in the vile, moth-eaten overcoat he wore in all seasons. I was thinking of the dubious mementos he left us with.

"Don't worry," said my good wife, "he won't stay in the apartment . . ."

"Thank God."

". . . But he asked if he could have the shed out back."

"I won't have it!" I shouted, putting my foot down. "I won't have him making a flophouse out of my storehouse."

"Julius," said Sophie in her watch-your-blood-pressure tone of voice, "he's been out there a week already."

I went down to the little brick shed behind the shop. The truth was that I seldom used it—only to dump the odd bolt of material and the broken sewing machines that I was too attached to to throw away. And Lazar's gifts. Though I could see through the window that an oil lamp was burning beneath a halo of mosquitoes, there was no answer to my knock. Entering anyway, I saw cobwebs, mouse droppings, the usual junk—but no Lazar.

Then I was aware of him propped in a chair in a corner, his burlap sack and a few greasy dishes at his feet. It took me so long to notice because I was not used to seeing him sit still. Always he was hopping from his real leg to his phony, being a nuisance, telling us we ought to get out and see more of the world. Now with his leg unhitched and lying across some skeins of mildewed cloth, I could have mistaken him for one of my discarded manikins.

"Lazar," I said, "in hospitals they at least have beds."

"Who sleeps?" he wanted to know, his voice straining up from his hollow chest. This was as much as admitting his frailty. Shocked out of my aggravation, I proceeded to worry.

"You can't live in here," I told him, thinking that no one would confuse this with living. "Pardon my saying so, but it stinks like Gehinom."[4]

3. Noodle dumplings stuffed with either chopped meat or cheese. They closely resemble Italian ravioli and Chinese won tons.

4. In Jewish and Christian eschatology, the abode of the damned in the afterlife.

I had observed the coffee tin he was using for a slop jar.

"A couple of days," he managed in a pathetic attempt to recover his native chutzpah,[5] "and I'll be back on my feet again. I'll hit the road." When he coughed, there was dust, like when you beat a rug.

I looked over at one of the feet that he hoped to be back on and groaned. It might have been another of his curiosities, taking its place alongside of the boar's tusk and the cypress knee.

"Lazar," I implored, astonished at my presumption, "go to heaven already. Your organs and limbs are waiting there for a happy reunion. What do you want to hang around this miserable place anyway?" I made a gesture intended to take in more than the shed, which included the whole of the dilapidated Pinch with its empty shops and abandoned synagogue. Then I understood that for Lazar my gesture had included even more. It took in the high roads to Iuka and Yazoo City, where the shwartzers[6] swapped him moonshine for a yard of calico.

"Heaven," he said in a whisper that was half a shout, turning his head to spit on the floor. "Heaven is wasted on the dead. Anyway, I like it here."

Feeling that my aggravation had returned, I started to leave.

"Julius," he called to me, reaching into the sack at his feet, extracting with his withered fingers I don't know what—some disgusting composition of feathers and bones and hair. "Julius," he wheezed in all sincerity, "I have something for you."

What can you do with such a man?

I went back the following afternoon with Dr. Seligman. Lazar told the doctor don't touch him, and the doctor shrugged like he didn't need to dirty his hands.

"Malkin," he said, "this isn't becoming. You can't borrow time the way you borrow gelt."[7]

Seligman was something of a neighborhood philosopher. Outside the shed he assured me that the old man was past worrying about. "If he thinks he can play hide-and-go-seek with death, then let him. It doesn't hurt anybody but himself." He had such a way of putting things, Seligman.

"But Doc," I said, still not comforted, "it ain't in *your* backyard that he's playing his farkokte[8] game."

It didn't help, now that the word was out, that my so-called friends and neighbors treated me like I was confining old Lazar against his will. For years they'd wished him out of their hair, and now they behaved as if they actually missed him. Nothing was the same since he failed to turn up at odd hours in their shops, leaving them with some ugly doll made from corn husks or a rabbit's foot.

"You think I like it," I asked them, "that the old fortz[9] won't get it over with?" Then they looked at me like it wasn't nice to take his name in vain.

Meanwhile Sophie continued to carry her noodle puddings and bowls of chicken broth out to the shed. She was furtive in this activity, as if she was

5. Nerve or gall (Yiddish).
6. A Yiddish term, often derogatory, for African Americans. "Iuka and Yazoo City": a town and a city, respectively, in Mississippi.
7. Money (Yiddish).
8. Screwed up, mixed up (Yiddish slang).
9. Fart (Yiddish).

harboring an outlaw, and sometimes I thought she enjoyed the intrigue. More often than not, however, she brought back her plates with the food untouched.

I still looked in on him every couple of days, though it made me nauseous. It spoiled my constitution, the sight of him practically decomposing.

"You're sitting shivah[1] for yourself, that's what," I accused him, holding my nose. When he bothered to communicate, it was only in grunts.

I complained to Sophie: "I was worried a flophouse, but charnel house is more like it."

"Shah!" she said, like it mattered whether the old so-and-so could hear us. "Soon he'll be himself again."

I couldn't believe my ears.

"Petrofsky," I confided at his lunch counter the next day, "my wife's as crazy as Lazar. She thinks he's going to get well."

"So why you got to bury him before his time?"

Petrofsky wasn't the only one to express this sentiment. It was contagious. Alabaster, Ridblatt, Schloss, they were all in the act, all of them suddenly defenders of my undying father-in-law. If I so much as opened my mouth to kvetch[2] about the old man, they told me hush up, they spat against the evil eye. "But only yesterday you said it's unnatural he should live so long," I protested.

"Doc," I told Seligman in the office where he sat in front of a standing skeleton, "the whole street's gone crazy. They think that maybe a one-legged corpse can dance again."

The doctor looked a little nervous himself, like somebody might be listening. He took off his nickel-rimmed spectacles to speak.

"Maybe they think that if the angel of death can pass over Lazar, he can pass over the whole neighborhood."

"Forgive me, Doctor, but you're crazy too. Since when is everyone so excited to preserve our picturesque community? And anyway, wouldn't your angel look first in an open grave, which after all is what the Pinch has become." Then I was angry with myself for having stooped to speaking in riddles too.

But in the end I began to succumb to the general contagion. I was afraid for Lazar, I told myself, though—who was I kidding?—like the rest, I was afraid for myself.

"Sophie," I confessed to my wife, who had been treating me like a stranger lately, "I wish that old Lazar was out peddling again." Without him out wandering in the boondocks beyond our neighborhood, returning with his cockamamie gifts, it was like there wasn't a "beyond" anymore. The Pinch, for better or worse, was all there was. This I tried to explain to my Sophie, who squeezed my hand like I was her Julius again.

. . .

Each time I looked in on him, it was harder to distinguish the immobile Lazar from the rest of the dust and drek.[3] I described this to Seligman, expecting medical opinion, and got only that it put him in mind of the story

1. The Jewish ritual of seven days of prescribed mourning after the death of a member of one's immediate family.

2. Whine or complain (Yiddish).

3. Trash, rubbish (Yiddish).

of the golem[4]—dormant and moldering in a synagogue attic these six hundred years.

Then there was a new development. There were bits of cloth sticking out of the old man's nostrils and ears, and he refused to open his mouth at all.

"It's to keep his soul from escaping," Sophie told me, mussing my hair as if any ninny could see that. I groaned and rested my head in my hands, trying not to imagine what other orifices he might have plugged up.

After that I didn't visit him anymore. I learned to ignore Sophie, with her kerchief over her face against the smell, going to and fro with the food he refused to eat. I was satisfied it was impossible that he should still be alive, which fact made it easier to forget about him for periods of time.

This was also the tack that my friends and neighbors seemed to be taking. On the subject of Lazar Malkin we had all become deaf and dumb. It was like he was a secret we shared, holding our breaths lest someone should find us out.

Meanwhile on North Main Street it was business (or lack of same) as usual.

Of course I wasn't sleeping so well. In the middle of the night I remembered that, among the items and artifacts stored away in my shed, there was my still breathing father-in-law. This always gave an unpleasant jolt to my system. Then I would get out of bed and make what I called my cocktail—some antacid and a shpritz[5] of soda water. It was summer and the rooms above the shop were an oven, so I would go out to the open back porch for air. I would sip my medicine, looking down at the yard and the shed—where Lazar's lamp had not been kindled for a while.

On one such night, however, I observed that the lamp was burning again. What's more, I detected movement through the little window. Who knew but some miracle had taken place and Lazar was up again? Shivering despite the heat, I grabbed my bathrobe and went down to investigate.

I tiptoed out to the shed, pressed my nose against the filthy windowpane, and told myself that I didn't see what I saw. But while I bit the heel of my hand to keep from crying out loud, he wouldn't go away—the stoop-shouldered man in his middle years, his face sad and creased like the seat of someone's baggy pants. He was wearing a rumpled blue serge suit, its coat a few sizes large to accommodate the hump on his back. Because it fidgeted and twitched, I thought at first that the hump must be alive; then I understood that it was a hidden pair of wings.

So this was he, Malach ha-Mavet, the Angel of Death. I admit to being somewhat disappointed. Such a sight should have been forbidden me, it should have struck me blind and left me gibbering in awe. But all I could feel for the angel's presence was my profoundest sympathy. The poor shnook,[6] he obviously had his work cut out for him. From the way he massaged his temples with the tips of his fingers, his complexion a little bilious (from the smell?), I guessed that he'd been at it for a while. He looked like he'd come a long way expecting more cooperation than this.

4. In Jewish folklore, an artificial human being endowed with life. The term is used in the Bible to refer to an incomplete or embryonic substance; therefore, *golem* is sometimes used as a synonym for monster.

5. A spray (Yiddish).

6. An unassertive, ineffectual person.

"For the last time, Malkin," I could hear him saying, his tone quite similar in its aggravation to the one I'd used with Lazar myself, "are you or aren't you going to give up the ghost?"

In his corner old Lazar was nothing, a heap of dust, his moldy overcoat and eye patch the only indications that he was supposed to resemble a man.

"What are you playing, you ain't at home?" the angel went on. "You're at home. So who do you think you're fooling?"

But no matter how much the angel sighed like he didn't have all night, like the jig was already up, Lazar Malkin kept mum. For this I gave thanks and wondered how, in my moment of weakness, I had been on the side of the angel.

"Awright, awright," the angel was saying, bending his head to squeeze the bridge of his nose. The flame of the lamp leaped with every tired syllable he uttered. "So it ain't vested in me, the authority to take from you what you won't give. So what. I got my orders to bring you back. And if you don't come dead, I take you alive."

There was a stirring in Lazar's corner. Keep still, you fool, I wanted to say. But bony fingers had already emerged from his coatsleeves; they were snatching the plugs of cloth from his ears. The angel leaned forward as if Lazar had spoken, but I could hear nothing—oh, maybe a squeak like a rusty hinge. Then I heard it again.

"Nu?"[7] was what Lazar had said.

The angel began to repeat the part about taking him back, but before he could finish, Lazar interrupted.

"Take me where?"

"Where else?" said the angel. "To paradise, of course."

There was a tremor in the corner which produced a commotion of moths.

"Don't make me laugh," the old man replied, actually coughing the distant relation of a chortle. "There ain't no such place."

The angel: "I beg your pardon?"

"You heard me," said Lazar, his voice became amazingly clear.

"Okay," said the angel, trying hard not to seem offended. "We're even. In paradise they'll never believe you're for real."

Where he got the strength then I don't know—unless it was born from the pain that he'd kept to himself all those weeks—but Lazar began to get up. Spider webs came apart and bugs abandoned him like he was sprouting out of the ground. Risen to his foot, he cried out,

"There ain't no world but this!"

The flame leaped, the windowpane rattled.

This was apparently the final straw. The angel shook his melancholy head, mourning the loss of his patience. He removed his coat, revealing a sweat-stained shirt and a pitiful pair of wings no larger than a chicken's.

"Understand, this is not my style," he protested, folding his coat, approaching what was left of my father-in-law.

Lazar dropped back into the chair, which collapsed beneath him. When the angel attempted to pull him erect, he struggled. I worried a moment that the old man might crumble to pieces in the angel's embrace. But he was

7. So? or Well? (Yiddish).

substantial enough to shriek bloody murder, and not too proud to offer bribes: "I got for you a nice feather headdress . . ."

He flopped about and kicked as the angel stuffed him head first into his own empty burlap peddler's sack.

Then the worldweary angel manhandled Lazar—whose muffled voice was still trying to bargain from inside his sack—across the cluttered shed. And hefting his armload, the angel of death battered open the back door, then carried his burden, still kicking, over the threshold.

I threw up the window sash and opened my mouth to shout. But I never found my tongue. Because that was when, before the door slammed behind them, I got a glimpse of kingdom come.

It looked exactly like the yard in back of the shop, only—how should I explain it?—sensitive. It was the same brick wall with glass embedded on top, the same ashes and rusty tin cans, but they were tender and ticklish to look at. Intimate like (excuse me) flesh beneath underwear. Forthe split second that the door stayed open, I felt that I was turned inside-out, and what I saw was glowing under my skin in place of my kishkes[8] and heart.

Wiping my eyes, I hurried into the shed and opened the back door. What met me was a wall, some ashes and cans, some unruly weeds and vines, the rear of the derelict coffee factory, the rotten wooden porches of the tenements of our dreary neighborhood. Then I remembered—slapping my forehead, stepping gingerly into the yard—that the shed had never had a back door.

Climbing the stairs to our apartment, I had to laugh out loud.

"Sophie!" I shouted to my wife—who, without waking, told me where to find the bicarbonate of soda. "Sophie," I cried, "set a place at the table for your father. He'll be coming back with God only knows what souvenirs."

1986

8. Guts, intestines (Yiddish).

ART SPIEGELMAN
b. 1948

Before the publication of *MAUS I,* Art Spiegelman drew irreverent, dark comic strips for "zines," underground publications on specialized topics. Circulated through informal networks, zines were enthusiastically embraced by many subcultures, notably teenagers and "Generation X-ers" who felt alienated from mainstream culture. Spiegelman first tentatively explored the legacy that the Holocaust left on his parents and himself in a comic called *Prisoner of the Hell Planet,* published in 1972 in *Funny Animals* (a comic strip) and *Short Order Comix.* The Hell Planet to which Spiegelman refers should be read as a metaphor for life with his parents: Vladek, his father, overbearing, miserly, and obsessive; Anja, his mother, melancholy and suffering from survivor's guilt. In fact, the event that prompted the creation of *Prisoner of the Hell Planet* was Anja's suicide in 1968.

MAUS, a Survivor's Tale appeared in 1986; five years later, Spiegelman published *MAUS II, a Survivor's Tale: And Here My Troubles Began,* the remainder of his and Vladek's story. In comic-book form, drawing the Germans as cats, the Jews as mice, and the Poles as pigs, Spiegelman illustrates his father's experiences in Nazi-occupied Europe and at Auschwitz. While doing this, he tells his own story of growing up as a child of survivors.

MAUS took Spiegelman from the subterranean world of zines to the bright lights of literary prominence. The irony of this transformation does not escape Spiegelman, who says in *MAUS II,* "No matter what I accomplish, it doesn't seem like much compared to surviving Auschwitz." Although portraying the Holocaust in a comic strip first invited suspicion, *MAUS*'s readers soon realized that Spiegelman had represented the Holocaust, as well as its aftermath, in an ingenious and forceful manner. The comic-strip form, with its side-by-side illustrations as well as text, all appearing simultaneously, allow Spiegelman to occupy at least two places at the same time—a fitting analogy for Spiegelman's emotional state, which he believed to be divided between his father's past and his own present. In the excerpt below, taken from *MAUS II,* Spiegelman uses the form to juxtapose his own success, guilt, and fame with the horrors that his father witnessed and experienced.

The critical and popular reaction to the *MAUS* texts has been overwhelmingly positive. In a country where representations of the Holocaust are numerous, variable in quality, and hugely controversial, *MAUS* and *MAUS II* have emerged as watershed texts, especially in their depiction of the trials of the "second generation"—a term used to denote the children of Holocaust survivors. Lawrence Langer, a prominent critic of Holocaust art, wrote that in *MAUS,* Spiegelman writes "with restraint and a relentless honesty, sparing neither his father nor himself. . . . Perhaps no Holocaust narrative will ever contain the whole experience. But Art Spiegelman has found an original and authentic form to draw us close to its bleak heart."

After the publication of *MAUS,* Spiegelman returned to writing comic strips for zines, but he also contributes regularly to more mainstream publications and has illustrated several *New Yorker* covers. He lives and works in New York City.

From MAUS II, a Survivor's Tale: And Here My Troubles Began

Tell our viewers what message you want them to get from your book?
a message? I dunno...
I-I never thought of reducing it to a message. I mean, I wasn't trying to CONVINCE anybody of anything. I just wanted—
Your book is being translated into German...
Many younger Germans have had it up to HERE with Holocaust stories. These things happened before they were even born. Why should THEY feel guilty?
Who am I to say?...
But a lot of the corporations that flourished in Nazi Germany are richer than ever. I dunno... Maybe EVERYONE has to feel guilty. EVERYONE! FOREVER!
Okay... Let's talk about Israel...
If your book was about ISRAELI Jews, what kind of animal would you draw?
I have no idea. ...porcupines?
Excuse me...
Artie, baby. Check out this licensing deal. You get 50% of the profits. We'll make a million. Your dad would be proud!
HUH?
MAUS
YOU'VE READ THE BOOK
NOW BUY THE VEST!
So, whaddya WANT— a bigger percentage? Hey, we can talk.
I want... ABSOLUTION. No...No... I want... I want... my MOMMY!
Could you tell our audience if drawing MAUS was cathartic? Do you feel better now?
WAH!

whew.
they're gone. Sometimes I just don't feel like a functioning adult.
I can't believe I'm gonna be a father in a couple of months.*
My father's ghost still hangs over me.
*NADJA MOULY SPIEGELMAN. BORN 5/13/87
It's 9:30 p.m. already. I've gotta head uptown for my appointment with Pavel.
Pavel is my shrink. He sees patients at night.
He's a Czech Jew, a survivor of Terezin and Auschwitz. I see him once a week.
His place is overrun with stray dogs and cats.
Hi Art. Come on in.
Can I mention this, or does it completely louse up my metaphor?
So, how are you feeling?
Completely messed up. I mean, things couldn't be going better with my "career," or at home, but mostly I feel like crying.
I can't work. My time is being sucked up by interviews and business propositions I can't deal with.
But even when I'm left alone I'm totally BLOCKED. Instead of working on my book I just lie on my couch for hours and stare at a small grease spot on the upholstery.
FRAMED PHOTO OF PET CAT. REALLY!

Somehow my arguments with my father have lost a little of their urgency... and Auschwitz just seems too scary to think about... so I just LIE there...
It sounds like you're feeling remorse-maybe you believe you exposed your father to ridicule.
Maybe. But I tried to be fair and still show how angry I felt.
Even so, EVERY boy when he's little, looks up to his father.
That sounds true, but its hard for me to remember..
Mainly I remember ARGUING with him... and being told that I couldn't do anything as well as he could.
And now that you're becoming successful, you feel bad about proving your father wrong.
No matter what I accomplish, it doesn't seem like much compared to surviving Auschwitz.
But you weren't in Auschwitz...you were in Rego Park.
Maybe your father needed to show that he was always right-that he could always SURVIVE-because he felt GUILTY about surviving.
maybe.
And he took his guilt out on YOU, where it was safe... on the REAL survivor.
um...Tell me, do you feel any guilt about surviving the camps?
No... just sadness.

So, do you ADMIRE your father for surviving?
Well... sure. I know there was a lot of LUCK involved, but he WAS amazingly present-minded and resourceful...
Then you think it's admirable to survive. Does that mean it's NOT admirable to NOT survive?
whoosh.
I-I think I see what you mean. It's as if life equals winning, so death equals losing.
Yes. Life always takes the side of life, and somehow the victims are blamed. But it wasn't the BEST people who survived, nor did the best ones die. It was RANDOM!
Sigh. I'm not talking about YOUR book now, but look at how many books have already been written about the Holocaust. What's the point? People haven't changed...
Maybe they need a newer, bigger Holocaust.
Anyway, the victims who died can never tell THEIR side of the story, so maybe it's better not to have any more stories.
Uh-huh. Samuel Beckett once said: "Every word is like an unnecessary stain on silence and nothingness."
Yes.
On the other hand, he SAID it.
He was right. Maybe you can include it in your book.

My book? Hah! What book?? Some part of me doesn't want to draw or think about Auschwitz. I can't visualize it clearly, and I can't BEGIN to imagine what it felt like.
What Auschwitz felt like? Hmm... How can I explain?...
BOO!
YIII!
It felt a little like *that*. But ALWAYS! From the moment you got to the gate until the very end.
So, what part of your book are you trying to visualize?
My father worked in a tin shop near the camp. I have no idea what kind of tools and stuff to draw. There's no documentation.
Let's see. There would be a cutter - like a giant paper cutter - and maybe an electric drill press or two.
How do you KNOW that?
Oh, I worked in a tool and die shop in Czechoslovakia when I was a kid.
But it's getting late now, and I still have to walk my dogs.
Okay. I'll see you in a week...
Gee. I don't understand exactly why...
but these sessions with Pavel somehow make me feel better...
Maybe I could show the tin shop and not draw the drill press. I hate to draw machinery.

And so...
CLIK
...THEN, WHEN I CAME OUT FROM THE HOS-PITAL, RIGHT AWAY SHE STARTED AGAIN THAT I CHANGE MY WILL!
PLEASE POP. THE TAPE'S ON. LET'S CONTINUE...
I WAS STILL SO SICK AND TIRED. AND TO HAVE PEACE ONLY, I AGREED. TO MAKE IT LEGAL SHE BROUGHT RIGHT TO MY BED A NOTARY.
LET'S GET BACK TO AUSCHWITZ..
FIFTEEN DOLLARS HE CHARGED TO COME! IF SHE WAITED ONLY A WEEK UNTIL I WAS STRONGER, I'D GO TO THE BANK AND TAKE A NOTARY FOR ONLY A QUARTER!
ENOUGH! TELL ME ABOUT AUSCHWITZ!
sigh
YOU WERE TELLING ME HOW YOUR KAPO TRIED TO GET YOU WORK AS A TINSMITH...
YAH. EVERY DAY I WORKED THERE RIGHT OUTSIDE FROM THE CAMP...
THE CHIEF OF THE TINMEN IT WAS A RUSSIAN JEW NAMED YIDL.
BAH! YOU'RE NO TINSMITH. YOU CAN'T EVEN CUT IT RIGHT.
BUT THIS IS HOW I'VE ALWAYS DONE IT!...
I'VE ONLY BEEN A TINSMITH FOR A FEW YEARS. IF YOU SHOW ME HOW YOU WANT IT CUT I CAN LEARN QUICKLY.
HAH! YOU NEVER DID AN HONEST DAY'S WORK IN YOUR WHOLE LIFE, SPIEGELMAN! I KNOW ALL ABOUT YOU...
I DON'T KNOW WHERE FROM HE HEARD STORIES ABOUT ME.
YOU OWNED BIG FACTORIES AND EXPLOITED YOUR WORK-ERS, YOU DIRTY CAPITALIST!
HE WAS A COMMU-NIST, THIS YIDL.
PFUI! THEY SEND DREK LIKE YOU HERE WHILE THEY SEND REAL TINMEN UP THE CHIMNEY.
WATCH OUT. I'VE GOT MY EYE ON YOU!
I WAS AFRAID. HE COULD REALLY DO ME SOMETHING.

WITH THE OTHER BOYS THERE, I GOT ALONG FINE.
DON'T WORRY...YOU JUST HAVE TO KNOW HOW TO HANDLE YIDL...
BRING HIM A FEW EGGS, SOME BUTTER OR CHEESE...
YOU'LL SEE. HE'LL SING A DIFFERENT TUNE.
HA! AND WHERE DO I GET ALL THIS FOOD?
JUST KEEP YOUR EYES OPEN. YOU CAN ORGANIZE THINGS WITH THE POLES HERE.
POLES FROM NEARBY THEY HIRED TO WORK ALSO HERE - NOT PRISONERS, BUT SPECIALIST BUILDING WORKERS...
(PSST-I CAN GET YOU A FINE GOLD WATCH FOR A POUND OF SAUSAGE AND SIX EGGS.)
(AGREED.)
THEY HAD NOTHING, ONLY FOOD FROM THEIR FARMS. THEY WERE HAPPY TO MAKE EXCHANGES.
THE HEAD GUY FROM THE AUSCHWITZ LAUNDRY WAS A FINE FELLOW WHAT KNEW WELL MY FAMILY BEFORE THE WAR...
FROM HIM I GOT CIVILIAN CLOTHINGS TO SMUGGLE OUT BELOW MY UNIFORM. I WAS SO THIN THE GUARDS DIDN'T SEE IF I WORE EXTRA.
HERE YIDL. I'VE GOT A BIG PIECE OF CHEESE FOR YOU.
A GIFT? VERY NICE, SPIEGELMAN.
AND WHAT ELSE DO YOU HAVE THERE? A LOAF OF BREAD? YOU'RE A RICH MAN!
WAIT! I NEED THAT TO PAY OFF THE GUY WHO HELPED ME ORGANIZE THE CHEESE!
HMPH.
HE WAS SO GREEDY, YIDL, HE WANTED I RISK ONLY FOR HIM EVERYTHING. I TOO HAD TO EAT.

EVERYBODY WAS SO HUNGRY ALWAYS, WE DIDN'T KNOW EVEN WHAT WE ARE DOING...
IN THE MORNING FOR BREAKFAST WE GOT ONLY A BITTER DRINK MADE FROM ROOTS.
I WOKE BEFORE EVERYBODY TO HAVE TIME TO THE TOILET AND FIND STILL SOME TEA LEFT.
ONE TIME A DAY THEY GAVE A SOUP FROM TURNIPS. TO STAND NEAR THE FIRST OF THE LINE WAS NO GOOD. YOU GOT ONLY WATER.
MIX IT! MIX IT!
NEAR THE END WAS BETTER - SOLID THINGS TO THE BOTTOM FLOATED.
BUT TOO FAR TO THE END IT WAS ALSO NO GOOD
..BECAUSE MANY TIMES IT COULD BE NO SOUP ANYMORE.
AND ONE TIME EACH DAY THEY GAVE TO US A SMALL BREAD, CRUNCHY LIKE GLASS.
THE FLOUR THEY MIXED WITH SAWDUST TOGETHER - WE GOT ONE LITTLE BRICK OF THIS WHAT HAD TO LAST THE FULL DAY.
MOST GOBBLED IT RIGHT AWAY, BUT ALWAYS I SAVED A HALF FOR LATER.
AND IN THE EVENING WE GOT A SPOILED CHEESE OR JAM. IF WE WERE LUCKY A COUPLE TIMES A WEEK WE GOT A SAUSAGE BIG LIKE TWO OF MY FINGERS. ONLY THIS MUCH WE GOT.
IF YOU ATE HOW THEY GAVE YOU, IT WAS JUST ENOUGH TO DIE MORE SLOWLY.

EACH MORNING AND EVENING THEY MADE AN APPEL. THEY COUNTED THE LIVE ONES AND DEAD ONES TO SEE IT WASN'T ANY MISSING...
WE STOOD SOMETIMES THE WHOLE NIGHT WHILE THEY COUNTED AGAIN AND AGAIN.
ON OUR APPELS IT WAS ONE OLD GUY THERE, ALWAYS HE WAS COMPLAINING...
I DON'T BELONG HERE WITH ALL THESE YIDS AND POLACKS!
I'M A GERMAN LIKE YOU!
I HAVE MEDALS FROM THE KAISER. MY SON IS A GERMAN SOLDIER!
ONLY THEY HIT HIM AND THEY LAUGHED.
WAS HE REALLY A GERMAN?
WHO KNOWS. IT WAS GERMAN PRISONERS ALSO... BUT FOR THE GERMANS THIS GUY WAS JEWISH!
ON ONE APPEL HE DIDN'T STAND SO STRAIGHT AND A GUARD DRAGGED HIM AWAY. I HEARD HE PUSHED HIM DOWN AND JUMPED HARD ON HIS NECK...
OR THEY SENT HIM TO THE GAS, I DON'T REMEMBER, BUT THEY FINISHED HIM AND HE NEVER ANYMORE COMPLAINED.

1991

CHARLES BERNSTEIN
b. 1950

"Out of fear of being opaque to one another, we play the charade of comprehensibility. . . . To be comprehensible at all is to censor all that is antagonistic, anarchic, odd, antipathetic . . . anachronistic, other." Bernstein, the leading theorist of Language poetry and a prolific poet, has championed difficulty and discontinuity in poetry, for it requires readers "to be actively involved in the process of constituting [the text's] meaning." Radical deconstruction of traditional routes of poetic meaning, subversion of conventional narrative and syntax, debunking of the false consciousness of individualism prevalent in the European American poetic tradition—these acts are all part of the Language poets' project; through Bernstein's lectures and books, they have been central influences on experimental poetry in this country and abroad for a generation.

Bernstein's recent book *My Way* (1999) reveals his evolving sense of Jewish identity, which he has come to slowly and tentatively, inspired in part by his daughter's Bas Mitzvah. Bernstein recalls that his "parents were assimilationists who nonetheless had a strong Jewish and Zionist identification. As for many in their generation, this made for interesting contradictions. We were loosely kosher in the 'beef fry' years, but in other years, the bacon fried plentifully and tasted sweet." Critic Marjorie Perloff tells us that "these contraditions come to animate a brilliant and densely dialogic poetry. He is unique in his mix of intellectual passion, black humor, and his unflinching refusal to accept sentimental solutions." The dialogic relation is evident in the poem excerpted here, adapted from an oral history related by his father, where Bernstein's exploration of idiom and syntax takes precedence over the poem's narrative sequence.

A native New Yorker, Bernstein attended Harvard, where he studied with philosopher Stanley Clavell. He has written nineteen books of poetry and two prose books. He was coeditor, with Bruce Andrews, of the journal *L=A=N=G=U=A=G=E* and is currently David Gray Professor of Poetry and Letters at the State University of New York, Buffalo, where he is also executive editor of the Electronic Poetry Center.

From Sentences My Father Used

[*Casts across otherwise unavailable fields*]

Casts across otherwise unavailable fields.
Makes plain. Ruffled. Is trying to
alleviate his false: invalidate. Yet all is
"to live out," by shut belief, the
various, simply succeeds which. Roofs that
retain irksomeness, gets sweep, I realize
slowly, which blurting reminds, or how
you, intricate in its. This body, like a
vapor, to circumnavigate. Surprising
details that hide more than announce, shells
codifiers to anyway granules, leopards, folding
chairs. Shunning these because of a more

promising hope of forgetfulness, I
can slip back in, see the wire coil making its
steady progress, peer at the looks flashed in
my face. Best leave that alone, & not
make any noise either, lie by the pool
absorbed in its blue. *It is our furniture that is*
lacking and our fortune than we are powerless.
The history of my suffering: useless and. "Like
we would have it today." Silk hat. Which I
never expressed at the time. My sister
Pauline, my brother Harry. Was very well
ah to me it was sad. That could have aggravated.
That may have brought on. The impression I
got is everybody. Or I should say well groomed.
But in appearances. Apoplexy. Any chance of
accumulating money for luxuries. Never even
challenged, never thought—that was the atmosphere
we found ourselves in, the atmosphere we
wanted to continue in. Exchange Buffet. Which
is very rare. Which I hear is not so apparent. Which
blows you away. Like the GE is here. We
don't fear this. It will quiet down. Now I was not
a fighter & I would run away but they
surrounded me & put eggs in my hat & squashed
them & I came home crying & my mother said
what are you crying for if you go to the barber shop
you'd have an egg shampoo & here you got it
for nothing. Muted, cantankerous, as the bus puffing
past the next vacant question, jarring you to close
it down a little more, handle the space with. "Now
I'm going to teach you how to sell goods." No rush
or push. We just conformed because of the respect
we had for each other. Sky scraped by borders, telling
you which way, I had better advise, or otherwise
looney tunes appear in the hall &, glass in hand, you
debate the enclosures. A sultry phenomenon—drained
of all possibility to put at ease, but heat soaked all the
same. Recursive to a fault. Lips eroded, tableware
carelessly placed, as if the haphazard could restore
the imagination. *I told you before*: even current
things: the advancement of medicine, the new
chemicals that were coming up, the cures that were
starting to break through. Patent leather shoes. In a
gentle way. I wasn't very, I didn't have a very, my
appearance wasn't one of, that one could take, well I
didn't make the. Nothing stands out. Nice type of
people. Rather isolated. Pleasant. I had the same dream
constantly: swinging from chandelier to chandelier.
Crystal. In a crowd of people. Just local. In
shame. Closeouts, remnants. I don't remember
too much. Gad was on my back everyday. I always
figured: what I could lose. Those were my values.

To me they were good values. I didn't want to
struggle. & I could live frugally. I didn't want
to get involved. I didn't care for it. Necessity made
the. Which can't be helped. *Meeting us on our*
journey, taking us away. Hooks that slide past
without notice, only to find out too late that all
the time that transportation was just outside the
door. Sitting there. I felt badly about it but never
made a protest for my rights. We never thought of
that. I kept in short pants: what was given we
ate. Nobody had to tell me this. Everything
went into the business: being able to take advantage
of an opportunity, create an opportunity. It was just
a job I had to do. We were separated all the time. No
rowdyism, no crazy hilarity. Impelled sometimes beyond
hands, that forces otherwise in a manner
of. Interesting conclusions leaving you stripped
of subsistence, trimmed beyond recognition, & all the
time the tree-lined roads—perfectly spaced—mock
the inner silence that voids all things. To take a step—
"I had to"—leading without gap to a treasury
of ambitions. "In here" I am whole. Or goes over piles
of rocks—cowboy, pharaoh, bandit—stealing looks
across the street so often crossed but never lingered
in. With a sense of purpose divorced from
meaning. Strictly misrepresenting by it this loom
of enclosure, a path that opens onto a field, lost on
account of open space. A canvas of trumped up
excuses, evading the chain of connections. As so far
bent on expectation. "Don't stay in here, then."
The plane swoops down low over the city, the gleaming
lights below waken the passengers to the possibilities
of the terrain, a comfortable distance above & back
into the clouds. Leaving this place, so hugely exiled
for whatever bang of misprision you take the time
out for, a cacophany of shifts, tumbling beside the
manners you've already discarded, falling
among—in place of—them. Months sink into
the water and the small rounded lump
accumulates its fair share of disuse. Dreadfully
private, pressed against the faces of circular
necessity, the pane gives way, transparent,
to a possibility of rectitude.

1980

EDWARD HIRSCH
b. 1950

"Passionate attention is prayer, prayer is love / Savor the world. Consume the feast with love," Edward Hirsch writes in his fifth volume of poems, *On Love* (1998). Hirsch's lyrical, expressive poems—distinguished by sheer loveliness—reflect his belief that poetry's lasting gift is emotion. Such strong emotion is evidenced in his rendering of *The Village Idiot* as well as in his dramatic monologue in the voice of his grandfather in the poem *Oscar Ginsburg*. Both of these poems recall an earlier era of Jewish life, the Old World that Hirsch says he can sometimes see staring back at him in the mirror. In that world, too, Hirsch says, "Eros is the strongest sword of poets."

Born in Chicago, Hirsch attended Grinnell College and received a graduate degree from the University of Pennsylvania. *For the Sleepwalkers* (1981), his first book, was nominated for a National Book Award, and his second, *Wild Gratitude* (1986), where *The Village Idiot* first appeared, won the National Book Critics Circle Award in 1986. Literary critic Harold Bloom called Hirsch's 1994 collection *Earthly Measures* "utterly fresh, canonical and necessary." About *On Love*, James Longenbach, a critic for the *Yale Review*, wrote, "At once, rapturous and controlled, in this book, Edward Hirsch takes the risk of becoming a major American poet."

The author of five books of poetry as well as the nonfiction *How to Read a Poem and Fall in Love with Poetry* (1998), Hirsch won a MacArthur Award in 1998. He teaches at the University of Houston.

The Village Idiot

No one remembers him anymore, a boy
who carried his mattress through the town at dusk
searching for somewhere to sleep, a wild-eyed
relic of the Old World shrieking at a cow
in an open pasture, chattering with the sheep,
sitting alone on the front steps of the church,
gnawing gently at his wrist. He was tall
and ungainly, an awkward swimmer who could swim
the full length of the quarry in an afternoon,
swimming back on his back in the evening, though
he could also sit on the hillside for days
like a dim-witted pelican staring at the fish.
Now that he is little more than a vague memory,
a stock character in old stories, another bewildering
extravagance from the past—like a speckled seal
or an auk slaughtered off the North Atlantic rocks—
no one remembers the day that the village children
convinced him to climb down into an empty well
and then showered him for hours with rocks and mud,
or the night that a drunken soldier slit his tongue
into tiny shreds of cloth, darkened with blood.
He disappeared long ago, like the village itself,
but some mornings you can almost see him again
sleeping on a newspaper in the stairwell, rummaging

through a garbage can in the alley. And some nights
when you are restless and too nervous to sleep
you can almost catch a glimpse of him again
staring at you with glassy, uncomprehending eyes
from the ragged edges of an old photograph
of your grandfather, from the corner of a window
fogging up in the bathroom, from the wet mirror.

1986

Idea of the Holy[1]

(*New York City, 1975*)

Out of the doleful city of Dis[2]
rising between the rivers

Out of the God-shaped hole in my chest
and the sacred groves of your body

Out of stars drilled through empty spaces
and Stones in My Passway[3] at four a.m.

All those hours studying under the lamp
the First Cause and the Unmoved Mover[4]

the circle whose circumference is
everywhere and whose center is nowhere[5]

the Lord strolled under the oak tree at Mamre[6]
at the hottest moment of the day

the Lord vacated a region within himself
and recoiled from the broken vessels[7]

a God uncreated or else a God withdrawn
a God comprehended is no God[8]

1. The title of the poem derives from *The Idea of the Holy* (1917) by the German historian of religion Rudolf Otto (1869–1937).
2. A city in the underworld of Dante's *Inferno*.
3. A reference to a song by legendary blues musician Robert Johnson.
4. The concept of the First Cause, often attributed to Aristotle, claims that every event has to have a cause—i.e., has to have moved as a result of something else other than itself. Therefore, something must have started the motion of the universe. According to Aristotle, this motion could not be infinite, and at some point we reach the unmoved mover, the thing that started the motion that cannot itself be in motion. Although Aristotle makes no theological claims, later theologians—Saint Thomas for Christians, Maimonides for Jews—took Aristotle's ideas and applied them to the Divine.
5. This is philosopher, mathematician, and religious mystic Blaise Pascal's (1623–1662) definition of the infinite universe, taken from his *Pensées* (1670).
6. A grave near Hebron, a city south of Jerusalem that was one of the favorite dwelling places of Abraham. (See Genesis 18.)
7. Kabbalist Isaac Luria (1543–1572) taught that God created a space where He was absent, thereby making room for the world. Luria also spoke of the catastrophe that he called "Shevirath ha-Kelim" (the Breaking of the Vessels).
8. From Gerhard Tersteegen (1696–1769), a German Protestant and an advocate of "Spiritual Pietism" who is most famous for writing hymns.

Out of subway stations and towering bridges
Out of murky waters and the wound of chaos

Out of useless walks under fire escapes
Be friends to your burning[9]

I saw the sun convulsed in clouds
and the moon candescent in a ring of flame

souls I saw weeping on streetcorners
in a strangeness I could not name

O falling numinous world at dusk
O stunned and afflicted emptiness

After three days and nights without sleep
I felt something shatter within me

then I lay down on my cot motionless
and sailed to the far side of nothing

1994

Oscar Ginsburg

Ladies and Gentlemen, Friends and Strangers:
I stand as a man with spectacles on his nose
(as Isaac Babel[1] said) and autumn in his heart—
a family man, an immigrant, an unknown poet
who scribbles lyrics in the backs of books
about the fair Jerusalem of erotic love.

I never would deliver a commentary on love,
though I affirm its textual strangeness,
a subject taken up by madmen, lovers, poets
who have filled hundreds—thousands—of books
with a Keatsian "holiness of the Heart's
affections,"[2] a prayer-book the beloved knows.

Eros is a fiery secret everyone knows
or should know. Cut open my pilgrim heart
and you'll find the sentiments of strangers:
De l'Amour, Liber Amoris, Women in Love,[3]
all the upper registers of romantic poets . . .
(Love, for Jews, is nothing if not bookish.)

9. From a poem by Ṣūfī poet Jalāl ad-Dīn ar-Rūmī (1207–1273).
1. Russian writer (1894–1941).
2. "I am certain of nothing but of the holiness of the Heart's affections and the truth of Imagination," English Romantic poet John Keats (1795–1821) wrote in a letter to Benjamin Bailey, November 22, 1817.
3. Hirsch refers to three renowned works about love: Stendhal's *De l'Amour* (On Love [1822]), William Hazlitt's *Liber Amoris* (Free Love [1823]), and D. H. Lawrence's *Women in Love* (1920).

A practical woman opened me up like a book
and recited me backwards like a Hebrew poem.
I fell deeply—even desperately—in love
with my wife, a lovely pragmatic stranger
who always wore spectacles on her nose
in matters concerning the human heart.

I speak the backward language of my heart:
"Reprove a man of sense, and he will love
thee" (Proverbs), and she reproved my books,
my airiness, my empty purse which—heaven knows—
I could never fill for my beloved stranger,
who preferred playing cards to reading poems.

And yet Eros is the surest sword of poets—
drawn across beds, cutting through books.
I have known what the migrant heart knows
("O, never say that I was false of heart")[4]
about the steadfast passions of such love
between tender enemies, intimate strangers.

Who knows—but someday the book of my heart
may be inscribed by a stranger, my daughter's
son, brooding about the strangeness of love.

1998

4. William Shakespeare, Sonnet 109, line 1.

MIRIAM ISRAEL MOSES
b. 1950

Miriam Israel Moses is primarily known as a playwright, a reputation that she established while holding down more traditional jobs: as a sales representative and a collection agent, and, since 1997, the executive director of the Civil Service Commission for the city of Seattle. She has also published short fiction and a volume of poetry, *Arabesque* (1996).

Her first musical piece, *Reflections*, became an anchor production at the Colonnades Theatre Lab in New York, where she was composer in residence from 1973 through 1979. Moses also wrote the book, music, and lyrics for her best-known musical, *Intimate Friends*, which premiered on the West Coast in 1987. Her newest play, *Eye of the Storm*, will open in 2000.

Born in New York City to Orthodox Sephardic parents who had survived the Holocaust, she did not learn the story of their ordeal until her father's death in 1983. It was after attending her father's funeral that she began writing *Survivors and Pieces of Glass*; it took her over a decade to complete the work. The excerpt reprinted here tells of a young girl meeting her mother's relatives just after her mother has died. The presence of her mother's sister, whom she has heard about all her life, offers her great consolation, especially when they share cultural traditions, which Moses, as a Sephardic Jew, is careful to underline as different than those of the larger Ashkenazic community. The style of *Survivors and Pieces of Glass* may remind the reader of the cadences and mannerisms of Gertrude Stein's work.

From Survivors and Pieces of Glass

It may certainly be assumed that much of this never really happened, but then it may just as certainly be assumed that much of it really did happen, for I no longer know about realities. Realities are for me the reflected memories found in shattered pieces of glass that hold illusions of what is real and imagined. This story is mine whether it is real or imagined, and so some of this story is my life even though it may certainly be assumed that at least some of it is only imagined, but then at least some of it is real.

It must have been during the second World War of the twentieth century but I never looked up the date. It was the day before Passover, sometime during the second World War and everyone was out shopping for special things. The Passover Seder Plate is filled with six significant special things. Then there are separate plates to hold more of the special things because the significant things are ceremonial and the separate plates are for passing around so that everyone can eat the six special things at six special times during the Seder.

And so everyone was out and about buying special things in Salonika. Somehow in my mind it must have been a perfect sunny day in Salonika, Greece, where a Mediterranean springtime must be sunny. It was a sunny warm day where the coming twilight draped itself in perfect picturesque highlights over the houses of the peaceful thriving seaport village, the prosperous ghetto city of the once and almost forever Sephardic Jews.

It must have been a joyful time and as people passed each other on the streets and in the squares they raised their hands in greeting saying "*Buenas entradas de fiestas!*"[1] The women were shopping and laughing I think, they were wearing scarves around their heads and gossiping and laughing as they passed each other. It was almost sundown and it was time for *minchah/ maariv*[2] and these Jews were religious Jews and the men prayed three times each day and the women prayed in affirmations through all the days of their lives. So it may certainly be assumed that it was a sunny warm day in Salonika, Greece on the Mediterranean the day before Passover in this twentieth century of World War II.

It must have been a perfect sunny day when the danger was all in the past. There could not have been any rumblings or thunder or signs of wrath. No. There could not have been any indication of malice in the air. Well, not to hear it told. Not to hear that part of it that I was told. Not the way that I remember it being told by my mother, without the sunny day and without the conversations, just the shopping for special things for Passover in the middle of World War II, just the shopping for the special things used in the ceremony that celebrates our release from slavery and our return to the

1. Ladino: "Happy entry into the Passover festival" [author's note].

2. Afternoon and evening prayers [author's note].

promised land, just the celebration that raises us to trust in the will of G-d who will deliver us from our suffering.

I can see then my mother, sitting in her shop where they called her the woman with "*manos de oro*."[3] Her adept fingers placed finishing touches on the beautiful dress she was making for her younger sister with the sun golden hair that I have never seen and whose name I never knew, who was my aunt before I was born and I cannot go on. The horror is only so bad as the beauty that was described in the lost looks of my mother's eyes so many years later when she told me only small parts of the story and I filled in the rest because I do not know if she was at the shop and I do not know if she was finishing a dress for her golden sister who was like a wisp of cloud in sunny sky on that day and every other day. But I know my mother's hands and I know the way she sang while she sewed and I know how she broke thread in her mouth without once losing a note of her melodies of sailors lost on the sea and golden sisters waiting for love.

Her mother came to her. Her mother was younger to her than mine was to me. My grandmother is what she would have been had she not stopped before I started and I know her name because it was given to me and she must be dead because we cannot name after the living and her name was Miriam.[4] She was only fifteen years old when she was married to my mother's father whose name was Israel and his name was not told to me until long after my mother died. Israel was given to me as my middle name and I thought it was as an affirmation of the promised land. I never knew of its real purpose until its derivation was explained to me by my mother's brother, my Uncle Eli, on the first night of *shivah*[5] for my father which was almost nine years after the death of my mother. I never asked about it because I didn't want to know any more of it and I didn't know all of it and what I did know was too hard to know and that is more than enough to know.

The German soldiers came. It may certainly be assumed that this is an insurmountable reality. My mother's mother who would have been my grandmother but wasn't because she was before me and I was not there went to my mother at her shop and said that there were some truths that needed to be told. One of the truths that needed to be told was that my mother was a born American Citizen and so was her brother my Uncle Eli. One of the truths that needed to be told was that my mother's family had once lived in the golden land of America and my mother and my uncle were born during that time. One of the truths that needed to be told was that, like so many fathers and brothers in that time and from that place, my mother's father had once escaped to America with my mother's mother because, like so many other Jews from that time and place, the men refused to be drafted into the armies of Greece and of the other countries that refused to make them citizens of the worlds they were expected to die for. It is not the same to die for being a Jew.

And so one of the truths that did not need to be told was that the German soldiers had come once before in the first World War of the twentieth century, and my mother's family, like so many other families from that time and from that place, were Sephardic Jews and they were not Ashkenazi Jews.

3. Ladino: Hands of gold [author's note].
4. In many Sephardic families children *are* named after living relatives [Linda Lewis's note].
5. A mourning ritual for Jews, usually lasting a week (Hebrew).

They spoke Spanish and they did not speak Yiddish and they did not eat gefilte fish and bagels and their Sabbath dinner was beans and rice with meat and marrow bones and it was not chicken and potatoes and matzah ball soup.[6] And so when they came to America where all Jews are the same Jews, they were placed with the other Jews who were Ashkenazi Jews and not Sephardic Jews. And some of the Ashkenazi Jews did not believe that the Sephardic Jews were real Jews because they did not speak Yiddish and all real Jews that they believed were real Jews spoke Yiddish. So some of the Ashkenazi Jews accused the Sephardic Jews of being imposter Jews, for it may certainly be assumed that many people aspire to successfully impersonate Jews.

So it was that in America my mother's family, like so many other families from those times and from those places, could not speak to the other Jews in their Jewish language, or find their foods or their books or their songs or their lives and so they returned willingly to their non-citizen status in their beloved Salonika when the first World War which was supposed to be the last World War of the twentieth century ended.

And one of the final truths that needed to be told when the insurmountable reality of the second coming of the German soldiers became an inescapable truth was that my mother and her brother had to report to separate doors from the doors through which the rest of their family walked with yellow stars sewn onto the outsides of their jackets and jewelry sewed into the inside linings of their clothes. But there is more to this story and I don't know it except for strands of fragments and broken pieces of glass strung together in the mind of a child which still the adult struggles to wear with dignity and grace instead of anger.

Happily they went to the freight trains and to the relocation ditches and the lamp shades and jewelry of gold fillings and wedding bands to be together as families in places where real death is preferable to life with the memory of it. We cannot say that. We cannot say that and we cannot answer that. We cannot say that and we cannot answer that and we cannot know that. But the alive ones who I loved were never alive here and this I know, or they disguised themselves very well and prepared for their deaths in sacred fashions. Only they prepared me to survive. The child must survive. They taught me every skill necessary to survival and none of the skills of life.

So there was a year somewhere during the twentieth century of World War II when there was a wooden boxcar and there were three women in it and I am certain that this was real though I do not know when or where in the World War this took place. And I have met the three women. One was my mother and there was Dora and also Violetta. It was a cold place and it was splintered dry wood and as the train traveled and stopped each day the three women went out into the empty cold not knowing where they were or who they were or why they were at all except to collect what food they could and to hear once a gypsy seer tell my mother that she would walk soon down a red carpet to a rich place and, in a manner of speaking, she did.

And there was the time of three women in a boxcar sometime during the second World War of this century when they had no clothes but the clothes they wore and so Violetta developed pneumonia and emphysema because

6. Moses refers to the traditional foods of the Jews from Eastern Europe.

they were good girls and washed their underwear each day and dressed again in the wet clothes. But Violetta did not die completely.

After three months in the wooden boxcar death express that picked up and delivered the condemned and already dead to the extermination camps, and I do not know how long this really was or what the route of the train really was, the three women were taken to what was before the war a resort in France called Vitelle Vogue that was transformed as all things are transformed in war into a prison holding camp with food that was occasional and a stolen rotten potato as the standard daily fare. So after the moving nowhere of the death-crate boxcar, there was no place but a holding place. And this place was of brick and barracks with blanketless beds of boards and barbed wire fences and many gestapo[7] guards with trained dogs and rifles trained.

The holding camp in France was for a year and I do not know how long it really was or whether it was wood or brick or barracks but there were these three women and my mother was one and Dora and Violetta were the other two and my living torment could not have been felt there as life itself was not felt because reality was not really known until later and then later reality changed again and again and again like this fragmented story of made-up pictures that I have painted from the hollow reflections of my mother's eyes and the longing in the sound of her voice as it remembered itself still echoing soprano through the Greek choir. Only in my life it intoned the Kaddish[8] and the Kaddish was sung to me as a child to help me fall asleep until my mother could sing no more and pray no more when she decided that real death was better than the praise of it.

And it was a year from the perfect sunny day before Seder[9] in Salonika or maybe it was longer since the war was longer, that the diplomats successfully negotiated a one for three trade of the valuable foreign-raised, born American and British citizens for the not so valuable Nazi prisoners of war. So Violetta was sent to England and my mother and Dora were shipped to the promise of happiness and luxury at last in America, where they really did walk down a red carpet to streets that are paved with gold and that must be true because my mother told me that the streets were paved with gold. I cannot still see the glittering concrete of New York City without knowing that the glass chips that scrape and cut the skin of every child who plays there are diamonds set in gold for emperors and queens.

And Dora came to the United States with my mother and Violetta was sent to England where she was put in a hospital and there she met a Dutch soldier named Freddie whom she married and they went to live in Holland and they had a son and a daughter the same ages as my older brother and sister. My mother and my father often wrote to Violetta and Freddie telling them about all of the important occasions in our lives and Freddie and Violetta wrote back telling of the same occasions in their lives, but my father and mother never wrote to Violetta and Freddie to tell them that my mother was dying.

From sunny Salonika to filthy nowhere to a camp on the French Mediterranean to a transatlantic cruise to Ellis Island and red carpets and gold and

7. Abbreviation for Geheime Staatspolizei, or secret state police (German); the terrorist arm of the Nazis, used to crush all who were suspected of disloyalty or who were deemed "degenerate" or otherwise unfit for society.
8. Jewish prayer for the dead.
9. Celebratory ritual meal at Passover.

diamond rough streets, my mother began her journey as a survivor when she was born in America, in a building on the corner of Broome and Allen near Delancey Street[1] in an apartment that had its own bathroom in 1920 which is the year that my mother was born with all the rights and privileges of a born American citizen. But they weren't happy in the great America, my mother's parents, they were Sephardic Jews and they were not Ashkenazi Jews and they were accused of being imposter Jews and they wanted to go home where they would at least be treated like real Jews and so they did and so they were.

So it was apparently in the same year as my mother's birth in America that my father, who was born in Salonika almost ten years before the birth of my mother, began studying in Alexandria, Egypt, where the wealthier Salonika sons did that and his specializations were higher mathematics and languages. At these he excelled. Though to hear it told about the sunny day before Passover it would seem that there was not even a rumble, when it was the time of the second coming of the German soldiers my father knew that he should not return to Salonika and so, as an interpreter who spoke seven languages, he joined the American Air Force under an American name and became an American Citizen and he was sent to England where he learned to speak English and after the second World War of this century he moved to New York City and became first a dishwasher and then an ILGWU[2] piece-rate presser in a variety of garment district sportswear factories. He was a non-combatant then and remained so until he died.

So it was also in New York that my mother was living in the home of Rabbi Alberto Matarasso who was a great Sephardic Rabbi, a renown[ed] and dedicated scholar, so famous and so loved and so respected and so completely an atheist as a result of all the killing and the dying and the already dead, and he introduced my mother to my father because she was almost over twenty-five years old which meant certain spinsterhood and my father was a good and pious man from the same town of Salonika and they would know how to be married to each other so they were and love grew between them to what extent it could.

There are three of us, their children, and I am the youngest. I knew the names of my father's parents who would have been my grandparents if they had not stopped before I started or if I had been there which I was not. Jacob and Dulce, my older brother and sister, acknowledge by their names the certain but uncertain fact of the death of my father's family. When I was growing up my father sent checks to his old address in Salonika to help his unmarried sister have a dowry and the checks were never returned and I don't know if they were ever cashed or by whom if they were, but that is real because my mother told me about it one day to try to make me understand that my father was really a very loving man and it was just that he could not give himself to me. Then and even now it made me angry because there was so little for the living that I hated living with all the dead in every face and every shoulder and every kiss.

During the first night of the *Shivah* for my father after the evening *minyan*[3] left our house in New York, my mother's brother, my Uncle Eli, his second

1. That is, on the Lower East Side of New York City.
2. International Ladies' Garment Workers' Union.
3. A group of ten men needed to observe mourning rituals.

wife my Aunt Marilyn, my mother's friend from the boxcar Dora, and her husband Jack, and my sister and I, sat around the dining room table and Dora and my Uncle Eli told us some of the story of the death train and some of the story of the holding camp in Vitelle Vogue and I wrote some of it down.

Although they were separated, my Uncle Eli was eventually sent to the same holding camp at Vitelle Vogue as my mother and Dora and Violetta. My Uncle had a stolen uniform that allowed him to sneak in and out of the camp and his mission was to go to Paris where he changed from his uniform into civilian clothes with an American Flag where his yellow star should have been to signify that he was an American Citizen. And he was conducting negotiations at the Swiss Embassy to establish Swiss Citizenship for 100 Polish Jews who were being held in a different section of the same camp at Vitelle Vogue because everyone knew that Polish Jews did not have the same trade value as American Jews and British Jews, and everyone knew that the Polish Jews would be killed.

My mother knew that my Uncle was going to Paris and she and Dora kept hearing rumors that they were going to be sent soon to America, so somehow, through some unexplained network, she sent word to my Uncle that she wanted him to buy her a pair of red shoes in Paris so that she could have them when she got to America. My Uncle received my mother's message and although it was within the World War and it was never really explained how, he was able to buy the red shoes and smuggle them back to my mother in the camp and she did have them when she came to America.

But my uncle was captured in Paris before his mission was completed and when the hundred Polish Jews learned that their only hope had been captured, they all jumped from the windows of their barracks to their certain deaths. It was two days before D-Day when my uncle was captured and he survived and so it may certainly be assumed that the 100 Polish Jews would have survived too. And now I have been to Paris and on my first day in Paris I walked along the Champs Elysées and I purchased a new pair of blood red shoes so that I would have them to wear in America and although I wore them on the Champs Elysées, I have never been able to bring myself to wear them in America.

And there are so many more people and so many more stories. All of the members of the Sephardic Jewish Brotherhood of America carrying all those Spanish, Portuguese, Greek, Turkish, French, Arabic and Hebrew surnames held proudly from before the Inquisition that make them always and unmistakably intertwined in these feelings. Thirty-two men with hollow eyes and surnames like Alhadeff, Davidas, Barocas, Benaroya, Mizrahi, Soury, Benardete, Angel, Matarasso, de Sola Pool, Gadol, Levy, Ezrati, Calvo, Cardozo, Nessim, Besso, Farhi, Behar, Shaloum, Maimon, Perahia, Mendes, Benezra, Nahoum, Rousso, Sustiel, Moché, Almelech, Toledano, Eskanazi, DeLeon, meeting on the morning of the third Sunday of each month to continue an organization that once helped Sephardim like my father and like so many other survivors adjust and assimilate to life in the United States, but now has lost almost all of its original purposes except to give a bit of tzedakah,[4]

4. Charity (Hebrew).

a few scholarships, and mainly to engage in the purchase of large blocks of cemetery plots so that the survivors from the same places may be buried in the same places within the old traditions and within the old ways.

The Brotherhood was home to Lily Assael who we called Miss Lily, and whose great achievement was surviving the war and teaching music to young Sephardim like me and also like Murray Perahia[5] when we were children. She had small hands and tattooed arms and she survived Aushwitz because she could crochet fine socks and hats for the German soldiers and officers and more important, she could play concert piano for the soldiers and officers and, most useful of all, she could play the accordion which enabled her to lead the marching band that accompanied the already dead Jews on their final march to the showers. And so Miss Lily always tried to teach her female students how to crochet and to convince all of her piano students to learn how to play the accordion. And although most of us declined to learn to play the accordion my sister who no longer remembers how to crochet very well and I have never stopped learning how to play the piano and I have never stopped entertaining the German soldiers and officers.

And so even my great love of music has always been a great love of death and survival and I learned it well until it almost destroyed me. But when the Nazis come again, as they always do, I know that I have learned it all very well and I will be ready. I know all of the fatal fanfares and I will play them for the Nazis and again for the Jews, and again I will survive my death. Yet, how can I survive what has not happened to me? Because for me what really is already happened before me and somehow I just missed being there on that perfect sunny day before Seder in Salonika during the second World War of this century.

But finally in these tellings some of the horror is gone. I no longer dream of all those dream of all those dead ribcages and thighbones held together by crusted brown dead flesh that I watched with my family after dinner on public television when I was a child. And I wondered which of the baked burnt bony bodies belonged to my family and I wanted to jump into the heaps of carcasses and be with them in their deaths because to hear it told, on that sunny day before Seder in Salonkia during the second World War of this century, their lives were happier than mine had ever been and I would rather have been dead with their memories than alive with my own.

And so it was after twenty-five years of my life that my mother died and at that time Violetta and Freddie came to the United States to visit so that Violetta could be reunited with my mother and with Dora. Violetta telephoned from her hotel and my grieving orthodox father who knew that they were coming answered the phone during the second night of *shivah* for my mother, which the Orthodox are not allowed to do, and I heard his side of the conversation.

"Ah, Violetta, ¿como esta?

¿Lena? Ayer mos enterramos a Lena."[6]

There was a silence and I found myself smiling with my father as if we'd played a practical joke on someone. My mother did not want Violetta to know about her five year cancerous comatose respirator driven deathlife. Perhaps

5. Concert pianist, recording artist, and musical scholar (b. 1947).

6. Ah, Violetta, how are you? Lena? Yesterday we buried Lena (Ladino).

she thought she would recover and perhaps she thought Violetta would not come at all if she knew. And my father said no more to Violetta and he held the phone out to me as he suppressed the almost embarrassed smile that was escaping through his eyes in answer to my more overt conspiratorial expression.

And so I spoke to Violetta for the first time as if I had always known her and as if we had shared so many memories because we did share them and my gladness in hearing her real voice as I had always imagined it to be was a part of the happiness and excitement that was within the smile of my words. Speaking in English the words that she already understood but could not fathom or absorb in Ladino[7] I gave her again the certain knowledge of my mother's final ending and of our shared grief and peace in this real truth.

And Violetta hesitated in the face of my mother's real death and thought perhaps that she would not come to our home and observe the Shivah with my family and with Dora and with Dora's husband Jack, but it was our destiny to be together in this time of real death and so she and Freddie came to our home that night for the real reunion in life that had always been the real dream of these three women, and my mother was one and Dora and Violetta were the other two.

And Dora and Violetta were together in life, and the spirit of my mother was with them too as I was with them in my sharing of this joy. And I explained to Violetta with Dora's affirming eyes nodding her knowing and complete support, that my mother did not want Violetta to know that she was sick and dying. Perhaps my mother was afraid that Violetta would come only to see her finally die after surviving a hate greater than cancer, and perhaps my mother was afraid that Violetta would not come if she knew that she would see my mother really dying for the utter certainty of mortality can defy the will to survive. And Violetta understood my mother's futile hope and the survivors' dilemma and she understood this death and she understood our need to celebrate my mother's liberation with her.

"You know what I cannot get in Holland?" Violetta announced while we violated the Shivah and sat on chairs[8] at the dining room table after both the Sephardic and Hasidic minyans left for the evening eating the dessert that she and Freddie brought, "I cannot get a good dish of *bamyah*."[9]

So I told her about a terrific restaurant in Brooklyn that served plates of *bamyah* more delicious than even my mother's and we drove in a car from my parents' home in Forest Hills Queens to Park Slope in Brooklyn and ate *bamyah* in an unkosher restaurant during the *shivah* and then we drove to Dora's home in Bayside Queens so that Violetta could see Dora's American home and meet her oldest American daughter Vivian.

And so in this gathering and in this laughter and in this reunion of all of us who seemed to have always known each other in life and in death, my mother could not have been better honored. So Violetta did not mourn my mother in any of the traditional ways and Dora, who sat with my mother's comatose body for all the days of the death-life they knew so well, Dora celebrated on that night too, and so did I.

7. The language of Sephardic Jews, which resembles Spanish.
8. Customarily, during shiva, mourners sit on hard wooden or cardboard boxes.
9. A dish of okra, spices, and fresh tomato sauce [adapted from author's note].

And now there must be a way of ending. It is time for a way of ending. It was just over twenty years ago that the magical night of the *shivah* reunion between Dora and Violetta and the spirit of my mother through me took place. I took several photographs during that evening of mourning and put them away in a box. After hearing of the certain death of Dora's oldest daughter Vivian in 1995, I sent copies of the pictures to her and to her husband Jack with a Chanukah card, and Dora wrote back to me saying that these pictures of our coming together, which was only three weeks after the death of Dora's youngest child, my friend Yale, brought back many wonderful memories of happier times.

And this is the real truth of my story for within these tellings are the memories of happier times, when each moment is remembered for its own sake and not held captive to the moments before and after. And it may certainly be assumed that what is remembered is real, and what is remembered may not be the same as what is known or what really happened, but what is remembered is held always within moments of time, like fragments of light on pieces of glass that reflect their truths on all of us whose memories are linked forever to the memories of those who survived, those who died, those who live, and to the memories of those who will follow us. And so we shall never forget ourselves in this life and in this death for each of us even as broken and shattered pieces of glass still reflects the whole prism of light, the whole of what is possible in life.

1997–1998

MELVIN JULES BUKIET
b. 1953

Melvin Jules Bukiet has written two novels and two collections of short stories, and is the editor of the anthology *Neurotica: Jewish Writers on Sex* (1999). His first short-story book, *Stories of an Imaginary Childhood* (1992), envisions the life of a boy in a prewar Polish shtetl. In his second collection, *While the Messiah Tarries* (1995), where *The Library of Moloch* originally appeared, Bukiet relocates to New York City to deepen his rendering of Jewish life, especially the Holocaust. The son of a Holocaust survivor himself, Bukiet, like Art Spiegelman, represents the "second generation." But by critically looking at subjects often considered sacred in Holocaust studies, his depiction of that event takes unconventional form. In his novel *After* (1996), for instance, Bukiet describes a time immediately after the war when survivors did not leave the camp, but stayed to run the black market. His portrayal of the survivors does not contain the usual sympathetic elements.

Similarly, the story included here contains a nasty and unsympathetic survivor as part of a larger satire of the way in which American scholars have "studied" the Holocaust. Reminiscent of Ozick's *The Shawl,* wherein Rosa Lublin, a Holocaust survivor, is badgered by an insensitive academician, *The Library of Moloch* features a professor who makes videotapes of original testimony. Obsessed by his subject, he believes that in these testimonies he will find the meaning of life. Critic Andrew Furman has written that "through his mischievous theological imagination, Bukiet engages the most serious quandaries that beset Jews amid his often bleak post-Holocaust landscapes."

The Library of Moloch[1]

Three hundred faces stared, blinked, squinted, and otherwise engaged the camera while recounting the most awful moments of the century.

"Smoke, that is the first thing I remember, that and the body of my little sister."

"Yes, they hung the village elders by their beards."

"Oh, the experiments. I had forgotten. Of course, the experiments. What was it you wanted to know? What was it *they* wanted to know?"

The library was a four-room suite of offices in the base of a gothic dormitory in which aspiring lawyers lived, ignorant of the stories that the folks with branded arms told underneath them.

One room of the suite contained a receptionist's desk, a couch, and coffee table where academic journals gathered dust. The second room was a dustless repository of videotape disks set upon rows of sleek metal shelving, along with two monitors for viewing them. Never had both monitors been used at the same time, but the initial grants to establish the library were generous.

Then there was the director's office, and the testimony room where they actually produced the videotapes. This room had the air of a dental chamber where the patient reclined in a large padded chair, the videotape machine directed at the face like an X-ray tube, aiming to penetrate the skin to the soul. There was always a cool young technician fiddling with the dials on an imposing black console with blinking red lights and fluctuating meters. These interns from the university's School of Communication Arts were more interested in the quality of sound reproduction than the meanings of the sounds reproduced. Attending the meaning, however, was a doctor, whose gentle probing elicited the words, although here it was a doctor of letters who conducted the procedure. Delicate as he was, there was also the occasional wince and cry of pain.

Other libraries have taken lesser tasks upon themselves, to contain and construe the physical properties of nature or the intellectual produce of man. The Library of Moloch sought no less than a moral explication of the universe.

Fortunately, it had excellent source material. All that remains from the Crusades, for example, are a few moldy documents. Likewise, the other episodes of vast and imponderable iniquity, the Reign of Terror or the Conquest of Mexico, have faded from human memory, and hence perished in all but legend. There may be articles about Tamerlane or Gilles de Rais in the yellowing journals on the coffee table, but their ravages no longer have the pulse of life.[2] The contemporary library has one invaluable resource that researchers into the more distant past do not, the victims. That was its

1. An ancient Semitic deity to whom children were sacrificed. The name is often used to suggest an evil or greedy deity.

2. Bukiet refers to historical events and persons characterized by barbarism and savagery.

avowed purpose, to find the victims of Moloch, to record them, to preserve their suffering, to remit immortality in return for the chronicle of their woe.

They had three hundred faces on file, nearly a thousand hours, tens of thousands of deaths described in ferocious detail. The library was a mausoleum, its librarians gravediggers. As for the individuals whose lives and memories were condensed onto half-inch tape, wound onto spools, stacked onto shelves—the hell with them.

Dr. Arthur Ricardo, English born, American bred, headed the project. He was a highly civilized gentleman, with many diverse interests. He enjoyed chamber music, Oriental rugs, and nineteenth-century economic theory. The latter was a family hobby, because he was a nonlineal descendant of David Ricardo, the eminent mercantile essayist and apostate. In addition to his rarified pursuits, Dr. Ricardo was an avid moviegoer who regaled his intellectual friends with tawdry tales of Hollywood excess. How he found his life's calling in the Library of Moloch is a tale in itself. His specialty was medieval literature, but he realized that his students were more interested in iron maidens and auto-da-fés than they were the quest for the grail.[3] Only if the grail was hidden within an iron maiden had they any chance of finding it.

At the moment when he was wrestling with his charges' gruesome misreadings of Ariosto,[4] there was a scandal at his institution, the academy that housed the library. An elderly professor who was respected by all in his field (thermodynamics) was determined to have been a wartime collaborator. Nobody accused him of any personal wrongdoing, but he had signed a loyalty oath and he withheld knowledge of this when he sought to enter America. Clearly the man needed to be punished. Equally clearly, he had lived an honorable life since his youthful indiscretions. He was, in fact, a leader of the physicians for nuclear responsibility movement. Ricardo's sympathies were with the professor, but a squat little man appeared unbidden at the provost's inquiry. He demanded to be heard. "I worked at the mountain," he said, meaning the underground silos where the rockets the venerable professor had designed fifty years ago were produced, where scientists labored in isolation while slaves died to prove the learned men's theories.

Ricardo was not present when the man spoke, but a video recording of the speech circulated, at first covertly and then, by mass demand, at public screenings. The tape exerted a bizarre fascination. The professor was hounded into retirement.

"Imagine," Ricardo said to his class, "what we could do with the personal testimonies of the prisoners of the Inquisition, what that would tell us about the nature of faith in that era."

But one student said, "Can't we extrapolate backward from this witness? Does human nature change?"

At first, Ricardo wanted to dismiss the query. The first tenet of his life was progress, implying the perfectability of man. But the question bothered him.

3. According to medieval legend, the cup used by Christ at the Last Supper. "Iron maidens": boxes in the shape of a woman that are lined with spikes which impale the enclosed victim when the lid is shut. "Auto-da-fés": literally, acts of faith; hisorically, pronouncements of judgment by the Inquisition followed by the execution of the sentences by the secular authorities; broadly, the burning of heretics.

4. Ludovico Ariosto (1474–1533), an Italian poet most remembered for his epic poem *Orlando Furioso*.

He had to admit that if human nature did change, it most certainly did so for the worse to just the degree that his generation's atrocities superseded those of the Middle Ages. Compared to the artifacts of the twentieth century, iron maidens were couture and racks[5] no more than chiropractic devices. The stories of that one man who "worked at the mountain" were sufficient proof.

And there were many more stories. The man who gave evidence was the tip of the iceberg. There were others who worked the mines and others who stoked the fires. Who knew how many of these refugees from the land of brimstone were walking the streets, and each time one clutched his heart and collapsed to the pavement another storehouse of history died with him. Ricardo spoke to the videotaper, and together they conceived of the library. The university was eager to balance the scales of public opinion that had been tipped by the scandal. A board of prestigious names lined up to support the project. Grants were expedited, space allocated. Funding flowed.

Ricardo placed advertisements in ethnic newspapers, and contacted organizations that aided survivors. They tended to stick together. It was difficult to overcome their distrust of strangers at first, but their very cohesiveness made further testimonies easier. One by one, the men and women who lived through the war came to him. And he listened.

"Fire, a column of fire into the sky. It was night. The column must have been a hundred feet high. Maybe two hundred. I don't know. I'm no Galileo."[6]

"Food, the lack of food. Hunger so great we would eat anything, grass, poison ivy, we would suck the juices from pieces of wormy wood. And you know what, Junior's cheesecake never tasted so good."

"The diseases, the scabs, the sores. We used to urinate on our wounds to anesthetize them. No, that's the wrong word. Anesthesia is what you do to the brain. My nephew's an anesthesiologist in Boston. Antibiotic? Antihistamine? Anti-something."

The more he heard, the more Ricardo needed. He grew insatiable. As the killers were driven to kill more and more, he wished to hear more and more of those they had been unable to kill. There were fifty thousand some of them, many more if one included those who hid in the woods, escaped eastward, or merely toiled away the war years in the brutal and often deadly labor camps scattered throughout the continent. Oh, he would tape them too, but it was the fifty thousand who had inhabited the capitols of death that he hunted, begged, cajoled, and, if necessary, bribed into telling their stories. He was like a collector who must attain not merely one of each species, but each and every one of the particular species he collects. To miss just one would mean an elemental loss.

"We arrived, and these men were beating us as soon as we arrived. With bayonets or gun barrels, screaming *Raus! Raus!*[7] That means 'Move quickly!' There were dogs, tearing at people, and everyone was filing past this desk and most everyone was going to the left except for a few big guys who were going to the right. So I shouted, 'Healthy. Twenty. Carpenter,' and I started to the right. I was puny, sixteen, and a student, but I started to the right,

5. Instruments of torture on which bodies are stretched.
6. Galileo Galilei (1564–1642), Italian astronomer and physicist.
7. Get out! or Go away! (German).

and a soldier knocked me down. I got up, and started that way again, and he knocked me down again. Well, I got up and started that way again, and the started after me when the officer in charge said, 'Let him be. He'll die anyway.' " The man looked into the camera and snorted, "Hah!"

It was interesting, despite their experience they were optimistic. Or was it because of their past that they were optimists, because they were able to conquer adversity, because ultimately they had triumphed. They had homes now, and businesses and children, and were able to follow the course of their lives like ordinary human beings, yet those who listened to them were devastated and came to believe in the inevitable doom of a species capable of such enormity.

Dr. Ricardo in particular suffered since his work at the library commenced. Yet the more he suffered, the greater his passion for his self-appointed mission. He ignored his students as he expanded his collection. One hundred, two hundred, three hundred tapes on the wall, a thousand hours of horror, and he knew them all by heart. His wife was eager to have children, but he would not breed. The tapes were his children.

Ricardo's eyes widened at the stories of misery, at the rivers of blood which ran from the tongues of the witnesses, at the mountains of ashes heaped up beneath the videotape camera, mountains to obscure the eye of the camera, to bury the Library of Moloch.

Most witnesses told their stories voluntarily. These stories were equivalent to their souls yet they were willing to donate them to the Library of Moloch because they believed that to tell was to verify a past that had become dreamlike even to themselves. And after all, they were people of the book. Of course, the form was strange, but they had faith that this "tape" was a newfangled kind of a book, and they were willing to move with the times.

Yet some were suspicious. They had been convinced to go to the library by their children or coaxed by Dr. Ricardo, who had obtained their home phone numbers.

One old lady arrived wearing a large rhinestone brooch on a highly textured brocade dress. Her hair was cut short in a golden helmet. She could have been a dentist's receptionist, or a dentist's mother. When the tape started to roll, and Ricardo began by asking her to tell him "a little about yourself," she said, "Pardon me, but why do you wish to know?"

"Isn't that self-explanatory?"

"I never did understand the obvious. It usually hurt too much."

Ricardo was taken aback; he was forced to define the library's purpose. "To prevent such a thing from ever happening again."

"Ah, so you believe that my warning will keep armies from crossing borders, railroads from chugging down the tracks, fires from burning. I was not aware that I had such power."

"Well, not just your warning."

"Everybody's. Mine and Max Adelstein's and Dora Schwartz's. Poor Dora. What a responsibility. And her with pleurisy."

"Well, don't you think it is important"—and he called up a phrase from the survivors' own organizations, a deliberate redundancy that struck them as biblical in its admonition—"to remember. Never to forget."

"Ah," she nodded understandingly. "Never to forget, you say. To remember, you say. Did you ever think that we might prefer to forget?"

"But as a survivor, you have an obligation to—"

"You know, I never liked the word, 'survivor,' it suggests too much personal ability. There was no ability. There was luck. We are not survivors, but merely remainders, or the remains. And you are jackals, feasting on the last tasty flesh that sticks to our bones. Tell me, is it good?"

"That is terribly unfair. I am sympathetic."

"Leeches. Vampires. You cannot get more blood from our loved ones, so you're sinking your teeth into us. I do not think you are unsympathetic. I think you are jealous, Herr Doktor Professor."

Ricardo said, "I wish you would not call me that," his clipped words emphasizing the last of the British accent he had shed as a child.

"And what charmed world do you inhabit where wishes are granted, Herr Doktor Professor?"

"Enough! I will not be insulted. If you insist, we will stop this session."

"Oh, so you will judge the validity of my story on whether I have the proper respect for you, Herr Doktor Professor?" The tiny lady squirmed delicately in her comfortable chair, her grandmother's eyes gleaming as she removed her glasses and rubbed them on her sleeve.

Ricardo surrendered. "You are right. We cannot judge. We are not here to judge."

The old lady made a gesture, a hand floating horizontally across an empty channel. It was the rod of the shepherd who winnows his flock by determining which pass beneath it and which do not. In the Yom Kippur prayer, the U-nisaneh Tokef, that image is a symbol of God's judgment for the upcoming year, who shall live and who shall die. It was also used as a deliberate parody in the land of evil, only instead of a gnarled shepherd's rod, a sleek leather riding crop was used, and the little ones, too little to reach that glistening leather while standing on their toes so as to make their topmost curls quiver, never had the chance to be whipped with it. Their slaughter was immediate.

"So, what occurred after you were deported?"

She answered this and the other questions he posed with brisk efficiency. But then, after she described the American soldier who "liberated" the eighty pounds that were left of her, she said, "And where were you during the war, Herr Dok—"

"I was young."

"So was I," she said. "I was young and in love and in Europe."

"Bala Cynwyd."

"What?"

"It's a suburb of Philadelphia."

"A suburb? Of Philadelphia?" Her voice was so skeptically inflected that she might as well have said, "A cathedral? In Vatican City?"

He bowed his head. "They call it the Main Line."

"How nice."

Her tone angered him. "It was. It was very nice. And I feel fortunate, but I do not feel ashamed. All right?"

"Fine by me." She lifted both her palms.

He said, "I don't have a gun."

"You don't need one. You have a camera."

"And what is that supposed to mean?"

"Nothing. Ignore me."

He wished he could. He had gotten what he wanted, another tape on the shelf, another cache of horror. The interview was over, but he could not leave it alone. "Jealous of what? Jealous of suffering? Jealous of death?" He tried to imitate the scornful laugh of one of his previous subjects. "Hah."

For the first time, Ricardo entered onto the record as more than an interlocutor from behind the camera, and the operator looked at the old lady as if for instruction or authorization to swivel the camera to view the professor's distress. She merely gazed into the lens with complete equanimity. Then she said, "There are two separate, inviolate realms. One is memory."

Ricardo answered as if in a trance, "And the other?"

She didn't answer, and it drove the doctor crazy. What was it that she wasn't telling him? What was it that none of them had told him? What was missing from his library? He mentally reviewed the names on the shelves. They were arranged alphabetically although they were also cross-categorized by age, sex, the nature of the torture endured, and the kind of response—from sorrow to anger to hatred to mystical contemplativeness. Yet something was missing.

And then it struck him. What bound and limited the library was that all of its subjects were victims. Where were their victimizers?

Amidst all of the workings of the man-made Hades, its transportation and extermination systems, recounted in detail for the librarians who spurred the informants to unearth even the tiniest additional tidbit concerning the kingdom of darkness, there was plenty about, but nothing from the lords of the infernal regions.

Of course, there was the legitimate desire to deny these men or their female counterparts credence. We do not want to hear their stories; we may find out how similar to ourselves they are. Besides which, the evildoers were hardly forthcoming. Though they pursued their crimes with vigor and pleasure, they were nonetheless aware that their actions were heinous. One archvillain even said that theirs was an episode which would remain hidden. But he was wrong. The library was intent on proving that. Maybe society had failed the victims. And politicians had failed them. The clergy had failed them. But the librarians would not.

Dr. Ricardo was sure that his register of martyrs hallowed them, and that his recordings of their lives saved them. Unfortunately, the beneficiary of his largesse was not convinced. The old lady not only refused to recognize his charity, she dared to question his role. "Watch out," she said. "There is only one sentence for those who tamper with forbidden mysteries."

"Do not threaten me."

"That's not a threat. It's a prophecy."

"Well, like it or not, we are in the archival era. This library does not exist in order to examine experience. Here experience exists in order to be examined."

The old lady stood as he ranted, and tottered away on the heels that brought her height to five feet shy, but the man who held the technological rod that measured her value in the new world did not notice.

When he was finished, Dr. Ricardo was alone with his roomful of gray cylinders. The camera was off, and the lady was gone. He sat in her chair, still warm, and stared at the empty lens of the videotape machine. Looking down, he noticed that the arm of the chair had been scratched clear through to the stuffing, a mixture of straw and compressed fibers. Obviously one of the interviewees had been so tormented, his or her fingernails punctured the supple leather surface.

The library had money enough to repair the damage or replace the chair. But Dr. Ricardo was curious whose memories evoked such a reaction. He supposed he would never know. The cameras focused on the subjects' faces while he focused on the words.

He reached into his breast pocket and removed the pack of cigarettes he had purchased earlier in the day. He had smoked for years, stopped for years, and recommenced when he started his series of interviews.

"The fences were electrified. This was a blessing. One could always kill oneself when the pain grew too tremendous. Many people availed themselves of the facility."

Dr. Ricardo lit a cigarette and inhaled. The very process was soporific. So he fell asleep, and twisted in the soft contours of the chair, his head filled with images of his parents' home in Bala Cynwyd, outside of Philadelphia, ringed with barbed wire, on fire. Ashes from his cigarette dropped to the exposed stuffing.

Soon Dr. Ricardo wore a crown of flames, yet still he slept.

The flames spread. They rode across the seam of the carpeting on the floor and caught at the papers on his desk.

The fire passed into the storage room, and climbed the shelves. There the cylinders buckled under the heat, and they popped open, the tapes writhing like snakes in a burning cave, and the words of the witnesses escaped, and the pictures created by their words escaped. The guard towers, the barbed wire, the fires blackening the sky, escaped into the air along with the smoke.

Throughout the dormitory, the young law students woke with shrieks of terror. Their dreams were tainted; their beds turned to pyres. They staggered outside in their pajamas, clutching their seared case books.

Finally, Dr. Ricardo also woke, coughing up burned gray phlegm, sputtering. His precious tapes, the wall of evil that he wished to preserve, was being consumed before his eyes. He tamped out what he could, but he could not extinguish the blaze.

The librarian might have been able to save himself, but there was one more question he had yet to ask. He grabbed at the last tape on the shelf, the one that served as a bookend because the secretary had not had time to file it. His fingers blistered from the touch, but he jammed the cassette into the monitor whose cord was a glowing copper filament. Nevertheless, the machine worked.

The lady appeared on television against a background of flames. "Pardon me," she said, "but why do you wish to know?"

He punched the device's fast-forward mechanism. There was a blur, and when he lifted his finger, the lady seemed to smile as she said, "I do not think you are unsympathetic. I think you are jealous, Herr Dok—"

He hit the bottom again, and left his finger there for what seemed like an eternity. He lifted it to see her silence and hear his own voice from off-screen, "Jealous of what? Jealous of suffering? Jealous of death?" But where he expected to hear himself give a last, resounding, "Hah!" there was only continued silence. The machine may have been damaged by the flames, which rose up the curtains. He could hear sirens.

Suddenly the lady answered, "Yes, jealous."

"What?"

"Jealous of the Holocaust."

In his delirium, he wondered if fire was the fate of all libraries. First there was the Library of Alexandria with the wisdom of the ancient world, and now, the Library of Moloch containing what its keeper truly believed was the wisdom of the modern world. Perhaps, he thought crazily amid the mounting flames, this fate was not inappropriate, for Moloch was the fire god to whom children were routinely sacrificed. Moloch, the Lord of Gehenna,[8] lived outside of Jerusalem in what was truly the valley of the damned, forever exiled in sight of the heavenly city.

He started to answer the flickering screen, but she would not allow him an opening.

"Jealous of having a reason to hate. Jealous of tragedy, because your life is no Charleston. Jealous of a people who refuse to submit to the impurities that surround them, Jealous of those who adhere to a broken covenant. Jealous of the sacred. So here you have it, Herr Doktor, so enjoy!"

"I do not understand."

"My poor professor. You know, the killers never understood us either. 'How,' they asked themselves, 'can these people meet our eyes? How can they persevere no matter the punishment we inflict?' Mind you, they were sophisticated; they knew that it was not merely the scourging of the body of the community, but the anguish of being compelled to acknowledge that animals like them shared the same cruel flesh we did, breathed the same vile air. But that was the part that made it easy. We knew we were looking at God."

"How could you tell?"

"Because God is made in the image of man. We met Him a long time ago, in Spain and Rome and Egypt, and more genteel spots. We saw Him in a topcoat and derby ducking into Whitehall. And we saw Him in Washington, too. The truth is, He is everywhere, but only we can recognize Him, because we are old friends. We know His story."

"Can . . ."

"Of course I can introduce Him to you. And now, my good fellow, prepare to meet your maker, for those who enter the Holy of Holies are condemned to burn. I told you. I told you, there are two inviolate realms."

That was it, that was what he had turned the videotape on in order to hear. That was the lesson for which he risked his own immolation in order to learn. "What are they?" he screamed at the tape, as the flames kissed his feet, and cracked his knees that were as immovable as if they were lashed to a stake.

Although the screen itself had begun to melt with the intensity of the heat, the image was calm. "I told you. One is memory."

8. Hell.

"And the other—the other, please! The other!"
The lady answered, "Theology."

1995

JACQUELINE OSHEROW
b. 1956

Born in Philadelphia, educated at Harvard and Princeton, Jacqueline Osherow stands out as one of the most gifted poets of her generation as well as the most enmeshed in the traditions of Judaism. In one poem after another, Osherow revitalizes images from the Bible, the landscapes of Israel, the sounds and cadences of the Yiddish language, and the ruins of the Holocaust. In the tradition of Wordsworth, Osherow's poems are often long, reflective pieces that seem to take on the pace of life, slowly acquiring moment and momentum. Her poetry challenges the reader to scale great intellectual heights; at the same time, her skillful metrics make the works masterpieces of form. In her long poem *Conversations with Survivors,* published in a 1994 collection of the same name, Osherow gives us the survivor Fany, "who always wears a turquoise turban" and who wins the lottery by playing the number tattooed on her arm. Her fourth book, *Dead Men's Praise* (1999), takes its title from Jacob Glatstein's poem *Dead Men Don't Praise God* and includes a reworking of the Psalms.

In the poems selected here, Osherow labors to save the Yiddish language (*Ch'vil Schreibn a Poem auf Yiddish*), obliterated, she observes, by the Holocaust. In *Ponar,* the poet imagines a world in which Jewish suffering has been erased and the great cultural institutions of Vilna still stand. In *Brief Encounter with a Hero, Name Unknown,* Osherow wonders, but ultimately can never know, how a female prisoner in Auschwitz had the courage to murder an SS man.

Osherow has published four books of poetry, has won a Guggenheim Fellowship and a National Endowment for the Arts fellowship, and has been anthologized widely. She teaches at the University of Utah, where she also directs the graduate program in creative writing.

Ponar[1]

In the world to come, the forests won't have secrets.
Leaves will fall on soil made of leaves,
Stems, mud, sand, the usual substances
And everything that happens will be heard for miles:
Leaves rattling, trees falling, gunshots.

1. A reference to Panory, a resort about five miles from Vilna, which was used as a Nazi extermination site. From 1941 to 1944, about 100,000 people were executed there.

Only there will be no gunshots.
We are talking about the world to come.

And the people in Ponar will brush off the dirt
And return to the twenty-seven libraries
And sixty study halls of the Vilna[2] synagogue
To run the gamut in their youth organizations
From right-wing Zionism to left-wing Zionism[3]
And mimeograph avant-grade poetic tracts
On the beauty of the aspens at Ponar.

Mostly, they'll learn Mishnah[4] and Gemara[5]
At the oversubscribed lectures of Rabbi Akivah,[6]
Who, though he was slaughtered like a beast
In the marketplace, according to the Midrash,[7]
Was not hindered in the world to come
From astounding even Moses with his insights.

Not just the rabbis and the rich will study,
But butchers, tailors, shoemakers, musicians;
The air itself, weighted down with ash,
Will rifle through the aspens' skittish pages
For commentaries on the sacred texts
Derived from half-revealed illuminations
Lost before they could be copied down

Along with murals, stories, recipes,
Chemical formulae, dress patterns,
Melodramas, new prime numbers, poems
Crowded together in the rare, dark soil
That polishes the aspens' tarnished silver
To prepare a setting for the alef-bet[8]

Or perhaps to make each leaf a tiny mirror
To shine, in miniature, an unclaimed face
Dreaming calmly to the world to come
Until it fills with gold and falls again—
This time gently—to its waiting place
And rests its secrets on the cluttered earth
Shaded by the forest at Ponar.

1994

2. The capital of Lithuania from 1323 to the present. Before World War II, it was a center of culture for Eastern European Jewry.
3. Zionism is a movement in which the goal is to establish and preserve the State of Israel for the Jewish people.
4. The study of oral Jewish law, mostly a matter of memorization and recapitulation. The word comes from the Hebrew *shanah,* "repeat."
5. One of two inexact names for the Talmud, the collection of teachings that consist of commentary on and discussions of the Torah.
6. The foremost scholar of his age, Rabbi Akivah (50–135) was also a patriot and martyr who exercised a strong influence on the development of sacred Jewish texts.
7. The Jewish literary tradition in which scholars interpret—and fill in—Scriptural writings in order to elucidate or bring out the morals or lessons of biblical stories.
8. Alphabet (Hebrew)

Brief Encounter with a Hero, Name Unknown

It could have been a matter of modesty
It could have been the gold sewn in your dress
You might even have feared for your chastity
Maybe it was simple recklessness

Perhaps you couldn't part with that one dress
Once rumpled by a skillful, knowing beau
Or were wearing it to hide a gaping abscess
Or were pregnant and ashamed to let it show

Maybe you'd seen a Western dubbed in Polish
Or Yiddish or Czech or whatever it was you spoke
And remembered some hokey John Wayne[1] flourish
That downed four outlaws at a single stroke

Maybe you were an unexceptional girl
Who'd gone crazy on the claustrophobic ride
Maybe you had had a lovers' quarrel
And, for days, been contemplating suicide

You could have been a fighter in the woods
And drilled this tactic over and over and over
Who knows? Perhaps you thought you'd beat the odds
Maybe it wasn't even the right maneuver

My father-in-law mentioned it in passing
When I asked how well he'd known his SS[2] boss
(His job in Birkenau[3] had been delousing;
They also used the Zyklon B[4] for lice)

And he named one Schillinger, SS
And told how he had watched Schillinger die
When a new woman, ordered to undress
(You were going to the gas chamber, apparently)

Instead grabbed hold of Schillinger's own gun
And killed three other guards along with him
Such things, says my father-in-law, were common
(Needless to say, in seconds you had joined them)

It could have been a matter of modesty
It could have been the gold sewn in your dress
You might even have feared for your chastity
Maybe it was simple recklessness

1996

1. Movie actor of the 1940s, 1950s, and 1960s who was known for his portrayal of cowboy heroes in American Westerns (1907–1979).
2. An abbreviation of *Schutzstaffel* (literally, "protection echelon"), Hitler's elite guards that evolved into a paramilitary group, responsible for carrying out many of the policies of the Final Solution (German).
3. An extermination camp annex of Auschwitz, Nazi Germany's largest concentration camp.
4. A poisonous gas used by the Nazis in the gas chambers at Auschwitz and other camps.

Ch'vil Schreibn a Poem auf Yiddish[1]

I want to write a poem in Yiddish
and not any poem, but the poem
I am longing to write,
a poem so Yiddish, it would not
be possible to translate,
except from, say, my bubbe's[2]
Galizianer[3] to my zayde's[4] *Litvak*[5]
and even then it would lose a little something,

though, of course, it's not the sort of poem
that relies on such trivialities, as,
for example, my knowing how to speak
its language—though, who knows?
Maybe I understand it perfectly;
maybe, in Yiddish, things aren't any clearer
than the mumbling of rain on cast off leaves . . .

Being pure poem, pure Yiddish poem,
my Yiddish poem is above such meditations,
as I, were I fluent in Yiddish,
would be above wasting my time
pouring out my heart in Goyish[6] metaphors.

Even Yiddish doesn't have a word
for the greatness of my Yiddish poem,
a poem so exquisite that if Dante[7] could rise from the dead
he would have to rend his clothes in mourning.
Oh, the drabness of his noisy,
futile little paradise
when it's compared with my Yiddish poem.

His poems? They're everywhere. A dime a dozen.
A photocopier can take them down in no time
but my Yiddish poem can never be taken down,
not even by a pious scribe
who has fasted an entire year
to be pure enough to write my Yiddish poem,

which exists—doesn't he realize?—
in no realm at all
unless the dead still manage to dream dreams.

It's even a question
whether G-d Himself
can make out the text of my Yiddish poem.

1. I want to write a poem in Yiddish (Yiddish).
2. Grandmother's (Yiddish).
3. A Jew born in Galicia, Poland.
4. Grandfather's (Yiddish).
5. A Jew born in Lithuania.
6. Gentile (Yiddish).
7. I.e., Dante Alighieri (1265–1321), great Italian poet, author of *The Divine Comedy*.

If He can, He won't be happy.
He'll have to retract everything,
to recreate the universe
without banalities like "firmament" and "light"

but only out of words extracted
from the stingy tongues of strangers,
smuggled out in letters made of camels,

houses, eyes, to deafen
half a continent with argument
and exegesis, each refinement

purified in fire after
fire, singed almost beyond
recognition, but still
not quite consumed, not even
by the heat of my Yiddish poem

1996

ALLEGRA GOODMAN
b. 1967

Highly acclaimed at a remarkably young age, Allegra Goodman has published two collections of short stories and a novel. Her second collection, *The Family Markowitz* (1996), secured her reputation, drawing praise for its keen observations and distinctive voice. A *Los Angeles Times* best-seller and a *New York Times* notable book of the year, this collection of interwoven stories, many of which originally appeared in the *New Yorker,* follows three generations of a secular Jewish family as it comments on the persistence of religious and familial ties in contemporary American culture. In the story reprinted here, *The Four Questions,* the reader finds that the issues that had dominated the experience of second-generation American Jews undergo a reversal in the third generation. In the second generation of Jewish American immigrants, offspring turn their back on the Old World obsessions of their immigrant parents, including religious rituals—witness Nathan Zuckerman, for instance, the prodigal son in so many of Philip Roth's novels.

Goodman's work provides a counterpoint to the prodigal children; her characters, second-generation Jewish Americans, are themselves parents, and their worries no longer center around the children's drifting away from Jewish faith. Instead, in the Markowitz family, assimilated parents worry about their daughter Miriam's increasing religious fervor, while Miriam scolds them for trivializing the true significance of Passover.

Allegra Goodman was born in Brooklyn but grew up in a small Jewish community in Honolulu, where her parents taught at the University of Hawaii. She recalls that she wore a floral muumuu at her Bas Mitzvah. At seventeen, she published her first short story in *Commentary*. As a twenty-one-year-old Harvard senior, Goodman published a dazzling first book, the collection of semiautobiographical stories *Total Immersion* (1989), described by the Literary critic Sanford Pinsker as "unflinchingly honest and easily intimate." *Total Immersion* earned Goodman the Whiting Foundation Writer's Award in 1991. Seven years later, Goodman published the widely acclaimed *Family Markowitz*. Her most recent book, the novel *Kaaterskill Falls* (1998), closely observes a sect of Hasidic Jews summering in the Catskill Mountains and was nominated for a National Book Award.

Drawn to neither textual innovation nor postmodern theorizing, Goodman has been characterized as a storyteller from the "old school," who jumps through no flaming literary hoops, but instead places herself squarely amid the tradition of other Jewish storytellers. Reminiscent of masters like Isaac Bashevis Singer, whose novel title *The Family Moskat* must have influenced the title of her own collection, Goodman renders the lives of American Jews with penetrating detail, and intimate observations. In *Kaaterskill Falls*, she expands upon a recurring theme in her work—how the sacred coexists with the pedestrian concerns of the workaday world. Ultimately, she decides that the two can exist only side by side and in relation to the other.

Goodman lives in Cambridge, Massachusetts, with her husband and two children.

The Four Questions[1]

Ed is sitting in his mother-in-law Estelle's gleaming kitchen. "Is it coming in on time?" Estelle asks him. He is calling to check on Yehudit's flight from San Francisco.

"It's still ringing," Ed says. He sits on one of the swivel chairs and twists the telephone cord through his fingers. One wall of the kitchen is papered in a yellow-and-brown daisy pattern, the daisies as big as Ed's hand. The window shade has the same pattern on it. Ed's in-laws live in a 1954 ranch house with all the original period details. Nearly every year since their wedding, he and Sarah have come out to Long Island[2] for Passover, and the house has stayed the same. The front bathroom is papered, even on the ceiling, in brown with white and yellow flowers, and there is a double shower curtain over the tub, the outer curtain held back with brass chains. The front bedroom, Sarah's old room, has a blue carpet, organdy curtains, and white furniture, including a kidney-shaped vanity table. There is a creaky trundle bed to wheel out from under Sarah's bed, and Ed always sleeps there, a step below Sarah.

In the old days, Sarah and Ed would fly up from Washington with the children, but now the kids come in on their own. Miriam and Ben take the shuttle down from Boston, Avi is driving in from Wesleyan, and Yehudit, the youngest, is flying in from Stanford.[3] She usually can't come at all, but this year the holiday coincides with her spring break. Ed is going to pick her up at Kennedy tonight. "It's coming in on time," Ed tells Estelle.

"Good," she says, and she takes away his empty glass. Automatically, instinctively, Estelle puts things away. She folds up the newspaper before Ed gets to the business section. She'll clear the table while the slower eaters

1. A reference to the questions in the Passover Haggadah that initiate the Seder. Traditionally, the youngest (most often male) child at the gathering asks the questions, which prompts answers from the elders. The questions will be stated several times in the text.

2. A suburb east of New York City.

3. A university in California. "Wesleyan": a university in Middletown, Connecticut.

are contemplating seconds. And, when Ed and Sarah come to visit and sleep in the room Sarah and her sister used to share, Ed will come in and find that his things have inexorably been straightened. On the white-and-gold dresser, Ed's tangle of coins, keys, watch, and comb is untangled. The shirt and socks on the bed have been washed and folded. It's the kind of service you might expect in a fine hotel. In West Hempstead it makes Ed uneasy. His mother-in-law is in constant motion—sponging, sweeping, snapping open and shut the refrigerator door. Flicking off lights after him as he leaves the room. Now she is checking the oven. "This is a beautiful bird, Sarah," she calls into the den. "I want you to tell Miriam when she gets here that this turkey is kosher. Is she going to eat it?"

"I don't know," Sarah says. Her daughter the medical student (Harvard Medical School) has been getting more observant every year. In college she started bringing paper plates and plastic utensils to her grandparents' house because Estelle and Sol don't keep kosher. Then she began eating off paper plates even at home in Washington. Although Ed and Sarah have a kosher kitchen, they wash their milk and meat dishes together in the dishwasher.

"I never would have predicted it," Estelle says. "She used to eat everything on her plate. Yehudit was always finicky. I could have predicted she would be a vegetarian. But Miriam used to come and have more of everything. She used to love my turkey."

"It's not that, Mommy," Sarah says.

"I know. It's this orthodoxy of hers. I have no idea where she gets it from. From Jonathan, I guess." Jonathan is Miriam's fiancé.

"No," Ed says, "she started in with it before she even met Jon."

"It wasn't from anyone in this family. Are they still talking about having that Orthodox rabbi marry them?"

"Well—" Sarah begins.

"We met with him," Ed says.

"What was his name, Lowenthal?"

"Lewitsky," Ed says.

"Black coat and hat?"

"No, no, he's a young guy—"

"That doesn't mean anything," Estelle says.

"He was very nice, actually," Sarah says. "The problem is that he won't perform a ceremony at Congregation S.T."

"Why not? It's not Orthodox enough for him?"

"Well, it's a Conservative synagogue. Of course, our rabbi wouldn't let him use S.T. anyway. Rabbi Landis performs all the ceremonies there. They don't want the sanctuary to be treated like a hall to be rented out. Miriam is talking about getting married outside."

"Outside!" Estelle says. "In June! In Washington, D.C.? When I think of your poor mother, Ed, in that heat!" Estelle is eleven years younger than Ed's mother, and always solicitous about Rose's health. "What are they thinking of? Where could they possibly get married outside?"

"I don't know," Ed says. "Dumbarton Oaks. The Rose Garden.[4] They're a couple of silly kids."

4. The formal gardens on the grounds of the White House. "Dumbarton Oaks": a mansion known for its gardens in Georgetown, Washington, D.C., where negotiations for the creation of the United Nations took place.

"This is not a barbecue," Estelle says.

"What can we do?" Sarah asks. "If they insist on this rabbi."

"And it's March already," Estelle says grimly. "Here, Ed"—she takes a pink bakery box from the refrigerator—"you'd better finish these eclairs before she gets here."

"I'd better not." Ed is trying to watch his weight.

"It's a long time till dinner," Estelle warns as she puts the box back.

"That's okay. I'll live off the fat of the land," says Ed, patting his stomach.

"I got her sealed matzos, sealed macaroons, vacuum-packed gefilte fish."[5] Estelle displays the packages on the scalloped wood shelves of her pantry.

"Don't worry. Whatever else happens, the boys are going to be ravenous. They're going to eat," Sarah assures her mother. They bring the tablecloth out to the dining room. "Remember Avi's friend Noam?"

"The gum chewer. He sat at this table and ate four pieces of cake!"

"And now Noam is an actuary," says Sarah.

"And Avi is bringing a girl to dinner."

"She's a lovely girl," Sarah says.

"Beautiful," Estelle agrees with a worried look.

In the kitchen Ed is thinking he might have an eclair after all. Estelle always has superb pastry in the house. Sol had started out as a baker, and still has a few friends in the business. "Are these from Leonard's?" Ed asks when Sol comes in.

"Leonard's was bought out," Sol says, easing himself into a chair. "These are from Magic Oven. How is the teaching?"

"Well, I have a heavy load. Two of my colleagues went on sabbatical this year—"

"Left you shorthanded."

"Yeah," Ed says. "I've been teaching seven hours a week."

"That's all?" Sol is surprised.

"I mean, on top of my research."

"It doesn't sound that bad."

Ed starts to answer. Instead, he goes to the refrigerator and gets out the eclairs.

"Leonard's were better," Sol muses. "He used a better custard."

"But these are pretty good. What was that? Was that the kids?" Ed runs out to meet the cab in the driveway, pastry in hand. He pays the driver as his two oldest tumble out of the cab with their luggage—Ben's backpack and duffel, Miriam's canvas tote and the suitcase she has inherited, bright pink, patched with silver metallic tape, dating from Ed and Sarah's honeymoon in Paris.

"Daddy!" Miriam says. "What are you eating?"

Ed looks at his eclair. Technically all this sort of thing should be out of the house by now—all bread, cake, pastry, candy, soda, ice cream—anything even sweetened with corn syrup. And, of course, Miriam takes the technicalities seriously. He knows she must have stayed up late last night in her tiny apartment in Cambridge, vacuuming the crevices in the couch, packing

5. Traditional foods served at Passover. "Matzos": unleavened bread. "Gefilte fish": literally, stuffed fish (Yiddish); ground fish that has been mixed with eggs, matzo meal, and seasoning, formed into small ovals or a large loaf, simmered in stock, and served cold. Once the stuffing for fish, it is now the dish itself.

away her toaster oven. He finishes off the eclair under her disapproving eyes. He doesn't need the calories, either, she is thinking. She has become very puritanical, his daughter, and it baffles him. They had raised the children in a liberal, rational, joyous way—raised them to enjoy the Jewish tradition, and Ed can't understand why Miriam would choose austerity and obscure ritualism. She is only twenty-three—even if she *is* getting married in June. How can a young girl be attracted to this kind of legalism? It disturbs him. On the other hand, he knows she is right about his weight and blood pressure. He hadn't really been hungry. He'll take it easy on dinner.

Meanwhile, Ben carries in the bags and dumps them in the den. "Hi, Grandma! Hi, Grandpa! Hi, Mom!" He grabs the TV remote and starts flipping channels. No one is worried about Ben becoming too intense. He is a senior at Brandeis,[6] six feet tall with overgrown ash-brown hair. He has no thoughts about the future. No ideas about life after graduation. No plan. He is studying psychology in a distracted sort of way. When he flops down on the couch he looks like a big, amiable golden retriever.

"Get me the extra chairs from the basement, dear," Estelle tells him. "We've been waiting for you to get here. Then, Sarah, you can get the wineglasses. You can reach up there." Estelle is in her element. Her charm bracelet jingles as she talks. She directs Ben to go down under the Ping-Pong table without knocking over the boxes stacked there; she points Sarah to the cabinet above the refrigerator. Estelle is smaller than Sarah—five feet two and a quarter—and her features are sharper. She had been a brunette when she was younger, but now her hair is auburn. Her eyes are lighter brown as well, and her skin dotted with sun spots from the winters in Florida. "Oh—" she sighs suddenly as Miriam brings a box of paper plates from the kitchen. "Why do you have to—?"

"Because these dishes aren't Pesach[7] dishes."

Estelle looks at the table, set with her white-and-gold Noritake china. "This is the good china," she says. "These are the Pesach dishes."

"But you use them for the other holidays, too," Miriam tells her. "They've had bread on them and cake and pumpkin pie and all kinds of stuff."

"Ooo, you are sooo stubborn!" Estelle puts her hands on her tall granddaughter's shoulders and gives her a shake. The height difference makes it look as though she is pleading with her as she looks up into Miriam's face. Then the oven timer goes off and she rushes into the kitchen. Sarah is washing lettuce at the sink. "I'll do the salads last," Estelle tells her. "After Ed goes to the airport." Miriam is still on her mind. What kind of seder[8] will Miriam have next year after she is married? Estelle has met Miriam's fiancé, who is just as observant as she is. "Did you see?" she asks Sarah. "I left you my list, for Miriam's wedding."

"What list?"

"On the table. Here." Estelle gives Sarah the typed list. "These are the names and addresses you asked for—the people I need to invite."

Sarah looks at the list. She turns the page and scans the names, doing some calculations in her head. "Mommy!" she says. "There are forty-two people on this list!"

6. A university in Waltham, Massachusetts.
7. Passover (Hebrew).
8. Ceremonial meal to observe the first night or first two nights of Passover (Hebrew).

"Not all of them will be able to come, of course," Estelle reassures her.

"We're having one hundred people at this wedding, remember? Including Ed's family, and the kids' friends—"

"Well, this is our family. These are your cousins, Sarah."

Sarah looks again at the list. "When was the last time I saw these people?" she asks. "Miriam wouldn't even recognize some of them. And what's this? The Seligs? The Magids? Robert and Trudy Rothman? These aren't cousins."

"Sarah! Robert and Trudy are my dearest friends. We've known the Seligs and the Magids for thirty years."

"This is a small family wedding," Sarah tells her mother. "I'm sure they'll understand—"

Estelle knows that they wouldn't understand.

"I think we have to cut down this list," Sarah says.

Estelle doesn't get a chance to reply. Avi has arrived, and he's standing in the living room with Ed, Miriam, and Ben. She stands next to him: Amy, his friend from Wesleyan. Estelle still holds back from calling her his girlfriend. Nevertheless, there she is. She has gorgeous strawberry-blond hair, and she has brought Estelle flowers—mauve and rose tulips with fancy curling petals. No one else brought Estelle flowers.

"They're beautiful. Look, Sol, aren't they beautiful?" Estelle says. "Avi, you can take your bag to the den. The boys are sleeping in the den; the girls are sleeping in the sun room."

"I don't want to sleep in the den," Avi says.

"Why not?" asks Estelle.

"Because he snores." Avi points at his brother. "Seriously, he's so loud. I'd rather sleep in the basement."

Everyone looks at him. It's a finished basement and it's got carpeting, but it is cold down there.

"You've shared a room with Ben for years," Sarah says.

"You'll freeze down there," Estelle tells him.

"I have a down sleeping bag."

"You never complained at home," Sarah says.

"Oh, give me a break," Ben mutters under his breath. "You aren't going to have wild sex in a sleeping bag in the basement."

"What?" Ed asks. "Did you say something, Ben?"

"No," Ben says, and ambles back into the den.

"I don't want you in the basement," Estelle tells her grandson.

"Can I help you in the kitchen, Mrs. Kirshenbaum?" asks Amy.

Estelle and Amy make the chopped liver. The boys are watching TV in the den, and Ed and Sarah are lying down in the back. Miriam is on the phone with Jon.

"Did you want me to chop the onions, too?" Amy asks Estelle.

"Oh no. Just put them there and I'll take out the liver, and then we attach the grinder—" She snaps the grinder onto the KitchenAid and starts feeding in the broiled liver. "And then you add the onions and the eggs." Estelle pushes in the hard-boiled eggs. "And the schmaltz."[9] She is explaining to Amy all about chopped liver, but her mind is full of questions. How serious is it with Avi? What do Amy's parents think? They are Methodist, Estelle

9. Rendered chicken fat (Yiddish).

knows that. And Amy's uncle is a Methodist minister! They can't approve of all this. But, then, of course, how much do they know about it? Avi barely talks about Amy. Estelle and Sol have only met her once before, when they came up for Avi's jazz band concert. And then, suddenly, Avi said he wanted to bring her with him to the seder. But he's never really dated anyone before, and kids shy away from anything serious at this age. Avi's cousin Jeffrey had maybe five different girlfriends in college, and he's still unmarried.

Amy's family goes to church every Sunday. They're quite religious. Amy had explained that to Estelle on the phone when she called up about the book. She wanted Estelle to recommend a book for her to read about Passover. Estelle didn't know what to say. She had never dreamed something like this would happen. If only Amy weren't Methodist. She is everything Estelle could ever want. An absolute doll. The tulips stand in the big barrel-cut crystal vase on the counter. The most beautiful colors.

By the time Ed goes off to the airport, everything is ready except the salad. They dress for dinner while he is gone.

"Do you have a decent shirt?" Sarah asks Ben, who is still watching television. "Or is that as good as it gets?"

"I didn't have a chance to do my laundry before I got here, so I have hardly any clothes," Ben explains.

"Ben!" Estelle looks at him in his red-and-green-plaid hunting shirt. Avi is wearing a nice starched Oxford.

"Maybe he could borrow one of Grandpa's," Miriam suggests.

"He's broader in the shoulders than I am," says Sol. "Come on, Ben, let's see if we can stuff you into something."

They wait for Ed and Yehudit in the living room, almost as if they were expecting guests. Ben sits stiffly on the couch in his small, stiff shirt. He stares at the silver coffee service carefully wrapped in clear plastic. He cracks his knuckles, and then he twists his neck to crack his neck joints. Everyone screams at him. Then, finally, they hear the car in the driveway.

"You're sick as a dog!" Sarah says when Yehudit gets inside.

Yehudit blows her nose and looks at them with feverish, jet-lagged eyes. "Yeah, I think I have mono," she says.

"Oh, my God," says Estelle. "She has to get into bed. That cot in the sun room isn't very comfortable."

"How about a hot drink?" suggests Sarah.

"I'll get her some soup," Estelle says.

"Does it have a vegetable base?" Yehudit asks.

"What she needs is a decongestant," said Ed.

They bundle her up in the La-Z-Boy chair in the den and tuck her in with an afghan and a mug of hot chocolate.

"That's not kosher for Pesach," says Miriam, worried.

"Cool it," Ed says. Then they sit down at the seder table.

Ed always leads the seder. Sol and Estelle love the way he does it because he is so knowledgeable. Ed's area of expertise is the Middle East, so he ties Passover to the present day. And he is eloquent. They are very proud of their son-in-law.

"This is our festival of freedom," Ed says, "commemorating our liberation from slavery." He picks up a piece of matzo and reads from his New

Revised Haggadah:[1] " 'This is the bread which our fathers and mothers ate in Mitzrayim when they were slaves.' " He adds from the translator's note: " 'We use the Hebrew word *Mitzrayim* to denote the ancient land of Egypt—' "

"As opposed to modern-day Mitzrayim," Miriam says dryly.

" 'To differentiate it from modern Egypt,' " Ed reads. Then he puts down the matzo and extemporizes. "We eat this matzo so we will never forget what slavery is, and so that we continue to empathize with afflicted peoples throughout the world: those torn apart by civil wars, those starving or homeless, those crippled by poverty and disease. We think of the people oppressed for their religious or political beliefs. In particular, we meditate on the people in our own country who have not yet achieved full freedom; those discriminated against because of their race, gender, or sexual preference. We think of the subtle forms of slavery as well as the obvious ones—the gray areas that are now coming to light: sexual harassment, verbal abuse—" He can't help noticing Miriam as he says this. It's obvious that she is ignoring him. She is sitting there chanting to herself out of her Orthodox Birnbaum Haggadah, and it offends him. "Finally, we turn to the world's hot spot—the Middle East," Ed says. "We think of war-torn Israel and pray for compromises. We consider the Palestinians, who have no land to call their own, and we call for moderation and perspective. As we sit around the seder table, we look to the past to give us insight into the present."

"Beautiful," murmurs Estelle. But Ed looks down unhappily to where the kids are sitting. Ben has his feet up on Yehudit's empty chair, and Avi is playing with Amy's hair. Miriam is still poring over her Haggadah.

"It's time for the four questions," he says sharply. "The youngest child will chant the four questions," he adds for Amy's benefit.

Sarah checks on Yehudit in the den. "She's asleep. Avi will have to do it."

"Amy is two months younger than I am," Avi says.

"Why don't we all say it together?" Estelle suggests. "She shouldn't have to read it all alone."

"I don't mind," Amy says. She reads: " 'Why is this night different from all other nights? On other nights we eat leavened bread; why on this night do we eat matzo? On other nights we eat all kinds of herbs; why on this night do we eat bitter herbs? On other nights we do not dip even once; why on this night do we dip twice? On other nights we eat either sitting up or reclining; why on this night do we all recline?' "

"Now, Avi, read it in Hebrew," Ed says, determined that Avi should take part—feeling, as well, that the questions sound strange in English. Anthropological.

"What was that part about dipping twice?" Amy asks when Avi is done.

"That's when you dip the parsley into the salt water," Ben tells her.

"It doesn't have to be parsley," Sarah says. "Just greens."

"We're not up to that yet," Ed tells them. "Now I'm going to answer the questions." He reads: " 'We do these things to commemorate our slavery in Mitzrayim. For if God had not brought us out of slavery, we and all future generations would still be enslaved. We eat matzo because our ancestors did not have time to let their bread rise when they left E—Mitzrayim. We eat

1. Book containing the story of the biblical Exodus as it must be told during the Seder (Hebrew).

bitter herbs to remind us of the bitterness of slavery. We dip greens in salt water to remind us of our tears, and we recline at the table because we are free men and women.' Okay." Ed flips a few pages. "The second theme of Passover is about transmitting tradition to future generations. And we have here in the Haggadah examples of four kinds of children—each with his or her own needs and problems. What we have here is instructions on how to tailor the message of Passover to each one. So we read about four hypothetical cases. Traditionally, they were described as four sons: the wise son, the wicked son, the simple son, and the one who does not know how to ask. We refer to these children in modern terms as: committed, uncommitted, unaffiliated, and assimilated. Let's go around the table now. Estelle, would you like to read about the committed child?"

" 'What does the committed child say?' " Estelle reads. " 'What are the practices of Passover which God has commanded us? Tell him or her precisely what the practices are.' "

" 'What does the uncommitted child say?' " Sol continues. " 'What use to you are the practices of Passover? To you, and not to himself. The child excludes him- or herself from the community. Answer him/her: This is on account of what God did for me when I went out of Mitzrayim. For *me*, and not for us. This child can only appreciate personal gain.' "

" 'What does the unaffiliated child say?' " asks Sarah. " 'What is all this about? Answer him or her simply: We were slaves and now we are free.' "

" 'But for the assimilated child,' " Ben reads, " 'it is up to us to open the discussion.' "

"We can meditate for a minute," Ed says, "on a fifth child who died in the Holocaust." They sit silently and look at their plates.

"It's interesting," says Miriam, "that so many things come in fours on Passover. There are four questions, four sons; you drink four cups of wine—"

"It's probably just coincidence," Ben says.

"Thanks," Miriam tells him. "I feel much better. So much for discussion at the seder." She glares at her brother. Couldn't he even shave before he came to the table? She pushes his feet off the chair. "Can't you sit normally?" she hisses at him.

"Don't be such a pain in the butt," Ben mutters.

Ed speeds on, plowing through the Haggadah. " 'The ten plagues that befell the Egyptians: Blood, frogs, vermin, wild beasts, murrain, boils, hail, locusts, darkness, death of the firstborn.' " He looks up from his book and says, "We think of the suffering of the Egyptians as they faced these calamities. We are grateful for our deliverance, but we remember that the oppressor was also oppressed." He pauses there, struck by his own phrase. It's very good. "We cannot celebrate at the expense of others, nor can we say that we are truly free until the other oppressed peoples of the world are also free. We make common cause with all peoples and all minorities. Our struggle is their struggle, and their struggle is our struggle. We turn now to the blessing over the wine and the matzo. Then"—he nods to Estelle—"we'll be ready to eat."

"Daddy," Miriam says.

"Yes."

"This is ridiculous. This seder is getting shorter every year."

"We're doing it the same way we always do it," Ed tells her.

"No, you're not. It's getting shorter and shorter. It was short enough to begin with! You always skip the most important parts."

"Miriam!" Sarah hushes her.

"Why do we have to spend the whole time talking about minorities?" she asks. "Why are you always talking about civil rights?"

"Because that's what Passover is about," Sol tells her.

"Oh, okay, fine," Miriam says.

"Time for the gefilte fish," Estelle announces. Amy gets up to help her, and the two of them bring in the salad plates. Each person has a piece of fish on a bed of lettuce with two cherry tomatoes and a dab of magenta horseradish sauce.

Sarah stands up, debating whether to wake Yehudit for dinner. She ends up walking over to Miriam and sitting next to her for a minute. "Miriam," she whispers, "I think you could try a little harder—"

"To do what?" Miriam asks.

"To be pleasant!" Sarah says. "You've been snapping at everyone all evening. There's no reason for that. There's no reason for you to talk that way to Daddy."

Miriam looks down at her book and continues reading to herself in Hebrew.

"Miriam?"

"What? I'm reading all the stuff Daddy skipped."

"Did you hear what I said? You're upsetting your father."

"It doesn't say a single word about minorities in here," Miriam says stubbornly.

"He's talking about the modern context—"

Miriam looks up at Sarah. "What about the original context?" she asks. "As in the Jewish people? As in God?"

Yehudit toddles in from the den with the afghan trailing behind her. "Can I have some plain salad?" she asks.

"This fish is wonderful," Sol says.

"Outstanding," Ed agrees.

"More," says Ben, with his mouth full.

"Ben! Gross! Can't you eat like a human being?" Avi asks him.

"It's Manishevitz Gold Label," Estelle says. "Yehudit, how did you catch this? Did they say it was definitely mono?"

"No—I don't know what it is," Yehudit says. "I started getting sick on the weekend when we went to sing at the Jewish Community Center for the seniors."

"It's nice that you do that," Estelle says. "Very nice. They're always so appreciative."

"Yeah, I guess so. There was this old guy there and he asked me, 'Do you know "Oyfn Pripitchik"?'[2] I said, 'Yes, we do,' and he said, 'Then please, can I ask you, don't sing "Oyfn Pripitchik." They always come here and sing it for us, and it's so depressing.' Then, when we left, this little old lady beckoned to me and she said, 'What's your name?' I told her, and she said, 'You're very plain, dear, but you're very nice.' "

2. *The Hearth*, an old Yiddish song that was usually sung to children to teach them the alphabet.

"That's terrible!" Estelle says. "Did she really say that?"

"Yup."

"It's not true!" Estelle says. "You should hear what everyone says about my granddaughters when they see your pictures. Wait till they see you—maid of honor at the wedding! What color did you pick for the wedding?" she asks Miriam.

"What?" Miriam asks, looking up from her Haggadah.

Ed is looking at Miriam and feeling that she is trying to undermine his whole seder. What is she doing accusing him of shortening the service every year? He does it the same way every year. She is the one who has changed—becoming more and more critical. More literal-minded. Who is she to criticize the way he leads the service? What does she think she is doing? He can remember seders when she couldn't stay awake until dinner. He remembers when she couldn't even sit up. When he could hold her head in the palm of his hand.

"I think peach is a hard color," Estelle is saying. "It's a hard color to find. You know, a pink is one thing. A pink looks lovely on just about everyone. Peach is a hard color to wear. When Mommy and Daddy got married, we had a terrible time with the color because the temple was maroon. There was a terrible maroon carpet in the sanctuary, and the social hall was maroon as well. There was maroon-flocked wallpaper. Remember, honey?" she asks Sol. He nods. "Now it's a rust color. Why it's rust, I don't know. But we ended up having the maids in pink because that was about all we could do. And in the pictures it looked beautiful."

"It photographed very well," Sol says.

"I'll have to show you the pictures," Estelle tells Miriam. "The whole family was there and such dear, dear friends. God willing, they'll be at your wedding, too."

"No, I don't think so," says Ed. "We're just having the immediate family. We're only having one hundred people."

Estelle smiles. "I don't think you can keep a wedding to one hundred people."

"Why not?" Ed asks.

Sarah clears the fish plates nervously. She hates it when Ed takes this tone of voice with her parents.

"Well, I mean, not without excluding," Estelle says. "And at a wedding you don't want to exclude—"

"I don't think it's incumbent on us to invite everyone we know to Miriam's wedding," Ed says crisply. Sarah puts her hand on his shoulder. "It's not even necessary to invite everyone *you* know."

Estelle raises her eyebrows, and Sarah hopes silently that her mother will not whip out the invitation list she's written up. The list with forty-two names that, mercifully, Ed has not yet seen.

"I'm not inviting everyone I know," Estelle says.

"Grandma," Miriam says, looking up. "Are you inviting people to my wedding?"

"Of course not," says Estelle. "But I've told my cousins about it and my dear friends. You know, some of them were at your parents' wedding. The Magids. The Rothmans."

"Whoa, whoa, wait a second," says Ed. "We aren't going to revive the guest list from our wedding thirty years ago. I think we need to define our terms here and straighten out what we mean by immediate family."

"I'll define for you," Estelle says, "what I mean by the family. These are the people who knew us when we lived above the bakery. It wasn't just at your wedding. They were at *our* wedding before the war. We grew up with them. We've got them in the home movies, and you can see them all forty-five years ago—fifty years ago! You can go in the den and watch—we've got all the movies on videotape now. You can see them at Sarah's first birthday party. We lived within blocks; and when we moved out to the Island and left the bakery, they moved too. I still talk to Trudy Rothman every day. Who has friends like that? We used to walk over. Years ago in the basement we hired a dancing teacher, and we used to take dancing lessons together. Fox trot, cha-cha, tango. We went to temple with them. We celebrated such times! I think you don't see the bonds, because you kids are scattered. We left Bensonhurst[3] together and we came out to the Island together. We've lived here since fifty-four in this house. We saw this house go up, and their houses were going up, too. We went through it together, coming into the wide-open spaces, having a garden, trees, and parks. We see them all the time. In the winters we meet them down in Florida; we go to their grandchildren's weddings—"

"But I'm paying for this wedding," Ed says.

At that Estelle leaves the table and goes into the kitchen. Sarah glares at Ed.

"Dad," Avi groans. "Now look what you did." He whispers to Amy, "I warned you my family is weird."

"I'm really hungry," Ben says. "Can we have the turkey, Grandma? Seriously, all I've had to eat today was a Snickers bar."

In silence Estelle returns from the kitchen carrying the turkey. In silence she hands it to Sol to carve up. She passes the platter around the table. Only slowly does the conversation sputter to life. Estelle talks along with the rest, but she doesn't speak to Ed. She won't even look at him.

Ed lies on his back in the trundle bed next to Sarah. She is lying on the other bed staring at the ceiling. Every time either of them moves an inch, the bed creaks. Ed has never heard such loud creaking; the beds seem to moan and cry out in the night.

"The point? The point is this," Sarah tells him, "it was neither the time nor the place to go over the guest list."

"Your mother was the one who brought it up!" Ed exclaims.

"And you were the one who started in on her."

"Sarah, what was I supposed to say—Thank you for completely disregarding what we explicitly told you. Yes, you can invite everyone you know to your granddaughter's wedding. I'm not going to get steamrollered into this—that's what she was trying to do, manipulate this seder into an opportunity to get exactly who she wants, how many she wants, with no discussion whatsoever."

"The discussion does not have to dominate this holiday," Sarah says.

3. A neighborhood in Brooklyn, one of New York City's five boroughs.

"You let these things go and she'll get out of control. She'll go from giving us a few addresses to inviting twenty, thirty people. Fifty people."

"She's not going to do that."

"She knows hundreds of people. How many people were at our wedding? Two hundred? Three hundred?"

"Oh, stop. We're mailing all the invitations ourselves from D.C."

"Fine."

"So don't be pigheaded about it," Sarah says.

"Pigheaded? Is that what you said?"

"Yes."

"That's not fair. You don't want these people at the wedding any more than I do—"

"Ed, there are ways to explain that, there are tactful ways. You have absolutely no concept—"

"I am tactful. I am a very tactful person. But there are times when I'm provoked."

"What you said about paying for the wedding was completely uncalled for."

"But it was true!" Ed cries out, and his bed moans under him as if it feels the weight of his aggravation.

"Sh," Sarah hisses.

"I don't know what you want from me."

"I want you to apologize to my mother and try to salvage this holiday for the rest of us," she says tersely.

"I'm not going to apologize to that woman," Ed mutters. Sarah doesn't answer him. "What?" he asks into the night. His voice sounds to his ears not just defensive but wronged, deserving of sympathy. "Sarah?"

"I have nothing more to say to you," she says.

"Sarah, she is being completely unreasonable."

"Oh, stop it."

"I'm not going to grovel in front of someone intent on sabotaging this wedding."

Sarah doesn't answer.

The next day Ed wakes up with a sharp pain in his left shoulder. It is five-nineteen in the morning, and everyone else is sleeping—except Estelle. He can hear her moving around in the house adjusting things, flipping light switches, twitching lamp shades, tweaking pillows. He lies in bed and doesn't know which is worse, his shoulder or those fussy little noises. They grate on him like the rattling of cellophane paper. When at last he struggles out of the sagging trundle bed, he runs to the shower and blasts hot water on his head. He takes an inordinately long shower He is probably using up all the hot water. He imagines Estelle pacing around outside wondering how in the world anyone can stand in the shower an hour, an hour and fifteen minutes. She is worried about wasting water, frustrated that the door is locked, and she cannot get in to straighten the toothbrushes. The fantasy warms him. It soothes his muscles. But minutes after he gets out, it wears off.

By the time the children are up, it has become a muggy, sodden spring day. Yehudit sleeps off her cold medicine, Ben watches television in the den with Sol, and Miriam shuts herself up in her room in disgust because watching TV violates the holiday. Avi goes out with Amy for a walk. They leave right after lunch and are gone for hours. Where could they be for three hours in West Hempstead? Are they stopping at every duck pond? Browsing in every strip mall? It's a long, empty day. The one good thing is that Sarah isn't angry at him anymore. She massages his stiff shoulder. "These beds have to go," she says. "They're thirty years old."

"It would probably be more comfortable to lie on the floor," Ed says. He watches Estelle as she darts in and out of the kitchen setting the table for the second seder. "You notice she still isn't speaking to me."

"Well," Sarah says, "what do you expect?" But she says it sympathetically. "We have to call your mother," she reminds him.

"Yeah, I suppose so." Ed heaves a sigh. "Get the kids. Make them talk to her."

"Hey, Grandma," says Ben when they get him on the phone. "What's up? Oh yeah? It's dull here, too. No, we aren't doing anything. Just sitting around. No, Avi's got his girlfriend here, so they went out. Yeah, Amy. I don't know. Don't ask me. Miriam's here, too. Yup. What? Everybody's like dealing with who's going to come to her wedding. Who, Grandma E? Oh, she's fine. I think she's kind of pissed at Dad, though."

Ed takes the phone out of Ben's hands.

"Kind of what?" Rose is asking.

"Hello, Ma?" Ed carries the cordless phone into the bedroom and sits at the vanity table. As he talks, he can see himself from three angles in the triptych mirror, each one worse than the next. He sees the dome of his forehead with just a few strands of hair, his eyes tired, a little bloodshot even, the pink of his ears soft and fleshy. He looks terrible.

"Ed," his mother says, "Sarah told me you are excluding Estelle's family from the wedding."

"Family? What family? These are Estelle's friends."

"And what about Henny and Pauline? Should I disinvite them, too?"

"Ma! You invited your neighbors?"

"Of course! To my own granddaughter's wedding? Of course I did."

"Ma," Ed snaps. "As far as I'm concerned, the only invitations to this wedding are going to be the ones printed up and issued by me, from my house. This is Miriam's wedding. For her. Not for you, not for Estelle. Not for anyone but the kids."

"You are wrong," Rose says simply. Throughout the day these words ring in Ed's ears. It is he who feels wronged. It's not as if his mother or Sarah's mother were contributing to the wedding in any way. They just make their demands. They aren't doing anything.

Miriam is sitting in the kitchen spreading whipped butter on a piece of matzo. Ed sits down next to her. "Where's Grandma?" he asks.

"She went out to get milk," says Miriam, and then she bursts out, "Daddy, I don't want all those people at the wedding."

"I know, sweetie." It's wonderful to hear Miriam appeal to him, to be able to sympathize with her as if she weren't almost a doctor with severe theological opinions.

"I don't even know them," Miriam says.

"We don't have to invite anyone you don't want to invite," Ed says firmly.

"But I don't want Grandma all mad at me at the wedding." Her voice wavers. "I don't know what to do."

"You don't have to do anything," Ed says. "You just relax."

"I think maybe we should just invite them," Miriam says in a small voice.

"*Oy*," says Ed.

"Or some of them," she says.

Someone rattles the back door, and they both jump. It's just Sarah. "Let me give you some advice," she says. "Invite these people, invite your mother's people, and let that be an end to it. We don't need this kind of *tsuris*."[4]

"No!" Ed says.

"I think she's right," says Miriam.

He looks at her. "Would that make you feel better?" She nods, and he gets to give her a hug. "I don't get to hug my Miriam anymore," he tells Sarah.

"I know," she says. "That's Grandma's car. I'm going to tell her she can have the Magids."

"But you make it clear to her," Ed starts.

"Ed," she says, "I'm not making *anything* clear to her."

At the second seder, Estelle looks at everyone benignly from where she stands between the kitchen and the dining room. Sol makes jokes about weddings, and Avi gets carried away by the good feeling, puts his arm around Methodist Amy, and says, "Mom and Dad, I promise when I get married I'll elope." No one laughs at this.

When it's time for the four questions, Ed reads them himself. " 'Why is this night different from all other nights? On other nights we eat leavened bread. Why on this night do we eat matzo?' Ben, could you put your feet on the floor?" When Ed is done with the four questions, he says, "So, essentially, each generation has an obligation to explain our exodus to the next generation—whether they like it or not."

That night in the moaning trundle bed, Ed thinks about the question Miriam raised at the first seder. Why are there four of everything on Passover? Four children. Four questions. Four cups of wine. Lying there with his eyes closed, Ed sees these foursomes dancing in the air. He sees them as in the naive illustrations of his 1960s Haggadah. Four gold cups, the words of the four questions outlined in teal blue, four children's faces. The faces of his own children, not as they are now but as they were nine, ten years ago. And then, as he falls asleep, a vivid dream flashes before him. Not the children, but Sarah's parents, along with the Rothmans, the Seligs, the Magids, and all their friends, perhaps one thousand of them walking en masse like marathoners over the Verrazano Bridge.[5] They are carrying suitcases and ironing boards, bridge tables, tennis rackets, and lawn chairs. They are driving their poodles before them as they march together. It is a procession both majestic and frightening. At Estelle's feet, at the feet of her one thousand friends, the steel bridge trembles. Its long cables sway above the water. And as Ed

4. Troubles, aggravation (Yiddish).
5. The bridge that connects Brooklyn and Staten Island, two boroughs of New York City.

watches, he feels the trembling, the pounding footsteps. It's like an earthquake rattling, pounding, vibrating through his whole body. He wants to turn away; he wants to dismiss it, but still he feels it, unmistakable, not to be denied. The thundering of history.

1996

Jews Translating Jews

Whenever any poet translates another, an act of furtherance and renewal takes place. If the translator is an American Jew and the other language is Hebrew or Yiddish or, indeed, any tongue spoken elsewhere by Jews, then possibly that act pushes forward a little the ever-deferred messianic hope ingrained in Judaism.

Kol omer davar b'shem omro mevia geula l'olam. The Hebrew (here transliterated) of the Babylonian Talmud tells us: "Whoever speaks a word in the name of its speaker, brings redemption to the world." This saying, from Megillah 15a, is taken to hold for translation. Specifically, it refers to Queen Esther bringing news from Mordecai to Ahasuerus that averts the king's assassination, whereupon she reveals her Jewishness and saves her people (Esther 2.22). So an act of translation may carry redemptive force. Except sometimes. A more recent source, the Yiddish and early modern Hebrew poet Chaim Nachman Bialik (1873–1934), claimed that reading a translation is like kissing a bride through the veil.

Bialik is famously seconded by Robert Frost: "Poetry is what gets lost in translation." And by the Italian *traduttore/traditore*, "translator/traitor"—or, more rhythmically and idiomatically, "render/bender." And by countless other gainsayers. Yet this chutzpah goes on, from generation to generation. "You translate poems? Isn't that dreadfully difficult?" To which one would respond like the Seabees of World War II, those dogged construction battalions laying pontoon bridges over the Rhine: "The difficult we do immediately, the impossible takes a little longer."

From time immemorial, the matter of translation has preoccupied Jews. Babel's hubris and disaster, a myth found in many cultures, was crystallized for the Judeo-Christian West in Genesis (11.1–9). "Everyone on earth had the same language." Then the people built a city and a tower to reach unto heaven, "And the Lord said, 'If, as one people with one language for all, this is how they have begun to act,' " there'll be no stopping them. So the Lord confounded their language and did "scatter them . . . over the face of the whole earth." Hence we speak thousands of tongues: multilingual, multinationed, richly disunited. Hebrew calls that city Babel, akin to Babylon, the Israelites' place of exile—which is to say that, for Jews, exile implies the need for translation. *Trans-late* = *carry across*. The word *Hebrew* itself, *Ivri*, denotes a "crossing-over" people: Abraham out of Ur to Canaan, Moses through the Red Sea to Sinai, Joshua across the Jordan into the promised land, the Israelites back from Babylon to Zion, Spain's Jews fleeing the Inquisition, Europe's seeking Palestine or America.

After Babel George Steiner called his 1975 tour de force on the philosophical, linguistic, and literary elements of translation. After Babel, translation tracks the steps of a people persisting in Diaspora for whom language—whether mother tongue or holy tongue—often forms their only homeland. Even in postexilic Eretz Yisrael, as the common people gradually ceased understanding Hebrew, translation and interpretation came into play. We have this one magnificent biblical moment after the return from Babylonian captivity to Jerusalem:

> The entire people assembled as one man in the square before the Water Gate, and they asked Ezra the scribe to bring the scroll of the Teaching of Moses with which the Lord had charged Israel. On the first day of the seventh month, Ezra the priest brought the Teaching before the congregation, men and women and all who could listen with understanding. He read from it, facing the square before the Water Gate, from the first light until midday, to the men and the women and those who could understand; the ears of all the people were given to the scroll of the Teaching. Ezra the scribe stood upon a wooden tower made for the purpose. . . . Ezra opened the scroll in the sight of all the people, for he was above all the people; as he opened it, all the people stood up. Ezra blessed the Lord, the great God, and all the people answered, "Amen, Amen," with hands upraised. Then they bowed their heads and prostrated themselves before the Lord with their faces to the ground. . . . They read from the scroll of the Teaching of God, translating it and giving the sense; so they understood the reading.
>
> Nehemiah . . . , Ezra the priest and scribe, and the Levites who were explaining to the people said to all the people, "This day is holy to the Lord your God: you must not mourn or weep," for all the people were weeping as they listened to the words of the Teaching.
>
> He further said to them, "Go, eat choice foods and drink sweet drinks and send portions to whoever has nothing prepared, for the day is holy to our Lord. Do not be sad, for your rejoicing in the Lord is the source of your strength." The Levites were quieting the people, saying, "Hush, for the day is holy; do not be sad." Then all the people went to eat and drink and send portions and make great merriment, for they understood the things they were told. (Nehemiah 8.1–12)

In a later period, at the weekly Torah or prophetic lesson, a targeman or meturgeman would stand next to the reading desk and immediately translate orally into vernacular Aramaic, often weaving commentary around the original text. Notably, those early Jewish translators were enjoined not to lean against the desk, but to stand deferentially off; not to look into the Torah as if the Targum were *there*; not to speak louder than the reader, but to declaim in the same pitch. And we have a rabbinic dictum about the targumists who made written versions of Scripture: "He who translates quite literally is a liar, while he who adds anything is a blasphemer." This might well baffle modern translators.

According to legend, Ptolemy, in the third century B.C.E., brought seventy-two elders of Israel, six from each tribe, to Alexandria to translate the Torah into Greek. This plus later biblical books became known as the Septuagint, having huge influence on Jewry's Hellenistic Diaspora (as well as serving Christian churches). And the medieval period, in Spain and elsewhere, saw immense production of translations from Arabic and Latin into Hebrew: theology, philosophy, grammar, mathematics, medicine, and other sciences. Jews during Spain's Muslim (and then Christian) centuries lived with some tolerance, comfort, strength, but also grave insecurity—which helps explain an epigram by Judah ben Solomon Al-Harizi (ca. 1170–1235), a Hebrew-language poet who wandered from his native Spain:

> The broadest land's too tight a squeeze
> To give two foes an ample space,
> Meantime a very narrow place
> Can hold a thousand friends with ease.

Al-Harizi translated into Hebrew Maimonides' *Guide for the Perplexed* as well as secular Arabic poetry. Samuel Hanagid, Ibn Gabirol, Moses Ibn Ezra, Judah Halevi, Abraham Ibn Ezra, besides occasionally translating from Arabic, "translated" Arabic and Spanish poetic forms into Hebrew verse. On the threshold of the Italian Renaissance, Immanuel ben Solomon of Rome translated Dante and composed Petrarchan-style sonnets in Hebrew. The story is proverbial: when in Diaspora, do as your hosts do—but with a Jewish bent . . . and then some. Spain's medieval Jewish poets do write of war, love, and wine, but they also explore Judaic lore and yearn for Zion.

In the modern Diaspora, as in Alexandria, translation does not move out of, but into the vernacular. Take the special case of Bible translation (a field that itself occupies a vast dimension). Moses Mendelssohn, leader of eighteenth-century German Jewry (and grandfather of composer Felix Mendelssohn), translated the Torah into High German—an act of Jewish Enlightenment—and published this text in Hebrew characters, as distinct from Martin Luther's hegemonic German Bible. After World War I, Martin Buber and Franz Rosenzweig, again translating the Bible, attempted to convey its Hebraic voice through innovative, renovative German diction, syntax, rhythm. With Nazism's takeover, the publishing house of Schocken Books doughtily began a series of slim volumes (1933–38) promoting Jewish culture: first Buber and Rosenzweig's rendering of Isaiah 40–55 entitled *The Consolation of Israel,* then Rosenzweig's version of Judah Halevi's songs of Zion, Buber's Hasidic tales in German, and the Hebrew author S. Y. Agnon's stories, translated by Gershom Scholem and Nahum Glatzer. All this to infuse Hebraic spirit into the body of German Jewry and into their mother tongue. (After the Shoah, however, and the end of any German-Jewish symbiosis, Scholem could only tell Buber that his Bible translation formed "the tombstone of a relationship that was extinguished in unspeakable horror.")

Philosopher Franz Rosenzweig (1886–1929), who wrote *The Star of Redemption* and led the first Jewish Lehrhaus, or study institute, remained acutely conscious of the dynamics between translation and Diaspora Jewishness. On his wedding trip, he translated the Hebrew Grace after Meals, but he would hide it from a guest who knew any Hebrew because "the least comprehended Hebrew word yields more than the finest translation." Rosenzweig calls Diaspora Jewry's need to translate Hebrew sources into the native tongue "our predicament" and accepts it: "We cannot avoid this path that again and again leads us out of what is alien and into our own." Thus Jewish spirituality abides in Hebrew per se, yet that spirit may have to pass through the body of our vernacular. Perhaps this paradox resolves if translation, as Rosenzweig says, points us back toward the source.

While it is true that Judaic essentials inhere within Hebrew and Yiddish sources, it is also true that Bible, theology, and liturgy do not occupy the whole domain of translation. Rosenzweig's sense of "our predicament," of the bending path "into our own," also has much to do with nonreligious literary translation from any language. Why, then, might a Jewish writer—Emma Lazarus, Cynthia Ozick, Franz Rosenzweig, Paul Celan—want to bring another Jewish writer into English or into German? In most times and places, Jews have not felt completely *zu Hause*, at home. Frequently marked, if not actually demonized, as the "other," they might well want to prove that difference, to test and contemplate it, by voicing some "other" writer's work in their own local tongue, especially since their birthright to that tongue has, at various times and places, been called into question.

Migrant or marginal as they have tended to be, for better and worse, Jewish writers often move inevitably between languages. Celan, for instance, learning German at home, Romanian at school, and Russian under occupation, translated the German-speaking Czech Jew Franz Kafka into Romanian and the Russian Jew Osip Mandelstam into German—Kafka and Mandelstam being his presiding spirits as much for their hedged and nuanced Jewishness as for their brilliant writing. "I consider translating Mandelshtam into German to be as important a task as my own verses," Celan once said. In his case, that task meant transfusing something new, some cleansing strangeness, into a German language recently corrupted by Nazi-Deutsch such as *Endlösung* ("Final Solution"), *judenrein* ("Jew-free"), *Sonderbehandlung* ("Special Treatment"). Nothing so drastic bears on the at-homeness of Jewish writers within American English. Yet in translating, they may feel themselves (literally) endorsing a strangeness, a Judaic otherness that nonetheless reroots them, reconnects an affiliation.

Incidentally, two major fields of translation do not figure in these considerations—prose and the Bible—not for lack of significance, but because a brief survey can more pointedly explore the options and effects involved in translating poems.

The poems in this section come in rough chronological order by their original author.

Emma Lazarus (1849–1887) first made translations of Heinrich Heine (and Victor Hugo) in her teens, but these were melancholy, Romantic lyrics, harmonizing with her own sentiment, not the German Jew's poetry of bitterness and anger such as Heine's *Rabbi of Bacharach* or *To Edom.* The same held true when Lazarus, years later, published a full collection, *Poems and Ballads of Heinrich Heine* (1881). But in contrast to the poetry inside, her introduction to that collection stresses Heine's "ineradicable sympathy with things Jewish," calling him "an enthusiast for the rights of the Jews" who "buried himself with fervid zeal in the love of his race" and died "a poor fatally-ill Jew." Then, in *Songs of a Semite* (1882), which manifests her outrage at recent pogroms in Russia and Germany, Lazarus does include some imitations of Heine, depicting anti-Semitism with keen irony. And soon afterward, in an article on him, she identifies his Jewish "sympathy of race, not of creed," quoting his tribute that Jews have remained *Menschen*, human beings, "in spite of eighteen centuries of persecution and misery." So Lazarus ended up confirming her own Jewish autonomy in endorsing Heine's. During the 1880s, she was also speaking out indignantly for a Jewish homeland, a revival of Zion. She had already translated (via German) Ibn Gabirol, Moses

Ibn Ezra, and Judah Halevi, including Halevi's *Longing for Jerusalem.* In 1883, having rendered a fervent poem by Judah Al-Harizi on renewing God's Covenant, she noted something new: "I have translated this from the original Hebrew—& so am very proud of it as my first effort!"

Until well after World War II, it is hard to find other American Jewish poets translating fellow Jews—anyone like Joseph Leftwich, whose *Yisrōel* (1933) and *Golden Peacock* (1939) introduced Yiddish literature in England, or A. M. Klein, who translated Bialik and others in Canada. Some such work did appear, mainly from Hebrew, but seldom by distinguished writers. Charles Reznikoff, above all, was fruitfully open to Hebrew poetry, whence his deft version of Halevi's song to Zion. And, doubtless, other instances exist that have not come to light. As teenagers in Chicago, Isaac Rosenfeld and Saul Bellow made a spoofing Yiddish version of T. S. Eliot's *The Love Song of J. Alfred Prufrock.* Then in 1953 they each translated stories by Isaac Bashevis Singer; this may mark a new American awareness, an access to secular Jewish tradition by way of first-rate literary translation. Marie Syrkin, Robert Friend, Sarah Zweig Betsky, and Aaron Kramer were among the earliest to translate from Hebrew and Yiddish poetry.

During the 1960s, the pace picked up, as it did for translation at large, with journals such as *Modern Poetry in Translation* in England and *Delos* in the United States. In *The Modern Hebrew Poem Itself* (1965), admirably edited by Stanley Burnshaw, T. Carmi, and Ezra Spicehandler, writers from Bialik to Dahlia Ravikovitch were "discussed into English." Irving Howe and Eliezer Greenberg's *Treasury of Yiddish Poetry* (1969), a sequel to their 1954 anthology of Yiddish stories, joined leading American poets with Yiddish ones: John Hollander with Moyshe-Leyb Halpern, Mani Leyb, Avrom Reyzen, Itzik Feffer; Cynthia Ozick with David Einhorn, H. Leyvik, Chaim Grade; Adrienne Rich with Celia Dropkin, Kadya Molodowsky, Devorah Fogel; Armand Schwerner with Peretz Markish; Jerome Rothenberg with Melech Rawitch; Stanley Kunitz with Israel Emiot; Irving Feldman with Isaiah Spiegel (some of these appear elsewhere in this anthology). Through such matchmaking, various voices otherwise inaudible—women, exiles, pre-Shoah immigrants, innovators, victims of Stalin and Hitler—were heard in an increasingly monolingual country.

Eventually, more poets reached out elsewhere and to other languages. Not every one would echo Robert Mezey's sense of his Uri Zvi Greenberg translations: "I wish I could claim them entirely, they are certainly the best things I have written." But perhaps they all felt a "shock of recognition" such as Melville experienced in reading Hawthorne: "Genius, all over the world, stands hand in hand, and one shock of recognition runs the whole circle round." Shirley Kaufman, transplanting her life to Israel, brings alive in English the partisan-poet Abba Kovner's Vilna and Sinai, and the Ukrainian-born Amir Gilboa's traumatic revision of Abraham and Isaac. Ruth Feldman transmits Primo Levi's blasphemous 1946 *Shema.* C. K. Williams gravitates to Avraham Sutzkever, whose Yiddish lyric voice persists after the Vilna ghetto for more than fifty years. Chana Bloch takes on the Bible-haunted Ravikovitch, a sabra, and also catches the idiomatic humor and passion of Yehuda Amichai, who fled Germany for Palestine in 1936. Joachim Neugroschel brings within earshot Else Lasker-Schüler, who left Germany and died in Jerusalem. (When asked by a Hebrew writer if he might translate her German lyrics, she replied: "But they really *are* written in Hebrew!") Stephen

Berg and S. J. Marks, helped by a native Hungarian, translate Miklós Radnóti, whose wife found him in a mass grave, poems in his overcoat pocket. John Felstiner tries for the quotidian, reiterated death-camp rhythm of Celan's *Deathfugue* (1944–45), which exposes Nazism's orchestrated genocide. David Unger reaches out to a Peruvian, Isaac Goldemberg. And Peter Cole evokes the courtly, battle-tried, fatherly presence of Samuel Hanagid perfecting Hebrew within a Muslim nation.

Incidentally, one distinctive case of matchmaking, seemingly made in heaven, arises when writers translate themselves, or work in two languages, or compose bilingually. Jewish American literature has nothing so accomplished as Nabokov's or Beckett's dual brilliance. But, like the Israeli Amichai, Russian émigré Joseph Brodsky turned to translating or writing some poems in English, having been named America's poet laureate. Autotranslation has not always succeeded happily. But the bilingual verses of Irena Klepfisz, shuttling between English and Yiddish the way many Latina/o poems do between English and Spanish, make for telling recognitions as they knit two cultures.

If poetry is not, or not merely, what gets lost in translation but what gets gained, then what is it that gets gained in transactions between American and foreign poets? Naturally, Jewish writers have not turned only to coreligionists. Witness Louis Zukofsky's Catullus, Stanley Kunitz's Voznesensky and Akhmatova, Richard Howard's Baudelaire, Anthony Hecht's Aeschylus and Sophocles, Muriel Rukeyser's and Eliot Weinberger's Octavio Paz, Allen Mandelbaum's and Robert Pinsky's Dante, just to mention a few. But when Jews do translate Jews, why do they? What have they stood to gain?—besides, of course, the elation that inheres in this exacting craft, in getting something right, as well as the primary cognitive gain: "I myself understand a poem," Rosenzweig remarked, "only when I have translated it." Several motives come to mind, coinciding variously, and they all might take the motto that Walter Benjamin prized from Karl Kraus: *Ursprung ist das Ziel*, "Origin is the goal"—a motto that holds as well for the recuperative process of translation itself.

Perhaps foremost, in opting for poets who by reason of time or circumstance stand closer to Scripture, translators have brought themselves and their readers into touch with the Bible and Judaic tradition. *Schreiben als Form des Gebetes*, Kafka once jotted in his notebook—"Writing as a form of prayer." For Jewish writers, translating a biblically charged poem can become a form of—and take the place of—prayer.

Israel, no less than Holy Writ, compellingly draws American Jews. They need to know what it feels like to live in a country where Jews predominate, enemies daily threaten, and Hebrew fills the streets. So Miriyam Glazer renders a Yona Wallach poem about what emerges from Hebrew's gendered nouns and verbs. Or in a time of crisis and loss, it may matter to align one's voice with Amichai's on "the War Dead":

et hayeled hachai tsrichim
lenakot b'shuvo mimischak

it's the living child we need
to scrub when he's back from play.

Finding a cadence in English, to move through syntax and line break, can mean growing answerable, responsive, almost participant.

To translate poets who survived or did not survive the European Jewish catastrophe asks for acute attentiveness and keeps patent the atrocious loss. If the Romanian-born Israeli Dan Pagis took twenty-five years after the Shoah before writing his quintessential vignette *Katuv b'iparon bakaron hechatum* (Written in Pencil in a Sealed Boxcar), those lines should probably be urged upon people whose families were not equally at risk:

kan bamishloach hazeh
ani chava
im hevel b'ni
im tiru et b'ni hagadol
kayin ben adam
tagidulo sh'ani

here in this transport
I Eve
with Abel my son
if you see my older son
Cain son of Adam
tell him that I

Possibly the human family feels as drastically ruptured in English as in Hebrew since it stems from the one myth, the founding text long common to Diaspora and Zion alike. But the plural addressee of Pagis's *tagidulo* gets lost: "tell [ye] him." That is to say, English cannot inflect the verb to show that Eve has something to tell a great many people, even unto the present generation, about her son's murder. And does the silence cutting short her last words, *tagidulo sh'ani*—do our questions suspended in that silence after "tell him that I"—resound the same in English as in Hebrew?

As for the Eastern European and immigrant dimension of Jewish experience: even if it seems to have relapsed as a source and recourse, as the vital stuff of contemporary literary creation, nevertheless American translators since the war have regained more and more of their inheritance. And Cynthia Ozick's story *Envy; or, Yiddish in America* rings with the cry of an immigrant poet to a young American woman: "Translate me!" Yet those scales may be balancing. The translation of Singer's writings, in itself a cottage industry, led to the Nobel prize. The efforts of numerous other translators and scholars, the ingathering and redisseminating of crumbling Yiddish books, the songfests and theater, the proliferating Klezmer bands and camps, the guided tours of Manhattan's Lower East Side and of Eastern Europe, the shtet on CD-ROM—does all this bespeak mere nostalgia or a kind of restitution? Maybe it will always be too soon to disentangle such things.

Whatever else may be said for Jewish American poets and other translators, they have brought striking new voices and a salutary strangeness into this country's literary bloodstream, at times into its mainstream. Some years ago, the New York Yiddish poet Jacob Glatstein complained: "I have to be aware of Auden yet Auden need never have heard of me." Translators have helped dissolve a little the dominant Christian strain in modern American poetry, from Eliot, Auden, and Stevens to Lowell and Frost. Or, rather, the admixture of Judah Halevi and Samuel Hanagid into American poetry, of Halpern and Glatstein, Mandelstam and Celan has moved us toward deep common ground. Witness Walter Benjamin, who himself died before crossing the border to freedom in 1940, in his essay *The Task of the Translator:* "Translation kindles from the endless renewal of languages as they grow to the messianic end of their history."

Note: Throughout this section, the year given at the bottom left of the poem indicates the date of the original poem's publication; at the bottom right, the date of the traslation's publication.

EMMA LAZARUS
1849–1887

Longing for Jerusalem

by Judah Halevi[1]

לִבִּי בְמִזְרָח, וְאָנֹכִי בְּסוֹף מַעֲרָב —
אֵיךְ אֶטְעֲמָה אֵת אֲשֶׁר אֹכַל וְאֵיךְ יֶעֱרָב?
אֵיכָה אֲשַׁלֵּם נְדָרַי וֶאֱסָרַי, בְּעוֹד
צִיּוֹן בְּחֶבֶל אֱדוֹם וַאֲנִי בְּכֶבֶל עֲרָב?
יֵקַל בְּעֵינַי עֲזֹב כָּל טוּב סְפָרַד, כְּמוֹ
יֵקַר בְּעֵינַי רְאוֹת עַפְרוֹת דְּבִיר נֶחֱרָב.

O city of the world, with sacred splendor blest,
My spirit yearns to thee from out of the far-off West,
A stream of love wells forth when I recall thy day,
Now is thy temple waste, thy glory passed away.
Had I an eagle's wings, straight would I fly to thee,
Moisten thy holy dust with wet cheeks streaming free.
Oh, how I long for thee! albeit thy King has gone,
Albeit where balm once flowed, the serpent dwells alone.
Could I but kiss thy dust, so would I fain expire,
As sweet as honey then, my passion, my desire!

1879

1. Halevi (ca. 1075–1141), Hebrew poet and philosopher, was born in Spain and probably died in Egypt, though legend has it he died in Jerusalem. His well-known verses actually begin: "My heart is in the East / and I in the uttermost West." The first section of Charles Reznikoff's translation follows them closely. Lazarus did this and other adaptations of medieval Hebrew poets from German versions.

[I know not what spell is o'er me]

by Heinrich Heine[1]

I know not what spell is o'er me,
That I am so sad to day;
An old myth floats before me—
I cannot chase it away.

The cool air darkens, and listen,
How softly flows the Rhine!
The mountain peaks still glisten
Where the evening sunbeams shine.

The fairest maid sits dreaming
In radiant beauty there.
Her gold and her jewels are gleaming.
She combeth her golden hair.[2]

With a golden comb she is combing;
A wondrous song sings she.
The music quaint in the gloaming,
Hath a powerful melody.

It thrills with a passionate yearning
The boatman below in the night.
He heeds not the rocky reef's warning,
He gazes alone on the height.

I think that the waters swallowed
The boat and the boatman anon.
And this, with her singing unhallowed,
The Lorelei hath done.

1881

1. Heine (1797–1856), German poet, was born in Germany and died in Paris. This popular lyric to the Lorelei, or Siren, was declared an anonymous folksong by the Nazis.
2. Paul Celan's *Deathfugue* echoes this line.

CHARLES REZNIKOFF
1894–1976

[My heart in the East[1]]

by Judah Halevi

My heart in the East
and I at the farthest West:
how can I taste what I eat or find it sweet
while Zion
is in the cords of Edom[2] and I
bound by the Arab?
Beside the dust of Zion
all the good of Spain is light;
and a light thing to leave it.

And if it is now only a land of howling beasts and owls
was it not so
when given to our fathers—
all of it only a heritage of thorns and thistles?
But they walked in it—
His name in their hearts, sustenance!—
as in a park among flowers.

In the midst of the sea
when the hills of it slide and sink
and the wind
lifts the water like sheaves—
now a heap of sheaves and then a floor for the threshing—
and sail and planks shake
and the hands of the sailors are rags,
and no place for flight but the sea,
and the ship is hidden in waves
like a theft in the thief's hand,
suddenly the sea is smooth
and the stars shine on the water.

Wisdom and knowledge—except to swim—
have neither fame nor favor here;
a prisoner of hope, he gave his spirit to the winds,
and is owned by the sea;
between him and death—a board.

1. There was some question in my mind if I should try to use rhyme as Jehuda Halevi did or at least follow his rhythms. Franz Rosenzweig, translating him into German, said it was sheer laziness not to do both. Perhaps. But the reproduction of a meter in another language does not necessarily have the effect it had in the original: rhyme and rhythm stirring in the Hebrew may be cloying and merely tiresome in English; it may be light instead of grave and so clever as to be nothing else. And it is of interest to note that Jehuda Halevi himself said (Jewish Publication Society's edition, p. xxii): "It is but proper that mere beauty of sound should yield to lucidity of speech" [Reznikoff's note].

2. The land across the Jordan River; biblically, Israel's eternal enemy.

Zion, do you ask if the captives are at peace—
the few that are left?
I cry out like the jackals when I think of their grief;
but, dreaming of the end of their captivity,
I am like a harp for your songs.

1959

PETER COLE
b. 1957

[Your manuscript shines]

by Samuel Hanagid[1]

And he had me copy in my youth and promised me compensation for every notebook, and I sent him what I'd copied and then he wrote me the following:

Your manuscript shines
like inlays of emerald,
its margins arranged
like a robe well-embroidered,
a feast for the eyes
like a tree's first figs,
its scent like myrrh on the perfumed bride.

Read and inscribe
and focus your heart on the Law of the ark
and its curtain—
as you add,
I'll add to your fee: Yehosef,
write with an iron pen in your book,

and be written within me,
and not on my skin.
Love for you
to the walls of my heart
and its chambers is held:
my rebukes have been open, my love concealed.

1996

1. Hanagid (993–1055), Hebrew poet, scholar, statesman, military leader, was born and died in Spain. He educated his sons in poetry and had them copy out his verses.

JOACHIM NEUGROSCHEL
(b. 1938)

Hagar and Ishmael[1]

by Else Lasker-Schüler[2]

Abraham's little sons played with seashells
And sailed the boats of mother-of-pearl;
Then Isaac anxiously leaned against Ishmael

And sadly they sang, the two black swans,
Such gloomy notes about their gaudy world,
And Hagar, expelled, quickly kidnapped her son.

Shed her great tears in his small tears,
And their hearts rushed like the holy source,
And even outstripped the ostriches.

But the sun burnt harshly on the desert,
And Hagar and her boy-child sank into the yellow hide,
And bit their white teeth in the hot sand.

1913 1979

1. In Genesis 16 and 21, when Sarah was barren, her Egyptian maidservant Hagar bore Abraham's son, Ishmael. After Sarah gave birth to Isaac, she had Abraham expel Hagar and Ishmael to the desert. God intervened to save them.
2. Lasker-Schüler (1869–1945), German poet, was born in Germany, emigrated to Switzerland in 1933, and then to Jerusalem.

STEPHEN BERG AND S. J. MARKS
b. 1934 1935–1991

The Seventh Eclogue[1]

by Miklós Radnóti[2]

Do you see night, the wild oakwood fence lined with barbed wire,
and the barracks, so flimsy that the night swallowed them?
Slowly the eye passes the limits of captivity
and only the mind, the mind knows how tight the wire is.
You see, dear, this is how we set our imaginations free.
Dream, the beautiful savior, dissolves our broken bodies
and the prison camp leaves for home.

1. A poem expressing nostalgia for pastoral peace and simplicity; made famous by Virgil. Steven Polgar collaborated on these translations.
2. Radnóti (1909–1944), Hungarian poet, was born in Budapest and murdered in a mass grave after a forced march. In 1946, his body was exhumed, and his wife found his last poems in the pocket of his greatcoat.

Ragged, bald, snoring, the prisoners fly
from the black heights of Serbia to the hidden lands of home.
Hidden lands of home! Are there still homes there?
Maybe the bombs didn't hit, and they *are*, just like when we were "drafted"?
Next to me, on my right, a man whines, another one lies on my left. Will they go home?
Tell me, is there still a home where they understand all this?

Without commas, one line touching the other,
I write poems the way I live, in darkness,
blind, crossing the paper like a worm.
Flashlights, books—the guards took everything.
There's no mail, only fog drifts over the barracks.

Frenchmen, Poles, loud Italians, heretic Serbs, and dreamy
Jews live here in the mountains, among frightening rumors.
One feverish body cut into many pieces but still living the same life,
it waits for good news, the sweet voices of women, a free, a human fate.
It waits for the end, the fall into thick darkness, miracles.

I lie on the plank, like a trapped animal, among worms. The fleas
attack again and again, but the flies have quieted down.
Look. It's evening, captivity is one day shorter.
And so is life. The camp sleeps. The moon shines
over the land and in its light the wires are tighter.
Through the window you can see the shadows of the armed guards
thrown on the wall, walking among the noises of the night.

The camp sleeps. Do you see it? Dreams fly.
Frightened, someone wakes up. He grunts, then turns in the tight space
and sleeps again. His face shines. I sit up awake.
The taste of a half-smoked cigarette in my mouth instead of the taste
of your kisses and the calmness of dreams doesn't come.
I can't die, I can't live without you now.

Lager Heidenau, in the mountains above Zagubica
July, 1944 — 1972

Postcard[1]

by Miklós Radnóti

4

I fell next to him. His body rolled over.
It was tight as a string before it snaps.

1. Radnóti's title for his last four poems was actually *Picture Postcards*.

Shot in the back of the head—"This is how
you'll end." "Just lie quietly," I said to myself.
Patience flowers into death now.

"Der springt noch auf,"[2] I heard above me.
Dark filthy blood was drying on my ear.

Szentkirályszabadja
October 31, 1944

1970

2. That one's still stirring (German). Radnóti saw his comrade shot; he himself was shot a few days later.

C. K. WILLIAMS
b. 1936

A Load of Shoes

by Avraham Sutzkever[1]

The cartwheels rush,
quivering.
What is their burden?
Shoes, shivering.

The cart is like
a great hall:
the shoes crushed together
as though at a ball.

A wedding? A party?
Have I gone blind?
Who have these shoes
left behind?

The heels clatter
with a fearsome din,
transported from Vilna
to Berlin.

I should be still,
my tongue is like meat,
but the truth, shoes,
where are your feet?

The feet from these boots
with buttons outside

1. Sutzkever (b. 1913), Yiddish poet, was born in Belorussia and grew up in Vilna, where he was a partisan fighter. He lives in Israel.

or these, with no body,
or these, with no bride?

Where is the child
who fit in these?
Is the maiden barefoot
who bought these?

Slippers and pumps,
look, there are my mother's:
her Sabbath pair,
in with the others.

The heels clatter
with a fearsome din,
transported from Vilna
to Berlin.

Vilna ghetto, January 1, 1943 1989

SHIRLEY KAUFMAN
b. 1923

Isaac

by Amir Gilboa[1]

Early in the morning the sun took a walk in the woods
with me and my father
my right hand in his left.[2]

A knife flashed between the trees[3] like lightning.
And I'm so scared of the fear in my eyes facing blood
on the leaves.

Father[4] father come quick and save Isaac
so no one will be missing at lunchtime.

It's I who am butchered, my son,
my blood's already on the leaves.
And father's voice was choked.
And his face pale.

1. Gilboa (1917–1984), Hebrew poet, was born in the Ukraine and died in Israel. He emigrated to Palestine in 1937, but his family perished in the Ukraine.
2. A reference to the Song of Songs 2.6: "His left hand was under my head, His right hand embraced me."
3. Gilboa's Hebrew for "trees" and "knife" echo the same words in the Bible story of the binding of Isaac (Genesis 22).
4. "Father" might also be rendered "Papa" or "Daddy."

I wanted to cry out, struggling not to believe,
I tore my eyes open
and woke.

And my right hand was drained of blood

1963 1979

#28 My Little Sister[1]

by Abba Kovner[2]

My sister sits happy
at her bridegroom's table. She does not cry.
My sister will do no such thing:
what would people say!

My sister sits happy
at her bridegroom's table. Her heart is awake.
The whole world drinks
kosher chicken soup.

The dumplings of unleavened flour
were made by her mother-in-law. The world is amazed
and tastes the mother's dessert.

My sister-bride sits. A small dish
of honey before her. Such a huge crowd!
Father twisted
the braids of the hallah.[3]

Our father took his bread, bless God,
forty years from the same oven. He never imagined
a whole people could rise in the ovens
and the world, with God's help, go on.

My sister sits at the table in her bridal veil
alone. From the mourners' hideout
the voice of a bridegroom comes near.
We will set the table without you;
the marriage contract will be written in stone.

1967 1973

1. This poem, from a sequence entitled *My Little Sister,* alludes to the wedding motif in the Song of Songs—"We have a little sister" (8.8)—and also to a young girl Kovner recalls from the Vilna ghetto.
2. Kovner (1918–1987), Hebrew poet, was born in Russia and grew up in Vilna, where he was a partisan leader. He died in Israel.
3. Braided loaf of bread eaten on the Sabbath and at the wedding meal.

RUTH FELDMAN
b. 1911

Shema[1]

by Primo Levi[2]

You who live secure
In your warm houses,
Who, returning at evening, find
Hot food and friendly faces:
Consider[3] whether this is a man,[4]
Who labours in the mud
Who knows no peace
Who fights for a crust of bread
Who dies at a yes or a no.
Consider whether this is a woman,
Without hair or name
With no more strength to remember
Eyes empty and womb cold
As a frog in winter.
Consider that this has been:
I commend these words to you.
Engrave them on your hearts
When you are in your house, when you walk on your way
When you go to bed, when you rise:
Repeat them to your children.
Or may your house crumble,
Disease render you powerless,
Your offspring avert their faces from you.

January 10, 1946 — 1976

1. Hebrew for "Hear," evokes the watchword of Judaism, "Hear, O Israel: The Lord our God is one Lord" (Deut. 6.4, King James version) and its succeeding injunctions, "And these words, which I command thee this day, shall be in thine heart . . ." (Deut. 6.6, King James version).
2. Levi (1919–1987), Italian author, was born and died (probably by suicide) in Italy. Liberated from Auschwitz, he wrote this poem shortly after reaching home in Italy.
3. Levi's "Consider . . ." also echoes the Inferno of Dante's *Divine Comedy* (26.118 ff.), where Ulysses urges his men: "Think of your breed; for brutish ignorance / Your mettle was not made; you were made men, / To follow after knowledge and excellence."
4. The phrase "whether this is a man" (*Se questo è un uomo*) became the title of Levi's 1958 memoir (retitled, in paperback, *Survival in Auschwitz*).

JOHN FELSTINER
b. 1936

Deathfugue

by Paul Celan[1]

Black milk of daybreak we drink it at evening
we drink it at midday and morning we drink it at night
we drink and we drink
we shovel a grave in the air where you won't lie too cramped
A man lives in the house he plays with his vipers he writes
he writes when it grows dark to Deutschland your golden hair Margareta[2]
he writes it and steps out of doors and the stars are all sparkling he whistles his hounds to keep close
he whistles his Jews into rows has them shovel a grave in the ground
he commands us play up for the dance

Black milk of daybreak we drink you at night
we drink you at morning and midday we drink you at evening
we drink and we drink
A man lives in the house he plays with his vipers he writes
he writes when it grows dark to Deutschland your golden hair Margareta
Your ashen hair Shulamith[3] we shovel a grave in the air where you won't lie too cramped

He shouts dig this earth deeper you lot there you others sing up and play
he grabs for the rod in his belt he swings it his eyes are so blue
jab your spades deeper you lot there you others play on for the dancing

Black milk of daybreak we drink you at night
we drink you at midday and morning we drink you at evening
we drink and we drink
a man lives in the house your goldenes Haar Margareta
your aschenes Haar Shulamith he plays with his vipers

He shouts play death more sweetly this Death is a master from Deutschland
he shouts scrape your strings darker you'll rise up as smoke to the sky
you'll have a grave up in the clouds where you won't lie too cramped

Black milk of daybreak we drink you at night
we drink you at midday Death is a master aus Deutschland
we drink you at evening and morning we drink and we drink
this Death is ein Meister aus Deutschland his eye it is blue
he shoots you with shot made of lead shoots you level and true
a man lives in the house your goldenes Haar Margarete
he looses his hounds on us grants us a grave in the air
he plays with his vipers and daydreams der Tod ist ein Meister aus Deutschland

1. Celan (1920–1970), German-speaking poet, was born in Romania and died by suicide in Paris. Celan composed this poem in 1944–45.
2. An allusion to the German heroine in Goethe's *Faust*.
3. A reference to the Hebraic maiden in the Bible's Song of Songs.

dein goldenes Haar Margarete
dein aschenes Haar Sulamith

1948 1995

Psalm

by Paul Celan

No one kneads us again out of earth and clay,
no one incants our dust.
No one.

Blessèd art thou, No One.
In thy sight would
we bloom.
In thy
spite.

A Nothing
we were, are now, and ever
shall be, blooming:
the Nothing-, the
No One's-Rose.

With
our pistil soul-bright,
our stamen heaven-waste,
our corona red
from the purpleword we sang
over, O over
the thorn.

1961 1995

CHANA BLOCH
b. 1940

Jews in the Land of Israel

by Yehuda Amichai[1]

We forget where we came from. Our Jewish
names from the Exile give us away,
bring back the memory of flower and fruit, medieval cities,
metals, knights who turned to stone, roses,
spices whose scent drifted away, precious stones, lots of red,

1. Amichai (b. 1924), Hebrew poet, was born in Germany and lives in Israel.

handicrafts long gone from the world
(the hands are gone too).

Circumcision does it to us,
as in the Bible story of Shechem[2] and the sons of Jacob,
so that we go on hurting all our lives.

What are we doing, coming back here with this pain?
Our longings were drained together with the swamps,
the desert blooms for us, and our children are beautiful.
Even the wrecks of ships that sunk on the way
reached this shore,
even winds did. Not all the sails.

What are we doing
in this dark land with its
yellow shadows that pierce the eyes?
(Every now and then someone says, even after forty
or fifty years: "The sun is killing me.")

What are we doing with these souls of mist, with these names,
with our eyes of forests, with our beautiful children,
with our quick blood?

Spilled blood is not the roots of trees
but it's the closest thing to roots
we have.

1971 1986

Deep Calleth unto Deep[1]

by Dahlia Ravikovitch[2]

In Jerusalem I had my days of roses.
(What is Jerusalem but a hive of old houses?)
I came there young and returned, years later,
strange even to myself.
Alone, in a house that wasn't mine,
I lifted my eyes to the hills
to see if help had come.

Clouds lashed at each other,
dark cypresses rustled beneath me—
Suddenly a weird flash of sun

2. In the ancient Canaanite city of Shechem (now Nablus), a chieftain of the same name took Dinah, Jacob's daughter, "and lay with her by force" and then asked to wed her. Jocob's sons agreed only if the males of the city were first circumcised like the Jews. When that was done, Jacob's sons Simeon and Levi slew all the males (Genesis 34).

1. This poem echoes Psalm 42.7 (King James Version): "Deep calleth unto deep at the noise of thy waterspouts: all thy waves and thy billows are gone over me"; and Psalm 121.1 (King James Version): "I will lift up mine eyes unto the hills."

2. Ravikovitch (b. 1936), Hebrew poet, was born and lives in Israel.

swooped down
from the ends of the West.

And my longings flooded me,
sawed in my head like a cricket,
swarmed like hornets—

I was that drunk.

1976

1978
revised 1989

DAVID UNGER
b. 1950

The Jews in Hell

by Isaac Goldemberg[1]

As the story goes,
the Jews bought for themselves
a private spot in hell.

In the first circle,
Karl Marx sits on a wooden bench
using his hand as a fan.
The prophet Jeremiah
fights off the heat by singing psalms.

In the second circle,
Solomon carefully studies
the stones from His Temple.
On some yellowing rolls of paper,
Moses draws hieroglyphics.

Christ dreams of Pontius Pilate
in the third circle.
Freud's clinical eye
follows every move he makes.

In the fourth circle,
Spinoza[2] edits
a history of the Marranos.[3]

1. Goldemberg (b. 1945), Peruvian author, was born in Peru and lives in New York City.
2. Baruch Spinoza (1632–1677), heretical Dutch Jewish philosopher and theologian.
3. Medieval Spanish and Portuguese Jews who were compelled to convert to Christianity, but who remained Jews in secret.

In the fifth circle,
Jacob wrestles with a devil.
Cain and Abel
treat each other like brothers.

In the sixth circle,
Noah rides drunk on a zebra.
Einstein searches for atoms
in the space between rocks.

In the final circle,
Kafka tilts his telescope
and bursts out laughing.

1973

1979

Selected Bibliographies

GENERAL

Jewish History

For general information on Jewish history and religion, consult H. H. Ben-Sasson's *History of the Jewish People* (1976) and R. S. Werblowsky and Jeffrey Wigador's *Encyclopedia of the Jewish Religion* (1965). For background on Jewish religion and culture in Eastern Europe, see the excellent anthology of primary sources edited by Lucy Dawidowicz, *The Golden Tradition: Jewish Life and Thought in Eastern Europe* (1967); see especially Dawidowicz's comprehensive introduction. *The Encyclopaedia Judaica* (1971–72), the standard source on Jewish culture, history, and religion, is also a good starting point though it does not list lesser known writers.

For particular information on Jewish history in the United States, an excellent and highly readable resource is the multivolume *Jewish People in America* (1992), edited by Henry L. Feingold: *A Time for Planting: The First Migration (1654–1820),* by Eli Faber; *A Time for Gathering: The Second Migration (1820–1880),* by Hasia R. Diner; *A Time for Building: The Third Migration (1880–1920),* by Gerald Sorin; *A Time for Searching: Entering the Mainstream (1920–1945),* by Henry L. Feingold; *A Time for Healing: American Jewry since World War II,* by Edward S. Shapiro. This set also contains fine notes and bibliographies. Gerard Sorin, author of the third volume in this set, has also written a concise one-volume history, *Tradition Transformed: The Jewish Experience in America* (1977). Morris U. Schappes has two informative works, *A Documentary History of the Jews in the United States* (1952) and *A Pictorial History of the Jews in the United States* (1958). The preeminent scholar in early Jewish American history, Jacob Rader Marcus, has written and edited many important works on the history of the Jews in America. We especially recommend *United States Jewry (1776–1985),* a multivolume work presenting an excellent overview of the topic (1990, 1991, 1993). We also suggest Marcus's *Critical Studies in American Jewish History* (1971). *The American Jewish Experience* (1986), edited by Jonathan Sarna, is a strong and useful collection of essays that covers several historical periods. A recent authoritative resource on women, who have consistently been omitted from the official histories of Jewish life and culture, *Jewish Women in America: An Historical Encyclopedia* (1997), edited by Paula E. Hyman and Deborah Dash Moore, is also extremely valuable to students and scholars.

Bibliographies

Bibliographical sources for Jewish American literature include Bruce Nadel's *Jewish Writers of North America: A Guide to Information Sources* (1981), an excellent resource that supersedes many previous checklists and bibliographies. It covers 118 poets, fiction writers, dramatists (Canadian and American), with headnotes and occasional critical annotations. For a useful and recent source of essays by a variety of authors, see *Contemporary Jewish American Novelists: A Biocritical Sourcebook* (1997), edited by Joel Shatzky and Michael Taub; this book also contains good bibliographical sources. Gloria Cronin's *Jewish American Fiction Writers: An Annotated Bibliography* (1991) contains listings of both primary and secondary sources for many writers for whom no individual bibliographies exist. Stanley F. Chyet's "American Jewish Literary Productivity: A Selected Bicentennial Bibliography," in *Studies in Bibliography and Booklore* (Winter 1975–76), provides annotations, anthology information, and bibliographies.

Jews in American Literature and the Jewish American Writer

Of the many general resources for the study of Jews in American literature, we first recommend Louis Harap's *Image of the Jew in American Literature: From Early Republic to Mass Immigration* (1974) and his three-volume history of Jewish American writing, completed in 1987: *Creative Awakening, In the Mainstream,* and *Dramatic Encounters.* Allen Guttmann's *The Jewish Writer in America* (1971) remains a stimulating analytical history that explores the options of assimilation, ethnic nationalism, and radical change in society. Leslie Fiedler's early and illuminating essay "The Jew in the American Novel" is reprinted in Fiedler's *Collected Essays,* vol. 2 (1971). *The Dictionary of Literary Biography* has many useful volumes, especially number 28, *Twentieth-Century American Jewish Fiction Writers* (1984), edited by Daniel Walden. Lewis Fried's *Handbook of American-Jewish Literature: An Analytical Guide to Topics, Themes, and Sources* (1988) is also recommended to the student.

A groundbreaking collection of essays by Jewish writers and scholars has been edited by Hana Wirth-Nesher: *What Is Jewish Literature?* (1994). It contains several essays focusing on the Jewish American literary experience. The forthcoming *Cambridge Companion to Jewish American Literature,* edited by Hana Wirth-Nesher and Michael Kramer, promises to be an important contribution to scholarship and will examine Jewish American literature by period and genre.

For general thematic and theoretical discussions of Jewish American literature, there is a plenitude of excellent sources. We recommend especially Robert Alter's *Defenses of the Imagination: Jewish Writers and Modern Historical Crises* (1977), as well as Lawrence Langer's *The Holocaust and the Literary Imagination* (1975). In the *Harvard Guide to Contemporary American Writing* (1979), edited by Daniel Hoffman, Mark Shechner's essay on Jewish writers is well worth reading. Lynn Davidman's and Shelley Tenenbaum's *Feminist Perspectives on Jewish Studies* (1994) has also made important contributions to the discussion of women in the field. Sanford Pinsker's *Jewish American Fiction (1917–1987)* (1992) thoroughly covers many important texts of the twentieth century. Irving Malin's collection *Contemporary American Jewish Literature: Critical Essays* (1973) will also acquaint the reader with important trends and issues in the field.

In the past several years, many new collections of Jewish and Jewish American writing have emerged: *The Oxford Book of Jewish Stories* (1998), edited by Ilan Stavans; *Writing Our Way Home: Contemporary Stories by Jewish American Writers* (1992), edited by Ted Solotaroff and Nessa Rapoport; and *American Jewish Fiction: A Century of Stories* (1998), edited by Gerald Shapiro. Steven Rubin's collection *Telling and Remembering: A Century of American Jewish Poetry* (1997) is one of the most comprehensive and accessible contributions to the study of Jewish American poetry.

Special Topics in Literary Study

Diane Matza's collection *Sephardic American Voices* (1997) is the first anthology that collects this literature. Similarly, Alan Mintz's *Hebrew in America: Perspectives and Prospects* (1993) is a unique source of critical essays.

Sources for the study of Yiddish literature are much more numerous. The two Yiddish encyclopedias for literature include biographies and bibliographies for most Yiddish writers: *Leksikon fun der nayer yidisher literatur* (1956–1981), and *Leksikon fun der yidisher literatur, prese, un filologye* (1928) by Zalmen Reyzen. The two landmark anthologies of Yiddish prose and poetry, Irving Howe and Eliezer Greenberg's *Treasury of Yiddish Stories* (1953, 1954, 1989) and *A Treasury of Yiddish Poetry* (1969, 1976), contain many fine works by Yiddish writers, and although American themes are not always prominent, the introductions to these texts provide excellent background material. *American Yiddish Poetry* (1986), collected by Benjamin and Barbara Harshav, bilingual and brilliant, is a fine source that includes an excellent critical and historical introduction, as well as biographical and bibliographical entries. The only anthology of American Yiddish fiction in translation is *New Yorkish and Other American Yiddish Stories* (1995), translated and edited by Max Rosenfeld. The only anthology of female Yiddish prose writers in translation is *Found Treasures: Yiddish Women Writers* (1994). Edited by Frieda Forman et al., it includes an excellent introduction by Irena Klepfisz.

LITERATURE OF ARRIVAL, 1654–1880

The documents used in the first part of this section, specifically those from the years 1654 to 1820, were taken from three crucial works on early American Jewish history: Morris U. Schappes's *Documentary History of the Jews in the United States* (1952, 1971) and Jacob Rader Marcus's *American Jewry: Documents* (1959). Haim Karigal's sermon was collected and introduced in Abraham Karp's *Beginnings: Early American Judaica (1761–1845)* (1975) and appears in full in that collection, which also includes several other original and hard-to-find documents from this period, including Myer Moses's oration to the Hebrew Orphan Society (1806).

For general information on this period, volume 1 of the series *Jewish People in America*, Eli Faber's *A Time for Planting: The First Migration (1654–1820)* (1992), offers a comprehensive and invaluable overview. Jacob Rader Marcus also edited many other books about this period; *American Jewish Woman: A Documentary History* (1981) may be especially interesting to some. Jonathan Sarna's influential *The American Jewish Experience* (1986) includes a helpful chapter on "The American Colonial Jew," and Howard M. Sachar's *A History of the Jews in America* (1992) is also useful.

Virtually no literary critical work in print discusses the writers in this earliest period. In a historical context, only Haym Salomon has attracted any attention. Students interested in doing further reading about him may consult a 1930 biography by Charles Edward Russell, *Haym Salomon and the Revolution*, or a more recent work, Shirley Milgrim's *Haym Salomon: Liberty's Son* (1979).

To be appreciated, the literature written by Jews in America during the years from 1820 to 1880 needs first to be contextualized historically. The great historian of Jews in America during the early period is Jacob Rader Marcus, whose multivolume history *United States Jewry (1776–1985)* presents an excellent overview of the culture and the history in the second volume, *The Germanic Period* (1991), and the third, *The Germanic Period, Part* 2 (1993).

Hasia R. Diner's *A Time for Gathering: The Second Migration, 1820–1880* (1992) is a reliable and succinct study. Parts 1 and 2 of *The American Jewish Experience*, edited by Jonathan D. Sarna (1986), contain articles on Jews in America during this period that set the stage for the study of the literature. Another useful collection of articles on the period is the second volume of *Critical Studies in American Jewish History*, edited by Marcus (1971).

Three standard encyclopedias contain information especially on Jews. A fourth focuses on Jewish women in America. Most readily available is *Encyclopaedia Judaica* (1971–72), now also available on CD–ROM. However, this work does not contain some of the more obscure writers, who were better known earlier in the twentieth century. *The Jewish Encyclopedia* (1906) is an excellent source for information on early-nineteenth-century Jewish personages, as is the *Universal Jewish Encyclopedia* (1939–43). More recently, *Jewish Women in America: An Historical Encyclopedia* (1997), edited by Paula E. Hyman and Deborah Dash Moore, provides information on women, who have consistently been left out of the official histories of Jewish life and culture.

Finding the authors and the literature of this early period is complicated. Anthologies such as Morris U. Schappes's *A Documentary History of the Jews in the United States, 1654–1875* (1950, 1952, 1971) and Jacob Rader Marcus's *The American Jewish Woman: A Documentary History* (1981) provide brief selections of many writers in many genres and are good places to start. Other anthologies that present some of the writers of this period are *Four Centuries of Jewish Women's Spirituality* (1992), edited by Ellen M. Umansky and Dianne Ashton, and *Sephardic American Voices* (1997), edited by Diane Matza.

Few of these authors have been published in scholarly or critical editions or had their works collected. Many of their writings are available only in the forms in which they were originally published. One exception is a scholarly edition of diaries kept by a young Jewish woman who lived through the Civil War in the South, *The Civil War Diaries of Clara Solomon: Growing Up in New Orleans (1861–1862)* (1995), edited and with an informative introduction by Elliot Ashkenazi. One can of course go directly to the periodicals and newspapers of the period to find these authors' works, such as the mid-nineteenth-century publications *The American Israelite* (1854–96), *The Occident* (1843–69), *The Asmonean* (1849–58), and *The American Hebrew* (1879–88). Many manuscripts, letters, and papers are found in archival collections, such as the American Jewish Archives, in Cincinnati, Ohio, the American Jewish Historical Society, in Waltham, Massachusetts, and local historical societies or synagogue archives.

Because many of these writers have been considered more as historical phenomena than as literary figures, there is little literary criticism of their works. With the exception of Emma Lazarus, whose poetry has recently received more critical attention, most of the other writers have been considered in terms of their biographies and historical roles. One exception is Diane Lichtenstein's *Writing Their Nations: The Tradition of Nineteenth-Century American Jewish Women Writers* (1992), which considers the literature from the perspective of gender studies.

Anonymous

The poem *Miriam* was published anonymously in *The American Israelite* 5.2 (July 16, 1858): 14.

Rebecca Gratz

The only published volume of Rebecca Gratz's work is *Letters of Rebecca Gratz* (1929), edited by David Philipson. Gratz's uncollected and unpublished papers are located in the American Jewish Historical Society, Brandeis University, Waltham, Massachusetts; among the Gratz Family Papers at the American Philosophical Society, in Philadelphia, Pennsylvania; and among the Gratz Family Papers in the Henry Joseph Collection at the American Jewish Archives, Hebrew Union College, in Cincinnati, Ohio.

The one book-length study of Gratz is Dianne Ashton's excellent biography, *Rebecca Gratz: Women's Judaism in Antebellum America* (1997). Ashton's entry on Gratz in *Jewish Women in America: An Historical Encyclopedia* (1997), edited by Paula E. Hyman and Deborah Dash Moore, presents a succinct summary of Gratz's life. David Philipson's introduction to *Letters of Rebecca Gratz* (1929) provides useful details and anecdotes, while Leo Hershkowitz's entry on the "Gratz Family," in the *Encyclopaedia Judaica*, volume 7 (1971), is also informative.

Emma Lazarus

Morris U. Schappes edited *Emma Lazarus: Selections from Her Poetry and Prose* (1967), the standard edition of Lazarus's writings. Also important is *Poems of Emma Lazarus in Two Volumes* (1888), which includes a substantial introductory essay by Josephine Lazarus, the poet's sister. Other works by Lazarus that have been reissued are *An Epistle to the Hebrews* (1887, 1987), *Disraeli, the Jew: Essays by Emma Lazarus* (1882, 1993), and *Admetus* (originally published in 1871).

H. E. Jacob's *World of Emma Lazarus* (1949) and Eve Merriman's *Emma Lazarus: Woman with a Torch* (1956), a full-length study of Lazarus, are useful though somewhat dated. Dan Vogel's *Emma Lazarus* (1980) is useful. Diane Lichtenstein's entry on Lazarus in *Jewish Women in America: An Historical Encyclopedia*, edited by Paula E. Hyman and Deborah Dash Moore (1997), cogently summarizes Lazarus's life and works, drawing from Lichtenstein's fuller treatment in *Writing Their Nations: The Tradition of Nineteenth-Century American Jewish Women Writers* (1992). Shira Wolosky's article "An American-Jewish Typology: Emma Lazarus and the Figure of Christ," in *Prooftexts* 16 (1996): 113–25, presents an essential and illuminating reading of the poetry. Sue Levi Elwell's entry on Josephine Lazarus, Emma's eldest sister and an essayist in her own right, in *Jewish Women in America: An Historical Encyclopedia* (1997) and Jacob Rader Marcus's *The American Jewish Woman: A Documentary History* (1981) provide additional information.

Isaac Leeser

Isaac Leeser published some fourteen titles, including several multivolume works; one is currently in print, his translation of the Bible, *The Twenty-Four Books of the Holy Scriptures* (1849, 1998). His *Collected Discourses*, in 10 volumes (1867), contains most of his sermons. Leeser's early works include his translation of *Johlson's Instruction in the Mosaic Religion* (1830), *The Jews and the Mosaic Law* (1833), *Hebrew Spelling Book* (1838), *His Catechism* (1839), and *The Claims of the Jews to an Equality of Rights: Discourses* (1841). These works, as well as issues of the periodical *The Occident* (1843–69), are found only in research libraries. His translations of *The Pentateuch*, Hebrew and English, in 5 volumes (1845, 1857), and of the Ashkenazic and Sephardic prayer books—*Daily Prayers, German Rite* (1848) and *Portuguese Prayers* (1837, 1857)—are also rare, as are his later writings—*Dias' Letters* (1859), *The Inquisition and Judaism* (1860), and *Meditations and Prayers* (1864).

Although Leeser is mentioned frequently in historical studies, such as the second volume of Jacob Rader Marcus's *United States Jewry, 1776–1985, The Germanic Period* (1991), he has not yet merited a full-length biography. A fairly recent essay on Leeser is the excellent study by Bertram Wallace Korn, "Isaac Leeser: Centennial Reflections," in the second volume of *Critical Studies in American Jewish History* (1971), edited by Jacob Rader Marcus. Entries by Mayer Sulzberger in the *Jewish Encyclopedia* (1904) and Jack Riemer in *Encyclopaedia Judaica* (1971) provide biographical and bibliographical information on Leeser.

Nathan Mayer

Nathan Mayer published two novels: *The Fatal Secret; or, Plots and Counterplots. A Novel of the Sixteenth Century Founded on Facts* (1858) and his Civil War novel *Differences: A Novel* (1867). Before it appeared as a book, *The Fatal Secret* was serialized in Isaac Mayer Wise's Cincinnati weekly, *The Israelite*. Our selection, chapter 46, appears in volume 5, number 5 (Aug. 6, 1858), pp. 33–34. None of Mayer's work has been reprinted or reissued until the present anthology.

There is little information on Mayer's life and work. The one biographical article on him was published in *The Universal Jewish Encyclopedia* (1942), edited by Isaac Landman; in that same encyclopedia the article about his father, Isaac Mayer, provides further information on the son. These two pieces draw on earlier sources, Hyman Morrison's *Early Jewish Physicians in America* (1929) and Solomon R. Kagan's *Jewish Contributions to Medicine in America* (1939). Isaac Mayer Wise's memoir, *Reminiscences* (1901, 1945), translated and edited by David Philipson, comments in passing on Nathan Mayer.

Adah Isaacs Menken

Adah Isaacs Menken published one book of poetry, *Infelicia* (1868), which has not been reissued. Individual poems are reprinted in the following anthologies: *Judith, Myself,* and *Hear, O Israel!* in *The American Jewish Woman: A Documentary History* (1981), edited by Jacob R. Marcus; *Judith* in *American Women Poets of the Nineteenth Century* (1992), edited by Cheryl Walker; and *Drifts That Bar My Door,* in *Four Centuries of Jewish Women's Spirituality* (1992), edited by Ellen Umansky and Dianne Ashton.

Two biographies of Menken have been published: Paul Lewis's *Queen of the Plaza: A Biography of Adah Isaacs Menken* (1964) and Wolf Mankowitz's *Mazeppa: The Lives, Loves and Legends of Adah Isaacs Menken* (1982). Alan Ackerman's entry on Menken in *Jewish Women in America: An Historical Encyclopedia* (1997), edited by Paula E. Hyman and Deborah Dash Moore, is informative. Ellen M. Umansky's and Dianne Ashton's introduction to Part II of *Four Centuries of Jewish Women's Spirituality* analyzes Menken's work in the context of nineteenth-century Jewish women's writing, while Shira Wolosky's article "Women's Bibles: Biblical Interpretation in Nineteenth-Century American Women's Poetry," forthcoming in Wolosky's *Poetry and Public Discourse, The Cambridge History of American Literature*, vol. 3, edited by Sacvan Bercovitch, places Menken's poetry in the context of American women poets.

Penina Moïse

Although Penina Moïse's collection of poems, *Fancy's Sketch Book* (1833), and of hymns, *Hymns Written for the Use of Hebrew Congregations* (1856), have not been reissued, selections from them are available in several more recent anthologies. Moïse's poem *Miriam* and short story *The Convict* were first published in *The Charleston Book: A Miscellany in Prose and Verse* (1845), edited by William Gilmore Simms, a facsimile of which was reprinted, with introduction and notes by David Moltke-Hansen and Harlan Greene (1983). Seven of her poems have been reprinted in Jacob Rader Marcus's *The American Jewish Woman: A Documentary History* (1981). Three poems from the *Hymnal of Penina Moïse* (1856) were reprinted in *Four Centuries of Jewish Women's Spirituality* (1992), edited by Ellen M. Umansky and Dianne Ashton; and two in *Sephardic American Voices* (1997), edited by Diane Matza.

There is no book-length study of Moïse's life and work, but information can be found in the following articles: Jay M. Eidelman's entry on her in *Jewish Women in America: An Historical Encyclopedia* (1997), edited by Paula E. Hyman and Deborah Dash Moore; the entry on Moïse in the *Dictionary of American Biography*; Jacob Rader Marcus's *The*

American Jewish Woman: A Documentary History (1981), and Ellen M. Umansky's "Piety, Persuasion, and Friendship: A History of Jewish Women's Spirituality" and Umansky and Dianne Ashton's "1800–1890, Stronger Voices," in *Four Centuries of Jewish Women's Spirituality* (1992), edited by Umansky and Ashton. Shira Wolosky's article, "Women's Bibles: Biblical Interpretation in Nineteenth-Century American Women's Poetry," places Moïse in the context of American writers.

Mordecai Manuel Noah

Aside from the play included in this anthology—*The Fortress of Sorrento: A Petit Historical Drama in Two Acts* (1808)—only one other of Mordecai Manuel Noah's plays has been reprinted in recent decades: *She Would Be a Soldier; or, The Plains of Chippewa* (1819) was reissued in *Dramas from the American Theatre, 1762–1909* (1966), edited and introduced by Richard Moody. Noah's other published plays—*Paul and Alexis; or, The Orphans of the Rhine* (1812), *The Grecian Captive; or, The Fall of Athens* (1822), *Marion; or, The Hero of Lake George: A Drama in Three Acts* (1822)—and pamphlets can be found in the American Culture Series and the Early American Imprints series of microfilm, available from University Microfilms and the American Antiquarian Society. The text of Noah's play *Yusef Caramalli; or, The Siege of Tripoli*, performed in New York City, on May 15, 1820, was not preserved. Noah's travelogue *Travels in England, France, Spain and the Barbary States in the Years 1813–14 and 15* (1819) may be available on microfilm. A brief family history, *Nunes's Story*, is reprinted in *Sephardic American Voices* (1997), edited by Diane Matza. Hermon Press reprinted *The Book of Jasher* (1972).

The standard biography of Noah is Jonathan D. Sarna's superb *Jacksonian Jew: The Two Worlds of Mordecai Noah* (1981), which includes an exhaustive "Bibliographic Essay" on both primary and secondary sources. Other accessible sources on Noah include Abraham J. Karp's catalogue for an exhibition at the Yeshiva University Museum, *Mordecai Manuel Noah: The First American Jew* (1987); Richard Moody's introduction to Noah's *She Would Be a Soldier; or, The Plains of Chippewa*, in *Dramas from the American Theatre, 1762–1909* (1966); and an article on him in the *Encyclopaedia Judaica* (1971).

Isaac Mayer Wise

Isaac Mayer Wise's memoir, in the translation by David Philipson, *Reminiscences* (1901; 2nd ed., 1945), makes for delightful reading. His other books, printed in the middle of the nineteenth century, are harder to find and of more historical than literary interest, such as *History of the Israelitish Nation* (1854), the prayer book *Minhag America* (The American Rite) (first published in 1857, some editions in Hebrew alone, some with English and some with German translations), the theological study *The Cosmic God* (1876), and *Pronaos to Holy Writ* (1891). His weekly newspaper *The Israelite* (later *The American Israelite*), published beginning in 1854, is available on microfilm.

Two biographies of Wise are M. B. May's *Isaac Mayer Wise* (1916) and J. G. Heller's *Isaac M. Wise* (1965). Heller's book includes an extensive bibliography. For quicker reference, the entry on Wise in the *Encyclopaedia Judaica* is useful. Jacob Rader Marcus's second and third volumes of his *United States Jewry, 1776–1985—The Germanic Period* (1991) and *The Germanic Period, Part 2* (1993)—discuss Wise's contribution as a Jewish leader and writer.

THE GREAT TIDE, 1881–1924

In order to appreciate the literature of this period, one must place it in an historical context. The richest, deepest, and most comprehensive cultural history of the Eastern European Jewish immigrants in America is *World of Our Fathers: The Journey of the East European Jews to America and the Life They Found and Made* (1976) by Irving Howe, with Kenneth Libo. The standard history of the Jews in America is Jacob Rader Marcus's *United States Jewry, 1776–1985: The East European Period and the Emergence of the American Jew*, volume 4 (1993), and a standard survey of Jewish history is *A History of the Jewish People* (1976), edited by H. H. Ben-Sasson. One can read more about the culture the immigrants left behind in *The Golden Tradition: Jewish Life and Thought in Eastern Europe* (1967), a collection of essays translated from Yiddish and with an excellent introduction by Lucy Dawidowicz. Other books that treat the history and culture of the Eastern European Jewish immigrants are Ronald Sanders's *The Downtown Jews: Portraits of an Immigrant Generation* (1969, 1976), Milton Meltzer's *World of Our Fathers: The Jews of Eastern Europe* (1976), and *The American Jewish Experience* (1986), edited by Jonathan Sarna. Susan A. Glenn's *Daughters of the Shtetl: Life and Labor in the Immigrant Generation* (1990) examines the roles of immigrant women in the family and the garment industry. Two essays in *Jewish Women in Historical Perspective* (1991), edited by Judith R. Baskin, present historical issues from the perspective of gender: Paula E. Hyman's "Gender and the Immigrant Jewish Experience in the United States" and Ellen M. Umansky's "Spiritual Expressions: Jewish Women's Religious Lives in the Twentieth Century United States." Hutchins Hapgood's *The Spirit of the Ghetto: Studies of the Jewish Quarter of New York* (1902, 1966) offers insights into the Jewish authors from a contemporary point of view.

Translations of American Yiddish literature are

most readily found in anthologies. *American Yiddish Poetry: A Bilingual Anthology* (1986), edited by Benjamin and Barbara Harshav, is the only recent anthology devoted to American Yiddish poetry; it presents each of the seven modernist poets in selections of translations facing the Yiddish originals. The other recent scholarly anthology is *The Penguin Book of Modern Yiddish Verse* (1987), edited by Irving Howe, Ruth R. Wisse, and Khone Shmeruk, which offers eighteen American Yiddish poets among a total of thirty-nine poets, with translations facing the Yiddish originals. *An Anthology of Modern Yiddish Poetry* (3rd ed., 1995), selected and translated by Ruth Whitman, includes seven American poets out of fourteen, also in a bilingual setting. A number of anthologies contain only the English translations. The most famous of these is *A Treasury of Yiddish Poetry* (1969, 1976), edited by Irving Howe and Eliezer Greenberg, which includes some twenty-five to thirty American Yiddish poets among its total of fifty-eight, and a worthwhile introduction. *A Century of Yiddish Poetry* (1989), selected and translated by Aaron Kramer, presents over 125 poets, approximately half of whom may be considered American. *Voices within the Ark: The Modern Jewish Poets* (1980), edited by Howard Schwartz and Anthony Rudolf, includes forty-four Yiddish poets, of whom twenty wrote in America. The self-published *American Yiddish Poetry: An Anthology* (1967), selected and translated by Jehiel B. Cooperman and Sarah H. Cooperman, presents sixty-nine American poets in English only. *The Golden Peacock: An Anthology of Yiddish Poetry* (1939), edited and translated by Joseph Leftwich, includes some sixty-eight American Yiddish poets. The Yiddish poet Samuel J. Imber's anthology, *Modern Yiddish Poetry* (1927), presents translations of poems by his modernist peers *en face* with transliterated Yiddish texts.

American Yiddish short stories and novellas in translation appear in a number of anthologies as well. The only anthology that focuses exclusively on American Yiddish prose writers is *New Yorkish and Other American Yiddish Stories* (1995), translated and compiled by Max Rosenfeld. *A Treasury of Yiddish Stories* (1953, 1954, 1989), edited by Howe and Greenberg, includes twelve American prose writers. *Found Treasures: Yiddish Women Writers* (1994), edited by Frieda Forman et al., contains stories by nine American Yiddish writers. *The Tribe of Dina* (1989), edited by Irena Klepfisz and Melanie Kaye/Kantrowitz, includes poems and stories by three women Yiddish writers.

One of the five works in *A Shtetl and Other Yiddish Novellas*, edited by Ruth R. Wisse (1986), is by an American Yiddish author, Joseph Opatoshu. *America and I: Short Stories by American-Jewish Women Writers* (1990), edited by Joyce Antler, includes four writers in English from this period.

Only three collections of Yiddish plays exist in English translation. *God, Man, and Devil: Yiddish Plays in Translation* (1999), translated and edited by Nahama Sandrow, is an excellent volume. Joseph Landis has translated and edited two fine anthologies of Yiddish plays: *The Great Jewish Plays* (1974), which contains three plays by the Yiddish American playwrights Sholem Asch, Peretz Hirshbein, and David Pinski, and *Three Great Jewish Plays* (1986), which reprints the Asch and Pinski plays.

Encyclopaedia Judaica is the standard reference on Jewish culture, literature, and history, and contains entries on many of the authors in this section. Two Yiddish encyclopedias present biographies and bibliographies for most of the Yiddish writers: *Leksikon fun der nayer yidisher literatur* (New York, 1956–81) and Zalmen Reyzen's *Leksikon fun der yidisher literatur, prese, un filologye* (Vilna, 1928). Three recent reference works in English present information on many Jewish American authors: *Jewish-American History and Culture: An Encyclopedia* (1992), edited by Jack Fischel and Sanford Pinsker has articles on Yiddish and English poetry and literature; *Handbook of Jewish-American Literature: An Analytical Guide to Themes and Sources* (1988), edited by Lewis Fried, has articles on literature as well; *Jewish Women in America: An Historical Encyclopedia*, edited by Paula E. Hyman and Deborah Dash Moore (1997), presents biographies and bibliographies of many of the women authors, as well as surveys of Jewish and Yiddish literature. *The Oxford Companion to Women's Writing in the United States* (1995), edited by Cathy N. Davidson and Linda Wagner-Martin, includes a series of articles on Jewish American writing.

The introductory essays in the anthologies of poetry, prose, and drama listed above provide good critical surveys of the literature. Harshav's introduction to *American Yiddish Poetry* offers an especially cogent view of the Introspectivist poets. Howe's introduction to *A Treasury of Yiddish Stories* is excellent, as is Wisse's introductory material in *A Shtetl and Other Yiddish Novellas*. Several books survey modern Yiddish literature and include many of our authors: A. A. Roback's *The Story of Yiddish Literature* (1940), Sol Liptzin's *The Flowering of Yiddish Literature* (1964) and *The Maturing of Yiddish Literature* (1970), and Charles Madison's *Yiddish Literature: Its Scope and Major Writers* (1971). Wisse's *A Little Love in Big Manhattan: Two Yiddish Poets* (1988) is a superb study of the Yunge and their contemporaries. Norma Fain Pratt's "Culture and Radical Politics: Yiddish Women Writers in America," Kathryn Hellerstein's "Canon and Gender: Women Poets in Two Modern Yiddish Anthologies," Sheva Zucker's translation of Shmuel Niger's "Yiddish Literature and the Female Reader," Laura Wexler's "Looking at Yezierska," and Carole S. Kessner's "Matrilineal Dissent: The Rhetoric of Zeal in Emma Lazarus, Marie Syrkin, and Cynthia Ozick," all in *Women of the Word: Jewish Women and Jewish Writing* (1994), edited by Judith R. Baskin, pertain to the Jewish American literature of our period. Nehama Sandrow's *Vagabond Stars: A World History of Yiddish Theater* places American Yiddish theater in a larger context, as does Lulla Rosenfeld's *Bright Star of Exile: Jacob Adler and the Yiddish The-*

atre (1977). *Hebrew in America: Perspectives and Prospects* (1993), edited by Alan Mintz, gathers excellent articles on American Hebrew literature.

Mary Antin

Mary Antin's first book, *From Plotzk to Boston*, was published in 1899 and was reissued with an introduction by Pamela S. Nadell (1985). Her second and most famous book, *The Promised Land*, first published in 1912, has been reissued in an edition with an excellent introduction and notes by Werner Sollors (1997), which includes her essay "How I Wrote 'The Promised Land,'" originally published in the *New York Times Book Review*. Antin's third book, *They Who Knock at Our Gates: A Complete Gospel of Immigration*, was published in 1914. In 1912 and 1913, Antin published short stories in the *Atlantic Monthly*—*The Amulet, The Lie,* and *Malinke's Atonement*—the last of which was reprinted in Joyce Antler's *America and I: Short Stories by American-Jewish Women Writers* (1990). Antin's correspondence has been published in *Selected Letters of Mary Antin* (2000), edited by Evelyn Salz.

The most useful study of Antin is Sollors's introduction to his edition of *The Promised Land*. Also worth reading are Michael Kramer's "Assimilation in *The Promised Land*: Mary Antin and the Jewish Origins of the American Self," *Prooftexts* 18.2 (May 1998); Pamela Nadell's entry on Antin in *Jewish Women in America: An Historical Encyclopedia* (1997), edited by Paula E. Hyman and Deborah Dash Moore; and Evelyn Salz's "The Letters of Mary Antin: A Life Divided," *American Jewish History* 84 (1996).

Sholem Asch

Although at least twenty-four volumes of Sholem Asch's novels and plays were translated into English during the twentieth century, very few if any are in print today. Beginning with the translation of *America* (1918), Asch's fiction was brought into English by a number of American and British translators. The most distinguished among these were Willa and Edwin Muir, a British Gentile couple famous for translating Tolstoy and Dostoevsky. They translated Asch's *Three Cities* (1933), *Salvation* (1934, 1968), and *Mottke the Thief* (1935). Maurice Samuel, an American writer and scholar, translated two of Asch's Christological novels, *The Nazarene* (1939) and *The Apostle* (1943), as well as *What I Believe* (1941) and *Children of Abraham: The Short Stories of Sholem Asch* (1944). A. H. Gross translated *East River* (1946, 1983). Elsa Krauch translated *Three Novels: Uncle Moses, Khaim Ledere's Return, Judge Not* (1938). Asch's other works in translation are *In the Beginning* (1925), *Kiddush Ha-Shem* (Sanctification of the Name) (1926), *Shabbati Zevi* (1930), *The War Goes On* (1937), *Song of the Valley* (1938), the controversial ecumenical statement *One Destiny* (1945), *The Burning Bush* (1946), *Tale of My People* (1948), *Mary* (1949), *Moses* (1951), *A Passage in the Night* (1953), *The Prophet* (1955), and *From Many Countries: Collected Short Stories* (1958).

In Yiddish, two editions of his *Gezamelte shriftn* (Collected Writings) appeared, one in Warsaw (ca. 1926) and the other in New York (1923–38). A volume of fiction was reissued in Buenos Aires in 1972, *Fun shtetl tsu der groyser velt* (From the Shtetl to the Great World). The play *Got fun nekome: a drame in dray aktn* (God of Vengeance: A Drama in Three Acts), first published in Vilna in 1907, has been published in three English translations: by Isaac Goldberg (1916); by Joseph Landis, in both *The Great Jewish Plays* (1974) and *Three Great Jewish Plays* (1986); and by Joachim Neugroschel, in *Der Pakn Treger/The Book Peddler* (1996).

To date, there is no biography or critical study in English devoted to Sholem Asch. Basic information about his life and works can be found in English in *New Encyclopaedia Britannica* (1995), Charles Madison's *Yiddish Literature: Its Scope and Writers* (1968, 1971), A. A. Roback's *The Story of Yiddish Literature* (1940), and in Yiddish in *Der leksikon fun der nayer yidisher literatur*, volume 1 (1956), and in Zalmen Reyzen's *Leksikon fun der yidisher literatur, prese, un filologye*, volume 1 (1928). Two forthcoming works treat Sholem Asch: a collection of essays, *Sholem Asch Reconsidered*; and a chapter in Anita Norich's *A Time for Every Purpose: Jewish Culture in America during the Holocaust*.

A Bintl Briv

The only collection in English translation of the *Forverts* column *A bintl briv* is the volume selected for this anthology, *A Bintel Brief: Sixty Years of Letters from the Lower East Side to the "Jewish Daily Forward"* (1971), compiled, edited, and introduced by Isaac Metzker with a foreword by Harry Golden, and translated by Diana Shalet Levy and Bella S. Metzker. One can find many other examples of *A bintl briv* in back issues of the *Forverts* (*Jewish Daily Forward*), published since 1897 by the Forward Association in New York City, and available on microfilm at YIVO Institute for Jewish Research in New York and other scholarly institutions.

Irving Howe writes cogently about *A bintl briv* in *World of Our Fathers* (1976), as do Ronald Sanders in *The Downtown Jews* (1976) and Jules Chametzky in *From the Ghetto: The Fiction of Abraham Cahan* (1977).

Abraham Cahan

Cahan wrote fiction for about twenty-five years, from 1891–92 until 1917, some in Yiddish, but mostly in English. His first published book in English was a novella, *Yekl: A Tale of the New York Ghetto* (1896), followed by a volume of short stories, *The Imported Bridegroom and Other Stories of the New York Ghetto* (1898)—both reissued in a single volume in 1970. His other novels are *The White Terror and the Red: A Novel of Revolutionary Russia* (1905) and *The Rise of David Levinsky* (1917). *David Levinsky* has been reissued several times, most recently in 1960 with a fine introduction by the historian John Higham and in 1993 with excellent notes and introduction by Jules Chametzky. Between 1899 and 1901, Cahan also published six stories in leading journals such as *Century, Cosmopolitan, Scribner's*, and *Atlantic*.

A complete bibliography of all these publications plus a listing of his fiction in Yiddish, many of his articles in English, and chief secondary works on him can be found in Jules Chametzky's *From the Ghetto: The Fiction of Abraham Cahan* (1977), which also provides analyses of all the Yiddish and English fiction and many of his critical essays. The best bibliographies are Ephrim Jeshurin's *Abraham Cahan Bibliography* (1941), which lists his work in Russian, Yiddish, and English, and Sanford E. Marovitz and Lewis Fried's "Abraham Cahan (1860–1951): An Annotated Bibliography," *American Literary Realism 1870–1910* 3.3 (Summer 1970), which lists and annotates all his English work.

There are exemplary articles about Cahan listed in Chametzky, the best of which are a review of *David Levinsky* by John Macy in 1917 and essays by Isaac Rosenfeld, "America, Land of the Sad Millionaire" (*Commentary*, Aug. 14, 1952), and Leslie Fiedler, "Genesis: The American Jewish Novel Through the Twenties," *Midstream* 4 (Summer 1958). Excellent studies of Cahan appear in Irving Howe's *World of Our Fathers* (1976) and, especially, in Ronald Sanders, *The Downtown Jews* (1969). As yet there is no definitive biography. The indispensable source for his life is Cahan's autobiography, five volumes in Yiddish, *Bleter fun mayn leben* (Pages from My Life) (1926–31), the first two volumes of which have been translated and are available as *The Education of Abraham Cahan* (1964).

Celia Dropkin

Celia Dropkin's Yiddish poems were published first in *In heysn vint, lider* (In the Hot Wind: Poems) (1935) and in a posthumous expanded edition that includes her short stories, *In heysn vint, Poems, Stories, and Pictures* (1959). There is as yet no volume of translations of her poetry or fiction into English. Gilles Rozier and Viviane Siman have translated her poems into French, *en face* with the Yiddish originals, in *Dans le vent chaud: Bilingue yiddish-francais* (In the Hot Wind: Bilingual Yiddish and French) (1994), and included an excellent introduction. Translations of individual poems or small groupings of poems have been published in a number of anthologies: by Adrienne Rich in *A Treasury of Yiddish Poetry* (1969), edited by Irving Howe and Eliezer Greenberg; by Howard Schwartz in *Voices within the Ark: The Modern Jewish Poets* (1980), edited by Howard Schwartz and Anthony Rudolf; by Ruth Whitman in *Penguin Book of Modern Yiddish Verse* (1987), edited by Howe, Ruth R. Wisse, and Khone Shmeruk; and by Ruth Whitman in Whitman's *Anthology of Modern Yiddish Poetry* (1995). Shirley Kumove's translation of the short story *The Dancer* appeared in *Found Treasures: Stories by Yiddish Women Writers* (1994), edited by Frieda Forman.

No book-length study of Dropkin's life and works has been published. Three essays in Yiddish provide information on the poet: Sasha Dillon's "Vegn Tsilye Dropkin" (About Celia Dropkin), in *In heysn vint, Poems, Stories, and Pictures* (1959), and the entries on Dropkin in *Leksikon fun der nayer yidisher literatur*, volume 2 (1958), and in Zalmen Reyzen's *Leksikon fun der literatur, prese, un filologye*, volume 1 (1926). In English, a critical treatment of Dropkin's life and work is the entry on her by Kathryn Hellerstein in *Jewish Women in America: An Historical Encyclopedia* (1997), edited by Paula Hyman and Deborah Dash Moore. Anita Norich's article "Yiddish Literature," also in *Jewish Women in America*, provides additional information.

Two critical articles have been published, both in *Gender and Text in Modern Hebrew and Yiddish Literature* (1992), edited by Naomi B. Sokoloff, Anne Lapidus Lerner, and Anita Norich: Janet Hadda's "The Eyes Have It: Celia Dropkin's Love Poetry" presents a psychoanalytic reading of Dropkin's poems; Kathryn Hellerstein's "From *Ikh* to *Zikh*: A Journey from 'I' to 'Self' in Yiddish Poems by Women" treats Dropkin's poetry in the context of poems by other women Yiddish writers.

A bibliography in Yiddish of Dropkin's publications, by Ephrim Jeshurin, "Tsilye Dropkin: Bibliografye" (Celia Dropkin: Bibliography), is appended to *In heysn vint, Poems, Stories, and Pictures*.

David Edelshtadt

At least two collections of the Yiddish poems of David Edelshtadt were published early in the twentieth century, both called *Shriftn* (London, 1909 and 1910, and New York, 1911). Translations of individual poems into English include four by Aaron Kramer (*To the Muse, My Testament, My Final Wish, From My Journal*), in *A Century of Yiddish Poetry* (1989), edited by Kramer, and two by Joseph Leftwich (*We Are the Hated and Driven* and *My Testament*) in *The Golden Peacock* (1939), edited by Leftwich.

The best bio-bibliographical articles on Edelshtadt in Yiddish are the entries in Zalmen Reyzen's *Leksikon fun der yidisher literatur, prese, un filologye*, volume 2 (1928), and by Leyb Vaserman in *Leksikon fun der nayer yidisher literatur*, volume 6 (1965). There is no full-length treatment of Edelshtadt's work in English, although a number of works treat Edelshtadt in passing, including A. A. Roback's *The Story of Yiddish Literature* (1940), Sol Liptzin's *The Flowering of Yiddish Literature* (1964), Charles Madison's *Yiddish Literature: Its Scope and Writers* (1968), Irving Howe's *World of Our Fathers* (1976), and the article on Yiddish poetry by Kathryn Hellerstein in *Jewish-American History and Culture: An Encyclopedia* (1992), edited by Jack Fischel and Sanford Pinsker.

Edna Ferber

Extremely prolific over a long career, Edna Ferber published her first novel, *Dawn O' Hara: The Girl Who Laughed*, in 1911 and her last, *The Ice Palace*, about Alaska, in 1958. Among her better-known works are *Fanny Herself* (1917), *The Girls* (1921), *So Big* (1924), *Show Boat* (1926), *Cimarron* (1930), *Saratoga Trunk* (1941), and *Giant* (1952). These last five were gathered in *Five Complete Novels* (1984). She also published several collections of short stories and was co-author with George S. Kaufman of five stage plays, among them *The Royal Family* (1928), *Dinner at Eight* (1932), and *Stage Door* (1941). *A Peculiar Treasure* is a first autobiography (1939); *A Kind of Magic* (1963) is a second, written in her old age.

Biographies and bibliographies are scarce. Roger Dickinson's *Edna Ferber: A Biographical Sketch with a Bibliography, with Many Quotations from Edna Ferber's Autobiographical Articles* (1925) gained interest because of the Pulitzer Prize she won for *So Big*. More recent studies are Mary Rose Shaughnessy's *Women and Success in American Society in the Works of Edna Ferber* (1977) and Julie Goldsmith Gilbert's *Ferber: A Biography* (1978).

Useful critical articles are by Paule Reed in *Dictionary of Literary Biography 9: American Novelists, 1910–1945* (1991) and Steven P. Horowitz and Miriam J. Landsman, "The Americanization of Edna: A Study of Ms. Ferber's Jewish American Identity," *Studies in American Jewish Literature* (1982).

Moyshe-Leyb Halpern

Although Moyshe-Leyb Halpern's three books were published in several editions earlier in the century, *In nyu york* (1919, 1927, 1954), *Di goldene pave* (1924, 1954), and the two-volume *Moyshe-Leyb Halpern*, introduced by Eliezer Greenberg (1934), none is in print today. One book-length selection of translations, accompanied by the Yiddish originals, was published in 1982, *In New York: A Selection*, translated, edited, and introduced by Kathryn Hellerstein. The most extensive selection of Halpern's poems, published *en face* with English translations by Benjamin Harshav and Kathryn Hellerstein, is in *American Yiddish Poetry: A Bilingual Anthology* (1986), edited by Benjamin and Barbara Harshav. Another fine selection of Halpern's poems in Yiddish, with translations by John Hollander and Leonard Wolf, is in *The Penguin Book of Modern Yiddish Verse* (1987), edited by Irving Howe, Ruth R. Wisse, and Khone Shmeruk. A much briefer bilingual selection of several Halpern poems is in Ruth Whitman's *Anthology of Modern Yiddish Poetry* (1994). Anthologies that include selections of Halpern's poems in English translation only are Howe and Greenberg's *Treasury of Yiddish Poetry* (1969, 1976), Joseph Leftwich's *The Golden Peacock: An Anthology of Yiddish Poetry* (1939, 1944), Howard Schwartz and Anthony Rudolf's *Voices within the Ark* (1980), and Aaron Kramer's *Century of Yiddish Poetry* (1989).

The only book-length study in English of Halpern is Ruth R. Wisse's superb *A Little Love in Big Manhattan: Two Yiddish Poets* (1988), which compares Halpern with Mani Leyb. Irving Howe's chapter on Yiddish poets in *World of Our Fathers* (1976) includes an illuminating discussion of Halpern. Kathryn Hellerstein's introduction to *In New York: A Selection* and her article "The Demon Within: Moyshe-Leyb Halpern's Subversive Ballads," *Prooftexts* 7 (Fall 1987) are useful, as are the introductions by Harshav (*American Yiddish Poetry*), Howe, Wisse, and Shmeruk (*Penguin Book of Modern Yiddish Verse*), and Howe and Greenberg (*A Treasury of Yiddish Poetry*).

In Yiddish, the best sources are Eliezer Greenberg's introduction to the poems, *Moyshe Leyb Halpern* (1934), and his book, *Moyshe leyb halpern in ram fun zayn dor* (Moyshe-Leyb Halpern in the Context of His Generation) (1942), as well as Yitzkhak Kharlash's entry on Halpern in *Leksikon fun der nayer yidisher literatur*, volume 3 (1963). Ephrim Jeshurin compiled an extensive biographical bibliography for the 1954 edition of *In nyu york*.

Horace M. Kallen

Horace M. Kallen's important essay "Democracy versus the Melting Pot: A Study of American Nationality" appeared originally in two installments of *The Nation*—100 (2590) (Feb. 18, 1915); and 100 (2591) (Feb. 25, 1915). He followed this with "Nationality and the Hyphenated American," *Menorah Journal* 1 (April 1915). His most significant book is *Culture and Democracy in the United States: Studies in Group Psychology of the American Peoples* (1924). But his other works on Judaism, Zionism, cultural pluralism, and philosophy are noteworthy. These include *Zionism and World Politics: A Study in History and Social Psychology* (1921), *Judaism at Bay: Essays towards Adjusting Judaism in Modernity* (1932), and *Cultural Pluralism and the American Idea: An Essay in Social Philosophy* (1956). Besides his own philosophical works, he edited William James's *Some Problems in Philosophy: A Beginning of an Introduction to Philosophy* (1911) and a collection of lectures delivered at the New School for Social Research, *Freedom in the Modern World* (1928).

Susanne Klingenstein has an exceptional section called "The American Ideas of Horace Meyer Kallen (1882–1974)" in her *Jews in the American Academy, 1900–1940* (1992). Werner Sollors deals expertly with Kallen's ideas in *Beyond Ethnicity: Consent and Descent in America* (1986) and in "A Critique of Pure Pluralism," *Reconstructing American Literary History* (1986), edited by Sacvan Bercovitch.

Mani Leyb

Only one of Mani Leyb's fourteen books is in print—*Yingl tsingl khvat*, originally published in Yiddish with illustrations by the Russian formalist El Lissitzky, in 1922, reissued as a children's book with a translation into English by Jeffrey Shandler (1986). The two-volume posthumous collection of Mani Leyb's poems, *Lider un baladn* (Poems and Ballads) (1955), which includes a bibliography of Mani Leyb's works by Ephrim H. Jeshurin, can be found in some university or research libraries. His early books include *Baladn*, *Lider*, and *Yidishe un slavishe motivn* (Jewish and Slavic Motifs), three major books, all published in 1918, and a number of chapbooks published around the same time that were intended for children—*Der fremder; der shlof* (The Stranger; Sleep) (1918), *Gazlonim* (Bandits) and *Di noyt* (Need) (1918), *Dos lidl fun broyt* (The Song of Bread) and *Dray malokhim* (Three Angels) (1918), *Blimelekh krentselekh* (Blossoms and Wreathes) (1918), *Kinder-lider* (1918), *In a vinterdiker nakht* (1918), *Viglider* (Lullabies) (1918), and *Yingl tsingl khvat* (1922). *Vunder iber vunder: lider, baladn, mayselekh* (Wonder upon Wonder: Poems, Ballads, Tales) (1930) is a fourth large book, followed by a biography for children of Mendele Moykhr Sforim (1936), and a book of children's poems, *A maysele in gramen fun dray zin mit a mamen* (A Tale in Rhymes about Three Sons and Their Mother) (1937). A collection of his stories, *A. Kuprin: dertseylungen*, appeared in 1920. Mani Leyb also co-edited the miscellany *Indzl* (1918) and the 1925 monthly by the same name, as well as a collection of works about the writer *Dovid Ignatov*. Several of his poems were set to music and published in the 1920s and 1930s.

Translations of Mani Leyb's poems into English include thirteen poems, translated by John Hollander and Marie Syrkin, in the *Penguin Book of Modern Yiddish Verse* (1987), edited by Irving Howe, Ruth R. Wisse, and Khone Shmeruk, and twelve poems, translated by Hollander, Syrkin, Miriam Waddington, and Nathan Halper, in *A Treasury of Yiddish Poetry* (1969), edited by Howe and Eliezer Greenberg.

The only full-length critical treatment of Mani Leyb (alongside Moyshe-Leyb Halpern) in English is Ruth R. Wisse's *A Little Love in Big Manhattan: Two Yiddish Poets* (1988). Irving Howe's *World of Our Fathers* (1976) discusses Mani Leyb. In Yiddish, Mani Leyb plays a role in Reuven Iceland's autobiography, *Fun unzer friling* (From Our Springtime) (1954). Mordechai Yafe's entry in *Leksikon fun der nayer yidisher literatur*, volume 5 (1963), presents the biographical and bibliographic basics.

H. Leyvik

Two two-volume editions of Leyvik's collected works appeared in 1940: *Ale verk fun H. Leyvik* and *Ale verk*. Leyvik's poetry is best represented in twenty-eight translations by Benjamin and Barbara Harshav in *American Yiddish Poetry: A Bilingual Anthology* (1986). Six of Leyvik's poems, translated by Meyer Schapiro, Cynthia Ozick, and Robert Friend and facing the Yiddish, are included in the *Penguin Book of Modern Yiddish Verse* (1987), edited by Irving Howe, Ruth R. Wisse, and Khone Shmeruk. Three poems appear in Ruth Whitman's bilingual *Anthology of Modern Yiddish Poetry* (1995). In English only, one finds ten titles by Leyvik, including a long selection from his verse drama *The Book of Job*, in *A Treasury of Yiddish Poetry* (1969), edited by Howe and Greenberg; the translations are by Ozick, Schapiro, Marie Syrkin, and Leonard Wolf. Joseph Leftwich includes fifteen of Leyvik's poems in translation in *The Golden Peacock* (1939), while Aaron Kramer includes seven in *A Century of Yiddish Poetry* (1989). Joseph C. Landis's translation of Leyvik's drama *The Golem* is in *Three Great Jewish Plays* (1986), edited by Landis.

In Yiddish, Yitskhok Karlash's entry on Leyvik in *Leksikon fun der nayer yidisher literatur*, volume 5 (1963), provides a great deal of biographical and bibliographical information on Leyvik. Harshav's biographical note in *American Yiddish Poetry* is an excellent summary. Levi Shalit's entry on Leyvik on the CD–ROM edition of the *Encyclopaedia Judaica* is also useful. Howe, in *World of Our Fathers* (1976), and Wisse, in *A Little Love in Big Manhattan* (1988), provide insightful glimpses of Leyvik.

Anna Margolin

Anna Margolin's only book of poems, *Lider* (Poems), was published in 1929. A scholarly edition of *Lider* was edited and introduced by Abraham Novershtern (1991). Margolin herself edited an anthology, *Dos yidishe lid in amerike—1923: antologye* (The Yiddish Poem in America—1923: Anthology) (1923). There is no volume of Margolin's poems in English translation, although one by Shirley Kumove is reportedly in progress. However, a number of translations of Margolin's poems have been published in English anthologies and journals. Translations by Adrienne Rich can be found in *A Treasury of Yiddish Poetry* (1969), edited by Irving Howe and Eliezer Greenberg; by Marcia Falk in the *Penguin Book of Modern Yiddish Verse* (1987), edited by Howe, Ruth R. Wisse, and Khone Shmeruk; by Adrienne Cooper in *The Tribe of Dina: A Jewish Women's Anthology* (1989), edited by Melanie Kaye/Kantrowitz and Irena Klepfisz; by Aaron Kramer in *A Century of Yiddish Poetry* (1989); by Joseph Leftwich in *The Golden Peacock: An Anthology of Yiddish Poetry* (1939); and by Ruth Whitman in *An Anthology of Modern Yiddish Poetry: Bilingual Edition* (1995).

Novershtern's introduction to *Lider* (Poems) (1991), " 'Who Would Have Believed That a Bronze Statue Can Weep': The Poetry of Anna Margolin," translated from the Yiddish by Robert Wolf, provides an excellent critical assessment of Margolin's life and work. More limited biographical and bibliographical information is available in Yiddish from a contemporary's point of view in Zalmen Reyzen's entry on "Lebensboym, Roza (Anna Margolin)," in the *Leksikon fun der yidisher literatur, prese, un filologye*, volume 2 (1927), while Mordechai Yafe's entry on Margolin in the *Leksikon fun der nayer yidisher literatur*, volume 5 (1963), provides a retrospective account. In English, Sarah Silberstein Swartz's article in *Jewish Women in America: An Historical Encyclopedia* (1997), edited by Paula Hyman and Deborah Dash Moore, is a succinct treatment of Margolin's life. Anita Norich's entry on Yiddish literature in *Jewish Women in America: An Historical Encyclopedia* places Margolin in the context of other women writers. Adrienne Cooper's note prefacing her translations in *The Tribe of Dina* is informative. Norma Fain Pratt's article "Anna

Margolin's *Lider*: A Study in Women's History, Autobiography, and Poetry," *Studies in American Jewish Literature* 3 (1983), reads Margolin's biography through her poems. Two articles by Kathryn Hellerstein, "From *Ikh* to *Zikh*: The Journey from 'I' to 'Self' in Yiddish Poems by Women," *Gender and Text in Modern Hebrew and Yiddish Literature* (1992), edited by Naomi B. Sokoloff, Anne Lapidus Lerner, Anita Norich, and "Translating as a Feminist: Looking at Anna Margolin," *Prooftexts* (Winter 2000), consider Margolin's poems critically.

Moyshe Nadir

Moyshe Nadir is said to have published one book in English, *Peh el peh* (Mouth to Mouth), and translated Sholem Aleichem's comedy *Shver tsu zayn a yid* (It's Hard to Be a Jew) into English. His many books in Yiddish include a dramatic verse comedy—*Rivington strit: Poeme* (Rivington Street: Long Poem) (1936); a translation of a play by G. Hauptmann—*Der ayngezunkener glok: drama in finf akten* (The Sunken Bell: Drama in Five Acts) (1929); critical essays—*Mayne hent hobn fargosen dos dozike blut: vegn bikher un teater* (My Hands Have Spilled This Very Blood: About Books and Theater) (1919); *Humor, kritik, lirik: fragmentn fun farshtarbetn tsu der karakteristik un zikhrones* (Humor, Criticism, Lyrics: Fragments That Characterize and Memorialize the Dead), edited by Shmuel Rozshanski (1971); journals and miscellanies edited by Nadir—*Der yidisher gazlen* (The Jewish Bandit) (1910–11) and *Fun mentsh tsu mentsh* (From Person to Person) (1916, 1919); many volumes of stories, poems, and parodies—*Mayselekh mit a moral: un oysgetrakhte zakhn* (Tales with a Moral and Imagined Things), *In vildn vertervald* (In the Wild Wordwoods), and *Kum shpatsiren gelibte, un fliterflirt* (Come Stroll, Beloved, and Flirt) (all published in 1919); *Moyshe nadirs zeks bikher* (Moyshe Nadir's Six Books) (1928); the posthumous *Moyde-ani: lider un proze, 1936–1943* (I Confess: Poems and Prose) (1944), which includes a foreword by the poet L. Faynberg and an autobiographical introduction by Nadir himself; *Nadirizmen: aforizmen, paradoksn, vertshpil, poetishe fraze* (Nadirisms: Aphorisms, Paradoxes, Wordplay, Poetic Phrases), edited by the Yiddish actor Hertz Grosbard (1973); and *A tog in a gortn* (A Day in a Garden), (1975).

In Yiddish, biographical information is found in the general references: Zalmen Reyzen's *Leksikon fun der yidisher literatur, prese, un filologye*, volume 2 (1927), Borekh Rivkin's *Yidishe dikhter in amerike* (Yiddish Poets in America) (1947), and Leyb Vaserman's article on Nadir in *Leksikon fun der nayer yidisher literatur*, volume 6 (1965), which includes a bibliography. In English, Irving Howe's *World of Our Fathers* (1976) treats Nadir in passing, while Ruth R. Wisse's *A Little Love in Big Manhattan: Two Yiddish Poets* (1988) presents a fuller picture of the writer.

Sidney L. Nyburg

Sidney L. Nyburg published several works of fiction: *The Final Verdict: Six Stories of Men and Women* (1915); *The Conquest* (1916); *The Chosen People* (1917); *The Gates of Ivory* (1920); and, about Baltimore, *The Buried Rose: Legends of Old Baltimore* (1932). As Stanley F. Chyet, in a most useful introduction to a 1985 reprint of *The Chosen People*, observes, only that book "is of particular Jewish interest." Nyburg's article "Jewish Ideals in a Changing World," *Menorah Journal* 4.2 (April 1918), is, however, astute and interesting. For biographical information, in a very lean field, Chyet relies on *The National Cyclopedia of American Biography*, volume 147 (1965). Otherwise, little is easily available on Nyburg.

Joseph Opatoshu

Midway through Joseph Opatoshu's life and career, the most prestigious Yiddish publisher in Vilna, B. Kletskin, issued a multivolume collection of all the author's works, *Ale verk fun Yoysef Opatoshu* (1928), from the tenth volume of which the two stories in this anthology are drawn. An edition of selected works, *Gezamlte verk* (1926–36), appeared around the same time. Opatoshu continued to publish for decades after that, such as *Der letster oyfshtand: roman in tsvey bikher* (The Last Revolt: A Novel in Two Books) (1948–55) and *Ven poyln iz gefaln* (When Poland Fell) (1943). Opatoshu's *Yidish un yidishkayt: eseyen* (Yiddish and Jewishness: Essays) appeared in 1949, and *Yidn-legende: un andere dertseylungen* (Legends of the Jews and Other Stories), in 1951.

In English translation, Opatoshu's 1917 novella *Romance of a Horse Thief*, translated by David Roskies, is found in *A Shtetl and Other Yiddish Novellas* (1986), edited by Ruth R. Wisse. Two short stories, *May the Temple Be Restored* and *The Eternal Wedding Gown*, translated by Bernard Guilbert Guerney, are in Irving Howe and Eliezer Greenberg's *Treasury of Yiddish Stories* (1973). A collection of Opatoshu's short fiction, *A Day in Regensburg*, was translated by Jacob Sloan (1968). Moshe Spiegel's translation of the 1948–55 novel *The Last Revolt* (1952, 1956) followed upon Isaac Goldberg's translation of the 1922 novel *In Polish Woods* (1938).

Much has been written about Opatoshu in Yiddish. Nachman Mayzel wrote a biography, *Yosef Opatoshu: zayn lebn un shafn* (Joseph Opatoshu: His Life and Creation) (1937). *Opatoshu bibliografye* (Opatoshu Bibliography) (1947) provides a thorough listing of his works and of works about him in Yiddish. The entries in Zalmen Reyzen's *Leksikon fun der yidisher literatur, prese, un filologye* (1928) and in *Leksikon fun der nayer yidisher literatur*, volume 1 (1956), provide summaries of the biography and the bibliography.

In English, Howe and Greenberg's introductory material in *A Treasury of Yiddish Stories* (1973) presents a brief note on Opatoshu and a discussion of his work in the context of Yiddish fiction, and Howe's chapter on "The Yiddish Word" in *World of Our Fathers* (1976) expands upon this topic. Opatoshu makes numerous appearances in Wisse's *A Little Love in Big Manhattan: Two Yiddish Poets*

(1988), which brings him to life among his contemporaries.

Avrom Reyzen

At least two comprehensive editions of Reyzen's writings were published during his lifetime: the twelve-volume jubilee edition of *Ale verk* (All the Works) (1916–17) and the fourteen-volume *Gezamlte shriftn* (Collected Writings) (1916, 1928). Reyzen published his memoirs, *Episodn fun mayn lebn* (Episodes of My Life), between 1929 and 1935. The short story included here, *Equality of the Sexes,* translated by Max Rosenfeld in *New Yorkish and Other American Yiddish Stories* (1995), was first published as *Glaykhkayt* (Equality), in *Gezamlte shriftn* (Collected Writings) (1916). Other stories by Reyzen in English translation include *The Poor Community* and *The Big Succeh,* both translated by Charles Angoff; *Tuition for the Rebbe,* translated by Anne and Alfred Kazin; and *The Recluse,* translated by Sarah Zweig Betsky, all in Irving Howe and Eliezer Greenberg's *Treasury of Yiddish Stories* (1973). Most recently, Curt Leviant has translated, edited, and introduced a collection of Reyzen's short stories, *The Heart-stirring Sermon and Other Stories* (1992).

Poems by Reyzen in English translation can be found in the *Penguin Book of Modern Yiddish Verse* (1987), edited by Irving Howe, Ruth R. Wisse, and Khone Shmeruk; in Howe and Greenberg's *Treasury of Yiddish Poetry* (1969); and in *The Golden Peacock* (1939), edited by Joseph Leftwich.

Detailed biographical and bibliographical information on Reyzen in Yiddish can be found in his brother Zalmen Reyzen's *Leksikon fun der yidisher literatur, prese, un filologye,* volume 4 (1929), and in Elihu Shulman's entry on Reyzen in *Leksikon fun der nayer yidisher literatur,* volume 8 (1981). Leviant's introduction to *The Heart-stirring Sermon and Other Stories* is useful. Howe's *World of Our Fathers* (1976) contextualizes Reyzen within his times.

Joseph Rolnik

Joseph Rolnik's books of poems in Yiddish include, in chonological order, *Afn zamdikn veg* (On the Sandy Road) (1913), *Lider* (Poems) (1915), *Tsum shtern Noyd* (1922), *Lider* (Poems) (1926), *Naye lider* (New Poems) (1935), and *A fenster tsu dorem* (A Window to the South) (1941). His *Geklibene lider* (Selected Poems) came out in 1948, and his *Zikhrones* (Memoirs), in 1954. In 1980, Rolnik's *Geklibene lider* (Selected Poems) was published in Hebrew, with the Yiddish texts facing the translations.

In English translation, five poems translated by Irving Feldman were included in the *Penguin Book of Modern Yiddish Verse* (1987), edited by Irving Howe, Ruth R. Wisse, and Khone Shmeruk, *en face* with the Yiddish poems. Previously, five poems translated by Lucy Dawidowicz with Florence Victor and by Harvey Shapiro were published in Howe and Greenberg's *Treasury of Yiddish Poetry* (1969). In 1939, Joseph Leftwich included his translations of fourteen poems by Rolnik in *The Golden Peacock.*

Biographical and bibliographical information can be found in Yiddish, in *Yoysef Rolnik, der dikhter un zayn lid: ophandlungen vegn zayn shafn* (Joseph Rolnik, the Poet and his Poetry: On his Work) (1961) and in Eugene Orenstein's entry on Rolnik in *Leksikon fun der nayer yidisher literatur,* volume 8 (1981). Howe discusses Rolnik briefly in *World of Our Fathers* (1976), as does Wisse in *A Little Love in Big Manhattan: Two Yiddish Poets* (1988).

Morris Rosenfeld

Numerous editions of Rosenfeld's collected works appeared throughout the twentieth century. For example, *Shriftn* (Writings) came out in six volumes between 1908 and 1910. In 1912, the *Forverts* published *Gevehlte shriftn fun Morris Rozenfeld* (Morris Rosenfeld's Selected Writings) in three volumes. Half a century later, *Oysgeklibene shriftn: lider, esseyen, felyetonen* (Selected Writings: Poems, Essays, Sketches) was published through the YIVO in Buenos Aires (1962, 1969).

The first English translations of Rosenfeld's poems were *Songs from the Ghetto,* with prose translations by Leo Wiener facing the Yiddish texts transliterated into a German typeface (1898, 1900). The facsimile of this landmark volume was reprinted in 1970. *Morris Rosenfeld: Selections from His Poetry and Prose,* edited by Itche Goldberg and Max Rosenfeld, was published in 1964.

Aaron Kramer's *Century of Yiddish Poetry* (1989) contains ten translations of Rosenfeld's poems. Joseph Leftwich included eight translations in *The Golden Peacock* (1939). The *Penguin Book of Modern Yiddish Verse* (1987), edited by Irving Howe, Ruth R. Wisse, and Khone Shmeruk, includes one Rosenfeld poem. Howe and Greenberg's *Treasury of Yiddish Poetry* (1969) contains five translations by Aaron Kramer and by Raphael Rudnick and Joseph Singer.

The best Yiddish sources on Rosenfeld's biography and bibliography are Berl Cohen's entry in the *Leksikon fun der nayer yidisher literatur,* volume 8 (1981), and Zalmen Reyzen's in *Leksikon fun der nayer yidisher literatur, prese, un filologye* (1928). Edgar J. Goldenthal's *Poet of the Ghetto: Morris Rosenfeld* (1998) is the first full-length study in English on this central poet. Shorter treatments of Rosenfeld occur in A. A. Roback's *Story of Yiddish Literature* (1940), Sol Liptzin's *Flowering of Yiddish Literature* (1964), Charles Madison's *Yiddish Literature: Its Scope and Writers* (1968, 1971), Howe's *World of Our Fathers* (1976), and Kathryn Hellerstein's entry on Yiddish poetry in *Jewish-American History and Culture: An Encyclopedia* (1992), edited by Jack Fischel and Sanford Pinsker.

I. J. Schwartz

I. J. Schwartz published at least sixteen books in Yiddish, including poems and translations. His most famous work, *Kentoki: poeme* (Kentucky: Epic), was originally published in Yiddish in 1925. In 1952, he published his autobiographical poem, *Yunge yorn:*

poeme (Childhood). *Geklibene lider* (Selected Poems) came out in 1961, and *Lider un poeme* (Poems and Epics) in 1968.

Schwartz's first publications were translations—of a section of John Milton's *Paradise Lost, Der farloyrener gan-eydn, fragment* (Fragment of *Paradise Lost*), which was published in *Dos naye lebn* (March–April 1911), and a book, *Geklibene verk fun Vilyam Shekspir* (Selected Works of William Shakespeare) (1918). Six years after *Kentoki*, he published a book of his translations of the great medieval Spanish Hebrew poets—*Unzer lid fun shpanye: di goldene shpanish-hebreyishe tkufe: Shloyme Ibn-Gvirol, Moyshe Ibn-Ezre, Yehude Haleyvi* (Our Poetry from Spain: The Golden Spanish-Hebrew Epoch: Solomon Ibn-Gvirol, Moses Ibn-Ezra, Judah Halevi) (1931). Then came *Lider un poemen, Hayim Nahman Bialik* (Poems and Epics: Haim Nachman Bialik) (1935), a volume collecting the great modern Hebrew poet's original Yiddish poems and Schwartz's Yiddish translations of Bialik's Hebrew poems. The following year, Schwartz translated and edited a collection of contemporary Hebrew poetry written in Palestine, *Erets-yisroel, 1936* (The Land of Israel, 1936). Another anthology of Hebrew poetry in Schwartz's Yiddish translations was published in 1942—*Hebreyishe poezye: antologye* (Hebrew Poetry: Anthology). Schwartz published his translations of Bialik's essays, lectures, letters, and two short stories in *Shriftn, Hayim Nahman Bialik* (Writings) (1946). Two collections of traditional Jewish texts, in Schwartz's Yiddish translations, followed: *Sefer ha-shabat; Shabes in yidishn lebn durkh ale doyres* (The Book of the Sabbath: The Sabbath in Jewish Life throughout the Generations) (1947) and *Moyshe rabeynu, loyt medresh un agodeh* (Moses Our Teacher, According to Midrash and Aggadah) (1953). Finally, Schwartz's translations of the poetry and writings of Bialik's contemporary, another major Hebrew poet, Saul Chernikovsky, *Lider un idilyes fun sha'ul tshernikhovski*, were published in 1957.

The only complete translation of Schwartz's American epic is Gertrude W. Dubrovsky's *Kentucky* (1990), which includes an informative critical and biographical introduction. An excerpt from *Kentucky* and *In the End-of-Summer Light*, translated by Seymour Levitan, were published in the *Penguin Book of Modern Yiddish Verse* (1987). Three lyric poems are included in Joseph Leftwich's *Golden Peacock* (1939). Two translations by Etta Blum of selections from *Kentucky* are in Howe and Greenberg's *Treasury of Yiddish Poetry* (1969). Aaron Kramer's *A Century of Yiddish Poetry* (1989) contains four poems by Schwartz.

Dubrovsky's introduction to her translation of *Kentucky* (1990) is the best source in English on the poet's life and work. Howe's *World of Our Fathers* (1976) and Ruth R. Wisse's *A Little Love in Big Manhattan: Two Yiddish Poets* (1988) provide additional information. In Yiddish, the entries in Zalmen Reyzen's *Leksikon fun der yidisher literatur, prese, un filologye*, volume 4 (1928), and Elihu Shulman's entry on Schwartz in *Leksikon fun der nayer yidisher literatur* (1981) provide additional information. Ephrim H. Jeshurin compiled a bibliography of Schwartz's works in *Y. Y. Shvarts, A. Raboy: pionern in amerike* (1964).

Yente Serdatsky

Yente Serdatsky's single collection of novellas, one-act plays, short stories, tales, and legends, *Geklibene shriftn* (Collected Writings) (1913), is hard to come by. Serdatsky's *Unchanged*, translated by Frieda Forman and Ethel Raicus, is included in *Found Treasures: Stories by Yiddish Women Writers* (1994), edited by Frieda Forman, Ethel Raicus, Sarah Silberstein Swartz, and Margie Wolfe. Her article *Di yunge hobn dos vort* (The Yunge Have Their Say) appeared in *Tsukunft* (June 1908). Some of her one-act plays are *Shpileray* (Games), in *Tsukunft* (August 1913), *Ah, di libe!* (Oh, Love!), in the *Forverts* (June 11, 1921), *Di Grine* (The Greenhorn Woman), in the *Forverts* (Oct. 18, 1921), and *Eyferzukht* (Sexual Jealousy), in the *Forverts* (Jan. 23, 1922).

Yiddish sources for information on Serdatsky's life and works include Benjamin Ellis's entry in *Leksikon fun der nayer yidisher literatur*, volume 6; Zalmen Reyzen's entry in *Leksikon fun der nayer yidisher literatur, prese, un filologye*, volume 2 (1927); and two works by Shea Tenenbaum, his memoir, *Ayzik Ashmeday* (1964), and his essay about Serdatsky, *Di kenign fun yunyon skver* (The Queen of Union Square), in his collection *Geshtaltn baym shraybtish* (Figures at the Desk) (1969).

In English, Dorothy Bilik's entry on Serdatsky in *Jewish Women in America: An Historical Encyclopedia* (1997), edited by Paula E. Hyman and Deborah Dash Moore, expands upon the information presented in the notes on Serdatsky in *Found Treasures*. Norma Fain Pratt's article, "Culture and Radical Politics: Yiddish Women Writers in America, 1890–1940," in *Women of the Word: Jewish Women and Jewish Writing*, edited by Judith R. Baskin (1994), discusses Serdatsky in the context of other women writing in Yiddish. Ruth R. Wisse, in *A Little Love in Big Manhattan: Two Yiddish Poets* (1988), presents a memorable sketch of Serdatsky. But it is Sheva Zucker's "Yente Serdatsky, Lonely Lady of Yiddish Literature," *Yiddish* 8.2 (1992), that gives us a clear sense of this author's contribution.

Lamed Shapiro

Four of Lamed Shapiro's short stories in English translation appear in Irving Howe and Eliezer Greenberg's *Treasury of Yiddish Stories* (1973): *White Challah*, translated by Norbert Guterman; *Eating Days*, translated by Bernard Guilbert Guerney; and two translated by Howe and Greenberg, *Smoke* and *The Rebbe and the Rebbetzin*. A fifth story, *New Yorkish*, appears in *New Yorkish and Other American Yiddish Stories* (1995), translated by Max Rosenfeld. David G. Roskies includes Shapiro's *The Cross*, translated by Joachim Neugroschel, and *White Challah*, translated by Norbert

Guterman, in *The Literature of Destruction: Jewish Responses to Catastrophe* (1989). The original Yiddish of *White Challah* was published in Shapiro's *Di yudishe melukhe un andere zakhn* (1919, 1929). This entire collection was translated into English, edited, and introduced by Curt Leviant, under the title *The Jewish Government and Other Stories* (1971).

Biographical and bibliographical information on Shapiro is available in Yiddish in Sh. Miller's "Biografishe notitsn" (Biographical Notes), the introduction to the posthumous volume of Shapiro's work, *Ksovim* (1949); David Roskies' entry on Shapiro in *Leksikon fun der nayer yidisher literatur*, volume 8 (1981); and Zalmen Reyzen's entry in *Leksikon fun der nayer yidisher literatur, prese, un filologye*, volume 4 (1928). In English, Roskies places Shapiro in the context of other pogrom writers in *Against the Apocalypse: Responses to Catastrophe in Modern Jewish Culture* (1984), while Irving Howe in *World of Our Fathers* and Ruth R. Wisse in *A Little Love in Big Manhattan: Two Yiddish Poets* (1988) consider Shapiro in the context of his contemporaries, the Yunge writers.

Fradl Shtok

Fradl Shtok published one collection of short stories in Yiddish, *Gezamlte ertseylungen* (Collected Stories) (1919), and one novel in English, *Musicians Only* (1927). Samplings of her poems were gathered in Yiddish anthologies of the day, such as M. Bassin's *Finf hundert yor yidishe poezye* (Five Hundred Years of Yiddish Poetry) (1917) and *Yidishe dikhterins: anthologye* (Yiddish Women Poets: Anthology) (1928), edited by Ezra Korman.

Shtok's poetry is included in only one of the English anthologies, Joseph Leftwich's *Golden Peacock: An Anthology of Yiddish Poetry* (1939), which presents three poems. Two short stories have been published in English translation: *The Shorn Head*, translated by Irena Klepfisz, in *The Tribe of Dina* (1989), edited by Melanie Kaye/Kantrowitz and Irena Klepfisz, and *The Veil*, translated by Brina Menachovsky Rose, in *Found Treasures: Stories by Yiddish Women Writers* (1994), edited by Frieda Forman, Ethel Raicus, Sarah Silberstein Swartz, and Margie Wolfe.

Sources in Yiddish on Shtok's life and works include Berl Cohen's entry in *Leksikon fun der nayer yidisher literatur*, volume 8 (1981), and Zalmen Reyzen's entry in *Leksikon fun der nayer yidisher literatur, prese, un filologye*, volume 4 (1927). The one strictly biographical source in English is Ellen Kellman's entry on Shtok in *Jewish Women in America: An Historical Encyclopedia* (1997), edited by Paula E. Hyman and Deborah Dash Moore. Three essays present critical views of Shtok's works in the context of other Yiddish writers: Kathryn Hellerstein's "Canon and Gender: Women Poets in Two Modern Yiddish Anthologies," in *Women of the Word: Jewish Women and Jewish Writing* (1994), edited by Judith R. Baskin; Irena Klepfisz's "Queens of Contradiction: A Feminist Introduction to Yiddish Women Writers," in *Found Treasures: Stories by Yiddish Women Writers* (1994), edited by Forman et al.; and Norma Fain Pratt's "Culture and Radical Politics: Yiddish Women Writers in America, 1890–1940," also in Baskin's *Women of the Word*.

The Yankee Talmud

The two selections of the Hebrew parodies of the Talmud are from Gershon Rosenzweig's *The Tractate America* (New York: A. Ginzberg, 1892) and Abraham Kotlier's *The Tractate "The Ways of the New Land"* (Cleveland: J. Zelig, 1893). There is an entry on Rosenzweig in the *Encyclopaedia Judaica* CD–ROM edition, but nothing on Kotlier. Hutchins Hapgood describes Rosenzweig in *Spirit of the Ghetto* (1902), as does Irving Howe in *World of Our Fathers* (1976). A scholarly article in German, "Gerson Rosenzweigs Massekhet Amerika—Eine Talmudparodie," by Dagmar Börner-Klein, in *Frankfurter Judaistische Beitrage* 25 (1998), presents a critical reading of Rosenzweig's parody of the Talmud and of Jewish life in America.

Yehoash

A sampling of Yehoash's prodigious output includes his collected poems, *Gezamelte lider*, issued in a 1st edition in 1907, in a 2nd edition in 1910, and in a 3rd edition in 1917. His three-volume memoir, *Fun Nyu-york biz rehoves un tsurik* (From New York to Rehovoth and Back), was published in 1917. In 1926, a year before his death, Yehoash co-authored with Hayim Spivak *Yidish verterbukh*, a Yiddish dictionary of Hebraic words and names. Yehoash's Yiddish translation of the Hebrew Bible, the Tanakh, *Torah, Nevi'im, uKhetuvim* (Torah, Prophets, and Writings), was published in full only after Yehoash's death, in 1939 and 1941.

Much has been written about Yehoash in Yiddish, but the best place to begin is with Hayim-Leyb Fuks's entry on him in the *Leksikon fun der nayer yidisher literatur* (Biographical Dictionary of Modern Yiddish Literature), volume 4 (1961). This article and the extensive bibliography of Yehoash's works, *Yehoash: A bibliografye fun zayne shriftn* (1944), by Bertshi Witkewitz (Bernard Witt), refer the reader to other articles and books about the poet in Yiddish. Irving Howe, in *World of Our Fathers* (1976), A. A. Roback, in *The Story of Yiddish Literature* (1940), Sol Liptzin, in *The Flowering of Yiddish Literature* (1964), and Charles Madison, in *Yiddish Literature: Its Scope and Major Writers* (1971), all consider Yehoash's place in Yiddish literature. There is, however, no book-length study of Yehoash in English.

Anzia Yezierska

Many of Anzia Yezierska's books are back in print. *Bread Givers: A Struggle between a Father of the Old World and a Daughter of the New*, originally published in 1925, has been reprinted, with an introduction by Alice Kessler-Harris (1975, 1984). *Hungry Hearts*, originally published in 1920, was reissued as *Hungry Hearts and Other Stories* (1985) and then yet again in *How I Found America: Collected Stories of Anzia Yezerskia* (1991). This book opens with an introduction by Vivian Gornick and contains all of Yezierska's published short stories, including the whole of *Hungry Hearts, Children of Loneliness* (1923), and seven uncollected stories. Yezierska's autobiography, *Red Ribbon on a White Horse*, with an introduction by W. H. Auden, originally published in 1950, was reprinted in 1981. The novel *Salome of the Tenaments* (1923) was reprinted in 1992, with an introduction by Gay Wilentz, who included, too, a bibliography of Yezierska's works and works about Yezierska. *The Open Cage: An Anzia Yezierska Collection* (1979) is arranged thematically and draws stories from *Hungry Hearts, Children of Loneliness*, and *Red Ribbon on a White Horse*, as well as three of her stories of old age. This volume also includes a beautiful afterword by Yezierska's daughter, Louise Levitas Henriksen. *Arrogant Beggar* (1927) and *All I Could Never Be* (1932) have not been reissued.

Along with the introductions to the various reissued volumes by Gornick, Wilentz, and Auden, as well as the afterword by Henriksen, Kessler Harris's introductions to *Bread Givers* and *The Open Cage* set Yezierska in a context. Henriksen, with Jo Ann Boydson, wrote a biography of her mother: *Anzia Yezierska: A Writer's Life* (1988). Carol Schoen's *Anzia Yezierska* (1983) is a book-length study of the writer. Sara Horowitz's entry on Yezierska in *Jewish Women in America: An Historical Encyclopedia* (1997), edited by Paula E. Hyman and Deborah Dash Moore, and Tobe Levin's entry in *Jewish American Women Writers: A Bio-Bibliographical and Critical Sourcebook* (1994), edited by Ann Shapiro et al., present her life and work with clarity. Jules Chametzky's entry on Yezierska in *Notable American Women: The Modern Period* (1980) is a concise summary of her life and work. Norma Rosen wrote a novel, *John and Anzia: An American Romance* (1989), a fictional retelling of the romance between John Dewey and Yezierska.

JEWISH HUMOR

Some helpful collections and works are Nathan Ausubel's *Treasury of Jewish Humor* (1951); Sarah Blacher Cohen's *Jewish Wry: Essays on Jewish Humor* (1987); *Encyclopedia of Jewish Humor: From Biblical Times to the Modern Age* (1969), edited by Henry D. Spalding; *Encyclopedia of American Humorists* (1988), edited by Steven H. Gale; Harry Golden's *Golden Age of Jewish Humor* (1972); Henry D. Spalding's *Treasure Trove of American Jewish Humor* (1976); William Novak and Moshe Waldoks's *Big Book of Jewish Humor* (1981); and Rabbi Joseph Telushkin's *Jewish Humor: What the Best Jewish Jokes Say about the Jews* (1992).

Woody Allen

Woody Allen has written, directed, and acted in more than twenty films—his signature films include *Bananas* (1971), *Play It Again, Sam* (1972), and the science-fiction-inspired masterpiece *Sleeper* (1973), from his early comic phase; *Annie Hall* (1977), *Manhattan* (1979), and *Stardust Memories* (1980) from a middle vintage period; works of technical virtuosity like *Zelig* (1983) and *The Purple Rose of Cairo* (1985); and later eclectic work that includes *Radio Days* (1987) and *Mighty Aphrodite* (1995). His collections of essays, stories, and parodies are *Getting Even* (1971), *Without Feathers* (1975), and *Side Effects* (1980). A recording exists of *The Nightclub Years, 1964–1968*.

There is a vast body of critical works on individual films and on Allen's entire work or aspects of it. Biographies include L. Guthrie's *Woody Allen: A Biography* (1978) and Eric Lax's *Woody Allen: A Biography* (1991). A good short appraisal and bio-bibliography is Nancy Pogel's *Woody Allen* (1987). Joanna E. Rapf's entry on Allen in the *Encyclopedia of American Humorists* (1988) usefully lists critical works, including Foster Hirsch's *Love, Sex and the Meaning of Life* (1984) as well as several articles from the *New York Times Magazine*, by Richard Schickel (Jan. 7, 1973), Nathalie Gittleman (April 22, 1979), and Caryn James (Jan. 19, 1986).

Allen has a large following in Europe. Robert Benayoun's *The Films of Woody Allen* (1986) has been translated from the French. Significant recent studies in this country are Annette Wernblad's *Brooklyn Is Not Expanding: Woody Allen's Comic Universe* (1992), Sam B. Girgus's *The Films of Woody Allen* (1993), David Desser's *Jewish American Filmmakers: Traditions and Trends* (1993), and Richard Aloysius Blake's *Woody Allen: Profane and Sacred* (1995). Excellent articles by Gerald Mast, "Woody Allen: The Neurotic Jew as American Clown," and Mark Shechner, "Dear Mr. Einstein: Jewish Comedy and the Contradictions of Culture," are in *Jewish Wry: Essays on Jewish Humor* (1987), edited with a major introduction to the subject by Sarah Blacher Cohen.

Groucho Marx

Grouch Marx's films include *The Cocoanuts* (1929), *Animal Crackers* (1930), *Horsefeathers* (1932), *Duck Soup* (1933), *A Night at the Opera* (1935), *Room Service* (1938), *The Big Store* (1941), *A Night in Casablanca* (1946), and *Love Happy* (1949). Groucho appeared in films without his brothers from 1947 until 1968, none as popular or distinguished as the classic works. His books are *Groucho and Me* (1959); *Memoirs of a Mangy Lover* (1963); *The Groucho Letters* (1967); and *Groucho Marx and Other Short Stories and Tall Tales* (1993), edited by Robert S. Baber.

Biographies are Arthur Marx's *Son of Groucho* (1972); Joe Adamson's *Groucho, Harpo, Chico, and Sometimes Zeppo: A History of the Marx Brothers and a Satire on the Rest of the World* (1973); Charlotte Chandler's *Hello, I Must Be Going: Groucho and His Friends* (1978), a lengthy biography published one year after his death. *Encyclopedia of American Humorists* (1988), edited by Steven H. Gale, can be profitably consulted.

Critical appraisals appear spottily in reviews and appreciations; one of the few book-length treatments is W. D. Gehring's *Groucho and W. C. Fields: Huckster Comedians* (1994), part of a series on popular culture.

FROM MARGIN TO MAINSTREAM IN DIFFICULT TIMES, 1924–1945

Several basic sources of bibliography, biography, works, and critical reception are useful for the following section—among them *Contemporary Authors, Dictionary of Literary Biography*—especially volume 28, *Twentieth-Century American-Jewish Fiction Writers* (1984), edited by Daniel Walden—and *Twentieth Century Authors. Jewish Writers of North America: A Guide to Information Sources* (1981), edited by Ira Bruce Nadel; *Encyclopedia of American Humorists* (1988), edited by Steven H. Gale; *Jewish American Fiction Writers: An Annotated Bibliography* (1982), by Gloria L. Cronin et al.; and *Contemporary Jewish-American Novelists: A Bio-Critical Sourcebook* (1997) by Joel Shatzky and Michael Taub are also helpful. Useful, too, is *Handbook of American-Jewish Literature: An Analytical Guide to Topics, Themes, and Sources* (1988), edited by Lewis Fried.

For understanding the period as a whole, decade by decade and major events, there are for the 1920s Frederick Lewis Allen's *Only Yesterday* (1931), Loren Baritz's *The Culture of the Twenties* (1970), and Lynn Dumenil's *The Modern Temper: American Culture and Society in the 1920s* (1995). For the 1930s, Daniel Aaron's *Writers on the Left* (1961) remains indispensable—Aaron also edited, with Robert Bendiner, *The Strenuous Decade: A Social and Intellectual Record of the 1930s* (1970). Also readable and useful are Richard H. Pells's *Radical Visions and American Dreams: Culture and Thought in the Depression Years* (1973) and a collection of primary documents, *Culture and Commitment, 1929–1945* (1973), edited by Warren Susman.

Studies of the war years and Franklin Delano Roosevelt's presidency abound. Good syntheses are Sean Cashman's *America in the Twenties and Thirties: The Olympian Age of Franklin Delano Roosevelt* (1989) and Michael C. Adams's *The Best War Ever: America and World War II* (1994).

Older historical and sociological works provide valuable background. Morris U. Schappes's *Documentary History of the Jews in the United States* (1952), Oscar Handlin's *The Uprooted* (1951), and *Race and Nationality in American Life* (1957), John Higham's *Strangers in the Land* (1955) and *Send These to Me: Jews and Other Immigrants to Urban America* (1975), and Milton Gordon's *Assimilation in American Life* (1964) remain germane. More recently, Werner Sollors's *Beyond Ethnicity* (1986), Jack Fischel and Sanford Pinsker's *Jewish-American History and Culture* (1992), and Gerald Sorin's *Tradition Transformed: The Jewish Experience in America* (1997) are to be recommended.

For specifically Jewish American concerns in this period, Henry L. Feingold's *A Time for Searching: Entering the Mainstream 1920–1945* (1992) is unsurpassed. This volume is the fourth in a five-volume series, the Jewish People in America, of which Feingold is the general editor, sponsored by the American Jewish Historical Society and published by The Johns Hopkins University Press. An interesting account by a bilingual writer whose Yiddish poetry is represented in this anthology is Judd L. Teller's *Strangers and Natives: The Evolution of the American Jew from 1921 to the Present* (1968).

The condition of Jewish writers broadly considered receives careful attention in Allen Guttmann's *The Jewish Writer in America: Assimilation and the Crisis of Identity* (1971) and in *After the Tradition: Essays on Modern Jewish Writing* (1969), by Robert Alter, one of the deepest thinkers on the subject. How Jews have been represented in literature is covered by Solomon Liptzin in *The Jew in American Literature* (1966), which brings the story up to Abraham Cahan, while Bryan Cheyette's *Between "Race" and Culture: Representations of the Jew in English and American Literature* (1996) carries it further. Louis Harap's three-volume literary history, published in 1987, is valuable. Especially helpful is the second volume, *Dramatic Encounters: The Jewish Presence in Twentieth-Century American Drama, Poetry, Humor*.

Special subjects relevant to the period, dealt with in many serious works, are the Holocaust, women and the family, politics, and aspects of the media. David Wyman's *Paper Walls* (1968) and *The Abandonment of the Jews* (1984) are searing and essential accounts of the U.S. government's failure to act significantly to save Jews. Deborah Lipstadt's *Beyond Belief: The American Press and the Coming of the Holocaust* (1985) provides a revealing analysis of the press, and her later book, though about more recent thought and action, *Denying the Holocaust: The Growing Assault on Truth and Memory* (1993), should be required reading. An unusual work is Herbert A. Straus's *Jewish Immigrants of the Nazi Period in the USA* (1978), which contains bibliography, a guide to oral histories, and articles about emigration from Germany.

Paula Hyman has edited, with Steven M. Cohen,

The Jewish Family: Myths and Reality (1986) and has written *Gender* and *Assimilation in Modern Jewish History* (1995); in addition, she coedited *The Jewish Woman in America* (1976) and, with Deborah Dash Moore, *Jewish Women in America: An Historical Encyclopedia* (1997). Moore is also the author of *At Home in America: Second Generation New York Jews* (1987), another indispensable study. An earlier work to be recommended is Sol Gittleman's *From Shtetl to Suburbia: The Family in the Jewish Literary Imagination* (1978). Also worth consulting is Sylvia B. Fishman's *Follow My Footprints: Changing Images of Women in American Jewish Fiction* (1992).

A group that has aroused great interest, politically and culturally, known as the "New York Intellectuals," was primarily Jewish, with roots in the 1930s and 1940s. Several good studies have been written on this group, among them Alexander Bloom's *Prodigal Sons: The New York Intellectuals and Their World* (1986) and Alan M. Wald's more penetrating political analysis, *The New York Intellectuals: The Rise and Decline of the Anti-Stalinist Left from the 1930s to the 1980s* (1987). Carol S. Kessner's *The "Other" New York Intellectuals* (1994) broadens the category to include less alienated, less secular Jewish intellectuals of the period. Memoirs of participants should be consulted, among them those by William Phillips, an editor of the *Partisan Review*, and Joseph Freeman, *An American Testament* (1936).

Finally, Sarah Blacher Cohen's *From Hester Street to Hollywood: The Jewish American Stage and Screen* (1983) and *Jewish Wry: Essays on Jewish Humor* (1987) are judiciously edited volumes on these subjects. And one must acknowledge the role of sports in Jewish American life and imagination, if only in a single fine essay, Eric Solomon's "Jews, Baseball, and the American Novel," *Arete* 1.2 (Spring 1984).

Hortense Calisher

Hortense Calisher is the author of eleven novels, six collections of short stories, and two autobiographies, *Herself: An Autobiographical Work* (1972) and *Kissing Cousins: A Memory* (1988). Her first book was a collection of stories, *In the Absence of Angels* (1951); some of her better-known novels are *The New Yorkers* (1969), *On Keeping Women* (1977), and *In the Palace of the Movie King* (1993). A good representation of her work is available in *The Collected Stories of Hortense Calisher* (1975) and, in a Modern Library edition, *The Novellas of Hortense Calisher* (1997).

Marcia Littenberg has a succinct biography of Calisher and a bibliography of her work and of works about her in *Jewish American Women Writers: A Bio-Bibliographical and Critical Sourcebook* (1994), edited by Ann A. Shapiro, and there is a useful entry on Calisher by Caroline Matalene in *Dictionary of Literary Biography*, volume 2 (1978). A valuable full-length study is Kathleen Snodgrass's *The Fiction of Hortense Calisher* (1992), and a sampling of critical views can be found in *Jewish Women Fiction Writers* (1998), edited by Harold Bloom.

Edward Dahlberg

Edward Dahlberg's novels are *Bottom Dogs* (1929), *From Flushing to Calvary* (1932), *Those Who Perish* (1934), and *The Olive of Minerva; or, The Comedy of a Cuckold* (1976). Two autobiographical works are *Because I Was Flesh: The Autobiography of Edward Dahlberg* (1964) and *The Confessions of Edward Dahlberg* (1971). Among his other works are *Do These Bones Live* (1941), which was revised as *Can These Bones Live* (1960); *The Sorrows of Priapus* (1957), with drawings by Ben Shahn; and *The Carnal Myth: A Search into Classical Sensuality* (1968). *The Edward Dahlberg Reader* is edited with a good introduction by Paul Carroll (1967), and a useful collection, *Bottom Dogs, From Flushing to Calvary, Those Who Perish, and Hitherto Unpublished and Uncollected Works* (1976) contains his first published story, from 1922.

Ira Bruce Nadel's *Jewish Writers of North America: A Guide to Information Sources* (1981) is a good and convenient source of bibliographical information. Major bibliographies are Harold Billings's *A Bibliography of Edward Dahlberg* (1971) and *Edward Dahlberg: A Tribute* (1970), edited by Jonathan Williams, originally published in *Triquarterly* 19 (Fall 1970), which contains perceptive and interesting appreciations. Charles L. De Fanti, Jr. is the author of *The Wages of Expectation: A Biography of Edward Dahlberg* (1979).

Critical works include *Edward Dahlberg: American Ishmael of Letters: Selected Critical Essays* (1968), edited by Harold Billings, and Fred Moramarco's *Edward Dahlberg* (1970).

Kenneth Fearing

The volumes of Kenneth Fearing's verse are *Angel Arms* (1929), *Poems* (1935), *Dead Reckoning* (1938), *Afternoon of a Pawnbroker* (1943), *Stranger at Coney Island and Other Poems* (1948), and *Collected Poems* (1940). Since his death two collections have been published, *New and Selected Poems* (1986) and *Complete Poems* (1994), edited, with notes and introduction and bibliographical material, by Robert M. Ryley.

Fearing's novels and psychological thrillers include *The Hospital* (1939), *Dagger of the Mind* (1941), *Clark Gifford's Body* (1942), *The Big Clock* (1946), and *The Loneliest Girl in the World* (1951). *The Big Clock* was made into a film in 1948, directed by John Farrow and starring Charles Laughton. It has become a cult classic. A remake, *No Way Out*, with Kevin Costner, was released some twenty years later. As a novel it continues in print and is included in *American Noir of the 1930s and 40s* (1997), selected and edited by Robert Polito.

Aside from Mary M. Lay's entry in the *Dictionary of Literary Biography*, volume 9 (1981), which concentrates on plot summaries of the novels, an interesting recent assessment of Fearing is Rita

Bernard's *The Great Depression and the Culture of Abundance: Kenneth Fearing and Nathanael West and Mass Culture in the 1930's* (1995), which traces positions congruent with Walter Benjamin and contemporary theorists of postmodernism. A number of his poems are given intelligent, sympathetic readings and put in context in M. L. Rosenthal's *Modern Poets* (1960), and Fearing's poetry is briefly but usefully discussed in Willard Thorp's *American Writing in the Twentieth Century* (1963).

Daniel Fuchs

Daniel Fuchs published three novels, many short stories, and numerous screenplays. His novels are *Summer in Williamsburg* (1934), *Homage to Blenholt* (1936), and *Low Company* (1937), all reissued as *Three Novels* (1961) and *The Williamsburg Trilogy* (1972). Some of Fuchs's stories are collected in *Stories* (along with works by Jean Stafford, John Cheever, and William Maxwell) (1956); *West of the Rockies* (1971); and *The Apathetic Bookie Joint* (1979). His screenplays or adaptations, often in collaboration with other screenwriters, are *The Big Shot* (1942), *The Hard Way* (1943), *Between Two Worlds* (1944), *The Gangster* (based on his novel *Low Company*, 1947), *Hollow Triumph* (1948), *Criss Cross* (1949), *Panic in the Streets* (1950), *Storm Warning* (1951), *Taxi* (1953), *The Human Jungle* (1954), *Love Me or Leave Me* (1955), *Interlude* (1957), and *Jeanne Eagels* (1957).

Fuchs wrote a warm and informative account of his family life, army service in World War II, and work as a Hollywood writer—with an especially vivid description of Jerry Wald, the Warner Brothers producer he sometimes worked with—in *Contemporary Authors Autobiography Series*, volume 5 (1987). Useful sources of biographical and bibliographical data are in Gabriel Miller's entry on Fuchs in *Dictionary of Literary Biography*, volume 28, *Twentieth-Century American-Jewish Fiction* (1984), edited by Daniel Walden, and the entry in *Contemporary Jewish-American Novelists: A Bio-Critical Sourcebook* (1997), edited by Joel Shatzky and Michael Taub.

An early perceptive article on his fiction is Irving Howe's "Daniel Fuchs: Escape From Williamsburg," *Commentary* (Aug. 1948). More recent full-length studies are Gabriel Miller's *Daniel Fuchs* (1979) and Marcelline Krafchick's *World Without Heroes: The Brooklyn Novels of Daniel Fuchs* (1988).

Jacob Glatstein

The most comprehensive selection of Glatstein's poems is found in *American Yiddish Poetry: A Bilingual Anthology* (1986), edited by Benjamin and Barbara Harshav, with translations by Benjamin Harshav, Barbara Harshav, and Kathryn Hellerstein, *en face* with the Yiddish originals. A fine but smaller selection of his poems, also facing the Yiddish texts, is in the *Penguin Book of Modern Yiddish Verse* (1987), edited by Irving Howe, Ruth R. Wisse, and Khone Shmeruk. English translations also appear in *A Treasury of Yiddish Poetry* (1969), edited by Howe and Eliezer Greenberg, and in other anthologies.

Several book-length translations of Glatstein's selected poems have been published, some with the Yiddish texts facing the English translations. These include Richard Fein's *Selected Poems of Yankev Glatshteyn* (1987), Etta Blum's *Poems of Jacob Glatstein* (1970), Ruth Whitman's *Selected Poems of Jacob Glatstein* (1972), and Barnett Zumoff's *I Keep Recalling: The Holocaust Poems of Jacob Glatstein* (1993). Nathan Guterman's translation of *Ven yash iz gekumen* is called, in English, *Homecoming at Twilight* (1962), and includes a forward by Maurice Samuel. A. Zahaven translated *Ven yash iz geforn* as *Homeward Bound* (1969).

Much has been published on Glatstein in Yiddish, but the student should begin with the entry by Zeyndl Diamant in *Leksikon fun der nayer yidisher literatur*, volume 2 (1958), for biographical and bibliographical basics. In English the only book-length study of Glatstein's life and works is Janet Hadda's excellent *Yankev Glatshteyn* (1980). Benjamin Harshav's introductory essay, "American Yiddish Poetry and Its Background," in *American Yiddish Poetry*, includes a substantial critical treatment of Glatstein's life and work as a modernist. Informative critical articles on particular aspects of Glatstein's work include Leah Garrett's "The Self as Marrano in Jacob Glatstein's Autobiographical Novels," *Prooftexts* 18.3 (Sept. 1998); Kathryn Hellerstein's "The Paradox of Yiddish Poetry in America," *La Rassegna Mensile di Israel* 62.1–2 (Jan.–Aug. 1996); Abraham Novershtern's "The Young Glatstein and the Structure of His First Book of Poems," *Prooftexts* 6.2 (May 1986); and Jan Schwarz's "Yankev Glatshteyn's *Ven yash iz geforn* as a Condition and Redefinition of the American Yiddish Novel," *Yiddish* 10. 1 (1995).

Michael Gold

Gold's best-known work is *Jews without Money* (1930), often reissued and translated into other languages. Other books, mostly stories and collections of articles, are *Life of John Brown* (1924), *The Damned Agitator and Other Stories* (1929), *120 Million* (1929), and *Money* (1929). His articles for the *Daily Worker* and other pieces are in *Change the World!* (1937) and *The Hollow Men* (1941). A useful collection is Michael B. Folsom's *Mike Gold: A Literary Anthology* (1972). His plays include *Hoboken Blues* (1928), *Fiesta* (1929), and, with Michael Blankfort, *Battle Hymn* (1936), which was produced by the Federal Theater Project.

Richard Tuerk, "Michael Gold (Irwin Granich)," *Dictionary of Literary Biography*, volume 28, *Twentieth-Century Jewish-American Fiction Writers* (1984), edited by Daniel Walden, is a good compact life and survey of the work. Daniel Aaron's *Writers on the Left: Episodes in American Literary Communism* (1961) is the best account of the ambience in which Gold flourished and polemicized. Charles Angoff's *The Tone of the Twenties and Other Essays* (1966) can be profitably consulted. The most favorable assessment of Gold in the Cold War era is Michael B. Folsom's "The Education of Michael Gold," in *Proletarian Writers of the Thirties* (1968), edited by David Madden (Folsom's piece also appears in his 1972 anthology, cited above).

Paul Goodman

Of some forty books, including six novels, four collections of short stories, many volumes of poetry and songs and literary theory, eighteen plays, and works on psychology, city planning, education, and other nonliterary subjects, the following should show Paul Goodman at his most interesting and characteristic. *Parents Day* (1951) is a novel with illustrations by his brother Percival, a noted professor of architecture. *The Empire City* (1959) collects three novels set in New York that display his anarchist and libertarian views in lively fashion. Many short stories and poems have been collected and published in volumes edited by Taylor Stoehr: *The Break-Up of Our Camp: Stories 1932–1935* (1978)—which is based on an earlier (1949) edition; *A Ceremonial: Stories 1936–1940* (1978); *The Facts of Life: Stories 1940–1949* (1979); *The Galley to Mytilene: Stories 1949–1960* (1980); and *Collected Poems* (1973), with a memoir by George Dennison. Stoehr has also edited Goodman's essays: *Creator Spirit Come!: The Literary Essays of Paul Goodman* (1977) and *Crazy Hope and Finite Experience: Final Essays of Paul Goodman* (1994).

Goodman collaborated on writing songs with the composer Ned Rorem. Some of these are only in limited editions, with such titles as *Paul's Blues* (1984)—containing songs composed in 1947—and *Rain in Spring* (1956). He also wrote a biography of Franz Kafka, *Kafka's Prayer* (1947). Goodman's nonliterary work brought him fame and occasional notoriety. *Communitas: Means of Livelihood and Ways of Life* (1947) was a thoughtful essay on city planning, written with his brother Percival. *Growing Up Absurd: Problems of Youth in Organized Society* (1960) was perhaps his most influential work. *The Community of Scholars* (1962) dealt critically with higher education in the United States. *Drawing the Line* (1962) collects some political essays. *Making Do* (1963) was very widely distributed and read in paperback editions.

Adam and His Work: A Bibliography of Sources by and about Paul Goodman (1911–1972) is by Tom Nicely. There is no full-scale biography. Partial bibliographies and data on his life are in Kingsley Widmer's *Paul Goodman* (1980) and in *Artist of the Actual: Essays on Paul Goodman* (1986), edited by Paul Parisi. An astute appreciation and analysis of Goodman's significance as a social thinker in urbanized America is in Lewis Fried's *Makers of the City* (1990).

Stanley Kunitz

Stanley Kunitz's books of poems include *Passing Through: The Later Poems, New and Selected* (1995); *Next-to-Last Things: New Poems and Essays* (1985); *The Poems of Stanley Kunitz, 1928–1978* (1979); *The Testing Tree* (1971); *Selected Poems, 1928–1958* (1958), which won the Pulitzer Prize; and *Passport to the War* (1940). *A Kind of Order, a Kind of Folly: Essays and Conversations* (1975) contains reflections both on his own work and on that of other poets. He co-translated from the Russian *Orchard Lamps* by Ivan Drach (1978), *Story under Full Sail* by Andrei Voznesensky (1974), and *Poems of Akhmatova* (1973).

Much of his work has been in editing. He edited *The Essential Blake* (1987), *Poems of John Keats* (1964), and The Yale Series of Younger Poets (1969–77). He was an editor of the volumes on *American Authors, 1600–1900, A Biographical Dictionary of American Literature* (1938), *Twentieth-Century Authors: A Biographical Dictionary of Modern Literature* (1942, 1961), and *Twentieth-Century Authors: First Supplement* (1955)—all good sources for American Jewish authors as well.

Books about Kunitz's work are Marie Henault's *Stanley Kunitz* (1980) and, by a fellow poet, Gregory Orr's *Stanley Kunitz: An Introduction to the Poetry* (1985). *A Celebration for Stanley Kunitz: On His Eightieth Birthday* (1986), edited by Howard Moss, contains contributions by other poets and former students. Mark Wunderlich's "Interview with Stanley Kunitz," *American Poet* (Fall 1997), appears on the web site of the American Academy of Poets.

Meyer Levin

Meyer Levin's work over fifty years reflects his three large interests: Chicago, where he grew up and worked as a reporter; Judaism and the Holocaust; and Israel and Zionism—with the diary of Anne Frank as a fourth concern that dominated much of his later life. His first and second novels, *Reporter* (1929) and *Frankie and Johnnie: A Love Story* (1930, revised as *The Young Lovers* in 1952), are Chicago stories, as are *The Old Bunch* (1937) and his most popular book, *Compulsion* (1956)—the story of the Leopold and Loeb case, later made into a film. *Citizens* (1940) is a documentary report on the 1937 killing of ten strikers on the picket line at Republic Steel in Chicago. His books on Judaism, broadly considered, include *The Golden Mountain* (1932), tales of the Baal-Shem-Tov, later republished as *Hasidic Tales* (1966); *The Story of a Synagogue* (1959); and *Eva* (1959), the story of a Holocaust survivor. He co-authored *The Story of the Jewish Way of Life* (1959) and *God and the Story of Judaism* (1962). His Zionist or Israel-based work includes *My Father's House* (1947)—the story of Jewish survivors' efforts to reach Palestine—*The Story of Israel* (1967), *The Settlers* (1972), and *The Harvest* (1978).

His deep involvement with Anne Frank, whose diary he brought to the world's attention, and what he viewed as the misrepresentation of her life and fate—the playing down of her Jewishness—in the Broadway play is evident in *The Fanatic* (1964), a fictionalized account of the issues, and in the aptly titled *Obsession* (1973), a more straightforwardly autobiographical account. His own play, *Anne Frank*, was performed in Israel in 1966 and at Brandeis University in 1972. He also dramatized *Compulsion* in 1957 and produced five mostly Zionist-oriented screenplays.

Basic bibliography and a good short account of his life, work, and reception are contained in Alyce Sands Miller's entry in *Dictionary of Literary Biography*, volume 9, *American Novelists 1910–1950* (1981), supplemented by Mashey M. Bernstein's *Dictionary of Literary Biography*, volume 28, *Twentieth-Century American-Jewish Fiction Writers* (1984).

Useful critical appraisals are in Sol Liptzin's *The Jew in American Literature* (1966); Allen Guttmann's *The Jewish Writer in America* (1971); Bruno Weiser Varon's "The Haunting of Meyer Levin," *Midstream* 22 (1976); Samuel I. Bellman's "The Literary Creativity of Meyer Levin," *Jewish Book Annual* (1975); and Webster Schott's "Meyer Levin: A Novel and a Talk," *New York Times Book Review* (Feb. 19, 1978). An important recent work is Ralph Melnick's *The Stolen Legacy of Anne Frank: Meyer Levin, Lillian Hellman, and the Staging of the Diary* (1997).

Ludwig Lewisohn

Ludwig Lewisohn was incredibly productive over the course of his long life, so one can list only a selection of his most interesting and representative works. The 1984 *Dictionary of Literary Biography*, volume 28 (on twentieth-century Jewish American authors) entry by Ralph Melnick lists forty-one books (novels, memoirs, literary studies, polemics), thirty-five "other" (translations, anthologies, introductions and editions, monographs), and fifty-five selected periodical publications. Melnick completes the monumental task of surveying Lewisohn's work in his indispensable two-volume *The Life and Work of Ludwig Lewisohn* (1998). A representative sampling of Lewisohn's work should include his first (and badly received) novel, The *Broken Snare* (1908); but his most important novels are *Don Juan* (1923), *The Case of Mr. Crump* (1926)—republished as *The Tyranny of Sex: The Case of Mr. Crump* (1947)—and *The Island Within* (1928), which was originally published in England in 1927 as *The Defeated* and is regarded by many critics as his most significant work. His important autobiographical works are *Up Stream: An American Chronicle* (1922), *Israel* (1925), and *Mid-Channel: An American Chronicle* (1929). Works on Judaism, Zionism, and Jewishness include *A Jew Speaks: An Anthology from Ludwig Lewisohn* (1931), edited by James Waterman Wise, *The American Jew: Character and Destiny* (1950), and *What Is This Jewish Heritage?* (1954; rev. ed. 1964). He also has books on American literature, German literature and drama, and French poets.

Besides Melnick's biography, mentioned above, there is also a useful review of the life and work in Seymour Lainoff's *Ludwig Lewisohn* (1982). Milton Hindus is a major commentator on Lewisohn, in his introduction to *What Is This Jewish Heritage?* (rev. ed. 1964) and in "Ludwig Lewisohn: From Assimilation to Zionism," *Jewish Frontier* 3 (Feb. 1964). David Singer has published three significant articles, "Ludwig Lewisohn and Freud: The Zionist Therapeutics," *Psychological Review* 58 (Summer–Fall 1971); "Ludwig Lewisohn: A Paradigm of American-Jewish Return," *Judaism* 14 (1965); and "Ludwig Lewisohn: The Making of an Anti-Communist," *American Quarterly* 23 (Dec. 1971). A fine appraisal of Lewisohn's work, especially of *The Island Within*, is Evelyn Avery's "Ludwig Lewisohn," *Dictionary of Literary Biography*, volume 9, *American Novelists 1910–1945* (1981). Very important and interesting chapters on Lewisohn are in Werner Sollors's *Beyond Ethnicity* (1986) and Susanne Klingenstein's *Jews in the American Academy, 1900–1940: The Dynamics of Intellectual Assimilation* (1991).

Letters and other papers of Lewisohn's are held at the Columbia University library and in libraries at Hebrew Union College in Cincinnati, Brandeis, and the College of Charleston.

A. Leyeles

The most extensive representation of A. Leyeles's poems appears in *American Yiddish Poetry: A Bilingual Anthology* (1986), edited by Benjamin and Barbara Harshav, in English translations by Benjamin and Barbara Harshav facing the Yiddish originals. The selection spans his entire career. This same anthology also includes selections of Leyeles's prose, written in collaboration with Yankev Glatshteyn and B. Minkoff, translated by Anita Norich and Benjamin Harshav as "Documents of Introspectivism (1919–1947)." The *Penguin Book of Modern Yiddish Verse* (1987), edited by Irving Howe, Ruth R. Wisse, and Khone Shmeruk, includes three poems, translated by Leonard Wolf and by John Hollander. Leyeles is represented with one poem in Aaron Kramer's *A Century of Yiddish Poetry* (1989), two poems tranlated by John Hollander in Irving Howe and Eliezer Greenberg's *Treasury of Yiddish Poetry* (1969), and five poems in Joseph Leftwich's *The Golden Peacock* (1939).

In Yiddish, his books of poems are *Labirint* (Labyrinth) (1918), *Yungharbst* (Young Autumn) (1922), *Rondeaux un andere lider* (Rondeaux and Other Poems) (1926), *Fabius Lind* (1937), *A yid oyfn yam* (A Jew at Sea) (1947), *Baym fus fun barg* (At the Foot of the Mountain) (1957), and *Amerike un ikh* (America and I) (1963). His verse dramas include *Shlomo Molkho* (1926) and *Asher Lemlen* (1928). His essays are collected in *Velt un vort* (World and Word) (1958).

Benjamin Harshav's introductory essay, "American Yiddish Poetry and Its Background," and biographical notes in *American Yiddish Poetry* provide the best critical assessment in English of Leyeles and his work. Sol Liptzin writes informatively on Leyeles in *The Maturing of Yiddish Literature* (1970); his entry ("Aaron Glanz") in the CD–ROM edition of *Encyclopaedia Judaica* is also useful. In Yiddish, biographical and bibliographical information is found in Mordkhe Yafe and Hayim-Leyb

Fuks's entry on Leyeles in *Leksikon fun der nayer yidisher literatur*, volume 5 (1963). Shorter critical discussions of Leyeles are found in Howe's *World of Our Fathers*, Charles Madison's *Yiddish Literature: Its Scope and Major Writers* (1971), and Ruth R. Wisse's *A Little Love in Big Manhattan* (1988).

Arthur Miller

Arthur Miller is mostly known and celebrated for his numerous and well-received plays, written and produced over six decades. The best-known—and often revived—are *All My Sons* (1947), *Death of a Salesman* (1949), *The Crucible* (1953), and *A View from the Bridge* (1955). Plays that deal with Jewish and Holocaust themes include *Incident at Vichy* (1964), *Playing for Time* (1985)—a dramatization of Fania Fénelon's 1977 book, later a television film, about her time at Auschwitz—and *Broken Glass* (1994). There is an early *Collected Plays* (1958) and *The Portable Arthur Miller* (1971), with an introduction by Harold Clurman, updated with an introduction by Christopher Bigsby in 1995.

Miller's books, in addition to the published versions of many of his plays, include the novel *Focus* (1945), attacking anti-Semitism (a 1984 edition has an introduction by Miller); *I Don't Need You Any More: Stories by Arthur Miller* (1967); and an autobiography, *Timebends: A Life* (1987). There are also *Arthur Miller and Company: Arthur Miller Talks about His Work in the Company of Actors, Designers, Directors, Reviewers and Writers* (1990), edited by Christopher Bigsby; and *The Theatre Essays of Arthur Miller* (1994), edited by Robert A. Martin, with an introduction by Martin and a foreword by Miller.

Most criticism deals with his work for the theatre. Recent studies include David Savran's *Communists, Cowboys, and Queers: The Politics of Masculinity in the Work of Arthur Miller and Tennessee Williams* (1992); and Alice Griffin's *Understanding Arthur Miller* (1996), a treatment of most of his plays. An older work by an astute critic worth consulting is Benjamin Nelson's *Arthur Miller: Portrait of a Playwright* (1970). The *Cambridge Companion to Arthur Miller* (1997) includes an essay on "The Holocaust, the Depression, and McCarthyism: Miller in the Sixties," by Janet N. Balakian; an article by Malcolm Bradbury on Miller's fiction; and an extensive, up-to-date bibliographical essay by Susan Haedicke.

Clifford Odets

Clifford Odets's most characteristic plays of the 1930s—*Waiting for Lefty* (1934), *Awake and Sing!* (1935), *Till the Day I Die* (1935), *Paradise Lost* (1935), *Golden Boy* (1937), and *Rocket to the Moon* (1937)—are all in the Modern Library edition *Six Plays of Clifford Odets* (1939), with a preface by the author. Later plays in published form are *Clash by Night* (1942), *The Big Knife* (1949), and *The Country Girl* (1951).

His screenplays are *The General Died at Dawn* (1936), *None but the Lonely Heart* (1944), *Deadline at Dawn* (1946), *Humoresque* (1946), *Sweet Smell of Success* (1957), *The Story on Page One* (1960), and *Wild the Country* (1961).

The Time Is Ripe: The 1940 Journal of Clifford Odets, with an introduction by William Gibson, was not published until 1988 and is a fascinating document, with its view of Odets's state of mind on the eve of his final departure for Hollywood.

Clifford Odets: An Annotated Bibliography (1990) by Robert Cooperman is very useful. William W. Demasthes's *Clifford Odets: A Research and Production Sourcebook* (1991) is equally important for production information. Worth consulting are the *Dictionary of Literary Biography*, volume 7, *Twentieth-Century American Dramatists* (1981) and *Dictionary of Literary Biography*, volume 26, *American Screenwriters* (1984).

Critical Essays on Clifford Odets (1991), edited by Gabriel Miller, contains good appraisals in an accessible form, but the best are still by Harold Clurman, Odets's colleague and principal director at the Group Theater in the 1930s, in his introduction to a re-issue of *"Waiting for Lefty" and Other Plays* (1993) and in *The Fervent Years* (1975), his brilliant and readable re-creation of the Group and its significance.

S. J. Perelman

A good place to start appreciating S. J. Perelman is *The Best of S. J. Perelman* (1947) and *The Most of S. J. Perelman* (1958, 1980), a collection of 123 pieces, with a foreword by Dorothy Parker. A string of books followed his first, *Dawn Ginsbergh's Revenge* (1929), whose titles give a good indication of his wry, punning, often sardonic wit: *Parlor, Bedlam and Bath* (1930), with Quentin Reynolds; *Crazy Like a Fox* (1944); *Acres and Pains* (1947), debunking the pleasures of country life; and *Westward Ha! or, Around the World in Eighty Clichés* (1948), one of his many comic travel books. There are also *The Ill-Tempered Clavichord* (1952), *The Road to Miltown; or, Under the Spreading Atrophy* (1957), *The Rising Gorge* (1961), and *Baby, It's Cold Inside* (1970).

Of the eight plays he wrote or collaborated on, only *One Touch of Venus* (1943), co-authored with Ogden Nash, music by Kurt Weill, was a real success, although *Sweet Bye and Bye* (1946), co-written with Al Hirschfeld (who did wonderful caricatures and illustrations for many of Perelman's works), music by Vernon Duke, lyrics by Ogden Nash, is fine. He also wrote or collaborated on eleven screenplays, of which *Monkey Business* (1931) and *Horse Feathers* (1932), early vehicles for the Marx Brothers, and *Around the World in Eighty Days*—for which he shared an Academy Award—are notable.

Steven H. Gale's "Sidney Joseph Perelman: Twenty Years of American Humor," *Bulletin of Bibliography* 29 (Jan.–March 1972), lists books and short essays between 1940 and 1960. Gale updates this to include almost all of Perelman's publications as well as critical and scholarly assessments in *S. J. Perelman: An Annotated Bibliography* (1986). There is a biography by Dorothy Hermann, *S. J. Perelman: A Life* (1986). *The Last Laugh* (1981) contains some autobiographical material, along with an introduction by Paul Theroux; and Jay Martin's *Nathanael West: The Art of His Life* (1970) contains much on Perelman and his wife, Laura, who was West's sister. *Don't Tread on Me: The Selected Letters of S. J. Perelman* (1987) is edited by Prudence Crowther.

Douglas Fowler's entry on Perelman in *Encyclopedia of American Humorists* (1988) is a good brief account, as is Steven H. Gale's entry in *Dictionary of Literary Biography*, volume 11, *American Humorists, 1800–1950* (1982). Gale has also edited *S. J. Perelman: Critical Essays* (1991). Fowler has a good short bio-critical study in *S. J. Perelman* (1982).

Among good articles by serious critics are Robert Alter's "Jewish Humor and the Domestication of Myth," in *Veins of Humor* (1972), edited by Harry Levin; Louis Hasley's "The Kangaroo Mind of S. J. Perelman," *South Atlantic Quarterly* 72 (Winter 1973); J. A. Ward's "The Hollywood Metaphor: The Marx Brothers, S. J. Perelman, Nathanael West," *Southern Review* 12 (July 1976), and Sanford Pinsker's "Jumping on Hollywood's Bones: How S. J. Perelman and Woody Allen Found It at the Movies," *Midwest Quarterly* 21.3 (Spring 1980).

The following tributes upon his death are noteworthy: Russell Davies's "S. J. Perelman: 1904–1979," *New Statesman* 98 (Oct. 26, 1979); and Woody Allen, Caskie Sinnet, and John Hollander's "Perelman's Revenge, or the Gift of Providence, Rhode Island," *Listener* 102 (Nov. 15, 1979).

Charles Reznikoff

Among Charles Reznikoff's books, many of which he printed and published himself at the beginning of his career, are *Rhythms* (1918); *Poems* (1920); *Uriel Acosta: A Play and a Fourth Group of Verse* (1921); *Nine Plays, Five Groups of Verse* (1927); *By the Waters of Manhattan* (1930); *Jerusalem the Golden, Testimony, In Memoriam: 1933* (1934); *Going To and Fro and Walking Up and Down* (1941); *Inscriptions: 1944–1956* (1959); *By the Waters of Manhattan: Selected Verse* (1962); *By the Well of Living and Seeing and The Fifth Book of the Maccabees* (1969); *Family Chronicle* (1969); and *Holocaust* (1975). *Early History of a Sewing-Machine Operator* (1936) was a collaborative effort with his father and mother, the second part of a family chronicle; a first part had been included in *By the Waters of Manhattan*. *Testimony: The United States 1885–1890: Recitative* (1965) and *Testimony: The United States 1891–1900: Recitative* (1968) are interesting compilations of "found" poem/stories that document individual human disasters from legal records. *The Manner "Music"* (1977) is a novel with an introduction by Robert Creeley. *Poems 1918–1936: Volume I of the Complete Poems of Charles Reznikoff* (1976) and *Poems 1937–1975: Volume II of the Complete Poems of Charles Reznikoff* (1977), edited by Seamus Cooney, were published after the poet's death.

"The Objectivist Poet, Four Interviews," with an introduction by L. S. Dembo, *Contemporary Literature* 10 (Spring 1966), includes an interview with Reznikoff. Milton Hindus published *Charles Reznikoff: A Critical Essay* (1977) and edited *Charles Reznikoff: Man and Poet* (1984), a biographical/critical volume with bibliography. *Selected Letters of Charles Reznikoff, 1917–1976* (1997), edited by Milton Hindus, also has bibliographical material. *The Dictionary of Literary Biography*, volume 28, *Twentieth-Century American-Jewish Fiction Writers* (1984), contains an essay on Reznikoff by Sanford Pinsker.

Edwin Rolfe

Edwin Rolfe's books of poems are *To My Contemporaries* (1936)—reviewed widely by, among others, Kenneth Fearing, Harold Rosenberg, Muriel Rukeyser—*First Love and Other Poems* (1951), and *Permit Me Refuge* (1956). He also published *The Lincoln Battalion: The Story of Americans Who Fought in Spain in the International Brigades* (1939) and was co-author of a mystery novel, *The Glass Room* (1946).

All of these in addition to listings of uncollected poems, reviews of his work, and his many articles for the *Daily Worker, New Masses*, and *Partisan Review* are in Cary Nelson and Jefferson Hendricks's "Edwin Rolfe: A Working Bibliography," *Edwin Rolfe: A Biographical Essay and Guide to the Rolfe Archive at the University of Illinois at Urbana-Champaign* (1990), an invaluable resource. *Collected Poems* (1993), with a long, analytical, and informative essay by the editor, Cary Nelson, is equally important.

Isaac Rosenfeld

Isaac Rosenfeld's output was limited, with much of his work done in reviews and essays for periodicals. The one book he published in his lifetime was the quasi-autobiographical novel of his growing up in Chicago, *Passage from Home* (1946). A collection of his essays is *An Age of Enormity* (1962), edited with an introduction by Theodore Solotaroff. His stories are collected in *Alpha and Omega* (1966).

Bonnie Lyons provides a good appraisal in her entry in *Dictionary of Literary Biography*, volume 28, *Twentieth-Century American-Jewish Fiction Writers* (1984). Mark Shechner edited *Preserving the Hunger: An Isaac Rosenfeld Reader* (1988). The volume includes both a perceptive and illuminating introduction by Shechner and a touching foreword by Saul Bellow. See also Steven J. Zipperstein, "The First Loves of Isaac Rosenfeld," *Jewish Social Studies* 5.1–2 (Fall 1998–Winter 1999), and a forthcoming biography by the same author.

Leo Rosten

Among his many books, Rosten's best-known works are humorous and linguistic. *The Education of H*Y*M*A*N K*A*P*L*A*N* (1937) had a sequel, *The Return of Hyman Kaplan* (1938), and a much later reprise, *O Kaplan, My Kaplan* (1976). *Joys of Yiddish* (1968) has been very popular and influential. It was followed by *Hooray for Yiddish!:*

A Book about English (1982), which offers Jewish wit, humor, vocabularies, and its influence upon English. His *Many Worlds of L*E*O R*O*S*T*E*N* (1964) is aptly named and includes memoirs, social commentary, "and sundry entertainments never before published." He wrote three sociological studies of Hollywood during his time there as a screenwriter, including *Hollywood: The Movie Colony, the Movie Makers* (1941).

Gloria L. Cronin's entry on Rosten in *Encyclopedia of American Humorists* (1988) is an excellent short biography and literary analysis. Her selected bibliography recommends Ellen Golub's entry in *Dictionary of Literary Biography*, volume 11, *American Humorists 1800–1950* (1982), and various reviews of the Hyman Kaplan books. There is no biography; nor are there any book-length studies.

Henry Roth

Henry Roth's *Call It Sleep* was first published in 1934, its best-selling paperback edition in 1960. Of interest is a 1991 reissue of the novel with an introduction by Alfred Kazin and an afterword by Hana Wirth-Nesher. Roth published a small number of stories in the 1950s and 1960s, but no additional novels until the four volumes of *Mercy of a Rude Stream*: volume 1, *A Star Shines over Mt. Morris Park* (1994), and volume 2, *A Diving Rock in the Hudson* (1995), appeared while he was still alive; volumes 3 and 4, *From Bondage* (1996) and *Requiem for Harlem* (1998), appeared posthumously.

His interesting published stories (after some juvenilia), which he sometimes called parables, are *Somebody Always Grabs the Purple, New Yorker* 16 (Mar. 28, 1940); *Petey and Yokee and Mario, New Yorker* 32 (July 14, 1956); *At Times in Flight, Commentary* 28 (July 1959); *The Dun Dakotas: Story, Commentary* 30 (Aug. 1960); and *The Surveyor, New Yorker* 42 (Aug. 6, 1966). A fascinating book that collects Roth's short works, interspersed with revealing interviews with the editor, is *Shifting Landscapes: A Composite, 1925–1987* (1987), edited by Mario Materassi.

Bonnie Lyons is a reliable commentator on Roth's work, life, and reception, in an early study, *Henry Roth, the Man and His Work* (1976), and in her entry on him in *Dictionary of Literary Biography*, volume 28, *Twentieth-Century Jewish-American Fiction Writers* (1984), edited by Daniel Walden. An early bibliography is Debra B. Young's "Henry Roth: A Bibliographical Survey," in the special Henry Roth issue of *Studies in American Jewish Literature* 5 (Spring 1979), which also contains many useful articles.

A classic source of the Roth revival is Leslie A. Fiedler's "Henry Roth's Neglected Masterpiece," *Commentary* 30 (Aug. 1960). Superb articles in the 1980s are Bruce Robbins's "Modernism in History, Modernism in Power," in *Modernism Reconsidered* (1983), edited by Robert Kiely and John Hidebidle, and Wayne Lesser's "A Narrative's Revolutionary Energy: The Example of Henry Roth's *Call It Sleep*," Criticism 23.2 (Spring 1981). In the 1990s some valuable books on Roth were James Berman's *Landscape, Silence, and Revelation: Modes of Symbolic Acculturation in Henry Roth's "Call It Sleep"* (1990); Julie Hopson Eastlake's *The Literary Reputation of Henry Roth* (1990); and a splendid collection, *New Essays on "Call It Sleep"* (1996), edited by Hana Wirth-Nesher. Wirth-Nesher's introduction to the volume develops the importance of multiple languages—chiefly Hebrew, Aramaic, and Yiddish—in the novel, and Werner Sollors contributes an illuminating synoptic essay.

Muriel Rukeyser

Theory of Flight (1935), foreword by Stephen Vincent Benet, was Rukeyser's first book of poems. *U.S. 1.* (1938) and *The Soul and Body of John Brown* (1940) were other early volumes. Among her many books of poems are *The Green Wave* (1948), *Selected Poems* (1951), *Breaking Open* (1973), *The Gates: Poems* (1976), and *The Collected Poems/ Muriel Rukeyser* (1978).

One Life (1957) is a life of Wendell L. Willkie; *Body of Waking* (1958) translates poems from the Spanish of Octavio Paz.

Rukeyser's work has been appearing anew, edited and introduced by younger woman poets. *The Orgy: An Irish Journey of Passion and Transformation* (1965, 1997) has a preface by Sharon Olds. *The Life of Poetry* (1974, 1996) has a new foreword by Jane Cooper and includes bibliographical references. Kate Daniels edited *Out of Silence: Selected Poems/Muriel Rukeyser* (1992), also including bibliographical material. Jan Heller Levi edited *A Muriel Rukeyser Reader* (1994), with a foreword by Adrienne Rich.

The Poetic Vision of Muriel Rukeyser (1980) by Louise Kertesz, foreword by Kenneth Rexroth, is a full-length critical and interpretive study with bibliography. *A World That Will Hold All the People* (1996) by Suzanne Gardinier has a sensitive chapter of the same name which discusses Rukeyser's life and work from a politically sympathetic point of view.

Delmore Schwartz

Delmore Schwartz's books of poems include *Vaudeville for a Princess and Other Poems* (1950), *Summer Knowledge: New and Selected Poems* (1959), *What Is to Be Given: Selected Poems* (1976), and *Last and Lost Poems by Delmore Schwartz* (1979).

Volumes of stories, or of mixed content, are *The World Is a Wedding* (1938, 1948) and *In Dreams Begin Responsibilities* (1938). *In Dreams Begin Responsibilities* (1978), edited and with an introduction by James Atlas, has a somewhat different table of contents from the earlier title.

Shenandoah and Other Verse Plays (1992) is edited and introduced by Robert Phillips.

Selected Essays of Delmore Schwartz (1970), edited by Donald A. Dike and David Zucker, contains an appreciation by Dwight MacDonald.

Letters of Delmore Schwartz (1984) was selected and edited by Robert Phillips; *Delmore Schwartz and James Laughlin: Selected Letters* (1993), edited by Phillips, contains bibliographical material. *Selections. Portrait of Delmore: Journals and Notes of Delmore Schwartz, 1939–1959* (1986) was edited and has an introduction by Elizabeth Pollet.

Some books about Schwartz are *Delmore Schwartz* (1974), by Richard McDougall, which contains a bibliography; *Delmore Schwartz: The Life of an American Poet* (1977), by James Atlas, also with a bibliography; and *The Middle Generation: The Lives and Poetry of Delmore Schwartz, Randall Jarrell, John Berryman, and Robert Lowell* (1986), by Bruce Bawer. *The Heavy Bear: Delmore Schwartz's Life versus His Poetry* (1996) is a published lecture by poet John Ashbery.

Karl Shapiro

Among Karl Shapiro's many books of poems are *Person, Place and Thing* (1942); *V-Letter and Other Poems* (1945); *Essay on Rime* (1945); *Trial of a Poet: And other Poems* (1947); *Poems of a Jew* (1958); *The Bourgeois Poet* (1964); *Collected Poems 1940–1978* (1978); and *New and Selected Poems 1940–1986* (1987). A recent selection is *The Wild Card: Selected Poems Early and Late* (1998), edited by Stanley Kunitz and David Ignatow with a foreword by Kunitz and an introduction by M. L. Rosenthal. Shapiro's two-volume autobiography is *Poet: An Autobiography in Three Parts* (1988). *Contemporary Authors Autobiography Series*, volume 6 (1988), also contains an account of his life as a poet. Some of Shapiro's volumes of essays are *Beyond Criticism* (1953), reprinted as *A Primer for Poets* (1965); *In Defense of Ignorance* (1960); *To Abolish Children and Other Essays* (1968); and *The Poetry Wreck: Selected Essays 1950–1970* (1975).

Bibliographies are *Karl Shapiro: A Descriptive Bibliography, 1933–1977* (1979), by Lee Bartlett, with a checklist of criticism and reviews; *Karl Shapiro: A Bibliography* (1960), with a note by Shapiro. *Karl Shapiro* (1981), by Joseph Reino, contains criticism and interpretation. *The Dictionary of Literary Biography*, volume 48, *American Poets 1880–1945*, has a useful essay by Ross Labrie. *The Contemporary Poet as Artist and Critic* (1964), edited by Anthony Ostroff, contains comments by other poets (Adrienne Rich, Donald Justice, others) on a section of *The Bourgeois Poet* and Shapiro's response. Karl Malkoff's "The Self in the Modern World: Karl Shapiro's Jewish Poems" is in *Contemporary American Jewish Literature* (1973), edited by Irving Malin.

Irwin Shaw

Irwin Shaw was a prolific writer of fiction, plays, and screenplays from the mid 1930s until the 1980s. He made his reputation first as a playwright with the antiwar one-act *Bury the Dead* (1936), followed by an antifascist play, *The Gentle People: A Brooklyn Fable* (1939) (adapted from a story), and *The Assassin: A Play in Three Acts* (1946). His early stories were equally popular, *"Sailor of the Bremen," and Other Stories* (1939), *"Welcome to the City," and Other Stories* (1942), and *"Act of Faith," and Other Stories* (1946). Collections are *Mixed Company: Collected Short Stories* (1950) and *Short Stories: Five Decades* (1984), which includes sixty-three of the eighty stories he had published by then and an appreciative and balanced foreword by Alfred Kazin. His novels include *The Troubled Air* (1951), which attacked the McCarthyism that was blacklisting people working in radio; *Lucy Crown* (1956); *Rich Man, Poor Man* (1970) and *Beggarman, Thief* (1977), which became the basis for a popular television mini-series; *Evening in Byzantium* (1973); and *Nightwork* (1975). These last four novels were collected in *Four Complete Novels* (1981). Probably his best-known novel was *The Young Lions* (1948), the parallel stories of a young Jew in the American army and a German officer during World War II that was made into a film in 1958 starring Marlon Brando as the German. Between 1936 and 1968 Shaw also wrote the screenplays for fourteen films, among them *Commandos Strike at Dawn* (1942), *The Hard Way* (1942, with Daniel Fuchs and Jerry Wald), *Act of Love* (1953), and *Desire under the Elms* (1958).

James R. Giles's "Irwin Shaw," *Dictionary of Literary Biography*, volume 102, *American Short Story Writers*, second series (1991), is a good compact source for the life, work, and reception. Michael Shnayerson's *Irwin Shaw: A Biography* (1989) is a fuller treatment. Notable critical works are John W. Aldridge's *After the Lost Generation* (1951), in which *The Young Lions* is trashed as superficial, and Leslie A. Fiedler's "Irwin Shaw: Adultery: The Last Politics," *Commentary* 22 (July 1956). A judicious view is contained in the full-length study by James R. Giles, *Irwin Shaw* (1983).

Tess Slesinger

Tess Slesinger produced a small body of work—nine stories, two books, eight screenplays for films produced—and though there is not a great deal written about her, her talent and achievement were always recognized and valued. Her books are *The Unpossessed* (1934) and *Time: The Present, a Book of Short Stories* (1935), which was enlarged as *"On Being Told That Her Second Husband Has Taken His First Lover," and Other Stories* (1971). Her stories appeared originally in *Pagany*, the *New Yorker*, *Vanity Fair*, and elsewhere. Her motion pictures are *His Brother's Wife* (1936); the Academy Award-winning *The Good Earth* (1937); *The Bride Wore Red* (1937); *Girls' School* (1938), adapted from her 1935 story *The Answer on the Magnolia Tree*; *Dance, Girl, Dance* (1940); *Remember the Day* (1941); *Are Husbands Necessary?* (1942); and *A Tree Grows in Brooklyn* (1945), with her second husband, Frank Davis.

Kim Flachmann's "Tess Slesinger," in *Dictionary of Literary Biography*, volume 102, *American Short Story Writers, 1910–1945* (1991), is a good basic bibliography. There is no full-scale biography. Critical articles include Shirley Biagi's "Forgive Me for Dying," *Antioch Review* 35 (Summer 1977); Janet Sharistanian's "Tess Slesinger's Hollywood Sketches," *Michigan Quarterly Review* 18 (Summer

1979); and Lionel Trilling's "Young in the Thirties," *Commentary* (May 1966).

Gertrude Stein

If one were to limit a bibliography to about one-fourth of Gertrude Stein's most characteristic and interesting work—stories, poems, plays, operas, correspondence, and essays on a variety of subjects (art, writing and language, money)—the following might qualify: her first published book, *Three Lives* (1909); *Tender Buttons* (1914); *The Making of Americans* (1925), the long novel about her family from which the excerpt in this anthology is taken; *A Lyrical Opera Made by Two to Be Sung* (1928); *Four Saints in Three Acts* (1929), with the composer Virgil Thomson; *How to Write* (1931); *Matisse, Picasso and Gertrude Stein* (1932); *The Autobiography of Alice B. Toklas* (1933), ostensibly the story of her companion, one of her most accessible and certainly most popular books; *Lectures in America* (1935), idiosyncratic lectures on money and other subjects, given on a triumphal tour of the United States; *Everybody's Autobiography* (1937); *Brewsie and Willie* (1946); *The Mother of Us All* (1947); and *Last Operas and Plays* (1949). There is a *Selected Writings* (1946), edited by Carl Van Vechten, whose correspondence with Stein is in *The Letters of Gertrude Stein and Carl Van Vechten, 1913–1946* (1986), edited by Edward Burns. Other letters are in *Correspondence and Personal Essays* (1977). There is also a volume of *Previously Uncollected Writings* (1974).

Robert A. Wilson has compiled *Gertrude Stein: A Bibliography* (1974); Howard Greenfield has written *Gertrude Stein: A Biography* (1973); and there is an unusual photobiography, *Gertrude Stein: In Words and Pictures: A Photobiography* (1994), edited by Renate Stendahl. Ray Lewis White has usefully provided *Gertrude Stein and Alice B. Toklas: A Reference Guide* (1984). Several works deal with the art and literary circles Stein moved in: James R. Mellow's *Charmed Circle: Gertrude Stein & Company* (1974); Janet Hobhouse's *Everybody Who Was Anybody* (1975); John Malcolm Brinnin's *The Third Rose: Gertrude Stein and Her World* (1961, 1987).

Efforts to deal with her large output in small compass are in Michael Hoffman's *Gertrude Stein* (1976) and Bettina Liebowitz Knapp's *Gertrude Stein* (1990). Specific aspects of her life and concerns are dealt with in Norman Weinstein's *Gertrude Stein and the Literature of Modern Consciousness* (1970); J. Rule's *Lesbian Images* (1975); G. F. Copeland's *Language and Time and Gertrude Stein* (1975); M. A. De-Kove's *Different Language* (1983); R. K. Dubnick's *The Structure of Obscurity* (1984); and Diane Souhami's *Gertrude and Alice* (1991).

J. L. Teller

J. L. Teller's four books of poems in Yiddish are *Simboln* (Symbols) (1930), *Miniaturn* (Miniatures) (1934), *Lider fun der tsayt* (Poems of the Age) (1940), and *Durkh yidishn gemit* (In a Jewish Mood) (1975). Forty-five of Teller's poems, the Yiddish text facing the English translations by Benjamin and Barbara Harshav, are published in *American Yiddish Poetry: A Bilingual Anthology* (1986), edited by the Harshavs. Six poems, translated by Grace Shulman, are included in the bilingual *Penguin Book of Modern Yiddish Verse* (1987), edited by Irving Howe, Ruth R. Wisse, and Khone Shmeruk. Three of Teller's poems, translated by Gabriel Preil and Howard Schwartz, appear in *Voices Within the Ark* (1980), edited by Schwartz and Anthony Rudolf. Two of Teller's many political books in English are *Scapegoat of Revolution* (1954) and *Strangers and Natives: The Evolution of the American Jew from 1921 to the Present* (1968).

The entry on Teller in the *Leksikon fun der nayer yidisher literatur*, volume 4 (1961), presents the basic biographical and bibliographical facts. Benjamin Harshav's introductory essay on the Teller poems in *American Yiddish Poetry* presents a rich and nuanced portrait of the poet and his work.

Berish Vaynshteyn (Weinstein)

Berish Vaynshteyn's six books of Yiddish poems are *Amerike: poeme* (America: Long Poem) (1955), *Basherte lider* (Destined Poems) (1965), *Brukhvarg* (Broken Pieces, Debris) (1936), *Homeryad: Poeme* (Homeriad: Long Poem) (1964), *In dovid hamelekhs giter: poeme* (In King David's Domains: Long Poem) (1960), *Lider un poemen* (Poems and Long Poems) (1949), and *Reyshe: poeme* (Reyshe: Long Poem) (1947). He edited *Opklayb: yerlekhe antologye fun lider in farsheydene tsaytshriftn b'meshekh dem fargangenem yor* (Selection: Annual Anthology of Poems from Various Periodicals in the Past Year) (1955). Twenty of Vaynshteyn's poems, in English translation by Benjamin Harshav, Barbara Harshav, and Kathryn Hellerstein, are included in *American Yiddish Poetry: A Bilingual Anthology* (1986), edited by Benjamin and Barbara Harshav, and three poems, translated by Leonard Wolf, are included in the *Penguin Book of Modern Yiddish Verse* (1987), edited by Irving Howe, Ruth R. Wisse, and Khone Shmeruk. Two volumes of Vaynshteyn's works have been translated into Hebrew: *Homeryadah: poemah* (Homeriad: Long Poem) (1964), translation by Naftali Ginton, and *Sefer ha-shirim* (Book of Poems) (1967).

Strangely, there is no entry for Vaynshteyn in the *Leksikon fun der nayer yidisher literatur*. Benjamin Harshav's introductory essay to Vaynshteyn's poems, in *American Yiddish Poetry*, is most informative about the earlier poems. Sol Liptzin provides perspectives on the later poems in *The Maturing of Yiddish Literature* (1970). Leonard Prager's entry on "Weinstein, Berish," in the *Encyclopaedia Judaica* CD–ROM version, is also informative.

Nathanael West

West's novels, all published in the 1930s, are small in number and size, but two of them, *Miss Lonelyhearts* (1933) and *The Day of the Locust* (1939), are regarded by many critics as masterpieces. His other two novels, *The Dream Life of Balso Snell* (1931) and *A Cool Million: The Dismantling of Lemuel Pitkin* (1934), have been published together as *Two Novels by Nathanel West* (1963). There are *The Complete Works of Nathanael West* (1991) and, in the Library of America series, *Novels and Other Writings* (1997), which includes unpublished writings and fragments and letters. This edition is the most up-to-date and is highly recommended.

There are bibliographies by William White, *Nathanael West: A Comprehensive Bibliography* (1975), and Dennis P. Vannatta, *Nathanael West: An Annotated Bibliography of the Scholarship and Works* (1976), with a foreword by Jay Martin. Martin, a major West critic, is the author of *Nathanael West: The Art of His Life* (1970) and editor of *Nathanael West: A Collection of Critical Essays* (1971). Noteworthy critical works on West include Victor Comerchero's *Nathanael West: The Ironic Prophet* (1964); James F. Light's *Nathanael West: An Interpretive Study* (1971); and Randall Reid's *The Fiction of Nathanael West: No Redeemer, No Promised Land* (1971).

Louis Zukofsky

Louis Zukofsky's poems are available in *Complete Short Poetry/Louis Zukofsky* (1991), with a foreword by Robert Creeley, which completes the ongoing body of work previously gathered in *All the Collected Short Poems, 1923–1958* (1965) and *All the Collected Short Poems, 1956–1964*, (1966). *"A"* (1978) is Zukofsky's twenty-four-part poem, composed over nearly fifty years. His translations of the Latin poet Catullus are included as one section in "A." Prose works by Zukofsky include *Prepositions: The Collected Critical Essays* (1968) and *Bottom: On Shakespeare* (1963).

Autobiographical material can be found in *Autobiography* (1970), a volume of fifteen poems set to music by Celia Zukofsky. Some of Zukofsky's letters have been published in *Pound/Zukofsky: Selected Letters of Ezra Pound and Louis Zukofsky* (1987), edited by Barry Ahearn.

There are useful bibliographies in *Louis Zukofsky, Man and Poet* (1979), edited by Carroll F. Terrell. This volume also contains valuable biographical/personal information about the poet and numerous important critical essays. Those by David Schimmel and M. L. Rosenthal have particular reference to Zukofsky's Jewishness. *A Bibliography of Louis Zukofsky* by Celia Zukofsky was published in 1969.

Interesting work on Zukofsky has been appearing. *Zukofsky's "A": An Introduction* (1983), by Barry Ahearn; *Louis Zukofsky and the Transformation of a Modern American Poetics* (1994), by Sandra Kumamoto Stanley; *Louis Zukofsky and the Poetry of Knowledge* (1998), by Mark Scroggins; *Apocalypse and After: Modern Strategy and Postmodern Tactics in Pound, Williams, and Zukofsky* (1995), by Bruce Comens—all suggest that literary sensibilities, which have not always been sympathetic, now may have caught up with the poet's work. Marjorie Perloff's "Barbed Wire Entanglements: The New American Poetry 1930–32" brilliantly supports that idea (www.wings.buffalo.edu/epc/authors/perloff/).

ACHIEVEMENT AND AMBIVALENCE, 1945–1973

Several early, concise, and useful views of mainly postwar Jewish American literature occur in introductions to anthologies: Irving Howe and Eliezer Greenberg's *Treasury of Yiddish Stories* (1954) and *Treasury of Yiddish Poetry* (1969); Saul Bellow's *Great Jewish Short Stories* (1963); Irving Malin and Irwin Stark's *Breakthrough: A Treasury of Contemporary American-Jewish Literature* (1964); Abraham Chapman's *Jewish-American Literature* (1974); Irving Howe's *Jewish-American Stories* (1977); and Howard Schwartz and Anthony Rudolf's *Voices within the Ark: The Modern Jewish Poets* (1980).

More recent anthologies include Melanie Kaye Kantrowitz and Irena Klepfisz's *Tribe of Dina: A Jewish Women's Anthology* (1986); Benjamin Harshav and Barbara Harshav's *American Yiddish Poetry* (1986); Irving Howe, Ruth Wisse, and Khone Shmeruk's *Penguin Book of Modern Yiddish Verse* (1987); Theodore Solotaroff and Nessa Rapoport's *Writing Our Way Home: Contemporary Stories by American Jewish Writers* (1992); and Steven J. Rubin's *Telling and Remembering: A Century of American Jewish Poetry* (1997).

Representative critical studies are Leslie Fiedler's *Waiting for the End* (1964) and *Fiedler on the Roof* (1990); Robert Alter's *After the Tradition: Essays on Modern Jewish Writing* (1969); Allen Guttmann's *The Jewish Writer in America: Assimilation and the Crisis of Jewish Identity* (1971); *Contemporary American-Jewish Literature* (1973), edited by Irving Malin; Ruth Wisse's *The Schlemiel as Modern Hero* (1980); Murray Baumgarten's *City Scriptures: Modern Jewish Writing* (1982); Alan Berger's *Crisis and Covenant: The Holocaust in American Jewish Fiction* (1985); Louis Harap's *In the Mainstream* (1987); Norman Finkelstein's *The Ritual of New Creation: Jewish Tradition and Contemporary Literature* (1992); Alan Berger's *Children of Job: American Second-Generation Witnesses to the Holocaust* (1997); and valuable works by Sanford Pinsker, Mark Shechner, and others. The *Dictionary of Literary Biography*, volume 28 (1984) and others, *Contemporary Literary Criticism*, and *Contemporary Authors* also contain entries on Jewish American writers, as do the Chelsea House collections of criticism, edited by Harold Bloom. Richard Howard's fine collection *Alone with America* (1971) includes essays on Feldman, Ginsberg, Hecht, Hollander, Levertov, Rich, and Simpson.

On the relatively little-studied topic of Jewish American poetry, there is Gary Pacernik's *Memory and Fire: Ten American Jewish Poets* (1989); Jonathan Barron and Eric Selinger's *Jewish American Poetry: A Collection of Essays* (2000); and several thought-provoking essays: Harold Bloom's "The Sorrows of American-Jewish Poetry," *Commentary* (March 1972); John Hollander's "The Question of American Jewish Poetry," *Tikkun* 3.3 (1988); Allen Grossman's " 'The Sieve' and Remarks toward a Jewish Poetry," *Tikkun* 5.3 (1990).

Journals such as *Commentary, Studies in American Jewish Literature, Modern Judaism, Judaism, Prooftexts, Midstream, Tikkun,* and *Jewish Social Studies* can also be consulted.

Among recent works by Sephardic writers are Andre Aciman's *Out of Egypt: A Memoir* (1994); Ruth Behar's autobiographical study, *Translated Woman: Crossing the Border with Esperanza's Story* (1993); Jack Marshall's book of poems, *Sesame* (1993); Victor Perera's autobiographical *Rites: A Guatemalan Boyhood* (1986, 1994); and Stanley Sultan's novel *Rabbi: A Tale of the Waning Year* (1977). The Jewish feminist journal *Bridges* published an excellent issue devoted to *Sephardic Women Writers* (7.1 [Winter 1997–98]).

There are a number of studies on Sephardic Jews in America, such as Marc Angel's *La America: The Sephardic Experience in the United States* (1982) and *Sephardim in the Americas* (1993), edited by Martin Cohen and Abraham D. Peck. David Burns's *Sephardic Studies: A Research Bibliography* (1981) is useful, as is Diane Matza's "A Bibliography of Materials on the National Background and Immigrant Experiences of the Sephardic Jews in the United States, 1880–1924," *The Immigration History Newsletter* 19.1 (May 1987).

Several articles of literary criticism regarding Sephardic American literature have been published in recent years. They include Louise Mirrer's "Reinterpreting an Ancient Legend: The Judeo-Spanish Rape of Lucretia," *Prooftexts* 6.2 (May 1986); and two articles by Ada Savin: "The Burden and the Treasure: Victor Perera's Sephardic Family Chronicle," *Prooftexts: Jewish-American Autobiography, Part 2*, edited by Janet Hadda and Hana Wirth-Nesher, 18.3 (Sept. 1998); and "Sephardic Jewish-American Literature," in *New Immigrant Literatures in the United States: A Sourcebook* (1996), edited by Alpana Knippling.

Saul Bellow

Saul Bellow's major novels include *The Victim* (1947), *The Adventures of Augie March* (1953), *Seize the Day* (1956), *Herzog* (1964), *Mr. Sammler's Planet* (1970), and others. His most recent novel is *Ravelstein* (2000). His short story collections include *Mosby's Memoirs* (1968), *Him with His Foot in His Mouth* (1984), and *Something to Remember Me By* (1991). He also published a play, *The Last Analysis* (1965), and a collection of nonfiction essays, *It All Adds Up* (1994). Gabriel Josipovici edited *The Portable Saul Bellow* (1974).

Biographical sources are Tony Tanner's *Saul Bellow* (1965); Ruth Miller's *Saul Bellow* (1991); Peter Hyland's *Saul Bellow* (1992); a memoir by his long-time agent, Harriet Wasserman, *Handsome Is* (1997); an interview in the *Paris Review Interviews*, 3rd series (1968), and *Conversations with Saul Bellow* (1994), edited by Gloria L. Cronin and Ben Siegel.

Critical studies include Sarah Blacher Cohen's *Saul Bellow's Enigmatic Laughter* (1974); *Saul Bellow: A Collection of Critical Essays* (1975), edited by Earl Rovit; *Saul Bellow: A Mosaic* (1992), edited by L. H. Goldman, Gloria L. Cronin, and Ada Aharoni. Gloria Cronin also assembled an annotated bibliography (2nd ed., 1987).

Irving Feldman

Irving Feldman's poetry collections are *Works and Days* (1961), *The Pripet Marshes* (1965), *Magic Papers* (1970), *Lost Originals* (1972), *Leaping Clear* (1976), *New and Selected Poems* (1979), *Teach Me, Dear Sister* (1983), *All of Us Here* (1986), *The Life and Letters* (1994), and *Beautiful False Things* (2000). A collection of critical essays is *The Poetry of Irving Feldman* (1992), edited by Harold Schweizer.

Allen Ginsberg

Allen Ginsberg's generous output is available in many forms—poetry, journals, interviews, tapes, videos, pictures. His principal poetry collections include *Howl* (1956), *Empty Mirror* (1960), *Kaddish and Other Poems* (1961), *Reality Sandwiches* (1963), *Wichita Vortex Sutra* (1967), *Planet News* (1968), *The Fall of America* (1972), *Collected Poems, 1947–1980* (1984), *White Shroud* (1986), and *Selected Poems, 1947–1995* (1996). Also available are his *Journals: Early Fifties, Early Sixties* (1977), *Journals Mid-Fifties, 1954–1958* (1995), plus some valuable remarks by Ginsberg in Donald Allen's *The New American Poetry* (1960), a revealing interview in *Paris Review Interviews*, 3rd series (1968), and *Allen Verbatim: Lectures on Poetry, Politics, Consciousness* (1974), edited by Gordon Bell.

Biographies include Jane Kramer's *Allen Ginsberg in America* (1969); Barry Miles's *Allen Ginsberg* (1989); Michael Schumacher's *Dharma Lion: A Biography of Allen Ginsberg* (1992); and Steven Watson's fascinating *Birth of the Beat Generation* (1995). *On the Poetry of Allen Ginsberg* (1984), edited by Lewis Hyde, has representative critical essays, and Bill Morgan compiled a bibliography, *The Works of Allen Ginsberg, 1941–1994* (1995). Ginsberg archives are located at Columbia and Stanford universities.

Chaim Grade

Much of Chaim Grade's writing remains untranslated from Yiddish. Nonetheless, his poetry has appeared in anthologies such as Ruth Whitman's *Anthology of Modern Yiddish Poetry* (1966), Irving Howe and Eliezer Greenberg's *Treasury of Yiddish Poetry* (1969), and Howe, Ruth R. Wisse and Khone Shmeruk's *Penguin Book of Modern Yiddish Verse*

(1987). His fiction in English includes *The Well* (1967), *The Seven Little Lanes* (1972), *The Agunah* (1974), *The Yeshiva* (1976), *Rabbis and Wives* (1982), and the richly moving memoir *My Mother's Sabbath Days* (1986). There is a film of *My Quarrel with Hersh Rasseyner* (*The Quarrel*, directed by Eli Cohen, 1992).

Anthony Hecht

Anthony Hecht's books of poetry include *A Summoning of Stones* (1954), *The Hard Hours* (1967), *Millions of Strange Shadows* (1977), *The Venetian Vespers* (1977), *The Transparent Man* (1990), *Collected Earlier Poems* (1990), and *Flight among the Tombs* (1996). He also published critical essays in *Obbligati* (1986), lectures in *On the Laws of Poetic Art* (1995), and various translations.

Critical studies of Hecht are Norman German's *Anthony Hecht* (1989) and *The Burdens of Formality* (1989), edited by Sydney Lea.

John Hollander

Since his first published book of poetry, *A Crackling of Thorns* (1958), John Hollander has published sixteen additional books of poems, his most recent being *Figurehead & Other Poems* (1999). Hollander's other works include *Movie Going and Other Poems* (1962), *Book of Various Owls* (1963), *Visions from the Ramble* (1965), *The Quest of Gole* (1966), *Types of Shape* (1969), *The Night Mirror* (1971), *Town and Country Matters* (1972), *The Head of the Bed* (1974), *Tales Told of the Fathers* (1976), *Reflections on Espionage* (1976), *Spectral Emanations* (1978), *In Place* (1978), *Blue Wine and Other Poems* (1979), *Looking Ahead* (1982), *Powers of Thirteen* (1983), *In Time and Place* (1986), *Harp Lake* (1988), *Selected Poetry* (1993), *Tesserae and Other Poems* (1993), and *The Gazer's Spirit: Poems Speaking to Silent Works of Art* (1995). Hollander is also the author of many critical works, including *Vision and Resonance: Two Senses of Poetic Form* (1975), *The Figure of Echo: A Mode of Allusion in Milton and After* (1981), *Melodious Guile: Fictive Pattern in Poetic Language* (1989), *Rhyme's Reason: A Guide to English Verse* (1989), and *The Poetry of Everyday Life* (1998).

Irving Howe

Besides books on Sherwood Anderson (1951), William Faulkner (1952), and Thomas Hardy (1967), Irving Howe published his literary critical essays in *Politics and the Novel* (1957, 1987, 1992), *A World More Attractive* (1963), *Decline of the New* (1970), *The Critical Point* (1973), and *Selected Writings, 1950–1990*. He cofounded and edited the magazine *Dissent* (1953–93).

He also edited numerous books dealing with literature, politics, society, often from a Democratic Socialist point of view. A major achievement was to edit, singly or with Eliezer Greenberg and others, a string of anthologies of Jewish literature, mainly Yiddish, including *A Treasury of Yiddish Stories* (1954, 1989), *A Treasury of Yiddish Poetry* (1969), *Voices from the Yiddish: Essays, Memoirs, Diaries* (1972), *Jewish-American Stories* (1977), *Ashes Out of Hope* (1978), and *The Penguin Book of Modern Yiddish Verse* (1987). Howe's magisterial *World of Our Fathers* (1976), on East European Jews in America, was followed by two documentary accounts of Jews in America.

Howe wrote an "intellectual autobiography," *A Margin of Hope* (1982), and he appears in a film on the New York intellectuals, *Arguing the World* (1997). A critical biography is Edward Alexander's *Irving Howe: Socialist, Critic, Jew* (1998).

David Ignatow

David Ignatow published *Poems* in 1948. Among his later volumes are *Say Pardon* (1961), *Figures of the Human* (1964), *Rescue the Dead* (1968), *Facing the Tree* (1975), *Leaving the Door Open* (1984), and others, including *I Have a Name* (1996), plus the collections *Poems, 1934–1969* (1970) and *New and Collected Poems, 1970–1985* (1987). Also in print are *The Notebooks of David Ignatow* and *Open between Us*, both edited by Ralph J. Mills, Jr.; *The One and the Many: A Poet's Memoirs* (1988); and selected letters, *Talking Together* (1992), edited by Gary Pacernik. A lively interview with Ignatow can be found in *Paris Review* 21.76 (Fall 1979). *Meaningful Differences* (1994), edited by Virginia R. Terris, contains essays on his poetry and prose.

Shirley Kaufman

Shirley Kaufman has published several volumes of poetry, including *The Floor Keeps Turning* (1970), *Gold Country* (1973), *Looking at Henry Moore's Elephant Skull Etchings in Jerusalem during the War* (1977), *From One Life to Another* (1979), *Claims* (1984), *Rivers of Salt* (1993), and *Roots in the Air: New and Selected Poems* (1996). She co-edited *The Defiant Muse: Feminist Poems from Antiquity to the Present* (1999) and has published selected translations of Abba Kovner, Amir Gilboa, and Judith Herzberg.

Alfred Kazin

Alfred Kazin's books of criticism concentrate on American literature: *On Native Grounds* (1942), *The Inmost Leaf* (1959), *Contemporaries* (1962), *Bright Book of Life* (1973), *An American Procession* (1984), *A Writer's America* (1988), *Writing Was Everything* (1995), *God and the American Writer* (1997). Equally revealing are his own autobiographical writings: *A Walker in the City* (1951), *Starting Out in the Thirties* (1965), *New York Jew* (1978), and *A Lifetime Burning in Every Moment* (1996).

Denise Levertov

Denise Levertov's prolific run of poetry collections makes a poem in itself: *The Double Image* (1946), *Here and Now* (1957), *Overland to the Islands* (1958), *With Eyes at the Back of Our Heads* (1959), *The Jacob's Ladder* (1961), *O Taste and See* (1964), *The Sorrow Dance* (1967), *Relearning the Alphabet* (1970), *To Stay Alive* (1971), *Footprints* (1972), *The Freeing of the Dust* (1975), *Life in the Forest* (1978), *Candles in Babylon* (1982), *Oblique Prayers* (1984),

Breathing the Water (1987), *A Door in the Hive* (1989), *Evening Train* (1992), and *Sands of the Well* (1996).

Levertov's telling essays on poets and poetry can be found in *The Poet in the World* (1973), *Light Up the Cave* (1981), and *New and Selected Essays* (1992). Christopher MacGowan edited *The Letters of Denise Levertov and William Carlos Williams* (1998), and Jewel Spears Brooker edited *Conversations with Denise Levertov* (1998). Levertov also wrote a fine sequence of personal "memories and suppositions," *Tesserae* (1995). Her archive is at Stanford University.

Studies of Levertov's work include Linda W. Wagner's *Denise Levertov* (1967); Harry Marten's *Understanding Denise Levertov* (1988); *Critical Essays* (1990), edited by Linda Wagner-Martin; *Denise Levertov: Selected Criticism* (1993), edited by Albert Gelpi; and a bibliography, *Denise Levertov* (1988), by Liana Sakelliou-Schultz.

Philip Levine

Philip Levine's earlier works include *On the Edge* (1961), *Silent in America: Vivas for Those Who Failed* (1965), *Not This Pig* (1968), *5 Detroits* (1970), *Thistles: A Poem Sequence* (1970), *Pili's Wall* (1971), *Red Dust* (1971), *They Feed They Lion* (1972), *1933* (1972), *New Season* (1975), *On the Edge and Over: Poems Old, Lost, and New* (1976), *The Names of the Lost* (1976), *7 Years from Somewhere* (1979), *Ashes: Poems New and Old* (1979), *One for the Rose* (1981), *Don't Ask Philip Levine* (1981), *Selected Poems* (1984), *Sweet Will* (1985), *A Walk with Tom Jefferson* (1988), *New and Selected Poems* (1991), *What Work Is* (1991), *The Bread of Time: Toward an Autobiography* (1994), and *The Simple Truth: Poems* (1994). *The Mercy* (1999) is Levine's most recent book of poetry.

In 1991 Christopher Buckley assembled an authoritative collection of criticism on Levine and his poetry entitled *On the Poetry of Philip Levine: Stranger to Nothing*.

Ephraim E. Lisitzky

The only volume of Ephraim E. Lisitzky's writings translated into English is his 1949 autobiography, *Eleh toledot adam* (This Is the History of a Man): *In the Grip of Cross-Currents*, translated from the Hebrew by Moshe Kohn, Jacob Sloan, and Gershon Gelbart (1959).

The entry on Lisitzky in the *Encyclopaedia Judaica*, volume 11, provides biographical and bibliographical information. Several essays in *Hebrew in America: Perspectives and Prospects* (1993), edited by Alan Mintz, refer briefly to Lisitzky, as does Gershon Shaked's essay "The Beginnings of Hebrew Literature in America," translated and edited by Evelyn Ben-Shim and Ruth Toker, in *Identity and Ethos: A Festschrift for Sol Liptzin on the Occasion of His 85th Birthday* (1986), edited by Mark H. Gelber.

Norman Mailer

Besides three film scripts, a play based on *The Deer Park*, and miscellaneous work, Norman Mailer's principal writings include *The Naked and the Dead* (1948); *Barbary Shore* (1951); *The Deer Park* (1955); *Advertisements for Myself* (1959); *The White Negro* (1959); *The Presidential Papers* (1963)—essays and commentaries; *Cannibals and Christians* (1964); *An American Dream* (1965); *Miami and the Siege of Chicago: An Informal History of the Republican and Democratic Conventions of 1968* (1968); *The Armies of the Night* (1969); *The Prisoner of Sex* (1971); *The Executioner's Song* (1979); *Ancient Evenings* (1983); *Tough Guys Don't Dance* (1984); *Harlot's Ghost* (1991); *Portrait of Picasso as a Young Man: An Interpretive Biography* (1995); *The Gospel According to the Son* (1997); *The Time of Our Time* (1998).

Useful bibliographies can be found in *Contemporary Authors*, volumes 11–12 (1974) and Andrew Gordon, "Norman Mailer," in *Dictionary of Literary Biography*, volume 28 (1984). Joel Schatzky and Michael Taub's *Contemporary Jewish-American Writers: A Bio-Critical Sourcebook* (1997) is good on critical reception. More extensive biographical matter can be found in Hilary Mills's *Mailer: A Biography* (1982); Peter Manso's *Mailer: His Life and Times* (1985); Carle E. Rollyson's *The Lives of Norman Mailer: A Biography* (1991); and, most interesting, Adele Mailer's *The Last Party: Scenes from My Life with Norman Mailer* (1997), by the former Adele Morales, Mailer's second wife, whom he stabbed, dangerously but not lethally, with a penknife.

Criticism includes *Norman Mailer: A Collection of Critical Essays* (1972), edited by Leo Braudy, which has essays by, among others, Diana Trilling, James Baldwin, Richard Poirier, and an interview by Steven Marcus. *Contemporary American-Jewish Literature* (1973), edited by Irving Malin, contains the fine essay by Helen Weinberg, "The Activist Norman Mailer." Other useful critical works include Huck Gutman's *Mankind in Barbary: The Individual and Society in the Novels of Norman Mailer* (1975); Nigel Leigh's *Radical Fictions and the Novels of Norman Mailer* (1990); Robert Merrill's *Norman Mailer Revisited* (1992), an updating of an earlier 1978 book; and Michael K. Glendon's *Norman Mailer* (1995).

Bernard Malamud

Bernard Malamud's forte, his short stories, appear at their best in *The Magic Barrel* (1958), *Idiots First* (1963), *Pictures of Fidelman* (1969), and *Rembrandt's Hat* (1973), as well as *Complete Stories* (1997). Most readers still consider Malamud's *The Assistant* (1957) his finest novel, along with *The Fixer* (1966), a fictional retelling of the 1911 Beilis blood libel. Other novels are *The Natural* (1952), *A New Life* (1961), *The Tenants* (1971), *Dubin's Lives* (1979), and *God's Grace* (1982). *Talking Horse* (1996), edited by Alan Cheuse and Nicholas Delbanco, collects valuable talks and essays by Malamud. Lawrence M. Lasker edited *Conversations with Bernard Malamud* (1991).

Leslie A. Field and Joyce Field edited *Bernard*

Malamud and the Critics (1970) and *Bernard Malamud: A Collection of Critical Essays* (1975). Other studies include Jeffrey Helterman's *Understanding Bernard Malamud* (1985); *Bernard Malamud* (1986), edited by Harold Bloom; *Critical Essays on Bernard Malamud* (1987), edited by Joel Salzberg; and Edward A. Abramson's *Bernard Malamud Revisited* (1993).

Kadya Molodowsky

In Yiddish, Kadya Molodowsky's major collections of poems are *Kheshvendike nekht: lider* (1927); *Dzshike gas: lider* (1933, 1936); *Freydke: lider* (1935, 1936); *In land fun mayn gebeyn: lider* (1937); *Der melekh dovid aleyn iz geblibn* (1946); a chapbook, *Malokhim kumen keyn yerushalayim: lider* (1952); and *Likht fun dornboym: lider un poeme* (1965). She edited an anthology of Holocaust poems, *Lider fun khurbn: antologye* (1962), and her children's poems were reissued in *Martsepanes: mayselekh un lider far kinder* (1970). Substantial selections from all these volumes in English translation, *en face* with the Yiddish originals, are available in *Paper Bridges: Selected Poems of Kadya Molodowsky* (1999), translated, edited, and introduced by Kathryn Hellerstein.

Molodowsky's children's poems have been translated into Hebrew by the poets Nathan Alterman, Leah Goldberg, Fanya Bergshteyn, and Avraham Levinson, in *Pithu et hasha'ar: shirei yeladim* (1945, 1979), and by Mirik Snir, in *Ugat hapelaim* (The Miracle Cake) (1999).

Molodowsky's fiction in Yiddish includes the novels *Fun lublin biz nyu york: togbukh fun rivke zilberg* (1942) and *Baym toyer, roman* (1967) and a collection of short stories, *A shtub mit zibn fentster* (1957). Two translations of Molodowsky's fiction have been published: Irena Klepfisz's translation of *The Lost Shabes* is in *The Tribe of Dina* (1989), edited by Klepfisz and Melanie Kaye/Kantrowitz, and Ethel Raicus's translation of *A House with Seven Windows* is in *Found Treasures* (1994).

Biographical and bibliographical information about Molodowsky is the focus of Kathryn Hellerstein's critical introduction to *Paper Bridges*. Other useful articles include Hellerstein's "In Exile in the Mother Tongue: Yiddish and the Woman Poet," in *Borders, Boundaries, and Frames: Essays in Cultural Criticism and Cultural Studies (Essays from the English Institute)* (1995), edited by Mae G. Henderson, Irena Klepfisz's "*Di mames, dos loshn*/The mothers, the language: Feminism, *Yidishkayt*, and the Politics of Memory," *Bridges* 4.1 (Winter/Spring 1994), Anita Norich's entry on Yiddish literature in *Jewish Women in America: An Historical Encyclopedia* (1997), edited by Paula Hyman and Deborah Dash Moore, F. Peczenik's "Encountering the Matriarchy: Kadye Molodowsky's *Women Songs*," in *Yiddish* 7.2–3 (1988), Norma Fain Pratt's "Culture and Radical Politics: Yiddish Women Writers in America, 1890–1940," in *Women of the Word: Jewish Women and Jewish Writing* (1994), edited by Judith R. Baskin, and Sheva Zucker's "Kadye Molodowsky's 'Froyen Lider,' " in *Yiddish* 9.2 (1994).

Howard Nemerov

The Collected Poems of Howard Nemerov (1977) covers volumes such as *The Salt Garden* (1955), *Mirrors and Windows* (1958), *The Blue Swallows* (1967), and *Gnomes and Occasions* (1973). The year of his death saw *Trying Conclusions: New and Selected Poems* (1991); *A Howard Nemerov Reader* also appeared in that year. Nemerov early on wrote several novels and published short stories as well as an autobiography, *Journal of the Fictive Life* (1965), and valuable literary essays: *Poetry and Fiction* (1963), *Reflexions on Poetry and Poetics* (1972), *Figures of Thought* (1978), *New and Selected Essays* (1985). Critical studies include Peter Meinke's *Howard Nemerov* (1968), Julia A. Bartholomay's *The Shield of Perseus* (1972), William Mills's *The Stillness in Moving Things* (1975), and Ross Labrie's *Howard Nemerov* (1980).

Tillie Olsen

Tillie Olsen's reputation is based mainly on the stories in *Tell Me a Riddle* (1961), then on the valuable novel *Yonnondio: From the Thirties* (1974) and her striking meditation on women authors, *Silences* (1978). She also published an essay-photograph collection, *Mothers and Daughters* (1987), with Julie Olsen Edwards and Estelle Jussim. Olsen's letters are at Stanford University. Critical work on her includes Mickey Pearlman's *Tillie Olsen* (1991), Mara Faulkner's *Protest and Possibility in the Writing of Tillie Olsen* (1993), Joanne S. Frye's *Tillie Olsen* (1995), Constance Coiner's *Better Red* (1995), and Nora Ruth Roberts's *Three Radical Women Writers* (1996).

George Oppen

George Oppen's volumes of poetry are *Discrete Series* (1934), *The Materials* (1962), *This in Which* (1965), *Of Being Numerous* (1968), *Alpine* (1969), *Primitive* (1978), *The Collected Poems of George Oppen, 1929–1975* (1975), and *Seascape: Needle's Eye* (1972). Rachel Blau DuPlessis edited Oppen's fascinating *Selected Letters* (1990), and Mary Oppen wrote an autobiography of their marriage, *Meaning a Life* (1978). *George Oppen: Man and Poet* (1981), edited by Burton Hatlen, brings together valuable essays.

Cynthia Ozick

Cynthia Ozick's fiction consists of novels, novellas, and short stories: *Trust* (1966), *The Pagan Rabbi* (1971), *Bloodshed and Three Novellas* (1976), *Levitation* (1982), *The Cannibal Galaxy* (1983), *The Messiah of Stockholm* (1987), *The Shawl* (1989), *The Puttermesser Papers* (1997), plus *A Cynthia Ozick Reader* (1996), edited by Elaine Kauvar. Her equally strong essay collections on literature and related themes are *Art and Ardor* (1983), *Metaphor and Memory* (1989), *What Henry James Knew* (1993), and *Fame and Folly* (1996). Critical work includes *Cynthia Ozick* (1986), edited by Harold Bloom; Sanford Pinsker's *The Uncompromising Fic-*

tions of Cynthia Ozick (1987); Lawrence S. Friedman's *Understanding Cynthia Ozick* (1991); Elaine M. Kauvar's *Cynthia Ozick's Fiction* (1993); and Sarah Blacher Cohen's *Cynthia Ozick's Comic Art* (1994).

Grace Paley

Grace Paley's reputation rests firmly on three short-story collections: *The Little Disturbances of Man: Stories of Women and Men at Love* (1959), *Enormous Changes at the Last Minute* (1974), and *Later the Same Day* (1985), along with *Collected Stories* (1994). Her poetry appears in *Leaning Forward* (1985) and *New and Selected Poems* (1992), and other writings in *Just As I Thought* (1998). Gerhard Bach and Blaine H. Hall edited *Conversations with Grace Paley* (1997). Critical work includes Neil David Isaacs's *Grace Paley* (1990), Jacqueline Taylor's *Grace Paley* (1990), and Judith Arcana's *Grace Paley's Life Stories* (1993).

Gabriel Preil

While Gabriel Preil's Hebrew poetry is published in Israel, one collection has appeared in English: *Sunset Possibilities* (1985), translated by Robert Friend. Yael S. Feldman wrote *Modernism and Cultural Transfer: Gabriel Preil and the Tradition of Jewish Literary Bilingualism* (1986).

Carl Rakosi

In his *Collected Poems* (1986), Carl Rakosi rearranged the work that had appeared in such volumes as *Selected Poems* (1941), *Amulet* (1967), *Ere-Voice* (1971), *Ex-Cranium* (1975), and *History* (1981). Andrew Crozier, whose interest spurred Rakosi to take up poetry again after a twenty-seven-year hiatus, edited the early work in *Poems, 1923–1941* (1995). In addition, we have Rakosi's *Collected Prose* (1983). Michael Heller wrote *Conviction's Net of Branches: Essays on the Objectivist Poets and Poetry* (1985) and edited an essay collection, *Carl Rakosi: Man and Poet* (1993).

Philip Roth

After his first book, *Goodbye Columbus and Five Short Stories* (1959), Philip Roth wrote twenty-five or so novels over four decades. Among the most highly regarded are *Portnoy's Complaint* (1969), *The Professor of Desire* (1977), *The Ghost Writer* (1979), *Zuckerman Unbound* (1981), *Zuckerman Bound* (1985), *The Counterlife* (1987), *Operation Shylock* (1993), *Sabbath's Theater* (1995), and *American Pastoral* (1997). His most recent novel is *The Human Stain* (2000). He also published *Reading Myself and Others* (1975), a collection of essays; *The Facts: A Novelist's Autobiography* (1988); and a fine memoir of his father's death, *Patrimony* (1991). George J. Searles edited *Conversations with Philip Roth* (1992).

Critical studies include Sanford Pinsker's *"The Comedy That Hoits": An Essay on the Fiction of Philip Roth* (1975); *Philip Roth* (1986), edited by Harold Bloom; *Reading Philip Roth* (1988), edited by Asher Z. Milbauer and Donald G. Watson; Murray Baumgarten and Barbara Gottfried's *Understanding Philip Roth* (1990); and Alan Cooper's *Philip Roth and the Jews* (1996). Bernard F. Rodgers, Jr. compiled *Philip Roth: A Bibliography* (2nd ed. 1984).

Emma Adatto Schlesinger

Emma Adatto Schlesinger's memoir, *La Tía Estambolía,* first published in *Midstream* magazine in February 1981, was reprinted in the anthology *Sephardic American Voices: Two Hundred Years of a Literary Legacy* (1997), edited by Diane Matza. Schlesinger previously wrote a master's thesis at the University of Washington on Sephardic folklore (*A Study of the Linguistic Character of the Seattle Sephardi Folklore,* 1938).

Kate Simon

Kate Simon's autobiographical *Bronx Primitive: Portraits in a Childhood* (1982) was quite successful and has since been followed by two sequels detailing her childhood in the Bronx, *A Wider World: Portraits in an Adolescence* (1988) and *Etchings in an Hourglass* (1990).

Louis Simpson

Louis Simpson's *Collected Poems* (1988) included books such as *A Dream of Governors* (1959), *At the End of the Open Road* (1963), *Adventures of the Letter I* (1971), *Searching for the Ox* (1976), and *Caviare at the Funeral* (1980). Later volumes are *In the Room We Share* (1990) and *There You Are* (1995). He also wrote a novel, *Riverside Drive* (1962), and literary criticism, including *Three on the Tower: The Lives and Works of Ezra Pound, T. S. Eliot and William Carlos Williams* (1975), *A Revolution in Taste: Studies of Dylan Thomas, Allen Ginsberg, Sylvia Plath and Robert Lowell* (1978), *A Company of Poets* (1981), and *Ships Going into the Blue* (1994).

In *North of Jamaica* (1972), Simpson wrote perceptively about coming to the United States, and he published another memoir, *The King My Father's Wreck* (1995).

Critical studies include Ronald Moran's *Louis Simpson* (1972); William H. Roberson's *Louis Simpson: A Reference Guide* (1980); and *On Louis Simpson: Depths beyond Happiness* (1988), edited by Hank Lazer.

Isaac Bashevis Singer

A great deal of Isaac Bashevis Singer's prolific work has been translated into English. Among the novels are *The Family Moskat* (1950), *Satan in Goray* (1955), *The Magician of Lublin* (1960), *The Slave* (1962), *Enemies, a Love Story* (1972), *Shosha* (1978), and *Shadows on the Hudson* (1998). His *Collected Stories* (1982) are drawn from such volumes as *Gimpel the Fool* (1957), *The Spinoza of Market Street* (1961), *Short Friday* (1964), *The Séance* (1968), *A Friend of Kafka* (1970), and *A Crown of Feathers* (1973); there is also *An Isaac Bashevis Singer Reader* (1971). His children's stories, illustrated by Maurice Sendak and others, are particularly popular: *Zlateh the Goat* (1966); *When Shlemiel Went to Warsaw* (1968); *Naftali the Storyteller and His Horse, Sus* (1976).

Singer's absorbing memoirs of his Polish and American experience are *In My Father's Court* (1966); *A Day of Pleasure* (1969), with Roman Vishniac's photos; and *Love and Exile* (1984). Richard Burgin edited *Conversations with Isaac Bashevis Singer* (1985); also available is Singer's *Nobel Lecture* (1979).

Biographies are Dorothea Straus's *Under the Canopy* (1982); Clive Sinclair's *The Brothers Singer* (1983), on Isaac and his author brother Israel Joshua; and Janet Hadda's *Isaac Bashevis Singer: A Life* (1997). Critical studies include Irving Malin's *Critical Views of Isaac Bashevis Singer* (1969), with a bibliography; Edward Alexander's *Isaac Bashevis Singer* (1980); Lawrence S. Friedman's *Understanding Isaac Bashevis Singer* (1988); and *Critical Essays on Isaac Bashevis Singer* (1996). David Neal Miller compiled a *Bibliography of Isaac Bashevis Singer, 1924–1949* (1983). Singer's papers are at the University of Texas (Austin).

Gerald Stern

At the age of forty-eight Gerald Stern released his first volume of collected poems, *Rejoicings: Selected Poems, 1966–72* (1973). His works before that collection included *Pineys* (1971) and *The Naming of the Beasts* (1972). After *Rejoicings*, he published *Lucky Life* (1977), *The Red Coal* (1981), *Paradise Poems* (1984), *Lovesick* (1987), *Selected Essays* (1988), *New and Selected Poems* (1989), *Leaving Another Kingdom* (1990), *Two Long Poems* (1990), *Bread without Sugar: Poems* (1992), *Odd Mercy* (1995), and *This Time: New and Selected Poetry* (1998). Stern's most recent work is *Last Blue: Poems* (2000).

Studies devoted to Stern include Jane Somerville's *Gerald Stern: The Speaker as Meaning* (1988) and her *Making the Light Come: The Poetry of Gerald Stern* (1990). Additionally, Peter Stitt discusses Stern in *Uncertainty & Plenitude: Five Contemporary Poets* (1997).

Lionel Trilling

Lionel Trilling's copious writings cover a wide range of American, British, and European literature, as well as the work and influence of Sigmund Freud, and also include his own fiction. He introduced, edited, and contributed to numerous books and to journals such as *Menorah Journal*, the *New Republic*, and *Commentary*. His chief essay collections are *The Liberal Imagination* (1950), *The Opposing Self* (1955), *Freud and the Crisis of Our Culture* (1955), *A Gathering of Fugitives* (1956), *Beyond Culture* (1965), and *The Last Decade* (1979), edited by Diana Trilling. He published a novel, *The Middle of the Journey* (1947), and Diana Trilling edited *Of This Time, of That Place and Other Stories* (1979).

Trilling sometimes wrote autobiographically for periodicals, and his wife, Diana, published a memoir, *The Beginning of the Journey* (1993). Critical studies include Nathan Scott's *Three American Moralists* (1973), on Trilling, Mailer, and Bellow; *Art, Politics, and Will* (1977), edited by Quentin Anderson, Stephen Donadio, and Steven Marcus; Robert Boyers's *Lionel Trilling* (1977); William M. Chace's *Lionel Trilling* (1980); and Mark Krupnick's *Lionel Trilling and the Fate of Cultural Criticism* (1986). Thomas M. Leitch compiled a bibliography, *Lionel Trilling* (1993).

Malka Heifetz Tussman

Six volumes of Malka Heifetz Tussman's poetry were published in Yiddish: *Lider* (Poems) (1949), *Mild mayn vild* (Mild My Wild) (1958), *Shotns fun gedenken* (Shadows of Remembering) (1965), *Bleter faln nit* (Leaves Do Not Fall) (1972), *Unter dayn tseykhn* (Under Your Sign) (1974), and *Haynt iz eybik* (Now is Ever) (1977). Two books of her poems have been published in English translation, *Am I Also You?* (1977) and *With Teeth in the Earth: Selected Poems* (1992), both translated, edited, and introduced by Marcia Falk. Tussman's poems have been included in several anthologies: Benjamin and Barbara Harshav's *American Yiddish Poetry: A Bilingual Anthology* (1986), with twenty translations by Kathryn Hellerstein *en face* with the Yiddish originals, and Irving Howe, Ruth R. Wisse, and Khone Shmeruk's *The Penguin Book of Modern Yiddish Verse* (1987), where five translations by Marcia Falk also face the Yiddish texts. *Voices within the Ark* (1980), edited by Howard Schwartz and Anthony Rudolph, includes nine of Tussman's poems, translated by Marcia Falk. One or two poems are included in other anthologies, such as *The Other Voice: Twentieth-Century Women's Poetry in Translation* (1976), edited by Joanna Bankier, Carol Cosman, Doris Earnshaw, et al., and Aaron Kramer's *A Century of Modern Yiddish Poetry* (1989).

Marcia Falk's introductory essays to *Am I Also You?* and *With Teeth in the Earth* are good summaries of Tussman's life. Two essays by fellow Yiddish poets, both in the Israeli Yiddish quarterly *Di goldene keyt* (The Golden Chain), provide insight into Tussman's work: M. Litvine's *"Dos poetishe verk fun malke kheyfets-tuzman"* (The Poetic Work of Malka Heifetz Tussman) (1976) and Avraham Sutzkever's eulogy *"Haynt iz eybik (tsum toyt fun malke kheyfets tuzman)"* (Today Is Forever—On the Death of Malka Heifetz Tussman) (1987). Zeynvl Diamant's entry in the *Leksikon fun der nayer yidisher literatur*, volume 3 (1960), supplies biographical and bibliographical background. Two essays by Kathryn Hellerstein, "A Question of Tradition: Women Poets in Yiddish," in *Handbook of American-Jewish Literature* (1988), edited by Lewis Fried, and "From *Ikh* to *Zikh*: A Journey from 'I' to 'Self' in Yiddish Poems by Women," in *Gender and Text in Modern Hebrew and Yiddish Literature* (1992), edited by Naomi B. Sokoloff, Anne Lapidus Lerner, and Anita Norich, offer readings of Tussman's poems.

Elie Wiesel

Most of Elie Wiesel's work is written in French, his adopted language, and translated into English by his wife, Marion, and others. His autobiographical memoir *Night* (1960) remains his best-known book. It was followed by a series of novels: *Dawn* (1961),

The Accident (1962), *The Gates of the Forest* (1966), *The Town beyond the Wall* (1967), *A Beggar in Jerusalem* (1970), *The Oath* (1973), as well as *Ani Maamin* (1973) and *Zalmen, or the Madness of God* (1974).

Wiesel's lectures on Hasidic and biblical figures at New York's 92nd Street Y gave rise to *Souls on Fire* (1972) and *Messengers of God* (1976), along with other books. His nonfiction includes *The Jews of Silence: A Personal Report on Soviet Jewry* (1966) and the essay collections *Legends of Our Time* (1968), *One Generation After* (1970), and *A Jew Today* (1978).

From the Kingdom of Memory (1990) contains reminiscences. Wiesel's two memoirs are *All Rivers Run to the Sea* (1995) and *And the Sea Is Never Full* (1999). *Harry James Cargas in Conversation with Elie Wiesel* came out in 1976. Critical studies include Michael Berenbaum's *The Vision of the Void* (1979), John Roth's *A Consuming Fire* (1979), Ellen S. Fine's *Legacy of Night* (1982), and Robert McAfee Brown's *Elie Wiesel* (1983). *Confronting the Holocaust: The Impact of Elie Wiesel* (1978), edited by Alvin Rosenfeld and Irving Greenberg, also has a good bibliography.

WANDERING AND RETURN: LITERATURE SINCE 1973

For a general historical and sociological overview of this period, two texts provide wide background materials: Arthur Hertzberg's *The Jews in America* (1989) and Edward Shapiro's *A Time for Healing: American Jewry since World War II* (1992). A more recent and controversial book, J. J. Goldberg's *Jewish Power: Inside the American Jewish Establishment* (1997), describes the many avenues by which Jewish Americans have participated in national and international political life. Alan Dershowitz's *The Vanishing American Jew* (1997) is also an important and controversial book, as is Michael Goldberg's *Why Should Jews Survive*? (1995); both of these books have reached a general as well as academic audience. A valuable essay collection, *Insider/Outsider: Jews and Multiculturalism*, edited by David Biale et al. (1998), examines the role of Jewish Americans in the current debate about multiculturalism.

Several anthologies of contemporary Jewish American literature are valuable, among them Steven Rubin's *Telling and Remembering* (1997), which is a wonderful and up-to-date collection of twentieth-century Jewish American poetry; similarly, Ted Solotaroff and Nessa Rapoport's anthology of Jewish American short fiction, *Writing Our Way Home* (1992), provides thorough coverage of the contemporary period.

Critics have just begun to mine this period for analysis and discussion. While not dealing with many of the writers included here, Norman Finkelstein's *The Ritual of New Creation: Jewish Tradition and Contemporary Literature* (1992) is a good sourcebook for a discussion of what Jewish American literature is, as is Mark Shechner's *After the Revolution: Studies in the Contemporary Jewish American Imagination* (1987). Sarah Blacher Cohen has written a great deal about contemporary women writers. Most recently, her *Making a Scene* (1997), a book about Jewish American women playwrights, provides names of many authors we could not include here. Andrew Furman's *Israel in the Imagination of Jewish American Writers* (1997) discusses both writers included here and some not. One of the more intriguing publications in the last few years has been Emily Miller Budick's *Blacks and Jews in Literary Conversation* (1998), which provides an extensive discussion of ethnic identity.

Several bibliographic sources exist: *Feminist Perspectives on Jewish Studies* (1994), edited by Lynn Davidman and Shelly Tenenbaum; *Handbook of American-Jewish Literature: An Analytical Guide to Topics, Themes and Sources* (1988), edited by Lewis Fried; and Gloria Cronin's *Jewish-American Fiction: An Annotated Bibliography* (1991).

Max Apple

Max Apple's compositions range from the satirical—*The Oranging of America, and Other Stories* (1976), *The Propheteers: A Novel* (1987)—to the autobiographical—*Roommates: My Grandfather's Story* (1994), *I Love Gootie: My Grandmother's Story* (1998). His other fictional works include *Zip: A Novel of the Left and Right* (1978), *Three Stories* (1983), and *Free Agents* (1984). Apple has also edited *Southwest Fiction* (1981). There have been no collections of or single-volume texts of criticism about Apple's work.

Charles Bernstein

Charles Bernstein's creative work ranges from poetry to prose to visual art; his primary texts are *Asylums* (1975), *Parsing* (1976), *Shade* (1978), *Poetic Justice* (1979), *Senses of Responsibility* (1979), *Controlling Interests* (1980), *Disfrutes* (1981) *The Occurrence of Tune* (1981), *Stigma* (1981), *Islets/Irritations* (1983), *Resistance* (1983), *Veil* (1987), *The Sophist* (1987), *Four Poems* (1988), *The Lives of the Toll Takers* (1989), *Rough Trades* (1989), *A Poetics* (1992), *Dark City* (1994), and *My Way: Speeches and Poems* (1999).

Linda Reinfeld's *Language Poetry: Writing as Rescue* (1992) is an authoritative guide not only to the work of Bernstein specifically but to "language" poetry in general.

Harold Bloom

Harold Bloom has edited hundred of books and written a score; many of the most important are in the field of British Romanticism and poetic theory. These include *Shelley's Mythmaking* (1959), *The Visionary Company: A Reading of English Romantic Poetry* (1961), *Blake's Apocalypse* (1963), *Yeats* (1970), *Romanticism and Consciousness: Essays in Criticism* (1970), *The Ringers in the Tower: Studies in Romantic Tradition* (1971), *The Anxiety of Influence: A Theory of Poetry* (1973), *A Map of Misreading* (1975), *Poetry and Repression: Revisionism from Blake to Stevens* (1976), *Figures of Capable Imagination* (1976), *Wallace Stevens: The Poems of Our Climate* (1977), *Agon: Towards a Theory of Revisionism* (1982), and, most recently, *Shakespeare: The Invention of the Human* (1998). He has also published several books about Judaism, including *Kabbalah and Criticism* (1975), *The Flight to Lucifer: A Gnostic Fantasy* (1979), *The Strong Light of the Canonical: Kafka, Freud, and Scholem as Revisionists of Jewish Culture and Thought* (1987), *Poetics of Influence* (1989), *Ruin the Sacred Truths: Poetry and Belief from the Bible to the Present* (1989), *The Book of J* (1990), *The American Religion: The Emergence of a Post-Christian Nation* (1992), *The Gospel of Thomas: The Hidden Sayings of Jesus* (1992), and *Omens of Millennium: The Gnosis of Angels, Dreams, and Resurrection* (1996). In 1994, he published a controversial overview of the so-called great books: *The Western Canon: The Books and School of the Ages*.

Critics have only gently approached Bloom's work. For an overview of Bloom's poetic theories, look at Graham Allen's *Harold Bloom: Poetics of Conflict* (1994), David Fite's *Harold Bloom: The Rhetoric of Romantic Vision* (1985), and Robert Moynihan's *A Recent Imagining: Interviews with Harold Bloom, Geoffrey Hartman, J. Hillis Miller, Paul De Man* (1986).

E. M. Broner

E. M. Broner's primary works include *Journal-Nocturnal and Seven Stories* (1986), *Her Mothers* (1975), *A Weave of Women* (1978), and *The Lost Tradition: Mothers and Daughters in Literature* (1980). Broner's other works, *The Telling* (1993) and *The Women's Haggadah* (1994), as well as the autobiographical *Mornings and Mourning* (1994) and *Ghost Stories* (1995), meditate on the role of women in Judaism.

Melvin Jules Bukiet

Melvin Bukiet's novels include *Sandman's Dust* (1986), *Stories of an Imaginary Childhood* (1992), *While the Messiah Tarries* (1995), *After* (1996), and his most recent work, *Signs and Wonders: A Novel* (1999).

E. L. Doctorow

E. L. Doctorow has written many important as well as popular novels. His two earliest books, *Welcome to Hard Times* (1960) and *Big as Life* (1966), established him as a rising talent, though it was not until he published *The Book of Daniel* (1971) that his literary reputation was established. His blockbuster *Ragtime* (1975) became a *New York Times* best-seller, a movie, and a Broadway play. *Loon Lake* (1980), *World's Fair* (1985), and *Billy Bathgate* (1989), the last also made into a film, were also well-received by the popular audience as well as literary critics. His *Three Complete Novels* was published in 1994, *The Waterworks* also in 1994, and *City of God* in 2000. Additionally, in 1984 Doctorow published a collection of stories, *Lives of the Poets*, and in 1996 he authored the play *Drinks before Dinner*.

There have been several important books of criticism about Doctorow, the most notable of which is Diane Johnson's *Terrorists and Novelists* (1982). Also interesting is Christopher Morris's *Models of Misrepresentation: On the Fiction of E. L. Doctorow* (1991), John Williams's *Fiction as False Document: The Reception of E. L. Doctorow in the Post-Modern Age* (1996), Douglas Fowler's *Understanding E. L. Doctorow* (1992), and John Parks's *E. L. Doctorow* (1991)—all provide important commentary about Doctorow's use of history and fiction. Michelle Tokarczyk has compiled *E. L. Doctorow: An Annotated Bibliography* (1988).

Bruce Jay Friedman

Bruce Jay Friedman has published much commercially successful and popular fiction, including *Stern* (1990), *Far from the City of Glass and Other Stories* (1963), *A Mother's Kisses* (1963), *Black Humor* (1965), *Black Angels* (1996), *The Dick* (1970), *About Harry Towns* (1974), *Steambath* (1971), *The Lonely Guy's Book of Life* (1984), *Let's Hear It for a Beautiful Guy and Other Works of Short Fiction* (1984), *Tokyo Woes* (1985), *The Current Climate* (1989), *The Slightly Older Guy* (1995), *The Collected Short Fiction of Bruce Jay Friedman* (1995), and *A Father's Kisses* (1996). Though Friedman has not attracted the attention of many literary critics, in 1974 Max Schulz edited *Bruce Jay Friedman*, a collection of critical essays on Friedman's work.

Allegra Goodman

Allegra Goodman has published three books: *Total Immersion* (1989), a collection of short stories; *The Family Markowitz* (1996), a novel; and *Kaaterskill Falls* (1998), also a novel.

Allen Grossman

Allen Grossman's many works include *A Harlot's Hire* (1962), *The Recluse* (1965), *Poetic Knowledge in the Early Yeats* (1969), *And the Dew Lay All Night upon My Branch* (1973), *The Woman in the Bridge over the Chicago River* (1979), *Of the Great House* (1981), *Against Our Vanishing: Winter Conversations on Poetry and Poetics* (1981), *The Bright Nails Scattered on the Ground* (1986), *The Sighted Singer: Two Works on Poetry for Readers and Writers* (1991), *The Ether Dome and Other Poems New and Selected* (1991), *The Philosopher's Window and Other Poems* (1995), and *Schoolroom: Lessons in the Bitter Logic of the Poetic Principle the Long* (1997).

Alan Williamson's *Introspection and Contemporary Poetry* (1984) focuses on Grossman's work.

Edward Hirsch

Edward Hirsch is the author of six books of poetry, including *For the Sleepwalkers* (1981), *Wild Grati-*

tude (1986), *The Night Parade* (1989), *Earthly Measures* (1994), and *On Love* (1998). He is also the author of *How to Read a Poem* (1999).

Irena Klepfisz
Irena Klepfisz is the author of several books: *Keeper of Accounts* (1982), *Different Enclosures* (1985), and *A Few Words in the Mother Tongue: Poems Selected and New, 1971–1990*, with an introduction by Adrienne Rich. She is also the author of *Dreams of an Insomniac: Jewish Feminist Essays, Speeches, and Diatribes* (1990). Edited by Klepfisz with Melanie Kaye/Kantrowitz is *The Tribe of Dina: A Jewish Women's Anthology* (1989). With Rita Febel and Donna Nevel, Klepfisz edited *Jewish Women's Call for Peace: A Handbook for Jewish Women on the Israeli/Palestinian Conflict* (1990).

Mark Mirsky
Mark Mirsky's works range from his first set of novels, *Thou Worm Jacob* (1967), *Proceedings of the Rabble* (1971), *Blue Hill Avenue* (1972), *The Secret Table* (1975), *My Search for the Messiah* (1977), and *The Red Adam* (1989), to his more recent work as both literary critic—*The Absent Shakespeare* (1994)—and, along with David Stern, anthologist—*Rabbinic Fantasies: Imaginative Narratives from Classical Hebrew Literature* (1998).

Miriam Israel Moses
Miriam Israel Moses's *Survivors and Pieces of Glass* appeared in the Winter 1997/98 issue of *Bridges*. In addition to publishing short stories in various journals, she has published a volume of poetry, *Arabesque* (1996), and is the author of several musicals and plays.

Jacqueline Osherow
Jacqueline Osherow has published four books of poetry: *Looking for Angels in New York* (1988), *Conversations with Survivors* (1993), *With a Moon in Transit* (1996), and *Dead Men's Praise* (1999).

Marge Piercy
Not only an acclaimed poet, teacher, and lecturer, Piercy has been a popular success as well; her *Gone to Soldiers* (1987) was a bestseller in that year. Piercy's volumes of poetry include *Breaking Camp* (1968), *Hard Loving* (1969), *To Be of Use* (1973), *Living in the Open* (1976), *The Twelve-Spoked Wheel Flashing* (1978), *The Moon Is Always Female* (1980), *Circles on the Water* (1982), *Stone, Paper, Knife* (1983), *My Mother's Body* (1985), *Available Light* (1988), and *Mars and Her Children* (1992), *The Art of Blessing the Day: Poems with a Jewish Theme* (1999), and *Early Grrrl: The Early Poems of Marge Piercy* (1999). Her novels include *Going Down Fast* (1969), *Dance the Eagle to Sleep* (1970), *Small Changes* (1973), *Woman on the Edge of Time* (1976), *The High Cost of Living* (1978), *Vida* (1982), *Braided Lives* (1982), *Fly Away Home* (1984), *Summer People* (1989), *He, She and It* (1992), *The Longings of Women* (1994), *City of Darkness, City of Light* (1996), *What Are Big Girls Made Of?* (1997), and *Storm Tide* (1998).

The primary criticism on Piercy's work is contained in Magali Cornier Michael's *Feminism and the Postmodern Impulse: Post-World War II Fiction* (1996), Kerstin W. Shands's *The Repair of the World: The Novels of Marge Piercy* (1994), Sue Walker and Eugenie Hammer's *Ways of Knowing: Critical Essays on Marge Piercy* (1984), Pia Thielmann's *Marge Piercy's Women: Visions Captured and Subdued* (1986), Margarete Keulen's *Radical Imagination: Feminist Conceptions of the Future in Ursula Le Guin, Marge Piercy, and Sally Miller Gearhart* (1991), and Patricia Doherty's *Marge Piercy: An Annotated Bibliography* (1997).

Robert Pinsky
Praised for the musicality of his recent translation, *The Inferno of Dante* (1994), Pinsky has enjoyed the rare blend of academic as well as popular success. His books of poetry include *Sadness and Happiness* (1975), *An Explanation of America* (1979), *The History of My Heart* (1984), *Poetry and the World* (1988), *The Want Bone* (1990), *The Figured Wheel: New and Collected Poems, 1966–1996* (1996), and *Jersey Rain* (2000). *The Sound of Poetry* (1998) is a volume on poetic terminology and a guidebook to poetic verse. He is also the editor, with Massie Dietz, of *Americans' Favorite Poems* (1999).

Willard Spiegelman's *The Didactic Muse* (1989) is the first book of criticism published on Pinsky's work.

Chaim Potok
Chaim Potok is the author of many works of fiction. His first novel, *The Chosen* (1967), was an immediate bestseller and quickly brought him fame. *The Promise* (1969), Potok's second novel and a sequel to his first, and *My Name Is Asher Lev* (1972) officially established his writing career. Since then Potok has published a diverse set of works, from fiction to Jewish history: *In the Beginning* (1975), *The Book of Lights* (1981), *Wanderings: Chaim Potok's History of the Jews* (1978), *Davita's Harp* (1985), *The Gift of Asher Lev* (1990), *I Am the Clay* (1992), *The Tree of Here* (1993), *The Sky of Snow* (1994), *The Gates of November: Chronicles of the Slepak Family* (1996), and *Zebra and Other Stories* (1998).

Edward Abramson's *Chaim Potok* (1986) is a collection of criticism on Potok's work.

Tova Reich
Tova Reich is the author of several works of fiction: *Mara* (1978), *Master of the Return* (1988), and *The Jewish War* (1995).

Adrienne Rich
Adrienne Rich's massive body of work includes *A Change of World* (1951), *Poems* (1952), *The Diamond Cutters and Other Poems* (1955), *Snapshots of a Daughter-in-Law: Poems, 1954–1962* (1963), *Necessities of Life* (1966), *Leaflets. Poems, 1965–1968* (1969), *The Will to Change: Poems, 1968–1970* (1971), *Diving into the Wreck: Poems, 1971–1972* (1973), *Of Woman Born: Motherhood as Experience and Institution* (1976), *Twenty-One Love*

Poems (1977), *The Dream of a Common Language: Poems, 1974–1977* (1978), *On Lies, Secrets, and Silence: Selected Prose, 1966–1978* (1979), *A Wild Patience Has Taken Me This Far: Poems, 1978–1981* (1981), *Sources* (1983), *The Fact of a Doorframe: Poems Selected and New, 1950–1984* (1984), *Blood, Bread, and Poetry: Selected Prose, 1979–1985* (1986), *Your Native Land, Your Life* (1986), *Time's Power Poems, 1985–1988* (1988), *An Atlas of the Difficult World: Poems, 1988–1991* (1991), *Collected Early Poems, 1950–1970* (1993), *What Is Found There: Notebooks on Poetry and Politics* (1993), *Dark Fields of the Republic, Poems, 1991–1995* (1995), *Selected Poems, 1950–1995* (1996), and *Midnight Salvage, Poems, 1995–1998* (1999).

Rich's work has inspired an impressive amount of critical attention, ranging from countless masters' theses and doctoral dissertations to full texts dedicated to her work: Paula Bennett's *My Life a Loaded Gun: Female Creativity and Feminist Poetics* (1986), Margaret Dickie's *Stein, Bishop, and Rich* (1997), Claire Keyes's *The Aesthetics of Power: The Poetry of Adrienne Rich* (1986), Wendy Martin's *The American Triptych: Anne Bradstreet, Emily Dickinson, Adrienne Rich* (1984), Jane Roberta Cooper's *Reading Adrienne Rich* (1984); Alice Templeton's *The Dream and the Dialogue: Adrienne Rich's Feminist Poetics* (1994); and Margaret Dickie's *Stein, Bishop, & Rich: Lyrics of Love, War, & Place* (1997).

Jerome Rothenberg

Jerome Rothenberg has won acclaim for his two-volume anthology of contemporary poetry: *Poems for the Millennium:The University of California Book of Modern and Postmodern Poetry:From Fin-de-Siecle to Negritude (Vol. 1)* (1994) and *Poems for the Millennium: The University of California Book of Modern and Postmodern Poetry (From Postwar to Millennium) (Vol. 2)* (1998).

Rothenberg's massive collection of work consists of many other anthologies as well as his own poetry, including *White Sun Black Sun* (1960), *The Seven Hells of the Jigoku Zoshi* (1962), *Sightings I–IX* (1964), *The Gorky Poems* (1966), *Between: 1960–63* (1967), *Conversations* (1968), *Poems 1964–1967* (1968), *Poland/1931* (1974), *Poems for the Game of Silence, 1960–1970* (1971), *A Book of Testimony* (1971), *Esther K. Comes to America* (1973), *Seneca Journal 1: A Poem of Beavers* (1973), *The Cards* (1974), *The Perk and the Pearl* (1975), *Seneca Journal: Midwinter* (1978), *Seneca Journal* (1978), *Abulafia's Circles* (1979), *B.R.M.TZ.V.* (1979), *Numbers and Letters* (1980), *Vienna Blood* (1980), *The Dada Strain* (1983), *New and Selected Poems, 1970–1985* (1986), *Khurbn and Other Poems* (1989), *An Oracle for Delfi* (1994), *Pictures of the Crucifixion: Poems* (1995), *Seedings and Other Poems* (1996), and *A Paradise of Poets: New Poems and Translations* (1999).

Many critics have written about the poet/anthologist. Several complete works are dedicated to his work: Gavin Selerie's *Jerome Rothenberg* (1984); Paul Sherman's *In Search of the Primitive: Reading David Antin, Jerome Rothenberg, and Gary Snyder* (1986); and Harry Polkinhorn's *Jerome Rothenberg: A Descriptive Bibliography* (1988).

Art Spiegelman

Most widely known for his *MAUS, a Survivor's Tale: My Father Bleeds History* (1986) and *MAUS II, a Survivor's Tale: And Here My Troubles Began* (1991), Art Spiegelman has created a body of work that evidences the wide array of influences on his unique brand of illustrated narrative. His other works include *The Complete Mr. Infinity* (1970), *The Vicar Viper of Vice, Villainy, and Vickedness* (1972), *Zip-a-Tune and More Melodies* (1972), *Ace Hole, Midget Detective* (1974), *Language of Comics* (1974), *Work and Turn* (1979), *Every Day Has Its Dog* (1979), *Two-Fisted Painters Action Adventure* (1980), *Raw* (1990), *Raw 2: Required Reading for the Post-literate* (1991), *Raw 3: High Culture for Lowbrows* (1991), *History of Commix* (1996), *Open Me—I'm a Dog!* (1997), *Comix, Essays, & Scraps from MAUS to Now* (1998), and *The Wild Party* (1999).

Steve Stern

Steve Stern is the author of several works of fiction largely concerned with Jewish assimilation and the anomaly of the Jew in the South. His novels include *Isaac and the Undertaker's Daughter* (1983), *The Moon and Ruben Shein* (1984), *Lazar Malkin Enters Heaven* (1986), *Mickey and the Golem: A Child's Hanukkah in the South* (1986), *Hershel and the Beast* (1987), *Harry Kaplan's Adventures Underground* (1991), and *A Plague of Dreamers* (1994).

PERMISSIONS

Woody Allen: *The Scrolls* from WITHOUT FEATHERS by Woody Allen. Copyright © 1974 by Woody Allen. Reprinted by permission of Random House, Inc.

Max Apple: *The Eighth Day* from FREE AGENTS by Max Apple. Copyright © 1984 by Max Apple. Reprinted by permission of HarperCollins Publishers, Inc.

Sholem Asch: GOD OF VENGEANCE (Act 1) by Sholem Asch, translated by Joachim Neugroschel. Reprinted by permission of Georges Borchardt, Inc. for Joachim Neugroschel. Originally appeared in DER PAKN TREGER Number 23, Winter 1996. Translation copyright © 1996 by Joachim Neugroschel.

Saul Bellow: *Something to Remember Me By*, Copyright © 1990 by Saul Bellow, first published in ESQUIRE Magazine, from SOMETHING TO REMEMBER ME BY by Saul Bellow. Used by permission of Viking Penguin, a division of Penguin Putnam Inc. and The Wylie Agency.

Irving Berlin: Lyrics of *God Bless America* by Irving Berlin. © Copyright 1938, 1939 by Irving Berlin. © Copyright Renewed 1965, 1966 by Irving Berlin. © Copyright Assigned to Winthrop Rutherford, Jr., Anne Phipps Sidamon-Eristoff, and Theodore R. Jackson as Trustees of the God Bless America Fund. International Copyright Secured. All Rights Reserved. Used by Permission.

Charles Bernstein: Copyright © 1999 Charles Bernstein. An excerpt from *Sentences My Father Used* in CONTROLLING INTERESTS (New York: Roof Books, 1980). Used by permission of the author.

Leonard Bernstein, Stephen Sondheim: *America* from WEST SIDE STORY. © Copyright 1956, 1957, 1959 by Amberson Holdings LLC and Stephen Sondheim. Copyright Renewed. Leonard Bernstein Music Publishing Company LLC, Publisher. Reprinted by permission of Boosey & Hawkes, Inc., Sole Agent.

A BINTL BRIV (A Bundle of Letters): Selections from BINTEL BRIEF, edited by Issac Metzker. (Schocken, Doubleday). Reprinted by permission of Jane Brenner.

Chana Bloch: Dahlia Ravikovitch, trans. Chana Bloch, *Deep Calleth Unto Deep* from THE WINDOW. Copyright © 1989 by Chana Bloch. Reprinted with the permission of The Sheep Meadow Press. Translation *of Jews in the Land of Israel* from SELECTED POETRY OF YEHUDA AMICHAI (1986). Reprinted by permission of the translator.

Harold Bloom: *Introduction* from THE BOOK OF J. Copyright © 1990 by David Rosenberg and Harold Bloom. Reprinted by permission of Grove Weidenfeld.

Jerry Bock: *If I Were a Rich Man*—Sheldon Harnick, Jerry Bock. Copyright © 1964—Alley Music Corp. and Trio Music Company, Inc. Copyright renewed and assigned to Mayerling Productions, Ltd. and Jerry Bock Enterprises for the United States and to Alley Music Corp., Trio Music Company, Inc. and Jerry Bock Enterprises for the world outside the United States. Used by permission. All rights reserved.

E. M. Broner: From *The Birth* from WEAVE OF WOMEN by E. M. Broner, Copyright © 1978 by E. M. Broner. Reprinted by permission of Henry Holt and Company, LLC.

Melvin J. Bukiet: *The Library of Moloch* from WHILE THE MESSIAH TARRIES, copyright ©1995 by Melvin Jules Bukiet, Reprinted by permission of Harcourt Brace & Company. First appeared in ANTAEUS.

Abraham Cahan: *A Ghetto Wedding* by Abraham Cahan from YEKL AND THE IMPORTED BRIDEGROOM AND OTHER STORIES OF YIDDISH NEW YORK, Dover Publications, Inc.

Hortense Calisher: *The Rabbi's Daughter* from THE COLLECTED STORIES OF HORTENSE CALISHER. Reprinted by permission of Donadio & Olsen, agents for the Estate of Hortense Calisher.

Peter Cole: translation of *Your Manuscript Shines* from SELECTED POEMS OF SHMUEL HANAGID (1996). Copyright © 1996 by PUP. Reprinted by permission of Princeton University Press.

Edward Dahlberg: *Chapter IX* by Edward Dahlberg, from BECAUSE I WAS FLESH. Copyright © 1954 by Edward Dahlberg. Reprinted by permission of New Directions Publishing Corp.

E. L. Doctorow: *Heist* from HEIST by E. L. Doctorow. Reprinted by permission of International Creative Management, Inc. © by E. L. Doctorow.

Celia Dropkin: all poems are previously unpublished translations by Kathryn Hellerstein from Celia Dropkin, IN HEYSN VINT (New York: 1959). Copyright 2000 by Kathryn Hellerstein. Reprinted by permission of the translator.

David Edelshtadt: *To the Muse* and *My Testament* by David Edelshtadt from A CENTURY OF YIDDISH POETRY, ed. and trans. Aaron Kramer (New York: Cornwall Books, 1989). Reprinted by permission.

Kenneth Fearing: *Dirge*, *Beware*, and *Afternoon of a Pawnbroker* from KENNETH FEARING: COMPLETE POEMS, ed. by Ryley. Reprinted by permission of The National Poetry Foundation.

Irving Feldman: *Psalm* and *The Pripet Marshes*. Reprinted from NEW AND SELECTED POEMS, The Viking Press © 1979. Reprinted by permission of the author.

Ruth Feldman: *Shema* from COLLECTED POEMS by Primo Levi, translated by Ruth Feldman and Brian Swann. English translation copyright © 1988 by Ruth Feldman and Brian Swann. Reprinted by permission of Faber & Faber Inc., an affiliate of Farrar, Straus & Giroux, LLC.

John Felstiner: *Deathfugue* and *Psalm* from PAUL CELAN: POET, SURVIVOR, JEW (Yale University Press, 1995), translated by John Felstiner. Reprinted by permission of the translator.

Edna Ferber: Chapter 3 from FANNY HERSELF. Reprinted by permission of the Estate of Edna Ferber.

Bruce Jay Friedman: *When You're Excused, You're Excused*, copyright © 1963 by Bruce Jay Friedman, from THE COLLECTED SHORT FICTION OF BRUCE JAY FRIEDMAN by Bruce Jay Friedman. Used by permission of Donald I. Fine, an imprint of Penguin Putnam Inc.

Daniel Fuchs: *A Hollywood Diary*. Copyright © 1979. From THE APATHETIC BOOKIE JOINT by Daniel Fuchs. Reproduced by permission of Routledge, Inc.

Allen Ginsberg: ALL LINES from *Footnote to Howl* from COLLECTED POEMS 1947–1980 by Allen Ginsberg. Copyright © 1955 by Allen Ginsberg. Copyright Renewed. Reprinted by permission of HarperCollins Publishers, Inc. *Hymnn: IV & V* and *Part II* from *KADDISH* from COLLECTED POEMS 1947–1980 by Allen Ginsberg. Copyright © 1959 by Allen Ginsberg. Copyright Renewed. Reprinted by permission of HarperCollins Publishers, Inc.

Jacob Glatstein: *1919, Autobiography, We the Proletariat, Good Night, World, Without Jews, Resistance in the Ghetto,* and *The Joy of the Yiddish Word* from AMERICAN YIDDISH POETRY: A BILINGUAL ANTHOLOGY, translated by Benjamin Harshav and Barbara Harshav. Copyright © 1986 The Regents of the University of California. Used with the permission of the University of California Press.

Michael Gold: *Fifty Cents A Night* from JEWS WITHOUT MONEY, reprinted by permission of the Evelyn Singer Agency.

Allegra Goodman: *The Four Questions* from THE FAMILY MARKOWITZ by Allegra Goodman. Copyright © 1996 by Allegra Goodman. Reprinted by permission of Farrar, Straus & Giroux, LLC.

Paul Goodman: *A Memorial Synagogue* by Paul Goodman. Copyright © 1977 by Sally Goodman. Reprinted from THE BREAK-UP OF OUR CAMP: STORIES 1932–1935 with the permission of Black Sparrow Press.

Chaim Grade: *My Quarrel with Hersh Rasseyner* by Chaim Grade, Milton Himmelfarb, translator, from A TREASURY OF YIDDISH STORIES by Irving Howe and Eliezer Greenberg. Copyright © 1953, 1954, 1989 by Viking Penguin, renewed © 1981, 1982 by Irving Howe and Eva Greenberg. Used by permission of Viking Penguin, a division of Penguin Putnam Inc.

Rebecca Gratz: From LETTERS OF REBECCA GRATZ. Published 1929 by the Jewish Publication Society. Used by permission.

Allen Grossman: *Part IV, Poland of Death* by Allen Grossman, from THE ETHER DOME. Copyright © 1991 by Allen Grossman. Reprinted by permission of New Directions Publishing Corp.

Moyshe-Leyb Halpern: *Memento Mori* by Moyshe-Leyb Halpern, translated by John Hollander from THE PENGUIN BOOK OF MODERN YIDDISH VERSE by Irving Howe, Ruth R. Wisse and Khone Shmeruk. Copyright © 1987 by Irving Howe, Ruth Wisse, and Khone Shmeruk. Introduction and Notes © 1987 by Irving Howe. Used by permission of Viking Penguin, a division of Penguin Putnam Inc. *Memento Mori* (Yiddish and transliteration) from IN NYU YORK by M. L. Halpern. Reprinted by permission of Isaac Halpern. *Isaac Leybush Peretz* from IN NEW YORK: A SELECTION, trans. Kathryn Hellerstein. Used by permission of the Jewish Publication Society. Copyright 1982. *Memento Mori, In the Golden Land, Zlochov, My Home,* and *My Only Son,* from AMERICAN YIDDISH POETRY: A BILINGUAL ANTHOLOGY, translated by Benjamin Harshav and Barbara Harshav. Copyright © 1986 The Regents of the University of California. Used with the permission of the University of California Press.

Lorenz Hart & Richard Rodgers: *Bewitched*, by Lorenz Hart and Richard Rodgers. © 1941 (Renewed) Chappell & Co. Rights for Extended Renewal Term in the United States controlled by the Estate of Lorenz Hart (administered by WB Music Corp) and Family Trust U/W Richard Rodgers and Family Trust U/W Dorothy F. Rodgers (administered by Williamson Music). All Rights Reserved. Used by permission. WARNER BROS. PUBLICATIONS U.S. INC., Miami, FL 33014. *My Funny Valentine*, by Lorenz Hart and Richard Rodgers. © 1937 Renewed Chappell & Co. Rights for Extended Renewal Term in the United States controlled by the Estate of Lorenz Hart (administered by WB Music Corp.) and Family Trust U/W Richard Rodgers and Family Trust U/W Dorothy F. Rodgers (administered by Williamson Music). All Rights Reserved. Used by Permission. WARNER BROS. PUBLICATIONS U.S. INC., Miami, FL 33014.

Anthony Hecht: *The Book of Yolek* from THE TRANSPARENT MAN by Anthony Hecht. Copyright © 1990 by Anthony Hecht. Reprinted by permission of Alfred A. Knopf, a Division of Random House, Inc. *The Room* from COLLECTED EARLIER POEMS by Anthony Hecht. Copyright © 1990 by Anthony E. Hecht. Reprinted by permission of Alfred A. Knopf, Inc.

Edward Hirsch: *Idea of the Holy* and *Oscar Ginsberg* from ON LOVE by Edward Hirsch. Copyright © 1998 by Edward Hirsch. Reprinted by permission of Alfred A. Knopf, a division of Random House, Inc. *The Village Idiot* from WILD GRATITUDE by Edward Hirsch. Copyright © 1985 by Edward Hirsch. Reprinted by permission of Alfred A. Knopf, Inc.

John Hollander: *Adam's Task, The Ninth of Ab*, and *The Ziz* from SELECTED POETRY by John Hollander. Copyright © 1993 by John Hollander. Reprinted by permission of Alfred A. Knopf, Inc.

David Ignatow: *The Bagel, Autumn Leaves, Europe and America, In Limbo*, and *God Said* from DAVID IGNATOW: POEMS 1934–1969 © 1970 by David Ignatow, Wesleyan University Press by permission of University Press of New England.

Shirley Kaufman: *His Wife, Bunk Beds,* and *Stones* from ROOTS IN THE AIR © 1996 by Shirley Kaufman. Reprinted by permission of Copper Canyon Press, P. O. Box 271, Port Townsend, WA 98368. Translation of *Isaac*, copyright © Shirley Kaufman. First published in THE LIGHT OF LOST SUNS: SELECTED POEMS OF AMIR GILBOA, 1974, New York, Persea Books, Inc. Abba Korner, *My Little Sister, part* 28 translated by Shirley Kaufman, from MY LITTLE SISTER:

FIELD TRANSLATION SERIES # 11. Copyright © 1986 Oberlin College Press. Reprinted by permission of the publisher. Lines from *The Western Wall* from THE FLOOR KEEPS TURNING by Shirley Kaufman. Copyright © 1970, University of Pittsburgh Press. Reprinted by permission of the poet.

Alfred Kazin: *The Kitchen* from A WALKER IN THE CITY, Copyright 1951 and renewed 1979 by Alfred Kazin, reprinted by permission of Harcourt Brace & Company.

Jerome Kern and Oscar Hammerstein II: *Ol' Man River*. Words and Music by Jerome Kern and Oscar Hammerstein II © Copyright 1927 Universal-Polygram International Publishing, Inc., a division of Universal Studios, Inc. (ASCAP) Copyright Renewed. International Copyright Secured. All Rights Reserved.

Irena Klepfisz: *Fradel Shtok* and the dedication from *Bashert* published IN A FEW WORDS IN THE MOTHER TONGUE: POEMS SELECTED AND NEW (1971–1990) (Portland, OR: The Eighth Mountain Press, 1990). © 1990 by Irena Klelpfisz. Reprinted by permission of the author and publisher.

Stanley Kunitz: *Father and Son*, copyright 1944 by Stanley Kunitz, *Foreign Affairs*, copyright © 1958 by Stanley Kunitz, and *Quinnapoxet*, copyright 1979 by Stanley Kunitz, from THE POEMS OF STANLEY KUNITZ 1928–1978 by Stanley Kunitz. Reprinted by permission of W. W. Norton & Company, Inc.

Tony Kushner: Excerpt from ANGELS IN AMERICA. Copyright © 1992, 1993 by Tony Kushner. Used by permission.

Denise Levertov: *Candles in Babylon* by Denise Levertov, from CANDLES IN BABYLON. Copyright © 1982 by Denise Levertov. *Illustrious Ancestors* by Denise Levertov, from COLLECTED EARLIER POEMS 1940–1960. Copyright © 1958, 1979 by Denise Levertov. Reprinted by permission of New Directions Publishing Corp. *The Jacob's Ladder* by Denise Levertov, from POEMS 1960–1967. Copyright © 1961 by Denise Levertov. All reprinted by permission of New Directions Publishing Corp.

Meyer Levin: All selections are from THE OLD BUNCH by Meyer Levin. Reprinted by permission of the Carol Publishing Group, Inc.

Philip Levine: *On a Drawing by Flavio*, *Sources*, and *Zaydee* from NEW AND SELECTED POEMS by Philip Levine. Copyright © 1991 by Philip Levine. Reprinted by permission of Alfred A. Knopf, Inc. *The Sweetness of Bobby Hefka* from WHAT WORK IS by Philip Levine. Copyright © 1991 by Philip Levine. Reprinted by permission of Alfred A. Knopf, Inc.

Mani Leyb: *Hush, I Am, They, A Plum, Strangers, Odors, To the Gentle Poet*, and *Inscribed on a Tombstone* by Mani Leyb, translated by John Hollander, and *Hush* by Mani Leyb, translated by Marie Syrkin from THE PENGUIN BOOK OF MODERN YIDDISH VERSE by Irving Howe, Ruth R. Wisse and Khone Shmeruk. Copyright © 1987 by Irving Howe, Ruth Wisse, and Khone Shmeruk. Introduction and Notes Copyright © 1987 by Irving Howe. Used by permission of Viking Penguin, a division of Penguin Putnam Inc.

A. Leyeles: *The God of Israel, New York, Fabius Lind's Days,* and *Shlomo Molkho Sings on the Eve of His Burning* from AMERICAN YIDDISH POETRY: A BILINGUAL ANTHOLOGY, translated by Benjamin and Barbara Harshav. Copyright © 1986 The Regents of the University of California. Used by permission of the University of California Press.

H. Leyvik: *Sanatorium* by H. Leyvik, from A TREASURY OF YIDDISH POETRY by Irving Howe and Eliezer Greenberg, © 1969 by Irving Howe and Eliezer Greenberg. Reprinted by permission of Henry Holt and Company, Inc. *Clouds Behind the Forest, To America,* and *Song of the Yellow Patch* by H. Leyvick, translated by Benjamin and Barbara Harshav, AMERICAN YIDDISH POETRY: A BILINGUAL ANTHOLOGY. Copyright © 1986 The Regents of the University of California. Used by permission of the University of California Press. *How Did He Get Here? (Spinoza Cycle, No 2)* from AN ANTHOLOGY OF MODERN YIDDISH POETRY, translated by Ruth Whitman. Reprinted by permission of the translator. *Sacrifice* by H. Leivick, translated by Robert Friend, from THE PENGUIN BOOK OF MODERN YIDDISH VERSE by Irving Howe, Ruth R. Wisse, and Khone Shmeruk. Copyright © 1987 by Irving Howe, Ruth Wisse, and Khone Shmeruk. Introduction and Notes Copyright © 1987 by Irving Howe. Used by permission of Viking Penguin, a division of Penguin Putnam Inc.

Ephraim Lisitzky: Selections from IN THE GRIP OF CROSS-CURRENTS by Ephraim Lisitzky, translated from the Hebrew by Moshe Kohn and Jacob Sloan (New York: Block,1959). Reprinted by permission of the publisher.

Frank Loesser: *Adelaide's Lament* from GUYS AND DOLLS. Copyright 1949, 1950, 1951, 1953 Frank Music Corp. Copyright renewed 1977, 1978, 1979, 1981 Frank Music Corp. Reprinted by permission of the Hal Leonard Corporation.

Norman Mailer: *Responses and Reactions I and II* reprinted from COMMENTARY, December 1962 and August 1963, by permission; all rights reserved. Copyright © 1962 by Norman Mailer for *Responses and Reactions I* and Copyright © 1963 by Norman Mailer for *Responses and Reactions II*. Reprinted by permission of The Wylie Agency.

Bernard Malamud: *The Last Mohican* and *The Magic Barrel* from THE COMPLETE STORIES by Bernard Malamud. Copyright © 1997 by Ann Malamud. Reprinted by permission of Farrar, Straus & Giroux, Inc.

Anna Margolin: *Dear Monsters, Epitaph* by Anna Margolin, translated by Marcia Falk from THE PENGUIN BOOK OF MODERN YIDDISH VERSE by Irving Howe, Ruth R. Wisse, and Khone Shmeruk. Copyright © 1987 by Irving Howe, Ruth Wisse, and Khone Shmeruk. Introduction and Notes Copyright © 1987 by Irving Howe. Used by permission of Viking Penguin, a division of Penguin Putnam Inc. *My Ancestors Speak* by Anna Margolin, translated by Adrienne Cooper, from THE TRIBE OF DINA by Melanie Kaye/Kantrowitz and Irena Klepfisz ©1986, 1989 by Melanie Kay/Kantrowitz and Irena Klepfisz. Reprinted by permission of Beacon Press, Boston. *A City by the Sea* translated by Adrienne Rich from A TREASURY OF YIDDISH POETRY by Irving Howe and Eliezer Greenberg, © 1969 by Irving Howe and Eliezer Greenberg. Reprinted by permission of Henry Holt & Company, Inc. *I Was Once a Boy, Mother Earth,* and *Forgotten Gods* are all previously unpublished translations by Kathryn Hellerstein. Copyright 2000 by Kathryn Hellerstein. Reprinted by permission of the translator.

Groucho Marx: [*We Were Brothers Before You Were*]. *On Intellectual Property: A Marxist Brief* from NEW YORK TIMES, WEEK IN REVIEW, 10/12/97, page 2. Reprinted by permission of the Estate of Groucho Marx. Introduction to the article by I. Molotsky. Introduction reprinted by permission of The New York Times.

Samuel Menashe: Lines from *Promised Land*, from THE NICHE NARROWS. *New and Selected Poems* by Samuel Menashe. Published by Talisman House, Jersey City, NJ. Copyright © 2000 by Samuel Menashe. Reprinted by permission of the poet.

Arthur Miller: *Monte Sant' Angelo* from I DON'T NEED YOU ANYMORE. Copyright © 1951 in HARPERS Magazine. Copyright renewed in 1979 by Viking/Penguin. Reprinted by permission of International Creative Management, Inc.

Mark Mirsky: *Memory Candle* first appeared in KEREM, Spring 1995. Reprinted by permission of the author.

Kadya Molodowsky: *God of Mercy* by Kadya Molodowsky, translated by Irving Howe, from THE PENGUIN BOOK OF MODERN YIDDISH VERSE by Irving Howe, Ruth Wisse, and Khone Shmeruk. Copyright © 1987 by Irving Howe, Ruth Wisse, and Khone Shmeruk. Introduction and Notes Copyright © 1987 by Irving Howe. Used by permission of Viking Penguin, a division of Penguin Putnam. *Alphabet Letters* and *Letters from the Ghetto* from PAPER BRIDGES (1999), by Kadya Molodowsky. Reprinted by permission of Wayne State University Press. *The Lost Shabes* by Kadya Molodowsky, translated by Irena Klepfisz, from THE TRIBE OF DINA by Melanie Kay/Kantrowitz and Irena Klepfisz ©1986, 1989 by Melanie Kaye/Kantrowitz and Irena Klepfisz. Reprinted by permission of Beacon Press, Boston.

Miriam Israel Moses: Excerpts from *Survivors and Pieces of Glass* from BRIDGES, Winter 97/98. Reprinted by permission of the author.

Moyshe Nadir: *The Man Who Slept Through the End of the World* by Moyshe Nadir, translated by Irving Howe, from A TREASURY OF YIDDISH STORIES, edited by Irving Howe and Eliezer Greenberg. Copyright © 1953, 1954, 1989 by Viking Penguin, renewed © 1981, 1982 by Irving Howe and Eva Greenberg. Used by permission of Viking Penguin, a division of Penguin Putnam Inc.

Howard Nemerov: *Lot's Wife, A Song of Degrees,* and *Nicodemus* from COLLECTED POEMS OF HOWARD NEMEROV. Reprinted by permission.

Joachim Neugroschel: translation of *Hagar and Ishmael* by Else Lasker-Schuler from VOICES WITHIN THE ARK (1980). Used by permission of Joachim Neugroschel. Translation © 1979 by Joachim Neugroschel.

Clifford Odets: *Awake and Sing* from WAITING FOR LEFTY AND OTHER PLAYS by Clifford Odets. Copyright © 1933, 1935 by Clifford Odets; copyright renewed © 1961, 1962 by Clifford Odets. Used by permission of Grove/Atlantic, Inc.

Tillie Olsen: *Tell Me A Riddle*, from TELL ME A RIDDLE by Tillie Olsen. Introduction by John Leonard. Copyright © 1956, 1957, 1960, 1961, by Tillie Olsen. Introduction Copyright 1994, by Dell Publishing. Used by permission of Delacorte Press/Seymour Lawrence, a division of Bantam Doubleday Dell Publishing Group, Inc.

Joseph Opatoshu: *Brothers* by Joseph Opatoshu is a previously unpublished translation by Kathryn Hellerstein, in ALE VERK FUN YOYSEF OPATAOSHU: BIANKE UN ANDERE DERTSEYLUNGEN (Vilna: Farlag B. Kletskin, 1928). Copyright 2000 by Kathryn Hellerstein. Reprinted by permission of the translator.

George Oppen: *Disasters, If It All Went Up in Smoke,* and *The Occurrences* by George Oppen, from COLLECTED POEMS, NEW AND EXPANDED, copyright © 2000 by Linda Oppen. Reprinted by permission of New Directions Publishing Corp. *Psalm* and *Exodus* by George Oppen, from COLLECTED POEMS. Copyright © 1975 by George Oppen. Reprinted by permission of New Directions Publishing Corp.

Jacqueline Osherow: *Brief Encounter with a Hero, Name Unknown* from WITH A MOON IN TRANSIT by Jacqueline Osherow. Copyright © 1996 by Jacqueline Osherow. Used by permission of Grove/Atlantic, Inc. *Ch'vil Shreiben a Poem Au Yiddish* from DEAD MEN'S PRAISE by Jacqueline Osherow. Copyright © 1999 by Jacqueline Osherow. Used by permission of Grove/Atlantic, Inc. *Ponar* from CONVERSATIONS WITH SURVIVORS by Jacqueline Osherow. Used by permission of University of Georgia Press. *The Yiddish Muses* from LOOKING FOR ANGELS IN NEW YORK by Jacqueline Osherow. Used by permission of University of Georgia Press.

Cynthia Ozick: *Envy; or, Yiddish in America* from THE PAGAN RABBI AND OTHER STORIES by Cynthia Ozick. Copyright © 1971 by Cynthia Ozick. Reprinted by permission of Alfred A. Knopf, Inc. *The Shawl* from THE SHAWL by Cynthia Ozick. Copyright ©1980, 1983 by Cynthia Ozick. Reprinted by permission of Alfred A. Knopf, Inc.

Grace Paley: *A Conversation with My Father* from ENORMOUS CHANGES AT THE LAST MINUTE by Grace Paley. Copyright © 1974 by Grace Paley. Reprinted by permission of Farrar, Straus & Giroux, Inc. *The Loudest Voice* from THE LITTLE DISTURBANCES OF MAN by Grace Paley. Copyright © 1956, 1957, 1958, 1959 by Grace Paley. Used by permission of Viking Penguin, a division of Penguin Putnam Inc. *In This Country, But in Another Language, My Aunt Refuses to Marry the Men Everyone Wants Her To* from LATER THAT SAME DAY by Grace Paley. Copyright © 1985 by Grace Paley. Reprinted by permission of Farrar, Straus & Giroux, Inc.

Dorothy Parker: *Résumé* copyright 1926, 1928, renewed 1954 © 1956 by Dorothy Parker, from THE PORTABLE DOROTHY PARKER by Dorothy Parker, Introduction by Brendan Gill. Used by permission of Viking Penguin, a division of Penguin Books, USA, Inc.

S. J. Perelman: *Nathanael West: A Portrait* from THE MASSACHUSETTS REVIEW, Winter/Spring 1965. Copyright 1933 by S. J. Perelman. First published in CONTEMPO, III. *Waiting for Santy: A Christmas Playlet* from PASKUDNIKS AND NO GOODNIKS. Copyright 1936 by S. J. Perelman. First published in THE NEW YORKER. Both reprinted by permission of Harold Ober Associates Incorporated.

Marge Piercy: *Maggid* and *The Ram's Horn Sounding* from THE ART OF BLESSING THE DAY by Marge Piercy. Copyright © 1999 by Middlemarsh Inc. Reprinted by permission of Alfred A. Knopf, a Division of Random House, Inc.

Robert Pinsky: *The Night Came* and *Visions of Daniel* from THE WANT BONE by Robert Pinsky. Copyright © 1990 by Robert Pinsky. Reprinted by permission of The Ecco Press. *Avenue* from THE FIGURED WHEEL: New and Collected Poems 1966–1996 by Robert Pinsky. Copyright © 1996 by Robert Pinsky. Reprinted by permission of Farrar, Straus & Giroux, LLC.

Chaim Potok: Excerpt from MY NAME IS ASHER LEV by Chaim Potok. Copyright © 1972 by Chaim Potok. Reprinted by permission of Alfred A. Knopf, Inc.

Gavriel Preil: *I Am Not in New York, The Eternal Present, Moving, Van Gogh. Williamsburg* from SUNSET POSSIBILITIES by Gavriel Preil. Used by permission of The Jewish Publication Society. Copyright © 1986.

Carl Rakosi: *Israel, Services*, translation of *Meditation* by Moses Ibn Ezra, translation of *Meditation* by Ibn Gabirol, and translation of *Song* by Judah Halevi from THE COLLECTED POEMS OF CARL RAKOSI. Reprinted by permission of the National Poetry Foundation.

Tova Reich: *The Lost Girl*, originally published in HARPER'S. Reprinted by permission of the Georges Borchardt Literary Agency.

Avrom Reyzen: *Equality of the Sexes* in NEW YORKISH AND OTHER AMERICAN YIDDISH STORIES, translated by Max Rosenfeld. Reprinted by permission of the Sholom Aleichem Club Press.

Charles Reznikoff: *Russia: Anno 1905, Building Boom, A Short History of Israel, Notes and Glosses: XI, Te Deum, [The invitation read . . .], I went to my grandfather's* (*From Early History of a Writer: 15*) and translation of *My Heart is in the East* from *Jehuda Halevi's Songs to Zion*. Copyright © 1977 by Marie Sykin Reznikoff. Reprinted from POEMS 1918–1975: THE COMPLETE POEMS OF CHARLES REZNIKOFF with the permission of Black Sparrow Press.

Adrienne Rich: Part 10 of *Eastern War Time*, from AN ATLAS OF THE DIFFICULT WORLD: Poems 1988–1991 by Adrienne Rich. Copyright © 1991 by Adrienne Rich. Part VII of *Sources*, and *Yom Kippur 1984* from YOUR NATIVE LAND, YOUR LIFE: POEMS BY ADRIENNE RICH. Copyright © 1986 by Adrienne Rich. *Trying to Talk with a Man* and five lines from *For Ethel Rosenberg* from THE FACT OF A DOORFRAME: POEMS SELECTED AND NEW, 1950–1984 by Adrienne Rich. Copyright © 1984 by Adrienne Rich. Copyright © 1975, 1978, by W. W. Norton & Company, Inc. Copyright © 1981 by Adrienne Rich. All used by permission of the author and W. W. Norton & Company, Inc.

Edwin Rolfe: *Epitaphs* (2) and *Elegia* from COLLECTED POEMS. Copyright 1993 by the Board of Trustees of the University of Illinois. Used with the permission of Mary Rolfe and the University of Illinois Press.

Joseph Rolnik: *Poets, Home from Praying*, and *The First Cigarette* by Joseph Rolnik, translated by Irving Feldman, from THE PENGUIN BOOK OF MODERN YIDDISH VERSE by Irving Howe, Ruth R. Wisse, and Khone Shmeruk. Copyright © 1987 by Irving Howe, Ruth Wisse, and Khone Shmeruk. Introduction and Notes copyright © 1987 by Irving Howe. Used by permission of Viking Penguin, a division of Penguin Putnam Inc.

Isaac Rosenfeld: *The Situation of the Jewish Writer* from THE CONTEMPORARY JEWISH RECORD. Reprinted by permission.

Morris Rosenfeld: *Corner of Pain and Anguish, My Little Son*, and *Walt Whitman (America's Great Poet)* by Morris Rosenfeld from A CENTURY OF YIDDISH POETRY, ed. and trans. Aaron Kramer (New York: Cornwall Books, 1989). Reprinted by permission of the publisher.

Rosenfeld & Green: *Confronting the Holocaust* by Rosenfeld & Green published by Indiana University Press. Reprinted by permission of the publisher.

Leo Rosten: *Mr. K*a*p*l*a*n and Shakespeare* from THE EDUCATION OF H*Y*M*A*N K*A*P*L*A*N by Leonard Q. Ross, copyright 1937 by Harcourt Brace & Company and renewed 1964 by Leo C. Rosten. Reprinted by permission of the publisher.

Henry Roth: *The Cellar* from CALL IT SLEEP by Henry Roth. Copyright © 1934, renewed © 1962 by Henry Roth. Introduction copyright © 1991 by Alfred Kazin. Afterword copyright © 1990 by Johns Hopkins University Press. Reprinted by permission of Farrar, Straus & Giroux, Inc.

Philip Roth: *Eli, the Fanatic* from GOODBYE, COLUMBUS. Copyright © 1959, renewed 1987 by Philip Roth. Reprinted by permission of Houghton Mifflin Co. All rights reserved. *Femme Fatale* from THE GHOST WRITER by Philip Roth. Copyright © 1979 by Philip Roth. Reprinted by permission of Farrar, Straus & Giroux, LLC.

Jerome Rothenberg: *Cokboy* by Jerome Rothenberg, from POLAND/1931. Copyright © 1974 by Jerome Rothenberg. *Dibbukkim* by Jerome Rothenberg, from KHURBN AND OTHER POEMS. Copyright © 1989 by Jerome Rothenberg. Both reprinted by permission of New Directions Publishing Corp.

Muriel Rukeyser: *Boy with His Hair Cut Short* and *Paper Anniversary* from THE COLLECTED POEMS OF MURIEL RUKEYSER, McGraw-Hill, New York City, 1978, by permission of International Creative Management. *More of a Corpse Than a Woman* and *Letter to the Front, 7*, from A MURIEL RUKEYSER READER, W. W. Norton & Company, New York City, 1994. Copyright © William Rukeyser.

Emma Schlesinger: *La Tía Estambolía* from SEPHARDIC AMERICAN VOICES, ed. by Diane Matza. Originally published in MIDSTREAM. Copyright © 1981 by The Theodor Herzl Foundation, Inc. Reprinted by permission.

Delmore Schwartz: *In Dreams Begin Responsibilities* by Delmore Schwartz, from IN DREAMS BEGIN RESPONSIBILITIES. Copyright © 1961 by Delmore Schwartz. Reprinted by permission of New Directions Publishing Corp. *The Ballet of the Fifth Year, Summer Knowledge*, and *The Heavy Bear Who Goes With Me* from SUMMER KNOWLEDGE: NEW AND SELECTED POEMS, 1938–1958. Copyright © 1959 Delmore Schwartz. By arrangement with the Estate of Delmore Schwartz.

I. J. Schwartz: from I. J. Schwartz, *Kentucky*, translated by Gertrude W. Dubrovsky (Tuscaloosa and London: U of Alabama Press, 1990): *Blue Grass, Litvaks*, and *Again Litvaks*. Used by permission.

Yente Serdatzky: *Unchanged* by Yente Serdatzky, translated by Frieda Forman and Ethel Raicus, in FOUND TREASURES: STORIES BY YIDDISH WOMEN WRITERS, eds. Frieda Forman et al. 1994, Second Story Press, Toronto. Reprinted by permission of the publisher.

Karl Shapiro: *Israel, Lord, I Have Seen Too Much, My Grandmother, Sunday, New Guinea,* and *The Alphabet* from COLLECTED POEMS, 1940–1978. Copyright © 1978, 1987 Karl Shapiro, by arrangement Wieser & Wieser Inc., New York, NY.

Lamed Shapiro: *White Chalah* by Lamed Shapiro, trans, by Norbert Guterman from A TREASURY OF YIDDISH STORIES by Irving Howe and Eliezer Greenberg. Copyright © 1953, 1954, 1989 by Viking Penguin, renewed © 1981, 1982 by Irving Howe and Eva Greenberg. Used by permission of Viking Penguin, a division of Penguin Putnam Inc.

Irwin Shaw: *Lament of Madame Rechevsky*. Reprinted with permission. Copyright © Irwin Shaw. Originally published in SHORT STORIES OF FIVE DECADES, Delacorte Press.

Fradl Shtok: *The Shorn Head, Sonnet, A Winter Echo*, and *Dusks* are all previously unpublished translations by Kathryn Hellerstein. Copyright 2000 by Kathryn Hellerstein. Reprinted by permission of the translator.

Kate Simon: *The Movies & Other Schools*, from BRONX PRIMITIVE by Kate Simon. Copyright © 1982 by Kate Simon. Used by permission of Viking Penguin, a division of Penguin Putnam Inc.

Louis Simpson: *A Story About Chicken Soup* from AT THE END OF THE OPEN ROAD © 1963 by Louis Simpson, Wesleyan University Press by permission of University Press of New England. *Dvonya* reprinted by permission of Louis Simpson. Copyright © 1971 by Louis Simpson from ADVENTURES OF THE LETTER I.

Isaac Bashevis Singer: *Gimpel the Fool* and *The Séance* from THE COLLECTED STORIES by Isaac Bashevis Singer. Reprinted by permission of Farrar, Straus & Giroux, Inc.

Tess Slesinger: *Missis Flinders* from THE UNPOSSESSED by Tess Slesinger (The Feminist Press, 1984).

Gustaf Sobin: lines from *Odèss* from TOWARDS THE BLANCHED ALPHABETS by Gustaf Sobin. Copyright © 1998 by Gustaf Sobin. Reprinted by permission of the poet.

Art Spiegelman: excerpt from MAUS II: AND HERE MY TROUBLES BEGAN by Art Spiegelman. Copyright © 1986, 1989, 1990, 1991 by Art Spiegelman. Reprinted by permission of Pantheon Books, a division of Random House, Inc.

Gertrude Stein: Excerpt from MAKING OF AMERICANS: THE HERSLAND FAMILY by Gertrude Stein, copyright 1934 by Harcourt Brace & Company and renewed 1962 by Alice B. Toklas, reprinted by permission of the publisher.

Gerald Stern: *Lucky Life*, copyright © 1977 by Gerald Stern from THIS TIME: NEW AND COLLECTED POEMS BY GERALD STERN. *Sixteen Minutes*, from ODD MERCY: POEMS BY GERALD STERN. Copyright © 1995 by Gerald Stern. Both reprinted by permission of W. W. Norton & Company, Inc.

Steve Stern: *Lazar Malkin Enters Heaven* by Steve Stern. Reprinted by permission of the author.

J. L. Teller: *Sigmund Freud at the Age of Eighty-Two, Of Immigration*, and *New York in a Jewish Mood* from AMERICAN YIDDISH POETRY: A BILINGUAL ANTHOLOGY, translated by Benjamin Harshav and Barbara Harshav. Copyright © 1986 the Regents of the University of California. Used by permission of the University of California Press.

Lionel Trilling: *Freud and Literature* by Lionel Trilling. Copyright © 1959 by Lionel Trilling, first printed in THE LIBERAL IMAGINATION. *Isaac Babel* by Lionel Trilling Copyright © 1965 by Lionel Trilling, first printed in BEYOND CULTURE. Both reprinted with the permission of The Wylie Agency, Inc.

Malka Heifetz Tussman: WITH TEETH IN THE EARTH (Wayne State, 1992), trans. Marcia Falk: *With Teeth in the Earth & Water Without Sound*. All other poems from AMERICAN YIDDISH POETRY: A BILINGUAL ANTHOLOGY, translated by Benjamin Harshav and Barbara Harshav. Copyright © 1986 the Regents of the University of California. Used by permission of the University of California Press.

David Unger: translation of *The Jews in Hell* by Isaac Goldemberg from VOICES WITHIN THE ARK (1980). Used by permission of David Unger. Translations © 1979 David Unger.

Berish Vaynshteyn: *Earth, On the Docks,* and *Lynching* from AMERICAN YIDDISH POETRY: A BILINGUAL ANTHOLOGY, translated by Benjamin Harshav and Barabara Harshav. Copyright © 1986 The Regents of the University of California. Used with the permission of the University of California Press.

Nathanael West: from *A Cool Million* from THE COMPLETE WORKS OF NATHANAEL WEST by Nathanael West. Copyright © 1957, renewed 1985 by Farrar, Straus & Giroux, Inc. Reprinted by permission of Farrar, Straus & Giroux, LLC.

Elie Wiesel: *Why I Write* from CONFRONTING THE HOLOCAUST edited by Rosenfeld & Green (Indiana: Indiana University Press). Reprinted by permission of the publisher. Excerpts from NIGHT by Elie Wiesel. Copyright ©1960 by MacGibbon & Kee. Copyright renewed ©1988 by The Collins Publishing Group. Reprinted by permission of Hill and Wang, a division of Farrar, Straus & Giroux, Inc.

Berish Vaynshteyn: *Earth, On the Docks,* and *Lynching* from Benjamin Harshav, Barbara Harshav, AMERICAN YIDDISH POETRY: A BILINGUAL ANTHOLOGY. Copyright © 1986 The Regents of the University of California. Used with the permission of the University of California Press.

Nathanael West: from *A Cool Million* from THE COMPLETE WORKS OF NATHANAEL WEST by Nathanael West. Copyright © 1957, renewed 1985 by Farrar, Straus and Giroux, Inc. Reprinted by permission of Farrar, Straus and Giroux, LLC.

Elie Wiesel: *Why I Write* from CONFRONTING THE HOLOCAUST edited by Rosenfeld & Green (Indiana: Indiana University Press). Reprinted by permission of the publisher. Excerpts from NIGHT by Elie Wiesel. Copyright ©1960 by MacGibbon & Kee. Copyright renewed ©1988 by The Collins Publishing Group. Reprinted by permission of Hill and Wang, a division of Farrar, Straus & Giroux, Inc.

C.K. Williams: translation of *A Load of Shoes*, by Avraham Sutzkever from THE LITERATURE OF DESTRUCTION edited by David Roskies. Copyright 1989 by the Jewish Publication Society. Reprinted by permission of David Roskies.

THE YANKEE TALMUD: from *The Tractate "America"* by Gershon Rosenzweig and *The Tractate "The Ways of the New Land"* by Abraham Kotlier, translated by David Stern. Reprinted by permission of the translator.

Yehoash: *Amid the Colorado Mountains* and *Woolworth Building* by Yehoash from A CENTURY OF YIDDISH POETRY, ed. and trans. Aaron Kramer (New York: Cornwall Books, 1989). Reprinted by permission of the publisher. *Lynching* and *Yang-Ze-Fu* by Yehoash, from A TREASURY OF YIDDISH POETRY by Irving Howe and Eliezer Greenberg © 1969 by Irving Howe and Eliezer Greenberg. Reprinted by permission of Henry Holt and Company, Inc. *Rachel's Tomb* by Yehaosh, is a previously unpublished translation by Kathryn Hellerstein. Copyright 2000 by Kathryn Hellerstein. Reprinted by permission of the translator.

Anzia Yezierska: *Children of Loneliness* from HOW I FOUND AMERICA: COLLECTED STORIES OF ANZIA YEZIERSKA. Copyright © 1991 by Louise Levitas Henriksen. Reprinted by permission of Persea Books, Inc.

Louis Zukofsky: *A8* and *A12* from A, pp 89, 148–150. Copyright (c) 1993 by Celia and Louis Zukofsky. Reprinted by permission of the Johns Hopkins University Press. *Fifth Movement: Autobiography* from COMPLETE SHORT POETRY, pp 15–18. Copyright Paul Zukofsky. Reprinted by permission of the Johns Hopkins University Press.

Every effort has been made to contact the copyright holders of each of the selections. Rights holders of any selections not credited should contact W. W. Norton & Company, Inc., 500 Fifth Avenue, New York, NY 10110, in order for a correction to be made in the next reprinting of our work.

Index of Translators

Index